DARK NEST

By Troy Denning

STAR WARS

DARK NEST

THE JOINER KING
THE UNSEEN QUEEN
THE SWARM WAR

Troy Denning

SCIENCE
FICTION

STAR WARS: DARK NEST I: THE JOINER KING Copyright © 2005 by Lucasfilm Ltd. & ® or ™ where indicated. All Rights Reserved. Used Under Authorization. Printing History: LucasBooks/Del Rey paperback, August 2005.

STAR WARS: DARK NEST II: THE UNSEEN QUEEN Copyright © 2005 by Lucasfilm Ltd. & ® or ™ where indicated. All Rights Reserved. Used Under Authorization. Printing History: LucasBooks/Del Rey paperback, October 2005.

STAR WARS: DARK NEST III: THE SWARM WAR Copyright © 2006 by Lucasfilm Ltd. & ® or ™ where indicated. All Rights Reserved. Used Under Authorization. Printing History: LucasBooks/Del Rey paperback, January 2006.

First SFBC Science Fiction printing: January 2006.

Cover art by Cliff Nielsen.

Published by arrangement with:
The Random House Publishing Group
A division of Random House, Inc.
1745 Broadway
New York, NY 10019

Visit The SFBC at http://www.sfbc.com
Visit Del Rey at http://www.randomhouse.com/delrey/
Visit the official Star Wars website at http://www.starwars.com

ISBN 0-7394-6330-6

Printed in the United States of America.

CONTENTS

THE STAR WARS NOVELS TIMELINE

33 YEARS BEFORE STAR WARS: A New Hope

Darth Maul: Saboteur*

32.5 *YEARS BEFORE STAR WARS: A New Hope*

Cloak of Deception
Darth Maul: Shadow Hunter

32 *YEARS BEFORE STAR WARS: A New Hope*

STAR WARS: EPISODE I
THE PHANTOM MENACE

29 *YEARS BEFORE STAR WARS: A New Hope*

Rogue Planet

27 *YEARS BEFORE STAR WARS: A New Hope*

Outbound Flight

22.5 *YEARS BEFORE STAR WARS: A New Hope*

The Approaching Storm

22 *YEARS BEFORE STAR WARS: A New Hope*

STAR WARS: EPISODE II
ATTACK OF THE CLONES

Star Wars Republic Commando:
Hard Contact
Triple Zero

21.5 *YEARS BEFORE STAR WARS: A New Hope*

Shatterpoint

21 *YEARS BEFORE STAR WARS: A New Hope*

The Cestus Deception
The Hive*

20 *YEARS BEFORE STAR WARS: A New Hope*

MedStar I: Battle Surgeons
MedStar II: Jedi Healer

19.5 *YEARS BEFORE STAR WARS: A New Hope*

Jedi Trial
Yoda: Dark Rendezvous

19 *YEARS BEFORE STAR WARS: A New Hope*

Labyrinth of Evil

STAR WARS: EPISODE III
REVENGE OF THE SITH

Dark Lord: The Rise of Darth
Vader

10-0 *YEARS BEFORE STAR WARS: A New Hope*

The Han Solo Trilogy:
The Paradise Snare
The Hutt Gambit
Rebel Dawn

5-2 *YEARS BEFORE STAR WARS: A New Hope*

*The Adventures of Lando
Calrissian:*
Lando Calrissian and the
Mindharp of Sharu
Lando Calrissian and the
Flamewind of Oseon
Lando Calrissian and the
Starcave of ThonBoka

The Han Solo Adventures:
Han Solo at Stars' End
Han Solo's Revenge
Han Solo and the Lost Legacy

STAR WARS: A New Hope YEAR 0

STAR WARS: EPISODE IV
A NEW HOPE

0-3 *YEARS AFTER STAR WARS: A New Hope*

Tales from the Mos Eisley
Cantina
Star Wars: Galaxies: The Ruins
of Dantooine
Splinter of the Mind's Eye

3 *YEARS AFTER STAR WARS: A New Hope*

STAR WARS: EPISODE V
THE EMPIRE STRIKES BACK

Tales of the Bounty Hunters

3.5 *YEARS AFTER STAR WARS: A New Hope*

Shadows of the Empire

4 *YEARS AFTER STAR WARS: A New Hope*

STAR WARS: EPISODE VI
RETURN OF THE JEDI

Tales from Jabba's Palace
Tales from the Empire
Tales from the New Republic

The Bounty Hunter Wars:
The Mandalorian Armor
Slave Ship
Hard Merchandise

The Truce at Bakura

6.5-7.5 YEARS AFTER STAR WARS: A New Hope

X-Wing:
Rogue Squadron
Wedge's Gamble
The Krytos Trap
The Bacta War
Wraith Squadron
Iron Fist
Solo Command

8 *YEARS AFTER STAR WARS: A New Hope*

The Courtship of Princess Leia
A Forest Apart*
Tatooine Ghost

9 *YEARS AFTER STAR WARS: A New Hope*

The Thrawn Trilogy:
Heir to the Empire
Dark Force Rising
The Last Command

X-Wing: Isard's Revenge

11 *YEARS AFTER STAR WARS: A New Hope*

I, Jedi

The Jedi Academy Trilogy:
Jedi Search
Dark Apprentice
Champions of the Force

12-13 *YEARS AFTER STAR WARS: A New Hope*

Children of the Jedi
Darksaber
Planet of Twilight
X-Wing: Starfighters of Adumar

14 *YEARS AFTER STAR WARS: A New Hope*

The Crystal Star

16-17 *YEARS AFTER STAR WARS: A New Hope*

The Black Fleet Crisis Trilogy:
Before the Storm
Shield of Lies

Tyrant's Test

17 *YEARS AFTER STAR WARS: A New Hope*

The New Rebellion

18 *YEARS AFTER STAR WARS: A New Hope*

The Corellian Trilogy:
Ambush at Corellia
Assault at Selonia
Showdown at Centerpoint

19 *YEARS AFTER STAR WARS: A New Hope*

The Hand of Thrawn Duology:
Specter of the Past
Vision of the Future

22 *YEARS AFTER STAR WARS: A New Hope*

Fool's Bargain*
Survivor's Quest

25-30 YEARS AFTER STAR WARS: A New Hope

The New Jedi Order:
Vector Prime
Dark Tide I: Onslaught
Dark Tide II: Ruin
Agents of Chaos I: Hero's Trial
Agents of Chaos II: Jedi Eclipse
Balance Point
Recovery*
Edge of Victory I: Conquest
Edge of Victory II: Rebirth
Star by Star
Dark Journey
Enemy Lines I: Rebel Dream
Enemy Lines II: Rebel Stand
Traitor
Destiny's Way
Ylesia*
Force Heretic I: Remnant
Force Heretic II: Refugee
Force Heretic III: Reunion
The Final Prophecy
The Unifying Force

35 *YEARS AFTER STAR WARS: A New Hope*

The Dark Nest Trilogy:
The Joiner King
The Unseen Queen
The Swarm War

*An ebook novella

DRAMATIS PERSONAE

Alema Rar; Jedi Knight (female Twi'lek)
Ben Skywalker; child (male human)
C-3PO; protocol droid
Cal Omas; Galactic Alliance Chief-of-State (male human)
Cilghal; Jedi Master (female Mon Calamari)
Gorog; mastermind (Killik)
Han Solo; captain, *Millennium Falcon* (male human)
Jacen Solo; Jedi Knight (male human)
Jae Juun; captain, *XR808g* (male Sullustan)
Jagged Fel; commander, Chiss task force (male human)
Jaina Solo; Jedi Knight (female human)
Leia Organa Solo; copilot, *Millennium Falcon* (female human)
Lowbacca; Jedi Knight (male Wookiee)
Luke Skywalker; Jedi Master (male human)
Mara Jade Skywalker; Jedi Master (female human)
R2-D2; astromech droid
Raynar Thul; crash survivor (male human)
Saba Sebatyne; Jedi Master (female Barabel)
Tahiri Veila; Jedi Knight (female human)
Tarfang; copilot, *XR808g* (male Ewok)
Tekli; Jedi Knight (female Chadra-fan)
Tenel Ka; Queen Mother (female human)
Tesar Sebatyne; Jedi Knight (male Barabel)
Welk; crash survivor (male human)
Zekk: Jedi Knight (male human)

THE JOINER KING

For Curtis Smith
Who invited me to play in the Galaxy Far, Far Away
A long, long time ago

ACKNOWLEDGMENTS

Many people contributed to this book in ways large and small. Thanks are especially due to: Andria Hayday, for advice, encouragement, critiques, and much more; James Luceno for being such a fun target for idea-bouncing; Enrique Guerrero for his suggestions and our many useful Chiss discussions; Shelly Shapiro and all the people at Del Rey who make this so much fun, particularly Keith Clayton and Colleen Lindsay; Sue Rostoni and the wonderful people at Lucasfilm, particularly Howard Roffman, Amy Gary, Leland Chee, and Pablo Hidalgo. And, of course, to George Lucas for opening his galaxy to the rest of us.

PROLOGUE

The feeling had returned, a sense of desperation that burned in the Force like a faraway star, clear and bright and beckoning. Jaina Solo found her gaze straying through the justice ship viewport, out into the blue-flecked void that hung behind the slowly spinning cylinder of Detention Center *Maxsec Eight*. As before, the sensation came from the direction of the Unknown Regions, a call for . . . what? And from whom? The touch was too wispy to tell. It always was.

"Jedi Solo?" The inquisitor stepped closer to the witness rail. "Shall I repeat the question?"

A tall, stiff woman with a shaved head and deep lines at the corners of her gray eyes, Athadar Gyad had the brusque demeanor of a retired military officer. It was a common affectation among petty Reconstruction Authority bureaucrats, even when the only notation in their service record was a decades-old planetary conscription number.

"When you boarded the *Night Lady* with Jedi Lowbacca and—"

"Sorry, Inquisitor. I did hear the question." Jaina shifted her gaze to the accused, a massive Yaka with an expressionless, near-human face. He wore an engraved Ithorian skull on the lateral cover of his cybernetic implant. "Redstar's crew tried to turn us away."

A glint of impatience showed in Gyad's gray eyes. "They attacked you with blasters, isn't that correct?"

"Right."

"And it was necessary to defend yourselves with your lightsabers?"

"Right again."

Gyad remained silent, tacitly inviting her witness to elaborate on the battle. But Jaina was more interested in the sense of desperation she felt in the Force. It was growing stronger by the moment, more urgent and frightened.

"Jedi Solo?" Gyad stepped in front of Jaina, blocking her view out of the inquest salon. "Please direct your attention to me."

Jaina fixed the woman with an icy stare. "I thought I had answered your question."

Gyad drew back almost imperceptibly, but continued her examination as though there had been no resentment in Jaina's voice. "What were you wearing at the time?"

"Our cloaks," Jaina said.

"Your Jedi cloaks?"

"They're just cloaks." Jaina had stood at enough witness rails in the last few years to know that the inquisitor was trying to bolster a weak case with the mystique of her Jedi witnesses—a sure sign that Gyad did not understand, or respect, the Jedi role in the galaxy. "Jedi don't wear uniforms."

"Surely, you can't mean to suggest that a criminal of Redstar's intelligence failed to recognize—" Gyad paused to reconsider her phrasing. Tribunal inquisitors were supposed to be impartial investigators, though in practice most limited their efforts to presenting enough evidence to lock away the accused. "Jedi Solo, do you mean to suggest the crew could have legitimately believed you to be pirates?"

"I don't know what they believed," Jaina said.

Gyad narrowed her eyes and studied Jaina in silence. Despite Luke Skywalker's advice after the war to avoid involving the Jedi in the mundane concerns of the new government, the challenge of rebuilding the galaxy obliged much of the order to do just that. There were just too many critical missions that only a Jedi could perform, with too many dire consequences for the Galactic Alliance, and most Reconstruction Authority bureaucrats had come to view the Jedi order as little more than an elite branch of interstellar police.

Finally, Jaina explained, "I was too busy fighting to probe their thoughts."

Gyad let out a theatrical sigh. "Jedi Solo, isn't it true that your father once made his living as a smuggler?"

"That was a little before my time, Inquisitor." Jaina's retort drew a siss of laughter from the spectator area, where two of her fellow Jedi Knights, Tesar Sebatyne and Lowbacca, sat waiting for her to finish. "And what would that have to do with the price of spice on Nal Hutta?"

Gyad turned to the panel of magistrates. "Will you please instruct the witness to answer—"

"Everyone knows the answer," Jaina interrupted. "It's taught in half the history classes in the galaxy."

"Of course it is." The inquisitor's voice grew artificially compassionate, and she pointed to the Yaka captive. "Would it be possible that you identify with the accused? That you are reluctant to testify against a criminal because of your father's own ambivalent relationship with the law?"

"No." Jaina found herself squeezing the witness rail as though she meant to crimp the cold metal. "In the last five standard years, I've captured thirty-seven warlords and broken more than a hundred smuggling—"

Suddenly the sense of desperation grew more tangible in the Force, more clear and familiar. Jaina's gaze turned back to the viewport, and she did not finish her answer.

"Wait."

Tahiri Veila raised a hand, and the two Yuuzhan Vong standing before her fell silent. The two groups of spectators watched her expectantly, but she remained quiet and stared into Zonama Sekot's blue sky. Over the last few weeks, she had begun to sense a distant foreboding in the Force, a slowly building dread, and now that feeling had developed into something more . . . into anguish and panic and despair.

"*Jeedai* Veila?" asked the smaller of the speakers. With one blind eye and a lumpy, lopsided face, he was one of the Extolled, a disfigured underclass once known as the Shamed Ones. They had earned their new name by rising up against their upper-caste oppressors to help end the war that had nearly destroyed both the Yuuzhan Vong and the civilized galaxy. "Is something wrong?"

"Yes." Tahiri forced her attention back to the group. Their blue-rimmed eyes and leathery faces seemed more familiar to her than the reflection of the blond-haired women she saw in the mirror every morning—but that was hardly a surprise, considering what had happened to her during the war. She was as much Yuuzhan Vong now as she was human, at least in mind and spirit. "But it doesn't have anything to do with this. Go on."

The Extolled One—Bava, she remembered—bowed deeply, intentionally lowering himself to her height.

"As I was saying, *Jeedai* Veila, four times this week we have caught Sal Ghator and his warriors stealing from our gardens."

Tahiri cocked her brow. "*Your* gardens, Bava?" La'okio was supposed to be a communal village, an experiment where the contentious castes of Yuuzhan Vong society would learn to work together—and to trust each other. "I thought the gardens belonged to everyone."

"We have decided that every grashal is also allowed to plant an extra plot for itself." Bava sneered in Ghator's direction, then continued, "But the warriors are too lazy to work their own ground. They expect us to do it for them."

"We cannot do it for ourselves!" Ghator objected. Half a meter taller than Tahiri and nearly three times her mass, he still bore the tattoos and ritual scarrings of a former subaltern. "We are cursed by the gods. Nothing we plant will grow."

Tahiri fought back a sigh. "Don't tell me you've separated by caste again. You're supposed to be living in mixed groups."

As Tahiri spoke, she felt the familiar touch of a Chadra-Fan searching for her in the Force, wanting to know if she also sensed the growing strength of the *feeling*. She opened herself to the contact and focused her thoughts on the mysterious fear. Tekli was not particularly strong in the Force, and what Tahiri perceived as a clarion call would seem barely a whisper to the little Chadra-Fan. Neither of them bothered to reach out for their companion Danni Quee; Force-sensitive though she might be, so far Danni had proven numb to the sensation.

"Living in mixed grashals is unclean," Ghator said, drawing Tahiri's attention back to the problems in La'okio. "Warriors cannot be asked to sleep on the same dirt as Shamed Ones."

"Shamed Ones!" Bava said. "We are Extolled. We are the ones who exposed Shimrra's heresy, while you warriors led us all to ruin."

The blue rim around Ghator's eyes grew wider and darker. "Beware your tongue, raal, lest its poison strike you dead."

"There is no poison in truth." Bava sneaked a glance in Tahiri's direction, then sneered, "You are the Shamed Ones now!"

Ghator's hand sent Bava tumbling across the rugrass so swiftly that Tahiri doubted she could have intercepted it had she wanted to, and she did not want to. The Yuuzhan Vong would always have their own way of working out problems—ways that Danni Quee and Tekli and perhaps even Zonama Sekot itself would never fully comprehend.

Bava stopped rolling and turned his good eye in Tahiri's direction. She returned his gaze and did nothing. Having risen from their outcast status through their efforts to end the war, the Extolled Ones were proving eager to find another caste to take their place. Tahiri thought it might be good to remind them of the consequences of such behavior. Besides, the *feeling* was growing stronger and clearer; she had the sense that it was coming from someone she knew, someone who had been trying to reach her—and Tekli—for a very long time.

Come fast . . . The voice arose inside Tahiri's mind, clear and distinct and eerily familiar. *Come now.*

The words seemed to fade even as Jacen Solo perceived them, sinking below the threshold of awareness and vanishing into the boggy underlayers of his mind. Yet the message remained, the conviction that the time had come to answer the call he had been feeling over the last few weeks. He unfolded his legs—he was sitting cross-legged in the air—and lowered his feet to the floor of the meditation circle. A chain of soft pops sounded as he crushed the tiny blada vines that spilled out of the seams between the larstone paving blocks.

"I'm sorry, Akanah. I must go."

Akanah answered without opening her eyes. "If you are sorry, Jacen, you must *not* go." A lithe woman with an olive complexion and dark hair, she appeared closer to Jacen's age than her own five standard decades. She sat floating in the center of the meditation circle, surrounded by novices who were trying to imitate her with varying degrees of success. "Sorrow is a sign that you have not given yourself to the Current."

Jacen considered this, then dipped his head in acknowledgment. "Then I'm not sorry." The call continued in the Force, a needle-sharp pang that pulled at Jacen deep inside his chest. "And I must go."

Now Akanah opened her eyes. "What of your training?"

"I'm grateful for what you have shown me so far." Jacen turned to leave. "I'll continue when I return."

"No." As Akanah spoke, the meditation circle exit vanished behind a vine-strewn wall. "I cannot permit that."

Jacen stopped and turned to face her. "Illusions aren't necessary. If you don't wish me to return, I won't."

"What I don't wish is for you to leave." Akanah floated over to him and lowered her own feet. She was so immersed in the White Current that even the delicate blada leaves did not pop beneath her weight. "It's too soon. You're not ready."

Jacen forced himself to remain patient. After all, he was the one who had sought out the Fallanassi. "I have completed many trainings, Akanah. What I have learned is that every order believes *its* way is the only way."

"I am not speaking of monks and witches, Jacen Solo. I am speaking of you." Her dark eyes caught his gaze. "Your feelings on this are unclear. Someone calls, and you go without knowing why."

"Then you feel it, too?"

"No, Jacen. You are as clumsy in the Current as your uncle. Your feelings leave ripples, and ripples can be read. Does the call come from your brother?"

"No. Anakin died in the war." It had been eight years, and Jacen could finally speak those words with some measure of acceptance, with some recognition of the purpose his brother's death had served in the Force. It had been the turning point in the war, when the Jedi finally learned how to fight the Yuuzhan Vong—and not become monsters themselves. "I've told you that."

"Yes, but is it *him*?" Akanah stepped closer to Jacen, and his nostrils filled with the scent of the waha plants that grew in the temple bathing pool. "After someone sinks beneath the Current, a circle of ripples remains behind. Perhaps it is the ripples you sense."

"That does not make what I feel any less real," Jacen countered. *"Sometimes, the effect is all we can know of the cause."*

"Do you remember my words only so you can use them to spar with me?" Akanah's hand came up as though to bat him across the ear, and his own hand reflexively rose to block. She shook her head in disgust. "You are a dreadful student, Jacen Solo. You hear, but you do not learn."

It was a rebuke to which Jacen had grown accustomed during his five-year search for the true nature of the Force. The Jensaarai, the Aing-Tii, even the Witches of Dathomir had all said similar things to him—usually when his questions about their view of the Force grew too probing. But Akanah had more reason than the others to be disappointed in him. Striking another would be anathema to any Adept of the White Current. All Akanah had done was lift her hand; it had been Jacen who interpreted the action as an attack.

Jacen inclined his head. "I learn, but sometimes slowly." He was thinking of the two apparitions he had already seen of his dead brother, the first when a cavern beast on Yuuzhan'tar used one to lure him into its throat, the second on Zonama, when Sekot had taken Anakin's form while they talked. "You think I'm giving form to this call, that I impose my own meaning on the ripples I feel."

"What *I* think is not important," Akanah said. "Still yourself, Jacen, and see what is really in the Current."

Jacen closed his eyes and opened himself to the White Current in much the same way he would have opened himself to the Force.

Akanah and the other Adepts taught that the Current and the Force were separate things, and that was true—but only in the sense that any current was different from the ocean in which it flowed. In their essential wholeness, they were each other.

Jacen performed a quieting exercise he had learned from the Theran Listeners, then focused on the call. It was still there, a cry so sharp it hurt, in a voice he remembered and could not identify . . . *come . . . help . . .* a male voice, but one he recognized as not belonging to his brother.

And there was something else, too, a familiar presence that Jacen *did* know, not sending the call, but reaching out along with it. Jaina.

Jacen opened his eyes. "It's not Anakin . . . or his ripples."

"You're certain?"

Jacen nodded. "Jaina senses it, too." That was what his sister was trying to tell him, he knew. Their twin bond had always been strong, and it had only grown stronger during his wanderings. "I think she intends to answer it."

Akanah looked doubtful. "I feel nothing."

"*You* aren't her twin." Jacen turned and stepped through the wall-illusion hiding the exit, only to find Akanah—or the illusion of Akanah—blocking his way. "Please ask the Pydyrians to bring my ship down from orbit. I'd like to leave as soon as possible."

"I am sorry, but no." Akanah's eyes caught his gaze again and held it almost physically. "You have the same power I once sensed in your uncle Luke, but without the light. You must not leave before you have found some."

Jacen was stung by her harsh assessment, but hardly surprised. The war against the Yuuzhan Vong had brought the Jedi a deeper understanding of the Force—one that no longer saw light and dark as opposing sides—and he had known before he came that the Fallanassi might find this new view disturbing. That was why he had hid it from them . . . or thought he had.

"I'm sorry you disapprove," Jacen said. "But I no longer view the Force in terms of light and dark. It embraces more than that."

"Yes, we have heard about this 'new' knowledge of the Jedi." Akanah's tone was scornful. "And it troubles my heart to see that their folly now rivals their arrogance."

"Folly?" Jacen did not want to argue, but—being one of the first advocates of the new understanding—he felt compelled to defend his views. "That 'folly' helped us win the war."

"At what price, Jacen?" Akanah's voice remained gentle. "If the Jedi no longer look to the light, how can they serve it?"

"Jedi serve the Force," Jacen said. "The Force encompasses both light and dark."

"So now you are beyond light and dark?" Akanah asked. "Beyond good and evil?"

"I'm no longer an active Jedi Knight," Jacen answered, "but yes."

"And you do not understand the folly in that?" As Akanah spoke, her gaze seemed to grow deeper and darker. "The arrogance?"

What Jacen understood was that the Fallanassi had a rather narrow and rigid view of morality, but he did not say so. The call was continuing to pull at him inside, urging him to be on his way, and the last thing he wanted to do now was waste time in a debate that would change no one's mind.

"The Jedi serve only themselves," Akanah continued. "They are pompous enough to believe they can use the Force instead of submitting to it, and in this pride they have caused more suffering than they have prevented. With no light to guide you, Jacen, and the power I sense in you, I fear you will cause even more."

The frank words struck Jacen like a blow, less because of their harshness than because of the genuine concern he sensed behind them. Akanah truly feared for him, truly feared that he would become an even greater monster than had his grandfather, Darth Vader.

"Akanah, I appreciate your concern." Jacen reached for her hands and found himself holding only empty air. He resisted the temptation to find her real body in the Force; Adepts of the White Current considered such acts intrusions just short of violence. "But I won't find my light here. I have to go."

ONE

Evening had come to Unity Green, and the first hawk-bats were already out, dipping down to pluck yammal-jells and coufee eels from the rolling whitecaps on Liberation Lake. On the far shore, the yorik coral bluffs that marked the edge of the park had grown purple and shadowed. Beyond them, the durasteel skeletons of the rising skytowers gleamed crimson in the setting sun. The planet remained as much Yuuzhan'tar as Coruscant, and in many ways that would never change. But it *was* at peace. For the first time in Luke Skywalker's life, the galaxy was truly not at war—and that counted for everything.

There were still problems, of course. There always would be, and today several senior Masters were struggling to address the chaos that Jaina and four other young Jedi Knights had caused by abruptly abandoning their duties and departing for the Unknown Regions.

"Lowbacca was the only one who completely understood the biomechanics of the *Maledoth*," Corran Horn was saying in his throaty voice. "So, as you can see, the Ramoan relocation project has ground to a complete standstill."

Luke reluctantly shifted his gaze from the viewport to the council room's speaking circle, where Corran stood using a laserwand to highlight the holographic projection of a huge Yuuzhan Vong slaveship. The Jedi order had been hoping to use the vessel to evacuate the population of a dying world.

Corran flicked the laserwand, and the holograph switched to the image of blast-pocked asteroid miner. "The situation in the Maltorian mining belt is deteriorating as well. Without Zekk there to lead the hunt, Three-Eye's pirates have the run of the system. Raw material shipments have fallen by fifty percent, and RePlanetHab is trying to buy them off."

"That's one circuit we need to kill now," Mara said. Seated in the chair next to Luke's, she was—as usual—the first to cut to the heart of the matter. That was one of the things Luke most admired about her; in a time when the smallest decision carried ramifications that even a Columi dejarik champion could not predict, his wife's instincts remained steady and true. "If rehab conglomerates start buying off pirates, we'll have marauders popping up all over the Core."

The other Masters voiced their agreement.

"Fine," Corran said. "Where do we find a replacement for Zekk?"

No one rushed to answer. The Jedi were spread too thin already, with most Jedi Knights—and even some apprentices—already assigned three tasks. And as the ranks of the greedy and the selfish grew ever more adept at manipulating the Galactic Alliance Senate, the situation seemed increasingly desperate.

Finally, Kyp Durron said, "The Solos should be finished on Borao soon." Dressed in threadbare cape and tunic, wearing his brown hair long and shaggy, Kyp looked as though he had just come in from a long mission. He always looked like that. "Maybe RePlanetHab will be patient if they know they're the Solos' next assignment."

The silence this time was even longer than the last. Strictly speaking, the Solos were not available for assignments. Han wasn't even a Jedi, and Leia's status was completely informal. The council just kept asking them to help out, they just kept doing it, and every Master in the room knew the order had been exploiting the Solos' selfless natures for far too long.

"Someone else needs to contact them," Mara finally said. "It's getting so bad that Leia cringes whenever she sees Luke's face on the holocomm."

"I can do it," Kyp offered. "I'm used to making Leia cringe."

"That takes care of Maltoria," Corran said. "Now, what about the Bothan ar'krai? Alema's last report suggested that Reh'mwa and his fundamentalists had a line on Zonama Sekot's location. They were provisioning the *Avengeance* for a scouting mission into the Unknown Regions."

A subtle eddy in the Force drew Luke's attention toward the entrance. He raised a hand to stop the discussion.

"Excuse me." He turned toward the foyer and immersed his mind completely in the Force until he recognized one of the presences coming toward them, then said, "Perhaps we should continue this later. We don't want Chief Omas to know how concerned we are about Jaina's departure."

"We don't?"

"No." Luke rose and started toward the door. "Especially not when he's bringing Chiss."

Luke stopped in the foyer area, where a simple wooden bench and two empty stone vases sat opposite the door, arranged to subtly calm visitors and make them feel welcome. Barely a moment passed before the door hissed open and a young apprentice came to a surprised halt directly in front of Luke.

"M-master S-skywalker!" the young Rodian stammered. He turned and raised and spindly-fingered hand toward the door. "Chief Omas and—"

"I know, Twool. Thank you."

Luke nudged the youth back into the corridor with the other apprentice, then stepped into the doorway and found himself looking at Chief of State Cal Omas and a trio of blue-skinned Chiss. With a wrinkled face and sagging jowls, the Chiss in front was probably the oldest Luke had ever seen. The two in the rear were clearly bodyguards—tall, strong, alert, and dressed in the black uniforms of the Chiss Expansionary Defense Fleet.

"Chief Omas," Luke said. The strains of Omas's office showed in his hollow cheeks and ashen complexion. "Welcome."

"You're expecting us." Omas cast a pointed glance into the conference room. "Good."

Luke ignored the hint and bowed to the elderly Chiss.

"And Aristocra . . ." It took a moment for the name to rise to the top of Omas's mind, where Luke could sense it without being overly intrusive. "Mitt'swe'kleoni. It's a pleasure to make your acquaintance."

The Chiss's red eyes narrowed to crimson lines. "Very impressive. It's not easy to gather identity files on Chiss aristocracy."

"We haven't." Luke smiled and continued to block the door. "You and your bodyguards are welcome to come inside, once you have removed your hidden weapons."

Omas cringed visibly, but Luke did not move. Even had he not perceived the concealed weapons through the Force, he still would have made the request. These *were* Chiss, after all.

"As you know," Luke continued, "the only weapons allowed in the Jedi Temple are lightsabers."

Mitt'swe'kleoni smiled like an old man caught sipping something against his doctor's orders, then pulled a small hold-out blaster from his boot and passed it to a bodyguard.

"My bodyguards will wait in the corridor," he said. "I can see they wouldn't be of much use in a room full of Jedi."

"There would be no need." Luke stepped aside and waved the two statesmen toward the conference circle. "Please join us."

As they crossed the room, Mitt'swe'kleoni kept sneaking glances at its appointments—the automated service kitchen, the small forest of rare trebala plants, the flowform chairs—and the arrogance vanished from his demeanor. It was not a reaction Luke liked to see. The new Temple had been a gift from the Galactic Alliance, pressed on the Jedi when—in a desperate attempt to manufacture a symbol of progress—the faltering Reconstruction Authority had moved the seat of government back to Coruscant. In most regards, the relocation had failed as spectacularly as it had deserved. But the Temple, a stone-and-transparisteel pyramid designed to harmonize with the new face of postwar Coruscant, never failed to impress with its regal scale and Rebirth architecture. It also served as a constant reminder to Luke of his greatest fear, that the Jedi would start to perceive themselves through the eyes of others and become little more than the guardians of a grateful Galactic Alliance.

At the conference area, the Jedi Masters rose to greet their guests.

"Everyone knows Chief Omas, I think." Luke motioned Omas into a chair, then took Mitt'swe'kleoni by the elbow and guided him into the sunken speaking circle. "This is Aristocra Mitt'swe'kleoni from the Chiss empire."

"Please use my core name, Tswek," the Aristocra instructed. "It will be much easier for you to pronounce correctly."

"Of course," Luke said, continuing to look at the council. "Tswek has some disturbing news for us, I believe."

Tswek's wrinkled brow rose, but he no longer seemed surprised by Luke's "intuition." "Then you know the purpose of my visit?"

"We can sense your apprehension through the Force," Luke said, avoiding a direct answer. "I assume it concerns our Jedi in the Unknown Regions."

"Indeed it does," he said. "The Chiss Ascendancy requires an explanation."

"An explanation?" Corran was not quite able to conceal his indignation. "Of what?"

Tswek pointedly ignored Corran and continued to stare at Luke.

"The Jedi have many voices, Aristocra," Luke said. "But we speak as one."

Tswek considered this a moment, then nodded. "Very well." He turned to Corran. "We demand an explanation of your actions, of course. What happens on our frontier is no concern of yours."

Despite the wave of confusion and doubt that rippled through the Force, the Jedi Masters remained outwardly composed.

"The *Chisz* frontier, Aristocra?" Saba Sebatyne, one of the newest Jedi Masters, asked.

"Of course." Tswek turned to the Barabel, his brow furrowed in thought. "You don't know what your Jedi Knights have been doing, do you?"

"All of our Jedi are well trained," Luke said to Tswek. "And the five under discussion are very experienced. We're confident they have good reason for any action they've undertaken."

A glint of suspicion showed in Tswek's crimson eyes. "So far, we have identified *seven* Jedi." He turned to Omas. "It appears I have no business here after all. Obviously, the Jedi involved in this matter are acting on their own."

"Involved in *what* matter?" Kyp asked.

"That is of no concern to the Galactic Alliance," Tswek said. He bowed to the council at large. "My apologies for taking so much of your time."

"No apologies are necessary," Luke said. He considered dropping the name of Chaf'orm'bintrani, an Aristocra he and Mara had met on a mission some years earlier, but it was impossible to know how this would be received. Chiss politics were as volatile as they were secretive, and for all Luke knew Formbi's had been one of the five ruling families that had mysteriously disappeared while the rest of the galaxy fought the Yuuzhan Vong. "Anything in which our Jedi Knights involve themselves concerns this council."

"Then I suggest you do a better job supervising them in the future," Tswek said. When Luke did not step out of his way, he turned to Omas. "I'm quite finished here, Chief."

"Of course." Omas shot Luke a look imploring him to stand aside, then said, "An escort will meet you at the Temple entrance. I believe I need to have a word with these Jedi."

"In that case, I'll thank you for your hospitality now." Tswek bowed to the Chief, then started for the door. "I'll be returning to the Ascendancy within the hour."

Omas waited until the Aristocra was gone, then scowled at Luke. "Well?"

Luke spread his hands. "At this point, Chief Omas, you know more than we do."

"I was afraid of that," Omas growled. "Apparently, a team of Jedi have involved themselves in a border dispute with the Chiss."

"How can that be?" Mara asked. Luke knew that she meant the question literally. Before departing, Jaina had sent the council a set of destination coordinates that she and the others had calculated by triangulating the direction from which the mysterious call had come. An astronomical reconnaissance had revealed not even a star in the area, and certainly no indication that the coordinates would be of interest to the Chiss. "Their destination was over a hundred light-years from Ascendancy space."

"Then our Jedi *are* out there," Omas said. "What in the blazes for? We can't spare *one* Jedi at the moment, much less seven."

Mara's green eyes looked ready to loose a stream of blaster bolts. "*Our* Jedi, Chief Omas?"

"Forgive me." The Chief's voice was more placating than apologetic; Luke knew that, in his heart, Omas considered the Jedi as much servants of the Galactic Alliance as he was. "I didn't mean to imply anything."

"Of course not," Mara said, in a tone that suggested he had better be serious. She turned to the rest of the council. "Mitt'swe'kleoni said *seven* Jedi. What do we make of that?"

"This one only countz five." Saba lifted her hand and began to raise her taloned fingers. "Jaina, Alema, Zekk, Lowbacca, and Tesar."

Kyp added two fingers. "Tekli and Tahiri?"

Omas frowned. "How could you know that? I thought they were with Zonama Sekot in the Unknown Regions."

"They're supposed to be," Corran said. "But, like the others, they're also Myrkr survivors."

"I don't understand," Omas said. "What does this have to do with the Myrkr mission?"

"I wish we knew," Luke said. Undertaken in the middle of the war with the Yuuzhan Vong, the Myrkr mission had been as costly as it had been successful. Anakin Solo and his strike team had destroyed the enemy's Jedi-killing voxyn. But six young Jedi Knights had died in the process—including Anakin himself—and another was missing and presumed lost. "All I can tell you is that for several weeks, Jaina and the other survivors of that mission reported feeling a 'call' from the Unknown Regions. On the day they left, that call became a cry for help."

"And since we know Tenel Ka is still on Hapes," Mara explained, "it seems likely the extra Jedi are Tekli and Tahiri."

Nobody suggested that Jaina's brother, Jacen, might be one of the extras. The last anyone had heard, he had been somewhere on the far side of the galaxy, sequestered with the Fallanassi.

"What *about* Zonama Sekot?" Omas asked. Zonama Sekot was the living planet that had agreed to serve as home to the defeated Yuuzhan Vong. "Could the call have come from it?"

Luke shook his head. "Zonama Sekot would have contacted me directly if it needed our help. I'm convinced this has something to do with the mission to Myrkr."

Omas stayed silent, waiting for more of an explanation, but that was all Luke knew.

Instead, Luke asked, "What did Mitt'swe'kleoni tell you?"

Omas shrugged. "He demanded to know why the Galactic Alliance had sent its Jedi—*his* words—to interfere in a Chiss border dispute. When he saw how surprised I was, he demanded to speak to you."

"This is bad," Mara said. "Very bad."

"I agree," Omas said. "Either he thinks we're all lying—"

"Or he believez our Jedi Knightz have gone rogue," Saba finished. "In either case, the result will be the same."

"They'll try to solve the problem themselves," Omas said. He ran a hand through his thinning hair. "How hard will this be on them?"

"Our Jedi Knights can take care of themselves," Luke said.

"I know *that*!" Omas snapped. "I'm asking about the Chiss."

Luke felt Mara's ire rise, but she chose to overlook Omas's tone and remain silent. Now was a poor time to remind him that the Jedi did not expect to be addressed as though they were unruly subordinates.

"If the Chiss take action against them, Jaina and the others will attempt to defuse the situation . . . for a time," Luke said. "After that, it depends on the nature of the conflict."

"But they won't hesitate to meet force with force," Mara clarified. "Nor would we ask them to. If the Chiss push things, sooner or later Jaina is going to bloody their noses."

Omas paled and turned to Luke. "You need to put a stop to this, and soon. We can't let it come to killing."

Luke nodded. "We'll certainly send someone to—"

"No, I mean *you* personally." Omas turned to the others. "I know the Jedi have their own way of doing things. But with Jaina Solo leading those young Jedi Knights, Luke is the only one who can be sure of bringing them home. That young woman is as headstrong as her father."

For once, nobody argued.

TWO

A silver splinter shot across the *Falcon*'s bow, three kilometers ahead and hanging just below the clouds, then disappeared into a fog bank almost before Han Solo realized what he had seen.

"Did you see that?" As Han spoke, he kept both hands on the control yoke. With fangs of gray mist dangling beneath a low gray sky and spires of vine-covered yorik coral rising from a floor of undulating forest, Borao was a dangerous planet to map. Deadly, even. "What's another ship doing here? You told me this planet was abandoned."

"It is abandoned, dear." Leia glanced at the console in front of the copilot's seat, then shook her head in disgust at the static-filled array. "The sensors can't get a reading through these ionized clouds, but we *know* what kind of vessel that was."

"And you say *I* jump to conclusions!" Despite Han's protest, his heart was sinking. Since the Derelict Planet Reclamation Act had passed, there seemed to be more survey ships in the galaxy than stars. "It could have been a smuggler or a pirate, you know. A place like this would make a good hideout."

Leia studied her display screen for a moment, then shook her head. "Not a chance. Have a look."

The view from the stern vidcam appeared on his display, showing the knobby little cone of a Koensayr mapping skiff. It was in the middle of his screen, dead center.

"He's following us!"

"So it would seem," Leia answered. "The good news is he hasn't been there long, or I'd have seen him. With our long-range sensors blinded, I've had the exterior cam views rotating across my display."

"Good thinking." Han smiled at Leia's reflection in the cockpit canopy. She had thrown herself into her role as the *Falcon*'s second in command with the same devotion she brought to everything she did, and now a finer YT-1300 copilot could not be found anywhere. But there was an uneasy tension beneath her regal bearing, a restlessness in her big brown eyes that sometimes made the post seem too small for her. And Han understood. Any woman who had inspired a rebellion and shepherded a galactic government through its infancy might find life a little cramped aboard a tramp freighter—even if she had too much class to say so. "That's what I love about you."

Leia smiled brightly. "Smart as well as beautiful?"

Han shook his head. "You're a really good copilot." He pushed the throttles forward, and the forested ridges below began to flash past in a verdant blur. "Maximize the rear shields. Koensayr just delivered a fleet of armed mappers to RePlanetHab, so things might get rough."

Leia only stared at the throttles. "Han, what the blazes are you doing?"

"I'm tired of getting kicked around by these RePlanetHab pilots. It makes me look old."

"Don't be ridiculous," Leia said. "You're barely in your mid-sixties."

"That's my point," Han said. "Just because a guy goes a little gray at the temples, people think he's slowing down. They think they can push him around—"

"Han, nobody thinks you're slowing down." Leia's voice grew soft. "You have at least forty good years left. Maybe even fifty, if you take care of yourself."

A prim electronic voice sounded from the comm station behind Leia. "And may I point out how difficult it would be to see the gray in your hair from another vessel?" C-3PO leaned forward, pushing his golden head into Han's peripheral vision. "Whatever the reason other pilots have for thinking you've slowed down, sir, I'm quite sure your hair color has nothing to do with it."

"Thanks, Threepio," Han growled. "Maybe you ought to disconnect those vocabulator circuits before someone probes them with a plasma torch."

"A plasma torch!" C-3PO cried. "Why would anyone do that?"

Han ignored the droid and took the *Falcon* into a wisp of low-hanging cloud. Normally, he would have circled around it to avoid the small risk of hitting one of the strange spires the Yuuzhan Vong had left scattered across the planet. But that would have required a second mapping run around the other side, and they simply did not have the time—not if they wanted to beat these claim jumpers at their own game.

When the *Falcon* came out the other side without crashing into anything, their passenger gasped in relief and pushed his T-shaped head between the seats.

"Captain Solo, there is no sense placing your ship at risk." Ezam Nhor spoke with the mouths on both sides of his arched neck, giving his Ithorian voice a mournful stereo quality. "DPRA regulations state that when two parties file simultaneous claims, the Reconstruction Authority must give preference to the one with greater resources. My people do not have the means to match even a small rehabitation conglomerate, much less one like RePlanetHab."

"You're young, so maybe you don't know this," Han retorted. "But I don't usually obey regulations."

An uneasy wheeze shot from both sides of the Ithorian's throat.

Leia laid her hand over Han's. "Han, I hate losing to these world grabbers as much as you do, but Ezam is right. The Ithorians don't have—"

"Look, we can do this," Han said. A vast fog bank appeared on the horizon, its misty hem dragging in the treetops. "Borao isn't an easy world to map, and we have a big head start."

"And?"

"And the Reconstruction Authority has to log every claim it receives." Han eased the control yoke back and started to climb above the oncoming fog bank. Risking a small wisp of cloud was one thing, but even he would not fly blind through who-knew-how-many kilometers of dense fog. "If I can talk Lando into sponsoring us, we still have a chance. All we have to do is transmit our map first."

Leia remained silent.

"Okay, so it's a small chance," Han said. "But it's better than nothing. And it's not like we haven't bet on long-shots before."

"Han—"

"Besides, maybe Luke can swing us some support from Cal Omas," he added. "That would—"

"Han!" Leia laid her hand on his and pushed the control yoke forward again, ending their climb. "We don't have time to waste recalibrating the terrain scanners."

"Are you crazy?" He studied the atmosphere ahead with a nervous eye. "You are. You're crazy."

"I thought you wanted to win this thing?"

"I do," Han said. "And to do that, we need to stay alive."

"Captain Solo makes an excellent point," C-3PO said. "Without our sensors working properly, our chances of hitting an abandoned watchtower in those clouds are approximately—"

"Don't quote me odds, Threepio," Leia said. "I need to concentrate."

She focused her attention on the gray curtain ahead, and whorls of fog began to peel away from the center. Han started to make a wisecrack about having a weather-Jedi for a copilot, then recalled what Leia had said to C-3PO and thought better of it. Her training was still casual at best, and if she said she needed to concentrate, it was probably smart to believe her.

By the time they reached the fog bank, Leia had opened a long channel down the center—a very narrow channel, not much wider than the *Falcon* itself.

C-3PO's electronic voice split the tense silence. "Oh, my!"

"Quiet, Threepio!" Han barked. "Leia needs to concentrate."

"I'm aware of that, Captain Solo, but the route she is clearing has opened a small path through the ionic interference. We seem to be receiving an insystem comm transmission from Master Durron."

"Take a message," Han ordered. In the canopy reflection, he saw a furrow crease Leia's brow, and blankets of fog started to spill back into the channel. "And stop bothering us!"

"I'm sorry, Captain Solo, that's quite impossible. The ionic interference seems to be returning, and our reception is too distorted for me to record. If you were to climb a few hundred meters, I could use the static scrubbers to enhance the signal."

"Not now!" The fog closed in completely. Unable to see past the end of the cockpit anyway, Han looked over to Leia. "If this is too much—"

"It's not too much, if you'll just leave me alone!" she snapped. "Do you want to win this thing or not?"

"All right. No need to get touchy."

Han turned his gaze forward, and the fog parted again.

"Much better," C-3PO said. "Thank you, Princess Leia. Master Durron seems quite upset."

Kyp's voice came over the comm speakers, scratchy and distorted. ". . . melt your circuits from the inside!"

"Take it easy, kid. You're on," Han said. "And this had better be good."

"When are you going to stop calling me kid?" Kyp asked.

"Soon," Han promised. "Look, we're kind of busy here, so if that's all you need to know—"

"Sorry," Kyp said. "I wish this could wait, but I'm only passing through on my way to Ramodi."

"The baradium ring?" Han asked. "I thought Tesar Sebatyne was supposed to handle that."

"*Supposed to* is right." Kyp paused a moment. "Something came up."

"Bigger than smuggling baradium?"

"Hard to say," Kyp said. "When you're done here, the council needs you and Leia to take over in the Maltorian system."

"Nice of them to ask," Han grumbled into the comm mike.

"That's what I'm doing now," Kyp said. "The council doesn't give orders—especially to you two."

"Could've fooled me," Han said. "What happened to Zekk? Is he okay?"

There was a long pause, and Han thought they might have lost the signal.

"Kyp?"

"Zekk's fine," Kyp said. "But something came up, and he had to leave."

Alarms started to go off inside Han's head. Jaina had told them about the mysterious call that she and the other strike team members had been feeling from the Unknown Regions.

"Listen"—Kyp's voice crackled over the comm—"we didn't want to ask you again, but this is important. RePlanetHab is about ready to start paying Three-Eye off."

"I'll have to talk it over with Leia." Given who was currently trying to steal Borao out from beneath them, Han was not sure either one of them would be eager to help RePlanetHab with its pirate problem. "Redstar's tribunal ought to be just about over, and we were hoping to catch up with Jaina for a few days before she goes out again."

There was another long silence, and this time Han decided to wait Kyp out. A blurry sliver of green murk appeared at the end of the fog channel that Leia was holding open. Her gaze remained dead ahead. Han hoped that she was actually seeing; that she had not sunk so deeply into her trance, she would fail to notice the hazy stripe of darkness ahead.

Finally, Kyp said, "Uh, seeing Jaina might be a problem."

"Don't tell me," Han said. "Something came up." The hazy strip ahead thickened into a sharp, distinct streak. "Something in the Unknown Regions, I'll bet."

"Well . . . yes."

"Thanks for letting us know," Han snorted. Normally, he tried not to worry about Jaina's assignments. As a top fighter pilot and leading Jedi Knight, his daughter could handle almost anything the galaxy threw her way. But the Unknown Regions were different. The Unknown Regions were home to a hundred terrors too terrible to imagine—or so he had been told. "What's the situation?"

"We don't know, exactly," Kyp said. "But there's no reason to worry. Master Skywalker has taken Mara and Saba to investigate."

Now Han *was* worried. To draw three Masters away when the Jedi were already spread too thin, the problem had to be serious.

"All right, kid," Han said. The dark streak at the end of the fog channel had grown sharp enough to identify as a yorik coral spire. "What *aren't* you telling us?"

"Nothing."

Han remained silent, and finally Kyp asked, "Did I mention the Chiss?"

To Leia's credit, she did not look away from the forward viewport—but she did lose her concentration. The fog came rolling back into the channel ahead of the *Falcon,* and Han lost sight of the spire. He jerked back on the throttles . . . then felt a sudden stab of neck pain as something slammed the ship forward. A cacophony of damage alarms erupted from the control console. Han's gaze flew to the status lights of the most critical systems.

"What was that?" Nhor asked from behind him. "Did we crash?"

"Not exactly," Han answered. Over the comm, he said, "Stand by, kid. We're a little distracted here."

"Copy." Kyp sounded relieved to have a few moments to formulate his explanation. "Take your time."

Once Han had confirmed that all vital components were still operational, he called up the view from the stern vidcam and saw nothing but static.

"Something hit us from behind."

"The mapping skiff?" Leia asked.

"It *was* following us," Han said. "I hate that."

"Oh, dear," C-3PO said. "I hope there aren't any casualties!"

"It would serve them right," Han growled. He activated the intercom and ordered Leia's Noghri bodyguards, Cakhmaim and Meewalh, into the cannon turrets. "Don't shoot anything. Just tell me what you see back there."

Han glanced over at Leia and saw by the tension in her lips that she had heard every word of the conversation between him and Kyp. He closed the intercom, then returned to his comm mike.

"Okay, kid. Tell us about the Chiss."

"It's not as bad as it sounds." Kyp told them about Aristocra Tswek's visit and Cal Omas's "suggestion" that Luke handle the matter personally, and then said, "Master Skywalker knew you'd be worried, so he asked Cilghal to fill you in when you asked for the Maltorian dossier. I really wasn't—"

The *Falcon* shuddered, and another damage alarm sounded. Cakhmaim reported that, despite its damage, the mapping skiff was firing at them.

"Then shoot back!" Han ordered. "Kyp, you'll have to—"

"Standing by," Kyp acknowledged. "Be careful."

"I've got a better idea." Han pushed the throttles forward and accelerated into the fog, then asked Leia, "Can you do that fog thing again?"

"Yes," Leia said. A low rumble reverberated through the *Falcon* as Meewalh and Cakhmaim unleashed the big laser cannons. "But why not climb out of here and fight where we can see?"

Han allowed himself a sly grin. "Didn't you see that spire up ahead?"

"I saw it," Leia said. A smile as sly as Han's came to her lips. "I like the way you think, flyboy."

"How does he think?" Nhor asked. "What are we doing?"

"You'll see," Han said. "Just hold on."

Leia turned her attention back to the fog, and soon the verdant finger of a vine-covered spire could be seen jutting up at the end of the channel. If Han did not break until the last second, the mapping skiff following them would have no time to avoid a crash.

Nhor finally saw what they were planning.

"No!" He shrieked the word with both mouths. "You mustn't! Tell your gunners to stop firing!"

"Stop firing?" Han repeated. The spire was as wide as his hand now, and he was beginning to see dark patches of coral showing through the curtains of vine. "Are you crazy? They're shooting at *us*."

"It doesn't matter." Nhor's voice remained shrill with panic. "My people could never inhabit a planet won through murder."

"It's not murder," Han objected. "They started this. We're just defending ourselves."

"There is a difference between defending and killing," Nhor said.

Han began to grow impatient. "Look, if that's the way you feel, the Ithorians are never going to find a planet." The spire had grown as large as his arm; another five seconds, and the mapping skiff wouldn't have a chance. "In this galaxy, you've got to fight for what you need."

"My people believe there has been too much fighting already." Nhor paused, then said, "This isn't your choice to make, Captain Solo. If you kill our rivals, the Ithorians will not come anyway."

"Han, Ezam's right," Leia said. Her gaze remained fixed on the fog, but she reached over and gently clasped his arm. "We just can't win this one."

Han could hear in the edginess of Leia's voice that she wanted to keep going as much as he did. The war had made both of them harder—less forgiving and more determined to win at any price— and sometimes that made him wonder if the Yuuzhan Vong had won after all. Certainly, they had changed more in the galaxy than a few thousand planets.

"Okay." Han pulled the control yoke back, and the *Falcon* began to climb free of Borao's clouds. "The world grabbers win again."

"Sorry to hear that," Kyp said over the comm. "But you'll have a freer rein in the Maltorian belt. There are no gray areas with Three-Eye."

"Not so fast, kid. We haven't said we're going."

"But Jaina—"

"Is in the Unknown Regions," Han said. "That's the point. Give us a second."

Leia muted the comm mikes, then asked, "What are you thinking?"

"You *know* what I'm thinking," Han said. Though he would never have said so, Han wished he had gone after Anakin to Myrkr. He knew it would have made no difference and maybe even gotten them both killed, but he still wished he had tried. "You're thinking the same thing."

"I suppose I am." Leia sighed. "You know there's no sense going after them."

"Them?" Han asked. "Jaina and Lowie and—"

"And Jacen." Leia's eyes were closed, and her face was raised toward the stars. "It feels like he's on the move, too."

"*Another* reason to go," Han said. "Five years is too long."

"You know we'd just be going for ourselves," Leia said. "Our kids are better at this sort of thing than we are now."

"Yeah," Han said. "But what else do we have to do? Stick our necks out for RePlanetHab? Look for another abandoned planet just so they can steal it out from under the Ithorians?"

Leia closed her eyes, perhaps reaching out to their children through the Force, or maybe only searching her own heart for guidance. Finally, she opened her eyes again and reactivated the channel.

"Sorry, Kyp, we can't help you," she said. "Han and I have other plans."

THREE

The unknown object lay directly ahead of *Jade Shadow*, a crooked oval of darkness the size of a human thumb. Sensor readings suggested a body about as dense as ice, which would have been a rare—though not impossible—thing to find floating around loose in the interstellar void. But infrared measurements placed the core temperature at somewhere between warm and sweltering, and the spectrograph showed a halo of escaped atmosphere that suggested living inhabitants.

Mara had already sensed as much through the Force. She could feel a strange presence within the object, diffuse and ancient and utterly huge. There were also other, more familiar life-forms—smaller, distinct, and somehow enclosed within the haze of the larger being. But there was no hint of Jaina or the other strike team members, nor of the urgent summons they had reported from these coordinates.

Mara glanced at an activation reticle in the front of the cockpit. A small section of the *Shadow*'s plexalloy canopy opaqued into a mirror, and she turned her attention to Luke and Saba Sebatyne, who were seated high behind her in the copilot's and navigator's chairs.

"Time to reconnoiter?" she asked.

"What's reckon . . . recoin . . . wreckoy . . . ?" The question came from behind Luke's chair, where a freckle-faced boy with red hair and fiery blue eyes stood peering around the edge of the flight deck hatchway. "What's that?"

"*Reconnoiter*, Ben. It means take a look." A smile came to Mara's heart at the sight of her son, but she forced a stern tone. "Aren't you supposed to be playing with Nanna?"

"Nanna's game module is for little kids," he complained. "She was trying to make me play Teeks and Ewoks."

"And why aren't you?" Luke asked.

"I turned her off."

"How?" Mara asked. "Her power switch is hidden under her neck armor."

Ben looked away as casually as a young boy could. "I tricked her into bending down and showing it to me."

"Turning Nanna off wasn't very nice," Mara said. "Her circuits are pulse-shielded. How do you think she's going to feel after an emergency shutdown?"

"Stupid." Ben's answer was almost gleeful. "I've only done it to her three times before."

A loud siss of amusement escaped the pebbled lips of Saba Sebatyne, causing Ben to shrink back through the hatchway—and almost muffling Luke's exclamation of alarm. "You have?"

Ben nodded, but his wide eyes remained fixed on Saba's lumpy face. Luke reached around the corner and pulled him onto the flight deck itself.

"Promise me you won't do that again," Luke said. Mara could feel how worried he was by Ben's mischievousness. They had long ago decided against having someone else raise their son while they crisscrossed the galaxy attending to their duties as Jedi Masters, but they both knew their choice would require an extraordinary amount of discipline from their young son. "Nanna can't protect you if you shut her down."

"If she's that stupid, how can she protect me anyway?" Ben countered. "A Defender Droid's not supposed to be dumber than her kid."

Rather than explaining the complexities of utter-devotion programming, Mara said, "Ben, answer your father. Or would you rather stay at the academy next time he and I go on a trip?"

Ben pondered his decision for a moment, then blew out a long breath. "Fine." He turned to Luke. "I promise."

"Good," Luke said. "Maybe you should go reactivate her."

"But we're *there*!" Ben pointed out the forward viewport, where the unknown object remained hidden in its darkness. "I want to see Jaina!"

"Jaina isn't here anymore," Mara said.

"How do you know?"

"The Force," Mara explained. "If she were here, your father and I would feel it."

"Maybe not. You don't feel everything."

"We would feel Jaina," Luke said. "She's not here."

"Now do as your father says." Mara hooked her thumb toward the main cabin. "Go power up Nanna and stay with her until we figure out where Jaina is."

Ben didn't argue, but neither did he turn to go.

"If Ben doesn't wish to go, this one will watch him." Saba spun her chair around and winked a slit-pupiled eye at him. "He can sit on her lap."

Eyes widening, Ben spun on his heel and disappeared down the access corridor. Saba sissed in amusement, but softly and slow, and Mara thought maybe the Barabel's feelings were hurt. Maybe.

"Don't let it bother you, Saba," Mara said. "Even we don't understand what's happening with him these days."

Saba blinked at Mara's reflection—twice. "He is hiding from the Force," she said. "This one is surprised you and Master Skywalker have not noticed."

"We have," Luke said. "What we don't understand is why. He started to close himself off after the war."

"Ben says he wants to be like his uncle Han and do things the hard way," Mara added. "But I think there's more to it than that. This has lasted too long to be a phase."

Mara did not add *and he's gotten too good at it,* perhaps because of how much that thought frightened her. She had to concentrate hard and long to find the Force in her son, and sometimes Luke had trouble sensing Ben's presence at all.

"Interesting." Saba licked the air with her long tongue, then turned to look down the access corridor. "Perhapz he did not like how the war felt."

"Perhaps not," Luke said. "We tried to shield him from it, but it just wasn't possible."

"There was too much happening in the galaxy," Mara said, surprised to find herself feeling almost defensive. "The Force was too filled with anguish."

"And so were we," Luke said. "That's what really worries us, Saba . . . maybe he's hiding from *us.*"

"Then you have nothing to worry about," Saba said. "Ben will not hide from you forever. Even this one can see how attached he is to his parentz."

Luke thanked her for the reassurance, then asked R2-D2 to bring up an infrared image of the unknown object. What looked like a collection of palpitating blood cells appeared on Mara's display screen. Each cell had an irregular white heart surrounded by a pink halo, and they were all connected by a tangled web of flowing red dashes.

"It looks like a network of housing modules," Mara observed.

"And it feelz like a rangi mountain," Saba added.

"Now we're getting somewhere," Luke said. "By the way, what *are* rangies?"

"Very tasty—and the feeling is mutual!" Sissing hysterically, Saba rose and turned to leave the flight deck. "This one will take the StealthX and reconnoiter."

"Better hold tight," Mara said. On the infrared display, a string of tiny white circles was flaring to life near the center of the unknown object. "At least until we know what those are."

The circles began to swirl and grow larger. Mara didn't even try to count the number, but there had to be over a hundred of them. More tiny circles blazed into existence and shot after the others. She initiated a series of automated systems checks to warm the *Shadow*'s battle circuits.

"Lower—"

The *Shadow*'s retractable laser cannons dropped into firing position as Luke anticipated Mara's order. She armed the proton torpedoes and opened the firing-tube doors.

"Artoo, tell Nanna to put Ben in his crash couch," Luke ordered.

R2-D2 tweetled a protest.

"Nobody said they *were* shooting," Luke said. "We just want to be ready."

R2-D2 added another warning.

"Really?" Luke responded. "That many?"

Mara glanced at the corner of her display and saw a counter quickly adding numbers.

"Five hundred?" she gasped. "Who sends five hundred craft to investigate one intruder?"

R2-D2 chirped testily, then Mara's screen displayed a message telling her to have some patience. He was still trying to assemble vessel profiles. Identifying who had sent them would have to wait.

"Sorry," Mara said, wondering when she had started to be intimidated by astromech droids. "Take your time."

R2-D2 acknowledged, then added a note about the propulsion systems the vessels were using.

"Rockets?" Luke asked in disbelief. "As in old nuclear rockets?"

R2-D2 tweeted irritably. The note on Mara's display read, *Chemical rockets. Methane/oxygen, specific impulse 380.*

Luke whistled at the low number. "At least we can run, if we have to."

"Jedi?" Saba began to siss again. "Run?"

The image on Mara's display melded into a single infrared blob. She looked up and saw a small cloud of twinkling stars between the *Shadow* and the unknown object. As she watched, the swirling cloud grew steadily larger and brighter. Soon the stars resolved into two parts, yellow slivers of rocket exhaust and brilliant green bursts that looked a lot like strobe beacons.

Mara engaged the ion drive actuator. "Does this make sense to *anyone*?" She began to turn, giving the *Shadow* some running room. "With all that evasive maneuvering, that *has* to be a combat—"

R2-D2 began to whistle and trill urgently.

Mara checked her display, then asked, "What old blink code?"

R2-D2 buzzed in impatience.

"*Imperial?*" Mara looked out the side of the canopy. The swarm had drawn close enough now to reveal the sleek, dart-shaped hulls of a small fighter craft stretched between the green nose strobes and the yellow rocket tails. In the closest vessel, she could barely make out a pair of curved antennae pressed against the interior of a low cockpit canopy, and there were two bulbous black eyes peering out at her. "As in *Palpatine's* Empire?"

R2-D2 squawked a peevish affirmative.

"Then tell us what they're saying," Luke ordered. "And stop talking to Mara that way."

R2-D2 warbled a halfhearted apology, then the message appeared on Mara's display.

Lizil welcomes you . . . Please all arrivals may please enter through the central portal please.

FOUR

The nearer the *Falcon* drew to her destination, the more mystified Leia became. The thumb-sized oval of darkness they had found when they emerged from hyperspace—at the coordinates they had wheedled out of Corran Horn, who was supervising operations in Luke's absence—was now a wall of murk that stretched to all edges of the cockpit canopy. But the terrain scanners showed a jumble of asteroids, iceballs, and dustbergs ranging from a hundred meters across to several thousand, all held together by a web of metal struts and stony tubes. Though the structure had not yet collapsed under its own gravity, a rough guess of its mass was enough to make Leia worry.

The *Falcon*'s escorts—a swarm of small dartships being flown by *something* with antennae and big, bulbous eyes—suddenly peeled off and dispersed into the surrounding darkness. A jagged array of lights came to life ahead, hooking along its length toward a single golden light at the end.

"That must be the guidance signal the dartships told us to watch for," Leia said. The terrain schematic on her display showed the lights curving over the horizon of a small carbonaceous asteroid located on the cluster's outer edge. "Follow the amber light. And slow down—it could be dangerous in there."

"In where?"

Leia sent a duplicate of the terrain schematic to the pilot's display. Han decelerated so hard that even the inertial compensators could not keep her from being pitched into her crash webbing.

"You sure about this?" he asked. "It looks about as safe as a rancor's throat down there."

The image on their displays was that of a jagged five-kilometer mouth surrounded by a broken rim of asteroids, with dark masses of dust and stone tumbling down into the opening in lazy slow motion. Though the scanner's view extended only two thousand meters into the chasm, the part it did show was a twisted, narrowing shaft lined by craggy protrusions and dark voids.

"I'm sure." Leia could feel her brother's presence somewhere deep inside the jumble of asteroids, calm, cheerful, and curious. "Luke knows we're here. He wants us to come in."

"Really?" Han turned the *Falcon* toward the lights and started forward. "What'd we ever do to *him*?"

As they passed over the array, Leia began to catch glimpses of a black, grainy surface carefully cleared of the dark dust that usually lay meters thick on carbonaceous asteroids. Once, she thought she saw something scuttling across a circle of light, but Han was keeping them too far above the asteroid to be certain, and it would have been too dangerous to ask him to go in for a closer look. She trained a vidcam on the surface and tried to magnify the image, but the shaft was too dusty and dark for a clear picture. All she saw was a screenful of gray grains not too different from sensor static.

They were barely past the first array when two more came to life, beckoning the *Falcon* deeper into the abyss. The ship bucked as Han avoided—only half successfully—a tumbling dustberg, then a frightened hiss escaped Leia's lips as the jagged silhouettes of two small boulders began to swell in the forward viewport.

"Don't sit there hissing." Han's gaze remained fixed on his display, where the resolution of the terrain schematic was not fine enough to show the two objects. "Tell me what's wrong."

"There!" Leia pointed out the viewport. "Right there!"

Han looked up from his display.

"All right, no need to get all worried." He calmly flipped the *Falcon* on her side and slipped between the two boulders an instant before the pair came together, then went back to watching his display. "I had my eye on them."

Han's voice was so cocky and sure that Leia forgot for a moment that this was not the same brash smuggler who had been running her defenses since she was still fighting the Empire—the man whose lopsided grins and well-timed barbs could still raise in her a ruddy cloud of passion or a red fog of anger. He was wiser now, and sadder, maybe a little less likely to hide his goodwill behind a cynical exterior.

"Whatever you say, flyboy." Leia pointed at the light arrays, the ones she had decided would be too dangerous to investigate. "I want to do a close pass on one of those."

Han's eyes widened. "What for?"

"To see what kind of technology we're dealing with here." Leia put on a flirtatious pout, then asked in an innocent voice, "That isn't too risky for you, is it?"

"For me?" Han licked his lips. "No way."

Leia smiled and, as Han angled toward the array, shunted extra power to the particle shields. Maybe the challenge of nap-of-terrain flying down a dark, twisting shaft filled with flotsam would help snap Han out of his touchy mood.

Han weaved past a dozen obstacles, working their way across the abyss toward the second array of lights . . . and that was when C-3PO, returning from a postjump hyperdrive check, arrived on the flight deck.

"We're crashing!"

"Not yet," Han growled.

"Everything's under control, Threepio." Leia's attention was focused on the asteroid ahead, where the lights had begun a slow flashing as the *Falcon* approached. "Why don't you go back and continue supervising the maintenance checks?"

"I couldn't possibly, Princess Leia!" C-3PO placed himself in the navigator's chair behind Han. "You need me in the cockpit."

Han started to reply, but stopped when a ball of frozen gas came floating across the *Falcon*'s path.

"You see?" C-3PO demanded. "Captain Solo nearly missed that object!"

"I *did* miss it," Han snapped. "Otherwise you'd be plastered across the canopy right now."

"What I meant was that you failed to see it until the last moment," C-3PO explained. "Do be careful—there's a rather large one coming toward us from forty-seven point six-six-eight—"

"Quiet!" Han swung around an oblong megalith the size of a heavy cruiser, then added, "You're distracting me."

"Then perhaps you should have your synapses checked," C-3PO suggested. "Slow processing time is indicative of aging circuits. There's another object at thirty-two point eight-seven-eight degrees, inclination five point—"

"Threepio!" Leia spun around to glare at him. "We don't need help. Go to the main cabin and shut down."

C-3PO's chin dropped. "As you wish, Princess Leia." He stood and half turned toward the exit. "I was only trying to help. Captain

Solo's last medical evaluation showed a reaction time decrease of eight milliseconds, and I myself have noticed—"

Leia unbuckled her crash webbing.

"—that he seems to be growing—"

She rose and hit the droid's circuit breaker.

"—rather hesiii t a a a."

The sentence trailed off into a bass rumble as C-3PO lost power.

"I think it's time to get his compliance routines debugged." She pushed the droid into the seat in front of the navigation station and strapped him in. "He seems to be developing a persistence glitch."

"No need." The *Falcon* shot to the right, then shuddered as a dustberg burst against its shields. "Nobody listens to droids anyway."

"Right—what does Threepio know?" Leia kissed Han on the neck, then returned to her own seat.

"Yeah." Han smiled the same hungry grin that had been making Leia's stomach flutter since Palpatine was Emperor.

Han swung the *Falcon* in behind the lights and began a steep approach toward the surface. The array began to flash more brightly, illuminating the rough, silvery surface of a metallic asteroid. On the ground behind the first beacon, Leia saw the swirling lines of a closed iris hatch, made from some tough membrane that bulged slightly outward under the pressure of the asteroid's internal atmosphere. The light itself was held aloft on the end of a conical, meterlong stand that seemed to be crawling across the surface of the asteroid on six stick-like legs. At the forward end of the apparatus, the lenses of a large ovoid helmet reflected the glow of the next beacon in line.

"Bugs!" Han groaned and shook his head. "Why did it have to be bugs?"

"Sorry," Leia said. Han normally avoided insect nests—something to do with a water religion he had once started on the desert world of Kamar. Apparently, a mob of angry Kamarian insects had tracked him down months after his hasty departure, taking him captive and demanding that he turn Kamar into the water paradise he had shown them. That was all Leia knew about the incident. He refused to talk about how he had escaped. "It'll be okay. Luke seems to feel comfortable with them."

"Yeah, well, I always knew the guy was a little strange."

"Han, we have to go in," Leia said. "This is where Jaina and the others came."

"I know," Han said. "That's what *really* gives me the creeps."

They reached the end of the array and passed over the insect holding aloft the amber light; then Leia glimpsed a second iris hatch and they left the asteroid behind. Far ahead, spiraling down the walls of the ever-narrowing passage, three more beacon lines flared to life. Han stayed close to the walls, showing off for Leia by following the contour of the conglomeration's unpredictable topography.

After a time, the arrays began to grow hazy and indistinct as the dust, being slowly drawn inward by the conglomeration's weak gravity, thickened into a gray cloud. Han continued to hug the wall, though now it was to make it easier for the terrain scanner to penetrate the powdery fog.

A nebulous disk of golden light appeared at the bottom of the shaft. As its glow brightened, Leia began to see meter-long figures in insect-shaped pressure suits working along the passage walls, dragging huge bundles across asteroid surfaces, repairing the stony tubes that held the jumbled structure together, or simply standing in a shallow basin and staring out at her from behind a transparent membrane.

"You know, Han," she said, "this place is starting to give *me* the creeps."

"Wait till you hear a pincer rap," Han said. "Those things will really ice your spine."

"Pincer rap?" Leia glanced over at the pilot's seat, wondering if there was something Han wasn't telling her. "Han, do you recognize—"

Han cut her off. "No—I'm just saying . . ." He raised his shoulders and shuddered at some memory he had kept buried their entire married life, then finished, "It's not something you want to experience. That's all."

The dust cloud finally began to thin, revealing the disk of light below to be a bulging hatch membrane more than a hundred meters across. Several dozen insects were scuttling away from the middle of the hatch, oozing a thick layer of greenish gel from a valve at the rear of their pressure suits. Han eased back on the throttles, then—when the portal showed no sign of opening—brought them to a stop twenty meters above the center.

The insects reached the edge and turned around, the lenses of their dark helmets turned up toward the *Falcon*. Soon, the gel began to bleed off in green wisps.

"What are they waiting for?" Han turned his palms up and gestured impatiently. "Open already!"

Once the gel had evaporated, the insects returned to the center of the portal and began to mill about aimlessly.

"Is there *anything* on the comm channels?" Han asked.

Leia double-checked the channel scanner. "Only background static—and not much of that." She did not suggest trying to comm the *Shadow*. Some insect species were sensitive to comm waves, a fact that had led to some tragic misunderstandings in the early days of contact between the Verpine and the rest of the galaxy. "I could wake Threepio. He might be able to tell us something about who we're dealing with here."

Han sighed. "Do we have another choice?"

"We could sit here and wait for something to happen."

"No," Han said, shaking his head wearily. "You can't outwait a bug."

Leia rose and flipped the droid's circuit breaker. After the light had returned to his photoreceptors, he sat turning his head back and forth as he calibrated himself to his surroundings, then finally fixed his gaze on Leia.

"I *do* wish you would stop doing that, Princess Leia. It's most disorientating, and one of these times my file allocation table will be corrupted. I could lose track of my personality!"

"Wouldn't that be too bad," Han replied.

"Threepio, we need your help," Leia said, allowing the droid no time to process Han's sarcasm. "We're having trouble communicating with the indigenous species."

"Certainly!" C-3PO responded cheerily. "As I was saying before you debilitated me, I'm always happy to help. And you are certainly aware that I'm fluent in—"

"Over six million—we know," Han interrupted. He pointed outside. "Just tell us how to communicate with the bugs."

"Bugs?" C-3PO stood and turned toward the roiling mass of insects. "I don't believe those are bugs, Captain Solo. They appear to be a sentient hybrid of coleoptera and hymenoptera, which often use complex dances as a means of communication."

"Dances? You don't say!" Han returned his hands to the control yoke and throttle. "So what are they telling us?"

C-3PO studied the insects for a moment, then emitted a nervous gurgle and moved forward to the control console.

"Well?" Han demanded.

"How odd." C-3PO continued to study the creatures. "I have no record of this happening before."

"Of *what* happening?" Leia stepped to the droid's side. "What are they saying?"

"I'm afraid I can't tell you, Princess Leia." C-3PO kept his photoreceptors focused below her eyes. "I have no idea."

"What do you mean, *no idea*?" Han demanded. "You're always bragging about how many forms of communication you're fluent in!"

"That's quite impossible, Captain Solo. Droids are incapable of bragging." C-3PO returned his attention to Leia. "As I was explaining, my memory banks contain no record of this particular language. However, syntactic analyses, step comparisons, and pattern searches do suggest that this is, indeed, a language."

"You're sure?" Leia asked. "It couldn't be random wandering?"

"Oh no, Mistress Leia. The pattern and period of circulation bear a statistical correspondence that is quite significant, and the recurring oblique head bobs suggest a syntax far more sophisticated than Basic—or even Shyriiwook." C-3PO turned back to the viewport. "I'm quite sure of my conclusions."

"Then let's hear 'em," Han demanded. "Who are these guys?"

"That's what I'm trying to explain, Captain Solo," C-3PO said. "I don't know."

They all fell quiet, C-3PO carefully documenting the mysterious dance while Leia and Han tried to see how this fit into the mystery of why the survivors of the Myrkr mission had been summoned here. None of it made any sense. It seemed almost impossible that the insects could have any tie to the Myrkr strike team. And even Leia could feel that they were not strong enough in the Force to send the call Jaina and the others had reported.

C-3PO suddenly stepped away from the canopy. "I've identified the basic syntactical unit! It's really quite simple, a matter of positioning the abdomen at one of three levels to indicate whether a step is—"

"Threepio!" Han interrupted. "Can you tell us why they're not opening the door?"

C-3PO tipped his head slightly. "Why, no, Captain Solo. To do that, I'd have to understand what they're saying."

Han groaned. "What's wrong with the Imperial blink code those dartships were using?"

"Unfortunately, their pressure suits don't seem to be equipped with strobes," C-3PO explained. "But I *am* making progress with their dance-language. For instance, I've established that they're repeating the same message time after time."

"*Exactly* the same message?" Leia asked.

"Of course," C-3PO said. "Otherwise, I would have said similar—"

"Long or short?"

"That's quite impossible to say," C-3PO said. "Until I can establish the average number of units it requires to express one concept—"

"How long does it take to repeat the message?" Leia peered out at the bulging hatch, studying its membranous segments. "Seconds? Minutes?"

"Three point five-four seconds, on average," C-3PO said. "But without a context, that datum is entirely worthless."

"Not *entirely* worthless." Leia returned to the copilot's seat. "Edge us ahead, Han. I want to see something."

As Han complied, Leia stared out at the bulging hatch, looking for any flaw in her thinking. The insects suddenly arranged themselves in the center of the membrane, then started to scuttle toward the edge and ooze green gel again.

"Keep going," Leia said. "I know what they've been saying."

"That's quite unlikely!" C-3PO objected. "Even I don't have enough data to establish a grammar—much less attempt an accurate translation."

Instead of arguing, Leia reached for the glide switches that controlled the *Falcon*'s shields. Han eyed her hand warily, but continued forward. When the hatch began to bow inward, Leia lowered the shields, and a moment later the flexible membrane was sucked tight against the *Falcon* by the external vacuum.

Han let out a breath, then said to Leia, "Good call."

"Yes, Princess Leia, it was quite an extraordinary translation." C-3PO sounded crushed. "In how many forms of communication did you say you are fluent?"

FIVE

Luke felt as though he had swallowed a jug of minnows. Ben had turned an alarming hue of green. Mara, who could normally whirl-dance for hours in weak gravity, held her jaws clamped tight against the possibility of an embarrassing eruption. The Skywalkers were hardly micro-g novices, but their stomachs were rebelling at the utter *strangeness* of the asteroid colony—at the sticky gold wax that lined the corridors, at the constant thrum of insect sounds, at the endless parade of six-limbed, meter-high workers scurrying past on the walls and ceiling.

Saba, however, seemed entirely comfortable. She was moving along in front, trotting along a wall on all fours, her head swinging from side to side and her long tongue licking the sweet air. Luke suspected that the heat and mugginess reminded her of Barab I, but maybe she just liked the way her hands and feet squished into the corridor's wax lining. Barabels, he had noticed, took pleasure in the oddest things.

They came to a cockeyed intersection, and Luke stopped to listen to a strange pulsing sound that was rumbling out of a crooked side tunnel. It was muted, eerie, and rasping, but there was a definite melody and rhythm.

"Music," he said.

"If you're from Tatooine, maybe," Mara said. "The rest of us would call that a rancor belch."

"This one likez it," Saba said. "It makez her tail shake."

"I've seen squeaky thrust impellers make your tail shake," Mara said. She pointed at the floor, where a steady flow of booted feet had worn the wax down to the stone. "But it is popular. Let's check it out."

They started up the passage, and Ben asked, "Is this where Jaina is?"

"No," Luke said. Ben had been repeating the same question since they had emerged from hyperspace. "I told you, she's not in the asteroid colony."

"Then where is she?"

"We don't know." Luke looked over his shoulder at Ben. "That's what we're trying to find out."

Ben considered this a moment, then said, "If you don't know where she's at, then maybe she *is* here, and maybe you just don't know it."

This sent Saba into a fit of sissing. "He has you there, Master Skywalker."

Ben retreated behind his mother, and Luke found himself worrying about the boy's strange fear of Saba. They had made a point of exposing him to friends of many species early in his life, and only Saba still seemed to frighten him.

Luke smiled patiently, then explained, "Ben, if Jaina were here, I would feel her in the Force."

"Oh."

Surprised that Ben was willing to drop the matter with that, Luke added, "But I do feel Aunt Leia. She's here with Uncle Han."

Saba stopped on the wall ahead and peered back down at Luke. "The Soloz are *here*? This one thought they were going to hunt Three-Eye."

"So did this one." Luke could not quite keep the displeasure out of his voice. "Apparently, they decided it was more important to join us."

"And they have every right," Mara said. "*We've* seen Jaina more than they have in the past year, and with Jacen still off chasing Force-lore . . . Han and Leia must be lonely." She ruffled Ben's hair. "I would be."

"I know," Luke said, feeling guilty now for his irritation. He had grown so accustomed to everyone doing as the council asked that he tended to forget that it had no formal authority; everyone— especially the Solos—served at their own pleasure. "They've already done more than we have a right to ask."

"And what of Three-Eye?" Saba asked. "Who will stop her?"

"It might not be a bad thing to let the Reconstruction Police handle that one until we find Jaina," Luke said. "After that, the council can send her and Alema back with Zekk. It shouldn't take the three of them long to clean up the problem."

"*If* they will go." Saba continued up the corridor shaking her head. "This one is beginning to doubt the wisdom of our council. Every pack needz a longfang, or itz hunters will scatter after their own prey."

"The Jedi are a different kind of pack," Luke said, following after her. "We're an entire pack of longfangs."

"A *pack* of longfangz?" Saba let out a trio of short sisses and disappeared around a bend. "Oh, Master Skywalker . . ."

As they continued up the passage, the music grew clearer. There was an erratic chirping that struck Luke as singing, a rhythmic grating that passed for percussion, a harsh fluting that provided the melody. The overall effect was surprisingly buoyant, and Luke soon found himself enjoying it.

After about fifty meters, the passage opened into a cavernous, dimly lit chamber filled with rough-looking spacers. The music came from a clear area in the center of the room, where a trio of stick-like Verpine stood playing beneath the chemical glow of a dozen waxy shine-balls. Luke found himself studying their instrument, trying to imagine how they made so many different sounds sharing only one string.

"Astral!" Ben left Mara's side and started into the cantina. "This is gonna blast!"

Mara caught him by the shoulder. "Not a chance."

He gave her a knowing smirk, for they had left Nanna behind to help R2-D2 watch the *Shadow*. "You can't leave me out here alone. I'm only eight."

"What makes you think you'll be alone?" Mara nodded Luke toward the cantina, then said to Ben, "You and I will stand watch out here."

Luke and Saba stepped through the door. The usual assortment of riffraff spacers—Givin, Bothans, Nikto, Quarren—were gathered in the middle of the room, sitting on synthetic stone benches and holding their drinks in their laps. A few hard cases, such as the Defel "shadow Wraith" hiding in the corner and a Jenet hoodlum holding court on the far side of the chamber, sat apart from the group. Many of the patrons were listing in their seats, but there was none of the latent hostility that usually permeated the Force in spaceport cantinas.

Luke followed Saba to the service area, where a distracted Duros stood at the end of a long bank of beverage dispensers. There was no counter or ordering station, nor anything that looked like a payment terminal, but a soft clicking noise was coming from a darkened alcove beneath the middle dispenser. As they drew near, the clicking stopped and a worker insect emerged from the alcove. It stared up at them for a moment, then handed an empty cup to both of them and retreated into its alcove.

Luke and Saba studied the unmarked dispensers for a moment, then Saba hissed in frustration. She walked over to the inattentive Duros and thrust her mug into his hands.

"Bloodsour."

The Duros swung his noseless head around sharply, then saw he was being addressed by a Barabel. The blue drained from his face.

"Don't have bloodsour," he said in his flat Duros voice. "Only membrosia."

"Will this one like it?"

The Duros nodded. "Everyone likes membrosia."

"Then I'll have the same," Luke said, passing his mug over.

The Duros studied Luke's face for a moment, clearly struggling to place it in some context other than a pair of well-worn flight utilities.

"I'm just a pilot," Luke said, reinforcing the Force illusion he was using to disguise himself. "A *thirsty* pilot."

"Sure."

The Duros turned to the nearest dispenser and filled both mugs with a thick amber liquid, then returned the cups. Luke pulled a ten-credit voucher from his pocket, but the Duros waved it off.

"Nobody pays here."

"Nobody payz?" Saba echoed. "This one doesn't believe you."

A hint of indignation permeated the Force, then the Duros shrugged and looked back to the Verpine musicians.

Saba studied him for a moment, then glanced at Luke. "This one is tired. She will find a seat."

She took a sip from her mug, then started to work her way deeper into the cantina. The Duros looked as though he wished Luke would join her, but Luke remained where he was, pouring camaraderie and goodwill into the Force. The Duros' aloofness did not melt until Saba raised a storm of angry jabbering by taking an empty seat in front of an Ewok.

"*This* should be interesting." The Duros grinned. "That little Ewok has a death mark in ten systems."

"You don't say." Luke took a sip of membrosia. It was sweet and thick and potent, warming him from his toes to his ear tips. He allowed himself a moment to savor the sense of well-being that came with the intoxicating heat, then asked the Duros, "Have you been here long?"

"Too long," the Duros said. "Turns out Lizil doesn't use processing chips, and now I can't get a cargo out."

"Is that a common problem?"

"Common, but not a problem." The Duros waved his hand vaguely in the direction of the membrosia dispensers. "Everything's free, and you can stay as long as you want."

"Very generous," Luke said. "What's the catch?"

"Isn't one," the Duros said. "Except you get used to it, and then you don't *want* to leave."

"That sounds like a catch to me," Luke said.

"Depends on how you look at it," the Duros admitted. "Especially if you have obligations at home."

"Why don't you just take your chips back to the known galaxy?" Luke asked. "With so many manufacturing worlds destroyed by the war, the Galactic Alliance is desperate for processing chips."

"Too dangerous." The Duros cocked his big head toward Luke. "You wouldn't want some kriffing bounty hunter to catch you with these particular chips."

"Ah," Luke said. Lando and Tendra had put up a million-credit reward for a load of specialized processing chips that had been hijacked on its way to Tendrando Arms' new rehab-droid factory. "That makes sense."

"Void-breathing right it does," the Duros said. "Already had five Jedi come through on my tail. That's when I decided to dump the load."

Luke tried not to wince at the loss of the vital chips. "You're sure the Jedi were looking for *you*?"

"Who else would they be looking for?" The Duros shook his head, then said, "I knew Calrissian had pull with the Jedi, but who'd have guessed it was *that* strong?"

"Not me," Luke answered. He stepped closer to the Duros and lowered his voice. "Were they fairly young? A couple of humans with a Barabel and a Wookiee?"

"And a Twi'lek." The Duros' voice grew suspicious, and he began to ease away from Luke. "How'd you know?"

"I've got a little problem of my own with them," Luke said. "And I don't want to find them waiting at my next stop. Know where they went?"

The Duros watched the Verpine band for a moment, no doubt trying to find a way to work an angle for himself. Luke poured a little more goodwill into the Force, and finally the Duros shook his head.

"Sorry," he said. "You'd need to ask Lizil."

Before Luke could ask how to find Lizil, he realized someone new was coming up behind him. The person seemed both to have her own presence in the Force and to be a part of the larger, diffuse essence that permeated the entire asteroid colony. He turned to find a striking Falleen female approaching, her scaly skin almost as green as a male's. She acknowledged Luke with a polite nod, then stopped before the Duros.

"Tarnis, we have a cargo for you," she said.

The Duros took a sip of membrosia and tried to appear calm. "To where?"

"The Horoh nest," the Falleen answered. "You'll be given a load to take home, of course."

Tarnis's eyes grew round—at least by Duros standards. "Done."

When the Duros did not instantly start for the exit, the Falleen said, "It requires immediate departure. Lizil is already loading the *Starsong*."

"No problem." Tarnis placed his mug on the floor. "I'll just gather my crew—"

"We're gathering them now." The Falleen started toward the exit. "They'll meet you in the hangar."

"Right behind you," Tarnis said. He started after the Falleen, shaking his head in amazement. "Finally!"

Seeing that he had been forgotten in the excitement, Luke used the Force to slow the Duros down, then cleared his throat.

"Oh, yeah." Tarnis took the Falleen's arm and gestured toward Luke. "This fellow wants to talk. I can find my own way to the hangar."

The Falleen barely slowed. "We're very busy." She glanced over her shoulder, but avoided Luke's eyes. "Enjoy the hospitality of the nest."

When Luke reached out to probe her feelings, he experienced a deep sense of worry. Her scales rippled in alarm; then an enormous, murky presence rose inside her mind and pushed him out so forcibly that he stumbled into a membrosia dispenser.

As Tarnis and the Falleen walked out the exit, Mara peered around the corner, checking to be certain the surprise she had felt was nothing to be alarmed about. Luke smiled and turned around to display the new membrosia stain on the back of his utilities, then watched intently as Tarnis and the Falleen disappeared down the corridor.

Once the pair were far enough ahead that she would not be noticed following, Mara took Ben's hand and started down the corridor, talking as though they were just a mother and son returning to their vessel.

Luke worked his way to the cantina center and sat on a bench next to a pair of Ishi Tib. He remained quiet for a few moments, pretending to listen to the music but actually reaching out in the Force to search for eavesdropping devices. He was not quite certain what had happened over at the membrosia dispensers, but he felt certain that the Falleen's arrival had been no coincidence. Lizil—whoever that was—had not wanted Tarnis to talk about Jaina and the others.

After a few minutes, Luke finally felt confident that he could ask his questions in peace. He began to pour out feelings of comradery and goodwill, and it wasn't long before the nearest Ishi Tib turned toward him.

"My name is Zelara." She pointed at her companion, who swiveled her eyestalks around and gently clacked her beak. "This is Lyari. She likes you."

Luke smiled back. "Thank you."

Zelara batted the lids of her yellow eyes. "*I* like you."

"That's very nice." He eased off the good feelings, then said, "Actually, I'm looking for some friends—"

"*We'll* be your friends," Lyari said. She came around to Luke's other side, then slipped her stubby hand through the crook of his arm. Her breath smelled heavily of membrosia. "I've never felt this way about a human before."

"Me, either." Zelara took Luke's other arm. "But this one is cute, even with the recessed eyes."

"Ladies, that's just the membrosia talking." Luke sensed Mara already returning to the cantina. She did not feel angry or frightened, but she was frustrated; she had lost the Duros and his escort. "I'm looking for a group of young travelers who came through here. There would've been at least two humans, a Twi'lek, a Barabel—"

"And a Wookiee?" Lyari asked.

"Then you've seen them," Luke said.

Lyari opened her beak in a sort of smile. "Maybe."

"Maybe not," Zelara added. She began to tug at the chest closures on Luke's utilities. "Let us have a look inside, and we'll tell you."

Luke caught her hand. "It probably wouldn't be a good idea for us to—"

"Come on, bright boy." Lyari reached for closures a little farther down. "Give us a chance."

"No." Luke put enough Force behind the word to prevent Lyari from ripping open his utilities. "That would never work."

"Why not?" Zelara demanded.

"Because I have lips and you have beaks, for starters."

Zelara spread her eyestalks. "You'd be surprised what a girl can do with her beak."

"Let me show you," Lyari said. She caught Luke's nose in her beak and gave it a tug.

"Ouch!" Luke reached up and freed his nose. Other people were starting to look in their direction, and that was exactly what he *didn't* want. "Please, ladies. Just tell me what you know about my friends."

Zelara ripped his chest closures open, revealing Luke's under-shirt. "First you show, then—"

Mara's astonishment hit Luke like a Force hammer, and he failed to hear the rest of Zelara's comment. He turned toward the exit and saw Mara swinging her hand down to cover their son's eyes.

"Who's that?" Lyari asked, following his gaze.

"My wife."

"Wife?" the Ishi Tib repeated in unison. They jumped to their feet, Zelara crying, "You didn't tell us you were mated!"

"And he's got a fry, too!" Lyari exclaimed.

The outburst caused the Verpine musicians to fumble over a string of notes, and several annoyed patrons turned to suggest that Luke and the Ishi Tib take their personal lives to a quiet corner.

Mara rolled her eyes, then shook her head and dragged a very reluctant Ben around the corner.

Luke sent her a feeling of reassurance, trying to make sure she knew there was a good explanation. He received an impression of amused doubtfulness in reply, then he heard Saba sissing from across the room and realized he might never live this one down. He shook his head in disgust, then closed his utilities and looked up at the Ishi Tib.

"Will you *please* sit?"

Zelara put a hand on her hip. "I don't think so."

"You just forget about us, you double-spawner." Lyari shooed him toward the exit. "You'd better go catch your mate and that little fry."

"As soon as you answer me." Luke grabbed both Ishi Tib by their wrists and pulled them down. "When did you see my friends? The Wookiee and the Barabel and the others?"

"When they were here," Zelara answered coolly.

"Which was?" Luke put the Force behind his question, pressuring her to answer.

"I don't know." Zelara turned to Lyari. "When was that?"

"Who can remember? They only stayed a day."

Luke started to pressure Lyari to think back, then realized that someone else was approaching. As with the Falleen who had led Tarnis away, the newcomer appeared to have a double presence in the Force, except that the individual essence felt much more menacing and powerful than had the Falleen's. Luke turned and, when he saw a blocky shadow with red eyes and white fangs approaching, nearly reached for his lightsaber.

The Defel watched Luke's hand until it dropped back to his side, then turned to the Ishi Tib. "The nest has secured a barrel of fresh Tibrin salts," he rasped. "We are preparing an immersion tank now."

"For us?" Zelara gasped.

"Where?" Lyari demanded.

The Defel offered a shadow-furred arm to each of them. "We'll escort you."

"First, answer my question," Luke said, putting the weight of the Force behind his command.

Lyari started to stop and look back, but the Defel pulled her forward.

"Come, ladies." His eyes flared red. "The immersion tank is growing cool."

The same murky presence Luke had felt before rose against him. It was not a Force attack, merely an enormous exertion of will. Had he wanted to, Luke could have found another way to maintain his hold, but that would have meant drawing even more of the mysterious entity's attention to himself than he already had.

Besides, Saba was on her way over, a furry little Ewok at her side. It was the Ewok she had sat in front of earlier, with a single white stripe running diagonally across a stocky body that was otherwise as black as space. They stopped in front of Luke and stood there sissing and chortling together.

"Go ahead," Luke said. "Get it out of your system now. Who's your friend?"

"Tar . . . Tarfang," Saba laughed. "He sayz he can help us find our friendz . . . if you are finished chasing Ishi Tib."

SIX

Save for the lining of golden wax, the rows of shine-balls stuck to the ceiling, the random tunnel openings, and the lack of even a vague sense of up or down, the interior of the spherical hangar resembled all the spaceports Han Solo had visited on a thousand unknown, out-of-the-way planets scattered across the galaxy. There was the usual collection of battered transports, the usual cargo of stolen goods on open display, the usual dregs-of-their-species smugglers bustling in and out of their vessels, working harder to make dishonest livings than they would have at honest jobs.

Han felt a swell of nostalgia rise inside, and he found himself missing the days when he could debark in such places and know that nobody was going to mess with him and the Wookiee. Of course, now he had a Jedi Knight wife, a pair of Noghri, and a refitted battle droid to back him up, but it just wasn't the same. Chewbacca had been his co-conspirator as well his best friend, a pain-in-the-neck conscience at times but also a comrade-in-arms who understood the betrayals and disappointments that had turned Han into the wary, bitter smuggler he'd been when Leia came along and rescued him from that aimless life.

"At least we've solved one mystery," Leia said. She pointed at a duraplast pallet filled with crates labeled RECONSTRUCTION AUTHORITY—SANITATION. "That may explain why it's been so hard to track down the RA supplies shrinkage."

"I don't know," Han said. He eyed the giant bugs that seemed to be crawling across every surface. "This pile of rocks isn't big enough to take everything that's disappearing."

The more Han watched the activity around the transports, the more he felt his skin crawl. The bugs were marching in and out of the vessels completely unescorted, off-loading cargo, foodstuffs, even vital ship's tools, and stacking them at the base of the boarding ramps. Instead of stopping the insects, the crews were doing the same thing in reverse, on-loading huge stoneware crocks, balls of multicolored wax, and many of the same tools and foodstuffs the bugs were unloading. And nobody seemed upset about working at cross purposes. In fact, save for the care they took to avoid crashing into each other, they barely seemed to notice one another at all.

Han spied the sleek gray wedge of a *Horizon*-class space yacht resting about halfway up the "wall" of the docking vault, its landing struts sunk well past their feet in the waxy substance that coated the chamber. The boarding ramp was lowered and a big Tendrando Arms Defender Droid was standing beside it, her massive torso and systems-packed limbs at odds with her cherubic face and smiling mouth.

"There's the *Shadow*," Han said. He brought the *Falcon*'s nose around and started toward an open berthing space on the wall next to Mara's ship. "Let's go say hello."

Leia shook her head. "It doesn't feel like there's anyone aboard."

"No?" Han scowled; it wasn't like Mara to leave the *Shadow* open and unattended—although with Nanna there, that wasn't really the case. Basically a bodyguard version of Lando's successful YVH battle droid crossed with a TD Nanny Droid, the Defender was more than capable of guarding the ship. Even the bugs seemed to realize that; every now and then, one would stop by and sweep its antennae across the ramp, but they never attempted to enter. "Probably in the cantina already."

Han swung the *Falcon*'s stern "up" along the wall and landed in the open berth. The struts sank into the wax and seemed to hold the ship fast, but he fired the anchoring bolts anyway. Microgravity could be tricky; it was impossible to tell which way it was pulling until something started to slide.

Han rose and strapped on his blaster. "Okay, let's go see Nanna. Maybe she can fill us in."

They lowered the boarding ramp and reeled back as a wave of warm, too-sweet air rolled through the hatchway. The vault was filled with a blaring cacophony of ticking that immediately sent a rivulet of sweat rolling down Han's spine. Half a dozen bugs appeared at the bottom of the ramp and started to board. They had deep orange thoraxes, pale blue abdomens, and feathery, meter-long antennae. Han's stomach turned queasy, but he started down to meet them.

Leia caught him by the arm. "Han? What's wrong?"

"Nothing." Han swallowed hard, then continued down the ramp. He was not going to be intimidated by a memory of the Kamarians. Besides, these guys were only about waist height, with four skinny arms, scrawny legs, and a stubby set of mandibles better suited to steadying loads than rending flesh. "I'm okay."

Han stopped midway down the ramp. He folded his arms across his chest and assumed a stance wide enough to block the ramp, then forced himself to glare down at the lead bug. In addition to the smooth green balls of its two main eyes, it had a trio of ocular lenses atop its head, leaving him uncertain as to which set of eyes he should meet.

"Where do you fellows think you're going?"

The lead bug stared up, ticking its mandibles nervously, and emitted a soft drumming from its chest.

"Burrubbubbuurrr, rubb."

It dropped to all sixes, lowering itself to about knee height, then dipped its antennae politely and shot between Han's legs.

"Hey!" Before the bug could continue up the ramp, Han spun around and caught it by the undersized wings on its back. Some insects had a habit of hiding eggs wherever they could, and he didn't want any infestations aboard the *Falcon*. "Hold on!"

The bug spun its head around to meet Han's gaze, then pointed at his hands and gently clacked its mandibles. *"Ubburr buurr ub."*

"Captain Solo," C-3PO said helpfully, "I do believe the insect is requesting that you release it."

"You understand this stuff?" Han asked.

"I'm afraid it's only an educated guess," C-3PO said. "This form of their language is as obscure as the dance—"

"Then not a chance."

"Han," Leia said, "I don't sense any danger here. Until See-Threepio figures out how to communicate—"

"I *am* communicating." Han fixed his gaze on the nearest of its eyes and said, "I don't know who you think I am, but no one boards the *Falcon* until *I* say so."

The other five bugs dropped to all sixes, then slipped to the underside of the ramp and continued toward the hatchway.

"No!" Han flipped the insect he was holding off the ramp, then started after the others. "Stop them!"

The Noghri stepped in front of Leia and placed themselves squarely in the door, crouched for action. The bugs swung back to the ramp's upper side and tried to squeeze aboard the *Falcon* anyway. The first pair were knocked away by a pair of quick Noghri kicks.

The remaining trio of insects stopped where they were and dropped into a six-limbed crouch. Their antennae fell flat against their heads, and a soft little *"rrrrrrrr"* began to come from their chests. Someone else might have described the sound as meek, but Han knew better than to assume. Bug minds did not work the same way as those of other species.

BD-8, the Solos' battle droid, appeared behind the Noghri and pointed his blaster cannon over Meewalh's shoulder. "Do not be alarmed!" With the full jacket of laminanium armor and red photoreceptors in a death's-head face, he still resembled the YVH droid from which he had been refitted. "Intruders identified. Permission to fire?"

"No!" Leia snapped. "Stand down! Return to leisure station."

"Leisure station?" BD-8's tone grew doubtful as the other bugs continued up the ramp. "Ma'am, we're being boarded!"

"We're *not* being boarded," Leia said.

"Not if I can help it!" Han said.

He snatched another of the bugs and, in the low gravity, sent it spinning twenty meters across the hangar. Cakhmaim and Meewalh removed the last two, grabbing a mandible and executing quick twists that sent the insects tumbling away.

Han nodded his approval. "See?"

A bitter odor began to waft up from the floor. Han looked down to see two of the dislodged bugs standing beside the ramp on their four front limbs, their abdomens raised so they could squirt greenish fluid on the sides of the ramp.

"What the garzal?" Han cried.

"Ubbub bubbur," the bugs drummed.

"Bubbur yourselves!"

Han raised his arms to shoo them away. They continued to squirt, and C-3PO picked that moment to interrupt.

"Captain Solo, we seem to have another visitor."

The droid pointed past Han's shoulder.

Han turned around to find a tall, bald-headed figure with large, buggy eyes and a pair of thick tusks approaching the *Falcon*'s boarding ramp. In his hands, he carried a rag and a spray canister.

"Great," Han said. "Now an Aqualish."

"That can't be good," Leia said. The Aqualish were an aggressive species known across the galaxy for picking fights—and jumping into the middle of them. "What's he want?"

"To wash the viewports, it looks like," Han said. The Aqualish reached the base of the ramp and started forward toward the bugs. "What do you want, Fangface?"

The nickname was despised by Aqualish, but it was better to take an aggressive tone with them. They were less likely to start a fight with someone who did not intimidate easily.

"Nothing, friend." The Aqualish spoke in the gravelly voice typical of his species. "Just to help you out."

Han and Leia exchanged puzzled glances. *Friend* was not usually a word you heard from an Aqualish.

"We're not your friends," Han said.

"You will be."

The Aqualish waited until the bugs finished squirting, then shooed away the one on his side of the ramp and sprayed a harsh-smelling foam over the same area.

"That stuff better not be corrosive," Han warned.

Aqualish could not smile—the need had probably never arisen during their evolution—but this one lifted his head and managed to seem like he was.

"It's not." He tossed the spray canister to Han. "You need to clean that mess up."

The Aqualish pointed at the far side of the ramp, where the other worker had squirted its goo, then started to wipe the area he had already coated. Han sprayed a thick layer of foam over the side of the ramp, filling the air with a smell somewhere between rotting fruit and burned synfur.

"Tell me again what I'm doing?"

"When you tossed the workers off, they marked you," the Aqualish explained. He tossed Han the rag. "Now you have to start over, or they'll call their soldiers and tear your ship apart to see what you're hiding."

"Start over?" Leia asked.

"Transacting," the Aqualish explained. "Isn't that why you're here?"

"Uh, maybe," Han said. "You mean like trading, right?"

"More like taking," the Aqualish said. "They take what they want. You take what you want. Everybody's happy."

The insects started up the ramp again.

"Boarding imminent," BD-8 reported. "Permission to—"

"No!" Leia said. "Stand down."

Han finished wiping the foam away, then stood up to find the six insects lined up on the ramp below.

"They're not going to lay eggs or anything?" he asked.

"No, they only do that in the heartcomb," the Aqualish assured him. "Just let them bring out whatever they want, then take back whatever you want to keep. It's a lot easier—and safer."

"If you say so." Han stepped aside to let the bugs pass. "Okay?"

The lead worker responded with a single mandible clack, which was simultaneously echoed by the rest of the squad.

"That would be an affirmative," C-3PO offered helpfully.

The bugs started up the ramp.

Han jumped down beside the Aqualish and returned the spray canister and rag. "Sorry about that Fangface stuff." He reached for his money. "What do I owe you for the help?"

"Nothing, friend." The Aqualish waved a dismissing hand. "It happens to everyone the first time."

"Really?" Han's mind began searching for angles, trying to figure out what kind of swindle the Aqualish was trying to pull. "Hope you don't mind me saying so, but you're a pretty helpful guy for your kind."

The Aqualish watched the last bug disappear into the *Falcon,* then nodded. "Yeah. I don't get it, either." He turned and started back toward his own vessel. "This place just makes me feel good."

Han, Leia, and the others spent the next hour returning to the *Falcon* most of what the bugs carried off. At first, the work was confusing and frustrating—especially after they had carried the same crate of protein packages aboard for the seventh or eighth time. But eventually order emerged, with the ship's crew leaving anything they could bear to part with at the foot of the ramp and stacking whatever they wanted to keep in the forward hold. Toward the end, the bugs even started to add balls of wax and jugs of some amber, sweet-smelling spirit to the *Falcon's* stack.

Finally, the only item under contention was *Killik Twilight,* a small moss-painting that had once hung outside Leia's bedroom in House Organa on Alderaan. Designed by the late Ob Khaddor—one of Alderaan's foremost artists—the piece depicted a line of enigmatic insectoid figures departing their pinnacle-city home, with a fierce storm sweeping in behind them. Han had no idea why the bugs were so taken with it—apart from the subject matter—but every time he put it on the *keep* stack, an insect would deposit a jug of spirits or a shine-ball in its place and carry it back down the ramp again. Han was about ready to start exterminating. The painting was Leia's most prized possession, and he'd almost died trying to recover it for her on Tatooine.

A bug emerged from the *Falcon* carrying *Killik Twilight* in its four arms and stopped about halfway down the ramp, peering over the top of the frame. Han, waiting at the bottom, folded his arms and sighed.

"Come on," he said. "Let's get it over with."

Instead of continuing down the ramp, the worker jumped to the floor and disappeared behind the disordered heap of crates and spare tools stacked next to the *Falcon*.

"Hey!"

Han rushed to the other side to cut off the bug's escape, but it was nowhere to be seen. He glanced back at its buddies—waiting for this last bit of "transacting" to be completed—but they only turned their oblong eyes away and pretended not to notice. Han sneered, then knelt down to peer behind the *Falcon*'s landing struts.

Nothing.

"Blast!" Han slowly turned, his pulse pounding as he searched for the bug. Halfway up the hangar wall, he saw the Skywalkers emerging from a passage with Saba Sebatyne and a black-furred Ewok, but no sign of the thief. "Huttslime!"

"Han?" Leia appeared at the top of the boarding ramp, her arms loaded with provisions that she and the others were stowing again. "What's wrong?"

"Nothing," Han answered. "The bugs are getting sneaky."

Leia put her load aside. "Define *sneaky*, Han."

"Nothing to worry about." A soft rustle sounded from the transaction pile. Han peered over a stack of raw protein packages and saw a slender insect foot sliding behind a crate of Endorian brandy. "I've got everything under control."

Han slipped around the stack of packages, then pulled the crate aside and found the worker bug cowering with *Killik Twilight* in its four hands.

"*Uub urr,*" it thrummed.

"Yeah? Two can play that game."

Han pulled the painting from its grasp, then turned to find Ben rushing up ahead of Luke and the others.

"Uncle Han!" He raised his elbow in an old smuggler's greeting Han had taught him. "Dad said you were here!"

"Good to see you, kid." Han touched his elbow to Ben's. "I'd love to talk, but I'm in the middle of a contest of wills."

Leaving Leia to slow down the bug and greet Luke and the others, Han carried the painting onto the *Falcon,* then knelt on the floor and opened a smuggling compartment.

"That's a funny place to put Aunt Leia's painting," said Ben, who had followed him aboard.

"Tell me about it," Han said. He slipped the painting into the compartment, closed the cover, and stood. "Now let's go see your mom and—"

The bug appeared in the corridor, sweeping its antennae along the floor. It passed Han with a polite rumble, then stopped and began to pry at the secret panel. When the compartment would not open, it sat down and began to clack its mandibles.

"All right! You don't have to call your buddies." Han knelt on the floor beside the bug. "Just get out of my way."

Han opened the panel. The insect pulled the painting from the compartment and turned to leave, then let out a startled rumble when it found Saba and her Ewok companion coming up the corridor. The Ewok snatched the painting from the bug's hands, turned it over, and spat on the back.

"What the blazes!" Han turned to Saba. "Is this guy a friend of yours?"

"Tarfang and I have made no killz together," Saba said. "But he can help us."

"Yeah?" Han watched doubtfully as Tarfang placed the painting on the floor. "How?"

The Ewok glared up at Han and jabbered something in the squeaky language of his species, then motioned Han and the others toward the boarding ramp.

"Listen up, Cuddles," Han said, "I don't know who you think you are, but on the *Falcon*—"

"Uncle Han, look!"

Ben pointed at *Killik Twilight.* The bug stood holding the painting in its hands, running its antennae over the back where the Ewok had spit. It repeated the gesture several times, then emitted a sad little hum and returned the painting to the smuggling compartment.

Han looked back to Tarfang. "How'd you do that?"

The Ewok's only answer was an indignant snort. He spun around and started for the boarding ramp, no longer seeming to care whether Han or anyone else followed.

"Touchy little fellow, isn't he?"

"Tarfang is not a nice being." Saba started after the Ewok. "But his captain can help us find Jaina and the otherz."

Han caught up to her outside, where C-3PO informed them that Luke and the others had gone on ahead with Tarfang. Despite Saba's assurances that *Killik Twilight* was perfectly safe now that someone had spit on it, Han asked the Noghri to stay with the painting.

They dropped Ben at the *Shadow* with Nanna, then joined Luke, Mara, and Leia outside the blast-pocked, carbon-scored disk of a small YT-1000 transport. A smaller cousin to Han's own YT-1300, the YT-1000's cockpit sat atop the hull where the *Falcon*'s upper laser cannon turret was located; there was no lower turret at all. For defense, the vessel had only four short-range blaster cannons spread evenly along the rim of its hull.

"That thing *flew* here?" Han gasped.

An indignant Ewok voice chuttered from inside the vessel's shadowy entrance.

"He says it came straight from Regel Eight," C-3PO translated.

Tarfang stepped into the light and jabbered at Han some more.

"I'm certainly glad we don't fly on this ship!" C-3PO said. "He says not everyone has credits to waste on repairs!"

Leia stepped to Han's side. "We apologize, Tarfang." She flashed one of her old diplomat's smiles, a bland show of teeth that could have meant anything. "Han didn't mean to insult you."

"Yeah," Han said. "I was just amazed by your bravery."

Tarfang eyed Han for a moment, then growled deep in his throat and waved them up the ramp.

Han turned to Luke and Mara. "You sure about this?"

"Not really," Luke said. He smiled and clapped Han on the shoulder. "We weren't expecting you and Leia."

"Yeah, well . . . *anybody* can bust up a pirate ring," Han said. "But Jaina—we figured you'd need the help."

"We might," Mara said with a laugh. She kissed him on the cheek. "Good to see you, Han."

They exchanged greetings all around, then climbed the boarding ramp into a surprisingly tidy air lock with all proper emergency equipment neatly stowed in a transparisteel rescue locker. Beyond the hatch, the interior of the main access corridor was lit only by two of the waxy shine-balls the bugs used for illumination. By the green glow, Han could see that the durasteel floor panels had been sanibuffed a little *too* well. There was a telltale shadow where the "invisible" seams came together over the smuggling compartments.

Tarfang was waiting a few steps up the corridor. He grunted and waved them into the main cabin. Given the ship's dim lighting, Han expected to find some fierce, dark-loving being like a Defel waiting inside.

Instead, kneeling in front of an open engineering panel was a little jug-eared Sullustan in a set of carbon-smeared utilities. He was
busy soldering powerfeeds to a new master control board, though
Han could not imagine how even a Sullustan could see to work by
the light of the single shine-ball stuck to the wall above him.

Tarfang went to the Sullustan's side and, coming to attention,
cleared his throat.

"Go on." The Sullustan spoke without looking away from his
work. "I'm listening."

Tarfang launched into a lengthy explanation, gesturing at Saba
and Luke even though the Sullustan's attention remained fixed on the
control board. Finally, the captain finished the attachment he was
working on and turned to his visitors.

"I'm Jae Juun, captain of the *XR-eight-oh-eight-g*."

"*XR-eight-oh-eight-g*?" Han asked. "What kind of name is
that?"

"It's a Galactic Alliance registration number, of course." Juun
frowned and squinted in the direction of Han's voice, but Han was
standing well back in the shadows, where even a Sullustan's sensitive
eyes would have trouble with the contrast between light and darkness. "You haven't heard of the *XR-eight-oh-eight-g*?"

"Should we have?" Leia asked.

Juun pasted on a small Sullustan smirk. "Not if I've been doing
my job."

"You're succeeding beyond your wildest dreams," Han said.

Leia grabbed the back of his elbow and squeezed in warning, but
the Sullustan merely smiled in pride.

"Tarfang tells me you're looking for someone to help you catch
your friends."

"To find them," Luke corrected.

"I see. Well, it makes no difference." Juun cast an annoyed
glance in Tarfang's direction. "I'm afraid my first mate sometimes
exceeds his authority."

Tarfang asked something in a disbelieving tone.

"It's not the mate's responsibility to raise funds," Juun replied.
"You let me worry how we're going to pay for that vortex stabilizer."

"A warp vortex stabilizer?" Han asked. "For a YT this old? It
can't be easy to come by one of those out here."

"Not at a fair price," Juun agreed. "I've had one brought in, but
I'm two hundred credits short of the shipping fees."

"Not if you help us, you're not," Han said, stepping into the
light. "We can pay you the two hundred credits."

Juun's mouth fell. "I knew that was your voice!" He turned to Tarfang. "Why didn't you tell me Han Solo was with them?"

Tarfang sneered in Han's direction and prattled an answer.

"Yes, but this is *Han Solo*!" The Sullustan rose and thrust a hand out. "The *XR-eight-oh-eight-g* follows all your procedures, and I've memorized all your combat maneuvers from the history vids."

"Uh, I wouldn't trust everything I see in those holovids," Han said, allowing the Sullustan to shake his hand. "Now, about that help . . ."

"I'd like to help you." Juun's voice grew disappointed, and he turned back to his work. "But it wouldn't be proper."

"Proper?" Han echoed. That particular word encompassed everything he hated about Sullustans. "Why not?"

"Because I have an arrangement with our hosts, and evidently they don't want you to find your friends."

Tarfang groaned and slapped his brow.

"We can't ignore the wishes of our business partners," Juun said to the Ewok. "We have a deal."

"A deal you can't keep until you find two hundred credits," Han said. "How long are they willing to wait?"

"We *are* facing a bit of a dilemma," Juun admitted.

"What if we were to buy a copy of your charts?" Luke asked.

Juun shook his head. "My charts wouldn't help you. Your friends went to Yoggoy."

"And you don't know where Yoggoy is?" Luke asked.

"Nobody does," Juun said. "The Yoggoy are very proud and secretive. They hide the location of their nest from outsiders."

Saba glared down at Tarfang. "Then why did you say you could help us find our friendz?"

Tarfang jabbered an answer.

"Because the *XR-eight-oh-eight-g* has been assigned a cargo for Yoggoy," C-3PO translated, "and when a ship is assigned a cargo for Yoggoy, it is also assigned a Yoggoy to serve as its navigator for the trip."

"Fine," Leia said. Even she seemed to be losing patience. "Help us get a cargo, and we'll pay you for consulting."

Tarfang rattled off a long response, which C-3PO translated as, "Tarfang suggests you simply give Captain Juun the money. They'll check on our friends and give us a report when they return."

"Sure they will." Han turned to the others, then nodded toward the door. "We're wasting our time here."

Luke motioned Han to wait, his gaze fixed on Tarfang. Han realized for the first time that Mara was no longer with them; under circumstances like these, she had an uncanny knack for slipping away unnoticed.

Finally, Luke turned back to Han. "Tarfang's not trying to swindle us, Han. He really does want to work out an honest deal."

Tarfang snarled something at the Jedi Master.

"He wasn't stealing your thoughts," C-3PO said to the Ewok. "Master Luke is not a thief."

Tarfang whirled on the droid and yapped a command.

"Very well. But I wouldn't blame him if he used his lightsaber on you." C-3PO turned to Luke. "Tarfang is threatening to remove your eyes if you do that again."

"Oh, *that* scares him," Han said to the Ewok. "You want to make a deal? Here it is: two hundred credits to get us a cargo."

To Han's surprise, it was Saba who answered. "He can't."

"Why not?"

"Because Lizil wouldn't allow it," Luke said. "He—or she—doesn't want us to find Jaina and the others."

"They," Juun corrected.

Luke frowned. "What?"

"*They*," Juun said.

The Sullustan continued to work, soldering what looked like the rear hold powerfeed onto the main cabin output. Han would have said something, but he had long ago learned never to tell another captain how to maintain his own ship. Besides, anyone who looked at the *Falcon*'s main control board would probably have just as many doubts about his work as he was having about Juun's.

"Lizil isn't their leader." Juun looked up from his work, dragging the hot tip of his soldering iron across the flux-inhibitor circuitry. "Lizil is *them*."

"They all share one name?" Leia asked.

"In a sense, but it's more than that. The way they think of it, they're all Lizil together. Lizil is the nest, but so are all of the members."

"They don't have an individual sense of identity?" Leia asked.

"I think that's so," Juun said. "But I'm not really current on my xenobiological definitions."

Tarfang chortled something helpful sounding.

"Master Tarfang says that it's only important to remember that when you say *Lizil,* you might be talking about the entire nest or any of its members."

Tarfang chattered something impatient.

"And you'll never be sure which," C-3PO added.

"Cozy," Han said. "So why doesn't Lizil want us to find Jaina?"

When Juun hesitated, Tarfang let out a long, urgent chitter.

"But nobody said it *wasn't* secret," Juun countered.

"You are being rockheaded," Saba rasped. "Something is only secret if—"

"Hold on," Han said to Saba. The Sullustan mind was as stubborn as it was methodical, and the Barabel would only delay things by browbeating Juun. "It *is* a bit unclear."

Saba glared at Han out of one dark eye.

"There are your implied agreements and your tacit obligations." Han turned to Juun. "Am I right?"

The Sullustan nodded rapidly. "Only captains understand these things."

"True," Han said. "But aren't you smugglers, too?"

Tarfang grunted an affirmative.

"There you have it, then," Han said. He looked back to Juun. "You have to answer me."

"I do?"

"Yeah." Han allowed some of the impatience he was feeling to show in his voice. "The Smuggler's Code says so."

Juun looked back to his work and casually asked, "The Smuggler's Code?"

"Item seven?" Han prompted. "*I swear to help other smugglers, as long as it don't cost* me?"

"Yes, of course." Juun's beady-eyed gaze flicked back and forth across the master control board. It was impossible that he actually knew the Smuggler's Code—Han was making it up—but nothing embarrassed most Sullustans more than admitting they did not know proper procedures. "Item seven. I'd almost forgotten."

"I think that clears things up," Leia said. She flashed Han an approving smile, then sat on her haunches beside Juun. "So what's Lizil trying to hide?"

Juun began to solder the forward loading door's powerfeed to the forward loading door's control circuit. "You have seen the Joiners?"

Han expected Leia to shake her head, but she seemed to sense something from her brother and allowed Luke to respond for her.

"You mean Lizil's translators?"

"Not translators," Juun said. "*Joiners.* They're Lizil, too."

Saba lowered her scaly brow. "How can that be?" she rasped. "Most of them do not even have six limbz!"

"It doesn't matter," Juun said. "They've been absorbed."

"Absorbed?" Han was having trouble following the conversation now, probably because he had not yet seen any of these "Joiners." "Absorbed *how*?"

"Mentally, I suspect," Luke said, keeping his eyes on Juun. "Is it some sort of brainwashing?"

Juun shrugged. "All I know is that when someone spends too long in a nest, he gets absorbed."

"You're saying that my daughter thinks she's some kind of bug?" Han demanded, taking a step forward. "And you *weren't* going to tell me?"

Juun jumped up and stepped behind Leia. "It's not my fault!"

"Take it easy, Han," Luke said. "We don't know that has happened."

"Do we know it hasn't?" Han countered.

"Now *you* are being a rockhead," Saba said. "We know nothing, not even where they are."

Saba's intervention reminded Han that he and Leia weren't the only ones with a child at risk. Her son, Tesar, was one of the Jedi Knights who had followed Jaina into the Unknown Regions.

"Sorry. I don't know what came over me." Han touched Saba's back—then swallowed hard, remembering that touching a Barabel uninvited was a good way to lose an arm. "Sometimes, I forget they're Jedi."

"Not to worry." Saba thumped a scaly hand down on his shoulder. "This one forgetz sometimez, too."

A moment of silence hung in the air as they recalled all they had lost at Myrkr, Anakin and Bela and Krasov and the others, and Han thought he could almost feel Saba reaching for him in the Force, trying to lend him the strength to have faith in his daughter's abilities, to recall that she was a Jedi Knight and an ace star pilot and a hero as big in her war as he and Leia had been in theirs. It was not an easy thing for a father to keep in mind, but it was true, and—as Leia always said—in truth there was strength.

"All right already," Han said, motioning Juun back to the control board. "You can go back to work. I'm better."

Leia gave him an understanding wink, then turned back to Juun. "What does Lizil need with a group of Jedi Knights?"

"I don't know," Juun said. "But they left with Unu."

"Unu?"

"The central nest," Juun said. "Your daughter and the others were met by an escort of Unu guards."

"*More* bugs?" Han had a sinking feeling. "Great."

"Then there's an *organization* of nests?" Leia asked Juun.

The Sullustan nodded. "The Colony."

Han thought he was beginning to understand. "How big?"

Juun pulled a datapad from beneath his utilities, then began punching keys. "I have heard three hundred and seventy-five names."

Luke whistled. "Enough to stretch from here to the Chiss frontier. Now this is beginning to make some sense."

"How do you figure?" Han asked.

"The situation isn't complicated," Leia said. "The Colony is rubbing borders with the Chiss empire. It's pretty clear why the central nest might want a team of Jedi Joiners on their side—especially this particular team."

"Jedi commandos are good equalizers," Han agreed. "But what I want to know is how the Colony got them to come out here in the first place."

Several moments passed with no answer, and finally their gazes began to drift toward Juun. Tarfang's eyes darted from one to the other of them, and finally he jabbered an angry denial.

"Tarfang asks that you stop looking at them," C-3PO said. "He denies any involvement."

"That's not what we were implying," Leia said.

"But we do need your help," Luke said to Juun. "*Han* needs your help. We must find our Jedi Knights."

Juun considered this for a moment, then said, "Perhaps there *is* a way. There's room in the forward hold. If we hide you in there—"

"Forget it," Han said. "We're flying our own ships."

"I'm afraid this is the only practical way," Juun said. "I'll be relying entirely on the guide myself."

Han shook his head.

"Han, I know it'll be crowded," Luke said. "But it sounds like the best plan."

"No, Luke," Han said, discreetly eyeing the control board. "It really *doesn't*."

Luke's gaze darted to the board and away again almost immediately, but he was not quick enough to escape Juun's notice.

"Why are you looking at the control board?" he demanded. "You don't trust me to maintain my own ship?"

"Well, you did slip with your solder." Han stooped down and pointed at a silver line angling across the board. "You're going to have a short running across your flux inhibitors."

Juun studied the line, then said, "It's nothing to worry about. I followed all the proper procedures."

"Yeah, but you slipped—"

"It's more than adequate. I'll demonstrate." Juun slipped the master plug onto the supply prongs, then waved Tarfang to the far side of the cabin. "Close the main breaker."

"Juun, I don't think that's a good—"

A sharp *clack* echoed across the room. Han barely managed to close his eyes before the ship erupted into a tempest of bursting lamps and sizzling circuits. Leia and the others cried out in shock. When the crackling continued, Han pulled his blaster and, opening his eyes to what looked like a indoor lightning storm, shot through the wire array just above the master plug.

The popping and buzzing quickly died away, and the main cabin was again plunged into its previous green dimness. Juun dropped to his knees in front of the control board.

"Not again!"

"What did I tell you?" Han asked.

Tarfang returned to the group and studied his crestfallen captain a moment, then looked Han in the eye and spoke sharply.

"He says the cost just doubled, Captain Solo," C-3PO said. "You must pay for the damages you caused."

"*I* caused?" Han protested. "I told him not to—"

"We'll be glad to replace the wire array Han destroyed saving the *XR-eight-oh-eight-g*," Leia interrupted. "And we'll do anything else we can to help Captain Juun complete his repairs . . . per item seven of the Smuggler's Code."

"You bet," Han said, catching Leia's strategy. "It's not as bad as it sounded, or the smoke would be a lot thicker."

Juun looked up, his small eyes round with wonder. "This is covered under item seven?"

"Oh, yeah," Han said. "But we're flying our own ships."

"I'm sure we can think of a way to follow Captain Juun." Luke spoke in a tone that suggested he had already solved this problem. "We may need to install a couple of pieces of equipment when we repair the wire array."

Tarfang raised a lip, then jabbered a demand.

"What kind of equipment?" C-3PO translated.

"The secret kind," Luke said, glaring at the Ewok.

Tarfang lowered his furry brow and glared back for a moment, then finally said something that C-3PO translated as, "Captain Juun will be taking a big risk. It'll cost you."

"Fine," Luke said. He stepped close to Juun and Tarfang, and suddenly he seemed as large as a rancor. "But you know who we are. You understand what it will mean if you try to double-cross us?"

Tarfang shrank back, but Juun seemed untroubled.

"Double-cross Han Solo?" the Sullustan asked. "Who'd be crazy enough to do that?"

SEVEN

Down in the valley, the Taat were scavenging along the floodplain, their thoraxes glowing green in Jwlio's hazy light. With the rest of their foraging territory brown and withering from a Chiss defoliant, the workers were stripping the ground bare, leaving nothing in their wake but rooj stubble and mud. It was a desperate act that would only deepen their famine in the future, but the insects had no choice. Their larvae were starving *now*.

In the midst of such poverty and hardship, Jaina Solo felt more than a little guilty eating green thakitillo, but it was the only thing on the menu tonight. Tomorrow, it would be brot-rib or krayt eggs or some other rarity more suitable to a state dinner than a field post, and she would eat that, too. The Taat would be insulted if she did not.

Jaina spooned a curd into her mouth, then glanced around the veranda at her companions. They were all seated on primitive spit-crete benches, holding their bowls in their laps and using small Force bubbles to keep the dust at bay. Despite the gritty winds raised by the tidal pull of Qoribu—Jwlio's ringed gas giant primary—the group usually took their meals outdoors. No one wanted to spend more time than necessary in the muggy confines of the nest caves.

After the curd had dissolved, Jaina tapped her spoon against the bowl. "Okay," she asked. "Who's responsible for this?"

One by one, the others raised their gazes, their faces betraying various degrees of culpability as they examined their thoughts over the last week or so. Shortly after arriving, the team had discovered that whenever they talked about a particular food, the Taat would have a supply delivered within a few days. Concerned about squandering their hosts' limited resources, Jaina had ordered the group to avoid talking about food in front of the Taat, then to avoid mentioning it at all.

Finally, Tesar Sebatyne flicked up a talon. "It may have been this one."

"*May* have been?" Jaina asked. "Either you said something or you didn't."

Tesar's dorsal scales rose in the Barabel equivalent of a blush. "This one *said* nothing. He thought it."

"They can't eavesdrop on thoughts," Jaina said. "Someone else must have slipped."

She glanced around the group, waiting. The others continued to search their memories, but no one recalled talking about food.

Finally, Zekk said, "I'm just happy it's thakitillo instead of some skalrat or something." Seated on a bench next to Jaina, he wore his black hair as long and ragged as he had in his youth, but that was all that remained the same. A late growth spurt had turned him into something of a human giant, standing two meters tall, with shoulders as broad as Lowbacca's. "I thought Barabels liked to catch their own food."

"When we can, but this one was thinking of our last meal aboard *Lady Luck,* and he alwayz tastes thakitillo when he rememberz Bela and Krasov and . . ." Tesar trailed off and glanced briefly in Jaina's direction, quietly acknowledging the bond of grief they had come to share through the Myrkr mission. ". . . the otherz."

Even that gentle reminder of her brother's death—even seven years later—brought a pained hollow to Jaina's chest. Usually, her duties as a Jedi Knight kept her too busy to dwell on such things, but there were still moments like these, when the terrible memory came crashing down on her like a Nkllonian firestorm.

"So maybe the Taat *are* eavesdropping on our thoughts," Tahiri said, bringing Jaina's attention back to the present. "If we're sure no one said anything, that has to be it."

Lowbacca let out a long Wookiee moan.

"I suppose we *will* have to avoid thinking about food," Jaina agreed. "We're Jedi. We can't keep eating like Hutts while the Taat larvae starve."

"It certainly takes the fun out of it," Alema Rar agreed. The Twi'lek slipped a spoonful of thakitillo into her mouth, then bit into a curd and curled the tips of the long lekku hanging down her back. "Well, *most* of the fun."

Zekk ate a spoonful, then asked, "Does it bother anyone that they're listening to our thoughts?"

"It *should*," Jaina replied. "We should feel a little uneasy and violated, shouldn't we?"

Alema shrugged. "*Should* is for narrow minds. It makes *me* feel
welcome."

Jaina considered this for a moment, then nodded in agreement.
"Same here—and valued. Zekk? You brought it up."

"Just asking," he said. "Doesn't bother me, either."

"I feel the same," Tekli agreed. The furry little Chadra-Fan
twitched her thick-ended snout. "Yet we avoid the battle-meld now
because we dislike sharing feelings among ourselves."

"That's different," Tahiri said. "*We* get on each other's nerves."

"To put it mildly," Jaina said. "I'll never forget how that blood
hunger came over me the first time Tesar saw a rallop."

"Or how twisted inside this one felt when Alema wanted to nest
with that Rodian rope-wrestler." Tesar fluttered his scales, then
added, "It was a week before he could hunt again."

Alema smiled at the memory, then said, "*Nesting* wasn't what I
had in mind."

Lowbacca banged his bowl down on the bench next to him,
groaning in distaste and weary resignation. After the war, Jaina and
the other strike team members had begun to notice unexplained
mood swings whenever they were together. It had taken Cilghal only
a few days to diagnose the problem as a delayed reaction to the Jedi
battle-meld. Their prolonged use of it on the Myrkr mission had
weakened the boundaries among their minds, with the result that
now their emotions tended to fill the Force and blur together whenever they were close to each other.

Sometimes Jaina believed the side effect was also the reason so
many strike team survivors found it difficult to move on with their
lives. Tenel Ka was doing well as the Hapan queen, and Tekli and
Tahiri seemed to regard Zonama Sekot as both a friend and a home,
but the rest of them—Jaina, Alema, Zekk, Tesar, Lowbacca, even
Jacen—still seemed lost, unable to maintain a connection with anyone who had not been there. Jaina *knew* that was why she had failed
to reconnect with Jagged Fel during their desperate rendezvous when
he had still been serving as Chiss liaison to the Galactic Alliance. She
loved him, but she'd just grown increasingly distant from him. From
everyone, really.

Sensing that she had let her dour mood affect the others, Jaina
forced a smile. "I *do* have some good news," she said. "Jacen is
coming."

As she had hoped, this lifted spirits instantly—especially those of

Tahiri, who shared a special kinship with Jacen by virtue of the time they had spent in Yuuzhan Vong torture dens.

But it was Alema—always quick to take an interest in males—who asked, "Can you tell how soon?"

"It's hard to say," Jaina answered. No one bothered to ask if she had actually spoken to her twin brother; there was no HoloNet in the Unknown Regions—and even if there had been, they were too close to the Chiss frontier to risk being overheard by a listening post. "But it feels like he's made it past whatever was delaying him."

"How will he find the Colony?" Tahiri asked. Though she could certainly sense Alema's interest in Jacen as clearly as Jaina did, she seemed more amused by it than irritated. "Tekli and I would have been lost without Zonama Sekot's help."

"I left a message for him with the coordinates of the Lizil nest," Jaina said. "So, assuming he tries to comm . . ."

She let the sentence trail off when she felt a sudden alarm. The sense did not ripple or grow or rise. It simply appeared inside Jaina, instantly full-blown and strong, and at first she thought she was feeling something inside her brother. Then bowls of thakitillo began to clack down on the spitcrete benches, and her companions started to rise and reach for their lightsabers.

"You feel it, too?" Jaina asked no one in particular.

"Fear," Zekk confirmed. "Surprise."

Lowbacca rawwled an addition.

"Resolve, too," Jaina agreed.

"What the blazes?" Tahiri asked. "It's like the Taat were a part of the meld, too."

"Maybe they're more Force-sensitive than we thought," Alema suggested.

Jaina gazed around, searching the faces of her companions for any indication that the sensation had felt even remotely like a normal Force perception to someone else. She found only looks of confusion and doubt.

A familiar rumble rose deep inside the nest. Long plumes of black smoke began to shoot from the exhaust vents above the hangar cave, then a cloud of dartships poured into the air above the valley and began to climb toward Qoribu's ringed disk.

"Looks like another defoliator squad coming in." Jaina was almost relieved as she started toward their own hangar. After the unexpected feeling of alarm, she had feared something worse. "Let's turn 'em back."

EIGHT

The wreck was a CEC YV-888 stock light freighter. Jacen could see that much from its tall hull, and from the stubs of the melted maneuvering fins on the rear engine compartment. The crash had occurred sometime within the last decade. He could guess that much from the faint odor of ash and slag that still wafted down the flowery slope from the jagged crater rim. But the vessel's hull was too thickly covered in insects for him to be certain this was *the* ship, the one that would explain why he and Jaina and the others had been called so deep into the Unknown Regions.

Jacen waited for a throng of thumb-sized insects to scurry past on the enclosure wall, then placed a hand on top and vaulted over. A harsh rattle rose behind him as other, larger visitors pulsed their wings in disapproval. He paid no attention and started up the slope, feeling his way with the Force to avoid stepping on any tiny beings hidden in the flora. The Colony species came in an enormous variety of sizes and shapes, and any insects he happened to crush on monument grounds were more likely to be other visitors than foraging bugs.

Jacen's guide, a chest-high insect who had been waiting at the Lizil nest to serve as his navigator, scurried to his side and began to rumble objections.

"You're the one who said we didn't have time to wait in line," Jacen reminded him.

"*Rububu uburu,*" the guide responded. With a yellow thorax, green abdomen, and bright red head and eyes, it was one of the more colorful strains that Jacen had seen. "*Urb?*"

"I told you," Jacen answered. "I might know this ship."

Jacen reached the crash crater and climbed to the rim. Ten meters below, in the crash bottom, a sagging tangle of heat-softened durasteel so covered in crawling insects that it took a moment to realize he was looking at a small starship bridge. The vessel had crashed upside down.

The guide thrummed impatiently.

"Not yet." Jacen pointed at a place near the bow where a dozen Jawa-sized insects were sticking their antennae through a twisted rip in the hull. "Ask the ones near that breach to clear a space. I need to see if I can read its name."

"*Ub Ruur.*" [The Crash.]

"I need to know the name of the *freighter*," Jacen explained. "It's written on the side of the hull. In letters."

Like most species of intelligent arthropods in the galaxy, the Colony insects recorded their language in pheromones instead of writing, but Jacen felt certain the Joiners would have explained the concept of letters.

"*U.*" The guide curled its antennae forward. "*Burubu ru?*"

"Maybe," Jacen said uncertainly. He was relying the Force and his empathic connection with other life-forms to infer his guide's meaning, and he could not always be sure that he understood all the nuances. "But we'll certainly be on our way sooner than if I have to piece the letters together through their legs."

The guide clacked its mandibles in frustration. It drummed its chest loudly, then the insects near the rip began to mill about in confusion. Jacen did not understand what they got out of crawling over the wreck, but insects were very tactile creatures, and he suspected they were establishing some sense of connection to it. Finally, a space began to clear where Jacen had requested. The durasteel was so caked with carbonization that he could barely make out a handful of dark, upside-down letters.

. . . ACH . . ON F . . . ER

"*Tachyon Flier,*" Jacen said. It was the ship in which the strike team had planned to depart the Myrkr system—until they were betrayed by two Dark Jedi they had rescued from the Yuuzhan Vong. Jacen turned to his guide. "What happened to the people aboard that ship?"

"*Bu ruub ubu buubu,*" the guide said.

"And he'll keep waiting until I have my answer."

"*Ubu buubu ru ruubu.*" [Unu must not be kept waiting.]

"Your rules," Jacen answered. "Not mine."

Seeing no easier way down, Jacen stepped off the rim and used the Force to slow his descent. The insects on his side of the *Flier* watched in stunned silence as he caught hold of the rip in the hull and brought his fall to a gentle stop.

The guide boomed a question from above.

"The people who brought this ship here had a friend of mine with them," Jacen said. "I'm not leaving here until I know what happened to him."

"*Rur ruru rr ubu buubu bub!*" the navigator drummed.

"*I* don't wish to see Unu at once." Jacen knew he was being rude, but he had learned from the Fallanassi to see through the illusion of authority, to free himself of the expectation of blind obedience by respecting his own desires first. "It makes no difference to me if Unu can't wait."

Jacen pulled himself up and peered through the hull breach. The *Flier*'s presence certainly lay at the heart of the mysterious summons that had brought him here, but that told him little. Before he allowed himself to be drawn farther along this current, he needed to find out what had happened aboard the ship. He needed to know *who* had called the strike team survivors here . . . and why.

The interior of the vessel was dark and acrid smelling, lit only by the shafts of light pouring through several dozen hull breaches. A few of the holes were large and twisted, like the rip beneath the vessel's name, and had probably resulted from the crash. The rest were oblong, small, and surrounded by the metal spatter-beads associated with hits from Yuuzhan Vong plasma cannons. The *Tachyon Flier* had clearly taken a beating as it left the Myrkr system. It was surprising the ship had held together long enough to fly into the Unknown Regions.

As his eyes grew attuned to the dim light, Jacen realized that he was looking into the hold area. The adjustable cargo decks had left their tracks in the crash and fallen into what had been the top of the ship, burying the bridge and crew quarters beneath a tangle of twisted, half-melted durasteel. Seeing that no insects were crawling over the inside of the ship, he closed his eyes and listened for any stirrings in the Force that might explain their reluctance to enter. He heard the whisper of a long-spent inferno and the faint scream of twisting metal, but nothing to alarm him now.

Jacen swung a leg up and slipped into the *Flier*'s hold. The acrid smell grew stronger. It was more than just ash, it was carbonized synthplas and iron slag and charred fibercrete. He slid down the hull, calling on the Force to hold himself against the wall and slow his descent. About two-thirds of the way to the bottom, he came to the jumble of decks and stopped, then used a Dathomiri Force spell to kindle a sphere of bright light.

A chorus of sharp *clacks* sounded above, and Jacen looked up to see a carpet of insects large and small crawling down the hull behind him, their feathery antennae sweeping the surrounding durasteel. Worried his invasion of a sacred site might be considered an outrage, Jacen touched them through the Force. He felt astonishment, curiosity, a little wariness, but no anger or indignation.

"Be careful," Jacen called, a little puzzled by their willingness to follow *him* into the vessel. "It might not take much to shift the debris down here."

The insects answered with the full range of thrums, chirps, and thuds.

Jacen used the Force to slide several tons of cargo deck into a secure position, then walked over to the edge and discovered the reason for the insects' earlier reluctance to enter the wreck. Several large exoskeletons lay crushed beneath a twisted cross-brace. Though the rest of the jumble was every bit as tangled as it had appeared from above, Jacen could now see that many decks had fallen against each other, creating a tent effect that might have protected the bridge from being crushed—at least from above.

Jacen turned to the insects. "I'd appreciate it if everyone stayed here for now."

The insects gave a confirming *clack*. Floating his sphere of Force light behind him, Jacen threaded his way down to what had been the underside of the bridge, where the metal was buckled and discolored from a conflagration below.

Jacen began to fear the worst.

Seeing no convenient hatch in the vicinity, he ignited his lightsaber . . . and was startled by the sudden clicking of mandibles behind him. He glanced over his shoulder and found a long ribbon of golden eyes reflecting the glow of his Force light and green lightsaber.

"I asked you to wait," Jacen said.

"*Uu rrrruub.*" The thrum set up a sympathetic vibration in the jumble above, inducing a long metallic scream as a deck edge slid down an underbrace. "*Brrr brru!*"

"I am being careful." Jacen used the Force to stabilize the twisted metal above their heads. "Just be quiet."

The swarm rustled its agreement—then clicked madly as he plunged his lightsaber blade into the floor of the bridge.

"I'm sorry to disrespect the Crash," he said. "But my friend may be down there."

"*Bru bur, ruu,*" a ghostly pale insect informed him.

"Obviously." Jacen continued to cut. "I still need to find him."

This occasioned a flurry of thrumming and clicking among the other insects.

"No." Jacen began to feel sick, though it was impossible to say whether this was from the smell of melting metal, the stale stench rising from below, or the insects' question. "I'm not going to eat his remains."

The insects continued to clack and drum. They seemed to be debating whether he should be allowed to continue if he wasn't going to return his friend to the Song. But Jacen was inferring as much as translating, and there was so much he did not know about the Colony that it was equally possible they were talking about eating *him*. He shut the words out and tried to hear through the Force, as the Theran Listeners had taught him, and was relieved to sense that they were arguing over whether *they* should eat the dead.

Jacen finished cutting, then used the Force to lift two disks of metal out of the hole he had cut in the double-floored deck. The smell of ash grew overwhelming, and rustling filled the air as the insects eased forward behind him. Jacen lowered his light through the hole and felt his heart sink.

The cabin below had been so incinerated that only the twisted remains of a row of double bunks, hanging upside down on the far wall, identified it as the crew's quarters. What had once been the ceiling lay barely two meters below, blackened, crumpled, and strewn with ash and twisted metal. The remains of several mattresses lay in the corner beneath the bunks, half burned and covered in black mold.

Being careful to avoid touching the white-hot edges, Jacen dropped through the hole and found several shattered tranqarest vials under one of the half-burned mattresses. Under another, he found a melted lump of casing and circuitry that might once have been Lowbacca's translation droid, Em Teedee. He tried to pick it up and discovered it had been fused to the floor.

Under a third mattress, he found the singed remains of one of the molytex jumpsuits the strike team had worn on their mission to Myrkr. There were four slashes across the chest, where Raynar had been wounded before being put aboard the *Flier*.

A series of soft patters sounded from the middle of the cabin. Insects began to swarm over the "floor" and walls, sweeping their an-

tennae over the bunks and other debris and raising a choking cloud
of ash. Jacen made his way forward through the galley and wardroom, dropping into a crouch as the space between the crumpled
ceiling and the old floor grew too short for him to walk upright. The
walls and other surfaces in these rooms were covered with a thick
layer of pink powder, the residue of a fire-fighting foam.

On the bridge, the foam lay so thick that he kicked up clouds of
pink dust as he moved. The canopy that had once enclosed the flight
deck on three sides was buckled and broken, with dirt spilling
through long rents in the transparisteel. A string of gray emergency
patches ran diagonally across the forward view-screen, roughly parallel to a line of destruction that had left the navicomputer, sublight-
drive control relays, and hyperspace guidance system in a burned
shambles. It was no wonder the ship had crashed; the Dark Jedi crew
had done well to escape the Myrkr system at all.

The crash webbing at all the flight deck stations hung down beneath the chairs in a melted tangle, but a faint drag mark beneath the
pilot's and copilot's seats led through the foam residue toward the engineering cabin. Jacen dropped to his knees to peer through the cockeyed hatchway, and his nostrils filled with the caustic stench of
charred bone.

Jacen began a slow breathing exercise. The harsh smell burned
his nostrils at first and threatened to make him nauseous, but as he
centered himself in the Force and slowly detached from his emotions,
the odor grew less biting, its implications less painful. He placed a
hand on the wall and imagined it growing warm under his touch.

The staleness seemed to fade from the air inside the wreck, then
the smell of old soot turned to the acrid bite of smoke. Jacen's eyes
started to water as he looked back through the Force. His lungs were
racked by an endless fit of coughing, and the cabin grew hot and orange. Where he was touching the wall, his palm began to sting and
blister. He held it in place and looked over his shoulder.

The flight deck was hidden behind a curtain of smoke and
rolling flame. Geysers of fire retardant rose from the ceiling nozzles,
creating swirling ghosts of pink fog. Howls of human anguish
drowned out the scream of buckling metal.

A single figure crawled out of the smoke, hairless and coughing and
blistered raw. His face was unrecognizable, but four gashes ran diagonally across his chest, the wound hanging half open where the fleshglue
had dissolved in the heat. One hand trailed behind, dragging a pair of
levitated shapes along by their cloak collars. The two shapes were still
burning, writhing in the air and flailing against each other in their pain.

Smoke began to rise from beneath Jacen's palm, and the smell of cooking flesh filled the air. He kept his hand pressed against the wall. Pain no longer troubled him. Pain was his servant; he had learned *that* from Vergere.

The crawling figure reached the hatchway and paused, turning in Jacen's direction. The face was too scorched and swollen to recognize, but the eyes belonged to Raynar, questioning and proud and so terribly naïve. The two of them locked gazes for a moment, then Raynar cocked his head in confusion and started to open his mouth . . .

Jacen pulled his hand from the wall. The figures vanished instantly, returning him to a flight deck filled with the stale smell of ash and clouds of pink dust.

An insect brushed its antennae over his scorched hand. *"Rur-rrrruu,"* it drummed in concern. *"Urrubuuuu?"*

"Yes, it does hurt." Jacen smiled. "It's nothing."

He removed a small canister from his equipment belt and sprayed a coating of synthflesh over his palm. Raynar had been the misfit of their childhood group, trying a little too hard to fit in and often the butt of jokes for his arrogance and showy clothes. He had never impressed anyone as exceptional Jedi material, and there had been a few conversations in which fellow candidates had expressed reservations about his judgment and initiative. Yet what Raynar had done on the *Flier*, risking his own life to save those who had betrayed his friends and abducted him, was the essence of being a Jedi Knight. Jacen doubted he would have done the same thing—and *Jaina* would have stayed to watch them burn. Given what the theft of the *Flier* had meant—that Anakin would certainly die of his wounds—Jacen might even have joined her.

Floating his Force light ahead of him, Jacen crawled into the engineering cabin and followed Raynar's trail through a cramped maze of toppled equipment. The stench of charred bones grew stronger, and Jacen feared he would only find their burned remains trapped in some dead-end corner, or simply lying in the middle of the aisle where Raynar had succumbed to smoke inhalation. His fears began to seem justified when he started to find scorched bones in the middle of the aisle—first, a few finger and toe and hand bones, then a forearm and a shin, then finally a femur. The space between the floor and ceiling grew smaller and smaller, and he had to drop to his belly, and he began to sense the residue of Raynar's panic in the Force.

Then Jacen came to the shoulder blade, lying half buried in a pile of dirt that had poured in through a rent in the hull, and he knew. He began to dig, pulling the soft dirt under his body and pushing it back with his feet, and a moment later he felt a welcome draft of fresh air. Raynar had reached an exit—but in what condition? Had he survived? Had either of the others?

His chest tight with hope and fear, Jacen belly-crawled through the hole, out into the bottom of the crater . . . and was surprised to find his guide waiting. In its hands, the insect held a new starfighter helmet and flight suit.

"*Ubu rrru ubb.*" Without waiting for Jacen to stand, the guide offered the helmet and suit to him. "*Urru bu.*"

Jacen stood. "Why would I need a starfighter helmet?" Instead of taking either item, he began to brush himself off. "I fly a skiff."

The guide raised one of its four hands toward the crater rim, where one of the Reconstruction Police's new XJ5 X-wings sat with an open cockpit.

Jacen had a sinking feeling. "I'm *happy* with my skiff."

The guide thrummed a long explanation, which seemed to assert that he would be much happier serving the Colony in a ChaseX than his skiff, which the Colony was already using to ferry a group of Togot pilgrims back to the spaceport.

Jacen did not bother to demand its return. He had already learned that the Colony insects had no real understanding of private property. The skiff would be put to use—and, fortunately, well maintained—until he was ready to track it down again.

"Why would I want to serve the Colony?" Jacen asked. "Especially in a combat craft?"

A membrane slid over the guide's bulbous eyes and rose again, and it continued to hold the helmet and flight suit out to Jacen.

"It's a simple question," Jacen said. "If the Colony expects me to kill people, you'd better be able to tell me why."

The guide cocked its head in incomprehension, and Jacen knew he was asking too much. As social insects, Colony residents obviously had a very limited sense of self—and absolutely no concept of free will. He might as well have been asking a beldon to take him fishing.

Always the preacher. The voice was the same that had come to Jacen back in Akanah's teaching circle—save that now the words were raspy and booming instead of faint and wispy. *You still think too much, Jacen.*

"I usually find it preferable to catastrophic blunders," Jacen said. The voice was so harsh and deep he found it even more difficult to place. It might have been Raynar—or it might have been Lomi or

Welk or someone else altogether. "You seem to know me. You couldn't believe I would just start killing for you."

We do know you, Jacen, the voice said, not unkindly. *We know what you* will *fight for.*

As the voice spoke, an immense murky presence rose inside Jacen's mind, overwhelming his defenses so quickly he had no chance to shut it out. In the midst of the presence, he saw Jaina and the others, their faces filled with surprise and revulsion and pity. They were all in their flight suits, haggard and travel-worn, but healthy enough and unafraid.

They *serve the Colony, Jacen,* the voice said. *Will you join them? Will you help your sister?*

Jacen did not answer, even in his thoughts. A day ago, he had felt Jaina growing small and cold in the Force, the way she always did before a battle. But there had been no indication afterward of anything alarming, not even the usual weary sorrow that always came of taking lives. He reached out to her, probing to see if there was anything amiss. She responded with a welcoming warmth that let him know she was looking forward to seeing him.

But there was more, just a hint of the murky presence that had pushed its way into Jacen's mind—not hostile or ominous or threatening, just there.

The guide drew Jacen's attention back to it by pressing the helmet and flight suit into his hands. *"Buu buur urub ruuruur."*

Jacen pushed the equipment back into the guide's hands. "I haven't said I'm going."

"Buu rurr. Ubu ur."

"Perhaps," Jacen allowed. The murky presence had withdrawn from his own mind, once again leaving him solely with his guide. "Once I've found out what happened here."

He squatted on his haunches and ran his fingers through the dirt, searching for any sign that Raynar and the others had died here. When he found no more large bones, he pictured the raw and blistered face he had seen on the flight deck, then called on the Force again, trying to reach into the past and learn what had become of Raynar.

But this time, the Force opened itself to him in its own way. Instead of the smoke and scorched flesh he had smelled on the flight deck, the odor it brought down to him was fresh and fragrant and familiar, a smell he had known since childhood.

Jacen looked up at the crater rim and was puzzled to find an image of his mother there, frowning across the gap at the *Flier's* blast-pocked hull. She was wearing a white blouse with a brown skirt and vest that reminded Jacen of his father's swashbuckling style, right down to the holstered blaster hanging on her hip. There were some new strands of gray hair and a few more laugh lines around her mouth, but she looked healthy and content, and Jacen's heart leapt at the sight of her. The last time he had seen her face had been over five standard years ago, before leaving on his odyssey of self-discovery, and he was astonished at the joy even a vision of it brought to him.

Jacen swallowed his surprise and tried instead to simply concentrate on what the Force was revealing to him. He knew that she was not actually standing there *now*, but at some other time. And, since his mother was the only figure he could see, she was probably the link to discovering what had become of Raynar.

She turned to someone he could not see, then asked, "What happened to the crew?"

There was a pause while she listened to the reply. Jacen could imagine only one thing that would bring his parents this deep into the Unknown Regions, the heart of the Colony itself. They had to be looking for the strike team.

His mother looked back to the *Flier*. "I mean the rest of the crew. We *know* Raynar survived."

Jacen had his answer, but he was not ready to release the vision—not yet. He looked up at his mother's image, reaching out to her in the Force to strengthen their contact.

"Hello."

Her gaze dropped toward Jacen's voice, then she furrowed her brow and reached out, as though grasping for someone's arm. "Jacen has been here."

Has. So they were still behind him.

The guide snapped its mandibles next to Jacen's ear. "*Bubu ruu bu?*"

"No one. Sorry." Continuing to hold the vision through the Force, Jacen finally took the helmet and flight suit. "Okay. Where am I going?"

The guide replied that Jacen wouldn't recognize the name of the system. It was on the Chiss frontier.

Up on the crater rim, the vision of his mother frowned. "Jacen? I'm having trouble hearing you."

Jacen ignored her and continued to speak to the guide. "Humor me. In case something happens and I need to find my own way."

The navigator spread its antennae. "*Burubu,*" it answered. "*Ur bu Brurr rubur.*"

"Jacen?" His mother's face grew pale. "How? You're not—"

"I'm fine, Mom," he said. "I'll see you soon."

The guide turned a bulbous eye toward the crater rim.

"Qoribu," Jacen said, looking up at his mother. "In the Gyuel system."

NINE

As the *Falcon* dropped toward the mottled pinnacles below, Leia found herself straining against her crash webbing, almost gasping at the bustling vastness of the Colony's central nest. The Yoggoy towers, brightly adorned in wild splashes of color, stood hip-to-hip across the entire planet, and the air was so thick with flying vehicles that she could barely see the surface.

"Kind of looks like old Coruscant," Han said, speaking to Leia and—over the comm—to Luke, Mara, and everyone else aboard the *Shadow*. "So big—and all that bustle."

Leia continued to strain forward over her controls, peering out the lower edge of the canopy. As the *Falcon* descended, she began to see that while the pinnacles came in every size, they were all distinctly cone-shaped, and they all had horizontally banded exteriors—like the insect spires in *Killik Twilight*.

She started to say as much, then decided she was letting her imagination run wild. Cones were a basic geometric form. Creating them out of mud rings was probably as common among intelligent insects as was erecting stone rectangles among social mammals.

"I'm gonna blast that can of corrosion back to quarks!" Han said.

Leia glanced over to find Han frowning at his tactical display, then checked her own screen and saw that the *XR808g*'s transponder code had disappeared. "Did Juun land already?"

Han shook his head. "The little earworm shut off his transponder."

Knowing better than to ask if Han had remembered to run a code search, Leia activated her throat mike.

"We've lost the *Exxer*."

The report was greeted with a troubled silence. Right now, the *XR808g* was their only hope of locating Jaina and the others.

"Any ideas?" Han asked. "I'd like to find these kids *before* they become a bunch of bughuggers."

"That's not going to happen." Even over the cockpit comm, Luke's voice was calm and reassuring. "They're Jedi."

"What's that have to do with the price of spice on Nal Hutta?" Han demanded.

"They're too strong, Han," Mara said. "Especially Jaina."

"Yeah?" Han asked. "If they're so strong, how'd that Force-call drag them all the way out here in the first place?"

The troubled silence returned.

Leia reached over and laid her hand over Han's. "It'll be all right, Han. I can still feel them out there. They're not Joiners."

"Yet," Han grumbled. Over the comm, he asked, "How about those ideas?"

"Try a code search," Luke suggested helpfully.

Han rolled his eyes.

Leia smiled at him, then said to Luke, "Thanks for the suggestion. We've already tried that."

"No need to worry," Mara said. "We haven't lost them."

"We haven't?" Leia asked. Before the *XR808g* left Lizil, Han and Juun had hidden a subspace transceiver beneath the cockpit and linked it to the navicomputer. Each time the *XR808g* initiated a jump, the transceiver automatically encoded the galactic coordinates and broadcast them to the *Shadow* and *Falcon*—but that didn't help them now, when they were already *at* those coordinates. "I don't understand."

"Give me a second." Mara remained silent for a moment, then said, "Be ready to take a fix, in case Juun is smarter than he looked."

Han raised his brow. "I don't recall planting a homing beacon on the *Exxer*."

"Because *you're* not the sneaky one—despite all reports to the contrary," Mara commed. "Ready?"

Leia smiled and prepared a navigation lock. "Ready." A red dot began to blink in the upper corner of the tactical display. "Got it."

Leia activated the lock, and Han swung the *Falcon* around behind the red dot. Yoggoy traffic proved an unimaginable free-for-all, with muscle-powered balloon-bikes competing for airspace against dilapidated cloud cars and modern airspeeders. Thick-waisted rocket planes flashed past in all directions, packed to bursting with goggle-eyed insects and trailing oily plumes of smoke. Battered space freighters eased their durasteel hulks down into the mess, descending through the traffic toward the haze-blanketed towertops below.

A stubby little rocket plane shot out from under a cargo blimp off to starboard and began to climb, coming for Leia's side of the cockpit.

"Rodder!" Han cursed, and the *Falcon* took a sudden skip upward. "Watch where you're going!"

"Don't get so upset," Leia said. "We have plenty—"

A thirty-meter insect shuttle flashed into view from beneath Leia's side of the cockpit, headed straight for the little rocket plane.

"Oh, my!" C-3PO said from the navigator's station. "That was too close—"

"Hard to port," Leia interrupted. "Now, Han!"

"Port?" Han shot back. "You're crazy!"

Leia glanced over and saw the mountainous hull of a giant transport gliding past above the *Falcon*'s forward mandibles.

"Oh—" Leia slapped the crash alarm, bringing the inertial compensators to maximum, priming the fire-suppression systems, and setting off a cacophony of alerts farther back in the vessel. "Brace yourself!"

"Dead stop!" Luke's voice came over the comm. "Dead stop!"

Han already had his hand on the throttles—but before he could pull them back, the shuttle was diving and the rocket plane was climbing past the *Falcon* almost vertically, so close that Leia could have reached out and grabbed the pilot's antennae.

Han casually slipped his hand off the throttle and deactivated the crash alarm. "No need to get all excited." His hands were shaking as badly as Leia's, but she saw no use in pointing that out. "I've got it under control."

"Yes," C-3PO agreed. "It's fortunate that you were wise enough to do nothing. It gave the other pilots time to respond to your error."

"*My* error?" Han replied. "I was flying straight and level."

"Quite so, but the others are all following sine wave trajectories," C-3PO said. "And may I point out that any system functions optimally only when all elements use the same equations?"

A two-seater rocket plane dropped in ahead of the *Falcon* and bobbed along pouring fumes into their faces, then swerved aside to reveal the bulbous shape of a balloon-bike coming at them head-on. Han rolled into an inverted dive and spiraled past beneath it.

"Now you tell me," Han said.

"Watch it back there," Leia warned the *Shadow*. "And have Artoo plot a sine wave trajectory for us—a *safe* one."

"We'll send it up in a moment," Mara promised.

The moment went by, then two, then several. Finally, when her nerves could stand no more close calls—and no more of Han's grouching—Leia commed back to the *Shadow*.

"Uh, we didn't receive that trajectory."

"We're trying," Luke said. "Artoo's sort of locked up."

"Locked up?" Han asked. "An *astromech*?"

"He's been acting strange lately," Luke explained. "All we got before he went blank was *not safe, not safe, not safe*."

"Oh, dear!" C-3PO exclaimed. "It sounds as though he's trying to resolve an unknowable variable. We're doomed!"

"Yeah?" Han waved at the traffic outside the forward viewport. "Then how come none of *them* are crashing?"

C-3PO was silent for a moment, then said, "I wouldn't know, Captain Solo. Their processors certainly aren't any better than Artoo's."

"They don't *need* processors." Leia was thinking of Luke's description of the cantina where Saba met Tarfang, of how the mysterious Joiners had arrived to lead away any patron with whom he struck up a conversation. "It was pretty clear that the Lizil can communicate telepathically. Maybe the Yoggoy can, too."

"Probably," Mara agreed. "And since *we* don't have any Yoggoy navigators aboard—"

"We're flying blind!" Han finished. "Better bring the shields to maximum, Leia. We're going to get some bug spatter."

"Perhapz not," Saba commed from the *Shadow*. "Leia, have you been doing your reaction drill?"

Leia felt a stab of guilt. "When there's been time."

Saba was kind enough not to remind her that she was supposed to *make* time for her training. That was the obligation of a Jedi Knight—though Leia, in all honesty, had a hard time thinking of herself as anything other than an eternal apprentice. Perhaps that was why she found it so hard to find training time.

"Do the drill now," Saba said. "But instead of stingerz, imagine the remote is shooting vesselz at you."

Leia started a breathing exercise, then closed her eyes and opened herself to the Force. She immediately felt something swooping down on them from above.

"Down and starboard," she said.

The *Falcon* continued on the same course.

"Han—"

"Are you crazy?" he interrupted. "With your eyes open, maybe. But not . . ."

The *Falcon* dropped five meters, and Leia opened her eyes to see the swollen underbelly of a big Gallofree transport gliding over them.

"*Now* you will . . . listen . . . to your nestie!" Saba was sissing hysterically. "Mara is *flying* with her eyes closed."

"Who isn't?" Han gave Leia a quick nod. "Whatever you say, dear."

Leia closed her eyes again and began to call directions. At first Han emitted an alarming string of oaths and gasps, but gradually the sensations grew more concrete—and Han's willingness to follow the blind more ready. Within the hour, they were bobbing and dodging along more or less steadily behind the *XR808g*.

Finally, Han said, "Looks like he's going to ground."

Leia opened her eyes to see the tracking blip drifting down toward the middle of the display, its color deepening to red as the *XR808g* lost altitude. She looked out the canopy and found the distinctive wafer of a YT light freighter in the distance ahead, descending into the hazy labyrinth of insect pinnacles. Traffic remained heavy above the spires, but there were only a handful of drifting balloon-bikes and slow-moving airspeeders among the towers themselves.

"We'll take point," Leia commed. "Why don't you fly top cover?"

"It's a plan," Luke answered.

As the *Falcon* descended, Leia saw that the mottled colors decorating the pinnacles had been created by pressing colored pebbles into the exterior walls. The effect was remarkably calming. If she watched them out of the corner of her eye, or allowed her gaze to go unfocused, the bright blotches of color reminded her of a meadow in full bloom—and, she realized, of the elaborate mosaics inside the spires depicted in *Killik Twilight*.

"Could it be?" she gasped.

"Could be anything," Han answered. "So let's be ready. Send Cakhmaim and Meewalh to the cannon turrets, and tell Beady to go to ready standby."

They followed the *XR808g* down to within a hundred meters of ground level, where the balloon-bikes and airspeeders gave way to rivers of racing landspeeders, speeder bikes, and dangerous-looking rocket carts steered exclusively by Yoggoy pilots. Pedestrians were forced to scurry along the tower bases, hanging on the walls sideways if they were insects or keeping themselves tightly pressed against the foundations if they were bipeds.

Juun began to fly erratically, making last-second turns and doubling back on his own trail. If not for the tracking blip, Leia would have lost him a dozen times in half an hour. Finally, they swung onto a large curving boulevard and began to circle a massive complex of fused towers sheathed in an eye-pulling mosaic done in every imaginable shade of red. The *XR808g* eased steadily toward the interior lanes, then abruptly dropped to ground level and disappeared into the dark mouth of a huge, barrel-vaulted gateway.

"That kreetle!" Han said. "I should've blasted him when I had the chance."

Leia immersed herself in the Force, then reported, "It looks more dangerous than it feels."

"You sure?" Han gave her a sidelong look. "No offense, but I *know* how much time you have to practice that Jedi stuff."

"Would it make any difference if I wasn't sure?"

Han gave her that crooked grin of his. "What do you think?"

He eased the yoke forward and swung the *Falcon* into the murky gateway. Leia activated the forward maneuvering lights, illuminating the interior of a huge, winding passage covered in a wavy pink-and-yellow mosaic. The tunnel was longer than Leia had expected, and each time the ship rounded a new bend, they sent a swarm of insects scurrying for the vault edges.

After a couple of minutes, they emerged in a small, flower-shaped plaza enclosed by a dozen fused towers. The mosaics were bright and disorienting, with solid bands of color gradually paling from deep amber at ground level to pure white at the pinnacletops. At the far side of the area, the *XR808g* sat on its landing struts, its boarding ramp already dropping into position.

Han brought the *Falcon* to within twenty meters and set her down with the missile launchers facing the *XR808g*. "Cakhmaim, Meewalh, be ready with those cannons," he ordered over the intercom. "Ready—"

"Prepared to open fire, Captain," the droid reported.

"Not *yet*," Leia said, unbuckling her crash webbing. "Only if they shoot first."

"Survival rates decrease thirty-two percent for combatants firing in reaction," BD-8 objected.

"We're not shooting first." Han strapped on his BlasTech holster. "Just stand ready to look tough."

"Look tough?" BD-8 inquired.

"Intimidation mode one," C-3PO clarified. He turned to Han. "You really should use the standardized terms with the BD series. Their tactical overlays leave little processing power for semantic analysis."

Han rolled his eyes. "Yeah, maybe I'll read the manual someday."

He led the way off the flight deck, and they descended the boarding ramp to find Juun scurrying toward them in a torn tunic.

"Han! Princess Leia!" he called cheerfully. "I was afraid we'd lost you!"

"Sure you were," Han replied coldly. He stopped a few steps from the end of the ramp and rested a hand on his holstered blaster. "Your transponder just happened to go on the blink?"

"Of course not!" Juun said. "Our guide disabled it. After the last jump, he found the subspace transceiver."

BD-8 came up behind Leia and glared over her shoulder, clicking and whirring loudly. Juun stopped three meters away and gawked up at the battle droid. Leia tried to get a read on his truthfulness, but she felt only alarm and confusion.

Juun raised his hands. "Please! It wasn't my fault!"

Leia glimpsed movement on the tower walls behind him, then saw several tiers of insect soldiers stepping into view. They looked much like Lizil workers, except they were the size of a Wookiee, with meter-long mandibles and scarlet carapaces covering their backs. The undersides of their thoraxes were bright gold, and their eyes were a deep, haunting purple. In their four hands, they each carried a crude electrobolt assault rifle and a short, thick-shafted trident. It took an instant to realize they were standing on small terraces instead of midair, for human eyes found it difficult to interpret the subtle interplay of hue and shadow that defined each belt of the wall mosaic.

"That does it!" Han said, reaching for his holster. "I'm gonna blast you myself."

The edges of Juun's cheek folds turned blue. "What for?"

"What for?" Han waved his blaster at the surrounding walls. "For leading us into a trap!"

Juun's eyes went wide. "I did?"

Leia reached out to the insects above, searching for any hint of hostile intentions, and felt none.

"Don't play dumb," Han said to Juun. He aimed his blaster at the Sullustan's knees. "It just makes me mad."

Leia reached over and covered Han's blaster hand. "Put that thing away!" she whispered. "It isn't what it looks like."

"Then what is it?" Han continued to glare at Juun.

"We'll have a better chance of finding out if you keep that thing in its holster."

Han allowed her to push the blaster down, but BD-8 was harder to convince.

"Situation serious," the droid reported. "Suggest withdrawal to transport. Permission to lay covering fire?"

"Denied!" Leia and Han said simultaneously.

"Okay," Han said to Juun. "Maybe it's not what it looks like. Where's Tarfang?"

Juun remained at a distance. "In the medbay. When our guide found the transceiver, there was a little fight."

Leia began to have a sinking feeling. "What about the guide? It's not—"

Her question was drowned out by the sudden thunder of insect drumming. The three lowest rows of soldiers raised their carapaces, then stepped off their terraces and added to the tumult the roar of hundreds of beating wings. Leia heard BD-8 ask something she could not understand and ordered him to stand down on general principles—though she did pluck the lightsaber off her belt and start easing back toward the *Falcon*'s boarding ramp.

Juun scurried over to join them, his round ears red with alarm. The soldiers continued to swirl overhead in a dark mass for several seconds, then glided to the plaza floor and formed a tightly packed cordon around the *Falcon* and *XR808g*.

"Situation critical," BD-8 reported. "Permission to return to stand ready?"

"G-granted," Leia said.

The soldiers thrummed their chests in a single deafening boom, then brought their feet together and snapped their weapons to the attention position against their thoraxes. On the far side of the *XR808g*, the cordon parted to admit a small parade of insects of many different body shapes, ranging in size from that of Leia's thumb to somewhat larger than an X-wing. Most seemed to be simple variations on the standard Colony pattern, with feathery antennae, large bulbous eyes, and four arms and two legs. But some had exaggerated features, such as one with slender, two-meter antennae ending in fuzzy yellow spheres, another with five large eyes instead of the usual two large and three small, and several that walked on four legs instead of two. One of the largest had a coat of sensory bristles so thick it looked like fur.

In the center of the procession walked an imposing, melt-faced man with no ears or hair and a mere bulge for a nose. His brows had fused into a single knobby ridge, and all his visible skin had the shiny, stiff quality of a burn scar. He wore purple trousers with a scarlet cape over a gold chitin breastplate.

"Who's the fashion victim?" Han asked Juun.

"I think it's the Prime Unu." Juun's voice was almost a gasp. "*Nobody* ever sees him."

"The Prime Unu?" Leia asked.

"You might consider him the chief of the Colony," Juun whispered. "He's doesn't rule it, at least not the way most species think of ruling, but he's the heart of the whole thing."

"Sort of the king bee, huh?" Han asked.

Leia felt Luke reaching out to her from above, alarmed by the growing trepidation he had been sensing in her. She filled her mind with reassuring thoughts.

The Prime Unu stopped in front of the *XR808g*, and two of his companions boarded the battered freighter. Leia reached out in the Force, trying to gauge his intentions, and found the same double presence that she had come to recognize in the Joiners of the Lizil nest. But the individual element of his presence felt stronger than most and—to her surprise—somehow familiar. Leia allowed her thoughts to roam freely over the past, seeking their own connections to that familiarity.

Her mind went first to the Jedi academy on Yavin 4, during a time when Anakin was still too young to attend and jealous of his older siblings. The memory brought with it a flood of emotion, and Leia found herself struggling to retain her composure—to avoid the torrent of grief and remembrance that always threatened to sweep her away when she thought of her lost son.

Her mind was telling her that the Prime was tied to her children—particularly Anakin—and she could not help hoping that the Prime *was* Anakin; that her son had somehow survived the Myrkr mission after all, and the funeral on Hapes had been some other young man's.

But that was fantasy. Had it been Anakin standing next to the *XR808g*, Leia would have *known*. She would have felt it in her bones.

Her thoughts wandered to another memory, on Eclipse, where Cilghal and Danni had learned to jam Yuuzhan Vong battle coordinators. The Jedi were meeting in a lab, with the milky splendor of the galactic core pouring down through the transparisteel ceiling. Cilghal was explaining that she had discovered where the enemy was growing the deadly voxyn that had been attacking the Jedi across the galaxy.

. . . *a full-grown ysalamiri,* the Mon Calamari was saying, and suddenly Leia felt an enormous, murky presence in the Force pressing her away from the Prime. She looked up and found him staring in her direction, his blue eyes shining like a pair of oncoming blaster bolts. Leia raised her chin and held his gaze. Her vision grew dark around the edges, and soon she could see nothing but his eyes.

He winked and looked away, and Leia felt herself falling.

"Whoa!" Han caught her under her arms. "What's wrong?"

"Nothing." Leia allowed Han to hold her as her vision returned to normal. "The king is Force-sensitive."

"Yeah?" Han replied. "I've never seen you react that way before."

"Okay, he's *very* Force-sensitive." Leia gathered her legs beneath her. "We might know him."

"You're kidding." Han studied the Prime for a moment, then shook his head. "Who is it?"

"I don't know yet," Leia said.

A pair of insects emerged from the *XR808g* carrying the Yoggoy guide that Juun had been assigned. The chitin of its thorax was pitted and charred, three of its limbs hung beside its body loose and swinging, and both of its antennae had been broken off. The Prime pressed his melted brow to the insect's, then raised the remains of a three-fingered hand and began to stroke the stumps of its antennae.

"An *Ewok* did that?" Han asked Juun.

The Sullustan nodded. "Tarfang is not the gentle soul he seems."

A contented *boom* reverberated from the chest of the wounded guide, and the Prime stood and started toward the *Falcon*. It was impossible to read the expression behind his grotesque mask of a face, but the briskness of his pace suggested how he felt about what he had just seen.

"The king doesn't look very happy," Leia said. "Maybe you should wait aboard the *Falcon*, Captain Juun."

"That won't be necessary," Juun said. "The guide assured me there would be no—"

The Prime raised two fingers and pointed at the *Falcon*'s laser cannons. There was a *thunk* as the turrets broke their collar locks, then the muffled scream of grating servomotors.

"Hey!" Han protested.

The turrets continued to rotate—tearing up their internal maneuvering mechanisms—until the cannons faced aft.

"Hostile action under way," BD-8 reported. "Permission to—"

The Prime raised a finger toward him, and the request ended in a garbled blast of static. The harsh smell of melting circuits filled the air, then the droid crashed to the ground. Han glanced over his shoulder.

"Bloah!" he gasped. "Can *Luke* do that?"

"Maybe I'll wait aboard the *Falcon* after all," Juun said.

The Sullustan turned and raced up the boarding ramp—and the Prime surprised Leia by letting him. The ghastly figure crossed the last few steps and stopped in front of the Solos, towering over Han by a good third of a meter. For a moment, he stood glaring down, his breath coming in audible wheezes that suggested badly damaged lungs, his blue eyes sliding back and forth between their faces.

Then Cakhmaim and Meewalh appeared at the top of the boarding ramp with power blasters in hand. Leia started to order the Noghri to stand down, but she was no match for their reflexes. They shouldered their weapons and yelled for the Solos to drop to their bellies.

The Prime flicked his wrist, and both Noghri went tumbling back into the *Falcon*'s main corridor. He stared in their direction for a moment, no doubt checking to make sure they would not surprise him later, then turned back to Leia and Han.

"Captain Solo." His voice was a deep, gravelly rasp that made Leia's throat close with empathic pain. "Princess Leia. We weren't expecting you." He glanced skyward, where Luke and Mara were still circling onstation in the *Shadow*. "Nor the Masters Skywalker."

"Sorry about that," Han retorted. "We tried to comm, but it turns out there's no HoloNet in the Unknown Regions."

"No HoloNet." The Prime's upper lip quivered, straining to smile, but not quite able to break free of its scar-tissue cast. "We hadn't considered that."

He turned away and walked under the *Falcon*, craning his inflexible neck around awkwardly to inspect the ship's belly. He made a complete circuit like this, pausing beneath the cargo lift, rising on his toes to peer at the seals around the missile tube doors, kicking the landing struts. Finally, he reached up and touched the carbon-scored hull.

"We never liked the black," the Prime said. "White is better. White is your color."

Leia's mind flashed back to the Yavin 4 visit, to a handsome blond-haired boy lying unconscious on the floor after being bitten by Jacen's crystal snake—a handsome boy dressed in the haughty scarlet, gold, and purple of the Bornaryn shipping empire.

"Raynar?" she gasped. "Raynar Thul?"

TEN

"Raynar Thul is no more," Raynar said. He was squatting on his haunches in the heart of the Prime Chamber, high atop a circular dais where he would always be visible to the hundreds of insect attendants that followed wherever he went. His long arms were hanging over his knees with the backs of his hands resting slackly on the ground before him, and his blue eyes were riveted, unblinking, to Luke's face. "We are UnuThul."

"How strange, then, that I still sense Raynar Thul's presence within yours," Luke said.

He found it difficult to meet Raynar's gaze, not because of those unblinking eyes or the ghastliness of the face that held them, but because of the conflicting emotions they aroused—elation that Raynar had survived his abduction, regret over what had happened afterward, anger and anguish that so many others had failed to return at all . . . especially his nephew Anakin. He still woke up nights praying that it had been just a bad dream; that there had been a better way to stop the voxyn and he had never been asked to authorize the mission to Myrkr at all.

But Luke was careful to keep those feelings hidden, buried deep inside where they would not show in the Force and complicate a discussion already sure to be difficult and full of emotion for both sides.

"Raynar Thul may be in hiding," Luke said carefully. "But he is not gone. I feel that clearly."

"We are surprised, Master Skywalker, that you cannot feel the difference between a ghost and a man." The same murky presence that Luke had felt in the Lizil cantina rose within Raynar's body, not forcing Luke out, but preventing him from feeling anything else. "Raynar Thul vanished with the Crash."

"And then UnuThul was born?"

"The Kind are not born, Master Skywalker," Raynar said. "An egg drops, a chrysalis is spun."

"You mean there was a metamorphosis?" Leia asked. Along with Mara and Saba, she was sitting cross-legged with Luke on the dais floor. Han, of course, could not be talked into sitting. He was pacing the edge of the dais, keeping a wary eye on the attendants below and grumbling about the heat and mugginess and too-sweet smell of the nest. "Is that the story on the walls?"

Leia gestured at the colorful mosaics that decorated the interior of the Prime Chamber, and Raynar's eyes flashed in delight, a pair of blue embers flaring back to life in that melted wreck of a face.

"You are as observant as we recall, Princess," he said. "Others are not usually observant enough to perceive the Chronicle."

"The Chronicle?" Luke asked.

Raynar pointed over Luke's shoulder, where a red streak arced down the domed ceiling to a white smear opposite the main entrance to the chamber.

"A star wagon fell from the sky," Raynar said.

As Luke twisted around to look, he glimpsed the blocky hull of an overturned YV-888 light freighter protruding above the rim of a still-smoking crater. But as soon as his gaze fell directly on it, the image dissolved into the same blur of semi-random color that had been there before.

"I don't see anything," Han complained.

"Only a wall of rockz," added Saba, whose Barabel eyes were incapable of seeing nearly half the colors in the design.

"You can't look directly at it," Mara explained. "It's like one of those air-jellies on Bespin. It only shows up when you look away."

"Oh, yeah," Han said.

Saba hissed in frustration.

Luke let his gaze slide to the next image and glimpsed Raynar kneeling over a wounded insect, his palms pressed to its cracked thorax.

"No, Master Skywalker. Over there." Raynar pointed to a pinkish blotch on the adjacent wall, eliciting a loud rustle as all the insects in the chamber turned to look in the direction he was pointing. "The Kind do not order such things in the same way you Others do."

When Luke turned his head, he saw a scorched figure lying in the bottom of the crash crater, surrounded by waiting insects.

"Beside the star wagon Yoggoy found Raynar Thul, a scorched and dying thing," Raynar continued. "We climbed down to wait for the Last Note so we could share his flesh among our larvae."

Raynar pointed across the room again, to another mosaic depicting the insects carrying him toward a small enclave of spires similar to those in the city outside.

"But he touched us inside, and we were filled with the need to care for his body."

The next image showed Raynar's burned body in the bottom of a large six-sided basin, curled into a fetal position and tended by two human-sized insects.

"We built a special cell, and we fed him and cleaned him like our own larvae."

Luke had to slide his glance past the following scene three times before he could be sure of what he was seeing. The mosaic showed only Raynar's face, surrounded by the walls of a much smaller cell, his neck craned back and his mouth gaping open to accept a meal from a nearby insect.

"After a time, Raynar Thul was no more."

The picture he pointed to next showed Raynar rising from the cell much as he was now, a knobby, faceless, melted memory of a man, arms crossed across his chest, feet together and pointed downward, eyes shining beneath his heavy brow like a pair of cold blue moons.

"A new Yoggoy arose."

The following image showed Raynar splinting the leg of a wounded insect, and the one after that showed several Yoggoy tending to an entire chamber of sick and injured nest members.

"We learned to care for the infirm."

Several pictures showed the Yoggoy nest expanding and growing, with Raynar supervising the construction of irrigation aqueducts and a drying oven.

"Before, only the nest mattered. But Yoggoy is smart. Yoggoy learned the value of the individual, and Yoggoy grew stronger."

Then came the crucial set of images. The first showed Raynar trading with other nests for food and equipment, the second depicted several insects from different nests gathered around listening to him, and in the third he was leading an even larger group of insects—all different in color, size, and shape—off to start their own nest.

"The Unu was created," Raynar said.

Before he could point to another mosaic, Leia asked, "What exactly is the Unu? The governing nest?"

Raynar tilted his head and gave a short, negative click. "Not in the way you think. It the nest of the nests, so that Yoggoy may share our gift with all of the Kind."

"Yeah?" Han asked. "And how's that work?"

"You would not understand," Raynar said. "No Other would."

There was more, an attack by a disapproving nest, a time of starvation as the flourishing nests stripped their worlds bare, the beginning of the Colony as the Kind began to spread across local space. But Luke paid little attention. He was struggling with what he had learned already, with the fear that Raynar remained as lost to them as ever, and that Jaina and the others would soon be just as lost—and with the growing alarm he felt over what the young Jedi Knight had become. Jedi should not be leaders of galactic civilizations; it was too easy to abuse the power they wielded, too easy to use the Force to impose their will on others.

He felt Mara touching him through their Force-bond, urging him to keep his disapproval in check.

To Raynar, she said, "What happened to the Dark Jedi who abducted you?"

Raynar lowered his fused brow. "The Dark Jedi?"

"Lomi and Welk," Luke prompted. He was careful to keep his disapproval well buried within himself, in case Raynar could sense his feelings better than he could Raynar's. "The Jedi whom you rescued on the Myrkr mission."

"Lomi and Welk . . ." Raynar's eyes grew restless. "They were . . . trouble. You say they abducted us?"

"They stole the *Flier* with you aboard," Mara said. "You must have figured this out by now. They tricked Lowbacca into leaving the ship, then stole it while you were unconscious inside."

As Mara spoke, Raynar's gaze kept sliding away from her face, then back again, and his presence in the Force grew confused as well. The familiar part, the part Luke recognized, rose repeatedly to the surface, only to be swallowed a moment later by the murkier, more powerful essence that confronted him every time he tried to probe a Colony member.

After a few moments, Raynar said, "We remember the Crash, but not the Dark Jedi. We think they . . . they must be dead."

"You don't remember them on the *Flier* at all?" Luke asked. "You must have seen them before you crashed."

The murky presence rose inside Raynar and pushed Luke out with such power that he felt as though he were falling.

"We remember the Crash," Raynar said. "We remember flames and pain and smoke, we remember fear and loneliness and despair."

The finality in Raynar's voice brought a tense silence to the dais—a silence that Han broke almost instantly when he whirled on Raynar with an outstretched finger.

"What about Jaina and the others?" he demanded. "Do you remember *them*?"

"Of course," Raynar said. "They were our friends. That is why we called them."

"*Were*?" Han stepped toward Raynar. "Has something happened? If you're trying to make Joiners of them—"

"Han!" Leia stopped Han with a gesture—she was probably the one person in the galaxy who could do that—then turned to Raynar. "Well?"

"Jaina and the others are well." Raynar addressed himself to Han. "But they were Raynar Thul's friends. We are unsure how they feel about *us*."

"You haven't answered the question," Luke observed.

"The Colony has need of them," Raynar replied. "Only Jedi can prevent a war with the Chiss."

Han started to complete the threat he had made earlier, but Leia quickly rose and drew him to the edge of the dais.

"The Chiss have told us that there is a border conflict," Luke said. "But not why."

Raynar's scar-stiffened face showed twitches of suspicion. "We do not know why. The system we have entered is over a light-year from the nearest Chiss base, and we have established nests only on food sources. Their explorers are alone on all the ore planets. We have even offered to work in their mines, in exchange for food and supplies."

"Let me guess," Han said from the edge of the dais. "The Chiss aren't interested?"

"Worse. They have poisoned our food worlds." He tilted his disfigured head and made a clicking sound deep in his throat—a sound that was echoed by the tapping mandibles of the attendant insects below. "Our nests our starving, and we do not understand why."

Luke found Raynar's confusion odd. "You're only a light-year from their border. You don't think they might be worried about your intentions? Or want to claim the system for their own?"

"The Colony is not stopping them," Raynar said. "They are free to take what they need."

"As long as you're free to take what you need?" Leia asked.

"We do not need the same things," Raynar answered. "There is no reason to fight."

"No reason you can see," Mara said. Luke sensed that she was as mystified as he was by Raynar's blindness to Chiss territorial concerns. "Maybe we should go take a look at what's happening there. Where is this system?"

Raynar's unblinking gaze shifted to Mara. "You wish to go there?"

"You said you needed help," Luke reminded him. "Perhaps we can resolve the situation."

"We know what we said."

Raynar's eyes grew very dark around the edges, and suddenly Luke could see nothing else. The murky presence began to reach into his mind, trying to push its way inside his thoughts to read his intentions. Luke was astonished by its power and had to reach deeply into the Force to bolster his own strength. Though the probe was hardly subtle or refined, it felt as though it were being driven by a thousand Raynars, and he feared for a moment that in his surprise he would be overwhelmed by its sheer might.

Then he felt Mara pouring her own strength into him, and Saba and even Leia. Together they pushed the dusky hand back. Luke found himself looking once again into the blue, lidless eyes of their host, and he finally began to comprehend just how difficult it was going to be to reach Raynar Thul.

"What are you waiting for?" Han demanded, apparently not noticing his companions' sweaty brows and trembling hands. "Tell us where the system is . . . unless you're afraid of what we'll find."

"We have nothing to fear from you, Captain Solo. Jaina and the others are free to leave anytime they wish." Raynar floated to his feet, then tipped his head to Luke and the other Jedi. "As are you, Master Skywalker. We will assign a guide to escort you back to the Lizil nest."

"We won't be going back to the Lizil nest. Not yet." Luke met Raynar's eyes, this time ready to meet a probe with a Force wall of his own. "We came to investigate what Jaina and the others are doing."

"You're welcome to stay on Yoggoy as long as you like," Raynar said. "But we're sorry. You can't see our Jedi."

"*Your* Jedi?" Han snarled. "When the Core goes dark!"

Leia motioned Han back, then stepped toward Raynar, her chin raised in challenge. "Why not? Because we'll discover you haven't been entirely honest? Because the Chiss are more in the right than you're telling us?"

"No." Raynar's mouth straightened, perhaps in an attempt at a smile. "Because we know how good you are, Princess Leia—and because you serve necessity instead of virtue."

"Just hold on," Han objected. "Leia has been out of politics for a long time. This is just *us*."

"Really?" Raynar turned to Luke. "What do the Jedi seek?"

"Peace," Luke answered instantly.

"Peace in the Galactic Alliance," Raynar amended. "We know where the new Jedi Temple has been built."

"That doesn't mean we are the Galactic Alliance's servants," Luke said.

"Master Skywalker, remember who Raynar Thul's parents were. We *know* how money works." Raynar stood. "You must bow to the needs of those who pay your bills—and, at the moment, the Galactic Alliance needs you to turn your back on what is right."

"Right from whose viewpoint?" Luke countered, also standing. "Right and wrong, good and evil, light and dark—most of the time, they are illusions that prevent us from perceiving the greater reality. The Jedi have learned to distance themselves from these illusions, to seek the truth beneath the words. Let us go—"

"No."

Raynar stepped toward Luke, and suddenly the dark presence returned, pressing against him, trying to push him toward the edge of the dais. Luke opened himself to the Force and pushed back, standing firm until Raynar came toe-to-toe with him, and they stood glaring into each other's eyes, two strangers who had been, in another life, Master and pupil.

"We have heard about this new Force of yours," Raynar said. "And we despair. The Jedi have grown blind to the dark side itself."

"Not at all," Luke said. "We have learned to see it more clearly than ever, to recognize that the dark side and the light side spring from the same well—inside *us*."

"And which side is it that wishes to find Jaina and the other Jedi Knights?" Raynar asked. "The side that knows what is right? Or the side that serves the Galactic Alliance?"

"The side that the serves the will of the Force," Luke answered. "Everywhere."

"Then you will serve it best by leaving Jaina and the others to settle this," Raynar said. He turned his back on Luke and started toward the steps. "As we said, you are welcome to stay on Yoggoy as long as you like."

"I'll bet," Han said, going after him. "And when we get to be Joiners—"

"Thank you." Leia grabbed Han's arm and jerked him back. "We look forward to learning more about the Colony. After we have, perhaps we can discuss this further?"

Raynar stopped on the top step and glanced back, his scorched face tipped at a slight angle. "Perhaps, but you won't change our mind, Princess. We know you too well." His gaze shifted back to Luke. "We know you *all* too well."

ELEVEN

Were it not for the golden gleam of C-3PO's head—bobbing along through a forest of feathery antennae as he questioned their guide about the Colony languages—Leia would never have been able to tell which scarlet-headed insect they were following. The route back to the hangar was swarming with Kind, and at least half of them were Yoggoy, proud and bustling and identical in every way she could see to the guide that had been assigned to escort them.

The passage took a sharp bend, and Leia lost sight of C-3PO. Waving the others to follow, she started to walk faster.

"What's the hurry?" Han said, catching her by the arm. "We could use a few minutes alone."

"Alone?" Leia tipped her head at the steady stream of insects clattering past. "Take a look around!"

Han was careful to avoid doing as she suggested, but gave a little shudder anyway. "You know what I mean. Without Raynar's spy listening in. I've got a plan."

"Planz are good," Saba agreed from the back of the group.

"But we don't want to look suspicious," Mara said. She waved the group forward again, and they set off with Leia and Han in the lead, Luke and Mara next, and Saba bringing up the rear. "Let's keep moving while we talk."

"I'm pretty sure I can talk Juun into giving us a copy of that list of nests on his datapad and any charts he *does* have on the Colony," Han said. "Between that and your Jedi senses, it shouldn't take us that long to figure out where Jaina and the others are. After all, Raynar practically told us where to look—a light-year or so from the frontier."

"*If* he was being honest," Mara said. "He was always clever, but now . . . we should be careful. This new Raynar is a lot more formidable than the kid we remember. I have a feeling he's already ten steps ahead of us."

"And *that's* why we should accept his offer to stay on Yoggoy for a while," Leia said. They rounded the bend in the corridor, and Leia spotted C-3PO's golden head fifteen meters ahead—far enough away that no matter how good the guide's ears were, it should be impossible to eavesdrop over the clicking and thrumming that filled the passage. "We need to learn as much about Raynar—and the Colony—as he knows about us."

"We know enough," Han grumbled. "We know that Raynar joined minds with a bunch of bugs, and that if we don't get to Jaina and Jacen and the others soon, the same thing's going to happen to them."

"Han, we have time," Luke said. "A Jedi's mind is not easily dominated."

"Oh, yeah?" Han glanced back. "*Raynar* was a Jedi."

"A much younger and inexperienced Jedi—and a grievously wounded one," Mara said. "Luke and Leia are right. We need to answer some questions before we go."

"Yes," Saba said. "This one would like to know why they are lying about the Dark Jedi."

Mara nodded. "I noticed that, too."

"Even *I* picked up on it," Han said. "But I don't see what difference it makes to finding Jaina and the others."

"*That's* what we need to find out," Leia said. Han's mind ran as straight as a laser bolt when he was worried about his children—and she loved him for it. "Trust me, we're better off knowing if Lomi and Welk are mixed up in this."

"And we need to talk to Raynar some more," Luke added. "I don't want to leave him here like that. I'm sure Cilghal knows someone who can repair that burn damage."

"*That* choice may not be ourz," Saba said. "He is the heart of the Colony. This one does not think the Kind will let him go easily."

"Even if he wanted to, which he won't," Mara said. "Power is addictive, and he's the king bee of a galactic empire."

"If power was the only appeal, we might have a chance," Leia said. The passage divided about twelve meters ahead, and C-3PO and the guide vanished down the right branch without looking back. "But Raynar is *responsible* for the Colony. It wouldn't exist without him, and he won't abandon it lightly."

"Now I *really* have a bone to pick with those Dark Jedi," Han said. "And with Raynar, too. Why couldn't he just let bugs act like bugs?"

"Because he's a Jedi." Luke sounded almost proud. "And he was trained in our old tradition—to serve life and protect it, wherever he found the need."

"Yeah, well, he won't be protecting much life when that border conflict gets out of hand," Han said.

"Yes, now many more livez are at risk," Saba said. "Nature is cruel for a reason, and Raynar has upset the balance."

"The law of unintended consequences," Mara said. "That's why it's better not to intervene. A modern Jedi would have held himself apart and studied the situation first."

"And we're sure that's a good thing?" Leia asked. She was as surprised as anyone to hear herself asking this question, for the war had hardened her to death in a way that she would not have believed possible twenty years before. But the war was over, and she was *tired* of death, of measuring victory not by how many lives you saved, but how many you took. "How many beings would have died while a modern Jedi studied the situation?"

Luke's confusion filled the Force behind her. "Does it matter? A Jedi serves the Force, and if his actions interfere with the balance of the Force—"

"I know," Leia said wearily. "I just miss the days when all this was simple."

Sometimes, she wondered whether the tenets of this new Jedi order were an improvement or a convenience. She worried about what had been sacrificed to this new god Efficiency—about what had been lost when the Jedi abandoned their simple code and embraced moral relativism.

They came to the divide in the passage and started down the right-hand branch. C-3PO and the guide were waiting about five meters ahead.

"*Buruub urub burr,*" the guide droned.

"Yoggoy asks that you please try to keep up," C-3PO translated.

"*Rurr bururu ub Ruur.*"

"And she politely suggests that you start your investigations at the Crash," C-3PO continued. "That way, you can see for yourself that UnuThul is not lying about the Dark Jedi."

"*Urr buub ur bubbu.*"

"Or anything else."

Leia's stomach tightened in surprise, but she wasted no effort trying to figure out how the insect knew what they had been discussing.

Instead, she smiled calmly and said, "That sounds like an excellent idea, Yoggoy. Thank you for the suggestion."

By the time they reached the hangar a few minutes later, another Yoggoy was waiting for them with a battered hoversled.

"Burru urr burrr ubb," it explained, pointing toward the *Shadow* with one of its four arms. *"Burrrr uuu!"*

"Oh, dear!" C-3PO exclaimed. "It seems that when Yoggoy attempted to collect Ben, Nanna threatened to open fire!"

"I apologize, Yoggoy," Luke said, addressing the driver. "But why were you trying to collect Ben?"

The driver drummed an excited explanation.

"Because you and Mistress Skywalker said it would be good for him to see the Crash," C-3PO translated. He tipped his head, then added, "As a matter of fact, Master Luke, I do recall hearing you say that only one point seven minutes ago."

"Yes, but how—"

"Collective mind," Leia said, suddenly understanding how their guide had been eavesdropping on their conversation earlier. "What one Yoggoy hears—"

"—they all do," Han finished. "Kind of a new twist on being bugged, isn't it?"

"It certainly is," Leia said. As the constant stream of insects droned past, Yoggoy had been eavesdropping on them one word at a time. She took Han's hand and stepped aboard the hoversled. "As I said, we have a lot to learn about the Colony."

The others climbed aboard as well. They stopped at the *Shadow* to pick up Ben and Nanna, then began a harrowing ride—it was very nearly a flight—through the congested avenues that wound through the skyscraping spires of the Yoggoy nest.

An hour later, they were still in the "city," standing in a long line of insects and Joiners outside the Crash. The site seemed part tourist attraction and part shrine, with thousands of insects waiting patiently in line, looking across a low stone wall up toward a wrecked light freighter. The crater slope was mottled with wadla and lyris and a dozen other kinds of flowers that Leia did not know, and the air was heavy with the vanilla tang of bond-inducing pheromones. Even the constant drone of several thousand drumming, ticking insect pilgrims had a strangely soothing effect.

Despite the ambience, Leia was growing increasingly uneasy. She felt as though the half-buried YV-888 were still burning down through the atmosphere, as though something huge were about to come smashing down atop her head. And the other Jedi felt it, too. She could sense Luke's disquiet through the Force and see Mara's wariness in the sudden economy of her gestures. Even Saba seemed tense, watching the surrounding insects out of the corner of her eye and testing the air with her forked tongue.

Or maybe the Barabel was just getting hungry.

Leia stretched out into the Force, hoping to learn more. But reaching into the immense, diffuse presence that pervaded the insect nests was like looking into a room filled with smoke. There was something going on, but it was impossible to tell what.

The Skywalker–Solo group finally reached a gate in the stone wall, where their escort motioned them to stop and wait.

"Would anyone object to our visit, Yoggoy?" Leia asked. She still found it a little awkward to address every insect in a nest by the same name, but it certainly cut down on the need for introductions. "I keep having the feeling we're not welcome here."

Yoggoy rumbled a reply.

"Yoggoy assures you that your feeling is wrong," C-3PO said. "Everyone is welcome to partake of the Crash."

"Partake?" Han asked. "What are we going to do, eat the dead?"

"*Uburu buu,*" Yoggoy replied. "*Bubu uu.*"

"There weren't any dead," C-3PO translated. "She apologizes."

"Uh, thanks," Han said. "But no need. I wasn't hungry anyway."

Leia felt a gentle tug through the Force. She turned slowly and found herself looking at her sister-in-law's slender face.

"Do you think Ben's too young for this?" Mara asked. Her green eyes slid toward her right shoulder, indicating to Leia that she was asking another question entirely. "I don't want him to see anything that would scare him off space travel."

"I'm old enough!" a small voice said from Luke's side. "Nothing's going to scare me."

"That's a good question," Leia said, ignoring Ben's protest. "I guess it depends on what we see."

As Leia answered, she was looking past Mara's ear toward a large, single-colored insect ten places back in the line. So blue it was almost black, it stood nearly the height of a man, with short bristling antennae and barbed, sharply curved mandibles. She could not tell whether its huge, bulbous eyes were focused on the Solo–Skywalker party, but when her gaze lingered an instant too long, the creature slipped out of sight behind a tan-and-gray insect the size of a landspeeder.

"We'll just have to keep an eye out," Leia said, "and take off if this starts to look disturbing."

"How disturbing can it be?" Han asked, clearly oblivious to what the two women were really talking about. "This wreck is seven years old. I'll bet he sees worse stuff on the newsvids."

"Every day," Ben agreed. Clearly eager to be on their way before his parents changed their mind, he turned to their guide. "Why are we standing here? I wanna see the Crash!"

The guide thrummed an explanation.

"Yoggoy assures you that we'll see it soon, Master Ben," C-3PO said. "But we must wait—"

"*Rurubur ur.*" The guide extended one of her lower hands to Ben.

"Oh. Apparently it's our turn—"

Before Nanna could stop him, Ben grabbed the insect's hand and dragged her up the slope at a sprint.

"Ben!" Nanna squawked, her repulsor-enhanced legs hissing as they propelled her enormous mass past Leia. "Stay with the group!"

Mara shook her head, then turned to Han. "You seem to be rubbing off on my kid, Solo. Were yours this headstrong?"

Han and Leia shared a glance, and they both nodded.

"Anakin," Han said. "If I said no, he had to find out why."

As Han spoke, a familiar sadness came to his face, and his eyes dropped. There was an awkward silence while everyone wondered what to say next, and Leia finally began to understand why there seemed to be such a bond between her husband and their nephew. Like Anakin, Ben was headstrong, fearless, and curious, with a clever mind and a quick wit, and he insisted on dealing with life on his own terms.

After a moment, Mara reached over and squeezed Han's forearm. "I just hope Ben grows up to be as fine a man as Anakin was. Nothing could make me more proud."

"Thanks." Han looked up the slope—probably to disguise the glassiness that had come to his eyes—then added, "He will."

They followed Ben to the rim, then found themselves looking into the bottom of the crater. Ten meters below sat a cockeyed box of heat-softened durasteel, somewhat flattened in the bottom and so covered in crawling insects that they could barely tell the vessel had landed bridge-down. The hull was pocked with the oblong holes made by plasma cannons, and there were several long, twisted rips that were probably a result of the crash itself.

"It looks like they flew through a plasma storm just leaving the Myrkr system," Luke said. "I'm surprised they made it out."

"Corellian engineering," Han said with pride. "A CEC ship will keep going until it hits something."

"Not always a good thing, especially when that something is a planet," Leia said.

She turned toward their escort, running her glance over the surrounding crowd, and noticed several dark blue insects similar to the one she had caught watching them earlier. It seemed to her that their huge eyes were all looking toward the Solo–Skywalker group, but that was hardly unusual. Most species of intelligent insect had an unsettling tendency to stare.

Leia reached out to Luke and sensed that he had noticed the blue insects, too, then asked their guide, "What happened to the crew?"

The guide used an upper hand to point at the base of the ship, where a pile of dirt lay slumped against the smashed bridge. Descending through the pile, toward a jagged rent in the hull, was a half-meter burrow that felt oddly familiar to Leia, as though she had seen it before—or somehow knew where it led.

The insect began a lengthy explanation, which C-3PO translated: "That is where Yoggoy found Raynar Thul. He was badly burned and barely alive."

Leia forced her attention back to the guide and said, "I mean, what happened to the *rest* of the crew?" She knew what Yoggoy was going to say—that there had been no one else—but when confronted with an obvious lie, a good interrogator kept asking the same question in different ways, trying to find a seam that she could pry open to expose the truth. "We know *Raynar* survived."

A familiar touch came to Leia through the Force, one that she knew instantly and certainly to be her son's, and she found herself looking away from their puzzled guide into the bottom of the crater. There, standing outside the burrow in a dirt- and soot-stained flight suit, was Jacen.

Or, rather, a vision of Jacen. The *Flier*'s hull was still visible behind him, as was the mouth of the burrow.

He smiled and said, "Hello."

The blood drained from Leia's head, and she had to grab Han's arm to steady herself. "Jacen's been here."

"What?" Han peered into the crater. "I don't see anything."

Luke saved her the trouble of explaining. "The Force, Han. She's having a vision."

Han's voice immediately grew wary. "Great. Just what we need. First, Force-calls, now Force-visions."

"Quiet, Solo," Mara said. "Don't interfere."

Jacen said something Leia could not hear, then a helmet and X-wing flight suit appeared in his hands.

"Jacen," Leia said, frowning. "I'm having trouble hearing you." Jacen spoke again, but still she could not hear him.

"Jacen?" Leia felt the color drain from her face. "How? You're not—"

"I'm fine, Mom," he said. "I'll see you soon."

"Uh-oh," Han said beside Leia. His hand tightened around her arm. "Looks like someone's been listening in."

Leia glanced over and saw three more deep blue insects pushing through the crowd gathered along the crater rim. They were clearly coming toward the Solo–Skywalker group, but Leia was not ready to leave yet. Jacen was still standing in the bottom of the crater, looking up at her.

"Qoribu," he said. "In the Gyuel system."

Leia wanted to ask him to repeat it, to be sure she had heard correctly, but Han was pulling her away, following Nanna down the crater slope through a swarm of astonished insects. Ben was in the droid's arms, while Luke, Mara, and Saba flanked her on three sides. Leia and Han were in the rear.

It took Leia a moment to see why they had suddenly grown so concerned. More blue insects had appeared, pushing through the crowd from all directions, not really attacking, just clacking their mandibles and staring. The rest of the Kind seemed unconcerned; they stepped aside politely, then continued to stare up at the Crash.

Leia drew her own lightsaber and activated it. "Threepio, what are they saying?"

"They're not saying anything that makes sense," C-3PO said. "They're just repeating *is it is it is* . . ."

Their guide rumbled an explanation.

"What a relief!" C-3PO said. "Yoggoy says they're just curious about us."

"Bugs are *never* just curious," Han said. He drew his powerful BlasTech DL-44. "Especially when they're hungry."

"*Ubrub ubru Ruur!*"

"They just want to see the Crash!"

"Then how come they're coming after *us*?" Mara demanded.

They reached the bottom of the slope and found the gate blocked by blue-black insects. Nanna shifted Ben to one arm and opened the other at the elbow, revealing her built-in blaster cannon.

"That means move," Han said, stepping past Nanna to confront the insects in front of them.

The insects began to crowd forward to meet him.

"The *other* way."

Han raised his blaster pistol and flicked the power setting from stun to lethal.

"Not yet, Han." Luke glanced in Han's direction, and Han's hand slowly fell to his side. "Let me handle this."

"Then you'd better handle it quick," Leia said, looking back up the crater slope. Two dozen of the blue insects had emerged from the mass and were slowly creeping closer. "It's getting crowded back here."

Leia felt a brush of reassurance from Luke, then an astonished booming erupted behind her. She glanced back to see several dozen insects hanging in midair, their legs and arms wiggling wildly as they attempted to make contact with the ground. The group began to move forward again, and she backed out the gate under the dangling insects. Luke was standing to one side, holding his hands palms-up above his shoulders.

"Not bad," she said.

"Impressive, even."

Luke winked at her, then turned toward the rest of the blue insects, who were still attempting to follow. He lowered one of his hands and stretched it toward them . . . and the insects immediately began to back away, dipping their heads and clacking their mandibles.

"They're apologizing, Master Luke," C-3PO said. "They didn't mean to make you feel hunted."

"No harm," Luke said. He waited until Leia, C-3PO, and their guide were past, then lowered the first group of blue insects down inside the gate. "As long as the feeling doesn't come back anytime soon."

They followed Mara and Nanna back to the lot where Yoggoy had left their transport, then climbed aboard the battered hover-sled. Their guide slipped behind the controls and turned her head all the way around to the passenger compartment, then thrummed a question.

"Yoggoy asks what you would like to see next," C-3PO said.

"The *Falcon*," Han said.

"*Rurr ur uu buubu.*"

"Yoggoy suggests a stop at a membrosia vault," C-3PO said. "You seem rather tense."

"That's 'cause I am," Han growled. "And getting—"

"I think we've seen enough for one day," Leia said tersely. She could tell that the other Jedi shared the same feeling she did, for they were still holding their lightsaber handles in their hands and scanning the surrounding area. "I think we'd all like to go straight back to our vessels."

"*Ububu.*"

The guide slipped the hoversled into motion so quickly that Leia and the others were knocked into their seats, and a moment later they were gliding onto a broad, traffic-choked boulevard flanked by looming insect spires.

The uneasy feeling Leia had been experiencing only grew worse. She slid forward and leaned over the low wall separating the driver's compartment from the passengers.

"Yoggoy, who were those blue insects?"

"*Ububub bur?*"

"The blue Kind who accosted us at the Crash," C-3PO explained helpfully. "Actually, they were more of a deep indigo, if that helps."

"*Bubu bur ub.*"

"Why of course there are blue Kind," C-3PO protested. "We just saw them at the Crash!"

"*Ur ub bur.*"

"What do you mean you don't remember that?" C-3PO demanded. "We all saw them."

The street ahead suddenly grew clear, and the unease Leia had been feeling blossomed into full-fledged danger sense.

"Stop the hoversled!" Leia cried.

Mara's approach was more direct. She was already leaping over the driver's wall, wresting the controls from their guide. She brought the hoversled to an instant halt, drawing a chorus of surprised *oofs* from Leia and the others.

"Not good," Han said, coming forward. "Bad, even. These streets never—"

Leia did not hear the rest of Han's observation, for suddenly her danger sense was turning somersaults in her stomach and Mara was backing the hoversled up the street. When their guide protested and tried to retake the controls, Mara used the Force to push the insect off the hoversled.

"Mom!" Ben cried. "You just dumped—"

A deafening crackle echoed through spiretops, then chunks of mosaic-covered wall began to rain down on both sides of the boulevard. Leia instinctively turned to protect Ben, but Nanna already had him on the deck, shielding him with her laminanium-armored body. Luke and Saba were standing beside the droid, using the Force to push falling rubble away from the hoversled.

Realizing that she still had a little honing to do before her instincts were up to full Jedi speed, Leia tipped her head back and began to look for chunks of falling building.

"Assailants at forty degrees!" Nanna reported.

The droid's arm rose and opened at the elbow. The entire hoversled shuddered as the warrior-nanny cut loose with her blaster cannon.

"Astral!" Ben yelled, peering out from under her arm.

Nanna gently pushed his head back, then fired again. More pieces of wall crashed down in the street, and Leia glimpsed the inky shape of half a dozen dark blue insects diving for the interior of the tower.

"Did you see that?" Han raised his blaster pistol and began to fire into the dust. "Kriffing bugs!"

In the next instant, the hoversled pivoted around and started up the avenue away from the ambush.

"They were trying to kill us!" Han cried from the floor of the hoversled. He hauled himself up and, as Mara swung down a side street and left the billowing dust behind, caught Leia's eye. "*Now* can we try my plan?"

TWELVE

For the first twenty minutes of the trip to the hangar, Han remained silent about Mara's piloting. She was racing down the insect-choked boulevard, using the Force to weave and jink and at times bounce through the traffic as though she were flying an X-wing instead of an ancient hoversled with a repulsor drive that sounded like it might come apart at any second, and most of the time he was just too scared to talk. But when she suddenly swung into a packed alley and slowed to a more sustainable speed, he could not help himself.

"Don't tell me you're losing your nerve," he said, leaning over the half wall into the pilot's compartment. "We've got to get back to the ships before Raynar finds out we survived!"

Mara continued at the same sane speed. "He already knows."

"The collective mind," Leia reminded him. "What one Yoggoy knows, they all do."

"Great." Han's stomach began to churn. "There ought to be a nice bunch of bugs waiting when we get back to the hangar."

"Maybe not," Luke said. "I can't believe Raynar would turn on us like that. He was one of the most earnest students at the academy."

Han and Leia shot Luke simultaneous looks of astonishment.

"*Raynar Thul is no more,*" Han quoted. "He's one of *them* now. UnuThul. A Joiner."

"Raynar's still in there," Luke said. "I felt him."

"Yeah? Well, it's the other guy I'm worried about," Han said. They left the alley, flashed across a boulevard, and shot into another alley. Han had no idea where they were—their guide had stuck to the main boulevards on the way to the Crash—but he assumed Mara knew where she was going. Jedi were not the only ones who could trust the Force. "And if his bugs try knocking another building down on us, I'm gonna blast him."

An amused twinkle came to Luke's eye, and Han suddenly realized how ridiculous his declaration must have sounded after describing how easily Raynar had destroyed BD-8, disabled the *Falcon*'s laser cannons, and neutralized Leia's Noghri bodyguards.

"Or something."

"Of course, dear," Leia said, patting his arm. "But I don't think that will be necessary. Raynar had to know that attack would never work—not with *three* Jedi Masters aboard."

"And a Jedi Knight of much experience." Saba nodded at Leia, though it was impossible for Han to guess whether this was a gesture of agreement or to indicate whom she meant. Barabels were *blasted* hard to read. "This one thinkz it was just a warning, a way to make us to leave."

"I hate giving in to bullies," Han said. "But I'll make an exception in this case. We can use the Force and Juun's datapad to track down the twins."

Leia nodded. "I think it's time to move on. We've found what we came for."

"We have?" Han asked.

"The Force-vision," Luke surmised. "What did you see?"

"Just Jacen," Leia said. "But he gave me the name of a planet and a system. I don't recognize them, but maybe Juun—"

"Jacen *told* you the system name?" Mara asked from the pilot's seat.

"That's right," Leia said. "He looked straight at me and said it. Why?"

"That is a strange kind of vision," Saba said.

"More of a sending," Luke agreed. "But across time instead of space."

The three Masters fell silent, leaving Han and Leia to look at each other in puzzlement.

Finally, Han said, "I don't get it. What's the problem?"

"I've never heard of a Jedi using the Force that way," Luke said.

"So he's creative," Han asked. "He's my kid. What'd you expect?"

"I think I understand," Leia said, beginning to sound worried. "The future is always in motion . . ."

"But not *yourz*," Saba said. "When Jacen spoke acrosz time, you became destined to be there."

"He fixed your future," Luke said. "At least for those few moments."

Leia was silent for a moment, then said, "Well, I seem to have survived it. And my future is my own again."

"I don't like it," Mara said. "Not at all. What exactly was he learning while he was gone?"

It was a good question—one Han had been asking himself since Jacen was a teenager.

Mara brought them out of the alley onto a busy avenue of zooming landspeeders and almost managed to keep up by pushing the repulsor drive beyond its top rating. The avenue snaked through the brightly decorated insect spires for perhaps five kilometers, then spilled onto the great boulevard that encircled the Unu's complex of red towers, and a few minutes later the hoversled was sliding down the long golden throat of the Prime Hangar.

The bugs were clattering about their business, durafilling micropitted hulls, off-loading bales of some spicy-smelling resin, tapping rivets on starships that should have been scrapped when the Empire was a glimmer in Palpatine's eye. Han began to hope that Saba was right about the attack—that it had just been an impolite invitation to leave.

Then they reached the bay where the *Falcon* and *Shadow* had been left, and Mara stopped short.

A trio of rocket shuttles had been squeezed between the two vessels. Maintenance crews were busy stringing webs of fueling hoses across the entire alcove, thwarting all hope of a quick departure. Even worse, Raynar was standing at the foot of the *Falcon*'s ramp, surrounded by an entourage of bug attendants and huge Unu soldiers. He was looking toward their end of the bay, clearly awaiting their return.

"So much for thinking he was just sending us a warning," Han said. "I really hate being right all the time."

Meewalh and Cakhmaim, who had remained behind to watch the ships and begin repairs on the *Falcon*'s weapons turrets, were peering out from the top of the ramp. The pair hadn't made much progress. Both sets of the blaster cannons remained pointed at the ship's aft.

"We should send the Noghri to fetch Tarfang and Juun," Leia said softly. "Do you think I can risk a comm call?"

"We'll have to," Han whispered. "Unless Jacen gave you coordinates to go with that name."

"Just the name," Leia said.

"I don't think this will come to a fight," Luke said. He rose and joined Han behind Mara, hiding Leia so she could comm the Noghri without being seen. "But Ben, you—"

"I know . . . stick close to Nanna," Ben said. "I know."

"Right," Luke said, smiling. "Nanna, get Ben aboard either ship as quickly as you can."

"But don't try anything pushy," Han advised. "You'll only get a brain-melt."

"I am not programmed to be pushy, Captain Solo," Nanna said.

"Will we get to shoot that blaster cannon in your arm again?" Ben asked enthusiastically.

"Only if someone threatens your life," Nanna said. "You know all my routines are strictly defensive, Ben."

Mara threaded the hoversled through the tangle of fueling lines, but had to stop ten meters from the *Shadow* because a rocket shuttle blocked their way. Nanna immediately took Ben and headed for the boarding ramp, which was still down because of the bugs' mistrust of closed doors. Everyone else remained on the hoversled, their hands out of sight and grasping their weapons, their gazes fixed on Raynar and his entourage.

Han felt as though he were aging a week for each second it took Ben to reach the *Shadow*. By comparison, Luke and Mara seemed downright calm. And why shouldn't they? Having seen all the times Han and Leia's kids had been kidnapped or threatened when they were supposedly hidden safely away, Luke and Mara had decided that—short of an actual battle—Ben would *always* be safer if they kept him close. So they had repeatedly rehearsed with Ben exactly what to do in circumstances like these, and weekly "protect-the-kid" drills were standard procedure for all traveling companions. Given whom they usually traveled with—Jedi Knights and veteran soldiers—Han thought they had probably made the right decision.

When Mara failed to start the hoversled toward the *Falcon*, Raynar cocked his earless head in bewilderment, then started across the hangar floor.

"That's my signal," Mara said. "I'm out of here."

She stepped out of the pilot's station and, still moving casually, started up the *Shadow*'s boarding ramp. Raynar's eyes followed her progress, but he made no attempt to stop her. That was good, since it meant Han didn't have to blast him yet.

Han slipped into Mara's place at the pilot's station, then frowned as he tried to pick out a path to the *Falcon*. This was going to be difficult, at least until Mara distracted them with her blaster cannon—provided Raynar didn't twist that around as he had the *Falcon*'s turrets. Han's palms started to sweat, and he began to wish he hadn't left their thermal detonators aboard the ship. Nothing distracted a big, bad, all-powerful enemy like one of those little silver balls rolling around at his feet.

Raynar stopped two paces from the hoversled. "Was anyone injured?"

"No," Han answered. "Sorry to disappoint you."

"Disappoint us?" Raynar's eyes grew confused. "When you left Yoggoy to be crushed, we thought someone must have been—"

"Yeah, well, sorry about the guide, but that's what happens when you start dropping buildings on people," Han said. Daring to hope that Raynar would actually make this easy, he gestured toward the *Falcon*. "Do you mind? We need to clean up."

Raynar lowered his melted brow, then shifted his gaze to Luke and Saba, who were waiting at opposite ends of the hoversled with their hands hidden behind the durasteel sides. His scarred lips twitched in a mockery of a smile.

"Of course." Raynar gave no discernible command, but a path opened through the soldier bugs at his back. He stepped onto the hoversled beside Han. "You believe the building collapse was an attack?"

"It wasn't exactly friendly." Trying to hide his uneasiness, Han started the hoversled toward the *Falcon*. "And we saw your killer bugs."

"Killer bugs?" Raynar asked.

"They were solid blue—dark blue," Saba said from the back of the sled. "They blasted the wallz just before we passed beneath."

"You're mistaken," Raynar said. "If any of our nests had attacked you, we would have known."

Saba rose and came forward, and Han was a little unnerved to realize that she was not large enough to loom over Raynar the way she did most beings. "This one saw the ambusherz with her own eyez. Ben's Defender droid killed two."

"The Kind did not lose anyone in the accident," Raynar said.

"It was no accident," Han snapped, beginning to grow angry. "Someone tried to kill us. You, I'm thinking."

"If we wanted to kill you, we would not make it look like an accident," Raynar said. "We would just do it."

They reached the *Falcon*. Han stopped the hoversled, then faced Raynar and found himself staring at the underside of a white-blotched chin.

"Remember who you're talking to, kid," he said. "This is *Han Solo*. I've been sticking my finger in the eyes of two-credit dictators like you since before I broke your mother's heart, so show a little respect when you threaten me. And don't lie. I hate that."

Raynar was no more intimidated than he had been by Saba. He simply glared down at Han, his breath coming in slow, angry rasps.

Luke leaned close to Leia and whispered, "Han dated Raynar's mother?"

"You'd be surprised at the women Han's dated. I always am." Leia stepped to Raynar's side, then said, "You must admit the collapse looks suspicious. If it was an accident, how did the Yoggoy nest know to evacuate the area? And what about the blue Kind we saw? The ones we *killed*?"

Raynar's breathing softened to a wheeze, and he turned to face Leia. "The only dead Kind we have found at the site was your guide."

"The otherz must have taken the bodiez," Saba said. "There were more than the onez Nanna killed."

"You were mistaken," Raynar said. "The dust was thick, the rubble was still falling. What you saw were shadows."

"Who're you trying to convince here?" Han demanded. He glanced at the attendant bugs, wondering whether they could have more say than he realized. Perhaps *they* were the reason Raynar was trying to deny the Colony's responsibility. Perhaps they didn't approve of murdering guests. "Because *we* know what we saw."

Raynar turned back to Han. "Eyes can deceive, Captain Solo. What you say you saw is impossible."

"Or our interpretation of it." Luke's voice was thoughtful. "What if it wasn't the Kind who attacked us at all?"

"Others aren't allowed to wander Yoggoy alone," Raynar said. "We would know even if someone else attacked you."

"What if you didn't know they were here?" Leia asked.

Raynar's eyes narrowed in thought, then he shook his head in a gesture that—for a change—seemed more Raynar than insect. "You said Yoggoy was warned to evacuate. Why would Others do that?"

"And if they did, you'd certainly know they were here," Luke said.

Han frowned at Luke. "Don't tell me you're buying this?"

"Not that it was an accident," Luke said. "But that Ray—er, UnuThul—believes it was."

Leia caught Han's eye, then gave a curt nod that suggested he should believe it, too. "I think we can all agree on that much," she said. "If the Colony wanted us dead, they wouldn't have given up after one try. The attack was supposed to look like an accident, which means somebody was trying to hide it from the Unu."

"We're glad you believe us, Princess," Raynar said. "But there's no evidence to support your theory."

"How could you know?" Han demanded. "There hasn't been time. The attack was less than thirty minutes ago!"

"Yoggoy workers have already cleared much of the rubble," Raynar answered. "The only body they have—Kind or Other—is your guide's. The evidence suggests the towers just collapsed. We are sorry it happened when you were about to pass beneath them."

"Does that happen often?" Leia asked. "That a spire just collapses?"

"Once, when there was a quake," Raynar said. "And sometimes storms—"

"Not what I asked," Leia said, stepping off the hoversled. "Let me show you something."

She took Raynar's meaty hand, then led him up the boarding ramp into the *Falcon*. Han followed with Luke and Saba, but fortunately only a small part of Raynar's entourage—the bug with the really long antennae and another covered in furry bristles—joined them. They caught up to Leia and Raynar in the Solos' sleeping quarters. The pair were standing in front of the bunk, staring at the famous moss-painting hanging on the wall.

"This is *Killik Twilight*," Leia said to Raynar. "Do you recognize anything?"

"Of course," Raynar said. "Lizil was very excited about the painting."

Raynar stepped to the side of double bunk—the Solos had installed it when they had realized the *Falcon* was going to be their primary home—then leaned closer to the painting and began to run his gaze over every detail.

"Thank you for showing it to us," he said. "We wanted to ask, but our meetings have gone so badly that we didn't want to presume."

Han raised his brow. Maybe there was less Raynar left in that seared body than he thought. The Raynar Thul whom Han remembered had been a decent-enough kid, but his wealthy family had never taught him to do anything *but* presume.

Leia appeared less stunned than Han by Raynar's politeness. She smiled graciously, then said, "Sometimes, art helps us know each other better. Do you know what this painting depicts?"

Raynar nodded. "It shows an arm of the Lost Nest." He still did not look away. "We remember it well."

"The Lost Nest?" Luke asked.

"*Remember* it?" Han gasped. "It's ancient!"

Raynar finally tore his gaze from the moss-painting.

"We remember the *nest*." He fixed his eyes on Leia. "When humans came to Alderaan, they called it the Castle Lands. But we knew the nest as Oroboro. Our Home."

Han shook his head in disbelief. He liked to say that all bugs were alike, but not even he had assumed that the Kind and the Killiks were actually the same. Sure, they shared the same general body shape and had the same number of limbs, but beyond that, the Kind looked like the Killiks in the painting about as much as humans looked like Aqualish. The towers, on the other hand, were another matter. In both the painting and the Yoggoy nest, they were crooked cones with distinctly banded exteriors.

Leia did not sound surprised at all. "So the Killiks didn't go extinct, as everyone supposed. They simply left Alderaan thousands of years ago."

"You seem less surprised at that than Lizil was to see a painting of Oroboro," Raynar said.

"I've had my suspicions since we arrived at Yoggoy," Leia replied smoothly. She turned back to the painting. "Archaeologists have dated the oldest of those spires to twenty-five thousand standard years."

"Correct," Raynar said. "The Celestials emptied Oroboro ten thousand generations ago—that would be twenty thousand years, as humans measure time."

Han wanted to ask who the Celestials were—and what Raynar meant by *emptied*. He also wanted to ask if a Killik generation really passed at the rate of one every two years. But he could see by the set of his wife's jaw that she was pursuing her own line of questioning.

"And yet, only three towers had collapsed before Alderaan was destroyed," Leia said. "No maintenance or repairs, exposed to the elements all that time, and only three collapse. But here, a tower just happens to collapse as we're about to pass by. Do you see where I'm going with this?"

"There is more gravity here than on Alderaan," Raynar countered. "And the ground does not make such strong spitcrete."

"This was still the first tower to collapse for no apparent reason," Luke reminded him.

"There is always a first, Master Skywalker." Raynar turned back to *Killik Twilight* and began to study it. "We cannot explain what happened. Please accept our apologies."

Han exchanged looks of frustration with Luke and Leia, but Saba—who did not truly understand the concept of apology—made a distasteful grating sound in her throat.

"This one does not want your apology, young Thul. She does not eat humanz." She glanced out into the corridor, where Raynar's duo of assistant Killiks stood waiting. "And she has never cared for the taste of insectz, either."

Raynar's head snapped around so quickly that Han feared he was about to have bloody Barabel scales flying all over his sleeping quarters.

"Take it easy, kid. You remember how Barabels are." Han took Raynar by the arm and started forward. "Sorry for the misunderstanding, but we still need to get under way. Why don't you tell us about these Celestials on the way out?"

"If you like." Raynar allowed himself to guided into the corridor. "It was after we built Qolaraloq—you Others call it Centerpoint Station. The Celestials were angry—"

Saba stumbled into Han's back as he stopped dumbfounded in the corridor.

"You're saying Centerpoint was built by *Killiks*?" Leia gasped. Finally, she sounded like something had surprised her.

Instead of answering, Raynar abruptly stopped. "We need to see the aft hold. Your Noghri are abducting Captain Juun and his first mate."

Han winced inwardly. "Abducting? What makes you say that?"

The muffled whine of an angry Sullustan drifted up the access corridor. ". . . *will* not be quiet! Let me see Captain—"

Juun's voice fell silent, but Raynar was already out the cabin door. Han turned to Leia. *"Abducting?"*

Leia shrugged. "I told Cakhmaim to bring Juun and Tarfang to the *Falcon*. I guess they didn't want to come."

"A misunderstanding," Luke said. "We'd better go explain."

Luke led the way into the access corridor, and they caught up to Raynar and his attendants outside the aft hold. Raynar hit the touch pad, then scowled when the hatch did not open and raised his palm toward it.

"Wait!" Han leapt to the control panel and punched in the override code. "Just be patient."

The door slid open to reveal Meewalh and Cakhmaim holding the *XR808g*'s two crew members. With one of Meewalh's arms clamped around his throat and her other hand covering his mouth, Juun was at least still conscious. Tarfang was another matter. Still casted and bandaged from his fight with the Yoggoy guide, the Ewok was lying unconscious in Cakhmaim's lap, with a freshly swollen eye and two new bare patches of fur.

"It's not what you think," Han said. "I can explain."

"That won't be necessary, Captain Solo." Raynar made a humming sound deep in his throat, then turned and fixed Han with his unblinking gaze. "Just tell us why you are suddenly in such a hurry to leave."

"Uh . . ." The truth was the last thing Han could tell him, but he knew how good Jedi were at detecting lies—and whatever Raynar was now, he had *started out* a Jedi. "What makes you think we're in a hurry?"

Raynar's noseless face grew stormy, and Han began to feel a dark weight pressing down on him inside.

It was Leia, as usual, who came to his rescue. "We have no wish to insult the Colony," she said, "but we don't feel safe here."

Raynar turned to her, and the dark weight lifted.

"You are safe. We promise."

"We don't believe you," Han said. That much was completely true. "Either you're lying—"

Leia's face paled. "Han—"

Han raised a hand, then continued. "Or you have no idea what's happening. Either way, we're out of here."

Raynar's eyes grew so soft that they made Han think of the poor, confused kid whom the other Jedi trainees used to heckle for dressing so funny.

"Very well. You have always been free to come or go as you wish." He turned toward the Noghri, who were still holding Juun and Tarfang captive. "The same applies to Captain Juun and his copilot. Will you be leaving with Captain Solo?"

Meewalh glanced at Leia. When she nodded, the Noghri removed her hand and arm from Juun's mouth and throat. The Sullustan bustled to his feet and, glaring at Han, brushed himself off.

"I'll have to think about it," he said. "Tarfang doesn't care for being kidnapped."

Han's stomach turned cold. Without Juun and his datapad, their chances of finding Jacen and the others before they turned into a bunch of Joiners went way down. Their only recourse would be to make their way to the Chiss frontier and start jumping from system to system.

Luke stepped toward Juun. "We weren't trying to kidnap you." He spoke in a soft monotone. "We were just—"

One of the bristly Killiks slipped forward to block Luke's way, and Raynar said, "It would be better if Captain Juun made up his *own* mind, Master Skywalker."

"Look, we were worried about him." Han addressed Raynar,

but he was watching Juun out of the corner of his eye. "We thought you were trying to kill us, and since he and Tarfang were the ones who helped us find this place—"

Juun's small mouth dropped in alarm. "Don't remind him!"

"Sorry—honest mistake," Han said. He felt guilty about forcing the Sullustan's hand, but Juun's days running Colony cargo had come to an end when their guide found the transceiver that had helped the *Falcon* follow him to Yoggoy. "We were kind of worried about you. But if you *want* to stay here—"

"I'm not leaving without the *XR-eight-oh-eight-g*," Juun said. He looked at Tarfang, who was still unconscious. "And you'll have to lend me a copilot until Tarfang's better."

Han faked a scowl. "Getting kind of pushy there, aren't you, fella?"

"You owe it to me," Juun said. "Item twenty-two in the Smuggler's Code."

Han sighed, then turned back to Raynar. "There you have it," he said. "I guess we're stuck with 'em."

THIRTEEN

The Jedi pilots rounded the brightly striped mass of the gas giant Qoribu and found themselves staring into the turquoise brilliance of the planet's huge star, Gyuel. Jaina blinked instinctively, and by the time her eyes opened again, her astromech droid had darkened the StealthX's canopy tinting. She saw the hawk-winged silhouettes of four inbound defoliators sweeping in just meters above Qoribu's dazzling ring system, racing for the gap between the moons Ruu and Zvbo on initial approach for a dispersal run. With a four-squadron escort of clawcraft, the Chiss were clearly determined to reach their targets this time.

Rather than break comm silence, Jaina opened herself to the battle-meld and immediately knew her wingmates had done the same. Sometimes they could hear one another's thoughts through the meld, but more often they simply *knew* what their fellows were thinking . . . what they were doing. And the connection had only grown stronger since coming to Qoribu. During battles, they sometimes came perilously close to sharing minds.

Jaina focused her thoughts on the impending clash. The Chiss were coming hard this time. The Jedi had to disable those defoliators quickly and withdraw before the fight turned bloody.

Jaina sensed disapproval and knew that Alema favored a more forceful approach, one that would leave the Chiss with no illusions about the consequences of attacking the Colony's food supply. And she was not alone. Others were outraged as well. Instead of attacking outright—a violation of the Ascendancy honor code, which prohibited an unprovoked first strike—the Chiss were trying to starve the Qoribu nests into retreat. Tesar, Tahiri, even Jacen believed that the

Chiss were engaged in a campaign of species cleansing and deserved to get their noses bloodied.

Only Zekk did not agree. Jedi saw similar cruelties everywhere they were called in the galaxy. But it was their responsibility to remain dispassionate, to cut through the veil of obscuring emotion and find the core of the problem. If they allowed themselves to seek retribution rather than peace, how could they bring a lasting solution to *any* conflict?

As much as Jaina wanted to make the Chiss pay for the lives they were taking, she had to agree with Zekk. So far, this had remained a low-intensity conflict. But if the Jedi turned it into a killing fight, that would end. A simple border clash would erupt into all-out war, and the carnage would be staggering.

The Chiss task force entered the gap between Ruu and Zvbo. Two of the four defoliators left the main formation with their clawcraft escorts and turned toward the moons. They were met by clouds of defenders, from the Saras nest on Ruu and the Alaala on Zvbo. Too small to be visible at even this relatively short distance, the dartships were nevertheless numerous enough to spread hazy stains of gray across Gyuel's blue face.

Jaina had barely formulated a plan to meet them before Tahiri shot ahead in the sleek little skiff that Zonama Sekot had grown for her. A living ship, its three-lobed hull glowed a deep, sea green against the star.

Jacen followed a moment later in his ChaseX, which, like Tahiri's living ship, could not be concealed from the Chiss sensors. The Jedi all understood what Jaina intended. Tahiri, who was not subject to StealthX comm restrictions, opened a channel to the Taat dartships still swarming around Jaina and the other StealthXs.

"ReyaTaat, bring the dartships and follow us. We need to make this look real."

"We are to create a diversion?" A Chiss Joiner who insisted on being called by both the nest name and her own, ReyaTaat freely admitted that she had been sent by Chiss Intelligence to spy on the Qoribu nests. Her allegiance had changed—she claimed—when the Taat discovered her hiding in near starvation and started to bring her food. "The stealth fighters will divide and strike the defoliators by surprise?"

"Something like that."

Though all of the Qoribu nests seemed to have complete faith in Reya, the Jedi were less trusting, and Tahiri was not about to reveal their plan.

When neither the dartships nor Reya's little scoutcraft started after her, Jacen added, "You need to come *now*. You're drawing attention to the StealthXs."

"Taat is not happy with this plan," Reya said. "The Chiss have changed tactics, and the nest worries they are trying to lure the Jedi into a trap."

Jaina's suspicions about Reya began to deepen, and Tahiri asked, "The nests worry, or you do?"

"We speak for the nests in this," Reya said. "And we know the Chiss."

"You *are* the Chiss." Tahiri's skiff slowed, and she added, "Maybe you're less worried about the Jedi than about your old friends."

"We are *Taat*," Reya insisted. "But we were Chiss once, and we understand how dangerous it is to underestimate them."

The Saras dartships met the first defoliator and swallowed it in a cloud of gray, whirling slivers. The defoliator continued toward Ruu's amber disk, engulfed in a halo of silver sparkles as the insect pilots hurled their tiny fighters against its shields. The Force grew heavy with anguish and admiration for their sacrifice, and Jaina was surprised to feel her own throat closing with emotion. Usually, she felt nothing when she entered battle, not fear or excitement or dread. Usually, she was too focused on the fighting to experience any emotions at all.

The Chiss clawcraft circled back and began to make runs along the length of the defoliator's hull, driving the Saras dartships off and giving the larger vessel time to refresh its shields. The StealthXs had to make their move *now*, or they would never reach the defoliators in time. Jaina pushed her throttles forward and broke for the amber moon, Ruu. Tesar, the second best pilot on the team, started for Zvbo, while Zekk, Alema, and Lowbacca all began a high arcing maneuver that would drop them down on the last two defoliators.

"ReyaTaat, the Jedi are starting their run." Jacen's voice was sharp. "And we're not going to be much of a diversion alone."

There was a moment of silence, then a vague tide of alarm rose in the Force. "Slow down!" Reya commed. "The dartships can't catch you!"

Jaina checked her tactical display and found a blue cloud of Taat dartships sweeping up from the bottom of the display, following Reya's little scout-lancet after Tahiri. At the top of the screen, both Chiss defoliators were fully engulfed in swarms of Saras and Alaala, with the curved horizons of Ruu and Zvbo hanging high in the corners. The main body of the Chiss task force remained in the center of the display, the clawcraft escorts hanging back just far enough to make the last two defoliators an inviting target.

What were they up to?

Jaina's astromech changed scale, and suddenly her tactical display was a mass of "friendly" blips—the Saras dartships—whirling around the defoliator she had targeted. The friendly blips were winking out by the dozens.

Jaina checked her estimated time to attack. Five seconds, but she sensed that Tesar needed seven. She armed two proton torpedoes, then added a sweeping curve to her approach and came in behind the battle.

Outside her cockpit, space was a tightly wound ball of orange rocket trails swirling around the blue glow of the defoliator's big ion drives. A pair of dartships blossomed in scarlet as they exploded against the shields of an oncoming clawcraft, but a third collided with its wing.

The clawcraft pilot lost control and went corkscrewing into Ruu's thin atmosphere. Assuming he survived the crash, Jaina knew, he would be taken into the Saras nest and treated as a welcome guest. Unless they were clearly being attacked, none of the Qoribu nests seemed to have any real concept of *enemy*.

Jaina tried to pick a route through the mad tangle of dartships, but it was like trying to avoid drops in a rainstorm. Two seconds from her launching point, a Saras bounced off her shields, and her canopy went black to prevent her from being blinded by the white flash of an exploding rocket.

By the time the tinting paled an instant later, three Chiss clawcraft were coming at Jaina head-on, pouring a steady torrent of cannon bolts in her general direction. She did a half-roll slip, taking two hits on her forward shield as she passed through the third fighter's stream of fire, then loosed her first torpedo.

Nothing if not well trained, the Chiss adjusted their aim instantly, targeting on the weapon's origination point. Jaina's forward shields flared into a white wavering wall of heat, and shrieking overload alarms filled the cockpit. She released the second torpedo and jinked hard to port. More Chiss brought their craft to bear, barely grazing her with a blue inferno that was nevertheless enough to bring her shields down with a final, warning screech. The air grew acrid with the smell of fused circuits, and warning messages that Jaina could not read through the smoke began to scroll down her status display.

"Just keep the masking systems up, Sneaky," Jaina ordered her droid, taking the StealthX through an unpredictable coil of reversing rolls. "If those guys get a sensor read on us, we'll really be in trouble."

The droid replied with a cynical whistle.

Jaina continued to maneuver until, a second later, the torrent of cannon fire ceased for an instant and she knew the Chiss had been momentarily blinded by her passing torpedoes. She pushed the stick up and to the left, circling out of the dartship tangle as quickly as she could and climbing for the stars, where her dark craft would not be silhouetted against Qoribu's scintillating rings.

A pair of bright dots flared through the smoke in Jaina's cockpit, and she leaned closer to her tactical display. Two shrinking circles of light indicated that her proton torpedoes had detonated where she intended, just behind the defoliator's thrust nozzles. The big ship was already beginning to swing off course, rising into a tight banking turn that would carry it into Qoribu's gravity well if the crew did not regain control soon.

Jaina allowed herself a moment of self-congratulation—just so her wingmates would know she had completed her assignment— then the Saras swarm began to drift back toward Ruu, leaving the crippled defoliator to recover control and flee. Even now, after two months of living and fighting with the Taat, Jaina was awed by the insects' complete lack of spite. Once a threat had been turned away, they never attempted to cause it more harm.

Jaina's admiration was mirrored in the Force by that of the other Jedi, and her thoughts turned to the other three defoliators.

"Give me an overall sitrep, Sneaky. And clean this smoke out of the cockpit." Jaina finally realized that she was reflexively using the Force to keep from coughing. "I can barely see my display."

A valve hissed open and cleared the air, then Jaina was hit by a wave of shock so sudden and powerful it reminded her of the time her X-wing had been blown from under her at Kalarba. She automatically began a systems sweep, but knew before her gaze reached the life-support readout that the alarm had come to her through the meld, from the three Jedi she had sent to stop the middle two defoliators.

The tactical display showed the other three defoliators also drifting dead in space. But a new vessel had appeared on the far side of the battle, well positioned to prevent the Taat—and Jedi—from returning to their home nest. It was simultaneously bleeding clawcraft into space and sweeping the area with tractor beams, gathering up dartships like flitnats in a net.

"*Victory*-class Star Destroyer." Jaina turned toward the battle zone and poured on velocity. "Where did *that* come from?"

Sneaky let out a defensive tweet, then replayed a high-speed version of the last ten seconds of tactical record. The vessel had simply appeared a few moments ago, *after* the Jedi had disabled the defoliators. Jaina grew instantly cold and emotionless inside.

"Cloaked."

She wasted no time asking herself why she had failed to anticipate the tactic—capable enemies *always* surprised you—but her thoughts did leap to the implications. Had the Star Destroyer been an escort, it would have revealed itself as soon as the nests moved against the defoliators. Instead, it had waited until the Jedi launched their proton torpedoes—betraying both their presence and their general location. It had come for *them*—using their own subterfuge against them.

It had been one of Jag Fel's favorite tactics, when they had flown together against the Yuuzhan Vong. Jaina reached out toward the Star Destroyer, searching for his familiar presence, but could not find him among all the beings on the vessel—at least not in the middle of the battle.

A burst of dismay swept through the Force, then a soft growl arose inside Jaina's head. Lowbacca was caught in one of the tractor beams. She wondered how bad, then had a brief vision in which dartships were flying past in a black, swirling wall and the cockpit was filled with the screaming whine of overloaded fusial thrust engines.

Jaina felt Tesar reaching out to Lowbacca, urging him to hold on until he and Jaina could get there. They might be able to shut down the tractor beam if they could destroy its generators. But none of the Jedi knew what the tractor beam generators on a Chiss Star Destroyer looked like . . . or where to find them.

Lowbacca thought they were being foolish; that they would only get themselves captured by trying something so risky. The best way to help him was to avoid falling into the Chiss trap themselves.

A swell of anger rose in the Force. Jaina was still too far from the battle to see anything more than a hazy cloud of dartships silhouetted against Qoribu's gleaming rings, but the tactical display showed more than a dozen clawcraft swarming Jacen and Tahiri, methodically herding them toward the Star Destroyer's tractor beams. Supported by a throng of Taat, they were fighting back valiantly, opening one hole after the other in the enemy formation. The Chiss always managed to cut them off and drive them back toward the sweeping tractor beams.

Then a clawcraft designator vanished. Another turned yellow and spiraled through the ring system and out of the system. Jaina felt Alema and Zekk urging Tahiri and Jacen to accelerate through the gap. Two of three clawcraft moving to cut them off also lost control and flew out of the battle, then Tahiri and Jacen were free, pulling away from their pursuers and weaving a crooked path among the few enemy fighters still in a position to attack.

Tahiri's gratitude flooded the Force, but quickly changed to astonishment when a clawcraft behind her exploded in a flash of static. A second one vanished an instant later, then a third turned yellow on Jaina's display and broke into two parts.

Tahiri's shock was overpowered by Alema's glee, then almost instantly by Zekk's righteous fury.

This is wrong! Zekk raged. He was furious with Alema; she was killing for revenge!

But Alema did not think so. She felt she was only killing to teach them a lesson, to make them understand there were consequences.

Jaina added her anger to Zekk's. Alema had violated the unspoken rules of the conflict. She had killed without purpose. When the Chiss reviewed their battle vids, they would feel bound to retaliate in kind.

Alema didn't care, and Taat seemed to agree. The hundreds of dartships not yet swept up in the tractor beams began to coalesce in tightly knit balls, moving with eerie precision into the path of oncoming clawcraft. Chiss fighters began to explode as though they were crashing into asteroids. The conflict was turning into an all-out battle.

Sensing Jaina's alarm, Tahiri opened a comm channel. "ReyaTaat, call off the dartships! Our last attacks were mistakes."

"They did not feel like mistakes," Reya countered. "They felt good."

"This battle is getting out of hand," Tahiri responded, echoing Jaina's feelings. "Reya was Chiss. She *knows* what will happen if you continue."

Reya fell silent, but the dartships continued to attack. Jaina found her frustration with Alema growing. The Twi'lek was a fine pilot, but she was too wild, too quick to surrender to the pearl of hatred that had been accreting inside her since the death of her sister, Numa. Now Alema's anger would spread across the Gyuel system like a nova blast.

When the Taat continued to attack, Jacen said, "ReyaTaat, the

Chiss will return with bigger ships. They'll attack the nests directly, and Taat will be destroyed. *All* the Qoribu nests will be destroyed."

"What difference does it make? Our nests are already dying." Reya's voice grew icy. "But Lowbacca must not be captured."

The Force resonated with agreement—none of the Jedi wanted to see their friend captured—but Lowbacca was calling the shots. He was the one in trouble.

"Lowbacca can take care of himself," Tahiri said. "And if he is captured, what the Taat are doing now will only hurt him."

"Lowbacca *won't* be captured," Reya said. "The Colony does not wish it."

The Taat continued to place themselves in front of their enemies, but instead of pursuing Tahiri and Jacen all the more ferociously, the clawcraft peeled away, giving them a clear route to freedom. Jaina exhaled in relief. At least Jag—or whoever was commanding this task force—still had the sense to back off before the conflict escalated.

Then a new tractor beam shot out from the Star Destroyer, capturing Tahiri, Jacen, and—judging by their surprise and anger—Alema and Zekk. Jaina cursed at the same time she heard Tesar's irate hiss in her ears. It was not easy to lock on to a wildly dodging spacecraft visually, but if a beam crew knew the comm frequency being used by the target, they could follow the carrier wave straight to their victim. And while Reya had not initiated the contact with Tahiri, she *had* kept the young Jedi talking until the clawcraft dispersed.

Jaina was close enough to the battle now that she could see the laser cannons flashing inside the whirling cloud of dartships. Four waving fingers of darkness marked the areas where the tractor beams were sweeping the Taat out of space, slowly pulling them toward the Star Destroyer. The vessel itself resembled a gray version of the Empire's old *Victory*-class Star Destroyers, save that it was a little sleeker, longer, and narrower, with a conical hull that gave it a menacing, needle-like appearance. It was impossible to tell where the bridge was located—it was not in the Chiss nature to reveal such a crucial detail just for the looking—but a dome-shaped bulge amidships probably housed the cloaking equipment that had masked the vessel's approach.

Jaina dropped the nose of her StealthX and started a fast approach toward the bow of the Star Destroyer, then felt Tesar's excitement starting to mount as he initiated his own run. An image of his view of the ship appeared in the back of her mind. He seemed to be approaching from the opposite end, more or less head-on toward Jaina. They would have to be careful to avoid a collision.

"Sneaky, give me a ten-mag view of the area around the root of the nearest tractor beam," Jaina ordered.

Risky or not, she could not let the Chiss reel in four Jedi.

Over the comm, Reya said, "We will have you free in a minute, friends."

Not kriffing likely, Jaina thought. Half of the Taat were already being sucked toward the Star Destroyer's capture bays, and the rest were too busy hurling themselves in front of clawcraft to disable any tractor beams.

"Help is coming." Reya's voice was reassuring. "The Mueum are almost here."

The timely assurance raised the hair on the back of Jaina's neck. Recalling Taat's uncanny ability to sense what foods she and the other Jedi were longing for, she began to wonder what else Reya could sense.

Tesar began to think Reya was a better spy than they had thought. Projecting his thoughts openly into the battle-meld, he wondered if he should eliminate her.

Jaina had the mental image of Tesar selecting Reya's lancet as a primary target, but realized instantly that the Barabel was only trying to test whether Reya knew what was happening in the battle-meld. He was passing over the stern of the Star Destroyer and could not have targeted her if he wished.

When Reya did not fall for the ploy, Jaina checked her tactical display and found a blue storm of Mueum dartships cascading down from the direction of Eyyl and Jwlio—just as promised.

"Sneaky, do an EM sweep of the hull," Jaina ordered. She still did not see how the arrival of the fresh swarm was going to save Lowbacca and the others. "We might get lucky and locate an energy output that will tell us where those generators are."

Sneaky whistled an acknowledgment, then the image on her display switched to a rectangular portal set into a field of gray durasteel. The tractor beam itself was invisible, save for a few distortion ripples that suggested it was a very powerful beam indeed—one designed to drag in unwilling ships. As Jaina had feared, the portal was protected by a grid of blue energy—a repulsor screen designed to prevent someone from disabling the beam by dropping a piece of ordnance into it. The Chiss were far too good to overlook something that obvious.

"Go to five mag," Jaina ordered.

The beam portal grew small in her display, and the white cave of a capture bay appeared beneath it. Jaina could see a pair of weapons turrets flanking a transparisteel viewing panel set high in the inner-most wall, but no hint of the tractor beam generator.

Sneaky piped a warning, and Jaina looked up to see the Star Destroyer stretched out before her like the long gray plain of an empty speeder lot. The beam cannons, big and small, remained silent in their sunken firing pits—a sure sign that the gunners still had not detected the approaching StealthXs.

"Anything on that EM sweep, Sneaky?" Jaina asked.

The droid tootled a negative, and Jaina sensed that the same was true for Tesar. It was beginning to look like they would have to do this the hard way. The Jedi would have to eject and destroy their ships.

Tahiri did not want to leave her living ship. It was a gift from Zonama Sekot . . . and it was a friend.

But her only other choice was to let herself be captured—and Jaina forbade that. She would go EV with Jacen and everyone else. Ten seconds.

Lowbacca did not have ten seconds. Five—if he was lucky.

Three, then.

"Give us eight!" Reya pleaded. No doubt now about whether she could read their emotions in the Force. "The Mueum are almost here."

Sure—enough time for your friends to capture Lowbacca's StealthX, Jaina thought. Two seconds.

Tesar urged Jaina to wait. The Mueum *were* attacking.

Jaina glanced at her display and saw a single, tightly packed arrow of Mueum designators driving through a screen of Chiss clawcraft like a blaster bolt through a tunic. The Star Destroyer opened up with all bearing batteries, hitting the mass with a devastating fusillade that would have torn a minor moon in half.

The Mueum did not even slow down. Long furrows of dartships vanished into fiery nothingness, and the swarm simply flowed into the open spaces, shrinking a little, but continuing toward the Star Destroyer amidships.

"No, Reya!" Jaina ordered. "Stop them!"

Lowbacca went EV, and Jaina lost all hope of bringing the conflict back under control. The Mueum took another volley of laser cannons and continued on as before, coalescing into a single black harpoon aimed at the heart of the Chiss Star Destroyer. Lowbacca's StealthX detonated in the mouth of the capture bay, taking with it fifty square meters of deck and several dozen dartships, but doing nothing whatsoever to interrupt the tractor beam.

Jaina rolled away from the Star Destroyer and started firing, trying to force as many clawcraft as possible away from Tahiri and the other captured Jedi. Tesar dropped in behind Jaina, firing to kill as a string of brave Chiss pilots jumped on her tail.

Finally, the Mueum reached the Star Destroyer. On her tactical display, Jaina glimpsed the lead dartships crashing into the vessel's particle shields, vaporizing themselves in an ever-broadening circle of light and fire. She thought for one moment that the suicide attack would come to no more than that; that the entire Mueum swarm would simply smash itself against the powerful Chiss shields.

Then the shields crackled, flashed, and fell. The Mueum assault smashed into the hull in a conflagration of rocket fuel and fire and burned through within seconds. Bodies and equipment began to tumble from the breached hull, but the swarm continued to pour through, streaming through the inner hull and spreading along the corridors to all the hidden corners of the vessel. Within moments, long tongues of flame began to lick out of the gun turrets, and towers of white fire started to shoot from the discharge vents.

A wave of explosions shook the Star Destroyer, and the hull began to come apart. Jaina was shaken by an all-too-familiar wave of anguish and fear, then a rip seemed to open in the Force as the huge vessel began to disintegrate from the inside.

The tractor beams sputtered into nothingness, and a sense of relief permeated the Force as Tahiri and Alema and Zekk finally regained control of their craft. A Chiss fighter appeared in front of Jaina, coming at her head-on and pouring angry streams of blaster bolts more or less in her direction. Jaina returned fire automatically, and she did not notice how her hand was shaking until after the clawcraft exploded.

Jaina reached out for Lowbacca and felt him drifting away, frightened and awed and lonely.

We'll find you! she promised. But he would have to stay open to the meld, he would have to help them find him.

She'll be doing well, Lowbacca thought, *just to save herself.*

FOURTEEN

After a week of travel and three off-course jumps, the dark-banded surface of Qoribu's night side was finally swelling in the *Shadow*'s forward viewport, biting an ever-larger crescent from the blue-green sun behind it. The planet was girded by a spectacular ring system, and the dusky shadows of its penumbra were brightened by a litter of twinkling moons, but Luke's gaze kept drifting to the velvet void beyond, to a few bright stars where the Chiss frontier hung stretched like the web of some dark, deadly spider better left undisturbed.

The Chiss prided themselves on never being the aggressor people. By their own law, they never attacked first. Their military doctrine took the edict even farther, decreeing that an enemy must attack them within Ascendancy space before they responded. So Luke did not understand how the Chiss had ended up in a border conflict when both sides acknowledged that the Colony was still over a light-year from the border.

Perhaps doctrine had changed. After all, the war with the Yuuzhan Vong had changed almost everything else. And Luke knew from his last journey into the Unknown Regions that there were things happening out here that the Galactic Alliance still did not understand. The number of Chiss ruling houses been reduced from nine to four for some unknown reason, and the Empire of the Hand had mysteriously vanished. So it certainly seemed possible the Chiss had changed their doctrine.

Still, Luke doubted that the Chiss would abandon their most basic tenet—the prohibition against attacking first. The law had stood for a thousand years, and Thrawn—the Chiss Grand Admiral who had nearly defeated the New Republic single-handedly—had been exiled from the Ascendancy for violating it.

To Luke, there was only one logical conclusion. The Colony had brought this conflict on itself—or Raynar had.

Just the thought of what Raynar had become filled Luke with guilt and sorrow. The Myrkr mission had cost his nephew Anakin and six other young Jedi their lives, and Raynar had suffered horribly, alone and with no reasonable hope of rescue. Could he be blamed for becoming the entity that he was now?

"It was war," Mara said softly from the pilot's seat. She glanced up at the activation reticle in the canopy, then looked at Luke in the section that mirrored over. "You're not responsible for what happened. Billions of good people were lost."

"I know that," Luke said. The blue star was completely hidden behind Qoribu's dark side now, and the yellow ring system looked as though it encircled a ghost planet. "But Raynar isn't lost. I may be able to bring Raynar back."

"You dream big, Skywalker," Mara said, shaking her head. "But it's not going to happen this time. For better or worse, Raynar is entwined with the Colony. I doubt that they *can* be separated."

"You're probably right," Luke said. "But something here feels wrong."

"Define *wrong*," Mara ordered. "Something to do with Raynar?"

"Maybe. It frightens me when Jedi become emperors."

"The galaxy had a bad experience with that," Mara admitted. "But Raynar is hardly another Palpatine. He seems very concerned about his, uh, people."

"For now," Luke said. "But how long before power becomes the end instead of the means?"

"So it's your job to set it right?" Mara asked. "We have enough to worry about in the Galactic Alliance."

"The galaxy is larger than the Galactic Alliance."

"And the Jedi can't be responsible for all of it," Mara retorted.

There was a long silence while they continued the discussion on a deeper, more intimate level, wrapping themselves around the other's viewpoint, trying to understand completely, but also searching for a way to consolidate what seemed to be opposing opinions. Such moments were one of the secret buttresses of their marriage. They understood how they fit together, how each had strengths and insights that complemented the weaknesses and blind spots of the other, and they had learned early in their relationship—during a desperate, three-day hike fleeing Imperials in a vornskyr-filled forest—

that their future always looked brighter when they relied on each other.

But this time there seemed no way to reconcile their concerns. Jedi resources were already stretched too thin to try separating Raynar from the Colony, even if Luke could convince the rest of the council that it was the right thing to do. Yet he could not escape the feeling that something important had fallen out of balance; that his Jedi Knights were busy plugging vac holes while their ship flew down a black hole.

"Life was a lot simpler when we could just draw a lightsaber and cut the bad guy down to size," Luke said.

Mara smiled. "Simpler—not necessarily easier."

They were close enough to Qoribu now that its moons had begun to resolve into colored shapes, from twinkling yellow specks to creamy fist-sized disks. Luke counted twenty-five different satellites glimmering in the penumbral grayness to either side of the gas giant's murky face, and the navigation display revealed another thirty hidden in the complete darkness of umbra.

Luke reached out in the Force. A diffuse insect presence blanketed six different moons, all currently clustered together near the penumbra's outer edge. Jaina and most of the other Jedi seemed to be on a moon near the center of the group, and—to his great relief—they exhibited only a hint of the Joiner double presence. But Lowbacca was floating a little behind the group, just inside Qoribu's pitch-black umbra, frightened and alone amid a mass of Chiss presences.

One of the Jedi in the main group stirred beneath Luke's Forcetouch, then extended a welcoming embrace.

Luke recognized Jacen's presence, but before he could respond with his own feeling of warmth, his nephew's voice sounded inside his head.

Hurry.

Jacen seemed more concerned than alarmed, and Luke had the clear impression that things were about to get crazy. He raised a hand to point toward the moon with their Jedi, but Mara was already swinging the *Shadow*'s nose toward it. He would have liked to open a hailing channel and raise Jaina on the comm, but there were certain to be Ascendancy listening posts all over the system—and the less the Chiss knew about who was approaching, the better.

"Faster." Saba's voice came over a vessel-to-vessel tight-beam channel that would be difficult for the Chiss to intercept; she was aboard the *XR808g* serving as Juun's copilot until Tarfang recovered. "It feelz like our Jedi Knightz are preparing a battle rage."

"You heard him, too?" Luke asked. "Jacen?"

"Yes." Saba's breathing began to grow heavy and deliberate. "It felt like they were about to go crazy. They must have found a great evil, or Tesar would never awaken the Hungry One."

"The Hungry One?" Mara echoed. "Take it easy, Saba. I don't think *crazy* means the same thing to humans as to Barabels."

Saba's breathing slowed. "No?"

"It just means unpredictable," Luke said, amazed at how little he *still* understood Barabels. "A bit out of control."

"Unpredictable?" Saba's voice returned to normal. "What a relief. This one does not like to set her mind aside."

Grimacing at the thought of a Barabel robbed of all restraint, Luke brought up a tactical display and found a trio of frigates drifting in unpowered orbit near Lowbacca's presence. They were being tended by a swarm of rescue craft, with a shield of clawcraft fighters hovering between them and the Killik-occupied moons. Floating just above the ring system were several massive chunks of flotsam that gave Luke a very bad feeling.

"Artoo, give me a composition analysis on that debris in the middle of the Chiss task force."

R2-D2 tweeted an listless acknowledgment, and a moment later the analysis appeared in an inset on Luke's screen. The flotsam was metallic, irregular, and mostly hollow. Starship pieces. Luke started to comment that there had been a battle, but stopped when he heard a pair of small feet slapping onto the flight deck behind him.

"Hurry!" Ben cried from the door. "Jacen needs us!"

Luke turned to find his son charging forward in his night tunic, his red hair still pillow-mussed and his eyes bleary with sleep.

Luke opened his arms. "You heard Jacen?"

Nanna clomped onto the deck behind him. "I apologize. He woke and jumped up before I could get to him." She extended her hand, saying to Ben, "Come back to bed. It was only a dream."

Luke motioned her to wait. "It wasn't." He hoisted Ben onto his knee. "We heard Jacen, too."

Ben's mouth dropped open. "You did?"

"Yes," Luke answered. "Through the Force."

This brought a flash of alarm to Ben's eyes.

"It's okay, Ben," Mara said in a soothing voice. "There's nothing to be scared of. You touched the Force all the time, when you were younger."

"During the war, I know." Ben stretched his arms toward Nanna. "I wanna go back to bed."

Luke didn't lift him toward the droid. "You're sure? We're coming up on Qoribu now."

Ben's face lit briefly in delight when he glanced forward, but he quickly turned back to Nanna. "I'm still tired."

"Really?" Luke frowned inside, but passed Ben to the droid. "We'll wake you when we see Jacen and Jaina."

"Okay." Ben buried his cheek on Nanna's synthflesh shoulder and looked away.

After the droid had taken him off the flight deck, Luke said, "He's afraid of it."

"Clearly." Mara's voice was sharp, but Luke sensed it was only because she was worried about Ben. "Maybe he thinks the Force is why his cousin and so many other Jedi died?"

"Maybe," Luke said. "It would be nice to have a reason we understood."

"But you don't think that's it."

"I guess not," Luke said. "When it comes to anything else, he's just too adventurous and confident, sometimes even reckless."

Noting that the *Falcon* was already drifting into a standard defensive formation while Juun's *XR808g* continued to speed ahead, Luke opened a tight-beam channel to both vessels.

"Not so fast, *Exxer*," he said. "Until we know what that battle was about—"

"There was a battle?" Juun gasped.

"Check your readouts," Han commed from the *Falcon*. When he received only dead silence in response, he added, "You *do* have the standard reconnaissance suite?"

"We have two pairz of electrobinocularz," Saba informed them, acting as the *XR808g*'s copilot. "And only one of us is small enough to use them."

As Han chided the Sullustan for this lack, Mara said to Luke, "Heads up. What's that?"

Luke checked his tactical display and found a torrent of Killik dartships streaming out of Qoribu's shadow. Frowning because he had not sensed any nests in that area, he turned to ask R2-D2 to double-check the readings—and found the little droid leaning against his interface arm, slowly twisting the information buffer back and forth in the socket. Alarmed at how the droid seemed to be deteriorating, Luke promised himself that he would schedule some maintenance time and looked out the forward viewport instead.

It took only a moment to see the sensors were not mistaken. An elongated oval of tiny white flecks was pouring into the gray shadows of the planet's penumbra, moving to position itself in front of the six moons where Luke *had* sensed Killiks.

"This isn't standard procedure," Juun said. The *XR808g* continued toward the Killik moons. "They must be nervous because of the battle."

"Then what are you doing?" Han asked. "Shouldn't we slow down?"

"The sooner they see us, the better," Juun said. "Once they realize we're only flying transports, they'll return to their usual routine. Insects are very advanced. They always follow standard procedure."

Luke wasn't so sure. He reached out to the dartships and sensed . . . nothing definite, only the same vague uneasiness that he had felt before the tower collapsed on Yoggoy. He knew that Mara felt it, too.

"Captain Juun, I think you should come back," Luke commed. "We can't feel those pilots in the Force."

"You place too much faith in your ancient sorcery, Master Skywalker," Juun said. "In *Running the Blockade: Escape from Yavin,* Captain Solo clearly illustrated the value of a confident approach."

"What'd I tell you about those history vids?" Han warned. "The Force isn't just some hokey religion. This stuff works."

"So does procedure, Captain Solo," Juun said. "That's why you're paying me the big credits. Let me do my job."

The dartships continued to stream out of the umbra, gathering in a wall of swirling, flickering orange between them and the Killik moons. The *XR808g* accelerated.

"Captain Juun, I think you should reconsider." Though Luke spoke more forcefully, he resisted the temptation to tell Saba to take control of the *XR808g*. The Jedi may have developed a ruthless streak during the war, but they still stopped short of fomenting mutiny. "After the attack on Yoggoy—"

"What attack?" Juun asked.

"The building collapse," Saba rasped.

"But that was determined to be an accident."

"Not by us, it wasn't," Han answered.

The *XR808g*'s running lights began to flash in ancient blink code. Luke looked to his display, but instead of the translation he had expected, he found only the blip-storm of approaching dartships.

"Artoo!"

R2-D2 emitted a surprised clunk, then trilled a short question.

"The *Exxer*'s blink code, that's what!" Luke said. "How about a translation?"

R2-D2 droned wearily, and the translation began to scroll across the screen.

This is the XR808g, flagship of JuunTaar Commercial, with two sister ships bearing supplies for the Jedi warriors. Please signal your intention to provide safe escort.

"*JuunTaar Commercial?*" Han complained over the comm. "*Flagship?* I didn't think Sullustans *had* that much imagination."

Luke looked back to R2-D2. "Any answer from the Killiks?"

R2-D2 tweeted a sharp no.

The dartships began to stream toward the *XR808g*, bleeding a swath of orange rocket flame through Qoribu's shadow.

"Juun, get out of there now!" Han's voice made the comm speakers pop. "Time to cut and run . . . or you're fired!"

Juun was already swinging around, but the dartships put on a burst of speed and shot across the last few kilometers in an eye-blink, engulfing the *XR808g* in a whirling cloud of rocket light and splinter-shaped hulls. Luke felt a sudden spike of Sullustan fear and Barabel anger, then bursts of silver light began to erupt around the transport.

Juun's voice came over the S-thread emergency channel. "Urgent, urgent." His voice was terrified but steady. "This is Captain Jae Juun of the *XR-eight-oh-eight-g* requesting immediate assistance. We are under attack just off Qoribu in the Gyuel system, coordinates—"

"Enough procedure, already!" Han said over the normal comm. "We *know* the situation."

"Copy," Juun said. The channel crackled as the *XR808g*'s shields fell, then the comm erupted into a steady, deep rumble. "Uh, we just lost our drives. Request plan update."

"I'll be there in a minute," Han commed. "Just sit tight."

"Cop—"

The signal disintegrated into a series of loud bangs, and the *Falcon* started forward.

"We'll take this one, *Shadow*," Leia commed. "Hang here and cover our stern."

"Why don't you cover *our* stern?" Mara suggested. "You're better armed."

"Because the *Shadow* has *yacht*-class drive units," Han said. "If you latch onto that transport, it'll take you a week to get moving."

"You have us there," Mara admitted.

The *XR808g*'s blaster cannons began to fire indiscriminately, blowing whole swaths clear of dartships, and the anger that Saba had been pouring into the battle-meld turned to hunt-glee.

"We're going in," Leia commed. "Just keep your ion drives hot. We may have to scoot out of here in a hurry."

"Copy." Luke was just as worried about Han and Leia as he was about Juun and Saba. The *Falcon* packed a powerful punch and boasted military-grade shields, but her legendary speed would not be available if she was dragging along a transport almost as large as she was. "Just be as fast as you can."

"Check that," Mara said. "I think you're scaring them off."

Luke glanced at his tactical display and saw that the dartships were swinging away from the *XR808g*, leaving the *Falcon* a clear path to rescue Juun and Tarfang.

"Maybe those guys aren't as homicidal as we thought," Luke said. "Could this be a communications problem?"

"It wasn't a communications problem when that tower fell," Mara said. "And I don't like the way those dartship pilots feel."

"Shadowy," Luke agreed. "Like they're hiding in the Force."

The dartships hooked around and began a ferocious acceleration on a course opposite the *Falcon*'s, back toward the pitch blackness of Qoribu's umbra.

"They're sure in a hurry," Luke said.

He switched scales, searching for any sign that the Chiss were moving against the Killiks, or the Killiks gathering for an assault on the Chiss. Everything looked quiet on both fronts. The dartship swarm split into two groups, one accelerating at twice the rate of the other.

"I didn't know methane rockets could provide so much thrust," Mara said. "None of this makes sense."

R2-D2 beeped, then scrolled a message across their displays.

These Killiks are flying hydrogen rockets.

By the time the *Falcon*'s tractor beam had caught hold of the *XR808g*, a two-kilometer gap had opened between the two sets of dartships. The swarms continued to accelerate toward the planet's umbra until the faster one was past the *Shadow*, then both groups pivoted around and came shooting back for a flank attack.

"Look sharp!" Luke warned. "They're coming back for us."

"See 'em," Leia replied coolly. "Thanks."

The *Falcon* began to accelerate, but hardly with her usual speed. She was dragging the *XR808g* along, drawing it in slowly because the two transports were so close in size. Working any faster, Luke knew, meant risking the tractor beam's grasp—or smashing the derelict into the *Falcon*.

The dartships continued to close, and it quickly grew apparent the *Falcon* could not outrun them without setting the *XR808g* adrift. Luke started to suggest that they let Juun and Saba go EV so the *Shadow* could pick them up on the way past, but the slow swarm suddenly stopped and began to form a wall between the *Shadow* and the *Falcon*. The second, faster swarm continued to pursue the *Shadow* from behind.

"*This* doesn't look good," Mara said. "Artoo, start plotting escape vectors."

The droid tweedled an acknowledgment and went to work.

"They drew us in," Mara said. "I'm ashamed."

"They're going to a lot of trouble to get us," Luke said. "What I want to know is why."

That was the question he held in his mind as he reached for Jacen and Jaina in the Force. Raynar had been unwilling—or unable—to discuss the Yoggoy attack honestly, but Luke felt sure his niece and nephew would prove much more open.

In reply, he received only an impression of confusion.

"Same story as on Yoggoy," Mara observed. "Nobody knows anything."

R2-D2 tweeted an announcement. The *Shadow* lacked enough current velocity to escape unscathed. No matter which way they turned, the fast swarm would have a thirty-second window of attack—and that assumed the *Shadow* suffered no damage to her drive units.

Nanna's voice came over the intercom. "Shall I take Ben to the docking bay?"

"Not yet," Mara said.

"I really think you should take Ben and flee in the StealthX, Master Skywalker," the droid insisted. "The *Shadow*'s odds of survival are—"

"Certain," Mara growled. Her gaze slid across the mirrored canopy toward Luke. "Right?"

"Right," Luke said. They had rehearsed just this situation many times. "We're fine."

Closing his mind to external distractions, Luke began a focusing exercise, breathing in through his nose, filling his belly diaphragm with air, then exhaling slowly out his mouth. He barely felt the *Shadow* shudder as the first dartships began to pelt her shields with balls of primitive chemical explosives, and when Han's voice came over the comm, he heard the words only with his ears.

"Uh, why aren't you on an escape vector? Is Artoo on the blink again?"

"Negative that," Mara answered. She lowered the *Shadow*'s blaster cannon and began to fire indiscriminately into the cloud of swirling dartships. "We're okay."

"You don't look okay," Han said. "We'll cut the *Exxer* loose and circle back to—"

"Nega*tive*!" Mara snapped. "You do that, we'll never get free of these pests. Keep going—and don't look back. Luke has a trick up his sleeve."

"Copy." It was Leia this time. "If you're sure."

"We're sure." Mara closed the channel, then—as the *Shadow*'s shuddering worsened—added, "I think."

Luke was sure. By then, he had opened himself wide to the Force, and it was pouring in from all sides, filling him with a maelstrom of power, imbuing his whole body with its energy.

A bang sounded back in the engineering bay as a power circuit overloaded, then the lights dimmed as R2-D2 redistributed shield power. Luke felt a surge of anxiety from Mara, but pushed it to one side so he could concentrate on the task at hand. He formed an imaginary picture of the *Shadow*'s exterior, then expanded it into the Force, moving it from his mind out into the cockpit.

Mara turned around and inspected the image carefully, then said, "Looks good."

Luke continued to enlarge the image, extending it into every corner of the vessel, taking his time to absorb the attributes that made up the *Shadow*'s sensor signature. He began to grow tired, but ignored his fatigue and expanded the illusion until it covered the entire ship like an imaginary skin.

Another bang sounded in the engineering bay. This time, before R2-D2 could redistribute power, the sound was followed by the muffled thuds of several hull hits. Mara hit the crash alert, closing all airtight doors and activating the pressure stop-loss systems, then spoke over the intercom.

"Nanna, get Ben into his vac suit."

"I've already done that," the droid responded. "We're waiting at our evacuation station now. Perhaps you should come—"

"Nanna, you short-circuit!" Ben's voice said. "We're fine. Dad said so!"

Trying not to be distracted by his son—or by the steadily growing shudder of the barrage of dartship attacks—Luke brought to mind another image of the *Shadow,* this time with a black, star-speckled veneer that resembled the emptiness of deep space. Instead of absorbing the ship's sensor signature, however, he blanketed it with a layer of cold emptiness.

Once the illusory skins were in place, he carefully adjusted them, drawing the masking image tight against the hull here, pushing the counterfeit out a little there. The effort of maintaining both illusions began to deplete the energy running through him, so Luke opened himself up completely, using his fear for Ben's life, his anger at the insects that were threatening it, to draw more Force into himself. Every centimeter of his body began to nettle with its sting, and a faint aura arose from his skin.

A third bang sounded from the engineering bay.

"How about that decoy, Skywalker?" Mara asked. "Our shields can't take—"

Luke released the outer skin. "Go!"

Mara shoved the throttles to overload, then, half a second later, shut down the drives. The *Shadow* slid out of her double and—still masked by the dark veneer Luke had constructed—glided quietly away from the Force illusion.

The shuddering stopped. Luke continued to maintain both illusions, the Force pouring through him like fire, burning more fiercely every moment. He was drawing more energy than his body was conditioned to endure, literally burning himself up from the inside. It was not really a dark side act—to a modern Jedi, the dark side was more a matter of intent than deed—but it felt that way to him. According to Mara, this was what happened to Palpatine, and Luke believed her. He could feel himself aging—his cells weakening, the membranes growing thin and the cytoplasm simmering, the nuclei coming apart.

The air around him began to crackle with static.

R2-D2 extended a fire extinguisher and started toward Luke, squealing in alarm.

"It's okay, Artoo!" Mara said. "He knows how far to push it. He's not going to ignite."

I hope, she added silently.

On Luke's tactical display, the illusionary *Shadow*—the real one was not visible even to her own sensors—was slowly drifting toward the bottom of the screen, still surrounded by a cloud of attacking dartships. A small inset was counting down the seconds remaining until the Force-cloaked *Shadow* would be far enough from the dartships to restart the drives and flee. The way Luke was hurting, thirty seconds seemed like an eternity.

"We're bringing Juun and Saba aboard now," Leia commed. Her voice was filled with the concern that Luke felt in the Force. "Do you need help?"

They could not answer for fear that the dartships would notice the comm waves and discover the *Shadow*'s true position. Instead, Mara reached out to Leia through the Force, trying to assure her that everything was fine. Though the message would have been clearer coming from Luke, his body was starting to tremble and spark, and he needed all his concentration just to fight his exhaustion.

The *XR808g* began to drift away from the *Falcon* on the tactical display, and the Solos started a sweeping turn back toward the "battle." Luke felt Mara protesting through the Force, but the *Falcon* only began to pick up speed. Leia was angry with them for trying to be heroes; the situation wasn't *that* bad.

"Stang!" Mara cursed. "That—"

"Moommmm!" Ben called, peeking around the corner. He was in his vac suit, with the helmet visor open. "Dad says we're not supposed to say *stang*."

"Your father's right," Mara said. "Aren't you supposed to be at your evacuation station with Nanna?"

"We were, but then the shuddering stopped and . . ." Ben's gaze drifted over to Luke's glowing, anguished form, and his eyes bulged with horror. "What's wrong with Dad?"

"Nothing. I'll explain later." Mara activated the intercom. "Nanna—"

The droid appeared behind Ben. "Master Ben!" She swept him up and retreated aft. "The drill is *never* over until we hear the all-clear."

Luke's skin felt as dry as a Tatooine lake, and tiny haloes of golden light were starting to appear around his fingertips. The *Falcon* was on a straight heading and accelerating toward the dartships. The inset on the tactical display showed three seconds, two . . .

Mara brought the sublight drives back online. Luke let the illusions drop and slumped into his chair, his skin prickling and his hair standing on end as the last of the Force energy left his body.

Han's voice came immediately over the comm. "What the blazes?" The *Falcon* made a hard turn away from the confused dartships. "Did you just tele—"

"Didn't I tell you not to look back?" Mara asked, her voice still that of a reproving mother. "Now fall in behind us and stay there."

"Uh, sure." Han sounded more confused by her tone than he had been by the sudden change in the *Shadow*'s location. "Whatever you say."

The comm went silent, and Mara let out a breath. "Chubba. Don't tell me I just talked to Han like he was a—"

"It's okay," Luke assured her. "At heart, he's just an overgrown kid anyway."

She activated a mirror section and looked back at him. "How're you feeling?"

"Like I grabbed a powerfeed," he said. "Why is that so much harder than pushing a Star Destroyer around?"

Mara smiled. "Just don't make a mess on my flight deck."

Feeling in danger of doing just that, Luke started to rise—then caught a glimpse of himself in the mirrored section of canopy. His face was puffy and wrinkled, his skin sallow and dry, his eyes sunken and baggy and rimmed in red. He was starting to look like Palpatine.

Not by half, Mara assured him through the Force.

"But get some rest," she said aloud. "If you push that stuff too hard, there's no telling what might happen."

FIFTEEN

The AWOL Jedi stood waiting in front of their makeshift squadron, a small eye of calm in a frenetic storm of insect activity. The Knights were still wearing their rumpled flight suits, staring at the *Shadow* and *Falcon* as they landed. Tesar and Zekk had the good grace to wear guilty expressions as well, but Jaina and Alema merely looked defiant. Jacen and Tahiri betrayed no emotion at all.

Mara took her time closing down the ship's systems, allowing their suspense to build—and giving herself a few moments to search the cavernous hangar for any hint of danger in the Force. There was no chance that Jaina or any of the others had been involved in the assault on the *Shadow*, but *someone* had attacked her family—and that someone had certainly *looked* like Killiks. Unlike Luke, she was utterly convinced that Raynar Thul would do anything he thought necessary to keep Jaina and the others in the Colony—even if that meant ambushing his old friends.

Finally, when she could not find even a hint of danger, Mara joined the others in the *Shadow*'s main cabin. Despite a twenty-minute rest trance, Luke still looked like an escapee from a spice mine, with sallow skin and red-rimmed eyes. Ben was bright-eyed and eager to meet his cousins. He kept looking from his father to the door.

Mara took his hand from Nanna. "Ben, you understand that we have important business with Jaina and the others, don't you?"

"I'm not a Gamorrean, Mom," he said. "I know we wouldn't come all the way out here if it was *unimportant* business."

"Good. You can say hello to your cousins, but then Nanna will take you to stay with Cakhmaim and Meewalh on the *Falcon*." She looked to Nanna. "Ask them to lock down the ship—I don't care if it *does* offend the Killiks."

"I was about to suggest the same thing myself," Nanna replied.

Mara nodded, then opened the boarding hatch to the cloying, fuel-laced mugginess of the big hangar. Ben was off like a blaster bolt, racing down the stairs and throwing himself into Jaina's arms. She laughed and gave him a warm hug.

"Nice to see you, too, Ben," Jaina said. She stepped back and ran an appraising eye over him. "You've grown."

"It's been a whole year." He smiled mischievously, then added, "Boy, are you guys in trouble!"

Mara, who was still only halfway down the stairs, cringed inwardly, but Jaina only smiled.

"I imagine we are."

"Well, I hope they don't take away your lightsaber or anything."

This caused Jaina's eyes to flash, but Ben didn't seem to notice. He turned to Jacen, who had matured into a handsome man with a thick beard and brooding brown eyes, and seemed unable to decide what he should do next.

Jacen smiled and extended his hand. "Hello, Ben. I'm your cousin Jacen."

"I know you." Ben took the hand and shook it. "You went away when I was two. Did you find it?"

The question puzzled Jacen less than it did Mara. "Some of it," Jacen answered.

Ben's face fell. "So you're going back?"

"No." Jacen's tone changed to that of a person addressing an equal. "What I haven't found, I doubt I ever will."

Ben nodded sagely, then glanced toward the *Falcon,* only now lowering her boarding ramp. "I have to go, but we can talk later."

"Yes," Jacen said. "I'll look forward to that."

Ben took Nanna's hand and started toward the *Falcon,* leaving nothing but an awkward silence between Mara and the AWOL Jedi. Though Luke was the informal leader of the Jedi Order, they had decided that she would be the one to confront them and put them on the defensive. That would leave Luke free to assume the role of judge, mentor, or friend—whatever was needed.

Mara stopped a few steps away and studied the young Jedi Knights in silence, meeting each of their unblinking gazes in turn, trying to gauge their moods but finding only the unreadable durasteel of veteran killers. She did not recall when they had grown so hard.

The Yuuzhan Vong had come, and it seemed to Mara that they had gone almost overnight from being teenage Jedi-in-training to seasoned warriors. After what they had seen in battle—after what they had *done*—it seemed ludicrous to think of them being "in trouble."

Jaina tolerated the scrutiny for only a few seconds, then stepped forward to give Mara a tentative hug. "*This* is a surprise."

"I'm sure," Leia said, arriving from the *Falcon* with Han, C-3PO, and Saba. "Raynar didn't make it easy for us to find you."

The glance of silent thanks that Leia flashed to Jacen did not go unnoticed by Jaina or the others, but Mara saw no sign that anyone seemed upset by it.

"Raynar is afraid you'll try to take us back." Tahiri Veila said. Over the last five years, she had matured into a sinewy blond woman—so much so that Mara might not have recognized her, if not for her bare feet and the three vertical scars the Yuuzhan Vong had left on her forehead. "And isn't that why you've come?"

"It's good to see you, too, kid," Han taunted. "What do you say we let Luke answer that and just say hello?"

Tahiri's face melted into an expression of joy and chagrin. "Sorry—we were kind of in the middle of something." She opened her arms and went to Han, giving him a big, Wookiee-style hug. "It *is* good to see you, Han."

When she started rubbing her arms across his back, Han shuddered and looked vaguely nauseated. Tahiri released him with a grin and embraced Leia as well, and the awkwardness finally faded between the two generations of Jedi. Han and Leia hugged Jacen and Jaina long and hard, fondly telling them both they had a lot of explaining to do and making them promise to do so later aboard the *Falcon*. Then the group exchanged greetings all around, and when they were done, Jaina quickly seized the initiative again.

"So what *are* you doing here? Without us, I didn't think the council would have any Jedi to . . ."

The sentence trailed off as her eyes drifted back to Luke's weary face, and her expression changed to one of dismay and fear.

"What's wrong?" she asked. "Are you sick?"

"I'm fine—just a little worn," Luke said. "We came to, um, *talk* about what's going on here."

Jaina's relief was obvious—as was that of her companions. Only Jacen's expression did not change—and he had seemed unconcerned in the first place. He had been gone five years, and still he seemed less surprised than anyone by Luke's temporary appearance.

Though Mara was being careful not to stare, Jacen gave her a small smile, letting her know that he had sensed her scrutiny. There was nothing menacing in the gesture, but it sent a cold prickle down her spine. As Palpatine's assassin, her life had often depended on her ability to hide her thoughts—both physically and in the Force. Yet Jacen had sensed her attention casually, the way he might have caught a young woman studying him from afar.

Mara pretended not to notice and kept her gaze riveted on Jaina. "You've let down the entire order," she said, deliberately forcing the younger Jedi to try to excuse their actions. "Losing one of you would have been bad enough, but there's no way we could fill the holes left by all five of you."

As Mara had expected, Jaina would not be intimidated. "Then how could the order spare *four* Jedi to come 'talk' to us?"

"The council felt the situation warranted it," Luke said. "And now the order is short *nine* Jedi."

"Situation, Master Skywalker?" Tesar rasped. "Has something happened?"

"You first," Mara demanded. This was not the way the council normally dealt with its Jedi Knights, but she did not want this group taking advantage of Luke's patience—or his regret over the outcome of the Myrkr mission. "What, exactly, are you *doing* here?"

Jaina and the others shared a moment of silent communion, then, to everyone's surprise, Alema Rar stepped forward.

"We're trying to prevent a war," she said. "Isn't that what Jedi are supposed to do?"

Luke would not be baited into making this a discussion. "Go on."

Zekk spoke next. "You know about the call we'd all been feeling . . ."

Luke nodded.

And Tahiri continued, "It wasn't something we could ignore, especially at the last."

"We *had* to come," Tesar rasped. He looked to his mother. "It was like the Mating Call. We could think of nothing else until it was answered."

They stopped, as if that had answered the question.

"That explains *why* you came," Leia said. "It doesn't explain what you're *doing*."

A chest-high Killik with a green thorax and tiny wings came over and brushed Jaina's arm with an antenna, then thrummed something with its chest.

"She says the StealthXs are fed and rested," C-3PO translated proudly.

"Fueled and armed," Jaina corrected. She ran her arm down the Killik's antenna, then said to it, "Thanks. We'll be leaving shortly."

"Lowie had to go EV," Zekk explained. "We're getting ready to bring him back."

"With shadow bombs?" Mara asked. She pointed to a rack of proton torpedoes being dragged away from the StealthXs by several Killiks. Even from ten meters away, it was apparent that the propellant charges had been replaced with packed baradium. "That's not exactly rescue equipment."

"We might need to create a little diversion," Alema admitted.

"No kidding?" Han scoffed. "You mean to get past all those Chiss?"

"Nobody's going anywhere." Mara directed this to Jaina. "Not until we have some answers. Things are too far out of control."

Jaina's face grew hard. "I'm sorry, but I'm not leaving Lowie out there another minute—"

"Lowbacca has dropped into a Force-hibernation," Luke interrupted. His eyes were half closed, his chin raised. "He's safe for now."

Jaina scowled and looked as though she wanted to argue, but she knew better than to doubt her uncle's word.

"The sooner we get those answers, kid, the sooner we get to Lowbacca," Han said.

Jaina and the others exchanged a few tense looks, then she nodded. "Fine. You want to see what this is about, come with us."

She led the way deeper into the hangar cavern, past rack after rack of dartship berths. Stacked a staggering fifteen berths high, they were strewn with fueling lines and swarming with Killik technicians. Their technology was unsophisticated, but the insects were incredibly efficient, working a dozen at a time in cramped spaces that would have had just two human technicians throwing hydrospanners at each other. The fuel-tinged air was permeated by a low, rhythmic rumble that sounded like machinery, but Mara soon realized it was coming from the creatures themselves.

She turned to Tahiri, who was walking beside her, and asked, "That sound . . . are they singing?"

It was Alema—walking at Luke's side—who answered. "It's more like humming."

"They do it when they concentrate," Tesar added. "The harder they work, the louder it growz."

"It's their part in the Song of the Universe," Tahiri explained.

"Doesn't sound like any song *I've* ever heard," Han said from a step ahead of Mara. "In fact, I've heard more rhythm in a bantha stampede."

"That's because you can't hear the whole song," Zekk explained helpfully. "Only insect species hear it all."

"Yeah?" Han scowled and turned to Jacen. "Can *you* hear it?"

"No." Jacen flashed an imitation of Han's roguish smile. "Then again, I've only been here about a month."

"Relax, Dad," Jaina called from the front of the group. "We don't hear it, either."

Han let out an audible sigh of relief, then Jaina suddenly stepped into an empty berth and ducked down a waxy passage that led out the back.

C-3PO stopped outside the berth. "That doesn't look like a proper corridor, Mistress Jaina."

"You could always stay here, Threepio," Han said, watching six Killik workers carry a damaged dartship past. "I'll bet these guys are always looking for spare parts."

"I was just commenting, Captain Solo."

C-3PO dropped into an awkward crouch that was half squat and half hunch, and they all followed Jaina into the passage.

"Sorry about this," Zekk said from behind Mara. "They weren't thinking of larger species when they dug these tunnels."

"No problem. We're not that old." Mara was bent over nearly double, so Zekk had to be crawling on all fours. "Where are we going?"

"You'll see," he said. "We're almost there."

The Force ahead grew heavy with pain and fear, and the humid air began to smell of blood, burns, and bacta. A moment later, they emerged into a large oblong chamber lined by hundreds of hexagonal wall bunks. In the open areas of the room, hand-sized Killik healers were swarming over casualties from both sides, spitting antiseptic saliva into their wounds, spinning silk sealant into cracked chitin, slipping tiny pincers into torso punctures to pull shrapnel from internal organs. Low purrs of gratitude reverberated from the chest plates of the insect patients, but the Chiss—those who were still conscious—were staring at the creatures in horror.

As the rest of the group stepped into the chamber behind Mara, a green triage nurse rushed over and brushed its antennae across Jaina's arm, then looked at Luke and thrummed a question.

"Oh, dear," C-3PO said. "She doesn't seem to know what's wrong with Master Luke!"

"Nothing's wrong with him, Taat," Jaina said to the insect. "We're all fine. We just wanted to see the infirmary."

The triage nurse stepped closer to Luke and scrutinized him with its bulbous gaze, then clicked its mandibles doubtfully.

"I'm sure." Jaina glanced at Mara. "Right?"

"Oh, yeah," Mara said. Even had there been something wrong with him, she would not have trusted the insects to fix it—not after what had become of Raynar.

"I'm just a little burned out," Luke assured the Killik.

The nurse spread its antennae in doubt, then scurried off to hold down a screaming Chiss. The patient did not seem pleased to have three Killik healers rummaging around inside his torso.

"They are not being cruel," Tesar said. "But the Taat are very stoic. They don't use anesthesia themselvez."

"And when they have it available for other species, they never get the dosage right," Jaina added. "They've decided that it's just faster and safer to do without."

"I'll bet," Han said, eyeing the carnage. "Because it kind of looks like they're enjoying it."

"They're not," Zekk assured him. "The Kind are the most gentle and forgiving species I've ever met."

"They have no malice," Alema added. She pointed to a nearby bunk, where a trio of Killik nurses clung to the wall, hovering over a half-conscious Chiss, holding a casted leg in traction. "Once the fighting's over, they care for their attackers as their own. They don't even imprison them."

"I can't imagine that works very well with *Chiss*," Leia said. "What happens when the prisoners attack?"

"Their escortz bring them here for evaluation," Tesar rasped. "They think other speciez are aggressive only because they can't stomach pain. So they look for the *source* of the pain . . ."

"Eventually, the Chiss figure it out and stop attacking," Tahiri said.

"Yeah, well, a little bug-probing would stop *me*," Han said. His gaze was fixed on a Killik healer, whose four limbs were straddling a Chiss face as it extracted something from the patient's red eyeball. "At least until I could escape this creep show."

"Dad, the Chiss don't need to *escape*," Jaina said. "They're free to leave whenever they like, if they can find a way."

Han nodded knowingly. "There's always a catch."

"Always," Alema agreed.

"But it's not what you think," Zekk added.

"The Chisz won't take back their MIAz," Tesar finished.

"I'm sure," Mara said. The young Jedi Knights' habit of talking fast and completing each other's thoughts was beginning to make her edgy. It was almost as if they were sinking into a permanent battle-meld. "I can't imagine the Chiss are much for prisoner exchanges."

"Oh, we're not talking about exchanges," Jaina said.

"The Chiss won't take them back at *all*," Tahiri explained.

"Before we got here, they used to steal transports and try to go back on their own," Alema said. "The Chiss just turned them away."

"How awful for them," C-3PO said sympathetically. "What happens to prisoners now?"

"A few hitch rides out, then who knows what happens to them," Jaina said. "Most end up staying with the nest."

Alarm bells began to ring inside Mara's head. She glanced toward the heart of the chamber, where Tekli and several Chiss medics had set up a makeshift surgical theater beneath the jewel-blue glow of a dozen shine-balls, then looked back to Jaina.

"Doesn't that worry you?" Mara asked.

"No," Zekk said, frowning. "Why should it?"

"Because they're *Joiners*," Han said. "They don't have their own minds."

"Actually, they have *two* minds," Jacen said, speaking for the first time since entering the infirmary. "They still have their own mind, but they share the nest mind as well."

Han grimaced, but Mara was relieved. At least *Jacen* still sounded as though he were considering matters from outside the Killik perspective. Maybe his odyssey had given him an extra resistance to the Killik influence . . . or maybe he had just arrived later than the others. Either way, it made him an asset when dealing with the rest of the strike team.

After a moment, Han said, "You'd better not be trying to tell me this is a *good* thing."

"It's not a good thing or a bad thing, Dad," Jacen replied. "It just *is*. What disturbs you is that the Will of the nest mind is more powerful than the will of the individual mind. They appear to lose their independence."

"Yeah." Han's eyes flashed to Jaina and the other young Knights. "That disturbs me. A lot."

"And it would certainly disturb the Chiss," Leia said. "They would feel very threatened by anything that limits their self-determination."

"That doesn't justify speciecide," Jaina countered.

"Speciecide is a harsh accusation," Luke said. The calmness of his voice, and the fact that he had been even more quiet than Jacen so far, commanded the attention of the entire group. "It doesn't sound like the Chiss. They have very strict laws regarding aggression—especially outside their own borders."

"You don't *know* the Chiss." Alema's voice was full of bitterness. "They keep Kind prisoners in isolation cells in a free-drifting prison ship and starve them to death."

"How can you know that?" Leia asked. "I can't see the Chiss letting anyone inspect their prisons."

"A Chiss Joiner revealed it," Jacen explained.

"The prison ships I believe," Mara said. "But I can't see the Chiss starving *any* prisoner. Their conduct codes wouldn't bend that far."

"The starvation is incidental," Jacen said. "The Chiss are *trying* to feed their prisoners."

"It can't be that hard to figure out what bugs eat," Han said.

"Not what, Dad—*how*," Jacen said. Motioning the group after him, he started toward the infirmary's main entrance. "Come on. This whole problem will make more sense if I just show you."

Jacen led the group into a huge, wax-lined corridor bustling with Killik workers. Most were bearing large loads—beautiful jewel-blue shine-balls, multicolored spheres of wax, wretchedly small sheafs of half-rotten marr stalks. But some carried only a single small stone, usually quite smooth and brightly colored, and these insects moved slowly, searching for the perfect place to affix their treasure amid the scattered groupings on the walls.

"So this is how they make the mosaics," Leia commented.

"One pebble at a time," Jaina said. "Whenever one of the Killiks comes across a pretty stone, she stops whatever she's doing and rushes back to the nest to find the perfect place. It can take days."

Mara was surprised to hear a tone of awe in her niece's voice; normally, Jaina was too preoccupied with tactics or readiness drilling to even *notice* art.

"*She?*" Leia asked. "The males don't contribute to the mosaics?"

"There aren't many males," Zekk explained.

"And males only leave their nest when it's time to establish a new one," Alema added.

The corridor branched, then ended a short time later at the brink of a huge, sweet-smelling pit so dimly lit that Han would have plunged over the edge had Jaina not caught him with the Force and pulled him back. Mara and the other Jedi had more warning. The

Force inside the chamber ached with a hunger so fierce that they instinctively hesitated at the entrance.

"This is the busiest place in the nest," Jacen said over the din of clacking mandibles and drumming chests. "The grub cave."

As Mara's eyes adjusted to the dimness, she saw that the chamber was swarming with Killiks, all carefully crawling over an expanse of hexagonal cells. Half the cells were empty, a handful were sealed beneath a waxy cover, and the rest contained the thick, squirming bodies of Killik larvae.

Each larva was being attended by an adult, who was either carefully cleaning its head capsule or feeding it small pieces of shredded food. As the group watched, a nearby larva ejected a brown, sweet-smelling syrup. The adult grooming it unfurled a long, tongue-like proboscis and quickly sucked up the fluid, then burped and turned to leave the chamber. A new Killik quickly took its place.

"Blast!" Han sounded as though he might imitate the larva. "Don't tell me that was dinner."

"It's not that unusual," Jacen said. He guided them to one side of the entrance, so they would not impede the constant flow of Killiks entering and leaving the nursery. "There are bees and wasps across the entire galaxy that feed this way. It produces a very stable social structure."

Han turned to Leia. "Didn't I tell you this would happen? We let him have too many weird pets when he was a kid."

"But it does explain why the Chiss captives are starving," Mara surmised, ignoring Han's joke. "Without larvae, the prisoners can't eat."

"You make it sound like an accident, and it's not." Zekk's voice was sharp with outrage. "The Chiss are trying to starve all of the Qoribu nests into leaving."

"But they can't leave." Alema's voice was bitter. "Even if they had someplace to go, each nest would need a vessel the size of a Star Destroyer, and it would take months to prepare. They'd have to build a whole new nest inside the ship."

"That's not the answer, anyway," Jaina said. "This isn't Chiss space. The Killiks are innocent victims here."

"Victims, possibly," Mara said. She was growing alarmed by the wholehearted naïveté with which her niece and the others appeared to be embracing the Killik cause. "But hardly innocent."

Jaina's eyes flashed at the challenge, but her voice remained steady. "You don't know the situation. This system—"

"I know that on the way in here, the *Shadow* was jumped by Kil-liks," Mara said.

"The trouble you had on the way in?" Jacen asked. "I've been wondering about that."

"So have we," Han said dryly.

"And you think it was Killikz?" Tesar asked.

"We know what a dartship lookz like," Saba said. "But these were better than the craft that met us at Lizil. These were powered by hydrogen rocketz."

"Hydrogen?" Zekk echoed. "That can't be right."

He exchanged a confused glance with the others, then Jaina explained, "We've been trying to get them to convert to hydrogen rockets, but they produce the methane themselves."

"What are you saying?" Leia demanded. "That those weren't Killik dartships attacking the *Shadow*? Or that we're making this up?"

The young Jedi Knights all looked uncomfortable, then Tahiri finally said, "We're saying none of this makes sense. The Kind wouldn't attack you, you wouldn't lie, none of the Kind nests have hydrogen rockets—"

"And those blast craters in my hull armor didn't get there by themselves," Mara finished. She kept her gaze fixed on Jaina. "Do you think maybe you're wrong about these insects?"

Jaina met her gaze squarely. "That's just not possible." She motioned a passing Killik over, then asked, "Our friends were attacked by a swarm of flying hydrogen rockets. Are any of the nests—"

An earnest thumping began to resonate from the Killik's chest.

"She claims it was the Chiss, pretending to be Kind," C-3PO translated. "They're trying to make the Protectors leave."

"It *wasn't* Chiss," Mara said. "I could see the pilots. They were insects."

The Killik drummed a reply, and C-3PO translated, "There are a lot of space-faring insects in the galaxy. The Chiss could have hired some."

"Not very likely," Leia said. "The Chiss are arrogant . . . elitist."

"These were Killiks," Luke agreed. "We're not mistaken."

A series of sharp booms reverberated from the Killik's chest.

"She asks if there's *anything* you will believe?" C-3PO translated.

"The truth," Mara answered.

The Killik rumbled a short reply, then dropped to all sixes and started down the corridor at a trot.

"She said she doesn't know the truth," C-3PO said. "And she sees no reason to think of one, since you won't believe it anyway."

Luke turned to Jaina. "We've seen enough. Take us back to the hangar."

"Not yet," Jaina said. "You still don't understand—"

"We understand all we need to." Luke glanced at Mara and Saba, silently asking if the council's representatives had reached a consensus. When they both nodded, he took a step back so he could address all of the AWOL Jedi. "The situation here is as confused as it is volatile, and your team has lost the neutrality required of Jedi Knights. The Masters ask for your return to Coruscant."

Mara cringed inwardly. Like Kyp, Corran, and several other Masters, she believed the Jedi Order should command the obedience of its Jedi Knights, rather than "ask" for it. Luke preferred to allow the Jedi Knights their independence, saying that if the Jedi Order could not trust the good judgment of its members, then the Masters were failing at their most important job. Being first among equals, Luke's opinion held sway.

Jaina was quick to seize on the opening, of course. "Is it *our* neutrality the council is worried about—or the Galactic Alliance's relationship with the Chiss?"

"At the moment, it's *you* we're worried about." Luke's voice was as warm as it was firm. "Any Jedi should recognize the importance of maintaining good relations with the Chiss. The sectors they patrol for us along the border are the *only* ones free of piracy and smuggling."

"The Jedi are not servants of the Galactic Alliance," Alema countered.

"No, we aren't," Luke agreed.

As he spoke, Killiks were beginning to gather in the corridor, clambering up onto the walls and ceiling. Mara did not sense anything threatening in the Force—it was closer to grim concern, if she was reading the insects' emotions correctly—but she reached out to Saba and Leia, subtly suggesting they move to a more defensible position.

"But a peaceful Galactic Alliance is the strongest pillar of a peaceful galaxy," Luke continued. "And the Jedi *do* serve peace. If the Reconstruction fails and the Galactic Alliance sinks into anarchy, so does the galaxy. The Jedi will have failed."

"What happened to defending the weak?" Zekk demanded. "To sacrificing for the poor?"

"Those are worthy virtues," Luke said. "But they won't stop the galaxy from sinking into chaos. They aren't the duties of a Jedi Knight."

"So we abandon the Killiks for the good of the rehab conglomerates snapping up our part of the galaxy?" Jaina asked. "Isn't that how Pal—"

"Don't say it!" Mara stepped toward her niece, drawing a rustle from the ceiling and walls as the Killik spectators shrank back. "It's bad enough to desert your posts and make us come out here looking for you. Don't you dare make that comparison. Some things I won't tolerate even from you, Jaina Solo."

Jaina's eyes widened in shock. She stared at Mara for a long time, clicking softly in her throat, hovering between an apology and an angry retort that everyone present knew would open a rift between the two women that could never be closed again. To his credit, Luke did not intervene. He simply stood quietly, patiently waiting to see what decision Jaina would make.

Finally, Jaina's face softened. "That was a thoughtless thing for me to say. I didn't mean to suggest that Uncle Luke was anything like the Emperor."

Mara decided to take that as an apology. "I'm glad to hear it."

"And we're not going to abandon the Killiks." Luke glanced up as the Killiks thrummed their approval, then looked to the rest of the strike team. "But I'm worried about you—all of you."

"You've lost your objectivity and you've taken sides," Mara said, sensing what Luke wanted from her. "You're openly fighting on the Killiks' side—and that means you have no chance at all of solving the problem."

"Frankly, you're half Joiners now," Luke said. "I think you should to return to Coruscant with us at once. All of you."

The bitter scent of an alarm pheromone filled the air, and the corridor erupted into such a panicked din of drumming and clacking that Mara's hand went automatically to her lightsaber—and so did the hands of Leia and Saba. The color drained from Han's face, and he casually hooked his thumb in his belt above his blaster. But Luke's hands continued to hang at his sides, and the only sign that he showed of hearing the tumult was the patience he displayed in waiting for it to die down.

When it was possible to hear again, he continued as though he had never been interrupted. "We saw what became of Raynar, and the order just can't afford to lose any Jedi Knights right now."

"What about the Killiks?" Tahiri asked. "Without us here, the Chiss will have a free rein to—"

"This one will stay," Saba said. "Until Master Skywalker can arrange to speak with Aristocra Tswek, she will let the Chisz know the Jedi are still watching."

"Alone?" Tesar asked.

Saba nodded. "Alone."

Tesar grinned, then thumped his tail on the floor and bumped skulls with his mother. "Good hunting."

Mara looked to Jaina. "And the rest of you?"

Jaina exhaled loudly, then looked from the floor to Leia. "You've been awfully quiet, Mother."

"I'm not a Master."

"I know," Jaina said. "So what do you think?"

Leia's brow rose, and she appeared almost as shocked as Mara felt. "You're asking *me* what to do?"

"Don't look so surprised," Jaina said. "I *know* how you and Dad feel about the Galactic Alliance. You're the only ones here who don't have an agenda."

"Oh, I have an agenda." Leia smiled. "Your father and I *did* come all the way out here to make sure you and Jacen are safe."

Jaina rolled her eyes. "Like *that's* going to happen. Just tell me what you think."

Leia didn't even hesitate. "Jaina, I think you're just making the situation here worse."

"Worse?" Alema demanded. Her lekku were writhing. "What do you know? You've only been here—"

Jaina glanced at the Twi'lek out of the corner of her eye, and Alema fell silent.

"Thank you," Leia said. "As I was saying, your presence is a provocation to the Chiss. They're only going to press harder, and you'll end up starting a war that might have been averted."

"Averted?" Tahiri asked. "How?"

"I don't know how—not yet," Leia admitted. "But I can tell you how it *won't* be averted: by destroying Chiss task forces. They'll just start sending bigger flotillas."

"They already have."

Jaina turned to her fellows to discuss the matter—or so Mara thought. Instead, they merely looked at each other for a couple of seconds, then the Killiks suddenly let out a single disappointed boom and began to disperse. Tesar, Jacen, and Tahiri started up the corridor.

"We'll go," Tahiri said.

"So will Tekli," Tesar added.

"That's half," Mara said, raising her brow to Jaina and the remaining two. "What about you three?"

"We *four*," Jaina corrected. "You forgot to count Lowbacca."

SIXTEEN

Far below the *Falcon,* the golden expanse of Qoribu's largest ring swept past, a vast river of sparkling rubble that curved under the purple moon Nrogu and faded into the twilight murkiness of the planet's dark side. In the distance, just beyond the ghostly green crescent of the moon Zѷbo, the first tiny darts of Chiss efflux were tracing a crazy lacework against the star-flecked void.

"We're coming into visual range now," Leia reported. "It looks like the search is spreading. I see ion trails to all sides of the ring— some up to thirty degrees above."

"Wonderful." Han's tone was sarcastic. "The Chiss are going to be in a *great* mood."

"What leads you to believe that?" Juun asked. He was in the port-side passenger's seat, annoying Han by constantly peering over his shoulder. Fortunately, Tarfang had been sent back aboard the *Shadow,* where Tekli would be able to tend to his wounds. "Because they're having trouble finding survivors from their starship?"

"How'd you guess?" Han's voice was even more sarcastic.

"Procedure," Juun answered proudly. "They've increased their search radius, and why would Chiss search protocols be any different from our own?"

"You're one smart Sullustan."

"Thank you." Juun beamed. "Coming from Han Solo, that is an enormous compliment."

"Yeah," Han said. "Sure."

He pulled back on the yoke, and the *Falcon* began to climb away from the ring. Immediately, Leia felt the curiosity of their escorts— Jaina, Saba, Alema, and Zekk—rise in the Force.

"Our StealthXs are wondering what you're doing," Leia reported. "To tell the truth, so am I."

"*We* don't have stealth technology," Han explained. "And as bad as things are going for the Chiss, if they catch us trying to sneak in, they're liable to blast first and not bother with questions."

"Like the Talu insertion in the Zsinj campaign," Juun declared. "The *Falcon* will act as a decoy while the StealthXs penetrate the enemy's perimeter."

"Not really," Han said.

"No?" Juun sounded crestfallen. "Why not?"

"Because you can't stuff a Wookiee into a StealthX cargo compartment," Han said. "So we're just gonna fly in there and fetch Lowbacca ourselves."

"And the Chiss are going to permit that?" Juun gasped.

"Sure." Han glanced over at Leia, then said, "Leia is gonna talk 'em into it."

"I am?" Leia waited for Han to elaborate, then finally realized he was counting on her to come up with a plan. "This should be interesting."

"Very," Juun said. "I'm looking forward to seeing how you do it."

"Me, too," Leia said.

Leia set her doubts aside and reached out to Jaina and the others in the Force, trying to lay out Han's plan without the benefit of words. Though she had participated in a handful of battle-melds toward the end of the war, she was not very practiced in the sort of empathic broadcasting used to communicate with StealthX pilots, and the sentiments she felt in reply ranged from confusion to concern. Growing more frustrated with each failure, she finally stopped trying and concentrated on two words: *Trust me.*

The four pilots seemed instantly reassured and spread out behind the *Falcon,* flying along the dark bands in the ring so their craft would not be silhouetted against the glittering rubble. Leia shook her head, thinking that she needed to spend more time practicing.

The Force filled with encouragement.

"Jaina and the others seem okay with the new plan," Leia reported. Though Saba was in charge of the Jedi in the StealthXs, Leia's bond with her daughter was so much stronger that the clearest communication came from her. "I think."

"Good." Han leveled off ten kilometers above the planet's ecliptic and took the *Falcon* into the gray dusk of its penumbra. "But doesn't all this seem a little easy to you?"

"Not really," Leia said. "We still haven't seen how the Chiss are going to respond, and—"

"Not them," Han said. "Jaina. She doesn't give up that easily."

"I'm sure she just realized you were right," Juun offered. "Any daughter would listen to a father of *your* experience."

"I'm afraid humans are more complicated than that," Leia said before Han could respond. Sooner or later, even a Sullustan would recognize the sarcasm in Han's voice, and she did not want to see Juun crushed again. It had been bad enough when they had shut off the tractor beam and let the *XR808g* float free. "And Jaina is more complicated than most. She's as stubborn as her father."

"Thanks." Han sounded genuinely proud. "She's got something up her sleeve, I know it."

"Probably," Leia agreed. "But at the moment, all that matters is recovering Lowbacca. After we've kept our end of the bargain, we can take her home by force, if necessary."

"By force?" Han looked down his nose at her. "We haven't had that option since she was ten. This is *Jaina,* remember? Sword of the Jedi?"

"I remember," Leia said. "But I'll always be her mother. I can still do what needs to be done."

Han studied her for a moment, then grinned and nodded. "Yeah, Princess, I'll bet you can."

"*We* can," Leia corrected. She could sense that Han did not entirely agree with her; that now *he* was the one hiding something up his sleeve. "We're in this together, nerf herder. This won't be like the time you left me to deal with that unwashed vent crawler she brought home."

"Honey, that was Zekk," Han said.

"I know who it was," Leia said. "If not for me, Jaina would have ended up living in the undercity with him. It was all I could do to get him into the Jedi academy so she'd stay there."

"Okay," Han said. "But Jaina's not thirteen anymore. She's older than you were when I met you, and twice as bantha-headed. If she doesn't want to go—"

"You're *not* suggesting we let her stay," Leia said. "I know you better than that."

"I'm *suggesting* we might not have a choice." Han took a breath, then spoke again in a calmer voice. "I don't get it, either. Why anyone would risk their neck to save a bunch of overgrown anthills is way beyond me. But Jaina really wants this. I saw it in her eyes when Luke asked her and the others to return home."

"Saw what?" Leia asked, wondering what Han was up to. This did not sound like the same man who had just flown across half the Unknown Regions to prevent his daughter from becoming a "bughugger." "Because all I saw was disappointment and defiance."

"Exactly," Han said. "She's not going to give this up. She's probably never felt anything this pure."

"You're not making any sense, Han."

"Look, Jacen and Jaina were raised on deals," Han explained. "They grew up watching us struggle to hold the New Republic together, making bargains and playing politics."

"Because *we* were the established order," Leia said, feeling a bit defensive. "It's more complicated to preserve the status quo than to overthrow it. You write your plans in shades of gray."

"That's what I mean," Han said. "Everything was a compromise for those kids. They never had anything simple to fight for."

"They had the Dark Jedi and the Diversity Alliance," Leia countered. "They had the Yuuzhan Vong. That was all pretty clear."

"And all of it was stuff to fight *against*," Han said. "I'm talking about something to fight *for*, something pure to build. None of these young Jedi Knights has ever had that."

Leia was beginning to see what Han was driving at. "You mean they didn't have the Rebellion."

"Right," Han said. "The Killiks are peaceful underdogs, minding their own business in neutral territory, and the Chiss are trying to starve them out. I can see how Jaina might think that's a pretty clearcut case of the weak needing protection from the strong. Heck, it almost makes *me* want to fight for them."

Leia frowned, wondering if her husband was showing the first signs of becoming a Joiner. "But you don't, do you?"

Han rolled his eyes. "I said *almost*." His tone was a little sharp and defensive. "I'm just talking about how *Jaina* might see things."

"What a relief," Leia said. "I thought for a minute you were going to say we had to let her and the others stay with the Colony."

"When black holes shine," Han scoffed. "What I'm *saying* is we have to make them think it's *their* choice. I don't want to take that spark away. Jaina finally has the same look in her eye that you did when I rescued you from the Death Star."

Trying not to read anything into the word *did*, Leia objected, "You *didn't* rescue me." The debate was an inside joke with them, a way of reliving their past, when their own dreams had been so pure and uncomplicated. "You fell for Darth Vader's trick and led the Imperials straight to Rebel base at Yavin Four."

"No," Han corrected. "I lured the Death Star into the Rebel trap. If not for me, that thing would still be flying around the galaxy."

"Really?" Juun gasped from the navigator's seat. "They didn't mention *that* in *Special Delivery*."

Han blinked slowly, then twisted around in his seat. "Are you still here?"

"Of course," Juun replied to Han. "A crew member never leaves the flight deck without permission."

"You're not a crew member," Han said.

Outside the forward viewport, Leia noticed a cluster of tiny blue halos beginning to swell in the darkness of Qoribu's shadow. She checked the tactical display and found two flights of Chiss starfighters heading their way.

"Han!" Leia grabbed Han's shoulder. "Company!"

By the time Han turned around, the halos were large enough to show the spidery silhouette of the clawcraft cockpits and weapons-arms.

"Finally." Han gestured at Leia's comm microphone. "What are you waiting for? Talk to 'em."

In the dream, Lowbacca was down in the Shadow Forest with his uncle Chewbacca, racing along the dark wroshyr branches toward the green wall that was the Well of the Dead. Though the Well's tangled boundary of foliage was no farther than two hundred meters ahead, the two Wookiees never reached it. They just kept running, tearing through curtains of sloth-moss, jumping the long kkekkrrg rro claws that swung up to slash at their ankles. Every dozen meters, Chewbacca would lay a mighty hand on Lowbacca's shoulder and rumble encouragement. But the words were never clear, and the only comfort came in the familiarity of his uncle's heavy touch.

But this time, the touch was not Chewbacca's. It was just as familiar, but lighter, and on the inside and it did not feel like a Wookiee at all.

It felt like a human. Like a *female* human.

Jaina.

When did she learn to climb wroshyr trees?

"You've what?" the Chiss voice demanded over the comm.

"I repeat," Leia answered, "we've come to assist your search for survivors."

"*Jedi* survivors?" the voice asked.

The six clawcraft had taken up escort positions behind the *Falcon*. With Leia occupied on the comm, Han had barely persuaded the Noghri not to hand-crank the as-yet-unrepaired cannon turrets around to face the starfighters.

"Negative," Leia replied. "All Jedi are accounted for. We've come to assist in the search for Chiss survivors."

"Really." The officer sounded disbelieving. "The Chiss Ascendancy has adequate resources in place. You may return to your own base at once."

Leia took a deep breath. She glanced over at Han and pointed at the throttles, signaling him to be ready to make a break for it, then said, "That's clearly not true."

There was a long pause, during which time the *Falcon* passed by Zvbo's ghostly crescent and slipped into the full darkness of Qoribu's umbra.

Finally, the Chiss asked, "Did you just call me a liar, *Falcon*?"

"We can see the search operation is going poorly," Leia said. "You've expanded your radius to an area your flotilla couldn't cover properly in a week, and the situation is rapidly growing worse. So please don't insult me by telling us you have the situation under control."

"Very well." The officer's voice turned icy. "Then I will simply instruct you to leave the area at once. Your assistance is not desired."

Han made a turning motion, but Leia shook her head. She was just getting started.

"Negative," she said. "We're continuing on to assist."

"Now you are the one insulting *me*," the officer said. "Whatever your interest is here, I doubt it is Chiss casualties. Turn back, or you *will* be fired upon."

"I really doubt that," Leia said. "If you don't know who flies the *Millennium Falcon,* I'm sure your superiors do. The Chiss are not going to fire on a former New Republic Chief of State and Luke Skywalker's twin sister—not over a few moons that aren't even inside their own territory."

A flurry of red cannon bolts flashed past and lit the *Falcon*'s canopy.

"Shouldn't we ob-b-bey?" Juun stammered. "He s-seems very serious!"

"You've got a lot to learn about security patrols," Han said. "If he had been serious, we'd be sucking vac right now."

"I see." Juun's tone was one of sudden enlightenment. "You have a copy of their procedural manual!"

Han let his chin drop and shook his head.

A moment later, the officer finally grew tired of waiting for Leia's protest. "That was your only warning. The next time, we fire for effect."

"Just how many Jedi *would* you like in this system?" Leia retorted. Her threat was far more empty than the officer's, since even if there had been enough Jedi Knights to carry it out, Luke would never use the Jedi in retaliation. "This is no longer an unauthorized operation. Master Skywalker has already taken half of our Jedi Knights and started back to the Galactic Alliance. I'm sure your superior wouldn't want my brother's report to the Jedi Order and Chief of State Omas to be influenced by another unfortunate incident. Wouldn't it be better to allow us to assist, as a gesture toward continuing to resolve this thing?"

There was a short silence, then the Chiss asked, "Which Jedi Knights departed with Master Skywalker?"

Leia smiled. It was an obvious honesty test, with the Chiss asking for information their spies had probably already supplied.

"Luke and Mara took Tesar Sebatyne, Tekli, my son Jacen, and Tahiri Veila," Leia said. "We plan to take the rest with us when we go."

"You give your word?" the Chiss asked.

"Certainly, if your commander will give *his* word that the Chiss will cease their attempts to force the Colony to depart Qoribu," Leia answered. She doubted the standoff would be resolved so easily, but it was worth a try. "In any case, we will be leaving a senior Jedi to monitor the situation."

There was another pause, then the Chiss said, "Obviously, I lack the authority to negotiate on behalf of the Ascendancy."

"Obviously," Leia said.

"But the offer will be passed to the appropriate Aristocra. Until then, we are honored to accept your offer of assistance. Please proceed to the coordinates I transmit and begin a two-kilometer grid search."

"Copy," Leia said. "And thank you for allowing us to help."

"My commander asks me to express his gratitude for your assistance," the officer replied. "Out."

The coordinates appeared on the navigation display.

"We're not going to find anyone up there," Juun complained. "That's practically out of orbit!"

"Juun," Han said. "You're supposed to be a smuggler."

"I *am* a smuggler." A catch came to Juun's voice. "At least I was until I lost the *XR-eight-oh-eight-g*."

"Then you should know we're not going anywhere near there." As Han spoke, he was swinging the *Falcon* away from Qoribu's dark mass onto a heading that would carry them generally toward the area they had been assigned. "We just gotta make it look good."

Lowbacca opened his eyes to a vast banded darkness and was instantly back above Qoribu, shivering inside the cold stink of his EV suit, anchored to a ronto-sized hunk of ice and dust in the planet's ring system. The blackness around him was filled with blue needles of ion discharge—Chiss rescue ships still searching for survivors—and a steady rain of battle debris was plunging into the gas giant's thick atmosphere, igniting a spectacular display of crimson cloud-blossoms.

Jaina continued to touch Lowbacca through the battle-meld, helping him push back the loneliness and despair that she herself had experienced when she went EV at Kalarba. Alema assured him they would reach him soon. Zekk worried about his life-support status. The heads-up display inside Lowbacca's helmet showed low batteries, no water, and thirty minutes of air—three times that if he returned to a hibernation trance. Another presence urged him to stay alert and be ready.

Lowbacca thought for a moment this last presence was Tesar, but it felt older, fiercer, less familiar . . . *Saba!*

Be ready! There would be only one chance.

Lowbacca disengaged his tether-line safety sleeve and poised his thumb over the quick release gate. He was ready.

With his other hand, he pulled himself down to the iceball, then grabbed the anchoring bolt and used it to slowly spin around, looking for the telltale halo of an approaching vessel. He saw only the ion trails of craft passing on the oblique, and that puzzled him. Jaina and the others would be coming in StealthXs, but they were even more cramped than standard XJs. How were they going to pick him up . . .

The question vanished from Lowbacca's mind. There was a dark shape about a hundred meters ahead, its canopy and one weapons-arm protruding above the sea of iceballs that formed Qoribu's ring system.

It was probably just an empty wreck. Or maybe Lowbacca was seeing things. His EV suit was automatically holding his oxygen consumption at a minimum, feeding him just enough air to keep him functional, and hallucinations were common under such circumstances. Jaina had told him she spent several hours talking to Yoda when she went EV. Unfortunately, she had not been able to understand anything he said because he spent the whole time speaking in Gamorrean.

Lowbacca slowly spun himself toward Qoribu, keeping a careful watch at ring level. He found another dark shape about the same distance away, this time pointed in his direction, standing on edge with two weapons-arms protruding above the surrounding surface. A flash of entry fire on Qoribu briefly lit the cockpit, silhouetting a helmeted head.

The cold suddenly began to seep into Lowbacca's bones. He reached out with the Force, extending his awareness in all directions, and found himself surrounded by living presences.

Chiss presences.

Leia set their new waypoint and transferred it to Han's display. "There, I think."

Han glanced down at his screen. "You think, or you're sure?"

"*Sure?*" The word emerged from Leia's dry throat in a high-pitched croak. "What do you think? The coordinates just popped into my head."

The navigation schematic showed a yellow destination icon hanging on the inner edge of Qoribu's ring, about as far from the *Falcon*'s assigned search area as it was possible to get.

"Sorry for asking," Han said. "But we're only going to get one shot at this."

When Han continued on their current trajectory, Leia sighed and reached out to her daughter, then began to recite the coordinates in her mind.

But Jaina was in no mood to be bothered. Leia sensed only an overwhelming urgency and determination—and perhaps an irritated admonishment to stop wasting time.

"Han, just go. Something's not right."

"Okay." Han swung the *Falcon* toward the new waypoint, then pushed the throttle forward and activated the intercom. "Battle stations back there. This might get rough."

"Battle stations?" Juun gasped. "Do you remember that your cannon turrets are nonfunctional? Your gunners won't be able to hit a thing!"

"Have some faith, Shortwave," Han said. "You'd be surprised what Noghri hit when they can't aim."

"This has happened before?"

"Sure," Leia said, only half listening. "It seems like something's always broken down just when you need it most."

To her surprise, the Chiss did not immediately demand to know why the *Falcon* had drifted off course. In fact, she detected no sign they had even noticed. Thankful that Raynar had not felt threatened by their sensor dish, Leia locked it on their destination and began a passive analysis of the vicinity.

"The Chiss are being awfully quiet," Han said. "Better take a sensor reading on our destination—but don't go active. We don't want to give away where we're going."

"Good idea," Leia said, vaguely affronted that Han had felt it necessary to tell her the copilot's job. "There are some unusual mass concentrations in the vicinity, but no EM or propulsion emanations."

Han glanced over and gave her a crooked grin. "You've been reading my mind again, haven't you?"

"Princess Leia does that?" Juun sounded worried—or embarrassed. "She reads minds?"

"Sure," Han said. He frowned at the Sullustan's reflection in the cockpit canopy. "All the best copilots do."

Leia found the Juun's embarrassment a little disturbing, but decided it was better not to contemplate the source. The Sullustan had probably been admiring her procedure or something.

"Speaking of mind reading, I can't get that infrared reading you were thinking about," Leia said. "Too much background radiation from Qoribu."

"Not good," Han said. "And the Chiss aren't sending—"

C-3PO clumped onto the flight deck. "Captain Solo, you seem to have forgotten about the cannon turrets when you declared battle stations," the droid said. "We should probably turn around now, before anything unfortunate happens. It would be much safer."

"Juun!" Han barked. "Do you know where the circuit breaker is on a threepio droid?"

"Of course."

"If he says another word about turning around or being doomed, trip it."

"Aye, Captain."

"Please don't," C-3PO said. "My poor circuits have already been overstressed by the deterioration of Captain Solo's reflexes, and the current folly isn't helping matters."

Juun stood on his chair.

C-3PO stepped away. "There's no need for that," he said. "I'll be the routine of bravery, I assure you. Go ahead. Fly us straight into that planet, and you won't hear another word from me."

"Tempting offer," Han grumbled.

Finally noticing the *Falcon*'s direction—or bothering to address it—the Chiss flight controller opened a channel.

"*Millennium Falcon*, this is Rescue One. Explain your course deviation."

Leia reached forward to open a reply channel, then thought better of it and lowered her hand. "Let's see if they're serious."

"The Chiss?" Han asked. "You want to see if the *Chiss* are serious?"

"I have a feeling," Leia said. "Just—"

"—trust me," Han finished. "I know."

Juun's eyes widened. "Does everyone on this ship read minds?"

"Why, no," C-3PO confessed. "I don't."

The *Falcon* continued toward the web of ion trails crawling across Qoribu's dark face for another second, then the Chiss controller's voice came over the comm again.

"*Millennium Falcon*, I ask again. Explain your course deviation."

Leia glanced over. Finding Han's eyes narrowed in thought, she knew they were thinking the same thing.

"They're afraid of scaring us off," she said.

Han nodded. "It's a setup."

"*Millennium Falcon*, if you fail to reply—"

"Sorry about that," Han said, activating his own microphone. "We've been kind of busy up here."

"Doing what?"

Before replying, Han glanced over and mouthed their daughter's name. Leia nodded and, allowing her alarm and suspicion to rise to the surface, reached out to Jaina.

"Uh, we think we've spotted some survivors," Han said into the comm. "That's why we weren't answering—been busy getting the recovery equipment ready."

"We haven't detected any survivors on your course," the Chiss said.

"We're closer," Han said. "And, uh, you don't have a Jedi on board."

"A *Jedi* found them?" There was a short pause, then the Chiss said, "Very well. Carry on with our gratitude."

Han closed the channel. "That does it—they're playing us," he said. "Did you warn Jaina?"

"She already knew." Leia's stomach felt as empty and cold as the darkness outside the canopy. "She doesn't care."

Lowbacca could not see the StealthXs, of course, but he could feel them. They were no more than a thousand kilometers away, converging on him from four sides, coming in fast and hard.

No! Lowbacca thought into the meld. He fixed his gaze on the nearest of the clawcraft, then imagined its laser cannons flashing to life as his rescuers swooped in to pick him up. *Ambush!*

Jaina's laughter echoed in his mind. But Saba seemed more curious. Lowbacca's meld-connection was not as strong to the Barabel as it was to Jaina and the other strike team members, but he felt sure she was wondering how many clawcraft there were, whether the StealthXs could take them all. Lowbacca had never wanted to lie more than he did at that moment, to see a friendly face smiling down at him from a StealthX cockpit. But his rescuers had no chance of success. There had to be an entire wing of clawcraft hiding in the rubble around him, all waiting for a shot at the Jedi rescue team.

Jaina wished he would stop exaggerating, but Saba seemed sorry, and it was clear she did not like the thought of abandoning him. Lowbacca wasn't worried. Clearly, the Chiss knew where he was.

Jaina's frustration filled the Force, and Saba's anger rose in reply. But Lowbacca could sense Jaina still approaching, feel her arming her weapons and selecting targets, determined to draw the Chiss off en masse. The Sword of the Jedi was not one to give up easily, not while there remained one sliver of hope.

Lowbacca knew what he had to do. He turned his wrist up, then opened the safety cover on the inside sleeve of his EV suit and revealed the emergency beacon activator.

"This is going to be bad, Han," Leia said.

"How bad?" Han armed the concussion missiles.

"Worse than that."

Jaina had lost too much during the war—Anakin, Chewbacca, Ganner, Ulaha, and on and on. She was determined to lose no more.

Then the steady *ping* of an emergency beacon sounded from the *Falcon*'s emergency speaker, and Leia looked down to see a bright yellow EV designator blinking over their waypoint. The tactical display instantly grew white with clawcraft, and Jaina's frustration changed to shock.

"Lowie!" Leia gasped, saddened and relieved at once. "Thank you."

She experienced a brief moment of warmth through the Force, then the feeling was lost as Lowbacca grew distracted and broke contact.

Han looked over expectantly. "Well?"

"It's over," Leia said. She reached out to Jaina and sensed her daughter's disappointment—and Saba's lingering fury at having had her orders disobeyed. "They're on their way back."

"Sounds like a good idea." Han swung the *Falcon* around to join them, then added, "The rescue team did everything it could. I hope Jaina knows that."

"Me, too, Han," Leia said. "But I don't think—"

She was interrupted by the Chiss flight control officer. "*Millennium Falcon,* what is the status of your survivors?"

"Survivors?" Leia was confused for a moment, but that confusion quickly turned to anger as she recalled the excuse Han had made and realized she was being mocked. "I'm sure you've figured that out, Rescue One."

There was a slight pause, then a deep and familiar voice sounded from the comm speaker. "My apologies, Princess Leia. I just wanted to confirm my understanding of the situation."

Leia's jaw fell, and she looked over to find Han having trouble keeping his own mouth closed.

"Jag?" she gasped. "Jagged Fel?"

"Indeed," the reply came. "It wasn't our intention to gloat."

"Jag!" Han cried. "What are you doing here?"

"That would fall under the heading of military intelligence, Captain Solo," Jag replied. "But rest assured, the Jedi Wookiee has been recovered. He'll be treated with all the rights and privileges due any enemy combatant—as will the rest of your rogue Jedi, when we capture *them.*"

SEVENTEEN

In every base, there was a place like this, someplace dark and hot and deserted where a Barabel could go to hunt and clear her mind, someplace filled with the smell of local soil and the rustlings of alien prey. Saba was deep below the Taat nest, creeping down a crevice at a speed only a reptile would recognize as motion, her darting tongue stinging with the acrid odor of Jwlio's fractured bedrock, her mouth filled with the bitter taste of Jaina's insubordination.

Master Skywalker had allowed his niece to take part in the rescue mission only on the condition that Saba was in command. Yet when matters had grown difficult, Jaina had submitted—as always—only to her own emotions. Saba did not consider herself worthy to question Master Skywalker's judgment, but she *did* fail to understand his wisdom in permitting the disorderliness that encouraged such behavior. Disobedience led to chaos, and chaos led to ineffectiveness.

The crevice opened into a cavity ahead, and the faint odor of meat that Saba had been following grew stronger. All her thoughts went instantly to the hunt, for the prey was often near its litter. She did not know what she was stalking, of course, but the smell suggested another predator. Herbivores rarely dragged fresh carcasses back to their lairs.

To her Barabel eyes, which saw well into the infrared spectrum, the entrance looked like a dark diamond opening into the cool gleam of Jwlio's bedrock. She crept another step forward and heard the soft scratch of movement inside the lair. She waited, every muscle tensed to pounce on anything that poked its head out. She had been careful to mask her own odor by rubbing her scales in crevice dust, but such efforts were never entirely successful—and a worthy quarry usually smelled the predator long before the final attack.

Another rustle sounded from the cavity. Saba started steadily forward, a tenth of a meter at a time. If the prey had not fled or showed itself by now, it was not going to. The musty odor grew stronger, with just a hint of Killik sweetness, and she came to the entrance. The edge dropped away into a cold darkness that gave her the impression of a sizable emptiness. She stopped there for ten heartbeats, listening and testing the air with her tongue, twenty, fifty, a hundred.

No more rustles.

Saba slipped over the edge and crawled down a fissured rock face into a three-meter hollow. She could not sense any other presences in the area, but the spines along her dorsal ridge had risen on end, and that usually meant something exciting was about to happen. She continued across a floor of jumbled stones, licking the air, following her tongue toward the musty odor ahead. A few steps later, Saba peered over a boulder and found the source of the rustles.

A flat stone ahead was littered with about two dozen cuticle exoskeletons, all empty and split down the spine from molting. They ranged in size from smaller than Saba's thumb to a little larger than her hand, and they were so light that even the unfelt movement of the cavern air made them quiver and rustle. Scattered among the empty shells were dozens of small bones, enough to make six or seven wabas. Most were stripped of their flesh and cracked open, but a handful in the center of the pile still had some meat on them.

Fresh meat.

Sensing that she was closing on her prey, Saba activated a glow rod and went over to the exoskeletons. They were a familiar dark blue, but with thick knobby chitin like that of Raynar's guards. Starting to feel puzzled—and therefore short-tempered—Saba blew aside several of the smallest ones and shined her light into a tail-width cleft that ran a meter down the center of stone. It had been precisely cut, as though by a laser saw—or perhaps a lightsaber.

Her prey was growing more interesting.

The cleft held four hexagonal cells, each about five centimeters in diameter and constructed of Killik spitcrete. One of the cells remained covered by a plug of dusty wax, but the other three were empty.

A soft rustle rose as the empty exoskeletons were stirred by an air movement so gentle Saba did not feel it. She flicked out her tongue and tasted a bitter hint of apprehension, but felt nothing in the Force except a faint stirring of her danger sense. Strange prey.

Her tail twitching with anticipation, she scraped the last cell open, using the talon of her smallest finger to pluck out the insect egg inside. It was withered, gray, and dry—not worth eating.

The bitterness in the air grew stronger. The scales between Saba's shoulder blades rose in excitement, and she swept her tail around in a swift arc that ended in a knee-crunching impact. Her prey landed with the crisp slap of a practiced warrior, winning Saba's instant respect by not crying out in either pain or surprise. She spun on her haunches, snatching her lightsaber off her utility belt, bringing it around from the direction opposite her tail.

A crimson blade sizzled into existence and blocked, then a Force wave blasted her across the chamber into the wall opposite. The air left her lungs as her skull slammed against stone and a ring of darkness formed around the edges of her vision. She could see only her prey's red lightsaber and his seated silhouette. She felt nothing in the Force from him, only the same vague danger as before.

Now, *this* would be prey worth taking.

The shadow man returned to his feet and remained where he was, gathering himself to continue or arrogantly waiting for Saba to ask who he was. First mistake. Saba sprang, sissing in delight, ignoring the murk in her head, bringing her arms around in a vicious overhand slash. Her prey—she wasted no time wondering who he was—limped two steps back, then brought his crimson blade up and stopped her swing cold.

Saba brought a knee around, driving for his rib cage, and felt like she had struck a statue. He slipped a palm-heel under her guard and caught her in the chin, sent her staggering back.

Strong, too.

Saba kicked a fist-sized stone off the floor, then used the Force to hurl it at his head and followed it in with a cut at his knees. He pivoted past the stone and met her attack, catching her blade on his and sweeping it up in a disarming counterarc, power-fighting against a Barabel and *winning*.

At the top of the arc, Saba released her lightsaber and raked her claws down in a vicious one–two slash, the first strike opening her prey's face from temple to jaw, the second strike slicing an eye apart. He whirled away, still silent but screaming in the Force, and planted a spinning stomp kick in Saba's belly. She went with the blow, rolling into a quick backflip and losing half a meter of tail to his lightsaber.

This time, the shadow man gave her no time to recover. A fork of blue lightning crackled from his hand and caught Saba square in the chest. Every nerve in her body became a conduit of blazing agony, and she dropped her to her knees, teeth gnashing, scales dancing, muscles clenching—paralyzed.

Continuing to hold the Force lightning on her with one hand, the shadow man limped forward. In the light of his red lightsaber, Saba saw her prey clearly for the first time. Dressed in an amalgam of black plastoid armor and blue Killik chitin, he was surprisingly gaunt, with a sinewy frame and a twisted posture that looked ready to collapse beneath his humped shoulder. His face was even more melted and shapeless than Raynar's, just two eyes and a lipless slash in a scarred oval of flesh, and one of his arms was as much insect as human, turning tubular and chitinous at the elbow before ending in a hooked pincer.

Raynar and the Killiks had lied, Saba realized. Welk, at least, had also survived the Crash.

The Dark Jedi stopped a meter and a half away. Having learned the folly of hesitation, he brought his arm up quickly, swinging at Saba's neck—then pitched backward as her Force shove buckled his injured knee. His lightsaber scraped along Saba's skull, flooding her mind with a pain so hot and blinding that she could not tell whether the Force lightning had stopped. She sprang anyway and slammed into his chest, driving her prey the last half a meter to the ground, clutching blindly at his weapon arm, biting into his throat.

Her fangs barely sank two centimeters. She tried to rip the wound open, but lacked the strength to keep her jaw clamped and came away only with a mouthful of blood.

Still, the bite took her prey by surprise. She found herself in the grasp of the Force, flying back through the darkness. She reached out, calling her lightsaber to hand, and had it in her grasp when she hit the cavern wall.

Fighting off a black curtain of unconsciousness, Saba slid down the wall and landed on her feet. Her vision was blotchy at best, and she could not even hear the customary *snap-hiss* as she ignited her lightsaber. She sprang at her prey anyway, covering the distance in three short bounds, and nearly lost her balance when she landed in his blood.

Welk retreated two meters and leveled another fork of Force lightning at her. She deflected it with her lightsaber and pivoted past, sissing in excitement. It was turning into a good hunt, a *very* good hunt. She rushed to close the distance. He brought his lightsaber to a middle guard and retreated another step.

Saba attacked high, but her reflexes were fading and his

lightsaber flashed up to block. He retreated another step. She launched a spinning advance, bringing her blade around in a shoulder slash, whipping her bloodied tail around at his legs.

She was smooth but slow. He blocked the shoulder slash and hopped over the tail sweep, then rolled his blade over Saba's in an *excellent* block-assault conversion.

The attack might have opened her throat, had there been a way for him to block Saba's trailing foot. As it was, she swept his feet from beneath him and continued into a second spin, bringing her lightsaber down across his pincer-arm, then planting a foot on his remaining arm and rolling her blade around to add a neck wound to the arm he had just lost.

That was when Saba's blotchy vision proved costly. She sensed something flying at her from behind and turned to look, but saw only dark against dark.

The rock slammed into her head wound, and then she was kneeling on the floor, her lightsaber in a high guard, with no recollection of how she had landed there. Her sight was worse than ever, narrowed to a tiny circle, and her senses of smell and taste had gone the way of her hearing.

This was becoming a hunt to remember.

Seeing nothing ahead but a narrow cone of rock, Saba stretched into the Force and felt more danger than before. It seemed to have her surrounded, as though her prey had extended his presence over the entire chamber. She began to weave her lightsaber in a blind defensive pattern and rose. Something spongy and warm landed on her shoulder beneath her head wound. She hoped it wasn't her brains.

Saba began to spin in a slow circle, and finally her narrow cone of vision fell on her quarry, fleeing toward the cavern wall at a fast limp, blood pouring from his neck wound, the cauterized stump of his severed arm waving useless in the air.

Good. The prey was weakening.

Saba shut down her lightsaber and bounded after him, her heart pounding in anticipation of the final kill. She reached the cavern wall three steps behind him . . . and hissed in surprise as something landed on her back and pierced her neck scales with a sturdy proboscis.

She reached over her shoulder and felt a creature about the size of her head. Cursing her fading senses, she pulled it off and found herself looking into the dark eyes of a small blue-black Killik.

It spread its mandibles, and a stream of brown fluid shot from its tiny mouth. Saba barely turned away in time to protect her eyes. The slime instantly began to eat away at her cheek scales.

Acid.

Saba felt her dorsal spines rise and knew another attack was coming. She dropped into a crouch, and a small boulder slammed into the slope above. She jumped out of the way as it rolled back toward her, then, holding the Killik at arm's length, glanced up to see Welk glaring down at her in disbelief. Saba jammed her lightsaber against the Killik's abdomen and activated the blade.

The discharge that followed was not quite an explosion. She lost only two fingertips instead of an entire hand. The fireball did little more than scorch her scales and bedazzle her eyes, but . . . exploding Killiks?

When Saba looked up again, Welk had started climbing for an exit crevice. She sprang after him and collapsed to her knees two steps later, feeling weak and nauseous. She touched the bite on her neck and found it already swollen and oozing.

Venom?

What kind of bugs were these? Saba should have stopped and gone into a healing trance. But her prey was wounded and escaping, and if she let him go, he would only be that much harder to track and capture next time. She continued her pursuit.

Her muscles obeyed reluctantly, stiffly, as though she were dropping into a hibernation—without the sleep. She drew the Force into her, calling on it to strengthen her, to burn the poison from her body, and staggered after her quarry.

Saba was only three meters behind when a second proboscis pierced her leg. She glanced down and found another small Killik latched onto her calf. She plucked it off and, holding it so it could not release its corrosive bile in her direction, tossed it high into the air.

The insect extended two pairs of wings, then spread its mandibles and came diving back at her, weaving and dodging past her flashing lightsaber to alight on her chest. Before Saba could grab it, the Killik's head dipped, and its proboscis pierced her scales. She plucked it off and held it away from her, trying to decide how to kill it without losing any more fingers.

Saba sensed another boulder flying in her direction. Still holding the insect at arm's length, she pivoted around and reached for the stone in the Force, redirecting it up the hill toward her prey. Her effort was rewarded with a dull *thud* and a cry that seemed equal parts surprise and pain.

The little Killik drummed its chest, then began to squirm and flap its wings, trying to escape. Saba caught a handful of wing and tore it off, *then* tossed the insect into the air.

Her reflexes were so slowed by the paralyzing poison that, by the time she ignited her lightsaber, the insect had already hit the ground. It took three strikes before she finally detonated it.

Saba turned instantly upslope, but her prey had already vanished into his exit crevice. Feeling half dead from poison already and not wanting to take yet another shot of venom, Saba remained motionless for a long time, trying to listen through her deafness, trying to taste the air with her dead tongue, trying to see outside her narrow cone of vision. She felt nothing, only the dark loneliness of the underworld.

Recalling that there had been three cells and only two Killik attacks, Saba went to the escape crevice and peered inside.

Nothing.

Her prey was gone, and so was the third Killik.

Every Barabel instinct urged her to continue the pursuit, to follow the quarry's blood trail until she ran it to ground. But the rational part of her mind knew better. A hunter needed a quick wit and sharp senses, and Saba's injuries had taken a toll on both. She was slow and beginning to tremble, and soon she might not be able to move at all.

Besides, Saba had a sinking feeling that the third Killik had left the nest early, and she could think of only one reason it would have done so: the departure of *Jade Shadow*.

EIGHTEEN

"Ben!"

Mara's voice came over the *Shadow*'s intercom so sharp and loud that Luke nearly dropped the micropoint he was holding in R2-D2's deep-reserve data compartment.

"Ben, come to the galley this instant!"

"Uh, that might not be such a good idea," Luke said into the intercom. He flipped up his magnispecs and looked across the utility deck to where Ben sat, surrounded by crate covers and spacing rods, covered head-to-toe in servomotor lubricant. "At least not until he's had a good saniscrubbing. He's on the utility deck with me."

"Doing what?" Mara demanded.

Luke caught Ben's eye and pointed his chin toward the intercom wall unit.

"Working on my Killik," Ben said meekly. His expression struck Luke as both guilty and worried. "Nanna said I could."

"Stay where you are!"

Luke cocked a brow at his son. "It sounds serious."

Ben nodded. "I guess."

"Any ideas?"

Ben returned to working on his "Killik" droid. "Maybe."

Deciding they would *both* find out what was troubling Mara in a minute, Luke returned to the sequestered sector he had found on one of R2-D2's deep-reserve memory chips. Judging by the tarnished break in the service circuit, the fault had occurred years—maybe decades—earlier, and had been entirely benevolent until a microscopic sliver of casing bridged the break. Given that R2-D2 had been functioning well with the fault for most of his service life, Luke was wondering how long it had been since anything was written to the sector.

The access hatch iris opened next to Luke, and Mara stepped through with an empty gelmeat container in her hand. Her irritation was obvious in the briskness of her step—and in the turbulent aura she projected in the Force.

"Hold on a second, Artoo," Luke said, setting the micropoint on the workbench. "This looks important."

R2-D2 tweedled a worried response.

"Of course you're important," Luke said. "But I need a break anyway. I'll want to be sure my hands are steady."

R2-D2 whistled his encouragement.

Luke started across the deck toward his wife and son, where Ben was still sitting inside his crate-cover Killik shell, looking up at Mara.

"Did Nanna say you could have a whole can of gelmeat, young man?" Mara asked.

Ben's eyes grew round. "She said I could have a slice."

"Does *this* look like a slice to you?" She held the empty container down for him to see.

Ben shrugged—rather bravely, Luke thought. "I thought she meant one *can*."

Luke felt Mara's patience snap. When she started to wave the container at Ben, he gave her a gentle Force tug and urged her to calm down.

Mara paused, collecting herself while she pretended to examine the container label.

"Nanna is the one who found the container, Ben," Mara said, handing it to him. "She says we've gone through a whole case since we left Jwlio—and I don't think anyone else eats this."

"Tesar might."

"Gelmeat?" Mara asked doubtfully.

"Maybe," Ben said hopefully. "He eats anything."

"Anything *alive*," Mara corrected. "But we could ask him. Should I have him come down?"

Ben hesitated, then shook his head. "No."

"I didn't think so." Mara's voice softened. "Ben, I don't know how you can eat all this without making a mess of my decks, but you have to stop. It'll make you sick."

"It's okay, Mom," Ben said, sounding relieved. "You don't have to worry about that. I haven't been *eating* it."

"You haven't?" Mara asked. "Then what have you been doing with it?"

Ben's expression grew worried again, and he reluctantly said, "Feeding it to my Killik."

Mara was silent for a moment, then she asked, "Ben, what did we say about lying?"

Ben's eyes dropped. "That if I lie, I have to stay with Kam and Tionne the next time you and Dad go on a mission."

"Right," Mara said. "Let's remember that."

"Okay," Ben said. "I didn't forget."

"Good." Mara stooped down and took the empty container from him. "And no more gelmeat."

Ben's eyes grew wide. "*None?*"

"Not until we get home." Luke hoped he sounded stern. "You've had enough to last you ten trips."

As he and Mara returned to the engineering station, he continued to feel a general irritation from her.

"Okay, this wasn't just about gelmeat," he said softly. "What's wrong? Tired of hearing about how much Tahiri and the others miss Jwlio?"

Mara shook her head. "It's not that."

"Tired of growling Ewoks?"

"It's not Tarfang, either," Mara said. "I'm not sure yet whether the Killiks are enemies or just dangerous friends, but I *am* certain we need to learn everything we can about them."

Luke remained silent, sensing more was to follow.

"It's just this uneasiness I have," Mara said. "I keep feeling like we're about to be attacked again."

Luke paused and consciously opened himself to the Force. "I can sense it, too, but not as strong as you. We could do another stowaway sweep."

"And find something we missed the last six times?" Mara shook her head and smiled. "Go back to your droid, Skywalker. You're just trying to get me into our cabin again."

"I'm predictable that way," Luke said. "But pay attention to this feeling. Whatever's causing it, you seem to have a special connection to it."

"Lucky me." Mara opened the hatch, then looked over her shoulder before stepping through. "And about that cabin."

"Yeah?"

"Maybe later."

R2-D2 trilled a worried objection.

"Don't worry," Luke said, chuckling. "I'm a Jedi Master. I can still concentrate."

He picked up his tools and carefully repaired the break in R2-D2's deep-reserve chip. Once the solder was cool, he flipped his magnispecs up again and turned to the diagnostic display above the workbench.

"All right, Artoo. Let's see what your deep-reserve memory shows now."

A list of headings and numbers began to scroll down the screen, but suddenly stopped as it approached the location of the repaired sector.

"Don't stop," Luke said. "I need to see if you can access that sector."

R2-D2 whirred a moment, then the scrolling resumed. The missing sector number appeared, but the descriptive heading looked like nothing but random characters.

"Stop," Luke said.

The scrolling continued until the heading vanished off the top of the screen, then stopped.

"Now your *response* time is slow," Luke complained. "Bring it back."

R2-D2 piped a question.

"The sector I've been trying to repair. Two twenty-two"

The list scrolled down until the lower half of the entry appeared at the top the screen.

"And you're having *roll* problems." Luke sighed. "It looks like you've got a bug in your system. I may need to get out the blast degausser."

The entry dropped toward the middle of the screen, one letter in the heading changing with each line it sank.

"Stop! Why are you randomizing the heading?"

The droid whistled a denial.

"You are, too," Luke said. "I saw the letters change."

R2-D2 whirred a moment, then displayed a message on diagnostic screen.

It must be encoded.

"Encoded?" Luke began to wonder if perhaps the sector had been sequestered on purpose. R2-D2 had seen a lot of action even before the Rebellion, and Luke was always curious about what secrets the little droid might have locked away. "Then slice it."

R2-D2 grated an objection.

"Artoo, you're an *astromech* droid," Luke said. "You have enough computing power to slice a triple-key, double-blind randomizer. I think you can solve a simple substitution code."

The droid buzzed in resignation, then began to whir and hum. A few moments later, the heading vanished altogether. Luke waited for it to return in legible form, then finally gave up and groaned.

"Don't tell me you lost the heading."

R2-D2 trilled an apology.

"No problem," Luke said, losing his patience with the little droid's excuses. He lowered his magnispecs. "I'll just fuse it to a sector that *is* in the directory."

R2-D2 withdrew his interface arm from the data socket and whistled in protest.

"Then plug back in and stop making this difficult," Luke said. "Let me see what's in that sector."

The droid warbled a question.

"*This* one."

Luke touched the tip of his soldering filament to sector 222 and was astonished to hear a tinny female voice erupt from the droid's speaker.

"Anakin . . ."

Luke caught a glimmer of moving light on the workbench. He flipped up his magnispecs, expecting to find the images of Tahiri and his dead nephew, Anakin, sharing a personal moment R2-D2 had caught with his holorecorder.

Instead, Luke found himself watching a beautiful, hand-sized, brown-eyed woman whom he did not recognize. She walked across the workbench, then stopped beside a sinewy young man dressed, as she was, in nightclothes.

"What's bothering you?" she asked.

The young man continued to look away from her. "Nothing."

"Anakin, how long is it going to take for us to be honest with each other?"

Luke's heart rocketed into his throat. He had not immediately recognized his father. He wanted to call out to Mara, to share with Leia what he was feeling . . . but he was too stunned. He simply continued watching.

The young man—Anakin—turned to face the woman. "It was a dream."

"Bad?"

Anakin looked over her head. "Like the ones I used to have about my mother . . . just before she died."

The woman hesitated, then finally asked, "And?"

Anakin's gaze fell. "It was about you."

The hologram crackled to an abrupt end, and an ominous humming arose deep inside R2-D2's internal workings. Luke flipped down his magnispecs and peered in to find the recording head bumping against his soldering filament as it attempted to access sector 222.

"Artoo!" Luke reached for the droid's primary circuit breaker. "Wait!"

The recording head stopped moving, but Luke did not lift the soldering filament.

"What are you doing?"

The droid reinserted his interface arm into the data socket, and Luke had to flip up his magnispecs to read the message on the diagnostics screen. He continued to hold the soldering filament in place.

I need to reformat sector 222. Those data are corrupted.

"Nothing looks corrupted to me." Luke could not understand why R2-D2 would try so desperately to hide 222's contents, but he had no doubt that was exactly what the droid was doing. "Who was that woman with my father?"

R2-D2 whistled two notes.

"The woman in the hologram," Luke said irritably. "Show it to me again."

R2-D2's holoprojector obediently came to life, displaying the familiar, three-dimensional figure of an Alderaanian Princess in an elegant white gown.

"Help me, Obi-Wan Kenobi," the figure said. "You're my only hope."

"Not *that* woman," Luke said. "I know my sister. The one talking to *Anakin*. Is that . . . is she my mother?"

A message appeared on the diagnostics display.

I don't know what woman you're talking about. That sector is defective. It should be sequestered.

"It *was* sequestered—probably on purpose."

Luke studied R2-D2 carefully, touching him through the Force. With most other droids, any hope of sensing the truth would have been lost to the indecipherable Force static generated by its system routines. But R2-D2 had been Luke's close companion for nearly three decades. The little droid's static aura was as distinctive to him as was the presence of Mara or Leia or Han.

After a moment, Luke sensed the direction his questions should take. "It didn't look like they knew you were holorecording. What were you doing? *Spying?*"

R2-D2 let out a squeal that Luke took to be a protest of denial—until it ended in a sharp crackle and a surge of electricity melted the filament Luke was using to protect sector 222. He jerked the wire free and started to rebuke the droid for his stubbornness, but one whiff of the acrid fumes pouring from the access panel told him this much damage was nothing the droid would do to himself. Luke used the Force to trip R2-D2's primary circuit breaker, then opened a second access panel to vent the interior of the casing.

When the smoke cleared, he flipped his magnispecs down and saw that every circuit within a millimeter of sector 222 had been melted. Worse, a bead of hot filament had landed on the sector itself. Luke tore his magnispecs off and hurled them against the wall.

"Kriffing slicers!" He could not help feeling that *someone* had gone to a great effort to prevent him from discovering his mother's identity, but of course that was just his disappointment. Whoever had booby-trapped R2-D2's spyware had done it for their own reasons—reasons important fifty years ago, but that hardly mattered now. "Kriffing history!"

"Dad," Ben's voice asked, "what's kriffing?"

Luke turned to find his son standing at his side, mouth agape at his father's unaccustomed display of anger.

"Nothing—a bad word," Luke said, calming himself. With a little luck—and the proper equipment—the memory chip could be restored and the booby trap bypassed. Things were never as bad as they seemed. "Your mother won't be happy I said it in front of you."

"Don't worry. I won't tell." An innocent smile came to Ben's small face. "Maybe I can have a tube of nerfspread?"

NINETEEN

With the dance-field glowing in the iridescent light of Qoribu's reflection and a thousand Taat swirling through the intricate patterns of the Little Dawn Rumble, Leia felt as though she had stepped a thousand centuries into Alderaan's past, when the Colony still ruled the planet and human expansion remained a dark storm on the galaxy's horizon. The Killiks were "singing" their part of the Song of the Universe as they danced, chirping melody through their tiny proboscises, tapping time with their mandibles, drumming bass in their chest cavities. Alien and primal though the music was, the performance was as flawless as anything Leia had ever heard in Harmony Hall on Coruscant, a thousand instruments played by a single artist.

"Now *that* is just not right," Han said, adding his own special counternote to the concert. "Why didn't she marry Jag Fel when she had the chance?"

"Be careful what you wish for," Leia said, following Han's gaze. "If we don't get her out of here soon, she might be spending more time than we like with Jag—being interrogated in his . . ."

Leia saw what Han had been looking at and let her sentence trail off. On the near side of the swarm, Jaina, Zekk, and Alema were frisking through the dance steps amid an eddy of dancers. The three Jedi were holding their hands above their heads, waving them in unison with the Killiks' antennae. Every few seconds, Jaina and Zekk would bow forward with the entire nest and rub forearms with the antennae of whatever insect they happened to be facing. Alema bowed as well, but rubbed lekku instead of arms.

"It does look a little . . . unnatural," Leia admitted.

"Not at all," C-3PO assured them. "It's a bonding dance, welcoming the birth of the new day. They perform it once a week, before they go to the Harem Cave to mate."

Stomach tightening in alarm—or perhaps it was revulsion—Leia turned to Han. "We'll talk to them as soon as the dance ends. You're okay with the plan?"

"For what good it'll do," Han grumbled. "Kidnapping her would be easier—and we both know how well *that* would work."

Leia grew exasperated with his pessimism. "Since when did you start worrying about the odds? You're starting to sound—"

She was saved from uttering the lethal *like Threepio* by the thunderous reverberation of an alarm rumble. She turned and found all the Killiks looking toward one of the passage entrances that ringed the dance-field. The insects were holding their antennae vertical and motionless, and their mandibles were spread wide in menace. Most of the Joiners were mimicking the gesture to the extent that their various anatomies allowed, but Alema was the only Jedi doing the same.

"That doesn't look good." Han turned to scan the sky. "Chiss?"

"I'll be happy to ask," C-3PO said.

He shot a burst of squelch at a nearby Killik.

"The Taat speak Bocce?" Leia asked.

"Why, yes, Princess Leia. I've yet to discover a language the Killiks *don't* understand. It seems they learn every language their Joiners know." A second Killik turned and answered C-3PO's question with a series of mandible clacks. "For instance, that was just Snutib click code."

"And?" Han asked.

"It was quite fluent," C-3PO said. "Though that particular dialect predates—"

"We're more interested in *what* it said," Leia clarified.

"My apologies." C-3PO sounded disappointed. "I believe it concerns Jedi Sebatyne."

"Saba?"

"Apparently, she appeared in the depths of the nest rather badly injured."

A knot of Taat emerged from the tunnel, tumbling and staggering as they attempted to keep ahold of a flailing mass of scales. The rest of the Killiks turned as one to look in Han and Leia's direction, then thrummed their chests.

"In fact, Taat is rather hoping that you might help calm down Master Sebatyne so their healers can close the small hole in her skull."

Han took off at a sprint, with Jaina and the other young Jedi forcing their way across the dance-field behind him. Leia asked Mee-walh to fetch the emergency medpac from the *Falcon*, then started running.

She arrived to find Saba strapped to a primitive stretcher, an elliptical slice of scalp and skull missing from one side of her head. Han was already standing at the Barabel's side, trying to quiet her.

"I know they're creepy looking," he was saying. "But settle down. They're trying to help."

"No!" Saba's eyes twitched as though she was trying to throw her head back and forth, but the head itself remained motionless. "Azzazzinz!"

Her lisp was more pronounced than usual—a bad sign, given the head wound. Leia also saw a number of other injuries—a circle of broken scales around her temple, some lost fingertips, a third of a tail missing, and some suspicious swelling on her neck and calf. Lying on the stretcher, strapped next to the injured tail, was something that hadn't come off Saba—a human bicep fused at the elbow to a chitinous Killik forearm.

A *blue* chitinous forearm.

The Killiks holding Saba drummed in protest.

"They point out that Jedi Sebatyne's brain is showing," C-3PO translated. "She's quite delusional."

C-3PO rose into the air and began to spin like a pinwheel.

"What? Stop! . . . Put me down, you overgrown newt!"

"Not . . . deluzional," Saba growled.

"Saba, it's okay." Leia reached out to the Barabel in the Force, trying to assure her that they did not doubt her. "We believe you."

C-3PO stopped spinning, and Saba's gaze shifted to Leia. The pupils of her eyes were hugely dilated. "Yezz?"

"Sure." Han let his gaze linger on the forearm. "*Something* happened to you. Anyone can see that."

"Why don't we take care of these wounds?" Leia wished Tekli had not left with Luke. She and Han had certainly patched up their share of wounds, but this was beyond their skill. "Then you can tell us about it."

"*Now,*" Saba insisted. "This one will tell you . . . now."

"Okay." Leia gestured to the Taat healers cowering on the edge of the sled. "As long as you'll let them work on you while we talk."

Saba narrowed a pebbly eye. "This one . . . thought you believed her."

"Saba, some of your wounds are cauterized," Leia pointed out.

"Does that mean you shouldn't trust anyone who carries a lightsaber?"

The Barabel snorted.

"Look, we've got some concussion missiles on the *Falcon*," Han said. "If they kill you, we'll blast the place."

"Blazt it?" Saba began to siss weakly. "You are alwayz joking!"

"He wasn't joking," Leia said. "Do we have a deal?"

Saba eyed the healers cowering on the edge of her stretcher, then nodded. "Deal."

She lowered C-3PO to the ground again.

"Thank goodness!" He clunked over to stand behind Leia, then said more softly, "They say she's been an impossible patient!"

A dozen Killik healers crawled onto her body and went to work, sterilizing her wounds and spinning silken bandages. As they labored, Saba recounted—in a halting voice—her discovery of the empty exoskeletons and the attack by Welk, then ended by noting that she had found *three* empty egg cells and killed only two immature assassins. She was worried that the third had left early to stow away aboard the *Shadow*.

One of the healers squatting over her opened skull purred an opinion, which C-3PO translated as, "Patients with head wounds often suffer from hallucinations."

"It waz no—"

"Allow me." Leia laid a calming hand on the Barabel's shoulder, then pointed to the arm lying next to Saba's truncated tail. "If it was a hallucination, how do you explain that?"

One of the Killiks holding the stretcher began to clack its mandibles.

"The healers sometimes make grafts for the injured," C-3PO translated. "In her delirium, Saba must have mistaken a Joiner for a Chiss. The nest is searching for his body now."

Saba raised her head. "It waz no—"

"Let us handle this, Hisser." Han motioned Saba down, then asked, "Then how'd she get delirious in the first place? Where'd all these wounds come from?"

It was one of the healers on her neck that answered.

"Oh, dear!" C-3PO exclaimed. "She says Saba must have fallen after she was poisoned."

"*Poisoned?*" Leia gasped.

"Did this one not mention . . . that?" Saba asked.

The healer on her head purred a comment.

"Head wounds often cause forgetfulness," C-3PO translated.

The Killik on Saba's neck added, "And they're very sorry about the poison. They hope you won't blast the nest."

"Blast the nest?" Leia looked to the healer that had spoken. "What's that mean?"

It was the healer on Saba's leg that thrummed an answer.

"It's a powerful neurotoxic venom," C-3PO said. "It causes permanent paralysis—and they have no antidote."

Saba cocked her brow up at Leia. "Told . . . you."

"You're not dead yet," Leia said. "How do you feel?"

"Worze than . . . it lookz."

Wondering if Saba had any idea how bad she looked, Leia turned to Han. "She might beat it with a healing trance, but—"

"We've got to take her back."

He looked as worried and frustrated as Leia felt. There was no question of *not* taking Saba back. The Barabel was clearly in danger of dying or being permanently paralyzed, and Cilghal—the Jedi Master-healer—had an infirmary and a lab back on Ossus that would have the best resources to help her.

Han turned to Cakhmaim. "Catch Meewalh and start prepping the *Falcon*."

The Noghri nodded and raced off toward the tunnel that led down to the hangar.

"And don't wake Juun up!" Han yelled as an afterthought. "The last thing we want is a Sullustan slowing things down with procedure."

Leia motioned the stretcher bearers after Cakhmaim. "Let's get her to the *Falcon*."

"Not zo . . . fazt," Saba said. The Killiks paid no attention to her and started across the dance-field after Cakhmaim. "The third az-zazzin . . . we muzt warn Mazter Zkywalker."

Leia exchanged a concerned look with Han, then said gently, "Saba, the *Shadow* is gone, remember? We won't be able to warn them until we reach Galactic Alliance space."

Jaina appeared alongside the litter with Zekk and Alema.

"Saba, are you *sure* about the assassins?" Alema asked. "It really doesn't sound like—"

The inquiry was cut short when the severed arm rose off the stretcher and hit the Twi'lek in the chest.

"Yezz . . . zure."

They reached the tunnel leading down to the hangar. Leia sent C-3PO on with the Killiks and Saba, then stopped at the entrance and turned to Jaina.

"How soon can you be ready?"

Jaina's jaw fell. "Ready?"

"Yeah, to leave," Han said, coming in on cue. "You can't have much stuff to pack."

Jaina continued to look shocked for a moment, then a shadow of her father's crooked grin came to her lips. "Nice try, guys."

"*Try?*" Han managed to sound outraged. "We had a deal!"

"You can't hold us to that!" Zekk cried.

Jaina raised a silencing hand to him. "Let me handle this, Zekk. I've had practice."

"Jaina," Leia said sternly, "we *did* go after Lowie."

"Don't try the Desilijic shift on me," Jaina said. "The terms were that we had to bring him back."

"Yeah, well, you should have told us your ex-boyfriend was sitting on him," Han countered. "You held back."

"Didn't know," Jaina said, "and it wouldn't matter if I did. Lowbacca's still out there. We're not going back without him."

As Jaina folded her arms, the gesture was simultaneously mimicked by the swarm of Killiks that had gathered around them. But Leia was not ready to give up.

"Jaina, you know you're only making the situation worse," she said. "The Chiss are escalating things because of your presence."

"That's right," Han said. "And you proved on the rescue mission that your judgment isn't exactly sound."

Jaina did a good job of maintaining a neutral expression, but Leia was too adept at reading faces to miss the glimmer of hurt that flashed through their daughter's eyes.

"Jaina, if you really want to help Lowbacca, you'll come back with us." Leia switched her gaze to all three Jedi. "You know the Chiss are an honorable people. Stop making the situation worse and give us a chance to work this out diplomatically."

Jaina and Zekk actually dropped their gazes, but Alema was ready with a response. "And while you're still trying to make contact, they'll send in a fleet of defoliators to finish what they began."

Jaina nodded. "Diplomacy is good," she said. "But it's better when there's something to back it up. Go ahead and make contact with the Chiss, but we're staying."

"That's one option," Leia allowed. "But I'm concerned that you really don't know who you're dealing with."

Jaina's scowl of confusion was mirrored by the other two Jedi.

"We're not talking about the Chiss," Han explained. "You three are in way over your heads here—unless you think Saba really *did* imagine those assassin bugs?"

Alema's eyes flashed at the word *bugs,* but she was the first to shake her head. "They were real."

"But they weren't Taat," Zekk added.

"That's one of the things we'll be working on," Jaina said.

"Until when?" Once again, Leia was unnerved by how easily the trio were finishing each other's sentences. "Until you become Joiners?"

Jaina and the others shared a glance, then Zekk said, "That depends."

"On what?" Han asked.

"On how quickly *you* convince the Chiss to stop," Alema finished.

"Maybe you'd better hurry back to the *Falcon,*" Jaina finished. "Especially if Saba is right about where that third assassin went."

Leia's stomach grew hollow and worried. Jaina was right about that much, at least. They did not have a lot of time to waste trying to talk the three Jedi into coming home.

And Han knew it, too. He stepped close to Jaina. "Jaina, listen to me—"

"I don't have to listen, Dad," Jaina said. "I can *feel* what you're thinking."

"We all can," Zekk added. *"No daughter of mine—"*

"—is going to become a bughugger," Alema finished.

"Hey, no fair!" Han objected. "Just because I don't like bugs doesn't mean I'm wrong. There's something sneaky going on here— and Raynar's in it up to his neck."

"You don't know that," Jaina said.

"This is the third time we've been attacked," Leia reminded her. "And Raynar *did* tell us he was afraid we'd try to take you away."

"Then he can stop worrying, because we're not going anywhere until the Chiss leave," Jaina said. "So hurry up and make that happen."

She opened her arms to embrace Han, but he stepped back shaking his head. "No, Jaina, I'm not giving this my—"

"I wasn't looking for your blessing, Dad." Jaina's voice had grown hard—not angry, just hard. "And I guess I'd be foolish to hope for anything else."

"If you're going to be ronto-brained about this, yeah," Han said. "I'll tell you what. You take Saba back in the *Falcon,* and your mother and I'll stay here to handle the Chiss."

"And recover Lowie," Leia added.

"You'd let me fly the *Falcon* home?" Jaina asked, cocking her head in an all-too-Killik-like fashion. "Alone?"

"Well, with Alema and Zekk," Han said. "Sure."

Jaina scowled. "Who do you think you're talking to, Dad? I know how you feel about insects." She turned her back on Han and held her arms out to Leia. "Mother?"

"I wish you'd listen to your father." Leia's chest grew heavy, for she could see Han's frustration with Jaina turning to anger. "You do know *you* might be the real prize in this conflict? Raynar isn't the earnest young man who went to Myrkr with you. He's desperate and lonely. I wouldn't be surprised if he had instigated the whole border conflict just to draw you—"

"Mom, sometimes you think too much." Jaina lowered her arms, then turned and started away. "You'd better get the *Falcon* off this moon. I'll try to warn Aunt Mara through the Force."

"Jaina!" Han barked.

Jaina ignored him.

Zekk said, "Do what you can with the Chiss. We'll keep things in check here."

He turned and started after Jaina.

"This isn't over, you know!" Han said to their backs. "We're going to come back."

Jaina waved over her shoulder, but Alema remained where she was, in front of the Solos.

"I'll be going with you," the Twi'lek said to Leia.

Jaina and Zekk both stopped and whirled around in surprise.

"You will?" Jaina asked.

"We didn't expect this," Zekk said.

"They'll need a guide," Alema explained. "They can't go back the same way they came without stopping at Yoggoy, and that may not be a good idea—at least not until we know who's behind these attacks."

Jaina scowled at the unexpected change of plan, but nodded and turned to her father. "Do you have room on the *Falcon*?"

"Sure," Han said. "Why don't you all come?"

TWENTY

Even curled into the primal egg position on the *Falcon*'s medbay bunk, staring dead ahead with glazed eyes, Saba looked more annoyed by her wounds than pained by them. Her pebbly lips were drawn back in a frozen sneer, with the tips of her forked tongue showing between her fangs, and the claws on her hands were fully extended. She held her bandaged tail wrapped tightly around her hindquarters, and if she was breathing at all, Leia saw no sign of it in her constricted nostrils and motionless chest.

"She looks like she's dying," Alema whispered over Leia's shoulder. "Is she dying?"

"I don't know." Leia checked the monitors and found a single spike on the cardio-line. There was a barely discernible upward slope on the respiratory chart. "I think it's just a healing trance."

"Well, she *looks* like she's dying," Alema said.

Saba's tongue shot out and snapped the air, drawing a surprised gasp from both Leia and Alema, then returned to its place between her teeth. The Barabel's eyes remained fixed and glazed.

"Healing trance," Leia concluded.

"Do you think she'll survive?"

Leia studied the silken bandage that covered half of Saba's skull. "With that head wound, anyone else would be dead already," she said. "But Saba's a Barabel. Who knows?"

Alema's only answer was a long, concerned silence.

After a time, Leia lowered the lights and told the medcomputer to alert her if anything changed in Saba's status.

As Leia drew the privacy curtain across the medbay, she asked,

"How about a nice mug of hot chocolate? We have some of Luke's special supply on board."

"Really? Hot chocolate!" Alema gasped. Always scarce, hot chocolate had become a true Hutt's pleasure after the Yuuzhan Vong reshaped seven of the eight planets capable of growing the rare pods necessary to produce it. "What about your duties in the cockpit?"

"Don't worry about that." Leia took the Twi'lek's arm and led her forward. The *Falcon* had just left Qoribu and was preparing to make its first jump to hyperspace, but Leia needed to find out what was really happening on Jwlio—and the sooner, the better. "Juun is filling in for me. Han's growing fond of the little guy."

Alema curled her lekku. "That's not the impression I get from Han."

Leia gave a knowing smile. "That's because *Han* doesn't realize it yet." They entered the main cabin. "Anyway, we have time. Have a seat."

Leia took several white, thumb-sized seeds from a storage box and placed them in the galley multiprocessor. She set the controls to DRY AND POWDER, then turned, placed a fist on her hip, and began to study Alema with the same slightly interested, slightly preoccupied expression that she had been using to soften up her subjects since her days as a junior Senator in the Old Republic.

Leia should have known it wouldn't work on Alema Rar. Lithe, beautiful, and averse to modest clothing, the Twi'lek was used to being stared at. She simply stared back, making Leia feel as though *she* were the one dressed only in a sideless chemise.

The multiprocessor chimed, allowing Leia to turn away gracefully. She added a lot of sweetener and a small amount of water, then set the controls to AGITATE AND HEAT.

"You have a complicated way of making hot-chocolate," Alema noted. "Usually, it just comes out of the dispenser nozzle"

"This is better," Leia said, turning back toward the Twi'lek. "Trust me."

"Of course," Alema said. "Is there a reason not to?"

Leia began to wonder who was being interrogated here. She waited until it was time to add the milk, then instructed the multiprocessor to heat slowly and joined Alema at the table.

"Okay." Leia assumed her best motherly tone and leaned in close. "So what is it?"

Alema frowned, but did not pull back. "What is *what*?"

"The reason you're here," Leia said. "We both know that Juun could have gotten the *Falcon* past Yoggoy."

Finally, a glimmer of doubt showed in Alema's face. Leia was tempted to probe her feelings through the Force, but suspected the Twi'lek would sense the intrusion and resent it.

Alema looked toward the multiprocessor. "Shouldn't you check the hot chocolate?"

"The unit will chime." Leia kept her gaze fixed on the Twi'lek's face. "I *saw* how Jaina and Zekk reacted, Alema."

"That doesn't mean—"

"You three could barely start a sentence without someone else finishing it," Leia said.

"It's the meld." Alema's answer came a little too quickly. "We really baked ourselves on the voxyn mission."

"That so?" Leia was far too experienced to miss the Twi'lek's attempt to change the subject, but she decided to play along—for now. "When did you start using the battle-meld with Killiks?"

Alema looked genuinely confused. "We haven't. What makes you think that? They're not even Force-sensitive."

"I know." Leia gave her a motherly smile. "But there *is* a mental connection, especially with you. I saw it at the dance."

Alema cast a hopeful look toward the multiprocessor, then seemed to realize that the bell would only delay the inevitable.

"Maybe there is," she said. "It's nothing you're aware of. You start feeling like you belong, then you sort of . . . suddenly you just seem to have a larger mind."

Leia began to wonder if there were any deprogrammers in the Galactic Alliance capable of handling eight Jedi.

"It's hard to describe." Alema must have sensed Leia's thoughts in the Force, because her tone was defensive. "You're aware of so much more. You see outside the nest when you're inside, or inside when you're outside. And what you feel—you feel *everything*."

"I've heard glitterstim is a lot like that," Leia commented dryly.

"This is even better," Alema said. "You don't get sick. It's completely harmless."

Leia was beginning to see why the Twi'lek's infatuation with Anakin had always made Han so nervous. Though the multiprocessor hadn't chimed yet, she returned to the galley and took two empty mugs from the cabinet, then placed a sliver of tangbark and a drop of orchid-bean extract in each.

"What's that?" Alema asked, joining Leia at the galley.

"Spice," Leia said.

Alema's eyes lit.

"Not that kind," Leia said. "Just flavoring."

The multiprocessor chimed. She filled both mugs, topped them with dollops of mallow paste—made from real mallow root—and handed one to Alema.

"You're wrong, you know," Leia said. "It's not harmless."

Alema glanced at her mug and looked confused.

"The Colony," Leia said. "Or have you forgotten the attack on the *Shadow*? And the tower collapse on Yoggoy?"

"You can't believe the Colony was responsible. Taat may not have healed Saba, but they saved her life."

"Taat's healers had to save Saba's life because someone else tried to take it."

"Not Killiks. Saba said she was attacked by . . ." Alema frowned, then finished, ". . . a man. You heard her."

"She thought it was Welk," Leia said, supplying the name Alema had not been able to recall. "Saba also said he was protecting a *Killik* nest. A nest with two dark blue Killiks." Leia paused, then demanded, "Who were they?"

"That part makes no sense," Alema said. "There are no blue Killiks—at least none we've seen here."

The denial would have been more convincing had Alema's eyes not slid away. Leia took a sip from her mug, savoring its silky sweetness as she pondered what the Twi'lek might be trying to conceal.

"It makes sense to *you*," Leia said finally. "But you don't want to tell me."

Alema took a sip of her drink, hiding from Leia behind the rim of her mug. "We're all upset about what happened to Master Sebatyne. Why would anyone hide information about that?"

"Obviously, because you're trying to protect the Killiks." Leia returned to the table and sat down, regarding the Twi'lek from across the cabin. "What I can't figure out is why you wanted to come with us. Are you afraid we're going to discover the secret they're trying to protect?"

"Very good." Alema raised her mug to indicate she was talking about the hot chocolate. "It *is* better this way."

Leia ignored the compliment. "Or maybe you're afraid that what happened to Master Sebatyne is going to happen to us?"

Alema raised her mug again, but she swallowed too quickly to enjoy what she was drinking.

"So that's it," Leia said. She could not help feeling a little hurt that her own daughter had not worried about her safety—but that was probably because Jaina knew that Leia and Han could take care of themselves . . . or so she told herself. "You're trying to protect us."

"Not at all." Alema came to join her at the table. "You don't need protecting—at least not from Killiks."

"The Chiss are afraid of *something*," Leia pointed out.

"Yes." Alema sat down next to Leia. "They're afraid the Galactic Alliance will learn what they've been doing in Qoribu."

"They're afraid of the *Killiks*," Leia said. "And you're hiding the reason. All of you are."

"There's nothing to hide," Alema said. "Chiss xenophobia is well documented. And where insects are involved, it's pure bigotry. Just because a life-form has six legs, they think they're free to smash it."

"Nice try," Leia said. "But we're not changing the subject."

The jump alert knelled softly, and the silky beverage in their mugs shuddered slightly as the *Falcon* slipped into hyperspace. Leia decided the time had come to start pushing.

"Alema, what were those insects Welk was protecting?"

Alema made a point of meeting Leia's gaze. "You know as much about that as anyone."

"Fair enough," Leia said. "I do have a theory. Those insects were exactly what Saba thought they were: Colony assassins."

Alema shook her head. "Why would the Colony need assassins?"

"Because Unu wants its own Jedi," Leia said. "And that means stopping *us*."

"No," Alema insisted. "The Colony would never murder anyone."

"Sure it would," Leia said. "That's why Raynar was willing to let us leave after we discovered Yoggoy's location. He didn't think we'd live long enough to reveal it to anyone else."

"He let you leave because he *trusted* you to keep the secret. Unu has nothing to do with the attacks on you and the *Shadow*. That was . . ."

Alema frowned again, as though she were trying to recall the name of Saba's attacker.

"Welk," Leia supplied. "I'm surprised you have so much trouble remembering the name of someone who betrayed you."

"It doesn't mean anything," Alema said. "You're flustering me with this nonsense about the Colony trying to kill you, that's all."

The excuse was just convenient enough to rouse Leia's suspicion. "I'm sorry. Maybe you can remember the name of Welk's Master? What was his name?"

"*Her* name," Alema said. "Good try, though."

"Do you recall her name?"

Alema thought for a moment, then asked, "What does this have to do with anything? They're both dead."

"Then it wasn't Welk who attacked Saba?" Leia asked.

Alema shook her head resolutely. "It couldn't have been. He died when the *Flier* crashed, along with . . . his Master."

Now it was Leia's turn to frown. The truth—at least Alema's memory of it—seemed to be changing before her eyes. "Then who was it?"

"It must have been a Chiss spy," Alema said.

"With a lightsaber?"

"He could have stolen it," Alema said. "Or found it."

"That's possible," Leia said carefully. "But wouldn't a simpler explanation be that Welk survived the Crash?"

Alema shook her head, and her tone grew ardent. "Raynar was the only one Yoggoy found at the Crash."

"That doesn't mean Raynar was the only one who survived," Leia insisted. "Didn't Jacen tell you? He was there. He saw Raynar pull both Welk and Lomi out of the crash."

"Jacen said that," she admitted. "But it's impossible. When the *Flier* crashed, he was on *Baanu Rass* with us. Or Vergere's prisoner on Coruscant."

"True," Leia said. "Still, he saw what happened at the Crash. I don't know how, but he did."

"He *said* he did." Alema stood and turned as though to leave, then whirled back toward the table. "That doesn't make it true."

Leia was puzzled by the strange reaction. "When I was at the Crash, he spoke to me—at the same time he was on Jwlio," she said. "So I tend to believe him."

"You would." Alema began to pace. "He's your son."

"And I've seen what he can do." Cautiously, Leia asked, "Why is it so important for you to believe Jacen is wrong?"

"Why is it so important for you to believe he *isn't*?"

"I'm trying to figure out who's been attacking us." Leia was speaking in a soft, nonthreatening voice . . . and wondering who exactly she was talking to. Maybe there had been more to that hopeful look than Leia imagined when Alema had mistaken the tangbark for glitterstim. "And I'm pretty certain Welk is involved. Possibly Lomi—"

"It doesn't matter what Jacen *thinks* he saw," Alema said. "They're both dead."

"And you know this?"

Alema nodded.

"How?" Leia asked.

"We . . ." Alema's face went blank, and she began to make loud clicking sound deep in her throat. "The Colony knows."

"The *Colony* knows." Leia made a point of letting her skepticism show. "Alema, what are you trying to protect us from?"

"*Nothing!*" The Twi'lek banged her fists on the table. "You have nothing to fear, if you will just do what we tell you!"

"We *who,* Alema?"

Alema's eyes widened, then she drew herself upright and stood at the table in shock, her mouth working but no sound coming from her lips. The Noghri appeared silently at the cabin entrance. Leia signaled them to wait with an eye flicker, then let the silence hang while she finished her hot chocolate.

Finally, she put the empty mug down and looked up. "Well, I'm happy to see you understand why that statement is so wrong."

"Of course," Alema said. "We . . . I . . . apologize."

She spun on her heel and left the cabin so quickly that the Noghri barely had time to step out of her way. Leia did not go after her. There would be plenty of time to tease the rest of the truth out of her on the trip back to Ossus, and Leia had learned enough for now. She closed her eyes and reached into the Force for Luke, hoping that this time her sense of him would be a little more solid, that she could impart to him some hint of the hidden danger that the *Shadow* might have carried back from Qoribu.

TWENTY-ONE

The four brains displayed above the medholo varied broadly in size and shape, the largest being oblong with only a slight downward bulge to join the brain stem, the smallest looking more like a withered pallie mounted on a pulsing mushroom stem. In three of the brains, bursts of activity were simultaneously blossoming in bright identical colors, then fading at exactly the same rate. Even more telling were the two-dimensional alpha waves crawling through the air beneath each hologram. Three of the patterns were indistinguishable, with matched frequencies and amplitudes. The fourth wave, located beneath the solid blue shape of a human brain, was alternating between dead flat and so wildly erratic that the peaks vanished into the holo above.

"Very funny, Jacen." Luke frowned toward the relaxi-chair where his nephew reclined, looking out through viewing window of a huge scanning hood. "Would you stop playing with the brain mapper?"

"Just making the point." The fourth brain went entirely white. "This won't tell you anything. You must decide for yourselves whether we can be trusted."

"Trust isn't the issue," Corran Horn said. Along with Luke, Mara, and several other Jedi Masters, he was standing in the isolation ward of the infirmary at the Jedi academy on Ossus, where they would be far from the prying eyes of the Galactic Alliance advisory council. "We're just trying to figure out what happened to you."

"It has nothing to do with Killikz," Tesar said.

"We overused the meld," Tahiri said.

"And now we can't stay out of each other's minds," Tekli finished.

Though Luke certainly knew about the problems the meld had

caused the strike team survivors, he suspected these new symptoms had more to do with Killiks than the meld. Still, that was a judgment better made by the Jedi order's Master healer.

Luke turned to Cilghal. "What do you think?"

The Mon Calamari looked at him out of one bulbous eye. "I think they are . . . mistaken."

"Mistaken?" Kyp Durron asked with his usual lack of tact. "Or lying?"

Tesar Sebatyne started to push his scanning hood off. "This one does not—"

"Easy, Tesar." Luke flashed Kyp a look of irritation. Now was hardly a good time to be testing Tesar's patience. The Barabel had felt his mother get wounded less than twenty-four hours earlier, and the only thing anyone knew about the circumstances was a vague sensation that Luke had felt from Leia suggesting that she was caring for Saba—and that he and Mara faced the same danger on Ossus. "I'm sure Master Durron didn't mean to impugn your honor."

Ignoring the opportunity for an apology, Kyp continued to look at Cilghal. "Okay, why do you think they're . . . *mistaken*?"

"Because the activity is in the wrong places."

Cilghal keyed a command, and a blobby structure about the size of a thumbtip began to glow deep within the hologram of Tahiri's brain.

"With the meld, the hypothalamus responds to emotional reverberations in the Force," Cilghal said. The blob began to swell and grow red. "Prolonged use—or very intense use—can enlarge it and make it hypersensitive. Melders can become so attuned to each other that their minds begin to read the reverberations much as transceivers read comm waves. That's when the meld slips into telepathy."

"What about the mood swings?" Corran asked.

Cilghal keyed another command. What looked like a wishbone with two long, curling tails appeared above the image of Tahiri's hypothalamus.

"As use is continued, the effect spills over into the rest of the limbic system, and melders begin to alter each other's emotions."

The Masters watched for a few moments as the "wishbone" grew thicker and darker. They were all aware of the risks associated with the meld, but this was the first time many had heard Cilghal's theory concerning the actual mechanism. Luke had the sense that some were looking inward, trying to guess how sensitive their own limbic systems might be growing.

Finally, Corran asked, "And where is the other kind of activity occurring?"

Cilghal keyed another command. A fibrous, cap-like structure about ten centimeters long appeared above Tahiri's limbic system and beneath both her cerebral hemispheres. It was, Luke noted, in a perfect position to act as bridge among all major sections of the brain.

"The structure of the corpus callosum has changed," Cilghal said. As she spoke, the hypothalamus and limbic system paled, and a hazy yellow fuzz formed in their place. "That haze you see is composed of free-dangling dendrites. It suggests that Tesar, Tekli, and Tahiri are sending impulses directly from one brain to another."

"And Jacen?" Mara asked.

"That's difficult to say." Cilghal glanced at Jacen, who sat beneath his hood, playing color games with the hologram of his brain. "But probably not, since he was there only a fraction of the time the others were."

"What about these impulses?" Kyle Katarn asked. With brown hair, brown eyes, and a tan shirt tucked into brown breeches, he looked like a farmer about to return to his fields instead of one of the Jedi order's most famous and skilled members. "Are you talking about Force impulses?"

Cilghal shook her elongated head. "Probably not. From what Master Skywalker said, the Killiks don't appear to be Force-sensitive." She stepped away from the controls, then continued, "I suspect the impulses are moving through their auras."

"Their *auras*?" Kenth Hamner asked. A tall Jedi with a deeply lined face and dignified bearing, he had a keen mind and a habit of skeptical inquiry. "I've always had the impression that auras were so much Fallanassi nonsense."

"Not at all," Cilghal said. "Every being is surrounded by an aura of subtle energies—heat, electric, magnetic, even chemical—some extending as far as ten meters. I have a multiband detector that can image your own, if you like."

"For now, we'll take your word for it," Luke said. At the moment, he was less interested in proof than in a working theory. "How confident are you?"

"Not confident at all," Cilghal said. "I'll have to perform some tests to verify my hypothesis."

"Tests are useless," Tekli said from inside her scanning hood. "They won't reveal anything."

"Our problem is the meld," Tahiri insisted.

"We need no testz to tell us that," Tesar agreed.

Luke and the other Masters exchanged uncomfortable glances,

their mutual concern growing sharper in the Force. The trio's insistence on blaming the meld was beginning to sound irrational.

Finally, Corran said, "Cilghal, you said their corpus ca—er—whatever-it-was had changed. How did that happen? Was that also caused by the auras?"

"Probably not," Cilghal said. "Most insects rely heavily on pheromones to regulate their lives, so that's where my suspicions fall first."

"That makes sense," Mara agreed. "The nests were soaked with pheromones."

"You're saying a *smell* changed our Jedi's brain structure?" Corran asked.

"Pheromones aren't just odors," Cilghal said. "They're very powerful chemicals. They trigger a wide range of behaviors—and physical changes—in nearly every animal in the galaxy."

"And they change your brain?" Corran repeated, still unconvinced.

"*Everything* changes your brain," Cilghal said. "Whenever you learn something new, or develop a skill, or make a memory, your brain grows new connections to store and access information. Under the right stimulus, it's very conceivable that parts of it could be completely modified."

"So," Mara asked, "spend enough time in the pheromone bath, and your brain rewires itself?"

"Exactly," Cilghal said. "Especially if the pheromones work through the nose. In most species, smell is a direct input to the brain."

"And you're sure these Jedi Knights are just *mistaken* about what's happened to them?" Kyp asked, raising the question again for no good reason Luke could see. "They couldn't be lying?"

"We are not lying!" Tesar stood, pushing his hood up and pointing a talon in Kyp's direction. "We do not lie!"

Concerned that Kyp was sensing something he had not, Luke reached out to Tesar and the others in the Force. He felt outrage, confusion, even a small hint of a Joiner's double presence—but no dishonesty. As far as he could tell, the trio believed they were telling the truth.

Luke sent a gentle Force-nudge urging Kyp to apologize, but the shaggy-haired Jedi ignored it and returned the glare Tesar was shooting in his direction.

"Then prove it," Kyp said. "Tell us why you agreed to come back from Qoribu."

The tip of Tesar's forked tongue darted between his lips, and the anger in his slit-pupiled eyes slowly changed to admiration.

"Very good, Master Durron," Tesar said. "We did not see that coming at all."

"I'm glad I still have something to teach," Kyp said. "Are you going to answer?"

"Of course," Tahiri said, slipping out from beneath her own hood. "All you had to do was ask."

"So we're asking," Mara said.

"We came to persuade the council to help the Killikz," Tesar said. "The Colony can only stop the Chisz through war."

"And the Jedi can bring other pressures to bear," Tahiri added. "It's best for everyone."

"That will be for the Masters council to decide," Kenth said. "And when it does, will you abide by our decision?"

"We aren't wrong about this," Tahiri dodged.

"The Chisz are committing xenocide," Tesar added. "We must intervene."

"Immediately." Tekli pushed her hood up and came to stand with the others, leaving only Jacen's brain—currently gold and pulsing—displayed on the medholo. "Aren't we bound as Jedi to protect the weak?"

"Jedi are bound by a great many duties, often contradictory," Kenth said. "Which is why we call Masters' councils. I ask again, will you abide by our decision?"

The trio fell silent, then Tahiri and Tekli dropped their eyes, and Tesar said, "That dependz on what the decision is."

Kenth and Corran recoiled visibly.

But Kyp Durron smiled. "Well, it's an honest answer."

"As much as that is possible for them," Cilghal said. She turned to Luke. "I don't like to question their integrity, Master Skywalker, but anything they tell us is suspect. We must assume their judgment has been compromised by the same power that called them away in the first place."

Tesar glared openly in Cilghal's direction. "You are saying we cannot be trusted?"

She met his gaze evenly. "You're not to blame, but yes—that's exactly what I'm saying."

Tesar looked from Cilghal to Luke to Kyp and back to Luke, then thumped his tail and retreated to his relaxi-chair.

Tahiri took his place. "We don't deserve this." She glared directly into Luke's eyes. "You have no reason to treat us like we're Sith."

"Probably not," Kenth said. "But until those mysterious attacks on Yoggoy and at Qoribu are explained, there's no harm in being safe."

"By all meanz," Tesar rasped from his chair. "This one would not want you to fear us."

Luke turned to Cilghal. "Perhaps you'd explain your concerns?"

The Mon Calamari nodded. "It's very simple. The meld always comes from the outside—you *know* you're listening to someone else's thoughts and reacting to someone else's emotions. But this . . . this *joining* feels like it comes from inside. The things our Jedi Knights see through it—or hear or smell or taste—seem like things they're sensing themselves. Even the thoughts they share seem to arise inside their own minds."

"So they don't know whether their thoughts are their own or someone else's?" Mara asked. Luke could sense that she was as concerned as he was, that she was afraid their young Jedi Knights were lost to the Colony already. "They can't just ignore outside thoughts, like we can in the meld?"

"I'm afraid that's correct," Cilghal said. "In all likelihood, it's impossible to know the difference."

The Masters studied Tahiri and the other young Jedi in silence, their faces betraying the same disappointment and concern and uncertainty that Luke felt. Cilghal could probably find a way to negate the changes to their brain structure. But the patients were clearly going to be uncooperative, and that would make recovery a long, difficult process.

Finally, Kenth said, "Well, that explains a lot. They certainly haven't been acting like themselves."

"Perhapz not," Tesar admitted. He leaned forward, being careful to remain seated and nonthreatening. "But that doesn't mean we are wrong about Qoribu."

"Ask Masters Skywalker," Tekli said. "They both saw Jwlio. *They* can tell you what the Chiss have done to the moon."

"Fair enough," Luke said. "Mara and I weren't on Jwilo long enough to gather many facts, but it *is* clear the Chiss are trying to drive the Killiks out of the system."

"And it's just as clear that the Killiks don't have the resources to leave," Mara added. "The way things are looking, the result will be war or extermination, probably both."

Tahiri beamed, Tesar assumed a reptilian grin, and Tekli brought her ears forward.

Then Corran asked, "Why?"

Tesar rose. "Why what?"

"Why are the Chiss doing this?" he asked. "They're xenophobic and secretive, but they're not expansionists. If they're trying to drive the Killiks away, they must have a reason."

"They are afraid the Colony will expand into their territory," Tesar said. "That is what their Joinerz say."

"There's more to it," Mara said. "If all the Chiss were worried about was border security, they'd just wait for a nest to pop up in their own territory, *then* attack."

"That's right," Luke agreed. "Something about the Killiks scares the Chiss so much they don't want them in the same sector as an Ascendancy system."

"You'd have to ask the Chiss about that," Tahiri said.

"We shouldn't need to," Kenth pointed out. "Isn't it the first duty of a Jedi to understand *both* sides of a conflict?"

Tahiri met his gaze with a raised chin. "We were occupied."

"Saving innocentz."

"And look what happened," Kenth said. "Both sides are closer to war than ever."

"Perhaps," Tekli said. "But our mistakes shouldn't condemn the Qoribu nests."

"And they shouldn't commit the Jedi to any action the Masters haven't authorized." Corran turned away from the trio and addressed the other Masters. "Our first concern must be the stability of the Galactic Alliance."

"No." Kyp Durron surprised everyone by stepping to Tahiri's side. "The Jedi are no one's mercenaries—not even the Galactic Alliance's. Our first concern, our only concern, is our own conscience. We must follow it wherever it leads."

Octa Ramis, who had remained silent until now, spoke up to agree with Kyp, then Kenth agreed with Corran, Kyp repeated his position, and the discussion degenerated into argument. Tahiri, Tekli, and Tesar remained silent, content to let their advocates argue their case. Luke glanced over at Jacen, who was continuing to create elegant swirls of light in his brain holo, and wished he were also free to ignore the argument. What he really wanted to be doing was looking for a slicer who could access that sequestered sector in R2-D2's memory, but personal business would have to wait. The argument among the Masters was rapidly growing more heated.

Luke eased his way into the middle of the knot.

"Enough." The tumult began to quiet, and he said, "This isn't the time for discussion. We're just here to have a look at Cilghal's tests and listen to our Jedi Knights' report."

An embarrassed silence fell over the room as the Masters contemplated their outbursts, then Kyp flushed and dropped his chin. "I let my emotions carry me away. I apologize."

"No need," Corran said, slapping his shoulder. "We were all a little excited."

"Master Skywalker is right," Kyle added. "We're just here to listen."

"You haven't listened to *me* yet."

Jacen sounded as though he were less than a meter from the group. But when Luke turned around, he found only the image of his nephew's brain floating above the holopad. Jacen himself remained seated in his relaxi-chair, eyes staring blankly out through the viewing window of his scanning hood.

"Okay, Jacen," Luke said. "We'd be very interested in hearing your report."

The hologram pulsed in a brilliant show of iridescent color, and the alpha line below it quivered in time to a deep, booming voice that was barely recognizable as Jacen's.

"Killiks are dangerous friends, but no one's enemy," the brain said. "The true danger lies not in *what* the Jedi do, but in their failure to act at all."

The effect was exactly what Jacen had intended. A thoughtful silence descended on the group, and the Masters' gazes turned inward as they searched for the deeper meaning in Jacen's words.

Luke walked over the control panel. "Very funny," he said, switching it off. "Didn't I tell you to stop playing with Cilghal's brain mapper?"

TWENTY-TWO

Han and Leia were alone in the cockpit, sitting together in one chair, watching the opalescent nothingness of hyperspace slide silently past. The jump was a long one, and there was no reason for them both to spend it on watch. But the flight deck was the one place on the suddenly crowded *Falcon* to find some discreet time together, and—after the way things had ended with Jaina—Han was glad they had. Somehow, it helped to know that Leia was as frightened for Jaina as he was—that she, too, was determined to find out what Raynar really had planned for their daughter, to return to Qoribu the minute they could, and to put a stop to it.

"You're in a better mood," Leia said.

"Talking to you, I guess," Han admitted. "How'd you know?"

"The humming. You never hum."

"Humming?" Han frowned. "I'm not humming."

"Really?" Leia cocked her head. "It certainly *sounds* like you are."

Han spun the seat around until he was facing the same direction Leia had been, then he heard it—a faint, undulating purr.

"That's not me." Han jumped up, dumping Leia onto her feet. "It's a coolant line!"

"A coolant line?" Leia slipped into the copilot's chair and began calling up status displays. "What happened to the alarm?"

"Good question." Han turned toward the back of the flight deck and started down the access corridor. "Disengage the hyperdrive and do a slow cool-down. I'll see what I can find out back in systems."

The hum grew steadily louder as Han advanced. By the time he entered the main cabin, it had risen to an irritating drone. He met the rest of his crew and passengers coming the other way. Cakhmaim and Meewalh were wide awake, but still pulling on their sleeveless robes. Alema and Juun were both bleary-eyed and dressed in their sleeping shifts, which, in Alema's case, was considerably more than she wore when she was awake.

C-3PO was also present and, of course, fully alert. "I don't believe I've ever heard the *Falcon* make a sound quite like this, Captain Solo. What is it?"

"Boiling coolant," Juun said through a yawn. He stretched his arms. "The hyperdrive must be—" The bleariness vanished from the Sullustan's bulbous eyes. "Bloah! The hyperdrive is overheating!"

A loud boom reverberated through the hull as the *Falcon* executed an emergency drop into realspace. The drone in the coolant lines became a loud, bubbling hiss.

Han pointed at Juun, then jerked a thumb toward the cockpit. "Take the navigator's station and get a fix on where we are. Threepio, take the comm station in case we need to send an emergency hail. Everyone else, with me."

Han led the way to the rear of the ship, then opened an access panel and peered in at the contorted tangle of valves and radiation-shielded conduits surrounding the unit itself. There was no need to ask for a thermoscanner to determine which lines were overheated. The lower inside conduit was bulging, glowing pale blue, and banging as if there were a profogg inside. Han activated the lighting and crawled into the sweltering cabinet, then traced the pipe up to the dark nook where it passed through the flow regulator. The diverter valve was stuck half closed, but Han could not see what had caused the malfunction—or why the sensor hadn't sounded an alarm.

"Meewalh, get me some burn gloves and a face shield."

Before he finished asking, the Noghri was passing the gloves and face shield into the cabinet.

As Han donned the equipment, Juun's voice came over the intercom. "Captain Solo, I haven't identified exactly where we are yet—"

"Well, keep working on it. I'm sure you can figure it out." Han rolled his eyes. "Let me know when you do."

"Of course," Juun said. "But I thought I should report—"

"Look, I'm kind of busy here," Han said. "So unless we're under attack, hold the reports until you're done."

There was a moment of silence, then Juun asked, "Do you want me to wait until we're *actually* under attack?"

"What?" Han turned, banging the side of his head on a strut. "Blast! What do you mean, *actually*?"

"Han, it looks like we're still in Colony territory," Leia said, breaking in. "We've got a swarm of dartships coming."

"Rodder!" Han nodded the Noghri toward the cannon turrets, then pulled on the second burn glove. "Okay, forget the cooldown. Recalculate the rest of the jump using three-quarter power and go. This shouldn't take long."

"You've found the problem?" Juun's voice was full of awe. "Already?"

"Even better." Han reached up to the regulator and shut down the damaged coolant line. "I've found a fix."

When Han pulled himself out of the cabinet, Alema was frowning down at him with her lekku crossed over her chest.

"Don't scowl at me," he said. "It gives you wrinkles."

The frown vanished at once. "Are you sure it's necessary to take this kind of risk?" she asked. "Those dartships are only coming to greet us. Their nest might even be able to help us make repairs."

"First, not all dartships are friendly." Han passed her his face shield, then pulled off his burn gloves. "Second, Saba can't wait for repairs—and maybe not Luke and Mara, either."

"And third?"

"There is no third."

"There's always a third," Alema said.

"Okay, third." Han passed her the burn gloves and, as the *Falcon* slipped back into hyperspace, concluded, "I'm the captain. It's safe if I say it is."

Alema shrank back. "Okay—just asking," she said. "Maybe we should check on Saba."

"You go ahead," Han said, wondering why the Twi'lek thought he was needed to check on the Barabel. *Bugs and bug-lovers,* he thought, *you can't trust either of 'em.* He had a sudden image of Jaina and Raynar rubbing forearms and shuddered. He closed the access panel and started forward. "I need to keep an eye on things in the cockpit."

Han had barely stepped onto the flight deck when Juun reported, "We have to recalibrate the warp controller. The heat buildup caused a performance spike in the number two nacelle, and we veered off course by seven one-thousandths of a degree."

"We don't have time," Han said. Recalibrating meant days of trial jumps, then he'd have to do it all again when they returned to the Galactic Alliance and repaired the problem. "Just run a compensation program."

"A compensation program?" Juun was aghast. "But procedure mandates recalibration anytime—"

"It also mandates obeying the captain's orders," Han said, slipping into the pilot's seat. "Just run the blasted program."

Juun was silent for a moment, then asked in a subdued voice, "Was the malfunction anything I should account for?"

Han softened. "Good question." He considered for a moment, mentally reviewing the entire coolant system in his mind. An *underactive* diverter could cause another performance spike, but probably not a closed one—especially not if the hyperdrive remained below maximum power. "I don't think so."

"You don't *think* so?" Juun repeated. "Didn't you identify the malfunction?"

"Didn't have time," Han said, growing irritated again.

"But if you haven't identified the problem, how can you know it's safe—"

"I *know*," Han growled. "Now, are you going to stop bothering me and run that program, or do I have to do it myself?"

"I'd advise you to choose the first option," C-3PO said. "When Captain Solo's voice assumes that tone, he has a nasty habit of tripping primary circuit breakers."

"It's okay, Jae," Leia said. "Han knows what he's doing."

"Oh, I realize that, Princess Leia," Juun replied. "I was only asking because I'd like to understand how Han Solo makes decisions."

"Wouldn't we all?" Leia replied.

Juun ran the compensation program, then they jumped back into hyperspace and spent the next quarter hour riding in silence, watching status readouts and listening for the faintest hum in the coolant lines. Finally, Han felt confident enough to pronounce the emergency passed. He sent Juun back to tell the others they could return to their bunks, then looked over to find Leia staring raptly into her display, biting her lower lip as she double-checked Juun's compensation parameters against status readouts.

She wore the same enthralled expression she'd often had as New Republic Chief of State, poring over a report on an initiative to feed hungry natives on Gottlegoob, or as Rebel leader studying a cruiser buildup on Farbog. It was a look Han had not seen since the end of the war with the Yuuzhan Vong, when the challenge of combat had faded to the drudgery of reconstruction and they had retreated into the *Falcon* to build a smaller, more private life together.

It was a look Han missed, and one he felt responsible for losing.

As much as he loved having Leia all to himself—finally—he knew she needed more out of life; she would never be happy flying around just having adventures. She needed to be doing important things, putting the galaxy back together and seeing to it that the megaconglomerates did not end up owning everything.

Seeming to feel the weight of his gaze—or perhaps sense it through the Force—Leia looked up from the columns scrolling down her display. "Something wrong?"

"Nothing," Han said. "I was just wondering . . ." He wanted to say *if you were happy*, but knew that would sound wrong—it would sound like *he* was unhappy. "Well, if . . ."

"Juun's parameters are very complete, if you're worried about that," Leia said. "We're not going to stay in the safety margin—but when do we ever?"

"Yeah," Han said. "That's kind of the point. Do you ever miss our old place back on Coruscant?"

Leia cocked her brow and remained silent, studying him like a worrt eyeing a kreetle.

"Having a whole bedroom suite to ourselves, and a real kitchen where we could cook real dinners?"

"That apartment is gone—along with everything else we might remember about that planet." Leia made a point of not looking at Han. "And I don't recall *you* doing much cooking."

"That doesn't mean I didn't like the food," he said. "And we could get another place. With the Reconstruction Authority trying to move the seat of government back—"

"What's this talk about moving into an apartment?" Leia asked. "I thought you loved living on the *Falcon*."

"I do," Han said. "But there's more to life than being happy!"

Leia frowned. "Han, you're starting to sound confused. Have you been seeing color flashes? Feeling dizzy? Having trouble hear—"

"I'm not having a stroke," Han interrupted. "I'm fine."

"Good." Leia returned to her status display. "So am I."

"And I'm *not* old," Han said.

"Did I say you were?"

Han activated his own display and went to work running sensor tests, trying to locate the fault that had prevented the safety system from detecting the coolant problem before it grew critical. An hour later, he had determined that all of the sensors on the coolant line were stuck at the optimum readings. It took another hour to determine that the number one nacelle readings were being repeated on the number two status bar. By itself, either malfunction was danger-ous; together, they could prove catastrophic.

"I don't know where we serviced the hyperdrive last time," Han said, "but the next time we're in the neighborhood, remind me to send them a concussion missile."

"Bad coolant?" Leia asked. Corrosive impurities were the cause of most coolant problems.

"Yeah, and that's not all," Han said. "Some short circuit ran a double status feed from the number two nacelle."

"Really?" Leia grew thoughtful. "I wonder what the chances of making those two mistakes are."

"Approximately one hundred twelve thousand to one, Princess Leia," C-3PO said helpfully. "The hangar staff at the Jedi Temple are generally quite proficient."

"*That's* where we got our last coolant change?" Without waiting for a reply, Han turned to Leia. "Something smell bad to you?"

"Very," she said. "The Temple would know by now if it had been using bad coolant. Someone would have warned us."

"Yeah," Han said. "It's gotta be something else."

"Sabotage?"

"That'd be my bet," Han said. "Threepio, find out how Saba's doing—and have Meewalh and Cakhmaim do another sweep of the ship. Tell them to look for droppings and bug tracks. That may be the only way we know they're here."

"They?" C-3PO asked.

"Killiks," Han said. "Stowaways."

The droid left to obey. Han turned to find Leia staring out the viewport with a distant expression. It was the same look he'd seen a dozen times, as she reached out in the Force and tried to warn Luke about the assassin bugs Saba had found.

He waited until her attention returned to the cockpit, then asked, "Any luck?"

"Luke's preoccupied with something about our family. I think he thought I was trying to tell him about Saba." Leia shook her head. "And I just don't have a strong enough connection with Mara."

"What about Jacen?"

"I don't know," Leia said. "I can't tell if he doesn't believe me or just doesn't understand."

"Blast," Han said. "We could us a little help here. If this is sabo-tage . . ."

Han let the sentence trail off, for a faint thread of blue had appeared ahead, stretched horizontally across the pearly void of hyperspace.

"Leia, do you see that?"

"What?"

Han pointed at the thread, which had thickened into a line of mottled colors ranging from white to dark purple. "Colors."

"Very funny," Leia said. "I'm sorry I called you old."

"No, really." Han jabbed his finger toward the line, which was now a finger-width band darkening toward sapphire. "Look."

Leia looked, and her jaw dropped. "Should that *be* there?"

Fangs of blue light began to flash out from both sides of the sapphire stripe.

"No," Han said.

"Then why hasn't the proximity alarm dropped us out of hyperspace?"

"You don't want to know."

By the time Han had a hand on the hyperspace disengage, the sapphire stripe had thickened into a braided grimace of purple and white, and the tips of the blue fangs were flashing clear up to the canopy. He pulled the control lever back to emergency override . . . and a muffled bang sounded deep in the *Falcon*'s stern.

"Han!" Leia demanded. "What don't I want to know?"

"Tell you in a minute." The entire ship began to buck and shudder, and an eerie chorus of whirs hummed up the access corridor. "Blast!"

Han reengaged the hyperdrive. The ship stopped shuddering and the whirs faded to silence, but the crimson blue ahead reached out and closed around the *Falcon*.

"Tell me, Han. *What* don't I want to know?"

"What is this?" a reedy voice asked from the back of the flight deck. "Have we flown into a nebula?"

Han was vaguely aware of Leia turning toward Juun's voice—but only vaguely. The blue teeth had become the interior of a white-veined mouth, and most of his mind was busy trying to figure out what to do next.

"You've flown into a nebula before?" Leia asked Juun.

"Of course—many times," Juun assured her. "But usually I disengage the hyperdrive and fly right back out."

"Not an option." Han eased the hyperdrive control lever back until he heard the first hint of a whir. It didn't take much. "We'll blow that bad coolant line when the shutdown temperature spikes."

"I thought you fixed that!" Juun complained.

"So did I." Han glanced up at Juun's reflection in the canopy. "Someone unfixed it."

If Juun noticed the fear in Han's voice, he hid it well. "Well, you can't just keep going. The gas friction will distort the continuum warp."

"Distortion won't kill us," Han said. The *Falcon*'s stabilizers would probably keep their warp within safe parameters. "It's the dust shell I'm worried about."

"Oh, yes." Juun's voice was forlorn. "The dust shell."

"How long?" Leia asked.

She was too good a copilot to need to ask what would happen when a vessel traveling through hyperspace tried to punch its way through the striated layers of dust and debris that hung inside an expansion nebula.

"That depends on how old the nebula is," Han said. Two-meter circles of white began to flash ahead of the *Falcon* as the first dust particles blossomed against her forward shields. "But not long enough."

"This is a young one," Juun agreed. "A *very* young one."

The whir finally went silent, and Han eased the control lever back until he heard it again. He was only prolonging the inevitable, but sometimes stalling was the only move you had.

"Han." There was a tremor in Leia's voice, and she was staring straight out the forward viewport. "Tell me the truth—are we going to die?"

"Can you do that fog-parting trick you used on Borao again?" Han asked. "And extend it to about twelve light-years?"

"I doubt it," Leia said.

"Then, yeah, we're probably gonna die."

"What a pity Tarfang isn't here!" Juun said.

Han scowled into the canopy reflection. "I thought you *liked* that mattball."

"Very much!" Juun exclaimed. "And I'm sorry his name won't be listed among those who died with Han Solo."

"Not so fast," Leia said. The dust particles were blooming fast and furious now, turning hyperspace almost solid white with microscopic novae. "If we're going to die anyway, there's nothing left to lose."

"I hadn't thought of it that way," Juun said. "But—"

"Watch and learn," Leia said.

She activated the *Falcon*'s attitude control system, then—before Han could stop her—spun the ship around so that it was traveling backward through hyperspace.

The white blossoms vanished, and for a moment, the *Falcon* felt as though she were simply traveling through hyperspace backward.

Then the nebula turned red and started to spiral away from the viewport. Han's stomach turned somersaults faster than a Jedi acrobat, and the *Falcon*'s hull began to wail and screech like a rancor in full rut.

"Ke . . . b . . . ff!"

Han could not understand Leia above the terrible clamor, but it was easy to guess what she was yelling. He eased the lever back another centimeter. There was no question of listening for the humming coolant line, so he decided to count to thirty and do it again. What did it matter? They were going to die anyway.

Then Leia did something *really* foolish . . . she fired the sublight drives.

The shrieking and wailing stopped at once, and suddenly it was the *Falcon* spinning instead of space. Han felt as though his heart were going to fly out between his ribs, and he lost his last three meals.

But incredibly, he was still alive to know how bad he was feeling. He realized he had lost his count and eased the control lever back some more.

The whir returned. It occurred to him that the *Falcon* had fallen otherwise silent—which meant they weren't being pelted by dust particles, which meant the sublight drives were blasting a hole through the dust shell. Han looked over to congratulate Leia. Her face was a meter wide and five centimeters tall.

Nice try, he said. It came out *yiiiiirt eeeeeciiiiN* in his own head. He doubted he would ever know how it sounded to Leia.

The whir vanished. He eased the control lever back. Leia's face went to a meter tall and ten centimeters wide. Something big exploded against the *Falcon*'s rear shields and the ship shook so violently that Juun—who had not strapped himself in—ended up splayed against the forward viewport.

Han eased the control lever back and took a long deep sniff, smelled only the sour barf of five different species—maybe a hint of verbobrain actuating gas—and eased the lever farther.

Leia's face shrank to half a meter on the diagonal, and Han said, *I love you, Princess, even if you drive like a . . .*

He didn't finish. The words came out *Eeeyyyyeeee wooooobe ooooooo*, which wasn't half bad, considering.

Han eased the control lever back again, and Juun slid down the canopy and disappeared behind the instrument console.

Then the proximity alarm went off, and the color outside the canopy went from blue to red to blue to whirling stripes of silver. Suddenly, Leia's face was the proper size and shape—still far too green, but at least oval and no more than twenty-five centimeters from chin to hairline—and Han felt even sicker than before.

That was when C-3PO came tumbling up the access corridor. "Doomed!" He crashed to a halt behind the navigator's chair, then fell to the deck, flailing. "We're doomed for sure!"

Han immediately knew they were going to make it. He took control of the *Falcon* and began to fire attitude thrusters, slowly bringing their spin under control. There was just a hint of coolant sweetness in the recycled air—enough to mean they would have to decontaminate the ship, but not so much they would die before they had a chance.

A pair of small hands appeared at the top edge of the control panel, and Juun pulled himself up to peer over the edge. "Real space?"

"Yeah." Han glanced out the viewport and saw nothing but the veined, red sky of a still-cooling nebula. "I think."

"It is," Leia said. "The proximity alarm dropped us out of hyperspace."

"And we survived?" Juun sounded almost disappointed. His sunken eyes swung toward Han. "That wasn't in any of the history vids. Did *you* teach her that?"

"No," Leia said. "And it hasn't worked yet. There's still one tiny problem."

"As long as it's tiny," Han said, eyeing the white static on his sensor screen.

"Well—not really tiny." Leia used the attitude thrusters to spin the *Falcon* around, bringing into view the green, rapidly swelling disk of the planet they were about to crash into. "It *was* big enough to drop us out of hyperspace."

TWENTY-THREE

Jacen dropped out of the tik tree to discover that even here, in the muggy heart of her private jungle garden, Queen Mother Tenel Ka was not alone. Seated in a small sunken courtyard with her rust-colored braids hanging down the back of her sleeveless frock, she was surrounded by twenty courtiers—mostly male and attractive, all attired in absurd, hand-tailored imitations of the Queen Mother's rustic fashion. Tenel Ka could have that effect on people.

Jacen crept up silently behind a camouflaged sentry who was patrolling the musky foliage along the garden wall—the last of the palace's many layers of security—and grasped the man's neck. The fellow tried to spin and yell the alarm, but went limp as Jacen sent a paralyzing jolt of Force energy through his spine.

Still alert to her Jedi instincts, Tenel Ka felt the disturbance and turned on her bench, revealing a classic profile even more stunning than the one in Jacen's memory. He expanded his presence in the Force so she would not be alarmed, then lowered the unconscious sentry to the ground and stepped out of the shrubbery.

Several courtiers cried out and sprang forward to shield Tenel Ka, and three more sentries emerged from the foliage along the garden wall. The two guards with clear angles zipped blasterfire in the intruder's direction, while the third called for help. Jacen deflected the bolts with his palms, then reached out with the Force and jerked the blaster rifles from their hands.

"Cease fire!" Tenel Ka ordered, a bit late. "Stand down!"

The guards, already rushing Jacen with their hand blasters half free of their holsters, reluctantly obeyed. The nobles complied far less reluctantly.

Once Tenel Ka was satisfied her orders were being followed, she leapt onto the courtyard wall and, smiling warmly, opened her arms. Jacen was not surprised to see that the right one still ended at the elbow. After the sparring accident that had claimed the limb, Tenel Ka had refused an artificial replacement, keeping the stump as a reminder of the arrogance that had led to the mishap.

"Jacen!" she cried. "Welcome!"

"Thank you." It warmed Jacen's heart to find such an enthusiastic reception. "It's good to see you again, Queen Mother."

As Jacen stepped forward to receive her embrace, half a dozen burly Hapans blocked his way. One of them, an icy-eyed noble with neck-length blond hair and no left hand, glanced back at Tenel Ka. "This man is a friend of yours, Queen Mother?"

"Clearly, Droekle." Tenel Ka pushed between Droekle and an even larger noble missing an entire forearm. "Would I wish to hug him if he weren't?"

She pressed herself tightly enough to Jacen's chest for him to tell that a lot had changed in the last five years—all for the better. Jacen hugged her back and, noting the noxious glowers from her male courtiers, tried not to smirk.

"I apologize for entering this way," Jacen said. "But your social secretary refused to announce me. He kept telling me you were unavailable."

Tenel Ka released him and took a step back, her expression darkening. "Which one? I must see that he's corrected."

"No need." Jacen allowed himself the hint of a smile. "He has been."

"Is that so?"

Tenel Ka waited for him to elaborate. When he did not, she shrugged and took his hand, then jumped into the sunken courtyard to face her slack-jawed courtiers. Jacen was astonished to see that more than half had lost parts of their arms.

"Jacen is one of my oldest friends." She squeezed Jacen's hand, then looked up at him with a mischievous grin. "He was the boy who cut my arm off."

Though Jacen and Tenel Ka had long ago come to terms with that terrible accident and had developed a friendship bordering on romance, even he was taken aback by the bluntness of the announcement. The courtiers were left stammering—which was exactly what he sensed Tenel Ka wanted. Pulling him toward the far side of the courtyard, she slipped her arm through his and leaned her head against his shoulder.

"I would like to catch up with my friend," she called back. "Please amuse yourselves."

She guided him onto a stone path that wound its way through the jungle alongside a small stream. Though the lush foliage and gurgling water made it seem as though they were alone, Jacen could sense the guards shadowing them in the brush—and the courtiers following them down the path, just out of sight one curve behind.

Guessing this must be the normal state of affairs for Tenel Ka, Jacen said, "Thank you for taking the time to see me, Queen Mother."

"No—thank *you* for coming," Tenel Ka said. "You cannot know how refreshing it is to speak with someone who is not trying to win my hand or coax something out of me."

Jacen felt instantly guilty. "Actually, I *did* come to ask a favor. A big one."

"I know." Tenel Ka squeezed his arm and leaned closer to him. "That changes nothing I said. Hapan nobles never *ask*. They *arrange* or *contrive* or—if I am lucky—merely *persuade*. You would not believe what they do to curry favor."

Jacen raised his brow. "The amputations?"

"*Fencing accidents.*" Tenel Ka snorted. The path came to a jungle pond, complete with a waterfall and a small island rising out of the green water. "To judge by the number of limbs being preserved in Hapan cryovats, most of my idiot nobles have no idea which end of a sword to hold."

They stopped at the edge of the pond, and Jacen leaned down so that his voice would not carry up the path. "You *do* know we're not alone, don't you?"

"Of course." Tenel Ka turned and raised her voice. "Be gone—or I will ask Jacen to take your other arms."

The nobles retreated quickly, but Jacen could sense the sentries continuing to lurk in the bushes.

Tenel Ka sighed. "There are some things even a Queen Mother cannot order." She slipped off her shoes, then turned toward the island. "Would you like to get your feet wet?"

"Why not?" Jacen eyed the twenty-meter distance to the island. "Only our feet?"

"Trust me." Pulling him along, Tenel Ka stepped out onto the water. Her feet sank only to the ankles. "Walk only where I walk, or it will be more than your feet."

Jacen did as she ordered and found himself standing atop a stone pier concealed just beneath the surface of the murky water.

"The Secret Way," Tenel Ka said. "It is an ancient Hapan defense—and it leads to the only place I can ever be truly alone."

"Why do you put up with them?" Jacen followed her along a jagged pathway of sharp, seemingly random turns. "Those idiot nobles, I mean?"

"They have their uses," Tenel Ka said. "I allow one to sit at my side, then watch to see who seeks him out."

"And that tells you what?" Jacen asked. "Who wants something from you?"

"Everyone wants something from me, Jacen." They reached the island and stepped onto a mossy path that, Jacen suspected, was rarely trodden by any feet but Tenel Ka's. "But the families who *don't* change alliances when I change favorites—I know those are the advisers I should listen to."

"It seems very . . . intricate," Jacen said.

"Calculated," Tenel Ka said. She led the way into a shielding copse of paan trees, then sat down on one end of the only bench. "It is the Hapan way, Jacen. There is a use for everyone."

Knowing it would not be proper etiquette to assume, Jacen did not sit on the other end of the bench. "Including me?"

Tenel Ka looked away. "Even you, Jacen." She patted the bench beside her, then said, "Now the houses of my suitors will be united against you. It would be wise to watch what you eat while you are here."

"Thanks," Jacen said. "But I won't be staying."

"Of course not." Tenel Ka continued to look away, but Jacen sensed tears in her voice. "What is it you need from us?"

"You felt Raynar's call?" Jacen asked.

"Yes. In the end, I had to keep myself locked in the palace. I didn't know who it was from. I thought maybe . . ." When Tenel Ka turned to face him, her gray eyes were clear and steady, but she had not bothered to wipe the tear tracks from her cheeks. "I have heard that a colony of Killiks is threatening Chiss space."

In that moment, the entire weight of the last five years' loneliness fell on Jacen's heart, and he wanted nothing more than to take Tenel Ka in his arms and kiss her.

Instead, he said, "It's a complicated situation."

Jacen went on to recount his journey into the Colony, from his arrival at Lizil to his exploration of the *Tachyon Flier* to joining Jaina and the rest of the strike team on Jwlio. Tenel Ka's gaze never strayed from his face, and he described his slowly dawning awareness that the Killiks shared a collective mind, what Raynar had become, and Cilghal's theories about how the pheromones altered the Joiners' minds. This drew a cocked brow from Tenel Ka, and for a while she seemed a young Jedi Knight again, her thoughts consumed by adventure and mystery rather than intrigue and politics. Jacen ended by reporting the mysterious attacks against his parents and aunt and uncle, and by noting that the Killiks claimed to have no memory of Lomi or Welk.

"The two of them just disappeared after the crash," Jacen finished. "The Killiks insist Raynar was the only one aboard the *Flier*, even though I *know* he dragged both Lomi and Welk out of the fire."

Jacen did not say exactly *how* he knew. There was no reason to go into the subtleties of Aing-Tii flow-walking right now. Tenel Ka sat in deep silence for several moments, then swung around, straddling the bench, and faced him.

"What became of Em Teedee?"

"Lowbacca's translator droid?" Jacen asked.

"He *was* on the *Flier* when it was stolen," she pointed out.

"I think he was destroyed in the fire," Jacen said. "I found a melted lump of metal that kind of looked like him."

Tenel Ka sighed. "Too bad. He could be a very annoying droid, but I know Lowie would have liked to have him back." Their gazes met, and neither hurried to look away. "So, you've come to ask me to leave here and help track down Lomi and Welk, before they create a whole legion of Dark Jedi?"

Jacen's heart leapt. "You could do that?"

Tenel Ka smiled, but her eyes turned sad. "No, Jacen. It was a joke."

"I see," Jacen said, also growing a little sad. "Am I required to laugh?"

"Only if you wish to avoid offending the Queen Mother."

"Never." Jacen laughed dutifully, then added, "You still have a lot to learn about jokes."

"So *you* say." Tenel Ka raised her hand and made an elaborate wave skyward. "Everyone *here* seems to think my jokes are quite funny."

"And you trust them?"

"Only the ones who don't laugh," Tenel Ka admitted. She swung her leg back over the bench and assumed a more regal pose. "All right, Jacen. I confess, I cannot guess. What is it you require of us?"

"A battle fleet," he said. "For the Colony."

Tenel Ka's face did not show the surprise that Jacen sensed from her in the Force. "That is a great deal to ask. The Hapes Consortium is a member of the Galactic Alliance."

"Does that mean the Galactic Alliance makes your decisions for you?"

Tenel Ka's gray eyes turned steely. "It *means* that we try to avoid angering Alliance friends."

"It's more important to prevent this war," Jacen said. "The Chiss are pushing too hard, and the Killiks couldn't withdraw if they wanted to. It's going to erupt into full-blown carnage, unless something happens to give the Chiss pause and the Colony a reason to be patient."

"And why should it matter to the Hapan people if a border conflict on the other side of the galaxy *does* become war?"

"Because it would end in xenocide, one way or the other," Jacen answered.

Tenel Ka turned and looked up into the paan trees, and Jacen sensed in the silence her Jedi instincts battling her duties as the Hapan queen.

"The Killiks are tied to the history of the galaxy in a way we don't understand yet," Jacen said. "They were living in cities before humans learned to build, and they were a civilization before the Sith were spawned. They were here when Centerpoint and the Maw were constructed—and they were driven from Alderaan by the beings who did it."

Though Tenel Ka's gaze remained in the treetops, her eyes widened, and Jacen knew he was reaching her.

"Tenel Ka, the galaxy will turn on what happens next," Jacen said. "And the Killiks are the pivot point. We need time to figure this out, because it could be total war—or true and lasting peace."

Tenel Ka finally turned to look at him. "What about the will of the Force, Jacen? Why not trust it?"

The reference to the Jedi's new understanding of the Force made Jacen think of Vergere—the lost Master who had opened their eyes to so much of that new understanding—and he smiled at the first truth she had taught him: *Everything I tell you is a lie.*

To Tenel Ka, he said, "Should I trust a river because it wants to run downhill?"

Tenel Ka frowned. "I am the one who asks the questions on Hapes, Jedi Solo."

Jacen chuckled. "Okay. The Force isn't a deity, Tenel Ka. It's not self-conscious, and it isn't capable of caring what happens to us. It's a flow. Its only will is to remove that which blocks it. When we facilitate that flow, when we allow it to run through us to others, we're in harmony. We're using the light side."

"And the dark side?"

"Is when we block that flow and turn it to our own ends," Jacen said. "We keep it from others. And when we release it too quickly, we turn it from a nurturing stream into a destructive flood."

"Didn't Vergere teach that our *intentions* make an act dark or light?" Tenel Ka asked.

"She did," Jacen admitted. "And she was telling the truth, from a certain point of view. If you have good intentions, you tend to let the Force flow through you. If not, you tend to bottle it up inside, and it starts eating away at your good looks."

Tenel Ka looked at him from the corner of one eye. "I prefer my truths to remain true from *all* points of view."

"Sorry," Jacen said. "The Force is too big."

"And this is what you learned in the five years you were gone?"

"The core of it, yes."

Tenel Ka studied the ground for a moment, then looked back at him. "It took five years to learn *that*?"

"There was a lot of travel time," Jacen said.

Tenel Ka smiled and rolled her eyes, then asked, "What about our Killiks? Is the Force flowing through them, or into them?"

"Too early to say," Jacen said. "Raynar has grown incredibly powerful in a short time."

"And that doesn't scare you?"

"Of course it does," Jacen said. "But right now, he's trying to *avoid* a war. I'll be a lot more frightened when he stops."

Tenel Ka nodded. "Fact." She stood and extended her hand. "I think my suitors have had enough time to plot your death."

"I'm glad I could bring them together."

"Yes, you have been very useful that way." They started down the moss path toward the water. "I hope you will stay the night. It would be even more effective."

Jacen slowed. "Tenel Ka . . ." He did not need to wonder exactly what she was asking; he could feel it in the Force. "I didn't come here to . . . to become your paramour."

"You won't. Paramours are playthings." She stopped in full view of the pond's far bank and gave him a long, warm kiss. "And I would never play with you, Jacen Solo."

Jacen was beginning to feel very carried along—and spending the night could only help his chances of getting the fleet. "Then I'll stay," he said. "But it can only be one night."

"One night is fine," Tenel Ka said. "One night will be very useful."

TWENTY-FOUR

The observation deck was as stately, luxurious, and hushed as one would expect aboard the Bornaryn Trading Company's mighty flagship, the *Tradewyn*. A curving wall of transparisteel enclosed the cabin on three sides, offering an expansive view of the vast cargo fleet waiting permission to descend into the thin atmosphere of a dusty orange planet. In the distance, a starfighter security screen was scratching a grid of blue ions across a star-flecked backdrop.

The luxurious cabin was the kind of place that always made Tesar drool with nervousness. He drew air through his fangs to dry them, then followed his human escort past a long beverage bar toward a woman and two men waiting at the front of the deck. It was a long trip made longer by the fact that they had all turned to watch his approach—and by his fear of depositing a glob of saliva on the expensive wroshyr-wood floor.

Now that he was actually here, twenty steps from the Thul family, Tesar could not understand what had possessed him to track down the Bornaryn merchant fleet. He had overheard Master Skywalker and several others discussing how much should be told to Raynar's mother about her son's fate. A few hours later, Tesar had felt compelled to find Aryn Thul himself, and a few hours after that he had sneaked off Ossus in a Jedi StealthX. It had not begun to seem like a bad idea until he had arrived outside the *Tradewyn*'s docking bay, taking the ship's watch officer by surprise and causing the consternation that had scrambled the fleet's starfighter screen.

Tesar's escort stopped in front of the three humans and bowed to the woman. "Madame Thul, may I present Jedi Sebatyne—*Tesar* Sebatyne."

Dressed in a blue shimmersilk gown, Madame Thul was gaunt and short, with long chestnut hair and a regal bearing. She wore a sash striped with scarlet, yellow, and purple.

"Tesar was one of the Jedi Knights who accompanied Raynar on the Mission." The escort stressed the word *Mission* just enough to make clear that this was how they referred to Raynar's disappearance. "He agreed to leave his weapons in a locker."

"Thank you, Lonn." Madame Thul lifted her chin and examined Tesar head-to-toe, lingering a moment on his brown Jedi robe and the empty lightsaber clasp on his utility belt. "I know the name."

Suspecting he was expected to speak now, Tesar drew more air to dry his fangs—creating a small hiss that caused Madame Thul to flinch. The dark-haired man behind her fingered the hold-out blaster in his pocket and took a single step forward.

"Sorry. This one did not mean to scare you." Tesar felt a drop running down his front fang and sucked air across his teeth again. "It is very warm in here."

Madame Thul raised a carefully thinned brow. "Something to drink?"

"Yes, that would be good."

Madame Thul waited a moment, then prompted, "Endorian port? Bespin sparkle? Talhovian ale?"

"Do you have nerf milk?" Milk always slowed the drool. "Which planet doesn't matter."

The shadow of a smile flicked across Madame Thul's lips, then she turned to her servant. "Milk for Jedi Sebatyne, Lonn. We'll have our usual."

The servant bowed and departed to collect the drinks.

Madame Thul gestured to the blond man at her side. "This is my late husband's brother, Tyko." She did not bother to introduce the bodyguard. "Now, what can Bornaryn Trading do for the Jedi?"

"Nothing." Sensing he should probably not just blurt out the news about Raynar to this frail woman, Tesar said, "This one is here with newz."

"News?" Tyko asked.

"About Raynar."

Tyko scowled and slipped half a step forward, moving to shield his sister-in-law. "Raynar died at Myrkr."

"Yes," Tesar said. "After a fashion."

"After a fashion?" Madame Thul gasped. "You mean he's alive?"

"After a fashion, yes," Tesar said, happy he had broken the news gently. "That is what I—"

"My son is *alive?*"

Madame Thul's knees buckled, and she would have hit the floor had Tesar not reached out and caught her beneath the armpits. He waited while the stunned bodyguard jerked his hand from the blaster pocket, then laid her back into the man's arms.

"S-sorry." Tesar sucked more air to dry his fangs. "This one did not mean to touch her. When he saw her falling, he just—"

"It's . . . it's okay. Thank you." Madame Thul glanced up at her bodyguard. "Perhaps we should sit down, Gundar."

"Of course."

Gundar returned Madame Thul to her feet and guided her toward a chair. Tesar started to follow, but Tyko put a hand on his chest.

Tesar reacted as most Barabels would to being touched by a stranger. He grabbed Tyko's wrist and pulled it past his face, bringing the elbow into perfect biting position.

"Stop!" Tyko cried. "What are you doing?"

Tesar looked down at the man out of one eye. "You did not challenge this one?"

"N-no!" Tyko was up on his toes, being held so that his feet barely touched the floor. "I just wanted to talk to you!"

"We *were* talking," Tesar pointed out.

"Alone." Tyko's eyes slid toward the krayt-leather couches where Madame Thul's bodyguard had deposited her. "Quietly."

"My brother-in-law is being protective," Madame Thul explained from her seat. Her blue eyes shifted to Tyko. "That's hardly necessary, Tyko. I'm sure I can judge for myself whether *Jedi* Sebatyne has come selling starlight."

"If he *is* a Jedi," Tyko said. "I doubt anyone here can tell one Barabel in a robe from another."

Tesar saw the doubt flash through Madame Thul's eyes and realized he might be asking the Thuls to take a lot on faith. He released Tyko's arm and turned toward the bar, where the servant had gathered their drinks on a silvertine tray. Tesar reached out with the Force and lifted the tray out of the servant's hands, then floated it over to Madame Thul.

Her surprise quickly turned to approval. "Thank you, Jedi Sebatyne." She removed a small crystal goblet filled with burgundy liquid, then shot her brother-in-law an amused look. "I think that establishes Tesar's bona fides quite sufficiently."

Tesar floated the tray over to Tyko.

"It would be hard to argue." Tyko took a golden-rimmed snifter that contained a clear yellow liquor.

Tesar took his milk, then returned the tray to the astonished servant and followed Tyko over to Madame Thul. He sat down on a padded tail-stool the bodyguard offered.

"Now, Jedi Sebatyne, tell me about my son," Madame Thul ordered. "What does *after a fashion* mean?"

"The ship he was aboard crashed in the Unknown Regionz," Tesar began. "There was a fire."

"Oh." Madame Thul reached for her brother-in-law's hand. "Go on."

"He was taken in by a nest of sentient insectz," Tesar said.

"The Killiks?" Tyko glanced at Madame Thul. "Our agents have been hearing reports of an insect colony in the Unknown Regions."

"They call themselvez the Kind," Tesar clarified. "Raynar'z nest is the Unu. It is the Colony'z king nest, and he is the Prime Unu."

"That doesn't surprise me." There was a touch of pride in Madame Thul's voice. "Raynar has always been such a natural leader."

"Always," Tyko agreed. "What exactly is the Prime? The chairman?"

"*Voice* would be closer," Tesar said. He started to explain how other species sometimes joined the collective mind of the Killiks, then felt a restraining influence and decided to leave it for later, when the Thuls would be better able to understand. "He representz the Colony, and sees that itz Will is done."

Tyko nodded as though he understood exactly what Tesar meant. "The operating officer. Not quite as high as the chairman, but more important in terms of real power."

"That hardly matters, Tyko," Madame Thul said. "We'll groom him to take my place when he returns home."

Madame Thul may have missed the alarmed flash in Tyko's eyes, but Tesar did not.

"This one does not think Raynar will return," he said. Part of Tesar still wanted to bite Tyko's arm off, but another part realized that it was important to avoid making an enemy of the man—to be certain Tyko understood that Raynar did not threaten his position. "Raynar is too important to the Colony."

"Of course he is," Madame Thul said, addressing Tesar. "How long will it take him to groom a replacement?"

"This one is sorry," Tesar said. "He is not making himself clear.

Raynar will not be returning. He has joined the Colony. He has become Unu. He has become the UnuThul."

"Are you really trying to tell me that my son has become an insect?" Madame Thul demanded.

"Not physically," Tesar said. "But, yes."

"By the Core!" Madame Thul studied him for a moment, then grew pale. "You're serious!"

Tesar nodded, and the purpose of his visit finally began to grow clear to him.

"Unu wishez to establish a relationship between the Colony and Bornaryn Trading," he said. "A *confidential* relationship."

"And *you're* the authorized agent?" Tyko asked.

Tesar considered a moment, then said, "For now."

Tyko accepted this with a nod, then turned to Madame Thul. "I've heard that there is large demand for the shine-balls and amber ale the independent smugglers are bringing back from the Unknown Regions."

Madame Thul seemed too shocked to reply. She merely nodded, then drained the contents of her goblet and held it up for the servant. "Lonn—"

"Of course, madame." Lonn took the empty goblet and replaced it with a full one. "I shall keep them coming."

TWENTY-FIVE

Even full hazmat gear could not prevent Alema from appearing immodest and just a little bit debauched. The suit she had selected was two sizes too small, stretched so tightly over her svelte curves that it was apparent she had decided to leave her underclothes—if she owned any—aboard the crippled *Falcon*. Leia shook her head in weary amusement, wondering whom Alema was hoping to attract on the deserted planet that had jerked them out of hyperspace. Then again, had *Leia* spent her formative years as a dancing slave in a Kala'uun ryll den—or merely been a Twi'lek female—she, too, might have felt comfortable only when on display.

Alema glanced back, no doubt feeling Leia's scrutiny through the Force. "Is something wrong?"

"Not really." Leia dropped her gaze to the Twi'lek's seat area. "Just wondering if that suit is going to split."

Alema craned around to look, then gave a roguish smile. "Only if I bend over."

Juun came down the access corridor holding Alema's utility belt and lightsaber. "You forgot this, Jedi Rar."

"I don't think we'll be needing weapons," Leia said. "The scan showed no animal life at all."

"Better to be safe," Juun said.

"Why, thank you, Jae." Alema raised her arms and let him buckle on the belt. When the short-armed Sullustan had to press his face against her stomach, she smiled and added, "You're always so considerate."

Silently cursing the Sullustan's growing infatuation with Alema, Leia had C-3PO fetch her own belt and buckled it on herself. After a thorough inspection of the *Falcon* had revealed no trace of insect stowaways, the Solos had been forced to turn their suspicions in other directions. Their plan had been to keep Alema separated from her weapons until Leia figured out whether she was the one who had been sabotaging the *Falcon*—but no one had told that to Juun, of course. He was the only other suspect.

Leia passed the Twi'lek four twenty-liter buckets, then lowered the boarding ramp. A cool wind was hissing across the marsh grass, carrying on its breath the fragrance of a carpet of nearby blossoms. Not far beyond, a ribbon of open water purled past, vanishing into the dark wall of a distant conifer forest.

"It's stunning!" Leia led the way down the ramp, carrying four empty buckets of her own. "It reminds me of Alderaan—unspoiled and beautiful."

"Yes, it's very . . . natural." Alema was looking above the forest, at a single jagged mountain silhouetted against the veined ruddiness of the nebular sky. "Not a bad place to crash—"

"Nobody crashed," Han said over their headsets. "And nobody's going to be marooned, either—if you two will get under the drive unit with those collection buckets."

"On our way." Under her breath, Leia added, "Hutt."

"I heard that."

"Good."

When Leia stepped off the ramp into the grass, the ground felt soft and spongy under her feet. She parted the grass and found water seeping up around her boot.

"We'll have to make this fast," Leia reported. "The ground's a little soft here."

"Ready when you are," Han replied.

Leia pulled on her hazmat hood and ducked under the *Falcon*. She tromped down the grass beneath the hyperdrive hull-access panel, then positioned her collection buckets under likely-looking leak points. Only when she finished did she notice that Alema was out beyond the boarding ramp, kneeling over a magenta blossom the size of a Wookiee's hand.

"Alema, we're kind of in a hurry here." Leia wondered if the Twi'lek was intentionally dawdling, hoping the *Falcon* would sink in the soft ground—and then she put the idea out of her mind. This was going to be dangerous enough without Alema sensing her suspicion through the Force. "We can look at flowers later."

"Sorry." Alema glanced in her direction, but did not rise. "Are you sure there are no animals here? No insects or birds or flying mammals?"

"The scan didn't reveal any," Leia said. "And I've seen nothing to suggest it was wrong."

"Interesting." Alema plucked the flower off its stem and brought it over to Leia. "If there are no insects or animals, what pollinates the flowers?"

Leia studied the blossom. Its structure was much the same as flowers across the galaxy, with a stamen, anther, and pollen.

"Good question," Leia said, surprised the Twi'lek had noticed. "I didn't think Ryloth had any true flowers."

"We have sex," Alema replied. "And males who want sex bring—"

"I get the picture," Leia said. "The answer is I don't know. Wind seems pretty inefficient, and that's about the only pollen-transfer agent I can see."

Han's voice came over their headsets. "If you two are done talking about the birds and the bees, I'd like to change out this coolant line—*before* the *Falcon* sinks to her belly."

"It's my fault." Alema's voice assumed the same purring quality she used with Juun. "I hope you can forgive me."

"That remains to be seen," Han said.

Leia winced at Han's cool tone, but saw no sign that Alema had sensed truth beneath his words. The Twi'lek simply retrieved her own buckets and positioned them beneath the *Falcon,* then curled her lekku into her hood and pulled it on.

"Ready."

Han grunted, and one corner of the hyperdrive hull panel sagged open. Toxic red coolant began to pour out. Leia quickly moved one of the buckets into position to catch the primary flow, then placed three others beneath adjacent drips.

It took only a minute to fill the first bucket. Alema passed an empty to Leia and moved the other one out of the way. They repeated the process four more times, carefully placing the filled buckets five meters away, where they were unlikely to be accidentally overturned.

Finally, the flow slowed to a drip, and Han said, "We're done. Just catch those last drips, and we'll be ready."

"Affirmative." Under her breath, Leia added, "For all the good it will do."

"Relax," Han said. "I can handle this repair. No problem."

The final drops of coolant fell from the hull panel. When they moved the last buckets aside, Leia was surprised to find the first little bit that had fallen on the flattened grass was evaporating before her eyes.

"Look at that," Leia said.

"It killed the grass," Alema observed. "That's to be expected."

"It should have killed a lot more," Leia replied. "And look at how fast it's drying up. It's not that hot—or dry—around here."

Alema shrugged. "Maybe the grass is absorbent." She glanced at the vast field surrounding the *Falcon,* then added, "I don't think we need to worry about the environmental damage."

They carefully wiped the access panel down with absorption pads, then Leia reactivated her throat mike.

"Okay, it's clean. You can close up now."

The panel hissed into place, then Han asked, "How much did you get?"

Leia eyed the buckets. "About a hundred and twenty liters."

"That's all?"

"Maybe one thirty," she said. "No more."

A disappointed sigh came over the headsets. "It'll have to do— but don't spill a drop. We need it all."

"Copy." Leia picked up a bucket, using both hands on the handle, and started for the *Falcon*'s ramp. "We'd better take it in one bucket at a—"

A liquid *thunk* sounded behind Leia, and she turned to find Alema holding a broken handle. At the Twi'lek's feet lay three overturned buckets, an eighty-liter pool of hyperdrive coolant slowly spreading across the ground.

"Alema!" Leia was trying to feel genuinely surprised, rather than disappointed, to avoid giving Alema any hint that this was exactly what she had expected. "What happened?"

"The handle broke," Alema said. "I'm—"

The Twi'lek's eyes grew large behind her faceplate, and suddenly she sprang toward the *Falcon*'s prow in a diving roll. An instant later, Meewalh and Cakhmaim dropped out of the ship's far-side air lock, their blaster rifles spraying stun bolts at the place Alema had just been standing.

Blasted Jedi danger sense.

Alema came up on her knees, her hazmat-gloved hands fumbling for her lightsaber.

"Did they get her?" Han asked over the headset.

Leia and Alema answered together. "No!"

The Noghri spun toward the *Falcon*'s prow and opened fire again, but Alema was already leaping behind a landing strut. Leia dropped her own bucket and started to circle behind the Twi'lek, fumbling at her lightsaber through the thick hazmat gloves.

"Wait!" Alema cried. "What's this about?"

"Spilled coolant," Han replied over the comm.

"It was an accident!"

"Sorry, kid," Han said. "We were watching on the hull cam. You broke the handle."

The four remaining buckets of coolant rose and went flying toward Meewalh and Cakhmaim. The Noghri dodged easily, but the maneuver gave Alema time to pull off her hood and gloves and snap her lightsaber off her belt.

Blasted telekinesis.

Leia pulled off her own gloves and hood, then grabbed her lightsaber and continued toward the prow. Though she felt certain that the Colony was behind Alema's treachery, Leia could not help feeling hurt, angry, and confused. Somehow, the Twi'lek's vulnerability felt like a betrayal in itself, and Leia could not help wondering whether Jaina had really been as surprised as she seemed when Alema announced her plans to return aboard the *Falcon*—or if her own daughter had known of the plan and kept silent about it.

Alema glanced in Leia's direction, but then Cakhmaim and Meewalh were fanning out toward her flanks, firing as they ran. The Twi'lek spun from her hiding place, her silver blade deflecting the Noghri's stun bolts back at them as she ran.

Han continued to chatter at Alema over the headsets. "What we can't figure out is *why*. What'd we ever do to you?"

"We told you," Alema insisted. "It was an accident!"

"You *kicked* over two buckets," Han said.

"We had no . . . choice." Alema launched herself through the air, flipping and corkscrewing closer to Cakhmaim, turning bolt after bolt in Meewalh's direction. "You betrayed the Colony!"

"*We* betrayed *them*?" Han was incredulous. "Saba's the one lying up there half dead."

"You see?" Alema landed. "You blame the Colony! We can't—" She directed one of Cakhmaim's stun bolts into Meewalh's chest. "—let you poison the Masters' council against us!"

Meewalh dropped to her knees, but kept firing. Leia ducked under the *Falcon*'s prow, ignited her own lightsaber at midguard, and raced to attack.

Alema did not even show Leia the respect of turning around. She simply raised a leg and planted a hazmat boot squarely in Leia's stomach and sent her flying back into a landing strut, then directed a second stun bolt into Meewalh and turned all her attention to Cakhmaim.

"How's it going down there?" Han asked.

"Aaaag . . ." Leia answered, trying to suck some air back into her lungs. "Ooog . . ."

"That good?"

Seeing that his blaster rifle was doing him more harm than good, Cakhmaim tossed it aside and drew his favorite weapon, a thin durasteel club connected by a hilt cord to a short sickle. Alema continued her advance more slowly, her lightsaber weaving a silver shield in front of her.

Leia really didn't want to turn this into a killing fight, but neither did she want to die marooned on an empty planet. She pointed to the bucket she had left near the boarding ramp and used the Force to send it flying at Alema, then pointed at Cakhmaim's discarded blaster rifle and sent *that* flying as well.

Alema pivoted away from the bucket and ducked the blaster rifle.

Then Cakhmaim was on her, club-and-sickle whirling, lashing sickle-low and club-high, then sickle-high and club-low, hands flashing as he switched from one weapon to the other. Alema fell back jumping, skipping, ducking, trying to land just one parry with her sizzling blade and send her attacker's weapons spinning away. Cakhmaim's reflexes were too quick for her. Every time she turned her wrists to intercept an attack, he reversed his whirling weapons and hit her where she was unprotected, clubbing her in the ribs, slashing her across the thigh, always forcing her to retreat.

Han continued to speak over the headsets. "Hang tight, Leia." His voice was strained, which was not surprising, given the length and diameter of the twisting access tunnel that led to the hyperdrive coolant drain. "Be there . . . anytime now!"

Leia pushed off the strut and rushed Alema with a heavy heart. Though she still intended to capture the Twi'lek alive if possible, she knew a killing fight when she found herself in one. She reached striking range and, activating her blade, swung for the head.

Alema had no choice but to drop to her haunches. Cakhmaim was all over the Twi'lek, catching her weapons-hand with the sickle and whipping it around, slashing the tendons that controlled her fingers. The lightsaber deactivated and went tumbling away. Cakhmaim brought his club around for a temple strike, but at the last instant must have glimpsed the sorrow in Leia's face and dropped it below the ear for a knockout blow.

Alema took full advantage of the switch, turning to take the strike on her lekku, then continuing around, bringing the palm of her good hand up under the Noghri's chin, putting the power of the Force into the blow and driving him off his feet. Cakhmaim's head hit the underside of the *Falcon* with a dull *clang*, then he dropped limply into the smashed marsh grass.

Leia slammed the butt of her lightsaber into Alema's head, striking to subdue but striking hard. The Twi'lek staggered and looked as though she might pitch forward. Leia cocked her arm to strike again . . . and felt one of the Twi'lek's legs catching her across the ankle, swinging through to sweep her off her feet.

Leia landed on the back of her head so hard that, even with the soft ground, her vision began to narrow. She braced a hand by her hip and instantly brought her feet under her, but Alema was already rolling to her feet, facing Leia, her good arm reaching out to call her lightsaber.

Leia reached out in the Force and tried to wrench the weapon away, but her head was spinning, and the lightsaber floated straight into Alema's hand. With both Noghri lying limp and helpless in the grass, Leia was on her own. She didn't like her odds. Her ankle was beginning to throb, and she wasn't sure she'd be able to stand on it.

"Han?"

"Almost . . . out."

A frightening darkness came to Alema's eyes, and she took one step toward Leia. "Put down your weapon, Princess. There's no need for us to fight. Without coolant . . ." The Twi'lek stopped midsentence, apparently realizing how she had been tricked, then said, "You have extra coolant."

Leia shrugged. The gesture felt like it would split her head. "We had to find out."

"You can still lay down your weapon," Alema said. "It would be better if you did."

Leia eyed the unconscious Noghri. If they had failed to take Alema by surprise, it seemed unlikely that Leia could win a lightsaber duel—even if Alema would be fighting with her off hand.

"You're right about one thing," Leia said. "There's no need for us to fight. I've been reaching out to Luke in the Force."

Alema remained where she was, about five steps from Leia—safely out of attack range, but close enough to spring.

"And?"

"And the Masters already know that something happened to Saba," Leia said. Her vision had returned to normal, but now her head was throbbing worse than her ankle. "They know the Skywalkers might have had a stowaway, too. My guess is they'll assume the Colony is responsible."

"You're lying."

"You're a Jedi Knight," Leia said. "You *should* know I'm not."

Alema's eyes narrowed, and Leia felt the Twi'lek probing her mind, searching for any hint of deceitfulness.

Leia made no attempt to resist. "The Colony's best chance to win the Masters' support—its *only* chance—is for you to go to Ossus *now* and explain what really happened."

Alema's lightsaber crackled to life.

"You won't win any friends for the Colony that way," Leia pointed out.

Alema shrugged.

"It doesn't *matter* to you?" Leia began to drag the Force into herself, preparing to pull herself to her feet the instant the Twi'lek even *looked* like she was going to advance. "I thought you sabotaged us because . . ."

Leia let the sentence trail off, suddenly realizing how badly she had misunderstood the situation. Alema did not *know* why she had sabotaged the *Falcon*. She thought she was protecting the Colony when she was actually damaging any chance it had of winning the Masters' sympathies . . . and why?

"Luke and Mara! Or . . . *Ben*?" Leia's heart felt like it would burst with rage. "You ungrateful—"

Alema sprang.

Leia activated her lightsaber and blocked the Twi'lek's first attack, then stretched out with the Force and used it to pull herself to her feet a dozen paces away. Alema started after her, coming fast but under control, and that was when a muffled *thud* reverberated from inside the *Falcon*—Han finally dropping out of the hyperdrive access tunnel into the aft service corridor.

Alema glanced up, and Leia had an idea.

"Han, I think she's figured us out!" Leia screamed into her headset. "She's looking toward the drive exhaust."

"The drive exhaust?" Han managed to make his confusion sound like alarm. "Well, stop her! If she cuts one of those—"

"Han!"

"Yeah?"

"Enough!" Leia said. Han certainly knew his own ship well enough to realize that the aft escape pod discharged a couple of meters forward of the drive exhaust, and she would just have to trust him to figure out the significance of that. "She has a headset, too. Remember?"

"All right . . . just stop her!"

Leia raised her lightsaber and charged. Alema looked first puzzled, then worried; then finally she pivoted away and blocked as Leia swung at her head.

Leia kicked wildly at the Twi'lek's leading foot, forcing her to step back, then swung again at the head. Alema blocked and stepped into the attack, trying to work her way past Leia to strike at the drive exhaust.

Leia attacked hard, smashing her knee into Alema's ribs, forcing herself not look toward the escape pod hatch, to not even *think* about it . . .

Alema surprised Leia with a spinning hook kick that caught her across the shins and sent her sprawling onto her face just centimeters from a pool of spilled coolant.

Han's panicked voice came over the headset. "Leia! Stop her!"

Leia looked up to find Alema racing past, only three steps shy of the pod hatch but a full meter off to one side. She locked her blade into the activated position, then rose to her knees and threw her lightsaber at the Twi'lek's shoulder.

Whether Alema sensed or heard the blade coming did not matter. She dodged away—and that was when the escape pod's outer hatch blew, catching the Twi'lek along her whole left side, buckling her knees and leaving her lying motionless in the grass.

By the time Leia scrambled to her feet and raced over to make sure Alema would not be getting up again, C-3PO was already riding the rear cargo elevator down with a hypo full of tranquilizer in his hand.

"Well done, Mistress Leia!" C-3PO said. "Captain Solo said all along that experience—"

"Give me that!" Leia snatched the hypo from the droid's hands and knelt down to inject the Twi'lek . . . then nearly fainted as a terrible pain shot up her leg. "Blast! If I'm going to make a habit of this, I really have to practice more."

TWENTY-SIX

At the near end of the academy training grounds, the youngest students were practicing Force leaps, stepping to the mark with knitted brows, then launching themselves one after the other over a three-meter cross ray. Most cleared the red beam with a simple arcing dive, then dropped into the landing area headfirst, relying on the safety repulsors to break their falls. But a few—especially from the more agile species—executed graceful somersaults and came down on their own feet. Some of the children in line noticed Luke and Mara emerging from the access tunnel and began to point and whisper, so Luke made a show of nodding approval as the next few jumpers cleared the beam.

"These are the Woodoos," Luke explained to their guest, Aristocra Chaf'orm'bintrani of the Chiss Ascendancy. "They're our youngest students."

"Your youngest?" A few centimeters shorter than Luke, the Aristocra was relatively small for a Chiss, with a blue angular face just beginning to sag with age. "How young are they?"

"The Woodoos are generally between five and seven years old, Formbi," Mara said, calling the Aristocra by his core name. "Though that varies by species—some mature at markedly different rates."

"Yes—well, we wouldn't have that problem in the Ascendancy." Formbi folded his hands behind his back and peered across the running track at the children. "Which one is your son?"

Luke felt the pang in his wife's chest as clearly as the one in his own, but when Mara answered, her voice betrayed no hint of her emotions. "Our son doesn't attend the Jedi academy."

"How strange." Formbi continued to watch the Woodoos. "My file lists his age as seven."

"Ben is withdrawing from the Force right now." As much as it pained him, Luke had no intention of hiding the fact. That would have implied he was ashamed, and he was not. "We don't know why."

Formbi turned. "I didn't know children could do that."

"Most can't," Mara said. "Ben demonstrated exceptional power from birth. This only confirms how gifted he is."

"I see," Formbi said. "I'm sorry, then, that he is choosing not to develop his potential."

"We're not," Luke said. He felt Mara's ire rising, but the smile on her face remained polite. Winning Formbi's cooperation was going to be difficult enough without allowing Chiss manners to become an issue. "Children must *want* to be at the academy to succeed. We don't force anyone to attend, and we do everything we can to encourage them to enjoy their time here."

"We can even arrange employment for their parents on Ossus—some are assistant trainers here at the academy," Mara said. "And we encourage students to develop at their own pace. So when Ben *is* ready, his natural capabilities will allow him to establish himself very quickly."

"I have no doubt." Formbi turned back to the training grounds, looking past the Woodoos to where the Rontos were practicing telekinesis by smashing giant bean bags against each other. "But I'm sure you didn't summon me here to discuss Jedi training techniques."

"As a matter of fact, we did," Luke said. They had also asked Soontir Fel to come, but he had politely declined, explaining it would not do for anyone on the Defense Fleet general staff to consort with Ascendancy enemies. "We want you to understand what goes into the training of a modern Jedi."

"Hoping to impress me so much that I'll persuade the Ruling Circle to let you handle the Qoribu problem?" Formbi asked.

"Precisely," Mara said. "And it was an invitation, not a summons."

"Funny," Formbi said. "Your message mentioned the Brask Oto."

"That's right," Luke said. The Brask Oto was a Chiss battle station he and Mara had saved during an earlier trip into Ascendancy territory. "We wanted you to know it was authentic."

Formbi smiled. "As I said—a summons. We Chiss always repay debts of honor." He waved a hand toward the interior of the training complex. "Please, impress me."

Luke led the way across the running track to the slidewalk that circled the inner fields, then heard an alarmed whistle behind them. He glanced back to find R2-D2 traversing a banked turn, one tread off the ground and perilously close to tipping over.

"Your droid seems rather intoxicated," Formbi observed.

"A memory fault is playing havoc with his systems." Luke reached out in the Force and carried R2-D2 over to the slidewalk. "I don't want it repaired until we find a way to extract some information stored on the chip."

Formbi watched with an amused expression as the droid settled onto the slidewalk behind him. "And this information is so valuable you must keep the droid with you at all times?"

Luke thought for a moment, then said, "Yes." The truth was that R2-D2 kept scheduling himself for a chip replacement, so Luke had decided to keep him nearby until the Galactic Alliance's best slicer, Zakarisz Ghent, arrived to bypass the security program protecting the memory chip. "It could solve a very old mystery for us."

"Then I wish you luck," Formbi said. He pointed to a circle of twelve-year-olds—Banthas—sitting cross-legged around a single happy-looking nerf, waving their fingers and sending the contented beast waddling back and forth among them. "What in space are they doing?"

"Mind tag," Mara explained. "It's how they develop their persuasive abilities."

Formbi gave her a sharp look. "I trust that's not how you intend to persuade me?"

"The technique only works on the weak-minded," Luke said.

"And no Jedi would ever consider a Chiss Aristocra to be weak-minded."

"Good," he said. "I was given to believe Jedi Knights are rarely fools."

"We generally try to train that out before anyone becomes a Jedi Knight, yes," Mara said.

"Then why do you insist on involving yourselves at Qoribu?" Formbi's voice was casual, as though it were only an idle question. "The conflict is of no concern to the Galactic Alliance."

"The Jedi serve the Force." Luke was keeping an eye on R2-D2, making sure he did not wander off. "Our concerns reach well beyond the Galactic Alliance."

Formbi's gaze grew hard. "Into the Ascendancy?"

"Into the Colony, at least," Luke said.

Formbi looked away, focusing his attention on a group of fourteen-year-olds who were using their lightsabers to bat live blaster bolts back and forth. These students had no nickname; once students built their first lightsabers, they were known simply as apprentices.

"You understand nothing about the Colony," Formbi said, almost absently. "If you did, you would leave it to us."

"We understand that what you're doing at Qoribu comes close to violating Chiss law," Mara said. "Unless the Ascendancy has bent from a thousand years of tradition?"

"A lot has changed in the Ascendancy." Formbi's voice grew resigned. "But not that. It remains unlawful for the Chiss to be the aggressor people."

"I've always admired that about the Ascendancy," Luke said.

"In truth, I find it rather quaint," Formbi replied. "But, having no desire to find myself exiled, I'll follow the law—even if it means the destruction of the Ascendancy itself."

A line of ten-year-old students appeared ahead, racing toward Luke and the others against the flow of the slidewalk. Formbi started to step aside so they could pass, but Mara used the Force to gently tug him back.

"Please, Aristocra," she said. "They'll be disappointed if we rob them of their chance to show off."

Formbi eyed the chubby Kitonak girl at the head of the line, then cocked his brow when she suddenly sprang off the slidewalk, turned a Force flip over his head, and landed gracefully—if somewhat heavily—behind him. The rest of the students followed suit, beaming in pride as they somersaulted over Luke and the others. Once Formbi grew accustomed to the game, he even encouraged the students by pretending to flinch before each one jumped.

"Thank you for indulging them, Aristocra," Luke said. "The dining halls will be buzzing tonight with how they actually drew a reaction from you."

"My pleasure," Formbi said. "As long as they understand the difference when they become Jedi Knights."

"They will," Mara said. "Chiss courage is legendary around here—which is why I'm so puzzled about your fear of Killiks."

"If you are puzzled, it is only because you are ignorant of the Colony's true nature."

"Then enlighten us," Luke said. "The sooner the Jedi understand the situation, the sooner we will find a solution and end our presence at Qoribu."

"And if there is no solution?"

"It would be better to discover that now," Luke said, "before any more of our Jedi become like Raynar."

Formbi frowned. "Who is Raynar?"

"Raynar Thul," Mara said. "He went MIA during the war. He was presumed dead, but apparently his ship crashed inside the Colony."

"A nest of Killiks rescued him and saved his life," Luke said.

"Saved his life?" Formbi sounded surprised. "When did this Raynar come up missing? About six years ago?"

"Close." Luke began to have a sinking feeling. "It was a little over seven."

"I see." Formbi's gaze turned inward. "That explains it."

"Explains what?" Mara demanded.

"The Defense Fleet reconnaissance corps has been watching the Colony for centuries," Formbi said. "It has been slowly expanding over time, but it wasn't considered a threat."

"Until recently," Mara surmised.

"Correct," Formbi said. "The insects—Killiks, as you call them—are clearly intelligent, but they've customarily shown little concern for life. When one was injured, its companions would simply abandon it, and when food grew scarce, whole columns would just wander off to die."

"And that changed six years ago," Luke said.

Formbi nodded. "The first satellite nests appeared on our border, and we began to notice an exponential population increase. Imagine our surprise when we learned that now they had hospitals to care for their ailing and were using interstellar trade to alleviate the cyclic food shortages that once kept their populations in check."

"And *that* frightened the Ascendancy into sending your defoliators to give nature a helping hand?" Mara asked.

"No." Formbi accepted the criticism in her question without visible emotion. "We didn't make that decision until later—after we had discovered how dangerous they were."

The slidewalk carried them past a sunken basin, where a group of adolescent apprentices stood meditating under the watchful eye of a training Jedi Knight. They were surrounded by twenty grown adults, who were shouting insults at them and pelting them with missiles ranging from kitchen leftovers to sting balls.

"My word!" Formbi gasped. "What kind of drill is that?"

"It's a centering exercise," Luke said proudly. He was counting on this part of the tour to persuade Formbi to speak on their behalf on the Chiss capital world, Csilla. "Young Jedi must learn to detach themselves from their emotions, to remain focused regardless of whatever they are feeling at the time."

"There are several other versions," Mara added. "A five-day fast while the rest of the academy feasts around them, a three-day swim in a warm bubble pool, an all-night tickle where they're forbidden to laugh."

"That may sound silly, but that's actually the most difficult test," Luke said. "And if they fail, they repeat the other exercises."

Formbi stared at them as though they had told him they were Sith Lords. "You people make the Ssi-ruuk look kind!"

"Jedi Knights often find themselves in tumultuous situations," Luke replied. "Their judgment must remain sound, no matter what they are feeling."

"Sound judgment is a warrior's best weapon," Formbi agreed. "Though I don't understand what the Jedi have against laughing."

The slidewalk carried them past the centering exercise, and R2-D2's presence began to fade. Luke looked back and, finding the confused droid facing the wrong direction, used the Force to lift him back to the group.

Mara was already grilling Formbi again. ". . . convinced the Ascendancy the Killiks are dangerous?"

Formbi hesitated a moment, then asked, "Do you recall our first meeting, when I welcomed you aboard the *Chaf Envoy* to examine the wreck of the Outbound Flight?"

"How could we forget?" Luke said. "The whole mission was a gambit to lure the Vagaari into attacking, so you could carry the war to them legally."

"The choice was theirs," Formbi said defensively. "But yes. And do you happen to remember how many ruling families there were at the time?"

"Nine," Mara said instantly. When it came to politics, she rarely forgot a fact. "But five years later, when we visited Csilla, the number was four. I assumed the discrepancy to be a result of a war with the Vagaari."

"Not directly," Formbi said. "But the Third Vagaari War did leave us with a labor shortage, and *that* led to the discrepancy."

"I'm afraid I don't understand," Luke said. "Were the losses of some families so heavy—"

"Several families began to hire entire nests from the Colony. It seemed the perfect solution. The insects were plentiful, industrious, and not averse to risk. This was a couple of years before your Raynar arrived, and they began to care about surviving." Formbi winced at how that sounded, then hastened to add, "Of course, we were careful not to take advantage."

"Of course." Luke had the unhappy feeling that he saw where this was leading. "Didn't you know about the Joiners?"

"We took precautions," Formbi said. "Very stringent precautions."

"That still didn't work," Mara surmised.

"They worked," Formbi replied. "Until someone started sabotaging them."

"The Killiks?" Luke asked.

Formbi frowned. "We value fools no more than the Jedi, Master Skywalker. The precautions remained solely under our control."

There was a moment of silence, then Mara asked, "And?"

"We don't really understand," Formbi admitted. "It may have been interfamily rivalries. All we know is that the precautions broke down, and before we realized it, two entire families had become Joiners."

"Only two?" Luke asked. "What about the other missing families?"

"Three of the families had become critically dependent on insect labor," Formbi replied. "There was a dispute over the best course of action."

"The Ascendancy had a civil war?" Luke gasped.

"Chiss do not have civil wars, Master Skywalker," Formbi replied. "We have disagreements. The matter was resolved before your visit to Csilla—though I do believe you were witness to some reverberations."

"The attack on Soontir Fel?" Mara asked. "I thought that concerned the aid he provided the Galactic Alliance against the Yuuzhan Vong."

"It is easy to disagree with the policies of someone who has destroyed your family," Formbi said. "Fel has a habit of being too merciful for his own good."

The slidewalk carried them to the training field that had been Luke's destination all along, a jumbled course full of traps, hazards, and obstacles. Two teams of senior apprentices—one team large and strong, the other small and quick—were running back and forth through the course, using long-handled rackets, stunblasters, and Force telekinesis to pass half a dozen crackling jet-balls to each other through the air. In the midst of the crashing bodies and acrobatic power plays, a single referee was struggling to maintain order.

Motioning Formbi and Mara along, Luke stepped off the slidewalk—then reached out with a mental hand and pulled R2-D2 to his side. Luke did not launch into a description of the game, however; he still had some questions about the trouble the Killiks had caused the Chiss Ascendancy.

"I'm beginning to see why the Ascendancy doesn't want the Colony encroaching on its frontier," Luke said. "Were the Killiks also responsible for the destruction of the Empire of the Hand?"

Formbi turned and, in a surprised voice, asked, "What makes you think the Empire of the Hand has been destroyed?"

Luke wasn't fooled for a moment. He could feel the Aristocra's dismay through the Force—and so could Mara.

"Baron Fel, for starters," she said. "He wouldn't have abandoned his duties while the Empire of the Hand stood."

"Perhaps it was merely absorbed," Formbi suggested.

"*After* being battered into nothingness," Mara said. "We know that Nirauan has been abandoned. Something must have happened."

Formbi sighed in resignation. "The Empire of the Hand served the purpose Mith'raw'nuruodo intended—though it was not against the Colony, as you suggest."

"The Vagaari, then?" Mara pressed. "The Yuuzhan Vong?"

"That's really all I am at liberty to say," Formbi answered wearily. "Except, perhaps, that the Colony is only one of the Terrors remaining to the Unknown Regions. Do not be surprised to see the Empire of the Hand rise again, when there is need."

"I see," Luke said, saddened to have confirmed what he had only suspected until now. "I know that three of the Fel children survived, but what of Chak—"

"Only *two* survived," Formbi said. "Jagged and Wyn. Chak, Davin, and Cherith are all dead."

"I'm sorry to hear that," Luke said. "I liked Chak very much."

"But what of Cem?" Mara asked, picking the question off the top of Luke's head. "Was she killed, too?"

"Cem?" A sly smile came to Formbi's mouth. "*Cem* is a son's name."

"Excuse me," Mara said. "We never actually met."

"I should think not." The smile grew wider and shiftier. "Cem would be the Fels' shadow child."

"Shadow child?" Luke asked.

"Publicly unacknowledged," Formbi explained. "Secret, in fact. It's a common Chiss precaution to keep enemies from wiping out an entire ruling family."

Luke began to have a guilty feeling in his stomach. "How secret?"

"Quite," Formbi replied. "In fact, this is the first time I've heard of a Cem Fel. I imagine *you* heard the name from Wyn."

"Jacen did," Mara replied. "How could you know?"

"Wyn is notorious for spilling secrets," he said.

"And now we've compounded it," Luke said. "I hope you'll hold the name in confidence."

"Of course." Formbi's voice was sincere. "And you shouldn't feel bad—Soontir Fel is a clever one. I often suspect that Wyn reveals only what he wishes her to."

"Thank you."

Luke returned the smile, hoping to conceal his doubt about the Aristocra's reassurances. He waved at the training field, where the small team had won control of all six jet-balls and was driving deep into opposition territory. "And now, perhaps you'd allow me to explain the game we're watching."

"Please," Formbi said. "It looks refreshingly riotous."

"We call it Skorch," Luke explained. "It's actually the referee who's being trained. Each team has a set of secret goals—such as collecting three balls or sending two into one goal and one into another—and it's the referee's job to discover those goals and see that both sides win."

"*If* that's possible," Mara said. "In some Skorch scenarios, the goals are mutually exclusive. Then the referee must see that both teams achieve an equivalent level of victory."

The referee, a black-furred Defel with eyes as red as Formbi's, popped up from behind a wall and sent a small Rodian sprawling. He intercepted the jet-ball that had been coming in her direction and sent it sailing toward the other end of the course.

"The referee can also arrange complete losses for both sides," Luke said. "Though that's a last resort. It's considered barely adequate."

"What an odd game," Formbi said.

R2-D2 emitted a discordant series of beeps, then raised his transceiver antenna and began to move off.

Luke scowled and called, "Artoo, come back here." When R2-D2 continued toward the Skorch field, Luke excused himself and caught up to the droid. "Didn't you hear me? We're in the middle of some very important business."

R2-D2 whistled a sharp reply.

"I'm sure your business is important, too," Luke said. "But you'll have to conduct it over there, with us."

R2-D2 pivoted on a tread, then tweedled a question.

"If it can't wait, you'll have to," Luke answered. "You're in no condition to wander around the training grounds alone."

Another question.

"Yes, on Ossus," Luke said. "Where did you think we were?"

R2-D2 gave a confused sigh, then reluctantly returned with Luke. Mara was explaining the theory behind Skorch as two players—a Wookiee and a Squib—wrestled with the Defel referee in an attempt to keep him from interfering with the game.

"The only rules are the ones the referee can persuade the players to accept," she was saying. "And his only rule is that he can't use his lightsaber on any of the players."

"It sounds like a dangerous game," Formbi observed. "How many students are killed playing it?"

"These are senior apprentices," Luke said. "They can take care of themselves."

"And there are always healing trances," Mara added.

"Healing trances are good," Luke agreed. "The idea is to teach our Jedi Knights to look for secret agendas and develop solutions that work for everyone." He turned to Formbi. "That's what we hope to do at Qoribu."

"Very noble." Formbi turned away from the game. "But I have seen nothing to convince me that you understand the Killiks any better than we do. Quite the opposite, in fact."

"We haven't had as long to study them as you have," Mara retorted. "But our senior scientist has already developed a theory about how Joiners are created—"

"And about how the Killiks' collective mind functions," Luke said.

"Which is?" Formbi asked.

Luke sensed that the question was a test. "We believe Joiners are created when Killik pheromones alter the basic structure of the corpus callosum," he said. "Those changes allow the Joiners to receive signal impulses directly from the Killik brains, which—we presume—have a similar capacity."

"And what is the transfer agent?"

Luke hesitated. He could sense that they were close to winning Formbi's support, but they were crossing from theory to guesswork here, and he did not want to undermine their progress by making a wild-sounding assertion.

Mara disagreed. He could feel her through their Force-bond, urging him to take the chance.

"We think the impulses are transferred through auras," Luke said. "But we're having trouble identifying exactly which part."

"All of them," Formbi said. "Heat, electric, magnetic, probably chemical—at least that's what *our* scientists think. But that doesn't explain the Will."

"The Will?" Mara asked.

"As far as we know, only individuals from the same nest share a truly collective mind," Formbi said. "Our scientists describe it as a sort of very advanced telepathy, where an individual has access to the thoughts and sense impressions of the entire nest."

Luke nodded. That was just as Tekli and Tahiri described the experience—though he was not going to admit *that* to Formbi. "That's what our investigations suggest."

"But insects from different nests must communicate with each other via language, just as we do," Formbi said. "The collective mind doesn't seem to extend far beyond the confines of the nest."

"Which is exactly what you'd expect, if the communication medium is their aura," Mara said. "To participate in the collective mind, an individual would always have to be within range of another insect's aura, and that one would have to be close to another—"

"Precisely," Formbi agreed. "The collective mind can extend over quite a large area, as long as the chain of insects remains unbroken."

R2-D2 began to beep for attention.

"Not now, Artoo," Luke said. He did not want to give Formbi time to reconsider what he was about to tell them. "Please continue, Aristocra."

Formbi glanced at the droid, then nodded. "But the entire *Colony* seems to be subject to a single Will. We've noticed that nests all across the sector are acting in concert, pursuing a single, unified purpose."

"Let me guess," Luke said. "Expanding the Colony."

"Very good," Formbi said.

"And this Will appeared about six years ago?" Mara asked. "When they started to develop hospitals and interstellar trade?"

"Right again," Formbi replied. "And, frankly, we're puzzled."

"How so?" Luke asked. "Perhaps we can help clear something up for you."

Formbi smiled. "Yes. Soontir suggested you would respond well to an information exchange, and we believe this mystery to be particularly well suited to the Jedi."

"We'll do what we can," Mara said, leaving out what exactly she meant by *can*. "Though, as I said before, we haven't had as long to study the Killiks as you have."

"That has been to your advantage, I assure you," Formbi said. "If you were wise, you would leave our part of the galaxy to us and avoid the Colony at all costs."

"We Jedi try to be brave as well as wise," Luke replied mildly. "Now, how can we be of service?"

"Our scientists are having trouble understanding how the Will exerts its hold over the entire Colony," Formbi said. "The distances involved are too great for it to function through their auras, as the collective mind does."

"Killiks aren't Force-sensitive, if that's what you're thinking," Luke said. "At least not the ones we've met."

"Would they need to be?" Formbi asked. "If each nest had just one Joiner who could feel the Will, wouldn't the entire nest be subject to it?"

"Possibly," Mara allowed. Luke felt her alarm growing as clearly as his own; it was growing all too obvious that Unu—Raynar's nest—was the source of what the Chiss were calling the Will. "But this central Will would have to be magnitudes stronger than the wills of the individual nests."

"And it could be," Luke said, recalling how powerful Raynar had grown in the Force. "A gifted Joiner might be able to draw on the Force potential of his entire nest."

"I thought you said that the Killiks aren't Force-sensitive," Formbi said.

"He did," Mara answered. "*Force-sensitive* means you have the ability to tap into the Force. *Force potential* is just another way of saying 'life energy.'"

"All living things generate Force energy," Luke explained. He was beginning to see that Formbi had played them—just as he had during the investigation of the Outbound Flight wreck. "But I suspect you already know that. The information is readily available on any HoloNet terminal in the Galactic Alliance."

"But it *is* good to have our theory vetted by the experts," Formbi said, still trying to maintain his charade. "And it seems a reasonable exchange, considering what I gave you."

"It would have been, if that's all you had come for." Luke turned back to the Skorch field, buying himself a moment to contain his rising emotions. The anger he felt was at himself, for failing to see Formbi's game early on, before they had told him about Raynar. "But you came looking for a name—for the source of the Will."

Formbi spread his hands and stepped to Luke's side. "You were the ones who summoned *me*."

On the Skorch field, the small team once again had control of all six jet-balls and were racing toward the large team's goal. The

Defel referee was limping after them with one furry arm synth-glued to his knee.

"You have what you came for," Mara said. "But it wouldn't be wise to act on the information."

Formbi looked at her in surprise. "Are you threatening me?"

"She's telling you that killing Raynar won't return the Colony to what it was," Luke said. "If you assassinate him, all you're going to have are a trillion angry insects who don't care if they die. The Jedi won't be able to save you."

"Actually, we weren't counting on that," Formbi said. "The Jedi have no business—"

R2-D2 emitted a piercing shriek, then began to bang back and forth on his treads until Luke looked down.

"Artoo, I said—"

R2-D2's holoprojector activated, and fuzzy image of Leia appeared on the ground in front of him. For a moment, Luke thought that it was the old message she had recorded for Obi-Wan—then he noticed that she was dressed in a white jumpsuit instead of a ceremonial gown, and her hair was falling loose down her back instead of being gathered in those ear-buns she used to wear.

"Luke?" Her voice was scratchy and barely audible. "Are . . . there?"

"Yes." Luke answered. "Artoo, where's this coming from?"

R2-D2 tweedled a sharp reply.

"I *know* it's being relayed through the Academy HoloNet transceiver," Luke said. He dropped to his knee. "Leia, where are you?"

"Luke?" Leia's image said. "Can't . . . you. But . . . important . . . Killik attacked Saba . . . stowaways on . . . think . . . after you and . . . maybe Ben."

"Stowaways?" Mara gasped. An image of their son holding an empty container of gelmeat flashed from her mind to Luke's, then she was racing toward the exit. "Ben!"

". . . careful," Leia's image said.

The image grew motionless, obviously waiting for a reply.

"Tell the comm officer to acknowledge and ask for a repeat," Luke instructed R2.

". . . tell if . . . ," Leia said. ". . . again later."

The image winked out, leaving R2-D2 buzzing in frustration.

"It's okay, Artoo. We heard enough." Luke turned to find Formbi eyeing him with an expression halfway between smugness and concern. "I'm afraid we'll have to cut our tour short."

"Of course," Formbi replied. "It sounds as though you'll be quite busy . . . as will I."

"Is that so?" Luke used the Force to summon a pair of apprentices out of the Skorch game to escort Formbi and look after R2-D2. "Can the Jedi be of any assistance?"

"Not really," Formbi said. "Chief of State Omas was kind enough to send an escort to accompany me to his office on Coruscant."

"I see," Luke said. "I assume you'll be discussing the situation at Qoribu."

Formbi smiled and dipped his head in acknowledgment. "*Discussing* would be the wrong word, I'm afraid."

TWENTY-SEVEN

Leia had heard it said that no captor could imprison a Jedi longer than the Jedi wished to be imprisoned, and she was beginning to understand how true that was. Even with Alema lying unconscious in the number two hold, with all four limbs shackled to cargo tie-downs and two angry Noghri guarding her with T-10 stun blasters, Leia constantly found herself limping back with a new way to confine their prisoner. Her head and ankle were throbbing harder by the minute, and the last thing she wanted was to start fighting the Twi'lek again.

Now Leia was holding a pair of LSS 1000-series Automatic Stun Cuffs from the security locker—highly illegal, of course, but standard equipment aboard the *Falcon*. After checking the vital-signs monitor on Alema's wrist to make sure the Twi'lek was still unconscious, Leia limped around behind her head.

A sudden shudder ran down Alema's lekku. Her eyes started to move beneath their lids, and she began to mumble in a frightened, high-pitched voice. At first, Leia thought the Twi'lek was crying out incoherently in a dream, but then she recognized a couple of Twi'leki words—those for "night" and "herald"—and realized Alema was actually talking in her sleep.

Leia turned toward the intercom panel. "Threepio, activate audio recording in hold two."

"As you wish, Princess," he said. "But I will need to leave Master Sebatyne unattended for a few moments."

"As long as she's still stable," Leia said.

"Oh, she's quite stable," C-3PO said. "Her vital signs have been hovering close to zero for hours."

A moment later, a red light activated on the intercom panel. Alema continued to mutter in her native language—something about "the Night Herald"—and her limbs began to jerk against their restraints. Leia glanced at the vitals monitor and saw that the Twi'lek had slipped into the REM state. She motioned for the Noghri to cover her, then squatted on her haunches and clamped the stun cuffs on Alema's lekku.

"You're a hard woman, Leia Solo," Han said, stepping into the hold. "I kind of like it."

"Just being careful," Leia said. She set the power to maximum, then slowly rose and backed away. "I doubt we could trick her twice."

"Sure we could," Han said. "Teamwork and treachery will beat youth and skill every time."

"Alema isn't that young—and I'd say she beats us handsdown in the treachery department," Leia said. She crossed the hold—emptied so Alema would have nothing to fling with the Force—and stopped at Han's side. "I thought you and Juun were plotting the next jump."

"We've been trying," Han said.

"Trying?" After repairing Alema's sabotage, they had emerged from the nebula to find themselves staring into the creamy heart of the Galactic Core, no more than twenty light-years from the Galactic Alliance. "You said we'd be on the Rago Run in one more jump."

"We will," Han said. "But every time we engage, the navicomputer detects a mass fluctuation and shuts us down."

"You're sure we're in the right place?" Leia asked. Worried about the possibility of an escape, she had insisted on supervising the security precautions while Juun filled in as copilot. "Jae didn't plot a bad jump?"

Han shook his head. "It's definitely the same place we stopped on the way out. Rago is five light-years ahead, and the star charts match what we stored in the navicomputer. The only difference is the fluctuation."

Leia cast a nervous glance at Alema, who was continuing to mumble and thrash against her restraints, then asked, "Could it be something coming down the Run toward us?"

"Sure," Han said. "If it had the mass of a battle fleet."

"I see what you mean."

Leia studied Alema for another moment, then checked the Twi'lek's vital signs again. The monitor showed her deep in the REM state, but Leia remained suspicious. She withdrew a hypo of tranqarest from her jumpsuit pocket and pressed it to Alema's neck.

"Whoa!" Han said. "She has a head wound!"

"She's young." Leia hit the injector and held it down until the hypo stopped hissing. "A little coma won't hurt her."

"Remind me not to get on your bad side," Han said.

Alema stopped thrashing and fell silent, and her vital signs dropped into the coma range. Leia thumped the Twi'lek on the eyelid just to be sure, then nodded when there was no reaction.

"Let's go see if we're still having that mass fluctuation."

Han raised his brow. "You think *she* was—"

"I don't know," Leia said. Leaving instructions for the Noghri to blast the Twi'lek at the first sign of trouble, she left the hold. "But it never hurts to be careful."

"You don't think you're overdoing it?"

"Han, she sabotaged the *Falcon* and gave me a beating," Leia said. "And there's every chance my message didn't get through to Luke and Mara. If the *Shadow* had a stowaway aboard—or if Tahiri and the others are as far gone as Alema—we might be too late already."

"Okay, there's that," Han said. "But—"

"Han, you *do* understand how good Alema is?" Leia stopped and turned him to face her. "How lucky we were to knock her out?"

"Yeah, I understand." There was barb to Han's voice. "But we've still got to keep her alive."

"Even if it means she might escape and blow us all to stardust?"

"Yeah, even if it means that," Han said. "Because what happened to her is probably happening to Jaina and Zekk, and maybe Cilghal can learn something from Alema to help us fix it."

"*That's* why you're so worried about her?" Leia was glad to hear the ruthlessness in his voice, to know that so many decades of strife and danger had only made him shrewder and more stubborn. "I was starting to think you'd gone soft."

She took Han's arm and started up the access corridor. They had lost so much during the war that it was impossible to believe they had come out stronger or happier. But they *had* emerged together, with a better understanding of each other and a bond that had survived the deaths of a son, a close companion, and more friends than Leia could name. No matter how alarming this latest crisis, no matter how frightened they were for Jaina, they would face it together— and together they would do whatever was necessary to prevail.

They reached the flight deck and found Juun staring at the navigator's display, so engrossed in star plotting and continuum calculations that he did not notice the Solos' presence. Leia could see that he was attempting a broad-spectrum variable analysis with a ten-decimal accuracy parameter. With his eyes bulging and his cheek folds flared in frustration, it looked like he would blow a circuit before the navicomputer did.

Leia brought her mouth close to Han's ear. "I hope you've been backing up our navigation log."

"You bet," Han said. "I knew what you were thinking the minute we realized we were coming down on an abandoned planet."

"Really." Actually, Leia had been too busy trying to cold-fire the repulsor engines to be thinking much of anything, but she wasn't going to admit that to Han. She didn't want him thinking Juun was a better copilot than she was. "Pretty sure of yourself, aren't you?"

"Yep." Han flashed a cocky grin. "*And* I charted everything in sensor range on the way out." The grin grew larger and cockier. "There might be another dozen stars inside the nebula."

"A dozen?" Leia gasped. Then, not wanting Han to see just how well he really did know her, she assumed a more subdued tone. "So there might be another five or six habitable planets, plus a few moons, if we're lucky."

"Five or six? There'll be a dozen—even two!" The indignation in Han's voice faded quickly to concern. "But will anyone *want* to colonize there? It's still outside the Galactic Alliance, and it's not easy to reach."

"The Ithorians will go right away," Leia said. "The world we came down on is perfect for them. And—given how they feel about violence—it's about the only chance they have of getting around the Reclamation Act."

"As long as the rehab conglomerates don't steal it out from under us again."

"The Reclamation Act doesn't apply outside the Galactic Alliance," Leia said. "Besides, who's going to tell them?"

Han nodded quietly at the navigator's station, where Juun was mumbling to himself and shaking his head in frustration. Finally, he banged the side of his fist into his temple and whined something in Sullustan that Leia did not quite catch.

"We'll just have to keep him close," she whispered. "At least until we've relocated the Ithorians."

Han let his chin drop. "You really know how to spoil the moment." He stepped on the flight deck and, peering at the display over Juun's shoulder, asked, "So, what have—"

Juun jumped out of his seat, the top of his head avoiding Han's chin only by virtue of his short stature, then spun to face them.

"What are you doing, sneaking up like that?"

Han raised his hands. "Easy. I wasn't trying to give you a power surge."

"Actually, Jae, we've been standing here talking for a couple of minutes." Leia leaned down to look at the display. "It appears you've been hard at work."

Juun relaxed somewhat. "I've been running a full gravitational analysis, per emergency troubleshooting procedure."

"Come up with anything besides a headache?" Han asked.

"Nothing that makes sense." Juun returned to his seat and began to call up columns of stellar deflection observations. "Light is definitely being distorted at a steadily increasing rate, which means that either there's a very large, completely invisible rogue body dead ahead—"

"Or something big is about to come out of hyperspace," Leia finished. "Did you do a rate-of-change analysis?"

"Of course." Juun typed a command and brought up a graph plotting angle of deflection against time. "According to this, space-time should be separating just about—"

Leia's hair stood on end, then an iridescent flash lit the interior of the cockpit, and tiny snakes of static electric began to drag-race down her neural pathways. The proximity alarm blared to life. She hurled herself toward the copilot's seat, but lost her footing and hung in midair for a moment, her eyes aching with the brilliance of the silvery flash ahead, her stomach swirling inside her like water down a drain.

Then Leia stumbled into the copilot's chair and found herself staring out the viewport at an immense, cylinder-studded crevice of durasteel whiteness. Her stomach rose toward her throat as Han put the *Falcon* into an emergency climb, and her ribs began to throb from an impact she did not remember receiving.

"What is it?" Han yelled.

Leia activated her tactical display and found the top half rapidly filling with transponder codes. It took her a moment to find the *Falcon*'s own code, surrounded as it was by others of a similar color.

"I . . . I think it's a battle fleet," Leia reported.

"Whose?"

A jagged line of familiar white ellipsoids appeared along the bottom edge of the viewport. Interspersed among them were about twice as many thin white arrows.

"Hapan." Leia did not bother to confirm her conclusion with a code search. She had seen the distinctive ships too many times—at

Dathomir, Corellia, and even Coruscant—to need corroboration. "Those are Novas and Battle Dragons."

"Yeah," Han agreed. "What are they doing out *here*?"

"Going to Lizil," Juun said. "What else?"

The comm channel crackled to life, and a voice with a thick Hapan accent said, "This is Hapes Battle Dragon *Kendall* hailing Galactic Alliance transport *Longshot*. Heave to and prepare for temporary impoundment."

"Impoundment!" Han maintained his course. "Better let them know who we really are."

Leia was already reaching for the transponder controls.

"*Longshot,* this is your last warning—"

"Battle Dragon *Kendall*." Leia activated the *Falcon*'s true transponder code. "This is Leia Organa Solo aboard the *Millennium Falcon*."

The Hapan voice grew more uncertain. "*Millennium Falcon?*"

"Yes," Leia said. "Sorry for the confusion, but we usually travel incognito. I'm sure you understand."

"Of course," the voice said.

"Good. If you'll assign us a safe vector, we'll move through and let you be on your way."

"I'm sorry, Princess. We have orders—"

"Then I suggest you let me speak to whoever issued them," Leia said. "Queen Mother Tenel Ka has been a frequent guest at my dinner table. I'm sure she would be unhappy to learn we were detained as a matter of . . . procedure."

A new voice came over the comm channel. "Princess Leia Organa Solo?" he asked. "The mother of Jedi Jacen *Solo*?"

"That's correct." Disturbed by the way the man had emphasized Jacen's last name, Leia reached out in the Force and was relieved to feel no sense that her son was anywhere in the fleet. "To whom do I have the honor of speaking?"

"Forgive me," the man replied. "I am Dukat Aleson Gray, ninth cousin to the Queen Mother and Duch'da to Lady AlGray of the Relephon Moons."

"Thank you," Leia said. "I'll remember you to the Queen Mother the next time we meet."

"You're very kind." Gray's tone was polite but doubtful. "I'm certain we can trust you to hold our encounter here in the strictest confidence."

"Of course," Leia replied. "We wouldn't want to jeopardize the Colony's reinforcements."

The comm fell silent.

"Blast, you didn't have to say *that*," Han groaned. "We know where they're going."

"But not *why*," Leia said. "If a war is breaking out, we need to know."

"Why?" Han asked. "We won't be able to tell anyone if we're stuck in the belly of a Battle Dragon."

Gray's voice came over the comm again. "Actually, our mission is closer to peacekeeping than reinforcing."

Leia shot Han a smug grin, then said, "Yes, that's what I was given to understand. Do you need navigation data to the Colony gateway?"

"That won't be necessary," Gray responded. "We have a course to the Lizil nest, and your son assured us that someone would be waiting—"

"Our *son*?" Leia interrupted.

"Yes." Gray sounded confused. "The Queen Mother's new consort. He was the one who, uh, *convinced* her to intervene."

A loud smack sounded from the pilot's seat. Leia glanced over to find Han holding his palm to his brow.

"You think you know him," Han said, shaking his head. "And then he tries to start a war."

TWENTY-EIGHT

The door slid aside, revealing the clean-lined interior of the Skywalkers' uncluttered Ossan cottage. Mara had grown so accustomed to the vague uneasiness she had been feeling in the Force that the sensation barely registered as she crossed the foyer. But this time she paid special attention, closing her eyes and letting her feet carry her toward where it seemed strongest.

"Mom!"

Mara opened her eyes and found Ben standing before her, on the other side of low table that was the living room's only furniture. The sliding wall panels that partitioned the house into rooms were all closed, so it was difficult to tell where he had come from. He pointed at her feet.

"Your shoes!"

Mara glanced down and saw she had neglected to leave her dusty boots in the foyer, as was the custom on Ossus.

"Never mind my shoes." She started around the table toward Ben. "Did you bring a pet back from Jwlio?"

Ben's eyes grew round. "A pet?"

"A Killik," Mara said. The uneasy feeling was as strong as ever, but she could not pinpoint a location. It seemed to be coming from Ben and from all around her. "Is that what you've been doing with all that gelmeat and nerfspread?"

"Aren't Killiks smart?" Ben asked.

"Smarter than I thought. Why?"

" 'Cause then she'd be a friend, not a pet."

Mara cocked an eyebrow. "*She*, Ben?"

Ben's mouth fell open, and he backed toward the kitchen. "I, uh . . . they're all—"

"Stay here." Mara started around the table. "Don't even *think* of moving."

"But, Mom—"

"Don't argue," she ordered. "Your father will talk to you later."

Mara stretched her awareness into the kitchen and sensed only Nanna inside, but that did not stop her from pulling her lightsaber.

"Mom, don't—"

"Quiet!"

Mara used the Force to slide a wall panel aside and found Nanna down on her knee joints, quietly brushing morsels of gelmeat onto a sheet of flimsiplast. The rest of the room appeared deserted.

"Nanna?"

The droid looked up, but was so flustered she continued to brush morsels, missing the flimsiplast and spreading them across the floor.

"Yes, Mistress Skywalker?"

Mara's eyes went to the three gelmeat containers lying empty on the preparation island.

"Don't worry," Nanna said. "Ben didn't eat all that."

"I hope not," Mara said. "That would be a good way to earn a memory wipe."

There was too much YVH droid in Nanna to be intimidated. "That won't be necessary. My nutritional programming is very up to date."

Mara pointed the handle of her lightsaber at the wrappers. "Then who ate that?"

The droid peered up at her. "I'm sorry. I can't say."

"Then how can you be sure it wasn't Ben?"

"I'm afraid you're misunderstanding," Nanna replied. "I know who ate the gelmeat. I'm the one who opened the food locker. I just can't tell you."

"*What?*" Mara used the Force to jerk the droid off her knees. "Explain yourself."

"It's a *secret*," Ben said from the edge of the kitchen. "You promised, Nanna."

"You can't have secrets from me," Mara said, holding the droid in the air. "I'm his mother."

"Under normal circumstances, of course not," Nanna agreed. "But where there is a danger to the child, my programming—"

"Danger to the child?" Mara demanded. "*What* danger?"

Nanna lowered her feet to the floor. "Ben said you would kill him if you found out what he was doing," the droid explained. "And I must say, considering how angry you are now, his fear certainly seems warranted."

"Ben?" When he failed to answer, Mara glanced back and found an empty doorway. She turned to go. "Ben! I said—"

Nanna started after her. "I'm sorry, Master Skywalker, but until you calm down I really must—"

Mara whirled on the droid. "Stand down, Beautiful Blaster."

The override code stopped the droid midstride, darkening her photoreceptors and dropping her chin to her chest.

"I'll handle this myself."

Mara continued into the living room and went straight to Ben's room, where he was busy pushing the closet panel closed.

"Ben, come away from there . . . now!"

Ben pressed his back to the closet. "It's not what you—"

Mara reached out with the Force and pulled him to her side, then grabbed his wrist and—keeping one eye on the closet door—knelt at his side.

"Ben, we just received a holo from Aunt Leia," she said. "She was worried that a Killik assassin might have stowed away aboard the *Shadow*. So if all that gelmeat you've been taking is for—"

"Gorog's no assassin!" Ben said. "She's my best friend."

"She's an insect, Ben."

"So? *Your* best friend's a lizard."

"Don't be ridiculous." Mara rose and pushed him behind her. "Aunt Leia is my best friend."

"Doesn't count," Ben said. "She's family. Saba is a lizard."

"Okay, maybe my best friend's a lizard."

Mara was both repulsed and terrified at the thought of her son developing a relationship with a Killik—especially given what Cilghal was learning about the Joiner bonding mechanism. But she was also beginning to worry about the psychological damage Ben might suffer if she slew his "friend" in front of him.

"If Gorog's your friend, tell her to come out nice and slow. We'll talk this—"

The muffled groan of a sliding wall panel sounded from two rooms over. Holding her lightsaber at the ready, Mara used the Force to open Ben's closet—and nearly ignited her blade when an empty exoskeleton tumbled into the room. It was about a meter high, with thick blue-black chitin and barbed mandibles half the length of Mara's arms.

"Ben!"

"I told you it wasn't what you thought."

"Stay here!"

Using the Force to slide the wall panels aside in front of her, Mara rushed two rooms over and found six black limbs—two legs and four arms—sticking out from under the low table that Luke used for a writing desk. The mandibles were protruding from one end, and the whole piece of furniture was trembling as though there were a groundquake.

Ben rushed up beside Mara.

"I told you to stay in your room," Mara said.

"I can't," Ben said. "Gorog's scared."

"Okay. Tell her to come out. Everything will be all right."

A low rumble reverberated from under the table.

"She doesn't trust you," Ben reported.

Mara actually looked away from the bug. "You speak Killik?"

"I don't speak it. I just understand it." Gorog drummed again, and he added, "She says you're a killer."

Coming from her son, the words felt like a vibroblade to the heart. "We talked about that, Ben. Sometimes I have to kill. Many Jedi Masters do."

Gorog rumbled something else, and it seemed to Mara that there was something sharp in the insect's rhythm, something spiteful and malevolent.

"Mom, what's cold blood?" Ben asked.

"Is that what she's saying?" Mara squatted down so she could look Gorog in the eye. Instead, she found herself staring at a dark sheaf of mandibles and mouthparts. "It means you kill when you don't have to. I don't do that."

The Killik slowly moved away, carrying the table along on her back and drumming incessantly.

"She says you killed lots of people when you didn't have to, for Palpytine," Ben said. "Mom, who's Palpytine?"

"Palpatine," Mara corrected automatically. She felt as though the Emperor were reaching across time to her yet again, as though to prove how foolish she had been to believe she could ever truly escape him. "A bad man I used to know. How does Gorog know his name?"

A stream of brown saliva shot out from under the table. Mara's reflexes were too quick for it to come near her face, but in the quarter second it took her to draw away, the insect came flying at her with the table still on its back. She activated her lightsaber instinctively—and heard Ben crying out over the crackle of the igniting blade.

"Don't!" Ben cried. "Please!"

Mara deactivated the blade in a pang of motherly concern and whirled into a spinning back kick instead, her foot landing high because she had to lift her leg above Ben's head. Instead of launching the Killik across the room, the attack simply knocked off the table and drove the insect to the floor.

A soft sizzle sounded from the wall beside Mara, and a sour, acrid smell filled her nostrils. She put down a hand to push Ben back, and Gorog slammed a mandible into her ankles, sweeping her from her feet.

Mara hit the floor flat on her back. The Killik stabbed a pair of sharp pincer-hands down on her shoulders and brought her head around, a hypo-shaped probosics pushing out between the mandibles, venom dripping from its tip. Mara smashed her lightsaber handle into the tube, folding it over and drawing a boom of pain from the Killik's chest cavity.

"*Mom!*" Ben cried.

"Go to your room!" Mara hooked her elbow around the arm on her shoulder and pulled, dropping Gorog to an elbow. "Now!"

The Killik reached for Mara's neck with its *other* two hands.

Mara drove her free hand up under the insect's jaw, then bridged on her shoulders and flipped it onto its back. She sprang instantly to her feet—and the Killik flexed a wing and flipped instantly to its feet.

Ben remained in the doorway, on the opposite side of the Killik from Mara.

"Ben, I'm very disappointed in you." Mara's shoulders were throbbing where the pincers had pierced them, and blood was running down the front of her jumpsuit. She could sense that Luke was only a couple of minutes behind her, but a lot could happen in two minutes—too much to be sure that she would not have to kill Ben's friend. "You need to start obeying me and go find your father."

"But you said to go to my—"

"Ben!" Mara brought her lightsaber up and started to circle toward him. "Just do as I say. You're in enough trouble already."

Ben's face grew pale, and the Killik began to pivot with Mara, keeping itself between her and her son. She thought for a moment the Killik meant to use Ben as a hostage, but it was careful to stay away from him—as though it, too, were worried he might be accidentally injured.

"Ben, I think Gorog wants you to leave, too."

Ben glanced at the Killik, then asked Mara, "Are you going to kill her?"

"Ben, *I'm* the one who's bleeding here."

"But you're a Jedi Master," Ben said. "It doesn't matter if a Jedi Master bleeds."

"You've been watching too many action holos," Mara said. Nevertheless, she hung her lightsaber on her belt. "But, okay, I promise—*if* you leave right now."

Gorog rumbled something that caused Ben to scowl.

"Maybe you should just be nice," he said to the Killik. "Then maybe Mom would let you stay."

Gorog thrummed, and Mara began to wish C-3PO were here to translate.

"She doesn't *always* lie," Ben protested. "Not even most—"

Gorog raised two hands and shooed him toward the door.

Ben sighed and left the room.

Mara waited until she heard the front door slide open, then said, "Thank you for that."

The Killik spread its mandibles and sprang. Mara caught it in the Force and slammed it into a support post. There was a sharp crackle, and when the insect dropped to the floor, one of its wings jutted out at an angle.

"I don't understand why you want to fight," Mara said. "Because you have *no* chance of winning—"

Gorog jumped across the room, mandibles snapping at head height. Mara rushed to meet the attack, then dropped into a slide, catching both ankles as she passed beneath the insect, spinning to her belly, twisting its legs around and slamming the Killik down on its back.

The insect flexed its good wing and landed back on its feet, but Mara was already driving an elbow into a tubular knee. The leg snapped with a sickening crackle, and the Killik dropped to the floor.

Mara grabbed the Killik's good leg and stood, jerking it up more or less upside down, then snake-locked her leg over the insect's and shoved against the joint.

"All right, that's enough," she said. "I promised Ben I wouldn't kill you—but I didn't say anything about hurting."

The Killik clacked its mandibles wildly, then released an acrid, foul-smelling vapor that filled Mara's eyes with cloudy tears and turned her stomach queasy and rebellious. She snapped the joint and attempted to launch herself out of danger with a departing thrust-kick, but the insect was already rolling into Mara's leg.

She landed facedown, her kicking leg trapped beneath the Killik. Four pincer-hands grabbed hold of her calf and began to pull, dragging her foot toward the clacking mandibles. Mara's own hand drifted toward her lightsaber, but she stopped short of pulling it free. This bug was not going to make a liar and a killer of her in her son's eyes. She reached forward, clawing at the wooden floor, trying to pull free, and only slipped farther beneath the insect.

Then Mara saw the table, lying on its side where it had fallen when Gorog attacked. She reached out with a mental hand, turned it end-on, and brought it sailing into the Killik's head.

The table connected with a spectacular *pop,* and Gorog's grasp loosened. Mara scrambled free and Force-sprang to her feet, then spun around to find the Killik collapsed on its belly, all six limbs trembling and shaking in convulsions. She rushed to its side and pulled the table away, revealing a ten-centimeter dent in the head where the edge had cracked the chitin.

"Stang!"

Mara pulled the comlink from her pocket and started to call for medical assistance—then noticed the Killik slowly drawing its trembling arms in toward its body, gathering itself to spring.

Mara slipped forward and brought her heel down on the dented chitin. "I said that was enough!"

Gorog collapsed again, unable to do anything but lie on the floor and tremble. Then Mara felt Luke urgently reaching out to her, warning her to be careful, urging her not to kill it.

Mara eyed the insect with spite in her heart. "What is it with you?"

A few seconds later, Luke came rushing in the door with half a dozen senior apprentices at his back.

"Mara, are you—"

"I'm fine, Skywalker." She took the hand he offered and glared down at the trembling insect. "But I'm getting awfully tired of people telling me not to squash that bug."

"Sorry about that, but the comm center just finished reconstructing some of Leia's message." Luke motioned the apprentices to secure the Killik, then added, "She says it could explode."

TWENTY-NINE

Reclining in long diagnostics chairs with their heads hidden beneath scanning helmets and their bodies swaddled in sensor feeds, the subjects of the experiment—Tahiri and the other Joiner Jedi Knights—reminded Luke of captives in an Imperial interrogation facility. It did not help that the Killik and Alema Rar, who had arrived aboard the *Falcon* just hours before, were heavily sedated and strapped in place with nylasteel bands. Even the isolation chambers in which the subjects were located—dark, gas-tight compartments with transparisteel doors—looked like detention-center cells.

"I'm sorry it's so dim in here, Master Skywalker," Cilghal said. She was standing behind a semicircular control station in a white laboratory smock, studying a data-holo comparing the brain activity of her subjects. "But it's better to have as little background stimulation as possible. It helps isolate their responses."

"I understand." Luke did not bother denying his revulsion. Cilghal could certainly sense his feelings through the Force, just as Luke could sense the excitement that had caused her to comm him in the first place. "And it's more than the darkness. The whole lab raises unpleasant associations."

"Yes, it does have a certain Imperial utilitarianism," Cilghal said. "I wish there had been time to design something less dismal, but this configuration was the quickest to assemble."

"Speed is important," Luke assured her. "It will only take Han a few days to repair the damage to the *Falcon*, and I'd like to have this thing figured out before he and Leia start back to the Qoribu system."

Cilghal studied him out of one bulbous eye. "You can't convince them to wait until we learn more?"

"Not with Jaina still there, not after what happened to Saba."

"Saba will recover, and Jaina . . ." Cilghal turned up the palms of her fin-like hands. "If Jaina would not return before, what makes them think she will listen to them *now*?"

"I don't know," Luke said. "But they're convinced we need to return to Qoribu as soon as possible . . . and I think I agree with them."

Luke had heard reports of Jacen's visit to Tenel Ka and rumors of unexplained Hapan fleet maneuvers, and Leia had told him flatly that the balance of power at Qoribu was about to shift. He and the other Masters were still debating if that was a good thing or bad, but events were clearly moving faster than the order's ability to deal with them. Whether the Jedi understood the Killiks or not, they had to take action soon.

After considering Luke's words for a moment, Cilghal said, "Then I should just tell you what I need and not waste time reporting failures."

Luke frowned at the hesitation . . . shame . . . he felt from the Mon Calamari. "If you think that's best," he said cautiously.

Cilghal turned to her assistants—a trio of apprentice healers—and sent them out of the room.

"That bad?" Luke asked.

"Yes." She pointed at the chambers holding Alema and Gorog. "I need to hurt them."

"*Hurt* them?"

"Inflict pain," she clarified. "Torture them, in truth. Not for long, and nothing that will injure. But it must be intense. It's the only way to test a critical hypothesis."

"I see."

Luke swallowed and forced himself to look through the transparisteel doors at the two prisoners. There was a time when he would not even have considered such a request—and when Cilghal would never have made it. But now that the Jedi had elected to embrace *all* of the Force, to utilize the dark side as Cilghal well as the light, nothing seemed off limits. They deceived, they manipulated, they coerced. To be sure, it was all done in the name of a higher purpose, to promote peace and serve the Balance, yet he occasionally felt that the Jedi were losing their way; that the war with the Yuuzhan Vong had turned them from their true path. He sometimes thought this must have been how Palpatine started, pursuing a worthy goal with any means available.

"Perhaps we should back up a little," Luke said. "Have you made any progress at all?"

"Of a sort." Cilghal pointed to her data-holo, which was basically a flat grid plotting each subject's name against various brain regions, with colored data bars above each square. As the level of activity changed, the bars rose and fell, changing colors and glowing more or less brightly. "As you can see, all of our subjects display similar levels of activity in their sensory cortices, which suggests they're experiencing the same physical sensations."

"And they shouldn't be?"

The corners of Cilghal's lips rose in a broad-mouthed grin. "Not really. The environment in each chamber is different—hot, cold, rank, fragrant, noisy, quiet."

Luke raised his brow. "Doesn't that confirm your theory about the corpus callosum receiving impulses from other brains?"

"It does." Cilghal pointed at four red bars near the end of Alema's and Gorog's data rows. "But look at this. The hypothalamus and limbic system are the center of the emotions. Alema's is correlating to Gorog's."

Luke noticed that this was true only of Alema and Gorog. The hypothalami and limbic systems of Tesar, Tekli, and Tahiri remained independent. Jacen's readings were, as usual, completely useless. He was playing with the brain scanner again, moving his color bars up and down in a rhythmic wave pattern. It was, Luke knew, a not-so-subtle form of protest; his nephew believed that the Jedi order should have more faith in its Jedi Knights than in Cilghal's instruments. Under normal circumstances, Luke would have agreed—but circumstances were not normal.

"Alema and Gorog are in a meld?" Luke asked.

Cilghal shook her head. "No. They're not *perceiving* each other's emotions, as Jedi do in a meld. Alema and Gorog are *sharing* emotions, the same way Tesar and the others are sharing sensations. This takes the collective mind a step deeper than we have seen before."

Thinking of the Will that Formbi had described, Luke reached out to Gorog in the Force and felt only the vague sense of uneasiness that—after the battle in the Skywalkers' cottage—he had come to associate with the blue Killiks that had been attacking them. But the data bars matched to Gorog's hypothalamic and limbic systems brightened to orange and started rising. So did Alema's.

"Interesting," Luke said. "This Killik is Force-sensitive."

"After a fashion," Cilghal said. "I believe she and other Gorog can use the Force to hide their presence—not only from us, but from other Killiks as well. What I need to find out is whether they can also use the Force to pass neural impulses to other members of the Colony—even those outside their own nest."

"And that's why you need to inflict the pain?" Luke asked.

Cilghal nodded. "I'll neutralize the numbing agent, but leave Gorog and Alema unable to move. If the pain is severe enough, Gorog will be motivated to reach out to the others, and we'll see the results on their graphs."

"And this will tell us . . . ?"

"Whether Gorog is also able to influence the others," Cilghal said. "We need to know that before we can begin thinking about countermeasures."

Luke's heart sank at the word *begin*. If Cilghal had not yet started to think about countermeasures, it seemed unlikely she would have any ready before the *Falcon* was repaired. And if Luke asked her to find some other way to test her hypothesis, unlikely became almost impossible.

Feeling just a little more lost inside, Luke nodded. "If there's no other way . . ."

"There isn't." Cilghal's sad eyes grew even sadder. "Not in the time we have."

She activated the electromagnetic shielding between the cells, and all the sensory cortex readings returned to independent levels. Alema's hypothalamic and limbic systems remained the same color and brightness as Gorog's, however.

Cilghal entered another command. A hypo dropped down from the ceiling panel and injected the neutralizing agent into a soft spot just below the Killik's mouthparts. A few seconds later, the insect's cortex activity began to fluctuate as its physical sensations returned. The hypo ascended back into the ceiling, and a flat-tipped probe took its place. Gorog's hypothalamic bar turned brilliant white, shooting to the top of the data-holo and staying there. So did Alema's.

"Gorog is angry with us," Cilghal observed.

"I don't blame her," Luke said.

He wanted to look away, but forced himself not to. If he was willing to sanction torture, then he had to make certain it never became easy.

Cilghal brought the probe down to where one of Gorog's upper arms joined the thorax, then sent an electrical charge through it. All six limbs—even the two casted legs—extended straight out and began to quiver. All of the insect's data bars brightened to white and rose to the top of the holo. Alema's limbic system continued to mirror the Killik's, but her sensory cortices remained quiet.

When the other subjects did not show a similar rise in the activity of their hypothalamic or limbic systems, Luke asked, "Is that enough?"

"Not yet. She must believe it will never end."

The Killik's mandibles clacked close, and its antennae began to whip madly back and forth. Luke reminded himself that this was the insect that had tried to turn his son against his wife, but that did not make torture feel right. Mara was spending every waking minute with Ben, trying to make him understand how the things that Gorog had said could be true and still not mean she was an evil person, and Luke knew that even *she* would not have approved of the insect's suffering.

Mara reached out to him in the Force, worried about Ben and curious about what was happening to Gorog.

Luke's stomach grew hollow with fear. Ben and Gorog were clearly joined—perhaps not as completely as Alema, but too much. A part of Luke wanted to kill the Killik right now, to punish it for trying to use his son against him, to sever the connection before it grew any stronger.

But a bigger part of Luke wanted to protect Ben, to spare him the anguish of knowing that his friend was in pain. He started to tell Cilghal to turn off the probe—then Tesar's hypothalamic bar began to rise. Tahiri's limbic system also began to show more activity, and Tekli exhibited steep rises in both.

A moment later, the trio's data bars vanished as they pushed off their scanning helmets and began to peel electrodes off their bodies. Unlike Alema and Gorog, they were not restrained.

"Okay, turn it off," Luke said. He could feel Mara growing more concerned about Ben. "There's no sense—"

Cilghal held up a hand. "Wait."

Gorog continued to clench her limbs to her chest and whip her antennae. Tekli, who as a healer was a little faster at extricating herself from the equipment, emerged from her chamber first.

"I'm sorry," she said, marching straight for the exit. "I need to use the refresher."

"Of course." Cilghal swiveled a dark eye in Luke's direction, and he felt her interest growing. "Take your time."

Tahiri emerged next. "You need to give us a break sometimes," she complained, walking over to the console. "I'm beginning to feel like I'm on a weeklong X-wing jump."

Tahiri's gaze drifted to the data-holo and lingered for a moment on Gorog's bars. Then she turned to Luke with her mouth twisted into a brutal grin.

"Looks like I'm not the only one who came out of the war part Yuuzhan Vong," she said. "What's next? Jedi tattoos?"

The comment stung Luke more than it should have—in large part because he could feel his wife growing more worried and angry as the experiment continued.

"This isn't for fun," Luke said. "We're—"

"Tahiri, are you feeling any pain?" Cilghal interrupted. "Is that why you came out here?"

Tahiri looked at the Mon Calamari as though she were a dimwit. "Cilghal, I'm half Yuuzhan Vong inside. The only thing pain would cause me is a religious experience."

"You're sure?" Cilghal asked. "You don't feel any at all?"

"This one feelz no pain, either, but that does not excuse what you are doing." Tesar emerged from his compartment trailing a dozen broken sensor wires. "This one is through with your gamez. He will not be party to a breaking."

He tore a handful of electrodes off his chest, threw them on the floor, and started toward the exit.

Tahiri watched him go, then looked back to Luke with the hardness of a Yuuzhan Vong in her green eyes. "Tesar and I must not be completely joined," she said. "*I'd* kind of like to stay."

"I think we're through," Luke said, wondering if the revulsion he felt was for the Yuuzhan Vong in Tahiri's personality, or for himself. "Isn't that right, Cilghal?"

"Yes, I have seen everything I need to."

She cut the power to the probe. Gorog's data bars returned to normal, and Mara gushed relief through the Force.

"We're through for today," Cilghal said to Tahiri. "Thank you."

As Luke watched the young Jedi Knight leave, he began to feel increasingly disappointed. He had no doubts now that Tesar and the others were completely under Raynar's control; that they had agreed to return to the Galactic Alliance only so they could sneak away from the academy—as they had all done at one time or another—and seek support for the Colony.

After the door had hissed shut, Luke shook his head and dropped onto a bench in front of the control panel. "I guess that tells us what we needed to know," he said. "They're all under control of the Colony's Will."

"Of a Will," Cilghal corrected. "Not *the* Will, as the Chiss believe."

Luke looked up. "You've already lost me."

Cilghal came out from behind the control console. "Like the Force itself, every mind in the galaxy has two aspects." She sat next to Luke on the bench. "There is the conscious mind, which embraces what we know of ourselves, and there is the unconscious, which contains the part that remains hidden."

Luke began to see where Cilghal was headed. "You're saying that since the war, the Colony has developed *two* Wills, one conscious and one subconscious."

"Not subconscious—*unconscious*," Cilghal corrected. "The subconscious is a level of the mind between full awareness and unawareness. We're talking about the *unconscious*; it remains fully hidden from the part of our mind that we know."

"Sorry," Luke said. "It's complicated."

"Just like every mind in the galaxy," Cilghal said. "This is an analogy, but it fits—and our experiment demonstrates just how closely. Alema and Gorog are controlled by the unconscious Will—the correlation of their emotional centers makes that clear."

"And Tekli, Tesar, and Tahiri are controlled by the Colony's conscious Will?" Luke asked.

"*Influenced* by," Cilghal said. "They have not fallen under the Colony's complete control. They still think of themselves as individuals."

"Then why did they end the experiment?"

"How often do *you* do something without truly understanding why?" Cilghal countered. "In every mind, the unconscious has a great deal of power—some psychologists even think it's absolute. So when Gorog was in pain, the Colony's unconscious Will influenced its conscious Will to end the experiment. Suddenly, Tekli had to use the refresher, Tahiri had to stretch—"

"And Tesar became angry with us."

"Exactly," Cilghal said. "Of the three, he was the only one who had even a vague understanding of his motivations. Barabels are usually in touch with their unconscious."

Luke thought of the mysterious attacks on him and Mara, and of the Killiks' absurd insistence that they had not occurred. "And the conscious Will wouldn't be aware of the unconscious Will, would it?"

"It *is* the nature of the unconscious mind to remain hidden," Cilghal said. "That is why the Gorog are so hard to sense in the Force. They use it to hide—not only from us, but from the rest of the Colony as well."

"Gorog is part of a secret nest," Luke said, making sure he understood what Cilghal was telling him. "The Colony wouldn't be aware of it—"

"And might well fool itself into believing it doesn't exist," Cilghal said. "We've more or less proved that, and it explains the Killiks' reaction to the attacks on you."

"It all makes sense, except for one thing—why does the secret nest keep attacking us?" Luke asked. "Raynar seemed to *want* our help."

"But Lomi and Welk are threatened by you." It was Jacen who asked this, his voice coming from the data-holo. "And *they're* the ones who control the Gorog nest."

"You know that for certain?" Luke turned toward the data-holo and, finding himself being addressed by a row of colored bars, frowned in irritation. "And I thought I told you to stop playing with Cilghal's brain scanner. Come out here, if you're going to be part of this conversation."

"I know that Raynar dragged Lomi and Welk out of the burning *Flier*." Jacen pushed the scanner helmet up and, now projecting his voice into the air in front of Luke, began to remove the electrodes attached to his body. "And *we* know that Saba was attacked by a disfigured Jedi Knight—almost certainly Welk. I'm willing to take a leap of faith and guess that Lomi survived, too."

"Yeah," Luke said. "I guess I am, too."

"Then only one question remains," Cilghal said. "Why did Alema join the Gorog, while the rest of you—"

"*Them*," Jacen corrected. "In case you haven't noticed, *my* mind remains entirely my own."

"Very well," Cilghal said. "Why did Alema join the Gorog, while everyone else joined the Taat?"

Luke knew the answer to that, and he wished he didn't.

"Because of Numa." He was remembering the time he had stood outside Alema's bacta tank, awash in the guilt the Twi'lek felt for allowing the voxyn to take her sister. "When Numa was killed, Alema turned a lot of her anger inward—and anger has always been fertile ground for the likes of Lomi Plo."

"You saw this coming, didn't you?" Jacen asked. He stepped out of the isolation chamber, pulling his tunic over his head. "Even before the mission to Myrkr, I mean."

Luke turned to look at the unconscious Twi'lek, held prisoner by nylasteel and tranqarest. "Not this—not Gorog," he said. "But I knew Alema would fall."

THIRTY

"Elders, welcome," Leia said, bowing.

She stepped away from the door and waved her Ithorian guests into the Rhysode Room. With a costly roo-wood serenity table surrounded by extravagant flowfit armchairs, the chamber was a conspicuous departure from the sparse décor of the rest of the Jedi academy. Being the designated receiving area of an institute that cordially discouraged visitors, it was also one of the least used rooms in the facility—and one that reflected the sensibilities of its Reconstruction Authority builders far more than it did those of the order itself.

"I hope you'll forgive the room," Leia said as the Ithorians filed into the foyer. "It's the best I could do under the circumstances."

Ooamu Waoabi—the eldest of the Ithorian elders—politely swung his ocular nodes around the room, his small eyes blinking gently as they observed the automated beverage dispensers, the state-of-the-art holotheater, the transparisteel viewing wall that overlooked the academy's training grounds and low-slung instruction halls.

"Your presence would make any room pleasant, Princess Leia." Waoabi spoke out of only one of the mouths on his throat, a reflection of the poor medical care aboard the Ithorian refugee cities. "But we thank you for your concern."

"And thank you for coming to Ossus." Leia could barely contain the excitement she felt—nor her fear that the Ithorians might balk at settling outside the Galactic Alliance. "I know it was an unexpected journey. But Han and I must return to the Unknown Regions as soon as the *Falcon* is ready, and there is something I wanted to discuss . . ."

Leia let her sentence trail off as a pair of black-clad Galactic Alliance bodyguards stepped into the foyer behind the Ithorians. The two women were not armed—only Jedi were permitted to carry weapons on Ossus—but their sinewy builds and supple grace suggested they did not need to be. Leia's hand dropped to her lightsaber, and she slipped between Waoabi and another Ithorian elder to confront the newcomers.

"May I help you?" she said.

"Yes." The first woman's cobalt eyes darted past Leia, scanning all corners of the chamber. "You can clear the room."

As the first woman spoke, the second was slipping past behind her, waving the feathery antennae of a threat scanner at various pieces of furniture and artwork. Leia glanced toward Han, but he was already placing himself squarely in the bodyguard's path, studying the scanner with feigned interest.

"Is that one of those new Tendrando Arms multisniffers Lando was telling me about?" Han pushed his head between the delicate antennae, pretending he wanted to see the data display—and ruining the instrument's calibration. "I've heard they can smell a gram of thermaboom at fifty meters."

Leia waited until the first bodyguard finally stopped looking past her, then said, "I'll be happy to clear the room when our meeting is finished. Until then, feel free to wait in the reception—"

"We have no time to wait." Cal Omas entered the room wearing a rumpled travel tunic as red as the veins in his bloodshot eyes. "This matter has taken too much of my time already."

"Chief Omas!" Leia's diplomatic skills must have been degenerating from disuse, for she could not quite conceal her shock. "What a surprise to see you here."

"I imagine." Omas started for the beverage station, walking straight past the Ithorian delegation and failing to acknowledge them. "Where's Luke?"

"I really don't know." Leia began to fume at the way he had slighted her guests. "Chief Omas, allow me to present Ooamu Waoabi and the Council of Ithorian Elders. We were about to begin a meeting—a meeting for which they have traveled a long distance on short notice."

Taking the hint, Omas set aside the glass of bwago juice he had been filling and returned to the Ithorians. "Elder Waoabi, a pleasure to see you again."

He bowed formally to Waoabi, then greeted each of the other elders by name, stumbling only when he came to the young Jedi liaison, Ezam Nhor. For a moment, Leia was impressed enough to recall why she had helped elect Cal Omas to the Chief's office in the first place.

Then Omas returned to the beverage station. "Forgive me for pushing in like this." He retrieved his bwago juice and took a sip. "But I've asked the senior Jedi to meet me here to discuss a matter of vital importance."

"And I'm afraid you're going to be disappointed," Luke said. He entered the room with Mara and, pausing to bow to the Ithorians, approached the Chief of State. "Most senior Jedi aren't available. Perhaps if there had been more notice . . ."

"If you hadn't been hiding here on Ossus, perhaps I would have been able to provide it." Omas gave Luke an icy glare. "As it is, *you* will have to do. Aristocra Formbi is demanding to know why the Galactic Alliance has sent a battle fleet to the Colony."

"Have we?" Luke's gaze remained fixed on Omas, but Leia felt his mind reaching in her direction, wondering what this had to do with her vague warning about the shift of power in the Colony. "I wasn't aware of that."

"Neither was I," Omas fumed. "Yet a Hapan battle fleet was seen at someplace called the Lizil nest."

"In the Colony?" Corran Horn asked, stepping into the room. "What's it doing there?"

"I was hoping someone *here* could explain." Omas's gaze swung to Leia. "Perhaps *you*?"

"I'm afraid not." Leia had been half expecting this. In the convoluted politics of the Hapan Royal Navy, there was sure to be some ambitious spy who saw an advantage in reporting the fleet's encounter with the *Falcon* to Galactic Alliance Intelligence. "They were in no mood to answer questions."

"*Who* was in no mood to answer questions?" Kyp asked, joining the group. He nodded to the Ithorians, from him the equivalent of a full diplomatic salutation, then ignored Omas and came to stand with Leia and Han. "The Hapans?"

"Yeah," Han said. "They wanted to intern us."

"*Intern* you?" Omas knitted his brow. "You *encountered* this fleet?"

Leia began to have a sinking feeling. "You didn't know?"

"No." Omas's voice was icy.

"I apologize," Leia said. "We gave our word not to reveal their presence."

"And you *kept* it?" Omas demanded.

"Some of us still honor our promises," Han said. "I know it's old-fashioned, but there you have it."

"The Galactic Alliance can't afford your promises right now," Omas retorted. "I only hope they haven't started a war."

"Leia had no choice," Luke said. "The word of one Jedi to another is binding."

Omas let his chin drop. "*Don't* tell me there were Jedi aboard those ships!"

"It was Tenel Ka's fleet, and *she* is a Jedi," Mara said. "Leia's word is as binding to Tenel Ka's agent as it would be to the queen herself."

The assertion was a stretch, since being honest with other Jedi was more of an unwritten policy than a formal code. And the concept of extending it to a Jedi's representatives was a new innovation entirely, but Leia appreciated the support. She started toward the conference area, initiating a subtle migration that she hoped would result in a shift of mood as well as location. Once she arrived, she turned and watched in silent amusement as Omas instinctively searched for the head seat at a round table. Now would have been a good time to ask the Ithorians to wait in the reception area, but she was not about to sanction the rude way Omas had burst into the chamber. If he did not want to discuss this in front of the Ithorians, *he* could be the one who asked them to leave.

"If you didn't know about our encounter with the fleet, Chief Omas, why did you think Han and I could tell you what it was doing in the Colony?" Leia asked.

"Because of your son." Omas finally took a chair across from her, his gaze lingering on the concentric black-circle, white-star inlay that repeated itself on the table's surface in ever-smaller renditions. "I thought Jacen might have told you why he arranged this."

"Jacen?" Han asked. He sat at Leia's right. "Last time I checked, he wasn't king of anything."

"No, but Tenel Ka dispatched the Hapan fleet shortly after his visit." Omas waited as Luke, Mara, and the other Jedi Masters also took seats at the conference table, allowing his gaze to linger on the Ithorians, then finally seemed to accept that the Jedi were not going to ask them to leave and simply turned back to the conference table. "I doubt it was a coincidence."

"It wasn't," Jacen said, breezing into the room. "I asked her to send a fleet to the Colony's aid."

Omas twisted around in his chair. "Why in the blazes would you do something like that?"

Instead of answering, Jacen stopped and greeted the Ithorians fondly, addressing several by name, then excused himself to go over to the conference area. The Ithorians, as perceptive as they were gentle, remained in the foyer area, awkwardly greeting Kenth Hamner, Cilghal, and the other Jedi Masters as they continued to trickle in.

Jacen took a chair at Omas's side, then said, "I am a Jedi. All you need know is that my reasons were sound."

The calming aroma of the roo wood must have been working, because Omas remained in his seat and looked across the table toward Luke. "I didn't realize Jacen was a Master."

"The opinions of all Jedi are valued in this room—even those who don't consider themselves members of the Jedi Order." Luke looked to Jacen. "Perhaps you'd explain to the Masters present?"

"If you like." Jacen's tone was cordial. "I was trying to prevent a war."

"*Prevent* one?" Omas demanded. "The Chiss—"

"Understand only power," Jacen interrupted. "And now the Killiks have some. The Hapan fleet will buy us the time we need to resolve this conflict."

"At the Galactic Alliance's expense," Omas said. "The Chiss are already threatening to withdraw their security patrols if we don't bring our Jedi under control."

Mara's eyes—and those of several other Masters—flashed at the word *our,* but Omas did not seem to notice. He turned back to Luke.

"And that's exactly what I want you to do, Master Skywalker," he said. "By force, if necessary. I want all of our Jedi, and the Hapan fleet, back inside Galactic Alliance borders by this time next month."

"Wouldn't it be better for *you* to talk to Queen Tenel Ka?" Leia asked. "She is, after all, the leader of a Galactic Alliance republic."

"*And* a Jedi," Omas countered. He lowered his eyes, then continued in a softer voice. "Frankly, she refuses to listen to me. She insists she is only doing what is right, and the discussion ends there."

"And perhaps ours should end here," Kyp said. He sat at Leia's left, looking across to where Luke sat at one tip of the conference table's largest inlaid stars. "Jedi don't answer to politicians."

"What?" This from Corran, who sat on the other side of Kyp. "Then who *do* we answer to? Ourselves?"

"Of course," Jacen replied calmly. "Who else can we trust to wield our power? We must follow our own consciences."

"That's very arrogant," Kenth Hamner said. He placed his hands on the table and leaned forward, looking Jacen directly in the eye. "It concerns me to hear *any* Jedi say such a thing . . . but you, Jacen?"

"It *is* sound public policy to place powerful factions like the Jedi under the control of a civil authority." Leia kept her voice reasonable and conciliatory. Whether Jacen knew it or not, he was digging at an old wound among the Masters, and she did not want the meeting to descend into another of the shouting matches that Luke had described over the Jedi's proper relationship to the government. "Even in those with the best of intentions, power corrupts."

"And so we place the burden of remaining pure on lesser shoulders?" Jacen pressed. "Mother, you've watched two governments collapse under the weight of their own corruption and inefficiency, and the third is sagging. Do you really believe Jedi should be the tools of such frail institutions?"

Leia was at a loss to respond. Jacen's question was almost rhetorical. He had been there when she declared that she was done with politics forever, and he knew better than anyone—probably even Han—how disheartened she had been by the ineptitude of the New Republic government. In truth, she almost agreed with what he was saying . . . and probably would have done so openly, had she known of a better way to run a galactic republic.

When Leia failed to answer, Jacen turned to Omas, who was flushing in speechless anger, and said, "I'm sorry if this offends you—"

"It offends *me*," Corran said. "The Jedi exist to serve the Galactic Alliance."

"Our duty is to the Force." Kyp's voice was calmer than Corran's, but harder. "Our *only* duty."

Kenth Hamner held his hand out toward Kyp, fingers forward in a conciliatory fashion. "I think what Corran is saying is that it's our duty to serve the Galactic Alliance, because serving the Alliance serves the Force."

"That so?" Han asked. He usually avoided ethics debates like the black holes they were, but this time even he could not restrain himself. "Because Corran made it pretty clear he thought the Jedi were just a bunch of Reconstruction Authority cops who ought to take their orders from Chief Omas like everyone else."

He winked at Jacen—which was exactly the wrong thing to do at that moment.

Corran glared blaster bolts at Han. "I think we are answerable to Galactic Alliance authority, yes."

"Even if it means war in another part of the galaxy?" Mara retorted. "Because Jacen's right about this. The Force extends beyond the Galactic Alliance—and so does our responsibility."

"Then let the rest of the galaxy pay your bills," Omas snapped.

"Until that happens, I expect the Jedi to put Galactic Alliance interests first."

A sudden silence fell over the conference table, with Corran and Kenth casting accusatory glances at Kyp and Mara, and Kyp and Mara studying Omas with knowing sneers.

After a moment, Luke said, "When the Alliance offered its support, it was with the explicit understanding that there were no conditions."

"In an ideal galaxy, that would still be true," Omas said. He met Luke's gaze without flinching—and with no regret or embarrassment for breaking his pledge. "But Galactic Alliance finances are stretched thin as it is. If we must suddenly replace the Chiss security patrols, the only way to afford the cost would be to slash the Jedi budget."

Kyp planted his elbows on a wedge of black tabletop and ran his gaze around the circle of Masters. "Well, at least the question is out in the open now. Are we mercenaries, or are we Jedi?"

Corran's eyes bulged, and the debate deteriorated into an open quarrel, with Corran and Kenth still arguing fiercely that the order's first obligation was to the Galactic Alliance, and Kyp and Mara stubbornly contending that Jedi should strive to bring justice and peace wherever the Force summoned them. Cringing at what the Ithorians must think of such a contentious display, Leia glanced over at the foyer area and found them standing there in polite silence, as overlooked and forgotten by the Jedi as they had been by the Galactic Alliance government for the last five years . . . and that was when a terrible thought struck her.

Leia had a solution to the Colony problem—a solution that meant cheating the Ithorians yet again.

The Masters' voices were growing sharp and loud, but Leia remained quiet. Her plan would please Omas more than it did her, and that in itself was almost enough to make her reject it. Once, she had held the Chief in high regard and helped place the war against the Yuuzhan Vong in his hands. But peace was often harder to manage than war. Over the last five years, Omas had made too many compromises, bowed to the demands of the moment so many times that he could no longer hold his head up high enough to see what was coming on the horizon.

And if Leia proposed her solution, she would be guilty of the same thing. She didn't know if she could do that, if peace would be worth seeing the defeated eyes of Cal Omas in her own face when she looked into the mirror every morning.

Finally, Luke had heard enough. "Stop!"

When Kyp and Corran continued to argue, he stood and sharpened his voice without raising it.

"Stop," he repeated.

Kyp and Corran slowly fell silent.

"Is this how Jedi resolve their disagreements?" Luke asked.

Both of the Masters' faces went red with embarrassment, and Corran said, "I'm sorry."

He was apologizing to Luke instead of Kyp, but that was more than Kyp did. He simply sank into his chair and, being careful to avoid Corran's eyes, stared blankly at the table's star-within-a-star inlay.

"Too bad," Han muttered. "I haven't seen a good lightsaber fight in ages."

Leia was about to kick Han under the table when he exclaimed, "Ouch!"

"Sorry." Mara looked past Han to Leia. "Just stretching."

"No problem," Leia said. Han's joke was too true to be funny; the rift in the Jedi order had been widened today, and she was beginning to wonder if it could ever be closed. "I was feeling a little cramped myself."

Luke allowed a tense silence to fall over the room, then sat down and turned to Omas.

"It may take some time to reach a consensus on your request, Chief Omas. As you can see, our decision is complicated by the fact that the Chiss are acting against the Killiks not because of what they *have* done, but because of what they *might* do."

Omas nodded gravely, his irresolute gaze gliding around the table, silently taking the measure of the Jedi who had defied him, trying to judge the resolve of those who had not. Finally, he came to Luke and stopped.

"Master Skywalker, I quite simply do not care," he said. "The Chiss's trouble with the Colony is no concern of ours. We can't put Galactic Alliance lives at risk just because a few Jedi feel bound by a quaint morality no one else understands."

Kam Solusar and Tionne arrived on the heels of the exchange. It had been over a year since Leia had seen either of them, but they looked much the same, Kam still wearing his white hair cropped close to the head and Tionne allowing her silver-white tresses to cascade over her shoulders. They had barely cleared the door before they drew up short, recoiling from the animosity in the Force with the horrified expressions of someone who had just stumbled upon a pair of mating Togorians.

Leia had not realized until she saw their alarm just how noxious the atmosphere in the room had grown. The rift in the council was widening before her eyes, opening a chasm that would only grow increasingly difficult for prideful Masters like Kyp and Corran to cross. Assuming that her idea was viable, and she felt sure it was, she had it in her power to close that rift—at the price of her own conscience.

Kam and Tionne took seats next to each other, on the opposite side of Cilghal from Luke.

"We were just discussing the situation at Qoribu," Luke said to them. "Chief Omas has informed us that Tenel Ka has dispatched a Hapan battle fleet to aid the Colony."

Tionne's pearlescent eyes grew wide. "That doesn't sound good."

"It gets worse," Corran said, scowling at Jacen. "A *Jedi* is responsible."

"He followed his conscience," Kyp said. "Which is more than I can say for half—"

"Actually," Leia said, cutting off Kyp's insult before it could be finished, "there may be a way for the Jedi to stop the war *and* earn the trust of the Chiss."

Han groaned, but everyone else turned to her with a mixture of relief and expectation in their eyes.

"Han and I discovered—"

"Uh, sweetheart?" Han grabbed her forearm. "Can I talk to you a minute?"

This did not please Omas. "Captain Solo, if you have discovered something useful to the Galactic Alliance—"

"Excuse me, Chief." Leia spun her chair around, placing her back to the table, then waited as Han did the same. "Yes, dear?"

Han's eyes bulged. "What in the blazes are you doing?"

"Stopping a war," Leia whispered. Knowing Han would only grow stubborn if he realized how much this was going to hurt her, she tried to hide her dismay. "Saving billions of lives, keeping the council together, preserving the Galactic Alliance. That kind of thing."

"Yeah, I know." Han jerked a thumb toward the Ithorians. "What about them? That world we found was perfect—"

"And it's perfect for the Killiks, too." She had a familiar queasiness inside, a heavy feeling that used to come whenever she was forced to make an unfair choice as the New Republic Chief of State. "We'll take care of the Ithorians another way."

"How?" Han asked. "Ask Omas to give them a planet?"

"No," Leia said. "*Make* him."

She turned around and smiled across the table at Omas.

"On the way home, Han and I discovered a small group of unin-habited planets." Leia waited for the murmur of surprise to fade, then said, "I think they might make a good home for the Qoribu nests."

A wave of disappointment filled the Force, and Leia could not help looking past Omas toward the foyer. The Ithorians were all staring silently in her direction, their eyes half closed in resignation—or perhaps it was sorrow. Still, when Leia met Waoabi's gaze, he merely tightened his lips and gave her an approving nod. No Ithorian would want to live on a world that had been bought with someone else's blood.

Leia directed her attention to Luke. "I propose that we move the Qoribu nests to these planets."

"*How?*" Jacen asked. "There are four nests in the system, each with at least twenty thousand Killiks, and you don't just *move* a Kil-lik nest. You have to rebuild it inside a ship, lay in stores—"

"I'm sure Tenel Ka will instruct her fleet to help with that," Leia said. "In fact, I'm rather counting on it."

Jacen's jaw fell, then he closed his mouth and nodded. "That could work."

"And it will look as though it's what the Jedi intended all along," Omas added. "Brilliant!"

"You're sure about this planet?" Luke asked Leia. "It's com-pletely deserted?"

"We should stop on the way back to the Colony and do a thor-ough sector scan." Leia glanced at Han, who nodded, then added, "But I'm sure. The astrobiology there is . . . unique."

"Well, then." Luke glanced around the circle, seeking and receiv-ing an affirmative nod from each of the council Masters. "We seem to have reached an agreement."

The bitterness began to fade from the Force, and the tension drained from the faces of the Masters.

"We'd better prepared to deal with the Dark Nest," Mara said. "It might not like this idea."

"Dark Nest?" Omas asked.

"The Gorog nest," Luke explained. "The Colony seems com-pletely unaware of it, so we've started calling it the Dark Nest."

"It's attacked us several times," Mara said.

"Why?" Omas asked.

Mara hesitated, clearly unwilling to tell the chief about the nest's personal vendetta against her, so Leia answered.

"We're not sure," she said. "The nest doesn't seem to want us involved with the Colony, so it's a good bet it will try to stop us."

"Maybe the Dark Nest *wants* war," Jacen suggested. "It sounds like the Colony was pushing up against Ascendancy territory even before their own worlds began to grow scarce. There must be a reason."

"I don't understand," Omas said. "I thought you persuaded Tenel Ka to send her fleet because the Colony is trying to *avoid* a war?"

"The *Colony* is," Cilghal said. "But the Dark Nest—"

"May have its own reasons to want a war," Leia said. She did not want to complicate Omas's view of the issue with a lengthy explanation of the Colony's unconscious motivations—or give him reason to doubt the Jedi's ability to resolve the crisis. "There's a bit of a, um, power struggle going on inside the Colony."

"Isn't there always?" Omas said, nodding sagely. Power struggles were something that every government official understood well. He turned to Luke. "Is this going to be a problem for us?"

"Only finding it," Mara said. "The Gorog are pretty secretive. So far, we've seen them on Yoggoy and Taat, but we have no idea—"

"Not a problem," Han interrupted. "I can find their nest."

"I don't know if that's even possible," Cilghal said. "The Gorog social structure may be quite different from other nests'. They may have parasite cells hidden among all the other—"

"I can find 'em—at least the, uh, *heart*," Han said, following Leia's lead in not mentioning Lomi and Welk by name. "Trust me."

"Fine." Luke turned to Chief Omas and added, "But we'll have to take along a Jedi team large enough to neutralize the nest. The Chiss will be alarmed—and nothing you say is going to reassure them."

"They'll be reassured when the Killiks leave Qoribu. I'll handle them until then—just don't take too long." Omas braced his hands on the table and rose. "Speaking of which, I'll be on my way—"

"Not so fast, Chief," Han said. "We haven't told you what this is going to cost."

"Cost?" Omas looked to Luke, who merely shrugged and directed the Chief back to Han. "Of course, the Galactic Alliance will be more than happy to compensate you for any expenses the *Falcon* incurred—"

"We're talking a lot more than that." Han pointed at Omas's chair, motioning him back down. "You see, Leia and I had something in mind for that group of planets, and we're not about to give that up just because you're afraid of what the Chiss think."

Omas scowled. "I'm sorry, I don't understand what you're saying."

"Borao," Leia said. "We want you to annul RePlanetHab's claim in favor of ours."

"You see, we were there first, and they kind of claim-jumped us," Han said. "It's been scorching my jets ever since."

"You want me to give you a *planet*?" Omas gasped. "In the Inner Rim?"

"Not us." Leia pointed over Omas's shoulder toward the Ithorians. "Our clients."

Omas spun in his chair, slowly, and faced the Ithorians—who were looking considerably less glum.

"I see," he said. "If the decision were mine alone—"

"Han, do you remember the coordinates of the new planet group?" Leia asked. "We were having that trouble with the navicomputer, and I'm not sure we made a backup of—"

"I'll see what I can do," Omas said, rising again. "But, you understand, I can't just *do* this. The Recovery Act is law—I'll have to push a special exception through."

"Then I suggest you hurry," Corran said, leaning back in his chair. "The Qoribu problem is time-sensitive, and I'm sure the Solos will want this matter resolved before they leave."

"That's quite impossible," Omas said.

When Corran merely shrugged, Omas turned to Kenth—who suddenly seemed far more interested in the training fields outside than in the Chief of State.

Omas sighed, then said, "But I *can* block RePlanetHab's claim." He turned to the Ithorians and added, "It may take a month or it may take ten, but I'll push this through. By this time next year, you'll have a planet of your own again. I give you my word as Chief of State."

"That's not much," Han said, also rising. "But it'll have to do."

"To the contrary, Captain Solo." Waoabi started forward, holding out his long-fingered hand to shake Omas's and accept the promise. "It is more than we have now. Thank you."

Waoabi's courtesy should have made Leia feel better, but it did not. Instead, she felt sad and sickened and a little bit soiled by the trade-off she had been forced to make.

Like it or not, she was suddenly back in politics.

THIRTY-ONE

A weight lay across Jaina's chest, and the inside of one ear was being warmed by a soft, pulsing growl. The dormitory air was filled with a comforting mélange of refresher soap and body smells from a dozen different species, but the predominant odor, familiar and musky and strongest, was human.

Male human.

Zekk.

Jaina reached down and felt his arm across her, and his leg a bit lower, then slowly turned her head. Through a lingering fog of membrosia excess, she saw the familiar chiseled features surrounded by a frame of shaggy black hair. Thankfully, he was still clothed.

The previous night came flooding back to her: Unu's arrival at Jwlio, the Dance of Union, the Taat drifting off into the Harem Cave, the Joiners leaving in twos and threes and fours, her hand in Zekk's . . .

Zekk's green eyes opened, and the smile on his face was replaced by a confused squint. He blinked two or three times, then glanced at the lightly-clothed female body over which he'd draped himself and raised his brow. Jaina sensed a distinct *click* in the back of his mind. His eyes slid away from hers, and she felt his emotions swinging from disbelief to bewilderment to guilt.

"Well," Jaina said, hoping to set a casual tone. "Interesting night."

"Yeah." Zekk pulled his arm and leg off of her body. "I—I thought it was a dream."

Jaina cocked her brow. "You're saying it wasn't?"

Zekk's eyes widened. "No, it was fun!" he said. "Great, even. I just . . . it just didn't feel real . . ."

Zekk let the sentence trail off, sharing his thoughts and emotions with Jaina directly via the meld—or perhaps it was the Taat mind—instead of trying to explain. He had loved her since they were teenagers, and he had imagined waking at her side countless times. But last night had not felt like *them*. They had been carried along on a wave of Killik emotion. He had sought her out in the rapture of the dance, even when he knew she did not share his feelings, and found himself leading her down into the dormitory with all the Joiners—

"Zekk, we didn't do anything," Jaina said. She could have answered him more quickly and clearly just by thinking, but right now she needed the sense of separation that came with speaking—even if it *was* an illusion. "It was just a little cuddling between friends. You have a problem with that?"

"No!" Zekk said. "I just feel like I took advantage."

Jaina clasped his forearm. "You didn't." She was genuinely touched by his concern—and truly relieved that it had been handsome, muscular, familiar Zekk who had taken her hand instead of Raynar. "We lost control there for a minute, but we got it back. I'm just glad Alema went home with Mom and Dad."

Zekk remained quiet.

Jaina propped herself up on an elbow. "Hey!" She punched him in the shoulder. "I know what you're thinking!"

"Sorry."

Zekk blushed and turned away, and Jaina felt him closing down emotionally.

"Zekk, you can't do that," she said. They had to keep the meld open between them, to constantly draw on each other's strength and resolve to remain their own little entity within the greater Taat mind. "And will you stop apologizing?" Jaina rolled her eyes, then reached for her jumpsuit. "I think I'm getting dressed now."

She sat up and, sensing someone behind her, pivoted to find Raynar on the busy walkway at the head of their sunken bed. Dressed in scarlet and gold and surrounded by his usual retinue of assorted Killiks, he was squatting on his haunches, staring down into the hexagonal sleeping cell with no discernible expression on his melted face. A sense of overwhelming awe arose inside Jaina—Taat's reaction to UnuThul's presence—and she felt her mouth broadening into an adoring grin.

She managed to wipe it away by reminding herself that this used to be *Raynar Thul*.

"Raynar—good morning." Jaina pushed her feet into the jumpsuit and continued to dress without embarrassment. There was not much sense in being modest when several thousand nestmates had access to your innermost thoughts. "Come down to see how the drones live?"

Raynar lowered his stiff brow. "Why do you call us Raynar when you know Raynar Thul is gone?"

"Raynar's still in there somewhere," Jaina said. "I can feel him."

Raynar glared down at her, then said, "Perhaps you are right. Perhaps a little Raynar Thul remains in us still." A glimmer of sadness appeared in his cold blue eyes. "And he will be sorry to see you go."

Jaina felt Zekk's alarm at the same time as her own.

"Go?"

"Your task here is done," Raynar explained.

"Really?" Jaina thrust her arm through a sleeve. "I hadn't heard the Chiss were gone."

As she said this, the image of a clawcraft reconnaissance patrol appeared in her mind—the scene being relayed to one of the tactical monitors in the Taat control room. The ships were silhouetted against Ruu's amber disk, flying just above the plane of Qoribu's golden ring system.

"It looks like they're still here to me," Zekk said, no doubt seeing the same thing in his mind's eye as Jaina did in hers. "So why would the Colony want us to leave *now*?"

"We wish you to return to the Galactic Alliance," Raynar said, dodging the question.

"What about our mission?" Jaina rose and closed her jumpsuit. "You brought us here to keep the peace."

Raynar stood. "Your starfighters are being fueled. We thank you for coming."

"You seem eager to be rid of us," Zekk said, zipping his own suit. "What's going on?"

"It's the Chiss." Jaina could not tell whether her inference came from her own mind, Zekk's, or Taat's, but she *knew* it was correct. "They're going to attack."

A short, very Raynar-like sigh escaped Raynar's lips. "There's nothing more you can do here. And we don't wish to involve Jedi in this fight."

"There isn't going to be a fight," Zekk said. "Jaina and I will turn them back."

"Not this time," Raynar said. "The Chiss intend to bring this to an end, and they won't be intimidated by Jedi tricks."

"There's no harm in trying." Jaina summoned her utility belt and began to buckle it on. She did not understand why the Chiss were suddenly changing strategy and launching a major assault, but in a war, some things you just did not have time to figure out. "Where are you expecting them? Zekk and I will—"

"No. We don't wish to risk the lives of our friends in this matter."

"What do you think we've *been* doing?" Zekk asked, buckling on his own belt. "We're here to keep the peace, and we're not leaving—"

"There is no longer a peace to keep," Raynar said. "And you *are* leaving."

Suddenly his voice felt like it weighed a thousand kilos, and the urge to do as he ordered grew almost overwhelming. There was more going on here than Raynar was telling.

Ambush.

The thought had barely flashed through Jaina's mind before a Taat in Raynar's retinue began to drum its chest. Raynar listened intently, then met Jaina's gaze and shook his head.

"You have always been too headstrong for your own good, Jaina. Do not try to figure this out, or—"

"It won't work," Zekk said, leaping to the same conclusion as Jaina. "If you destroy the Chiss fleet, the next one will only be bigger."

Raynar let his chin drop in another old-Raynar gesture. "Now you've done it." The urge to depart suddenly vanished. "Now you must stay."

"We weren't leaving without Lowbacca, anyway." Jaina sounded more certain than she was; Raynar's will had felt like it was more than a match for her stubbornness. "And Zekk is right. The Colony isn't strong enough to destroy the entire Chiss space force."

"That won't be necessary," Raynar said. "We only need to hold them off until the Hapans arrive."

"Hapans?" Jaina climbed out of the sleeping cell onto the walkway with Raynar, causing a soft clatter as his retinue scrambled to make room for her. "What are Hapans doing out here?"

"Defending the weak," Raynar said. "Jacen convinced Tenel Ka to send us a fleet."

At least now Jaina understood why the Chiss were attacking. They wanted to destroy the Qoribu nests before reinforcements arrived to complicate the job.

"Jacen convinced Tenel Ka, or *you* used Jacen to convince her?" Jaina was thinking of how Raynar had nearly forced her to leave just a few moments earlier—and of the irresistible call that had summoned her and the others to the Colony in the first place. "Your touch can be very compelling."

"Perhaps, but even *we* are not strong enough to control Jacen," Raynar said. "He has moved beyond our control—or anyone else's. You know that yourself."

Jaina could not argue. During Jacen's five-year journey, she had felt him growing steadily stronger in the Force—but also more distant and isolated, like a hermit retreating to his mountaintop. At times, he had seemed to vanish into the Force entirely, and at other times she had sworn he was floating just above her shoulder.

To tell the truth, it had given her the creeps. She had started to feel like she was sharing a twin bond with a different brother every few weeks—or like he was practicing to be dead or something.

"Jacen wouldn't send you a fleet," Zekk said. He jumped up onto the adjacent side of the sleeping cell, into the middle of a steady line of Joiners streaming past toward the communal refresher. They smoothly detoured down another walkway, and both the conversation and the morning parade continued unabated. "That could start a war between the Chiss and the Galactic Alliance."

"Or prevent one between us and the Chiss," Raynar countered. "Perhaps he is willing to run the risk."

"Even Solos don't like odds *that* long," Jaina said. "When Chiss feel threatened, they don't back off. They get mean and aggressive."

"You can't do this," Zekk added.

"What we cannot do is allow the destruction of the Qoribu nests." Raynar's retinue abruptly started for the exit, and he turned to follow. "Once the ambush begins, you will be free to fight or leave, as you wish. Until then, you remain our guests."

Jaina started after him. "Raynar!" When a pair of knobby-shelled bodyguards moved to cut her off, she used the Force to shove them into a sleeping cell, then said, "This is madness!"

Raynar continued moving away from her. "It is self-defense." Again, his voice grew heavy and commanding, and this time it contained an edge that suggested he would abide no more argument. "You will return to your proper barracks and remain there until the battle begins."

Jaina felt an overwhelming urge to obey, but there was a darkness in his tone that alarmed her, a hint of brutality so utterly alien to Raynar Thul that she knew it was not him alone speaking. She planted her feet on the walkway and, drawing on Zekk for the strength to resist the compulsion to start toward the barracks, touched Raynar in the Force.

The murky presence inside him was so caustic that she recoiled and would have lost contact had Zekk not bolstered her through their meld. Jaina began to feel her way through the bitter darkness, searching for Raynar's pride and idealism, trying to find the core of him that she sensed was still there.

"*They* want this war," she said. "They're the ones who convinced you to establish your nests so close to Chiss territory."

Raynar stopped, but did not turn around. "*They?* Who is *they?*"

"Your shipmates on the *Flier*." Zekk stepped past Jaina and, shuffling along the walkway, started toward Raynar. "Lomi and Welk."

"Lomi and Welk are dead."

Jaina found something pure and compassionate inside the Prime and touched it. "Then who attacked the *Shadow* on her way in?"

"Insect mercenaries hired by the Chiss," Raynar answered instantly.

Zekk stopped a step behind Raynar. "You have proof?"

"We have no time to look for proof." Raynar reluctantly turned around, and his retinue of insects began to file back toward the discussion. "We are too busy defending our nests."

Jaina sighed inwardly. It was the same circular logic they encountered every time they tried to investigate the mysterious attacks.

"What about the attack on Saba?" Zekk pressed. "I suppose you're going to tell me she attacked a Joiner by mistake, and he took her lightsaber away and wounded her?"

"Yes," Raynar replied. "That is the best explanation."

Jaina tightened her hold on the core of benevolence she had found. "Raynar, they're blinding you to the truth. The best explanation—"

"We are tired of telling you!"

The murky presence welled up inside Raynar and swallowed the pure center that Jaina was holding, and she found herself suddenly adrift in a void of biting darkness. Instinctively, she reached for Zekk and opened herself to their meld, but instead of his strength, all that came to her was cold, stinging shadow.

"Raynar Thul is gone," Raynar said.

Jaina felt herself turning. She tried to fight the compulsion, to lock her gaze on Raynar and keep it there, but she simply did not have the strength to fight him. She stepped away and started for the barracks.

"We are all that remains."

THIRTY-TWO

A long, golden arrow curved through the heart of the hologrammic flight control display, tracing the route of the stolen skiff from the repair hangar to its current location on the edge of Ossus's gravity well. The reckless manner in which the skiff had cut through the approach zone of the planet's primary spaceport suggested the pilot had been eager to get away from the Jedi academy as quickly as possible. But Luke had already known that. Escapees liked to move fast.

"Thirty seconds before she can jump," a flight controller reported. A large-headed Bith with an auditory data feed in one ear, he was seated at one of a dozen control stations surrounding the hologrammic display. "She still won't acknowledge our signal."

"Keep trying," Luke said. He could feel the anxiety of the XJ3 pilots trailing the skiff—a pair of young Jedi Knights flying their first security rotation. They were worried they would have to blast it out of space. "Do we know yet whether she has company?"

"Not with certainty," said the Bith's supervisor, a blue-skinned Duros woman named Orame. She stepped to an empty terminal and clacked a few keys. An inset of a repair hangar security vid appeared at the base of the flight control display. "But we did find this."

The inset showed Alema Rar striding through a darkened repair bay, two cases of food goods floating through the air ahead of her.

"We think that shadow—"

"Enhance the cases," Mara said. Along with Han, Leia, and several others, she had accompanied Luke up from the hangar floor as soon as the stolen skiff had streaked skyward. "Bring up a label, if you can."

The Duros typed a command, and the carton label filled the image.

"NUTROFIT GELMEAT," Mara read.

"She's stealing Gorog!" Ben cried.

The skiff's trajectory began to flatten as Alema prepared to enter hyperspace. The XJ3 pilots commed for permission to open fire, and Luke reached out to them in the Force, urging them to avoid disabling the vessel.

"Permission granted," Orame said over the comm channel. "Open fire."

The pilots hesitated. "But—"

"You heard the order," Luke said, still reaching out to the pilots through the Force, urging them let the skiff go. "Open fire."

The skiff's trajectory began to weave and wobble as it began evasive maneuvers.

"She's getting away!" Ben cried. "Stop her!"

"They have to be careful, Ben," Mara said gently. "Or they might hurt Gorog."

Ben considered this, then sighed and took her hand. "Let them go. I don't think Gorog wanted to stay anyway."

The skiff's trajectory reached the edge of Ossus's gravity well and vanished. The flight controller reported that the stolen skiff had entered hyperspace.

Han let out a sigh of relief. "Right on sch—"

"Not now," Luke interrupted, raising his hand to silence Han. He turned to Ben. "How did you know Gorog didn't want to stay? Do you still feel her in your mind?"

Ben closed his eyes, then nodded. "Sort of. She wants me to be happy."

Luke felt his own dismay mirrored in Mara. If Ben remained in touch with Gorog after she had entered hyperspace, it could only be through the Colony's Will. He was part Joiner—Dark Nest Joiner.

Mara had reached the same conclusion. Luke could feel her alarm and anger through the Force, and she was as quick as he was to realize that they could not discuss their plans in front of their son.

"Ben, maybe Nanna can take you to the pilots' lounge for some Fizzer," Mara said. "We have some things to discuss, then we'll find you there before we leave."

Ben made no move toward the door, where Nanna and C-3PO were waiting.

Luke frowned. "Ben, I'm sure you heard your mother."

Ben nodded. "I heard. But why do I have to stay behind on Ossus?" Without waiting for an answer, he turned to Han. "Is there going to be another war?"

Han grimaced, then said, "Not if we can help it, kid."

"And certainly not in this part of the galaxy," Mara added. "Why are you worried about that?"

"Because this is what you *do* when there's a war," Ben said. "You just dump me someplace with Masters Tionne and Solusar and then never even come to visit."

The accusation struck a pang in Luke's heart, and he felt Mara wince as well. They often wondered how much Ben's refusal to use the Force had to do with the separation anxiety he had suffered during the war with the Yuuzhan Vong, and Ben knew this particular complaint had an effect on them.

Even so, Mara refused to be manipulated by an eight-year-old. "Don't exaggerate, Ben. We had to keep you safe, and you know we came to see you every chance we had."

"Besides, they won't be gone long this time," Jacen said, stepping out from behind Han and Leia. "There isn't going to be a war."

Ben frowned. "How do you know that?"

"I *know*." Jacen flashed a crooked Solo smile. "Trust me."

Luke felt a sudden qualm in Mara, and though her eyes remained fixed on Ben, he sensed that her thoughts were on Jacen.

"Besides, you're not going to be alone," Jacen added. "I'll be here, too."

"You're not going back?" Ben asked.

"Not yet. The Masters are worried that *some* of us have spent too much time with the Killiks already."

"Tell me about it," Ben answered, rolling his eyes.

"So maybe you and I could hang out together?" Jacen glanced at Mara. "If that's all right with your mother."

"Of course." Mara answered with no outward hesitation, but Luke detected just a hint of apprehension, as though she did not quite trust the "new-and-improved" Jacen. "As long as Master Solusar thinks Ben is keeping up with his schoolwork—"

"No problem!" Ben's smile was as broad as a Hutt's. "School's easy."

"*And* as long as you obey Masters Tionne and Solusar," Mara warned Ben. "No secrets with Nanna, either."

"I can't do that anymore," Ben said. "Dad altered her program."

"Good." Jacen took Ben's hand and started for the door. "Why don't we get that Fizzer now?"

"Can I have kyleme?" Ben asked, not looking back. "A Blue Giant size?"

As soon as they were out of earshot, Han said, "Jacen has a knack with kids. Go figure."

"It's his empathy," Leia said. "I'm glad to see it's intact."

Leia left unsaid what Luke knew she was thinking: that after the war—after all Jacen had suffered at the hands of Vergere and the Yuuzhan Vong—she was surprised he had *any* empathy left.

Luke turned to Han. "Sorry to interrupt you earlier, but we don't know how much the Dark Nest might be able to glean from Ben's mind."

"No problem," Han said. "I got a little carried away when I saw how well the plan was working."

"I don't know why you're surprised," Leia said. "Alema is still a Jedi. Once Cilghal let her regain consciousness, there was never any question she could escape. The tricky part is going to be following her."

"How did you know which vessel she'd steal?" Mara asked.

"We didn't," Leia said. "We bugged them all."

"Speaking of bugs, we'd better get going," Han said. "That transmitter only has a subspace range of fifty light-years. We can't be too far behind when Alema hits Colony space, or we'll be stuck guessing where she went."

Luke followed Han and the others toward the door. Their intention was to follow Alema to the core of the Dark Nest, then undermine its influence over the Colony by eliminating Welk and—assuming she had survived the Crash—Lomi Plo. Cilghal and Jacen were convinced that at least Welk had survived—and that a Dark Jedi now led the Gorog in much the same way Raynar led the Unu. It was a somewhat ruthless plan, especially in the way it placed Alema's life at risk without her consent. But it seemed to Luke to be consistent with the nature of modern Jedi themselves. The war with the Yuuzhan Vong had taught the Jedi the folly of valuing sentiment over effectiveness, the wisdom of striking quickly and fiercely at the heart of a problem. Sometimes, Luke wondered whether it was a lesson the Jedi had learned too well; whether in defeating their enemies they had not become a little too much like them.

At the door, Han ran headlong into a short, gawky man with a heavily tattooed face and unruly blue hair. Without apologizing for—or even seeming to notice—the collision, the newcomer pushed past Han and stopped in front of Luke. R2-D2 followed close behind.

"Here you are," the man said. "I've been looking everywhere."

"I don't understand why, Ghent," Mara said. "We told you we were leaving on Jedi business."

Ghent furrowed his brow. "You did?"

"Several times." Luke saw Han tapping his wrist impatiently. "And we have to leave soon."

"Oh." Ghent's eyes dropped, then slid back toward R2-D2. "I guess this can wait."

"*What* can wait?" Leia asked. Luke had told her about the holo hidden in the sequestered sector in R2-D2's memory, and she was as eager as he was to learn more about the mysterious woman. "Did you find something?"

Ghent shook his head. "Just a few seconds of holo that I managed to relocate before I tripped a security gate. What I wanted to ask is if I could—"

"Holo of what?" Luke asked. "A brown-eyed woman?"

"That's right," Ghent said. "But it's really not very much. If I can—"

"Can you show it to us?" Leia sounded even more excited than Luke felt. "Before we leave?"

Ghent frowned. "Of course."

An uneasy silence fell as Luke and the others waited.

"Ghent, we want to see the holo," Mara said. "Now. As Luke said, we haven't got much time."

Ghent's brow rose. "Oh."

He squatted and inserted the plug of a homemade diagnostics scanner into one of R2-D2's input slots, then hastily typed a command. "Show them."

R2-D2 piped an objection, and Han groaned and looked at his chrono.

"Don't make me scramble your sector tables again," Ghent warned. "This time, I won't restore them."

R2-D2 let out a long, descending trill, then activated his holoprojector.

The hand-sized profile of the same brown-eyed woman that Luke had seen before appeared on the control room floor. She seemed to be standing alone, facing someone outside the hologram.

"Has Anakin been to see you?" asked a male voice.

"Wait a minute," Han said. "That guy sounds familiar."

"He should," Luke replied. The voice was much younger than when they had known him, but there was no mistaking its clarity and resonance. "That's Obi-Wan Kenobi."

Ghent tapped a key on his diagnostics scanner, stopping the holo. "Do you want to see this or not?"

"Of course—we're sorry," Leia said. "Please continue."

Ghent punched the key again, and R2-D2 restarted the holo from the beginning.

"Has Anakin been to see you?" Obi-Wan's voice asked.

"Several times." The woman smiled, then said, *"I was so happy to hear that he was accepted on the Jedi Council."*

"I know." Obi-Wan walked into the hologram, wearing a Jedi cloak with the hood down. He was still young, with a light brown beard and an unwrinkled face. *"He deserves it. He's impatient, strong-willed, very opinionated, but truly gifted."*

They laughed, then the woman said, *"You're not just here to say hello. Something's wrong, isn't it?"*

Obi-Wan's face grew serious. *"You should be a Jedi, Padmé."*

The name shot an electric bolt of excitement through Luke—and he could sense it had done the same to Leia.

"You're not very good at hiding your feelings," Padmé said.

Obi-Wan nodded. *"It's Anakin. He's becoming moody and detached."* His holoimage turned half away. *"He's been put in a difficult position as the Chancellor's representative, but I think it's more than that."* The image turned back to Padmé again. *"I was hoping he may have talked to you."*

Padmé's expression—at least what could be seen of it in the small hologrammic image—remained neutral.

"Why would he talk to me about his work?"

Obi-Wan studied her for a moment. *"Neither of you is very good at hiding your feelings, either."*

Padmé frowned. *"Don't give me that look."*

Obi-Wan continued to look at her in the same way. *"I know how he feels about you."*

Padmé's eyes slid away. *"What did he say?"*

"Nothing," Obi-Wan answered. *"He didn't have to."*

Padmé's face fell, and she turned and walked out of the hologram. *"I don't know what you're talking about."*

"I know you both too well." Obi-Wan followed her out of the frame. *"I can see you two are in love."*

There was no answer, and the hologram ended.

Luke could see Han biting his tongue, forcing himself to remain patient while the distance grew between them and Alema's skiff, but this was important—at least to him and Leia.

"That's all?" Luke asked.

Ghent nodded and tapped R2-D2's silver dome. "Artoo's block-ing me. When I tripped that security gate, he encrypted the rest of the data."

R2-D2 whistled an objection.

"It's not your place to decide what is good for Master Luke," C-3PO said. "You're only a droid."

R2-D2 trilled an angry reply.

"No, I *don't* know the secret you're keeping," C-3PO answered. "And if I did know, I'd tell Master Luke instantly."

R2-D2 responded with a low, slurpy buzz.

Luke frowned at the exchange, but turned back to Ghent. "Look. We've got about two minutes before we have to launch. Is there any way to see the rest now, without Artoo's cooperation?"

Ghent sighed. "Sure." He pulled his scanner plug out of R2-D2's input socket. "All I have to do is overwrite his personality sectors—"

The rest of Ghent's explanation was lost to R2-D2's screech of objection.

"Don't expect me to translate that," C-3PO said. "That's what happens to arrogant droids like you. I suggest you extend your coop-eration immediately."

R2-D2 trilled a sad refusal.

Luke glanced at the droid, then asked, "I mean *without* a per-sonality wipe."

"Not in two minutes—and maybe not in this lifetime," Ghent said. "This droid hasn't had a memory wipe in decades. His circuits are one huge personality fault."

"I know that," Luke said. "What about the spyware?"

Ghent looked confused. "Spyware?"

"The spyware that's keeping me from accessing those memo-ries." Luke was losing patience with the programmer. "The memo-ries concerning the woman we just saw?"

"Oh, *that* spyware," Ghent said. "There isn't any."

"There isn't?" Luke frowned. "Then how come Artoo won't give me access?"

Ghent sighed, sounding as exasperated as Luke felt. "That's what I'm trying to explain—"

"Maybe you can explain on the way to the pilots' lounge," Mara interrupted. She motioned them out the door. "We can finish talking on the way. We've still got a Twi'lek to catch, remember?"

"Right."

Luke was so excited by the hologram that he had let it over-shadow their mission for a moment. Anakin—his father—had been in love with a beautiful woman named Padmé. And Padmé did not look so different from Leia. Did they finally know their mother's name? He could sense that Leia thought so—but she was too afraid to say as much out loud. So was he.

Luke fell in beside Ghent. "You were explaining why Artoo won't let me access those memories?"

"Because he thinks he's protecting you," Ghent said. "He's a very stubborn droid."

"But you can get around that, right?" Leia asked. "I've seen you slice codes on units far more sophisticated than Artoo's."

Ghent turned around and looked at Leia as though she had asked for the name of the last girl he had tried to pick up in a cantina— they *never* told him their name.

"No," he said. "Artoo units were designed to military standards. That means their security protocols will destroy the data before they let it fall into unauthorized hands. If you try to force access, a doomsday gate will reformat the entire memory chip."

"And there's no way to beat that security without wiping Artoo's personality first?" Luke asked.

"I didn't say *that,*" Ghent said. "There's a way—but you'd have to help me, and you probably can't do it."

"Try us," Han said.

"Okay," Ghent said. "Bring me the Intellex Four designer's datapad."

"What for?"

"Because *he* had to have a way to access the data when his prototypes developed glitches like these," Ghent said. "And if he's like most droid-brain designers, that hatch became part of the Intellex IV's basic architecture. It's a very complicated computer unit, so there'll be a long list of passwords and encryption keys on that datapad."

"That shouldn't be too difficult, assuming it wasn't destroyed in a war," Luke said. "Who was this designer?"

Ghent shrugged. "Your guess is as good as mine. The Artoo was originally an Imperial design, and the Imperial Department of Military Research kept the identities of its top scientists secret."

"You must be joking," Leia said. "You want us to find this guy's datapad without knowing anything about him?"

"It's not quite that bad," Ghent said. "Do you remember when Incom's design staff defected to the Rebellion with the X-wing prototypes?"

"Of course," Leia said cautiously.

"Well, this guy was consulting with them on the Artoo interface," Ghent said. "And after the defection, Industrial Automaton never made another design modification to the Intellex Four."

"They were afraid to," Han surmised. "Because this guy was the only one who could do it right, and he had defected with the X-wing designers."

"No, not because he had defected," Leia said. She was studying Ghent intently. "If he had, we'd know who he was. Right?"

"Right," Ghent said. "He just disappeared."

Luke had a sinking feeling. "When you say disappeared, do you mean—"

"Nobody knows." Ghent turned to Leia. "That's what *disappeared* means, right? Nobody knows."

THIRTY-THREE

The sky had been dark for hours beneath clouds of dartships, roaring into the Taat nest to refuel and refresh life-support systems, roaring back out to await the arrival of the Chiss assault fleet. Jaina had given up trying to estimate how many craft the Colony had assembled for the ambush, but the number had to be over a hundred thousand. The Taat hangars alone were servicing six swarms an hour, and there were three other nests in the Qoribu system.

It makes us proud, Zekk said through the Taat mind. *No other species could mount such an operation.*

The Chiss will be surprised, Jaina agreed. Somewhere deep in her mind, she knew that this was a bad thing, that it would make her mission as a Jedi more difficult—but it did not feel that way to Taat. To Taat, it felt like their nests were finally going to be saved. *They will pay a terrible price.*

Good, Zekk said.

Good, Jaina agreed.

The roar of arriving dartships faded to a mere rumble, and the kilometer-long oval of a top-of-the-line Gallofree medium freighter descended out of the rocket smoke. The well-maintained hull was finished in the scarlet-and-gold flames of the Bornaryn Trading Company, with an escort of corporate E-wings providing security.

Jaina wondered what the vessel was doing so far from home, but Taat did not know. Unu wished the nest to welcome *Roaming Ronto,* and so Taat welcomed *Roaming Ronto.* Taat had heard, though, that similar vessels had landed on Ruu and Zvbo carrying a big surprise for the Chiss.

As the *Ronto* neared the nest, it adjusted course, heading out over the plateau toward the freight yard, where a swarm of Taat workers were already assembling to unload it. Jaina thought briefly about going to see the cargo, but Unu did not want that. Unu wanted her to enjoy the beauty of the nest from the veranda of the Jedi barracks.

That freighter should alarm us, Jaina said to Zekk. *It can only make war more likely.*

It's too late to stop the war, Zekk replied. *But we should try.*

Jaina started to rise, then suddenly felt too tired and dropped back onto her seat. *Maybe later.*

"Yeah," Zekk said aloud. *We'd rather sit here.*

There was something wrong with that, Jaina knew. Jedi were supposed to be dauntless, resourceful, resolute. They were supposed to accomplish the impossible, to keep trying no matter how difficult the mission.

They were supposed to have indomitable spirits.

Jaina felt a stirring deep down inside, in the place that had always belonged to her brother Jacen, and she knew he was with her, urging her to fight back, to throw off her lethargy, to break the Colony's hold on her and reach for that part of her that was just Jaina.

Jaina stood.

Where are you going? Zekk asked. *It doesn't feel like you need the refresher.*

"Get out of our—*my*—mind," Jaina said.

Jacen was urging her to remember how Welk and Lomi Plo had tricked the strike team on *Baanu Rass,* how they had stolen the *Flier* and abandoned Anakin to die. And now Jaina was allowing them to control her mind.

Jaina did not understand how that could be. The entire Colony knew that Raynar Thul was the only survivor of the Crash.

But Jacen seemed so sure. A black fury rose in Jaina's mind, the same black fury to which she had succumbed when she went to recover Anakin's body, and finally she felt able to act.

She wanted to find Welk and kill him. She wanted to find Lomi Plo and make *her* wish for death.

But first, there was duty. To let anger distract her was to let the Dark Jedi win. First, Jaina had to stop the war—*then* she could kill Lomi and Welk.

Jaina turned toward the hangar.

"Where are you going?" Zekk whined from his bench. "We can't do anything. It's too late."

Jaina opened herself to their meld, then reached out to him and let her anger pour from her heart into his.

I won't surrender to them. *I'm going to stop this war.*

Zekk's eyes widened, then turned a bright, angry green. He slammed his palms down and pushed himself to his feet.

"I'm with you," he said, catching up. "How are we going to do this?"

"Tell you later," Jaina said. She did not yet have a plan—and she had no intention of developing one until after they were away from the Taat nest. "For now, let's just concentrate on getting to our StealthXs."

They stepped into the sweet dampness of the wax-lined access tunnel and started down toward the hangar. As they progressed, Taat began to fill Jaina's mind with doubts about her intentions, to make her wonder if she would really be stopping the war—or merely sparing the Chiss a much-deserved defeat.

Jaina thought of Anakin, and her doubts vanished in the black fire of her anger.

Taat workers began to pour into the tunnel, all scurrying up a passage that led only to the Jedi barracks. Jaina and Zekk threatened them with word and thought, but the Killiks continued to clamber past, slowing the pair's progress to a crawl.

Zekk took the lead and began to muscle forward, using the Force to shove aside the Killiks ahead of him. More Taat poured into the tunnel, convinced they had some urgent errand in the Jedi barracks. Zekk continued to push ahead. Jaina added her Force powers to his, and the entire stream of insects began to slide backward down the tunnel.

The Killiks dispersed, and a strange resistance began to rise inside the two Jedi, a cold hand pushing at them inside their own bellies. Their limbs grew heavier, their breathing became labored, their pulses pounded in their ears. They leaned against the cold hand, and still it grew harder to move. Soon, their legs were too heavy to lift, their lungs were ready to burst, their drumming hearts drowned out their own thoughts. They came to a stop, hanging parallel to the floor, and the harder they tried to move forward, the more impossible it became.

They hung there for several minutes, testing their wills against that of the Colony, and only grew more tired. Jaina thought of how Lomi and Welk had betrayed Anakin, and she grew more determined than ever to avenge him—and less able to move.

Jaina began to despair. Her anger was no match for the Will of the Colony. She had to find another way.

The seed of a new plan came to Jaina, a plan that relied not on anger, but on love instead.

Jaina did not nurture that seed. Instead, she buried it deep down in her mind, in that part that was still *I* instead of *we*.

Keep trying, she urged Zekk. *Don't stop, no matter what.*

Never! he assured her.

Good.

Jaina let the pressure push her away from the hangar, back up the passage.

"Hey!" Zekk's voice was strained. "Where are you going?"

"The barracks," Jaina said. "I'm giving up."

"What!"

"I'm not as strong as you." It irked Jaina to say this, but it was the one way to be sure Zekk would continue to struggle. "I'll see you later."

As Jaina retreated up the passage, the pressure gradually diminished. Finally, she was able to simply walk back to the barracks. She could sense Zekk down near the hangar, feeling puzzled and angry and a little bit abandoned, but he remained determined not to quit, to show Jaina he was as strong as she believed.

Once Jaina reached the barracks veranda, she returned to her bench and began to contemplate the beauty of the Killik mind. Every member of a nest worked flawlessly with all the others, executing unbelievably complex tasks—such as refueling and restocking several thousand rocket ships an hour—in near-perfect harmony. There were seldom any of the accidents or shortages or confusion so common to any military operation—and there were never arguments or disagreements or territorial spats.

Would it truly be so bad if there *was* a war, and the Colony won? For once, there would be true galactic peace—no vying for resources, no clashes of interest, no territorial conquests, just all the peoples of the galaxy working together for the common good. Was that so wrong?

Jaina supposed that the fact that she did not see anything wrong with that meant she had become a true Joiner. She was only worried that the Colony could never win a war against the Chiss.

The Colony would have help, Taat assured her. An image came through the nest mind of the *Ronto* being unloaded. A dozen long streams of Killiks were pouring in and out of its cargo bays, working together to off-load the huge, telescoping barrels of at least a dozen turbolaser batteries.

The Chiss were going to be *very* surprised when they attacked. Maybe the Killiks could win this war after all.

Jaina decided to wait there on the veranda until Unu called for her. Sooner or later, there would be a mission that only a Jedi in a StealthX could do, and Jaina would be ready.

Then, when her mind finally went quiet and she knew that Taat and Unu were no longer paying her any attention, she pictured the handsome, square, scarred face of Jagged Fel. She held the image in her mind and performed a series of breathing exercises, focusing on the feelings they had shared while they were fighting the Yuuzhan Vong together—and during those few times they had managed to rendezvous after the war—then turned roughly toward where the Chiss staging area would be, somewhere outside the orbit of Qoribu.

While Jag was not Force-sensitive, Jaina had touched him through the Force many times while they were together, and she felt sure he would recognize the sensation of her presence brushing his. But he wouldn't trust her. He would think she was just another Joiner trying to lure him into a mistake. So she would have to convince him that he was discovering the ambush on his own—and she would have to do it before Taat realized what she was doing.

Jaina reached out to Jag in the Force and found his presence—distant and dim—somewhere ahead on Qoribu's orbital path, exactly where he would be if he was guarding the staging area for a Chiss assault fleet.

Come get me, lover boy, Jaina sent. Jag would not understand the words, of course, but would recognize the sentiment. She had used the same taunt many times when they sparred. *If you can.*

Jaina felt Jag start in surprise, then she caught a flash of anger as he recognized her touch. This wasn't a game! This was war, and . . .

His irritation suddenly changed to concern as it dawned on him why she had picked *that* particular day to reach out to him. Jaina sensed a rising tide of alarm, then lost contact as Jag drew in on himself.

THIRTY-FOUR

Qoribu's brightly striped orb hung sandwiched between the flat, twinkling clouds of two sizable space fleets. For now, both sides seemed content to avoid a battle, each hiding from the other behind the gas giant's considerable bulk. But they were also maintaining aggressive postures, keeping their sublight drives lit and their shields up, dropping reconnaissance patrols through the planet's golden ring system like airspinners from a Bespin raawk trawler.

"Good news," Han said, decelerating hard. As they had half expected, the homing beacon aboard Alema's stolen skiff had led them straight back into the middle of the Qoribu conflict. Though the standoff between the two fleets was certain to complicate their plans, Han could not have been more thrilled. After they destroyed the Dark Nest, he could track down Jaina and have her safely away from the Taat nest within hours. "We're just in time for the war."

"Why is that good news?" Juun asked from the navigator's station. "Are we planning to go back into smuggling?"

"No!" Leia said. She keyed a command on the copilot's console, and the tactical display began to light up with mass readings and vector arrows. "Han's smuggling days were over a long time ago."

Tarfang, still regrowing his fur after the head-to-toe clipping that had preceded a lengthy stay in the bacta tank, chittered a rude-sounding question.

"Tarfang wishes to inquire whether Princess Leia always answers questions on Captain Solo's behalf," C-3PO said.

Han did not bother to answer. He had brought Tarfang along only because Juun would not come without him, and he had brought Juun along because he was actually considering taking the Sullustan on as a copilot. After seeing how deftly Leia had resolved the crisis between the Jedi and the Galactic Alliance, it had finally grown clear to Han that he was blocking fate. Leia had been born to run things, and the wretched state of the Galactic Alliance Reconstruction was evidence enough of how badly she was needed. Thus he had made up his mind to step aside so she could follow her destiny . . . again.

Tarfang jabbered something else, which C-3PO translated as, "Tarfang says it is quite unfortunate that old age has broken your spirit, Captain Solo. Wars are good for smugglers. You might have been able to earn enough to replace the fine ship you tricked Captain Juun into sacrificing on your behalf."

This was too much. "First, I'm not old, and my spirit is fine." Han twisted around and wagged his finger at Tarfang. Without any fur, the Ewok reminded him of a womp rat with a short nose and no tail. "And second, *I'm* not the one who told Juun to outfly his cover. Getting that rustcan blown out from under him probably saved his life."

Tarfang started to yammer a reply.

"Later, you two," Leia interrupted. "Luke and Mara will be arriving soon, and we have work to do."

She pointed at the tactical display, which now identified the fleet hovering above Qoribu's northern pole as Hapan and the one at the southern pole as Chiss. While the Chiss appeared to be outnumbered more than two to one, Han knew appearances were deceptive. In all likelihood, they had a much larger force waiting just inside Ascendancy territory, ready to jump into battle the instant the enemy attacked. He only hoped that Dukat Gray—or whoever commanded the Hapan fleet—understood the basic deceptiveness of Chiss war doctrine.

Across the center of Qoribu ran a thick band of yellow bogey symbols.

"Dartships?" Han gasped.

"That's how it looks," Leia said. "The spectrograph suggests a methane-based fuel."

"There must be a million of 'em!"

"Closer to a hundred and fifty thousand, Captain," Juun said from behind him. "Plus a handful of freighters, blastboats, and four KDY orbital defense platforms."

Han raised his brow. "I wonder where *those* came from?"

Tarfang offered an opinion, which C-3PO reported as, "Smugglers."

Han ignored the Ewok and asked Leia, "Where's Alema?"

"Still working on that," she said. "I could use a little help."

"Yeah, sure," Han said. "All you have to do is ask."

A grid appeared over the bright band of bogey symbols strung across Qoribu's equator.

"Alema's skiff has to be somewhere in there, or we would have picked her up by now," Leia said. A quarter of the grid turned red. "Do an efflux search on the areas I'm assigning you. She's only a few minutes ahead, so her ion drives must still be active."

The homing beacon they had planted on the stolen skiff was only accurate to within a light-month, which left a lot of territory to search via normal sensors. Han brought up the first grid square and began to look for a telltale plume of hot ions. At this scale, the band of dartships resolved itself into a lumpy strand of swirling dots, with the gray disk of one of Qoribu's moons hanging just beneath the main area of activity.

After a moment of study, Han switched to the next grid and found several bogey symbols that turned out to be a Gallofree freighter and a pair of patrolling blastboats. As soon as he brought up the third grid, he was tempted to move immediately to the next one. The dartships in this area were spread so thin that he could make out the thin gold line of Qoribu's ring system and the irregular nugget of a small ice moon. But the thin Killik defenses here just did not feel right. Han brought the moon, Kr, to the center of his display and enlarged the scale.

A blue circle the size of a fingertip appeared in the screen center, slowly growing smaller as it traveled toward the moon.

"Got it!" Han began a mass analysis to confirm his suspicions, but he was sure enough of himself to transfer an inset to Leia's display. "This one's still moving insystem. It has to be her."

"Very good." Leia leaned across and kissed his cheek. "You win the reward."

"That's my reward?" Han complained. "I get that every day."

"That could always change, flyboy."

"Come on. You know you can't help yourself." Han flashed her his best arrogant smirk, then activated the intercom. "Battle stations back there. We might be going anytime."

"We know," Kyp replied. "We're Jedi."

"Oh, yeah." Han looked at the ceiling and silently cursed Kyp's arrogance. "I must be getting forgetful in my old age."

Meewalh informed him that she and Cakhmaim were also ready. Noghri were always ready.

When the mass analysis finally confirmed Han's guess, he turned to face Juun. "You two had better head to your battle station, too. You remember how it works?"

"Of course—you went over the procedure several times." Juun popped his datapad out of his vest pocket. "And I've recorded all your instructions right here, in case I forget."

"Uh, great." Han glanced away so Juun would not see him wince. "That makes me real confident."

"I'm happy to know that," Juun said. "But I do have one question."

Han counted to three, reminding himself that it was better for the Sullustan to ask his questions now rather than later, when they were being dive-bombed by a thousand dartships.

"Okay, shoot."

"Has this ever been tried before?"

Han and Leia exchanged looks of surprise, then Leia said, "I don't see how it could have been, Jae."

"Oh." Juun was silent for a moment, then said, "I have another question."

"No kidding," Han grumbled.

"Maybe we should make this the last one," Leia said. "I just felt Luke and Mara emerge from hyperspace."

"Of course." The Sullustan slipped out of his chair, and Tarfang did the same. "How do we know it's going to work?"

"Good question," Han said. He turned forward again and placed a tracking lock on Alema's skiff.

After a moment, Leia explained, "It was Han's idea, Jae."

"Oh, I see." Juun sounded satisfied. "Of course it will work."

Tarfang growled something doubtful, but Juun was already leading the way back toward the engineering station.

A moment later, the irregular, matte-black body of two StealthX starfighters pulled alongside the *Falcon,* and Han saw Luke's and Mara's helmet-framed faces looking over from the cockpits of phantom craft. Leia closed her eyes for a moment, reaching out to them in the Force, trying to get some sense of their intentions. After the Dark Nest attack on the *Shadow,* they had decided to return with only the *Falcon* and a couple of StealthX escorts. Since the *Falcon* was not equipped to carry fighters, Luke and Mara had been taking turns with the other two Jedi Masters on the mission—Kyp and Saba— ferrying the star-fighters through hyperspace.

Luke and Mara happened to be in the cockpit when the time came for the final jump to Qoribu, but Han suspected that Mara would have insisted on being one of the pilots to follow Alema into the Dark Nest. She was taking the whole assassin thing pretty personally.

Leia opened her eyes, then Luke and Mara accelerated away toward Kr. They remained visible for a moment, a pair of dark X's silhouetted against Qoribu's bright stripes, then shrank into invisibility.

"Luke wants us to hold here until they find the nest," Leia reported. "Then—"

"Excuse me," C-3PO interrupted. "But we have an unfortunate situation. We're being hailed by both Dukat Gray of the Hapan fleet *and* Commander Fel of the Chiss."

"Put Gray on first," Han said. "Fel is just going to—"

"No, shift them to a conference channel," Leia said. "Maybe we can promote a dialogue."

"Or a war," Han grumbled.

Gray's voice came over the speaker first. "Princess Leia, I demand an—"

"Who's this?" Fel demanded.

"Dukat Aleson Gray, Duch'da to Lady AlGray of the Relephon Moons," Gray responded.

There was a long silence.

"To whom am I speaking?" Gray demanded.

"Commander Jagged Fel," Fel replied. "Of the Chiss Expansionary Defense Fleet."

Another long silence.

Finally, Gray said, "I was attempting to comm Princess Leia and her crew. Have you boarded their vessel?"

"I was wondering if *you* had," Fel said.

"Of course not. Why would I comm a vessel I had boarded?"

"I don't know that you *are* comming them," Fel countered suspiciously. "Your signal is coming from the *Falcon*."

"*Your* signal is coming from the *Falcon*," Gray accused. "I warn you, I won't fall for any of your Chiss—"

"Pardon me, gentlemen," Leia said. "Your concern is touching, but I assure you, the *Falcon* remains under Han's command. Will you both activate Idol Smasher?"

Idol Smasher was an old encryption system the allies had used in the war against the Yuuzhan Vong. Outdated though it was, it was almost a certainty that both fleets would still have the decoding hardware available in their code room archives. Military cryptographers were notorious pack rats.

After a short pause, Gray said, "We'll need two minutes."

"We'll need one." Fel's tone was superior. "Please notify us when you're ready, Dukat."

Han glanced back at C-3PO, who was already plugging the necessary module into the comm station, and smirked.

"The *Falcon* is ready now."

The transmission light went out, then Leia said, "Trouble, Han."

Han looked back to the tactical screen and immediately began to warm the ion drives. The moon Kr was fast vanishing behind a cloud of dartships. As he watched, the spectrograph identified their propulsion as hydrogen-based.

"Dark Nest," he said. "Anything from Luke and Mara?"

"A little anxiety—they're not calling for us, yet."

"Tell them not to push it," Han said. "They're too old to play hero."

"Han, they're younger than you were at the Battle of Yuuzhan'tar."

"Yeah, well, I've got my luck," Han said. "All they have is the Force."

Fel's voice came over the comm. "Checking encryption."

"Well done, Commander!" C-3PO answered. "That took only thirty-three point seven seconds."

"Thirty-three point *four*—you neglected the transmission lag," Fel corrected. "I wanted to have a word with the Solos before Dukat Gray joined us."

"Jag, we're not going home." Han was keeping one eye on the tactical display and one on Leia, ready to start toward Kr the instant it looked like Luke and Mara were in trouble. "Jaina's in there, and—"

"Yes, I know," Fel said. "I think . . . actually, I'm *convinced* she saved our fleet."

Leia's jaw fell, but her voice betrayed no hint of her shock. "You find that surprising, Jag? The Jedi are here to stop a war, not choose sides."

"We've never doubted your intentions, Princess Leia," Fel said. "Only your province in being here—and your ability to resist the Colony's Will."

"Then Jaina has changed your minds?"

"She has opened *mine*," Fel corrected. "But that is very different from convincing Defense Fleet Command that the Jedi can neutralize the Killik threat."

"We understand your concern," Leia said. "Perhaps Defense Fleet Command would believe us if the Colony withdrew from Qoribu?"

There was a moment of stunned silence. On the tactical display, Kr had vanished beneath a yellow swarm of dartship symbols. Han shook an inquiring finger in the moon's general direction, but Leia shook her head. Luke and Mara still did not want any help.

Finally, Fel asked, "The Jedi can arrange that?"

"Testing encryption," Gray's voice broke in. "You've been talking without me."

"Encryption confirmed." In a tone that mimicked Gray's peevishness, C-3PO replied, "Though you *are* somewhat late."

"It was only two minutes twenty," Gray complained. "That's no excuse—"

"We were just catching up on old times," Leia said. "You may not be aware of it, but Commander Fel came *very* close to becoming our son-in-law."

As Leia spoke, her eyes grew wide, and she began to gesture frantically out the forward viewport. Han slammed the throttles forward, and the *Falcon* leapt toward Qoribu.

"Commander Fel, Dukat Gray, your tactical officers are about to tell you that the *Falcon* is accelerating toward the moon Kr at maximum power." Though Leia's face was pale, her voice remained calm. "I wanted to inform you both of the reason."

Leia briefed them on the Jedi discovery of the Dark Nest and their theory about the power it held over the rest of the Colony's collective mind. She even revealed the Order's fear that the nest was being controlled by the two Dark Jedi who had abducted Raynar Thul on *Baanu Rass*, keeping secret only the fact that the Dark Nest was also attempting to absorb Alema Rar.

"You're telling us that the Colony is ruled by a hidden nest?" Fel asked, incredulous.

"Only in the sense that any sentient mind is ruled by its own unconscious mind," Leia said. "*Influenced* might be a better term—though in the Killiks' case the influence is very heavy. We're fairly sure the Dark Nest is responsible for the Colony's decision to inhabit Qoribu."

"For what purpose?" Fel asked.

"To start a war," Han said. "And so far, you guys are playing right into their snappy little pincers."

"It would be foolish to assume you know our plans, Captain Solo."

"Your plans were clear enough when the Fleet of the Glorious Defender Queen arrived," Gray said. "You were maneuvering to attack."

"Obviously, I cannot discuss our plans with any of you," Fel said. "I assume that the Jedi have located this Dark Nest on Kr and intend to break its hold over the Colony?"

"You could say that," Han said. Kr was visible to the naked eye now, a fuzzy blue nugget about the size of a thumb. "If blasting it to bug parts counts."

"With just the *Falcon*?" Gray asked.

"We have more than the *Falcon*," Leia said. "Luke and Mara have already found the entrance to the nest."

"That explains the activity on Kr," Fel concluded. "The dartships seem to be swarming something."

Though the *Falcon*'s tactical display showed no indications of weapons activity, Han had no doubt that the Skywalkers were busy dodging dartships. He could see it in the tautness around Leia's eyes.

"Master Skywalker is under attack?" There was more excitement in Gray's voice than concern.

"There's no need for alarm, Dukat!" Leia commanded. "Luke and Mara can easily—"

A pair of Hapan Novas began to slip down the tactical display toward Kr. Han's heart rose into his throat.

"Uh, what are you doing there, Dukat?"

"Sending support," Gray said. "Queen Mother Tenel Ka would not be pleased if I allowed this Dark Nest to kill Master Skywalker and her husband—"

"Recall your vessels at once, Dukat," Fel said. "We cannot permit any Hapan capital ship to approach the orbital plane."

"It's a small force," Gray said. "Any fool can that see it poses no threat to—"

"Only a fool would allow his enemy to establish a forward position under the current circumstances," Fel replied. A Chiss Star Destroyer and half a dozen cruisers started upward to meet the Hapan trio. "And we Chiss are not fools."

"Oh, boy," Han said under his breath. "I've got a—"

"—bad feeling. I know," Leia finished. "Dukat Gray, leave this to us. We'll let you know if—"

A chain of tiny orange flashes suddenly flared along Kr's long axis as someone on the moon opened fire.

Two more Battle Dragons, accompanied by a dozen Novas, began to descend toward Qoribu's rings.

"The queen's fleet will not stand idly by while Master Skywalker is viciously attacked," Gray declared.

"Dukat Gray—"

That was as much as Leia could say before Fel started to talk over her.

"The Chiss have no wish to see Master Skywalker and his wife injured, either." A dozen Chiss cruisers joined the growing migration toward Kr. "But the Dark Nest is on *our* side of the rings. Allow *us* to support him."

"Out of the question!" Gray shot back. Han had known even before the reply that Fel's offer would never reach orbit. Gray cared more about being able to claim credit for rescuing Luke and Mara than whether they actually *needed* to be rescued. "The Chiss have made it clear they didn't want the Jedi here in the first place. We have no assurance that you wouldn't kill them yourselves."

"Perhaps not," Fel returned coolly. "But if you don't recall those vessels, I *can* assure you—"

"Dukat Gray," Leia said. "Sparking a clash with the Chiss is *not* going to win the Queen Mother's favor. I suggest you recall your vessels and wait until your aid is truly needed."

Another string of explosions lit Kr's face. "It's apparent to me that our aid *is* needed," Gray said. "And if we must fight the Chiss to deliver it, we will."

He closed the channel.

"Stubborn rodder!" Leia cursed. "Jag, you understand—"

"I'm sorry, Princess Leia," Fel said. The Chiss fleet began to stream upward on all sides of the planet. "But my superiors refuse to take the chance that this isn't a ploy. I suggest you avoid getting caught in the crossfire."

THIRTY-FIVE

A pillar of orange rocket exhaust arced out of Kr's frozen tangle of ethmane crystals, emerging from an ice-lined shaft more than a kilometer across. This column was far larger than any others Luke and Mara had seen, its heat raising a wall of steam as it bent toward the Skywalkers and streaked low over the moon's frozen surface.

Confident they had finally found what they were looking for, Luke and Mara banked away and began to accelerate, drawing the orange column after them. Luke would have liked to make a reconnaissance pass to be certain the huge shaft was the hangar opening he believed it to be, but Kr's tortured terrain and icy blue light neutralized the speed and camouflage of their StealthXs, and both of their starfighters had already taken too much of a beating to risk another confrontation.

Two seconds later, Luke's R9 astromech unit—sitting in for an operationally challenged R2-D2—sounded an attack alarm. Luke felt a start from Mara as an explosion rocked her StealthX; then his own starfighter gave a sharp double buck. The R9 pointedly informed Luke they were being ambushed by Gorog dartships, and the tactical display showed half a dozen of the little craft behind them, rising from the sensor-blocking depths of the frozen ethmane jungle.

Luke continued toward the *Falcon*, flying low over Kr's feathery jungle of ethmane crystals. Ideally, he would have climbed for open space where their StealthXs would have full advantage, but the tactical display showed a second swarm of dartships flying top cover, in perfect position to stop them.

The Skywalkers had traveled barely a kilometer when another column of dartships rose out of the ethmane jungle ahead.

Luke sensed Mara's alarm almost before his own. They had stayed a little too long, and now Gorog was boxing them in. The swarm spread out before them, creating an orange wall of rocket exhaust. The Skywalkers began to pour cannon fire into the swirling mass, trying to clear a lane for their StealthXs.

It was like trying to blast a tunnel through a cloud. Every time they created a hole, it filled instantly.

As the Skywalkers drew closer, the orange wall resolved itself into a pattern of fiery whirling disks, each with the black dot of a dartship at its heart. Mara continued to fire, and Luke followed her lead. The tactic clearly had no chance of success, but Mara had a plan. Luke was almost sure of it.

Finally, when the swarm was so close that the dartships had grown into tiny cylinders, glowing streaks of missile propellant began to reach out toward the Skywalkers. Mara took the lead and pulled up, a loose wing stabilizer shuddering under the strain. The two nearest swarms—the one blocking their escape and the one pursuing from behind—nosed up to give chase.

Stick close, she warned.

Suddenly Mara dropped the nose of her StealthX. Luke followed so quickly that he almost beat her, but the Dark Nest was not fooled. The dartships simply leveled off and continued to close on the Skywalkers.

Luke expected Mara to pull up again and outclimb their pursuers, gambling that the StealthXs could withstand a barrage of Killik chemical explosives long enough to fight through the top-cover swarm. Instead, she continued to dive. The ice jungle's feathery canopy came up rapidly. Luke began to wonder when she intended to pull up.

She did not.

A flurry of cannon bolts lanced out from Mara's StealthX, instantly superheating the ice crystals in front of her and filling Luke's forward view with brown steam. He switched to instrument flying and followed her through the cloud into the snarled depths of the ice jungle. Flash-frozen spires of ethmane stood at all angles, glowing translucent blue with Gyuel's distant light, reaching out to embrace each other with delicate arms of hoarfrost.

Mara flipped her StealthX up on edge and slipped between two ethmane pillars, then crashed through a curtain of frost and sent up a glittering cloud of ice particles. Luke ducked under a frozen arch, then shot ahead of Mara into the lead.

He offered his apologies through their Force-bond, along with an image of the loose stabilizer he had seen on her wing.

Whatever, she answered.

Luke felt a sudden compulsion to swing back toward the nest and wondered if his wife had gone crazy.

Mara urged him to think. Gorog expected them to run for the *Falcon*.

Luke quickly brought them around. It would be safer to go in the opposite direction . . . and sneak a look at the nest. He focused all his attention on the frozen jungle ahead and began a Jedi breathing exercise, allowing his mind to race forward through the ethmane spires, to find its own route down the twining passages and rolling channels. Time seemed to slow. He surrendered his steering arm to the Force, and his hand began to move of its own accord, guiding the StealthX into one shimmering gap after another, bobbing over blue curtains, ducking beneath long fronds of frost, blasting holes through impassable walls of ice.

Mara stayed close on his tail, almost joining her hand to his through their Force-bond, and thirty seconds later they shot through a small icy portal into an irregular blue shaft barely broad enough for Luke to bank the StealthX into a tight inside spiral.

Stang!

Luke felt Mara's fear through the Force, and his heart jumped into his throat. Then, as he continued his own spiral around the small shaft, he saw the jagged hole where her StealthX had bounced off the icy wall. His tactical display showed her still on his tail, but weaving badly.

Mara?

Fine! she answered.

Luke continued to bank, setting the StealthX up on one wing so that he could look up out one side of the cockpit and down out the other. He estimated they were about two kilometers deep, though that was impossible to confirm with instruments. This far down inside the frozen moon, the StealthX's sensor range extended only as far as the walls of frozen ethmane.

Below, the shaft continued to narrow and curved back under itself, concealing the nest entrance—assuming it was down there—behind a wall of blue ice. Aside from the walls, which had been polished smooth by the heat-and-freeze cycle of countless rocket launches, there was no sign of dartships.

Mara seemed worried by how quiet it was.

Luke didn't like it, either. Gorog would have left *something* to defend the nest. The hair on his neck began to rise, and he decided they had seen enough.

Mara, now directly opposite him on the other side of the shaft, agreed and started to climb. Her shields were flickering, and that loose stabilizer was flapping around beneath her wing.

Luke fell in behind her; then an attack alarm sounded and a laser cannon began to fire blue bolts up the shaft. He felt another jolt of emotion from Mara, this time anger, as her StealthX took a trio of hits. Her shields went down with the second, and the ends of both starboard wings vanished with the third.

Luke did not waste time looking at his tactical display. He simply dropped the StealthX into a dive and started firing and *then* saw the nose of Alema's stolen skiff, just slipping back out of sight. He continued to fire for a second longer, pouring his rage and disbelief at her through the Force, until the bend in the shaft vanished behind a curtain of ethmane steam. He sensed no shame or sorrow in the Twi'lek, only the enormous, murky presence of the Dark Nest.

When no more cannon bolts rose out of the fog, Luke pulled up into a tight banking turn that would allow him to keep an eye on the shaft in both directions. Mara was still above him, her StealthX crawling around the shaft in a wobbling circle, both starboard engines shut down and the stumps of her starboard wings vibrating badly.

Mara?

Everything good, she reported.

It didn't look good. Luke was about to tell her to try climbing when the mouth of the shaft—two kilometers above—began to brighten with the orange glow of dartship rockets.

Mara brought her StealthX out of its circle and fired at the icy wall, trying to punch through into the ethmane jungle beyond.

The stumps of her starboard wings tumbled away in a cascade of sparks and mini-explosions. Then she slipped into a spin and flashed past Luke, vanishing into the ethmane steam below.

Luke felt her stretching out to him, clinging to their Force-bond as she fought to bring the StealthX under control. He poured reassurance into their bond, trying to let her know that he would not abandon her, that he was coming right behind her. Then he reached for Leia in the Force, pouring out his alarm and picturing a crashing starfighter, and dived after Mara.

He caught up to Mara on the other side of the fog. She was using a combination of the Force and power manipulations to keep the StealthX under control, corkscrewing down the shaft in an ever-tightening spiral, pushing the damaged craft to its limits and a little beyond to stay ahead of the approaching dartfighters.

The shaft twined its way another seven kilometers into the ice moon, growing ever smaller and more twisted. Finally the squarish, cave-like opening of a launching bay appeared at the bottom of the shaft, perhaps a kilometer away.

Luke armed a pair of proton torpedoes, then urged Mara to do the same. They would need to give the *Falcon* something to look for.

With pleasure!

Mara stabilized her spin just long enough to send a pair of proton torpedoes streaking toward the cavern mouth. Under other circumstances, Luke might have felt a pang of concern knowing that Alema's skiff had entered the hangar only a short time before. But under these conditions—even understanding that she was under the control of the Dark Nest—he felt nothing. Whatever happened, the Twi'lek had brought it on herself.

A brilliant flash filled the cavern mouth as Mara's torpedoes detonated inside, and suddenly the last five hundred meters of shaft were filled with glittering ice shards. Luke activated his targeting computer, but between Mara's wildly gyrating StealthX and interference from the ethmane ice, he was unable to get a lock.

Mara. Luke moved his finger to the torpedo trigger. *Stay left.*

The first barrage of turbolaser fire fanned down from the Hapan batteries, and Kr was suddenly veiled behind a curtain of crimson energy. The Chiss answered with a volley of missiles, and a thousand propellant trails rose to bar the way forward. Han pulled up short and rolled the *Falcon* away from the sudden fury.

"No!" Leia's eyes were fixed on her display, where a navigation lock had been guiding them toward the detonation site of the Skywalkers' proton torpedoes. "Luke and Mara need help."

"And they won't get it if we fly into that mess," Han said. In fifty years of flying, he had never seen a battle this compact before. There had to be a hundred capital ships fighting over a moon only eighty kilometers long. "Even I'm not that good."

"Yes, Han, you are."

"Look, I'm not leaving," Han said. "We just have to find another way in."

Leia's voice grew sober. "Han, I think they're down."

"Down?" A leaden ball formed in Han's stomach. "What do you mean, *down*?"

"Crashed," Leia said. "They may need—"

Han swung the *Falcon* around and started back toward Kr.

"—extraction," Leia finished.

"How did that happen?" Han demanded. Space ahead had become a flashing sheet of turbolaser fire, striped at irregular intervals by growing lines of missile flame. "They're *Jedi*, blast it! In *StealthXs*! They were just supposed to find the nest and call *us*."

"Things go wrong even for Jedi." Leia's eyes were fixed out the viewport. "Threepio, break out the EV suits."

"EV suits?" C-3PO squealed. "If we go EV out *there*, we're doomed! The odds of surviving are . . . why, they're entirely incalculable!"

"Still better than with no suit," Han said. "Do as she says. We may need suits to recover Luke and Mara."

"As you wish, Captain Solo," C-3PO said. "But I really don't think we're going to survive long enough to reach them."

The sheet of flashing energy ahead brightened rapidly as the *Falcon* drew closer, and the canopy tinting darkened. Han looked to his instruments and found nothing but electromagnetic static, its density increasing as space ahead grew more brilliant.

"Sweetheart," Han asked as casually as he could manage, "do you think you can do that Jedi thing—"

"Quiet." Leia was already staring out the forward viewport with a faraway expression in her eyes. "I'm concentrating."

Han waited for instructions. Leia continued to concentrate.

A web of tiny efflux trails—all that was visible of the Chiss and Hapan starfighters vying for control of the attack routes—began to lace the darkened canopy. Even that faded when the *Falcon* entered the battle zone.

A shudder ran through the decks as Meewalh opened up with the belly turret against some hazard Han could not see. Then the attack alarms shrieked as cannon fire pounded their lower shields.

"Who was that?" Han demanded over the intercom.

Meewalh informed him it was a starfighter, but she had no idea whose. All she had been able to see was a blurry tail of ion exhaust.

"Uh, sweetheart?"

"*Concentrating!*"

The invisible fist of a turbolaser blast glanced off the *Falcon*'s port side, instantly overwhelming the shields and sending her spinning out of control. The cockpit erupted with damage alarms, and Leia began to scream.

It took Han a moment to realize she was finally giving him instructions. "Port! Go port!"

He steadied the *Falcon*—relieved to see that he still could—then swung hard to port.

"Threepio, give me a damage report."

The droid dropped an EV suit on the deck. "We'velostourauxiliaryaccelerationcompensator!" he babbled. "Andourportdockingringiscompromised. We'llnevergetoutofthisinonepiece!"

"The damage is minor," Saba said over the intercom. "This one will see to it."

Han frowned. Saba still had a piece of skull missing under that thick hide of hers. She had talked Luke into bringing her along only by threatening to come anyway, but he knew better than to protest. It just wasn't smart to question a Barabel's ability to do *anything*.

Leia ordered, "Climb!"

Han pulled back on the yoke and felt the *Falcon* buck as something exploded under her.

"Dive!"

Han pushed the yoke forward and was nearly thrown out of his seat as a turbolaser blast blossomed just to their stern.

"Starboard, gentle."

Han swung to starboard, and the red streak of a missile shot past the *Falcon*'s blackened canopy.

"Dead ahead, fast."

Han pushed the throttles into overdrive. The canopy grew suddenly transparent again, and still he could not see anything. There was only a thick brown fog, blossoming here and there with cannon fire and laced with the blue trails of starfighter ion drives.

"They melted it!" Han gasped. "They melted an entire—"

"Instruments, Han!"

Han glanced down and found the reassuring sight of a space battle on his tactical display. What looked to be about ten dozen squadrons of starfighters were whirling around Kr, maneuvering for position and pouring laserfire at each other. A single Chiss cruiser was sliding quietly around the moon's bulk, playing a game of moog-and-rancor with a pair of Hapan Novas.

Kr's surface, a sensor-blocking layer of frozen ethmane, was literally disappearing before their eyes. Every time a stray cannon blast struck ground, a thumb-sized area of ice vanished from Han's display.

Leia found the fading rad signature of the Skywalkers' proton torpedoes and reestablished their navigation lock. Han slipped the *Falcon* under the moon, streaking toward their destination only a hundred meters below Kr's jagged belly. Their goal lay about ten kilometers ahead of the Chiss cruiser, so he chose a slow, direct route that would take them past its weapons turrets at a respectable distance. In a battle like this, the only way *not* to get shot at was to make clear you were no kind of threat.

As the *Falcon* neared the cruiser, a flight of clawcraft dropped out of the fog to look her over.

C-3PO opened an emergency channel. "This is the *Millennium Falcon* hailing all combatants. We are neutral in this conflict. Please direct your fire away from us! I repeat: we are neutral!"

The clawcraft dropped back into the kill zone behind the *Falcon* and hung there. The navigation lock slowly drifted toward the center of the screen.

The stolen skiff was floating amid the rest of the wreckage, a pile of flattened durasteel flickering in the light of Mara's two functioning spotlights. There was no way to tell whether Alema and Ben's Killik "friend" had been aboard when the proton torpedoes eviscerated the launching bay, but Mara was betting the pair had escaped. So far, she had seen no signs of the Twi'lek's body among the scorched pieces of chitin tumbling past her canopy, and Alema was a *Jedi*. She would have sensed what was about to happen and raced for shelter.

Mara guided her ailing starfighter through a jagged breach in the launching bay's rear wall. Her spotlights stabbed through a dusty cloud of floating rubble, illuminating a maintenance hangar with a bank of shattered dartship berths on the far wall. She sealed her EV suit and dropped her StealthX to the deck, skidding to a lopsided landing between the broken remnants of two egg-shaped storage tanks.

Knowing that Luke would be covering her from his own craft, Mara sprang out of the cockpit and tumbled all the way to the ceiling, coming to a rest beside a spitcrete ridge that would have served the Gorog as a sort of upside-down catwalk. When no attacks came, she exchanged her lightsaber for her blaster and covered Luke while he landed.

A large part of her—the part that was Ben's mother—would have preferred him to rejoin the *Falcon* and come back with the Solos and the heavy artillery. But she had known from the moment her R9 died that would never happen; Luke would no more have left her alone than she would have him. Besides, this wasn't so bad. It had been her and Luke against a world more times than she could count, and they always won.

Luke took cover inside the shattered base of a storage tank, then Mara pushed off the ceiling and joined him. They were taking care to stay out of their StealthXs' spotlights, but there was enough ambient light to see his lips pressed tight together through his faceplate.

"What do you think?" Mara spoke over their suit comm. She wanted to keep her Force-senses clear for alerting her to danger. "Try to squeeze into your Stealth and sneak out?"

Luke shook his helmet. "There won't be any slipping past that dartship swarm out there. As a matter of fact . . ." He turned toward his StealthX and commed his R9. "Arnie, go find a dark corner and—"

The command came to a sudden end as the orange glow of rocket exhaust lit the launching bay entrance. Mara grabbed Luke's arm and kicked off the floor, using the Force to pull them toward a ruptured door membrane in the back of the maintenance hangar. Arnie started to tweedle a question, but the comm channel abruptly dissolved into static as a trio of bright flashes lit the chamber.

There was no boom, of course, but Mara suddenly grew uncomfortably warm inside her vac suit, and the shock wave hurled her and Luke headlong through the door membrane into the darkened utility passage beyond.

With no gravity or friction to slow them down, they did not stop until they slammed into a wall two seconds later. Mara hit back-first, driving the air from her lungs but not breaking anything she could feel. A sharp crack over the comm suggested that Luke had impacted on his helmet. She started to ask if he was okay, then sensed him wondering the same thing about her and knew he was.

"Check air and suit," Luke said, righting himself.

The reminder was unnecessary. The heads-up status display inside Mara's faceplate was already glowing, though she did not remember activating it.

"I'm good," she said. "You?"

"Have a hisser," he reported, indicating a small air leak. "But we'd better look for it later."

He pointed back toward the maintenance hangar. Thirty meters away, the orange glow of rocket exhaust was flickering against a section of curved tunnel, dimming and brightening as dartships landed and shut down their engines and more poured into the hangar behind them.

"I don't recall seeing any EV suits in the Taat hangars," Mara said hopefully.

"No—but a carapace is a good start on a pressure suit."

"Killjoy." Mara turned her wrist over and entered a four-digit code on her forearm command pad. The StealthX's self-destruct alarm began to gong inside her helmet, and the heads-up display on her faceplate began a twenty-second countdown. "Come on, Skywalker. Let's stay on the move until we hear from the *Falcon*."

Mara turned away from the hangar and started into the frozen darkness ahead.

THIRTY-SIX

The walls and floor were coated in a frozen black wax that absorbed the light from Luke's helmet lamp and made the passage seem even darker and murkier than it was. Every few meters, a fissure caused by the tunnel's sudden decompression ran all the way to the moon ice, sometimes exposing a short length of spit-crete piping or power conduit. There were none of the shine-balls that illuminated other Killik nests, nor any sense of order to its convoluted plan. The passages seemed to meander at random, twining around each other like vines, branching off at arbitrary intervals and rejoining the main passage without crossing any obvious destination between.

At the speed he and Mara were sailing through the darkness, using the Force to pull themselves along through the zero-g, Luke was growing badly disoriented. He no longer had any sense of whether they were traveling deeper into the moon or back toward the surface; whether ten meters of ethmane ice separated them from the hangar or a thousand. Were it not for the frozen beads of vapor that his leaky vac suit was leaving behind, he wasn't even sure he could have found his way back down the same passage.

Mara suddenly grabbed a crack in the wall and brought herself to a stop. Luke did the same and found himself looking at one of the bulging hatch membranes that Killiks used instead of air locks. A pull chain hung to one side of the hatch, attached to a set of valves positioned to spray sealing gel over the membrane before anyone tried to push through.

Mara didn't reach for the pull chain, and neither did Luke. Both their spines were prickling with danger sense, and they were all too aware of how difficult it was to sense Gorog in the Force.

"Ambush," Mara concluded. "They're starting to come after us."

"Starting?"

Luke looked around, and his helmet lamp illuminated a torrent of dartship pilots pouring around the bend, at most thirty meters away. Wearing their dartship canopies like carapaces, they were scurrying along every available tunnel surface, with their legs and arms sheathed in a shimmering fabric that bunched and gathered at the joints. They had no weapons other than their six limbs—but that would be enough if the swarm ever caught up.

There was no question of using the Force to hide. Whenever the Gorog lost sight of their quarry, they simply spread out, scrambling over every surface in every direction, literally hunting their quarry down by feel.

Luke began to pour blasterfire into the front ranks. Most bolts ricocheted off the canopies, while those that hit a limb simply activated a safety seal at the nearest joint. The insects just kept coming.

"Trouble," Luke said over the suit comm. Lightsabers would be more effective, but he *really* didn't want to go hand-to-hand with who-knew-how-many bugs. "Big trouble, in fact."

"Maybe not that big," Mara said.

"No?"

"They can't *all* be dartship pilots," Mara said. He felt rather than saw her nod at the bulging hatch membrane. "So they won't *all* be wearing pressure suits."

"You're right," Luke said. The first pilots were less than ten meters away now, but he holstered his blaster and grabbed his lightsaber. "Not that big."

They ignited their lightsabers, then pressed themselves against the tunnel wall and slashed a large X across the center of the hatch. The membrane blew apart, and their would-be ambushers went tumbling past on a tide of explosive decompression, crashing into the pilot swarm and bringing its advance to a tumbling, confused halt.

Once the torrent slowed, Mara floated through the tattered membrane into a corridor filled with flash-frozen Killiks. Luke followed a few meters behind, using the Force to pull himself along, shouldering aside Gorog warriors with heads painted in the dark spray pattern of decompression death.

"How's that hisser?" Mara asked.

Luke checked the heads-up display inside his faceplate. He was down to just fifteen minutes of air, and the loss rate was increasing.

"Fine for now."

He turned his helmet lamp back through the burst hatch and was relieved to illuminate only a small portion of the throng that had been pursuing them so far. About fifty of the insects were still coming, pushing their way up the body-choked passage toward him and Mara. The last dozen or so were scurrying in the opposite direction, vanishing into the darkness behind the hundreds of pilots that had already started back toward their dartships.

"But the next time we come to a pressure hatch, let's try to leave it intact," Luke said. "I think our rescue party is about to be delayed."

The navigation lock finally reached the center of the display. Relieved to note their Chiss escorts were still behind them—the cruiser was less likely to blast the *Falcon* to atoms that way—Han began a slow, spiraling descent into Kr's thickening fog. He would have liked to drop into a power dive and go screaming down to find Luke and Mara, but that would have looked suspicious. And when Chiss grew suspicious, they killed things.

"Let's see what it looks like inside that fog," Han said. "Activate the terrain scanners."

Leia brought the scanners online. Unlike ethmane ice, ethmane fog was almost as transparent to sensors as air, and a moment later the mouth of a broad funnel-like pit appeared on Han's display. The hole appeared to be a deep one, descending more than two kilometers before finally curving out of sight.

"Any sign of rescue beacons?" Han asked.

Leia shook her head. "None." She closed her eyes. "They're too deep."

"Deep?"

"Inside Kr," she said. "I think they're in the nest."

"*In* the nest?" Han felt like he was going to choke on his heart. "That's not funny, Leia."

"It gets less funny," she said. "Luke seems to think we'll meet a reception committee."

"You don't say." Han smiled. "Good."

"Good?" C-3PO demanded. "I don't see anything good about this situation at all. There's every chance that both Master Skywalkers will be killed by our baradium missiles!"

"Not really." Han pushed the *Falcon*'s nose down and dropped into a steepening dive. "For that to happen, we'd have to actually *fire* the baradium missiles."

"You don't intend to fire them?" C-3PO asked, growing even more alarmed. "Not even one?"

"No." Leia's tone was relieved. It had been her idea to bring the baradium missiles along, but she had spent most of the trip worried about how they were going to keep Alema clear when they fired the weapons at the nest. Han had not been quite so worried. "Not with Luke and Mara inside."

"But you won't be able to clear the nest!" C-3PO objected. "Without those missiles, the odds will be—"

"Easy, Threepio." The last thing Han wanted to hear was how bad the odds were. He was already having to hold the yoke tight to prevent his hands from shaking. "I wasn't counting on the missiles anyway."

"You weren't?"

"Of course not," he said. "They're baradium. You *never* get to shoot the baradium missiles."

"Oh." C-3PO grew calmer. "That's true. I have no record of one ever actually being launched."

They descended a thousand meters into the fog, then a Chiss voice crackled over the comm.

"*Millennium Falcon,* be advised that if you attempt to evade us, we *will* open fire."

"We're not evading," Han answered. "We're going in . . . and you're welcome to follow."

"Going in?" The ethmane ice was already beginning to make the comm signal scratchy. "Clarify."

"We have two Jedi pilots down inside the nest," Leia explained. "We're going to extract them."

The clawcraft reappeared on the *Falcon*'s tail. "We've detected no other craft—"

"Do you ever?" Han interrupted. "She said they were *Jedi* pilots—Luke and Mara Skywalker, to be exact. You coming or not?"

There was a moment's silence, then the two clawcraft began to drop back. "Your request lies outside our mission profile, but we have been authorized to wish you good luck."

"Thanks for nothing," Han grumbled.

"You're welcome," the Chiss replied. "We could have shot you down."

The *Falcon* continued to descend, then finally broke out of the fog into a twisting, ice-walled shaft that was much narrower than it had appeared on the terrain scanner. Han gasped and pulled the ship in a spiral so tight it was almost a spin.

"Oh, dear!" C-3PO cried.

"Relax, circuit-brain." Han spoke between clenched teeth. "I've got us under control."

"That isn't what concerns me, Captain Solo. We have a safety margin of point—"

"Threepio!" Leia barked. "What *does* concern you?"

C-3PO's golden arm stretched toward the viewport. "*That.*"

It took a moment for Han and Leia to see the faint orange glow building in the depths of the shaft.

"Okay." Leia sighed. "That kind of concerns me, too."

"Relax. Everything's under control." Han activated the intercom. "Juun, you ready back there?"

There was a short delay, followed by the electronic screech of someone speaking too close to the intercom microphone. "Yes, Captain, if you think this is going to work."

"It's going to work," Han said. He checked the power levels on the *Falcon*'s tractor beam and saw that they were holding at maximum. Still, he asked, "Are you *sure* you're ready?"

There was a short pause, then Tarfang jabbered something sharp.

"Tarfang assures you that he and Captain Juun are very prepared," C-3PO translated. "He adds that if your geejawed plan fails, it's your own fault; you shouldn't try to blame it on them."

"It's going to work," Han said.

He started to address the rest of his passengers, but Kyp cut him off.

"Of course we're ready." Kyp's voice came over the comm channel rather than the intercom, an indication that he was already in his vac suit and buttoned up tight. "We're Jedi."

Han glanced over at Leia. "I *hate* it when he does that," he growled. "*You* ready?"

She nodded gravely. "As soon as you tell me how you're going to get past that swarm."

Han grinned. "Who says I'm going to?"

They rounded a bend and, about two kilometers below, saw the first haze of the dartship swarm filling the shaft. Han pointed the *Falcon*'s nose at them and accelerated.

"Han?"

"Yeah?"

"You don't have to impress me." Leia pinched her eyes shut. "I've never thought you were fainthearted. Not even once."

Han chuckled. "Good. Just want to keep—"

Juun's voice came over the intercom. "Captain Solo, I have a question."

"*Now?*" Han asked. The swarm of dartships had thickened to a gray-and-orange cloud. "*Now* you have a question?"

"I can't find the activation safety," Juun said.

"There isn't one!" Han said. "Just activate . . . *now!*"

"But the CEC maintenance manual clearly states that every freight-moving apparatus shall have—"

"Flip the kriffing switch!" Leia yelled.

The shaft's blue walls vanished behind the swarm, and bolts of red energy began to streak down into the shaft as Cakhmaim and Meewalh cut loose with the quad laser cannons.

"That's an order!" Han added.

Juun flipped the switch.

The cabin lights dimmed, and every display on the flight deck winked out as cockpit power dwindled to nothing. Even the quad lasers started to dribble beams of blue light.

"Han?" Leia's voice broke with fear. "We don't have any status displays. I can't monitor our shields. Is it supposed to do that?"

"You bet," Han said proudly. "When I reversed the polarity of the tractor beam, I had to feed it every spare erg of power I could find."

All Han could see ahead was the cloud of dartships, so close now that he could make out individual exhaust trails curving toward the *Falcon*'s nose.

"But not the shields, right?" Leia said. Canopy bulges began to appear atop the closest dartships, some with antennae waving inside, and propellant trails began to stab out from the swarm. "Please tell me we're not drawing on the—"

A cone of iridescent energy shot out from beneath the *Falcon,* swallowing both the Gorog missiles and the swarm beyond. A series of fiery blossoms erupted as the missiles interpreted the repulsion beam as impact and detonated. The dartships were harder to defeat. The pilots increased power, and the cloud of ships hung in stasis, still struggling to ascend the shaft.

But as the *Falcon* continued to descend, the beam grew stronger. Soon the Killiks' primitive rocket engines began to overload and explode. Some dartships fell out of control and crashed, while others began to tumble back down the shaft. For several moments, Han and Leia continued to catch glimpses of dartships rolling around inside the beam, smashing into each other, spontaneously exploding, erupting against the pit's icy walls.

Han slowed their descent until the eruptions grew less frequent.

Finally, the boiling cloud of rubble dispersed, and nothing lay below them but a jagged star of darkness that had once been a dartship launching bay. He brought the *Falcon* to a full stop and activated the intercom.

"Okay, Juun, you'd better shut down before something blows up." Han looked over at Leia and winked, then added, "And shift that power diverter back to the shields."

THIRTY-SEVEN

The Battle Dragon and its escorts were floating nose-down above Qoribu's blast-tattered rings, trading fire with two Chiss cruisers as the Great Swarm swept down to join the fight. Jaina's and Zekk's cockpit speakers crackled to life with Hapan comm officers demanding explanations and Colony Joiners outlining Unu's plan, but the two Jedi paid the exchange little attention. They were two hundred kilometers behind the Swarm, with a third StealthX slaved to Jaina's controls, and their mission was completely independent of the Killik assault. UnuThul was still angry about the spoiled ambush, and he had planted one notion firmly in their minds before allowing them to launch: Jaina and Zekk were to find Lowbacca and leave.

The Great Swarm reached the Hapan fleet and swallowed it in a flickering cloud of rocket exhaust, then streamed past to engulf the maelstrom of starfighters battling for the crucial space midway between the two sides. The Chiss cruisers redoubled their fire. Brilliant bursts of crimson and sapphire blossomed inside the Great Swarm, three or four a second, but the Colony continued to descend, a dozen dartships vanishing every time a turbolaser struck. The Killiks did not even break formation.

Hoping to locate Lowbacca before they entered hostile territory, Jaina and Zekk quieted their minds and reached into the Force . . . and were so surprised that they gasped. Together.

That feels like Master Skywalker, Zekk said through their shared mind.

Both of them, Jaina confirmed. *And Mother and Kyp and others . . . hard to tell. Pretty shut down.*

Trying to hide, Zekk agreed. *But having a bad time. Wonder if Unu knows?*

UnuThul must know, Jaina replied. Though she and Zekk were hundreds of kilometers from the nearest Taat, and not currently in touch with the larger collective mind, they could still feel the Colony's Will. UnuThul was too powerful *not* to know when so many Jedi entered the system. *Wonder why Unu hid it from us.*

Unu's will began to press down on them, and their thoughts turned back to Lowbacca.

After a few moments of searching, they found their friend, groggy and confused and barely conscious, down below Qoribu's southern pole in the heart of the Chiss command group.

Drugged, Zekk said in their thoughts. *Not surprising.*

Predictable, Jaina agreed, growing impatient. *We'll have to move fast.*

Unu's will pressed down, and their hands grew too heavy to lift toward their throttles. Their turn would come later—once the Great Swarm prepared the way.

By the time the Colony's command ship—an outdated *Lancer*-class frigate operated by the Unu—appeared, the first dartships were closing with the cruiser escorts. Jaina's and Zekk's tactical displays turned white with propellant trails and did not darken again. The Chiss escorts flickered and vanished one after the other, and the Killik barrage fell on the cruisers themselves. Both vessels lost shields within seconds and withdrew under fire.

The lead cruiser took a drive hit and was overtaken. Its turbolasers continued to fire for another few seconds, then it suffered a hull breach and began to belch flame. Once its weapons had fallen silent, the Great Swarm stopped attacking and streamed after the surviving cruiser.

The Hapan squadron started to follow, moving to secure the hole the Killiks had opened in the enemy's lines, but Jaina and Zekk were in no mood to wait. They needed to retrieve Lowbacca *before* the Chiss withdrew to Ascendancy space.

Unu's will grew lighter, and Jaina and Zekk shot past the nearest Hapan Nova, passing so close to the bow that they saw the bridge pilot squinting at the shadowy silhouettes of their StealthXs.

The passage opened into a murky vault too large for Mara's helmet lamp to illuminate; the beam merely reached into the darkness and vanished. She shined the light at her feet and found a dark, ribbed slope strewn with membrosia balls. In places, the balls were heaped a meter high. Her spine felt prickly and cold, but that was nothing new. Her danger sense had been on overload since the moment they entered the nest.

Luke's blaster flashed behind her. A distant *peew-peew* sounded through Mara's helmet, suggesting that air pressure had been restored to at least this part of the nest. A quick check of the heads-up display inside her faceplate confirmed her guess.

"At least my hisser's no problem now." Luke opened his faceplate and continued to fire. "One less thing to worry about."

Mara glanced back and found a wall of six-legged dartship canopies scurrying up the passage. She used the Force to shove all but one of the insects back down the passage, clogging the tunnel while Luke concentrated on the leader. Half a dozen shots later, the canopy finally cracked, and a blaster bolt burst the pilot's head.

Mara allowed another Killik to come forward, and she and Luke repeated the maneuver once more before the insects in back turned around and started down the tunnel.

"Time to go," Mara reported, still speaking over her suit comm. "Trying to flank us again."

Luke finished the insect they had isolated, then they floated out into the weightless darkness. Fifteen meters in, Luke stopped and began to shine his helmet lamp around the chamber.

"Might be a good place to make a stand," he said. "Room to maneuver. With the Force, we'll have an agility advantage."

Mara swept her own lamp around the vault. Once in a while, she glimpsed a stretch of shapeless wax or a few membrosia balls resting on a dark, sloping wall. Otherwise, they seemed to be floating in empty air.

"Sounds good." Mara shined her light back into the passage from which they had come. She was surprised to find it completely empty. The dartship pilots were nowhere in sight. "Just one problem."

Luke turned to look as well. Mara sensed him reaching into the Force, then he said, "Han and Leia must be drawing them off. I think the *Falcon* is inside the nest."

Mara equalized her suit pressure, then retracted her faceplate and nearly gagged on the cloying rankness of the air. "You could have warned me," she complained. "What *is* that smell?"

"Maybe it's better not to know," Luke said. "Something rotting, I think."

"And I thought Lizil smelled bad."

As Mara spoke, a ball of membrosia drifted past, "falling" at an angle toward her knees. In contrast to the clear amber syrup of the

Lizil and Yoggoy nests, this liquid looked dark and muddy inside its wax container, with stringy clots of solids silhouetted in the glow of her helmet lamp.

Mara looked up toward the ceiling and thought for a moment she was only looking at an area of burnished wax. Then, as her eyes grew more accustomed to what she was seeing, she began to make out several speeder-sized Killik heads. All were deep, dark blue, and all were facing a two-meter tunnel opening.

"What the blazes?" Mara reached for her lightsaber. "Queens?"

"I don't think so," Luke said, sounding a little disgusted. "Membrosia givers. Look at the other end."

Mara ran her light along one of the Killiks' bodies, past a thorax clamped to the ceiling by six tubular legs running to a hugely swollen abdomen. About the size of a bantha, it was oozing cloudy beads of dark membrosia and crawling with tiny Gorog attendants, which carefully slurped up each drop and redeposited it in a waxy ball extruded from their own abdomens.

"Appetizing," Mara commented dryly. Neither the membrosia givers or their attendants seemed inclined to attack—no doubt because they were entirely lacking in combat ability. "What now? Start back?"

As Mara asked this, Alema Rar appeared in the tunnel above, still dressed in the skintight flight suit she had been wearing when she stole the skiff back on Ossus. Now the material was stained and rumpled in a way Alema would never have permitted before.

The membrosia givers extended short feeding tubes and began to clack their mandibles for attention, but Alema ignored them.

"Sorry," she said to Mara. "We can't let you leave."

"You can't *let* us?"

The sight of their betrayer made Mara's blood boil. She tried to remind herself that Alema was not entirely responsible for her actions—that the Twi'lek had unwittingly fallen under the Dark Nest's influence—but it didn't make her feel any less angry. She pulled her lightsaber from its belt hook, then glanced toward the empty tunnel that led back toward the hangars.

"From where I stand, you're in no position to stop us."

Alema gave a sly smile. "We believe we are."

A muffled rustling rolled up the tunnel, and a wall of Gorog warriors appeared in its mouth. Though they lacked the canopies that had protected the dartship pilots, they were much larger and armed with both tridents and electrobolt assault rifles. The rifles, Mara knew, were relatively feeble weapons, cheap and reliable but requiring three or four hits to take down most targets. Unfortunately, she did not think the Killiks were going to have any trouble massing their firepower.

A shrill chorus of *squeck-squecking* began to spread outward from the dark corners of the chamber, the sound of hundreds of Killik feet rushing across the sticky wax that lined the nest. Mara swept her helmet lamp over the walls and found them crawling with Gorog warriors, and the anger she felt toward Alema assumed an acid taint.

"Tell your masters they're about to wish they *had* died in the Crash." Mara slipped a fresh power pack into her blaster pistol. "We're coming for them."

Alema smirked, and Gorog warriors began to pour out of the tunnel behind her. "You will need more than lightsabers and blaster pistols, we think."

The *Falcon*'s darkened air lock slid silently open. The four YVH "bugcruncher" war droids—on loan from Tendrando Arms and specially programmed to Han's specifications—jumped into the pitch-black hangar. Next went the four Jedi—Kyp, Saba, Octa Ramis, and Kyle Katarn—in their combat-rated vac suits. Han was just glad he had convinced Meewalh and Cakhmaim to "help" Juun and Tarfang guard the *Falcon*, or he and Leia—bringing up the rear in standard-issue EV suits—would have had to follow *them*, too.

"I'm the captain of *Millennium Falcon*," Han grumbled into his faceplate. "That used to mean something."

A moment later, Leia took his wrist, and they jumped out of the air lock. She drew him along through the weightless darkness, using the Force to move them away from the *Falcon* so they would not need to activate their jet belts and make targets of themselves. To Han, it was like making his way through a cargo hold during an all-systems failure. He kept bumping into stuff, and stuff kept bumping into him.

Finally, the YVHs gave an all-clear and activated their thrusters, briefly illuminating the airless, flotsam-choked launching bay before they shot through a hole in the rear wall. Conversing through the Jedi battle-meld if at all, Kyp and the other Masters activated their green combat lamps and used the Force to pull themselves after the war droids. Leia drew Han by the wrist and followed. He felt like a little kid being dragged through a bad dream, what with all the loose bug heads and chunks of thorax chitin floating around.

As they passed through the hole, Leia's helmet lamp came on. Han activated his own light and found himself in a small repair hangar. The YVHs led the way into a small utility tunnel filled with Gorog bodies. Most of the insects had burst eyes and dark strings of tissue extruding from the breathing spiracles on their thoraxes—signs of a quick-but-painful decompression death.

Kyp motioned the rescue party forward, then activated his belt thruster and led the way up the passage. Glad to finally be under his own power, Han started his own thrusters and followed at Leia's side. The accumulation of insect bodies grew thicker as they advanced, and soon the group almost seemed to be swimming through them.

Han touched his helmet to Leia's so they could speak without breaking comm silence. "Luke and Mara did all this?"

"Kyp seems to think so."

"Huh." Han started to wonder who might need rescuing more—the Skywalkers or the bugs. "Nice of them to leave us a trail."

They passed through the tattered remains of a hatch membrane and continued deeper into the twisting warren of tunnels, following a steady trail of dead Gorog and gouged walls. Han began to think the Skywalkers had decided to hunt down Welk and Lomi Plo on their own.

The rescue party came to another hatch, this one intact, and progress slowed to a crawl as the bugcrunchers pushed through one by one. Kyp and Octa Ramis followed the droids, and suddenly the membrane grew bright with battle flashes.

"Enemy located," Bug One reported, terminating comm silence. "Engaging now."

Han armed the T-21 repeating blaster he had brought along as bug repellent, then started toward the membrane.

Leia put out a hand to stop him. "Not yet," she said over the comm. "Kyp's suit has been punctured."

She did not need to explain further. With Kyp's suit damaged, it would not be smart to draw more fire in the hatch's direction.

"Well, tell 'em to hurry up," Han said. "My trigger finger is getting itchy."

Leia's eyes slid away from Han's, looking past his shoulder back down the corridor.

Then Saba's faceplate suddenly loomed up behind Leia's head, her pebbly lips broadening into a huge, fang-filled smile.

"It will not itch for long, this one thinkz."

Han spun around, and his stomach sank.

Dozens of dartship canopies on legs were racing up the tunnel toward them. Han raised his T-21 and opened fire. One canopy shattered, but most of the bolts ricocheted off, melting holes into the

walls and filling the passage with an ever-thickening cloud of ethmane vapor.

Han slid over to stand shoulder-to-shoulder with Leia.

"Sweetheart . . ." He lowered his aim and began to blast Killik
legs. ". . . did I ever tell you how much I hate bugs?"

THIRTY-EIGHT

The Chiss were retreating in disarray, spiraling down below Qoribu's south polar region in a tangled vortex of ion trails, lacing space behind them with a ragged net of turbolaser fire. Jaina and Zekk spotted an opening and swung their StealthXs toward it. Before they could dart through, a pair of frigates managed to shift their fire and string the hole with streaks of energy.

Jaina and Zekk peeled away, the StealthX slaved to Jaina's controls lagging half a second behind. Silhouetted against the white backdrop of Qoribu's south pole, they were visible to any sensor operator with a tracking telescope, and it would be folly to attempt a penetration when they had so clearly been spotted. If they wanted to reach Lowbacca alive, they would have to try another approach.

Not as disorganized as they look, Jaina observed.

This is a show, Zekk agreed.

Jaina and Zekk checked their tactical displays. The screen showed only the portion of the battle not hidden behind Qoribu's mass. But what it did show clearly revealed the Chiss falling back in a crooked, disjointed line that was barely managing to stay ahead of the swarm's dartships. A couple of frigates and light corvettes were blinking with damage, but most of the cruisers, and all of the Star Destroyers and fighter carriers, were safely below Qoribu, milling about in the heart of the fleet.

A Bothan fade, Jaina remarked.

The Chiss probably have a different name for it, Zekk pointed out.

Probably, Jaina agreed.

They swung around in a crooked, uneven curve, ducking behind blossoming turbolaser strikes and changing their approach frequently to throw off anyone trying to track them by sight. But Qoribu's polar region was as vast as it was bright, and their StealthXs remained silhouetted against its whirling white clouds.

We should warn UnuThul, Zekk suggested.

Our help isn't wanted, Jaina replied. That fact made them feel sad and rejected and horribly, utterly alone. *Our mission is to—*

—retrieve Lowbacca and leave, Zekk finished. *But we're Jedi.*

Our first mission is prevent a wider war, Jaina agreed.

They were deliberating more than discussing, weighing both sides of the argument in a single shared mind, and an unhappy thought occurred to them.

What if they did nothing?

The Great Swarm would be destroyed—perhaps even the Hapan fleet, which was advancing behind the safety of the Killik dartships. Without the means to defend the Qoribu nests, the Colony would be forced to abandon them, or to find a way to evacuate. In either case, the Chiss would no longer feel threatened, and a greater war would be averted.

UnuThul might be killed, Zekk pointed out.

Would the Colony return to normal? Jaina wondered.

Impossible to know.

Impossible, Jaina agreed. *But maybe not a bad thing.*

Jaina and Zekk waited, expecting to feel Unu's Will pressing down on them, driving them to act in the Colony's best interest.

But they were out of contact with the Taat mind—cut off from it by distance as well as by Unu's anger—and UnuThul was too busy coordinating the overall battle to join their combatmeld. Jaina and Zekk's mind was their own—for now.

A hole appeared in the turbolaser net, and they accelerated toward it, aiming for a quartet of tiny blue circles that their R9 units assured them was a cruiser's sublight drive. If they could sneak up close enough, they could slip into the heart of the Chiss fleet by hiding near its exhaust nozzles, where the glare would blind anyone peering in their direction.

This feels wrong, Zekk said. *Like we're betraying the Colony.*

And UnuThul, Jaina added. *But we're Jedi.*

Jedi do what is necessary, Zekk agreed. *To prevent war.*

To keep the peace.

The cruiser was so close now that they could see the boxy outline of its engine skirt enclosing the bright disks of its four huge thrust nozzles. Turbolaser beams stabbed out all around them, but never close enough to suggest that the StealthXs had been spotted again. Jaina and Zekk continued to close the distance.

Then another unhappy thought occurred to them. *Welk.*

If UnuThul dies . . .

The possibility was almost too terrible to consider. If UnuThul died, Welk—or Lomi Plo, if she had survived—might become the new Prime Unu. They did not know what that would mean for the Colony, but it would certainly be bad for the rest of the galaxy. The Dark Jedi would use the Killiks for their own ends, perhaps even to draw the entire galaxy into a single collective mind.

Need to protect UnuThul, Zekk concluded.

Better warn him.

Jaina and Zekk were relieved. It was what they had wanted anyway. Maybe they had even convinced themselves it was the best thing when it was not, but their mind was made up. They reached out to UnuThul in the Force, urging him to open himself to their combat-meld.

Unu's will pressed down on them. Suddenly, rescuing Lowbacca seemed more important than stopping the Colony's attack. If Jaina and Zekk did not rescue their friend quickly, he would perish along with his captors when the Great Swarm destroyed the Chiss fleet.

Jaina and Zekk pushed back, but—being out of touch with the Taat mind—they had no way to explain the Chiss trap. All they could do was pour their alarm into the Force and urge UnuThul to join the combat-meld.

Unu's will grew heavier, and they began to believe it was not so important to reach UnuThul after all.

Afraid we're trying to trick them again, Zekk surmised.

Only the knowledge that Unu was wrong gave them the strength to resist, to continue reaching into the Force.

Finally, someone reached back—but it was Jaina's mother, not UnuThul. Jaina and Zekk stretched out toward her, inviting her into their battle-meld, and the situation grew a little clearer. Leia and the others were under attack. An image of dozens of blue-black Killik soldiers appeared inside their mind, swarming up a dark tunnel, pouring electrobolt fire toward them.

Jaina and Zekk were alarmed, but Leia did not seem frightened or worried. Why should she be? She and Han had been trapped in worse situations a hundred times.

Now Jaina and Zekk were really worried—and confused. They

did not know of any blue-black Killiks in the Qoribu system—nor of any nests with such gloomy walls.

Kr, Leia explained. *Secret nest.*

A nest could not be secret. Unu would know about it.

Welk? Leia reminded them. *Saba?*

Now Jaina and Zekk understood. Every time they had tried to investigate the assault on Saba, the Taat—and later UnuThul—had turned them aside. The Barabel had mistakenly attacked a Joiner, it was claimed, or she had fought a Chiss assassin.

Perhaps UnuThul had been attempting to hide the secret nest all along. Or maybe he just did not want to believe it existed.

Either way, the situation was worse than Jaina and Zekk had realized. They wanted to go to Kr to help Leia and the others, but if UnuThul died, the Dark Jedi would be close by, waiting to take over.

Leia seemed to understand. She was already withdrawing from the meld, urging them to be careful, assuring them that Luke and the other Masters had things well in hand on Kr.

When she was gone, Jaina and Zekk still felt no hint of UnuThul.

Have to do this the hard way, Jaina said.

Go back and make contact with Taat, Zekk agreed. *Then the Colony will know what we're thinking.*

Jaina and Zekk hesitated. Unu's will was a bantha sitting on their shoulders, pushing them toward Lobacca, toward the heart of the Chiss fleet.

Lowie can wait a few more minutes, Jaina said. *We'll come back for him.*

Lowie would understand, Zekk agreed. *Lowie is a Jedi.*

Jaina and Zekk rolled into simultaneous wingovers and reversed direction, pointing their noses back toward the Great Swarm. Unu's weight sank to their stick hands.

Only one problem with this plan, Zekk observed.

Jaina could feel Zekk fighting, as she was, to keep his controls dead center.

Not really. Jaina released her stick. "Sneaky, take us in."

The astromech took control of the StealthX, then chirped a question.

"To Unu's squadron." As Jaina spoke, Zekk was giving the same orders to his own astromech. The Taat were flying escort for UnuThul's flag frigate, so all the two Jedi needed to do to was rejoin the swarm, and the Taat mind would know everything they did. "And that command is non—"

"There is no need to desert our friend." UnuThul's gravelly voice reverberated over their comm speakers, but when Jaina and Zekk checked their reception meters, they discovered that their transceivers were not receiving a signal. "We will listen to your plea, but Unu will never let you stay. You have betrayed the Colony's trust—"

"It's not about us." Jaina was not quite certain what form of reply UnuThul could hear, so she simply spoke the words aloud. "We need to warn you."

"You're flying into a trap," Zekk added.

They took control of their StealthXs again, turned back toward the Chiss cruiser they hoped to use for cover. Lowbacca would not have to wait after all.

"This *is* about you," UnuThul insisted. "You are trying to save the Chiss fleet. Again."

"We're trying to save you," Jaina replied.

"It's a Bothan fade," Zekk added. "The Chiss are drawing you into the open."

"You studied battle tactics on Yavin," Jaina said. "You know what's going to happen when the fight moves beyond Qoribu's gravity well."

The boxy outline of the cruiser's engine skirt was again visible ahead. UnuThul remained silent as the brilliant circles of the thrust nozzles continued to swell in front of the StealthXs. Jaina and Zekk began to hope that they had convinced Unu of the danger.

Then UnuThul said, "It must be a coincidence. There were no Chiss in our tactics classes."

Jaina and Zekk knew better than to waste time pointing out the flaws in Unu's argument. Killik logic did not follow the same rules as that of most species—in fact, it did not follow rules at all.

Instead, Jaina asked, "Can the Colony really afford to take that chance?"

"When the Great Swarm reaches Qoribu's south pole, take a minute to regroup," Zekk suggested.

"You remember what will happen if we're right?"

"Of course," UnuThul said. "We have an excellent memory."

The comm speakers fell silent, leaving Jaina and Zekk feeling alone and shunned again, worried their pleas would go unheeded. The first tendrils of the cruiser's exhaust tail began to lick at their forward shields. Jaina and Zekk dropped below it and closed to within three hundred meters of the ship's stern. Their canopy tinting darkened to solid black, and they flipped their bellies toward the ion stream to protect the delicate sensor windows on top of the StealthXs' nose cones.

For the next thirty seconds, they remained on the fringes of the exhaust stream, following the cruiser toward the heart of the Chiss fleet. Jaina and Zekk tried to keep an eye on their tactical displays, but the ion interference rendered their screens almost unreadable. To discern anything, the R9s had to use a complicated algorithmic analysis to separate interference from true sensor returns.

Jaina and Zekk were beginning to think Unu had ignored their warning when the R9s announced that the Great Swarm had slowed. The eyes of the two Jedi Knights went to their tactical displays, desperately trying to infer a picture from the static on the screens. The astromechs reported that the Chiss retreat appeared to be growing even more disorganized.

Trying to tempt the enemy, Zekk observed.

Hope Unu sees that. To Sneaky, Jaina said, "Give us a simple schematic—"

Sneaky interrupted with a series of concerned tweets. Jaina looked out the canopy to see the cruiser swinging back toward Qoribu.

Baiting the trap, Jaina observed.

With our camouflage, Zekk complained. *Too many eyes watching now.*

Better find something else to follow in, Jaina agreed.

They dropped out of the exhaust stream. As their canopies grew transparent again, they found themselves surrounded by durasteel hulls ranging in apparent size from that of a finger to something closer to a Wookiee's arm.

Already deeper than we thought, Jaina observed.

Yeah, Zekk agreed. The static began to clear from their tactical displays. *But is that a good thing or—*

Blossoms of turbolaser fire lit the space around them. Jaina and Zekk surrendered their hands to the Force, and their StealthXs began to weave and bob, swinging wide before a strike exploded in front of them, climbing away from a beam even as it lanced out behind them.

Jaina's hand pushed the stick forward. The third StealthX—the one slaved to her controls—followed her into a dive and slammed into a blossom of fire behind her. Her R9 let out a sad whistle as it received the final data burst from its counterpart, then Jaina jinked starboard and Zekk juked port, and a trio of turbolaser strikes burst into a miniature sun between them.

Our boyfriend means business, Zekk observed.

Don't know that it's him. And it's old *boyfriend.*

Right. We're so over him.

We?

Jaina and Zekk dropped the line of thought there. It was just getting too creepy, with Zekk sharing everything that Jaina *still* felt for Jag, and Jaina sharing everything that Zekk still felt for her, and it didn't help matters that, at the moment, Jag was doing his best to kill them both.

He's just following orders, Zekk consoled.

He has to, Jaina agreed. *He's Chiss.*

They continued to dodge through the barrage, angling first one direction, then another, always working deeper into the fleet. Despite the loss of the third StealthX, they could still rescue Lowbacca. Zekk's storage compartment was filled with oxygen tanks, and there was an air feed running into the empty torpedo bay below his seat. Unfortunately for Jaina, she was the only one small enough to fit inside.

The Chiss brought more ships to bear, stringing kilometer-wide screens of crimson energy ahead of the StealthXs, hoping the elusive starfighters would simply fly into a strike. Jaina and Zekk rolled away from one beam and found another crossing their noses. Jaina pulled up hard, her astromech screeching alarms as the inertial compensator strained to keep the ship together. Zekk dropped his nose and squeezed past underneath, his StealthX shuddering and bouncing as its shields crackled and overloaded.

Enough! To her droid, Jaina said, "Sneaky, give us a one-second fuse and drop a shadow bomb . . . now!"

The droid tweeted its alarm, but obeyed.

Jaina gave the bomb an aftward Force shove, and a silver flash filled the space behind them. The shock wave hit an instant later, slamming both StealthXs forward and pushing their tails down. Jaina and Zekk did not right themselves. They simply poured on the power and shot away, doing anything they could to change course and location before the Chiss eyes tracking them recovered from the blinding flash of the shadow bomb.

The Chiss brought even *more* turbolasers to bear—but well behind and below the StealthXs. Jaina and Zekk were close enough now to feel Lowbacca's presence aboard a heavily armored Dreadnaught escorting the flagship. They closed formation and swung toward it, then finally had time to check their tactical displays.

Unu had listened to their warning. The Great Swarm remained at

Qoribu, spread out just beneath the southern pole, with the Hapans taking a supporting position behind the dartships. Meanwhile, the Chiss had given up trying to draw out the Colony and were smoothly dispersing into their own defensive wall, three layers deep and just out of Hapan turbolaser range.

Could have timed this better.

Going to be hot as a nova getting through that picket field, Zekk agreed.

The Dreadnaught's ion drives suddenly brightened, then Jaina and Zekk's heart sank as the ship turned and accelerated away from the fleet. The Chiss were not fools. Having lost track of their quarry, they had decided to remove the bait.

Could have timed this a lot better. Jaina's vision blurred with welling tears, and she and Zekk reached out to Lowbacca, trying to reach him through the stupor in which his captors were keeping him, trying to assure him that they would find him, urging him not to lose faith.

They felt a question struggling toward the top of Lowbacca's mind, then anger; then the Dreadnaught vanished into hyperspace and they felt nothing at all.

THIRTY-NINE

The chamber was choked with dead Gorog, and still more came, pushing through the bodies and floating globules of gore to press their assault, their electrobolt rifles stringing the darkness with bright ropes of silver. Luke was tumbling through the rancid air, somersaulting over forks of crackling energy and spinning away from thrusting tridents, his lightsaber tracing a green cage around him as the blade moved smoothly from defense to offense, from diverting electrobolts to cleaving dark chitin. Mara was twisting along three meters behind him, connected by an invisible Force tether, firing her blaster with one hand and wielding her lightsaber with the other. They were sinking deeper into a battle trance, becoming one with their weapons, becoming the hands of death . . . and drawing ever closer to Alema Rar.

Luke felt the warm prickle of danger sense and glimpsed a large band of Gorog gliding through the bodies to his right, the electrodes on their rifles already charged and glowing. Still rolling and twisting, fighting off attacks from every direction, he pointed at one of the membrosia givers on the ceiling and used the Force to pull it down— legs flailing and chest booming—into their line of fire.

Alema tried to wrench the creature free, but her grasp was no match for Luke's. The membrosia giver remained in the thick of battle, a shrill screech rising from its feeding tube, long gobs of membrosia shooting from its abdomen.

Alema spat a Twi'leki curse and ignited her lightsaber. Luke's chest tightened with cold anger—he had not thought her foolish enough to come for him—and he steeled himself to do what was necessary.

But Alema went straight to the membrosia giver, stunning Luke by sinking her lightsaber deep into the insect's thorax and dragging the blade along the insect's entire length. The two halves of the huge body drifted apart, and a deafening volley of electrobolt fire lit the darkness.

The Skywalkers ducked away, Luke protecting them with his lightsaber while Mara's blaster added more dead Killiks to the shell of bodies already shielding them.

"Getting dangerous . . . in here!" Mara observed.

"Looks like."

"Time to carry the fight to them." Mara stopped firing and reached for a fresh power pack. "Time to go after Welk." She slipped the pack into her blaster and resumed firing. "And Lomi Plo."

Luke risked a glance toward Alema, who was clearly in no hurry to engage the Skywalkers directly and was gliding back toward her tunnel.

"Hoping to wear us down," Mara observed.

Luke shook his head. "Protecting something," he said. "Or someone."

Take her, Mara ordered through their Force-bond. "I'll cover."

Luke moved to intercept, no longer dodging or twisting, just shouldering past Killik corpses and going after Alema. He was shocked by her ruthlessness, but hardly surprised. The line she had crossed was an invisible one, a matter of degree and intention rather than principle. Had another Jedi Knight made a similar sacrifice pursuing a Jedi goal, Luke might have condoned the act, even tried to console the individual and reassure her that it had been the best choice available.

And that made him wonder more than ever what the Jedi had become.

A trio of Gorog warriors zeroed in on Luke, forcing him into somersaults until Mara took them out. He arrived at the cutoff point after Alema, but close enough on her heels that she had to turn and face him. She showed no emotion on her face or in the Force, but she raised her lightsaber into a middle guard—the best initial defense for an outmatched fighter.

Luke continued to bat electrobolts aside, his lightsaber weaving a green cage around him, but he made no move to attack.

"Alema, this doesn't have to happen," he said. "You still have a home with us. Gorog persuaded you to betray the Jedi, but we *can* forgive you." Luke did not like what the war had done to the Jedi— what it had done to *him*—and he was determined to start *undoing* that right now. "Alema, reach out to me. I can help you find the way back."

"We don't want to come back!" Alema sprang, flying at Luke behind a whirling onslaught of slash and backslash. "Stop . . . interfering!"

Luke blocked and redirected her momentum, sending her tumbling into the body-choked darkness—and placing himself between her and the tunnel she had been guarding. He felt an inquiry from Mara, then glimpsed her pointing her blaster at the Twi'lek's back. He shook his head.

Be quick! Mara broke their Force tether, then launched herself into a wild gyre of sweeping blade-light and flashing blasterfire. *Han and Leia . . .*

Luke could sense the rest for himself. Han and Leia were almost there—and they would not be so forgiving. He began to retreat toward the tunnel, weaving and dancing as the electrobolts flew thick and fast around him. Alema started after him and had to slow down to dodge and block herself.

"Alema, your anger has made you vulnerable," Luke said. "Your sister's death made you angry, and the Gorog are using that anger to hold you."

"Numa was a warrior!" Alema snarled, readily shifting topics—as Luke had known she would—to the still-open wound of her sister's death. "She would defend the Colony!"

This time, she came at Luke under control, combining the flashing blades of a speed attack with the driving stomp kicks of a power assault. He switched to a one-handed grasp, parrying her strikes with his own lightsaber, slipping her kicks with a deft trunk twist, deflecting electrobolts with the palm of his free hand.

"Numa was wise." Luke continued to fall back, spinning around to slash open a pair of Gorog warriors foolish enough to charge him from behind. "She would have been the first to warn you against your anger."

Luke reached out for the Twi'lek, trying to embrace her in the Force and shield her from the Dark Nest's touch. "She would have been disappointed to see how you have surrendered to it."

Alema was too far gone. She attacked all the more furiously, shrieking her grief and rage in Twi'leki, slashing low and high, kicking right and left, her words as hard and angry as her blows. Time and again, Luke forced her to leave her body open for a killing blow he did not want to deliver, and time and again she failed to notice his mercy and spun around in another wild attack.

Then Luke felt an icy jolt of fear. He looked past Alema to see Gorog warriors closing on Mara from all sides, silver rays crackling at her so fast and furious she could not block them all. The first bolt burned a fist-sized hole in the thigh of her vac suit and filled the air with the stench of scorched durafiber. The second caught her in the chest, and Luke did not see the third. By then he was driving forward, pressing the attack and forcing Alema back toward Mara.

Suddenly the Twi'lek stopped, determined to stand her ground. Luke tapped her lightsaber aside, then used the Force to pull her hand toward him, drawing her off balance onto his own weapon. Her eyes widened, and the blade sliced down through her clavicle, deep into her shoulder.

Luke brought his boot up under her chin, snapping her head back, sending her arms flying out to her sides. She began to backflip away, her lightsaber slipping from her open fingers.

Luke summoned the weapon into his empty hand and continued toward Mara, who had disappeared inside a knot of Gorog. Her weapons were still flashing inside the snarl and her presence was burning hot in the Force, and that gave him hope. He reached out to Leia, urging her to hurry, then fell on the jumble with both lightsabers whirling.

The battle erupted into a tempest of hissing blades and shrieking blasters and crackling electrobolts. Luke opened a dozen thoraxes in a dozen strokes, then his back spasmed with the paralyzing heat of an electrobolt strike. Mara fired from somewhere inside the tangle of limbs and mandibles, and the acrid stench of melted chitin rose behind him. Luke stretched out with the Force, dragging Killiks away from Mara, hurling them into their fellow warriors or impaling them on crooked forks of energy.

Luke pulled himself toward a glimpse of red-gold hair, his lightsabers opening a path, filling the air with globules of insect gore. Twice, a mandible slipped through his defenses, one stabbing deep into his thigh, the other slipping a barb inside the face opening of his helmet. Both times, he slashed off the attackers' heads and moved on.

Finally, Luke came to Mara's whirling figure. Her vac suit had been burned to tatters, and she had half a dozen black circles where electrobolts had hit her. A faint aura of gold had arisen around her, a sign she was drawing on the Force to keep her exhausted, wounded body going.

Mara briefly locked gazes with Luke, then her green eyes slid away, looking overhead. Luke followed her line of sight and was surprised to see Alema Rar pulling herself into the tunnel mouth. Her left arm was floating at her side, a deep, gaping V where she had been cleaved.

Mara lowered her gaze again and continued her defensive whirl.

She batted away an electrobolt, then groaned, "This isn't really taking the fight to *them*."

"Not too late, though." Luke sent a flurry of electrobolts screaming back toward the Killiks that had fired them. "Got them overconfident now."

"Better make it look good, then."

Mara sent a dozen bolts screaming toward the Twi'lek. Luke did not see whether any hit. By then, the Gorog were pressing the attack again, and he was too busy defending himself and Mara to worry about Alema.

Leia's arms had become deadweights fifteen minutes into the fight, and she was able to wield her lightsaber now only by virtue of the strength Saba was lending her through the Force. Han had run out of power packs—she had not noticed when—and traded his T-21 for a pair of captured assault rifles, which he had taken to firing one in each hand. The bugcrunchers had taken so many hits that Bugs One through Three had exhausted their laminanium repair ingots. With the exception of Saba—who only seemed to grow quicker, stronger, and more joyful as the battle wore on—even the Jedi Masters were slowing, if the tattered condition of their combat vac suits was any indication.

And the Gorog just kept coming, blocking the way ahead, clattering out of side passages, rumbling up the tunnel behind the rescue team. A limitless swarm.

"Han!" Leia's lightsaber swept down to divert an electrobolt streaking toward his knee, then swung up to block one coming at her own head. Her arms were so numb she did not even feel them move. "Do those bugcrunchers have thermal detonators on them?"

"What do you think?"

"Use 'em."

"In *here*?" The assault rifle in Han's left hand ran low on power and began to shoot sparks. He let it float free. "That's crazy! If we blow a hole in this ice cube—"

"Use 'em!" Leia used the Force to pull a rifle out of a dead Gorog's hands and floated it up the corridor to Han. "I don't think we're going to reach Luke and Mara in time. And we're not doing very—"

"YVH bugcrunchers," Han said over the combat channel. "Go BAM. Use your detonators."

"BAM status requires authorization—"

"Do it!" Han shouted so loudly that his voice reverberated out of five other helmets. "Do it *now*!"

"Authorization code *do it now* accepted," Bug One said. The soft crump of the droid's grenade launcher sounded from the head of the line. "*By Any Means* status—"

A brilliant flash lit the corridor, and the rest of the report was lost to the earsplitting crackle of a thermal detonator.

The rescue team surged forward into the crater, and Bug Four called, "Proceed with all haste." A soft *crump* sounded as the droid launched his detonator. "Explosion imminent."

Leia and the others barely had time to start forward before a brilliant flash filled the corridor behind them. Leaving Bug Four to handle rear-guard duty, they followed Kyp and the other Masters forward. Another *crump* sounded from the front of the line. Another detonator exploded. The tunnel behind them filled with Gorog, and Bug Four launched a detonator.

"Blazt!" Saba shut down her lightsaber. "Where is the fun in that?"

Moving much faster now, they passed through another crater and started around the next corner—then stopped short when a deafening storm of electrobolt fire sent Bug One tumbling back into the adjacent wall. His armor was blasted down to the frame and his internal systems were hanging out, sparking and shooting green lubricant.

"Major eneeemyyy conceeeee . . ." He raised his arm, and a detonator floated out. "Deeeeee . . . eee . . . e . . ."

His systems shut down, leaving the detonator floating in front of him, its red warning light blinking the countdown.

"Misfire! Misfire!" Bug Two started toward the detonator. "Please seek—"

"Stand fast!" Leia ordered.

She raised her finger toward the detonator, but Saba or Kyp or someone had already sent it sailing around the bend. It detonated with a brilliant flash, then Bug Two led the charge forward.

When the rescue team followed, they found themselves entering a vast, murky vault filled with Gorog warriors. Leia could sense Luke and Mara a dozen meters above, hidden in a tangle of insects so thick and large she could not see the glow of their lightsabers.

"How about it, Saba?" Han asked. "That enough fun for you?"

Before the Barabel could answer, some of the Gorog recovered their senses and fired a volley of electrobolts. Leia's lightsaber came up automatically, as did those of Kyp, Saba, and the other Masters, but there were just too many strikes to block. She took a scalding hit in the shoulder and heard Han curse as he took one, then a pair of *crumps* sounded as Bug Two and Bug Three launched more detonators.

"Careful!" Kyp warned. "Master Skywalker—"

The rest was lost to a pair of earsplitting crackles, and Leia's sight flashed to white. The air shuddered as the bugcrunchers opened up with their blaster cannons. By the time her vision cleared, both droids had activated their thrusters and were shooting toward the combat tangle above. Kyp and the other Masters were close on their heels.

Leia looked over at Han. A hand-sized expanse of blistered flesh showed through a hole in the stomach of his vac suit.

"You all right?" he asked.

"Fine," Leia said. She started to remark that Han's wound looked worse than hers, but stopped when Jaina and Zekk touched her through the battle-meld, wondering what the blazes was happening and assuring her that help was coming. She grabbed Han's wrist. "Han, there's something I should tell you."

"Now?" He leaned down and kissed her on the lips. "I love you, too, but maybe—"

"Not that," Leia said. "I mean, it's Jaina. She's on her way."

"Here?" Han scowled. "Good thing or bad?"

Leia could only shrug and shake her head. "I'm pretty sure she and Zekk are Joiners."

Han let his chin drop. "Just shoot me—"

A volley of electrobolt fire crackled up the tunnel behind them. Bug Four retreated around the corner, armor smoking, a deep melt-crease along one side of his head.

"Okay—I didn't mean that."

Han dropped one of his electrobolt rifles and grabbed Leia around the waist, then activated his belt thrusters. They jetted toward the combat above, plowing through an ever-thickening morass of blood globules and drifting bodies. The largest part of the Gorog swarm had turned to face Kyp and the other Masters, but Luke and Mara were still trapped a few meters above the main combat, their lightsabers weaving brilliant snakes of color as they spun and slashed and killed.

Leia and Han were about halfway to the fight when she noticed that no Gorog were firing in their direction. Faced with a line of Jedi

Masters and bugcruncher droids, apparently Leia and Han just did not seem like much of a threat.

Leia *hated* being underestimated.

"That way!" Leia reached across Han's face, pointing away from the battle at an angle. "Flank 'em!"

"I was just about to think of that." Han turned in the direction Leia had indicated, then dropped his second assault rifle and drew his trusty DL-44 blaster. "Take the stick!"

Before Leia could ask for clarification, Han braced his blaster hand across his free arm and pointed the emitter nozzle at one of the Gorog attacking Luke and Mara.

"Are you crazy?" Leia cried. "You can't shoot into a hand-to-hand fight!"

"No kidding?" Han replied. "I didn't know that."

Leia grabbed Han in the Force and, as they continued to approach the battle, tried to steady him. He squeezed the trigger, and a bolt streaked up to blast a Gorog's head apart. He fired again, and an abdomen exploded. The third shot burned a hole through a warrior's thorax.

Han began to fire more rapidly now, always aiming for the perimeter of the battle. The two Masters used the Force to shove targets into his line of fire, and it was only a few seconds before the only Gorog between them and the Solos were dead ones.

Han stopped firing and waved them down. "Come on! Let's get outta—"

Luke and Mara shook their heads, then turned toward the ceiling and vanished into a tunnel surrounded by the five largest, ugliest Killiks Leia had ever seen.

"Hey!" Han yelled, still trying to wave them back. "The ship's *this* way!"

FORTY

Jaina and Zekk knew they were getting close to the launching bay when the broken cylinders of derelict dartships began to appear in the ethmane fog. They could feel Leia and the other Jedi somewhere beyond, deep within Kr, awash in a battle whirl of anger and fear and pain.

They followed the shaft around a bend and, in the fog below, saw the hazy star of a blasted-out launching bay. From inside came the silver flicker of a small-arms barrage, punctuated at intervals by the brilliant bursts of laser cannons. Jaina and Zekk stretched their Force-awareness into the battle. They felt only four living presences aboard the *Falcon*, the Noghri and two others they did not recognize.

As their StealthXs slipped through the entrance, forks of white energy began to crackle across their forward shields. Jaina and Zekk activated their forwards floodlights. The launching bay was filled with wrecked dartships and drifting insect parts. In the heart of the carnage floated the *Millennium Falcon*, taking fire from dozens of positions concealed in the flotsam. Perhaps two dozens insects in the chitin-and-insulfiber carapaces that served as Killik pressure suits had slipped inside the *Falcon*'s shields. They were blasting it with electrobolts at point-blank range, melting fist-sized pits into the hull armor.

Jaina and Zekk paused, struggling to grasp what they saw. Despite what they had sensed from Leia through the Force, they still found it difficult to believe that a nest of Killiks would attack the *Falcon* without reason . . . and all too easy to believe the *Falcon* might have provided a reason. Only the memory of the unprovoked attacks on the *Shadow* and Master Sebatyne earlier—and of the illogical explanations provided by the Colony—gave them the resolve to open fire.

Their laser bolts were blindingly brilliant in such a narrow space, and their canopy flash tinting went to black. Jaina and Zekk instinctively reached into the Force to locate their targets, but the only presences they felt were aboard the *Falcon*. They had to settle for counterfire, allowing their R9 units to control the laser cannons and target the source of each electrobolt.

It took longer, but the result was the same. The positions in the flotsam fell silent, leaving only the Killiks on the *Falcon*'s hull to contend with. Jaina and Zekk sealed their vac suits and moved their StealthXs deeper into the launching bay.

Before they could pop their canopies, the *Falcon*'s rear cargo hatch opened and two Noghri in vac suits dropped out of the vessel with a pair of T-21 repeating blasters. The hatch closed behind them, and they turned in different directions, twisting and spinning like Jedi, working their way around the hull, burning the Killiks off the ship. As much as it pained Jaina and Zekk to watch the deaths of so many Kind, they had to admire the artistry.

The Noghri had almost completed their hull cleaning when the *Falcon*'s ion drives glowed to life. Jaina and Zekk stretched their awareness into the ship again, trying to figure out why the two presences aboard would do such a thing.

They did not like what they felt.

"Help!" C-3PO's voice came over the emergency channel. "This Ewok is a criminal! He has the death mark on ten planets, and now he's attemptttiiiing . . . tooooo . . . steeeeeeaa . . ."

C-3PO's plea trailed off into a deep rumble as someone tripped his primary circuit breaker.

The *Falcon* spun her bow toward the exit. Still fighting the Killiks, the Noghri were thrown from the hull and began to drift.

Jaina swung her StealthX in behind her father's beloved freighter and armed a proton torpedo.

Zekk began to wonder if this was not overkill.

The specifications of the *Falcon*'s military-grade shields rose to the top of their mind, and Zekk understood. He armed a torpedo of his own.

They activated their targeting computers.

The *Falcon* stopped spinning—no doubt as target-lock alarms filled the cockpit.

A nervous Sullustan voice came over the comm channel. "This is Jae Juun, second mate of the *Millennium Falcon,* requesting the two unseen craft to deselect us as targets."

Jaina and Zekk did not comply.

The glow died from the *Falcon*'s ion drives. "This is Jae Juun, second mate of the *Millennium Falcon.* See-Threepio was mistaken. Our only intention was to move the ship out of . . . the line . . . What the bloah is *that*?"

Jaina and Zekk did not need to see past the *Falcon* to know what Juun was talking about. They could feel it in the growing pressure of Unu's will, in the growing weight inside them.

The *Falcon* slipped away from the exit, exposing the old *Lancer*-class frigate now blocking the way outside. A small, well-armed launch was gliding silently through the jagged entrance, nosing aside ruined dartships and tumbling pieces of Killik.

Unu's will grew crushing, compelling Zekk and Jaina to answer honestly—even before they sensed the question.

Who did this?

Mara and Luke were ten meters down a sticky, wax-lined tunnel, and every time Mara made the mistake of breathing, she came close to retching. The dank air stank worse than a Sarlacc's belch, a cloying mélange of decay, spice, and free ethmane. And the smell was only growing worse as they advanced.

"At least it keeps you from thinking about the burns," Luke said.

Mara's awareness of her wounds—half a dozen aching circles where electrobolts had burned thumb-sized craters into her flesh—returned. She drew a little more of the Force into herself, using it to reinvigorate exhausted muscles, to keep her pain-crippled body functional.

"That's what I love about you, farmboy," she said.

"I always look on the bright side?"

"Not really." Mara assumed a cynical tone. "You always know how to make a girl feel better."

The tunnel finally opened into a large vault where the air was so humid and hot that their faces grew instantly moist. An eerie whine permeated the chamber, barely loud enough to hear above the pounding of her own heart, and the Force grew heavy with the pain of the nearly dead.

Mara followed Luke into the vault, and suddenly she forgot the eerie sound, the horrible smell, even her own fiery pain. The entire chamber was lined by large hexagonal cells, some sealed with a wax cap, some containing a paralyzed Chiss captive curled around a Gorog larva. Many of the prisoners were dead and mostly devoured, with the barbed mandibles of a nearly developed larva protruding half a meter above the cell walls. Just as many remained alive, groaning weakly as larvae gnawed at their immobile bodies.

"I'm beginning to understand the Chiss point of view," Luke said. "I wonder if Raynar knows about this?"

"Maybe, on some—"

Mara's neck prickled with cold, and she spun around to find the wrong end of an electrobolt rifle illuminated in her lamp beam. Behind it, sighting down the stock, was a blue face framed by a pair of Twi'lek lekku.

Rather than taking half a second to ignite her lightsaber and another half a second to block, Mara pointed and released the Force energy she had been using to keep herself going. Her body erupted into pain and muscle tremors, but blue lightning shot from her fingertips and blasted the rifle, driving the stock back into the Twi'lek's mangled shoulder and crackling deep into the wound. Alema cried out and let the weapon slip from her hands, then went limp and floated away into darkness.

Mara felt a hint of uneasiness in Luke. "What?"

"Nothing," Luke replied. *Just thinking—*

Luke's lightsaber crackled to life and droned past Mara's ear, blocking what sounded more like blasterfire than another electrobolt. She sensed a second attack coming and activated her own blade, sweeping it up behind Luke's to bat away another string of bolts.

The blasterfire fell silent, but not before Mara could swing her helmet lamp toward its source. She glimpsed a hump-shouldered man with a half-melted face and one chitinous insect arm grafted to his shoulder; then he slipped out of the light.

"Force lightning." The man's voice was raspy and sharp. "We had thought Skywalker's Jedi considered themselves above that."

"We make exceptions." Again, Mara sensed a certain apprehension in Luke. She ignored it and swung her helmet lamp toward the voice, and again the dark figure slipped out of the light. "Especially in your case, Welk."

As Mara spoke, she and Luke moved apart, positioning themselves just within each other's reach, where they could still take advantage of overlapping fields of defense.

A soft flutter sounded above Mara's head.

"Hear that?" Mara asked.

"What?"

"I was afraid you didn't." Mara reached out in the Force but felt only a shadowy sense of danger, so vague and ambiguous she could have been imagining it. "There's something flying around over here."

"Welk?" Luke asked.

A string of blaster bolts erupted from Luke's other side, directly opposite the fluttering. He brought his lightsaber around and sent the bolts tearing back toward the source.

"I don't think so," Mara concluded.

She brought her own blade up, slashing through the darkness above her head, finding only dank air. Another flutter sounded behind her. She spun to attack and suddenly found herself in the Force grasp of someone else, twirling across the room and accelerating. Mara reached out, searching for her attacker. She felt only the horror and anguish that permeated the entire room.

Then she came to the wall, and a piercing agony blossomed low in her back. She looked down to find ten centimeters of mandible tip protruding from her abdomen, and the pain spread across her entire belly.

"Roddddder!"

The second mandible closed, driving a pair of barbs deep into the flesh above her hip.

"That *hurts*."

Mara reversed her grip on her lightsaber, and a flutter arose in the darkness at her side. Suddenly the handle grew stinging cold, then the blade started to sputter, flicker, and fade. Mara attacked anyway.

The blade sank two centimeters and sizzled out. The larva began to shake its head back and forth, its mandibles tearing at her inside.

"Mara?" Luke had activated his second lightsaber—the one he had taken from Alema earlier—and was advancing on Welk, batting the Dark Jedi's blaster bolts back at him. "Need the spare—"

"Fine here!" Mara returned her useless weapon to its clip. "Just take care of Welk."

Welk broke into an evasive tumble, firing as he moved and seldom going astray. Luke deflected a chain of bolts, but finished with his blades out of position and had to somersault away.

Trying.

Mara drew her blaster and put a bolt into the larva's head. It shook even harder, drawing an involuntary cry from her as a barb scraped something inside. She fired a second time, then heard a soft throb in front of her and brought her weapon around.

The handle grew icy cold, then a depletion alarm sounded. When she squeezed the trigger, she heard only the soft *pop* of a gas charge moving into the XCiter chamber.

"Neat trick," Mara said to the darkness. "It isn't going to save you."

The air pulsed above Mara's left shoulder. She swung her helmet lamp toward the sound and—as always—saw nothing. Then a prickle of danger sense raced up her spine, and she looked in the opposite direction. Gliding out of the darkness, just at the edge of her light, was a meter-high Gorog with thick chitin armor and overlong mandibles.

Even had she not seen the splint fused to its broken leg, Mara would have known that this was the assassin she had fought on Ossus. Much smaller than a typical Gorog warrior, it was coming at her in a fury, mandibles clacking, thorax drumming, crooked proboscis foaming.

Mara finally hesitated, confused, unsure, angry. The nest would be reaching out to Ben now, using the Force to share all that was happening here, to make him feel every Gorog death.

A puff of dank air brushed Mara's face. Her helmet grew biting cold and the lamp dimmed to darkness, then a soft *phoot* sounded from the direction of the approaching assassin bug. A glob of caustic-smelling acid hit the front of her ragged vac suit, and her flesh erupted with a new kind of burning.

Ben would have to get over it.

Opening herself completely to the Force, using her resolve to draw it in, Mara lifted her hand toward the assassin bug and squeezed. It popped with a long, sharp crackle and the rotten smell of dissipating methane.

A pair of blue bolts flashed up from Welk's direction and streaked into the smashed body. Mara had just enough time to push out with the Force and create a small bubble of protection before the assassin bug exploded.

In the orange light, floating just beyond arm's reach, she glimpsed a pale oval with little to suggest a face, only a few dark areas where there might have been a mouth and nose and eyes. Mara swung her hand toward it, but the blast light faded and the apparition was gone.

Luke barely felt the heat of the explosion, but the shock wave sent him cartwheeling into darkness. He kept his helmet lamp fixed on Welk's tumbling form and brought himself to a halt a few meters later. Welk slammed into a sealed cell and crashed through the wax cap.

Luke Force-plucked the blaster from Welk's hand and started toward him. He could feel that Mara was wounded but, at the moment, no longer under attack. The best thing he could do was keep the enemy too busy to worry about her—at least until Han and Leia arrived with the rest of the team.

Luke was still five meters away when Welk pulled his twisted body free of the cell. His black armor was smeared in yellow pulp, and the lipless slash of his mouth hung agape with what was either fear or disdain.

Luke reactivated his lightsabers.

The soft whiffle of wings sounded to his right, and the air suddenly grew as thick and heavy as water. He twisted toward the noise, but his body seemed to move in slow motion, and by the time he turned there was nothing to see but darkness.

A crimson blade ignited a few meters ahead, and Luke knew Welk was coming. He brought his lightsabers around in a cross guard and looked back toward the attack. Again, his actions seemed to take forever, and the glow of the crimson blade drew within striking range long before Luke was ready to defend.

The fight was about to get interesting.

Luke extended himself toward the glow, slamming his Force presence into Welk. It was like trying to push Qoribu out of orbit. Welk continued to come, bringing his blade around in a brazen full-reach attack.

Luke didn't even try to block. The Dark Jedi was strong—even stronger than Saba had said—but great strength was like great power. It seduced those who had it, lulled them into relying on might when other tools were better. Luke reversed tactics, pulling his attacker toward him. Welk tumbled forward, his hoarse voice croaking in alarm, his scarred face dropping toward Alema's silver blade.

The low throb of wings sounded overhead, and the hilt of Alema's lightsaber grew painfully cold as the thing causing the sound—he wondered if *that* could be Lomi Plo—drained the energy from its power cell. The blade sputtered and died.

Welk slammed into Luke headfirst, sending them both into an uncontrolled tumble. The Dark Jedi's crimson blade flashed past Luke's leg and burned a gouge into his shin, sending a fiery shaft of pain straight to the heart.

Luke righted himself, but he was still moving in slow motion, and Welk was already coming again. Luke reached out in the Force, bringing his thumb and forefinger together.

Welk's lipless mouth fell open. Dire gurgling sounds began to rise from his throat—and then Luke remembered Alema's sacrifice of the membrosia giver. Had *he* grown that casual about killing? So accustomed to the power he wielded that he would use it to kill when he had other means to defend himself?

Luke opened his fingers and released Welk.

The Dark Jedi's breathing returned to normal, but he stopped where he was, rubbing his throat and eyeing Luke in suspicion.

Skywalker! Mara's voice was a screech in the Force, but when she spoke aloud, it sounded weak and pained. "Are you crazy? Finish him!"

"Not that way," Luke answered. "The Force may have no light or dark side, but we do. We must choose."

"Right *now*?" Mara asked.

"*Especially* now."

Luke caught Welk's gaze, then—still moving slowly—raised his remaining lightsaber to high guard.

"Are you ready, son?"

"We are not your son!"

The Dark Jedi sailed forward, bristling at the condescension, striking at the flank Luke had left open.

Moving even slower than was necessary, Luke pulled his guard around and rotated away. A soft flutter sounded behind him. The hilt of his lightsaber grew cold—as Alema's had a moment earlier—and the blade died.

By then Luke had already released the weapon and accelerated to his best speed, slipping forward even as he twisted away from the attack. The sudden speed change caught Welk by surprise. Luke trapped the Dark Jedi's wrist in an X-block and continued to pivot smoothly away, forcing those hands into a tight circle and driving the lightsaber back up into Welk's stomach in one not-so-fast motion.

Welk let out a bloodcurdling scream and tried to deactivate the lightsaber, but Luke had his hand over the switch and now *he* was the strong one. He wrenched the handle free and ripped the blade out the Dark Jedi's side, then turned to face the attack he felt certain would be coming from Lomi Plo—and went spinning out of control when the air suddenly grew light and thin again and he could once more move at normal speed.

Luke saw the wall flashing past, coming up fast, barbed mandibles protruding where he was about to hit. He deactivated the lightsaber, then reached out in the Force and jerked the larva from its cell, slammed into it in midair, and tumbled off in a new direction.

This time he managed to stop himself before he hit another wall.

He reignited Welk's lightsaber and spun around with the crimson blade swinging—then felt a jolt of alarm and sensed Mara approaching out of the darkness.

"Hey, it's me!" Mara used the Force to push the weapon down. "Don't you recognize your own wife anymore?"

Luke deactivated the blade. "Sorry."

Being careful to keep the beam below her chin so he didn't blind her, Luke turned his helmet lamp in Mara's direction. Her Force aura had subsided to a mere blush, and the charred circles on her body reminded him of how much his own electrobolt wounds ached. But it was the jagged, triangular puncture wound in her right abdomen that he found most alarming. About the size of three fingers bunched together, it was smeared with grime and oozing dark blood.

"How are you feeling?"

"About as good as I look." As Mara spoke, her eyes were searching the darkness around them. "But I'll last until we can find Alema. Any idea where she's—"

A series of dull thuds reverberated through the chamber, followed by the fading light and dying crackle of the thermal detonators that had just discharged inside a wall across the chamber. An instant later, a pair of Han's YVH bugcruncher droids rode into the chamber on the blue-white tails of their propulsion thrusters and quickly swung toward the Skywalkers.

"Remain calm!" one ordered in its ultradeep, ultramale voice. "Remain stationary! Help is coming."

FORTY-ONE

The bolt burns had been smeared with bacta salve, the puncture wounds were covered with actibandages on both sides, and there was enough stericlean in the air to disinfect half the nest. All that could be done in the field, Leia had done, and still she did not like how her sister-in-law looked. Mara had an ashy complexion and a hint of blue in her lips, and her eyes were so sunken they looked like crash craters.

"We'll get you to the *Falcon* soon," Leia said. They were back in the membrosia chamber, where the worst of the battle had taken place, waiting for a pair of fresh vac suits for Mara and Luke. "Bug four should be returning anytime now."

"No hurry." Mara squeezed Leia's hand. "I've been hit worse than this."

"It's not *you* she's worried about," Han said. "If I don't get out of this place soon . . ."

Han let his sentence trail off, and Leia turned to find him shining his helmet lamp into the haze-filled darkness. The beam extended only about ten meters before terminating in a wall of floating Gorog corpses.

"What, Han?"

"I don't know." Han pointed into the carnage, then swung his helmet lamp away to reveal a faint golden glow snaking through the corpses and floating blood globules. "Trouble, maybe."

Leia reached out in the Force and felt a swarm of Killiks approaching in the company of three Joiners.

"It's Jaina and Zekk!" she said. "With Raynar."

"Like I said," Han muttered. "Trouble."

The golden glow resolved itself into a line of shine-balls being carried by a long column of Killiks in chitinous pressure suits of many different configurations. At the head of the procession came the hulking form of Raynar Thul, his vac suit helmet tucked under one arm, his scar-frozen face red with fury. Half a meter behind, Jaina and Zekk followed, looking more nervous than angry.

Leia waited as they approached, then bowed to Raynar. "Un-uThul, I'm sorry we must meet—"

"So are we," Raynar said. The battle-pitted form of Bug Four drifted out from among the mass of Unu following him. The droid's photoreceptors were dark, the seams of his body shell were smeared with soot, and he was surrounded by the acrid stink of scorched circuits. "Your droid murdered Unu."

Giving Leia no chance to respond, Raynar floated around her to the sides of Luke and Mara, and several hand-sized Killik healers poked their tiny heads up past the collar of his pressure suit. Leia started to go after him, but was stopped by a gentle Force tug.

"Wait with us," Jaina said from behind Leia. "Trying to explain now will only make Unu angrier."

"Thank you for the advice." Leia turned to face Jaina and caught the flash of several tiny eyes peering out of her collar, too. "Looks crowded in there."

Jaina stared into Leia's eyes. "Not really."

"It grows on you," Zekk said. He reached over and rubbed the backs of his fingers down Jaina's cheek.

"To tell the truth, we kind of like it," Jaina added.

"Oh," Leia said. "I would have thought all that creeping inside your suit would feel, um, *uncomfortable*."

Jaina and Zekk shook their heads in unison.

"Not at all," Jaina said.

"It makes us feel whole," Zekk added.

The trio spent an awkward moment looking at each other, Jaina and Zekk softly humming and clicking to themselves, Leia hiding her feelings behind a polite smile. Though she had already sensed in the Force what had become of her daughter and Zekk, actually seeing them behave like Joiners was almost more than she could bear. Her heart was dropping with every beat.

Finally, Jaina asked, "What are you doing here, Mother?" Little Killik healers began to crawl out of her suit and launch themselves into the darkness. "We thought you were going to open negotiations with the Chiss."

"I had another idea," Leia said. "One that might actually work."

Jaina and Zekk waited patiently for her to elaborate.

"There's no sense explaining it twice," Leia said. "Let's wait until Ray—er, UnuThul is available."

A hurt look came to the faces of Jaina and Zekk. Leia felt a pang of regret, but she did not apologize. Too much depended on her plan, and she could not risk having the pair speak against it before she had a chance to present it to Raynar.

"What about Dad?" Jaina asked quietly. She glanced toward Han, who remained with Luke and Mara but was looking over at his daughter and Zekk. "Is he still going to cut our tether for staying?"

"It may take some time for your father to accept this," Leia said. "He still has nightmares about whatever happened to him after that misunderstanding with the Kamarians."

"We're not Kamarians," Jaina objected. Zekk absentmindedly rubbed his forearm along the back of her neck, and Han made a sour face and looked away. "We're still his daughter."

"Just give your father some time," Leia said. She did not know how to explain—without offending Jaina and Zekk—what she knew in her heart: that Han was not as disappointed with Jaina as he was angry in himself; that he blamed himself for not protecting her from what she had become. "This is going to be hard for him."

"It will be hard on us all, we think," Zekk said.

Raynar slipped away from Luke and Mara—who were now crawling with Killik healers—and returned to Leia. He fixed his gaze on her, and suddenly her vision darkened around the edges. His blue eyes seemed the only lights in the chamber, and she felt an enormous, murky presence pressing down on her inside.

"*Now* you can explain this slaughter, Princess Leia," Raynar said. "Why did the Jedi kill all these Kind?"

"Quite simply, we had no choice," Leia said. "They were attacking Luke and Mara."

This drew a round of suit-muffled chest pulsing from the entourage of Unu.

"Strange," Raynar said. "This does not look like the Skywalkers' nest. Are you sure *they* were not the ones attacking?"

"It's complicated." Leia started to suggest they come back to that in a moment, but the presence in her chest grew heavy, and she found herself explaining more about the mission than might have been wise. "This nest was drawing the Colony into a devastating war. We hoped to undermine their influence so you would consider our peace plan."

Han's jaw fell. "Leia! How about a little tact?"

"We prefer her candor," Raynar growled. His burning eyes continued to hold Leia's gaze. "But this slaughter was pointless. Eliminating this nest can only turn us against your plan."

"Unfortunately, we had no choice." By the sound of Luke's voice—Leia remained unable to see anything but Raynar's eyes—he was floating over to insert himself into the conversation. "They were trying to eliminate *us*. It was self-defense."

"Self-defense?" Raynar sounded outraged. "The Kind fight only when *they* are attacked."

"Yeah," Han said. "You're a lot like the Chiss that way."

Raynar turned to glare at Han. Leia's vision returned to normal, and she found Han sneering confidently back at Raynar, looking as though he were staring down an Aqualish bar brawler instead of the leader of an interstellar civilization.

Leia slipped between the two. "Let me show you something." She addressed herself not only to Raynar, but to the entire Unu entourage. "You need to understand something about this nest, and then we can talk about whether the Colony truly wants peace."

Without waiting for permission, Leia turned toward the ceiling, leading Raynar, Han, and the Unu through the body-filled darkness toward the nursery entrance. Luke and Mara, who had stopped using the Force to compensate for their injuries, remained behind at the insistence of the Killik healers, and Jaina and Zekk stayed with them. Leia did not understand why, but there was a lot about her daughter and Zekk that she did not understand right now.

After a few moments, they reached the cave that Bugs Two and Three had blasted through the ceiling, and the smell of decay grew sickening. Kyp and the other Masters were inside the nursery gathering Chiss survivors and searching for Lomi Plo, so Leia opened herself to the battle-meld and urged them to have the bugcrunchers stand down.

"Bugcrunchers?" Raynar said.

Leia was a little surprised, since she could not sense Raynar's presence in the meld, but Han was nonchalant.

"No offense. We had to call 'em something."

Halfway through the cave, they found Saba waiting. Her vac suit and face scales were smeared with wax and offal from pulling Chiss out of larval cells, and the stench rising off her was enough to send a rustle of revulsion through the Unu.

Saba allowed Raynar and the entourage to stare at her for a moment, then said, "This one is sorry for her smell. The work in here is meszy."

"What *is* your work?" Raynar asked.

Saba looked to Leia before answering.

"It will be better if we just show you," Leia said, directing her comment more to Saba than Raynar. "Any sign of Alema yet?"

"None," Saba said. "Perhapz she was disintegrated in a detonator explosion."

"Maybe." Having seen for herself how acute the Twi'lek's danger sense was, Leia had her doubts. "What about Lomi Plo?"

Saba turned her palms up. "Vanished."

"Lomi Plo is dead," Raynar said, as if by rote. "She died in the Crash."

Saba glanced his way, gnashing her fangs, then looked back to Leia. "You are sure about this?"

Leia nodded. "Unu needs to see this." Silently, she added that it was *still* the only way to break the Dark Nest's hold on the Colony.

Saba shrugged, then led Leia and the others into the darkness of the nursery. The air was hot and dank and so filled with the stench of decay that Raynar gulped and the Unu rumbled their thoraxes. Kyp and the rest of the rescue team were working along the far side of the chamber, the beams of their helmet lamps sweeping across the wall but revealing little more than the hexagonal pattern of the nursery cells.

A few meters in, Leia stopped and swung her helmet lamp toward the nearest wall. The beam illuminated the half-devoured corpse of a Chiss prisoner, still curled around a squirming Gorog larva.

Raynar gasped, and the nearest Unu brought their mandibles together in shock. Han shined his helmet lamp on a second cell, and Saba a third. Both of those cells also contained the bodies of Chiss captives.

"What is this?" Raynar demanded.

"Looks pretty clear to me," Han said. As more Unu poured into the room with their shine-balls, the chamber brightened rapidly, and the true extent of the horror grew more apparent. "Kind of makes a fella see how the Chiss might have a point, doesn't it?"

Raynar whirled on Han. "You think *we* did this?"

"Not *you,* exactly," Leia said, silently cursing Han's biting humor. "The Dark Nest did it. The Gorog."

"Gorog?" Raynar's gaze drifted back to the gruesome sight in the cells. "What is this Dark Nest?"

"*This.*" Saba waved her arm at the murk around them. "The nest that keepz attacking us. The one that has been feeding on Chisz captivez. The one that made you build more nestz at Qoribu."

Raynar glowered at the Barabel. "The nests do not lead Unu. Unu leads the nests."

"Really?" Leia cocked her brow. "Then all this is *Unu's* doing?"

"No." Raynar's voice grew sharp. When his entourage began to clack and drum, he added, "This is not even a Colony nest. We do not *have* a nest on Kr."

Han looked around pointedly. "Funny. Looks a lot like that nursery on Jwlio—except for all the Chiss captives, of course."

"Actually, it can be a Colony nest," Leia said to Raynar. "And you *wouldn't* remember."

This drew an even louder protest from the Killiks, but Leia spoke over it. "Cilghal thinks the Dark Nest serves as a sort of unconscious for the Colony's collective mind. It would be able to influence the Kind without you knowing—just as the unconscious mind of most species influences *their* behavior."

"Impossible," Raynar said, far too quickly. "There are no Gorog in the Kind. How could the nest influence us?"

"The same way *you* influenced Jaina and the others when you called them to help the Colony," Leia replied. "Through the Force."

Raynar's voice grew soft. "Through the Force."

"That's right," Leia said. "The same way you convinced Tesar to visit Bornaryn Trading. The same way you convinced Tahiri and Tekli to argue the Colony's case to the Jedi Order."

Raynar's eyes flared in understanding, but Unu's protest rose to a crescendo. He closed his eyes as though trying to concentrate, but Leia could see in the twitching muscles of his face some internal struggle, some insect argument she would never understand. She began to have the unpleasant feeling she was attempting the impossible.

Leia glanced over at Saba and mouthed Welk's name. The Barabel's eyes narrowed, but she nodded and quickly slipped away.

At last, the insect din quieted, and Raynar opened his eyes.

"Even if you are right about the Dark Nest, conquering is not our way," he said. "The Kind seek only to live in harmony with the Song of the Universe."

"Yeah, well, you don't have to conquer something to take it over," Han said. "And the Dark Nest had more in it than just Killiks."

"I assume you remember the Dark Jedi," Leia pressed. "Raynar fought them as a young man at Yavin Four. And Welk and Lomi Plo abandoned the strike team on *Baanu Rass*."

Raynar studied her for a moment, then nodded. "We remember. And you think . . ." He let the sentence trail off as the Unu began to rustle and clack; then his voice grew stubborn again. "But you must be wrong. Welk and Lomi Plo died in the Crash."

"Then who is this?" Saba asked.

She emerged from shadows dragging Welk's badly slashed body. He was still dressed in his chitin-and-plastoid armor, with a new insect arm grafted to his shoulder. His face looked even less human than Raynar's, but he clearly wasn't Chiss:

Saba sent the corpse gliding toward Raynar's chest.

Han waited until the thing hit, then said, "He's got some pretty bad burn scars, but that tells you something right there."

Once it was in front of him, Raynar seemed riveted by the corpse, his blue eyes slowly sliding back and forth beneath his scarred brow, his breath coming in ever-raggeder rasps.

"Jacen investigated the Crash," Leia said. "He saw you pull Welk and Lomi out of the flames."

The Unu fell deathly quiet, and Raynar's gaze swung to Leia. "*Saw* us?"

"Through the Force," she clarified.

"Yes—we remember." Raynar nodded and closed his eyes. "He was there . . . on the bridge . . . for just a moment."

"You saw *Jacen*?" Han gasped.

"That's impossible," Leia said. "He would have had to reach across time—"

"We *saw* Jacen. He gave us the strength to continue . . . to pull them . . ." Suddenly Raynar stopped and turned toward the center of the nursery. "Where is Lomi?"

He had barely asked the question when the Unu entourage began to disperse across the nursery, their shine-balls illuminating the vault in a spray of whirling light.

"*Where is Lomi?*" Raynar repeated.

Relief washed over Leia like a Rbollean petal-oil shower. She had broken through to Raynar's memory. "Then you recall saving her?"

"We remember," Raynar said. "She was afraid that the Yuuzhan Vong would find us again, or that Anakin would come looking for her, or Master Skywalker. She was afraid of many things. She wanted to hide."

"Well," Han said, "that sure confirms Cilghal's theory."

"What theory?" Raynar asked.

"The way Cilghal sees it," Han said, "when a Killik nest swallows up someone who's Force-sensitive, the nest takes on some of his personality."

"In your case, the Yoggoy absorbed the value you place on individual life," Leia said. "They started to care for their feeble and provide for the starving, and it wasn't long before their success led to the creation of the Unu."

"That's much how we remember it," Raynar allowed. "But it has nothing to do with the Gorog."

"You said you remember pulling Welk and Lomi Plo out of the fire," Han pointed out. "But then they just disappeared."

"You said Lomi was afraid and wanted to hide," Leia added. "That was what Yoggoy absorbed from her. Isn't it possible that she also created a nest of her own—a nest hidden from everyone else?"

As Raynar considered this, the color seemed to drain from his face. "*We* caused this?"

"That's not what we're saying," Leia said. "Only that the Dark Nest is influencing—"

"If we saved Lomi and Welk, we are responsible."

An eerie tempest of clacking and muffled booming rolled through the nursery as the Unu again started to protest. Raynar turned from Leia and the others and slowly glided along the wall, peering into each cell he passed and shaking his head in despair.

"If we saved Lomi and Welk—"

Han caught up and took Raynar by the arm. "Look, kid, you couldn't have known."

Amazingly, Raynar did not send Han tumbling across the room or silence him with a gesture or even pull away. He merely continued to float along, seemingly unaware of Han at all, staring into the cells.

"If we saved Lomi and Welk, *we* did this."

"You should get a medal for saving them," Han said. "What happened later, that's not your fault."

That got Raynar's attention. He stopped and turned to Han. "This is not our fault?"

"No way," Han said. "All you did was save their lives. That doesn't make you responsible for what they did later."

"We are not responsible." Raynar's voice was filled with relief, and Unu's clacking died away. "That's right."

The spray of shine-ball light slowly began to contract back toward Raynar, and Leia felt Kyp reaching out to her, demanding an explanation, but she could not sense what he wanted explained.

"Maybe this is a Chiss ruse," Raynar said, talking more to himself than Han now. "It must have been a trick to convince the Jedi that the Colony is in the wrong."

Saba shined her helmet lamp into one of the cells. "To this one, it lookz like the trick was on the Chisz."

"The Chiss are ruthless," Raynar said. There was an ominous note of insistence to his gravelly voice. "They would sacrifice a thousand of their own kind to turn the Jedi against us."

"That doesn't explain the Gorog that attacked us on the way in," Leia said. She was alarmed by how Raynar was trying to reshape reality, by how he seemed to be searching for a story that worked. "They weren't Chiss—and neither are all these larvae."

"Yes, it was a very insidious plan," Raynar said. "The Gorog must have been brain-slaves. They were *forced* to fight—and to feed on Chiss volunteers."

"Perhaps," Leia allowed carefully. In a human mind, she would have called Raynar's thought process a psychotic break; in the collective mind of the Colony, she didn't know what to make of it. "But there is another explanation."

"The Chiss are creating Killik clones?" Raynar asked.

"I don't think so," Leia said.

The Unu entourage began to return, many of them drawing the helpless, wide-eyed forms of the Chiss survivors that the rescue team had been pulling out of the cells. Kyp and the other Masters were also approaching, pouring their displeasure into the battle-meld. Saba reached out to them, urging them to stand by, assuring them Leia was in control.

Thanks a lot, Leia thought.

"Do you remember what we were talking about?" Leia asked, continuing to address Raynar. "The Dark Nest?"

"Of course. Our memory is excellent." Raynar's eyes turned bright and angry. "Han said we were not responsible."

"That's right," Leia said. Her vision began to dim around the edges again, and the heavy presence she had experienced before returned to her chest. "But that doesn't . . . mean . . . ."

The murky weight inside grew heavier, and Leia began to understand that Raynar had been damaged as much on the inside as on the outside. Hopelessly marooned, in unimaginable anguish, dependent on a bunch of insects—the shock had just been too much. Raynar had dissociated from the situation, literally becoming UnuThul so he would not recall all the terrible things that had happened to Raynar Thul.

"We understand what *not responsible* means," Raynar said. "It means that just because the Dark Nest exists, we are not the ones who created it." He pointed to the nearest captive, a frightened-looking male wearing the black shreds of a CEDF gunnery officer's uniform. "The Chiss did."

The officer's face paled to ash, and his eyes grew even wider—the only signs of fear that his paralyzed body could still exhibit.

"What we do *not* understand," Raynar said, "is the purpose of this nest."

An unintelligible groan rose from the Chiss's throat, so weak and low that Leia took it to be more of a pained whimper than an attempt to speak.

"Tell us!" Raynar commanded.

The officer moaned again, but the noise sounded even less like words than before.

"We know you are lying." Raynar's tone was ominous, and the officer's face grew white. "Do not insult us."

"I don't think he means to," Leia said. She felt certain that the officer had not said anything at all; Raynar's shattered psyche was just imposing its own meaning on the Chiss's incoherent groans. "I'm sure he doesn't even know that the Chiss created this nest."

Raynar turned back to Leia. "You are *sure*?"

"Perhaps *confident* is a better word," Leia corrected. Again, the weight pressed down inside, and she knew she had to tell Raynar something he wished to hear—something that would make him agree to her plan. "What if the Chiss didn't even *know* they created the Dark Nest?"

"How could they create the Dark Nest without knowing it?" Raynar's voice was doubtful. "We don't see how that could work."

"By *accident*," Han said, picking up on Leia's plan. "That's the only way it could happen. The Chiss would never intentionally do something like this to themselves—not even to volunteers. They have too many honor codes."

"That's right," Leia said. The weight inside was decreasing. "Chiss society is defined by war. They're always fighting—against the Vagaari, the Ssi-ruuk, even each other."

"And the Qoribu nestz are filled with Chisz Joinerz."

Saba let the statement hang, leaving it to her listeners to draw their own conclusions. Under normal circumstances, it would have been perfect persuasive technique. But with Raynar, Leia did not want to take any chances. There were too many dangerous turns available to a dissociative mind—especially a dissociative *collective* mind.

"Remember what Han said about Cilghal's theory?" Leia asked.

"She believes that when a Killik nest absorbs a Force-sensitive being, the nestmates assume a portion of that being's personality."

"When the Yoggoy absorbed you," Han added, "they started to value individual life. When they absorbed Lomi Plo and Welk, they assimilated the desire for secrecy and—"

"We are not responsible for the Dark Nest!" Raynar protested. "Lomi Plo and Welk died in the Crash!"

"That's right," Leia said, cringing inwardly. "Welk and Lomi Plo died in the Crash."

It was growing more apparent that dragging Welk and Lomi Plo out of the burning *Flier* had been just too much for Raynar to bear; that whenever he remembered it, he also remembered how much *he* had suffered—and all that he had lost—by doing it.

Leia continued, "But the Yoggoy absorbed your respect for living things, and it wasn't long before their success led to the creation of the Colony."

"That is how we remember it," Raynar agreed. "But we do not see what that has to do with the Dark Nest—"

"Everything!" Saba waved her scaly arm at the nursery again. "Look at how many Chisz Joinerz they had!"

Raynar's eyes brightened with anger. "The Kind are not cannibals. Our nests do not feed on our own Joiners."

"*Something* happened in this nest," Saba pointed out.

"And the Chiss are bloodthirsty warriors," Leia added. It was a wild exaggeration, but one that Raynar would be eager to believe. "Really, I'm surprised this hasn't happened to the other Qoribu nests."

"This?" Raynar shook his head. "This could not happen to another nest of Kind."

"It happened here," Saba pointed out.

"Maybe there's some sort of balance point," Han added, feigning contemplation. "When a nest gets too many Chiss Joiners . . ."

He let the sentence trail off and turned toward Raynar, his expression growing steadily more concerned.

Raynar finished the thought. "It becomes a Dark Nest?" The Unu broke into a distressed drone, and he nodded. "That could explain what happened here."

"The Chisz *are* great believerz in secrecy," Saba offered helpfully.

"Yes." Raynar spoke with an air of certainty. "The Kind will take no more Chiss into our nests."

"That's one solution," Leia agreed. She caught Han's eye, and they shared one of those electric moments of connection that made her wonder if he was Force-sensitive after all. "But what are you going to do with all your prisoners?"

A nervous clatter rose among the Unu, and Raynar asked, "Prisoners?"

"*Chisz* prisonerz," Saba said. "As the war spreadz, you will have hundredz of thousandz. *Millionz.*"

"Only one thing *to* do." Han shook his head in mock regret. "Of course, that'll only make the rest of the Chiss fight that much harder."

Raynar turned to glare at Han. Leia found herself holding her breath, hoping she had not made a mistake reading Raynar's warped psyche—that he had not grown ruthless enough to accept Han's suggestion.

At last, Raynar said, "The Colony does *not* kill its prisoners."

"No?" Han returned the glare for a moment, then shined his helmet lamp on a half-eaten body. "That'll change soon enough."

The Unu entourage erupted into an angry buzz, but Raynar said nothing.

"Maybe it will not be so bad for the Colony," Saba said. She turned to address the Unu. "Soon, *all* your nestz will be like the Gorog. The Kind will become great fighterz."

"We do not wish the Kind to be great fighters," Raynar said. "We have seen what happens to great fighters. *Anakin* was a great fighter."

A pang of grief struck Leia, but she forced herself to continue. "I'm sorry, UnuThul. I don't see how you can avoid it."

"Too bad there's going to be a war," Han said. "If there wasn't, the Colony could set up some sort of buffer zone and keep the Chiss away from their nests."

"That might work," Leia said. "But Qoribu is too close to Chiss territory. The nests are bound to keep coming into contact with Chiss exploration and mining crews. Sooner or later, they'll reach the balance point."

"Qoribu is too close," Saba agreed. "The Colony would have to move itz nestz."

"Impossible," Raynar said. "It cannot be done."

"That's very unfortunate." Leia said this to the Unu entourage. "Because Han and I found this paradise world—"

"Several worlds, probably," Han added. "All empty, lush with foraging grounds, just waiting for a species to come along and claim them."

The entourage began to rustle with interest.

"Tell us more," Raynar said.

"It's in a subsector on the edge of Colony territory," Leia explained. "We didn't have time to do a complete survey, but the world we visited would be perfect for the Taat nest. There were at least two other habitable planets in the same system, with another dozen systems nearby that gave every indication of being just as profuse."

"We were thinking the Colony would want to have a look," Han said. "But if you guys aren't interested, there are still plenty of displaced species in the Galactic Alliance—"

"We are interested," Raynar said. "We always have need of new territory."

"Good," Leia said. "I'm sure the Chiss could be persuaded to stand down long enough for you to organize a relocation."

The corners of Raynar's mouth turned down. "I've told you, that is impossible. There's no way to transport the Qoribu nests. They are too large."

"Really?" Han flashed a smug smile, then asked, "So large they couldn't be temporarily rebuilt in the hangars and launching bays of, say, a few Hapan Battle Dragons?"

Raynar's jaw dropped. "The Hapan fleet would help us escape the Chiss?"

"Sure, why not?" Han retorted. "That has to be easier than *defending* you."

"And they would let us build *nests* in their Battle Dragons?"

"This one thinkz they would." Saba sissed in amusement. "In fact, she is *sure* of it."

The Unu thrummed their chests and tapped their mandibles for a long time, then Raynar finally said, "We understand what you are doing. You're just as bad as Jaina was."

"*Was?*" Han scowled and looked back toward the other room—the one he had departed without even greeting his daughter. "If you've—"

"Relax, Han." Leia touched Jaina through the Force, then said, "She's fine. She's still with Luke and Mara."

"Of course she is," Raynar said indignantly. "We *meant* that Jaina is no longer welcome in her nest."

Han raised his brow. "I've been kicked out of a few saloons in my time, but a nest? What'd she do?"

"She's too much like you," Raynar said. "She is stubborn and tricky, and she cared about nothing but preventing a war."

"You don't say." Han smiled proudly, then asked, "Does this mean she'll stop being a bughugger?"

Raynar's eyes flashed in anger, and Leia began to have visions of her carefully crafted peace initiative falling apart.

"Han," she said. "Remember, UnuThul hasn't agreed to our proposal yet."

"Well, he hasn't *disagreed,* either." Han turned to Raynar. "What's it going to be, kid? A nasty war and a Colony full of Dark Nests, or a free ride to a free world?"

The Unu erupted into a riot of chest drumming and antenna waving, but Han ignored them and kept his eye fixed on Raynar. The entourage kept the racket up for a few moments longer, then abruptly fell silent and began to stream out of the vault.

Leia frowned. "Are we to take that as a yes?"

"Of course," Raynar said. He rubbed his arm down the antennae of a small, red-eyed Killik about half the size of an Ewok, then turned and started after his nest. "Wasn't it *our* idea?"

EPILOGUE

At the far end of the long, slanting cylinder of spitcrete storage cells, a single Taat was clinging to a patch of durasteel wall, peering out through the hold's lone observation bubble at the golden-ringed mass of the planet Qoribu. With *Kendall*'s decks shuddering beneath the power of her sublight drives and the departure alarms chiming over the intercom, the other members of the nest were perched atop the cell covers, thrumming a soft, mournful song that made the hair rise on the back of Han's neck.

"Enchanting song," Mara said.

Peering in through the hatch with Han, Luke, Leia, and several others, she was seated in a hoverchair she probably did not need. The Killik healers had tended her goring wound so well that the Hapan surgeons had sent her straight to the bacta ward. Between her own healing trances and the month she had spent in the tanks, the only signs that remained of the fight on Kr were the dark circles beneath her eyes and a general haggardness—both of which, according to Leia, had less to do with her injuries than with having to call so heavily on the Force to keep herself going during the battle.

"It's an ancient Killik tune that goes back to the creation of the Maw," C-3PO said. "I'd—"

"Hold on," Han said. "The Killiks were there when the *Maw* was created?"

"Of course," C-3PO said. "According to their histories, they were the ones who built it."

"The Killiks?" Dukat Gray gasped. He took an unconscious step away from the hatch. "Truly?"

"I wouldn't count on it," Leia said. "Killik memories can be rather, uh, flexible."

"What about the song?" Mara asked again. "Can you translate, Threepio?"

"Of course," C-3PO said. "The air tides move us to a different place, the air—"

"Not quite, Threepio," Jaina said.

"It's more like this," Zekk added.

Together, they sang:

The cold wind carries us far from our nest,
The cold wind sweeps us where it may.
Cold wind, bear us out of danger,
Cold wind, carry us home again.

An uneasy silence fell over the group; then the underway alarms fell silent. *Kendall* gave a small jolt, and the bands of Qoribu began to grow smaller as the Fleet of the Defender Queen moved off. Han resisted the temptation to check on the *Falcon*'s status; she was isolated in a capture hangar, safely secured alongside the Jedi StealthXs and being guarded by two Noghri and the surviving pair of YVH droids. She would ride safely until the fleet reached the Killiks' new home.

Zekk said, "We are going to miss them."

"Them?" Han asked. He recalled what Raynar had said about Jaina and Zekk no longer being welcome in their nest, but the Colony's attitude about a lot of things had softened in the last month, and Jaina and Zekk had been spending most of their time with the Taat, helping build the temporary nest aboard *Kendall*. "The rings of Qoribu? The moons?"

"The *Taat*, Dad," Jaina said. "Our mission in the Colony—"

"—is over," Zekk finished.

"No kidding?" A smile as wide as a door crept across Han's mouth. "Great! That's just—" He felt his eyes growing watery, then threw his arms around Jaina and Zekk and pulled them close so they would not think he was going to cry. "I'm happy as a Jawa in a junkyard."

"Dad!" Jaina lifted her chin. "You didn't let us finish!"

"We're not coming home until . . ."

Zekk let the sentence trail off when a Hapan adjutant appeared at the edge of the group with a portable holocomm.

"Until when?" Han demanded.

"Later." Jaina nodded at the adjutant. "I think this could be important."

"Indeed." Gray turned toward the adjutant with an air of expectation. "Is the passenger aboard?"

The adjutant's reply was drowned out by a thundering Wookiee bellow from the other end of the access corridor. Lowbacca came bounding up the passage, his furry arms spread wide. Jaina and Zekk started to race off to meet him, but stopped a step away to look back over their shoulders.

"Dad, about that *until*," Jaina said, smiling.

"Just forget it," Zekk finished.

Then Lowbacca was on them, picking them up in his arms and complaining about the food in Chiss prisons.

Once the noise had died down a bit, the adjutant said, "Pardon me, Your Grace, but we're being hailed."

"Hailed?" Gray repeated. "Out here?"

"By the Chiss, Your Grace. Ship-to-ship."

Gray sighed. "Very well. I'll take it in—"

"I'm sorry." The adjutant looked as though he expected to be hit. "But the Aristocra wishes to speak to Master Skywalker."

Gray scowled at Luke, then swung his scowl over to the adjutant. "What are you waiting for?"

The adjutant paled, then knelt in front of Luke and activated the holocomm. The image of a Chiss of about Han's age appeared above the pad.

"Aristocra Formbi," Luke said immediately. "What a surprise."

"It shouldn't be," Formbi retorted. "Did you think Jagged Fel was overseeing this operation?"

"Not really," Luke said. "What can we do for you . . . that we haven't already?"

"Absolutely nothing," Formbi declared. "Commander Fel informs me that your sister was responsible for persuading the Killiks to depart Qoribu."

"For *negotiating* a truce," Leia said, stepping into the holocam's view. "The Chiss also made certain guarantees."

"Of course. A border guarantee and a promise of nonaggression. All Chiss doctrine, anyway."

"Explicit guarantees, nonetheless," Leia said.

Noting that Qoribu had now shrunk to a size such that the whole planet could be seen through the Taat's observation bubble, Han caught Leia's eye and made a winding motion with his finger.

Leia nodded, then said, "What is it you wished to say to me, Aristocra? We have time left before the fleet enters hyperspace, but we should be aware of it."

"Of course—forgive me," Formbi said. "First, I wished to congratulate you on your success. Without your talents, I fear this matter would have come to war."

"Thank you, Aristocra," Leia said. "But it took the involvement of a great number of people to resolve this conflict—Jagged Fel among them."

"Commander Fel will receive a promotion in recognition of his judgment here," Formbi said. "But is you who deserves our thanks. You have achieved peace in our time."

"The *Jedi* achieved this peace, Aristocra. I was just one of many who were involved." Qoribu's bands were now a colorless mass, and its rings looked like tiny ears protruding from the fattest part of its sphere. "And the second thing? We don't have much time."

"I wanted you to know that Commander Fel is responsible for the return of your Wookiee," Formbi said. "Had it not been for his objections—his very *vigorous* objections—the prisoner would have remained interned until we could be certain this peace is going to hold."

"Then it's a good thing you listened to Jag," Han said. "Keeping the Wookiee would have been a bad mistake."

"Yes, so Commander Fel informed me," Formbi replied calmly. "Be that as it may, I thought you should know that Commander Fel guaranteed your Jedi Knight's parole personally. We don't expect to see *any* Jedi back in our neighborhood soon, but if Lowbacca were to return, the Fel family would be responsible for repaying any damages he caused to the Ascendancy—and a Wookiee Jedi can cause quite a lot of damage, if our prison ship is any example."

"That's very kind of Commander Fel," Leia said. "Please thank him for us."

Jaina and Zekk appeared at Han's back. Lowbacca was towering over them from behind, more of an appendix to their pair than a third member.

"Dad," Jaina whispered.

"We'd like to talk to Jag," Zekk finished.

Han cringed at the thought of Zekk being a part of that particular conversation, but nodded and spoke into the holocomm.

"Is Jag there? We have someone here who wants to say thanks personally."

"Jaina, I presume." Without waiting for confirmation, Formbi said, "Let me check his availability."

Formbi turned and said something they could not hear to someone they could not see. A moment later, Jagged Fel's rugged face replaced Formbi's above the holopad. Han and the others stepped aside to let Jaina—and Zekk—move into the holocam's field.

"Jaina." He frowned, a little confused, and his gaze reluctantly shifted to Zekk. "And Jedi Zekk. I'd like to express my personal gratitude for . . . everything you did. Your efforts helped avert the war."

"You owe us no thanks for that," Zekk said.

"We were acting on everyone's behalf," Jaina said.

"Yes . . . of course." Jag's gaze drifted to Zekk again, and he seemed even more uncertain of himself. "Congratulations, then. You did it very well."

Han glanced out the observation bubble and saw that Qoribu had shrunk to a flattened, silver disk about the size of his thumb. He leaned down next to Jaina's ear.

"Get to the point," he whispered. "The jump is coming."

Jaina and Zekk nodded, then Jaina said, "Thanks for getting Lowbacca released. We were worried that we might have to come break him out."

"So were we." Jagged's tone remained deadpan. "I was not looking forward to that meeting."

"Neither were we," Zekk said.

"But we do look forward to seeing you again sometime soon," Jaina said.

"Under better circumstances," Zekk added.

"Both of you?" Jagged's gaze slipped back and forth between them. "Yes, I will look forward to that." He glanced away, his scarred brow betraying his disappointment—or perhaps it was revulsion. "Now, if you will excuse me, duty calls."

"Of course," Jaina said. "We'll be entering hyperspace soon ourselves. May the Force be with you."

"And with you." Jag shifted his gaze to Zekk. "*Both* of you."

The holocomm blinked out, then Jaina and Zekk turned away, the same crestfallen expression on both their faces. A shudder ran down Han's spine, but he did his best to hide it.

"Kind of sticks in the ol' throat, doesn't it?" he asked, flashing his best crooked, fatherly smile.

"Like we're going to choke on it," Jaina answered.

"But we'll survive." Zekk rubbed his forearm along Jaina's, and she began to make low clicking sounds in her throat. "We have each other."

Han had to look away.

Qoribu was a tiny, oblong circle of light now, glinting in the light of its blue sun, and the Taat's song was growing more forlorn and haunting by the minute. It seemed to him that he could actually feel their sadness himself, and he wondered if this was what it was like to sense something in the Force: to know a thing more clearly in one's heart than in one's head.

Zekk and Lowbacca stepped through the hatch into the temporary nest and began to rub their arms along Taat antennae.

Jaina lingered behind. "We think it will be better to say goodbye now," she explained. "It will only be harder if we wait until they make the new nest."

"Go on," Han said. "I don't have to watch."

Jaina smiled and kissed him on the cheek, then followed Zekk into the hold.

Dukat Gray irritated Han by coming to stand behind him and Leia. For a few moments, the Hapan seemed content to simply watch the two Jedi saying good-bye to their nest, but then he finally decided to ruin the moment completely.

"Aristocra Formbi may have been right about one thing, Princess."

"I find that hard to believe, Dukat," Leia said. "But perhaps I'm mistaken."

"If you will forgive me for saying so, I think you are," Gray said. "It *is* a pity you're not serving in the Galactic Alliance government. A diplomat of the talent and skill you displayed here could be of great service to the new government."

"Thank you, Dukat," Leia said. "Coming from you, that's a very informative suggestion."

Gray beamed, and Han's heart fell. The time had finally come for him to stop being selfish, to suggest that Leia return to her first love.

"Listen," he said. "I know you've missed being in the middle of things. Maybe it's—"

"Yes, it's time for a change," Leia said, cutting him off. "But *not* that way, Han. The last thing I want to do now is join a government—the Galactic Alliance's or anyone else's."

Han began to grow confused. "No?"

"No," Leia said. "I'm sick to death of compromising, of finding the workable solution instead of the right one."

"Okay," Han said cautiously. "What do you have in mind?"

"Following my heart—for a change," Leia said. She turned to Luke. "I've seen many changes in my life—"

"And brought about most of them," Luke said.

"Perhaps," Leia said. "And I've worn some very high titles."

"You deserved 'em," Han said, wondering where this was going.

"That wasn't what I was getting at. After all that, after all that I've seen and done, it always comes down to this." She pulled the lightsaber off her belt and hefted it in her palm. "To one Jedi, to one blade, standing against the darkness." She turned to Han. "I think it's time that I chose a new path."

"New path?" Han asked, growing worried now. "What do you mean, *new path*?"

"I've loved being your copilot, really," Leia said. "But the galaxy has changed. *I* need to change."

"Define *change*," Han said. "Because if this is about the snoring—"

"Don't you dare stop that *now*—I wouldn't be able to sleep!" Leia laughed, then turned to Luke. "I'm beginning to understand the Jedi's place in the galaxy—and to see my place in the Jedi."

Luke smiled. "You want to assume your place in the order."

Leia shook her head. "No—I want to *earn* my place in the order." She turned to Saba Sebatyne, who had been standing at the back of the group in typical reptilian silence. "I want to dedicate myself to becoming a proper Jedi."

"You *are* a proper Jedi," Saba said. "You have done more for the galaxy than any *ten* Jedi."

"You're not listening," Leia said. "Diplomacy didn't stop this war. *Jedi* did. I want to complete my training—and I want you to be my guide."

Saba's scaly brow rose almost as high as Han's, and Luke's, and Mara's.

"You want *this* one to guide *you*?" Saba asked carefully.

Leia nodded. "If you would consider it."

"*This* one?" Saba repeated.

"Yes," Leia repeated. "I want someone who will challenge me in unexpected ways. I want someone who will teach me what I *don't* know."

Saba's diamond-shaped pupils grew narrow as slits, and her forked tongue began to flick between her pebbly lips. She studied Leia for several moments more, then began to siss so hard that she had to grab her sides.

"That is a good one, Princesz. You really had this one—"

"I'm *not* joking," Leia interrupted.

Saba's hissing stopped. "Truly?"

Leia nodded. "Truly."

"Well, then." Saba glanced at Han. "It seemz this one has no choice."

"Not really," Han said. "And it's a lot better than the alternative."

"What alternative?" Saba asked.

Before Han could answer, the jump alarms chimed. A shudder ran through *Kendall*'s decks, then Qoribu's distant pinpoint of light winked out of existence. The Taat's mournful song came to an abrupt end, and the velvet light outside the observation bubble paled to the colorless blur of hyperspace.

THE UNSEEN QUEEN

For Doug Niles
A Treasured Friend

ACKNOWLEDGMENTS

Many people contributed to this book in ways large and small. Thanks are especially due to: Andria Hayday for advice, encouragement, critiques, and much more; James Luceno for brainstorming and ideas; Enrique Guerrero for his many fine suggestions; Shelly Shapiro and all the people at Del Rey who make writing so much fun, particularly Keith Clayton, Colleen Lindsay, and Colette Russen; Sue Rostoni and the wonderful people at Lucasfilm, particularly Howard Roffman, Amy Gary, Leland Chee, and Pablo Hidalgo. And, of course, to George Lucas for Episodes I through III.

PROLOGUE

Like thieves all across the galaxy, Tibanna tappers worked best in darkness. They slipped and stole through the lowest levels of Bespin's Life Zone, down where daylight faded to dusk and shapes softened to silhouettes, down where black curtains of mist swept across purple, boiling skies. Their targets were the lonely platforms where honest beings worked through the endless night de-icing frozen intake fans and belly-crawling into clogged transfer pipes, where the precious gas was gathered atom by atom. In the last month alone, the tanks at a dozen stations had been mysteriously drained, and two Jedi Knights had been sent to bring the thieves to justice.

Emerging into a pocket of clear air, Jaina and Zekk saw BesGas Three ahead. The station was a saucer-shaped extraction platform, so overloaded with processing equipment that it seemed a wonder it stayed afloat. The primary storage deck was limned in blue warning strobes, and in the flashing light behind one of those strobes, Jaina and Zekk saw an oblong shadow tucked back between two holding tanks.

Jaina swung the nose of their borrowed cloud car toward the tanks and accelerated, rushing to have a look before the processing facility vanished behind another curtain of mist. The shadow was probably just a shadow, but down here at the bottom of the Life Zone, heat and pressure and darkness all conspired against human vision, and every possibility had to be investigated up close.

Spin-sealed Tibanna gas had a lot of uses, but the most important was to increase the yield of starship weapons. So if somebody was stealing Tibanna gas, especially as much as had been disappearing from Bespin in recent weeks, the Jedi needed to find out who they were—and what they were doing with it.

As Jaina and Zekk continued to approach, the shadow began to acquire a tablet-like shape. Zekk readied the mini tractor beam, and Jaina armed the twin ion guns. There was no need to remark that the shadow was starting to look like a siphoning balloon, or to complain that the strobe lights were blinding them, or even to discuss what tactics they should use. Thanks to their stay with the Killiks, their minds were so closely connected that they scarcely knew where one began and the other ended. Even after a year away from the Colony, ideas and perceptions and emotions flowed between them without effort. Often, they could not even tell in whose mind a thought had formed—and it did not matter. They simply shared it.

A blue glow flared among the holding tanks, then a small tapper tug shot into view, its conical silhouette wavering against the pressure-blurred lights of the station's habitation decks. An instant later three siphoning balloons—the one Jaina and Zekk had spotted and two others—rose behind it, chased by long plumes of Tibanna gas still escaping from siphoning holes in the holding tanks.

Jaina opened fire with the ion guns, narrowly missing the tug, but spraying the station's central hub. Ion beams were safer to use around Tibanna gas than blaster bolts, since all they did was disable electronic circuitry, so the barrage did not cause any structural damage. But it did plunge two levels of habitation deck into a sudden blackout.

Zekk swung the tractor beam around and caught hold of a siphoning balloon. The tappers released it, and the balloon came flying straight at the cloud car. Zekk deactivated the beam immediately, but Jaina still had to swing wide to avoid being taken out by the huge, tumbling bag of super-cooled gas.

Jaina let out a tense breath. "Too—"

"—close!" Zekk finished.

By the time she brought the cloud car back around, the last two balloons were following the tug up into a dark, churning cloud. Jaina raised their nose and sent another burst of ionized energy streaming after the tappers, but Zekk did not reactivate the beam.

They agreed—the capture attempt had looked realistic enough. Now the quarry needed room to run. Jaina backed off the throttles, and they began a slow spiral up after the thieves.

A moment later, a fuzzy pinpoint of yellow appeared deep inside the cloud, rapidly swelling into a hazy tongue of flame that came shooting out into clear air almost before Jaina could bring the ion guns around. She pressed both triggers and began to sweep the barrels back and forth. She was not trying to hit the missile—that would have been impossible, even for a Jedi. Instead, she was simply laying a blanket of ionized energy in its path.

Zekk reached out and found the missile in the Force, then gently guided it into one of Jaina's ion beams. Its electrical systems erupted into a tempest of discharge lightning and overload sparks, then failed altogether. Once the tempest died down, Zekk used a Force shove to deflect it from the extraction platform. The dead missile plunged past, barely a dozen meters from the edge of the storage deck, then vanished into the seething darkness of the Squeeze Zone.

Jaina frowned. "Now, that was—"

"—entirely uncalled for," Zekk finished.

With all that supercooled Tibanna pouring out onto the storage deck, even a small detonation would have been enough to blow the entire platform out of the sky. But that had probably been the idea, Jaina and Zekk realized: payback for calling in Jedi—and a warning to other stations not to do the same.

"Need to get these guys," Zekk said aloud.

Jaina nodded. "Just as soon as we know who they're working for."

Judging they had allowed the thieves a large enough lead to feel comfortable, Jaina and Zekk stretched out into the Force in an effort to locate them. It was not easy. Even at these depths, Bespin was surprisingly rich in life, from huge gasbag beldons to their mighty velker predators, from vast purple expanses of "glower" algae to the raawks and floaters that scavenged a living from extraction platforms like BesGas Three.

Finally, Jaina and Zekk found what they were searching for, a trio of presences exuding relief and excitement and more than a little anger. The three thieves felt insect-like, somehow more in harmony with the universe than most other beings. But they remained three distinct individuals, each with a unique presence. They were not Killiks.

And that made Jaina and Zekk a little sad. They would never have changed the decision that had gotten them banished from the Colony. It had prevented the outbreak of a savage war, and they did not regret it. But being apart from Taat—the nest they had joined at Qoribu—was like being shut off from themselves, like being cast aside by one's sweetheart and friends and family without the possibility of return. It was a little bit like becoming a ghost, dying but not departing, floating around on the edges of the living never quite able to make contact. So they *did* feel a little sorry for themselves sometimes. Even Jedi were allowed that much.

"Need to get these guys," Jaina said, reiterating a call to action that she felt sure was more Zekk than her. He had never had much use for regrets. "Ready?"

Silly question. Jaina accelerated after the tappers, climbing up into a storm so violent and lightning-filled that she and Zekk felt as if they were back in the war again, fighting a pitched battle against the Yuuzhan Vong. After a standard hour, they gave up trying to maintain a steady altitude and resigned themselves to having their stomachs alternately up in their throats and down in their guts. After three hours, they gave up trying to stay right-side up and concentrated on just making forward progress. After five hours, they emerged from the storm into a bottomless canyon of clear, still air—only to glimpse the tappers entering a wall of crimson vortexes where two bands of wind brushed against each other in opposite directions. Amazingly, the tug still had both siphoning balloons in tow.

Jaina and Zekk wondered whether the tappers knew they were being followed, but that seemed impossible. This far down in the atmosphere, Bespin's magnetic field and powerful storms prevented even rudimentary sensor equipment from working. Navigation was strictly by compass, gyroscope, and calculation. If the tug was going through that wind wall, it was because it was on its way to deliver its stolen Tibanna.

Jaina and Zekk waited until the tappers had vanished, then crossed the cloud canyon and carefully accelerated into the same vortex. The wind grabbed them immediately, and it felt as if they'd been fired out of a turbolaser. Their heads slammed back against their seats, the cloud car began to groan and tremble, and the world beyond their canopy became a blur of crimson vapor and stabbing lightning. Jaina let go of the control stick, lest she forget herself and tear the wings of their craft by attempting to steer.

An hour later, Jaina and Zekk sensed the tappers' presences drifting past to one side and realized they had made it across the Change Zone. Still keeping her hand off the stick, Jaina pushed the throttles to full. The cloud car shot forward screaming and bucking; then the vapor outside faded from crimson to rosy, and the ride grew suddenly smooth.

Jaina eased off the throttles until the cloud car's repulsor drive finally fell silent, then began to circle through the rosy fog at minimum speed.

"Well, that was—"

"—fun," Zekk agreed. "Let's never do it again."

Once their stomachs had settled, Jaina brought the cloud car around and they crept back through the pink fog, unable to see a hundred meters beyond their noses, still using the presences of the tappers to guide them. It felt like they had overshot the thieves by a considerable distance, but it was impossible to say whether that distance was a hundred kilometers or a thousand. The Force did not have a scale.

After a quarter hour, they began to suffer the illusion that they were simply floating in the cloud, that they were not moving at all. But the instruments still showed their velocity at more than a hundred kilometers per standard hour, and it felt as if they were closing rapidly on their quarry.

Jaina wondered where they were.

Zekk said, "The gyrocomputer calculates our position as three-seven-point-eight-three north, two-seven-seven-point-eight-eight-six longitude, one-six-nine deep."

"Is that in—"

"Yes," Zekk answered. They were about a thousand kilometers into the Dead Eye, a vast region of still air and dense fog that had existed in Bespin's atmosphere at least since the planet's discovery.

"Great. Only nineteen thousand kilometers to the other side," Jaina complained. "Do the charts show—"

"Nothing," Zekk said. "Not even a marker buoy."

"Blast!" This, they said together.

Still, it felt like they were catching up to the tappers quickly. There had to be *something* out there.

"Maybe they've just stopped to—"

"No," Jaina said. "That gas was already—"

"Right," Zekk agreed. "They've got to—"

"And soon."

The stolen Tibanna gas had already been spin-sealed, so the tappers had to get it into carbonite quickly or see it lose most of its commercial value. And charts or no charts, that meant there was a facility somewhere in the Dead Eye. Jaina eased back on the throttles some more. It felt as if they were right on top of the thieves, and in this fog—

The corroded tower-tanks of an ancient refinery emerged from the pink haze ahead, and Jaina barely had time to flip the cloud car up on edge and bank away. Zekk, who was just as surprised but a lot less busy, had a moment to glance down through the open roof of a ruined habitation deck. The rest of the station remained hidden in the fog beneath, showing just enough ghostly corners and curves to suggest the lower decks had not fallen off . . . yet.

Focusing on the presences of the three Tibanna tappers, Jaina carefully spiraled down around the central tower complex while Zekk looked for ambushes. Much of the outer skin had long since rusted away, exposing a metal substructure caked and pitted with corrosion. Finally, the ruins of the loading deck came into view. Crooked arms of pink fog reached up through missing sections of flooring, and the docking berths were so primitive that they were serviced by loading ramps instead of lift pads.

A berth close to a missing section of floor held the conical tug Jaina and Zekk had been chasing. The vehicle was standing on three struts, with the boarding ramp lowered. The two siphoning balloons lay on the deck behind the tug, empty and flattened. There was no sign of the crew.

Jaina and Zekk circled once, then landed near the empty siphoning balloons. At once, they felt a rhythmic quiver—the station's repulsorlift generator was straining.

The hair rose on the back of Jaina's neck. "We need to make this fast."

Zekk had already popped the canopy and was leaping out onto the deck. Jaina unbuckled her crash webbing and followed him over to the tug, her lightsaber held at the ready but not ignited. The repulsorlift generator was in even worse condition than she had thought. The quiver was cycling up to a periodic shudder, and the shudder lasted a little longer and grew a little stronger every time it came.

Jaina and Zekk did not like the sound of that. It seemed odd that it should fail now, after so many centuries of keeping this station afloat. But perhaps power was being diverted to the carbonite freezing system—since that was clearly what the tappers were using this place for.

When they reached the tug, it grew apparent they would need to rethink that theory. They could feel the tappers inside the vessel, listless, far too content, almost unconscious. While Jaina stayed outside, Zekk ascended the ramp to investigate, and she received through their shared mind a complete perception of what he was finding.

The ramp opened onto an engineering deck, which—judging by the debris and nesting rags strewn about the floor—also doubled as crew quarters. It felt like the tappers themselves were on the flight deck, one level above. The air was filled with a cloying odor that Jaina and Zekk both recognized all too well, and the floor was piled high with waxy balls containing a dark, muddy liquid filled with stringy clots.

"Black membrosia?" Zekk asked.

There was only one way to be certain, but Zekk had no intention of tasting the stuff. After a brush with the dark side as a teenager, he held himself to a strict standard of restraint, and he never engaged in anything that even hinted of corruption or immorality.

So, after a last check to make sure nothing was creeping up on them out of the fog, Jaina ascended the boarding ramp. She picked up one of the balls and plunged her thumb through the wax, then withdrew it and licked the black syrup. It was much more cloying than the light membrosia of their own nest, with a rancid aftertaste that made her want to scrape her tongue . . . at least until her vision blurred and she was overcome by a feeling of chemical euphoria.

"Whoa. Definitely membrosia." Jaina had to brace herself against a wall, and she and Zekk were filled with a longing to rejoin their nest in the Colony. "Strong stuff."

Jaina could feel how much Zekk wanted to experience another taste—even through *her* mind—but the dark membrosia was almost narcotic in its potency, and now was hardly the time to have her senses dulled. She pinched the thumb hole shut and set the ball aside, intending to retrieve it on the way out.

"Bad idea."

Zekk used the Force to return the ball to the pile with the others. He could be such a zealot sometimes.

The image of a vast chamber filled with waxes of stringy black membrosia came to Jaina's mind, and she recalled where black membrosia came from.

The Dark Nest had survived.

"And we need to know—"

"Right." Jaina led the way up the ladder to the flight deck. "What Dark Nest membrosia is doing *here*."

"Yes—"

"And what it has to do with Tibanna tapping."

Zekk sighed. Sometimes he missed finishing his own sentences.

On the flight deck, Jaina and Zekk found three Verpine slumped at their flight stations in a membrosia-induced stupor. The floor surrounding all three tappers was littered with empty waxes, and their long necks were flopped on their thoraxes or over their shoulders at angles unnatural even for insects. The long fingers and limbs of all three were fitfully jerking, as though in a dream, and when the pilot managed to turn his head to look toward them, tiny sparkles of gold light appeared deep inside his bulbous eyes.

"Won't get any answers here for a while," Jaina said.

"Right," Zekk said. "But they didn't unload those siphoning balloons themselves."

Jaina and Zekk left the tug and returned to the siphoning balloons, then followed a new transfer hose over to a section of missing deck. The line descended through the hole and disappeared into the fog, angling down toward the top of the unipod—where the carbonite freezing facilities were usually located.

Jaina and Zekk looked at each other, silently debating whether it would be better to slide along the hose or work their way down through the central hub of the station . . . and that was when the repulsorlift generator finally stopped shuddering.

They felt their stomachs rise and hoped that they were just reacting to the sudden stillness—that the sudden silence was not the bad sign they feared.

Then the blue glow of a large repulsor drive flared to life below.

"Rodders!" Jaina cursed.

The blue glow of the departing vessel swung around, briefly silhouetting the hazy lance of the station's unipod, then quickly receded into the fog.

"They shut the generator down!" Zekk said.

Jaina and Zekk turned to race to their cloud car, then remembered the tappers and started for the tug instead.

Their knees buckled as the deck suddenly lurched upward beneath them; then a strut collapsed beneath the tug, and it tumbled across the platform. Jaina and Zekk were too confused to react—until they noticed that they were also starting to slide.

The station was tipping.

Jaina spun back toward their cloud car and found it sliding across the deck, rocking up on its struts and about to tumble over. She thrust an arm out, holding Zekk with her other hand, and used the Force to pluck the vehicle up and bring it over. She caught hold of the cockpit and started to pull herself inside, then realized Zekk was still a deadweight in her other hand.

He was staring toward a missing section of deck, holding his arm out. But his Force grasp was empty, and Jaina could feel how angry he was with himself for missing the tug.

"Get over it!" She pulled herself into the cloud car's cockpit, dragging him after her. "They're Tibanna toppers. They're not worth dying for!"

ONE

Woteba.

The last time Han Solo had been here, the planet had had no name. The air had been thick and boggy, and there had been a ribbon of muddy water purling through the marsh grass, bending lazily toward the dark wall of a nearby conifer forest. A jagged mountain had loomed in the distance, its pale summit gleaming against the wispy red veil of a nebular sky.

Now the air was filled with the aroma of sweet membrosia and slow-roasted nerf ribs, and the only water in sight was rippling down the face of an artificial waterfall. The conifer forest had been cut, stripped, and driven into the marsh to serve as log pilings beneath the iridescent tunnel-houses of the Saras nest. Even the mountain looked different, seeming to float above the city on a cushion of kiln steam, its icy peak almost scraping the pale-veined belly of the Utegetu Nebula.

"Interesting, what the bugs have done to the place," Han said. He was standing in the door of the glimmering hangar where they had berthed the *Falcon,* looking out on the nest along with Leia, Saba Sebatyne, the Skywalkers, and C-3PO and R2-D2. "Not so creepy after all."

"Don't call them bugs, Han," Leia reminded him. "Insulting your hosts is never a good way to start a visit."

"Right, we wouldn't want to insult 'em," Han said. "Not for a little thing like harboring pirates and running black membrosia."

He crossed a spinglass bridge and stopped at the edge of a meandering ribbon of street. The silver lane was packed with chest-high Killiks hauling rough lumber, quarried moire-stone, casks of blue-

water. Here and there, bleary-eyed spacers—human and otherwise—
were staggering back to their ships at the sore end of a membrosia
binge. On the balconies overhanging the tunnel-house entrances,
glittered-up Joiners—beings who had spent too much time among
Killiks and been absorbed into the nest's collective mind—were smiling and dancing to the soft trill of spinning wind horns. The only in-
congruous sight was in the marshy, two-meter gap that served as the
gutter between the hangar and the street. A lone insect lay facedown
in the muck, its orange thorax and white-striped abdomen half covered in some sort of dull gray froth.

"Raynar must know we've arrived," Luke said. He was still on
the bridge behind Han. "Any sign of a guide?"

The bug in the gutter lifted itself on its arms and began to drum
its thorax.

"I don't know," Han answered, eyeing the bug uncertainly.
When it began to drag itself toward the bridge, he said, "Make that
a maybe."

The Killik stopped and stared up at them with a pair of bulbous
green eyes. *"Bur r rruubb, ubur ruur."*

"Sorry—don't understand a throb." Han knelt on the street's
glimmering surface and extended a hand. "But come on up. Our
protocol droid knows over six million—"

The insect spread its mandibles and backed away, pointing at the
blaster on Han's hip.

"Hey, take it easy," Han said, still holding out his hand. "That's
just for show. I'm not here to shoot anybody."

"Brubr." The Killik raised a pincer-hand, then tapped itself between the eyes. *"Urrubb uu."*

"Oh, dear," C-3PO said from the back of the bridge. "She seems
to be *asking* you to blast her."

The bug nodded enthusiastically, then averted its eyes.

"Don't get crazy," Han said. "You're not that late."

"I think it's in pain, Han." Mara knelt on the street beside Han
and motioned the insect to come closer. "Come here. We'll try to
help."

The Killik shook its head and tapped itself between the eyes
again. *"Buurubuur, ubu ru."*

"She says *nothing* can help," C-3PO said. "She has the Fizz."

"The Fizz?" Han echoed.

The Killik thrummed a long explanation.

"She says it is very painful," C-3PO said. "And she would appreciate it if you would end her misery as soon as possible. UnuThul is waiting in the Garden Hall."

"Sorry," Han said. "I'm not blasting anyone this trip."

The Killik rumbled something that sounded like *rodder,* then started to drag itself away.

"Wait!" Luke extended his hand, and the Killik rose out of the mud. "Maybe we can rig an isolation ward—"

The rest of the offer was drowned out as Saras porters turned to point at their nest-fellow's frothy legs, drumming their chests and knocking the loads out of one another's arms. The Joiner dancers vanished from their balconies, and startled spacers staggered toward the gutter, squinting and reaching for their blasters.

Luke began to float the Killik back toward the bridge. It clacked its mandibles in protest and thrashed its arms, but its legs—hidden beneath a thick layer of froth—dangled motionlessly beneath its thorax. A steady drizzle of what looked like dirt specks fell from its feet into the gutter.

Han frowned. "Luke, maybe we'd better leave—"

A blaster bolt whined out from down the street, taking the Killik in midthorax and spraying a fist-sized circle of chitin and froth onto the hangar's milky exterior. The insect died instantly, but another uproar erupted on the street as angry spacers began to berate a wobbly Quarren holding a powerful Merr-Sonn Flash 4 blaster pistol.

"Ish not my fault!" The Quarren waved the weapon vaguely in Luke's direction. "Them Jedi wash the ones flyin' a Fizzer 'round."

The accusation diverted the angry looks toward Luke, but no one in the group was membrosia-smeared enough to harangue a party that included four beings dressed in Jedi robes. Instead the spacers staggered toward the hangar's other entrances as fast as their unsteady legs could carry them, leaving Han and the Jedi to stare at the dead Killik in astonished silence. Normally, they would have at least taken the killer into custody to await local law enforcement, but these were hardly normal circumstances. Luke just sighed and lowered the victim back into the gutter.

Leia seemed unable to take her eyes off it. "From the way those spacers reacted, this is fairly common. Did Raynar's message say anything about an epidemic?"

"Not a word," Mara said, standing. "Just that Unu had discovered why the Dark Nest attacked me last year, and we needed to discuss it in person."

"I don't like it," Han said. "Sounds more convenient all the time."

"We know—and thanks again for coming," Mara said. "We appreciate the backup."

"Yeah, well, don't mention it." Han returned to his feet. "We've got a personal interest in this."

Strictly speaking, the pirate harboring and membrosia running in which the Killiks were engaged was not Han and Leia's concern. But Chief of State Omas was using the trouble as a pretext to avoid keeping his side of a complicated bargain with the Solos, saying that until the nests of the Utegetu Nebula stopped causing so much trouble for the Galactic Alliance, he could not muster the votes he needed to give the Ithorians a new homeworld.

Han would have liked to believe the claim was just a big bantha patty, but someone had leaked the terms of the deal to the holopress. Now both the Solo name and the Ithorian homeworld had become linked in the public mind with the pirate raids and "tarhoney" dens that were blighting the frontier from Adumar to Reecee.

Once the street traffic had returned to normal, Luke said, "We seem to be out a guide. We'll have to find Raynar ourselves."

Han started to send C-3PO into the street to ask directions from a Killik, but Luke and the other Masters simply turned to Leia with an expectant look. She closed her eyes for a moment, then turned down the street and confidently began to lead the way deeper into the shimmering nest. Fairly certain that she knew exactly where she was going, Han fell in beside C-3PO and R2-D2 and followed the others in silence. Sometimes hanging out with Jedi was almost enough to make him feel inadequate.

For a quarter of a standard hour, the nature of Saras nest did not change. They continued to meet long lines of Killik porters coming in the opposite direction, to crave the roasted nerf they smelled in the air, to marvel at the iridescent sheen of the sinuous tunnel-houses—and to gasp at the purling beauty of the endless string of fountains, sprays, and cascades they passed.

Most of the Killik nests Han had visited had left him feeling creepy and a little sick to his stomach. But this one made him feel oddly buoyant and relaxed, perhaps even rejuvenated, as though the most pleasant thing in the galaxy would be sitting on a tunnel-house balcony, sipping golden membrosia, and watching the Joiners dance.

It made Han wonder what the bugs were up to *now*.

Gradually, the streets grew less crowded, and the group began to notice more froth-covered bodies in the gutter. Most were already dead and half disintegrated, but a few remained intact enough to raise their heads and beg for a merciful end. Han found himself torn between the desire to stop their suffering and a reluctance to do something so drastic without understanding the situation. Fortunately, Luke was able to take the middle road, using the Force to render each victim unconscious.

Finally, Leia stopped about ten meters from an open expanse of marsh. The street continued, snaking through a brightly mottled sweep of bog flowers, but the road surface turned dull and frothy ahead, and the ends of the nearby tunnel-houses were being eaten by gray foam. In the center of the field stood a massive spinglass palace, its base a shapeless mass of ash-colored bubbles and its crown a braided tangle of iridescent turrets swimming with snakes of color.

"Tell me that's not where Raynar was waiting," Han groaned. "Because there's no way we're going—"

"Raynar Thul could not be waiting there," a gravelly voice said from a nearby tunnel-house. "You should know that by now, Captain Solo. Raynar Thul has been gone a long time."

Han turned around and found the imposing figure of Raynar Thul standing in the tunnel-house entrance. A tall man with regal bearing, he had a raw, melted face with no ears, hair, or nose, and all of his visible skin had the shiny, stiff quality of a burn scar. He wore purple trousers and a cape of scarlet silk over a breastplate of gold chitin.

"Guess I'm a slow learner that way," Han said, smiling. "Good to see you again, uh, UnuThul."

Raynar came into the street. As always, he was followed by the Unu, a motley swarm of Killiks of many different shapes and sizes. Gathered from hundreds of different nests, they accompanied Raynar wherever he went and acted as a sort of collective Will for the Colony.

"We are surprised to see you and Princess Leia here." Raynar made no move to take the hand that Han extended. "We did not summon you."

Han frowned, but continued to hold out his hand. "Yeah, what's the deal with that? Our feelings were kind of hurt, seeing how we're the ones who gave you this world."

Raynar's eyes remained cold. "We have not forgotten." Instead of shaking hands, he reached past Han's wrist and rubbed forearms in a buggish greeting. "You may be sure of that."

"Uh, great." Han tried to hide the cold shudder that ran up his spine. "Glad to hear it."

Raynar continued to rub arms, his keloid lip rising into a faint sneer. "There is no need to be afraid, Captain Solo. Touching us will not make you a Joiner."

"Never thought it would." Han yanked his arm away. "You're just enjoying it way too much."

Raynar's sneer changed to a small, taut smile. "That is what we have always admired most about you, Captain Solo," he said. "Your fearlessness."

Before Han could respond—or ask about the gray foam eating the Saras nest—Raynar stepped away, and Han found himself being stared down by one of the Unu, this one a two-meter insect with a red-spotted head and five blue eyes.

"What are *you* looking at?" Han demanded.

The insect snapped its mandibles closed a centimeter from Han's nose, then drummed something sharp with its thorax.

"The Colony certainly seems impressed with your courage, Captain Solo!" C-3PO reported cheerily. "She says she is either looking at the bravest human in the galaxy—or the dumbest."

Han frowned at the bug. "What's that supposed to mean?"

The Killik looked away and walked past him, leading the rest of the Unu to join Raynar and the Skywalkers. Han motioned C-3PO and R2-D2 to his side, then shouldered his way through the softly droning mass to stand with Saba and Leia.

"I'm not liking the buzz around here," he whispered to Leia. "It's beginning to feel like a setup."

Leia nodded, but kept her attention fixed on the center of the gathering, where Raynar was already exchanging greetings with the Skywalkers.

". . . apologize for receiving you in the street," he was saying to Luke. "But the Garden Hall we built to welcome you was . . ." He glanced toward the marsh. ". . . destroyed."

"No apologies are necessary," Luke answered. "We're happy to see you anywhere."

"Good." Raynar motioned them up the street, toward a small courtyard only a couple of meters from the marsh. "We will talk in the Circle of Rest."

Alarm warnings began to knell inside Han's head. "Shouldn't we go someplace safer?" he asked. "Farther away from that froth?"

Raynar turned to Han and narrowed his eyes. "Why would we do that, Captain Solo?"

"Are you kidding me?" Han asked. "Why *wouldn't* we? I've seen what that foam does."

"Have you?" Raynar asked. Han's vision began to blur around the edges, and soon all that remained visible of Raynar's face were the cold, blue depths of his eyes. "Tell us about it."

Han scowled. "What do you think you're doing? Don't you try that Force stuff . . ." A dark weight began to gather inside his chest, and words began to spill out of Han of their own accord. "There was a bug outside our hangar covered in gray froth. It was disintegrating before our eyes, and now we get here and see the same thing happening to your—"

"Wait a minute!" Leia's voice came from in front of Han. "You think *we* know something about this 'Fizz'?"

"You and Captain Solo *are* the ones who gave us this world," Raynar said. "And now we know why."

"I don't think I like what you're saying." Han could still see only Raynar's eyes. "We pull your feet out of . . . the fire at . . . Qoribu, and . . ." The weight inside his chest grew heavier, and he found himself returning to the original subject. "Look, this is the first time we ever saw the stuff. It's probably some bug disease you guys brought baaarrggh—"

The weight became crushing, and Han dropped to his knees, his sentence ending in an unintelligible groan.

"Stop it!" Leia said. "This is no way to win our help."

"We are not *interested* in your help, Princess Leia," Raynar said. "We have seen what comes of your 'help.' "

"You must want something from us," Luke said. It sounded to Han as though Luke had also stepped in front of him. "You went to a lot of trouble to lure us here."

"We did not *lure* you, Master Skywalker." Raynar's blue eyes slid away. The weight vanished from inside Han's chest, and his vision slowly returned to normal. "Unu *did* discover why Gorog is trying to kill Mara."

"*Is* trying to?" Luke's tone was one of clarification rather than surprise. Gorog was a furtive nest of Killiks—called the Dark Nest by Jedi—that acted as a sort of evil Unconscious for the Colony's collective mind. The Jedi had attempted to destroy it last year, after it had precipitated the Qoribu crisis by secretly persuading Raynar to establish several nests on the Chiss frontier, but they had realized they had failed as soon as the Dark Nest's black membrosia began appearing on Alliance worlds. "We're listening."

"In good time," Raynar said. "We will tell you about the plot against Mara *after* you tell us about the Fizz."

He turned and started toward the Circle of Rest.

Han rose and stomped after him. "I told you, we don't know anything about that—and if you ever try that heavy-chest thing on me again—"

Leia took Han's arm. "Han—"

"—I'm going to buy myself a spaceliner," Han continued. "Then I'm going to start booking culinary tours—"

Leia's fingers bit into Han's triceps hard enough to stop him from uttering the fateful *from Kubindi,* and he turned toward her, scowling and rubbing his arm.

"Ouch," he said. She had spent the last year training under Saba, and even without the Force, her grasp could be crushing. "What'd you do that for?"

"Maybe we *do* know something," she said.

Han's frown deepened. "How do you figure?"

"Because we have Cilghal—and a state-of-the-art astrobiology lab," Leia said. "Even if we've never seen this stuff before, we can probably figure it out."

Raynar stopped at the Circle of Rest and turned to glare at them. "We want to know *now.*" His entourage began to clack and thrum thoraxes. "We will not stand for your stalling, Princess."

"I don't care for the way you're speaking to us, UnuThul." Leia met Raynar's gaze from where she was standing, about three meters down the street. "We've done nothing to deserve that tone."

"You cheated us," Raynar insisted. "You tricked us into leaving Qoribu and coming here."

"*Cheated* you?" Han exploded. "Now just a blasted—"

"I'm sorry," Leia interrupted. "But if that's the way the Colony feels, we have nothing to discuss."

She turned away and started back up the street toward the *Falcon.* Luke and the other Jedi instantly followed Leia's lead, and Han did likewise. This trip had become, he sensed, something of a test of Leia's progress toward becoming a full Jedi, and he was not going to mess it up for her—no matter how much he was aching to put that ungrateful bughugger in his place.

An indignant rumble sounded from the Unu entourage, and Raynar called, "Stop!"

Leia continued to walk, and so did Han and everyone else.

"Wait." This time, Raynar managed to sound as if he was asking instead of ordering. "Please."

Leia stopped and spoke over her shoulder. "These discussions can proceed only in an atmosphere of trust, UnuThul." She slowly turned to face him. "Do you think that's possible?"

Raynar's eyes flashed, but he said, "Of course." He motioned them back toward the Circle of Rest. "You may trust us."

Leia appeared to consider this for a moment, but Han knew she was only posturing. She and Han wanted these discussions as badly as Raynar did, and there was no way Luke was going to leave the planet without learning more about the Dark Nest's vendetta against Mara. No matter how crazy and paranoid Raynar sounded, they had to deal with him.

Leia finally nodded. "Very well."

She led the way back up the street, and Raynar waved them into the courtyard with the Unu. Basically a walk-in fountain, the Circle of Rest consisted of four egg-shaped monoliths arrayed in a semicircle, the open side facing the Garden Hall. All four had sheets of water rippling down the sides, and looking out from inside each monolith was the hologram of a blinking, smiling Joiner child or pucker-mouthed Killik larva. Han found the place oddly soothing—in a cold, creepy sort of way.

They joined Raynar in the center of the semicircle, where C-3PO immediately began to complain about the fine mist spraying them from all sides. Han silenced him with a quiet threat, then tried not to complain himself as the insects of the Unu began to crowd around.

"Perhaps I should begin by explaining why Han and I are here," Leia said. She looked from Raynar to his entourage. "If that's agreeable to you and Unu."

The insects clacked their approval, and Raynar said, "We approve."

Leia's smile was polite, but forced. "As you may know, after Han and I discovered these worlds inside the Utegetu Nebula, our first intention was to give them to refugees who are still looking for new homeworlds after the war with the Yuuzhan Vong."

"We have heard this," Raynar allowed.

"Instead, Chief of State Omas encouraged us to give them to the Colony, to avoid a war between you and the Chiss," Leia continued. "In return, he promised to secure a new homeworld for one of the refugee species we had hoped to settle here, the Ithorians."

Raynar's gaze drifted out across the marsh, to where the gray foam was steadily creeping higher up the Garden Hall. "We fail to see what that has to do with us."

"The arrangement has become common knowledge in the Galactic Alliance," Leia explained. "And people are blaming us and the Ithorians for the trouble your nests in the Utegetu Nebula are causing."

Raynar's eyes snapped back toward Leia. "What trouble?"

"Don't play dumb with us," Han said, unable to restrain his anger any longer. "Those pirates you're harboring are raiding Alliance ships, and that black membrosia you're running is eating the souls of whole species of Alliance insect-citizens."

Raynar lowered his fused brow. "The Colony kills pirates, not harbors them," he said. "And you must be aware, Captain Solo, that membrosia is gold, not black. You certainly drank enough on Jwlio to be certain of that."

"The Dark Nest's membrosia was dark," Luke pointed out. "And Alliance Intelligence has captured dozens of pirates who confirm that their vessels are operating out of the Utegetu Nebula."

An ominous rumble rose from the thoraxes of the Unu, and Raynar turned on Luke with blue eyes burning. "Pirates lie, Master Skywalker. And you destroyed the Dark Nest on Kr."

"Then why did you say *is*?" Saba demanded. "If it'z still hunting Mara, then it hasn't been destroyed."

"Forgive our exaggeration." Raynar returned his attention to Luke. "You destroyed *most* of the nest on Kr. What remains couldn't supply a starliner with black membrosia—and certainly not whole worlds."

"Then where is it all coming from?" Leia asked.

"You tell us," Raynar replied. "The Galactic Alliance is filled with biochemists clever enough to synthesize black membrosia. We suggest you start with *them*."

"Synthetic membrosia?" Han echoed.

He was beginning to feel as if they had had this conversation before. The Colony's concept of truth was fluid, to say the least, and its peculiar leader was incredibly stubborn. Last year, Raynar had literally had to be hit in the face by a Gorog corpse before he would believe that the Dark Nest even existed. It had been just as hard to convince him that the mysterious nest had been founded by the same Dark Jedi who had abducted him from *Baanu Raas* during the war with the Yuuzhan Vong. Now Han had the sinking feeling it would prove even harder to convince Raynar that the Utegetu nests were misbehaving.

Han turned to Luke. "Now *that*'s something we hadn't thought of—synthetic membrosia. We'll have to check it out."

"Uh, sure." Luke's nod could have been a little more convincing. "As soon as we get back."

"Good." Han turned back to Raynar. "And since you're so sure that the Utegetu nests *aren't* doing anything wrong, you shouldn't have a problem sharing a log of your legitimate traffic with the Galactic Alliance. It would really help them out with the pirate problem."

Raynar's eyes grew bright and hot. "We are telling the truth, Captain Solo—the *real* truth."

"The *Jedi* understand that," Mara said. "But the Galactic Alliance needs to be convinced."

"And Chief Omas is willing to make it worth your while," Leia added. "Once he's convinced that the Utegetu nests aren't supporting these activities, he'll be willing to offer the Colony a trade agreement. It would mean larger markets for your exports, and lower costs for your imports."

"It would mean regulations and restrictions," Raynar said. "And the Colony would be responsible for enforcing them."

"Only the ones you agreed to in the first place," Leia said. "It would go a long way toward bringing the Colony—"

"The Colony is not interested in Alliance regulations." Raynar signaled an end to the subject by stepping closer to Luke and Mara and presenting his back to Han and Leia. "We invited the Masters Skywalker here to discuss what Unu has learned about the Dark Nest's vendetta."

Leia refused to take the hint. "Strange, how you can remember the vendetta," she said to Raynar's back, "and still not know what's really happening here inside the nebula."

Raynar spoke over his shoulder. "What are you saying?"

"You know what she's saying," Han said. "The Dark Nest fooled you once—"

The air grew acrid with Killik aggression pheromones, and Raynar whirled on Han. "*We* are not the ones being fooled!" He glanced in Leia's direction, then added, "And we will prove it."

"Please do."

Leia's wry tone suggested she believed the same thing Han did—that it could not be done, because Raynar and the Unu *were* the ones being fooled.

Raynar smirked their doubts aside, then turned to Mara. "When you were the Emperor's Hand, did you ever meet someone named Daxar Ies?"

"Where . . ." Mara's voice cracked, and she paused to swallow. "Where did you hear that name?"

"His wife and daughter came home early." Raynar's tone grew accusatory. "They found you searching his office."

Mara narrowed her eyes and managed to put on a good impression of collecting herself. "Only three people could know that."

"And two of them became Joiners."

Luke reached out to steady Mara, and Han knew she had *really* been shaken.

"All right," Han said. "What's going on?"

"Daxar Ies was a . . ." Mara's hand slipped free of Luke's, and she forced herself to meet Han's and Leia's gazes. "He was a target."

"One of *Palpatine's* targets?" Leia asked.

Mara nodded grimly. Recalling her days as one of Palpatine's special "assistants" was not something she enjoyed. "The only job I ever botched, as a matter of fact."

"We would not call it *botched*," Raynar said. "You eliminated the target."

"That was only part of the objective." Mara was looking at Raynar now, *glaring* at him. "I didn't recover the list . . . and I left witnesses."

"You let Beda Ies and her daughter live," Raynar said. "You told them to vanish forever."

"That's right," Mara said. "As far as I know, they were never harmed."

"They were well protected," Raynar said. "Gorog saw to that."

"Wait a minute," Han said. "You're saying these Ies women joined the Dark Nest?"

"No," Raynar said. "I am saying they *created* it."

Han winced, and Leia's eyes flashed with alarm.

"I thought we already knew how the Dark Nest was created," Leia said. "The Gorog were corrupted when they absorbed too many Chiss Joiners."

"We were mistaken," Raynar said.

Han's wince became a genuine sinking feeling. To broker a peace between the Colony and the Chiss, Leia had been forced to bend the truth and contrive an origination tale for the Dark Nest that would make the Killiks want to stay far away from the Chiss. The Colony had readily embraced the new story, since it was less painful than believing one of its own nests could be responsible for the terrible things they had found in the Gorog nest. If Raynar and the Unu were trying to develop a new version now, it could only be because they wanted to renew their expansion toward Chiss territory.

"Look," Han said, "we've been through all that."

"We have new information," Raynar insisted. He looked back to Mara. "Mara Jade told Beda Ies and her daughter to vanish and never to be found. They fled into the Unknown Regions and took refuge with Gorog—before it was the Dark Nest."

"Sorry, but this story won't work for us," Han said. "You should have brought the Ies women up last year."

"We did not know about them last year," Raynar said.

"Too bad," Han said. "You can't just make up a new—"

"Han, I don't think they're making this up," Mara interrupted. "They know too much about what happened—at least the part about the Ies women."

"So what if the Ies girls did become Joiners?" Han asked. He was beginning to wonder whose side Mara was on. "That doesn't mean *they* created the Dark Nest. They could have joined some other nest, and the Colony would still know enough about them to put together a good story."

"The story we have put together is the truth," Raynar said. "When Beda and Eremay became Joiners, the Gorog absorbed their fear. The entire nest went into hiding. It became the Dark Nest."

Han started to object, but Leia took his arm.

"Han, it could be the truth," she said. "I mean, the *real* truth. We need to hear this."

"Yes," Saba agreed. "For Mara'z sake."

Han let his chin drop. "Blast it."

"You should not feel bad, Captain Solo," Raynar consoled. "We have believed the new truth for some time. Nothing you could say would make us change our mind."

"Thanks loads," Han grumbled. "That's a real comfort."

A flash of humor danced through Raynar's eyes, and he turned back to Mara. "We are sure you have figured out the rest," he said. "Gorog recognized you at the Crash last year—"

"And assumed I had come to find the list," Mara finished. "So they attacked first."

Raynar shook his head. "We wish it were that simple. Gorog wanted revenge. Gorog *still* wants revenge—against you."

"Of course." Mara did not even blink. "I killed Beda's husband and Eremay's father, and condemned *them* to a life in exile. Naturally they want me dead."

"They want you to suffer," Raynar corrected. "*Then* they want you dead."

"And you had to bring Mara and Luke all the way out here to tell them that?" Han asked. He could tell by their expressions that the Jedi—well, at least the *human* Jedi—were all convinced that Raynar was telling the truth. But something here smelled rotten to Han, and he had noticed the stench as soon as they arrived on the planet. "You couldn't have sent a message?"

"We could have." Raynar stared at Luke a moment, then turned and looked across the bog toward the froth-covered walls of the Garden Palace. "But we wanted be certain that Master Skywalker understood the urgency of our situation."

"I see." Luke followed Raynar's gaze out across the bog, and his face slowly began to cloud with the same anger that was welling up inside Han. "And Unu's Will isn't strong enough to change what Gorog feels?"

"We are sorry, Master Skywalker, but not yet." Raynar tore his gaze off the Garden Hall and faced Luke coolly. "Perhaps later, after we have stopped the Fizz and are less concerned with our own problems."

TWO

The interior of the hangar smelled of hamogoni wood and containment fluid, and the air was filled with the clatter and drone of Killik workers—mostly cargo handlers and maintenance crews—scurrying from one task to another. The *Falcon* sat a hundred meters down the way, looking deceptively clean in the opaline light, but berthed directly beneath one of the gray blemishes that were beginning to mar the hangar's milky interior.

Luke took the lead and used the Force to gently nudge a path through the frenetic activity. The companions were hardly fleeing, but they did want to launch the *Falcon* before Raynar had time to reconsider the agreement Leia had negotiated after his veiled threat against Mara—and before the blemishes on the ceiling turned into the same gray froth spreading over the exterior of the hangar.

"Looks like we're not the only ones eager to clear this bug hive," Han said, moving up beside Luke. "That Fizz must be even faster than it looks."

"This one does not think so," Saba said. In her hands, she was holding a sealed stasis jar containing a thumbsized sample of gray froth. "If it workz so fast, why would they stay to load their shipz?"

"I see you haven't spent much time around smugglers," Luke said. "They *never* leave without their cargo."

The boarding ramp descended, and Leia's longtime Noghri bodyguards, Meewalh and Cakhmaim, appeared at the top armed with T-21 repeating blasters.

"What a relief!" C-3PO clinked ahead and started up the ramp. "I can't wait to step into the sterilizer booth. My circuits itch just holding a record of that Fizz."

"Sorry, Threepio. Han and I need you and Artoo with us, to translate and look for patterns in the froth attacks." Luke stopped at the foot of the ramp and turned to Han and Leia. "If that's all right with you."

"No problem," Han said. He stepped closer and spoke in a whisper so low that Luke barely heard it. "We'll just wait until the boarding ramp starts to go up, then jump on. Leia can cold-start the repulsor drives, and we'll—"

"Han, we gave Raynar our word."

"Yeah, I remember." Han continued to whisper. "But we can do this. We'll be out of here before—"

"We're staying." Luke spoke loudly enough so that the eavesdroppers he sensed watching them would have no trouble overhearing. "A Jedi Master's promise should mean something."

Han glanced at the Saras cargo handlers loading moire-stone into the next ship over, and a glimmer of understanding came to his eyes. Each nest of Killiks shared a collective mind, so as long as there was a single Saras within sight of them, all of the Saras Killiks would know exactly what they were doing. And since the Unu included a delegate from the Saras nest, that meant *Raynar* would always know exactly what they were doing.

"I see your point," Han said. "We wouldn't want to double-cross *UnuThul*."

Luke rolled his eyes. "Han, you *don't* see."

The ease with which Alema Rar had fallen under the sway of the Dark Nest during the Qoribu crisis had prompted Luke to do a lot of soul searching, and he had come to the conclusion that the Jedi had been injured by the war with the Yuuzhan Vong in ways even more serious than the deaths they had suffered. They had embraced a ruthless, anything-goes philosophy that left young Jedi Knights with no clear concept of who they were and what they stood for, that blurred the difference between right and wrong and made them far too susceptible to sinister influences. And so Luke had decided to rebuild a sense of principle in the Jedi order, to demonstrate to his followers that a Jedi Knight *was* a force for good in the galaxy.

"If we leave now, it will make solving other problems with the Colony more difficult," Luke continued. He hated having to drag Han into his quest to revitalize the Jedi, but Raynar had agreed to allow Mara, Leia, and the others to leave peacefully only if Luke *and* Han remained on Woteba until the Jedi found a remedy for the Fizz. "We have to build some trust, or we'll only have *more* pirates and black membrosia coming out of these nests."

Han scowled. "Luke, you just don't understand bugs," he said. "Trust isn't that big in their way of seeing things."

"Captain Solo is quite correct." C-3PO remained halfway up the ramp. "I haven't been able to identify a word for 'trust' or 'honor' in any of their native languages. It really would be wiser to flee."

"Nice try, Threepio," Mara said, stepping to Luke's side. "But you may as well come back down here. We're staying."

As the droid clanked reluctantly down the ramp, Luke turned to Mara. He knew she could sense his unspoken plan as clearly as *he* sensed her anxiety, but this was one time he would truly be better off without her at his side.

"Mara, I think—"

"I'm not leaving here without you, Luke."

Leia touched Mara's elbow. "Mara, the Dark Nest wants you *dead*. Staying on Woteba will only make Luke and Han targets along with you."

Mara's eyes grew narrow and angry, but she dropped her chin and sighed. "I hate this," she said. "It makes me feel like a coward."

"Coward? Mara Jade Skywalker?" Saba snorted. "That is just rockheaded. Leaving is the best thing you can do for Master Skywalker and Han."

"Yeah, but before you go, I want to know who this Daxar Ies was," Han said. "I've never heard of him."

"You wouldn't have. He was one of Palpatine's private accountants," Mara answered. "He embezzled two billion credits from the Emperor's personal funds and stashed it in accounts all over the galaxy."

Han whistled. "Brave guy."

"Foolish guy," Saba corrected. "He believed he could deceive the Emperor?"

Mara shrugged. "You'd be surprised how many people believed that," she said. "And Daxar Ies was a strange man. All that money, and I found him living in a shabby twilight-level apartment on Coruscant. He never left the planet."

"Maybe he lost the list of accounts, or couldn't get to it," Leia suggested. "That would explain why you couldn't find it."

"Maybe," Mara said. "But the Emperor didn't think so. Ies knew where one of the accounts was. He made a withdrawal, and that's how I tracked him down."

Though Mara showed no outward sign of her feelings, Luke could sense how much she disliked talking about that part of her life, how angry she grew when she thought of how the Emperor had manipulated her trust—and how sad it made her to recall her victims. He took her in his arms, silently reminding her that that part of her life was long over, and kissed her.

"Go back to the academy," Luke said. "Cilghal will need you on Ossus, to tell her everything you can remember about the Fizz. Han and I will be fine."

Mara pulled herself back and forced a smile. "You'd better be telling the truth, Skywalker."

"This one will make sure of it." Saba passed the stasis jar to Mara. "She is also staying."

"No way," Han said. "You'll make the bugs think we're up to something. Raynar picked me to stay with Luke because he figured one Jedi Master would be more than enough to watch."

"And because he knowz you are disturbed by insectz," Saba said. "This one does not like the way this feelz, Han. Raynar is showing a cruel streak."

"So it seems," Luke said. He reached out with the Force, urging the Barabel to board the *Falcon* with the others. "But Han's right—we don't want to make the Killiks suspicious of us."

"If you wish, Master Skywalker," Saba said. "You are the long-fang here."

Saba took the stasis jar back from Mara, then turned and ascended the ramp with no further comment. In any other species, the abruptness might have indicated anger or hurt feelings. In a Barabel, it just meant she was ready to go.

Luke kissed Mara again and watched her start up the ramp.

Han hugged and kissed Leia, then stepped back with an overly casual air. "Be careful with my ship," he said to Leia. "I've finally got that hyperdrive adjusted just right."

Leia rolled her eyes. "Sure you do." She gave him a wistful smile, then said good-bye to Luke and started up the ramp. "I'll send Cakhmaim out with your bags."

"And please don't forget my cleaning kit," C-3PO called after her. "This planet is unsanitary. I feel contaminated already."

"Who doesn't?" Han asked.

Being careful to do nothing that would make the Killiks think they intended to flee, Luke and Han waited at the foot of the ramp until Cakhmaim returned with their bags and C-3PO's cleaning kit. Though Luke had not yet had a chance to outline his plan, he was fairly certain that Han had guessed it. He was going to search out the Dark Nest, determine how big a threat it posed to Mara and the Galactic Alliance, and find a way to destroy it for good.

Once Cakhmaim had passed them their bags, Leia raised the ramp and sounded the departure alarm. Luke, Han, and the droids backed away to a safe distance, then watched in silence as the *Falcon* lifted off without them and glided over the bustling floor. When it reached the hangar mouth, it paused briefly and flashed its landing lights in a complicated sequence of flashes and blinks.

R2-D2 let out an astonished whistle.

"I don't know why that should surprise you," C-3PO said. "Of course they're concerned about us."

"What did they say?" Luke asked.

"Be careful," C-3PO translated. "And don't let anything drip on the droids."

"Drip on the . . . ?" Han looked up. "Uh, maybe we'd better get out of here."

Luke followed Han's gaze and found the gray blemish on the ceiling beginning to blister. There was no froth yet, but a long shadow down the center suggested the surface would soon start bubbling.

Luke was about to turn toward the exit when his danger sense made the hairs on his neck stand upright. He did not sense anything unusual from the eavesdroppers who had been watching them—no hardening of resolve, no cresting wave of anger or gathering lump of fear. He remained where he was, pretending to study the blemish on the ceiling as he opened himself more fully to the Force.

But instead of expanding his awareness as he would normally do when searching for an unseen threat, Luke waited quietly, patiently, without motion. He was trying to feel not the threat itself, but the ripples it created in the Force around it. The technique was one he had developed—with his nephew, Jacen—to search for beings who could hide their presences in the Force.

"Uh, Luke?" Han had already taken a dozen steps toward the exit and was standing in the middle of a long column of Saras porters. The insects were swinging their line around him, rushing a load of five-meter hamogoni logs into the hold of a boxy Damorian SpaceBantha freighter. "You coming?"

"Not yet," Luke said. "Why don't you go on ahead and ask about a place to stay? I'll join you in a few minutes."

Han frowned, then shrugged. "Whatever you say."

"Perhaps Artoo and I should go with Captain Solo." C-3PO was two steps ahead of Han. "He's sure to need a translator."

But R2-D2 remained behind. Luke had been forced to remove a motivation module to preserve a secret memory cache that had surfaced last year, and now the little droid refused to leave his side.

As Han departed, Luke worked to quiet his mind, to shut out the booming and banging and whirring of the busy hangar, the swirling mad efficiency of the Killiks and filmy hot weight of the dank air, to sense nothing but the Force itself, holding him in its liquid grasp, lapping at him from all sides, and soon he felt one set of ripples that seemed to come out of nowhere, from an emptiness where he sensed only a vague uneasiness in the Force, where he felt nothing except a cold, empty hole.

Luke turned toward the emptiness and found himself looking under an old Gallofree Star Barge that was listing toward a collapsed strut. The shadows beneath its belly were so thick and gray that it took a moment to find the source of the ripples he'd felt, but finally he noticed a pair of almond-shaped eyes watching him from near the stern. They had green irises surrounded by yellow sclera, and they were set in a slender blue face with high cheeks and a thin straight nose. The thick tendrils of a pair of lekku curled back from the top of the forehead, arching over the shoulders and vanishing behind a lithe female body.

"Alema Rar." Luke let his hand drop to the hilt of his lightsaber. "I'm glad to see you survived the trouble at Kr."

" 'Trouble,' Master Skywalker?" The Twi'lek scuttled forward into the light. "That's a pretty word for it."

Alema was dressed in a Killik-silk bodysuit, the color of midnight and as close fitting as a coat of paint. The cloth was semitransparent, save for an opaque triangle that covered the sagging, misshaped shoulder above a dangling arm. Luke's danger sense had formed an icy ball between his shoulder blades, but both of the Twi'lek's hands were visible and empty, and the only weapon she carried was the new lightsaber hanging from the belt angled across her hips.

Luke began to quiet his mind again, searching for another set of unexplained Force ripples.

"Worried, Master Skywalker?" Alema stopped a dozen paces away and stared at him, her eyes as steady and unblinking as those of an insect. "There's no need. We're not interested in hurting you."

"You'll understand if I don't believe you."

Though Luke had noticed no other suspicious Force ripples, he pivoted in both directions, scanning the shadows beneath nearby ships, the churning Killik swarms, the hexagonal storage cells along the walls, and anywhere else an attacker might be lurking. He found nothing and turned back to Alema.

"I don't suppose you're here to ask the Jedi to take you back?"

"What an interesting idea." The smile Alema flashed would have been coy once, but now seemed merely hard and base. "But no."

Fairly confident now that Alema was not going to attack—at least physically—Luke moved his hand away from his lightsaber and advanced to within a few steps of the Twi'lek.

"Well, what are you doing here?" Knowing it would upset her and throw her off balance, Luke purposely allowed his gaze to linger on Alema's disfigured shoulder. "Just stopping by to let us know you and Lomi Plo are still alive?"

Alema gave a low throat-click, then said, "Lomi Plo died in the Crash."

"With Welk, I suppose."

"Exactly," Alema said.

Luke sighed in frustration. "So we're back to that, are we?" He had slain Welk during the fight at Qoribu, only a few minutes after he had cut Alema's shoulder half off, and he had good reason to believe that the apparition that had nearly killed *him*—and Mara—was what remained of Lomi Plo. "Alema, you were at Kr. You saw Welk before I killed him, and it had to be Lomi Plo who pulled you out of the nest at the end."

"You killed BedaGorog," Alema said. "She was the Night Herald before us."

"The person I killed was male." Luke suspected he was arguing a lost cause. The Dark Nest remained determined to hide the survival of Lomi Plo behind a veil of lies and false memories, and—as a sort of collective Unconscious for the entire Colony—it was adept at manipulating the beliefs of Joiners and Killiks alike. "He had a lightsaber, and he knew how to use it."

"BedaGorog was Force-sensitive." A lewd smile came to Alema's lips. "And as we recall, you did not take the time to check inside her pants before you killed her."

Luke let his chin drop. "Alema, you disappoint me."

"The feeling is mutual, Master Skywalker," Alema said. "We have not forgotten the slaughter at Kr."

"There wouldn't have been a slaughter if you had done your duty as a Jedi." Luke sensed a familiar presence creeping toward him, skulking its way under the stern of the old Star Barge, and realized that Han had returned to the hangar without C-3PO. "But you let your anger make you weak, and the Dark Nest took advantage."

Alema's unblinking eyes turned the color of chlorine. "Don't blame us for what—"

"I'll lay the blame where it belongs. As a Master of the Jedi council, that is *my* duty—and my privilege!" Hoping to keep Alema's attention too riveted on him to notice Han sneaking up behind her, Luke moved to within lightsaber range of the Twi'lek. "Now I ask you one last time to return to Ossus. I know it will be hard to face those you betrayed, but—"

"We are not interested in 'redemption' . . . or anything else you have to offer, Master Skywalker. We are here with—"

Alema stopped in midsentence and cocked her head, then reached for her lightsaber.

Luke had already extended his arm and was summoning the weapon to himself, literally ripping Alema's belt off her waist and leaving the Twi'lek with an empty hand as Han hit her in the flank with a stun bolt.

Alema dropped to her knees, but did not fall, so Han fired again. This time, the Twi'lek collapsed onto her face and lay on the hangar floor twitching and drooling. Han leveled the weapon to fire again.

"That's enough," Luke said. "Are you trying to kill her?"

"As a matter of fact, yeah." Han scowled at the setting switch on the barrel of his blaster, then thumbed it to the opposite position. "I could have sworn I had it set on full power."

Luke shook his head in dismay, then used the Force to turn the weapon's barrel away from Alema. "Sometimes I wonder if I still know you, Han. She's defenseless."

"She's a Jedi," Han said, "She's *never* defenseless."

Still, he flicked the selector switch back to stun, then stood behind the Twi'lek and pointed the barrel at her head. Luke removed her lightsaber from her belt, then squatted on the floor in front of her and waited until she started to come around—which was incredibly quickly, even for a Jedi.

"Sorry about that," Luke said. "Han's still a little sore about what you did to the *Falcon.*"

Alema opened one eye. "He always did carry a grudge." She struggled to bring Luke into focus, then said, "But perhaps you should make something clear to him. We are not at *your* mercy."

A tremendous clamor rumbled through the hangar as nearby insects began to drop their loads and scurry toward the Star Barge.

"You are at *ours.*"

Luke began to slap Alema's lightsaber against his palm, allowing his frustration to pass, trying to remind himself that the Twi'lek was not in control of herself, that it was impossible for her to separate her own thoughts from those of the Dark Nest. But Jaina and Zekk had found themselves in a similar situation, and they had not turned their backs on the Jedi. The difference was, they had *tried* to resist.

Finally, Luke tucked Alema's lightsaber into his belt and stood. "You could have fought this," he said. "Maybe you still can. Jaina and Zekk became Joiners, and yet they remained true to their duty."

"You place too much faith in others, Master Skywalker." Alema braced her good arm on the floor and pushed off, then brought her feet up beneath her. "That has always been your weakness—and soon it will be your downfall."

A cold shiver of danger sense raced up Luke's spine, and he resisted the temptation to ask Alema's meaning. This *was* the reason she had come to the hangar, he felt certain. She was trying to trap him, to draw him into some dark and twisted maze where he would become as lost as she was.

Unfortunately, Han did not have Jedi danger sense. "Too much faith? What's *that* supposed to mean? If something's going on with Jaina—"

Alema glanced over her shoulder at Han, pouting at the blaster still pointed at her back, then said, "We didn't mean to alarm you, Han. Jaina and Zekk are fine, as far as we know." She looked back to Luke. "We were talking about Mara. She has been dishonest with Master Skywalker."

"I doubt that very much." Luke saw what the Dark Nest was attempting, and he could not believe they would be foolish enough to try such a thing. Nobody was going to drive a wedge between him and Mara. "And even if I didn't, I would hardly take the Dark Nest's word over that of a Jedi Master."

"We have proof," Alema said.

"And I doubt *that*." Han glanced at her skintight bodysuit. "You don't have a place to put it."

"We're glad you're not too old to notice," Alema said. "Thank you."

"It wasn't a compliment."

The smile Alema flashed Han was both knowing and genuine. "Sure it was." She turned back to Luke, then glanced at R2-D2. "But we should have said *you* have proof."

Luke shook his head. "I really don't think so. If that's all you have to say—"

"Daxar Ies wasn't the Emperor's *accountant*," she interrupted. "He was an Imperial droid-brain designer." She glanced again at R2-D2. "He designed the Intellex Four, as a matter of fact."

Luke's mind raced back to the year before, to his discovery of the sequestered sector in R2-D2's deep-reserve memory, trying to remember just how much Alema might have learned about those events before fleeing the academy.

"Nice try." Han had clearly noticed her glance toward the droid as well. "But we're not buying it. Just because you heard someone say that Luke was looking for information on the Intellex Four designer—"

"Han, she couldn't have overheard that," Luke said. "She was already gone. We were in flight control when Ghent told us about his disappearance, remember?"

"That doesn't mean she didn't leave bugs all over the place," Han pointed out.

"We didn't—as we are sure your eavesdropping sweeps have already revealed." Alema continued to stare at Luke. "Do you want to find out more about your mother, or not?"

Luke and Leia had long ago guessed the woman in the records R2-D2 had sequestered—Padmé—might be their mother, but hearing someone else say it sent a jolt of elation through him . . . even if he *did* feel certain that the Dark Nest was counting on exactly that reaction.

Han was more cynical. "So Anakin Skywalker was making holorecordings of his girlfriend—I know a lot of guys who used to do the same thing. It doesn't mean she's Luke's mother."

"But it means she *could* be—and we can help Master Skywalker learn the truth." Alema shot Luke a sardonic smile. "Unless you prefer ignorance to knowing that Mara has been deceiving you. Daxar Ies was no accountant. He was the one being who could have helped you unlock the secret of your mother's past."

"Nice story," Han said. "Hangs together real well—until you get to the part where Daxar Ies is the Intellex Four designer. Why would the Emperor have his best droid-brain designer *killed*?"

Alema's face grew enigmatic and empty. "Who knows? Revenge, perhaps, or merely to keep him from defecting to the Rebels, too. That is not as important as the reason Mara lied to you about who he is."

"I'm listening." Even saying the words made Luke feel hollow and sick inside, as though he were betraying Mara by hearing the Twi'lek out. "For now."

Alema wagged her finger. "First, what *we* want."

"That does it," Han said. He thumbed the selector switch on his blaster to full power. "I'm tired of being played. I'm just going to blast her now."

Alema's gaze went automatically to Luke.

Luke shrugged and stepped out of the line of fire. "Okay, if you have to."

"Please . . . ," Alema said sarcastically. She flicked a finger, and the selector switch on Han's blaster flipped itself back to stun. "If you were really going to blast me, you wouldn't stand here discussing it."

"You're right." Han flicked the selector switch back to full power. "We're done dis—"

"Perhaps you will be more inclined to hear us out after we have proved that we can access the records," Alema said to Luke. She gestured at R2-D2. "May we?"

Luke motioned Han to wait. "May you what?"

"Display one of the holos, of course," Alema said. When Luke did not automatically grant permission, she glanced up and added, "If we wished to harm him, Master Skywalker, we would already have sprinkled him with froth."

Luke looked up at growing blister on the ceiling, then let out a breath. Alema was telling the truth about that much, at least—it would have been a simple matter to use the Force to pull some of the gray froth down on them. He nodded and stepped aside.

As the Twi'lek approached, R2-D2 let out a fearful squeal and began to retreat as fast as his wheels would carry him. Alema simply reached out with the Force and floated him back over to her.

"Artoo, please show . . ." She paused and turned to Luke. "What would you like to see?"

Luke's heart began to pound. He was half afraid that Alema's claims would prove hollow—and half afraid they would not. While he was extremely eager to find some way to retrieve the data that did not involve reprogramming R2-D2's personality, Luke was also keenly aware that the Dark Nest was trying to manipulate him to ends he did not yet understand.

"You choose."

Alema let out a series of throat-clicks. "Hmmm . . . what would *we* want to know if we had been raised without our mother?" She turned back to the beeping, blinking droid she was holding in the air before her. "We have an idea. Let's look for something that confirms the identity of Master Skywalker's parents, Artoo."

R2-D2 whistled a refusal so familiar that Luke did not even need a translation to know he was claiming to have no such data.

"You mustn't be that way, Artoo," Alema said. "We have your file security override code: Ray-Ray-zero-zero-seven-zero-five-five-five-Trill-Jenth-seven."

"Hey," Han said, "that sounds like an—"

"Account number, yes," Alema said. "Eremay was rather special—she barely knew her own name, but she never forgot a list of numbers or letters."

Artoo let out a defeated trill; then his holoprojector activated. *The image of a beautiful brown-haired, brown-eyed woman—Padmé—appeared before the droid, walking through the air in front of what looked like an apartment wall. After a moment, a young man's back came into the image. He seemed to be sitting on a couch, hunched over some kind of work that was not visible in the hologram.*

Without looking up, the young man said, "I sense someone familiar." The voice was that of Luke's father, Anakin Skywalker. "Obi-Wan's been here, hasn't he?"

Padmé stopped and spoke to Anakin's back. "He came by this morning."

"What did he want?"

Anakin set his work aside and turned around. He appeared tense, perhaps even angry.

Padmé studied him for a moment, then said, "He's worried about you."

"You told him about us, didn't you?"

Anakin stood, and Padmé started walking again. "He's your best friend, Anakin." She passed through a doorway, and the corner of a bed appeared in front of her. "He says you're under a lot of stress."

"And he's not?"

"You have been *moody lately," Padmé said.*

"I'm not moody."

Padmé turned around and faced him. "Anakin . . . don't do this again."

Her beseeching tone seemed to melt Anakin. He turned away, shaking his head, and vanished. "I don't know," he said from outside the image. "I feel . . . lost."

"Lost?" Padmé started after him. "You're always so sure of yourself. I don't understand."

When Anakin returned to the image, he was looking away, his whole body rigid with tension.

"Obi-Wan and the Council don't trust me," he said.

"They trust you with their lives!" Padmé took his arm and pressed it to her side. *"Obi-Wan loves you as a son."*

Anakin shook his head. *"Something's happening."* He still would not look at her. *"I'm not the Jedi I should be. I'm one of the most powerful Jedi, but I'm not satisfied. I want more, but I know I shouldn't."*

"You're only human, Anakin," Padmé said. *"No one expects any more."*

Anakin was silent for a moment, then his mood seemed to lighten as quickly as it had darkened a moment before, and he turned and placed a hand on her belly.

"I have found a way to save you."

Padmé frowned in confusion. *"Save me?"*

"From my nightmares," Anakin said.

"Is that what's bothering you?" Padmé's voice was relieved.

Anakin nodded. *"I won't lose you, Padmé."*

"I'm not going to die in childbirth, Anakin." She smiled, and her voice turned light. *"I promise you."*

Anakin remained grave. *"No, I promise you,"* he said. *"I'm becoming so powerful with my new knowledge of the Force that I'll be able to keep you from dying."*

Padmé's voice turned as grave as Anakin's, and she locked eyes with him. *"You don't need more power, Anakin. I believe you can protect me from anything . . . just as you are."*

This won a smile from Anakin—but it was a small, hard smile filled with secrets and fear, and when they kissed, it seemed to Luke that his father's arms were not embracing so much as claiming.

The hologram ended. R2-D2 deactivated his holoprojector and let out a long, descending whistle.

"No need to apologize, Artoo." Alema's eyes remained fixed on Luke. "The file you chose was excellent—wasn't it, Master Skywalker?"

"It served to illustrate your point," Luke allowed.

"Come now," Alema said. "It confirmed the identity of your mother—just as we promised it would. We're sure you would like to learn what became of her."

"Now that you mention it, yeah," Han said. "One file doesn't prove a thing."

"Nice try." Alema shot Han an irritated scowl. "But one sample is all you get. And we advise you not to try opening any files yourself. The access code changes with each use, and the file will be destroyed. When three files have been lost, the entire chip will self-destruct."

"That would be unfortunate, but not disastrous," Luke said. Though he had little doubt now that the woman in the holos was indeed his mother, his father's brooding nature had left him feeling uneasy inside—and a bit frightened for the woman. "Leia and I have learned a great deal from Old Republic records already. We're fairly certain that the woman in the holos is Padmé Amidala, a former Queen and later Senator of Naboo."

"Will those old records tell you what she looked like when she smiled? How she sounded when she laughed? Why she abandoned you and your sister?" Alema pushed her lip into a pout. "Come, Master Skywalker. We are only asking that you leave Gorog alone. Do that, and each week we will feed you one of the access codes you need to truly know your mother."

Luke paused, insulted that Alema could believe such a ploy would work on him, wondering if there had ever been a time when he could have seemed so unprincipled and self-serving to her.

"You surprise me, Alema," Luke said. "I would never place personal interests above those of the Jedi and the Force. You must know that—even if Gorog doesn't."

"Yeah, but that doesn't mean we're looking for trouble, either," Han added hastily. "We're just here to help with the Fizz. As long as the Dark Nest isn't bothering us, we won't bother it."

"Good." Alema trailed her fingertips across Han's shoulders, smirking as though she had won her concession. "That's all we can ask."

Han shuddered free of her. "Do you mind? I don't want to catch anything."

Alema cocked her brow, more surprised than hurt, then held her hand out to Luke. "If you'll return our lightsaber, we'll let you be on your way." She glanced at the ceiling, which was already starting to froth, then added, "We wouldn't want anything to happen to Artoo."

Luke took the weapon from his belt, but instead of returning it to Alema, he opened the hilt and removed the Adegan focusing crystal from inside.

"It pains me to say this, Alema." He began to squeeze, calling on the Force to bolster his strength, and felt the crystal shatter. "But you are no longer fit to carry a lightsaber."

Alema's eyes flashed with rage. "That means nothing!" Her lekku began to writhe and twitch, but she managed to retain control of herself and turned toward the door. "We'll just build another."

"I know." Luke turned his hand sideways and let the crystal dust fall to the floor. "And I'll take that one away, too."

THREE

The mourners wore gaily patterned tabards brighter than anything Cal Omas had ever imagined a Sullustan owning, but they approached the vault in somber silence, each masc setting a single transpariblock into the seamweld the crypt master had spread for him, each fem taking the weld-rake in her left hand and carefully smoothing the joints.

This being Sullust, and Sullustans being Sullustans, the tomb-walling ceremony followed a rigid protocol, with the crypt master inviting mourners forward according to both their social status and their relationship to the deceased. Admiral Sovv's younglings and seven current wives had placed the first blocks, followed by his grown children and the other husbands of his warren-clan, then by his blood relatives, his closest friends, the two Jedi Masters in attendance—Kenth Hamner and Kyp Durron—and the entire executive branch of Sullust's governing corporation, SoroSuub. Now, with only one gap remaining in the wall, the crypt master summoned Cal Omas forward.

Omas's protocol droid had warned him that before placing the last block, the person called upon at this point was expected to deliver a brief comment of exactly as many words as the deceased's age in standard years. This was not to be a eulogy—recounting the departed's life would have been considered an affront to those present, implying as it did that the other mourners had not known the dead person as well as they thought. Instead, it was to be a simple address from the heart.

Omas took his place in front of the vault and accepted the transpariblock. The thing was far heavier than it looked, but he pulled it close to his body and did his best not to grimace as he turned to face the assembly.

The gathering was huge, filling the entire Catacomb of Eminents and spilling out the doors into the Gallery of Ancestors. The throng contained more than a hundred Alliance dignitaries, but they went almost unnoticed in the sea of Sullustan faces. As the Supreme Commander of the force that had defeated the Yuuzhan Vong, Sien Sovv had been a hero of mythical proportions on Sullust, an administrator and organizer who rivaled the stature of even Luke Skywalker and Han and Leia Solo in other parts of the galaxy.

Omas took a deep breath, then spoke. "I speak for everyone in the Galactic Alliance when I say that we share Sullust's shock and sorrow over the collision that took the lives of Admiral Sovv and so many others. Sien was my good friend, as well as the esteemed commander of the Galactic Alliance military, and I promise you that we *will* bring those who are truly responsible for this tragedy to justice . . . no matter what nebula they try to hide within."

The Sullustans remained silent, their dark eyes blinking up at Omas enigmatically. Whether he had shocked the mourners with his suggestion of foul play or committed some grievous error of protocol, Omas could not say. He knew only that he had spoken from the heart, that he had reached the limits of his patience with the problems the Killiks were causing, and that he intended to act—with or without the Jedi's support.

After a moment, an approving murmur rose from the back of the crowd and began to rustle forward, growing in volume as it approached. Kenth Hamner and Kyp Durron scowled and peered over their shoulders at the assembly, but if the Sullustan mourners noticed the censure, they paid it no attention. There had already been rumblings about Master Skywalker's conspicuous absence from the funeral, so no one in the crowd was inclined to pay much attention to the opinions of a pair of bug-loving Jedi.

Once the murmur reached the front of the crowd, the crypt master silenced the chamber with a gesture. He had Omas hoist the heavy transpariblock into place, then invited the mourners to retire to the Gallery of Ancestors, where SoroSuub Corporation was sponsoring a funerary feast truly unrivaled in the history of the planet.

As Omas and the other dignitaries waited for the catacombs to clear, he went over to the two Jedi Masters. Kenth Hamner, a handsome man with a long aristocratic face, served as the Jedi order's liaison to the Galactic Alliance military. He was dressed in his formal liaison's uniform, looking as immaculate and polished as only a former officer could. Kyp Durron had at least shaved and sonismoothed his robe, but his boots were scuffed and his hair remained just unruly enough for the Sullustans to find fault on such a formal occasion.

"I'm happy to see the Jedi were able to send *someone*," Omas said to the pair. "But I'm afraid the Sullustans may read something untoward into Master Skywalker's absence. It's unfortunate he couldn't be here."

Rather than explain Luke's absence, Kenth remained silent and merely looked uncomfortable.

Kyp went on the attack. "You didn't help matters by suggesting that the Killiks were responsible for the accident."

"They were," Omas answered. "The Vratix piloting that freighter were so drunk on black membrosia, it's doubtful they ever *knew* they had collided with Admiral Sovv's transport."

"That's true, Chief Omas," Kenth said. "But it doesn't mean that the Killiks are responsible for the accident."

"It certainly does, Master Hamner," Omas said. "How many times has the Alliance demanded that the Colony stop sending that poison to our insect worlds? How many times must I warn them that we'll take action?"

Kyp frowned. "You know that the Dark Nest—"

"I *know* that I've been attending funerals all week, Master Hamner," Omas fumed. "I *know* that the Supreme Commander of the Alliance military and more than two hundred members of his staff are dead. I *know* who is responsible—ultimately, utterly, and undeniably responsible—and I know the Jedi have been shielding them ever since Qoribu."

"The Killik situation is complicated." Kenth spoke in a calming voice that immediately began to quell Omas's anger. "And inflaming matters with hasty accusations—"

"Don't you *dare* use the Force on me." Omas stepped close to Kenth and spoke in a low, icy tone. "Sien Sovv and most of his staff-beings are dead, Master Hamner. I will *not* be calmed."

"My apologies, Chief Omas," Kenth said. "But this sort of talk will only make matters difficult."

"Matters are already difficult." Omas lowered his voice to an angry whisper. "You told me yourself that Master Horn suspected this was more than an accident."

"I did," Kenth admitted. "But he hasn't found any evidence to suggest that the Killiks were the ones behind it."

"Has he found any evidence to suggest that someone else was?" Omas demanded.

Kenth shook his head.

"Maybe that's because it *was* only an accident," Kyp suggested. "Until Master Horn finds some proof, his suspicions are just that—suspicions."

"Taken with what we already know, Master Horn's suspicions are quite enough for *me*," Omas said. "The Killiks must be dealt with—and it's time that you Jedi understood that."

"Hear, hear!" a gurgly Rodian voice called.

Omas glanced over and found Moog Ulur—the Senator from Rodia—eavesdropping with several of his colleagues from barely an arm's length away. To be polite, the Sullustan dignitaries had moved off to a distance of a dozen meters or so—but, of course, Sullustans had better hearing.

Omas straightened his robes. "Gentlemen, I think it's time I made my way to the feast." He turned toward Ulur and the other Senators, then spoke over his shoulder to the two Masters. "Have Master Skywalker contact me at his earliest convenience."

FOUR

The Queen's Drawing Room smelled of emptiness and disuse, with the odor of polishing agents and window cleanser hanging so thickly in the air that Jacen wondered if the housekeeping droid needed its dispensing program adjusted. An octagonal game table rested in the center of the opulent chamber, directly beneath a Kamarian-crystal chandelier and surrounded by eight flow-cushion chairs that looked as though they had never been sat upon. The Force held no hint of any living presence, but the silence in the chamber was charged with a sense of danger and foreboding that made Jacen cold between his shoulder blades.

Jacen's nine-year-old cousin, Ben Skywalker, stepped closer to his side. "It's creepy in here."

"You noticed. Good." Jacen glanced down at his cousin. With red hair, freckles, and fiery blue eyes, Ben appeared typical of many boys his age, more interested in hologames and shock ball than in studies and training. Yet he had more innate control over the Force at his age than any person Jacen had ever known—enough to shut himself off from it whenever he wished, enough to prevent even Jacen from sensing just how strong in the Force he really might be. "What else do you feel?"

"Two people." Ben pointed through a door in the back of the room. "I think one's a kid."

"Because one has a smaller presence in the Force?" Jacen asked. "That's not always a guide. Sometimes, children have—"

"Not that," Ben interrupted. "I think one's holding the other, and she feels all . . . mushy."

"Fair enough." Jacen would have chuckled, save that he had already sensed through the Force that Ben was right, and he could not understand what Tenel Ka was doing alone in her chambers with a child. It had been nearly a year since their last meeting, but they had spoken several times since—whenever they could arrange a secure HoloNet connection—and Jacen felt certain that she would have told *him* if she had decided to take a husband. "But we shouldn't make assumptions. They can be misleading."

"Right." Ben rolled his eyes. "Shouldn't we get out of here? If a security droid catches us in here, this place is gonna be dust."

"It's all right," Jacen said. "The Queen Mother invited us."

"Then how come you used your memory rub on the guards?" Ben asked. "And why do you keep Force-flashing the surveillance cams?"

"Her message asked me to come in secret," Jacen explained.

"Asked *you*?" Ben furrowed his brow for a moment. "Does she know *I'm* coming?"

"I'm sure she has sensed your presence by now," Jacen said. Spies were so pervasive in the Hapes Cluster that Tenel Ka had asked him not to acknowledge her message, so there had been no opportunity to warn her that he would have to bring Ben along. They were supposed to be on a camping trip to Endor, and a sudden change in plans would have aroused suspicion. "But I know Tenel Ka will be happy to see you."

"Great." Ben cast a longing glance toward the security door behind them. "I'll be the one the security droid blasts."

A motherly voice spoke from the next room. "And why would I do that?"

A large droid with the cherubic face and padded, synthskin chest of a Tendrando Arms Defender Droid—similar to the one who guarded Ben when he was not with Jacen or his parents—stepped into the room. Her massive frame and systems-packed limbs were still close enough to the YVH war droids from which she had been adapted to give her an intimidating appearance.

"Have you been causing any trouble?"

"Not me." Ben glanced up at Jacen. "This was *his* idea."

"Good, then we'll get along just fine." The corners of the droid's mouth rose into a mechanical smile, then she turned her photoreceptors on Jacen. "Jedi Solo, welcome. I am DeDe One-one-A, a Tendrando Arms Defender—"

"Thank you, I'm familiar with your model," Jacen said. "What I don't understand is what Queen Tenel Ka needs with a child protection droid."

The smile vanished from DD-11A's synthskin face. "You don't?" She stepped aside and waved him forward. "Perhaps I should let the Queen Mother explain. She is expecting you in her dressing chamber."

The droid led them into an extravagant bedchamber dominated by a huge bed covered by a crown-shaped canopy. Around it were more couches, armchairs, and writing desks than ten queens could use. Again, the chamber smelled of cleanser and polish, and there was no indentation to suggest that the bed, pillows, or chairs had ever been used.

"Creepier and creepier," Ben said.

"Just be ready." Until Jacen knew what was causing the cold knot between his shoulder blades, he would have preferred to leave Ben somewhere safe—except he had no idea where 'safe' might be, or even if they were the ones in danger. That was the trouble with danger sense—it was just so blasted vague. "You remember that emergency escape I taught you?"

"The Force trick you said to keep really . . ." Ben fell silent and glanced at DD-11A, then his voice grew more subdued. "Yeah, I remember."

DD-11A stopped and swiveled her head around to stare down at Ben. "The Force trick that Jedi Solo said to keep really *what,* Ben?"

Ben's gaze slid away. "Nothing."

The corners of DD-11A's mouth drooped. "Are you keeping secrets, Ben?"

"I'm *trying* to," Ben admitted. "Jacen said—"

"No harm, Ben," Jacen interrupted. Defender Droids were programmed to be suspicious of children's secrets, and this particular Force trick was not one he cared to have investigated. He faced DD-11A. "The secrecy is a security precaution. The trick's effectiveness would be compromised if its nature was revealed."

DD-11A fixed her photoreceptors on Jacen for a moment, then extended a telescoping arm and took Ben by the shoulder. "Why don't you wait here with me, Ben? The Queen Mother wishes to see Jedi Solo alone first." The droid turned to Jacen, then pointed her other arm toward the far side of the chamber. "Through that door."

Jacen did not start toward the door. "I'd rather keep Ben with me."

"The Queen Mother wishes to speak to you alone first." DD-11A made a shooing motion with her hand. "Go on. We'll come along in few minutes."

When the cold knot between Jacen's shoulder blades did not seem to grow any larger, he nodded reluctantly. "Leave the doors open between us," he said. "And Ben—"

"I know what to do," Ben said. "Go on."

"Okay," Jacen said. "But mind your manners. Remember, you're in a queen's private chambers."

Jacen went through the door into a third room, this one much smaller and less opulent than the first two. One end was filled with shelves and clothing racks, mostly empty, and furnished with full-length mirrors, unused vanities, and overstuffed dressing couches. The other end held a simple sleeping pallet, of the kind Tenel Ka had preferred since her days at the Jedi academy, and a night table containing a chrono and reading lamp.

The Queen Mother herself was through the *next* door, leaning over a small baby crib in what was plainly a nursery. Her red hair hung over one shoulder in a loose fall, and she was dressed in a simple green robe with nursing flaps over both sides of her chest. When she sensed Jacen studying her, she looked up and smiled.

"You cannot see anything from there, Jacen. Come in." Tenel Ka was as beautiful as ever—perhaps even more so. Her complexion was rosy and luminous, and her gray eyes were sparkling with joy. "I have someone to introduce you to."

"So I see." It was all Jacen could do to hide his disappointment. Though he had long known that Tenel Ka's position would require her to take a Hapan husband, this was hardly the way he had expected her to break the news. "Congratulations."

"Thank you." Tenel Ka motioned him over. "Come along, Jacen. She won't bite."

Jacen went to the crib, where a round-faced newborn lay cooing and blowing milk bubbles at Tenel Ka. With hair so thin and downy that it still lacked color and a face more wrinkled than an Ugnaught's, she did not really look like anyone. But when the infant turned to squint up at Jacen, Jacen experienced such a shock of connection that he forgot himself and reached down to touch the child on the chest.

"Go ahead and pick her up, Jacen." Tenel Ka's voice was nearly cracking with excitement. "You do know how to hold a newborn, don't you?"

Jacen was too stunned to answer. He could feel in the Force—and in his heart—that the girl was his, but he could not understand *how.* The child could be no more than a week old, but it had been more than a year since he had even *seen* Tenel Ka.

"Here, let me show you." Tenel Ka slipped her one arm under the baby, cradling the head in her hand, then smoothly scooped the infant up. "Just keep a firm hold, and always support her neck."

Finally, Jacen tore his gaze away from the baby. "How?" he asked. "It's been twelve months—"

"The Force, Jacen." Tenel Ka slipped the baby into Jacen's arms. She groaned a couple of times, then returned to cooing. "I slowed things down. Life will be dangerous enough for our daughter without my nobles knowing *you* are the father."

"*You're* a father?" Ben's voice came from the doorway behind Jacen. "Astral!"

Jacen turned around, his daughter cradled in his arms, and frowned at Ben. "I thought you were waiting in the Royal Bedchamber with DeDe."

"You told DeDe you wanted to keep me with you," Ben countered. "You *asked* if I knew what to do."

"I meant if there was trouble, Ben."

"Oh." Ben came closer. "I thought you meant trip her circuit breaker."

"No." Jacen sighed, then turned to Tenel Ka. "Allow me to present Ben Skywalker, Your Majesty."

Ben took his cue and bowed deeply. "Sorry about your droid. I'll turn her back on if you want."

"In a minute, Ben," Tenel Ka said. "But first, stand up and let me have a look at you. I haven't seen you since you were a baby yourself."

Ben straightened himself and stood there looking nervous while Tenel Ka nodded approvingly.

"I apologize for bringing him unannounced," Jacen said. "But your message said to come immediately, and we were supposed to be on a camping trip while Luke and Mara are in the Utegetu Nebula."

"Jacen's my Master," Ben said proudly.

Tenel Ka cocked her brow. "In my day, apprentices did not address their Masters by their first names."

"It's an informal arrangement," Jacen said. Now was not the time to explain the complicated dynamics of the situation—that while Mara disapproved of much of the Force-lore Jacen had gathered on his five-year journey of discovery, she was truly grateful to him for coaxing Ben out of his long withdrawal from the Force. "I'm working with Ben while he explores his relationship with the Force."

Tenel Ka's eyes flashed with curiosity, but she did not ask the question Jacen knew to be on her mind: why Ben was not exploring that relationship at the Jedi academy like other young Force-adepts.

"So far, I'm the only one Ben feels comfortable using the Force around," Jacen said, answering the unspoken question. He looked at

Ben. "But I'm sure that will change once he realizes that the Force is our friend."

"Don't hold your breath," Ben replied. "I'm not interested in all that kid stuff."

"Perhaps one day." Tenel Ka smiled at Ben. "Until then, you're a very lucky young man. You could not ask for a better guide."

"Thanks," Ben said. "And congratulations on the baby. Wait until Uncle Han and Aunt Leia hear—they'll go nova!"

Tenel Ka furrowed her brow. "Ben, you mustn't tell anyone."

"I mustn't?" Ben looked confused. "Why not? Aren't you guys married?"

"No, but that isn't why. The situation is . . ." Tenel Ka looked to Jacen for help. ". . . complicated."

"We *are* in love," Jacen said. "We always have been."

"Fact," Tenel Ka said. "That is all that matters."

"But you're not married—and you had a baby!" Ben's eyes were wide and gleeful. "You guys are gonna be in *so* much trouble!"

Tenel Ka's voice grew stern. "Ben, you must keep this secret. The baby's life will depend on it."

Ben frowned, and the cold knot between Jacen's shoulder blades began to creep down his spine. Even Tenel Ka seemed to be growing pale.

"Ben can keep a secret," Jacen said. "But I think it's time to reactivate DeDe. Ben—"

"On my way." Ben turned and ran for the door.

"Bring her here," Tenel Ka called after him. "And tell her to arm all systems."

The baby began to mewl in Jacen's arms. He took a moment to forge a conscious link to Ben's Force presence, then slipped the child back to Tenel Ka.

"Is this why you asked me to come?" he asked.

"It is why I asked you to come *now*," Tenel Ka corrected. "This feeling has been growing worse for a week."

"And the baby is—"

"A week old."

Jacen's chest began to tighten with anger. "At least we know what they're after. Any idea who—"

"Jacen, I have kept myself in seclusion for months," Tenel Ka said. "And most of my nobles have guessed why. The list of suspects includes every family who has reason to believe the child does not carry their blood."

"Oh." Jacen had forgotten—if he had ever really understood—

just how lonely and perilous Tenel Ka's life really was. "So that would include—"

"All of them," Tenel Ka finished.

"Well, at least it's simple," Jacen said. "And I suppose *who* really doesn't matter at the moment."

"Correct," Tenel Ka agreed. "First we defend."

Jacen sensed a sudden confusion in Ben's presence, then saw him coming through the queen's dressing room with DD-11A close on his heels. There was nothing chasing them, but a muffled scurrying sound was arising behind them.

"Insect infestation!" DD-11A reported. "My sensors show a large swarm in the ceiling, advancing toward the nursery."

The baby began to cry in earnest, and Jacen pulled his lightsaber off his utility belt.

"Jacen, it's okay!" Ben cried. "It's Gorog!"

"Gorog?" Jacen began to still himself inside, trying to calm his anger so he could focus on the ripples he felt in the Force. "Are you sure?"

Ben entered the nursery and stopped. "Yeah."

"Who is Gorog?" Tenel Ka asked. The scurrying sound was drawing closer. "And what is he doing in my vents?"

"They," Jacen corrected. He found a set of ripples that seemed to be coming from a cold void in the Force and knew Ben was right. "*Gorog* is the Killik name for the Dark Nest."

"The Dark Nest?" Tenel Ka used the Force to depress a wall button, then turned to Ben. "Why is it okay to have the Dark Nest in my air vents?"

"They're not *in* your vents." Ben's eyes were fixed on the ceiling above the closing door. "Your vents are shielded and lined with security lasers."

Jacen's heart sank. For Ben to know so much about the insects' entry route suggested that even after a year apart, he remained sensitive to Gorog's collective mind—and perilously close to becoming a Joiner.

"Very well." Tenel Ka began to rock the baby gently, and her crying faded back to mewling. "What is the Dark Nest doing in my *ceiling*?"

"They have a contract." Ben furrowed his brow for a moment, then turned to Jacen. "I don't understand. They want to—"

"I know, Ben," Jacen said. "We won't allow it."

The scurrying noise stopped outside the nursery door, still in the ceiling, then rapidly built to a gnawing sound. Ben stared up toward the sound, his face pinched into a mask of fear and conflict.

"You can't!" He seemed to be speaking to the insects. "She's only a little kid!"

The gnawing grew louder, and the indecision suddenly vanished from Ben's expression. "They're almost through." He rushed to the rear of the nursery, though there was no exit there that Jacen could see, and began to pull at the sides of a tall shelving cabinet. "We have to get her out, now!"

"Ben, calm down." Jacen began to study the floor, reaching into the Force to see if there was anyone in the room below them. "Losing your head—"

"Ben, how do you know about the escape tunnel?" Tenel Ka interrupted. "Did you find it through the Force?"

"No," Jacen said, answering for Ben. Joiners had trouble separating their own thoughts from those of the collective mind of the nest. He used the Force to pull Ben away from the cabinet, then said, "Gorog told him."

Ben scowled. "No way!" He tried to go back to the cabinet. "I just knew."

"*Gorog* knew," Jacen countered. He activated his light-saber, then plunged it into the floor and began to cut a large circle. "And if *they* want you to open that door—"

"—*we* don't." Tenel Ka reached out with the Force and pulled Ben to her side. "Let us do this Jacen's way."

A loud metallic patter sounded inside the cabinet Ben had tried to open and quickly changed to a cacophony of scratching and scraping. Jacen continued to cut his circle in the floor, at the same time trying to puzzle out who had contracted the Dark Nest to attack Tenel Ka's child—and how. The Gorog were notoriously difficult to locate—the Jedi had not even been certain the nest had survived the battle at Qoribu until about three months ago—and experience suggested they were far too interested in their own agenda to accept an assassination contract for credits alone. So whoever had hired the nest possessed the resources to find it in the first place—and to provide whatever the Dark Nest had asked in return.

The gnawing above suddenly grew more distinct, and a section of ceiling dropped to the floor. Jacen lifted his free hand toward the hole, but DD-11A was already taking aim. As the first cloud of insects began to boil down into the room, her wrist folded down and discharged a crackling plume of fire.

Ben screamed and began to thrash about, trying to break free of Tenel Ka's Force grasp.

"Ben, stop it!" Tenel Ka ordered. The baby was wailing in her arm now. "We cannot let theeemmmargh—"

Tenel Ka's command ended in a startled cry as Ben whirled on her with an untrained but powerful Force shove. She slammed into the corner two meters above the floor, her head hitting with a sharp crack, her eyes rolling back and her shoulders slumping, but her arm never slackening beneath the crying baby.

Jacen used the Force to gently guide Tenel Ka to the floor, then turned to find Ben leaping toward DD-11A's upraised arm. His eyes were bulging and he was screaming at the droid not to burn his friends, and Jacen was too unnerved by his young cousin's anger—and the raw Force-strength he had displayed—to take the chance of being gentle. He extended his arm and used the Force to pull Ben into his grasp, grabbing him by the throat.

"Enough!" Jacen pinched down on the carotid arteries on the sides of the neck. "Sleep!"

Ben gurgled once; then his eyes rolled back in his head and he sank into a deep slumber that would not end until the Force command was lifted. There was a time, before Vergere and the war with the Yuuzhan Vong, when Jacen would have felt guilty for having to use such a powerful attack on a nine-year-old boy. But now all that mattered was protecting Tenel Ka and the baby, and Jacen felt nothing but relief as he laid his young cousin aside.

He cut through a few more centimeters of floor, and the ferrocrete substructure began to sag. He continued cutting until he judged that the droid's mass would be enough to fold the circle down like a trapdoor, then shut off his lightsaber and stepped to DD-11A's side.

The hole above the droid's head was rimmed with white foam from the palace's fire-suppression system, but the Gorog were not foolish enough to peer out of the same hole DD-11A had just blasted with flame. Instead Jacen could hear the insects scurrying past overhead, spreading out across the ceiling and beginning to gnaw in several different places.

"What do you have that can generate a good-sized fireball?" Jacen asked DD-11A.

"Grenades." The droid pivoted around to the other side of the hole and sprayed a stream of fire at a line of scurrying, blue-black shadows. "Two each, thermal, concussion, and flash—"

"That'll do. Here's what I want you to do."

Jacen outlined his plan, then gathered Ben in his arms and retreated to the corner with Tenel Ka and the baby. The Gorogs in the secret tunnel had scratched their way into the cabinet, and the tips of hundreds of tiny blue-black pincers were beginning to protrude through the thin line between the doors.

Jacen laid Ben beside Tenel Ka, then pointed. "DeDe!"

The droid swiveled around and poured flame into the crack. A trio of fire-suppression nozzles popped down to coat the doors with suppressant, but by then black wisps of smoke were already seeping out the back of the cabinet.

Jacen pulled his cloak off and held it in front of them at chin height.

"Okay, go!"

DD-11A's photoreceptors lingered on the cloak. "Your camouflage is inadequate. I can't leave the child with you."

"It's . . . fine." Tenel Ka's voice was groggy, but firm. "Do as Jacen commands."

Jacen was already immersing himself in the Force, allowing it to flow through him as fast as his body would allow.

Small pieces of plasrock began to rain from the ceiling. DD-11A raised her arm and began to spray flame into the holes, but openings were appearing faster than even a droid could target. Still, DD-11A did not move to obey.

"Now, Honeygirl!" Tenel Ka snapped.

DD-11A's head swiveled around. "Override command accepted."

The droid stepped into the sagging circle Jacen had cut in the floor. The flap gave way beneath her weight and folded down, and she crashed into the room below.

Jacen exhaled in relief, then glanced over his shoulder and touched the corner behind them, forming a complete sensory image of how the walls looked and smelled and felt, even of the nearly inaudible sounds coming from the pipes and ducts concealed inside, then looked forward again and quickly expanded the image into the Force.

The baby continued to cry.

Tenel Ka started to open one of her nursing flaps, hoping to silence the child by feeding her, but Jacen stopped her. He *needed* that crying.

Instead of *allowing* the Force to flow through his body, he began to use his fear and anger to consciously pull it through. His skin began to nettle and his head to ache, and still he continued to draw the Force, catching his daughter's wailing voice in the stillness of its depths, sending the sound streaming down through the floor after

DD-11A, not allowing it to return to the surface until it had overtaken the metallic clank of the droid's receding footsteps.

He was almost too late. The fire retardant had barely started to drip from the holes DD-11A had left in the ceiling before clouds of tiny blue-black Killiks began to drop into the room on their droning wings. They were much smaller than the assassin bugs that had attacked Mara and Saba the year before, only a little larger than Jacen's thumb. But they had the same bristly antennae and black bulbous eyes, and they all had long, venom-dripping proboscises protruding between a pair of sharply curved mandibles.

Instead of dropping down through the hole, the Gorog simply seemed to swirl about the room, gathering in an ever-darkening swarm, ignoring the hole in the floor and the sound decoys Jacen had arranged. They began to land on the cabinet that concealed the escape tunnel and on the surrounding walls, on the door that closed off Tenel Ka's dressing chamber, on the empty crib in the center of the nursery.

A few even came and landed on the cloak that Jacen was using as the basis of his Force illusion, and when a pair of Gorog started to hover in the air above the top edge of the cloak, he feared his plan would fail. The illusions he had learned to craft from the Adepts of the White Current were powerful, but even they would not keep an insect crawling in midair. Jacen began to think that he had overreached in planning to take out the entire swarm at once; he should have settled for leaving DD-11A behind to slow the assassins while he and Tenel Ka fled with Ben and the baby.

Then suddenly Tenel Ka's palm was there for the insects to land on, and the illusion held.

Jacen looked over and saw the baby floating on a cushion of Force levitation, her head resting on the stump of Tenel Ka's amputated arm and her feet kicking the empty air.

A tense moment later, the cabinet doors clanged open. The insects on Tenel Ka's palm and Jacen's robe sprang into the air, joining the black fog of Killiks that came growling into the nursery, and the whole boiling mass swirled down through the floor in pursuit of DD-11A and the sound of the baby's crying voice.

Jacen maintained the illusion until the last insect had followed, then continued to maintain it for another hundred heartbeats. When no sound in the room remained except the pounding of their own hearts, he waited *another* hundred heartbeats, his eyes scanning every dark corner of the nursery, searching the shadows for any hint of blue carapace, examining the Force for ripples with no tangible source.

An uneasy feeling remained in the Force, but the ripple pattern was too diffuse and confused for Jacen to locate the observers Gorog had almost certainly left to watch the nursery. Still, the swarm would catch up to DD-11A any instant and discover it had been fooled.

Jacen dropped his illusion, then reached out in the Force and began to pull the folded circle of floor back into place. The ferrocrete substructure rose with a loud, grating shriek, and he felt the Force ripple as the swarm reversed course.

A handful of blue-black insects rose into the air from the dark corners of the nursery and came streaking toward the corner. Tenel Ka's lightsaber sizzled to life behind Jacen, and one of the bugs burst into a yellow spray as she Force-smashed it against the wall.

Jacen finished pulling the floor section back into place, then flung his cloak up in front of the approaching insects and used the Force to pin them against the wall. The tough molytex lining lasted about a second before the tips of their slashing mandibles started to work through.

Jacen sprang across the room, Force-leaping over the crib, and smashed the insects beneath the pommel of his lightsaber.

A loud bang sounded from the corner as Tenel Ka's lightsaber ignited the methane sac the assassin bugs carried inside their carapaces as a final surprise. He glanced over to see Tenel Ka trying to blink the spots from her eyes, her lightsaber weaving a defensive shield in front of her. The baby lay crying in the corner behind her, and two more insects were flitting around her knees, trying to dodge past her guard to attack.

Jacen stretched out in the Force and nudged them both into the path of her turquoise blade. They detonated with a brilliant flash that left stars dancing before his eyes and the baby screeching louder than ever, but Jacen sensed no pain in the infant, only fear and alarm.

Realizing he still had not heard the *carumpf* of DeDe's first grenade, Jacen started to reach for his comlink—then heard a muffled drone building behind him and spun around to find the first Gorog crawling through the seam his blade had left in the floor.

"*Now*, DeDe!" Jacen screamed at the floor. He jumped into the center of the circle and began to drag his lightsaber along the seam, igniting the insects before they could take flight. "What's taking so—"

A sharp jolt struck Jacen in the pit of his stomach, then suddenly he found himself kneeling in the middle of the circle, surrounded by a curtain of yellow flame, the air filled with the naphthalene smell of a thermal grenade.

"About—"

He was jolted by another explosion, and this time he was unsurprised enough to feel the floor buck as more flames came shooting up through the seam.

"—time."

The floor bucked another time, then another, and suddenly white foam was showering down from the ceiling, smothering the smoke and the fumes beneath the soapy clean smell of flame retardant. A series of wet thuds sounded on the surrounding floor as the foam weighed down the handful of Gorog assassins that had escaped DD-11A's grenades.

The insects immediately turned toward the corner and began to scurry toward where Tenel Ka was kneeling with the baby and Ben. Jacen used the Force to sweep them all back toward him, then batted them into oblivion with a single stroke of his lightsaber. They exploded brilliantly, but Jacen did not allow himself to look away. He was too afraid of letting one of the creatures slip past his blade.

A moment later, with spots still dancing before his eyes, he turned toward the corner. "Are you okay?" he asked Tenel Ka. "Both of you?"

"We are fine," she answered. "It is Ben I worry about."

"Don't." Though Jacen knew Ben's behavior had not been the boy's fault, he could not quite keep the anger he felt out of his voice. "I don't think Gorog would hurt him. He's practically a Joiner."

"I am not worried about what Gorog did to him," Tenel Ka answered. "I am worried about those bruises on his throat."

Jacen stood, his vision clearing, and went to his young cousin's side. The impression of his thumb and forefinger were purple and deep, clearly made in anger, but Ben's breathing was regular and untroubled.

"There's no need to worry." Jacen placed his fingers over the bruises and touched Ben through the Force. "They'll fade in no time."

Tenel Ka frowned. "That is not the point, Jacen."

Jacen looked up. "Then what is?"

A globule of fire retardant dropped off the wall and splatted at Tenel Ka's feet. There were no insects inside, but she stomped on it anyway.

"Never mind. I will tell you later." She stepped past Jacen and started toward the door to her dressing room. "We need to leave here. If I know my grandmother, she already knows that her first attempt failed."

"Your grandmother?" Jacen lifted Ben in his arms and followed. "You think Ta'a Chume is behind this?"

"I *know* she is," Tenel Ka said. She stopped at the door and faced Jacen with narrowed eyes. "The only ones who know about the escape tunnel are the Queen Mother . . . and the *former* Queen Mother."

FIVE

The route to Cilghal's lab on Ossus was as meandering as any across the academy grounds, winding through a labyrinth of shrubbery and detouring past carefully planned vistas, following a path of tightly placed stepping-stones that deliberately forced walkers to slow down and contemplate the garden. Even so, Leia's gaze kept coming back to the stasis jar in her hands. The glob suspended inside was pulsating like a silvery heart, growing larger each time it expanded, trembling a little more noticeably each time it contracted. She shuddered to think what might happen if the mysterious froth exploded over the interior of the jar. Anything that throbbed inside a stasis field could probably eat its way through seven millimeters of nonreactive safety glass.

The path rounded a gentle bend, and a dozen meters ahead, the trapezoidal span of Clarity Gate framed a tranquil courtyard accented by a small fountain. Leia passed under the crosspieces without stopping, then turned toward an opening to one side of the fountain—and heard a disapproving hiss behind her.

"This one is shocked at the forgetfulnesz of her student," Saba rasped. "What must a Jedi do as she enterz the academy groundz?"

Leia rolled her eyes and turned to face the Barabel. "We don't have time to meditate right now, Master."

Saba blinked twice, then clasped her claws together and remained standing on the other side of the gateway.

"Really." Leia went back through the gate and tapped the side of the jar. "Look at this stuff."

Saba looked, then said, "That is no excuse for ignoring the rulez."

"We don't have *time* for rules," Leia said. "We need to get this jar to Cilghal."

"And the sooner you complete your meditationz, the sooner we will do that."

"Saba—"

A rumble sounded low in Saba's throat.

"*Master* Sebatyne," Leia corrected, "don't you think Luke would want us to hurry?"

The Barabel tipped her head and glared down at Leia out of one eye. "You are doing it again."

"Doing *what*?"

"*Reasoning*. That is a skill you have already mastered." Saba's tone grew stern. "What you have not yet learned is obedience."

"I'm sorry, Master." Leia was growing exasperated. "I promise to work on that later, but right now I'm more worried about this stuff getting loose inside the academy."

"It is when we are alarmed that meditation is most important." Saba reached for the stasis jar. "This one will hold the froth so you can concentrate."

Realizing that her determination was no match for a Barabel's stubbornness, Leia reluctantly yielded the stasis jar. She focused her attention on the fountain, watching its silver spray umbrella into the air, listening to it rain back into the pool, and began a Jedi breathing exercise. She grew aware of the crisp scent of anti-algal agents and the coolness of mist on her skin. But even that faded after a moment, and she was left with only her breathing to concentrate on . . . *in through the nose . . . out through the mouth . . .* and the knots inside her started to come undone.

Leia began to realize that she was not worried about the froth at all. She had seen on Woteba that it did not disintegrate anything instantly. Even if the glob were to explode inside the stasis jar, she would still have plenty of time to reach Cilghal's lab and contain it in something else.

What troubled her was Han—or, rather, Han's absence. She felt guilty about having to leave him on Woteba, especially to honor a promise *Luke* had made . . . and especially knowing how he felt about "bugs." Even more than that, everything just seemed wrong. It was the first time in years she had traveled more than a few hundred thousand kilometers without Han, and it felt as if a part of her was missing. It was as if an MD droid had removed the wisecracking part of her brain, or she had suddenly lost a third arm.

And Leia knew that her sister-in-law felt much the same about Luke. After landing on Ossus, the first thing Mara had done was head for the Skywalkers' apartment to see if Ben was back from his camping trip with Jacen. She had claimed she only wanted to be sure that the academy rumor mill did not alarm him with a tangled version of why Luke had not returned with the *Falcon,* but Leia had sensed the same hollow in her sister-in-law that she felt in herself. Mara had been trying to fill the uncomfortable void caused by leaving Luke behind, to reassure herself that her family's life would quickly return to normal . . . just as soon as Cilghal told them how to stop the froth.

Leia was about to end her meditation when it was ended for her by Corran Horn's throaty voice.

"Where's Master Skywalker?" Corran entered the small courtyard via a path leading from the academy administration building. He was dressed in breeches, tunic, and vest, all in various shades of brown. "The hangar chief said he didn't disembark from the *Falcon.*"

"Neither did Han," Leia said. Judging by the expression of shock that flashed across Corran's face, she had not quite managed to conceal the irritation she felt at being tracked down even before her legs had grown accustomed to Ossan gravity again. "They stayed on Woteba to guarantee our good intentions."

Corran lowered his thick brows. "Guarantee?"

"Woteba is having a Fizz problem." Saba lifted the stasis jar toward Corran's face.

He frowned at the silvery froth inside. "A Fizz problem?"

"It's corrosive . . . *very.*" Leia told him what was happening to the Saras and their nest, then added, "The Colony believes the Jedi knew about the problem all along, *before* we convinced them to relocate their nests from Qoribu."

Corran's face fell, and alarm began to fill the Force around him. "So Master Skywalker stayed behind to convince them we *hadn't?*"

"Not exactly." Leia began to grow alarmed herself. "And Han stayed, too. What's wrong?"

"More than I thought." He took Leia's elbow and tried to guide her toward a bench near the fountain. "Maybe I should go get Mara. She'll need to hear this, too."

Leia pulled free and stopped. "Blast it, Corran, just tell me what's wrong!"

Saba rumbled low in her throat, a gentle reminder to follow the rules.

"Sorry." Leia kept her eyes fixed on Corran. "Okay, *Master* Horn—tell me what the chubba is going on!"

Saba nodded approvingly, and Corran nodded cautiously.

"Very well. Chief Omas has been trying to get Master Skywalker on the HoloNet all morning. The Chiss are furious—transports are landing Killiks on planets all along their frontier." Corran's tone grew worried. "It's beginning to look like the Killiks have this whole thing planned out."

"Or the Dark Nest does." Leia turned to Saba, then pointed at the froth inside the jar. "Can you think of a better way to destroy our relationship with the Colony?"

"Perhapz," she said. "But the Fizz is working well enough. It has already turned Raynar and Unu against us."

"And now the Colony has Han and Luke for hostages," Corran said. Signaling them to follow, he turned toward the path that led toward academy administration. "Chief of State Omas needs to hear about this as soon as possible."

"No, he doesn't." Leia started toward the opposite corner of the courtyard, toward the path that led to the academy science wing. "We should handle this ourselves."

"I have no doubt we will," Corran said, speaking to Leia across several meters of paving stone. "But our first duty is to report the situation to Chief Omas."

"So the Galactic Alliance can start blustering and making threats?" Leia shook her head. "That will only polarize things. What we need to do is get this stuff to Cilghal so she can tell us how the Dark Nest is producing it—and give us enough proof to convince Raynar and Unu."

Corran scowled, but reluctantly started toward Leia's side of the courtyard.

"No," Saba said. She placed a scaly hand on Leia's shoulder and pushed her toward Corran. "This one will see to the froth. You may help Master Horn with his report."

"Report?" Leia stopped and turned back toward the Barabel. "Did you hear what I just said?"

"Of course," Saba said. "But you did not hear what *this* one said. It is not your place to question Master Horn'z decision."

This shocked even Corran. "Uh, that's all right, Master Sebatyne. Princess Leia is a special case—"

"Indeed. She knowz how to give orderz already." Saba's gaze shifted to Leia. "Now she must learn to take them. She will help you with your report, if you still think that is best."

"I *know* how to take orders," Leia fumed. "I was an officer in the Rebellion."

"Good. Then this will not be a difficult lesson for you."

Saba started down the path toward Cilghal's lab, leaving Leia standing beside Corran with a stomach so knotted in anger, it felt like she had been punched. She knew what Saba was doing—teaching her how to fight from a position of weakness—but *now* was not the time for lessons. The lives of her husband and her brother would be placed at risk if she lost, and Corran Horn could teach even Barabels a thing or two about stubbornness.

Once Saba was beyond earshot, Corran leaned close to Leia. "Tough Master," he observed in a quiet voice. "Did you really pick her yourself?"

"I did," Leia admitted. "I wanted someone who would challenge me in new ways."

"Hmm." Corran considered the explanation a moment, then asked, "Well, is training with her what you expected?"

"More rules and less sparring." Leia fell silent a moment, then grew serious. "Corran—Master Horn—you don't actually intend to send that report to Chief Omas, do you?"

Corran studied her for a moment, then said, "I always did." He started down the path toward academy administration. "Now that Saba's pulled rank for me, I guess there's no harm in admitting that I just didn't see any point in arguing with you about it."

Leia nodded. "Silence is not agreement." Feeling a little foolish for forgetting one of the first lessons she had learned as a Chief of State, she started to follow. "But you know what will happen when Chief Omas hears that Luke has been taken hostage by Killiks."

"He'll demand that they release him."

"And the Killiks will refuse. Then he'll threaten them, and they'll draw in on themselves, and we'll have no chance at all of convincing the Colony to withdraw from the Chiss frontier peacefully."

"If you were the Chief of State, you'd be free to handle it differently," Corran said. "But you're not. Cal Omas deserves to know what's happening."

"Even if it means sacrificing control of the Jedi order?"

Corran stopped. "What are you talking about?"

"I think you know," Leia said. "The Chief of State has been frustrated with the Jedi since the Qoribu crisis. He thinks we've put the good of the Killiks above the good of the Alliance. With Luke out of contact, you don't think Omas would jump at the chance to take control of the order and make sure our priorities are what he believes they should be?"

Corran frowned, but more in thought than alarm. "He could do that?"

"If the Jedi were divided, yes. I know how strongly you believe our mission is to serve the Alliance. But you *do* see how dangerous it would be for the order to fall under the Chief of State's direct control?"

"Of course. The will of the government is not always the will of the Force." Corran fell silent for a moment, then finally shook his head and started walking again. "You're worrying about nothing, Princess. Omas will never take direct control of the Jedi order."

Leia started after him. "You can't know that."

"I can," Corran insisted. "The Masters may disagree on a lot, but never that. It could lead to the Jedi becoming a political tool."

Leia followed him down a narrow promenade flanked by more cedrum trees, cursing Saba for insisting that they continue training even in the middle of a crisis. What did Saba expect her to do, hit Corran over the head with a rock? It would have been such a simple matter for the Barabel to pull rank on *him* instead of goading him into doing the same to her. After all, Corran was the newest Master, promoted on the basis of his actions during the war against the Yuuzhan Vong, the disruption of several pirate rings, and having trained an apprentice—a young Jedi named Raltharan whom Leia had never met. Saba, on the other hand, was a highly respected member of the Advisory Council who had produced more than a dozen highly skilled Jedi Knights before she had even *seen* Luke Skywalker.

The path descended to a shallow brook and continued across the water via a zigzag course of stepping-stones, but Leia stopped at the edge and simply stared at Corran's back. In sparring practice, Saba was always rasping at her to stop making things hard on herself; to save her own strength by using the attacker's against him.

Leia smiled, then called, "Master Horn?"

Corran stopped with his feet balanced precariously on two rocks. "There's no sense discussing this any further," he said, looking back over his shoulder. "My mind is made up."

"I know that." Leia looked to her side, where a winding stone-chip walkway snaked along the edge of the brook toward the academy residences. "But before you make your report, shouldn't you tell Mara? You owe that much to her, if you're determined to place her husband's life in danger."

"Danger?" Corran's face fell, his green eyes blazing with conflict as he realized that performing his duty to Chief Omas would mean betraying his personal loyalty to Luke. "Chief Omas wouldn't push things that far."

"I'm not the Master here," Leia said, shrugging. "You'll have to decide that for yourself."

Corran did not even need time to think. His chin simply dropped, then he swung a leg around and started back across the stepping-stones.

"You win," he said. "This isn't something I should decide on my own."

"Maybe not," Leia allowed.

Corran stepped off the last stone and gave Leia an exaggerated frown.

"No gloating at Masters," he said. "Hasn't Saba taught you anything?"

SIX

The big hoversled emerged from behind a massive hamogoni trunk and skimmed across the forest floor, crashing through the underbrush and weaving around bustling crews of insect loggers. Han slipped the landspeeder he was piloting behind a different trunk, this one at least twenty meters across, then stopped and took a moment to gawk around the grove of giants. Many of the trees were larger than Balmorran skyscrapers, with knee-roots the size of dewbacks and boughs that hung out horizontally like enormous green balconies. Unfortunately, most of those balconies were shuddering beneath the droning saws of Saras lumberjacks, and a steady cascade of branch trimmings was raining down from above.

"Okay, Han," Luke said. He was sitting in the passenger's seat beside Han, using a comlink and datapad to follow the tracking beacon they had planted on their quarry back in Saras nest. "The signal's getting scratchy."

Han cautiously moved the landspeeder out of its hiding place, then, when they saw no visible sign of their quarry, hurried after the hoversled. In mountainous terrain like this, a scratchy signal could quickly turn into no signal at all, so they needed to close the distance fast. He dodged past a crew trimming the sprigs off a log as big around as a bantha, then decelerated hard as something big and bark-covered fell across their path. A tremendous boom shook the landspeeder, rocking it back on its rear floater pads, and the route ahead was suddenly blocked by a wall of hamogoni log twelve meters high.

Han sat there, waiting for his heart to stop hammering, until a shower of boughs and sticks, knocked loose by the falling tree, began to hit the ground around them.

"Perhaps Master Luke should drive," C-3PO suggested from the backseat. "He has taken better care of himself over the years, and his reaction time is point-four-two second faster."

"Oh, yeah? If we'd been point-four-two seconds farther ahead, you'd be a foil smear right now." Han jammed the landspeeder into reverse and hit the power, then said to Luke, "Okay, I give up. How are these guys leading us to the Dark Nest?"

Luke shrugged. "I don't know yet." His eyes remained fixed on the datapad, as though he had not noticed how close they had just come to being crushed. "But the barrels they're carrying are filled with reactor fuel and hyperdrive coolant. Do you see anything out here that needs so much power?"

"I haven't seen anything on this whole planet that needs that much power." Han started the landspeeder forward again and began a hundred-meter detour around the fallen tree. "That doesn't mean our smugglers are headed for the Dark Nest."

"It's the best explanation I can think of," Luke said.

"Yeah? What would the Dark Nest do with hyperdrive coolant? And that much reactor fuel?"

"I don't know yet," Luke repeated. "That's what scares me."

Han rounded the crown of the fallen tree, drawing a cacophony of alarmed drumming as he nearly ran into a line of Saras loggers scurrying toward the tree from the opposite side. A few of the insects carried modern laser cutters, but most were equipped with primitive chain saws—or even long, double-ended logging saws powered by hand. C-3PO thrummed a polite apology; then the Killiks opened a hole in their line, and Han took the landspeeder over to where the hoversled had disappeared.

"Blast!" Luke said, still staring at his datapad. "We lost the signal."

"Don't need it," Han said. He swung the landspeeder onto a deep-cut track—it was not quite a road—that led in the same direction the smugglers had gone. "I'll follow my nose."

"Your nose?" Luke looked up, then said, "Oh."

They followed the track over a knoll, then found themselves looking into a valley of mud and giant tree stumps. The smugglers, four Aqualish and a flat-faced Neimoidian, were about three hundred meters down the slope, parked outside the collapsed stone foundation of what had once been a very large building. The Aqualish had hoisted one of their fuel barrels onto a hamogoni stump that was two meters high and as big around as a Star Destroyer's thrust nozzle. The Neimoidian—presumably the leader—was standing next to the barrel, talking to half a dozen Killiks. With bristly antennae, barbed, hugely curved mandibles, and dark blue chitin, they were clearly Gorog—the Dark Nest.

The Neimoidian held something up to the light, examining it between his thumb and forefinger, then nodded and slipped the object into a pouch hanging beneath his robes. The closest insect handed him something else, and he began to examine that.

Han ducked behind a giant stump and brought the landspeeder to a halt. "Sometimes I hate it when you're right," he said to Luke. "But I'm not crawling down any bug holes with you. I'm through with that."

Luke grinned a little. "Sure you are."

"I'm serious," Han warned. "If you go there, you're on your own."

"Whatever you say, Han."

Luke pulled a pair of electrobinoculars from the landspeeder console, then slipped out of the passenger's seat and disappeared around the side of the tree stump. Han shut the vehicle down and told C-3PO to keep an eye on things, then joined Luke behind a lateral root so high that he had to stand on his toes to peer over the top.

"Interesting," Luke said. He passed the electrobinoculars to Han. "Have a look."

Han adjusted the lenses. The Neimoidian was examining a reddish brown mass about the size of a human thumb, shaped roughly like a tear and so transparent that Han could see a tiny silver light glimmering in its core. After studying the lump a moment, the Neimoidian placed it in his pouch and held out his hand. The closest Gorog placed in it another globule, this one so cloudy that the Neimoidian did not even bother raising it to his eye before he tossed it aside.

"Star amber?" Han asked, lowering the electrobinoculars.

Luke nodded. "At least now we know where it's . . ." He spun toward their landspeeder, his hand dropping toward his lightsaber, then finished his sentence in a whisper. ". . . been coming from."

"Why are you whispering?" Han whispered. He pulled his blaster from its holster. "I *hate* it when you whisper."

Luke raised his finger to his lips, then slipped over the root they had been hiding behind and started around the stump, moving *away* from their landspeeder. Han followed, holding the electrobinoculars in one hand and his blaster in the other. The route took them into full view of the smugglers and the insects down the slope. Luke flicked his fingers, and the entire group turned to look in the opposite direction. Han would have accused him of cheating, except that just then C-3PO's voice came over their comlinks.

"Be careful, Master Luke! They're trying to come—"

The warning ended in string of metallic thunks. A loud boom echoed across the valley, and black smoke billowed up behind the stump. Han scrambled over another lateral root and raced the rest of the way around the stump behind Luke.

They came up behind the fuming wreckage of their landspeeder, which sat on the ground surrounded by a pool of fuel and cooling fluid that had spread halfway up the tree stump. C-3PO was standing two meters in front of the vehicle, looking scorched and soot-covered and leaning forward at the waist to peer around the tree stump. R2-D2 had jetted himself onto the top of the stump and was wheeling along the edge, using his arm extension to hold out a mirror and spy on something moving along around the base.

Luke signaled Han to continue around the stump, then Force-jumped up with R2-D2. Han crept up behind C-3PO.

"Back here, Threepio," he whispered. "What have we got—"

C-3PO straightened and turned to face him. "What a relief!" he exclaimed. "I was afraid they were going to come on you from behind."

A familiar scurrying sound rose from down the slope, just out of sight around the stump, and Han suddenly felt sick to his stomach.

"Thanks for the warning," Han growled. He thrust the electrobinoculars at C-3PO and raced for cover next to the stump. "Get back, *now*."

Han barely managed to kneel partway inside a small hollow before six Gorog Killiks scuttled into view. It was about what he had been expecting, but being right only made him more queasy. He just couldn't handle bugs, not since those crazy Kamarians had tracked him down on Regulgo . . . but he couldn't think about that now, not if he wanted to keep control of himself.

"Okay, fellas, stop right there. Drop those . . ." Han hesitated when he realized that it was not blaster pistols the insects were holding. ". . . shatter guns and tell me why you shot up my landspeeder."

The Gorog began to thrum, raising their weapons as they turned.

"You *know* why," C-3PO translated. "The Night Herald told you to stay out of Gorog's business."

"Too bad." Han leveled his DL-44 at the closest bug's head. "Now hold it right there."

They did not, of course, and Han put a blaster bolt through the first one's head the instant its shatter gun swung toward him. He burned another hole through the thorax of the second bug as it extended its weapon arm, then Luke dropped down behind the group with his lightsaber blazing. The blade droned a couple of times and two more Gorog fell, then the stump around Han erupted into acrid-smelling bark shards as the surviving insects squeezed off their first shots. Han fired back, Luke's blade whined again, and the last two insects collapsed.

Han stood, holding his blaster in both hands, and Luke lowered his blade and spun in a slow circle, examining each of the corpses. He had almost finished when he suddenly staggered, then abruptly shut down his lightsaber.

"Blast!"

"What's wrong?" Han started forward. "I didn't hit you with a stray, did I?"

Luke turned with a scowl. "I'm a little better than that, Han." He lifted his gore-slimed boot and scraped the sole across a Gorog mandible, then said, "They're all dead. I was hoping to get some answers out of them."

R2-D2 chirped something from the tree stump, then began to rock back and forth on his treads.

"What is it, Artoo?" Luke asked.

"He says you might be able to ask one of the six who were talking to the smugglers," C-3PO translated helpfully. "They're on the way up now."

"Yeah, but I don't think they're coming to talk to *us*," Han said.

After a quick scan of the area to make sure there were no other Killik surprise parties, Han and Luke returned to their original hiding place. The six Gorog were clambering up the slope with their weapons drawn. The four Aqualish smugglers had broken out G-9 power blasters and were kneeling on their hoversled, hiding behind the barrels of reactor fuel and aiming up the slope to cover the insects. The Neimoidian was fleeing toward the far side of the old building foundation.

"I've got the smugglers." Luke started toward the low end of the root. "Take the Gorog—and remember, we need one alive. I want to find out what that reactor fuel is for."

Han caught him by the arm. "Those bugs have shatter guns," he said. "Maybe we should just run for it. You know how the Dark Nest is. Once we're back over the hill with the loggers, they won't want to show themselves."

"I'm not worried, Han," Luke said. "You're covering me."

"Look, kid, I don't have their range," Han said. "And your lightsaber isn't that good against those pellets."

"It's okay. You'll do fine."

Luke moved along the root's length until it covered him only from the chest down. The hillside erupted into a river of blaster bolts and magnetically accelerated projectiles.

Han cursed Luke's misplaced optimism and began to fire back. His bolts either flew wide or crackled into nothingness before they reached their targets, but they gave the bugs something to think about. Most of the shatter gun pellets thumped harmlessly into the mud below them, and the few that didn't crackled past far overhead.

The power blasters were another matter. Their bolts sizzled into the other side of the root with unnerving accuracy, filling the air with smoke and wood chips. Han sent a couple of bolts their way just to see if he could startle the Aqualish into putting their heads down. They didn't even flinch, and smoke began to drift through holes on Han and Luke's side of the root.

Then Luke extended a hand toward the stump behind the smugglers, and the barrel they had already off-loaded rose into the air and came crashing down into the middle of the hoversled. Several of the containers broke, spilling hundreds of gallons of coolant and dozens of meter-long gray rods. The Aqualish stopped firing and jumped off the sled, fleeing after the Neimoidian.

The Gorog glanced over their shoulders, then began to drum their thoraxes in anger. Han thought for a moment that they would charge, but four of them simply fanned out across the slope to take up holding positions. The other two rushed back toward the hoversled.

"Are they crazy?" Han gasped. "Ten minutes with those rods in the open like that, and they'll start glowing."

"Gorog doesn't care. It *wants* that fuel." Luke stepped back into full cover behind the root. "If our tracking equipment still works—"

"Run for your lives!" C-3PO came around the tree stump at a full clank, waving the electrobinoculars Han had passed him earlier. "We're doomed!"

"Doomed?" Han stepped out to intercept the droid—then nearly lost his head as a shatter gun pellet came hissing past his ear. He stepped back into the shelter of the root, pulling C-3PO after him. "What are you talking about?"

C-3PO turned and pointed back toward the landspeeder. "The Fizz! It has the landspeeder!"

"The Fizz?" Han asked. "Out here?"

"Perhaps we brought it with us," C-3PO suggested.

An alarmed whistle sounded from above, then R2-D2 rolled off the edge of the stump and began to drop. He would have crashed on their heads had Luke not reached out with the Force and caught him.

Luke lowered R2-D2 to the ground, then leaned down. "What's wrong with you, Artoo? You could have hurt someone."

R2-D2 whistled a long reply.

"Artoo says it probably doesn't matter," C-3PO translated. "There's a seventy-three percent chance that we're disintegrating already."

"Come on." Though R2-D2 was not normally given to doomsaying, Han tried not to be shaken by his evaluation of the situation. Despite the temporary repairs Luke had done on the little droid's personality, he was still acting as strangely as a Defel in a tanning booth. "It can't be that bad. I was just up there, and I didn't see any froth."

R2-D2 chirped curtly.

"Artoo suggests you go see for yourself," C-3PO translated. "Though I don't think that's a very good idea. It's all over the ground."

"All over the ground?" Han frowned, thinking. "Under the landspeeder? Where all that fuel spilled?"

"Precisely," C-3PO said. "And spreading rapidly. Why, I wouldn't be surprised if the entire landspeeder was engulfed by now."

"Great." Luke turned and started back toward the landspeeder. "I left the tracking set in the front seat."

"Hold on." Han caught him by the back of his robe. "I don't think it's going to matter."

Luke stopped but didn't turn around. "It's not?"

"Not if what I'm thinking is right." Han holstered his blaster and extended his hand toward C-3PO. "Threepio, hand me the electrobinoculars."

The droid looked down as though astonished to discover he was still holding the viewing device, then extended his arm. "Of course, Captain Solo—though I really don't think they're a viable substitute for the tracking set. Once the hoversled passes out of your sight line, they'll be no good to you at all."

"I don't think that hoversled *will* pass out of my sight line."

Han peered over the edge of the root and found the Gorog rear guard still holding their positions. The other two had reached the hoversled and were using their bare pincers to throw the spilled fuel rods back into the cargo bed. Han flipped the electrobinoculars to full power, then lifted them to his eyes and began to study the ground beneath the hoversled.

Luke came to his side. "What are you looking for?"

"Tell you in a minute," Han said, "in case I'm wrong about this and need to make something up to keep from embarrassing myself."

A series of sharp bangs sounded as shatter gun pellets began to strike the root, jarring Han so hard that the eyepieces slammed against his cheekbones. He stopped bracing himself on the root and continued to peer through the electrobinoculars.

"Uh, Han, maybe we should find a better observation post," Luke said. "This is getting dangerous."

"I'm not worried, kid," Han said. "You can cover me."

"Very funny," Luke replied. "But my blaster's range isn't much better than yours."

"It's okay." Han continued to study the ground beneath the hoversled. "You'll do fine."

Luke sighed, but he pulled his blaster and began to return fire. He must have actually hit something, because the pellet impacts dwindled to almost nothing. Han's arms started to ache from holding the electrobinoculars up, so he braced his hands back on the root and continued to watch.

The Gorog had almost finished loading the hoversled when they suddenly dropped one of the fuel rods and leapt into the cargo bed. They carefully began to examine the others, and Han was confused for a moment, until they tossed another rod onto the ground. It landed almost perpendicular to him, so that he noted a silver sheen starting to glitter along one side of its dull gray surface.

Han smiled in satisfaction, then backed away from the root and passed the electrobinoculars to Luke. "Take a look."

They exchanged equipment, and Han began to trade fire with the sole member of the Gorog rear guard that Luke had not already killed. Somehow, Han's shots kept sizzling out about thirty meters shy of their target.

After a moment, Luke said, "So that's what you were talking about. The Fizz."

"Almost," Han said. "Look at what it's *not* on."

"You mean the rocks in that old foundation?" Luke asked.

"And the stumps," Han confirmed. "If it's in the ground around here, how come it's leaving all that stuff alone? How come it's only attacking our landspeeder, and that coolant, and those fuel rods spilled around their hover-sled?"

Luke lowered the electrobinoculars and turned to Han. "Contamination?"

Han nodded. "It only attacks what attacks Woteba," he said. "It's an environmental defense system."

SEVEN

The steamy spa air smelled of mineral mud and pore cleanser, and the soothing notes of a classic feegharp sonata were wafting out of the sound system, not quite masking the gentle whirring and tinking of the Lovolan Beauty Artist installed in one corner of the room. Reclining on the droid's built-in comfort chair was a mud-masked, seaweed-wrapped mummy whom Jacen assumed to be Tenel Ka's grandmother, Ta'a Chume. Her scalp was being kneaded by an undulating massage hood, while each of her eyelids was hidden beneath the translucent star of what looked like some small, tentacled sea creature. There was even a beverage dispenser that automatically swung a draw nozzle out to her lips, since both hands were enveloped inside automatic manicure gloves.

When Jacen sensed no other living presences nearby, he entered the spa. He passed a series of sunken basins filled with bubbling mud, water, and something that looked like pink Hutt slime, then stopped beside the droid. Ta'a Chume showed no sign of sensing his presence, and for a moment he considered whether simply ending her life might not be the surest way to protect his daughter. Certainly, the old woman deserved it. She had been liquidating inconvenient people since before Jacen and Tenel Ka were born, and currently she was under house arrest for poisoning Tenel Ka's mother. At one time, Ta'a Chume had even attempted to have Jacen's own mother assassinated.

But Tenel Ka had asked him not to kill the old woman, saying she would deal with her grandmother's treachery in her own way. Jacen suspected that meant a long and very public trial, in which Ta'a Chume might well escape conviction due to a lack of verifiable evidence—and Jacen was, quite simply, not willing to run that risk with his daughter's life.

Jacen took his lightsaber off its belt hook, but did not activate the blade. "I see you're making the most of your house arrest, Ta'a Chume."

A hole appeared in the mud mask as Ta'a Chume's mouth fell open, then she pulled out of the massage hood and raised her head. The sea creatures left her eyelids and slid down her cheeks, leaving trails of exposed skin in their wakes.

"Jacen Solo," Ta'a Chume said. "I'd ask how you sneaked into my private chambers—but that's what Jedi *do,* isn't it?"

"Among other things." Noting that she had not taken her hands out of the manicure gloves, he said, "You can signal for help all you like—your bodyguards won't be coming—but please don't attempt to point that hold-out blaster at me. I promised Tenel Ka I wouldn't kill you, and I'll be very angry if you make me break my word."

Ta'a Chume's eyes faded to paler shade of green, but she cracked her mud mask by forcing a superior smile. "What a pity—when I saw you standing there with a lightsaber, I thought my granddaughter had finally grown a spine."

"Had Tenel Ka lacked courage, you would have died never knowing I was here," Jacen said. "Instead she's willing to risk keeping you alive for a public trial. Her security team will be arriving soon. I've made sure they won't need to kill anyone to reach you."

The tension left Ta'a Chume's shoulders. "How very considerate of you." A cunning light came to her eyes, then she slowly removed her hand from the manicure glove and dropped a small hold-out blaster to the floor. "Would you mind telling me why?"

"You know why," Jacen said. Ta'a Chume was playing a game with him—he could feel it in her presence as clearly as he heard it in her voice—but what he could not figure out was the reason. "You tried to kill her daughter."

Ta'a Chume poured anger into the Force, but her voice grew aggrieved. "The Queen Mother has a child?" She drew her second hand out of the manicure glove and pressed her fingers to her temples. "And she did not even trouble to tell her own grandmother?"

Jacen scowled. "Your act isn't fooling me. I sense your true emotions in the Force."

"Then you must sense how shocked I am—and worried." Ta'a Chume put her hands down and turned to look at him, but her gaze lingered on his chest, running up and down the lapels, pausing at every wrinkle. "Certainly, I resent being imprisoned on the orders of my own granddaughter, but I'd never wish her harm—much less have anything to do with it!"

Jacen finally understood. "There is no spycam, Ta'a Chume." He pulled his robe open to show her that he had no equipment hidden underneath. "I'm here looking for answers to my own questions—not gathering evidence for Tenel Ka."

"That never crossed my mind, Jedi Solo, but I do hope that when you see my granddaughter again, you'll be good enough to pass along my concern for her and her daughter." Ta'a Chume looked up and batted her eyes at him. "By the by, you wouldn't happen to know who the father is, would you?"

The smirk in Ta'a Chume's voice was clear, as though she was taunting Jacen, telling him that he would never beat her at this particular game—and it made him angry.

"That would be me." Jacen stepped around behind the beauty droid and used the Force to pull Ta'a Chume back in the seat. "And I'm very determined to protect my daughter."

Ta'a Chume grew nervous. "What are you doing?"

"I'd like some answers, and we don't have long before the security team arrives."

Jacen pushed the scalp hood aside, then plunged his fingers into Ta'a Chume's red-dyed hair and began to massage her scalp.

"So we can do this the easy way . . ." He pressed his thumbs into the base of her skull, then sent a tiny charge of Force energy shooting through her brain. ". . . or we can do it the hard way."

Ta'a Chume gasped in pain, then said, "You're a Jedi! You can't do this."

"Sure I can," Jacen said. "The Jedi learned some new tricks during the war with the Yuuzhan Vong—or hadn't you heard?"

Jacen felt a warning jolt from Ben, whom he had left hidden with his skiff outside Ta'a Chume's estate, then heard the distant *crump* of the front gates being blown by Tenel Ka's security team.

Ta'a Chume's head twitched toward the sound, and Jacen knew that she believed her arresters would be her saviors—that if she could just hold out long enough, her secrets would remain safe. He sent another charge of Force energy into her mind.

This time he did not stop with a short surge. He continued to pour more Force energy into Ta'a Chume's head, pushing in behind it, expanding his own Force presence inside her mind. He was not as sure or strong with the technique as Raynar—in fact, he was not even sure it was the same technique—but he *was* good enough to overpower a surprised old woman who did not know how to use the Force.

A long cry escaped Ta'a Chume's lips; as it died away, Jacen felt her resistance crumble. Outside on the palace grounds, voices began to yell commands at Ta'a Chume's servants.

Jacen ignored the commotion and leaned close to Ta'a Chume's ear. "First, I want to know why."

Ta'a Chume tried to resist. "Why wha . . ." Jacen pushed harder, and she said, "You couldn't believe I would allow the child of two *Jedi* to claim the throne. Hapes will never be a Jedi kingdom!"

"I don't think that's Tenel Ka's intention."

"It is *your* intention that concerns me," Ta'a Chume said. "You've already persuaded Tenel Ka to involve a Hapan fleet in a matter of no concern to us. I won't allow you to make a Jedi tool of the Hapes Consortium."

"You see? That wasn't so hard. Now tell me about the Dark Nest."

"The Dark Nest?"

"The Gorog," Jacen clarified. It felt like she was genuinely confused. "The Killiks. How did you get them to go after the baby?"

Muffled crashing sounds started to rumble up through the palace itself, and Ta'a Chume began to hope again that she could hold out.

"I don't know . . ."

Jacen expanded his presence.

"They came to *me!*" she cried. "They were unhappy about Tenel Ka's interference at Qoribu, and they knew I had reason to want her dead."

The statement made sense. Hoping to expand its influence in the Colony—and to expand the Colony into Chiss territory—the Dark Nest had deliberately been trying to start a war with the Chiss Ascendancy. But he could feel Ta'a Chume fighting to hold back, struggling to leave something unsaid. He expanded further into her mind. She screamed, and something slipped, like a hand opening on a rope, but Jacen did not back off. He needed to know what the Dark Nest was doing.

"The Gorog . . . were wrong," Ta'a Chume said. "I don't want Tenel Ka dead . . . at least not . . . until I'm in a better position . . . to reclaim the throne."

"But your spies had told you about the baby," Jacen surmised. "And you wanted the baby dead . . ."

"So I told Gorog . . . that killing Tenel Ka's daughter would be even better." Ta'a Chume tried to stop there, but Jacen was pushing so hard that she barely had a hold on her own mind. "But they weren't doing it out of revenge. I had to strike a deal to save . . . to take the baby instead of Tenel Ka."

Male voices began to echo up through the building as Tenel Ka's security team started its ascent. Jacen had already made sure that they would encounter no resistance, so the climb would be a quick one, with each floor requiring only a cursory clearing before they climbed to the next.

"The deal terms?" Jacen asked.

Despite the apparent proximity of the security team, Ta'a Chume did not even try to resist. Her grasp on her mind was just too tenuous.

"They wanted . . . navicomputer technology," she said.

"Navicomputers?" Jacen could not imagine what the Dark Nest wanted with that particular technology. "To travel insystem?"

"No," Ta'a Chume said. "To go through hyperspace."

"Why?" Jacen asked. "Killiks don't build hyperspace-capable vessels. They hire transports."

"They didn't say, and I didn't ask," Ta'a Chume answered. "This was a political arrangement, not a marriage."

Jacen would have pressed harder, but he could feel that she was telling the truth, that she had not cared why the Gorog were interested in the technology—so long as Tenel Ka's baby was killed. He had to move his fingers away from Ta'a Chume's throat. They were beginning to squeeze.

A muted thump sounded from the outer door of Ta'a Chume's private wing, and a loudspeaker voice began yelling at her to deactivate the locks and lie down on the floor. Jacen's interview was coming to an end—and Ta'a Chume knew it. He could feel her starting to fight back, trying to claw her way back into control of her mind.

"Just one more question," Jacen said. "Will there be any more attacks on my daughter?"

"Not your daughter, no." Ta'a Chume was lying—Jacen could feel that she would never give up, and she hoped and expected that the Dark Nest never would, either—but he did not call her on it. There was more, something she was eager for him to know. "But your daughter should not be your only concern."

"I'm listening," Jacen said.

"I didn't rule Hapes for all those years by being a fool," Ta'a Chume said. "I knew you and Tenel Ka would figure out who attacked your daughter—and I knew you would come after me."

A loud bang sounded from the outer door of the wing.

"We're out of time," Jacen said. "Tell me why I shouldn't kill you now, or—"

"If I die, Tenel Ka is a target. If I am imprisoned, if I am disgraced . . . Tenel Ka is a target." Ta'a Chume eased her neck out of Jacen's hands, then twisted around to face him. "If you want your daughter to grow up with a mother, Jacen, you must spare me. That is the only way."

The anger that Jacen felt suddenly turned to something else—something cold and calculating.

"Not the only way," he said. "There is another."

He grabbed Ta'a Chume by the shoulder and pulled her back into the seat. Then, as the muted tramp of boots began to pound through the outer warrens of her living chambers, Jacen poured hot, crackling Force energy into her head, pushing hard with his own presence, violently, until they both blasted free of her brain and Ta'a Chume gave a last, falling shriek, plunging down into the depths of her mind, plummeting into the darkness of a soul that had never loved, that had cared only for power and wealth and control, leaving only a black fuming void ringed by torn neurons and seared dendrites and a shattered, broken brain.

And Jacen suddenly found himself outside Ta'a Chume, outside himself, a passive observer outside time itself, his presence filling the entire room, the entire palace, a witness to something he could not control. He saw the whole Hapes Cluster and the whole galaxy, and all of it was burning—not just the suns, but also the planets and the moons and the asteroids, burning, every speck of stone or dust solid enough to hold a sentient foot. And the fires were traveling from place to place on tiny flickering needles of ion efflux, being set by torches carried in the hands of men and Killiks and Chiss, and the inferno just kept growing brighter, until worlds blazed as brightly as suns and systems flared as brightly as novae, until sectors shined as brightly as the Core and the whole galaxy erupted into one huge eternal flame.

The flame vanished when a loud pounding began to echo through the spa door. "By the Queen Mother's order, unlock the door and lie down on the floor!"

Jacen stumbled away from the beauty droid feeling horrified and confused. He had experienced enough Force-visions to recognize what had happened, but he could not bring himself to accept what he had seen. Visions were symbolic, but the meaning of this one seemed clear enough to him. The galaxy was about to erupt into a war unlike anything it had ever seen before—a war that would never end, that would spread from world to world to world until it had consumed the entire galaxy.

And the Killiks were at the heart of it.

A sharp bang sounded from the spa entrance, sending the durasteel door flying into the opposite wall and filling the chamber with an impenetrable cloud of blue smoke. Jacen pushed the massage hood back down on Ta'a Chume's head and jumped into the sunken basin of mineral mud. He sank down to his chin and looked around him, taking careful note of the mud's surface, then carefully expanded that illusion into the Force—as he had learned from the Adepts of the White Current.

He was not quite finished when the eye-goggled, body-armored forms of a dozen Hapan security commandos charged into the room. They advanced in a bent-legged shuffle that seemed vaguely insect-like, then rushed over to the Beauty Artist, all twelve of them pointing their assault blasters at Ta'a Chume's unmoving form. When the old woman showed no sign of resistance, the squad leader reluctantly lowered his weapon and placed three fingers on her throat.

"She's alive." He handed his assault blaster to a subordinate, then leaned over Ta'a Chume and stared into her unmoving eyes. "But get Doc up here—I think she's had some sort of brain hemorrhage."

EIGHT

A two-story hologram of the planet Woteba hung in the projection pit a few meters beyond the command console, a nearly featureless reminder of just how valid Leia's fears really were. Han and her brother were trapped and alone on a half-known world, surrounded by insects answering to an enemy queen, and—judging by her sense of Luke's emotions in the Force—they did not even realize they were in trouble. That was what really worried Leia. Han and Luke could take care of themselves, but only if they knew there was a need.

"Maybe the Dark Nest isn't even *on* Woteba," Kyp Durron suggested. "What do we know about the other planets?"

"Only that they were all as deserted as Woteba before we helped the Killiks settle there." Leia swung her gaze toward the shaggy-haired Master. Along with Mara and Saba, they were in the Operations Planning Center in the Jedi Temple on Coruscant, conversing with several other Jedi via the HoloNet. "And fourteen were habitable."

"The Killiks weren't interested in detailed surveys," Mara explained. "All they wanted to know was which worlds were habitable. We have a basic planetary profile and not much else."

"Because they didn't *want* us to know too much." The comment came from Corran Horn's hologram, arrayed with several others on a shelf curving along the back edge of the control console. "To me, it's beginning to sound like the Killiks never intended to keep the peace with the Chiss."

"Don't confuse the Killiks with the Gorog," Jaina warned. She and Zekk were sharing the hologram next to Corran's, their heads touching above the temples and their unblinking eyes fixed straight ahead. "It was only the Dark Nest that wanted the war, not the Colony."

"Whoever wanted it *then,* the entire Colony is clearly involved *now,*" Corran countered. "And they have Master Skywalker to guarantee that we don't interfere with their plans again."

"You don't understand how the Colony's mind works," Zekk objected.

"It may look like the entire Colony is involved," Jaina added, "but the Dark Nest is the one behind this."

"Remember last time?" Zekk asked. "UnuThul summoned us to *prevent* a war."

"That is called a false flag recruitment," Kenth Hamner said from the end of the array. With Corran, Kenth had argued forcefully that the Killiks should be left to their own devices during the Qoribu crisis. "A valuable asset—a team of young Jedi Knights, shall we say—is convinced to undertake a mission under false pretenses."

"That's not how it was," Jaina said.

"Unfortunately, we can no longer afford to give the Colony the benefit of the doubt," Kenth said. "Until Master Skywalker and Captain Solo are safe, we must consider the evidence: despite the *fifteen* worlds we gave them—worlds that the Galactic Alliance's own beings desperately need—the Killiks are harboring pirates and poisoning the minds and bodies of our own insect species with black membrosia."

Jaina and Zekk spoke simultaneously. "That's just the—"

"Let me finish." Kenth did not raise his voice, but, even coming from a holopad speaker, his tone was as hard as durasteel. "Raynar Thul lured Master Skywalker into a trap so the Colony could take him hostage, and now the Killiks are provoking a confrontation with the Chiss. We have no choice but to assume the worst."

"Because the *Dark Nest* has taken control!" Zekk blurted.

A tight smile came to Kenth's hologram. "Precisely."

Jaina rolled her eyes. "Master Hamner, if you hold the entire Colony responsible—"

"—you're creating a self-fulfilling prophecy," Zekk added.

"And the Killiks *will* turn on us," Jaina finished. "Why don't you get that?"

"What I 'get,' Jedi Solo, is that you and Jedi Zekk still have an emotional attachment to the Killiks." The hologram wavered as Kenth's gaze shifted, and now his image seemed to be looking Leia straight in the eye. "Frankly, I question the wisdom of allowing these particular Jedi Knights to participate in the discussion at all."

"No one is more familiar with the Killiks than Jaina and Zekk." Leia purposely allowed some of the resentment she felt to creep into her voice. After what Jaina and Zekk had sacrificed to prevent the Qoribu conflict from erupting into a galactic war, Kenth Hamner did not have the right to cast aspersions on their loyalty. "They're our best hope of figuring out where the Dark Nest might be located."

"I understand that." A purple tint came to Kenth's image, indicating that he had closed the channel to all other participants and was now conversing only with the Operations Planning Center. "But there's something you don't know—something that we can't trust with your daughter and Zekk—or with any of the Jedi Knights who spent too much time with the Killiks."

Leia's blood began to boil. "Master Hamner, Jaina and Zekk have already demonstrated their loyalty to the order—"

Mara cut Leia short by reaching past her and suspending transmission to everyone else. "What is it, Kenth?"

"I apologize if I offended you, Princess Leia," Kenth said. "But Chief Omas asked me not to tell *anyone* in the order what I'm about to reveal. I hope you'll understand. It has a bearing on our discussion."

"Of course." Leia understood when she was being told that she wasn't going to hear something without a promise of confidentiality. "I won't reveal it to anyone. I give you my word."

"Thank you."

Kenth's head turned as he consulted something off cam. Kyp, Corran, and Jaina and Zekk, aware by the sudden silence from the Operations Planning Center that they had been cut out of the conversation, fell quiet and tried not to look impatient.

A moment later, Kenth's gaze returned to his holocam. "Sorry for that, but I wanted to check the latest. The Fifth Fleet has put out for Utegetu."

"The whole fleet?" Leia was stunned. Moving the Fifth Fleet would shift the responsibility for patrolling the entire Hydian Way to local governments—and that was not something Chief Omas would do lightly. "To do what?"

Kenth shook his head. "Those orders are sealed, but we can be certain they're trying to appease the Chiss. What concerns me is that I only found out by accident. Someone had forgotten to remove my name from the routing list. Chief Omas called personally to ask me to keep the information to myself."

"They don't want us to know?" Leia gasped.

"Clearly," Mara said. "Omas didn't like how the Jedi handled the Killiks last time—and you must admit things aren't going well now."

"Do they know about Han and Luke?" Leia asked.

"Not from me," Kenth answered. "But I doubt it would make any difference. Chief Omas was very adamant that we need to support the Chiss this time."

"Then time is chewing our tailz," Saba said. Standing behind Leia with Mara, she was also party to their private discussion. "We must get a team to Woteba *now*. Yez?"

"Agreed," Kenth said. "But—"

"Then we will discusz *that*," Saba said.

"I think we should," Kenth said. "But Jaina and Zekk—"

"—will not be told." Saba leaned over Leia's shoulder and reactivated the suspended channels. "Where do we look for the Dark Nest?"

Jaina and Zekk gave a simultaneous *cloq-cloq* of surprise, and the irritation they had shown at being left out of the conversation vanished from their faces. A blue dot appeared on Woteba's empty face, next to one of the few mapping symbols that the hologram already contained: Saras nest.

"You don't find Gorog," Jaina said.

"Gorog finds you," Zekk added. "But we know the nest will be watching Han and Master Skywalker."

"So we must watch them, too," Jaina finished.

Leia and Mara exchanged glances. They did not have time for "watching." The instant the Fifth Fleet entered the Utegetu Nebula, the Dark Nest would move against Han and Luke. The memory of the Kr nursery—where Luke and Mara had found thousands of Gorog larvae feeding on paralyzed Chiss prisoners—flashed through Leia's mind, and she firmly shook her head.

"Too risky," she said.

"They'll see us watching," Mara added. "And we can't let Lomi Plo escape this time."

"Isn't there a faster way we can find it?" Leia asked.

Jaina and Zekk considered this for several moments, then Jaina said, "Perhaps *we* could feel where their nest is—"

"—if we went to Utegetu."

"This one thought nobody could sense the Dark Nest in the Force," Saba rasped. "Especially Joinerz."

"Jaina and I might be different," Zekk said. "We were in the nest at Kr."

"So we know what Gorog feels like," Jaina added.

Leia frowned. "And what about that gang of Tibanna tappers you're supposed to be hunting?" She did not like the eagerness she heard in their voices, the desire to experience again the all-encompassing bond of a collective mind. "Cloud City's shipments are down ten percent."

"Lowie and Tesar can take over," Zekk said.

"They finally found out who was hijacking the Abaarian water shipments," Jaina added.

"Forget it," Mara said, issuing the command before Leia could—and adding to it the authority of a Master. "You two aren't getting within five parsecs of a Killik nest. Clear?"

Jaina and Zekk leaned away from each other, making clicking sounds in their throats and blinking in unison. "Clear," they said.

"We were only trying to help," Jaina added defensively.

"Sure you were," Leia said. "Anybody have any *real* ideas?"

"I don't think there is a way," Kyp said immediately. "We've tried to trace the black membrosia back to the source and never made it past the blind drops in the Rago Run. And with a collective mind, the Dark Nest will know if we start sniffing around the Utegetu Nebula too hard."

"Then maybe Jaina and Zekk are right," Corran said. "Maybe the best thing to do is to watch Han and Master Skywalker and just be patient."

"I thought we had already ruled that out." Though Leia's outward voice remained calm, inside she wanted to give him a Barabel ear-slap. The one thing they did not have was time—though, of course, Corran had no way of knowing that. He had not been a part of the private conversation with Kenth. "We'll just have to recover Luke and Han first, and hope they were able to find the Dark Nest on their own."

"No good," Kyp said. "That tips our hand. If the Dark Nest is watching them—"

"We *can* be discreet," Mara said in a tone that would abide no argument. "We're Jedi, remember?"

The rebuke in her tone made Corran wince, Kyp cock his brow, and Jaina and Zekk tilt their heads. There was a long moment of silence in which those who had not been privy to Kenth's secret were clearly trying to figure out why everyone else was in such a hurry.

Then a knowing light came to Kyp's brown eyes. "You're worried about your husbands!" He flashed a reassuring smile that came off as more of a smirk in the hologram. "That's only natural, ladies. But Han and Master Skywalker can take care of themselves. I've been in worse places than this with both of them, lots of times."

Mara sighed. "No, Kyp, that's not it."

"What Master Skywalker means is that we need to act quickly," Kenth said. "With the Colony provoking the Chiss again, the situation is too unpredictable. The sooner we resolve this, the less likely it is to blow up in our faces worse than it already has."

Corran nodded sagely. "Our reputation has already taken a bad hit, especially in the Senate."

Kyp looked doubtful. "That's it? You're worried that things might get a little messy?"

"Yes, Kyp, that's it," Leia said. "Except that if things get messy, they're going to get *very* messy. We need to prove to the Chiss—and everyone else—that the Jedi can be counted on."

Kyp considered this for a moment, then shrugged. "Okay. But we need a backup plan, because we're never going to get to Han and Luke without the Dark Nest knowing. Those bugs are good."

"Good?" Saba sissed in amused disbelief. "You spent too much of your life in the spice minez, Kyp Durron. There is too much methane in them. They taste like a—"

"I think he meant they were skilled observers, Master Sebatyne," Leia said. "I'm sure that Master Durron has never actually eaten a Gorog."

"No?" Saba's tail thumped the floor. "Not even a little one?"

"Not even a taste." Kyp was quick to change the subject. "Now, about our backup plan. I have one."

"That was easy," Corran said. "Will it work?"

"Of course," Kyp said. "We just take out Raynar and the Unu."

"Kill them?" Corran's tone was shocked.

Kyp grew thoughtful. "That would work, too, and it would be a lot easier than bringing Raynar back here alive—at least if he's as powerful as everyone says."

"You can't!" Zekk objected. "It would destroy the Colony!"

"Actually, it would only return the Killiks to their natural state," Mara corrected. "There *was* no Colony until Raynar came along."

"That's like saying there was no Jedi order until Uncle Luke came along," Jaina countered.

"You can't destroy an interstellar civilization just because it didn't exist ten years ago," Zekk added.

"Probably not," Kenth replied. "But when that civilization refuses to honor its agreements and live in peace with its neighbors, we may find ourselves duty-bound to try."

"I might argue with that," Corran said. "War is one thing. But assassination . . . that's not something Jedi *do*."

"Especially when you have a better way to handle the problem," Jaina said.

"Jaina," Leia said, "if you're talking about you and Zekk going back to the Killiks, forget it."

"Why?" Zekk demanded. "Because you're afraid you'll lose us the way you lost Anakin?"

Coming from Zekk's mouth instead of Jaina's, the question felt just bizarre enough that the dagger of loss it drove into Leia's chest did not find her heart. She retained her composure and studied her daughter's image in silence, but Jaina was too tough to be stared down over the HoloNet. She simply accepted Leia's glare with the unblinking eyes of a Joiner, then spoke in an even voice.

"We're sorry, Mother. That was uncalled-for."

"But we're still Jedi," Zekk added. "You can't stop us from doing what Jedi do."

Mara leaned close to the holocam and spoke in a sharp voice. "She isn't trying to—and you know it." She waited until the pair gave a grudging nod, then asked, "But if you can do this in a better way, let's hear it."

Jaina's and Zekk's eyes bugged in surprise. "You'd send us back?"

"*If* that was the best way," Mara said. "Of course."

Leia stiffened and would have objected, save that Saba sensed what she was about to do and gave a warning hiss. It had not been her place to tell Jaina and Zekk to forget returning to the Killiks, and now Mara had to waste valuable time correcting the mistake. After a lifetime of leadership in both politics and the military, Leia sometimes found it difficult to remember that in the Jedi order, she was technically just another Jedi Knight—and, as far as Saba was concerned, a fairly junior one at that.

After a few moments' silence from Jaina and Zekk, Mara prompted, "We're listening."

Jaina and Zekk furrowed their brows, then Jaina finally said, "We could talk to UnuThul."

"And say what?" Kyp demanded. "That he should make the Killiks stop harboring pirates and running black membrosia?"

"You said Gorog was controlling him," Zekk pointed out. "We could make him see that."

"Or watch him until Gorog shows herself," Jaina said. "Then follow her to her nest."

"Listen to yourselvez!" Saba said, leaning over Leia toward the holocam. "*That* is why you cannot go."

"I agree," Kenth said. "You're both outstanding Jedi. But when it comes to the Colony, it's clear that all you want is to return."

"You can't go back," Kyp agreed. "It would be bad for you and worse for us."

In the face of the Masters' opposition, Jaina and Zekk dropped their gazes. "Sorry," Jaina said.

"We'll go back to the Tibanna tappers."

As Zekk spoke, a hailing light activated on the command console. "It's just that—"

"Hold on," Leia said, relieved to have an excuse to cut off Zekk's plea. "Someone's trying to contact us on this end."

She opened a sequestered holochannel, and the pink, high-domed head of a Mon Calamari appeared over an empty holopad.

"Cilghal!" Leia said. "I wasn't expecting to hear from you so soon."

"Analyzing that froth turned out to be easier than we had feared."

"That's good news," Leia said.

"Not really," Cilghal replied.

"Is this something the whole planning group will need to hear?" Mara asked.

Cilghal's short eyestalks sagged. "Probably so."

Leia patched the Mon Calamari's channel into the network. "Cilghal has made some progress on the Dark Nest's froth."

"Actually, I doubt the Dark Nest is responsible for the froth," Cilghal said. "From what we know of Killik society, they have no nanotechnology abilities at all."

"Nanotech?" Kyp echoed. "As in molecule machines?"

"As in *self-replicating* molecule machines," Cilghal corrected. "The sample that Master Sebatyne gave me appears to be a terraforming system. From what I can tell, it's designed to create and maintain an environmental balance optimal for its creators."

"Yes," Saba said. "But what does it *do*?"

"I'm not sure we'll ever understand completely." Cilghal steepled her webbed fingers beneath her chin tentacles. "It's very advanced, far beyond any nanotechnology capabilities here in the Galactic Alliance."

Saba rasped in impatience.

"Basically," Cilghal continued, "the system consists of many different kinds of tiny machines. Some of those machines monitor the soil, the air, the water. When they detect a notable imbalance in the environment, they join together and become machines that disassemble the contaminants, molecule by molecule, then use that raw material to build more machines. That's what is happening when you see the froth."

"And these contaminants," Corran said. "They are . . . ?"

"Whatever lies outside the system parameters," Cilghal said. "Toxic spills, spinglass buildings, droids, Killiks—in short, anything in sufficient amounts that wasn't on Woteba when Leia and Han found it."

Leia's heart sank. Moving the Killiks to Woteba had felt a little too convenient all along, and now she knew there was a reason.

"This is great news!" Jaina said.

"The Colony isn't lying to us after all!" Zekk added.

"Don't start your victory rolls yet," Kyp warned. "Maybe the Killiks didn't make this stuff, but the Dark Nest is still using it to turn the Colony against us."

"Only until UnuThul understands what happened," Zekk said.

"Once we disable the nanotech, he'll see that we weren't trying to trick him," Jaina added.

"I'm afraid he's going to have to take our word for it," Cilghal said.

Jaina and Zekk frowned. "Why?"

"Because the system is probably worldwide, and it is certainly very resilient." Cilghal interlaced her fingers, then her hands dropped out of the hologram. "If the supernova didn't destroy it—"

"Supernova?" Corran asked. "What supernova?"

"The one that created the Utegetu Nebula," Leia clarified. There were many different kinds of nebulae, and most of them did not result from supernova explosions. "The Utegetu is a shell nebula."

"I see," Corran said.

"The blast would have destroyed all life on every planet within a dozen parsecs," Cilghal continued. "But my assistant's calculations suggest that the nebula is only a thousand standard years old."

"And you think the nanotech survived to restore Woteba and the other worlds," Leia surmised.

"Yes. Otherwise, the planets would still be dead." Cilghal glanced at something out of view, then said, "We calculate that it would have taken only a year or two for the first pockets of soil to become fertile again, and there would have been plenty of seeds trapped where the blast radiation wouldn't destroy them."

"But the animals wouldn't have lasted," Mara said. "They would have starved within months."

Cilghal nodded. "And that is how you end up with a cluster of empty paradise worlds."

"I don't suppose there's any chance of Raynar believing all this?" Corran asked.

"We'll certainly do our best to persuade him," Leia said. "But I suspect the Dark Nest will convince him that we're lying."

"What do you two think?" Mara asked Jaina and Zekk.

They were silent for a moment; then they reluctantly shook their heads.

"Unu has already put the Colony's plans in motion," Zekk said.

Jaina added, "It will be easier to believe the Dark Nest."

"Then we're back to where we started," Leia said. "Recover Han and Luke, then hope we can find the Dark Nest—and take it out this time."

When no one voiced an objection, Corran asked, "What about our backup plan? I just don't see assassinating Raynar as an option."

The discussion descended into an uncomfortable silence as they all considered their own interpretation of what it meant to be a Jedi. Not so long ago, during the war against the Yuuzhan Vong, they would not have hesitated to do *whatever* was necessary to safeguard the order and the Galactic Alliance. But Luke had been growing increasingly uncomfortable with that attitude, and over the last year he had quietly been encouraging Jedi Knights and Masters alike to contemplate just where the balance lay between good intention and wrong action.

Corran Horn, as usual in matters of conscience, came to his answer more quickly than most. "War is one thing, but taking out Raynar is murder."

"Maybe it's just because my husband is out there, but it seems more like self-defense to me," Mara said. "It feels like the Dark Nest is coming after us."

"It is more than a feeling," Saba said. "First there are the piratez and the black membrosia, then they lure Master Skywalker to Woteba, and now they are establishing Coloniez along the Chisz border. Who knowz what is next? They have been hunting us for a long time, and we have been asleep under our rockz."

"We've certainly given them the initiative," Kenth agreed. "And we need to win it back now. If that means taking Raynar out, so be it. Clearly, he intends to use Han and Master Skywalker as hostages, and that makes him a legitimate target."

"Even if he's under the Dark Nest's control?" Corran countered. "We can't be sure that he's responsible for his own actions."

"It doesn't matter," Kyp said. "You guys are really overthinking this. It's simple: Raynar is a Jedi, and now he's becoming a threat to the galaxy. He's our responsibility, and we have to stop him. *How* we do that matters a lot less than whether we still can."

The uncomfortable silence returned to the participants, and the eyes in all of the holograms vanished from sight as the Jedi on the other end stared at their respective floors.

Finally, Jaina and Zekk clicked several times in the back of their throats, then looked up and nodded.

"Master Durron is right," Jaina said.

"Raynar *is* our responsibility," Zekk added. "The Jedi must do whatever it takes to stop him."

NINE

A gentle Woteban breeze was wafting across the bog, cool and damp and filled with acrid wisps of the peat smoke rising from the chimneys of the nearest Saras tunnel-house. Close by, the serpentine skeletons of ten more structures were beginning to take shape beneath the bustling anarchy of Killik construction crews. A kilometer beyond, at the far edge of the nest expansion, more insects were moving hamogoni pilings off a steady stream of lumber sleds.

"Oh, boy," Luke said, eyeing all the new construction. "This is bad."

"Only if there are contaminants," Han said. "If there aren't any, it might be okay."

Their Saras escort, a chest-high worker that had been waiting to meet the logging sled on which they had hitched a ride back to the nest, thrummed a short question.

"Saras wishes to know what might be okay," C-3PO informed them. "And why you are so worried about contaminants."

"*Bur ru ub br urrb,*" the insect added. "*Rrrrr uu uu bub.*"

"Oh, dear," C-3PO said. "Saras says the nest has a perfectly sound method of disposing of toxins—it pumps them into the bog!"

"Great," Han growled. He turned to Luke. "We gotta get off this sponge before we start glowing or something."

"Let's talk to Raynar," Luke said. "Maybe once the Killiks understand what's happening, he'll consider our promise kept."

"*Urru buur rbur.*" Their escort waited as an empty lumber sled glided past and disappeared down a winding boulevard into Saras nest proper, then started toward the completed building. "*Ubu ruru buub.*"

"Raynar Thul is dead," C-3PO translated. "But UnuThul is waiting for us in the replica factory."

"Sounds like he's already heard part of it," Han said. "I just hope he doesn't blast the messenger when he hears the rest."

Luke led the others after the escort, through a large iris membrane into the throat of a twining, hangar-sized tunnel-house so filled with smoke and manufacturing fumes that the iridescent walls were barely visible. Along one wall stood a long row of peat-fired furnaces, serviced by hundreds of bustling Killiks. The middle of the chamber was filled with steaming vats, also surrounded by hundreds of Killiks. Along the far wall ran a serpentine workbench, flanked on each side by a seemingly endless Killik production line.

Luke stopped a few paces inside the door. Han let out a complaining cough, then leaned close.

"Better make this fast," he whispered. "It's a wonder this place hasn't been Fizzed already."

Luke did not reply, for Raynar had emerged from the swarm along the workbench and was coming toward them with a pair of spinglass sculptures in his hands. As usual, he was followed by the teeming Unu entourage. He stopped five paces away and stared at them expectantly, as though he assumed they would cross the remaining distance to him.

When they did not, there was a moment of tense silence.

Finally, Han demanded, "What's so important you couldn't let us hit the refresher first?" He pulled at his dirty tunic. "We're kind of ripe."

Raynar's scarred face seemed to harden. "We were worried you might be difficult to find later—if, for instance, you decided to get off this sponge before you 'started glowing or something.'"

Luke dipped his head in acknowledgment. "You've been keeping tabs on us through our escort," he said. "We thought as much. So you must also know we have no intention of leaving until *you* consider our promise kept."

"I have heard." Raynar's rigid lips pressed into an awkward smirk; then he turned to Han. "We apologize if our summons seemed abrupt, but we wished to thank you and Master Skywalker for discovering the star amber cheats. Saras did not realize they were taking something so valuable."

Raynar closed the last of the distance separating them, and Luke saw that the sculptures in his hands were spinglass replicas of *Millennium Falcon* and a T-65 X-wing.

Raynar turned to Luke first and presented him with the X-wing. "Unu wanted you to be the first to have one of these. It is an exact copy of the fighter you were flying when you destroyed the original Death Star."

More than a little stunned by the gesture, Luke accepted the sculpture with genuine gratitude. The piece was so intricately executed that Luke could identify both R2-D2 and the loose stabilizers the droid had been struggling to repair as he began the final assault run.

"Thank you," he said. "I'll treasure it."

"It's the first of a limited run commissioned by one of our business partners in the Galactic Alliance," Raynar said proudly. "Turn it over. It's numbered and signed by the artist."

Luke did as Raynar asked. Etched into the bottom was SARAS: 1/1,000,000,000. SECOND MISTAKE ENTERPRISES.

Luke nodded politely, then turned it back over. "I'm sure the line will be a great success."

"We think so, too," Raynar said. He turned to Han and gave him the replica of *Millennium Falcon*. "Also a first run."

"Thanks. Real nice." Han turned it over and inspected the artist's signature. "Second Mistake Enterprises?" He frowned, then looked back to Raynar. "Your partners wouldn't happen to be three Squibs named Sligh, Grees, and Emala?"

Raynar's eyes widened. "How did you know?"

"Leia and I had some dealings with them, back before you were born," Han said. Luke remembered something about a trio of Squibs being involved when *Killik Twilight* fell into Imperial hands during the war. "They've got a nose for fine artwork—supplied Thrawn for a while, as a matter of fact."

Raynar's voice grew suspicious. "Do not bother contacting them," he warned. "Our agreement is exclusive."

Han's brow rose. "Wouldn't dream of it." He nonchalantly passed the replica to C-3PO. "You guys were made for each other."

"Good." Raynar almost smiled. "They expect the value of the first pieces to grow exponentially. That's why Unu wanted you and Master Skywalker to have these two replicas, as a reward for helping Saras catch the star amber cheat."

"I appreciate it." Han furrowed his brow and cast a questioning glance in Luke's direction, then, when Luke nodded, he continued, "But the guy Saras caught wasn't exactly a cheat."

"It was something of an inside job," Luke added. "We'll tell you about it later, but first—"

"Tell us about it now," Raynar interrupted. "If you believe any of our transacting partners are not being honest with us, we wish to hear it."

"Actually, it isn't your partners," Luke said. "The Dark Nest has been the one taking the star ambers."

The Unu began to clack their mandibles, and Raynar lowered his melted brow. "The Neimoidian is a Joiner?"

"No," Luke said. "We think—"

"We *know*," Han corrected.

"It *looked* like the Neimoidian had a deal with Gorog," Luke compromised. "He was trading reactor fuel and hyperdrive coolant to them."

This drew a tumult of mandible clacking from Unu.

"Perhaps we were mistaken about the nature of the material," C-3PO suggested quietly. "Unu seems quite amused by the idea that the Colony owns a reactor."

"They wouldn't know," Han insisted. "Who can say what Gorog is hiding?"

"Of course we would know, Captain Solo! The Colony learns from its mistakes." Raynar fell silent for a moment, then spoke in a calmer voice. "But we will discuss your idea while I show you our production facilities, if that will make you feel better."

He extended a hand toward the furnaces.

Luke and Han exchanged glances. Luke said, "It might be better to do that—"

"Come!" Raynar insisted. "What are you afraid of? Killiks do not have accidents."

Luke exhaled in frustration, but reluctantly nodded and led the others after Raynar toward the furnaces.

Their first stop was a large, semicircular basin. Dozens of huge-headed Saras were standing around the curved end on all sixes, spitting out long streams of sticky white fiber and using their mandibles to feed it into the tub. On the other side of the basin, a steady procession of workers was gathering up large bundles of the dried fiber and carrying it off toward the furnaces.

"This is the materials pit," Raynar explained. He pointed at the spitting Killiks. "Saras's spinners produce the raw spin, and the workers take it to the furnaces to be melted down."

"Yeah, real interesting," Han said. "But about that reactor—have you actually *been* to Gorog's nest?"

Raynar's reply was curt. "Of course not. Gorog keeps its nest secret."

"Then you really can't know whether they have a reactor, can you?" Luke asked, picking up on Han's line of thought. "And it's probably a pretty big one, too, judging by how much fuel the Neimoidian had with him."

An uneasy murmur rolled through the Unu, then Raynar said, "If there was so much fuel, why didn't Saras find any when they captured the Neimoidian?"

"Because the fuel went the same place as our landspeeder and the 'Moid's guards," Han said. "The Fizz took it."

"And that's something we should discuss *now*." Luke's throat was aching from all the smoke and soot in the air; even without the Fizz, he would not have wanted to stay inside the building long enough for a complete tour. "The Fizz didn't just bubble up when those fuel rods happened to be there. It was *attacking* them."

Unu's drumming grew more agitated.

"Now they don't believe there ever was any fuel," C-3PO reported. "They're accusing us of making up the whole story."

Han rolled his eyes. "I knew this would happen." He turned to Raynar. "Look, it's been a long couple of days. If you don't want to listen—"

"Hold on, Han," Luke said. "We have evidence."

Han frowned. "We do?"

Luke nodded. "Probably." He turned to R2-D2. "Artoo, do you have a record of what happened in the forest?"

R2-D2 whistled a cheerful affirmative and began to project a hologram of the incident. The quality was not as good as what came out of a dedicated holopad, of course, but it was more than adequate to show the blue-black forms of several Gorog sneaking down a slope of hamogoni stumps. C-3PO's voice came from R2-D2's acoustic signaler, warning Luke and Han about the sneak attack. A pair of Gorog turned toward the holocam, and the scene grew confused as the battle played out.

A few moments later, it showed the Neimoidian smuggler fleeing his hoversled, while his Aqualish bodyguards remained behind, kneeling behind the barrels in the cargo bed and trading fire with Han and Luke. When one of the barrels suddenly rose and crashed back down, spilling its cargo, a murmur of surprise raced through the Unu entourage. R2-D2 added to the excitement by displaying a set of ionic-decay readings that left no doubt about the nature of the rods.

By the time the froth began to consume the rods a few minutes later, a stunned silence had fallen over Raynar and Unu. Luke waited until the Fizz had engulfed the hoversled, its cargo, and the Aqualish guards, then had R2-D2 shut down his holoprojector.

Raynar remained silent a long time, and even the cacophony inside the replica facility grew subdued. A stream of orange slag began to shoot out of one furnace and disappear down a waste tube through the floor, and Han groaned and made a winding motion with his finger.

Luke signaled him to be patient. The froth had appeared very quickly after the reactor rods were exposed in the forest, but slag was not nearly as toxic as reactor rods—or even hyperdrive coolant. It would take a lot more slag to trigger the Fizz. So Luke hoped, anyway.

Finally, Raynar raised his gaze. "We thank you for bringing this to our attention."

"Friends *should* be willing to tell each other difficult truths," Luke said, feeling encouraged by Raynar's reasonable tone. "It's only a theory at this point. But if we're right, the Fizz is going to keep attacking Saras."

The pronouncement sent a peal of nervous drumming through Unu. Raynar's eyes seemed to sink even deeper into their dark sockets, but he said, "Theory or not, we are listening."

"Good." Luke glanced down at R2-D2. "Start the holo where we left off."

The droid reactivated his holoprojector. Unu crowded closer, the insects in back climbing onto the shoulders of those in front, and within moments they were towering over Luke and his companions in a great, teeming mass. Luke squatted down beside the holo and shifted the X-wing replica to one hand.

"Look how the Fizz is attacking the hoversled and the fuel, but not the hamogoni trunk." He inserted his finger into the holo, pointing out the features as he named them, then moved to the stone foundation, where the Aqualish had collapsed. "The same here. It's attacking the bodyguards, but not the stones they're on."

A low, chattery rustle rose from Unu, and Raynar asked, "Are you saying that the Fizz does not attack anything native to Woteba?"

"Not quite," Luke said. R2-D2 continued to run the holorecording, and the hoversled and Aqualish began to disintegrate beneath the Fizz. "I'm saying it only attacks things that harm Woteba."

"And you think that is why the Fizz attacks us?" Raynar clarified. "Because we harm Woteba?"

"I think it attacks you *when* you harm Woteba," Luke corrected. "As long as you aren't hurting the environment, it remains inert."

The last bits of the hoversled and the Aqualish vanished. The froth quickly subsided, leaving only piles of brown dirt behind, and the forest in the holorecording returned to stillness.

R2-D2 shut down his projector, and when Raynar and Unu *still* remained silent, Han couldn't take it anymore.

"Well, that's our theory, anyway," he said. "There might be others that are just as good."

This brought Raynar out of his silence. "It is not a bad theory," he said. "It fits with what we have seen ourselves."

Luke felt like an immense weight had been lifted off his shoulders. He allowed himself a moment of self-congratulation—then a soft shudder, so faint it was barely perceptible, ran through Unu.

"Sometimes, Master Skywalker, we forget how clever you are." Raynar raised his hand and shook the stump of a gloved index finger toward Luke. "But not today."

"I don't understand," Luke said. Alarmed by Raynar's sudden hostility, he quieted himself inside and began to concentrate on the Force itself, on its liquid grasp, on its ripples lapping him from all sides. "You saw Artoo-Detoo's holo."

"We will not let you say we brought this on ourselves," Raynar said. "We *know* who is responsible."

"Not the Jedi," Luke said. It wasn't easy to match all the different ripples in the Force to an individual source—not with Saras and Unu obscuring the picture with their own hazy presences. "I promise you that."

The Unu mass began to disassemble itself and drop to the floor.

"Uh, maybe we should just forget the tour." Han began to ease toward the exit. "Thanks for the ship models. Really."

But Luke was not ready to give up. A familiar prickling had begun to rise between his shoulder blades, and he knew the Dark Nest was watching from the shadows, quietly reaching out to Raynar, carefully distorting the facts to put the Jedi in a bad light. Luke did not fight back. Instead he accepted his growing feeling of unease, allowing it to build into a chill along his entire spine, until the feeling had grown strong enough for him to have some sense of its source.

When Luke did not follow Han toward the exit, Han took his arm and began to pull. Raynar's eyes barely narrowed, but the Unu immediately moved to cut off their escape, mandibles spread.

"Uh, Luke?" Han said. "If you're going into a trance or something, now isn't the time. Really."

"Don't worry. Everything's under control." Luke passed the X-wing replica to Han, then pulled free and turned toward the nearest furnace, where there was a bantha-sized mound of dried spin he did not remember seeing a few moments before. "Just keep Raynar busy a second."

"Sure," Han said. "I'll let him explode my brain or something."

Luke used the Force to open a path through the Unu and started toward the heap. His entire back began to nettle with danger sense; then Han's voice rose behind him.

"You know what I don't get? The *pilot*. How do you get that kind of detail inside—"

"Out of my way!" Raynar roared.

But that was all the time Luke needed to pull his light-saber off his belt. He gathered himself for a Force leap . . . and that was when Alema Rar emerged from behind the spin mound, dressed in a midnight-blue jumpsuit with a plunging neckline and side slits.

"We are very impressed, Master Skywalker." Her lip curled into a smile that came off as more of a sneer. "But you won't need your lightsaber. We are not here to harm you."

"Is that so?" Luke deactivated his lightsaber—and allowed himself a small smile of triumph. Given the revulsion Raynar had shown on Kr when he saw the Dark Nest's slave-eating larvae, Luke felt certain that exposing the Dark Nest's presence now would redirect Raynar's hostility to where it belonged. "Then why were you hiding?"

"How could we have been hiding? We only just arrived." Alema started forward. "It came to our attention that we needed to correct a misunderstanding about what you saw in the forest."

"No misunderstanding," Han said. "We know what we saw."

"Do you?"

Alema slipped past Han without a second glance and continued toward Raynar. Luke tried to follow, but it was slow going. The mass of Unu seemed to part to let the Twi'lek pass, then crowd in behind her to gather in Luke's way.

"The rods *were* fuel rods, nobody is arguing that." Alema kept her gaze fixed on Raynar. "But maybe it was the *Jedi* who brought them to Woteba. Maybe Gorog discovered what you were doing and was there to intercept the reactor fuel."

"What?" Han cried. "That's backward. And a lie!"

Unu erupted into a tumult of clacking mandibles and booming thoraxes, and C-3PO reported, "Now Unu is saying *we* must have brought the rods!"

"That's ridiculous." Luke spoke in a calm voice, addressing Raynar directly, confident that Raynar's revulsion toward the Dark Nest would soon show itself. "Why would the Jedi bring reactor fuel to Woteba?"

Alema stopped two meters from Raynar. "Perhaps because you

know more about the Fizz than you're saying." Though her words were addressed to Luke, her gaze remained fixed on Raynar. "Perhaps the Jedi knew it would trigger the Fizz. Perhaps that is why they sent reactor fuel to *all* of the Utegetu worlds."

"Wait a minute!" Han gasped. "You're saying *all* the Utegetu worlds have problems with Fizz?"

"Yes." Raynar's tone was bitter. "All the worlds you traded to us are poisoned."

"I'm sorry to hear that," Luke said, finally coming up behind Alema. "But the Jedi didn't know—and we *didn't* send reactor fuel to any of the worlds. We have no reason to wish the Colony harm."

"You serve the Galactic Alliance, do you not?" Raynar asked. "And the Alliance feels threatened by our rise."

"How do you figure?" Han scoffed. "Because you're harboring a few pirates and running some black membrosia? That's O-class stuff. If you were inside Alliance territory, you'd barely be a crime syndicate."

Raynar's face began to twitch beneath its scars, and it grew clear that he was not going to turn on Alema—at least not without some nudging.

"UnuThul, Han is right," Luke said. "The Galactic Alliance would like the Colony to be a good neighbor, but it is *not* afraid of you. The Dark Nest has been using your own fear to deceive you."

Given the Killiks' fluid sense of truth and fact, Luke knew his argument would be a difficult one to make—but the alternative was to ignite his lightsaber and cut a path back to the spaceport.

"Perhaps you are the one who is being deceived, Master Skywalker," Alema said. She turned to look at him, her eyes now smoky and dark and as deep as black holes. "Perhaps Chief Omas and Commander Sovv haven't told you just how afraid of us they really are . . . and perhaps *they* are not the only ones deceiving you."

Luke tried to puzzle out the Twi'lek's implication, then gave up and frowned at her. "What's that supposed to mean?"

As soon as Luke asked the question, he began to feel smoky and raw inside, and a cloudiness came to the edges of his vision.

"Have you given any more thought to why Mara lied to you about Daxar Ies?" Alema asked.

"No," Luke said. "And I doubt Mara did lie."

But even as he said it, Luke began to see why Mara could have been reluctant to tell him. She knew how much learning more about his mother meant to him, and being the one who had deprived him of that opportunity would have weighed heavily on her conscience. She might even have found the prospect to be more than she could bear.

Alema stepped closer, then spoke in a coldly alluring voice. "Of course, we hope that you're right, Master Skywalker, but, for everyone's sake, it's important that you consider the possibility that you're wrong—that you're being deceived by those close to you."

"There *is* no possibility," Han growled.

"Then no harm will come of considering it." Alema kept her gaze fixed on Luke, and the cloudiness at the edges of his vision began to darken. "But Master Skywalker must make up his own mind. That is why we have decided to give him the next code."

R2-D2 gave a little squeal of protest, and Luke said, "I don't want it."

Alema's voice grew sultry and knowing. "Now who are you deceiving, Master Skywalker? It is not us." She turned to C-3PO. "Remember this sequence. Master Skywalker will want it later."

She started to rattle off a string of numbers and letters, but Han pushed in front of her.

"All right, that's enough," Han said. "He said he didn't—"

"It's okay." Luke pulled him away. "Alema's right."

Han turned to face him. "You're sure?"

Luke nodded. "A code sequence isn't going to hurt us."

He knew, of course, that the sequence *would* hurt him; the Gorog's Night Herald would not be giving it to him otherwise. But Luke wanted the code anyway, not because he believed anything he might learn from R2-D2's files could change his love for Mara, or even because the smoke inside him was growing darker and harsher and harder to ignore every moment. He wanted the code because it had frightened him—and if he allowed himself to be afraid of what he did not know, then the Dark Nest had already won.

After giving the rest of the code sequence to C-3PO, Alema turned to Luke.

"You are as brave as we recall, Master Skywalker." The Twi'lek sent a cold shiver through Luke by trailing a finger down his arm, then added, "We don't know what Mara is trying to hide from you, but we hope it has nothing to do with your mother's death. It would be very sad if Daxar Ies was not her only victim."

The suggestion rocked Luke as hard as she intended, leaving him stunned, his mind clouded by the acrid smoke that had been rising inside since he had given her that first opening.

Not so with Han.

"What?" he roared. In a move so fast that even Luke barely saw it, Han pulled his blaster and leveled it at the Twi'lek's head. "Now you've just gone too far."

Alema calmly turned to look down the barrel. "Come, Han." She flicked her finger in the air, using the Force to send the barrel of Han's blaster jerking toward the ceiling. "If you were going to pull the trigger, you wouldn't have wasted your one chance talking about it."

She turned her back on Han, then went over to Raynar, rose up on her toes, and kissed his scar-stiffened lips.

"We'll see you in our dreams." She remained there for a moment, then dropped back down and looked toward Luke and Han. "And keep a closer watch on these two. We can't have them stirring up any more Fizz with those reactor rods."

Raynar spent a moment studying Luke and Han over Alema's head, then nodded and released her hand without looking at her. She slipped past and moved off through the mass of Unu, and though Luke was careful never to take his eyes off her, he somehow missed the moment when she vanished from sight.

Once Alema was gone, Raynar said, "We have decided to keep a closer watch on you two. We cannot have you two stirring up any more Fizz with your reactor rods."

"You don't say?" Han's tone was sarcastic. "Does she tell you when to sanibrush your teeth and use the refresher, too?"

"She?" Raynar lowered his brow. "She *who*?"

"Alema Rar," Luke prompted. "The Night Herald?"

Raynar frowned, and Unu drummed their thoraxes.

"The Killiks seem to have no idea who you're talking about," C-3PO informed them. "Unu claims it has never met Alema Rar."

"*Burrurruru ubburr,*" one of the insects added. "*Uuubu burru.*"

"And everyone knows the Night Herald is just a myth you tell the larvae," C-3PO translated, "to make them regurgitate."

Han scowled and pointed his blaster at the ground in front of Raynar. "That myth was just standing there kissing you."

"Had we *ever* kissed Alema Rar, we are sure we would remember," Raynar retorted. "And we certainly were not *just* kissing her. Alema Rar is dead."

"Don't tell me," Han said. "She died in the Crash."

"Of course not," Raynar said. "She died at Kr, with the rest of the Dark Nest."

"Just great." Han let his chin drop. "Here we go again."

"We do not understand why you persist in this fantasy, but you are not going anywhere. That is the point." Raynar extended his hand. "You will give us your weapons."

Han's knuckles whitened around his blaster grip. "When Hutts ride swoops!"

"We would rather have it now," Raynar said. Han's blaster twisted free of his grasp and floated over, then Raynar turned to Luke. "Master Skywalker?"

Luke hated to yield his weapon—especially with Alema Rar running around loose—but he would have an easier time recovering it later than fighting to keep it now. He removed the focusing crystal from the handle—the Jedi equivalent of unloading a weapon before surrendering it—and handed both the crystal and the lightsaber over.

"A wise choice," Raynar said. A swarm of large, orange-chested worker insects began to gather around Luke and Han. "Saras will see you to your new quarters. Please do not force us to harm you by attempting to leave before Princess Leia returns with a way to stop the Fizz."

TEN

In the middle of the Murgo Choke hung the white wedge of an *Imperial*-class Star Destroyer, its hull lit by the harlequin blaze of four different suns. To its left hung two of the suns, an orange and yellow binary system well matched in both size and color. To its right hung an odd couple, a blue giant orbited by a crimson dwarf so small and dim Leia could barely tell it was there. And directly behind the Star Destroyer, stretched between the two sets of binary stars like the web of some enormous spider, was the sapphire veil of the Utegetu Nebula.

"You see? This one did not miscalculate!" Saba was perched on the edge of the *Falcon*'s copilot's chair, squinting out at the Star Destroyer. "We were *pulled* out of hyperspace."

"Maybe," Leia said. Threading its way between the two pairs of binary stars, the Murgo Choke was the trickiest of the many complicated hyperspace transits connecting the Rago Run to the Utegetu Nebula. "But there are a hundred things in the Choke more likely to revert us than the mass of a single Star Destroyer."

Saba hissed in annoyance. "The Star Destroyer'z *masz* did not pull us out—itz artificial gravity generatorz did. That is the *Mon Mothma* ahead."

Leia frowned at her tactical display, but the electromagnetic blast of the four stars was overpowering all the *Falcon*'s sensor and comm systems. She saw only a cloud of static on the screen.

"You can't know that," Leia said.

"This one findz your lack of faith disturbing, Jedi Solo." Saba ruffled her neck scales in what Leia had come to recognize as disappointment. "You must learn not to doubt your Master."

"You keep telling me to doubt everything," Leia pointed out.

"And do you listen?" Saba held her hand out. "You are a terrible student. Give me your lightsaber."

Leia shook her head. "The last time I did that, you hit me on the head with it. I had a knot for a week."

Saba's voice grew harsh. "So you are disobeying?"

Leia frowned. Saba kept saying that she needed to learn to obey—but Leia was not about to make the same mistake twice. She held out her own hand.

"First, give me *your* lightsaber."

Saba's eyes widened, then she began to siss. "You are so funny, Jedi Solo." She lowered her hand. "But at least you have learned *something*."

"Thanks," Leia said. "Now, how sure are you that's the *Mon Mothma* up there?"

"How sure are you that it is *not*?"

"This is no time for games, Master. I need to know."

"*Life* is a game, Jedi Solo," Saba said. "If you need to know, find out."

Leia let out her breath in exasperation, then reached into the Force. She felt Mara and three more Jedi StealthX pilots hanging off the *Falcon*'s stern. Because of the close tolerances involved in transiting the Choke, all five craft had needed to make their own jump calculations, and the likelihood of the entire flight making a mistake that brought them out so close together was practically nil. They had definitely been pulled out of hyperspace by an artificial gravity well.

But that still did not explain how Saba knew it was the *Mon Mothma* ahead. The Galactic Alliance had two *Imperial*-class Star Destroyers equipped with hidden gravity-well generators. Leia stretched out to the ship in the Force and felt the expected throng of life, but the concentration was too dense for her to recognize the presence of anyone in particular.

"Okay, we were interdicted," Leia said. "But I still don't see how you can be sure it's the *Mothma* up there. It could be the *Elegos A'Kla*."

"It is the *Mon Mothma*," Saba insisted. "But what does it matter?"

"It doesn't, really," Leia said. "Nobody in the Defense Force is going to interfere with a Jedi mission, but the *Mothma*'s commander, Gavin Darklighter, is an old family friend. He won't waste too much of our time."

"It would not be wise to place your trust in friendship, Jedi

Solo," Saba warned. "Chief Omas tried to keep the fleet'z departure from us, and now this. Commander Darklighter will have orderz."

"Probably," Leia said. "But you don't know Gavin Darklighter. He always finds a way to do the right thing."

She touched Mara and the other StealthX pilots in the Force, alerting them that she was about to get under way, then activated the *Falcon*'s sublight drives and started forward. The Star Destroyer quickly began to swell in the viewport, and the comm signals and sensor returns soon grew strong enough for the electronic scrubbers to clarify. Finally, the *Mon Mothma*'s transponder code appeared on the tactical display, surrounded by a large cloud of symbols denoting war-era XJ3 X-wings and Series 4 E-wings.

A comm officer's voice crackled over the cockpit speaker, so raw and scratchy that it was impossible to recognize the owner's species. *"Millennium Falcon,* be advised that the Utegetu Nebula is under blockade. Please reverse course."

"Blockade?" Leia made herself sound more surprised than she really was. "Under whose authority?"

"The Galactic Alliance's, obviously," the comm officer replied. "I ask again, please reverse course. All vessels attempting to enter or leave the nebula will be impounded."

Leia's blood started to boil. *"You* be advised that the *Falcon* is on a Jedi mission."

She began to angle ahead of the *Mothma*'s bow. The tactical display, still smudged with blank streaks and small patches of static, showed a squadron of XJ3s moving to intercept the *Falcon.*

Leia frowned, then said to the comm officer, "I trust you've been in the Defense Force long enough to understand the grief you'll face if you interfere with us."

"I know the consequences of ignoring my orders," the officer said. "This is your last warning. Continue to advance, and the *Falcon* will be impounded."

The Force grew electric with the outrage and surprise of Mara and the other StealthX pilots, but Saba was more contemplative. She flicked the air absentmindedly with her forked tongue, then activated her own microphone.

"We will consider your threat," she said. "Stand by."

"Stand by?" the officer echoed. "That is not—"

Saba closed the channel, then turned to Leia. "We should reverse course."

"And leave Han and Luke stranded on Woteba?" Leia asked. "Never!"

"Having no ship and being stranded are different thingz," Saba replied. "Master Skywalker is . . . he is *Master Skywalker*. He can find a way off Woteba anytime he wishez."

"But he *won't*," Leia objected. "He's waiting for us to return with a cure for the Fizz—and in the meantime, the Colony is provoking the Chiss again. We need to get him and Han off Woteba before a war breaks out."

Mara began to pour impatience into the Force, urging Leia and Saba to start their run.

Leia looked over at Saba.

Saba shook her head. "Not through the Murgo Choke. We cannot take a Star Destroyer."

"Take it?" Leia asked. "You think we're going to *attack* the *Mon Mothma*?"

"You know another way through the Choke?" Saba asked.

"Sure," Leia said. "We call their bluff."

Leia reached out to initiate the Jedi battle-meld and discovered that Mara and the other pilots had already opened it. Clearly in agreement with Leia, Mara was radiating confidence, reassuring them that the StealthXs were ready to drop in behind the XJ3s. Saba let out a hiss of resignation, then began rerouting extra power to the shields.

Leia reopened the comm channel to the *Mon Mothma*.

Before she could speak, the comm officer's angry voice came over the cockpit speakers. "*Falcon*, we have finished warning you. Slow and stand by for escort."

"Negative," Leia said. "Let me speak to Commodore Darklighter."

"Commodore Darklighter is unavailable," the officer replied.

Saba made a hissing sound deep in her throat, and Leia saw on her display that the XJ3 squadron had moved into firing position behind the *Falcon*.

"Kill your drives and stand by," the comm officer ordered, "or we *will* open fire."

Leia rolled her eyes. "You're not going to fire on the *Millennium Falcon* without Commodore Darklighter looking over your shoulder. Put him on *now*, or stand down and let us proceed with our mission."

Lock-alarms chimed in the cockpit as the XJ3s designated the *Falcon* a target. Leia could not believe that this would actually come down to being fired upon, but she began to juke and jink like a fighter pilot. It never hurt to be careful.

"You are certain they are bluffing?" Saba asked quietly.

"Nearly certain." Leia silenced the lock-alarms, and they quickly reactivated. The XJ3-wing pilots were selecting and deselecting the *Falcon*, repeatedly triggering the alarms in an effort to wear on the crew's nerves. "Almost, even."

A sense of satisfaction came to the battle-meld; Mara and the other StealthX pilots had slipped in behind the XJ3s without being noticed.

Saba switched her microphone to the ship's intercom. "Cakhmaim, Meewalh, shut down those quad cannonz."

"Good idea," Leia said. "The last thing we want is a shooting match with the *Mon Mothma*. It would only make Chief Omas believe that the Jedi have gone completely over to the Colony's side."

Saba gave her a sideways glance. "That, too."

Leia sensed through the meld that the Barabel's concern had been more immediate: they were not going to be much use to Han and Luke if they got blasted to atoms here.

"I find your lack of faith disturbing, Master," Leia said. "You must learn to trust your pilot."

Saba made a rasping sound low in her throat. "The pilot, this one trustz. It is her arrogant student that worriez her."

Leia laughed, then activated the intercom again. "Cakhmaim and Meewalh, when you're done in the turrets, go to engineering and power up Han's repulsor beam."

Saba raised her brow. "We are going to *push* the *Mothma* out of the way?"

"Hardly," Leia said. The repulsor beam was a special anti-dartship device Han had developed the year before by rigging the *Falcon*'s tractor beam so the polarity could be reversed. "But we may need to swat a few flitnats off our tail."

Leia reset the lock-alarms for what must have been the tenth time, and they did not reactivate. The XJ3s had stopped flicking their target selectors.

The meld began to fill with reptilian battle lust. "If this is a bluff, they are raising the stakez," Saba said. "It feelz to this one like they are about to open—"

Before Saba could say *fire*, eight of the XJ3s—four two-ship combat teams—broke into evasive loops and spirals, and the *Falcon*'s military comm scanner came alive with the alarmed voices of XJ3 pilots.

"Targeted! Targeted! . . . breaking right . . . breaking left . . . where are they? . . . still on me . . . can't shake him . . . find 'em, *find them!*"

Then a deep female voice announced, "StealthXs! We have StealthXs out here!"

Leia pushed the throttles past their safety stops, still angling ahead of the *Mon Mothma*'s bow. The tactical display showed the remainder of the XJ3s—the four craft that had been guarding the squadron's flanks—sliding into firing position and slowly closing to range.

Leia told the Noghri to activate the repulsor beam and dust two of the remaining starfighters off their tail.

"Only two?" Saba asked. "Why?"

"Just sending a message," Leia said. "Besides, we may need those XJs later."

The cabin lights dimmed, and the status displays winked out as every spare erg of the *Falcon*'s power was diverted to the repulsor beam. But unlike the first time they had used the device, the shields did not go down. When Han had decided that the repulsor beam was too handy to dismantle, Leia had insisted that they install a supplemental fusion unit so they wouldn't be quite so vulnerable to counterattack.

The *Falcon* gave a little jolt as the Noghri triggered the repulsor beam. Two of the XJ3s suddenly went out of control and veered toward the edge of the tactical display, and the comm scanner erupted into startled curses and a tense request for permission to open fire.

Gavin Darklighter's voice came over the comm an instant later. "Captain Solo, will you *please* stop kriffing around? Chief Omas is serious about this blockade."

Leia continued to accelerate, still jinking and juking. "Is that why he didn't inform the Jedi about it?"

Darklighter hesitated, and the *Falcon*'s lock-alarms whined again. Leia checked the tactical display and saw that the last pair of XJ3s had reached firing range. The rest of the squadron was still rolling and looping, either trying to recover from the repulsor beam or shake the StealthXs still threatening them with target-locks. Thankfully, there was no shooting.

"I apologize for the language, Princess," Darklighter finally said. "I was addressing Captain Solo."

"Han is unavailable," Leia replied. "I'm in command of the *Falcon* for now."

The channel fell silent for a long time, and Leia began to wonder if Darklighter had deliberately manipulated the admission out of her. He was a shrewd commander, and he would be analyzing even the tiniest scrap of information for hints as to the true nature of their mission. Normally, it would not have troubled Leia to share such information with a high-ranking Defense Force officer. But right now, the last thing she wanted was for anyone subordinate to the Chief of State to realize there was a power vacuum at the top of the Jedi order.

They passed in front of the *Mon Mothma*'s bow. The last pair of XJ3s remained on their tail, but Darklighter sent none of the other squadrons to cut off the *Falcon*—and that made Leia nervous.

"Keep an eye on the *Mothma*'s tractor beams," she said to Saba. "Let me know the instant any of them start to power—"

Leia felt a surge of alarm from Saba and knew the Star Destroyer was activating its tractor beams. She accelerated into an open, erratic spiral that would make it almost impossible for the beam operators to lock on to the *Falcon*.

The red cones of four tractor beams appeared on the tactical display, stabbing out from the *Mon Mothma*'s designator symbol to circle the *Falcon*. Leia aimed for the trailing edges of the beams, rolling and diving from one to the next, alert for the telltale hesitation that Han claimed always gave the operators away when they figured out the strategy.

An instant after the tractor beams appeared, Darklighter said, "I didn't . . . any offense, Princess." With the comm antenna constantly struggling to adjust to the *Falcon*'s gyrations, the signal had grown a little patchy. "Chief Omas has been . . . to reach Master Skywalker for a week. When there was no response, he decided the Jedi must be . . . the Killiks' side again."

Saba hissed, and Leia felt the same frustration rising in Mara and the other StealthX pilots that was welling up in her. She started to make a sharp reply—then realized what Darklighter was trying to do and remained silent.

"He is trying to provoke you," Saba agreed. She closed the channel, then set the comm unit to burst mode to prevent the *Mon Mothma*'s tractor beam operators from riding a comm wave back to the *Falcon*. "Do you still believe Commodore Darklighter is bluffing?"

"If he weren't, he'd be shooting by now," Leia said. She opened the channel to Darklighter again. "Nice try, Commodore. But if Chief Omas is claiming that the Jedi have betrayed the Galactic Alliance just because he can't reach Luke—"

"What's . . . supposed to assume?" Darklighter interrupted. "And now . . . only proving him right. Kill your drives or . . . open fire."

Leia hesitated. Darklighter was really raising the stakes this time.

If she refused to obey, he would either have to make good on his threat, or admit that it was a bluff. She reached into the battle-meld, urging Mara and the others to keep their fingers away from their triggers, then took a deep breath and activated her microphone again.

"I guess you'll have to open fire, Gavin. This is too important."

A long silence followed in which even the comm crackles seemed to be growing sharper. Leia angled back toward the center of the Choke, placing the last pair of XJ3s between her and the *Mon Mothma,* and the Star Destroyer's tractor beams flickered off. She felt a flash of approval from Mara and the StealthX pilots, then Darklighter's voice came over the comm again.

"Blast it, Princess! I'm not bluffing."

"Neither am I," Leia returned. Now that she was past the *Mon Mothma* and heading straight toward the blue curtain of the Utegetu Nebula, she was happy to keep talking. Every second carried her farther down the narrow alley between the two sets of binaries, closer to making that final jump to Utegetu. "Gavin, you know Luke. He would never betray the Galactic—"

"Nice try, Princess," Darklighter said. As the *Falcon* drew away from the *Mon Mothma,* the comm antenna was able to stay focused in one direction, and the signal grew stable again. "I won't let you stall your way out of this. You have ten seconds to kill your drives."

Leia glanced over at Saba. The Barabel was already on the intercom, warning the Noghri to be ready with the repulsor beam again.

"This is about Luke and Han, isn't it?" Darklighter asked. "They're still on Woteba. That's why Chief Omas can't reach Master Skywalker."

Apprehension filled the battle-meld. Darklighter's conjecture had been made over an open fleet channel, so there could be no doubt that it would be on Chief Omas's desk by this time tomorrow. Returning Luke to Alliance space had just become a bureaucratic race against Chief Omas.

"Commodore Darklighter, can we go to secure channel?" Leia asked. "In private?"

"I'm sorry, no." Darklighter's tone was sincere. "This is a matter of record. You have five seconds to kill your drives, Princess."

"Thank you for the warning, Commodore," Leia said. "No hard feelings."

Darklighter's voice grew genuinely alarmed. "Leia! I can't protect—"

Leia closed the channel, then slipped the *Falcon* out of her spiral pattern and returned to jinking and juking. It was just as hard for starfighter cannons to target, and she would make a lot more forward progress.

"Jedi Solo?" Saba asked. "What did Commodore Darklighter mean when he said this was a matter of record?"

"Just that he can't help us, I think," Leia said. "Admiral Bwua'tu must be aboard."

"*Nek* Bwua'tu?" Saba growled. "The Bothan who beatz the Thrawn simulator?"

"He *is* in command of the Fifth Fleet," Leia said. "But it doesn't matter. They're bluffing."

"And if they are not?"

"They *are*," Leia said. "And, anyway, there's a big difference between simbattle and the real thing. Don't worry."

"This one is curiouz, not worried." Saba's tone was even, but her irritation was pouring into the battle-meld. "She is *never* worried."

"Right—sorry."

The lock-alarms chimed, and the shield display flared yellow as they took an aft-port laser cannon hit.

"Still bluffing?" Saba asked.

"Yes, Master," Leia said. "We're still in one piece, aren't we?"

An instant later the *Falcon* gave a little jolt as the Noghri activated the repulsor beam, and a string of curses came over the comm scanner as the last pair of XJ3s tumbled away out of control. The battle-meld grew still and electric; the relationship between the Jedi and the Galactic Alliance had just changed in a way no one could foresee.

Leia checked the tactical display. The *Mon Mothma* was bleeding more squadrons into the Choke, while those that had been on-station were moving into screening formations in front of the StealthXs' last-known position. No one was coming after Leia and Saba, but the combat controllers were being careful to leave a clear firing lane between the Star Destroyer and the *Falcon*.

Mara reached out through the battle-meld, urging Leia and Saba to run for it. The StealthXs would have to hang back and sneak through later. They would rendezvous at Woteba.

Leia wished her good luck, then the canopy's blasttinting went black as the first turbolaser strike blossomed ahead. Her shoulders hit the crash webbing as the *Falcon* bucked through the shock wave, then space around them erupted into exploding clouds of color as the gunnery crews began to refine their targeting.

"Jedi So-o-lo!" Saba's voice jumped as each shock wave shook the *Falcon*. "Next time, you wi-ill listen to your Master!"

"Trust me!" Leia said. "They're just trying to make us believe they're serious."

"They are doing a good job," Saba said.

Leia swung the *Falcon* toward the blue giant. "We'll run for the big guy. The EM blast will interfere with their targeting sensors, and the gravity well will give us some acceleration."

Saba nodded her approval. "Go-od! You have done this before."

"Only forty or fi-if-ty times." Silently, Leia added, *Just never without Han.*

The ride smoothed out for a moment as the *Falcon* slipped out from under the Star Destroyer's firing pattern. The canopy tinting went black as the face of the giant sun slid across the forward viewport, and still its boiling mass shined through the transparisteel, warming their faces and stabbing at their eyes. Their sensors and comm units quickly fell victim to the star's electromagnetic blast, and even the ship's internal electronics began to flicker and wave.

Then the *Mon Mothma*'s gunnery crews found them again. A curtain of a turbolaser strikes erupted ahead, circles of red and orange so pale against the star's glare that they were barely visible. Leia pointed the *Falcon* at the closest blossom and surrendered her hands to the Force. The shields crackled with crimson energy as they passed through the dissipation turbulence, then the *Falcon* shuddered as they bounced through the shock waves.

The pilot's console lit up with damage indicators and critical warnings. There were broken seals, leaking ducts, misaligned gyros.

"Will you look at that?" Leia complained. "Han's going to kill me!"

Another blast bounced them sideways, and Saba said, "This one only hopez we last long enough to give him the chance."

Judging they had descended about as deep into the star's gravity well as they dared, Leia pulled up and started around the curve of its massive blue horizon. The *Mon Mothma* continued to pour turbolaser fire in their general direction, but the electromagnetic camouflage had finally confused their targeting sensors, and none of the strikes hit closer than within a kilometer or two of the *Falcon*.

The turbolaser strikes soon faded altogether, and Leia knew they had rounded the horizon and vanished from the *Mon Mothma*'s line of sight. She rolled the cockpit away from the blue giant and started to pull out of its gravity well.

The canopy grew clear enough that the red orb of the blue giant's tiny satellite star shined through the bottom of the forward viewport. The other binary set, the orange and yellow stars, were shining through top of the canopy, and the blue veil of the Utegetu Nebula was barely visible directly ahead.

Leia glanced down at her tactical display, silently urging the sensors to come online so they could plot their jump to Utegetu. There was no reason to be anxious—neither the *Mon Mothma* nor her fighters could catch the *Falcon* now—but something still felt wrong. She had a cold, queasy feeling in her stomach, and she could not escape the feeling that someone was watching.

"Saba, do you—"

"Yes," Saba said. "It feelz like we have raced into the shenbit'z den."

The nacelle temperatures were already 20 percent beyond specification, but Leia grabbed the throttles and began to push them even farther beyond the safety locks . . . and the *Falcon* decelerated as though it had hit a permacrete wall.

"What the—"

The last of Leia's exclamation was drowned out by the sudden screeching of proximity alarms and system alerts. The nacelle temperature shot past 140 and started toward 150, and the *Falcon* continued to decelerate.

Leia pulled the throttles back, then activated the intercom. "Cakhmaim, Meewalh, get into the cannon turrets and see—"

"Star Destroyer," Cakhmaim rasped. The *Falcon* began to slide sideways toward a point between the blue giant and its smaller satellite. "One of the new pirate hunters."

Leia used the attitude thrusters to spin the *Falcon* around, and saw that they were being drawn toward the distant wedge of a new version of the venerable *Victory*-class Star Destroyer. Mounted on its upper hull, in a turret nearly as large as the bridge itself, was one of the huge asteroid-tug tractor beams that Lando Calrissian had started selling the Defense Force to combat pirates and smugglers.

"Simbattle or not," Saba rasped, "this one thinkz maybe Admiral Bwua'tu *is* as good as they say."

ELEVEN

Han sat in his new quarters holding the model of the *Millennium Falcon* in his lap, running his thumbs over its silky surface, peering into the dark holes of the cockpit canopy, hefting its substantial weight in his hands. Sure, the workmanship was good, and there was something hypnotic about rubbing your fingers over the spinglass. But he could not imagine where the Squibs were going to sell a billion of these things. The stuff was hardly art—and with the galaxy still struggling to recover from the war against the Yuuzhan Vong, there were only so many people with credits to throw away on kitsch.

Someone was definitely being played here. But was the Colony playing the Squibs, or the Squibs playing the Colony, or both of them playing someone else?

Luke entered from his quarters, his eyes closed and his hands pressed to the iridescent spinglass, using the Force to search for a stress point in the exterior wall of their two-room prison. He did the same thing every hour or so, stopping in a different place and having R2-D2 use his utility arm to scratch a small x in the hard surface.

A few minutes later, they always heard a crew of Killiks scurrying over the same spot, reinforcing the outside of the wall with more spinglass. The barrier had to be close to a meter thick in places, but Han did not suggest that the xs were a waste of time. If Luke wanted to mess with Saras's mind, that was his business.

They both knew that Luke could break them out of their prison anytime he wanted—and Han suspected that Raynar knew it, too. Escape would be the easy part. But it would do them no good until they thought of a way to find the Dark Nest, and so Han and Luke were being patient—being patient and thinking hard and doing their best to look very bored.

Han flipped the model of the *Falcon* over again. There was no shift of weight inside, but that didn't mean anything. He had known a smuggler once who had molded his entire cargo of contraband explosives into landspeeder dashboards and walked them through Imperial customs with all the proper documentation.

Without opening his eyes, Luke said, "She's all right, Han."

"I know she is." Han put his ear close to the model and shook it, but heard nothing. "I still worry about her. It's not easy for her to be away from me this long."

"Is that so?"

"Yeah," Han said. "She has trouble sleeping if my snoring's not there to drown out the banging in the climate control lines."

Luke smiled. "Thanks for clearing that up." He returned to running his hand over the wall. "I've been wondering what she sees in you."

Though Han had not been dwelling on how much he missed Leia, he saw now that he had been thinking of her without realizing it—that he was *always* thinking of her, half expecting her to be there every time he turned around, imagining her voice in the distance whenever the tunnel-house fell silent, reaching out to her when he rolled over at night. And Luke had *known* all of that was going on in the back of Han's mind—just as Han knew that something similar was going on the back of Luke's.

Han spun around on his stool. "Did you just use a Jedi mind-reading trick on me?"

Luke stopped and looked puzzled. "We can't really do that, Han." he said. "Well, *most* of us can't."

Without having to ask, Han knew that Luke had been thinking of Jacen when he added that last bit. "I was afraid of that."

"Afraid of—" Luke stopped, then shook his head. "I don't think we're reading each other's minds, Han. We haven't been here long enough to become Joiners."

"Yeah? Then how come *I* know what you want for lunch today?"

"I don't see how Master Skywalker can be hungry already," C-3PO said from his place in the corner. "He just had breakfast."

"Threepio's right," Luke said. "It's too early to think about—"

"A nerfburger and hubba crisps," Han interrupted. "With a lurol smoothie to wash it down."

Luke furrowed his brow. "You're right, that *does* sound good. But I wasn't thinking about it until you . . . or was I?"

"It wasn't me," Han growled. "I hate hubba crisps."

Luke's face fell. "Raynar is trying to make Joiners of us."

"You think so?"

Luke was so upset that he failed to notice the sarcasm in Han's voice. "The Dark Nest must think the Colony will be able to dominate me and take control the Jedi order."

"Dominate *you*, Master Skywalker? Why, that's a perfectly absurd idea!" C-3PO cocked his head at the look of alarm on Luke's face. "Isn't it?"

Instead of answering, Luke went back to searching for stress points. "They've just been playing for time, Han. We've got to get out of here."

Han flipped the model over. "And do what?"

"You know what," Luke said. Find the Dark Nest.

Han remained on his stool. "How, exactly? The bugs know every move we make. The second we step outside our quarters, Saras is going to come running with about a thousand Killiks—and we don't have any weapons. We're better off just waiting until Leia and Mara get back."

Luke frowned. "Are you feeling all right, Han?"

"Fine," Han said. Actually, he was feeling great, now that he knew how they were going to find the Dark Nest, but he could not tell that to Luke. The walls had ears—well, *something* did. "Just in no mood to hear any ronto-brained escape plans."

He rose and went over to the door membrane. It was opaque and bonded shut by some gooey fiber the bugs had spun over the outside, but the spinglass surrounding it was so thin and translucent that Han could see the silhouette of their Saras guard standing watch outside.

He waved an arm to get the guard's attention. "Hey, open up! I need to talk to you."

The guard came over to the wall and pressed its orange thorax to the spinglass. A muffled thrum reverberated through the wall.

"Saras says she can hear you through the wall," C-3PO said, clunking over to translate. "And she is reluctant to open the door, since Master Skywalker was just talking about escaping."

Han shot an irritated look over his shoulder.

Luke shrugged. "It's not like they couldn't figure it out on their own."

"Yeah, okay." Han raised the *Falcon* model up. "Can you get in touch with the Squibs who are buying these?"

"*Mooroor oom.*" The bug's rumbling was so softened by the wall that the words seemed mumbled. "*Oomoor ooo.*"

"She seems to be saying that the Squibs aren't *purchasing* the line—they're handling it on consignment." C-3PO turned to Han. "I don't think that's wise. From what I recall, the Squibs we met on Tatooine weren't very trustworthy."

"*Ooorr?*" Saras demanded. "*Ooom?*"

"Don't worry," Han said, addressing the bug through the wall. "They won't pull anything on Raynar—"

"*OoomoMoom.*"

"Right, *UnuThul* has trading in his blood," Han said. "Besides, with the idea I've got, we're all going to make so much money the Squibs won't *want* to cheat you."

"I can't believe this, Han," Luke said, coming over to the door. "You're thinking about *money* at a time like this?"

"Yeah," Han said. When it came to money, Squibs could do the impossible. But he didn't say *that* aloud—he tried not to even think it.

Luke rolled his eyes, and Han scowled at him, hoping he would finally get the message. "Why don't you go input those code sequences Alema gave you or something?"

The anger that flashed in Luke's eyes suggested their minds were not all *that* connected. "That was low, Han, even for you."

"Sorry—didn't mean to rattle your cage," Han said. "Just let me make my deal. I'm trying to make the best of a bad situation here."

"Fine." Luke scowled at him, then stepped back shaking his head. "Don't let me stand in your way."

"When have I ever?" Han turned back to Saras. "Now, how long will it take you to get in touch with the Squibs?"

The bug drummed something short.

"She wants to know what your idea is," C-3PO said.

Han shook his head. "No way. I deal directly with the furbags on this."

"*Ooomoor.*"

The bug spread its four arms and began to back away from the wall.

"Okay, okay," Han said. "But if you steal the credit—"

"Han, will you just tell it?" There was a glint in Luke's eye that suggested he finally realized Han was up to something more useful than having R2-D2 scratch x's in the spinglass. "You're getting on my nerves."

Saras returned to the wall.

"All right—you're going to love this." Han held the model of the

Falcon up close to the wall. "You're going to produce a billion of these, right?"

Saras nodded.

"What if I signed some of them?" Han asked. "They'd be worth five times as much, and the publicity would help launch the entire line."

The bug was silent for a moment, then it clacked its mandibles and pointed at Luke. *"Moomor?"*

"She's inquiring whether Master Skywalker would also sign his models," C-3PO informed them.

"When Sarlaccs fly!" Luke said. "I'm a Jedi Master, not some cheap HoloNet personality."

"Sure, he'll sign," Han said. "If the price is right."

The bug thrummed something else.

"Oh, dear," C-3PO said. *"This* may be a deal killer."

"Let me decide that," Han said. "What is it?"

"Saras says you'd have to sign one percent of the production run," C-3PO said.

"No problem," Han replied.

"Ten *million* units, Han?" Luke asked. "That would take you the rest of your life."

"I *said* it's no problem," Han answered. Even if he were serious about the deal, he knew the Squibs were never going to *sell* ten million units. "Once we become Saras Joiners, anybody in the nest will be able to sign."

"Joiners?" Luke cried. "Han, that's not going—"

"Look, I'm as disgusted by the thought as you are," Han said. "But it's going to happen. We might as well take advantage of the situation."

"Moom!" the bug boomed.

It clacked its mandibles and began to back away from the wall, but Han shook his head and motioned it to the wall again.

"Not so fast, fella," he said. "I don't come cheap, you know."

"Could have fooled me," Luke muttered.

Saras stopped in the middle of the corridor that ran past their quarters. *"Oom morr?"*

Han shook his head. *"That,* I talk about with the Squibs." He backed away from the wall. "If they're interested, tell them to come see me."

The bug gave a noncommittal throb and retreated to the other side of the corridor.

Han returned to his stool, and Luke came and sat on the bunk next to him.

"You really think your autograph is worth that much?" Luke asked.

He held Han's eye a little longer than was necessary, and Han *thought* he could sense something more in the question.

"A million credits, at least," Han said. He passed the *Falcon* model to Luke, casually flipping it belly-up as he did so. "And *your* signature would go double that. Maybe triple."

"Triple?" Luke looked genuinely flattered. "Really?"

"At least," Han said. He had always been a little too repulsed to ask Jaina and Zekk much about how things had progressed when they started to become Joiners, but just in case Saras was starting to share his mind, too, he tried to keep his thoughts away from what he really intended to ask of the Squibs. "With all the 'Net the Jedi are getting regarding the Reconstruction, you're going to be as hot as a blue star right now."

"In that case, maybe I *should* consider it," Luke said. He casually flipped the model back over, and Han thought he felt a little jolt of surprise in the back of his mind—or maybe that was just wishful thinking. "But first, I think I'll take your other advice."

Han frowned. "My other advice?"

"About the code sequence Alema gave me," Luke said. "I think it's time I had a look."

Now Han *knew* Luke understood.

"You sure?" Han asked. He was fairly sure that Luke had not used the code sequence because he was afraid of what it might reveal about Mara—it might bolster Alema's suggestion that Mara was hiding something terrible from him. "I thought you didn't want to give her the satisfaction."

"I don't," Luke said. "That's why I have to do it now—*before* we become Joiners."

Han nodded. He knew what Luke was thinking because he was thinking it, too. It was almost a given that Gorog had spies watching them, and the last thing they wanted was for the Dark Nest to start thinking about what Han *really* wanted from the Squibs. So Luke was going to keep Gorog occupied by giving it something to gloat over.

Luke passed the model back to Han, then turned to R2-D2. "Artoo, come here."

R2-D2 gave a sad whistle and started for Luke's quarters.

"No, Artoo," Luke said. "Come over *here*."

R2-D2 disappeared through the door, quietly tweeting and beeping to himself.

"Artoo!" C-3PO called. "Are you *ignoring* Master Skywalker?"

R2-D2 gave a one-beep reply.

C-3PO recoiled as though he had been struck, then turned to Luke. "It appears that his compliance routines have failed completely. I'll go see if I can reset them."

"That's okay," Luke said. "I'll handle this myself."

He extended a hand toward his quarters, and an electronic squeal sounded from inside. A moment later, R2-D2 floated back into Han's quarters, his treads whirring and his utility arm scratching along the wall.

"Artoo-Detoo!" C-3PO said. "This is Master Skywalker's last request before he becomes a Joiner. The least you can do is honor it."

R2-D2 shot back a string of whistles and trills.

"Don't be ridiculous," C-3PO said. "Of course I'll recite the override sequence that Jedi Rar provided, if Master Skywalker asks me to. That's what a protocol droid does. He facilitates."

R2-D2 let out a long bleat as Luke lowered him the floor between the bunk and Han's stool.

"Well, *you're* certainly not doing him any favors by behaving this way," C-3PO replied. "And don't talk to me like that. I'll trip your primary circuit breaker myself."

"That's enough, Threepio," Luke said. "Just give him the sequence."

R2-D2 screeched in protest and swung his holoprojector away from Luke, and it seemed to Han that he felt the *Falcon* replica give a faint shudder of anticipation, so soft and brief that it could have been a flutter in his own pulse. He pretended not to notice and put the model aside, turning the cockpit so that it was only partially facing Luke, and C-3PO dutifully recited the code sequence.

R2-D2 emitted a long, descending whistle, and the hologram of a large, fountain-filled chamber appeared on the floor in front of Han. The viewing angle was from high in one corner, where a security cam might be mounted, and the only movement in the room was the water falling from the fountains.

"What nonsense is this, Artoo?" C-3PO demanded. "You didn't record this. You're not that tall."

R2-D2 tweedled a reply.

"A *stolen* file?" C-3PO cried. "Stolen on whose authority?"

R2-D2 answered with a short whistle.

"I don't believe you," C-3PO said. "Even Artoo units have restraints against that sort of thing."

"What sort of thing?" Luke asked.

"Artoo claims he downloaded this file on his own initiative," C-3PO said. "But now I know he's running us a corrupted feed. He claims this is from the internal security computer at the Jedi Temple, and we all know there is no room like this at the Jedi Temple."

R2-D2 whistled a correction.

"Oh," C-3PO said. "Now he claims it's from the *old* Jedi Temple."

"The Room of a Thousand Fountains," Luke said. "I've seen it mentioned in some of those records we recovered from the *Chu'unthor*."

R2-D2 began to trill a long, additional explanation.

"He adds that he had no choice," C-3PO translated. "It was during the Jedi Revolt, and his owner had stopped talking to him. They were about to leave on a mission to Mustafar, and he needed to update his friend-or-foe data."

The hologram continued to show the empty room, and Han began to think that the little droid had found one more clever way to keep his secret. Given the effect that secret was likely to have on Luke, Han almost hoped the droid had.

But R2-D2's acoustic signaler began to emit the tinny *pew-pew* of recorded blasterfire. Stray dashes of blue began to streak through the hologram, blowing fountains apart, burning holes in the walls, vanishing into the heights of the vaulted ceiling.

Dozens of children, dressed in simple Jedi robes and wearing a single braid on the sides of their heads, began to retreat into the room. The youngest, those under six or seven, simply tried to run or find a place to hide. The older ones were attempting to fight, using the Force to hurl benches and pieces of broken fountain at their attackers. Some were firing captured blaster rifles, while a few were trying to use their newly constructed lightsabers to ricochet bolts at the unseen enemy. For the most part, they failed miserably but bravely, deflecting half a dozen or a dozen attacks before one sneaked through and knocked them off their feet.

The teenagers came next, backing into the room with their lightsabers whirling, weaving a wall of flashing energy before a column of advancing infantry. Dressed in what appeared to be early stormtrooper armor, the soldiers assaulted ruthlessly, cutting down fleeing four-year-olds with the same brutal efficiency with which they slaughtered the Padawans.

Han had been just a boy in Garris Shrike's band of vagabonds when the Separatists tried to break away from the Old Republic, but he had seen enough of the war to recognize the finned helmets and independent joint covers on the white armor the soldiers wore.

"Clone troopers!"

R2-D2 gave a confirming tweet.

A huge Jedi with stooped shoulders and a gnarled face backed into view, anchoring the line of teenage defenders, his lightsaber sending bolt after bolt back at the attackers, lashing out to cut down one trooper after another. A pair of Padawans stepped in to support his flanks, and the entire line stopped falling back, the lightsabers of the young Jedi weaving an impenetrable wall of energy that—for a few short moments—allowed nothing past, not a blaster bolt, nor a clone trooper, nor even, it seemed to Han, a stray glance.

A blue lightsaber appeared at the edge of the holo, beating down the defense of the first Padawan and slashing through his torso, then slipping past the guard of the other one and cutting him down as well. The back of a blond head and a pair of caped shoulders appeared behind the blue blade and began to carry the attack to the stoop-shouldered Jedi.

The two stood battling toe-to-toe for only an instant before the caped figure slipped a strike and brought his own blade down on the defender's stooped shoulder, cleaving him deep into the torso. The Jedi's gnarled face paled with shock, and he collapsed in too much pain to scream.

The Padawans continued to battle on valiantly, but without the burly Jedi to anchor their line, they were no match for the sheer numbers assaulting them. Their defense collapsed, and the caped figure stepped aside, standing in seeming indifference as the clone troopers poured past to continue the slaughter of the children.

Han felt sickened and angered by what he was watching, but he also felt a little bit relieved. Mara would have been only a baby—and perhaps not even that—when the Jedi were slaughtered. Whatever Alema hoped to reveal with the code sequence, the scene they were watching could have nothing to do with Mara.

Finally, the last of the children had fallen, and the clones stopped firing. The caped figure studied the room for a moment, then gave a barely perceptible nod and turned back toward the entrance. The face that stared into the cam was clouded with anger, the eyes sunken and dark, the mouth set in a grim slash, but there was no mistaking who it belonged to.

Anakin Skywalker.

"That's enough, Artoo," Luke said. His face remained a mask of composure, but he rose and turned toward his own quarters. "Thank you."

R2-D2 deactivated his holoprojector, then emitted a long descending whistle and started to follow Luke through the door.

Han quickly rose and blocked the little droid's path. "Better stay put for a while," he said. "I'll handle this."

R2-D2 spun his photoreceptor toward C-3PO and trilled a long string of notes.

"I don't know why you're blaming *me*," C-3PO said. "I was only following instructions."

Han went to the doorway connecting his quarters to Luke's and found Luke floating cross-legged in the air, the backs of his wrists resting on his knees.

Without opening his eyes, Luke said, "I just need to center myself, Han."

"Yeah, that's what I figured." As Han spoke, he saw that Luke wasn't the only thing floating in the room. So were the stool, the bunk, and the X-wing replica Raynar had presented to him. The replica seemed to be trembling with excitement. "That was kind of rough in there, even on me."

"I'll be okay, Han," Luke said. "I just need to center myself."

"I'll bet," Han said. "What I don't get is how Alema knew what that code sequence was going to access. Even if she's telling the truth about that Daxar Ies character, she didn't say anything about him working on Artoo. There's no way he should have known what's in that memory sector Artoo's hiding."

"Oh, I'm quite certain he didn't," C-3PO said from behind Han. "The code Alema gave me was undoubtedly a universal key. Most droid-brain designers bury them in the circuitry architecture, as a safeguard against data lockouts and irreversible shutdowns. They simply force a unit to convert its most secure file to an open access file. In Artoo's case, that file was one incriminating him in the worst sort of data theft. No wonder he didn't want to reveal it!"

"That's great." Luke's eyes were still closed, but he was sitting on the floor now—as were the bunk, the stool, and the replica. "But I really need—"

"You said the code was a *universal* key?" Han said, turning around to face C-3PO. "You mean it could unlock all of Artoo's files?"

Artoo issued a sharp tweet, but C-3PO ignored him. "If we knew the basis for the code progression, of course. But not even Artoo knows that. It has self-changing variables, so unless we know the original algorithm and variables—"

"Okay, I get it." Han glanced back into the room, where Luke had given up trying to meditate and was simply sitting on the floor looking up at the doorway. "It's probably just as well."

A furrow came to Luke's brow. "Han—"

"All right, already." Han turned and shooed C-3PO away from the door. "Will you give the man some room? He needs to center himself."

"Han—"

"I'm going already."

"Han, that's not it." Luke closed his eyes. "I think it's time to close your deal."

"Already?" Han turned toward the door membrane. "I thought the Squibs would play it a little cooler than that."

Luke frowned. "I don't think it's the Squibs . . . You go on." He glanced down at the replica of his X-wing, then motioned Han out his door. "I need a minute to finish my meditations, but I'll be there when you need me."

Han turned toward the interior wall of his quarters, where a group of silhouettes was just growing visible through the translucent spinglass. Most of the figures were obviously Killiks, with shadows in their hands that suggested electrobolt assault rifles and Verpine shatter guns. But the two silhouettes in the center had only two arms each and carried no visible weapons. They were about Squib height, but a little too stocky and flat-faced.

A Saras guard pressed its thorax to the wall and boomed an order. "She's ordering us to step away from the door," C-3PO said.

Han looked around and held his arms out to his side. "Where do you expect us to go? We're already in the back of the room."

The guard drummed an acknowledgment, then it and several other bugs used their mandibles to snip and rip the outer seal away from the doorway. A moment later, the two silhouettes they were escorting pushed through the membrane into Han's quarters, bringing with them a sweet-smelling cloud of the bond-inducing pheromones that pervaded the jail.

The first figure was a jug-eared Sullustan in a tidy white flight suit resembling that worn by the captains of commercial starliners. The second was a furry little Ewok with a white stripe running diagonally across a body that was otherwise as black as carbon.

"*Tarfang?*" Han gasped. He shifted his glance back to the Sullustan. "*Juun?*"

The Ewok chuttered something sharp at Han, while the Sullus-tan merely braced his hands on his hips and looked around the cell shaking his head.

"Tarfang suggests that since you're an inmate and Captain Juun is the owner of a fine Damorian *Ronto*-class transport, you should address him as *Captain* Juun," C-3PO reported.

"A *Ronto*?" Han did not bother to hide the disdain in his voice. Rontos were among the slowest, ugliest, and least efficient of the light transports crisscrossing the galaxy. He frowned at *Captain* Juun. "What happened to that Mon Cal Sailfish I set you up with?"

"She was too expensive," Juun explained. "My weekly payments were customarily running a week and a half late."

Han frowned. "But you were making them, right?"

"Yes," Juun said. "With the appropriate interest, of course."

"And Lando took her back for *that*?"

Tarfang jabbered an explanation.

"Captain Juun was too clever to give him the chance," C-3PO translated. "He traded his equity for *DR-Nine-one-nine-a*—free and clear."

"*Someone* got a real bargain." Han did not bother to ask what the pair were doing on Woteba; *Ronto*-class transports were just too slow for the inventory-running contract he had talked Lando into giving Juun. "I don't suppose the Second Mistake Squibs are the ones who gave you this steal?"

Juun looked surprised. "How did you know?"

"Because I sent for them and *you* showed up," Han replied. "It doesn't take a genius to know you're in deep with them."

Juun nodded proudly. "They gave us a ten-standard-year freight-ing contract." In a softer voice, he added, "We're exclusive."

"No kidding," Han said. "Let me guess, expenses included?"

Tarfang twitched his nose, then leaned toward Han and gibbered something suspicious.

"Tarfang requests—"

The Ewok whirled on C-3PO and barked a single word.

"—er, he *warns* you against discussing this with them," the droid corrected. "It's the Squibs' own bad fortune if they agree to such a poor bargain."

Han raised his palms to the Ewok. "Hey, that's between you guys—and I don't see why I should clue them in to *anything*, if they're not interested in my deal."

"Hold on!" Juun's voice was alarmed. "What makes you think they're not interested?"

Han made a show of looking around his quarters. "I don't see them here."

"Only because they are important business beings," Juun explained, "and this is a detention center."

Tarfang chittered an addendum.

"And they mustn't let themselves be seen with a pair of . . . oh, my . . ." C-3PO paused, searching for a diplomatic interpretation, until the Ewok growled. "With a pair of *dustcrusts* like you and Master Skywalker."

"That's okay," Han said. "I understand."

"You do?" Juun's cheek folds rose in relief. "In that case, they've authorized me to make you a very generous offer—they'll pay you a millicredit for each replica you sign."

"A whole millicredit?" Han repeated. "That much?"

Juun nodded eagerly. "That's ten thousand credits in all," he said. "And they're even willing to pay a third in advance. Emala said to tell you they haven't forgotten what you did for them on Pavo Prime."

Han pretended to consider the offer. "I'm willing to talk about it—have a seat." He motioned them to his bunk, then retrieved the *Falcon* replica and sat across from them on the stool. "But first, I want to make sure I've got this straight. You guys are running replicas like this one back into the Galactic Alliance?"

"We've already made our first run," Juun said proudly, "a promotional delivery to the Fifth Fleet."

"To the Fifth Fleet?" Han's heart rose into his throat. What was the Dark Nest doing—going after the entire Galactic Alliance? "No kidding?"

Tarfang growled a few words.

"Tarfang warns you that their deal with Second Mistake is vac-sealed," C-3PO translated. "He advises you that even thinking about moving in on them is a waste of time."

Han turned to the Ewok. "Us moving in on you is the *one* thing you don't have to worry about right now."

Tarfang chortled a spiteful reply.

"That's right!" C-3PO translated. "You're stuck here in a rehab house getting—"

C-3PO broke off to shoot a question at Tarfang in Ewokese, then seemed to stiffen at the response.

"Oh, my—Tarfang says this is an acceleration facility! Saras brings criminals here to rehabilitate them quickly—by making them Joiners!"

The Ewok jumped up, standing on Han's bed and chuckling so hard he had to hold his belly.

"Keep it up, fuzzball," Han said. "This place is a vacation moon compared to where the Defense Force is going to lock you two."

Tarfang stopped laughing, and Juun asked, "Why would they lock us up?"

Before he answered, Han hesitated and started to glance back toward Luke's quarters.

"Go ahead, Han," Luke said from the door. "Show them."

Without saying anything more, Han raised the replica of the *Falcon* over his head and hurled it to the floor. The spinglass did not shatter so much as explode into a droning cloud of blue-black bugs about the size of Han's thumb.

Juun and Tarfang yelled in surprise and pressed themselves against the wall. Even Han cried out and tumbled off the stool backward as the swarm boiled into the air before him—he had been expecting to find a single hand-sized Killik inside the replica, not dozens of smaller ones.

The cloud began to arc toward Han, tiny droplets of venom glistening on the proboscises between their curved mandibles. He grabbed the stool and started to swing it up to bat them away—then felt Luke's hand on his shoulder.

"Stay down."

Luke stretched his arm out, and the swarm went tumbling across the room and splattered against the wall, leaving the ivory spinglass flecked with palm-sized stars of gore. The room fell abruptly silent, and the air immediately grew sickening with the smell of insect methane.

Luke pointed to Han's bag, sitting under his bunk. "Get some undershirts and wipe the wall down. I can only hold the illusion for a few minutes."

"Why *my* shirts?" Han demanded.

"Because mine are in the other room," Luke said. "And the illusion is only in here."

"Yeah—I'll bet you planned it that way." Han pulled the bag out from under the bunk, then pulled out two undershirts—all he had—and passed them to Juun and Tarfang. "Get busy."

Juun immediately went over to the wall, but Tarfang simply looked at the cloth and sneered.

Before the Ewok could ask the question that was almost certainly coming, Han pointed at him and said, "Because if you don't, I'm not going to tell you two how to fix the mess you've made for yourselves."

Tarfang chittered a long reply, which C-3PO translated as, "What mess?"

"Like the one we're cleaning up here—only a whole lot worse." Han pulled a spare tunic from his bag and went over to the wall. "I don't think the Defense Force is going to be very happy with you two when they figure out you were the ones who delivered a whole Ronto-ful of Gorog assassin bugs to the Fifth Fleet."

Juun's eyes grew even larger. "Tarfang, get over here!" Once the Ewok had jumped off the bunk, he turned to Han. "You can tell us how to fix *that*?"

"Sure," Han said. "Easiest thing in the galaxy—all you have to do is help us find the Dark Nest."

TWELVE

Leia and Saba stood shoulder-to-shoulder at the top of the boarding ramp, listening to a muffled string of beeps and chirps as the boarding party's slicer droid tried to outsmart the *Falcon*'s espionage-grade security system. The external monitors showed that the ship was surrounded by a full company of soldiers in full blast armor. Something did not feel quite right in the Force, as though the troops were nervous or hesitant about their orders, and Leia wondered if the commander could really believe that Jedi would attack Galactic Alliance troops.

"They feel frightened." There was a note of disdain in Saba's voice, for Barabels tended to regard fear as something felt only by quarry. "You are sure we should not draw our lightsaberz? Frightened prey is unpredictable."

Leia shook her head. "You're the Master, but I really think we need to defuse things. Somebody's going to get hurt if we keep pushing."

Saba glared down at Leia out of one eye. "*We* are not the onez pushing thingz, Jedi Solo."

Finally, the slicer droid stopped beeping and chirping. The monitor showed him releasing his interface clips from the wires dangling from the *Falcon*'s exterior security pad; then he turned to an officer and gave a dejected whistle.

"What do you mean you can't open it?" The security system speaker made the officer's voice sound a little tinny. "That's what you were designed for—to open ship hatches."

The droid beeped a short reply, which Leia knew would include an explanation of how the access code kept changing. The security system's first line of defense was an automatic reset anytime two incorrect codes were entered into the keypad. Its second line of defense was to never grant access from the outside when the keypad cover was removed.

"Well, try again," the officer ordered. "I'm not going to use a flash torch on the *Millennium Falcon*!"

The droid gave a weary whistle, then started to sort through the security wires again.

Leia turned to Saba. "I think we've made our point."

Saba nodded. "If you are sure about the lightsaberz."

"I am," Leia said. "They may be scared, but they wouldn't dare blast us."

Leia instructed Cakhmaim and Meewalh to stay out of sight, then released the safety-hold and palmed the toggle button on the wall. The seal broke with a hiss, and the ramp began to descend.

A surprised murmur arose out in the hangar. The captain barked an order, and when there was enough space to see, Leia and Saba found themselves surrounded by a semicircle of blaster barrels.

Once the ramp clanged into position against the durasteel floor, the officer stepped to the foot and looked up at them. He was young—no doubt straight from the academy—and so nervous he could barely bring himself to meet the gazes of Leia and Saba.

"You will p-place your hands on your heads." Despite his cracking voice, he was clearly being deliberately rude, ordering them about as though they were common pirates and neglecting to address them by any sort of title. "Descend the ramp slowly."

Leia heard Saba's scales rustle, then suddenly the Barabel's hand rose. "We are Jedi Knightz." The barrels of the blaster rifles began to swing away. "Point those somewhere else!"

Deciding it was better to follow her Master's lead than stand there looking confused, Leia raised her hand and used the Force to turn aside a trio of blaster rifles.

The officer paled and stepped away from the ramp. Behind him knelt two soldiers armed with bell-barreled Czerka HeadBangers—ultrapowerful riot guns designed to stun any target into submission.

"Oh, kr—"

That was as far as Leia made it before a blinding spark of silver lit the barrels of both weapons. Something like the head of a charging bantha hit her in the chest, then she felt herself go limp and start to fall, and the floor disappeared beneath her, sending her tumbling down into darkness.

* * *

The fall must have been a long one, judging by how Leia felt when she woke. The world was spinning. Her stomach was churning and her temples were pounding, and her body felt as if she'd run headlong into a dewback stampede. Her ears hurt . . . she could not even describe how her ears hurt, and some inconsiderate rodder was hammering words against her head.

"Princess Leia?"

The voice was familiar, but it was hard to place with all that lightning cracking through her head.

"Princess Leia?"

Hoping the Voice would give up and go away, she kept her eyes closed tight.

Instead, something popped in front of her face, and a smell like burning hyperdrive coolant blistered her nostrils. She reacted with a blind Force shove and heard a body thud off the far wall. The Voice groaned and thumped to the floor.

Then a second voice gasped, "Commodore Darklighter?"

"Don't!" Darklighter gasped. "I'm okay . . . I think."

"Gavin?"

Leia opened her eyes to the stabbing light of a silver sun, then let out an involuntary groan of her own. She tried to push herself up and discovered her hands were cuffed behind her.

"Just how angry are you trying to make me?"

"Please settle down, Princess," Darklighter said. "Wurf'al isn't under my command, and he's just looking for an excuse to activate those stun cuffs."

"Avke Saz'ula is my mother's uncle's third wife's cousin," a gravelly voice said. "I owe you."

Leia glanced toward the gravelly voice and, as her vision began to clear, saw the long-snouted silhouette of a young Bothan naval officer standing in the doorway of what was obviously a detention cell.

"Who's Avke Saz'ula?" she asked.

The fur rose on the Bothan's cheeks. "You Jedi are lower than skalworms!"

Leia looked to Darklighter, who was standing just inside the door. The first streaks of gray were beginning to show in his brown hair and goatee, but otherwise his rugged face looked much the same as it had through the thirty years Leia had known him.

"Do I *care* who Saz'ula is?"

"Jedi rabble!" Wurf'al raised his arm, pointing a stun-cuff remote at Leia.

Darklighter's hand immediately pushed the arm down. "How

would Admiral Bwua'tu feel about using unnecessary force on a co-operative prisoner?"

"I doubt it would upset him—he *is* my mother's uncle." Nevertheless, Wurf'al pocketed the remote. "But he would be upset about the delay. He has been waiting long enough for these prisoners to awaken."

Leia breathed a silent sigh of relief. The remote was for a pair of LSS 401 Stun Cuffs—not as sophisticated as the LSS 1000 Automatics she and Han carried aboard the *Falcon,* but just as powerful and painful.

Wurf'al stepped out of the doorway, then Darklighter extended a hand toward Leia. She ignored it and rose on her own, trading a little unsteadiness on her feet for the opportunity to put Darklighter on the defensive. Saba was waiting in the corridor outside, guarded by a squad of detention personnel and also restrained in stun cuffs.

She lifted her pebbly lips, showing her fangs in something more than a scowl. " 'We don't need our lightsaberz,' you said," she quoted. " 'They wouldn't dare blast *us.*' "

They had not exactly been blasted, but Leia wasn't about to argue a fine point like that with a Barabel. Instead she shot a frown at Darklighter. "I didn't think they *would.*"

Darklighter shrugged. "Wasn't my decision. Admiral Bwua'tu didn't even ask me to come over to the *Ackbar* until Saba was already starting to come around."

"You have only yourselves to blame for how you feel," Wurf'al said. "Admiral Bwua'tu anticipated that you would try to impress us with your Jedi sorcery and took appropriate measures."

The Bothan turned and started toward the front of the detention block.

Leia fell in beside Darklighter and quietly asked, "So who *is* Avke Saz'ula?"

"Gunnery officer aboard the *Avengeance,*" he whispered.

"Wonderful." Leia grimaced. The crew of *Avengeance* was currently occupying its own wing of *Maxsec Eight,* after the Jedi caught them attempting to locate the sentient world Zonama Sekot. During the war, the Bothans had declared an ar'krai—a death crusade—against the Yuuzhan Vong, and many of them remained determined to follow the invaders into the Unknown Regions and finish what they started. "A Bothan with a grudge."

"I *gave* you a chance to turn around," Darklighter whispered. "Don't blame me."

They reached the front of the detention block and were admitted into the central processing area, where the bust of another Bothan in an admiral's tunic sat in a display niche across from the watch desk. It was made from a pale, iridescent material that resembled Saras spinglass.

"I see Admiral Bwua'tu likes to remind his prisoners who's holding them," Leia said.

"That is my doing," Wurf'al said proudly.

"But he hasn't made you take it down," Saba observed.

"Of course not," Wurf'al said. "Admiral Bwua'tu knows what an inspiration he is for the crew of the *Admiral Ackbar*. They feel privileged to serve under an admiral who has risen from the obscurity of a birth on Ruweln to become the finest fleet commander the Galactic Alliance has ever seen."

"The finest?" Leia echoed, taking offense on behalf of her dead friend Admiral Ackbar. "Really? I wasn't aware that Admiral Bwua'tu has actually seen fleet action as a commander."

"He hasn't," Wurf'al said, apparently not noticing the irony in his answer. "But he defeats the Thrawn simulator every time."

"I'm relieved to know the Fifth Fleet is in such capable hands," Leia said, struggling to keep the sarcasm out of her voice. "By the way, where did you come by the bust? The material is very distinctive."

"It was a gift, from a shipping line grateful for our protection along the Hydian Way," Wurf'al said. "Now, if you don't mind, my mother's uncle the admiral is waiting for us."

Wurf'al nodded to the watch sergeant, who keyed a code into his console. A security cam dropped down from the ceiling and scanned the face of each person in the group—Wurf'al and guards included. After it had finished, a green light came on above the outer doors, and they slid aside.

Wurf'al led the group out into the corridor and down to a lift station, where they were confronted by another bust of Admiral Bwua'tu—this one sitting on a small plasteel pedestal. Leia and Saba exchanged glances, and even Gavin quietly rolled his eyes. They ascended the lift with Leia and Saba encircled by guards, then Wurf'al led them through a maze of corridors on the operations deck. As they walked, Leia began to feel a faint tickle between her shoulder blades, the same uneasy feeling she had experienced in the capture bay just before she and Saba were stunned into unconsciousness. She reached out and could tell that the Barabel felt it, too, but even Saba did not seem able to identify its source.

Finally, they came to another lift, this one guarded by a pair of human sentries wearing the uniform of bridge security.

Wurf'al stopped and reached for his comlink, but one of the sentries waved him off. "Go on up. He's waiting for you."

The fur on Wurf'al's cheeks flattened noticeably. "He's *waiting?*"

"Five minutes now." The second sentry reached behind him and hit a slap-pad, and the lift doors opened to reveal a squad from bridge security already waiting inside. "Better hurry. He sounded like he was in a mood."

Wurf'al waved Saba and Leia into the lift. "Go on. He's waiting!"

Leaving the detention guards behind, they joined the security squad in the lift and ascended into the bridge. The squad escorted them into a small briefing room containing a large conference table, a service kitchen with its own droid, and, in one corner, another bust of the great admiral. The large chair at the far end of the table was turned away from the entrance, toward a full-wall viewing panel currently displaying a thin crescent of jewel-colored sun along each edge, with the crimson web of the Utegetu Nebula stretched between.

The security squad guided Leia and Saba to the near end of the table, then took up positions behind them. Wurf'al and Darklighter stood behind chairs on the opposite sides.

A gritty Bothan voice spoke from behind the chair. "Please forgive the stun cuffs, but with you Jedi, we must do what we can to make an escape attempt inconvenient."

The chair spun around, revealing a dignified-looking Bothan with a weather-creased snout and graying chin fur. He was dressed in an immaculate white uniform draped in medals and gold braid, and he held his shoulders square without appearing rigid or tense. He acknowledged Leia with a glance and a nod, then addressed himself to Saba.

"We can remove them, if you'll give me your word as Jedi that you won't attempt to escape. I'm sure Chief Omas will instruct me to release you shortly."

"You are very trusting," Saba rasped, "for a Bothan."

Bwua'tu flashed a canine-baring smile. "Not really. It would be far easier for us to rely on your honor than to attempt holding two Jedi against their wills." He glanced at Darklighter. "And Commodore Darklighter assures me that if you and Princess Leia give your words, you will honor them."

"That is so," Saba said. "But we will not give you our wordz."

Bwua'tu nodded. "I didn't think so." He looked to Wurf'al. "It seems you'll have to hole the *Millennium Falcon*'s drive nacelles."

"*What?*" Leia cried.

"We'll keep you locked in your cells in stun cuffs, of course."

Bwua'tu's gaze shifted to Leia. "But we know better than to believe *that* will hold two Jedi. This is our best chance of preventing you from escaping."

"You can't do that!" Leia said.

"I'm quite certain we *can*," Bwua'tu replied. "I'm sure those Noghri we haven't been able to find will put up quite a fight, but I have no doubt we'll prevail in the end. If all else fails, we'll just use the capture bay battery on it."

"You would enjoy that, this one thinkz," Saba said. "Some revenge for your third wife'z cousin."

"Nonsense," Bwua'tu replied. "My clan relations have no more to do with this matter than the revulsion I feel for the Jedi's weakness in sparing the Yuuzhan Vong their just due. This is purely in the line of my duty as commander of the Fifth Fleet."

"I wonder if Gilad Pellaeon will see it that way?" Leia asked. With Sien Sovv dead, Pellaeon had agreed to come out of retirement until Chief Omas and the Senate appointed a new, permanent Supreme Commander. "You *know* how sticky Sullustans are about regulations."

"I do." Bwua'tu gestured at Darklighter. "That's why I had Commodore Darklighter consult with me on this. Holing the *Falcon*'s nacelles was *his* idea."

Leia's jaw dropped. "Gavin!"

"Sorry, Princess," he said. "But you *have* been trying to run a Galactic Alliance blockade."

Bwua'tu looked back to Wurf'al. "Why are you still here? You have your orders."

Wurf'al's fur flattened. "Sorry, sir." He passed the stun-cuff remotes to the leader of the security squad and turned toward the door. "On my way."

"All right," Leia said. "We give our words."

"*You* give your word," Bwua'tu said, looking to Saba. "What about Master Sebatyne?"

Wurf'al reached the door and left without waiting to be called back. Saba remained silent.

"Good," Bwua'tu said. "There is no regulation against enjoying my duty."

During her two decades of political service to the Rebellion and the New Republic, Leia had dealt with enough Bothans to know when one was bluffing. There was no tell-tale ruffling of the fur, no synthetic snarl. Bwua'tu was patiently waiting for Saba to make up her mind—and the gleam in his eye suggested that he hoped that she would remain silent.

"Saba, I don't think he's bluffing," Leia said.

"He is not," the Barabel said. "We will have to take one of the *Ackbar*'z message skiffz instead of the *Falcon*."

"I've no doubt you can," Bwua'tu replied. "But thank you for the warning."

Leia began, "Master Sebatyne—"

"If we give our word, we place Han and Master Skywalker at Chief Omas'z mercy," Saba interrupted. "That we cannot do."

"Master Sebatyne, I understand your concern."

As Leia spoke, she was reaching out to Saba in the Force, trying to make her see that Bwua'tu was not half as clever as he believed himself to be. He had asked for a very specific promise—that Leia and Saba not attempt to *escape*—so they could still make the rescue plan work, if they could find a way to get the supplies aboard the *Falcon* to Mara and the rest of the StealthX pilots without escaping.

"But you know how Cakhmaim and Meewalh are," Leia continued. "If something happens to the *Falcon,* they'll try to take out this whole Star Destroyer."

"There is no try." Saba flicked her tongue. "They *will*."

Bwua'tu drummed his clawed fingers on the table and looked at the door.

"We can't let that happen," Leia pressed. "You must give Admiral Bwua'tu your word."

Saba let out a long, harsh croak that actually made Bwua'tu recoil. "Very well. This one promisez."

Bwua'tu's bushy brows fell. "Finally, you surprise me." He looked to the leader of the security squad. "Release the stun cuffs."

The leader punched a code into the remote, and the stun cuffs opened on both Leia and Saba.

"Please, sit." Bwua'tu gestured to the chairs at their end of the table. "Would you like something from the service kitchen?"

"No, thank you." Leia's throat was raw with thirst, but Saba had drilled into her time and again that it was as important to maintain the Jedi mystique as it was to master the Force. "I'm fine for now."

"This one will have a membrosia." Saba used the Force to pull out a chair, then perched on the edge, wrapping her tail onto her lap. "Gold, of course."

Bwua'tu eyes narrowed. "This is a military vessel," he said stiffly. "Spirits of any sort are not allowed aboard."

"None?" Saba let out a disappointed snort. "Then this one hopez it will not be *too* long before you hear from Chief Omaz."

"As do I." Bwua'tu asked the droid to bring him a tall glass of iced fizzwater, then said, "There is one other matter we must attend to before I have you escorted to your new cabins."

"Aren't you forgetting something?" Leia asked.

Bwua'tu frowned. "That's highly unlikely."

"I think she's worried about the *Falcon,* sir," Darklighter said.

"Is she?"

The admiral depressed a hidden button on the tabletop, and the door opened to reveal Wurf'al standing at attention on the other side. The younger Bothan smiled at Leia and stepped back into the cabin.

"You keep your promises," Bwua'tu said, "and I'll keep mine."

So much for the Jedi mystique, Leia thought.

"Good." Saba rose. "Then we are done here. This one is ready to go to her cabin."

"In a moment," Bwua'tu said. "First, I want you to call your fellow Jedi in. We've been trying to reach them for three days—"

"Three days?" Leia gasped.

"You've been unconscious for four," Darklighter said.

"I'm afraid I overestimated your Jedi resiliency," Bwua'tu added. "I ordered the boarding party to set their HeadBangers to maximum. So you can see why we're growing concerned about your escort. They must be running out of air, water, and food by now."

"Maybe even power," Darklighter said. "I've heard that StealthXs draw down faster than the standard XJ series."

Leia glanced over to see how Saba wanted to play this—the Barabel *was* her Master—and received absolutely no hint, either in her expression or through the Force. Leia's choice.

Leia turned to Bwua'tu. "We *were* trying to run the blockade, you know." As she said this, Leia reached out to Mara in the Force and felt her somewhere nearby, deep in a Force-hibernation. "Has it occurred to you that our escort is already gone?"

"Frankly, no," Darklighter said. "I doubt they went to Woteba with no way to refuel before combat. No pilot would."

"By the way, we have removed your cargo to a safe location," Bwua'tu added. "I wouldn't want you to get any ideas about shooting a few fuel cells out to your friends without actually trying to *escape.*"

Leia's heart sank, but she was careful to maintain a neutral face. Bwua'tu did not know as much about Jedi as he believed. Mara and the others could stay in their StealthXs for another week by remaining in their Force-hibernation.

The question was whether Luke and Han could last that long.

"Okay, they're still out there," Leia admitted. "But I won't call them in."

Bwua'tu's brow rose in surprise. "Why not?"

"You must!" Darklighter said. "They're going to start going under pretty soon, and we can't find those StealthXs. We won't be able to save them."

"They are safer out there than they would be in here," Saba said. "We will not call them into danger."

Bwua'tu's nostrils began to flare. "Whatever my feelings about Jedi meddling in the ar'krai, I assure you they will be in no danger aboard the *Ackbar*!"

"Not from *you*," Leia said. She had vague sense of where Saba was trying to go with this, but could not tell whether the Barabel had sensed some new menace or was simply trying to play Bwua'tu. "Something is wrong on this ship. Master Sebatyne and I have been sensing it since we came aboard."

Bwua'tu pushed back in his chair. "Please—you're talking to a Bothan! I see what you're trying to do."

"We are trying to *protect* you," Saba growled.

"From what?" Bwua'tu demanded.

Saba and Leia looked at each other, then Leia admitted, "The Force is not yet clear on the matter."

"Then please let me know when the Force *does* become clear on the matter." Bwua'tu's tone suggested that he did not think that would ever happen. "Until then, do not attempt frightening my crew again. I assure you, it will do nothing to speed your release."

Darklighter said, "Admiral, that isn't what's happening here. If Princess Leia says she feels something wrong, then it bears investigating."

Bwua'tu turned to glare at Darklighter. "Is that your opinion, Commodore, or is there some General Defense Force Directive that I'm unaware of?"

Darklighter drew himself up straight. "Sir, that is my opinion."

Bwua'tu fell silent, and Leia thought for a moment they had convinced him of the danger.

Then the admiral stood. "Do you know what I think, Commodore Darklighter? I think you have allowed your friendship with Princess Leia to affect your judgment." His gaze shifted to Leia and Saba. "And now you are dangerously close to supporting her in fomenting unrest among my crew."

Darklighter's face paled. "Sir, that's not my intention—"

"You are a dangerously naïve officer to be flying one of my Star Destroyers, Commodore Darklighter," Bwua'tu said. "I suggest you return to it while it is still yours to command."

"Sir."

Darklighter drew himself to attention and saluted, then cast one last glance in Leia's direction before he turned and left the room.

Bwua'tu turned to Wurf'al. "I fear Commodore Darklighter may have misjudged the value of a Jedi's promise. Place them back in their stun cuffs and return them to the detention center."

"This isn't a ploy, Admiral," Leia said. "You're making a mistake."

"Perhaps, but it is mine to make." Bwua'tu returned to his chair and spun around to stare at the sapphire web of the Utegetu Nebula. "Tell your guard when you wish to call your friends in, Princess. Chief Omas will not be happy if they suffocate in the Murgo Choke."

THIRTEEN

It was afternoon in Unity Green and a fierce storm was rolling across Liberation Lake, raising three-meter white-caps and bombing the yammal-jells with fist-sized hail. In the flat light, the bluffs along the lake's far shore were barely visible, a mere band of darkness rising from the edge of the gray water. But the abandoned skytower project atop the cliffs was all too visible, a line of durasteel skeletons silhouetted against the flashing sky, twisted and bowing beneath the weight of the enormous yorik coral goiters hanging from their necks.

In many ways, Cal Omas viewed the skytower project—and the entire reconstruction of Coruscant—as emblematic of his service as Chief of State, a visionary undertaking being dragged down by the deadweight of selfish concerns and species rivalry. After the devastation wrought by the Yuuzhan Vong, rebuilding the galaxy would have been almost impossible under any circumstances. But doing it as the head of an alliance of semi-independent governments . . . he considered it a testament to his skill and hard work just to have kept the peace for six difficult years.

And now the Jedi were threatening even that one small accomplishment. They had been his most valuable asset for most of his tenure, able to eliminate criminal cabals with a single team of Jedi Knights, or to bring a pair of starving worlds back from the brink of war with the arbitration of a Master. Then the Killik problem had arisen in the Unknown Regions, and the Jedi order had become just one more problem, more deadweight threatening to bring the Galactic Alliance down around his ears.

Sometimes Omas truly did not know whether he was up to the job—whether *anyone* was.

A female voice spoke from the door to the council chamber. "Chief Omas, the Masters are here."

Omas turned away from the viewport. "Well, send them in, Salla. I *am* just a visitor in their Temple."

Salla, his personal assistant, twitched her whiskers in what someone unfamiliar with a Jenet might have mistaken for condescension, but which Omas knew was simply amusement.

"So you are." She stepped out of the door and waved the Masters inside. "I'm sure you heard Chief Omas."

"I'm sure he meant us to," replied the familiar voice of Kyp Durron. He marched into the chamber with the other Masters at his back, then stopped at the edge of the speaking pit. With a threadbare robe and unkempt hair, he was as raggedly groomed as always. "Thanks for letting us into our own council chamber, Chief."

Omas accepted the insolence with a smile. "Not at all, Master Durron. After all, the Reconstruction Authority gave the *entire* Temple to the Jedi."

Omas's irony might have been lost on Kyp, but not on Kenth Hamner. "And the Jedi are very grateful," he said. Though he usually dressed in a civilian tunic or his liaison's uniform, today he wore the same brown robes as the rest of the Masters. They obviously intended to present a united front. "We're all here as you requested, Chief Omas."

"And thank you for coming." Omas slipped into a comfortable flowform chair at one end of the speaking circle and motioned to the seats nearest him. "Please, sit. Can Salla get you anything from the service kitchen?"

The Masters all declined, of course. Omas had never seen a Jedi Master accept food or beverage when a confrontation was expected. It was part of their mystique, he thought—or perhaps they were simply more cautious than he realized.

"Very well."

Omas gestured again to the nearby seats, then waited in silence until the six Masters finally realized he was pulling rank on them and perched on the edges of the big flowform seats, their backs ramrod-straight and their hands resting on their thighs. Kyp took the seat nearest him. That was one of the things that had always troubled Omas about the rogue Jedi—he never backed down.

"We need to talk," Omas began. "Normally, I would bring a matter like this up with the six Masters who sit on the Advisory Council, but Masters Skywalker and Sebatyne seem to be unavailable. I've asked Masters Horn and Katarn to sit in their place."

"On whose authority?" Kyp demanded.

Omas raised his brow in feigned surprise. "No one's. I felt this discussion should include six Masters instead of four." He turned to Hamner. "Is that a problem?"

"Yes," Kyp blurted. "When you handpick—"

"It's fine," Hamner said, cutting Kyp off short. He shot the younger Master a warning glance, but the damage had been done. Corran furrowed his brow, and Katarn's brown eyes grew as hard as larmalstone. "We don't speak for the entire order, but we can certainly listen on its behalf."

Omas nodded. "That's all I ask." Knowing how easy it was for Jedi to read emotions, he tried not to gloat. He let his gaze drift toward Corran, then said, "First, I must start by saying how disappointed I am that you've been keeping Master Skywalker's absence from me. It has led me to imagine some very disturbing scenarios, I'm afraid."

Corran's gaze shifted.

But Kyp said, "Master Skywalker's whereabouts aren't your concern."

"Actually, they *are* his concern," Kyle Katarn said. He was still a slim and fit-looking man; his beard and hair were just beginning to show the first shocks of gray. "I'm sorry you felt we were keeping secrets from you, Chief Omas. The truth is that Master Skywalker's absence took us by surprise, and we were afraid you would try to take advantage of the situation."

"Take advantage?" Omas kept his voice pleasant. Divide, *then* conquer. It was one of the lessons he had learned by watching Admiral Ackbar. "By trying to usurp his leadership?"

"We know how upset you have been over the Killiks," Tresina Lobi said. A golden-haired Chev woman, Lobi resembled a pale-skinned human with obsidian eyes, a heavy brow, and a sloping forehead. "So, yes, we are concerned about your intentions."

"My intentions are to protect the Galactic Alliance," Omas said simply. "What the Jedi are doing places our relationship with the Chiss at risk—"

"We prevented an interstellar war!" Kyp interrupted. "We saved billions of lives!"

"That is in the past," Omas said, raising a hand to stop Kyp's protest. "I'm talking about the present. The Jedi are the last ones who need to be reminded of the havoc black membrosia is wreaking on our insect worlds. Shipping losses to the Utegetu pirates are approaching wartime levels—and do I really need to remind you of the death of Sien Sovv?"

"The Jedi are well aware of the trouble the Killiks are causing, Chief Omas," Katarn said. "That doesn't mean we are ready to surrender control of the order to you."

"The Jedi need leadership," Omas countered. "Surely, you all see that as clearly as I do. The situation just keeps growing worse. There's even a rumor that the Killiks tried to assassinate Queen Mother Tenel Ka!"

Though the Masters' expressions remained outwardly unreadable, their silence told Omas all he needed to know.

"Something else you have been keeping from me." He shook his head wearily, then looked out the viewport at the silhouettes of the distant skytowers, bowing and swaying in the wind. "My friends, we cannot go on like this. Too much depends on us."

"We all agree on that, Chief Omas," Corran said. "But we've discussed this, and we can't allow you to assume direct control of the Jedi order."

Omas nodded. "Of course. I'm not a Jedi."

"Actually, only Master Durron feels that has anything to do with it," Lobi said. "The problem lies in what you *are*—the Chief of State."

Omas frowned. "I don't understand."

"We can't allow the Jedi to become a tool of office," Hamner explained. "We are guardians as well as servants, and we cannot make ourselves beholden to the same authority we are pledged to watch."

"And, as the Chief of State, your concerns are too narrow," Kyp added. "You're only worried about the Galactic Alliance. The Jedi serve the whole galaxy—"

"The Force," Corran corrected.

"Right," Kyp said. "The point is, *we* have more to worry about. What's good for the Galactic Alliance isn't always what serves the Force."

"I see."

Omas grew thoughtful—though he was contemplating not the wisdom of what the Masters were saying, but the care they had taken to meet him with a united front. Bringing the Jedi back into the Alliance fold was going to be more difficult than he had anticipated.

After a moment, he looked Kyp directly in the eye. "This may surprise you, but I agree."

For once, the Masters appeared stunned.

"You do?" Kyp asked.

"Who am I to question the wisdom of the Jedi?" Omas replied. "But that doesn't mean my concerns can be dismissed. The Jedi are floundering, which means the Galactic Alliance is floundering—and that is something I cannot allow. We must do something."

"We *are* doing something," Kyp said. "Han and Master Skywalker are looking for the Dark Nest, and then we're going to destroy it."

"Like you did last time?" Omas asked immediately. "I'm sure you'll understand my complete lack of confidence in that plan. Dark Nest membrosia has ruined the economy of the entire Roche asteroid field, and—as you know better than I—Dark Nest assassins have apparently attacked the queen of an Alliance member-state."

The Masters fell into silent contemplation. Omas allowed them to ponder his words for a few moments, then decided the time had come to drop his bomb.

"And there is something you may *not* realize. After the Jedi intervention at Qoribu, the Chiss seem to believe that it is your responsibility to persuade the Colony to withdraw from their frontier. They've given you ten days to stop further migration into the buffer zone, and a hundred days to persuade the Killiks to withdraw the Colonists who are already there."

For the first time he could recall, Omas had the pleasure of watching the jaws of several Jedi Masters drop.

"Those aren't unreasonable terms," Hamner said.

"And a remarkable expression of trust, considering that they're Chiss." Omas allowed himself one small smirk. "Though, considering the order's disarray without Master Skywalker available to guide it, I'm wondering if it wouldn't be more honest to let them know that they're on their own."

All of the Masters gave voice to their disapproval and dismay, but Kyp was loudest. "That's not your decision to make!"

Omas fixed the shaggy-haired Master with his iciest glare. "To the contrary, Master Durron, it is very much my decision. The Chiss chose to transmit their demand through me, so how I respond is entirely at my own discretion. If I feel that the Jedi order isn't up to the task, then it is not only my right to tell them so, it is my duty."

Kyp began to work his mouth in soundless anger. Omas sighed, then slumped back in his chair. Hamner, who had nearly as much experience on the bureaucratic battlefield as Omas himself, was the first to realize that the Chief was waiting for them to open negotiations.

"What are you looking for, Chief Omas?" he asked.

Omas allowed himself a moment of dramatic silence, then spoke without straightening himself. "A leader."

"A leader?" Katarn asked.

Omas nodded. "Someone to take charge of the Jedi and handle this mess until Master Skywalker returns."

Kyp frowned, clearly suspicious. "Who?"

"One of you." Omas leaned forward. "Starting today. Beyond that, I really don't care. How about you?"

Kyp was just as astonished the other Masters. "Me?"

"You seem to have a very clear idea of what the Jedi should be," Omas said. "I think you'd make a fine leader. And, believe it or not, you and I want the same thing—a peaceful end to the Killik problem."

A distant light came to Kyp's eyes, and if he noticed the uncomfortable expressions on the faces of the other Masters, he did not show it.

"I suppose that's true," he said.

Hamner cleared his throat and sat forward. "No offense to Master Durron, but the Jedi order is led by a *council* of senior Masters. You know that, Chief Omas."

"Of course." As Omas replied, he was watching the light vanish from Kyp's eyes. "But we all know that Master Skywalker is first among the Masters. I'm merely suggesting that Kyp step up and take his place—just until Master Skywalker returns, of course."

"I see what you're doing—and it won't work," Kyp snarled. "Master Skywalker leads the Jedi."

"Not from Woteba, he doesn't," Omas replied. "And if you're counting on Princess Leia's rescue mission to bring him back soon, I'm afraid you're going to be waiting a very long time."

Omas had expected a feeling of alarm to fill the council room when he announced this, but the Masters disappointed him—as they were doing in so many ways, these days. They simply closed their eyes and fell silent for a moment.

Tresina Lobi was the first to open her eyes again and look at him. "Where is she?"

"I'm afraid Admiral Bwua'tu has impounded the *Falcon*." Omas forced an apologetic smile. "It seems Princess Leia and her friends were trying to run the Utegetu blockade."

"You interfered with their mission?" Katarn demanded. "You're putting Han and Luke in danger!"

"Not intentionally, I assure you," Omas said smoothly. "But these things happen when we keep secrets from each other."

"We've already explained that," Katarn said.

Omas shrugged. "It doesn't change what happened." He turned to Hamner. "Forgive me, but when I couldn't get Master Skywalker to return my messages, I assumed the worst."

"That we were going to help the Killiks move the Utegetu nests to the Chiss frontier?" Hamner asked. "We would never—"

"How am I to know what the Jedi would or would not do?" Omas nodded toward Kyp. "As Master Durron says, your concerns go beyond the Galactic Alliance. Mine do not—and the Jedi have placed our interests second before."

"A peaceful galaxy is in everyone's best interest," Kyp countered.

"And when you can guarantee *that*, the Galactic Alliance will gladly support a Jedi government." Omas allowed his anger to show. "Until then, we will look out for our own interests—and if that means arresting Jedi when they attempt to run our blockades, so be it."

"You're holding Jedi hostage!" Kyp snarled.

"Not at all," Omas said. "Admiral Bwua'tu is merely providing accommodations until we come to an agreement."

"There won't be one." Kyp rose and started for the door. "Not while you're still Chief of State."

"Master Durron!" Hamner jumped up to go after him. "That kind of talk is—"

"Kenth . . . Kenth!" Omas had to yell before Hamner stopped and turned toward him. "Let him go. He's not wrong, you know. I *am* forcing your hand."

Hamner let out a breath of exasperation, then said, "It had not escaped our notice, believe me."

"And I'm sorry." Omas's apology was sincere. "But it's time we started to work together again, don't you think?"

"It appears we have no other choice," Lobi said. Her eyes flicked down the line of Masters beside her. "Who are we going to elect our temporary leader?"

"Not so fast," Katarn said. "Before we go on, maybe we should see if anyone else intends to join Master Durron."

"Of course," Omas said. "I wouldn't want to force anyone to be part of this."

"That's very considerate of you," Cilghal said.

To Omas's surprise, she rose and started for the door. He waited until she was gone, then turned to Katarn.

"And what is your decision, Master Katarn?"

"Oh, I'm staying." Kyle extended his legs and folded his arms across his chest. "I wouldn't want to make this too easy on you."

"Of course not." Omas smiled. Now that he had brought the Masters in line, he needed a temporary leader who was incapable of uniting the Jedi in support of the Killiks—and who would have no choice but to yield the position once Luke Skywalker was allowed to return. After all, Omas was not trying to *destroy* the Jedi, merely keep them out of the way while the Chiss dealt with the Killiks. "Perhaps you would care to be the one who nominates Master Horn as the temporary leader of the order?"

FOURTEEN

The barrier field at the mouth of the Jedi academy's main hangar was still up, despite the fact that Jaina and Zekk and the other pilots of the rescue squadron sat sweltering in their cockpits, itching inside their flight suits and choking on the stale, vapor-tinged air that accumulated within any starfighter in the long minutes before it launched. Their StealthXs were fully fueled and armed, their repulsorlift drives activated, their jump coordinates plotted all the way to the Murgo Choke . . . and *still* flight control held them in the hangar.

Kyp Durron's voice came over their cockpit speakers. "Flight control, this is Rescue One." He was speaking from the seat of his own starfighter, transmitting under the only circumstance in which StealthX protocols authorized use of the comm system. "Request deactivation of the hangar shield *again*!"

"Rescue One, please stand by," control responded.

"We *have* been standing by," Kyp retorted. "Deactivate this hangar shield now, or I'll do it for you!"

Kyp bolstered the threat by arming his laser cannons, then floating his StealthX around to target the generator housings at the top corner of the barrier field.

During the tense silence that followed, Jaina and Zekk felt Jacen's presence in the twin bond between him and Jaina for the first time in weeks. He was reaching out to them—to Jaina, really, but it felt like *them*—urging them to wait.

Kyp's voice came over the comm unit again. "Control, you have five seconds. Five—"

"Rescue One, please stand by," control replied. "Someone is coming down to talk to you."

"I'm done talking," Kyp said. "Four."

Jaina opened a squadron-only channel. "Master Durron, we think it's Jacen."

"We felt him in the Force," Zekk added. "Urging us to wait."

"Don't tell me *he's* taking Horn's side!" Kyp said.

"You know better than that," Tahiri reproached. "The only side Jacen takes is the Force's."

"Toes is right," Tesar Sebatyne rasped, referring to Tahiri by her squadron call sign. "Jacen is above all this arguing."

Kyp sighed. "How long?"

Jaina and Zekk reached out to Jacen, sharing with him the impatience they were already feeling with the launching delay. A moment later, an image of the Jedi academy as seen from the air appeared on their mind. It was growing rapidly larger.

"Soon," Zekk said.

Kyp dropped his StealthX back onto its skids. "Okay. Everyone pop your tops and get some air." He switched back to the open channel. "Affirmative, control. We'll wait."

"You will?" Control sounded as surprised as she did relieved. Like most of the non-Jedi support staff caught up in the argument over Corran Horn's appointment as the temporary leader of Jedi order, she was just trying to carry on as usual . . . and failing miserably. "Thank you!"

The squadron popped their canopies and let out a collective sigh of relief as the relatively fresh air of the hangar flooded their cockpits.

Jaina and Zekk reached out to Jacen, trying to get some sense of what he was thinking. But he had drawn in on himself again, maintaining just enough presence in the twin bond to be sure the squadron was still waiting. That was typical Jacen. Since his return from his five-year journey to learn more about the Force, he seemed more determined to control his bond with Jaina and Zekk, more reluctant to share himself with them. It almost seemed as though he was trying to protect something from them.

Or protect *them* from something inside him.

That was probably the case, Jaina and Zekk decided. No one could suffer what Jacen had at the hands of the Yuuzhan Vong and remain completely whole. The torments Tahiri had suffered during her captivity had ultimately caused a personality split, and Jacen had been held prisoner far longer than she had—under even more brutal circumstances. What had shattered inside him was anyone's guess.

Jaina and Zekk would be patient. They would continue to hold the twin bond open, to share with him what he would not share with them. And when he finally came apart, they would be there to help him find the pieces. That was what nest-fellows did.

Jacen's presence was still somewhere far above the academy when the door to the main access corridor slid open. A moment later Corran Horn marched into the hangar with Kenth Hamner and several other Jedi following close behind. All were scowling, and all were heading straight for the rescue squadron.

Kyp twisted around to scowl at Jaina. "That's not Jacen."

"He's on his way," she said.

"He's too late." Kyp turned back around, then spoke over the squadron-only channel. "Button back up. We're leaving."

As the rest of the squadron started to lower their canopies, Kyp reactivated his repulsorlift drive.

"Put that craft back down!" Corran yelled.

He pointed at the hangar floor and yelled something else, but Jaina and Zekk's canopies were already down and they did not hear what he said.

Whatever it was, Kyp ignored it and turned the nose back toward the barrier field generator. "Control, this is my last warning."

Corran suddenly came bounding across the floor with an activated lightsaber. He landed beneath the nose of Kyp's StealthX, then reached up beneath the forward landing strut, slashed one of the hydraulic lines necessary to retract the gear, and leapt back just in time to avoid being hit with a spray of oily orange fluid.

"Nizzze move," Izal Waz commed over the squadron channel. "Didn't think Horn had that in him."

"Hold the chatter," Jaina commed. Izal Waz was one of the Wild Knights whom Saba Sebatyne had introduced to the Jedi order during the war with the Yuuzhan Vong, and he had a sharp tongue even by Arconan standards. "We don't need any zingers right now."

"Things are tense enough," Zekk added.

And getting tenser. Kyp had already returned his StealthX to the hangar floor and was climbing out of the cockpit. Jaina and Zekk and the rest of squadron reopened their canopies.

". . . wrong with you?" Kyp was yelling at Corran. "You could have gotten killed!"

"I ordered you to stop," Corran retorted.

"I heard you." Kyp dropped to the hangar floor and peered under the StealthX's nose. "And look what you did! That's going to set us back three hours."

"It doesn't matter," Corran said. "This mission isn't authorized."

Kyp looked up. "*I* authorized it."

He flicked his wrist, and Corran went sailing across the hangar back toward Kenth and the other Jedi. It was a particularly insulting dismissal, since Corran could not respond in kind, having never been able to master the skill of Force telekinesis.

The same was not true of Kenth Hamner. He extended his arm, and Kyp flew back against the hull of his StealthX and remained there, pinned.

"*You* were not appointed the leader of the Jedi order," Kenth said, leading Corran and the rest of the Jedi back toward Kyp. "Master Horn *was*."

"This is getting out of hand," Jaina commed over the squadron channel.

"Everybody out," Zekk added.

"But leave your lightsabers in your cockpits," Jaina finished.

"Leave our lightsabers?" Wonetun objected. Another Sebatyne-trained Jedi Knight, the powerfully built Brubb had a voice as raspy as his pitted hide. "They have *their* lightsabers."

"Doesn't matter," Jaina said.

"This *isn't* going to be a fight," Zekk added.

"*Yet,*" Tesar Sebatyne finished.

Before Jaina could rebuke the Barabel for contributing to the general chaos, Tesar was dropping out of his cockpit and striding across the floor toward the rapidly growing showdown. Lowbacca caught up to him an instant later, and they took flanking positions behind Kyp's shoulders. By the time Jaina and Zekk and the rest of the squadron reached the crowd, the argument was already in full roar.

". . . needs a leader," Kenth was saying. "And the Advisory Council confirmed Master Horn as the temporary leader of the Jedi order."

"The Advisory Council doesn't pick our leaders," Kyp retorted. "And even if it did, there were only two real Jedi representatives there!"

"Whose fault is that?" Tresina Lobi asked. "You and Cilghal left."

"Because it was a *bogus meeting*!" Kyp yelled. "Omas has just been waiting until Luke was out of the way to put somebody he could control in charge."

"No, my friend." Kenth spoke in a deliberately soft tone, at the same time pouring soothing emotions into the Force. "Chief Omas choose Master Horn deliberately, because he knew it would throw the order into convulsions."

"And he certainly succeeded," Corran said. "Look, I *know* I'm not the best person to lead the order—"

"At least we agree on something," Kyp interrupted.

"That's out of line, Master Durron," Kenth said evenly. "We need to be civil, or Omas has already succeeded."

An anticipatory lull fell over the argument.

After a moment, Kyp blew out his breath and said, "Fine. I apologize."

"Thank you, Master Durron," Corran said. "Now, as I was saying—"

"If I may," Kenth interrupted. "I believe I was speaking."

Corran raised his brow. "Sorry. Go ahead."

"Thank *you*." Kenth's politeness was exaggerated, but it was doing wonders to help calm the situation. He turned back to Kyp. "If you'll indulge me a moment, what I'm trying to point out is that Chief Omas is trying to neutralize the Jedi order so that he can take action against the Killiks."

"And keep the Chiss happy—we know," Kyp said. "So we ought to surprise him by sticking together."

"That's *two* points we agree on," Corran said.

"Great!" Kyp's enthusiasm was as exaggerated as Kenth's politeness. "We'll launch the rescue mission as soon as my StealthX is repaired." He eyed Corran. "Unless you're going to cut another hydraulic line."

"Only if I have to," Corran retorted. "Going off on a cockeyed rescue mission is exactly the *wrong* thing to do. We need to prove to Chief Omas that the Galactic Alliance has nothing to fear from us."

"By letting him hold Jedi hostage?" Tesar demanded. "Never!"

"Cooperation is both the fastest and the surest way to win their release," Tresina said. "We need to turn this situation around, and it arose in the first place because last time we chose the Colony over the Alliance."

"We chose peace over convenienzzze," Izal Waz said. "That is our duty."

"Our duty is to support the Alliance," Corran said, "even if we disagree with its leader."

"Our duty is to the Force," Kyp retorted. "Nothing else."

And they were off, voices rising and gestures growing sharp as they argued the same points they had been arguing since Kyp had called Jaina and Zekk and the rest of the rescue squadron back from their other missions. With a mother being "detained" by the Galactic Alliance and a father and an uncle trapped in the Utegetu Nebula, Jaina and Zekk's position was as firm as it was obvious. But they did not like seeing the order torn apart by the disagreement, either. They had spent literally their entire lives working to establish it, and the prospect of seeing it dissolve was only slightly less loathsome than the thought of letting Cal Omas control it.

They had to get Uncle Luke and Dad out of Utegetu.

After a few minutes, the debate grew so heated that when the hangar's barrier field went down, only Jaina and Zekk seemed to care. They turned and saw Jacen's sleek little Koensayr Starskiff gliding into the entrance.

The situation inside the hangar appeared even worse from the cockpit of Jacen's Starskiff than in the glimpses he had been stealing through his sister's eyes. Kyp's rescue squadron was more like a squadron and a half, including Tam Azur-Jamin, Kirana Ti, and half a dozen Barabel Jedi Knights from Saba's old Wild Knights squadron. Corran Horn's group was equally large, with two Council Masters, Tresina Lobi and Kenth Hamner, among them. The two sides were arguing fiercely, almost violently, and it was clear that no one was listening to anyone.

"What's all that about?" Ben asked from the copilot's seat. "It feels like they're ready to slug each other."

"They are," Jacen said. "It has something to do with a mission to rescue Master Sebatyne and my mother, and maybe your father and mine. It's a little unclear."

"To *rescue* them?" Ben cried. "What's wrong?"

"I don't know yet," Jacen said. "But don't worry about it."

"Why not?"

"Because *I'm* not." Jacen put the skiff down on the side of the StealthXs farthest from the argument. There was no use letting Ben actually *hear* what adult Jedi were capable of yelling at each other. "And I have two parents involved."

"That's a dumb reason," Ben said. "You never worry about anything."

"That's not true," Jacen said. At the moment, he was terribly worried about two people on the planet Hapes. "I just don't worry about things I can't control, and I fix things I *can* control."

"Can you fix what they're arguing about?"

"No one can fix what they're arguing about," Jacen said. "But everything is going to be okay. If your father or my parents needed help, I'd know about it."

"How?" Ben demanded.

Jacen looked over and said nothing.

"Oh, yeah," Ben said. "The Force."

By the time Jacen shut the craft down, Jaina and Zekk had left the argument and were picking their way through the StealthX squadron toward the Starskiff. Jacen grabbed Ben's travel bag, then lowered the boarding ramp.

Ben raced down the ramp and immediately confronted Jaina. "Where's Mom? What happened to Dad and Uncle Han and Aunt Leia?"

"Nothing—they're okay," Jaina said.

"Why do you think something has happened to them?" Zekk asked.

Ben pointed across the hangar. "Because you're arguing about whether to rescue them or not, aren't you?"

Jaina and Zekk raised their round eyes to Jacen.

"It's not my fault," Jacen said. "He could feel it in the Force. So can half the students in the academy, I'm sure."

They blinked—together—and looked back to Ben.

"It's not that kind of rescue mission," Jaina explained. "No one's in danger right now."

"The Killiks are sort of holding your father and Uncle Han," Zekk explained. "And we're, um, discussing whether we should allow that."

Ben considered this a moment, then frowned in suspicion. "Why aren't you talking about Mom and Aunt Leia?"

"Because they're in even less danger," Jaina said. "They're being held by the Galactic Alliance, on a Star Destroyer."

"So no one's in danger?" Ben asked.

"Not yet," Zekk said.

"Then what's everyone arguing about?" Ben shook his head in disappointment. "Dad wouldn't like that."

"There are a lot of things happening right now he wouldn't like," Zekk said. "That's why we're trying to get him back."

"But that's not something *you* should worry about," Jaina said. "Why don't you tell us about your trip?"

"Was it fun?" Zekk added.

"Uh, yeah." Ben hesitated for a moment, then frowned. "We went camping on the forest moon of Endor."

Jaina and Zekk gave simultaneous throat-clicks, then frowned and looked to Jacen.

"Ben, tell them about Moon Falls," Jacen prodded. He had given Ben two memory rubs already, but the boy was so strong in the Force that his mind kept resisting. "I don't think Jaina has ever seen them."

"It's awesome!" Ben said. "The upper lake drops over a ledge into the lower lake, and it's so far that the water turns to mist!"

"Tell them how wide the falls are," Jacen said. He casually began to ruffle Ben's red hair, using the Force to push the Endor trip deeper into the boy's mind, to block any lingering memory of their visit to Hapes. "And what happens when they face away from the planet."

"Right—the falls just stop!" Ben said. "I guess the planet pulls the lake back or something."

"And how wide are the falls?" Jaina asked.

"*Twenty* kilometers," Ben said. "You can't even see from one end to the other."

"Astral!" Zekk said.

"That's pretty big," Jaina said.

Though Jaina and Zekk were looking at Ben, Jacen sensed through his twin bond with Jaina that her attention—and Zekk's—was on him. He had hoped they would not notice what he was doing, but it hardly mattered. He could not endanger his daughter's life further by taking the chance that Ben would remember what had happened on Hapes, then let slip that Jacen was the father of the new heir to the Hapan throne.

Jaina and Zekk fell silent and simply stood waiting in the patient way of Joiners. Jacen was about to suggest that Ben tell them about their stay with the Ewoks when he sensed a familiar presence approaching the back of the hangar.

Relieved to have an excuse to get Ben away from his all-too-perceptive sister and her mindmate, he turned to Ben. "Can you tell me who's coming through that door?"

Ben furrowed his brow for a moment, then said, "It must be Nanna."

The door slid open, revealing the massive, systems-packed torso and cherubic face of Ben's Defender Droid, Nanna.

"Very good!" Zekk said.

"You can sense droids already?" Jaina asked.

"Naw!" Ben shook his head. "It had to be her—Jacen called her on the way in."

"Very resourceful!" Jaina laughed. "Using your mind is—"

"—even better than using the Force," Zekk finished.

"Go meet her." Jacen passed Ben's travel bag to him, then patted him on the back. "Tell her all about our trip to Endor."

"I will!" Ben piped. "See you, Jaina and Zekk!"

Jaina and Zekk said their good-byes, then, once Ben was out of earshot, turned to Jacen.

"Okay, what was *that* about?" Jaina demanded.

"What?" Jacen asked.

"The head rubbing," Zekk said. "We felt you using the Force."

"It was nothing." Jacen was not willing to tell even Jaina about his daughter—not when that meant he was also telling Zekk. "Ben saw something upsetting while we were away. I've been using a little Force trick I learned from the Adepts to block it."

"So you *didn't* go camping on Endor," Zekk surmised.

"We did—afterward." Jacen was telling the truth. He had needed *something* to take the place of Ben's Hapan memories. "I'll fill you in later. But first, what's that all about?"

He pointed at the argument.

"You *have* been out of touch," Jaina said. "Cal Omas appointed Corran Horn temporary leader of the Jedi order."

"Some of us don't like it," Zekk added.

Jacen continued to study the argument. "Does this have anything to do with the Colony?"

"Everything," Jaina said.

They told him the highlights, from Raynar blaming the Jedi for the Fizz attacks on the Utegetu nests to the Colony's return to the Chiss border. Then they summarized Cilghal's theory about the stuff being a self-replicating nanotech terraforming system, and what they knew about Leia and Saba's detention by the Galactic Alliance. They finished by describing Chief Omas's attempt to take control of the Jedi order by appointing Corran Horn its temporary leader.

"And you can see how well *that's* working," Jaina said. "Half the order thinks we need to mount rescue missions for Mom and Saba and Dad and Uncle Luke."

"And the other half thinks we need to support the blockade and intimidate the Colony into pulling out of the buffer zone," Zekk added. "Meanwhile, the Killiks are establishing nests all along the Chiss frontier."

Jacen felt the blood drain from his face, and he saw again the burning planets and the spaceships carrying flames from system to system, he saw the hands of humans and Chiss and Killiks setting those fires, saw the whole galaxy going up in one eternal blaze.

"Jacen?"

"What's wrong?" Jaina asked. "Jacen!"

"It's happening," Jacen gasped.

"*What's* happening?" Jaina demanded.

"Another war." Jacen was beginning to see what had to be done, why the vision had come to *him*. "An eternal one."

"All right, Jacen," Jaina said. "You're starting to scare us."

"Good," Jacen said. "Because *I'm* terrified."

He turned toward the argument still raging beyond the StealthXs, then touched Tesar in the Force and summoned him over.

The meaning of the vision was growing clearer to Jacen every moment. Ta'a Chume had attacked his infant daughter through the Dark Nest, just as the Dark Nest was attacking the Galactic Alliance through its black membrosia and its pirate harboring. The Force had shown him what was going to come of the Colony's actions—and it had shown him in the moment he was taking action to protect his daughter.

The Force wanted him to protect *its* child.

The Force wanted him to do to the Killiks what he had done to Ta'a Chume.

"Jacen?" Jaina asked. "Tesar said you—"

"Just a minute," Jacen said.

He summoned Lowbacca next, and then Tahiri, one at a time so their departure would go unnoticed by those in the argument.

Once they were all gathered around, he said, "I need your help. Now."

"Now?" Tesar asked. "Sorry. Master Durron needz us to rescue—"

"That isn't important."

"It's important to *us*," Tahiri said. "The Colony is holding Han and Master Skywalker hostage—"

"Free Uncle Luke or not, support Master Horn or oppose him, it makes no difference in the end." Jacen reached out to them all in the Force, trying to share with them the horror he had felt when he experienced that vision, offering them just a glimpse of the dark future he had foreseen. "I need you to do something that will make a difference."

Lowbacca groaned the opinion that Jacen should tell them what in space he was talking about.

"I had a vision."

The group grew quieter, and Tahiri whispered, "*That* can't be good."

"It isn't," Jacen said. "A war erupts between the Killiks and Chiss, and the Galactic Alliance is drawn into it."

"That is what we're trying to prevent," Tesar said. "That is why we must rescue Master Skywalker and put an end to the Galactic Alliance'z blockade."

Jacen met the Barabel's eye. "The war has already started—and the Killiks are the only ones who know it."

"The Killiks?" Jaina shook her head. "The Killiks are peaceful—"

"The Dark Nest *isn't*," Jacen said. He could see that the others were still too enamored of the Killiks to help him willingly, so he would have to explain things in terms they could accept. "The Dark Nest is leading the Colony astray again. The black membrosia, the Utegetu pirates, who knows what else—it's been working to destabilize the Galactic Alliance for months."

"Because they still want to expand into the Chiss frontier?" Tahiri asked.

"Because the Dark Nest still *wants a war* with the Chiss," Jacen corrected.

"This one is not so sure," Tesar said. "Why would the Dark Nest want a war with the Chisz?"

"The same reason they did last time," Tahiri said. "To conquer them."

"Remember how their larvae feed," Zekk said.

"It can't be easy to expand a nest when you need a constant supply of slaves to lay your eggs in," Jaina added. "A war is the ideal cover. When people disappear, they're casualties, not mysteries."

"Exactly," Jacen said. "Everything the Dark Nest has done has been designed to neutralize the things that prevented the war last time. The Galactic Alliance is so angry about the black membrosia and the pirates that it won't lift a finger to interfere with the Chiss."

Lowbacca nodded, then looked back toward the argument and growled that the Jedi had been neutralized as well.

Tahiri let out a breath, then asked, "So what do you want us to do, Jacen?"

"Stop the war." Jacen slowly drew a veneer of calm over his presence, projecting an aura of tranquillity into the Force that would prevent the others from sensing the lies he was about to tell. "In my vision, the war starts in earnest when the Chiss launch a surprise attack against the new Killik colonies."

"That makez no sense," Tesar objected. "Even Master Durron sayz the Chisz are waiting for the Jedi to make the Killikz withdraw."

Jacen used a smile to hide the grimace inside. This was something he had not heard about. "And how do we know this?"

Tesar remained silent and looked to Lowbacca and Tahiri, who merely shrugged.

"From the meeting where Master Horn was appointed our leader," Tahiri said.

"So we can assume that the information came from Chief Omas," Jacen said. "And he might or might not be telling the truth—as he knows it."

Lowbacca groaned a question.

"What I'm saying is that the information probably came from the Chiss themselves," Jacen said.

Jaina nodded. "And if they *were* planning a preemptive attack—"

"—they would want to keep the Galactic Alliance out of the way," Zekk finished.

"Exactly," Jacen said. "Chiss lie—visions don't."

Seeing the alarm in their faces—and sensing it in the Force even more clearly—Jacen fell quiet and allowed the others a few moments to contemplate what he was asking. With the Jedi essentially leaderless and in disarray, he had no doubts about their eventual decision. In times of turmoil, most people were eager to follow a being with a vision. Vergere had taught him that.

It was Tahiri, of course, who brought up the question that Jacen felt sure was nagging them all. "If the Dark Nest is *causing* all this trouble, why aren't we going after it?"

"Two reasons," Jacen said. "First, that's what Master Durron and his squad will end up doing, after they get Dad and Uncle Luke back."

"And second?" Tesar asked.

"We're either going to be in the middle of the war with the Chiss or stopping it," Jacen said. "The Dark Nest will be coming to *us* soon enough."

Jaina and Zekk nodded at this, then the group fell silent and studied each other for a few moments.

Finally, Jaina asked, "When do we leave?"

Jacen thought for a moment, running through different ways to furtively deactivate the barrier field—which had been raised again after his skiff entered the hangar—then pointed at the six nearest StealthXs. "We'll take those."

FIFTEEN

The pearly light had drained from the outer walls of their prison three hours earlier, and still Luke sensed no hint of Juun and Tarfang's approach. Maybe the Ewok had convinced his Sullustan captain that Han was swindling them, or maybe the pair had decided they were in so much trouble they would be better off just running and hiding. Maybe Raynar had learned of their plans and imprisoned them, too. All Luke knew for sure was that *DR919a* should have signaled them more than two hours ago, and they were still waiting.

"You going to move that savrip or what, Skywalker?" Han asked.

"What's the hurry?" Luke asked, pretending to study the hologrammic dejarik board R2-D2 was projecting between their stools. "It's not like we're going anyplace."

Han's eyes finally left the game. "That's no excuse to bore me to death," he said. "Besides, the time will go faster if you keep your mind on the game. We'll be out of here before you know it."

It was clear to both Luke and Han that they were talking about their escape plans and not the game, but that was as close to *relax, they're coming,* as Han could say aloud. Luke had sent the X-wing replica—and the Gorog spies it contained—back to Raynar, and a Saras guard had immediately taken up residence inside their cells. Even now, it was hovering behind Luke, watching the dejarik game with great interest.

Luke spent a moment actually studying the game, then said to R2-D2, "Leave my savrip where it is. Have my closest grimtassh attack Han's ghhhk, then make a surprise-kill attack on his houjix."

"Oh, my—that is quite an unorthodox move," C-3PO said. "Are

you sure you want to do it, Master Skywalker? If you defeat the gh-hhk and take the surprise attack on Captain Solo's houjix—"

"Butt out, chiphead," Han growled. He turned to R2-D2. "What are you waiting for? You heard the man."

Luke barely noticed as his grimtassh hopped over to Han's gh-hhk and took its place on the board. From what he could feel in the Force, Mara and Leia were fairly close to the Utegetu Nebula, but Mara had dropped into a deep Force-hibernation, and Leia seemed frustrated and impatient. Clearly, the *Falcon* had been delayed on her return trip, and Luke's patience with his "detention" had come to an end. If Juun and Tarfang did not show up soon, he was going to break out and go hunting for them.

Han sent a k'lor'slug over to assault the savrip Luke had neglected to move out of harm's way, then scowled at R2-D2 when the attack failed.

"What are you doing?" he demanded. "That was from behind! It's automatic."

"There *are* no automatic victories in dejarik," C-3PO said helpfully. "Even rear attacks have a one in ten thousand probability of failure."

"And Artoo expects me to believe he just *happened* to generate a failure when Luke makes a vac-headed move like that?"

R2-D2 emitted a defensive whistle.

"He says that Master Luke is distracted," C-3PO said. "He needs a handicap."

"I'm not *that* distracted," Luke said. "Do it over, Artoo—and use standard probabilities."

R2-D2 let out an annoyed whistle, then Luke's savrip vanished and was replaced by Han's k'lor'slug.

"That's more like it," Han said. "Now pay attention, Skywalker. The game is about to get interesting."

Luke barely watched as Han's k'lor'slug slinked over to attack his monnok. He was trying to connect the *Falcon*'s delay to Alema's attempts to make him doubt Mara. Clearly, the Dark Nest was trying to drive a wedge between him and his wife, probably to punish her for killing Daxar Ies. But he was beginning to suspect that there was another reason—that the attacks were also directed against him in some subtle way he had yet to understand.

"Luke?" Han said. "It's your move."

Luke looked up to find Han smirking at him across the hologram. Han had succeeded in taking control of the center of the board and now had Luke's ghhhk encircled, with no hope of escape.

"Artoo, have my strider retreat to the edge of the board."

"Retreat?" Han scowled. "You're sacrificing the ghhhk?"

R2-D2 whistled gleefully and did as Luke instructed, leaving Han's pieces almost alone in the middle of the board. Once Han took the ghhhk, he would be stuck with all his pieces facing center and no surprise-kill attacks available to change orientation. Luke, meanwhile, was scattered around the edge of the board, able to attack any of Han's pieces from behind.

Han took one look and kicked the hologram. Of course, all that happened was that his boot came down in the middle of the game.

"You sandbagged me again!" Han accused. "You were paying attention the whole time."

Luke shrugged. "Dejarik is an old Jedi game." As he spoke, Luke finally sensed the familiar presences of Juun and Tarfang streaking across Saras nest toward their prison. "Are we going to play it out?"

Han must have sensed Luke's rising excitement, because when Luke looked up, there was a glint in Han's eye that could not possibly have come from the belief that he could win.

"You bet," Han said. "I've still got a three-piece . . ."

Han let his sentence trail off as the guard suddenly stepped away from Luke and began to drum its thorax.

"Saras is ordering us to move away from the wall," C-3PO reported. "She seems to believe we're trying to—"

Luke sprang from his stool, already bringing his foot around in a crescent kick that sent the Killik stumbling into the wall. Han was on the insect before it could catch its balance, slamming his stool down across the back of its head with chitin-cracking force.

"—escape," C-3PO finished. He studied the unconscious Killik with a cocked head for a moment, then turned to Luke. "Pardon me, Master Skywalker, but *are* we making our escape attempt now?"

"No," Han growled. "We just thought we'd have some fun beating up our guards."

"Oh." C-3PO straightened his head. "In that case, you're going to have quite an exciting time. Saras was trying to tell you that there is a whole company of reinforcements coming up the ramp."

Luke and Han exchanged glances, then Han said, "I'll take 'em." He hefted his stool, then went into his own room and turned toward the hatch. "You just get that wall open."

Luke followed Han and went to the wall where he had been having R2-D2 scratch x's. He used his finger to connect four sets of x's together, tracing an imaginary asterisk on the wall.

By this time, the Saras reinforcements had arrived outside the cell. Luke could hear them snipping and ripping away the outer seal of the hatch, and he could see their silhouettes through the translucent wall, backlit by green shine-balls. They appeared to be holding Verpine shatter guns and electrobolt assault rifles.

"I've got it under control, Skywalker," Han said, sensing Luke's concern without having to turn around. "Just get that hole open."

The wall in Luke's room brightened with the blue glow of an exterior spotlight.

"Master Skywalker," C-3PO began. "I believe Captain Juun has arrived, and he seems to be signaling—"

"The wrong room, I know." Luke placed his palm in the center of the asterisk he had traced in Han's room, then began to pulse rapidly outward with the Force, setting up a kinetic vibration that would weaken the spinglass. "You and Artoo stand behind me."

"Behind you?" C-3PO asked. "I don't see what good that will do."

"Threepio!" There was a dull thump as Han smashed the stool into the head of the first Killik attempting to push through the hatch. "Just do it!"

"There's no need to shout, Captain Solo." C-3PO gestured to R2-D2, then went to stand where Luke had instructed. "I was merely going to point out that Captain Juun won't be extending the boarding ramp in the proper place."

"That's okay." Luke assumed a formal punching stance in front of the asterisk he had scratched. "We'll improvise."

He summoned as much Force energy as he could into himself, then drew his arm back and slammed a palm-heel into the center of the asterisk. His hand drove through the spinglass almost effortlessly, shattering it along the stress lines R2-D2 had etched into the wall.

Outside was the blocky, carbon-scored hull of Juun's *Ronto*-class transport, hovering twenty meters off the ground, with a boarding ramp butted against the wall outside Luke's room. A dark Ewok head peered out of the ship's hatch and began to jabber at Luke.

"Of all the audacity!" C-3PO said, peering around the side of the hole. "Tarfang says we made our hole in the wrong place. The *DR-Nine-one-nine-a* isn't going to move!"

A flurry of sharp plinking sounds broke out behind them as the Saras guards began to fire through the hatch wall with their shatter guns.

"Go!" Han turned away from the hatch and crossed the tiny room in two bounds. "Go nowwwww!"

Luke barely caught hold of Han's belt as he flew past. He pushed off the side of the hole, Force-leaping onto the *DR919a*'s boarding ramp. As they balanced there, shatter gun pellets began thunk into the hull beside them, creating a circle of fist-sized dents just three meters away.

"Blast!" Han turned to look back toward their prison. "That was too close—"

Han's exclamation came to a startled end as the *DR919a* began to bank away, the boarding ramp retracting with them still on it. He whirled toward the hatch and began to curse out Tarfang, but Luke did not hear what he said. C-3PO had appeared in the hole, pulling R2-D2 along by the astromech's grasper arm.

"Master Skywalker! Wait! Please don't—"

The droid's upper body abruptly flew forward, and he tumbled out of the hole, pulling R2-D2 along behind him.

"—ussss beeehinnnn—"

Luke extended a hand and caught the two droids in the Force, then nearly fell himself when the end of the ramp retracted into its stowage slot.

"Whoa!" Han grabbed Luke's arm and pulled him through the hatch. "You okay?"

"Of course not!" This from C-3PO, who was floating along with R2-D2 a couple of meters below the hatch. "I've been badly wounded! My systems might deactivate at any moment!"

Han guided Luke's free hand over to a grab bar inside the hatch, then knelt down to help the droids as Luke pulled them up with the Force. Once everyone was safely inside the *DR919a*, Han closed the hatch.

Juun's voice immediately came over the intercom. "Secure yourselves back there! I'm pushing the throttles to seventy percent!"

Han took a deep breath and looked genuinely scared. "May the Force be with us!"

A moment later, the *DR919a* shuddered and began to accelerate sluggishly. Han put his ear to the hull and listened for a moment, then sighed in relief and turned to inspect C-3PO's damage.

"Relax, Goldenrod," Han said. "It's an arm hit. You've got a few shorts and you've spilled a lot of hydraulic fluid, but you're not going to deactivate anytime soon."

C-3PO turned to Luke. "I'd feel much better if you would check me over, Master Skywalker. You know how Captain Solo always underestimates these things."

Han rolled his eyes but stood aside so Luke could have a look. There was a fist-sized hole in the back of the droid's arm, and dozens of internal wires had been cut, along with both hydraulic tubes. But none of that was going to be a problem—there weren't any critical systems in the limb.

"Han's right," Luke reported. "Just disable all functions in your right arm, and you'll be fine."

"What a relief!" C-3PO said. "After all I've been through, I thought I was headed for the scrap heap for certain."

R2-D2 whistled a gentle reproach.

"I'm hardly exaggerating," C-3PO said. "You have no idea what it's like to be wounded."

R2-D2 tweeted a contradiction.

"You do?" Luke gasped. He knelt beside the droid. "Where?"

R2-D2 spun his dome around, revealing a puncture the size of three fingers. When Luke peered into the hole, he saw Han's eye looking at him from the other side.

"That can't be good," Han said.

R2-D2 trilled a long reply.

"What do you mean it's not too bad?" C-3PO demanded. "Being unable to see is *very* bad!"

Tarfang threw a sympathetic arm around R2-D2's casing and started to guide the droid forward, keeping up a reassuring jabber as they moved.

"Thank you, Tarfang, but a visit to the Squibs really won't be necessary," C-3PO said, following along. "I assure you, Master Skywalker can afford to buy the finest *new* replacement parts."

They came to the *DR919a*'s flight deck. Extremely basic, it was little more than the forward end of the main deck with a couple of Sullustan-sized swivel chairs bolted in front of an instrument console. The viewport was barely large enough to justify the name, with the blue curtain of the Utegetu Nebula stretched across the micropitted transparisteel and the cragged peak of one of Woteba's high mountains protruding up in the foreground.

"Welcome aboard." Juun did not look away from his instruments as he spoke. "I'm sorry we were late, but the Saras are evacuating their nest, and the Squibs wanted us to pick up a load from the replica factory."

"*Evacuating* their nest?" Luke gasped.

"Yes, it's half empty already," Juun said. "They're surrendering it all to the Fizz."

"I don't like the sound of that," Luke said.

"Me either!" Han agreed. "I think they were going to leave us!"

"*We* wouldn't have left you, Captain Solo," Juun assured him. "We just had to avoid drawing suspicion. Now please take your seats and buckle in. Saras is sending a swarm of dartships after us."

Luke ignored the instructions and peered over the Sullustan's shoulder at the navigation display. It was filled with static, but a swirling mass of tiny dark dashes did seem to be rising from an amorphous blob of lights that might have been Saras nest.

"Can you outrun them?"

Tarfang barked something indignant, then waved a furry hand toward the passengers' seats at the rear of the deck.

"Of course—they're only rockets," C-3PO translated. "And the copilot reminds you to take your seats as Captain Juun instructed."

"In a second," Han said. He was squatting next to the copilot's seat, studying the navicomputer. "Hey, Jae, how come we're not jumping to the Murgo Choke?"

"There's a blockade," Juun answered. "We'll have to use the Mott's Nostril."

"The Mott's's Nostril?" Han objected. "That dumps us—"

"Hold on, Han."

Luke stood upright, then clasped his hands behind his back and thought for a moment, trying again to connect the *Falcon*'s delay to Alema's attempts to make him doubt his wife. Maybe the Dark Nest had just been trying to buy time, to keep him busy thinking about her instead of what was happening in the Utegetu Nebula.

Finally, Luke said, "I want to hear more about this blockade."

"Now?" Juun asked. "I'd be happy to tell you about it *after* we're safely away from the dartships."

Han frowned. "Tarfang said we could outrun them."

"Because we have a good head start," Juun said. "But if we don't jump soon, they'll catch us."

"Then please don't waste any more time arguing," Luke said. "Tell me about the blockade. This is important."

Juun let out a long breath, flapping his cheek folds in dismay. "The Galactic Alliance has blockaded the Utegetu Nebula. They're trying to prove that they're on the Chiss's side," he said quickly. "Okay? Can we jump now?"

Han ignored the question. "Don't tell me," he said. "The Colony is already expanding into the frontier again."

Tarfang chattered a few lines.

"Tarfang doesn't see why we're surprised," C-3PO reported. "What did the Jedi expect to happen when they cheated the Colony?"

"Who, exactly, is blockading the nebula?" Luke asked Juun. "The Fifth Fleet?"

Juun's jaw dropped. "How did you know?"

"Lucky guess," Han said. "And this would be the same Fifth Fleet you delivered that cargo of spinglass to?"

Juun nodded—slowly. "I guess so."

Han and Luke looked at each other slowly, then Han dropped to his knees beside the navicomputer.

"I'll set a course for the Choke."

"No." Luke shook his head. "So far, the Dark Nest has been playing us all like a bunch of Kloo horns, and the only way we're going to change that is find them and figure out what they wanted with all that reactor fuel and hyperdrive coolant."

Han sighed. "I was afraid you were going to say that."

"As was I," C-3PO agreed. "Perhaps it would be a good idea to drop off the wounded before you continue. Surely, R2-D2 and I won't be of much use to you in our condition, and we might slow you down."

"You'll be fine," Luke said. "You won't even have to get off the ship."

Han looked from the navicomputer to Juun. "Any idea where we should look?"

Tarfang chittered off a sharp string of syllables.

"I'm sorry, Tarfang," Luke said, taking a guess at what the cranky Ewok was saying. "But if you want us to get you out of trouble for delivering that spinglass to the Fifth Fleet—"

Tarfang barked a short reply, then pulled Han away from the navicomputer and began to program it himself.

"Pardon me, Master Luke," C-3PO said. "But Tarfang wasn't objecting. He was suggesting that we set a course for the Tusken's Eye."

"Why?" Han demanded.

Tarfang jabbered an explanation, but Juun beat C-3PO to the translation.

"Because that's where we've been taking all that Tibanna we've been running for the Squibs," he said. "And those pirates are hiding *something*."

SIXTEEN

Orbiting above a swirling atmosphere of yellow sulfuric clouds, Supply Depot Thrago was classically Chiss—austere, utilitarian, and bristling with defenses. In addition to the floating fuel tanks that Jacen and his team would soon be destroying, the tiny moon base was equipped with turbolaser platforms, a shield array, cannon turrets, hidden bunkers, and a clawcraft hangar with two entrances. The weapons platforms were arranged with overlapping fields of fire, and the bunkers and hangar had been concealed with typical Chiss cunning. Even for Jedi in StealthXs, this was going to be a difficult run—especially if they wanted to minimize their target's casualties.

It had to be done. The attack on Jacen's daughter had been only a single move in the Dark Nest's plan—a plan that would ultimately lead to the eternal war Jacen had seen in his vision. Probably, that was even what the Dark Nest intended, since its larvae fed on live captives.

Jacen was not foolish enough to believe he could stop the war. The Gorog had been waging it for months already, even if no one realized it. But he *could* prevent it from becoming the eternal war of his vision. All he needed to do was rouse the Chiss, to prod them into action before the Dark Nest completed its preparations.

Of course, once the Chiss went to war, they would not stop with one nest. They would destroy the entire species, wipe out every Killik nest they could find, and that was Jacen's plan. As long as there was a Colony, there would be a Dark Nest, and as long as there was a Dark Nest, his daughter's life would be in danger. He had sensed that much from Ta'a Chume. Gorog had promised to kill Tenel Ka's child, and she had believed the insects would make good on their word. So the insects had to go.

Unfortunately, Jacen could not say as much to Jaina and Zekk and Tesar and the others. They would argue that only the Dark Nest needed to be destroyed, that a whole species should not be condemned to protect one child.

They did not understand the Killiks the way Jacen did. The Colony had been harmless once, but Raynar and Welk and Lomi Plo had changed the insects. They had brought the knowledge of good and evil to an innocent species, had created a hidden aspect of the Colony's collective mind that would forever be obsessed with vengeance, hatred, and conquest. The Killiks had become an aberration, and they had to be destroyed. It was the only way to stop the eternal war.

It was the only way to save his daughter.

Jacen reached out to his companions in the Force, letting them know that the time had come to act. A big fuel tanker was gliding toward the supply depot, decelerating as it approached the gate, and it was a good opportunity for the strike team to slip through the shields.

As they opened the combat-meld, Jacen felt a sense of uncertainty from his sister and Zekk, and to a lesser extent from Tesar and Lowbacca. During the mission briefing that morning, they had all expressed reservations about launching a preemptive strike on the Chiss. The Ascendancy had laws against attacking first, so Jaina and Zekk had found it difficult to believe that the Chiss really intended to launch the surprise attack Jacen claimed he had foreseen.

It had been Tahiri who had pointed out that the Colony was technically in violation of the Qoribu Truce. The Killiks had moved colonists into the buffer zone, so the Ascendancy was free to attack anytime it wanted. And everything the strike team had seen over the last few days of reconnoitering suggested the Chiss *were* mobilizing for a major attack. They were moving assets forward, stockpiling fuel, ammunition, food, and spare parts, and running fleet maneuvers with live gunnery.

Of course, those were the same preparations the Chiss would make as a contingency plan. The strike team had seen nothing that pointed exclusively to a surprise attack, and even now, as they waited to move their StealthXs into position, Jacen could sense that Jaina and Zekk remained somewhat skeptical.

Jacen concentrated on the place within him that had always belonged to his sister, filling it with his own sense of certainty, hoping Jaina would interpret his confidence to mean he was sure about the surprise attack. He felt bad about using the twin bond to mislead his sister—but not as bad as he would feel if his vision became reality.

Jaina and Zekk's hesitancy began to subside, and Tesar and Lowbacca grew almost enthusiastic. Giving his companions no further chance to hesitate, Jacen activated his sublight drive and led the way down to the freighter. Though their StealthXs were almost as invisible to the naked eye as they were to sensors, the pilots took the precaution of approaching from directly behind, where there would be no viewing ports.

Once they had slipped up on the ship, they clustered together beneath the stern, tucked into the dark recess between the giant sphere of the vessel's number three cargo tank and the immense flare of its engine housings.

For several minutes, the Jedi had to float along in the shadows, able to see nothing but the swell of the cargo tank's gray skin, the colored glow of a handful of running lights, and, out the sides of their canopies, the star-flecked velvet of deep space. Then Jacen's astromech droid reported that a hole had opened in the shields, and the blue glow of an inspection light began to brighten space around the tanker.

Jacen flipped his StealthX upside down so that he could keep watch as they approached the supply depot. Since he could no longer see anything of the freighter except the round bellies of its four big fuel tanks, he had to trust Jaina to keep him in position by urging him to speed up or fall back.

It took only a few seconds before the supply depot's gate-platforms came into view. Floating vertically, they were basically crescent-shaped weapons platforms with shield generators instead of turbolasers. The inner edges were lined with cannon turrets, missile launchers, and plasma guns—all designed to defend against just the sort of infiltration the six Jedi were attempting. Shining out from behind the weapons were two semicircular banks of inspection lamps, arranged so that they would illuminate the entire girth of the freighter as it passed through the gates.

Jacen focused his attention on the vessel's port side and watched patiently as the inspection lamps lit up the exterior of the number two cargo tank. When the forward end of the number three tank slid under the light, he visually followed one of the beams back to its source, then reached out in the Force and pulled the cathode out of its mounting.

The lamp erupted into a brilliant spray of sparks, and a ten-meter section of the cargo tank was plunged into darkness. Jacen reached out to the team, then pushed his throttles forward and led the way through the gap. A backup lamp came online no more than five seconds later, but by then the Jedi and their StealthXs were safely inside the depot's shields, tucked in a dark cranny between the freighter's bow and its number one cargo tank.

The Chiss swept their inspection lights back and forth over the number three tank a few times, but there was no question of a reinspection. Kilometer-long freighters did not simply stop and back up. Even at the vessel's current low velocity, it would have taken the braking thrusters a full half kilometer to stop the vessel, and by then any infiltrators would be well inside the shields anyway.

But Jacen knew the Chiss well enough to realize what would come next. Although lamp cathodes did sometimes blow spontaneously, the Chiss were cautious. They would almost certainly make a flyby inspection. He kept the strike team in hiding only until the freighter had cleared the shields, then dropped out of the cranny and slowly began to move away, careful to keep the huge cargo tanks between the StealthXs and the well-armed gate-platforms.

A few moments later, half a dozen shuttles appeared around the freighter, carefully working their way forward and shining their spotlights into every nook and cranny on the vessel's exterior. Jacen let out a deep breath of relaxation, then led the strike team down through a zone of floating repair docks—mostly empty at the moment—and around a line of frigates and blastboat escorts beam-anchored to the tiny moon that served as the heart of the base.

The battle-meld suddenly filled with Jaina and Zekk's doubt, and Jacen sensed them worrying about the frigates. He reached out to the vessels in Force and did not feel anyone aboard. His IR sensors suggested that internal temperatures were well below freezing, and he knew that would make Jaina question whether the Chiss were really planning a massive surprise attack.

Jacen could think of a dozen reasons the frigates might be in cold storage. Perhaps they were being held in reserve, or maybe their crews had not yet arrived . . . he tried to reassure his sister that there were many possible explanations.

Jaina and Zekk only seemed to have more doubts about his vision, and Jacen was well aware that the empty vessels just did not support his claim that the Chiss were about to launch an assault. It would take a week to bring a cold frigate online. The reactor cores would have to be lit, the vessel's temperature raised slowly to avoid stressing the hull or superstructure. Several kilometers of mechanical lines would have to be bled and filled with the proper fluids. Provisions would have to be brought aboard and properly stowed. These vessels showed no indication of any of that.

Jacen projected an air of thoughtfulness into the meld, pretending to consider his sister's feelings while he watched the tiny moon grow larger and brighter. It was little more than a hubba-shaped lump of rock, barely ten kilometers from end to end and so blanketed in dust that its thousands of craters had a soft, almost featureless look to them.

The fighter hangar, their first target, was located inside a ridge between two particularly deep craters, with one entrance opening out of a crater slope on each side. The surrounding terrain was flecked with cannon turrets, indistinguishable from boulders except for the tired sentries Jacen could feel standing watch inside a handful of them.

Jaina and Zekk projected their hesitation into the meld more forcefully.

Jacen could sense where their line of thought was going—and he did not like it. Being careful not to let anyone else sense what he was doing, he reached out in the Force and touched the nearest sentry, urging the fellow to look up and pay attention.

Jaina and Zekk began to urge the team to pull up—

Too late. Jacen felt the sentry targeting him, then began to juke and jink as a flight of cannon bolts came streaming up from the side of the nearest crater.

Jaina and Zekk were furious, and all thought of calling off the mission vanished from the meld. Unless the strike team wanted to find itself in a very bad dogfight—while trapped inside the supply depot's shields—they had to proceed as planned.

Tesar, Lowbacca, and Tahiri barrel-rolled away and swung around to attack the hangar entrance in the far crater, while Jaina and Zekk fell in behind Jacen and banked around to make their attack run barely three meters above the floor of the near one. Cannon bolts and plasma bursts began to stab out from the sides of more boulders, but it was practically impossible for gunners to target what their sensors could not see, so most shots went wildly astray.

Jacen armed his glop bomb and ran the last hundred meters to the hangar mouth straight in, and bursts of cannon fire finally began to blossom on his forward shields. His astromech screeched a warning that the shields were about to go, and Jaina tried to move up and take the front position in the shielding trio. Jacen cut her off, then released his glop bomb and took two more forward hits as he stayed on course to guide it in.

Jaina's anger at his heroics scalded the combat-meld, then Jacen pulled up, climbing the crater wall slope so closely that his astromech began to screech about the belly shields. Jaina released her glop bomb behind him, then Zekk's feeling of triumph confirmed that he had seen at least one of the bombs detonate and fill the hangar mouth with its quick-hardening foam.

Jacen cleared the crater rim and felt Tesar rising exactly opposite him from the other crater. He spun his cockpit around and found himself flying almost wingtip-to-wingtip with the madly grinning Barabel. They held that position and corkscrewed away from the moon's surface, the rest of the team close on their tails and the Chiss gunners lighting space around them with bright blossoms of fire.

As soon as they were out of the gunners' range, Tesar led Lowbacca and Tahiri back through the frigates toward the tank fields near the upper reaches of the shields. Jacen took Jaina and Zekk and wheeled back toward the moon. The area around the fighter hangar was so clouded in dust that the craters were no longer visible. The gunners, unable to see anything, had finally given up firing.

Seeing that his front shields had fallen to zero, Jacen commanded, "Transfer half the available power to the forward shields."

His astromech bleeped a sharp reply, then displayed a message explaining that there *were* no forward shields. The generator had been blown off when Jacen ignored the droid's warning that they were about to fail.

Jaina moved into the lead position, with Zekk behind her, leaving Jacen to bring up the rear. He could feel his sister's irritation in the meld and knew that once the team returned to the Colony, Jaina and Zekk were going to have a long talk with him about flying as a team. Until then, he would have to hide behind *them*.

The darkness above turned a flashing, brilliant orange as Tesar and his squad attacked the floating fuel tanks. Jacen knew from their planning session that the trio would bypass any tank near which they sensed a living presence, but there was no question that most of the base's fuel supply would be destroyed. During their reconnaissance, they had counted more than five hundred tanks, each half a kilometer in diameter, and the only time any Chiss had been near one was when it was being dropped off by a transport.

Jaina led Jacen and Zekk a quarter of the way around the moon's surface toward a dust-covered hill that was the depot's primary ammunition dump. Instead of dropping close to the surface, this time they attacked from more than a kilometer above, each firing a two-stage bunker-buster torpedo.

The propellant trails had barely flashed to life before dozens of "boulders" on the hill suddenly came alive and began to pour fire up toward the attacking StealthXs. Jacen slipped in close behind Zekk, then turned his hand over to the Force and began to weave and dodge through the crimson blooms.

Then the bunker busters hit, raising a curtain of dust as their focused thermal detonators burned a meter-wide hole down through the roof of the dump. Half a second later the torpedoes' main warheads—simple proton bombs—descended through the same hole into the bunker interior. Normally, such bombs would explode instantly, but the strike team's were less deadly; they would spark and hiss for five minutes to give personnel time to evacuate the vicinity.

Once the dust cloud had risen high enough to obscure the gunners' aim, Jaina pulled up. She turned toward the second bunker, located about two kilometers away on the horizon of the little moon, and the trio instantly fired their second set of bunker busters. Again, as soon as the propellant trails flared to life, the Chiss laced the darkness with defensive fire. Jacen saw one torpedo flash out of existence as a laser cannon scored, but then the telltale curtain of dust rose from the bunker.

Jaina turned away, dropping around the edge of the moon toward the third and final dump. But she did not fire her last torpedo. It took Jacen a couple of seconds to see the problem. A small but bustling repair hangar had been built into the wall of a shallow crater below the ammunition dump. When the dump exploded, it would almost certainly bury the hangar beneath it.

Jaina and Zekk started to pull up without firing, but Jacen continued on course. Jaina and Zekk filled the meld with alarm and confusion. There were a hundred Chiss in that hangar who would not realize what was happening until it was too late.

Jacen adjusted his course toward the hangar. He would chase out the personnel; then Jaina and Zekk could take out the ammunition dump. The Chiss had to see that the Jedi were serious about stopping them, or they would simply continue with their plans.

But Jaina and Zekk did not seem to understand what he was planning—or perhaps they simply thought it was too risky. They continued to angle away from the attack.

Jacen adjusted his course back toward the ammunition dump, leaving Jaina and Zekk with two choices: chase the personnel out of the repair hangar—or leave them there to perish. It did not matter to

Jacen which option they chose; the Chiss would get the message either way.

The Chiss gunners opened fire, turning space ahead into a wall of flashing cannon bolts. Jacen yielded his stick hand to the Force and weaved his way through the barrage for another two seconds, then heard his astromech squeal as it took a hit. He locked on to the ammunition dump manually and fired his last bunker buster. An instant later he saw the telltale curtain of dust rise ahead and knew the torpedo had penetrated the ammunition dump.

Jaina and Zekk poured disbelief and outrage into the meld, but Jacen felt them roll in behind him then drop into the crater. Suddenly a tempest of Chiss panic filled the Force, and Jacen knew that a bunker-buster torpedo had landed outside the repair hangar and begun to sputter its warning.

Tesar began to pour triumph and relief into the Force, and Jacen looked up to see that the flames from the fuel fires were now boiling away into space. Tesar and his squad had brought the base shields down and were already streaking toward the rendezvous point. All that remained for Jacen and his squad was to escape the moon's defenses and follow.

Abruptly Jacen felt Jaina pouring her anger into their twin bond, punching at that empty place inside him that used to be hers. Never again, she was telling him, never again would she fly with him.

But Jacen had known that before the mission began. He pulled his stick back and climbed for the fiery sky.

SEVENTEEN

As the silver whorl of the Tusken's Eye swelled steadily in the forward viewport, Luke began to feel a cold ache in the pit of his stomach, a growing sense that he was being studied. He glanced casually around the *DR919a*'s flight deck and found his companions intent on their work, Juun holding the control yoke firmly in both hands, Tarfang taking sensor readings and calculating hazard locations, Han studying the vessel's main power-supply grid and muttering to himself in disgust. Whoever was watching him, it wasn't any of his companions.

"Captain Juun, what did you do with those replicas you had before you came for Han and me?" Luke was sitting cross-legged on the floor, assembling his spare lightsaber from components he kept hidden inside R2-D2. "Are they still aboard?"

Juun shook his head. "I thought the assassin bugs might interfere with your escape." He kept his eyes fixed forward as he spoke. "So I had Tarfang drop the entire cargo in the marsh."

"I was afraid of that," Luke said.

"I could have kept them?" Juun gasped.

"No way," Han said, looking up from his work on the power grid. "Dumping those bug houses is the first smart thing you've done in this mess."

Tarfang jabbered at Han.

"How unusual!" C-3PO said. "Tarfang agrees with you. He says their first mistake was helping us escape the rehab house. They would have been much better off leaving you and Master Skywalker to be Fizzed."

Tarfang chuttered an addendum.

"Oh dear—he says you also owe the Squibs a million credits," C-3PO said. "Captain Juun incurred the nondelivery penalty on your behalf."

"Fine. Tell 'em to put it on my account," Han said. He turned back to Luke. "So what's wrong with dumping the cargo?"

"Nothing. It just means the replicas aren't what I'm feeling." Luke still had the cold knot in his stomach, an ache that did not quite rise to the level of danger sense. "Someone's watching us."

Tarfang jabbered in Luke's direction.

"Of course someone is watching," C-3PO translated. "We're in pirate space."

"Not *that* kind of watching," Han said. "I think he means through the Force."

Juun's face fell. "The Dark Nest?"

"That's my bet," Han answered.

"They know we're coming?" Juun's alarm began to fill the Force. "The *DR-Nine-one-nine-a* isn't equipped for combat. Maybe we should turn around."

"Not yet." Luke looked out the forward viewport, where the silver whorl of the Tusken's Eye was shining so brightly that it really was beginning to look like the goggled eye of a Tusken Raider. "The Dark Nest may know we're here, but we still haven't found *them.*"

Tarfang barked a sharp reply.

"Tarfang says if anything happens to the *DR-Nine-one-nine-a,* you're paying for repairs," C-3PO said.

"Not a problem," Luke said.

"If there's anything left to repair," Han muttered, turning back to the main power-supply grid. "These shields couldn't stop a micrometeor."

"I'll see if I can improve our chances," Luke said.

He reached out in the Force and immediately felt the crew of a sizable spacecraft closing fast from somewhere ahead. The *DR919a* was just entering the inner wall of the nebula shell, where a miasma of glowing gas and dark dust limited visibility to almost nothing. There was little hope of getting a visual fix on the craft, or even of picking it up on the transport's rudimentary sensors. But the presences aboard the vessel were too clear in the Force to be from the Dark Nest, too distinctly individual to be Killiks, and too savage to be Alliance military personnel.

Luke glanced over at Han and mouthed the word *pirates.* Han's brow went up, and he nodded toward the entrance to the *DR919a*'s belly turret. Luke shook his head, motioning for Han to continue rerouting more power to the shields, then began to quiet his mind, shutting out the gentle beeping of R2-D2 running diagnostics on the ship's power grid, the steady chitter of Tarfang apprising Juun of navigation hazards, even the gentle whisper of his own breath.

Soon Luke was focused entirely on the Force, and he began to sense its ripples lapping over him, coming from the direction of his companions and the pirates—and from another place where he did not feel any presences at all, only a profound uneasiness in the Force. He turned toward the empty place and found himself staring into a wispy red corona that had appeared around the rim of the Tusken's Eye.

Luke reached into the corona with the Force, searching not for the Dark Nest, but for the hosts he knew it needed to grow its larvae. For a moment, he sensed only the same void as before—an absence too perfect in its emptiness to be genuine, a silence too pure in its stillness even for deep space. Then, gradually, the terror began to wash over him, the despair and suffering of thousands of paralyzed slaves being slowly devoured from the inside out.

Luke shuddered, shaken by his contact with their anguish, and vowed again to destroy the Dark Nest.

Then the corona blurred for a second, and a tiny silver crescent came into view, almost too faint to be seen through the crimson glow. Luke began to feel another set of presences, full of anger and savagery and selfishness—more pirates, no doubt.

No sooner had Luke spied the crescent than the ache in his stomach began to expand into the rest of his torso. The feeling was due to more than just being watched, he realized. Someone was touching him through the dark side, trying to distract—or perhaps even incapacitate—him. He took a few deep breaths, then called on the Force to fight off the growing chill.

"Luke?" Han asked. "You all right?"

Luke glanced over to see Han studying him with a concerned expression.

"I'm fine." Luke's answer was only partially truthful. "Somebody doesn't like me looking for the Dark Nest."

"Alema?"

"I don't think so," Luke said. "Too powerful to be her."

"I was afraid of that." Han did not bother to ask whether it was Lomi Plo. "Maybe we should turn back. You're not looking too great."

Luke frowned. "Han, are you starting to feel afraid?"

"Me? No way." Han looked back to his work a little too quickly. "Just worried about *you*, that's all."

"No need," Luke said. "We're just going to take a quick look at what's going on, then run for the Choke."

The wave of relief from Juun and Tarfang confirmed what Luke had already guessed: the Dark Nest was using the Force to project an aura of fear into the *DR919a*—perhaps into this entire area of space. Whatever she was doing in there, Lomi Plo did not want Luke—or anyone else—sneaking a peek.

Luke finished assembling his spare lightsaber, then went to the pilot's station and pointed over Juun's shoulder toward the silver crescent he had spotted earlier.

"Do you see that?" Luke asked.

Juun squinted out the viewport. "See what?"

Luke touched the Sullustan's mind through the Force, trying to project the image of the silver crescent he saw. "That sliver of light. It looks like a planet."

Juun gasped. "Where did that come from?" He frowned at his instruments, then peered over at Tarfang. "You need to adjust the calibration. We're not picking anything up, and I can *see* it."

Tarfang chittered something that sounded atypically like an apology, then studied the sensor controls and began to scratch the white stripe on his head.

"It's not the instruments." Luke touched the Ewok's mind, then said, "Try looking out the viewport first. That will help."

Tarfang glared over at Luke for a moment, as though he was suspicious of sorcery, then looked out the viewport and barked something that sounded a little bit like *chubba!*

Luke looked over Juun's shoulder at the sensor display. It showed that a white-clouded world lay dead ahead. The planet had more than a dozen moons, and it was orbiting around a fairly standard G-class star—the source of the silver glow that created the Tusken's Eye.

The screen also showed an old *Carrack*-class cruiser approaching from the direction of the planet, about a third of the way to the *DR919a*. It was escorted by a pair of blastboats, and not one of the vessels was broadcasting a transponder code.

"The pirates!" Juun said. "They've seen us!"

Tarfang began to plot an evasion route.

"Don't worry about the pirates," Luke said. He knew by the deepening chill in his stomach that the Dark Nest was still watching their ship, trying to make it turn back. "I'll handle them."

"You sure about that?" Han asked. "We *know* where the Dark Nest is now. It might be better to go to the Choke and get some help."

"We don't have time for that." Luke turned to Han. "You know those shivers running up your spine? That tightness you're feeling in your throat?"

Juun spun around, his cheek folds rising. "You feel it too?"

"No—with me, it's something different," Luke said. "But I know what you're feeling, because it's not real. Lomi Plo is trying to scare you off."

Tarfang chittered a long opinion.

"Tarfang says she is doing us a favor," C-3PO said. "And I must say I agree. Our chances of surviving a battle with that pirate cruiser are approximately—"

"Stow it, Threepio." Han was scowling and looking toward the planet. "She knows we've found her?"

"I'm fairly certain," Luke said. "She and I are having a sort of a shoving match."

"We know where the Dark Nest is, and she's *still* trying to make us turn back?"

"Isn't that what it feels like to you?" Luke asked.

"As a matter of fact, yeah." Han's eye grew angry and determined. "We'd better get close and take a good look, because whatever she's trying to hide isn't going to be there long."

Tarfang looked back and began to harangue them both.

"Tarfang remains *very* concerned about the pirates," C-3PO reported. "He points out that the laser cannons in the upper turret aren't working."

"The pirates won't get near us." Luke used the Force to fill his voice with reassurance. "Lomi Plo isn't the only one who can use Force illusions."

Luke opened himself wide to the Force, and it began to pour into him from all sides, filling him with a tempest of power until his entire body was suffused with its energy. Using the same technique he had used to save *Jade Shadow* from the Dark Nest's attack at Qoribu, he formed a mental image of the *DR919a*'s exterior and expanded it into the Force, moving it from his mind out into the cockpit.

Tarfang yapped in astonishment, then stood on his chair and poked a finger into the image.

"Does it look right?" Luke asked.

Tarfang studied it wide-eyed for few moments, then nodded and chortled his approval.

"Good. This next part is going to take a lot of concentration, so you'll have to follow Han's instructions for a while." Luke turned to Han. "You *do* remember what Mara and I did at Qoribu?"

"How could I forget?" Han answered. "Juun, we're going to need all the speed this tub can make. Open up those throttles."

"They *are* open," Juun protested. "The maintenance engineer on Moro Three said we'd be crazy to take them past seventy-five percent."

"Yeah?" Han slipped by Luke and grabbed both throttles, then shoved them past the safety stops. "Well, it's time to go crazy."

A low roar rose somewhere in the *DR919a*'s stern, and the deck began to shudder beneath their feet. Juun shrank in his seat, waiting for the ship to explode, and Tarfang launched into a torrent of angry chittering that left C-3PO at a loss to translate gracefully.

After a few seconds, the shuddering finally settled into a rhythmic rumble.

Juun seemed to relax a little. "That's enough, Tarfang," he said. "If Han Solo thinks we need to push the *Niner*'s drives twenty-two percent beyond spec, then we must take the risk."

Tarfang snarled a sharp reply, but by then Luke was too focused on his task to hear C-3PO's translation. He had extended the image of the *DR919a* into every corner of the vessel and was holding it there, taking his time and drawing into the image all the attributes that made up the transport's sensor signature. The effort wearied him a little, but he ignored his fatigue and expanded the illusion until it covered the entire ship like an imaginary skin.

The pirates hailed the *DR919a*. "Turn that kreetle barge around before we blast it out from under you!"

Han rushed to the comm station and took over from an indignant Tarfang. "Turn around? Gorog told us she wanted this load of hyperdrive coolant *yesterday*," he said. "You want us to turn around, talk to her."

"That was yesterday," a gravelly voice retorted. "You got ten seconds, then we open fire."

"Go ahead," Han said. "But I'd talk to Gorog first."

"*Talk* to Gorog?" A deep laugh came over the comm channel. "That's a good one. You got five seconds."

Luke brought to mind another image of the transport, this time with a stringy blue veneer that resembled the gas shell around them. Instead of drawing the *DR919a*'s sensor signature, however, he backed the image with a layer of cold emptiness.

Maintaining both illusions began to drain him, and he no longer had the energy to suppress the cold ache in his stomach. The chill began to seep through his body.

Lock-alarms began to sound as the pirates reached targeting range and prepared to make good on their threat.

"Uh, Luke?" Han said. "You *do* hear—"

"Shut down the drives in three, two . . ." Luke gave the outer skin a little extra push. "Now!"

Juun pulled the throttles back, then the image of the *DR919a* slid away, the counterfeit glare of its sublight drives forcing everyone on the flight deck to close their eyes. Luke angled the illusion off to port, as though the vessel were attempting to go around the pirates. Meanwhile, the *DR919a* remained cloaked by the second, camouflaging illusion. The lock-alarms fell silent, and the cold ache inside Luke slowly began to recede.

Tarfang howled in delight, then turned to Luke and began chuttering in excitement.

"I really don't think Master Luke is interested in giving up his position in the Jedi order," C-3PO interrupted.

Tarfang yapped sharply.

"Very well, I'll ask him." C-3PO turned to Luke and began to translate. "Tarfang would like to know if you're interested in joining the crew of the *Niner*. He's sure that Captain Juun would give you a full share. And with your talent, they could go back to smuggling and make a fortune."

Luke could barely spare the effort to throw a pleading look in Han's direction. The Force was pouring through him like fire, and it was all he could do to keep the two illusions intact.

"Threepio's right, Tarfang," Han said. "I've been making the same offer for years, and he just keeps talking about how much the galaxy needs him."

A flurry of streaks and flashes filled the forward viewport as the pirates opened fire on the counterfeit *DR919a*. Luke continued the illusion's gentle turn, keeping it well ahead of its attackers and drawing them farther away. His skin felt dry and papery, and waves of heat were rolling through his body as the cytoplasm inside his cells began to boil. He did not let up. During the past year, he and Jacen had been working on overload techniques, so he knew could endure the pain and fatigue almost indefinitely. His body would pay a steep price, aging a year in a matter of minutes, but he knew he would not collapse.

Finally, they could no longer see the pirate cruiser in the viewport, and the *DR919a*'s navigational display suggested the ship was well beyond turning back to intercept them. Luke continued to hide their real vessel while moving the decoy ever deeper into the miasma. There were still plenty of pirates ahead—and they were the least of the *DR919a*'s problems.

Han and R2-D2 returned to their work on the power grid, and the silver crescent ahead swelled steadily to a disk with one dark side, then to a hazy half-orb cloaked in white vapor. The cold ache in Luke's stomach had diminished to almost nothing, but had not faded completely. He hoped that was just residual, a spillover creeping into him through his connection to the illusion, but it could just as easily have been Lomi Plo trying to lure him into a false sense of security. There was no way to be certain. Luke just did not know enough about what she was doing to him.

As they drew close to the planet, the system's star assumed the form of an immense silver maelstrom sucking in vast quantities of nebular gas. The planet itself became an alabaster glow with no distinct edge, a cloud of white brightness surrounded by the dark flecks of a dozen moons.

The *DR919a*'s rudimentary sensor package could not penetrate the dense clouds in the planet's upper atmosphere, but the heavy concentration of ice crystals indicated an abundance of water below, and the world's general mass and size suggested a rocky core. The moons were easier to survey. They were all about eight kilometers long, egg-shaped, and radiating heat from a core area near their thick ends.

"Those aren't moons!" Han said, looking over Tarfang's shoulders. "They're nest ships!"

Luke immediately felt like a fool. Until that moment, he had believed the problem with the Utegetu nests was basically a misunderstanding; that Raynar and Unu had become upset over the Fizz and allowed their anger to place them temporarily under the sway of the Dark Nest. But there were fifteen nest ships here: one for each of the fourteen nests the Colony had established on the nebula worlds, plus an extra vessel for the Dark Nest. Even the Killiks could not have built such a fleet in only a couple of months. Either all of the Utegetu nests had been under the Dark Nest's influence for most of the last year, or Raynar and the rest of the Colony had been a part of the plan from the beginning. Luke felt betrayed either way.

Hoping the pirates would be fooled into believing their quarry had escaped into the nebular miasma, Luke gave the decoy a final burst of speed, then let it drop and turned to Han.

"I guess this answers . . . our question," Luke said. He still had to concentrate to speak, as he was continuing to hide the *DR919a*.

"It's pretty clear why they've been so desperate to trade for reactor fuel and hyperdrive coolant."

"Yeah—but I really wish it wasn't," Han said.

"Why?" Juun asked. "In the history vids, you're always saying that it pays to know who you're fighting."

"Didn't I tell you to stop watching those things?" Without answering Juun's question, Han turned back to the power grid. "We can get by without climate control for a while. And who needs air scrubbers?"

Tarfang jumped out of his chair and scurried toward Han, jabbering in alarm.

"Tarfang is inquiring whether you've lost your mind," C-3PO said. "Without the air scrubbers, carbon dioxide concentration will rise twelve percent an hour."

"No problem," Han said. "We're not going to last an hour."

Juun's eyes grew large, and he looked over his shoulder at Luke. "I don't understand."

"We have to stop them," Luke explained. The fiery pain inside had begun to subside when he stopped overdrawing on the Force, but the cold ache of Lomi Plo's attention remained with him. "We can't let a whole fleet of nest ships loose."

"They'll eat whole sectors bare," Han said. "Worse—they'll turn the natives into Joiners."

Juun let his jaw fall and was silent for a moment, then he suddenly started chuckling.

"You fooled me!" He shook his head and looked forward again. "The history vids didn't say you liked practical jokes!"

"We're not joking, Captain Juun," Luke said. They had now reached the planet, a huge disk of swirling white that filled most of their forward viewport. He could feel the presence of a large mass of pirates beneath the clouds, somewhere near the world's equator. "We really need to stop them."

"We—" Juun's voice cracked. He stopped to wet his throat, then tried again. "We do?"

"I don't like it much, either, Juun," Han said. "But that's what happens when you start hanging out with Jedi."

Han's tone was joking, but there was a core of truth to his words. Luke was acutely aware that he was the only one aboard who had volunteered for this mission. Everyone else had gotten caught up in it simply because they happened to be nearby when it became a necessity, and none of them was very well equipped to survive the job. When he thought about what might happen if he went through with this, he wondered if he really had the right to pull them along. But when he thought about what might happen if the Killiks dispersed across the galaxy . . . he wondered if he had the right *not* to.

The first of the "moons" began to swell in the forward viewport. At eight kilometers long, it was an ungainly vessel, with a stony hull, giant control fins, and two cavernous docking bays—one of which was currently launching a battered five-hundred-meter passenger liner. Luke ignored the liner and reached out to the nest ship through the Force. It was filled with Killiks—probably the Taat nest, judging by the stoic nature of their presence.

Almost instantly the cold ache in his stomach began to expand again as Lomi Plo reacted to the contact. Luke took a few deep breaths and called on the Force to push the ache back down, but this time he merely succeeded in stopping it from expanding any further. Lomi Plo was growing stronger as he drew nearer.

"Captain Juun, how tight is the Alliance's blockade?" Luke asked. "Will it prevent the Killiks from escaping in these ships?"

"Of course," Juun replied. "As long as the Killiks use the standard routes to leave the nebula."

"What about the nonstandard routes?" Han asked.

Tarfang chuttered and shook his head.

"Tarfang points out that the pirates have never used the standard routes," C-3PO translated. "And neither have the black membrosia smugglers."

"Forget the blockade, Luke," Han said. He let the power grid cover clang shut, then latched it in place. "You want this done, we've got to do it ourselves."

Luke sighed. "You're right." He turned to Juun and Tarfang. "I'm sorry, but I really need your help stopping these nest ships."

"*Stopping* them?" Juun twisted around in his seat. "How?"

"I don't suppose you've got a bunch of baradium on board?" Han asked.

Juun's eyes went wide. "You carry *baradium* in your stores?"

"Han is joking, Captain Juun," Luke explained. "And we don't need to disable *all* of the Killiks' ships. I only have to stop the one carrying the Dark Nest. They're the key to this."

Tarfang chittered a question.

"Tarfang still wants to know *how*," C-3PO said. "The *DR-Nine-one-nine-a* doesn't even carry concussion missiles."

"It has an escape pod, doesn't it?" Han asked.

"Of course," Juun said. "The pod is quite functional."

"Good." Luke did not have to ask to know that Han was thinking the same thing he was—with one exception. "Then all you have to do is get close and drop me off."

"*Us* off," Han corrected.

Luke shook his head. "This a Jedi mission, and we don't even have much in the way of weaponry. You'll just—"

"If you say *get in the way*, I'm going to Hutt-thump you," Han warned. "Leia would kill me if I let you die alone in there."

Luke sighed in resignation, then began searching for the Dark Nest again. Each time he made contact with one of the nest ships, the cold knot inside rose a bit higher into his chest. It wasn't long before he had to wage a constant Force battle just to keep the feeling in check.

They were just passing the third nest ship when Luke sensed a mass of pirate presences rising through the planet's clouds below.

"Be ready," he warned. "The pirates are coming up to cut us off."

Tarfang let loose with a long string of Ewokese invective.

"That's not fair," C-3PO said. "It's hardly Master Luke's fault that you haven't replaced the tail cannon."

"Don't sweat it," Han said. "If we have to open fire, we're starslag anyway."

Another nest ship appeared from behind the curve of the planet, and the anguish of the captives being devoured by the Gorog larvae grew clear and raw in the Force.

"There." Luke pointed at the vessel. "Do a flyby and we'll eject in the escape pod. Then head for the Murgo Choke and tell everything you know about this to the highest-ranking blockade officer you can find."

Tarfang began to gibber and shake his head.

"Tarfang doesn't think that is very wise," C-3PO translated. "The Defense Force is going to be looking for someone to blame about those replicas."

"And if you don't want it to be you two, then *you'd* better be the ones who sound the warning," Han said. "If you get there before anything bad happens, they might even give you a reward."

Tarfang's furry brow rose. "*Gabagaba?*"

"I'm sure it would be substantial," Luke said.

"Yeah, a thousand credits, at least," Han said. "You might be saving an entire fleet, after all."

"A reward would be nice," Juun said. "But that's not the important thing, Tarfang. It was our mistake, so it's our duty to correct it."

Tarfang groaned and let his head drop, but waved Luke and Han aft toward the escape pod.

"I'll keep the *Niner* cloaked as long as I can," Luke said, turning to go. "But once you're beyond interception range, get out fast. I need to devote—"

Luke's instructions were interrupted by the wail of *DR919a*'s proximity alarms. Juun shrieked, and Luke whirled around to see a blue streak of ion efflux lighting the forward viewport.

"Pirate ship?" he asked.

Juun could barely bring himself to nod.

"Relax—they missed," Han said. "Now that they're past—"

The proximity alarms screamed again, and this time Luke was thrown from his feet as the ship bucked. A loud boom rolled forward, then metal groaned in the stern and the sour smell of containment fluid began to fill the air.

Juun studied his console for a moment. "I can't believe it! We're not showing any damage."

"What a relief!" C-3PO said from where he had landed across the deck. "My calculations indicate that even if the impact was glancing, we were hit by something at least the size of a Corellian Engineering Corporation corvette."

"Uh, I wouldn't get too excited." Han rolled to his knees next to Luke. "I rerouted the damage control power to the shields."

Tarfang, who like Juun had been strapped into his seat, looked back and began to yap at Han angrily.

"Yeah?" Han rose and jabbed his finger in the Ewok's direction. "Well, we wouldn't even be here if I hadn't boosted that flit-field you two were calling shields."

A pirate frigate shot past between the *DR919a* and the Gorog nest ship, then wheeled around and opened fire with a small bank of turbolasers.

The bolts flashed past at least a kilometer overhead.

Luke returned to his feet and checked Juun's navigational display. He was relieved to see the rest of the pirate fleet—about thirty vessels, ranging in size from blastboats to frigates—executing much the same maneuver, all laying fire in a circle around a disabled blastboat floating several kilometers to their stern. His Force illusion was still working; the pirates had no idea where *DR919a* was and were attacking blindly in the hope of landing a lucky shot.

"I think the worst is over," Luke said. The Gorog nest ship was now directly in the center of the *DR9819a*'s viewport and rapidly beginning to swell. "But you need to pull up a little. I think the collision dropped our nose."

"I *am* pulling up," Juun gasped.

Luke glanced at the yoke and saw that the Sullustan had pulled it back almost into his lap. Tarfang unstrapped and started aft, sputtering in alarm and motioning to Han.

"Hey, it's not my fault," Han said, following. "I didn't touch the attitude thrusters."

The *DR919a* passed under the pirate frigate and continued toward the Gorog nest ship.

Han's voice came over the intercom. "It's only a smashed relay box. We'll have it fixed in . . ."

The rest of the sentence was drowned out by a sudden, painful pop in Luke's ears.

R2-D2 began to whistle in alarm, and C-3PO said, "Are you sure?"

R2-D2 tweeted in irritation.

"Oh, my!" C-3PO said. "Master Luke, Artoo says the ship is losing cabin pressure."

"I know." Luke's ears popped again. "Han—"

"Did you feel that?" Han said over the intercom. "We've got a hull breach!"

"Where?" Juun demanded. His eyes were glued to his damage control console. "I'm blind!"

"It doesn't matter," Luke said. The Gorog nest ship was filling the forward viewport now. "Even if you *could* seal off the breach, there's no time."

Juun looked up at him. "What are you saying?"

"I guess I owe you a new ship," Luke said. "If we live that long."

EIGHTEEN

In Leia's mind, daybreak was forever.

She was floating on the edge of a purling river, relishing the soft brush of a warm breeze on her face, watching Alderaan's sun stand on the canyon rim. She had been watching it for hours, days perhaps, and it never moved. That was the point of the meditation, to still all: thoughts, emotions, mind.

But the water was growing rough. There was anger between Jacen and Jaina, a feeling of betrayal and . . . acceptance. Leia reached out to them in the Force, hoping that her love might help them heal the chasm that divided them. They were so far away, so deep in the Unknown Regions, where only the Killiks and the Chiss could find them. This was all she could do for them. They had to rely on each other. They needed to take care of each other . . . for Leia, if not for themselves.

The sense of acceptance—Jacen—closed itself off, and Jaina's sense of betrayal began to grow less bitter. For Leia, she would watch over her brother.

Leia relaxed again, trying to return to her meditations, but the water started to lap at her, to lift her and pull her out into the current. She did not try to stay close to shore. There was a familiar warmth in the water's grasp, an honest strength that she recognized as her brother's presence in the Force. She surrendered to the river, and the canyon walls began to rush past. The yellow sun climbed high into the sky, the breeze vanished and the air grew still and stale, and suddenly Leia was back in her detention cell, sitting cross-legged on her bunk, staring at the same empty place on the wall that she had been watching for . . . she checked her chrono . . . eighteen standard hours.

Leia started to respond to Luke, but he had already sensed her return to the realm of the temporal and was warning her that something was escaping, that things were terribly wrong inside the nebula. She could sense that he was in some kind of turmoil, and that Han was with him—but not much more. Her heart rose into her throat, and she pictured Saras nest in her mind and wondered if they were still on Woteba.

The only reply was the overwhelming impression that a threat was coming, that Leia had to sound the alarm. She reached for more, trying to find out if Han and Luke were in danger and needed help, but all she sensed was a raw fear that might have been her own—and then Luke's presence was gone.

Leia remained on her bunk, taking a moment to collect her thoughts. Han and Luke were in the middle of a bad situation, and she could not help chastising herself for letting Bwua'tu detain her and Saba. She had remained imprisoned aboard the *Admiral Ackbar* out of concern for the deteriorating relationship between the Jedi and the Galactic Alliance, and now Han and Luke might pay the price.

But Luke had not asked her for help. He had contacted her as a Jedi Knight, directing her to take action on behalf of the order. She was to sound the alarm, and soon.

Leia started by reaching out to Mara, who was still in a Force-hibernation. Whether Leia and Saba convinced Bwua'tu of the danger or merely departed in the *Falcon,* Mara and the other StealthX pilots would need to be ready.

As soon as Leia had alerted Mara, she reached out to Saba and felt . . . nothing. Either the Barabel did not wish to be disturbed, or she was not awake. Leia hesitated to try again. Saba had once confided that when she sensed someone's presence while she was sleeping, she often awoke with a terrible urge to hunt them down.

Still sitting on her bunk with her legs folded, Leia reached out in the Force and grabbed the security cam hidden inside the ceiling light. She located the signal feed and pulled. A soft *clack* sounded from inside the fixture, and then she sensed the mild irritation of a guard stationed in the processing area at the front of the cell block.

Moving quickly now, Leia unfolded her legs and went to the door. She could not sense any living presences on the other side, but she felt sure there would be an EverAlert droid—a Justice Systems variant on Lando's highly successful YVH series—standing in the corridor between her cell and Saba's. She pressed her ear to the door, then looked up toward the side wall of her cell, fixing her attention approximately over the last cell on the block, and used the Force to project a loud *boom* into the ceiling.

A series of muffled hisses and metallic thunks sounded outside her door as a massive droid charged down the corridor to investigate the noise. Leia placed her hand over the magnetic lock she had seen when her door was open, then reached out with the Force and disengaged the internal catch. The door slid open with an all-too-audible hiss.

She stepped out and found the EverAlert swinging around to face her.

"Your cell door has malfunctioned." The droid planted its foot and began to bring up the heavy stun blaster in its right arm. "Return to your cell and remain—"

Leia flicked her finger at the EverAlert's head and used the Force to flip its primary circuit breaker. The switch lay hidden beneath its neck armor, but that was no hindrance to a Jedi.

"—staaaationaaaar . . ."

The droid's chin slumped against its chest, and the stun bolt it had been preparing ricocheted harmlessly off the floor.

A metallic *clank* sounded behind Leia as the blast door at the front of the cell block retracted. She spun around to see a pair of astonished guards standing on the other side of the threshold, their blaster pistols still holstered.

"Stang!" the older one said. "She's—"

Leia swept her arm in their direction, using the Force to jerk both guards forward. She slammed them into the blast door, then dropped them across the threshold so the cell block could not be sealed off without crushing them.

The older man, a grizzled human sergeant, snapped the comlink out of his sleeve pocket. His companion, a Duros with smooth blue skin and red eyes bulging in alarm, made the mistake of reaching for his blaster.

Leia reached out with the Force and slammed his head into the wall, then summoned the blaster from his open holster. By the time she got the muzzle pointed in the sergeant's direction, he was raising the comlink to his lips.

"Everything's fine here," she said, touching his mind through the Force. "There's no need for alarm."

"W-whatever you say, P-princess." The sergeant was careful to keep his finger away from the comlink's activation switch. "You're the one holding the blaster."

Leia sighed. She was going to have to work on her Forcepersuasion skills with someone besides Saba. Force intimidation was fine for Barabels, but humans needed something a little more subtle.

She gestured at the comlink. "Tell the watch officer—and no funny business. I'm a Jedi. I'll know if you use an alarm code."

The sergeant nodded, then activated the comlink. "Everything's fine here, Watch."

"Then how come she's holding a blaster on you?" came the tinny reply.

Leia looked up at the security dome in the ceiling. "Because Junior was dumb enough to reach for it." She pulled the power pack out of the blaster's handle, then tossed the pistol aside. "I'm not interested in harming anyone. I just need to talk to Admiral Bwua'tu. I have important information for him."

"Fine," the watch officer said. "Return to your cell and I'll ask for an audience."

"I'm not *asking*." Leia raised a hand toward the security dome, then located the power feeds in the Force. "And I'm not waiting. It's urgent."

She jerked the lines free, then stepped over to Saba's cell. Keeping one eye on the sergeant and his assistant, she placed her hand on the cold door and used the Force to disengage the internal catch.

The cell was empty, save for a couple of broken claws on the floor and a comlink lying on the bunk. A section of durasteel panel was hanging down at one end of the ceiling, leaving just enough room for a Barabel to squeeze through.

Leia summoned the comlink to her hand, then turned the volume down so that the sergeant and his assistant would not be able to hear Saba's end of the conversation.

"Master?" Leia whispered into the microphone.

There was a short pause, then Saba answered. "Blast! You scared them away."

"Scared who?" Leia asked.

"The gankerz," Saba answered. "This one is hungry."

"You couldn't have asked for a . . . never mind." The last thing Leia wanted to do was start a discussion about detention-center cuisine with a Barabel. "Can you meet me at the bridge? We need to talk to Bwua'tu."

"No." Saba touched Leia through the Force, initiating a combat-meld. "That will do no good."

"Saba, Luke reached out to me," Leia said. She opened herself to the meld, and an impression of vast openness appeared in her mind. "Something's happening in the nebula."

"Yes," Saba said. "The Killiks are leaving."

"And we must warn the fleet," Leia said. She recognized the vast openness as a hangar and realized that Saba was leaving the truth unspoken—no doubt because she feared some Alliance comm tech was eavesdropping on their conversation. "Luke was very clear about that."

"Bwua'tu won't believe you."

"We must try," Leia said.

The image of the *Falcon,* sitting on the hangar deck surrounded by a squad of Alliance troops, flashed through her mind.

"Then try," Saba said. "This one is still hungry. She is going to continue her hunt."

The slag that had once been the *DR919a* lay thirty meters in, an unrecognizable mass of blindingly bright metal glowing out from the crater it had blasted into the Gorog nest ship. A steady torrent of flotsam was pouring into the immense hole from the surrounding decks, dead Killiks and stony hunks of spitcrete and three lengths of twisted durasteel that looked suspiciously like turbolaser barrels. Gushing out of the surrounding walls were several cones of white vapor—air or water or some other vital substance shooting out of broken conduits into the cold vacuum of space.

Luke felt nothing from the crater itself, but the Force was filled with ripples from the surrounding area, all very sharp and erratic as stunned Gorog struggled to figure out what had just happened. Unfortunately, the confusion did not extend to Lomi Plo. She was still touching him through the Force, filling him with the same cold ache he had been experiencing since they entered the Tusken's Eye.

Luke stepped away from the escape pod's viewing port, then pulled up his tunic and turned his back to Han.

"Do it, Han."

"You sure about this?" Han asked. "Even on stun, at this range you're going to get burned."

"*Now,* Han!" Luke ordered. "Before Gorog starts to sort things out."

"All right," Han said. "No need to get—"

A searing pain exploded across Luke's back, and he dropped to his knees. Even calling on the Force to bolster himself, it took all of his willpower to remain conscious. He let the pain fill him, gathering it up and directing it down into the pit of his stomach where he felt Lomi Plo's chill touch.

Something released inside, like a knot coming undone, and the cold ache vanished all at once. Luke reached out to his companions, gathering their presences into a single bunch, then shut them all off from the Force.

They let out a collective gasp of surprise. Tarfang suddenly slumped down in his crash couch and began to babble in a frightened tone.

"Tarfang is convinced we died in the crash and don't know it yet," C-3PO explained. "And I must say, I feel something odd in my own circuits."

"I'm hiding us from Lomi Plo," Luke explained. He let his tunic down. His back was still racked with pain, but at least the cold weight inside had vanished. "With any luck, *she'll* think we died in the crash, too."

Tarfang eyed Luke warily, then sat up and began to jabber angrily, alternately pounding his fists and stabbing a furry finger at the air.

"I most certainly will *not* say that to Master Luke," C-3PO replied. "And I fail to see the harm if he *is* trying to make us feel better. It's certainly better than dwelling on a negative."

"We're *not* dead," Luke said between gritted teeth. He went to Juun's side and pointed out the pilot's viewport toward a section of deck hanging free just inside the rim of the crater. "Put the pod over there. We need to get out of this thing before Gorog sees it."

Juun dropped them into the crater. The temperature inside climbed rapidly as they drew closer to the molten remains of the *DR919a,* and the pod gave a noticeable jerk when it entered the nest ship's artificial gravity.

"Hoersch-Kessel gravity system," Han observed. "Boy are they going to regret that."

Tarfang chittered an indignant question.

"Tarfang would like to know what you think is wrong with—"

"Everything," Han said. "I just hope we can keep this rock from lighting its hyperdrive. I really hate what those g burps do to my joints."

Juun sat the pod down on the sagging edge of a deck section surrounded by antennas and dishes and data feeds, all of it very un-Killik-looking and all of it arranged around a half-melted relay station.

"They had help building these things," Han said, peering out the pod's viewport. "And a lot of it. That heat sensor looks Balmorran, and the signals package is definitely a Kuat Drive Yards Eavesdropper."

"Probably had help from the pirates—financed by the black

membrosia trade," Luke said. "But we'll sort that out later. Right now, we need to get to those hyperdrives."

"Good idea." Han opened the pod's survival pack and sprayed Luke's back with bacta salve, then passed him a blaster and took one for himself. "Any idea how we're going to get there through a nest full of bugs?"

"We're not going to go *through* them," Luke said. He pulled the top of his vac suit over his shoulders and began to seal the closures. "We're going to go around them."

Juun frowned and stopped short of pulling his helmet visor down. "I don't understand."

"Outside the ship." Luke secured his own helmet to the collar ring. "By crawling across the hull."

"I was afraid that's what you had in mind," Han said.

Luke lowered his visor, then picked up the heavy survival pack and turned toward the hatch. Han and the others sealed their own vac suits, then they all left the escape pod and started to push it toward the still-glowing crater.

A shudder ran through the deck. They all scrambled back, afraid it was about to collapse. But the deck remained where it was. While it was sagging slightly, it was clearly in no danger of falling, even with the heavy escape pod sitting just a meter or so from its edge.

The shuddering grew stronger. The severed lines and equipment dangling on the walls began to bounce around soundlessly, then Han's voice came over the vac suit comm system.

"We'd better wait awhile." He pointed out through the crater hole, where the pirates' unnamed planet was starting to glide by ever more rapidly. "I'm not sure I want to be crawling around outside when this thing goes into hyperspace."

NINETEEN

Leia found the command deck of the *Admiral Ackbar* to be as spotless, orderly, and efficient as the rest of the Star Destroyer. The mixed-species crew was both alert and focused, glancing up as she stepped out of the lift, then quickly returning to their tasks when they saw she was escorted by a detail from bridge security. Bwua'tu himself was in the Tactical Salon—the TacSal—at the back of the command deck, surrounded by his staff and studying a holodisplay of the Murgo Choke. An opalescent bust of the great admiral sat in a niche on the back wall, keeping a solemn watch over the entire deck . . . and causing a cold tingle in the middle of Leia's back.

The security detail stopped outside the TacSal, where the admiral's aide, Wurf'al, met Leia with a disapproving sneer. He gestured curtly for her to follow, and as they approached the holodisplay, Bwua'tu ended the discussion he was having with his staff to greet Leia with a smug grin.

"Princess Leia, you wanted to see me?"

"That's right, Admiral," Leia said. "Thank you for not making it difficult."

"Why should I?" Bwua'tu asked. "I'm as concerned as you are."

This surprised Leia. "You are?"

"Of course," Bwua'tu said. "Even if your friends in the StealthXs are carrying extra air scrubbers in their cargo compartments, they must be breathing their own fumes by now. I only hope it's not too late."

Leia's surprise changed to irritation. "My friends are fine. I came to warn you that the Killiks are about to contest your blockade."

"Truly?" Bwua'tu's expression remained smug, but Leia could

tell by the way his neck fur flattened that this news troubled him. "And this knowledge came to you while you were staring at the wall of your cell?"

"More or less," Leia said. "Luke reached out to me through the Force."

"Of course . . . your Jedi sorcery." Bwua'tu considered this for a moment, then asked, "Did your brother also reveal where to expect this threat—or what form it might take?"

"Unfortunately, no," Leia said. "Communication through the Force isn't usually that precise. All I could tell was that Luke is very concerned."

"I see."

Bwua'tu's gaze slid back toward the holodisplay, where the starfighter complement from both the *Admiral Ackbar* and the *Mon Mothma*—well over a hundred craft—were deployed in a double screening formation between the two Star Destroyers. The admiral seemed to forget Leia for the moment and lose himself in thought, then he abruptly looked back to her.

"Master Sebatyne is more adept with the Force, is she not?"

"She is," Leia said. "That's one reason she's a Master."

"Then perhaps Master Sebatyne could provide me with a more thorough report," Bwua'tu said. "Inform her that I require her presence on the command deck."

"I've already been in contact with Master Sebatyne, as I'm sure your comm officers have informed you." As Leia spoke, she was puzzling over what seemed an odd, almost desperate starfighter deployment. "She's unavailable at the moment."

"That's right," Bwua'tu said. "She's hunting gankers."

Leia shrugged. "There's no reasoning with her when she's hungry. Barabels like their meat fresh."

"As do we all," Bwua'tu said. "But there *are* no gankers aboard this ship, Princess Leia."

"Come, Admiral." Leia touched Bwua'tu through the Force and confirmed what she had already surmised: he did not believe a word she was saying. "There are *always* gankers aboard a capital ship."

"Not aboard my ship." Bwua'tu stepped closer and spoke in a low, gravelly voice. "Your plan is a good one, *Jedi* Solo, but you forget with whom you are dealing."

"My plan, Admiral?" Leia glanced back at the holodisplay and realized what she was seeing. The starfighters from the *Mon Mothma* were carefully working their way toward those from the

Admiral Ackbar, slowly weaving back and forth in a tight search pattern. "You think I'm trying to stage a diversion!"

"It will do your friends in the StealthXs no good, of course," Bwua'tu said. "But I *am* impressed with the tactical coordination you Jedi achieve with your sorcery."

"You give us too much credit." Leia stretched her Force-awareness into the Choke and felt the familiar presence of a StealthX battle-meld. Then Kyp Durron reached out to her, assuring her that his team would soon be coming to help her and Saba. Leia seethed inwardly; she hardly needed rescuing. But the idea that someone could believe she *did* made her think it had been a mistake to sit in a cell just to avoid further straining relations with the Galactic Alliance. "Until I saw your starfighter deployment, Admiral Bwua'tu, I didn't even know that Master Durron and his squadron were out there."

"Now you mock me, Jedi Solo." Bwua'tu sounded genuinely irritated. "The Rurgavean Sleight is obscure, but did you really think *I* would fail to recognize it?"

"Of course not." Leia racked her brain, trying to remember what the Rurgavean Sleight *was.* "But you must believe me. Luke's message is real. I'm not trying to distract you."

"For someone who is not trying, you are doing an exceptional job," Bwua'tu said. "If Master Sebatyne fails to report to the nearest officer within thirty seconds, the StealthX fuel will be destroyed. After that, we will move on to the *Falcon's* drive nacelles."

"What will it take to prove I'm telling the truth?" Leia had to struggle to keep an even voice. "Would you believe me if I called in both teams of StealthXs?"

Bwua'tu narrowed his eyes, contemplating her offer, then tapped a bent claw in her direction. "Well done, Princess. A classic slide into the Mandalorian Surrender."

Leia sighed. "I'm trying to *help* you, Admiral—not capture the *Ackbar.*"

A cold knot formed between Leia's shoulder blades as she spoke. She half turned, expecting to see Wurf'al or some other officer glaring in her direction. Instead she found herself looking into the vacant eyes of the admiral's bust.

"Admiral, I continue to sense something wrong aboard this ship." She pointed at the bust. "May I ask what kind of security scans were performed on that piece?"

"You may not," Bwua'tu said sternly. "I won't be distracted, Jedi Solo." He raised his hand and studied his chrono for a moment, then added, "And your thirty seconds have passed. Since we still have no sign of Master Sebatyne, I'll have to carry out my threat."

Wurf'al produced a comlink and passed it to the admiral. "Security Two, Admiral."

Bwua'tu kept his gaze fixed on Leia. "That would be the detail guarding your StealthX fuel."

"Go ahead," Leia said. She still had a bad feeling about the bust, but it seemed clear Bwua'tu would not listen while he thought she was trying to stage a diversion. "Perhaps it will convince you of my sincerity."

"As you wish." Bwua'tu activated the comlink. "Tibanna detail—"

The admiral stopped speaking when the comlink in Leia's sleeve pocket echoed his words.

Bwua'tu scowled and motioned Wurf'al to retrieve the device. Once Wurf'al had done so, the admiral raised his own comlink and spoke again.

"Tibanna detail, come in."

The call was repeated over the comlink in Wurf'al's hand—the same comlink that Saba had left for Leia to find on her bunk.

Bwua'tu raised his bushy brow and turned to Leia. "My compliments. It appears I am no longer in control of your StealthX fuel."

A loud sissing came over both comlinks.

Bwua'tu frowned, then spoke into his. "I wouldn't gloat, Master Sebatyne. I still control the *Falcon*."

This only drew more sissing.

Bwua'tu deactivated the comlink, then surprised her by not immediately ordering an attack on the *Falcon*'s drive nacelles. Instead he turned to his aide, Wurf'al.

"Send a detail to investigate what became of the squad guarding the StealthX fuel," he said. "And sound battle stations in the capture bay."

Before Wurf'al could acknowledge the order, the sharp wail of a proximity alarm sounded from the flight deck speakers.

"Contact cluster exiting hyperspace," an efficient female sensor officer announced. "No transponder codes, outbound from the nebula."

Fifteen black triangles—the tactical symbols for unknown vessels—appeared at the edge of the holodisplay, coming from the direction of the Utegetu Nebula. Instead of stopping to reconnoiter or plot their next jumps, as most starship fleets would do, they streaked straight toward the heart of the Murgo Choke at a substantial percentage of lightspeed.

Leia was still trying to comprehend what she was seeing when Bwua'tu began to rattle off orders. "Wurf'al, make that general battle stations."

"Sir!"

"Grendyl, recall all starfighters . . . Jorga, assign targets to turbolaser batteries . . . Rabad, have Commodore Dark-lighter bring the *Mothma* forward to support us . . . Tola, start a withdrawal toward the *Mothma* . . ."

The acknowledgments came faster than Leia could track them—"Sir . . . sir . . . sir . . . sir . . ."—and the flight deck erupted into a controlled frenzy as the officers jumped to execute their orders.

"Batteries five, nine, and seventeen have acquired targets, Admiral," a Duros gunnery officer reported.

"Well done, Jorga. Open fire."

"Open fire?" Leia gasped. "You don't even know—"

Bwua'tu raised a finger, warning her to remain silent. An instant later clouds of tiny black triangles began to stream from the fifteen larger vessels.

"Contacts launching fighters," the sensor officer announced.

Leia was stunned. The Killiks were not merely attempting to run the Galactic Alliance's blockade, they were going to *attack* it. Implications and ramifications raced through her mind in a mad swirl, and she was filled with the deepening fear that she was watching the outbreak of another galactic war—one born of desperation and misunderstanding, and all the more tragic for it.

The colored glare of an outgoing turbolaser barrage flashed through the viewport and lit up the *Ackbar*'s flight deck. A couple of seconds later the tactical display showed strikes against three different targets.

"Affirmative hits," the sensor officer reported. "No shields, damage unknown."

The unknown-vessel triangles began to assume three-dimensional shapes, each with a figure ranging between 7,952 and 8,234—its length in meters—shining inside it. They looked like fifteen egg-shaped rocks, all trailing stubby tails of ion efflux. The fighters were just clouds of tiny slivers, but an inset in one of the swarms displayed the image of what was basically a dartship mounted on an oversized ion engine.

"Interesting." Bwua'tu seemed to be speaking to himself. "The

Killiks have some new toys. I wonder what other surprises they may have brought us?"

Leia's thoughts went instantly to all the busts of Admiral Bwua'tu she had seen aboard the *Ackbar*. They resembled spinglass too much to be anything else. She turned toward the one watching over the TacSal and did not even need to reach out in the Force to know she was right. A bolt of danger sense shot down her spine, so cold and crisp that she broke into goose bumps.

Leia turned to Wurf'al. "Excuse me, Captain, where is the nearest disposal chute?"

"Disposal chute?" Wurf'al frowned as though he was going to question her need for one. Then the rest of the *Ackbar*'s batteries cut loose, filling the command deck viewport with a multihued glare and causing the overhead lighting to flicker and dim. He pointed absentmindedly toward a spotless cover-flap on the far wall. "There."

"Thank you."

Leia used the Force to slide the bust, which was about forty centimeters high, free of its mounting. A Mon Calamari lieutenant commander let out a startled cry as it drifted out of the niche, then stepped in front of Bwua'tu to shield him.

"Sorry to alarm you," Leia said. She floated the bust over to disposal chute and began to push it through the flap. "But this thing *has* to go."

"The admiral!" Wurf'al cried. He dived after the piece, jamming his arms into the chute up to his shoulders. "It's okay. I have him!"

Leia felt the barrels of several blasters swing her way. The petty officer in charge of her security escort warned, "Don't even think about moving, Princess."

She kept her hands in plain sight but did not otherwise acknowledge the threat.

Bwua'tu peered over the shoulder of the lieutenant commander in front of him, scowling first at Leia, then at Wurf'al.

"Captain, what the blazes are you doing with your arms down in a disposal chute?"

"Holding on to your bust, sir." A muffled clink sounded inside the chute. "Bloah!"

Bwua'tu frowned. "Captain?"

"Sorry, sir, but something—rodder!" Wurf'al suddenly straightened and pulled his arms out of the chute. His hands and wrists were covered in dozens of blue, thumb-sized insects. "They're biting!"

"They're Gorog!" Leia reached out in the Force and pulled the chute cover closed. "Dark Nest Killiks!"

Wurf'al dropped to his knees, screaming and trying to shake the insects off. Those that came free buzzed up to his head and alighted on his eyes. His screams grew primal, but the TacSal seemed frozen in its confusion, and even Leia was at a loss as to how to help the aide. After a couple of seconds he threw his head back and collapsed, a raspy gurgle coming from his throat.

The assassin bugs exploded into the air, spreading their wings and droning off in every direction.

"Commando raid!" Bwua'tu yelled.

He pulled his sidearm and blasted a Killik from the air. Half a dozen bolts sizzled past Leia's shoulder, taking out another insect. Then the rest of Bwua'tu's staff began to react, drawing their own blasters and lacing the air with fire.

They were not entirely effective. A Duros lieutenant commander slapped at his throat, then fell to the floor and began to convulse, and perhaps two dozen of the insects escaped out onto the command deck.

Once the shock of the initial assault wore off, Bwua'tu stepped over to the disposal chute and slapped the VOID button to suck the contents down into the *Ackbar*'s waste tanks.

"Well done, Princess." He slapped the button again. "What alerted you?"

Leia used the Force to flick an assassin bug away from his ear, then splattered it against the wall. "Jedi sorcery."

"Marvelous stuff." Bwua'tu eyed the blue-and-yellow smear, then looked past Leia to the petty officer in charge of her security escort. "You, take your detail and secure this deck."

"Sir. And the prisoner?"

"Prisoner?" Bwua'tu snorted. "She was *never* your prisoner, son. She was just being polite."

"Thank you, Admiral," Leia said. "I don't know what the Killiks are up to, but I hope you understand that the Jedi aren't—"

"Say no more." Bwua'tu raised a hand to stop her. "The Jedi may be idealistic fools, but they are not traitors—as you have already proven."

"I'm glad we understand each other." Leia tried not to bristle at being called a fool; under the circumstances, she was glad just to have earned Bwua'tu's trust. "If I might make a suggestion, Killik nests share a collective mind—"

"Of course." Bwua'tu turned to the intercom and opened a ship-wide channel. "Infiltration alert. Seal all hatches, blast anything with six limbs, and dump all statuary down the nearest disposal chute. This is not a drill."

Bwua'tu paused a moment to look out at the chaos on the *Ackbar*'s command deck—at least a dozen stations were empty while the crew fought the remaining assassin bugs—then returned to his place at the holodisplay.

"All right, people, we've got a battle to win," he said to the Tac-Sal staff. "Back to your stations."

Leia stepped to the holodisplay with his officers. Most of the Killik fleet was headed straight for *Mon Mothma* and the heart of the Choke, and clouds of insect starfighters were already boiling past the thin screen of Alliance defenders. But a small task force—five ships and several thousand dartships—was veering toward the *Ackbar,* preparing to intercept it and prevent it from reaching the *Mothma.*

Knowing how valuable any intelligence about one's foes could be in a battle, Leia oriented herself to the fighting, then turned toward the Killik ships and, one by one, began to reach out to them in the Force. She sensed the presence of a single Killik nest aboard each of the large ships, often accompanied by dozens or even hundreds of Joiners, and she even recognized the stoicism of the Taat and the artistic sensibilities of the Saras among the vessels headed for the *Mothma.* But when she came to the last ship of the group moving to intercept the *Ackbar,* she felt no presences at all, only an empty place in the Force.

"Something you wish to share, Jedi Solo?" Bwua'tu asked.

Leia looked up to find the Bothan studying her. She pointed at the image of the "empty" vessel in the holodisplay.

"I think that is the Dark Nest's ship," she said. "Of course, we don't know how the Killik fleet is organized, but that will be as close to a flagship as they have."

"I really shouldn't be surprised by what you Jedi can tell, but I am." Bwua'tu thought for a moment, then turned to the Mon Calamari captain who had tried to shield him earlier. "We won't show our hand *yet,* Tola."

"Very good, sir."

"But when that ship enters effective range, let's be ready to give it everything we have," Bwua'tu said. "Maybe we can surprise *them* for a change."

"Yes, sir," Tola said. "I'll have all batteries lock it in as a secondary target now."

"Good. Designate it Bug One." Bwua'tu turned back to the holodisplay, but said, "And one more thing. Have the capture bay stand down. All Jedi craft are free to come and go as they require."

Tola acknowledged the order, then turned to pass on the admiral's commands.

Leia smiled. "Thank you, Admiral," she said. "But if I can be of some service *here*—"

"I was thinking of your StealthXs, Princess," Bwua'tu interrupted. "They're going to need a place to refuel and rearm."

"They are?" Leia asked. "I mean, if the Jedi can be of any help—"

"They *will* be." Bwua'tu began to pace, but his gaze remained glued to the holodisplay. "Inform them that they're now under my command."

"Uh—"

"Is there a problem with that?" Bwua'tu demanded.

"No, sir," Leia answered. "Just thinking about the best way to let them know."

"The way that makes it clear. These are bugs with a plan, Princess." Bwua'tu stopped pacing and scowled along his snout at her. "We need to stop them here, or we won't stop them at all."

Leia swallowed. "I know that, Admiral. I'll do my best."

She closed her eyes, then stretched her Force-awareness out into the Choke. She found Mara and her team first, very calm and focused. A bright circle of ion glow, surrounded by the stern of a large rocky vessel, appeared in Leia's mind; they were sneaking up on a Killik ship. She filled her thoughts with good feelings about Admiral Bwua'tu and silently repeated the word *respect*.

Mara and the others seemed puzzled, but willing.

Leia reached out to Kyp's squadron next and was immediately engulfed in a conflagration of fear and exhilaration and anger, all blasting her at once. She allowed herself to sink into the emotional turmoil and began to glimpse flashes of exploding dartships and fiery white propellant trails.

Kyp's presence touched Leia, assuring her that he was on his way. She replied as she had with Mara, by filling her mind with good thoughts about Bwua'tu and silently urging Kyp to respect him.

Kyp poured indignation into the Force. Leia repeated the sentiment more strongly, trying to impress on him that the problem was the Killiks, not the Fifth Fleet. Kyp grew frustrated, but his stubbornness slowly gave way to willingness.

Leia opened her eyes in time to see Tola, the Mon Calamari, drop to his knees, gasping for breath and clawing at his throat. Bwua'tu glanced over and calmly smashed the butt of his blaster into the back of Tola's skull. There was the sound of crunching chitin, then the lieutenant commander pitched forward, a string of insect gore momentarily connecting his head to the admiral's blaster handle.

"Stay alert, people!" Bwua'tu ordered. "I can't have my staff dropping dead around me."

A pair of security guards stepped into the TacSal to carry the convulsing Mon Calamari away. Leia pushed aside the sorrow she felt for him, then caught Bwua'tu's eye.

"The StealthX crews have agreed." She pointed into the holodisplay, indicating the five Killik ships moving to intercept the *Ackbar*. "Mara's team—half a squadron—is somewhere behind this group, moving up on one of the ships."

Bwua'tu frowned. "What's her status? Mara's team can't be combat-ready after so long in space."

"They can make one attack run, but dogfighting is out of the question until they refuel," Leia said. "Other than that, they're good."

Bwua'tu looked doubtful.

"Trust me, Admiral." Leia smiled. "It's Jedi sorcery."

Bwua'tu snorted. "If you say so."

Leia pointed at a cluster of dartships that seemed to be gathered between the two groups of Killik ships for no apparent reason. "I think Master Durron's squadron is engaged here."

"On their way to free you and Master Sebatyne," Bwua'tu surmised. "We don't need them here. Have them withdraw toward the *Mothma*."

"It might be more precise if you spoke to our teams yourself." Leia went to the comm station and opened a channel to the StealthXs. "They can't acknowledge, but they'll hear your orders."

"Very well."

Bwua'tu stepped away from the holodisplay and told the StealthXs what he wanted. Leia felt acknowledgments from everyone except Mara, who seemed firmly opposed to abandoning the target she had already selected. When Leia allowed her bewilderment to rise to the surface of her mind, Mara flooded the meld with concern for Luke and Han.

"Everyone except Mara is a go," Leia reported. "Mara is going to stay with her current target. It has something to do with Luke and Han."

Bwua'tu cocked his thick brow. "*Something* is a rather imprecise term, Princess."

"I'm sorry, Admiral." Leia reached out into the Force, searching for her brother's presence, and felt nothing. "That's all I know."

Bwua'tu frowned, clearly unaccustomed to having his commands modified in this manner. "That will . . ."

He let the sentence trail off as the leading elements of the Killik fleet filled the holodisplay with flashes of light. *Mon Mothma*'s image changed to yellow, indicating that its shields were absorbing more energy than they could rapidly disperse. The *Ackbar*'s image remained blue.

"Enemy weapons are identified as turbolasers," the sensor officer reported. "Unknown manufacturer, but clearly Alliance technology."

"At least we know who the Tibanna tappers have been supplying," Bwua'tu observed. He turned to Leia. "Have Master Sebatyne prep the *Falcon* for launch. The StealthXs may need a mobile refueling platform."

Leia retrieved the comlink Saba had left on her bunk. "Master Sebatyne, would you prep the *Falcon* for launch? Admiral Bwua'tu may need it to refuel the StealthXs."

"It *is* prepped," Saba retorted. A muffled *phew-phew* sounded in the background. "But this one does not know how long we can keep it that way."

Leia frowned. "Is that the *Falcon*'s blaster cannon I hear?"

"Of course!" Saba replied. "Those little Gorog are everywhere!"

Leia started to report to Bwua'tu, but he was already at a wall display, punching codes into the control panel. He paused, then punched more codes and cursed. The screen never showed anything but static.

"These bugs are good," he growled. "They've been cutting our status feeds."

Leia activated the comlink again. "We're blind up here, Master. What can you tell me about the situation?"

"It'z bad!" Saba said. "If this one had not already disabled the capture bay batteriez, you wouldn't be talking to her now. The crew is down, and bugz are everywhere."

"Okay," Leia said. "Maybe you'd better launch now."

"Without *you*?" A rhythmic hissing came out of the comlink. "You are alwayz joking, Jedi Solo."

Saba closed the channel.

Leia looked up to find Bwua'tu speaking to a young Sullustan ensign wearing the double-lightning bars of the engineering staff.

"—didn't Captain Urbok inform me the *Ackbar*'s situation was this bad? Damage assessment is her responsibility."

"B-because she's dead, s-sir?" the lieutenant stammered.

"What about Lieutenant Commander Reo?"

"Also dead, sir."

Leia could sense Bwua'tu's anger building, but he maintained a civil tone. "And Lieutenant Aramb?"

"Paralyzed and unable to speak, sir," the ensign reported. "Apparently, the Killik venom isn't as effective against Gotals."

"Well, then, who *is* running engineering?" Bwua'tu demanded.

The Sullustan looked back toward the decimated command deck, then asked, "You?"

"Wrong, *Captain* Yuul." Bwua'tu pointed to the ship engineer's chair. "Now get to your station, get on the comm, and find out the condition of this ship!"

"Sir!"

As the Sullustan turned to obey, Bwua'tu looked to Leia and shook his head. "These Killiks are beginning to worry me, Princess. What other surprises do they have tucked under their chitin?"

Without awaiting a reply, he returned his attention to the holodisplay. The *Mon Mothma* was concentrating its fire on the lead ship, blowing off so many pieces that the thing looked more like an asteroid field than a capital vessel. But the Killik dartship swarms had already overwhelmed the Alliance fighter screens, and for every turbolaser strike the *Mothma* delivered, it took ten.

The *Ackbar* was faring better, at least outside the hull. Although space beyond the viewport was bright with turbolaser blossoms, the Killik gunners seemed to be having trouble accounting for the gravitational effects of the binary stars behind the Star Destroyer. Most strikes fell short or passed harmlessly below the *Ackbar*'s belly, and the few that landed were not powerful enough to seriously challenge its shields.

The *Mothma*'s likeness suddenly changed to red, indicating that it had suffered a shield breach. Bwua'tu sighed audibly, then turned to a female human who had been sticking close to his side.

"Grendyl, tell Commodore Darklighter to withdraw. Have all surviving Fifth Fleet starfighters disengage and meet him at Rendezvous Alpha."

Grendyl's eyes grew round. "Even *our* fighters, Admiral?"

"That's what I said, blast it!" Bwua'tu barked. "Is something wrong with those little pink flaps you call ears?"

An astonished silence settled over the surviving members of Bwua'tu's staff, and all eyes went to the holodisplay.

Bwua'tu took a breath, then said, "I apologize, Grendyl. That was uncalled for. Our unfortunate situation has put me rather on edge, I'm afraid."

"It's quite all right, sir." Her voice was about to crack. "I'll send the message at once."

"Thank you," Bwua'tu said. "And make it a direct order, to both Commodore Darklighter and the starfighter squadrons. I won't have them wasting valuable Alliance resources on pointless displays of bravery. The *Ackbar* is lost."

Grendyl brought her hand up in a smart salute. "Sir."

The rest of Bwua'tu's staff remained silent, staring into the holodisplay and contemplating the admiral's grim conclusion. The *Ackbar* was trapped with its back against a binary star, with five Killik capital ships and a swarm of several thousand fighters coming at it with nothing in the way except a few atoms of hydrogen. The situation was hopeless, and Bwua'tu was both astute enough to see that early on and sensible enough not to deceive himself or anyone else about their chances of escaping the trap.

Leia felt Saba urging her to return to the *Falcon,* but she remained where she was. Something did not feel right. The *Ackbar*'s turbolasers were hammering all five enemy ships coming toward it, but its own shields were barely flickering.

After a few moments, Bwua'tu said, "I think the time has come for our surprise." He went to the comm and opened a channel to the turbolaser batteries. "All batteries, switch targeting to Bug One. Acknowledge when ready."

The *Ackbar*'s turbolaser batteries fell silent for a moment, then the acknowledgments rolled in so fast that Leia could not keep track of them.

When the comm fell silent again, Bwua'tu said, "Fire on my mark . . . three . . . two . . . mark!"

Space beyond the command deck viewport grew brilliant with turbolaser fire, and the deck shuddered with kinetic discharge. They waited, breathless, during the instant it took the barrage to cross the vast distance and land. Bug One's symbol turned yellow on the holodisplay.

"Affirmative hits," the sensor officer reported. "Estimate ten percent loss of mass."

An enthusiastic cheer rose from the survivors in the TacSal and on the command deck.

Bwua'tu spoke into the comm. "Well done, gunnery! Odd-number batteries maintain fire—"

Leia did not hear the rest of what Bwua'tu said, for Mara was suddenly reaching out to her, full of alarm and worry for Luke and Han. Leia frowned, confused, and the image of a Killik ship appeared in her mind. There were several tiny figures on it, creeping across its broken surface, noticeable only because of the pinpoints of light coming from their helmet lamps. Then turbolaser fire began to rain down on it like a Nkllonian meteor storm, blowing huge, ragged holes into the ship's hull, hurling fountains of stone into space, and hiding the tiny figures behind a curtain of dust.

And then, suddenly, Leia felt Luke's presence, somewhere near Mara and even more alarmed.

Leia sprang to Bwua'tu's side. "Stop! Luke and Han are on that ship!"

Bwua'tu lowered his furry brow, as confused as Leia had been a moment ago. "What?"

"Luke and Han are on Bug One!" Leia explained. "That's why Mara wouldn't retarget earlier. She saw them!"

Bwua'tu's eyes widened. "You're sure?"

"I am," Leia said. "I just felt Luke in the Force—he must have been hiding before."

Bwua'tu narrowed his eyes. "I see." He thought for a moment, then returned to the comm. "Batteries ending in five or zero maintain fire on Bug One. All others return to normal targeting."

Leia frowned. "That's still ten batteries!"

"If your brother and husband are aboard that ship, they're either prisoners or stowaways," Bwua'tu said. "If they're prisoners, their best chance of escape lies in disabling the ship. If they're stowaways—"

"—we might draw attention to them by stopping the attack," Leia finished.

Bwua'tu nodded. "We'll make a fleet admiral of you yet, Princess."

They returned to the holodisplay. The tiny triangle of an unidentified vessel was just separating from Bug One and starting to accelerate toward the *Ackbar*.

"Sensors, give me a reading on that right *now*," Bwua'tu demanded. "What is it? A missile?"

There was a short pause, then the image changed to the triangular cylinder of an old Kuat Drive Yards frigate.

"New contact is confirmed as a *Lancer*-class frigate," the sensor officer reported. "Affiliation unknown."

Bwua'tu frowned, then looked toward Leia. "Can your sorcery be of any help, Princess?"

Hoping to sense Luke and Han aboard the frigate, she reached out to the vessel in the Force . . . and found Raynar Thul instead. She immediately tried to break contact, but as she withdrew, he followed, and an enormous, murky presence rose inside her mind. Her vision grew dark around the edges, and a dark weight began to press down on her, so heavy and cold and draining that her knees grew weak and buckled.

"Princess Leia?" Bwua'tu and Grendyl stepped to her side, their blaster pistols cocked to smash the first crawling thing they saw. "Where did it get you?"

"I'm . . ." Leia tried to rise and failed. "Not bugs . . . frigate . . ."

Bwua'tu frowned. "The frigate?" He pulled her up. "What about it?"

Leia wanted to answer, to tell him who was coming, but the dark weight inside was too much. She could not bring the words to mind, could not have spoken them even if they had come.

"I see," Bwua'tu said. "Grendyl, designate that vessel hostile . . . and make it a high-priority target."

A few moments later a turbolaser barrage streaked toward the frigate. A deep pang of sorrow washed over Leia as she awaited the coming explosion. Whatever Raynar had become among the Killiks, he had once been a Jedi and a close friend of her children, and she knew that his loss would leave her feeling empty and dismal.

Then, as the strike neared Raynar's vessel, the dark weight inside vanished, and Leia's strength surged back. Still gasping, she was about to report who was aboard, but the turbolaser barrage suddenly veered away and blossomed in empty space.

Grendyl cried out in astonishment, a murmur of disbelief rose from the survivors on the command deck, and Leia finally understood why the Killik gunners were such bad shots.

They weren't *trying* to hit the *Ackbar*.

When the second volley of turbolaser fire also veered away at the last instant, Bwua'tu narrowed his eyes and turned to Leia.

"What is it?" he asked. "Some sort of new shield?"

Leia shook her head. "It's Raynar Thul," she said. "And I think he's coming to take your ship."

TWENTY

The exterior of the nest ship was knobby and shadowed, a broken vista of narrow trenches zigzagging between giant blocks of spit-crete. Han knew that the blocks were almost certainly primitive heat sinks, necessary to keep the hull from cracking open in the extreme temperature swings of space. But that didn't make navigating around them any easier. The vessel's surface was like an immense spitcrete maze, stretching ahead almost endlessly, then suddenly vanishing against the blue brilliance of a massive crescent of ion efflux. Han felt as though he were walking into a sun—an impression supported by the droplets of sweat stinging his eyes and rolling down his cheeks. With the four real suns of the Murgo Choke blasting him in the side and shoulders, the *DR919a*'s cheap escape pod vac suits were not up to the task of cooling their occupants. He was afraid they would start melting soon.

Han stopped at the base of a heat sink—a spitcrete monolith two meters high—that Luke had scaled to study the terrain ahead, then tipped his helmet back so he could look up. There was another nest ship a hundred kilometers or so above, and a constant stream of tiny colored dashes came and went as it traded fire with an Alliance Star Destroyer somewhere inside the Murgo Choke.

Han activated his suit comm. "Are we there yet?"

"Almost, Han." Luke continued to study the horizon, one glove shading his helmet visor. "There's a square shadow at eleven that might be a thermal vent."

"Do you see any heat distortion above it?"

"No."

"Then we're not there." Han tried to keep his disappointment out of his voice—he did not want to encourage any more jabbering over the suit comm from Tarfang. "A hyperdrive for a ship this big is going to release heat for hours. When we get near a vent, we'll know it."

"I suppose." Luke turned to climb down, then suddenly tipped his helmet back to look over their heads. "Incoming! Get—"

Space turned white, and Luke's voice dissolved into the telltale static that meant a turbolaser strike was all too precisely targeted. Han tried to drop behind cover, but that was next to impossible in a stiff escape pod vac suit. He made it as far as bending his knees; then the nest ship hull slammed up under him, hurling him into the side of the heat sink. He tumbled down the surface and came to a rest at its base, the inside of his faceplate so smeared with perspiration that he could not tell whether he was lying facedown or face up.

The hull continued to buck and shudder, bouncing Han's nose against his faceplate, and the strike static grew deafening. He chinned his suit comm off so he could listen for the hiss that would mean his vac suit had been compromised, then slowly brought up his arms and determined that he was lying on his belly.

Han rolled to his back, then wished he hadn't. Space above was one huge, blurry sheet of turbolaser energy—most of it incoming—and filled with roiling spitcrete dust and tumbling chunks of heat sink . . . and something that looked like a half-sized vac suit, spinning out of control and waving its spread-eagled limbs.

Han activated his suit comm again and heard even more static. Some Alliance Star Destroyer was hitting them with everything it had. He stood and nearly got bounced free of the ship's artificial gravity himself, then came down hard beside C-3PO.

The droid turned his head and looked as though he was speaking. Fortunately, Han could not hear a word.

Trying to keep one eye on whoever it was floating off up there, Han rolled to a knee and, through the thickening haze of barrage vapor, found Luke about five meters away. Han scrambled over, then touched helmets so they could speak without the comm unit.

"Someone got bounced!" Han pointed toward the slowly shrinking figure. "We're losing him!"

Luke looked in the direction Han was indicating. "It's Tarfang."

"How can you tell?"

Luke pointed at a pair of shadows tucked behind a heat sink. "Juun and Artoo are over there."

He lifted his hand and used the Force to draw Tarfang's spinning form back down. The ship's artificial gravity caught hold of the Ewok about two meters above the surface. He landed hard, then bounced to his feet shaking his fist and jabbering behind his faceplate. When another close strike launched him off the hull again, Han had to think twice before he reached up and caught the Ewok by the ankle.

Tarfang noticed the hesitation. He glared vibrodaggers as he was pulled back down, but that did not prevent him from grabbing Han's utility belt and holding tight. Han tried again to activate his suit comm, but with space flashing like a Bespinese thunderstorm, all that came over the helmet speakers was strike static.

Luke did not need the comm. He simply stood and looked toward Han, and Han understood. They had to keep moving. Luke had used the Force, and now Lomi Plo could feel them coming.

They gathered Juun and the droids and started forward, following the spitcrete troughs between the heat sinks, zigzagging their way through the barrage with giant columns of shattered spitcrete and vapor shooting up all around. Within a few minutes, the turbolaser storm faded to a fraction of its former fury, but it remained fierce enough to make them fear for their lives. Several strikes landed so close that everyone was bounced off their feet, and twice Luke had to use the Force to pull someone back down into the nest ship's artificial gravity. The barrage haze grew steadily thicker, obscuring visibility to the point that Han came within a step of leading Tarfang and C-3PO off the edge of a cavernous blast hole.

Perhaps half a kilometer later, Luke stopped short and pointed toward a billowing column of dust and shattered spitcrete about fifty meters ahead. It was roiling with convection currents and rising at a steady rate.

"We're there, Han." Luke's voice was scratchy but understandable; under the lighter barrage, the electromagnetic static had diminished and no longer jammed their suit comms completely. "But be ready. I think we have a reception committee."

Tarfang stopped and planted his feet. "*Wobba jobabu!*"

"Don't worry," Luke said. "We'll have backup."

"Backup?" Han turned to look, peering through the barrage haze. "Out here?"

"Mara is keeping an eye on us from a StealthX," Luke explained. "I think she spotted our helmet lamps when she was sneaking up to attack the nest ship."

"She's in a StealthX?" Han asked. "And you still want to do this the hard way? Why don't we let *her* drop a shadow bomb down that thermal vent and jump this rock? We can trigger our rescue beacons and wait for a ride."

"That's not a bad idea, Han," Luke said. Something that sounded like chattering teeth came over the suit comm, and he turned toward the thermal vent. "I'd like you to take the others and do exactly that. It will make things easier for me."

"Easier *how*?" Han asked suspiciously. "I thought all we needed to do was blow the nest ship's hyperdrive, and Mara can do that a lot easier with a shadow bomb than we can with a lightsaber and two crummy blaster pistols."

"There's a complication," Luke said. "One we can't hit with a shadow bomb."

"A complication?" Han put his faceplate close to Luke's and saw that the Jedi Master was shivering uncontrollably. "You mean Lomi Plo?"

Luke turned to Han and nodded. "I should f-finish her off while I have the chance."

"I don't know who you think you're fooling, but it isn't me," Han said. "She's got ahold of you again, hasn't she?"

Luke sighed. "That doesn't mean you should stay."

"You come with us, and I won't," Han said.

"And m-make us all targets?" Luke shook his head. "I'm going to stay here and see this thing through."

"That makes two of us," Han said. He turned to Tarfang and Juun. "How about you two?"

Tarfang launched into tirade of angry jabbering, then renewed his grasp on Han's utility belt and shook his head. Juun merely stood there, blinking at them out of his helmet.

"Well?" Han asked.

When Juun's expression did not change, Han tapped the side of the Sullustan's helmet. Juun frowned and shook his head.

"I guess it's unanimous," Han said. "Juun can't risk jumping off this rock with a faulty comm. If his beacon fails, too, he'll be a goner out there."

"I wish you'd reconsider, Han."

"Yeah, and I wish we had a satchel full of thermal detonators and a few kilos of baradium," Han said. "But that's not going to happen. Let's go."

They started to move again. But instead of traveling straight toward the thermal vent, Luke carefully circled it. Every few meters, he would stop and remain motionless for five or ten seconds, then adjust his course and creep ahead even more slowly.

Finally, he motioned for a stop, then sneaked forward to peer around the side of a heat sink. Han followed and saw several dozen hazy, bug-shaped figures wearing the bulky carapaces that Killiks used as pressure suits. They were all crouching in ambush, still facing the direction he and Luke had been approaching from a few minutes earlier.

"Everybody be ready," Luke unhooked his lightsaber, then took the blaster pistol out of his utility belt and passed it to Tarfang. "Mara's making her run."

"Then what?" Han asked.

"Then Lomi Plo will have to show herself," Luke answered. "After we finish with her, we trip our rescue beacons."

"I'm holding you to that," Han said. He motioned Juun to stay with the droids and keep down—without a comm or a blaster, the Sullustan would be no good in the fight anyway—then twisted around to look up into space. "What's taking so—"

Luke jumped up and ignited his lightsaber, pointing the tip toward the hiding Gorog. In the same instant, the dark shape of a Jedi StealthX appeared behind the insects and began to stitch the nest ship's hull with fire from its four laser cannons. A curtain of spitcrete dust, hull chips, and bug parts boiled spaceward, and then the StealthX was gone, vanished against the star-flecked void.

A moment later a small line of pressure-suited Gorog came charging forward between the heat sinks, spraying electrobolts and shatter gun pellets ahead of them. Han returned fire, cursing in frustration as most of his bolts bounced harmlessly off the insects' carapace pressure suits. Luke simply made a sweeping motion with his hand, and one end of the Gorog line went tumbling into space.

Then brilliant spears of cannon fire began to stab down from space again, churning what remained of the insect line into an amalgam of chitin and gore. Han continued to fire, more to make sure Mara knew where he was than because he thought he was going to kill anything. In a moment the StealthX's dark shape swept past only a few meters from their hiding place, so close that Han could see Mara's head swinging back and forth as she selected her targets.

Han was still watching her when something tinked the back of his helmet. He spun around, half expecting to feel that painful final pop as a shatter gun pellet tore through his head, but there was nobody behind him except Juun and the droids.

The Sullustan pointed toward something on the other side of Luke. Han glanced over and found nothing but the usual barrage haze. Luke was standing just as he had a moment before, his lightsaber blazing and his attention fixed on the few would-be ambushers that had survived Mara's strafing runs so far.

Juun began to gesture violently, this time a little closer to Luke. Han looked again, saw nothing but dust, then spread his hands in a gesture of helplessness.

Juun beat his fists against his helmet, then leapt to his feet and raced in the direction he had been pointing.

"Look out, Luke!" Han warned over the comm. "You've got a crazy Sullustan—"

Luke whirled, bringing his lightsaber around in a high guard—then stopping cold in a flicker of sparks.

Han scowled. "What the—"

Luke suddenly doubled over in the middle, as though he had been kicked hard in the stomach. Then Juun slammed to a stop about a meter in front of Luke, his arms wrapping around something Han could not see.

Luke brought his blade up and hit nothing but air, then flipped the tip over his shoulder in a back-guard maneuver that resulted in another flurry of sparks. He followed this by dropping into a spinning leg sweep that caught whatever Juun was clinging to. The Sullustan's arms came loose, and he went rolling across the spitcrete into the side of a heat sink.

Han opened fire on the general area, and a flurry of blaster bolts flashed past his shoulder as Tarfang did the same. Most of their attacks did nothing more harmful than burn divots into the hull of the nest ship. But a couple of times, the shots were mysteriously deflected, and once Han thought he saw the flash of a scarred face, so haggard and misshapen that he could not be sure whether it was human or insect.

Luke danced back into the combat, slashing high and low with his lightsaber, missing more often than not, but spinning directly into the next attack, his blade sparking and flashing as it blocked and deflected the unseen strikes coming his way. Han and Tarfang scrambled after the fight, firing more or less where the Jedi was attacking, drawing just enough attention so that Luke could continue to drive the unseen enemy back.

They continued to press the attack for perhaps five or ten seconds; then a row of six-limbed figures wearing bulky Killik pressure suits emerged from the heat sinks. Han's heart rose into his throat—

he wondered if that was what Jedi danger sense felt like—and he stopped advancing.

"Uh, guys?" He glanced to each flank and saw that there were more bugs to each side. "Get down!"

There was a flurry of motion as the insects brought up their weapons. Han was already dropping to the hull. He landed on his side and kicked behind a heat sink; silver flashes began to dance across his faceplate while flying chips of spitcrete beat an irregular cadence on his helmet. He curled into a fetal ball and counted himself lucky.

A moment later Luke's voice came over the suit comm. "Cover!"

"What do you think I'm—"

Han's comm gave a sharp pop, then a series of sharp concussions reverberated through the hull. The sound of the chips striking his helmet was replaced at first by a dozen seconds of static, then by utter silence. He uncurled and carefully raised his head.

The barrage dust had thickened to a murky gray cloud, but it was not too thick to prevent him from seeing the brilliant streaks of Mara's laser cannons chasing off the Gorog survivors. Han rolled to his knees and turned in the other direction. The hull ended about three meters from where he was kneeling, opening into a deep, dark crater filled with flotsam, floating corpses, and shooting streams of vapor.

"Han?" Luke's voice came over the suit comm. "Are you okay?"

"That depends." Han stood and turned in a slow circle, then finally saw Luke coming toward him from about ten meters away. "Did you get Lomi?"

Luke shook his head. "I can still feel her."

"Then I'm about as un-okay as you can get." Han began a slow rotation, his blaster held ready to fire. "I *hate* being crept up on by stuff I can't see. Let's get back to where we left Juun."

"Why do you want Juun?" Luke asked.

"Because he can see her," Han said.

Luke stopped three paces from Han. "You're sure?"

"Didn't you see the way he tried to tackle her? Of course I'm sure." Han did not like the surprise in Luke's voice. "Does that mean something?"

"Yes," Luke said. "It means I'm wrong about Lomi Plo."

"Great," Han growled. He would have liked to suggest again that they leave the ship and activate their rescue beacons, but he did not want Luke telling him to go ahead on his own. He was afraid the temptation might be too much for him. "Wrong how?"

"I thought she was using some sort of Force blur to hide herself," Luke said. "But if Juun can see her, and *I* can't . . ."

When Luke let the sentence trail off, Han said, "Yeah, that scares me, too." He turned back the way they had come. "Maybe Juun can explain it."

"Wait a minute," Luke said. "What about Tarfang?"

"Tarfang?" Han took a quick look around, then tipped his helmet back. "Don't tell me he got bounced again!"

Luke was silent for a moment, then said, "He didn't. Tarfang is below us, inside the nest ship." He turned and looked toward one of the holes Mara's shadow bombs had knocked in the hull. "I think Lomi Plo has him."

TWENTY-ONE

With a cloud of assassin bugs droning behind them and elite Unu soldiers zipping shatter gun pellets down every side corridor they passed, Leia knew her small company was in trouble. They would never hold off the Killiks long enough to initiate the *Ackbar*'s self-destruct sequence.

What Leia did *not* know was how to break the news to Bwua'tu. They had been forced to abandon the command deck after a swarm of assassin bugs had erupted from the ventilation ducts. Since then, activating the self-destruct cycle had been the admiral's only concern, but the Killiks had foreseen the move. Every primary access terminal Leia and the others passed was damaged beyond all hope of a quick repair—usually by an electrobolt blast to the keypad.

Leia came to another intersection, and Bwua'tu's voice barked out from the middle of the group behind her. "Right!"

With the assassin bugs buzzing up the corridor behind them, there was no question of pausing to reconnoiter. Leia simply ignited her lightsaber—which Bwua'tu had retrieved from his wardroom vault as they fled the bridge—and led the charge around the corner.

Not surprisingly, there was a squad of Unu soldiers coming the other way. They were as large as Wookiees, with golden thoraxes and big purple eyes and scarlet carapaces covering their backs, and in their four pincer-hands they carried both shatter guns for ranged combat and short tridents for close fighting. They opened fire as soon as Leia rounded the corner, and the corridor broke into a cacophony of zipping and pinging.

Though lightsabers weren't much good at deflecting shatter gun attacks, Leia began to spin and whirl forward, slipping and dodging past the flying pellets with no conscious thought, surrendering herself to the Force and trusting it to guide her steps.

Her companions—a ragtag band of ship's crew whom she and Bwua'tu had been picking up along the way—raced into the corridor a step behind her and poured fire at the Killiks. No one hesitated to shoot past their shipmates or Leia. Twice, she had to deflect friendly blaster bolts, and once she nearly stepped in front of a shatter gun pellet to avoid being hit from behind. She did not blame her fellows for being reckless. There was just no time to be careful.

Leia reached the Unu soldiers and Force-shoved the nearest one into the Killik beside it. She lashed out with her lightsaber and separated the insect's head from its golden thorax, then whipped the blade back and opened another across the middle.

A pair of huge mandibles clamped down on Leia from the side, and then she saw a set of trident tines rising toward her chest. She used the Force to shove the weapon away, then deactivated her lightsaber, flipped the handle around, and reignited the blade as she pressed the emitter nozzle to her captor's thorax.

An ear-piercing shriek sounded in Leia's ear. She brought her foot up and kicked aside a shatter gun another Unu soldier was raising toward her, then flipped her lightsaber downward, slashing her captor open and bringing the blade up between the legs of her would-be attacker. Both insects collapsed with their lives flooding out of them.

Then Leia's companions reached the melee, and the battle erupted into a savage gun-and-pincer fight. Badly outmatched in size and strength, the *Ackbar*'s crew poured blaster bolts into the Killiks at point-blank range. The Killiks used one set of hand-pincers to fire their shatter guns and the other to slash and thrust with their tridents, sometimes using their mandibles to grab an attacker, sometimes whipping their mandibles around to knock someone off his feet.

Leia glanced back to check on Bwua'tu and found the admiral on her heels, as covered in insect gore as she was and firing a blaster pistol with each hand. His aide Grendyl was behind him, tossing a thermal grenade back into the approaching cloud of assassin bugs.

"Go!" Bwua'tu pushed Leia up the corridor. "There should be an access terminal ahead, outside the hatch!"

Leia spun and cut her way through a soldier-insect that had been winning a grapple-and-shoot fight with two Alliance ensigns. An orange light flashed behind them as Grendyl's grenade detonated, rumbling off the walls and filling the corridor with acrid fumes, then Leia stepped out of the fray into empty corridor.

Ten meters away, a cluster of much smaller Gorog soldiers—lacking carapaces and only about shoulder height—were rushing out of a side corridor to block a security hatch marked CAPTURE BAY ACCESS. With them was a slender Twi'lek female armored in blue chitin so closely formfitted that it looked like a body stocking. One arm was hanging limp beneath a sagging, misshapen shoulder—a result of her fight against Luke a year earlier at Qoribu—and as soon as she saw Leia, her full lips twisted into a contemptuous sneer.

"Alema Rar!" Leia said. "I've been looking forward to this."

Leia reached back and caught one of the last standing Unu soldiers in a Force grasp, then brought her arm forward and hurled the insect sideways down the corridor. She followed a few steps behind, using its body as a shield, listening to shatter gun pellets drum into its carapace.

A couple of moments later, she heard the *snap-hiss* of an igniting lightsaber, then a blade so blue it was almost black sliced the insect in half. Leia pressed the attack, leaping between the body halves as they dropped away, hitting Alema with a Force shove and bringing her own blade around in an overhand power strike.

Alema barely got her guard up in time, and sparks filled the air as the two blades met. Leia brought her foot up in a driving stomp kick that rocked the Twi'lek back on her heels, then rolled her lightsaber into a horizontal slash at Alema's limp arm.

Alema had no choice except to pivot away and bring her weapon around in a desperate block that left her sideways and out of position. Leia swung her foot around in a powerful roundhouse kick that caught the Twi'lek behind the knees and swept both legs.

Alema landed flat on her back, her mouth gaping and her green eyes wide with alarm. Leia allowed herself a small smirk of satisfaction—recalling how lopsided the combat had been in Alema's favor the last time they fought—then blocked a desperate slash at her ankles and slipped into a counter, angling the tip of her blade toward the Twi'lek's heart.

Before Leia could drive the thrust home, a thrumming mass of blue chitin hit her in the chest and bowled her over backward. She tried to bring her lightsaber up and found her arms pinned to her chest, then her attacker pressed the muzzle of a shatter gun to her ribs. She used the Force to push the weapon away, but then the insect's mandibles were clamped around her head, its needle-sharp proboscis darting toward her eye.

Leia shot her free hand up between its mandibles, catching the proboscis between two fingers and continuing to shove until it snapped. The Gorog let out a distressed whistle and bore down with its mandibles, and the edge of her face exploded into pain. But by then she was shoving at the insect with the Force, opening enough of a gap so she could bring her lightsaber up and slice her attacker in two.

Leia started to spring up—until a storm of blaster bolts streamed past overhead, tearing into a trio of Gorog at her feet. Half a dozen crew members rushed past and crashed into the wall of insects in a deafening cacophony of blows and small-arms fire, then Bwua'tu appeared at her side, reaching down to help her up.

"Princess! Are you—"

"Fine!" Leia brought her feet under her, automatically raising her lightsaber in a high block. "Get ba—"

Alema charged out of the melee, her lightsaber already descending for the kill. Leia caught the attack on her blade, then delivered a Force-enhanced punch to the Twi'lek's chitin-armored midsection.

It was like hitting a wall. She felt a bone snap in her hand, and she did not even drive Alema far enough away to buy space to stand. The Twi'lek brought her knee up under Leia's chin, snapping her head back with such force that her vision went black for a moment.

Leia lashed out with her free arm, hooking it around the knee that had just struck her, then launched herself into a back roll. Alema had to sprang in the opposite direction, executing a backflip, and they both came up on their feet facing each other. Leia's hand throbbed, but not so badly that it prevented her from grasping her lightsaber handle with both hands.

Bwua'tu and the rest of the crew members were behind Alema, pressing the attack on the Gorog and driving them back toward the capture bay. On the other side of the hatch, Leia sensed Saba and the Noghri, struggling to override the security system so they could join the battle. Coming down the corridor behind her, working their way through the smoke left by the Grendyl's grenade, Leia heard the distant drone of the surviving assassin bugs.

Alema studied Leia with narrowed eyes. "You've been practicing."

Leia shrugged. "A little."

"It won't matter," Alema sneered. "You're too old to start being a real Jedi now."

Leia raised her brow. "I think I need to teach you some manners."

Leia sprang forward, once again attacking the side with Alema's crippled arm. This time, the Twi'lek did not make the mistake of underestimating her opponent. She gave ground quickly, pivoting around so that her crippled side was protected.

Their blades clashed time and again, each Jedi augmenting their lightsaber strikes with Force shoves and telekinesis attacks, each trying to take advantage of the other's weakness. Leia's face had become so swollen that she could barely see out of one eye, and Alema kept circling to find a blind spot. As Alema tried to protect her weak side, Leia kept slipping toward it, forcing the Twi'lek to retreat toward the security hatch. All the time, the drone of the assassin bugs drew nearer.

Then Bwua'tu and the *Ackbar*'s crew began to overwhelm Alema's company of insect-soldiers, forcing them past her toward the access terminal. Though the Twi'lek's back was now to the main fight, as the admiral and his followers drew closer to the terminal, the knowledge came to her through Gorog's collective mind. Her eyes flashed with alarm, then she sprang back, locked her blade on, and hurled her lightsaber at Leia's legs.

Leia had no choice but to block low and pivot away, and in that second Alema pointed at Bwua'tu's spine and let loose a crackling stream of Force lightning. Leia started to grab the admiral in the Force, intending to jerk him out of the way, but his aide Grendyl was already leaping to protect him.

The lightning caught the woman full in the chest, hurling her back into Bwua'tu and knocking him to the deck.

Leia leapt at Alema, striking for the shoulders. The Twi'lek spun away . . . and launched Leia into a wall with a whirling back kick to the ribs.

The blunt clang of skull against durasteel sounded inside Leia's head. Her mind turned to gauze and she thought for a moment that the bloodcurdling howl assaulting her ears was her own. Then she noticed the meter-long segment of amputated lekku flopping around on the deck like a baagalmog out of water.

Leia looked up and found Alema trembling and screaming in pain, the cauterized stump of one nerve-packed head-tail ending just above her shoulder. But the Twi'lek's pain did not prevent her from releasing another stream of Force lightning—this time into the access terminal itself.

The unit exploded into a spray of sparks, pieces, and fumes. The security hatch gave the telltale hiss of a breaking seal, and Bwua'tu cried out in frustration.

Leia sprang to her feet and started toward Alema.

The Twi'lek was already stretching her arm up the corridor, calling her lightsaber back to hand. Leia heard the sizzle of the blade growing louder behind her and dropped into a deep squat as the weapon spun past overhead, then stabbed for Alema's heart.

The Twi'lek brought her blade down and blocked easily, then brought her foot up in a side-snap kick that caught Leia in the base of the throat. The blow was more painful than harmful, but Leia dropped to her seat, coughing and choking and trying to make it sound as though her larynx had been crushed. She could hear the drone of the assassin bugs only a few meters behind her and knew the time had come to end this fight—and she could see by the unreasoning fury in Alema's eyes that the wounded Twi'lek was primed for a mistake.

Leia rolled her eyes back in her head and let herself collapse to the floor. She heard Alema slide forward, then felt a knot of anticipation form in her stomach as the time approached to bring her blade slashing up through the Twi'lek's abdomen—and that was when Leia felt a surge of relief from Saba and the Noghri. A loud grating sounded from the security hatch, and she knew her Master and bodyguards had finally forced it open.

The pulsing whine of Meewalh's T-21 repeating blaster echoed down the corridor, then Alema's blade began to hiss and sizzle as it batted blaster bolts away. Leia opened her eyes to find the Twi'lek dancing along one wall of the corridor, just beyond reach and retreating into the droning cloud of assassin bugs.

When their eyes met, Alema's brow shot up in surprise. She flicked her lightsaber up in a brief salute, then gave Leia a spiteful sneer and fled out of sight.

Leia locked her blade on and spun around to throw her lightsaber, but the Twi'lek was nowhere to be seen.

Leia felt herself sliding across the deck, then realized Saba was using the Force to draw her away from the approaching cloud of assassin bugs. Cakhmaim and Meewalh appeared at her sides, spraying the corridor with blasterfire.

"Jedi Solo," Saba said. "Why are you lying on the floor at a time like this?"

Leia deactivated her lightsaber and stood with as much dignity as she could manage, considering how much her hand was beginning to hurt and how swollen her face was.

"I was laying a trap."

"Laying a trap?" Saba shook her head and began to siss hysterically. "You are beginning to sound just like Han."

TWENTY-TWO

The shadow bomb had opened a velker-sized hole in the hull of the nest ship, but the blast had penetrated only as deep as the second deck, where Luke now stood amid a tangle of devastation. The Force was too filled with ripples to tell where Lomi Plo had gone, but he knew by the cold knot in his stomach and the ache in his limbs that she was somewhere nearby, watching and waiting for the right moment to attack again.

Luke could sense Tarfang about thirty meters ahead, slowly moving away. Hearing the Ewok was even easier. Tarfang was chattering angrily into his suit comm, though it was anyone's guess whether he was cursing his captors, or Luke and Han.

Then Han's voice came over the comm as well. "All set here, Luke."

Luke looked up and saw Han and Juun two stories above, dimly silhouetted against the star-flecked void of space. C-3PO and R2-D2 were nowhere in sight; Han had left the damaged droids on the exterior of the ship, where they would be easy to retrieve on the way out.

Luke grasped Han and Juun in the Force and lowered them through the hole, being careful to keep them well away from any jagged edges or sharp protrusions. *DR919a*'s escape pod vac suits were about as flimsy as space suits came; one tear would be the end of the person inside. Once they were down, Mara's StealthX appeared in the breach and descended on its repulsorlifts, slowly spinning in a circle.

Luke kneeled at Juun's side and touched helmets so they could converse. "Did you see Lomi Plo up there, when she tried to sneak up on me?"

"I aw *omeding*," Juun said. Sound waves never carried well through helmets, and his nasal accent made the situation worse. "I did na know it wah *her* until you had the lisaber fight."

"Good enough," Luke said. He stood and turned toward Mara's StealthX, now settling onto the deck next to them, and activated his comm unit. "We're a little short on weapons."

Mara nodded inside the cockpit. A moment later the canopy opened, and she passed Luke the E-11 blaster rifle from the survival kit attached to her ejection module.

"What about destroying the hyperdrive?" she asked over her suit comm. "We can't let this nest ship leave the Choke."

"I know," Luke answered. "But we have to get Tarfang back first. I dragged him into this, and now I have to drag him out."

This drew an affirmative Ewok yap over the suit comm.

"We don't have much time," Mara warned. "And we're only going to have one chance to hit that thermal vent you and Han found. I'm down to my last shadow bomb, and the *Falcon* can't do this."

Luke nodded. He had felt Leia's relief as she and Saba escaped the *Ackbar*'s captors aboard the *Falcon,* and now they were on their way to the Gorog nest ship to retrieve him, Han, and the others. But the *Falcon*'s concussion missiles would not be accurate enough to reach the nest ship's hyperdrive—or powerful enough to destroy it even if they did.

"What about Kyp and all the other Jedi I sense out here?" Luke asked. "Maybe I should call them over to help."

"You could," Mara said. "But you'd have to countermand Admiral Bwua'tu's orders. He has them targeting the hyperdrives of the other nest ships. This one is my responsibility."

Luke raised his brow. "*Kyp* has been helping with this blockade?"

"Hardly," Mara scoffed. "It's complicated, but it all started when Leia and Saba were captured by the *Ackbar* on our way back to Woteba."

"An Alliance vessel arrested *Jedi*?"

"It gets worse," Mara said. "From what I've been able to pick up eavesdropping on comm traffic between the *Ackbar* and the *Mothma,* the Chiss have been holding the Jedi and the Galactic Alliance responsible for the Killiks' return to their border. Chief Omas tried to appease them by blockading the Utegetu nests, and to keep the Jedi from interfering, he placed Corran Horn in charge of the order."

Luke frowned. "Chief Omas doesn't choose Jedi leaders."

"That's what Kyp and his team thought," Mara said. "So they

commandeered a squadron of StealthXs to free you and Han from the Killiks, and Leia and Saba from the *Ackbar*. It's a mess."

"That's an understatement." Luke shook his head in frustration. He had always taught that Jedi should act in accordance with their consciences, trusting that the Force would lead them to do what was best for the order, the Alliance, and the galaxy. Clearly, his faith had been misplaced somewhere along the line. "Then why is Kyp—and everyone else—following Bwua'tu's orders now?"

"Because Leia urged us to," Mara said. "Nobody wants Killiks loose in the galaxy with these nest ships."

"At least everyone agrees on that much."

Luke had a terrible, hollow feeling in his stomach. In his efforts to build an order of self-directing Jedi, he had left the order itself adrift. No one had made a selfish or wrong decision—not even Chief Omas—but there had been no one to make them work together, no one to channel their energy in a single direction.

In short, there had been no leadership.

"Don't be too hard on yourself, Skywalker," Mara said. "You were stuck on Woteba."

"I remember," Luke answered. "But it shouldn't have mattered—not if I had prepared the other Masters properly."

Mara shook her head. "This is on Kyp and Corran and the rest of them. You can't be there every minute."

"No, but I *can* provide direction . . . and vision," Luke said. "If I had been doing that, the Masters would never have let Omas split them."

Han came over to stand beside the StealthX. "Maybe you two can talk command theory later," he said. "If we don't reach Tarfang before the bug queen drags him into a pressurized area, we'll never get him back."

"Sorry." Luke reached up and rested his glove on the sleeve of Mara's vac suit. "We've got to do this. I can't leave him."

Mara sighed. "I know—and so does Lomi Plo. She's trying to draw us in."

Luke smiled. "Her mistake."

"It better be," Mara said. "I'm not going to raise Ben alone."

"You won't have to." Luke patted her arm, then stepped away from the cockpit. "I promise."

Han started to follow Luke away from the StealthX, but Mara motioned him back toward the cockpit.

"Take this." She passed her lightsaber to Han. "If things get close, it will do you more good than a blaster."

Han's faceplate remained turned toward the weapon for a moment, then he nodded. "Thanks. I'll try not to cut up anything I shouldn't."

Mara smiled inside her helmet, but her eyes betrayed her concern. "After you three get Tarfang, jump on my wings," she said. "I'll lift you out of here fast, then go drop a shadow bomb down that thermal vent."

"Sure," Han said. "It'll be just like my swoop-riding days."

Once Han had stepped back, Mara closed the canopy and lifted the StealthX off the deck again. She turned in the general direction of Tarfang's presence, then activated the external floodlamps and began to creep forward.

Luke waved Juun to his side, then leaned down and touched helmets. "Stick close to me." He gave the blaster rifle from Mara's survival module to the Sullustan. "And when you see Lomi Plo, don't hesitate. Start blasting."

Juun's eyes widened inside his faceplate. "Me?"

"You want to save Tarfang, don't you?"

"Of course." Juun flipped the safety off. "I'd wo anywing."

"Good," Luke said. "Just remember: stick close."

He motioned Han to the StealthX's other flank, then started to follow the starfighter forward on his own side. The deck seemed to have been little more than a storage level. There were a few Gorog bodies, their eyes burst from sudden decompression, but most of the debris looked like broken waxes of black membrosia.

"These bugs are really starting to scare me," Han said over the comm. "This ship design is sturdy . . . really sturdy."

"Even with no shields?" Luke asked.

"Doesn't need 'em," Han said. "Every deck is a shield layer itself. Blast through one, and there's another just like it right below. Given the size of these bug haulers, you might have to go down a hundred decks before you hit anything important."

Luke had a sinking feeling. "What about Bwua'tu's plan?"

"Oh, that'll work," Han said. "All ships are weak in the stern—even these monsters. But those shadow bombs better go right down the thrust channels. If they hit a wall and detonate before they reach the hyperdrive itself, all they'll do is throw the bugs off course when they jump."

"I was afraid you'd say that."

Luke opened himself to the combat-meld, trying to impress on Kyp and the other pilots how important it was to be accurate when they targeted the other nest ships. He perceived a variety of emotions in response, from joy at sensing his presence, to gratitude for the advice, to frustration that the warning had come so late. The StealthXs were in the middle of their runs; some had already launched their bombs and were turning back to join the *Falcon* in coming after Luke and Han.

Luke poured reassurance into the meld; then the light from Mara's floodlamps fell on a section of spitcrete wall. A band of about twenty pressure-suited Gorog were nearing one of the leathery membranes Killiks used as air locks. They were holding—*struggling* to hold—a small, kicking figure in a vac suit.

Mara touched Luke through the Force, wondering if she should take a shot.

He gave her a mental nod, then warned Han, "Watch your eyes! Cannons!"

Luke averted his own gaze and reached down to cover Juun's faceplate, then Mara fired the StealthX's laser cannons. The flash was so bright that Luke's eyes hurt even looking at the floor.

When the light faded an instant later, he raised his gaze and found that the blast had destroyed not only the membrane, but much of the wall around it as well. Dozens of Gorog were spilling out through the gap, their limbs and bristly antennae flailing as they suffered swift but painful decompression deaths.

Many of the bodies tumbled into Tarfang's captors, knocking some off their feet and turning the band into a tangled knot. One of the Ewok's arms came free, and he began to thrash about so violently that the tangle became a snarl of whirling carapaces and flailing limbs.

Han rushed forward, firing half a dozen times before he traded the blaster pistol for Mara's lightsaber. When he ignited the blade, the gyroscopic effect of the arc wave caught him off guard, and he spun in a complete circle before bringing the weapon under control and slashing through a Gorog's midsection.

By the time Luke and Juun arrived, the Gorog had recovered from the initial shock of Han's attack and were turning to fight, their shatter guns rising to fire. Luke used the Force to sweep the barrels aside, then ignited his own lightsaber and opened four pressure suits in a single slash. Juun clung to his back, firing point-blank into any insect that made the mistake of trying to close from the sides.

With their mandibles and pincer-hands enclosed inside their carapace-like pressure suits, the Killiks were reduced to simple blows or using their shatter guns. Luke concentrated on the weapons, defending himself, Juun, and Han with his lightsaber and the Force, lopping off gun hands and deflecting aims.

That left Luke and his companions vulnerable to hand-to-hand attacks, and several times Luke was almost knocked off his feet when a carapace slammed into him or a flailing limb smashed into his legs. But Mara was watching their backs from the StealthX, using the Force to seize any bug wielding anything that looked sharp enough to tear their flimsy vac suits, then sending it crashing into a jagged stub of broken wall.

When they had carved the band down to the last half a dozen insects, Mara's lightsaber began to trace a frenzied, twirling, rolling pattern through the middle of the fight. Luke thought Han must have locked the blade on by accident and dropped the weapon. But then he caught a glimpse of orange vac suit behind the handle, and the lightsaber began to slice through Gorog pressure suits, dropping four insects in half as many seconds.

"Han?"

"Not me," Han answered over the suit comm. He appeared a couple of meters away from the lightsaber, picking himself up off the floor. "I got knocked over."

The lightsaber dropped another Gorog, then Luke cut the legs out from under the last insect as it spun around to fire its shatter gun.

Clinging to the lightsaber handle with both hands, being tossed around like a rag in sandstorm, was Tarfang. He was chattering in mad delight, swinging his legs around like a rudder, vainly attempting to counterbalance the weapon's gyroscopic effects.

Luke stepped in and blocked, bringing the wild ride to a sudden halt and allowing Tarfang's feet to drop back to the deck. He used the Force to deactivate the blade, then summoned the weapon out of the Ewok's trembling hands.

Tarfang stood wobbling for a moment, then drew his shoulders back, chittered something grateful sounding over the suit comm, and held his hand out for the lightsaber.

"Sorry," Luke said. "You'd better take the blaster."

Tarfang placed his gloves on his hips and snarled.

Then the StealthX's floodlamps began to dim, and Luke felt Mara's confusion through their Force-bond. Tossing the lightsaber to Han, he whirled toward the StealthX and saw nothing but the fading glow of the floodlamps.

Han stepped to Luke's side. "What is it?"

"Trouble!" Luke said. He gave Mara's lightsaber back to Han. "Lomi Plo is draining the energy from Mara's flood—"

He stopped in midsentence as Juun opened fire with the blaster rifle, aiming for a dark area just behind the StealthX's cockpit. A trio of bolts passed only a meter above Mara's canopy, then abruptly reversed course and came streaking back toward Juun.

The chill ache in Luke's joints was slowing his reflexes, so he would have never have been quick enough to save Juun had he not known that Lomi Plo would deflect the attack. But when she did, his lightsaber was already dropping into position, and one after the other he intercepted the bolts, batting them back toward their original target.

The first bolt was deflected toward the ceiling. The other two simply passed over the StealthX and vanished into the darkness beyond.

Mara twisted around in her seat, trying to see what they had been attacking, but the StealthX's floodlamps were already returning to their normal brightness. Lomi Plo had been forced to retreat.

"It's okay," Luke commed. "We're coming!"

He grabbed Juun by the shoulder and started toward the StealthX, but the Sullustan suddenly stopped and dropped to a knee, trying to look under the craft.

Luke knelt beside him and touched helmets. "Where is she?"

"Behind de strut." Juun's voice was muffled. "Don't you see her leg?"

"No," Luke said. "I *can't* see her."

"*You* can't see her, Madter Skywalker?"

"No, Jae," Luke answered. "*You're* the only one who can see her."

"But when you foughd her, you blocked her addacks."

"The Force was guiding my hand," Luke explained.

Juun was quiet for a moment, then asked, "And when she dent my shots back at me?"

"The Force was guiding my hand," Luke repeated.

Juun remained silent a moment longer, then exclaimed, "Madter Skywalker, you set me up!"

"I knew she would deflect your attacks," Luke admitted. "But I did block her attacks . . . and you said you'd do anything to save Tarfang."

"I suppose I did." Juun sounded disappointed in himself. "All wight. What now?"

"Start shooting again. We need to chase her away from the StealthX before she does any more damage."

Juun shouldered the blaster rifle, but did not open fire.

"What's wrong?" Luke asked.

"I can't dee her, either."

Luke's heart rose into his throat. "What do you mean? Did she move?"

Juun shrugged. "I don't know. Her leg just dort of disappeared—right in front of my eyes."

Han and Tarfang came and knelt beside them.

"Let's climb on that StealthX and get out of here!" Han urged over the suit comm. "If Lomi Plo darkened those lamps, it's because she doesn't want us to see the reinforcements coming up behind us."

"You're right." Luke rose and started to lead the way forward, circling out of the StealthX's line of fire. "But we need to be careful. She's still up there, and now Juun can't see her, either."

"Why not?" Han demanded.

"I don't know," Luke said. "When he realized *we* couldn't see her, he stopped . . ."

He let the explanation trail off, for he suddenly understood why Juun had lost sight of Lomi Plo.

"Doubt!" Luke turned to Han. "*Cloud your vision, doubt will.* Blast it! How many times did I hear that from Yoda?"

"Probably about as many times as I've heard that from you," Han said, sighing.

Luke ignored the barb. "That's how she's doing it, Han. She's using our doubts against us!"

"Only one problem with that theory," Han said. "I believe in her, and I can't see her, either."

Tarfang added a positive yap.

"It doesn't have to be doubt in *her,*" Luke said. They drew adjacent to the StealthX, and Mara began to back the starfighter toward the opening on its repulsor drive. "If Lomi Plo can sense any doubt in a mind at all, she can hide behind it."

Han fell quiet for a moment, then said, "That might explain why Alema was trying so hard to make you doubt Mara."

"I'm sure it does," Luke said. "And now that I know what she was trying to do, I know that it's without basis."

He glanced in the StealthX's direction and saw . . . nothing.

When Luke remained silent, Han seemed to sense his disappointment.

"It won't be that easy, kid," Han said. "Nobody knows how to twist up a guy inside better than a Twi'lek dancer. And Alema's got the Force to help."

Although Mara could hear their discussion over her own suit comm, she limited her response to the sharp sense of curiosity—it was almost suspicion—that Luke felt through their Force-bond. The idea of anyone, especially Alema Rar, sowing doubts about her in Luke's mind angered Mara, but she was trying not to be hurt—at least until they reached someplace where Luke could explain himself in private.

One of the StealthX's floodlamps suddenly exploded in a brilliant burst of light, then sparks began to flash off the starfighter's dark armor. A dozen forks of lightning lanced down from under the fuselage, and the repulsorlift drive began to emit a steady shower of sparks. The StealthX started to wobble.

Luke glanced back to see a line of pressure-suited Gorog swarming after them, pouring shatter gun fire into Mara's craft.

Mara opened fire with her laser cannons, filling the chamber with flashing light. The shatter gun fire dwindled off as the Gorog pursuers dived for cover or were blasted apart. Deciding the time had come to chance a meeting with Lomi Plo, Luke grabbed Juun by the shoulder and started toward the StealthX.

Then the cannon fire began to dim and grow erratic, and he knew that Lomi Plo had returned to the starfighter. She was somewhere on the StealthX, draining its power again—or worse.

Luke pushed Juun toward the hole through which they had entered the nest ship, then said, "Han, run for the breach!"

He activated his lightsaber and Force-leapt onto the upper wing of the wobbling StealthX. He advanced behind his whirling blade, trying to force an attack from his unseen foe.

The tactic succeeded almost too well. As he reached the engine next to the fuselage, Luke felt the Force moving his lightsaber down to block a knee strike. Then a loud *thunk* sounded in his helmet as a kick or elbow or *something* sent him cartwheeling off the nose of the craft.

He reached out and caught hold of the engine cowling, then swung down in front of the lower wing.

To his astonishment, Han was crawling onto the lower wing with Juun and Tarfang.

"What are you doing?" Luke demanded. "I said *run*."

"*You* run," Han said. "I'll take the cover."

A series of shatter gun pellets punctuated Han's point by sparking off the engine mount next to Luke's head. He glanced back and saw that the Gorog swarm had renewed its charge. With the StealthX's laser cannons out of commission, the Killiks were firing blindly around the starfighter, hitting whatever they could.

Mara shut down her last functioning floodlamp and accelerated backward toward the hull breach, the StealthX wobbling wildly and nearly dragging its overloaded wing on the deck. Tarfang filled the suit comm with howls of fear—or maybe it was excitement. Juun simply stared wide-eyed at Luke, his legs flapping off the wingtip like a pair of orange streamers until Han pulled him the rest of the way up.

Luke used the Force to do a twisting flip up onto the top of Mara's canopy, then began to advance behind his whirling lightsaber again. It took only an instant before his blade intercepted Lomi Plo's in another flurry of sparks. He pirouetted into a spinning hook kick that may as well have connected with pillar of durasteel. His foot stopped cold. Something hard smashed into his inner knee and sent pain lancing up his leg.

Still unseen, Lomi started to push Luke off the other side of the canopy. Then Luke saw Han's helmet and shoulders pop up behind her, and Mara's lightsaber came sweeping across the fuselage at ankle height.

Lomi stopped pushing. Sparks flashed as she blocked Han's attack and sent Mara's lightsaber skittering off the tail of the StealthX.

Luke sprang forward, slashing for the place where Lomi's midsection was sure to be, knowing that this was the death strike—then suddenly the StealthX was bucking and shuddering beneath him, and it was all he could do to Forcestick himself to the starfighter's fuselage.

"Hang on!" Luke yelled over the suit comm. "We're going up!"

The edge of a ruptured deck flashed past, followed by the breach in the vessel's hull, and suddenly the StealthX was out in space, wobbling and listing a dozen meters above the nest ship.

Han was still clinging to the wing with both hands, his legs floating free now that they had escaped the artificial gravity. Tarfang was clasping the barrel of a laser cannon with both hands, yowling wildly and fluttering his legs as though he were swimming.

But Juun was spinning off into space, his arms grasping at the void, his feet kicking at nothing. Luke caught the Sullustan in the Force and began to pull him back toward the wobbling StealthX.

Then his lightsaber began to flicker and fade, and a cold knot of danger sense formed between his shoulder blades. Luke did not even take the time to turn around. He simply stepped into a powerful back-stomp kick that caught his invisible attacker square in the chest.

Even with the Force reinforcing it, the kick was not powerful enough to launch Lomi off the StealthX—but it did save Luke's life. Her blade scraped across the equipment pod on the back of his vac suit, and he pivoted into the attack, bringing his arms around in a double block that first slammed, then trapped both of Lomi's arms.

Juun was still five meters from the StealthX, reaching for Tarfang's fluttering boots.

"Tarfang, hold still!" Luke ordered, using the Force to pull the Sullustan the rest of the way back to the wing. "My hands are full, and Juun needs . . . help!"

Tarfang continued to kick, but Juun caught hold of a boot anyway. The Ewok glanced back, saw his captain hanging on to his boot, and finally obeyed.

Something sharp and powerful smashed into the pit of Luke's stomach, taking him by surprise, since he still had both of Lomi Plo's arms trapped.

Mara wheeled the StealthX around, going for the thermal vent, and Luke almost lost his balance. C-3PO and R2-D2 flashed by below. They were still standing where Han had left them, C-3PO's photoreceptors following the StealthX as it passed overhead. One of Tarfang's hands came loose, and for a moment the Ewok and Juun were hanging from the cannon barrel by one hand.

Again, something sharp and powerful smashed Luke in the stomach—could it be a third elbow?—and this time it drove the air from his lungs. He kicked one of Lomi's legs, twisting the two arms he *did* have under control, trying to wrest her lightsaber free.

The third elbow slammed Luke another time. When he tried to fill his lungs again, it felt as if he were trying to suck down a chestful of gauze.

Luke was out of air.

He glanced at the status display inside his helmet and found only darkness. The slash across his equipment pod might have killed him after all. He tried one more time to wrench the lightsaber from Lomi Plo's hands, but he was losing his strength.

Then the gentle *clunk* of a launching shadow bomb pulsed through the fuselage. The StealthX bucked as they shot through the heat plume above the thermal vent. Lomi Plo immediately released her lightsaber and slammed Luke with a powerful Force shove, trying to rid herself of his grip so she could divert the bomb.

Luke almost came free . . . until he hooked a leg around one of Lomi's and slammed down on top of Mara's astromech. He used the Force to stick himself in place, then saw Han across from him, holding on with one hand and aiming Tarfang's blaster with the other. His lips seemed to be moving inside his helmet, but whatever he was saying remained unheard. Lomi's slash had disabled Luke's comm unit as well as his air recycler—or perhaps he was just slipping into unconsciousness.

A brilliant flash lit space behind them, then Mara banked the StealthX around and Luke saw Tarfang and Juun, still hanging onto the cannon barrel, silhouetted against a huge column of flame. It died down for a moment, then suddenly shot up again as a secondary explosion shot out of the thermal vent. Had there been any air left in Luke's lungs, he would have cried out in joy. At least they had disabled the Dark Nest's hyperdrive.

Mara stretched out to him through the Force, ordering him to hold on just a little longer. Luke was already doing just that. He could feel Leia and Kyp and the rest of the Jedi pilots touching him through the battle-meld, assuring him that help was close by. He began to calm his mind and his body, to slow his heartbeat and other natural processes in preparation for entering a Force-hibernation.

Then an unseen weight settled astride his chest and invisible fingers began to scratch at his helmet, attempting to open the faceplate or break a seal. Luke lashed out as best he could, but he was starting to grow dizzy, and his reactions were slow and weak. He heard an ominous *click* behind his ear, near the faceplate hinge, and reached out with the Force, trying to shove his attacker off.

Lomi shoved back, slamming his helmet into the top of Mara's canopy. Energy bolts streamed past his head as Han opened fire with the blaster, and finally Lomi turned her attention to deflecting the attack.

Mara urged Luke to hold on tight, and Han suddenly stopped firing. The StealthX flipped upside down, and Luke found himself looking down at the knobby hull of the nest ship, less than three meters away. He used the Force to pull himself even tighter to the fuselage, then glimpsed the blocky shape of a heat sink swelling in front of him. He tried not to waste his last breath on a scream.

Whether Lomi Plo jumped or was scraped off as they passed, Luke could not say. But in the instant beforehand, he saw two bulbous green bug eyes staring down at him through the transparent face panel of a Killik pressure suit. They were set in a melted female face with no nose and a pair of stubby mandibles where there should have been lower jaws. Luke would have sworn that when the mandibles opened, he could see a smiling row of human teeth . . . or maybe his oxygen-starved mind was merely beginning to hallucinate.

Then the weight vanished from inside his chest, too, and he was suddenly free of Lomi Plo, still using the Force to pin himself against the StealthX. He turned his head and saw Han wedged between the fuselage and the engine cowling, clinging to the shield generator mount with both hands, screaming something inside his helmet that Luke was just as glad he could not hear.

Mara suddenly flipped the StealthX right-side up again. A flight of dartships went streaming past overhead, then wheeled back around to attack. A dozen propellant trails streaked from their bellies. Mara ducked behind a boulder, and an instant later a series of orange flashes lit the heavens on the other side.

Luke's vision began to darken around the edges. He glimpsed the *Falcon* streaking past above, her repulsor beam already stabbing out to send the dartships tumbling on their way, then felt Leia and Saba touch him through the Force, urging him to hold on just a little longer, telling him that the *Falcon* was coming right behind him. Finally, Luke's vision went completely black.

But he did not fall unconscious. He reached out to Mara and Leia and Kyp and all of the other Jedi, even to Han and Juun and Tarfang, and their strength held him out of the abyss.

EPILOGUE

Outside the viewport hung eleven distant nest ships, a string of dark dots silhouetted against the sapphire curtain of the Utegetu Nebula. They were blocking the Murgo Choke, as though the Killiks believed that the small task force of cruisers and frigates with which the battered *Mon Mothma* had returned actually intended to launch an assault. Han fancied that he could even see a dark blur where the screen of dartfighters was deployed in front of the bug fleet. Their caution was somewhat reassuring, suggesting as it did a certain military naïveté. No commander in his right mind would attack the bugs' fleet with anything less than a three-to-one Star Destroyer advantage, and it would be weeks before the Alliance could assemble a battle group of that size.

Han only hoped that some genius on the general staff did not get the bright idea of trying to hold the bugs off with a couple of StealthX squadrons. So far, there was no indication that either Jaina or Jacen was anywhere near this mess—and that was just fine with him. They had both faced more death and treachery in their young lives than any ten Jedi should ever have to.

The door to the briefing room whispered open, and Han turned to see Gavin Darklighter emerging, his dress whites slightly rumpled after the long session inside. He paused long enough to run a hand through his dark hair, then he let out a deep breath and came to stand with Han.

When he didn't say anything, Han asked, "Any word?"

"Bwua'tu is still asking questions," Darklighter said. "He's fair for a Bothan, and your statement did a lot to exonerate them both. But I couldn't get a read on how he's going to handle having the *Ack-*

bar commandeered. Juun and Tarfang are a pretty convenient-looking pair of scapegoats."

Han nodded. "I figured that, but I was asking if you had heard anything about Luke." He gestured toward the guards at the lift station. "They won't let me leave the deck until I'm dismissed by Bwua'tu, and medbay is too busy—"

The lift doors started to open, and Luke's voice said, "We're fine, Han." He stepped into the corridor with Mara at his side. He looked as pale as a shaved wampa, but seemed alert enough and steady on his feet. "I told you that aboard the *Falcon*."

"No, what you said was '*ooormmgg fffff*,'" Han said, flashing a crooked smile. "Then you passed out."

"Did I?" Luke asked half seriously. "I don't remember."

"Yeah, you did," Han said. "I don't suppose the EmDee droids let you see Leia before you came up here?"

"Better than that," Mara said. She stepped aside, and Leia and Saba emerged from the rear of the lift. "They told us they needed the bed."

After the fight with Alema and her bugs, Leia's face was still swollen and so swaddled in bacta wrap that she looked like a Tusken bride. But the sight of her lifted Han's heart as it had not been lifted since the births of Anakin and the twins, and he went to her and took her hands—at least the one that wasn't in a cast—in his.

"Hello, beautiful."

Leia smiled—then winced. "You need to get your eyes checked, flyboy."

"Nope." Han kissed her on the lips . . . very, very gently. "I'm seeing better than ever."

Saba slapped her tail against the deck, then rolled her eyes and walked away sissing.

"Yes, well, we're glad to see both of you well again," Darklighter said. He motioned Leia toward a couch near the viewport, then turned to the guards stationed in front of the briefing room. "Inform Admiral Bwua'tu that Master Skywalker is available to make a statement."

The guard acknowledged the order with a salute, then disappeared through the sliding door.

"Thank you, Gavin," Luke said. "Juun and Tarfang risked their lives trying to warn the fleet about what was in those statues. I owe it to them to make certain Admiral Bwua'tu understands that."

"Han has already made a report," Darklighter said. "But hearing your account will certainly add weight to it."

Luke nodded, then went to the viewport and looked out at the string of nest ships. "How bad is it?"

"Not as bad as it could have been," Darklighter said. "The Killiks got out with four nest ships and the *Ackbar,* but the Dark Nest's ship is still here—along with ten others. I'll do what I can to make sure that the Jedi receive the credit they deserve in the official report to Chief Omas."

"Thank you," Luke said. "That will go a long way toward rebuilding the trust between us. We're going to need that, if we're going to prevent this from erupting into a full-scale war."

Darklighter looked uncomfortable. "I'm afraid we're running out of time for that, Master Skywalker."

"Chief Omas has already decided to go to war?" Leia asked.

"Not Omas," Darklighter said. "A courier arrived for Admiral Bwua'tu a short while ago. The Chiss are claiming that a group of Jedi launched a preemptive strike against one of their supply depots."

"That's impossible," Luke said quickly. "Jedi don't launch preemptive strikes!"

"Then a handful of Jedi loaned their StealthXs to some Killiks," Darklighter said. "The Chiss sent along a security holo from one of the ammunition dumps that was taken out. It shows a pair of StealthXs pretty clearly. And Jagged Fel seems convinced that one of the pilots was Jaina. He claims he recognizes her flying style."

"Jaina?" Han slapped his forehead. "Why would she do something like that?"

"That's what the Chiss would like to know," Darklighter replied. "Nobody was killed—and that convinces *me* that it was Jedi—so the Chiss aren't treating the attack as an act of war. But they *are* taking it as proof that they need to handle the Killiks themselves. They've declared the Qoribu Truce violated and are preparing to launch an assault to push the Colony back."

Han shook his head. "Jaina knows the Chiss better than anyone," he said. "She'd *know* how they would respond to a preemptive strike. Something stinks about that report."

"Actually, the preemptive strike can be a very sound tactic," a gravelly Bothan voice said. "Especially if you are trying to *provoke* a response."

Han looked over to see Bwua'tu stepping out of the briefing room. Juun and Tarfang followed a pace behind, their chests puffed out and smug grins on their faces.

"That's what I mean," Han said. "Jaina and Zekk are practically bugs themselves! She'd never do anything to make the Chiss launch a major attack against the Colony."

"I'd like to take your word for it, Captain Solo," Bwua'tu said, going to the viewport. "After all, you know your daughter better than I."

The admiral stared out at the nest ships in contemplative silence, then spoke without looking away from the viewport.

"Commodore Darklighter, have the task force launch all fighter squadrons and deploy in attack formation."

Darklighter's jaw dropped even farther than Han's. "*Attack* formation, sir?"

"You may choose which one, Commodore," Bwua'tu said. "I don't believe it will matter."

Darklighter made no move to obey. "May I remind the admiral that we barely have a ten-ship advantage over the Killiks, and that most of our vessels are significantly out-classed?"

"You just did." Bwua'tu turned to glare at Darklighter. "After the *Ackbar*'s capture, I may not be in command of the Fifth Fleet much longer. But until I am relieved, you *will* obey my orders. Is that clear, Commodore?"

Darklighter jerked to attention. "Sir!"

"Carry on," Bwua'tu said. "Report back when you are finished."

Darklighter pulled a comlink and stepped away to carry out the admiral's orders. Han, Luke, and the rest of their group exchanged nervous glances, clearly wondering what the Bothan could be thinking. Only Leia did not seem convinced that he had lost his mind; her expression was one more of curiosity than apprehension.

Either oblivious to their expressions or pretending not to notice, Bwua'tu turned to Luke.

"Captain Solo gave a glowing account of Juun's and Tarfang's actions once they learned the true nature of the statuary they delivered to my fleet. Would you concur?"

"I would," Luke said. "They aided our escape from the Saras rehabilitation house, lost their own vessel while investigating the Killik plans, and fought valiantly on the Gorog nest ship. It's unfortunate that my Artoo unit was damaged, or we would be able to provide documentation."

"That's quite unnecessary," Bwua'tu said. "The word of a Jedi Master is documentation enough."

An uncomfortable silence followed while the admiral continued to stare out the viewport—and while Han, Luke, and the others silently considered what they might be able to do to stop the attack on the nest ships and prevent the loss of yet more Alliance lives.

Finally, Darklighter returned and reported that the admiral's orders had been issued.

"Very good," Bwua'tu said. "I was very impressed with Captain Juun's and Tarfang's knowledge of our enemy. Sign them on as intelligence affiliates and see to it that they're assigned a scout skiff. Make certain it's stealth-equipped. I imagine they'll be doing a lot of work behind the lines."

Han and Luke exchanged surprised glances, then Luke asked, "Admiral, are you sure that's a good idea?"

Tarfang stepped over to Luke and let loose a long, angry string of jabbering—to which Bwua'tu replied in kind. After a short exchange, the admiral looked back to Luke with a scowl.

"Tarfang doesn't understand why you're trying to undermine him and Captain Juun," Bwua'tu said. "And frankly, Master Skywalker, neither do I. You seemed quite impressed with them a few moments ago."

"Captain Juun and Tarfang are very earnest," Luke responded. "But that doesn't mean they would make good intelligence agents. They can be, uh, rather naïve. I worry about their chances of survival."

Tarfang started to yap an objection, but Bwua'tu silenced him with a soft chitter, then turned back to Luke.

"So do I, Master Skywalker." Bwua'tu looked back out the viewport, where the task force frigates were beginning to move out toward the flanks. "I worry about us all."

Luke frowned, clearly at a loss as to what he could say to make Bwua'tu change his mind. Han caught Leia's eye, then nodded toward the admiral and raised his brow, silently asking if he was crazy. She flashed a reassuring smile, then gave a slight shake of her head.

"Trust me, Captain Solo," Bwua'tu said, speaking to Han's reflection in the viewport. "Your friends are capable of more than you think. They usually are."

"Uh, actually, I was worried about your attack orders," Han said. "You don't think that seems a little crazy?"

"I do," Bwua'tu said. "But right now, these bugs are unsure of themselves. More importantly, they are unsure of *us*."

"And we need to keep them that way," Mara said, approvingly.

"Precisely," Bwua'tu replied. "You Jedi tossed a hydrospanner into the Killiks' plan. They'll be wondering what else you can do, and I intend to use that doubt to make them believe they *lost* this battle."

Luke's brow went up. "And force a negotiation!"

Bwua'tu shot Luke a impatient frown. "Not at all, Master Sky-walker. I expect them to retreat."

"And if they don't?" Luke asked.

"Then I will have miscalculated . . . again." Bwua'tu turned to Han. "I've been thinking about your daughter's preemptive strike. By all accounts, she's a sound tactician. What do you think she would do if she *knew* the Chiss were preparing a major attack?"

Han's stomach sank. "How could she know something like that?"

Bwua'tu shrugged. "I have no idea. But if she *did*, a preemptive strike would be a stroke of genius. It would force the Chiss to attack before they were ready—or risk having their preparations disrupted completely. It might well be the Colony's only hope of survival."

"*Survival?*" Leia asked. "Didn't the Chiss message say they were only going to push the Killiks away from the frontier?"

"Yes, and their previous message said that they were going to let the Jedi handle the problem," Bwua'tu replied. "That's the trouble with Chiss messages, isn't it? You never know when they are telling the truth."

"Wait a minute," Han said. He couldn't believe what he was hearing—didn't want to, anyway. How many times would he face his children flying off to war? How many times *could* he? "You think this war is already *starting*?"

Bwua'tu nodded. "Of course. It started before their messenger left Ascendancy space." His gaze remained fixed on the viewport, where the task force cruisers were moving out in front of the formation. "The irony of it is, I believe the Chiss are worried that we'll side with the Killiks. Their message may be just a ruse to reassure us, to keep the Alliance from taking action until it's too late to save the Colony."

"This is just nuts!" Han said.

"Not nuts—scary," Mara said, her face falling. "What are the Chiss going to think when the *Admiral Ackbar* shows up on the Colony's side? It'll only confirm their suspicions. They'll think the Alliance *gave* it to the Killiks."

"Exactly," Bwua'tu said. "If I am right, this is going to be a very interesting war."

Leia closed her eyes for a moment, then reached out and squeezed Han's hand. "I'm afraid you are right, Admiral," she said. "Jaina and Jacen are in the middle of something bad. I can feel it."

Han's heart sank. *Not again, not so soon.*

Bwua'tu sighed. "I'm sorry to hear that, Princess." He turned to Darklighter again, then said, "Commodore . . . have all batteries open fire."

THE SWARM WAR

For David "DJ" Richardson
Good friend

ACKNOWLEDGMENTS

Many people contributed to this book in ways large and small. I would like to give special thanks to the following: Andria Hayday for her support, critiques, and many suggestions; James Luceno for brainstorming and ideas; Enrique Guerrero for his thoughts on the Chiss; Shelly Shapiro and Sue Rostoni for their encouragement, skillful editing, and especially for their patience; all the people at Del Rey who make writing so much fun, particularly Keith Clayton, Colleen Lindsay, and Colette Russen; all of the people at Lucasfilm, particularly Howard Roffman, Amy Gary, Leland Chee, and Pablo Hidalgo. And, of course, to George Lucas for sharing his galaxy with us all.

PROLOGUE

The bomb lay half buried in the red sand, a durasteel manifestation of the brutality and unreasoning fear of its makers. It had fallen from orbit in a long fiery tumble, then planted itself tail-first atop the dune opposite the nest. Its heat shield was still glowing with entry friction, and the casing was so carbon-scored that the marks emblazoned on its side could not be read. But Jaina and Zekk needed no identifiers to know they were staring at a Chiss megaweapon. The thing was the size of a beldon, with a bulge on its nose that could house anything from a baradium penetrating charge to the triggering laser of a planet-buster warhead.

When it grew clear that the bomb was not going to detonate—at least not *yet*—Jaina finally let out her breath.

"We need a better look at that thing," she said.

Along with Jacen, Zekk, and the other three Jedi on their team, she was standing in the mouth of the Iesei dartship hangar, gazing up three hundred meters of steep, sandy slope toward the bomb. Every couple of seconds, a turbolaser strike would crack down from orbit, melting a rontosized crater of pink glass into the dune and raising a ten-story plume of dust that often obscured their view.

"We need to know what the Chiss have up their sleeves," Zekk agreed.

"We *need* to get out of here," Jacen countered. "Or am I the only one who still feels the Force-call?"

"No—" Zekk said.

"—we feel it, too," Jaina finished.

The call had arisen a few hours earlier, in the middle of a StealthX assault that had failed to turn back the Chiss task force.

The summons was coming from the direction of the known galaxy, a sense of beckoning and urgency that was growing more powerful by the hour, calling the Jedi Knights back toward Ossus, demanding they return to the Academy at once.

"We *all* feel it," Tahiri said. She furrowed her scarred brow, then turned to Tesar and Lowbacca. "At least I think we do."

The Barabel and the Wookiee nodded in agreement.

"It iz hard to ignore," Tesar said.

"And we shouldn't try," Jacen replied. "Something bad must be happening for my uncle to summon us all like this. Even Luke Skywalker can't pull on the Force that hard without suffering for it."

"Maybe not," Jaina said. "But it will only take a few minutes to look at that bomb. I think we have time."

"It must be some kind of secret weapon," Zekk added. "We'll need an R-nine unit—"

"And some testing equipment," Tesar finished. He and Lowbacca started toward the interior of the near-empty hangar, where a few dozen Killiks with rosy thoraxes and green-mottled abdomens were bustling over the team's battered StealthXs—repairing and refueling, but not rearming. The StealthXs had run out of shadow bombs the previous day, and they had depleted the nest's store of actuating gas that morning. "We will collect it and catch up."

Jacen quickly moved to block their way. "No."

Tesar's neck scales rose and Lowbacca's fur bristled, and they glared down at Jacen without speaking.

"Think about it—they're *Chiss*," Jacen said. "It could be a trap. Maybe that bomb isn't meant to detonate until we're out there trying to examine it."

Tesar and Lowbacca clucked their throats and looked over their shoulders toward the bomb. They were not yet Joiners, but Jaina and Zekk could sense their thoughts well enough to know the pair were being influenced by Jacen's argument. And so was Tahiri, of course. She did not need to be a mindmate for Jaina and Zekk to know she had fallen under Jacen's sway. She was always rubbing her forearms over him, and whenever he looked her way, she suddenly had to blink.

Zekk let out a grudging chest rumble, then Jaina said, "We wish your thinking had been this clear at Supply Depot Thrago."

"We don't know that my thinking *was* unclear," Jacen said. "Not yet, anyway."

Zekk frowned. "Our raid was supposed to delay the war—"

"—not start it," Jaina finished.

Jacen shrugged. "The future is always in motion." He looked away, then added, "It's too late to undo what happened after the raid. We should respect Uncle Luke's summons and return to Ossus at once."

"And abandon Iesei?" Zekk asked. Jaina and Zekk had not been with Iesei long enough to join its collective mind—in fact, living with a nest other than Taat seemed to be weakening their own mental link—but Iesei felt like a sibling to them, and they were bound to it through the Will of the Colony. "With the Chiss preparing to land?"

"We won't save the nest by staying," Jacen said. "It's better to leave while we still can."

"Why are you in such a hurry?" Jaina asked.

When Jacen's only reply was a flash of anger, she tried to sense the answer through the Force-bond they shared as twins, but she felt nothing. And neither did Zekk, who still shared most of what she thought and felt. Since the raid on Thrago, Jacen had been shutting them both out—perhaps because Jaina and Zekk had grown so angry with him when he took a reckless shot and nearly turned the raid into a massacre. Or maybe Jacen was hiding something. Jaina and Zekk could not tell. They only knew that his withdrawal from the twin bond was one of the biggest reasons they no longer trusted him.

After a moment, Jacen finally replied, "I'm in a hurry because it's prudent. If we stay, all we can do is kill a few dozen Chiss—and what good would *that* accomplish?"

Jaina and Zekk had no answer. They knew as well as Jacen did that Iesei would be wiped out to the last larva. The Chiss assault force was just too large and well equipped to be stopped.

But there was still the bomb. If they could find out what it was, there was no counting the number of other nests they might save.

"Jacen, no one is keeping you here," Jaina said. "Leave whenever you want."

"We're going to look at that bomb," Zekk added.

Jaina turned to Tesar. "Give us a one-minute head start. If Jacen is right about this being a trick—"

"—we will know soon enough," Tesar finished. "Go."

Lowbacca added a groan assuring them that he and Tesar would be close behind.

Jacen finally opened their twin bond, flooding the Force with his alarm and concern. "Jaina! Don't—"

Jaina and Zekk ignored him. Jacen only opened the twin bond when he wanted something, and right now what he wanted was for them to leave the bomb and start home. They turned away, springing out of the hangar mouth and dropping five meters down the slope of the nest-dune. Almost immediately it grew apparent that the bomb was no trick. A ripple of danger sense prickled their necks, then a barrage of turbolaser bolts crashed down from orbit and pelted their faces with hot sand. They dived away in opposite directions and somersaulted down the slope half a dozen times, then rose to their feet and Force-leapt across a five-meter trough onto the opposite dune.

The turbolasers followed, filling the air with the fresh smell of ozone. The slope of the dune turned into a churning mass of sand, half spraying through the air while the rest growled down the slope in a series of eerie-sounding avalanches. Now working against gravity, Jaina and Zekk began to ascend toward the bomb in sporadic Force leaps. Sand scratched their eyes and filled their noses and throats, but they remained within the roiling cloud, trying to hide from the Chiss sensors and make themselves more difficult to target.

They were barely halfway to the bomb when they felt Jacen, Tahiri, and what remained of the Iesei nest racing up the slope behind them. The intensity of the barrage abruptly decreased as the Chiss gunners began to spread their fire, and the silhouettes of hundreds of Iesei appeared in the surrounding haze. The insects were scurrying up the hill on all sixes, their antennae waving as they overtook Jaina and Zekk.

A moment later the silhouettes of Jacen and Tahiri emerged from the sand cloud and came to Jaina's side.

"So the bomb *isn't* a trick," Jacen said. "This is still a bad idea."

"Then what are *you* doing here?" Zekk asked from behind Jaina.

"Looking after you two," Jacen said. "Uncle Luke won't be very happy if I go back without you."

Jaina frowned and started to protest; then a deafening bang echoed across the desert. The dune gave way beneath their feet, and the Jedi found themselves being swept down the slope in a giant sandslide.

For a moment Jaina and Zekk thought the Chiss gunners had finally hit the half-buried bomb. Then they heard the distant roar of engines and realized the bang had been a sonic boom. Jaina waved her hand, using the Force to clear a hole in the dust cloud. A black plume of entry smoke was blossoming against the yellow sky, descending from the dark sliver of the Chiss assault cruiser that was raining fire down on them.

"Drop ship!" Jaina shouted. "Be ready!"

"Iesei, take cover!" Zekk added.

An instant later, an endless string of silver flashes erupted from the head of the smoke plume. The Killiks pushed their heads into the sand and began to dig, while the Jedi used the Force to pull themselves free of the sandslide and yanked their lightsabers off their utility belts.

A blue cascade of cannon bolts began to sweep across the dune, its deep *thump-thump*ing an almost gentle counterpoint to the crashing roar of the turbolasers. Jaina and Zekk stood expectant for what seemed an eternity. There was no use trying to run or take cover. Drop ship weapons systems were designed to spread a carpet of death around their landing zones. Often, they laid fire as thick as twenty bolts a square meter.

An eerie chorus of squeals arose as the cannon strikes found the buried swarm of Iesei, and the haze grew heavy with the bitter smell of scorched chitin. More bolts began to sizzle down all around Jaina and Zekk, raising chest-high sand geysers and charging the air with static. They raised their lightsabers and yielded control to the Force, then started to whirl and dance across the dune, dodging incoming fire and deflecting it into the ground beside their feet.

Zekk took a cannon blast full on his blade and was driven to his knees. Jaina spun to his side and tapped two more bolts away, only to find herself badly out of position as a third dropped toward her head.

Zekk's lightsaber swept up just centimeters from her face, catching the bolt on the blade tip and sending it zipping across the dune. Jaina spun away from another attack and glimpsed Jacen and Tahiri standing back-to-back, Jacen holding his hand above their heads, cannon fire ricocheting away as though he held a deflector shield in his palm. *That* was something Jaina and Zekk had never seen before.

Then the fusillade was past, leaving in its place a slope of churned sand strewn with pieces of smoking chitin and flailing, half-buried Killiks. Jaina and Zekk started toward the crest again, but it was clear they would never reach it ahead of the Chiss drop ship. The sandslide had carried them to the bottom of the dune, and with most of the Iesei dead or dying, the turbolaser gunners were once again beginning to concentrate their fire on the Jedi.

Tesar and Lowbacca arrived from the hangar, Tesar floating an R9 unit behind him, Lowbacca carrying a rucksack full of equipment over his shoulder.

"This one does not like this," Tesar rasped. "Why do the Chisz send a drop ship instead of a fighter? Would it not be easier to hit the bomb with a missile than to recover it?"

"A concussion missile would leave pieces," Jaina said.

"And we can still learn a lot from pieces," Zekk added.

"If they want to protect their secret, they need to keep the bomb out of our hands completely," Jaina finished.

Lowbacca rowled another thought, suggesting that maybe the assault cruiser had run out of missiles. It had used thousands just fighting its way to the planet.

The drop ship completed its attack pattern, then stopped firing as it descended below the effective altitude for its fire-control apparatus. The vessel itself was a fiery wedge of ceram-metal composite at the tip of the smoke plume, no more than forty meters long and perhaps half that at the base. Jaina and Zekk and the others continued to ascend the slope in Force leaps, but there was no sign of any healthy Killiks—either the laser cannons had gotten them all, or the survivors were staying hidden.

The turbolaser strikes continued to come, obscuring the Jedi Knights' vision and slowing their progress, but failing to stop them entirely. It was difficult enough to hit moving targets from orbit, without those targets having the Jedi danger sense to warn them when a strike was headed their way.

The team was halfway up the slope when the turbolaser barrage suddenly ended. Jaina and Zekk would have thought the drop ship was landing, except that the roar of its engines continued to build. They used the Force to clear another hole in the dust cloud. The drop ship was much closer than it sounded, but that was not the reason the barrage had stopped.

High overhead, above the dispersing column of entry smoke, the tiny white wedge of a Star Destroyer was sliding across the sky toward the assault cruiser. Small disks of turbolaser fire were blossoming around both vessels, and a pair of flame trails were already angling down toward the horizon where two damaged starfighters had plunged into the atmosphere.

"Is that an *Alliance* Star Destroyer?" Tahiri asked, coming to Jaina's side.

"It must be," Tesar said, joining them. "Why would the Chisz fire on each other?"

"They wouldn't," Jaina said.

She and Zekk reached out to the Star Destroyer in the Force. Instead of the Alliance crew they had expected, they were astonished to feel the diffuse presence of a Killik nest.

A familiar murk began to gather inside their chests. Then Zekk gasped, "Unu!"

Lowbacca groaned in bewilderment, wondering how a nest of Killiks had come by a Galactic Alliance Star Destroyer.

"Who knows? But it can't be good." Jacen stopped at Jaina's side. "Maybe *this* is why Uncle Luke is trying to call us home."

"Maybe," Jaina allowed. The murk inside began to grow heavy, and the mystery of the Star Destroyer's arrival began to seem a lot less important than the bomb. "But we still have to find out what that bomb is."

"*We* do?" Jacen demanded. "Or UnuThul does?"

"We *all* do," Zekk said.

Jaina and Zekk continued toward the top of the dune. Without the barrage churning up sand and dust, the air was beginning to clear, and they could see the crimson wedge of the drop ship descending the last few meters to the sand. Its nose shield was still glowing with entry heat, and the multibarreled laser cannons that hung beneath the wings were hissing and popping with electromagnetic discharge.

Then the drop ship's belly turret spun toward the Jedi and began to stitch the slope with fire from its twin charric guns. Jaina, Zekk, and the others raised their lightsabers and started to knock the beams back toward the vessel. Unlike blaster bolts—which carried very little kinetic charge—the charric beams struck with an enormous impact. Several times Jaina, Zekk, and even Lowbacca felt their lightsabers fly from their grasps and had to use the Force to recall the weapons.

The Jedi Knights continued up the dune in sporadic leaps, taking turns covering each other, seeking the protection of craters or mounds of sand when they could, but always advancing toward the crest of the dune and the bomb. When it grew apparent that the turret guns would not be enough to hold them at bay, the drop ship dipped its nose to give the laser cannons a good firing angle. The blue-skinned pilot came into view through the cockpit canopy. Sitting in the commander's seat next to him was a steely-eyed human with a long scar over his right eye.

Jagged Fel.

Jaina stopped in her tracks, so astonished and touched by old feelings that a charric beam came close to sneaking past her guard. She had been the one to end their romance, but she had never quite stopped loving him, and the sight of him now—commanding the enemy drop ship—filled her with so many conflicting emotions that she felt as though someone had tripped her primary circuit breaker.

Fel's gaze locked on Jaina, and a hint of sorrow—or maybe disappointment—flashed across his face. He spoke into his throat mike; then Zekk's large frame slammed into Jaina from the side and hurled them both into the glassy bottom of a turbolaser crater.

Before Jaina could complain, Zekk's fear and anger were boiling into her. Suddenly she was rebuking herself for trusting Fel, then she and Zekk were wondering how she could have been so foolish . . . and how their minds could have come unjoined at such a critical moment.

Sand began to rain down from above. They felt the crater reverberating beneath them and realized the dropship's laser cannons had opened fire.

"You're—*we're*—supposed to be over him!" Zekk said aloud.

"We *are* over him," Jaina said. She could feel how hurt Zekk was by the tumultuous emotions that seeing Fel had raised in her, and that made her angry—at Fel, at herself, at Zekk. Did Zekk think she could *make* herself love him? "We were just shocked."

Zekk glared at her out of one eye. "We have to stop lying to ourselves. It'll get us killed."

"*I'm* not lying," Jaina retorted.

She rolled away from Zekk, then scrambled up the crater's glassy wall and peered over its lip toward the drop ship. As she had expected, a squad of Chiss commandos had dropped out of the vessel's belly. Dressed in formfitted plates of color-shifting camouflage armor, they were racing along the crest of the dune toward the unexploded bomb. Instead of the recovery cables or magnetic pads that Jaina had expected, they were carrying several demolition satchels.

Zekk arrived at Jaina's side and peered up the slope. They wondered for a moment why the Chiss would go to the trouble of landing a party to blow up the bomb. A few hits from the drop ship's laser cannons would have done the job more than adequately.

Then they understood. "Vape charges!" Zekk shouted.

The Chiss equivalent of thermal detonators, vape charges left nothing behind to analyze. They *disintegrated*. But they could not be delivered by missile. Like thermal detonators, they were infantry weapons. They had to be thrown or placed.

Jaina snaked a finger over the edge of the crater and pointed at one of the drop ship's laser cannons, then used the Force to scoop up a pile of sand and hurl it up the barrel. The weapon exploded, vaporizing one wing and ripping a jagged gash in the fuselage.

Fel's eyes widened in shock, and Jaina and Zekk lost sight of him as the drop ship rocked up on its side and flipped. It landed hard in the sand, and a chain of blasts shook the dune as the remaining laser cannons exploded. The vessel rolled back onto its belly and began to belch smoke.

A pang of sorrow shot through Jaina's breast, and Zekk said, "We can't worry about him, Jaina—"

"He wasn't worried about us," Jaina agreed. Her sorrow was quickly turning to rage—at Zekk and at herself, but most of all at Fel—and her hands began to tremble so hard she found it difficult to hold on to her lightsaber. "We know."

Now that the laser cannons had fallen silent, Jaina leapt out of the crater and led the charge toward the top of the dune. Half the Chiss commando squad stopped and started to lay fire down the slope, while the rest raced the last few meters to the bomb and began to string a linked line of vape charges around it.

Jaina and the other Jedi Knights continued their ascent, deflecting the charric beams back toward the Chiss who were working to set the charges. Four of these commandos fell before their fellows realized what the Jedi were doing, but the survivors were too well trained to lose focus.

By the time Jaina and the others neared the crest of the dune, the charges had been placed and the survivors were scrambling to rejoin their companions. The squad leader fell back behind the rest of the squad and began to punch an activation code into a signaling unit built into the armor on his forearm.

Jaina pointed in the leader's direction and used the Force to tear his hand away from the buttons, and the rest of the Chiss turned their charric guns on her.

Zekk stepped in front of Jaina, deflecting beam after beam into the leader's chest armor. The impact drove him back toward the wreckage of the drop ship, finally splitting his armor when he came to a stop against the hull.

Then Tesar and Lowbacca and Tahiri were among the surviving commandos, batting their charric beams aside, kicking their guns from their hands and ordering them to surrender.

The Chiss did not, of course. Apparently more frightened of becoming Killik Joiners than of dying, they fought on with their knives, their hands, leaving the Jedi no choice but to kill, amputate, and Force-shove. Intent on securing the triggering device, Jaina and Zekk circled past the brawl and started toward the squad leader, who lay crumpled and immobile beside the drop ship.

And that was when a loud groan sounded from the hull. Jaina and Zekk paused, thinking the craft was about to explode. Instead, it rolled away from them, revealing a dark jagged hole where the near wing had once connected to the fuselage.

Realizing someone had to be using the Force, Jaina and Zekk glanced over their shoulders and found Jacen looking in the drop ship's direction. He smiled, then nodded past them toward the vessel.

When Jaina and Zekk turned around again, it was to find a coughing, brown-haired human staggering out of the fuselage. He was covered in soot, and he looked so stunned and scorched that it seemed a miracle he was moving at all.

"Jag?" Jaina gasped.

She and Zekk started forward to help, but Fel merely stooped down and depressed a button on the dead squad leader's forearm.

The signaling unit emitted a single loud beep.

Fel did not even glance in Jaina and Zekk's direction. He simply turned away and hurled himself over the far side of the dune.

Jaina and Zekk spun back toward their companions. "Run!"

Jaina's warning was hardly necessary. The rest of the Jedi were already turning away from the confused commandos, Force-leaping toward the bottom of the dune.

Jaina and Zekk found Jacen and adjusted their own leap so they came down on the slope next to him.

"You planned that!" Jaina accused her brother.

"Planned *what*?" Jacen asked.

He leapt the rest of the way to the bottom of the dune, where he was joined by Tahiri, Tesar, and Lowbacca. Jaina and Zekk landed next to the group an instant later.

"The vape charges!" Zekk accused.

"You helped Jag!" Jaina added. As Jaina made her accusation, she and Zekk were turning back toward the bomb—now about three hundred meters above, still at the top of the dune. "You don't *want* us to recover this weapon!"

"That's ridiculous. I was only trying to save Jag's life." Jacen's voice was calm and smooth. "I thought you would thank me for that."

"Ask *Jag* to thank you," Jaina snapped.

She and Zekk raised their hands, reaching out to grasp the vape charges in the Force, but they were too late. A white flash swallowed the crest of the dune. They threw up their arms to shield their eyes, then heard a deep growl reverberating across the desert and felt the sand shuddering beneath their feet.

When they looked up, the top of the dune was gone—and so was the bomb.

ONE

Star Pond had calmed into a dark mirror, and the kaddyr bugs had fallen mysteriously silent. The entire Jedi academy had descended into uneasy stillness, and Luke knew it was time. He ended the meditation with a breath, then unfolded his legs—he had been floating cross-legged in the air—and lowered his feet to the pavilion floor.

Mara was instantly at his side, taking his arm in case he was too weak to stand. "How do you feel?"

Luke's entire body felt stiff and sore, his head was aching, and his hands were trembling. He tested his legs and found them a little wobbly.

"I'm fine," he said. His stomach felt as empty as space. "A little hungry, maybe."

"I'll bet." Continuing to hold his arm, Mara turned to leave the meditation pavilion. "Let's get you something to eat . . . and some rest."

Luke did not follow her. "I can last another hour." Through the Force, he could feel nearly the entire Jedi order gathered in the lecture hall, waiting to learn why he had summoned them. "We need to do this now."

"Luke, you look like you've been hanging out in wampa caves again," Mara said. "You need to rest."

"Mara, it's *time*," Luke insisted. "Is Ben there?"

"I don't know," Mara said.

Although their son was finally beginning to show some interest in the Force, he continued to shut himself off from his parents. Luke and Mara were saddened and a little disturbed by Ben's detachment, but they were determined not to push. The turmoil in the Force during the war with the Yuuzhan Vong had left him somewhat mistrustful of the Jedi way of life, and they both knew that if he was ever going to follow in their footsteps, he would have to find his own way onto the path.

"Does Ben really need to be part of this?" Mara's tone suggested the answer she wanted to hear.

"Sorry, but I think he does," Luke said. "Now that Jacen has convinced him that it's safe to open himself to the Force, Ben will have to make the same decision as everyone else. All the students will."

Mara frowned. "Shouldn't the children wait until they're older?"

"We'll ask them again when they become apprentices," Luke said. "I don't know whether I'm about to save the Jedi order or destroy it—"

"*I* do," Mara interrupted. "The Masters are pulling the order in ten different directions. You have to do this, or they'll tear it apart."

"It certainly looks that way," Luke said. With Corran Horn and Kyp Durron at odds over the anti-Killik policies of the Galactic Alliance, it seemed as though every Master in the order was trying to impose his or her own compromise on the Jedi. "But whether this is successful or not, it's going to change the Jedi order. If some students don't want to be a part of that, it's better for everyone to find out now."

Mara considered this, then sighed. "I'll have Nanna bring Ben over." She pulled out her comlink and stepped to one side of the pavilion. "And I'll let Kam and Tionne know you want the students there."

"Good. Thank you."

Luke continued to look out over the dark water. He had spent the last week deep in meditation, sending a Force-call to the entire Jedi order. It would have been easier to use the HoloNet, but many Jedi—such as Jaina and her team—were in places the HoloNet did not cover. Besides, Luke was trying to make a point, to subtly remind the rest of the order that all Jedi answered to the same authority.

And the strategy had worked. In every arm of the galaxy, Masters had suspended negotiations, Jedi Knights had dropped investigations, apprentices had withdrawn from combat. There were a few Jedi stranded on off-lane worlds without transport and a couple unable to suspend their activities without fatal consequences, but for the most part, his summons had been honored. Only two Jedi Knights had willfully ignored his call, and their decision had surprised Luke less than it had hurt him.

A familiar presence drew near on the path behind the meditation pavilion, and Luke spoke without turning around. "Hello, Jacen."

Jacen stopped at the entrance to the pavilion. "I'm sorry to disturb you."

Luke continued to look out on the pond. "Come to explain why Jaina and Zekk aren't here?"

"It's not their fault," Jacen said, still behind Luke. "We've had some, uh, disagreements."

"Don't make excuses for them, Jacen," Mara said, closing her comlink. "If you felt Luke's summons, so did they."

"It's not that simple," Jacen said. "They may have thought I was trying to trick them."

Luke finally turned around. "Tesar and Lowbacca didn't seem to think so." He had felt three other Jedi Knights return to Ossus along with Jacen. "Neither did Tahiri."

"What can I say?" Jacen spread his hands. "I'm not *their* brother."

Mara frowned. "Jacen, your sister used you as a pretext and we all know it. Let's leave it at that." She turned to Luke. "Nanna's on the way with Ben, and Kam says the students have all been waiting in the lecture hall since this morning."

"Thanks." Luke joined her and Jacen at the rear of the pavilion, then gestured at the path leading toward the lecture hall. "Walk with us, Jacen. We need to talk."

"I know." Jacen fell in at Luke's side, between him and Mara. "You must be furious about the raid on the Chiss supply depot."

"I was," Luke admitted. "But your aunt convinced me that if you were involved, there had to be a good reason."

"I was more than involved," Jacen said. "It was my idea."

"*Your* idea?" Mara echoed.

Jacen was silent a moment, and Luke could feel him struggling with himself, trying to decide how much we could tell them. He was trying to protect something—something as important to him as the Force itself.

Finally, Jacen said, "I had a vision." He stopped and looked into the crown of a red-fronded dbergo tree. "I saw the Chiss launch a surprise attack against the Killiks."

"And so you decided to *provoke* the Chiss just to be certain?" Luke asked. "Surely, it would have been better to warn the Killiks."

Jacen's fear chilled the Force. "There was more," he said. "I saw the Killiks mount a counterattack. The war spread to the Galactic Alliance."

"And *that's* why you attacked the Chiss supply depot," Mara surmised. "To protect the Galactic Alliance."

"Among other things," Jacen said. "I had to change the dynamics of the situation. If the war had started that way, it wouldn't have stopped. Ever." He turned to Luke. "Uncle Luke, I saw the galaxy die."

"Die?" An icy ball formed in Luke's stomach. Considering the turmoil the order had been in at the time, he was beginning to understand why Jacen had felt it necessary to take such dire action. "Because the Chiss launched a surprise attack?"

Jacen nodded. "That's why I convinced Jaina and the others to help me. To prevent the surprise attack from happening."

"I see." Luke fell quiet, wondering what *he* would have done, had he been in Jacen's place and experienced such a terrifying vision. "I understand why you felt you had to act, Jacen. But trying to change what you see in a vision is dangerous—even for a Jedi of your talent and power. What you witnessed was only *one* of many possible futures."

"One that I can't permit," Jacen replied quickly.

Again, Luke felt a wave of protectiveness from Jacen—protectiveness and secrecy.

"You were protecting something," Luke said. "What?"

"Nothing . . . and everything." Jacen spread his hands, and Luke felt him draw in on himself in the Force. "This."

They came to the Crooked Way, a serpentine path of rectangular stepping-stones, set askew to each other so that walkers would be forced to slow down and concentrate on their journey through the garden. Luke allowed Mara to lead the way, then fell in behind Jacen, watching with interest as his nephew instinctively took the smoothest, most fluid possible route up the walkway.

"Jacen, do you know that you *have* prevented what you saw in your vision?" Luke asked. He was meandering back and forth behind his nephew, absentmindedly allowing his feet to choose their route from one stone to the next. "Can you be certain that your own actions won't bring the vision to pass?"

Jacen missed the next stone and would have stepped onto the soft carpet of moss had he not sensed his error and caught his balance. He stopped, then pivoted around to face Luke.

"Is that a rhetorical question, Master?" he asked.

"Not entirely," Luke replied. He was concerned that Jacen had fixed the future again, as he had when he had reached across time and spoken to Leia during a vision at the Crash site on Yoggoy. "I need to be sure I know everything."

"Even Yoda didn't know everything," Jacen said, smiling. "But the future is still in motion, if that's what you're asking."

"Thank you," Luke said. Fearing dangerous ripples in the Force, Luke had asked Jacen not to reach into the future again. "But I still wish you hadn't acted so . . . forcefully."

"I had to do something," Jacen said. "And when it comes to the future, Uncle Luke, don't we *always* plot the next jump blind?"

"We do," Luke said. "That's why it is usually wise to be cautious."

"I see." Jacen glanced up the Crooked Way, where the steeply pitched roof of the lecture hall loomed behind a hedge of bamb-wood. "So you summoned the entire Jedi order to Ossus to do something cautious?"

Luke put on an exaggerated frown. "I said *usually,* Jacen." He let out a melodramatic sigh to show that he was not truly angry, then said, "Go on ahead. I can see that you're a disrespectful young nephew who delights in embarrassing his elders."

"Of course, Master."

Jacen smiled and bowed, then started up the Crooked Way, now taking the straightest possible line toward the lecture hall. Luke watched him go, wondering whether the jump he was about to make with the future of the order was any less bold—or blind—than the one his nephew had made in attacking the supply depot.

"You have to do *something*," Mara said, sensing the drift of his thoughts. "And this is the best choice."

"I know," he said. "That's what worries me."

Luke followed, taking his time, concentrating on the musky smell of the garden soil, deliberately focusing his thoughts on something other than the address he was about to give. He already knew what he needed to say—*that* had grown very clear to him as he learned more about the growing rift in the order—and overthinking it now would only interfere with the message. Better to let the words come naturally, to speak from his heart and hope the Jedi would listen with theirs.

By the time they reached the eastern gable of the lecture hall, a familiar calm had come over Luke. He could sense the Jedi waiting inside the building, tense with anticipation, all hoping that he could resolve the impasse that was threatening to tear the order apart. That much was clear, but he sensed more: frustration, animosity, even bitterness and rage. The disagreements had grown intense and personal, to the point that several Jedi Masters could barely stand to be in the same room.

Luke slid open the instructor's door and led the way down a

short, wood-floored hallway. As they approached the sliding panel at the end, the Jedi on the other side sensed their presence, and the low murmur in the auditorium died away.

Mara kissed Luke on the cheek, then whispered, "You can do this, Luke."

"I know," Luke said. "But keep a stun grenade handy just in case."

Mara smiled. "You won't need a grenade—they're *going* to be stunned."

She pulled the panel aside, revealing a simple but soaring auditorium with pillars of pale wood. The Jedi were gathered in the front of the room. Kyp Durron and his supporters were clustered near the left wall, and Corran Horn and his group were bunched along the right. Jacen and Ben sat in the middle with the Solos and Saba Sebatyne, while the students were interspersed in small groups along both sides of the center aisle.

Luke was shocked by how small the gathering looked. Including the students and Han, there were just under three hundred people in a hall that had been designed to hold two thousand—the academy's entire complement of Jedi and support staff. The vacant benches were a stark reminder of how small a bulwark the Jedi truly were against the dark forces that always seemed to be gathering in the unwatched corners of the galaxy.

Luke stopped in the middle of the dais and took a deep breath. He had rehearsed his speech a dozen times, but he still had more butterflies in his stomach than when he had faced Darth Vader on Cloud City. So much depended on what he was about to say . . . and on how the Jedi responded to it.

"Thirty-five standard years ago, I became the last guardian of an ancient order that had thrived for a thousand generations. During all that time, no evil dared challenge its power, no honest being ever questioned its integrity. Yet fall it did, brought low by the treachery of a Sith Lord who disguised himself as a friend and an ally. Only a handful of Masters survived, hiding in deserts and swamps so that the bright light that was the Jedi order would not be extinguished."

Luke paused here and exchanged gazes with Leia. Her face had been lined by four decades of sacrifice and service to the galaxy, yet her brown eyes still shined with the intensity of her youth. At the moment, they were also shining with curiosity. Luke had not discussed what he intended to say even with her.

He looked back to the other Jedi. "Under the guidance of two of those Masters, I became the instrument of the Jedi's return, and I have dedicated myself to rekindling the light of their order. Ours may be a smaller, paler beacon than the one that once lit the way for the Old Republic, but it *has* been growing, both in size and in brilliance."

Luke felt the anticipation in the Force beginning to shift toward optimism, but he also sensed concern rising in his sister. As a Force-gifted politician and a former Chief of State, she realized what he was doing—and she could see where it would lead. Luke pushed her worries out of his mind; he was doing this to save the order, not to aggrandize himself.

"We have been growing," he continued, "until now."

Luke looked first toward Corran and his supporters, then toward Kyp and his.

"*Now* we are threatened by a different enemy, one that I brought into our midst through my misunderstanding of the old practices. In my arrogance, I believed we had found a better way, one more in tune with the challenges we face in our time. I was wrong."

A murmur of soft protest rustled through the hall, and the Force near both Kyp and Corran grew unsettled with guilt. Luke raised his hand for silence.

"In the order I envisioned, we served the Force by following our own consciences. We taught our apprentices well, and we trusted them to follow their own hearts." Luke looked directly into Leia's troubled eyes. "It was a splendid dream, but it has been growing more impractical for some time now."

Luke returned his gaze to the other Jedi. "My mistake was in forgetting that good beings can disagree. They can evaluate all of the evidence and study it from every angle and *still* reach opposite conclusions. And each side can believe with pure hearts that only *their* view is right.

"When that happens, it's easy to lose sight of something far more important than who's right and who's wrong."

Luke fixed his eyes on Kyp, who managed to avoid looking away despite the color that came to his face. "When the Jedi are at odds with each other, they are at odds with the Force."

Luke shifted his gaze to Corran, who responded with a contrite lowering of the eyes. "And when the Jedi are at odds with the Force, they can't perform their duty to themselves, to the order, *or* to the Alliance."

The hall fell utterly silent. Luke remained quiet—not to build the suspense, but to give every Jedi time to reflect on his or her own part in the crisis.

Ben and the students were sitting very still, with their chins pressed to their chests. But their eyes were darting from side to side, looking for clues as to how they should respond. Tesar Sebatyne flattened his scales—betraying the shame he felt for helping precipitate the crisis, and Lowbacca slumped his enormous shoulders. Tahiri sat up straight and stared stonily ahead, her stiff bearing an unsuccessful attempt to disguise her guilty feelings. Only Leia seemed unaffected by the subtle chastisement. She sat with her fingers steepled in front of her, studying Luke with a furrowed brow and a Force presence so guarded he could not read her emotions.

When the mood in the hall began to shift toward regret, Luke spoke again. "I've meditated at length, and I've concluded that *how* we respond to a crisis—the one facing us now or any other—is far less important than responding to it together. Even with the Force to guide us, we're only mortal. We *are* going to make mistakes.

"But mistakes by themselves will never destroy us. As long as we work together, we'll always have the strength to recover. What we *can't* recover from is fighting among ourselves. It will leave us too exhausted to face our enemies. And *that* is what Lomi Plo and the Dark Nest want. It's the only way they can defeat us."

Luke took a deep breath. "So I'm asking each of you to rethink your commitment to the Jedi. If you can't place the good of the order above all else and follow the direction chosen by your superiors, I'm asking you to leave. If you have other duties or loyalties that come before the order, I'm asking you to leave. If you cannot be a Jedi Knight first, I'm asking you not to be a Jedi Knight at all."

Luke took his time, looking from one shocked face to another. Only Leia seemed dismayed—but he had expected that.

"Think about your choice carefully," he said. "When you are ready, come to me and let me know what you have decided."

TWO

A stunned silence still lay over the lecture hall as Leia stepped onto the dais and started after her brother. As a Jedi Knight, it was hardly her place to challenge a decree from the order's most senior Master, but she knew what Luke was doing . . . even if *he* did not. She entered the small corridor behind the dais, and that was when Han caught up and took her arm.

He slid the panel shut behind them, then whispered, "Hold on! Don't you want to talk this over before you quit?"

"Relax, Han. I'm not leaving the order." Leia glanced down the corridor, toward the golden light spilling out the entrance to the lecture hall's small library. Inside, calmly awaiting the storm, she could sense her brother's presence. "I just need to talk some sense into Luke before this gets out of hand."

"Are you sure?" Han asked. "I mean, you're not even a Master."

"I'm his sister," Leia retorted. "That gives me special privileges."

She strode down the corridor and entered the library without announcing herself. Luke was seated on a mat at the far end of the room, with a low writing table before him and the HoloNet access terminal at his back. Mara stood beside him at one end of the table, her green eyes as hard and unfathomable as an eumlar crystal.

When she saw Leia, Mara cocked her brow. "I doubt you're here to pledge your obedience to the order."

"I'm not." Leia stopped in front of the table and glared down at Luke. "Do you *know* what you've just done?"

"Of course," Luke said. "It's called the Rubogean Gambit."

Leia's aggravation gave way to shock. "You're taking control of the order as a ploy?"

"He has to do *something*," Mara said. "The order is falling apart."

"But the Rubogean Gambit?" Leia protested. "You can't be serious!"

"I'm afraid so," Luke said. "I wish I wasn't."

Leia reached out to her brother in the Force and realized he was telling the truth. He was filled with disappointment—in Kyp, Corran, and the other Masters, in himself, in her. The *last* thing he wanted was to take personal control of the order, but Mara was right. Something had to be done, and—as usual—it fell to Luke to do it.

Leia considered her brother's plan for a moment, growing calmer as she reflected on his other options—or rather, his lack of them.

Finally, she said, "Your provocation isn't strong enough. Most of the Jedi in that hall *want* you to take over. They won't resist you."

"I hope they'll change their minds once they reflect on it," Luke answered. "If not, then I'll *have* to take control of the order."

"For its own good." Leia's rusty political instincts began to trip alarms inside her head. "Do you know how many despots have said the same thing to me?"

"Luke is *not* a despot." Mara's voice grew a little heated. "He doesn't even *want* control."

"I know." Leia kept her gaze on her brother. "But that doesn't make this any less dangerous. If the gambit fails, you'll be reducing the order to a personality cult."

"Then let's hope my ultimatum helps the Masters find a way to work together again." Luke's eyes grew hard. "I will not let them tear the Jedi apart."

"Even if it means anointing yourself king of the Jedi?" Leia pressed.

"Yes, Leia—even if it means *that*."

Surprised by the sudden sharpness in her brother's voice, Leia fell into an uneasy silence. It was clear Luke had already made up his mind. That alone made her worry. He had reached his decision without seeking the benefit of her political experience—and the fact that she could think of no better plan made her worry even more.

When the silence became unbearable, Han stepped to the end of the table opposite Mara. "Okay, I'm lost. Will somebody please slow down and tell me what the blazes a Rubogean Gambit is?"

"It's a diplomatic ploy," Leia explained, relieved to have an excuse to break eye contact with Luke. "You distract your counterpart with a provocative assertion, hoping he's so upset that he doesn't notice what you're really doing."

"In other words, you pull a bait and switch." Han scowled at Luke. "So you *don't* want the Jedi to put the order first?"

"Actually, that's what I *do* want," Luke said. "Our problem now is that everybody puts the order last. Corran thinks we exist to serve the Alliance, and Kyp is convinced we should follow nothing but our own consciences. Meanwhile, Jaina and *her* team believe our first duty is to protect the weak from aggression."

"I'm with you so far," Han said. "Where I make a bad jump is the part where you take full control. If you don't want to be king of the Jedi, why are you using this swindle to slip it past everyone in the order?"

"Luke is trying to unite the Masters against him, Han," Leia explained.

"Yeah, I get that part." Han furrowed his brow, clearly even more skeptical of what was happening than Leia was. "But like I said, if Luke doesn't want to be king, why try slipping it past everyone?"

"Because being sneaky is the only way to convince the Masters I really want this," Luke said. "The threat has to be big—and it has to be *real*. If I'm too obvious, they'll know I'm trying to manipulate them, and it won't work."

Han thought this over for a moment, then said, "That makes sense. But it's still risky. How do you know they'll catch on to this Rubber Gambit or whatever it is?"

"Han, they're Jedi *Masters*," Mara said. "They caught on before Luke finished his speech."

Luke suddenly lifted his chin and looked past them toward the entrance to the library. "This will have to be the end of our discussion. The first Jedi is coming to tell me her decision."

A sad heaviness began to fill Leia's chest. "Of course."

She took Han's hand and turned to go. Danni Quee was already coming through the entrance, her blue eyes shining with unshed tears. When she saw Leia and Han already in the room, she stopped abruptly and looked a little flustered.

"I'm sorry." She started to withdraw. "I'll come back later."

"That's okay, Danni," Leia said. "We were finished here, anyway."

Leia started to lead Han past, but Danni put up her hand to stop them.

"Please don't leave on my account. This won't take long, and what I have to say isn't private." Without waiting for a reply, Danni turned to Luke. "Master Skywalker, I hope you won't think I don't value what I have learned with the Jedi because I came to this decision quickly, but I was never a true member of the order, and my future lies with Zonama Sekot. There is still so much to learn from her that I'd be lying to myself if I said that the Jedi came first. I wish you and the Jedi the best, but I'm going to return to Zonama Sekot."

"I understand, Danni." Luke rose and stepped around the table, then took her hands in his. "You were a tremendous help to the Jedi in our most desperate hour, but we've all known for some time that your destiny lies elsewhere. Thank you, and may the Force be with you always."

Danni smiled and wiped her eyes, then embraced Luke. "Thank *you*, Master Skywalker. And please come see us when you can. Sekot would enjoy visiting with you again."

"I will," Luke promised. "I'd enjoy visiting with her, too."

Danni released Luke and embraced Mara and Leia and Han, then left the room.

She was barely gone before Tenel Ka, the Queen Mother of Hapes, strode in. She held her dimpled chin high and her shoulders square, but the resolve in her eyes was more heartbreaking than reassuring.

Tenel Ka flashed Leia a sad smile, then turned to Luke. "Master Skywalker, I would like nothing more than to place myself entirely at the Jedi order's disposal." She bit her lip, then reached under the Jedi robe she had donned for her visit and removed her lightsaber from its clip. "And if there were only myself and my daughter to consider, perhaps I would.

"But that would be irresponsible. I am the sole able-bodied sovereign of an interstellar empire, and if I were to relinquish my throne, my nobles would spill lakes of blood fighting to take my place." She held out her lightsaber to Luke. "It is with great regret that I must surrender this. I simply cannot fulfill the duties of a Knight in the Jedi order."

"I understand." Luke accepted Tenel Ka's lightsaber, then pushed it back into her hand. "But please keep your lightsaber. You earned the right to carry it, and that can never be taken away."

Tenel Ka managed a sad smile. "Thank you, Master Skywalker. Your gesture means a great deal to me."

"Thank *you*, Queen Mother," Luke said. "You may have assumed other duties for now, but you carry within you everything that a Jedi Knight is. Perhaps one day you will be free to return to the order. There will always be a place for you."

Tenel Ka's smile turned more hopeful. "Yes, perhaps that is so."

She embraced Luke with her one arm, then surprised Leia by embracing her and Han. "You mean more to me than I will ever be able to tell, my friends. I am going to miss you both."

"Miss us?" Han replied. "This isn't forever, kid. We're going to visit, you know."

"That's right," Leia added, returning the Queen Mother's embrace. "Your security chief may not allow baby holos, but I still want to see your daughter—and if we have to come all the way to Hapes to do it, we will."

Tenel Ka stiffened in Leia's arms. "That would be . . . nice." She stepped back, her anxiety permeating the Force. "Be sure to let us know when you are coming, so we can arrange the proper security."

"Of course." Leia had to force herself not to frown. "Thank you."

Tenel Ka gave Leia and Han an uneasy smile, then turned her attention to Luke and Mara as well. "Good-bye. May the Force be with you all."

The Queen Mother spun and left the room so quickly that neither Leia nor anyone else had time to wish her the same.

Han frowned after her. "That was weird."

"Something about the baby," Leia said. "There's a reason she won't let anybody get a good look at it."

"Maybe she's embarrassed," Han said.

"Han!" Leia and Mara exclaimed together.

"Look, she still won't say anything about the father," he said. "I'm just saying that maybe there's a reason. Maybe she's not proud of the guy."

"You know, Han might be right," Luke said. "Not that she's embarrassed, but maybe there's something she doesn't want the galaxy to see. How would her nobles react if the heir to the Hapes throne was less than a perfect beauty?"

Leia's heart sank. "Oh, no. That poor woman."

"I'm glad you let Tenel Ka keep her lightsaber, Luke," Mara agreed. "She may need it."

They all stared out into the corridor after the Queen Mother, pondering the lonely circumstances of her life, wondering how they might be able to help, until another set of footsteps echoed down the passage. A moment later, Corran Horn appeared at the entrance to the library and bowed respectfully.

"Master Skywalker, would now be a good time to speak with you?" he asked.

"Of course." Luke glanced meaningfully in Leia and Han's direction, then returned to his mat behind the writing table and sat. "Come in."

Leia took Han's hand again and started past Corran. "Excuse us, Corran. We were just leaving."

"Please don't, at least not yet," Corran said. "I've already said this to the rest of the order, and I'd like you to hear it, too."

Leia glanced at Luke for permission, then nodded. "If you wish."

Corran went to the center of the room and clasped his hands behind his back.

"Master Skywalker, first I would like to apologize for the part I've played in this crisis. I can see now that in complying with Chief Omas's request that I become the order's temporary leader, I was playing directly into his hands."

"Yes, you were," Luke said.

Corran swallowed, then fixed his gaze on the wall behind Luke's head. "I assure you, it was never my intention to usurp anyone's authority, but when it grew clear how bad Jedi relations had grown with Chief Omas and the Alliance, I felt something had to be done. I can see now how badly mistaken I was."

"Mistakes are always easy to see in retrospect," Luke said mildly.

Corran glanced down at Luke, clearly uncertain how he was taking the apology. "But I *do* carry the good of the order utmost in my heart."

"Good," Luke said.

"That's why I think it might be best if I left." Corran's voice was choked with emotion. "My presence can only be a divisive element."

"I see." Luke braced his elbows on the writing table, then rested his chin on his steepled fingers. "Corran, isn't this the second time you have offered to leave the order for its own good?"

Corran nodded. "It is. After the destruction of Ithor—"

"Don't let there be a third," Luke interrupted. "I won't stop you next time."

Corran frowned, clearly confused. "Stop me?"

"Corran, you may have been naïve for believing the Yuuzhan Vong would honor their word, but *they* destroyed Ithor, not you," Luke said. "And the mistakes that led the Jedi into our current crisis are more mine than anyone else's. So please stop trying to shoulder the entire galaxy's guilt by yourself. To be honest, it makes you look a bit pompous."

Corran looked as though someone had detonated a stun grenade in his face. "Pompous?"

Luke nodded. "I hope you don't mind me telling you that in front of others, but you're the one who invited them to stay."

Corran glanced over at Leia and Han. "Of course not."

"Good," Luke said. "Then we're all settled? You're going to continue as a Jedi, and your loyalty to the order comes first?"

"Yes." Corran nodded. "Of course."

Luke smiled broadly. "I'm glad. We couldn't afford to lose you, Corran. I don't think you realize just how valuable you are to the order. The Jedi *do* have a duty to support the Galactic Alliance—far more than we have been—and nobody represents that viewpoint better than you do."

"Uh, thank you." Corran remained in the center of the room looking confused.

After a moment, Luke said, "That's all, Corran. Unless there's something else—"

"Actually, there is," Corran said. "I think the other Masters have all chosen to stay, as well. After I spoke with them, they asked me to tell you they would be waiting in the auditorium."

"They did?" Luke raised his brow and tried to avoid showing the satisfaction that Leia sensed through their twin bond. "I guess I should go hear what they have to say."

Leia stepped aside, then she and the others followed Luke into the auditorium. The room was even emptier than before, with Kyp, Saba, and the rest of the Masters gathered in a tight cluster near the front of the speaking dais, holding an animated conversation in barely civil tones. Tesar, Lowbacca, Tahiri, and Tekli were seated together a few rows back, trying not to be too obvious in their eavesdropping. Jacen sat on the opposite side of the aisle, appearing more interested in his conversation with Ben than in whatever the Masters were whispering about.

The rest of the order was gone—presumably sent away by the Masters so they could have a private conversation with Master Skywalker. The fact that Jacen, Tesar, and the others had been asked to stay suggested that the conversation was going to be about the Killiks. Apparently, Luke's plan had at least made the Masters willing to talk again. Leia doubted they would agree on anything, but talking was a start.

When Han saw the gathering of Masters, he hopped off the dais and held his hand out toward Ben. "It looks like we're going to be a little out of place at this meeting, partner. Why don't we go back over to the *Falcon* and work on that warp vortex problem I was telling you about?"

Ben's eyes lit up. He started to say good-bye to Jacen—until Kenth Hamner rose and spoke from among the Masters.

"Actually, Captain Solo, we'd like you to stay."

Han cast a worried look in Leia's direction, and she knew they were thinking the same thing: that Jaina and Zekk were going to be a big part of this conversation.

"Yeah, sure," he said. "Whatever you want."

Ben twisted his freckled face into a sour expression. "What about the *Falcon*'s vortex problem?"

"Don't worry about that, kid," Han said to him. "Vortex stabilizers don't fix themselves. It'll be there waiting when we're ready."

"Perhaps Ben's Defender Droid could take him home." Kenth glanced toward the speaking dais. "If that's acceptable to the Masters Skywalker?"

"Of course," Mara said. She looked toward the back of the hall. "Nanna?"

The big Defender Droid stepped out of the shadows, then extended her metallic hand and waited as Ben reluctantly shuffled up the aisle to join her.

Once the pair had left the hall, Kenth turned to Han. "Thank you for staying, Captain Solo. We know your affiliation is informal, but you're an important part of the order, and your opinion has always carried a great deal of weight with the Masters."

"Always glad to help," Han said cautiously. "So what's this about?"

"In a minute." Kenth waved Han toward a seat. Clearly, the Masters had come to an agreement about one thing—they were going to meet Luke's gambit with a united front. "First, we would like to ask how Master Skywalker sees family fitting into his new view of a Jedi's commitment to the order."

"I'm not saying we have to abandon our loved ones," Luke said, stepping between Leia and the Masters. "But obviously, any Jedi is required to be away from his or her family for extended periods."

When Luke remained between Leia and the Masters, she took the hint and stepped off the dais, then went to Han's side. They both sat on the bench with Jacen.

As Luke and the Masters continued to clarify just what Luke meant by "placing the order first," Han leaned close to Jacen's ear.

"Tenel Ka left the order," he whispered. "Thought you'd want to know."

"I already did," Jacen answered. "Uncle Luke didn't leave her much choice, did he?"

"It only formalizes what we've all known for some time," Leia said. Jacen and Tenel Ka had been close throughout their teenage years, and Leia did not want Jacen to allow Tenel Ka's departure to influence his own decision. "Tenel Ka's duties as the Queen Mother already prevent her from participating in the order in any meaningful way."

Jacen smiled and placed his hand on Leia's knee. "Mom, I'm not going to disappear again. I've already decided to stay."

Leia was so relieved that she suspected even Han could feel it, but she kept a straight face and said, "If that's what you think is best for you, dear."

Jacen laughed and rolled his eyes. "Mother, your feelings betray you."

"I suppose so." Leia grew more serious, then asked, "What has Tenel Ka told you about her daughter?"

"Allana?" Jacen's presence suddenly seemed to disappear from the Force, and his tone grew guarded. "What about her?"

"We mean, what is Tenel Ka hiding?" Han demanded. "Mention the kid, and she closes up like a rabclab in ice water."

"What makes you think Tenel Ka would tell *me* anything?" Jacen asked.

"She obviously *has,*" Leia said. "Or you wouldn't be trying to dodge our questions."

Jacen stared at the floor. Leia had the sense that he wanted to tell them, but was struggling with whether he had the right. Finally, he met Leia's gaze.

"If Tenel Ka finds it necessary to keep her daughter out of the hololight, I think we should trust that she has good reason."

Han looked past Jacen to Leia and nodded. "Luke was right."

Jacen's eyes widened. "About *what*?"

"About Allana," Leia said. "If she were, uh, *afflicted* in some way, Tenel Ka would need to keep the child hidden. The Hapans' obsession with beauty goes beyond the neurotic. I can't imagine what they might do if the heir to their throne was blemished."

The alarm in Jacen's expression began to fade. "Don't bother asking for details. I don't know them."

Leia could tell by the way Jacen avoided her eyes that he was lying, but she decided to let it go. He clearly felt that they were already asking him to betray a confidence, and pressing him any harder would only make him less forthcoming.

"We know all that we need to," Leia said. "I only hope Tenel Ka realizes we're here to help."

"Mom, Tenel Ka has more money than Lando, and dozens of Jedi friends," Jacen said. "I'm pretty sure she knows she can get all the help she needs."

"Hey, we're just worried about her," Han said. "Poor kid—whatever's wrong, I'll bet the problem came from the father."

Jacen frowned and was silent for a moment, then said, "I'm sure you're right, Dad. And if this is your way of asking if I know who the father is, it's not going to work."

Han pretended to be hurt. "You think *I'd* snoop?"

"I *know* you would," Jacen said. "That's the Zeltron Lead you just tried. You taught it to me when I was ten."

Han shrugged. "And I didn't think you were listening."

Leia's attention was drawn to the gathering of Masters by a sudden lull in their conversation. She looked up to find Luke seated on the edge of the dais, motioning everyone forward. As they all approached, she sensed a certain hopefulness in her brother's presence.

"The Masters have agreed that the order's first responsibility during any crisis is to respond in a coherent and united fashion," he said. "Now the question is, what are we going to do about the Killiks?"

"That's why we asked all of you to stay," Tresina Lobi said, turning to Leia and the others. "You know more about the Killiks than any of us, so your insights will guide our decision."

Luke nodded his agreement. "I'd like to ask Jacen to share his vision with the rest of us."

"Vision?" Corran asked.

"It's why I organized the attack on Supply Depot Thrago," Jacen explained, going to stand between the Masters and the dais. "I saw the Chiss launch a massive surprise attack against the Killiks."

Kenth frowned. "Surely, you didn't think that you could prevent—"

"Let him finish," Luke said, raising his hand to silence the Master. "Jacen's plan was desperate, but not unreasonable given the circumstances at the time—especially our own disarray."

Jacen continued, "What really frightened me about the vision was that the Chiss failed to destroy the Colony. Instead, I saw the Killiks mount a counterattack, and the war spread to the Galactic Alliance."

"Let me see if I understand this," Corran said, frowning in confusion. "You saw the war spreading to the Galactic Alliance, so you attacked the Chiss to keep that from happening? That sounds crazy, Jacen."

Jacen nodded. "It's convoluted, I know. But I felt we had to change the dynamic. Obviously, the Chiss are *still* attacking—"

"And the Galactic Alliance is *still* being dragged into the war." Kenth's tone was sharp. "Not only are we fighting in the Utegetu Nebula now we have the Chiss mobilizing against us because they think we gave the *Ackbar* to the Killiks. I don't see that your attack accomplished anything except to hasten the war—and make everything vastly more complicated."

"It convinced the Chiss they couldn't win with a quick strike," Han said, coming to Jacen's defense. "At least now there's *some* chance you can bring this mess under control before it erupts into a galaxywide bug stomp."

"Han is right," Corran said. "Besides, debating our past mistakes—whether or not they *were* mistakes—won't solve this problem. We need to talk about how we're going to stop this war before it gets out of control."

The Masters nodded their agreement, but fell silent and stared at the floor, clearly reluctant to launch into the same argument that had been threatening to tear the order apart for several months. After a few seconds, Corran, Kyp, and even Saba began to cast expectant glances toward Luke, clearly hoping he would take the lead. He remained silent, determined to force the Masters to work through the problem themselves and develop their own consensus.

Finally, Jacen spoke up. "I know how to stop the war."

Everybody's brow—including Leia's—went up.

"Why am I not surprised?" Kyp asked. He ran a hand through his unruly hair, pausing to scratch his scalp. "Okay, let's hear it. You seem to be the only one with any ideas."

Jacen stepped over next to Luke, placing himself squarely in front of the Masters. His determination hung heavy and hard in the Force. He was going to stop the war. Too much would be lost if he did not.

"We kill Raynar Thul."

"*What?*"

This was cried by several Jedi at once, among them Tesar Sebatyne and the other young Jedi Knights who had accompanied Jacen on the raid against Supply Depot Thrago. Even Leia found herself wondering if she had heard Jacen correctly.

"Did you see *that* in your vision, too?" Corran asked. He turned to the other Masters, shaking his head in disapproval. "We talked about this before."

Luke frowned. "We did?"

"When you and Han were captured on Woteba," Mara informed him. "It was our backup plan."

"And now it should be our primary plan," Jacen said calmly. "It's the only way to prevent the war."

"Go on," Luke said.

"Most insect species have an immense mortality rate," Jacen explained. "One egg out of a thousand might produce a larva that survives to become an imago and produce young of its own. When Raynar became a Joiner—"

"But killing Raynar would destroy the Colony!" Tesar rasped.

"I believe that's the point," Kenth said. "They *have* declared war on two other galactic civilizations."

Lowbacca roared an objection, protesting that the Dark Nest was causing all the trouble.

"Jacen has obviously given this a lot of thought," Luke said, raising his hands for quiet. "Why don't we hear him out?"

"Because hearing Jacen out is dangerous," Tahiri said, glaring at Jacen. "He says one thing and means another."

Coming from Tahiri, whom the Solos had considered practically their own daughter since Anakin's death, the comment was especially stinging. Leia would have admonished her for her rudeness, had Luke not done so first.

"That's enough!" Luke scowled first at Tahiri, then at Tesar and Lowbacca. "This debate is among the Masters, and when we *ask* for your opinion, you're going to give it in a civilized fashion. Is that clear?"

Tesar's scales stood on end and Lowbacca's fur ruffled, but they joined Tahiri in nodding. "Yes, Master."

"Thank you." Luke looked back to Jacen. "You were saying?"

"When Raynar became a Joiner, the Killiks began to value the lives of individual nest-members," Jacen continued. "Their population exploded, they began to strip their own worlds bare, and that's when the Colony was born and began to infringe on Chiss space."

"But will killing Raynar change that *now*?" Saba asked from the front bench. "The Killikz have already changed. This one does not see how removing Raynar will change them back."

"Because the change is a *learned* behavior." Jacen was obviously ready with his answer. "Raynar is the only element of their personality that *innately* values individual life."

"So we remove Raynar, and they unlearn the behavior?" Kenth asked.

"Exactly," Jacen said. "Raynar's ability to project his will through the Force is what binds the individual nests into the Colony. If we remove that, the nests will need to survive on their own."

"The nests will either return to their normal state or starve," Kenth said. "Either way, the problem takes care of itself."

"Not exactly," Corran said. "You're forgetting the Dark Nest. By all accounts, they're already running the Colony from behind the scenes. If we take out Raynar, what's to prevent Lomi Plo from taking over?"

"We have to take her and Alema Rar out, too," Jacen said. "I'm sorry, I thought that was a given."

When no one objected, Luke asked, "So everyone agrees on that much, then? The Dark Nest must be destroyed."

"Assuming we can," Han muttered. "We've tried that before, remember?"

"We've learned a lot since then," Jacen insisted. "This time, we'll succeed."

"I'm glad you're so confident, Jacen," Kyp said. "How about letting the rest of us in on the secret?"

"I already have," Jacen said. "We're going to eliminate Raynar and his nest, too."

This drew a pair of snorts from Tesar and Lowbacca, but a warning glance from Luke was enough to silence the two Jedi Knights.

"Now I'm really lost," Corran said. "If we have to destroy the Dark Nest anyway, why don't we just stop there and *reason* with Raynar?"

"I wish we could," Leia said. "But Raynar's mind was shattered by the *Flier*'s crash, and the Killiks have a very fluid concept of truth. When you put those two things together, you can't count on him to behave rationally. We only persuaded him to abandon Qoribu by convincing him that if he didn't, *all* of the nests there would turn into Dark Nests."

"That's true, Mother," Jacen said. "But the real problem is you *can't* destroy the Dark Nest without killing Raynar. As long as there is an Unu, there will be a Gorog."

"That'z zilly," Tesar scoffed.

"Not at all." Cilghal spoke in a soft voice that had a quieting effect on the whole argument. "I began to suspect the same thing myself when the Dark Nest reappeared in the Utegetu Nebula."

Corran, Kenth, and even Luke looked stunned.

"Why?" Luke asked.

"Do you remember our discussion about the conscious and unconscious mind?" Cilghal replied.

Luke nodded. "I believe you put it this way: 'Like the Force itself, every mind in the galaxy has two aspects.' "

"Very good, Master Skywalker," Cilghal said. "The conscious mind embraces what we know of ourselves, and the unconscious contains the part that remains hidden."

"I thought that was the subconscious mind," Corran said.

"So did I, until Cilghal explained it," Luke said. "The *subconscious* is a level of the mind between full awareness and unawareness. The *unconscious* remains fully hidden from the part of our minds that we know. Right, Cilghal?"

"You have an excellent memory, Master Skywalker," she said.

"Wait a minute, Cilghal," Kyp said. "You're saying that Jacen is actually right? That even if the Dark Nest didn't exist, the Colony would create one?"

"I am saying that Jacen's theory fits what we have observed," Cilghal replied. "To the extent that the Colony is a collective mind, it makes sense for it to create an unconscious. And you cannot destroy an unconscious mind without also destroying the conscious mind."

Cilghal paused and swiveled one bulbous eye toward Tesar, Lowbacca, and Tahiri. "I am sorry, but if this theory is correct, it is simply impossible to destroy the Dark Nest without destroying the Colony. One accompanies the other."

"Then Jacen's theory is wrong!" Tesar rasped.

"That is always possible," Cilghal admitted. "But it explains everything we have observed, and that makes it the best working theory we have."

"So we kill one of our own?" Corran shook his head harshly. "I can't believe that's our best option. It goes against everything I feel as a Jedi. We're not assassins, we don't betray our own, and we don't destroy entire civilizations."

"Corran, we talked about *that*, too," Leia reminded him. "It's because Raynar *is* a Jedi that we must act. He's become a threat to the galaxy, and it's our responsibility to stop him."

"I understand that he's a threat," Corran responded. "But if he's as shattered as you say, we shouldn't be trying to kill him—we should be trying to help him."

"May the Force be with you on *that*!" Han scoffed. "You'll need it. Raynar's more powerful than Luke, and he doesn't *want* your help."

Luke cocked his brow at Han's assessment of his relative strength, but looked more surprised than insulted and did not protest.

"Corran, think about what you're asking," Leia said. "Exactly *how* do you suggest we help Raynar? You know how difficult it is to hold a regular Jedi against his will, and Raynar's resources are immensely more vast. I'm afraid we have to face the reality of the situation."

"So you're agreeing with Jacen?" Corran asked. "You think our only choice is to kill Raynar?"

The question struck Leia like a kick in the stomach. She had known Raynar since he had come to the Jedi academy on Yavin 4 as the haughty child-heir to the Bornaryn Shipping Empire, then watched him mature into the sincere young man who had volunteered to accompany Anakin on the ill-fated strike mission to Myrkr. The thought of actually sending Jedi against him made her lips tremble with sorrow. But she had seen for herself, when the Killik fleet attacked in the Murgo Choke, that he had no such qualms about assaulting his former friends.

Leia nodded sadly. "Yes, Corran," she said. "I think Jacen is right. Our best option is to take out Raynar. In fact, it is our duty."

Corran's face reddened, and Leia knew the exchange was about to get rough.

"Our *duty*?" he demanded. "What about Jaina and Zekk?"

"What about them?" Han shot back.

"They're Joiners, too," Corran pointed out, still looking at Leia. "Will you be so eager to kill *them* when they take Raynar's place?"

Luke raised a hand in an effort to restore calm, but the damage had already been done. The question had heated even Leia's blood, and Han immediately went into full boil.

"They're not *going* to take Raynar's place!" Han shouted.

"You can't know that," Corran replied. "Jaina has always done as she pleases, and now she's with the Colony." He turned back to Leia. "So I want to know: will you say the same thing when we have to go after Jaina and Zekk?"

"That's a baseless question, and you know it!" Leia said.

"Not really," Kyle Katarn said. "I, for one, would find your answer relevant to Raynar's case."

"Huttwash!" Kyp protested. "Jaina and Zekk have already demonstrated that they're Jedi first. It's not relevant at all."

"Then why aren't they here?" Kyle pressed.

"Probably because they're trying to stop a *war*," Han retorted.

And they were off, voices rising, tempers flaring, gestures growing increasingly sharp. Corran continued to press the Solos about what they would do if Jaina and Zekk were running the Colony instead of Raynar. Han and Leia continued to insist it was a moot question, and Kyle, Kyp, and the rest of the Masters continued to line up on both sides of the issue, taking increasingly rigid positions.

Within minutes, it grew apparent that they had reached an impasse, and Leia sensed her brother's frustration building. His attempt to unite the Masters had failed miserably. They were no closer to reaching a consensus now than they had been while he and Han were trapped in the Utegetu, and even Leia could see the situation was only going to grow worse.

"Thank you."

Though Luke spoke softly, he used the Force to project his words into the minds of everyone present. The effect was immediate; the argument came to a sudden halt, and the entire group turned to face him.

"Thank you for your opinions." Luke stepped back onto the dais. "I'll consider them all carefully and let you know what I decide."

Kyp frowned. "What *you* decide?"

"Yes, Kyp," Mara said. She stepped toward him and locked eyes with him. "What *Luke* decides. Don't you think that's best?"

Kyp's brow rose, then he looked around him at the faces of the other Masters—many still flushed with the emotions of their argument—and slowly seemed to realize what Leia already had: Luke was taking control of the order.

Before Kyp found the breath to answer, Han turned and started up the aisle toward the exit, his boot heels clunking on the wood floor. Leia started after him, almost running to catch up. Luke seemed content to watch them go in silence, but not Saba.

"Jedi Solo, where are you going?" the Barabel demanded.

"With Han," Leia replied. "To get our daughter back."

"What about the order?" Saba asked.

Leia did not even turn around. "*What* order?"

THREE

The Yuuzhan Vong's attempt to reshape Coruscant into the image of their lost homeworld had brought many good things to the planet, and fresh y'luubi was one of the best. Taken from Liberation Lake no more than three hours before smoldering, it had a rich, smoky flavor that filled Mara's entire head with pleasure. She held the spongy meat on her tongue, allowing it to dissolve as she had heard was proper, and marveled at the succession of spectacular tastes. The flavor went from smoky to sweet to tangy, then ended with a sharp, spicy bite that made her mouth water for more.

"The y'luubi are unbelievably wonderful, Madame Thul," Mara said, addressing their host. She and Luke had barely been back on Coruscant for a week before Madame Thul arrived aboard the *Tradewyn* and sent a message to the Jedi Temple inviting them to dine with her.

"The whole meal is," Luke added. "Thank you again for insisting that we meet here."

Aryn Thul—Raynar Thul's mother and the chairwoman of the board of Bornaryn Trading—smiled politely. "I'm so pleased you're enjoying it." A gaunt, almost frail woman with gray hair and durasteel eyes, she carried herself with a dignity and grace appropriate to the shimmersilk gown and Corusca gem necklace she had chosen for their "casual" dinner. "I was told Yuza Bre is the finest restaurant on Coruscant."

"By all accounts," Mara said. "I understand reservations are usually required months in advance. I can't imagine why it's deserted tonight."

"You can't?" Tyko Thul asked. A large, round-faced man with

short graying hair and hazel eyes, he was the brother of Madame Thul's late husband—and the chief operating officer of Bornaryn Trading. He turned to Madame Thul and shared an arrogant smile. "It appears the Jedi are not quite as all-knowing as we are led to believe."

"We shouldn't judge that on the basis of a restaurant, Tyko. I doubt corporate acquisitions are very high on their list of concerns." Madame Thul turned to Mara. "As of this morning, the Yuza Bre is a Bornaryn property. Buying it was the only way to guarantee our visit would remain private."

"Buying a restaurant was hardly necessary, Madame Thul," Luke said in a guarded tone. "If there's something you need to discuss in private, I would have been happy to meet you aboard the *Tradewyn*."

Given the argument among the Masters over whether to eliminate Raynar, both Mara and Luke had found the timing of Madame Thul's dinner invitation suspicious. But Luke had been a friend of the Thuls since Raynar attended the Jedi academy on Yavin 4, and Mara had convinced him that *if* Madame Thul knew about the argument, declining the invitation would be viewed as evidence that he agreed with those who felt the only way to resolve the Killik crisis was to kill her son.

Madame Thul frowned. "Luke, we have been friends since before Bornan died." Her tone remained nonchalant, but Mara could sense her anger—and her fear—in the Force. "Surely, you know me well enough to realize that if I wish to discuss something with you, I will."

"Does that mean you don't wish to discuss *anything*?" Luke asked.

"It means that you aren't the primary reason I bought Yuza Bre." Madame Thul allowed herself a guilty smile. "This happens to be Chief Omas's favorite restaurant. As you can imagine, from now on, he is going to find it difficult to make reservations."

"That seems rather petty," Mara said. Madame Thul struck her as a woman who appreciated frankness, so she spoke bluntly. "And it's hardly likely to sway his attitude regarding the Colony."

Madame Thul shrugged, her blue eyes twinkling with mischief. "I have been trying to be heard on this for months, but that Jenet assistant of his refuses to schedule an appointment. This seems as good a way as any to make my displeasure known."

"I'm sure it will accomplish *that*," Mara said. "But if feeding y'luubi to the Skywalker family is how you show displeasure with the Jedi, I'm sorry to inform you it isn't working."

She smiled, expecting Madame Thul to do likewise and utter at least a polite little laugh. Instead, the chairwoman fixed her with a steely-eyed glare.

"I really don't understand, Mara." She turned to Luke. "Is there some reason I *should* be displeased with the Jedi?"

"That isn't for us to say," Luke answered. "You're certainly aware of the Jedi's role in the recent trouble between the Colony and the Alliance."

"Of course," Madame Thul said. "You were crucial in keeping the nest ships trapped inside the Utegetu Nebula."

"So the answer to your question depends on you, Chairwoman Thul," Mara said. "Where do your loyalties lie?"

It was Tyko Thul who answered. "Our loyalties lie where they always have—with Bornaryn Trading. We have outlasted three galactic governments . . . and we'll outlast this one."

"What about family?" Luke asked, addressing the question to Madame Thul. "I'm sure your loyalties also extend to Raynar."

"Our interests in the Colony are very important to us, yes." Madame Thul's voice grew icy. "Obviously, Bornaryn will do *whatever* we must to protect them—and at the moment, we are well positioned to be extremely effective."

"For example, Bornaryn has diversified into exotic starship fuels," Tyko added. "Just yesterday, we acquired Xtib."

A tense silence fell over the table. Xtib was the processing company that produced TibannaX, the special Tibanna isotope used in StealthX engines to conceal their ion tails.

After a moment, Mara raised her eyes and locked gazes with Tyko. "I hope you don't intend that as a threat, Chief Thul. We're a little short on patience these days."

"Is there a reason Bornaryn would *need* to threaten the Jedi?" Tyko asked, refusing to be intimidated.

"You're obviously aware of our discussions regarding Raynar," Luke said, rising. "Rest assured that the Jedi would never take such an action lightly, but we *will* do what we must to bring this war to a swift end."

"Thank you for your frankness, Master Skywalker." Some of the stateliness seemed to drain from Madame Thul's bearing, and she motioned for him to return to his chair. "I don't know why, but I do take some small comfort from the reluctance in your voice. Please stay and finish your dinner."

"I'm afraid that isn't possible," Luke said.

"But we *would* like to know how you came by your information," Mara added, also rising. Her stomach was knotting in anger, though not because of any threat Bornaryn Trading might pose to the Jedi's TibannaX supplies. Someone—almost certainly a Jedi—had betrayed the confidence of Luke and the order. "Who told you?"

Madame Thul lifted her brow. "You truly expect me to reveal that?"

"You really don't have a choice," Mara said.

"This is outrageous!" Tyko snapped.

He started to rise, but Mara flicked a finger in his direction, and he dropped back into his chair, paralyzed by her Force grasp. Gundar, the thick-necked bodyguard who had been doubling as their waiter, reached for his blaster and started to leave his station near the kitchen.

Luke wagged a finger at the hulking human, then used the Force to pin him against a wall and looked to Madame Thul.

"I take security breaches very seriously," he said. "Don't make me use the Force on you."

Madame Thul sighed, then looked away. "You mustn't be too hard on them," she said. "They were convinced they were doing the right thing."

"They always are," Mara said. "Who was it?"

"The Barabel and his Wookiee," Madame Thul said. "Tesar and . . . Lowbacca it was, I believe."

Mara could sense Madame Thul's truthfulness in the Force, but she still found it difficult to believe—if only because it proved just how deeply divided the order remained even *after* Luke's gambit.

"It makes sense." Luke sounded as defeated as Mara was shocked. "I had just hoped for better."

"If you are disappointed, perhaps you should look to yourself for the reason," Madame Thul suggested. "Tesar and the Wookiee have good hearts, Master Skywalker. They would not betray your confidence unless they believed they had no other choice."

"Or unless they were under the Colony's control," Mara said. She turned toward the restaurant's transparisteel wall and looked across the green glow of Victory Square, toward the golden sheen of the Jedi Temple's giant pyramid. "They *were* back among the Killiks for more than a month."

Luke's concern—or perhaps it was sorrow—permeated the Force-bond Mara shared with him, but he retained a neutral expression as he spoke to Madame Thul.

"Thank you for your hospitality," he said. "The y'luubi was beyond description. I'm sure the Yuza Bre will continue to prosper under Bornaryn's ownership."

"You really must leave?" Madame Thul asked.

"I'm afraid so," Luke said. "Until the troubles with the Colony are resolved, it's probably better for Bornaryn Trading and the Jedi to keep their distance."

Madame Thul nodded. "I understand. But before you go, I hope you'll allow me to make one gift to you—friend to friend."

Tyko's eyes widened. "Aryn, I don't think that's a good idea. We might still have a use—"

"I doubt it." Madame Thul scowled at her brother-in-law. "It's obvious that we're not going to sway Master Skywalker with a *droid,* so we may as well give it to him."

Mara frowned. "A droid?"

Madame Thul smiled. "You'll see." She turned to her bodyguard. "Gundar, you can bring in ArOh now."

Gundar activated a remote, and a terrible squealing arose in the kitchen. A moment later, an ancient R series astromech droid lurched into view, its locomotion system so corrupted and corroded that it resembled an ancient sailing ship zigzagging into a headwind. Someone had recently made an effort to polish its brass casing, but the tarnish along the crevices and seams was so thick, it looked like paint.

"An antique droid?" Mara asked.

"A very special antique." Madame Thul waited until the droid had wandered within arm's length of the table, then reached out and gently guided it to her side. "Master Skywalker, allow me to present Artoo-Oh, the original prototype for the R-two astromech line."

Luke's jaw fell. "The *prototype*?"

"So my systems supervisor assures me," Madame Thul said. "I'm told it contains the original Intellex Four droid brain. I hope it will prove helpful in working through Artoo-Detoo's memory problems."

"I'm sure it will!" Mara gasped. "Where did it come from?"

"An abandoned warehouse, apparently," Madame Thul said. "It was owned by Industrial Automaton, which Bornaryn recently purchased. Of course, their records were *almost* completely useless in locating the prototype."

"Industrial Automaton?" Mara asked. "Ghent said the Artoo was an Imperial design."

"Misinformation," Tyko said. "Imperial Intelligence waged a deliberate campaign to obscure the origin of all the Empire's vital military technology."

"Then the designer of the Intellex IV droid brain *wasn't* an Imperial?" Luke asked.

"Not when he worked on the R-series." Tyko shrugged. "Who can say what happened later? He might have become one, or he might have been forced into their service. All our historians could determine was that his identity has been deleted from all known databases regarding the R-series."

"But you have the prototype," Madame Thul said. "I hope you can find what you need there."

"I don't know what to say," Luke said. "Thank you!"

" 'Thank you' will be quite sufficient," Madame Thul said. "Every man should know his mother."

"I'm sure it will be very helpful," Mara said. "But what made you think of it? Artoo's memory problems aren't exactly common knowledge outside of the Jedi order."

Madame Thul smiled. "Tesar and the Wookiee," she said. "I told you—they have good hearts."

FOUR

With dozens of battered transports hanging on the wax-coated walls at every possible angle and swarms of orange worker-Killiks floating war cargo through the microgravity, the Lizil hangar looked even busier than the last time Han and Leia had visited. The largest available berth was a wedge near the top of the sphere, and even that looked barely big enough for the bulky *Dray*-class transport the Solos had borrowed from Lando to complete their disguise. Han rolled the *Swiff* onto its back and began to ease toward the empty spot.

Leia inhaled sharply, then activated the landing cams and studied the copilot's display. "Wait. Our clearance is only half a meter."

"That much?"

"Han, this isn't the *Falcon*."

"You don't have to tell *me*," Han said. "This big tub handles like an asteroid."

"I believe Princess Leia is suggesting you might not be adept enough with this vessel to berth in such a confined space," C-3PO offered from the back of the flight deck. "Your reaction speed and hand-to-eye coordination have degraded twelve percent in the last decade."

"Only when you're around," Han growled. "And quit telling me that. My memory is fine—and so's my driving, metal mouth."

"What I'm *suggesting*," Leia said, "is that it's a tight fit, and you promised Lando you wouldn't scratch his ship."

"And you think he believed me?"

"I *think* we should wait for a larger berth to open up," Leia said. "We're not going to win the Colony's confidence by causing an accident."

"We don't need their confidence." Han jerked a thumb toward the *Swiff*'s huge cargo bay. "When they see that big magcannon we've got back there, they're going to *beg* us to take it out to the front lines."

"That's quite unlikely, Captain Solo," C-3PO said. "Insect species rarely have a sense of charity, so it simply would not occur to them to appeal to your compassion."

"Han means they'll be eager to contract with us," Leia said. "Which is all the more reason to wait. We don't want to overplay our hand. Jaina and Zekk will still be in the front lines when we get there."

"*Wait?*" Han shook his head and continued to ease the *Swiff* toward the landing spot. One of the adjacent transports, an ancient Republic Sienar Systems *Courier*-class, had extended its boarding ramp into the space he intended to occupy, but he wasn't worried. The *Swiff*'s landing struts were far enough apart to straddle the ramp, and the Lizil workers streaming up and down the incline were used to dodging ships. "It could take days for another berth to open."

"It won't take more than an hour." Leia pointed out the top of the cockpit canopy. "That Freight Queen is making ready to leave."

Han looked, but instead of the Freight Queen, his gaze fell on a sharp-looking Mon Calamari Sailfish berthed directly "below" them in the middle of the hangar floor. The ramp was down, and there were two Flakax standing guard outside, keeping watch over a ragged mob of Verpine, Vratix, and Fefze who seemed to be waiting for an audience with the captain of the Sailfish. The sight sent a cold shudder down Han's spine. He did not like seeing that many different insect species gathered in one place—it made him think they were planning something.

Instead of admitting that—he knew Leia already thought he was paranoid when it came to bugs—he asked, "Is that a LongEye booster on the back of that Sailfish's rectenna dish?"

"How should I know?" Leia asked, frowning at the vessel. "And why would I care?"

"Because that's what Lando adds to the sensor package on all his ships," Han said. "Including that Sailfish he sold to Juun and Tarfang."

"The one they traded to the Squibs?"

"That one," Han confirmed.

Leia eyed the Sailfish for a moment, now clearly as interested in the vessel as Han was. Over the years, the Solos had crossed paths many times with the Squibs, an enterprising trio who liked to operate on the edge of any legal system to which they were subject. The last time, however, the trio had gone too far, helping the Killiks slip a swarm of commando bugs aboard the *Admiral Ackbar*.

Finally, Leia said, "I'm sure Defense Force Intelligence will be very interested in the answer—and what its connection might be to all those different insects loitering outside."

"So I'm not the only one who thinks that's weird," Han said.

"It really isn't that far out of the ordinary," C-3PO said. "When one considers that sixty-seven percent of the ship crews in this hangar are insects, it's barely a statistical deviation."

"Sixty-seven percent?" Han repeated. He looked around the hangar more carefully, paying more attention to the crews and their ships. As C-3PO had pointed out, there *were* an awful lot of bugs, and fully half of the vessels had been manufactured by Slayn & Korpil—a Verpine company. "This is beginning to give me the creeps."

"It could be just the war," Leia said. "Maybe the Killiks feel more secure dealing with insects."

"And that doesn't worry you?" Han asked.

"I said *maybe*," Leia replied. "We'll need to take a closer look."

"May I suggest you do that *after* we finish berthing?" C-3PO asked. "We seem to be in danger of setting down on top of another ship!"

Han glanced at his display and saw that one of the strutcams showed a landing skid poised to set down atop the Courier's dorsal observation bubble.

"Relax, chipbrain." Han fired an attitude thruster to spin the *Swiff* back into proper position. "It's a tight fit, so I'm using the Sluissi twist."

"The Sluissi twist?" C-3PO asked. "I have no record of that maneuver in my memory banks."

"You will in a second," Han said.

He fired another thruster to stop their rotation, then felt a faint shudder as the edge of the landing skid grazed the Courier's hull. The worker-bugs scattered, and an instant later the *Swiff* touched down and settled onto its struts. Han sank the anchoring bolts and instructed the ship's droid brain to initiate the automatic shutdown sequence, then looked over to find Leia staring out her side of the cockpit canopy.

"I didn't know Wasbo mandibles could open that wide!" Leia said.

"That *was* a great berthing." Han unbuckled his crash webbing, then went to the back of the flight deck. He turned in a slow circle, displaying the elaborate robes, long-haired wig, and white contact lenses he wore as part of his disguise. "Everything in place?"

"Very Arkanian," Leia said. "Just don't draw attention to your hands. That little finger still looks too thick."

"Yes, the disguise would be far better if you had *removed* your ring finger," C-3PO agreed. "Amputation always results in a more convincing four-fingered hand, and I calculate Lizil's current chance of recognizing us at fifty-seven point eight percent, plus or minus four point three percent."

"That so?" Han asked. "How about we disguise *you* as a one-armed cleaning droid?"

C-3PO drew his head back. "That hardly seems necessary," he said, inspecting the green patina that had been applied to his outer casing. "Droids seldom attract much attention anyway. I'm certain my costume will prove perfectly adequate."

"And so will Han's," Leia said, joining them. She was disguised as a Falleen female, with a face covered in fine green scales, beads and combs adorning her long hair, and a spiny dorsal ridge showing through her shape-hugging jumpsuit. "How do I look?"

"Good—great, even." Han flashed a lustful smile, openly admiring the athletic figure Leia was developing under Saba's rigorous training regimen. "Maybe we have time to—"

"What happened to getting our clearance to enter the war zone?" Leia interrupted. She pushed past him, shaking her head. "At least I know the artificial pheromones are working."

Han followed her aft, fairly certain that it wasn't the pheromones he was reacting to. He and Leia had been married for nearly thirty years, and not a day passed when he still did not ache for her. It was as though his attraction to her had been growing a little stronger every day, until one morning he had awakened to find that it was the force that held his galaxy together. It was not a feeling he really understood—perhaps the cause lay in his admiration of her spirit of adventure, or in his love for her as the mother of his children—but it was something for which he was deeply, immensely grateful.

"You're welcome," Leia said.

"What?" Han frowned. Now, whenever anyone read his thoughts, it made him worry he was on his way to becoming a Joiner. "I didn't say anything."

"Not aloud." Leia turned around and gave him a sly reptilian grin that he found rather . . . stirring. "But I'm a Jedi, remember? I sensed your gratitude through the Force."

"Oh . . . yeah." Han found it embarrassing to get caught being so sentimental, even by Leia—*especially* by Leia. "I was just thinking how grateful I was you wanted to come along."

"And I can tell when you're lying, too." The outer corners of Leia's reptilian brows rose. "And why *shouldn't* I have come? Jaina is my daughter, too."

"Take it easy—I didn't mean anything," Han said. "I was talking about that whole 'Jedi come first' thing Luke is pulling. It couldn't have been easy for you to leave with me."

"Luke has to do what he thinks is best for the order," Leia said, avoiding a direct answer to the question. "We have to do what we think is best for Jaina and Zekk. The two aren't mutually exclusive."

"Right," Han said. "But I get the feeling Luke and Saba would've felt a whole lot better about it if they had actually *sent* us to get Jaina and Zekk back."

"I'm sure they would have." Leia started toward the hatch again. "But I don't know if I can support Luke's decision to make himself Grand Master of the Jedi."

"Come on," Han said. "It's not like he had any other choice—and you know he'll do a good job."

"Of course," Leia said. "But what happens to the order when Luke is gone? That's a lot of power for one being to wield, and power corrupts. The next Grand Master might be more susceptible to its dark influence than Luke."

"Then you're worried about nothing," Han said. "You saw how the Masters were. Without Luke, the order won't last a year."

"I know," Leia said. "And that worries me, too."

They reached the main hatch, where Cakhmaim and Meewalh were waiting in their disguises. The Noghri were doing their best to waddle about and cock their heads in the characteristic expressions of curious Ewoks, but somehow they still looked far too graceful. Han slipped the voice synthesizer into his mouth, then turned and spoke to the Noghri in a deep, booming tone.

"Try to be a little clumsy," he said. "Maybe drop some stuff and trip once or twice."

The pair looked at Han as though he had asked Ewoks to fly.

"Well, do what you can," Han said.

He lowered the boarding ramp and nearly gagged on the clammy, too-sweet air that rolled through the hatchway. The cacophony of ticking and thrumming was even louder than the last time he was here. A dozen waist-high Killiks with deep orange thoraxes and blue abdomens appeared at the bottom of the ramp and started to ascend without requesting permission.

Han stepped aside and—gritting his teeth at their lack of ship etiquette—waved the bugs aboard. They brushed past him and immediately began to spread out through the *Swiff,* running their feathery antennae over every available surface and clacking their mandibles in interest.

Han waved them toward the stern. "This way, my friends," he said, trying to give his best impression of a down-on-his-luck Arkanian technolord. "We have something truly special for you."

Three of the Killiks thrummed their chests and came over, but the rest continued to explore the ship. Han motioned Cakhmaim and Meewalh to keep an eye on the others, then smiled and led the way back to the main cargo hold. Knowing the insects would investigate every meter of the ship, he and Leia and the Noghri had taken pains to shoot any hint of their true identity out the disposal tube, but he still had beads of nervous sweat trickling down his ribs. Given how things had gone in the Utegetu Nebula, it seemed unlikely that Lizil would react well to discovering who he and Leia really were.

When they reached the cargo hold, Han made a show of depressing the slap-pad that opened the hatch. "I present the Magcannon Max, the finest piece of magnetic coil artillery in the galaxy."

The three Killiks stepped through the hatch, then stopped inside and craned their necks back to stare up at the weapon's armored housing—all three stories of it. Han nodded to Leia, who went over to the base of the weapon and began a carefully rehearsed sales pitch in the sultry—if completely artificial—voice of a Falleen.

"The economical Magcannon Max delivers a planetary-defense-grade firepower in a self-contained package. With a fully shielded housing and an internal sensor suite, this naughty girl can find a bombarding Star Destroyer as easily as she can spill its guts."

Leia flashed a winsome Falleen smile, then turned to lead the way toward the weapon's giant, telescoping barrels. Instead of following, the Killiks turned to Han and began to thrum their thoraxes.

"They would like to know how they move a weapon of this size," C-3PO translated. "Does it have its own propulsion system?"

Han addressed the bugs directly. "*You* don't move it. We transport and install wherever you need it—even in the war zone." Han gave them a regal Arkanian smile. "Our service package is superior."

All three bugs turned and left the hold.

Han frowned and started after them. "So you'll take it?"

The last Killik in line turned and fixed Han with its bulbous green eyes. "*Rrrub uur.*" It shook its head emphatically. "*Buubb rruuur uubbu, rbu ubb rur.*"

"Oh dear," C-3PO said. "She says the Colony has no use for weapons emplacements. The Chiss are overrunning their worlds too fast."

The Killik started up the corridor again, chest rumbling.

"But the repeating blasters and thermal detonators in the secret weapons locker inside the wall behind the main engineering terminal will prove very useful," C-3PO translated. "Lizil has left a dozen shine-balls and fifty waxes of golden membrosia at the foot of the boarding ramp in exchange."

"That's all?" Han followed them to the ramp, where Cakhmaim and Meewalh were already bringing the shine-balls and membrosia aboard—still looking far too graceful for Ewoks. "We didn't come all the way—"

Han's objection came to an abrupt end when he found himself unable to continue down the ramp after the bugs, held immobile by the Force.

Leia came and took him by the arm. "Lord Rysto, there's no use forcing the situation," she cooed in her Falleen voice. "If Lizil doesn't want the gun, we'll just have to find another way to sell it."

Leia's words began to calm Han immediately. He was allowing his frustration to affect his judgment—and that could be very dangerous indeed, given how deep they were inside enemy territory.

Han placed his hand over Leia's. "Thank you, Syrule—you're right." He looked down toward the Mon Calamari Sailfish sitting below them in the middle of the hangar floor. "And I think I know just where to start looking."

FIVE

With most of the Jedi order off chasing pirates or reconnoitering for Admiral Bwua'tu in the Utegetu Nebula, the Knights' Billet on the tenth floor of the Jedi Temple was next to deserted. The only Jedi Knights present were the trio Luke had ordered to meet him here—Tesar, Lowbacca, and Tahiri—and the air had a stale, uncirculated smell. Tesar and Lowbacca were waiting in the conversation salon near the snack galley. Tahiri was in the exercise pen at the far end of the suite, working on a lightsaber form with thirteen fist-sized remotes whirling around her. Judging by the smoke haze visible through the transparisteel walls, the remotes' sting-bolts were set high enough to inflict burns.

Luke leaned close to Cilghal, who stood next to him with an armload of sensor equipment. "Can we do this in the salon?"

"We can detect aural fluctuations anywhere," she said, nodding. "But you know that won't answer your real question."

"It'll help," Luke said. "If their minds are still joined, then it's more likely they have fallen under Raynar's control."

"And if we find their minds *aren't* joined?"

"Then I'll know that telling Madame Thul about the debate over Raynar was their own choice," Luke said. "And I'll take action."

Luke led the way toward the salon. He could feel how concerned Cilghal was by his angry reaction to the Jedi Knights' betrayal, but he felt amazingly certain of himself. The other Masters had left him no choice but to play the Grand Master fully—to run the order as he thought best and demand full obedience from everyone in it.

As Luke and Cilghal drew near, Tesar and Lowbacca rose from the snack table where they were sitting and watched the two Masters approach with an unblinking, insect-like stare. They were both wearing their formal robes, but not their equipment belts or lightsabers. Tahiri remained in the exercise pen, concentrating on her lightsaber form and paying no attention to the arrival of the two Masters.

Luke motioned Cilghal and her equipment to the adjacent table, then took a seat opposite the pair and motioned them to sit. He did not summon Tahiri from the exercise pen. Madame Thul had not actually named Tahiri as one of the Jedi who had warned her about the plans to target Raynar, so Luke was content to let the young woman continue exercising—for now.

He remained quiet, studying the two Jedi Knights across the table while Cilghal completed her preparations. Nothing in the Force suggested they were under the Colony's control, but that meant little. Unless Raynar happened to be exerting the Colony's Will at that very moment, Luke suspected there would be nothing for him to sense.

Lowbacca watched Cilghal prepare her equipment, his scientific mind seemingly more interested in her calibrations than in the reason he had been recalled to the Jedi Temple. Tesar, on the other hand, was so nervous that he began to hiss and smack his lips in an effort to keep from drooling.

Finally, Cilghal nodded that she was ready. Luke did not bother to explain the equipment. Like all Jedi who spent more than a few days among the Killiks, Lowbacca and Tesar had submitted to dozens of aural activity scans as part of Cilghal's research.

"I'm sure you know why I ordered you to meet me here," Luke said.

Lowbacca nodded and groaned, saying that it probably had something to do with what they had told Aryn Thul.

"We can explain," Tesar added.

"I doubt it." Luke's tone was sharp. "But please try."

"We had no choice," Tesar said.

Lowbacca growled his agreement, reasserting the argument that destroying the Colony would be immoral.

"And so would assazzinating a friend," Tesar added. "Raynar was our hunt-mate. Killing him would be wrong."

"Maybe," Luke said. "But that decision isn't yours to make."

Lowbacca countered with a long, stubborn rumble.

"Jedi Knights *do* serve the Force," Luke answered. "But now they serve it through the Jedi order. We've seen what happens when everyone goes in their own direction. We paralyze ourselves, and our enemies flourish."

Lowbacca rowled the opinion that being paralyzed was better than following a yuugrr out on its limb.

Luke frowned. Yuugrrs were dim-witted predators famous for stealing Wookiee children out of their beds, then trying to shake their pursuit by going out on a thin limb. More often than not, the limb broke, plunging the yuugrr, the child, and sometimes the pursuers into the depths of the Kashyyyk forest.

"If you're calling me a yuugrr, I'm not sure I follow your analogy." It was a struggle for Luke to keep an even tone; he felt so betrayed by the pair that it required an act of will to remain interested in their reasons. "What's it supposed to mean?"

"Not that *you* are a yuugrr," Tahiri said, joining them. Sweat was still pouring down her face, and there were several holes where the remotes had burned through her jumpsuit and raised burn blisters. "You're *following* one—and you're taking the whole order with you. We had to do something."

"*We?*" Luke asked. He resisted the urge to send Tesar to fetch some bacta salve from the first-aid kit. This was no time to appear nurturing, and besides, Tahiri's mind still had enough Yuuzhan Vong in it that she probably enjoyed the pain. "Madame Thul didn't mention your name."

"Only because these two didn't tell me what they were doing." Tahiri shot Lowbacca and Tesar a dirty look. "Otherwise, I would have been right there with them."

Luke did not bother to hide his disappointment. "I appreciate your honesty, but I *still* don't understand."

"It's not complicated." Tahiri took a seat between Lowbacca and Tesar, rubbing her forearms against theirs in the Killik manner. "You listen to Jacen as though he were a senior Master, and his advice can't be trusted. He has his own agenda."

"*Jacen* isn't the one who broke confidentiality," Luke retorted. "And he doesn't know what I've decided about Raynar, either."

"But you do lizten to Jacen," Tesar rasped. "You cannot deny *that.*"

Lowbacca grunted his agreement, adding that both Luke and Mara gave more weight to Jacen's opinion than to anyone else's. They seemed to think, Lowbacca continued, that taking a five-year furlough made him a better Jedi Knight than the Jedi who had been serving the order and the Alliance all along.

"Jacen's experience is unique," Luke said. "We all know that."

Even to him this sounded more like an excuse than a reason. The truth was that he valued his nephew's opinion because of what Jacen had learned about other Force-using traditions—but also because Jacen was the only person whom Ben would trust to be his guide to the Force. And that certainly *did* make Jacen a favorite in the Skywalker family—they were parents, after all.

Luke glanced over at Cilghal, reaching out to her in the Force with a single question in mind. She raised a webbed hand and gave it an ambiguous flutter that Luke interpreted to suggest a moderate correlation in the aural activity of the three Jedi Knights—enough to suggest there was still a link, but certainly not the complete fusion typical of Joiners.

Luke returned his gaze to Tahiri and the others. "But I value your opinions just as highly. If Jacen has a different agenda, what is it?"

All three Jedi Knights let out nervous throat-clicks. Then Tahiri said, "We haven't been able to figure that out."

"But it had zomething to do with the attack on Supply Depot Thrago," Tesar said.

Lowbacca added a long growl noting that Jaina had refused to fly with her brother since the attack. She was convinced Jacen had deliberately been trying to provoke the Chiss.

"I'm sure he was," Luke said. "The way he explained it to me, that was the only way to prevent the Chiss from launching the surprise attack he saw in his vision."

Lowbacca and Tesar shot uncomfortable glances at each other, but Tahiri kept her unblinking eyes fixed on Luke.

"We think Jacen may be lying about his vision."

Luke's brow shot up. "I didn't sense any lies when he told *me* about it."

"Were you trying to?"

"Jacen is very good at hiding his emotionz," Tesar added.

Lowbacca nodded and grunted that half the time, even Jaina could not feel him in the Force anymore.

"Then *you've* caught him lying?" Luke demanded. "These are very serious charges."

"We haven't actually *caught* him," Tahiri said.

Lowbacca oorrwwalled a clarification, explaining that the facts just did not add up.

"The Chisz were still stocking the depot with fuel when we attacked," Tesar added.

"And there were half a dozen frigates mothballed there," Tahiri finished. "They hadn't even fired the main reactors."

"Your point being?" Luke was growing impatient with their innuendo. It was the favorite weapon of the character assassin, and he expected better of Jedi. "Had Jacen told you the Chiss surprise attack was imminent?"

Tesar and Lowbacca glanced at each other, then Tahiri shook her head. "No, Jacen never said *that*."

"But when the Chisz *did* attack, their assault was improvised," Tesar said. "They did not have enough forward support."

Lowbacca nodded emphatically, adding that the secret weapon they had deployed against the Iesei had obviously been rushed through development. Otherwise, the bomb would not have failed to detonate on its initial use.

"The failed bomb—and everything else you've told me—tends to *support* Jacen's vision, not cast doubt on it," Luke said. He had found the trio's report about the failed bomb as worrying as it was incomplete. Given the Chiss willingness to deploy Alpha Red during the last war—and to run the risk of wiping out the entire galaxy along with the Yuuzhan Vong—he viewed the mysterious bomb in a very ominous light. "Clearly, the Chiss *have* been making war preparations. Forcing their hand may have been the only way to salvage the situation."

"You're saying Jacen did the right thing?" Tahiri gasped. "Even if the Chisz were *not* ready to attack?"

Luke nodded. "Sometimes it's better to hit first—especially if you see the other guy reaching for a thermal detonator."

He stared into the unblinking eyes of each Jedi Knight for several moments, wondering where he could have gone so wrong in their instruction. Perhaps he had been too hesitant to impose his own values on such a diverse group of students, or perhaps he had failed to present them with enough moot dilemmas to develop a proper moral center. All he knew for certain was that he had failed them *somewhere,* that he had not prepared them to face the soul-corrupting ruthlessness of the war against the Yuuzhan Vong, or instilled in them the strength to withstand the power of Raynar Thul's Will.

After a few moments of silence, Luke stood and stared down at the three Jedi. "You are not going to blame Jacen for your actions. Even if he *had* lied about his vision—and I don't believe he did—what you did was inexcusable. In going to Madame Thul with this, you betrayed me, you betrayed the other Masters, and you betrayed the Jedi order."

The three Jedi Knights were not disconcerted in the slightest. Tahiri and Tesar met Luke's gaze with an unblinking glare that was somewhere between anger and disbelief, and Lowbacca let out a very Killik-like chest rumble that suggested he was more angry than remorseful.

"You are a fool to place your faith in Jacen!" Tesar rasped. "He is nothing but a shenbit in a snake'z skin. You trust him with your hatchling—"

Lowbacca snarled a warning to the Barabel, telling him that he was only going to make Luke angrier by mentioning *that*.

"Mentioning what?" Luke demanded.

"Nothing," Tahiri said. "We didn't see it for ourselves, so we don't even know if it's true."

"If *what's* true?" Luke demanded.

Lowbacca gave Tesar a sideways glare, then grooowled a long reply explaining that Jaina and Zekk had caught Jacen blocking some of Ben's memories.

"*Blocking* memories?" Luke asked.

"Ben saw something upsetting," Tahiri explained. "Jaina and Zekk caught Jacen using the Force to prevent him from remembering it."

Luke scowled, the anger he already felt rising to rage. "If you're making this up—"

"We are not," Tesar insisted. "Jaina and Zekk saw it. They saw Jacen rubbing Ben's brow and felt something in the Force."

Lowbacca weighed in with a low rumble, explaining that Jacen had told them it was a technique he learned from the Adepts of the White Current.

"I never heard of anything like that from them," Luke said. "What memory was Jacen trying to block?"

Tahiri shrugged. "You'll have to ask him—he's not much into sharing these days."

Luke could sense that Tahiri was telling the truth, but even without the Force he would have believed her. While Jacen had returned from his five-year sojourn with remarkable skills, he had also returned a far more mysterious person, often deflecting or flatly refusing to answer questions about his experiences. It was as though he believed that no one who had not taken such a retreat for himself was entitled to share in the wisdom it yielded.

"I'll certainly ask Jacen about the memory blocking," Luke said. "But I fail to see what that has to do with *your* betrayal."

Although he was still fuming inside—especially at the trio's efforts to deflect his anger onto Jacen—Luke paused to give them an opportunity to make the connection for him.

When they did not, he asked, "Then I am to assume that you're not suggesting Jacen has blocked *my* memory of something?"

Even Tahiri's eyes widened with shock, and Tesar said, "Yesz—I mean no—we have no reason to believe he has blocked *your* memoriez."

Luke looked to the other Jedi Knights for confirmation, then nodded when they remained silent.

"Very well," he said. "Before coming here today, I gave this matter a great deal of thought, and nothing you've said has convinced me I was wrong."

Lowbacca began to moan, asserting that everything they did was for the good of the order—

"I know that's what you think," Luke said, raising a hand to silence him. "But what *I* think is that you would rather believe Jacen has betrayed his family, friends, and the order than admit that the Colony is on the brink of plunging the galaxy into the eternal war he saw in his vision."

Tesar ruffled his scales. "That is zilly! We are not under the Colony'z influence!"

"I'm sorry, Jedi Sebatyne," Cilghal said, speaking for the first time since the discussion had begun. "But we can't know that for certain. Your minds *are* still connected, at least rudimentarily, and Raynar was able to exert a considerable influence over you even *before* you were exposed to the collective mind."

"So you're going to base your decision on the *possibility* that we're Joiners?" Tahiri stared at Luke as she asked this, her green eyes as hard and emotionless as olivon. "That's not like you, Master Skywalker."

"If you're asking me to give you the benefit of the doubt, you're right," Luke said. "There are many questions about *why* you betrayed the order, but there are none as to *whether* you did. You tried to influence my decision by bringing pressure to bear from Madame Thul."

The three Jedi Knights continued to stare at him, their emotionless eyes neither blinking nor flicking away as they awaited the rest.

"Your actions cast serious doubt on your desire to remain Jedi Knights," Luke said. "I suggest you go to Dagobah to reflect on the subject."

"*Dagobah?*" Tesar rasped. "You are sending us on *vacation?*"

"On retreat," Luke corrected. "To meditate on what it means to be a Jedi Knight."

Tahiri and Lowbacca exchanged glances, then Tahiri asked, "For how long?"

"Until I send for you," Luke replied. "And if you have any desire at all to remain members of the Jedi order, you *will* obey me in this. I'll take any failure—for any reason whatsoever—as your resignation."

SIX

Leia watched in confusion as Han started down the wall, picking his way through the crowded transaction hangar of the Lizil nest toward the suspicious Sailfish. With Defense Force Intelligence actively searching for the Squibs, the Lizil nest seemed a likely place for the trio to take refuge—and Han clearly intended to use that fact to find Jaina. What Leia did not understand was *how*—and, if she knew her husband, neither did Han.

Leia instructed C-3PO and the Noghri to stay with the *Swiff*, then descended the ramp and started after Han, her feet *squeck-squeck*ing in the soft wax that lined the interior of the nest. It took only a few steps before the microgravity, the lack of perspective, and the cloying smell began to unsettle her stomach. She clamped her jaws shut and focused her thoughts on Han, trying to guess what outrageous plan he was developing—and whether it had any chance of working.

A few steps later, Leia caught up to Han and leaned close. "Han, what are you doing?"

"Maybe *they're* interested in a Magcannon Max." Han pointed at the Sailfish, now close enough for a visual inspection. The black box behind the rectenna dish was, indeed, one of Lando's distinctive LongEye boosters. "It looks like they're dealers."

"Have you lost your *mind*?" Leia hissed. "We can't let the Squibs know we're here!"

"Sure we can," Han said. "They're not going to tell anybody."

"They're not?"

"No way." Han glanced around, then whispered, "Juun and Tar-fang used to work for those furry little backstabbers. And the last thing they want is for me to tell Lizil that it was *their* employees who helped me and Luke escape Saras on Woteba."

"You don't think they've already told Raynar?" Leia asked.

"Are you kidding?" Han asked. "These are *Squibs*. They'd never admit they played a part in anything that went wrong—especially something that fouled up the Dark Nest's plans."

Leia raised her brow—and felt the scales of her artificial Falleen face ripple in response. "And since they didn't admit it right away—"

"It'll look really bad if *we* tell the Killiks now," Han finished.

"That's what I like about you."

"Handsome as well as rich?" Han asked.

Leia shook her head. "Resourceful . . . and just a little bent."

She gave him a coy smile—then felt a small vibration between her shoulder blades as her disguise reacted to her expression and dispensed a shot of attraction pheromones. A sparkle of lust immediately came to Han's eyes, and he cast a longing glance back toward the *Swiff*.

"Easy, boy!" Leia hissed. *"Later."*

"Okay." Even in his Arkanian disguise, Han looked crestfallen. "Will you wear the costume?"

Leia had to resist the temptation to hit him, for they had reached the hangar "floor" and were in full view of dozens of bustling Lizil. They circled around an old Gallofree light transport, then pushed through the small crowd of insects waiting outside the Sailfish.

Leia followed Han to the foot of the boarding ramp, where they stopped in front of two huge Flakax guards. Standing a little taller than a Wookiee, with sharp beak-like proboscises, black chitinous shells, and long ovoid abdomens hanging beneath their thoraxes, the pair made truly intimidating sentries—especially since Flakax who left their homeworlds tended to become psychopaths.

"We're here to see the Squibs," Han said, hiding the fear that Leia could sense behind the bluster of an Arkanian technolord. "Tell them they still owe us for Pavo Prime."

The sentries' huge, compound eyes studied Leia and Han indifferently.

"It wouldn't be wise to keep us waiting," Leia pressed. "We happen to be old friends."

This drew a chorus of amused clacks and hisses from the insect crews waiting outside the Sailfish, and one of the Flakax held out a three-pincered hand.

"Appointment vouchers cost fifty credits each."

"Appointment vouchers?" Han repeated.

"You expect us to stand here for nothing?" the second Flakax demanded.

Leia stepped forward, craning her neck back to stare up at the Flakax's wedge-shaped head. "We don't need an appointment voucher," she said, using the Force to influence the insect's mind. "We're expected."

"They don't need a voucher," the first Flakax said. He stepped aside and motioned the Solos aboard. "The Directors are expecting them."

The second remained where he was, gnashing his mandibles and blocking the base of the ramp. "They are? *Now?*"

"Yeah." Han pulled a credit chit from his pocket. "What's the going price for being expected? Ten?"

The Flakax flattened his antennae. "Twenty-five."

"Twenty-five!" Han objected. "That's—"

"A paltry amount, not worth the effort to negotiate," Leia interrupted. "Why don't we just add it to the Directors' account, Lord Rysto? That way everyone will be happy."

"Very well." Han continued to glare at the Flakax, but passed the credits over and slipped back into the character of a haughty Arkanian. "If the Squibs object, I'll instruct them to bring the matter up with you."

The Flakax gave a little abdomen shudder, but stepped aside and waved Leia and Han through the Sailfish's air lock. The air aboard the vessel was stale and musky, and the broad oval corridors typical of Mon Calamari designs were so packed with weapons, power packs, and armor that it was only possible to walk single file. Leia followed Han into the forward salon, where a pair of Verpine pilots stood facing the interior of a large, curved table piled high with trinkets and gadgets. On the other side of the table, a single Lizil Killik stood behind three seated Squibs.

". . . grateful for the cargo," one of the Verpine was saying. "But we need more delivery time. If anything goes wrong, we won't make the date."

"What could go wrong?" the Squib on the left asked. With graying fur, a wrinkled snout, and red bags under his big brown eyes, Grees looked as though he had aged sixty years in the thirty that had passed since Leia had first met him. "Just follow the route we give you. Everything will be fine."

"It's the Chiss that concern us, Director," the second Verpine explained. "Tenupe is on the front lines, you know."

"That's why we saved this run for *you*," the Squib on the right said. One of his ears no longer stood up straight, instead lying at an angle like a broken antenna. And his voice was so harsh and raspy that Han barely recognized it as Sligh's. "We wouldn't trust just *anyone* with this, you know. We have placed our complete faith in you. Consider it a gift."

The two Verpine glanced at each other nervously; then the first said, "We've heard the Chiss are moving fast. What happens if they overrun the base before we deliver? There's no one else out there who would want your TibannaX—especially not so much."

Han's heart began to pound in excitement. As far as he knew, there was only one use for TibannaX: it was fuel for Jedi StealthXs.

"Ark'ik, you came to us begging for a cargo, but all you have done since we granted it to you is ask *What if this? What if that?*" Emala said. Seated between Grees and Sligh, her eyes were covered in a milky film, and the tip of her nose was cracked and bleeding. She shook her head sadly and looked away from the two Verpine. "Honestly, we are beginning to think you aren't grateful."

The antennae of both Verpine went flat against their heads. "No, we're very grateful, Director," Ark'ik said. "We just don't want to fail you."

"And we don't want that either," Sligh said. "We thought you two were ready to be major players in the war business. But if you're not interested . . ."

"*We'll* take the cargo," Han said, stepping into the cabin.

The first Verpine—Ark'ik—turned with fury in his dark eyes, but his anger swiftly changed to confusion as Leia slinked toward him in her Falleen costume.

"I hope you don't mind." She touched him through the Force, implanting the suggestion that she was only repeating what he already believed. "But you don't need this run. Too many things can go wrong."

"Mind? Why should we mind?" Ark'ik asked. "Too many things can go wrong—"

"Ark'ik!" The second Verpine slapped the first in the back of the head. "Fool! She's using her pheromones on you."

Leia did not bother to correct him. One of the reasons she had chosen a Falleen costume was that it would camouflage many of her Force manipulations as the result of pheromones.

"So?" Ark'ik asked his companion. "This run doesn't have anything to do with *our* fight anyway."

"So be quiet!" The second Verpine turned to the Squibs. "We'll take the run, Director—but we may need another wax. It's a long trip."

"Another wax?" Grees was immediately up and standing in his chair. "Who do you think you *are*? You'll take the three waxes we're giving you and be grateful."

"There's a war on!" Sligh added. "We're lucky we can get *any* black 'brosia out of the Utegetu."

The second Verpine let out a long throat rasp, then dropped his gaze. "Forgive us, Director. I didn't mean to be greedy."

Emala shook her head sadly. "You disappoint us, Ra'tre. We give you a chance to be a part of history, and you try to take advantage." She motioned toward a corridor, and a much younger Squib with red-brown fur and black ear tufts entered the salon. "Krafte will tend to the details. Be sure to tip generously. It makes his charts more accurate."

"Of course." Ra'tre bowed nervously. "Thank you!"

He took Ark'ik's arm and dragged him after the young Squib.

Once they were gone, Han joined Leia in front of the table. "Quite an operation you have here," he said. "Brokering war cargo *and* pushing black membrosia? The Hutts could learn a few things from you."

Emala sat up with pride. "You're not the first to say so."

"Not that it's any business of yours," Grees said. He leaned forward, his nose twitching and his eyes narrow. "Do we *know* you?"

Before Han could launch into his indignant act, the Killik standing behind the Squibs began to rumble its thorax—no doubt explaining that Lizil had already "transacted" with them.

Leia stepped closer to the Squibs' table. "Actually, you might remember us from Pavo Prime," she said. "And before that, we worked together on Tatooine."

"Tatooine?" Sligh reached across the table, then took Leia's hand and rubbed it across his cheek. His ears went flat against his head. "You!"

"*Brub?*" Lizil demanded.

"We're old friends." Leia kept her gaze fixed on the Squibs, who were all trying to slowly lower their hands out of sight below the table—no doubt reaching for their holdout blasters. Though the possibility had not occurred to her before, the trio would have good reason to assume that she and Han had come to retaliate for the part the Squibs had played in the capture of the *Admiral Ackbar*. "There's nothing to be upset about—isn't that right, Sligh?"

"We'll s-s-see," Sligh stammered.

"Just don't try anything," Grees warned. "You're not as quick as you used to be."

Lizil cocked its head and stared at Leia out of one bulbous green eye. *"Uuu rru buur?"*

"Sligh is nervous because we haven't seen each other in a long time," Leia said, taking a guess at what the insect had asked.

"And Sylune and I looked a lot different back then," Han added.

"I'm sure our appearance must be shocking," Leia said to the Squibs. "But there's no need to be alarmed. We're not here to start trouble—as long as no one else starts it, either."

She cast a meaningful glare at the Squibs' hands, and all three returned their palms to the edge of the table.

"Then why *are* you here?" Grees demanded. "Lizil already told you the Colony doesn't need a magcannon."

"Can't an old friend pay a social call?" Han smiled and fixed Grees with a threatening glare. "I just wanted to tell you that I ran into a couple of your contract employees not so long ago. They were a great help to me and a good friend of mine." He glanced at the Killik behind them. "I thought maybe I should tell you about it."

"No!" all three Squibs said together.

"We mean there's no need," Sligh added quickly. "We already know everything."

"You're sure?" Leia asked. "Even about how they—"

"We *heard*!" Grees said. He turned toward the same corridor from which Emala's son Krafte had emerged. On cue, a small female with silky black fur appeared. "Now we really are very busy. Seneki will see you out."

"That's all the time you have for your friends?" Han turned toward the black female and shooed her back toward the corridor. "I'm hurt!"

Seneki froze halfway into the salon and looked to Emala for instruction.

"Time is money," Emala said, waving Seneki forward. "You understand."

"Not really," Leia said. She held her hand out to Seneki—presumably Emala's daughter—and used the Force to hold her back, drawing a gasp of surprise from the young Squib. "But I'm beginning to think we really should talk about your employees. You could take a lesson from them in politeness."

The three Squibs sighed and looked at each other, then Emala shook her head and said, "You *know* how valuable our time is, and our schedule is very tight today. You'll just have to buy another—"

"Maybe we can make it worth your while," Leia interrupted.

"I doubt that," Sligh said. "If you'll just leave—"

"We're not leaving," Han growled. He turned back to Leia. "You were saying, Syrule?"

Leia smiled and propped her hand on her hip. "Well, I'm sure the Colony wouldn't want our magcannon to end up in the hands of the Chiss or the Galactic Alliance."

Lizil clacked its mandibles in a very definite "No!"

"Then maybe we should sell it to our old friends," Leia said. "I'm sure *they* could find a safe buyer for it—and that way, we would be free to run a load of cargo to Tenupe."

"Tenupe is in a war zone," Sligh said. "The Colony only allows insect crews to run supplies into war zones."

"So talk to them for us," Han said. "It looks like you've got plenty of pull around here."

"Ruruuruur bub?" the Killik asked.

"Lizil wants to know why you're so interested in Tenupe," Emala translated.

"We're not," Han answered. "It's the StealthXs we want to see."

The Squibs, who had almost certainly figured out that Han and Leia wanted to see Jaina and Zekk, rolled their eyes.

But Lizil asked, *"Bub?"*

"We have a client who could benefit from the technology," Leia answered. She smiled conspiratorially. "And I'm sure it would only *help* the Colony's war effort if the Galactic Alliance suddenly had to divert even more resources to chasing pirates in stealth ships."

Lizil's antennae tipped forward in interest; then the insect turned to Grees. *"Uubbuu ruub buur?"*

Grees sighed, then said, "Sure, we'll vouch for 'em." His sagging red eyes glared blaster bolts at Leia. "And if they disappoint you, we'll make sure they take their secrets to the grave with them."

SEVEN

Luke usually sensed when the outer door to his office suite in the Jedi Temple was about to open. Today, however, he was so engrossed in Ghent's work that he did not realize he had a visitor until someone stopped at the entrance to the inner office and politely cleared his throat. The micrograbber in Ghent's hand jerked ever so slightly, and a tiny *tick* sounded somewhere deep inside R2-D2's casing. The slicer uttered a colorful smuggler's oath—something about Twi'lek Hutt-slime wrestlers, which he had no doubt learned during his stint in Talon Karrde's smuggling syndicate. Then he slowly, steadily backed the micrograbber out of R2-D2's deep-reserve data compartment.

"That didn't sound good," Luke said. Without turning around, he motioned whoever was at the door to wait there. "How bad is it?"

Ghent turned his tattooed face toward Luke, his pale eyes appearing huge and bug-like through his magnispecs. With his unkempt blue hair and tattered jumpsuit, the scrawny man looked more like a jolt-head from the underbelly of Talos City than the Alliance's best slicer.

"How bad is what?"

"Whatever it is you're swearing about," Mara said. She was kneeling beside Ghent, holding a handful of ancient circuits they had taken from the R2 prototype Aryn Thul had given them. "It sounded like you dropped the omnigate."

"I heard it hit inside Artoo," Luke said helpfully.

Ghent nodded. "Me, too," he said, as though it were an everyday occurrence.

He retrieved a penglow from his tool kit and shined it down into R2-D2's casing, slowly playing the beam over the internal circuitry without answering the original question. Luke accepted the neglect as the price of genius and reluctantly turned toward the entrance to his office, where his nephew Jacen was waiting in his customary garb of boots, jumpsuit, and sleeveless cloak. Now that he had shaved off the beard he had grown during his five-year absence, he looked more than ever like his parents, with Leia's big brown eyes and Han's lopsided smirk.

"Twool said you wanted to see me." Jacen glanced toward Ghent and Mara. "But if I've come at a bad time—"

"No, we need to talk." Luke motioned him toward the outer office. "Let's go out here. I don't want to disturb Ghent."

"That's okay," Ghent said, surprising Luke by reacting to a remark that *wasn't* directed at him. "You're not disturbing me."

"I think Luke needs to talk with Jacen privately," Mara explained.

"Oh." Ghent continued to work, peering through his magnispecs into R2-D2's data compartment. "Doesn't he want to see if the omnigate works?"

"Of course," Luke said. The omnigate was a sliver of circuitry Ghent had found inside the prototype droid. Supposedly, it was a sort of hardware passkey that would unlock all of R2-D2's sequestered files. "You mean you're ready?"

"Almost," Ghent said. "And you'd better not leave. The omnigate is pretty deteriorated—it might not last long."

"You've figured out a way to unlock Artoo?" Jacen started across the room without seeking permission from Luke. "You can bring up a holo of my grandmother?"

"Sure." Ghent pulled his micrograbbers out of R2-D2's data compartment, then flipped up his magnispecs. "Either that or lose Artoo's entire memory to a security wipe."

"At least the risks are clear," Luke said, following Jacen back over to the slicer's side. This was hardly the reason he had sent for his nephew, but Jacen had almost as much right to see the lost holos as Luke himself. "Which is more likely?"

Ghent shrugged. "Depends on how much you trust the Thul woman. Her story makes sense."

Luke waited while Ghent's gaze grew increasingly distant . . . as it often did when the slicer actually had to discuss something.

After a moment, Luke prompted, "*But?*"

Ghent's eyes snapped back into focus, and he restarted the conversation where he had left off. "But if that isn't the real Intellex Four prototype in there, the omnigate will trigger every security system your droid has. We'll be lucky if *our* memories aren't erased, overwritten, and reformatted."

"So it depends entirely on whether Aryn Thul is being honest with us?" Mara asked.

"And on whoever sold *her* the prototype," Ghent said. "Droid antiquers are always getting crisped by counterfeit prototypes."

"That's one thing we don't have to worry about," Mara said. "Nobody is going to swindle Aryn Thul. That woman is a business rancor."

Luke turned to Jacen. "What do you think?"

Jacen finally looked surprised. *"Me?"*

"You have an interest in this, too," Luke said. The conversation he wanted to have with his nephew would be difficult enough, so it seemed wise to reassure Jacen that he was still held in high regard. "You should be part of the decision."

"Thanks . . . I think." Jacen furrowed his brow, then said, "Madame Thul certainly has reason to be suspicious of you—even angry. But I don't see any advantage to her in erasing Artoo's memory."

"So you think we should try?" Luke asked. The answer had been exactly what he *wasn't* looking for, relying as it did on calculation and logic instead of the insight and empathy that had been Jacen's special gifts before the war with the Yuuzhan Vong had changed him. "You want to take the chance?"

Jacen nodded. "I don't see that Madame Thul could gain anything by slipping you a counterfeit omnigate."

"That's not what Luke asked," Mara said, apparently sensing Luke's disappointment. "He wants to know how you *feel* about it."

"How I *feel*?" Jacen's eyes lit with comprehension. "That's a silly question. How do you *think* I feel?"

Luke smiled. "I'll take that as a go-ahead." He turned to Ghent and nodded. "Do it."

"Okay, nobody even breathe for a second." Ghent flipped his magnispecs down. "I need to seat the omnigate."

As Ghent lowered his micrograbbers into R2-D2's data compartment, Luke's heart began to beat so hard that he half feared the pounding would break the slicer's concentration. As much as he wanted to learn his mother's fate, more depended on the omnigate than filling the gaps in his family history.

During his stay on Woteba, the Dark Nest had insinuated that Mara might be trying to hide her involvement—during her days as the Emperor's Hand—in the death of Luke's mother. Of course,

Luke had realized even then that the insinuation was unfounded. But the known facts left just enough room to keep doubt alive, and doubt could be a very stubborn enemy . . . especially when it was bolstered by the Dark Nest.

Lomi Plo thrived on doubt. If she sensed any doubt in a person's mind at all, she could hide behind it in the Force and make herself effectively invisible. That was how she had nearly killed Luke the last time they met . . . and if he hoped to defeat *her* the next time, he had to cast aside all doubt—in Mara, in himself, in his fellow Jedi. To a greater extent than he had admitted to anyone except Mara, that was one of the driving forces behind his reorganization of the Jedi order. He simply could not allow any doubt in his mind about where it was going.

A few moments later, Ghent let out a sigh of relief and pulled the micrograbbers from the data compartment.

"Okay, you can breathe now," he said. "The gate is attached to the sequestered circuit."

He flipped Artoo's primary circuit breaker, and the little droid came to life with a sharp squeal.

"It's okay, Artoo," Luke said. "Ghent has just been working on those memory problems you've been having."

R2-D2 swiveled his dome around, studying the stacks of prototype parts surrounding him, then trained his photoreceptor on Ghent and beeped suspiciously.

"He didn't add anything you need to worry about," Luke said. "Now, show us what happened between my mother and father after he finished in the Jedi Temple."

Artoo started to squeak a refusal—then let out an alarmed whistle. He spun his photoreceptor toward Luke and reluctantly chirped a question.

"Your parameters are too vague," Ghent chastised. "He probably has a thousand files that fit that description."

"I mean after the file he showed to Han and me in the Saras rehabilitation center." Luke tried to remain patient; he suspected R2-D2 was just stalling to buy time to defeat the omnigate, but it was possible that the droid really did need a more specific reference. "It's the record you stole from the Temple's security system, where my father supervised the slaughter of the students."

Though Luke had already told Jacen and everyone else in his family about the record, he still felt a jolt in the Force as Jacen and the others were reminded that the deaths and screams of the innocents had actually been caught on holo.

When R2-D2 still failed to activate his holoprojector, Luke said, "I think my request is clear enough, Artoo. Stop stalling, or I *will* have Ghent wipe your personality. You know how important this is."

R2-D2 gave a plaintive chirp, then piped a worried-sounding trill.

"I'm *sure*," Luke said.

The droid emitted an angry raspberry, then tipped forward and activated his holoprojector.

The veranda of what looked like an elegant, old-Coruscant apartment appeared in the holo. Padmé Amidala rushed into view, followed closely by a golden protocol droid that looked very much like C-3PO. A moment later, Anakin Skywalker appeared from the opposite direction and embraced her.

"*Are you all right?*" Padmé asked, pulling back a moment later. "*I heard there was an attack on the Jedi Temple . . . you can see the smoke from here!*"

Anakin's gaze slipped away from hers. "*I'm fine,*" he said. "*I came to see if you and the baby are safe.*"

"*Captain Typho is here. We're safe.*" Padmé looked out of the holo, presumably toward the Jedi Temple. "*What's happening?*"

Anakin's response was muffled as the protocol droid blocked their view of Padmé and Anakin, then the droid asked, "*What is going on?*"

"Is that See-Threepio?" Jacen gasped.

Luke shrugged and motioned for quiet. He would solve the mystery of the golden protocol droid later, after he discovered what had become of his mother.

"*You can't be any more confused than I am!*" the golden droid said, replying to a string of squeaks and beeps from R2-D2.

He moved out of the way, and Anakin and Padmé came back into view.

"*. . . Jedi Council has tried to overthrow the Republic—*"

"*I can't believe that!*" Padmé exclaimed.

A furrow appeared in Anakin's brow. "*I couldn't either at first, but it's true. I saw Master Windu attempt to assassinate the Chancellor myself.*"

The golden droid's head filled the holo again. "*Something important is going on. I heard a rumor they are going to banish all droids.*"

R2-D2 beeped loudly in the hologram, and Mara hissed, "That *has* to be Threepio. No other droid is that annoying."

"*Shhhh . . . not so loud!*" C-3PO said in the holo. R2-D2 beeped more softly, then C-3PO's head disappeared from the holo again. "*Whatever it is, we'll be the last to know.*"

Padmé was seated on a bench near the edge of the veranda now. "What are you going to do?"

Anakin sat next to her, his face growing resolute. "I will not betray the Republic. My loyalties lie with the Chancellor and the Senate."

"What about Obi-Wan?" *Padmé asked.*

"I don't know," *Anakin replied.* "Many of the Jedi have been killed."

"Is he part of the rebellion?" *Padmé pressed.*

Anakin shrugged. "We may never know."

They both stared at the floor for a moment, then Padmé shook her head in despair.

"How could this have happened?"

"The Republic is unstable, Padmé. The Jedi aren't the only ones trying to take advantage of the situation." *Anakin waited until Padmé met his gaze, and his voice assumed a more ominous tone.* "There are also traitors in the Senate."

Padmé stood, and her expression grew uneasy. "What are you saying?"

Anakin rose and turned her to face him. "You need to distance yourself from your friends in the Senate. The Chancellor said they will be dealt with when this conflict is over."

"What if they start an inquisition?" *Padmé's tone was more angry than frightened.* "I've opposed this war. What will you do if I become suspect?"

"That won't happen," *Anakin said.* "I won't let it."

Padmé turned away from him and was silent for a time, then she said, "I want to leave, go someplace far from here."

"Why?" *Anakin seemed hurt by her suggestion.* "Things are different now! There's a new order."

Padmé refused to yield. "I want to bring up our child someplace safe."

"I want that, too!" *Anakin said.* "But that place is here. I'm gaining new knowledge of the Force. Soon I'll be able to protect you from anything."

Padmé studied him for several moments, her expression changing from disbelieving to disheartened as she contemplated his battle-sullied clothes. Finally, she let her chin drop.

"Oh, Anakin . . . I'm afraid."

"Have faith, my love." *Seeming to miss that it was* him *she feared, Anakin took her in his arms.* "Have faith, my love. Everything will soon be set right. The Separatists have gathered in the

Mustafar system. I'm going there to end this war. Wait until I return . . . things will be different, I promise."

Anakin kissed her, but he must have sensed the misgivings that Luke could see even in the tiny holo—the fear of what he was becoming—because he stopped and waited until she looked into his eyes.

"Please . . ." His voice assumed just a hint of command. "Wait for me."

Padmé nodded, lowering her eyes in surrender. "I will."

Anakin studied her for a moment; then, as he turned and approached R2-D2's position, the file ended.

Luke and the others remained silent for a moment, he and Mara and Jacen pondering Padmé's final words, trying to match her expressions to her tone. When she told Anakin that she was afraid, had she been thinking of the anti-war inquisition she had mentioned? Or of what the future held for *them*?

Mara was the first to break the silence. "No offense, Luke, but your father gives me the shudders."

"Why is that?" Jacen asked, sounding genuinely puzzled.

Mara raised her brow in surprise. "You didn't catch the subtext? That little threat when he told her to distance herself from her friends in the Senate?" She frowned. "I *know* you're more sensitive than that."

"What I saw was a man worried about his wife's safety," Jacen replied. "That's *all* I saw."

"You didn't find him a little controlling?" Luke asked. He was really beginning to worry about his nephew's emotional awareness; it was as though all of the tenderness had evaporated from his soul during his sojourn to explore the Force. "Even when he had completely dismissed her wish to go someplace safe?"

"He promised to keep her safe *there*." Jacen gave them a lopsided smile. "From what I've heard about Anakin Skywalker and his abilities, he was probably telling the truth."

"I guess that's one way of looking at it." Mara's tone implied that she chose to look at the exchange another way. "But maybe Luke and I are reading too much into it, as you suggest. There's not much detail in a holo that size."

"And maybe you have more context to place it in than I do," Jacen allowed. "I'm not saying it was the right thing—just that I understand what he was thinking."

"Good point—sometimes we forget that Anakin Skywalker was only human." Luke turned to R2-D2. "Artoo, show us the next—"

"Uh, you might not want to do that," Ghent interrupted.

Luke frowned. "Why not?"

Ghent frowned back. "Didn't I tell you that the omnigate is pretty . . ." He glanced at R2-D2, then apparently decided it would not be wise to mention how deteriorated the gate was in front of the droid. ". . . that it was *used*?"

"Yes," Mara said. "That doesn't explain why we shouldn't view the next file, though."

"In fact, it tends to suggest we *should*," Jacen said, "while everything is still working."

Ghent just stared at them blankly.

"Well?" Luke asked impatiently.

Ghent shrugged. "It's your omnigate, I guess."

Luke furrowed his brow, waiting for an explanation, but Mara—who knew the slicer far better from their days working for Talon Karrde—said immediately, "You'll have to tell us the problem, Ghent. Why is a *used* omnigate so risky?"

"Oh." He knelt beside R2-D2 and deactivated the droid again, then said, "You don't want to overheat a deteriorated gate. It's too easy to melt it."

"So we just have to wait for it to cool off?" Jacen asked.

"That would help," Ghent said.

"Only *help*?" Mara asked.

"Well, we're probably overheating the gate every time we use it," Ghent said. "It was in pretty bad shape."

"You're saying it's just a matter of time before it goes?" Mara clarified.

"Yeah—it could go the next time you use it, or the time after that," Ghent said. "I don't think it will last three times."

Luke exhaled in frustration. "Is there anything we can do about that?"

Ghent thought for a moment, then nodded. "I could try to copy its architecture."

"How risky is that?" Mara asked.

"It's not," Ghent said. "Unless, of course, I make a mistake."

"But then we'd have a backup in case the first gate melted?" Luke asked.

Ghent looked at him as though he had just asked a very foolish question. "Well, that *is* the idea of making a backup."

"Then why didn't you just say so in the first place?" Jacen demanded, growing uncharacteristically impatient with the communicationally challenged slicer. "What's the drawback?"

"Time," Ghent said. "It takes a lot of time—especially since I don't want to make a mistake."

"Time could be a problem," Luke said.

So far, he had been content to let the Jedi continue on the sidelines of the war, trying to rebuild Chief Omas's confidence in the order by hunting down pirates and adjudicating quarrels among the Alliance's member-states. But he was not willing to continue that approach forever. Sooner or later, the Jedi would need to take action . . . and a deepening tickle in the base of his head was beginning to suggest it would be sooner.

Luke hated to let his personal history interfere, but before the Jedi went into action, he needed to be free of his doubts. Mara had assured him that she had never been involved in anything concerning Padmé Amidala, and Luke believed her. But the possibility remained that the Dark Nest's insinuations were true: that Padmé might have lived under an alias for fifteen or twenty years, and that Mara—then Palpatine's assassin—might have been sent to track her down without knowing her true identity. If Luke were to have any chance at all of defeating Lomi Plo, he needed to know what had happened to his mother—to banish utterly from his heart the last ghost of doubt about Mara's involvement.

When Ghent merely continued to look at him without speaking, Luke sighed and asked, "How long would it take to build the backup?"

Ghent shrugged. "It'll be faster than trying to figure the algorithm and original variables for the universal key you used last—"

"Okay, I understand." Luke closed his eyes and nodded. "Copy it—but don't do anything that would prevent me from taking the original back and using it in an emergency."

"Emergency?" Ghent seemed confused. "How could looking at a bunch of old holos be an emergency?"

"It *could*," Mara told him. "You don't need to know why."

Ghent shrugged. "Okay." He flipped his magnispecs down and reached for his micrograbbers. "No problem with the emergency thing."

Luke waited until the slicer had started work, then turned to Jacen. "Let's move to the outer office and leave Ghent to his work."

"Oh yeah—the *conversation*." Jacen started toward the door, then stopped and glanced over his shoulder. "Aren't you coming, Aunt Mara? After all, you're the *really* angry one."

"I wouldn't say angry, Jacen."

"No?" Jacen gave her a crooked Solo smile. "*I* would."

EIGHT

The private hangar, hidden deep under several metallic asteroids on the rear side of the nest, appeared much more orderly than Lizil's main hangar. Two dozen Slayn & Korpil transports hung on the walls in neat rows, taking on everything from blaster rifles to concussion missiles to artillery pieces. There was no "transacting"; nothing was being removed from the vessels, and there was not a membrosia ball in sight.

Han swung the *Swiff* into an open berth near the exit membrane, using the attitude thrusters to stick the landing pads to the wax-lined floor extra firmly. The hangar was crawling with big bugs—Killik and otherwise—and he had no intention of firing the anchoring bolts until he was sure a quick departure would not be needed.

"We sure picked the wrong disguises for this job," Han said, eyeing the bustling swarm. "I don't see anything that isn't a bug anywhere."

"That's odd, Captain Solo," C-3PO said. "I don't see any bugs at all. The Verpine are a species of mantid, the Fefze are more closely related to beetles, and the Huk are much closer to vespids than—"

"I don't think Han actually meant *bugs,* Threepio," Leia interrupted. "He was using the term pejoratively."

"He was?" C-3PO asked. "Might I suggest that this is a particularly poor time to insult insects, Captain Solo. You and Princess Leia seem to be the only mammals in this hangar."

"Like I hadn't noticed," Han grumbled. He unbuckled his crash webbing and initiated the shutdown cycle, but remained in his seat staring out the forward canopy. "Leia, do you notice anything strange about the Killiks loading those transports?"

"Now that you mention it, yes," Leia said. "They really don't look like Lizil."

"That, too," Han said. Unlike Lizil workers, these Killiks were nearly two meters tall, with powerful builds, blotchy gray-green chitin, and short curving mandibles that looked like bent needles. "But *I* was wondering why there aren't any coming *down* the ramps."

Leia studied the ships for a moment, then said, "Good question."

"Actually, the answer is rather clear," C-3PO said. "Those Killiks aren't loading the transports, they're boarding them."

"It certainly appears that way," Leia agreed. "The Chiss may be in for a big surprise."

"A surprise?" C-3PO said, missing the obvious as only he could. "What sort of surprise?"

"You *did* notice all those S and K transports hanging out in the entrance tunnel?" Han asked.

"Of course," C-3PO said. "All one hundred twenty-seven of them."

Han whistled. He had not thought it was so many. "Okay, let's say each one of those tubs can transport three hundred bugs . . . that's close to forty thousand troops, counting these ships."

"A full division," Leia said. "That's going to be a very *nasty* surprise for the Chiss—especially if the Killiks strike someplace they're not expecting."

"Oh, dear," C-3PO said. "In that case, perhaps we should return to our own territory and send a messenger to warn Commander Fel."

"Not a chance," Han said, rising. "The Chiss are on their own—at least until we get our daughter back."

He led the way back to the aft hold, where Meewalh and Cakhmaim were waiting with the hoods of their Ewok disguises tucked under their arms. The huge Magcannon Max that had once been stowed here was gone, now headed for a pirate base somewhere in the Galactic Alliance. If Lando's engineers could be trusted, the weapon would blow itself apart the first time it was live-fired.

Han instructed the Noghri to put on their Ewok heads. After he and Leia checked their own disguises—Arkanian and Falleen—he turned to the cargo lift controls and was puzzled to find a pair of Fefze staring at him from the external monitors. The black, meter-high beetles were standing beneath the cargo lift, staring up into the vidcam, frantically waving their forward legs for the cargo lift to be lowered.

"What now?" Han demanded. He turned to C-3PO. "Didn't Grees say his Flakax goons would be the ones meeting us?"

"I believe his precise words were 'Tito and Yugi will be there to take care of you,'" C-3PO reported. "And he *was* pointing at the Flakax at the time."

"So what do these two want?" Han asked.

Leia closed her eyes a moment, then said, "Let them in. I think we know them."

"*Know* them? If I'd ever met a puker, I'd remember." Han was referring to the Fefze habit of regurgitating food paste whenever they grew frightened. "You're sure about this? I don't want to spend the rest of the trip in a stinky—"

"Han, their presences are familiar." Leia reached past him and depressed the lift control. "Let them in."

The lift had barely touched down before the Fefze scrambled over the safety rail and began gesturing for it to be raised again. Han glanced at Leia uncertainly, then—when she nodded—brought the two insects up. The pair's antennae had barely risen above floor level when one of them began jabbering in muffled Ewokese.

C-3PO shot something back in the same language, then turned to Han.

"You were quite justified in your reluctance to let them aboard, Captain Solo. I haven't been spoken to quite so rudely since the *last* time we had dealings with that dreadful Ewok."

"Ewok?" Han went over to the lift. "I think I'd rather have the bug."

The Fefze jumped onto the deck of the hold, then reared up on its rear legs and began to flail its forelegs about haphazardly. A moment later, its head popped off and fell to the floor, revealing another head inside—this one black and furry, with large dark eyes and little round ears.

"Tarfang!" Leia exclaimed, coming to Han's side. "What are *you* doing here?"

Tarfang began to chitter rapidly, waving his remaining Fefze legs excitedly.

"Oh, dear," C-3PO said. "He says if he tells you, he will have to kill you."

The Ewok added two more syllables.

"Your choice," C-3PO translated.

"That's okay," Han said. The last time they had seen Tarfang, Admiral Bwua'tu had just offered him and Jae Juun positions as military intelligence affiliates. "We can guess."

The second Fefze joined them and began to flail its arms around, as had Tarfang. Han reached over and twisted the head off, exposing a bug-eyed face with grayish, dewlapped cheeks.

"Juun!" Han slapped the Sullustan on the back of his costume. "I'm glad you're still alive, old buddy—and a little surprised, too!"

"Yes, all of our missions are very dangerous," Juun said, beaming. "Admiral Bwua'tu always sends Tarfang and me when the mission is likely to be fatal."

"You certainly appear to be beating the odds," Leia said. "How can we help?"

Tarfang pattered something impatient.

"He says they're here to help *us*," C-3PO translated.

"The Squibs have put a death mark on your heads," Juun explained. "Over a thousand credits—*each*."

"What?" Han scowled. "That doesn't make any sense."

Tarfang twattled a sharp reply.

"That's hardly fair," C-3PO replied. "It's been nearly two decades since Captain Solo had a death mark on him. He has every right to be frightened."

"I'm not scared," Han said. "I just don't believe it. We have a deal with the Squibs."

"And *they* have a deal with Tito and Yugi," Juun said. "Tito said we could eat your brains if we helped."

"Did they say *why* the Squibs want us killed?" Leia asked.

Juun shook his head. "Only that it wouldn't be much of a job, because you'd never see it coming."

The Sullustan pulled his Fefze head back on, then turned toward Tarfang, who had noticed the two Noghri in their Ewok disguises and gone over to glare at them.

"Tarfang, let's go," Juun said. "The Flakax are already on their way."

Instead of retrieving the head of his own disguise, Tarfang let out an angry yap and shoved Meewalh. She reacted instantly, dropping the Ewok to the deck with a foot sweep and landing atop him in a full straddle-lock that left him completely immobilized.

"Tarfang!" Juun snapped. "What are you doing? We have to leave before the stingers arrive."

Tarfang burbled an angry reply, purposely spraying saliva into the face of Meewalh's costume.

"I don't care if it *is* an insult," Juun replied. "We don't have time for this. If we blow our cover, Admiral Pellaeon will never know where this division is going."

Han's brow shot up. "*Pellaeon* asked for this mission?"

"Uh, er, I'm really not at liberty to—"

"Yeah, sure," Han said. "What I don't get is why the GA's Supreme Commander would be that interested in a bug division headed for Chiss space."

"I do," Leia said. "If Pellaeon can tell the Chiss where these Killiks are headed, he just might convince them that the Galactic Alliance isn't siding with the Colony. It's a long shot, but it's probably the galaxy's best chance to avoid a three-way war."

Tarfang let out a long, fading gibber, and Cakhmaim moved over to threaten him with a stun stick—not that it was necessary, with Meewalh still straddling him.

"It doesn't look like you'll be killing anyone to me," C-3PO said to the Ewok. "Princess Leia's bodyguards appear to have you very well under control."

"Relax," Han said. "Your secret is safe with us—and you've got to get out of here before the trouble starts."

He motioned for the Noghri to release Tarfang. Meewalh growled low in her throat but quietly slipped off the Ewok.

Tarfang's eyes darted from one Noghri to the other, and it seemed to Han that he was trying to estimate his chances of launching a successful attack while still lying on the floor.

"Your devotion to operational security is admirable," Leia said, using the Force to set the Ewok back on his feet. "But Captain Juun is right. We don't pose a threat to your mission, and you *do* need to be going."

Han picked up the head of Tarfang's Fefze disguise and plopped in place before the Ewok could utter more threats, then shoved him onto the cargo lift with Juun.

"The next time we see Gilad, we'll be sure to tell him how brave you two are," Han said. "And thanks for the warning—we owe you."

Cakhmaim activated the lift, and the two spies dropped slowly out of sight.

Han went to Leia's side. "Now, *that* was a surprise."

"What? That they lasted this long?" Leia asked. "Or that they'd risk their lives to help us?"

Han shook his head. "That they're crazy enough to come back to this place in bug costumes."

"You're right." Leia reached up adjusted Han's wig. "That *is* crazy."

Han frowned. "It's different for us," he said. "We're good at this stuff."

"Sure we are," Leia said. "That's why the Squibs are trying to kill us."

"Yeah, I don't get that," Han said. "We had a deal."

"Maybe they don't like us having something on them," Leia suggested.

Han shook his head. "That doesn't make sense. The Squibs know we can't tell Lizil anything without exposing ourselves. Trying to take us out just adds to the chances we'll be caught, and they know we'd try to settle the score by telling Raynar who helped me and Luke on Woteba."

"Maybe they think they can kill us before we talk," Leia said.

"They're arrogant, not stupid," Han countered. "Even taking us by surprise, there's a big chance we'll survive. Any way you look at it, attacking us *here* is a risk."

"Then it doesn't make sense," Leia said. "They should be trying to cover for us, not kill us—at least while we're still in the nest."

"Right." Han rubbed the synthetic skin of his disguise, then said, "So they're trying to hide something—something big enough to risk angering Raynar."

"Something to do with the black membrosia?" Leia asked.

Han thought for a moment, then shrugged. "I can only think of one way to find out."

"Ask the Flakax?" Leia asked.

"May I point out that Flakax males are noted for being unhelpful and rude?" C-3PO asked. "I really don't think they're going to tell you much. Perhaps it would be better to leave before they arrive."

"Too late." Leia closed her eyes for a moment. "They're here—and they feel very dangerous."

Han went to the control panel and checked the external monitors. The two Flakax had arrived with four Verpine assistants. They were each bearing a crate labeled GREEN THAKITILLO or BROT-RIB or some other delicacy that the Squibs had pressured the Solos into carrying as part of the agreement to help them reach Jaina and Zekk in the war zone.

"Six of 'em," he reported. "All carrying crates."

"Their weapons are probably in the crates," Leia said. "I'll take care of those first."

"Right," Han said, motioning Cakhmaim and Meewalh to follow him. "We'll get the drop on them from behind."

C-3PO started to clunk away in the opposite direction. "I'm sure you don't want me in the way. I'll wait on the flight deck until you sound the all-clear."

"Good idea," Leia agreed. "Keep a watch on the external monitors."

"And if it looks like any Killiks are coming this way, get out there and stall," Han said. "We can't have the bugs stumbling on this fight any more than the Squibs can. It could blow our chances of joining the convoy."

"Stall?" C-3PO stopped at the threshold and let his head slump forward. "Why am I always assigned the dangerous tasks?"

Han drew his blaster pistol—a 434 "DeathHammer," which Lando had given him to replace the trusty DL-44 that Raynar Thul had taken on Woteba—then he and the Noghri each slipped into one of the cramped crawlways hidden behind the service hatches in the back of the hold.

Han sat in the dark, waiting and thinking about how Leia's devotion to her Jedi training had changed things between them. There had been a time—not that long ago—when he would never have agreed to let her stand bait. But now, even the Noghri recognized that her Force abilities were adequate protection. She radiated a calm confidence that seemed as unshakable as the Core, as though her Jedi studies had restored the faith she had lost in the future after Anakin died.

Han was glad for the change. Leia had always been his beacon star—the bright, guiding flame that had kept him on course through so many decades of struggle and despair. It was good to have her brightening the way again.

The soft whir of the cargo lift sounded from the other side of the service hatch and sent a chill racing down Han's spine. He had not been thinking about his experience with the Kamarians when he squeezed into the crawlway to set up an ambush, but the darkness and the cramped confines and the likelihood of a bug fight set his pulse to pounding in his ears. It had been over forty years, but he could still feel those Kamarian pincers closing around his ankles, hear his nails scraping against the durasteel as he tried to keep them from dragging him out of his hiding place . . .

Han grabbed his earlobe and twisted, *hard,* trying to break out of his thought pattern with pain. His hands were already shaking, and if he let the memory progress into a full-fledged flashback, he would end up lying there in a ball while Leia and the Noghri dealt with the Flakax.

The lift clunked into place, and Leia's muffled voice sounded through the service hatch. "Are these the crates the Squibs, er, the *Directors* wanted us to take to Tenupe?"

"Right." The Flakax ended his answer with a throat-click. "Where do you—queen's eggs!"

Han pushed open the service hatch and saw the heads of all six insects turned toward the far corner of the hold, where the crate Leia had just Force-ripped from the pincers of the first Flakax was crashing into the wall. It broke open, spilling a rifle version of the Verpine shatter gun and a variety of thermal grenades.

"Why, that doesn't look like green thakitillo," Leia said.

She pointed at the box in the second Flakax's arms. That crate, too, went flying, and the insects finally recovered from their shock. The four Verpine ripped the tops off their crates. Before they could pull their weapons from the boxes, Cakhmaim and Meewalh opened up with their stun blasters and dropped all four from behind.

Han leveled his DeathHammer at the Flakax. "Take it easy, fellas," he said. "No one has to get—"

The pair launched themselves at Leia, clacking their mandibles in fury and spewing a brown fume from their abdomens. Han fired twice, but their chitin was so thick and hard that even the Death-Hammer's powerful bolts did little more than blast fist-sized craters into it.

Leia vanished beneath the two creatures, and Han stopped firing. The chances of hitting Leia were just too great, especially when all he could see through the growing haze of brown fume was thrashing arms and swinging insect heads. He called for Cakhmaim and Meewalh and raced forward. As he gulped down his first breath of bug vapor, his nose, throat, and lungs erupted into caustic pain.

Within two steps, his eyes were so filled with tears he could no longer see. A step after that, he grew weak and dizzy and collapsed to his hands and knees, coughing, retching, and just generally feeling like a thermal grenade had detonated inside his chest. He crawled the last three meters to the fight and reached up to press the muzzle of his blaster to the back of a greenish thorax.

With its large compound eyes and a fully circular field of vision, the Flakax had already seen Han coming. It caught him in the head with a lightning-quick elbow strike. The DeathHammer bolt went wide, ricocheting off the deck before it burned a hole through the wall.

Then a muffled *snap-hiss* sounded from beneath the insect, and Han was nearly blinded when the tip of Leia's lightsaber shot up through the Flakax, just a few centimeters from his nose. He barely managed to roll out of the way as the blade swept toward his face, opening the thorax from midline to flank and spilling bug blood all over Lando's deck.

"Hey, watch—" Han had to stop and cough, then finished, "—that thing!"

Han staggered to his feet and pointed his blaster in the general direction of the tear-blurred melee in front of him, trying to separate his wife's shape from that of the Flakax attacking her.

Then Cakhmaim and Meewalh came leaping in, hacking and gasping as they slammed into the writhing pile. An instant later the two Noghri went flying in the other direction, riding the surviving Flakax as Leia used the Force to send it tumbling across the hold.

"Han!" Leia's voice sounded as raw and burning as Han's felt. "Are you—"

"Fine." He reached down and pulled her to her feet. "Why didn't you do that in the first place?"

"Hard to concentrate with those . . . mouthparts snapping in your face." She deactivated her lightsaber and led Han after the Noghri and the Flakax. "Why didn't *you* blast them?"

"I *did*," Han said. "Someone ought to make armor out of those bugs."

"Han!" Leia coughed. "They're sentient beings!"

"Fair is fair," Han countered. "If they get to wear it, so should we."

They stepped out of stink cloud to hear Cakhmaim and Meewalh snarling as they continued to wrestle with the second Flakax. Han wiped the tears from his eyes and found the bug lying facedown on the deck with the two Noghri sitting astride it, still in their Ewok disguises. Cakhmaim had the insect's arms pinned together behind its back at the elbow, while Meewalh was holding its ankles, pulling its legs back against the hip joints every time it tried to open the gas duct in its abdomen.

Leaving Leia to deal with the fray, Han secured the unconscious Verpine and stowed the impressive array of weaponry the insects had brought aboard. By the time he had finished, Leia and the Noghri had the Flakax kneeling with its arms bound behind its back and its abdominal gas duct plugged with a piece of cloth.

Leia waved the tip of her lightsaber in front of the insect's head, causing the facets of its compound eyes to quiver and rustle as they followed the glow.

"Which one are you?" she asked. "Tito or Yugi?"

"Tito!" The Flakax sounded insulted. "I'm the handsome one. Everyone knows."

"Yeah, those eyes of yours are really something," Han said. "Now, why don't you explain why you were going to kill us?"

Tito spread his mandibles in the buggish equivalent of a shrug. "Thought it would be fun."

"Obviously," Leia said. "We're talking about the *other* reasons."

"We know the Squibs put you up to this," Han pressed.

Tito cocked his head to the side, turning one bulbous eye toward Han. "You know that, you know why."

"Stop playing dumb," Han said. "You understand what we're asking. The Squibs want us dead for a reason. What are they trying to hide?"

The Flakax's mandibles spread wide, and a yellow mass of regurgitated *something* shot out and covered Han's chest. "Kill me now. Better than what the Directors will do, if I break my quiet swear."

"Quiet swear?" Han repeated. "You mean like a vow of silence?"

Tito tried to raise his abdomen, straining to clear the plugged gas duct. Cakhmaim drove the point of his elbow down on the nerve bundle where the thorax connected, and the abdomen dropped to the deck again.

Leia turned to Han. "I thought those crime vows were supposed to be reciprocal?"

"They are," Han said, seeing where Leia was headed. "But you know the Squibs."

Tito's head swung from Han to Leia and back again, and finally he could no longer resist asking, "The Directors?"

Han and Leia exchanged looks, then Han asked, "Should we tell him?"

Leia shook her head. "It would just be cruel, since we're going to have to kill him anyway."

"What would be cruel?" Tito asked.

Meewalh pressed her blaster to his head, but Tito seemed a lot more concerned about what they were keeping from him than the likelihood of being killed.

"Tell!"

Han frowned. "You're sure you want to know? No one likes to die knowing they've been set up."

Tito began to work his mandibles. "*How?*"

"You don't want to know," Leia said. She turned to Meewalh. "Go—"

"Wait!" Tito said. "You tell me, I tell you."

Meewalh asked if she should fire.

"Not yet." Leia frowned down at the prisoner. "You're sure you want to know? It'll just make you angry."

"*Really* angry," Han said. "You just can't trust Squibs."

"Flakax *never* get angry," Tito said. "Never get *anything*. Have no useless feelings like humans."

"Okay," Han said. "I'll give you a hint. Aren't you curious about how we knew you were coming?"

Tito turned one eye toward Leia. "Squibs not tell you. They want you dead."

"That's right." Leia made a small motion with her hand, then added, "And we're not the only ones."

Tito spread his antennae. "They want *us* dead, too?"

"That's the way we hear it," Han said. "Before the Verpines, the Squibs asked a couple of Fefze to help you, right?"

"How you know?"

"Because they're the ones who sold us the warning about you," Leia said. "And we're not the only ones they were asked to kill."

Tito clattered his mandibles. "Fefze kill Flakax? That is funny." He turned to Meewalh. "I much amused. You pull trigger now."

"It's not *that* funny." Leia made another motion with her hand. "Remember, you were going to be fighting *us*."

"I don't suppose you noticed the thermal detonator in the brot-rib crate?" Han asked. He had not found any thermal detonator when he stowed the weapons that had spilled from the crate, but that hardly mattered. Han could always produce one from their own stores and claim the Squibs had slipped it into the box when Tito was looking the other way. "Even a Fefze could set a detonator and take off while you were busy fighting *us*."

"Though, of course, I think the Verpine were a much better choice," Leia said, casting an eye at the unconscious insects. "They're so much more technological."

Tito considered this for a moment, then let out a long throat rattle. "The Directors broke their own swear!"

"That's the way it looks, isn't it?" Han replied.

Leia nodded. "And now that we've kept our part of the bargain—"

"The Directors want you dead because Lizil isn't sending you to Tenupe, like they promise," Tito said. "Lizil told them, 'Two-legs are more use in Alliance. Send them with convoy.'"

Han's jaw fell. "Wait a minute! You're saying this convoy is headed for *Alliance* territory?"

Tito clacked his mandibles shut, then looked from Han to Leia. "Maybe."

Leia's brow rose, now with shreds of Falleen disguise hanging from it after the fierce fight. "No wonder they want us dead!"

"Yeah," Han said. If this convoy was headed for Alliance space, there could only be one purpose for all the war cargo they had seen being loaded. "The Colony is supporting a coup—maybe a whole string of them!"

"I think so." Leia's gaze grew troubled, and she slowly turned to Han. "Somebody has to warn Luke."

Han nodded. "I know. Maybe we can find—"

He caught himself and stopped short of saying *Juun and Tarfang,* then took Leia by the elbow and led her away from their prisoner.

Leia did not even wait until they reached the front of the hold. "Han, we have to do this ourselves."

"We're busy," Han said.

"Think about all the Alliance insects we've seen here," Leia pressed. "Verpine, Flakax, Fefze, Vratix, Huk."

"I *have* been thinking about them," Han said. "I've been thinking about them a *lot.*"

"If those governments fall, the Defense Force will be so busy in Alliance territory that it won't be able to keep the pressure on in Utegetu—much less carry the war to the rest of the Colony." Leia stopped and turned him to face her. "You know we can't trust this to Juun and Tarfang, Han."

"Of course we can!" Han said. "You heard Juun. Bwua'tu believes in those two."

"But do *we*?" Leia asked. "Even assuming they would be willing to disregard their orders on our say-so, are you ready to place the Alliance in their hands?"

"It'd serve the Alliance right," Han grumbled. "The rehab conglomerates are claim-jumping everything anyway."

"At least the rehab conglomerates aren't spreading the war," Leia said. "And that's what will happen if we let the Colony overthrow the Alliance's insect governments."

Han let his chin drop to his chest, wondering why it always came down to him and Leia, why they always had to be the ones in the right place at the wrong time.

"Well, I guess there was never any doubt," Han said.

Leia frowned. "Doubt?"

"About going back," Han said. "You *still* have to do the right thing. You just can't help yourself."

Leia thought about this a moment, then nodded. "I guess that's true. I just couldn't live with myself if we let the Colony topple those governments."

"Well, don't be too hard on yourself," he said. "With a Squib death mark on our heads and the Killiks determined to send us back to the Alliance, we didn't have much chance of reaching Tenupe anyway."

"Not this time," Leia agreed. "But we'll be back."

"Yeah, there's always next time." Han allowed himself a moment to curse the universe, then nodded toward Tito and the Verpine. "What about them?"

"We can't take them back as prisoners," she said. "Especially not Tito. He's not all that psychopathic for a homeless Flakax, but that will change now that his buddy is dead. We just can't take the chance."

"Then I guess there's only one thing to do," Han said, starting back toward the insect.

Leia caught him by the arm. "Han, you're not going to—"

"Yeah, I am." Han disengaged his arm. "I'm going to send him back to the Squibs."

NINE

With an artificial waterfall purling in the corner and a school of goldies swimming laps in the catch pond, the conversation area of Luke's outer office was designed to encourage a peaceful, relaxed exchange. The lighting was soft and warm, the floor was sunken to separate it from the rest of the office, and the padded benches were arranged at an oblique angle so that any negative energy arising from a discussion would not fly directly at the conversers.

All of this was, unfortunately, wasted on the current situation. Jacen had chosen to remain standing, feet spread and arms crossed in front of him, facing off against Luke and Mara both. Sensing that Jacen knew exactly why he had been summoned, Luke wasted no time coming to the point.

"Jacen, your fellow Jedi Knights had some very disturbing things to say about the raid on the Chiss supply depot."

Jacen nodded, his expression unreadable. "I imagine."

"They claim that it was very clear the Chiss weren't preparing for a surprise attack," Luke pressed. "They believe you started the war unnecessarily."

"They're wrong."

When Jacen did not elaborate, Mara asked, "Okay—what do you know that *they* don't?"

"Just what I saw in my vision," Jacen said. "I couldn't let the Chiss attack on their own terms. I had to force their hand."

Luke could not sense a lie in his nephew's words—in fact, he could not sense anything at all because Jacen had closed himself off from the Force. He was trying to hide something.

"Jacen, I've never liked being lied to," Luke said, acting on instinct. "And I absolutely refuse to tolerate it now. Tell me the truth or leave the order."

Jacen recoiled visibly, then seemed to realize he had betrayed himself and began to study Luke in slack-jawed surprise.

"Don't think about it," Mara ordered. "Just do it."

Jacen's shoulders slumped, and his gaze shifted to the pool at the base of the waterfall. "It doesn't change what had to be done, but I did have to alter one detail of my vision to persuade Jaina and the others to help me."

Luke had a sinking feeling inside, more disappointment than anger. "*Which* detail?"

Jacen hesitated, then said, "In my vision, I didn't see who attacked first. I just saw the war spreading, until it had consumed the entire galaxy."

"So you thought you would just go ahead and get things started?" Mara asked, incredulous. "What were you *thinking*?"

"That the war *was* already started!" Jacen retorted. "The Colony had been attacking us—the Jedi and the Alliance—for months. All I did was wake everyone up to the fact."

Given what he and Han had discovered on their trip to Woteba, Luke could hardly argue the point. In addition to the fleet of nest ships the Colony had been constructing inside the Utegetu Nebula, it was now clear that the Killiks had caused many of the problems plaguing the Galactic Alliance, by harboring pirates, providing a market for the Tibanna tappers, and aiding the smugglers of black membrosia.

But that was hardly an excuse for provoking the Chiss into an attack.

"Jacen, what you did was wrong," Luke said. "And I suspect you know it, or you wouldn't have needed to trick your sister and the others into helping you."

"What else was I *supposed* to do?" Jacen demanded, turning on Luke with heat in his eyes. "You were trapped on Woteba, Mom and Mara were stuck in the Murgo Choke, and Masters Durron and Horn had the entire Jedi order locked in a contest of wills."

The reply hurt because it was so true—and because the breakdown had been Luke's failure.

"I understand, but that's never going to happen again." Luke locked eyes with his nephew and put some durasteel in his voice. "And neither will something like the trick you pulled on your sister and the others. Is that clear?"

Jacen let out a breath of exasperation, but nodded. "The next time, I'll come to you."

"And if Luke's not available?" Mara asked.

"I'm sure he'll have designated someone to oversee the order in his absence." Jacen gave Luke a wry smile. "I'm not the only one who learns from his mistakes."

"Let's hope not." Luke reached out and was unhappy to find his nephew still closed off from the Force. "Now, what else are you hiding?"

Jacen was not surprised this time. He merely nodded, then said, "It has nothing to do with the Jedi—and I wouldn't be hiding it if it wasn't very important."

"Does it explain why you want to kill Raynar so badly?" Luke pressed.

Jacen smirked. "That's no secret," he said. "I want to kill Raynar because it's the only way to stop the war. Lowie and Tesar *don't* want to because he was our friend at the academy."

"You don't think they're being influenced by Raynar?" Mara asked.

Jacen considered this for a moment, then shrugged. "If Raynar had known what we were considering, sure. But they're not complete Joiners, so it's hard to believe they would've been in close enough contact for him to know that the Masters were discussing his death."

Luke nodded. Raynar had already proven—when he originally summoned Jaina and the others to the Colony's aid—that he could use the Force to exert his will over non-Joiners. But Cilghal's experiments had established that he was not able to read minds—even Joiner minds—over long distances any better than Jedi could communicate through the Force. It was all feelings and notions; at the most, Raynar would have felt a vague sense of danger and unease.

"Good," Luke said, relieved Jacen had not seized such an obvious opportunity to cast doubts on the judgment of his rivals. At least he was still trying to be fair and balanced in his actions. "That's the way I understood the situation, too."

"Of course," Jacen added, "now that Tesar and Lowie have told Madame Thul about the debate, we can assume Raynar has been informed via more conventional means."

Luke frowned. "How do you know about *that*?"

"Tesar and Lowie?" Jacen's gaze flicked away, and he could not quite hide his frustration with himself. "I didn't realize it was supposed to be a secret."

"*We* haven't told anyone about it," Luke said. "And since I sent the three of them to Dagobah to consider whether they truly want—"

"You sent Tahiri, too?" Jacen gasped. "But she didn't tell Madame Thul *anything*!"

It was Mara's turn to frown. "And how would you know *that*?"

Jacen hesitated a fraction of a second, then seemed to realize he had made a mistake and said, "Tahiri and I still talk."

"About what Lowie and Tesar are doing?" Mara demanded. "Is she *spying* for you?"

"We *talk*," Jacen insisted. "Sometimes their names come up."

"I can't believe this!" Luke rolled his head back and shook it in despair. Had matters really gotten so out of hand that the order's Jedi were *spying* on one another? "Maybe I should send *you* to Dagobah to join them."

"*I* didn't betray the Masters' confidence," Jacen replied evenly. "But if that's your decision, of course I'll go."

"I'll think about it," Luke said darkly. "In the meantime, no more spying. If we can't trust each other, we don't have a chance of pulling together."

"Actually, spying *builds* trust." Jacen was quoting a maxim that Luke had often heard Leia use as the New Republic's Chief of State. He must have sensed Luke's displeasure, because he quickly added, "But it looks like I won't be talking to Tahiri anytime soon, anyway."

"Thank you," Luke said.

"You're welcome," Jacen said. He glanced toward the exit. "If that's all, I really should be—"

"Nice try," Mara said, blocking Jacen's exit. "I still want to know what you're hiding."

Jacen did not even pause before he shook his head. "I'm sorry. I can't tell you."

"Does it involve what you did to Ben?" Mara's voice grew as sharp as a vibroblade, for she had been even more alarmed than Luke when he reported what Lowie and Tesar had told him. "Blocking his memories?"

Jacen did not seem as surprised as he should have. "Not at all," he said. "I did that to protect him."

"From what?" Mara demanded.

"We were sleeping near an Ewok village when a Gorax attacked," he explained. "Before we could get there, it had wiped out half the village and was heading home."

Luke felt Mara's ire fading. Gorax were primate behemoths,

standing as tall as the trees on the forest moon, and they were well known for their brutal natures. "I see. You were afraid the memory would traumatize him."

"No, actually not," Jacen said. "Ben knows better than most kids his age that the galaxy is filled with monsters, so I'm sure he could have handled what he saw with a little adult guidance."

"You're more confident of that than I am," Luke said. "Did he feel their deaths in the Force?"

Jacen nodded. "And he sensed what the Gorax's captives were feeling, too."

Mara's hand went to her mouth.

Luke asked, "So that's why you blocked—"

"No," Jacen said. "I blocked Ben's memory to keep him from recalling what *I* did."

"What *you* did?" Luke asked.

"Ben started to scream that I had to save the Ewoks, and that drew the Gorax's attention," Jacen explained. "But I couldn't take him into the fight with me, and I could sense another Gorax in the forest behind me—"

"So you couldn't leave him alone," Mara finished.

Jacen nodded. "I used the Force to hide us."

When Jacen remained silent, Luke prompted, "And?"

"And Ben was very sensitive that night," Jacen continued. "He felt what happened to the prisoners in the cave."

"*That's* what you didn't want him to remember," Mara said.

"By morning, he was already beginning to withdraw from the Force again," Jacen said. "He's still young; I think he blames it for the bad things he feels in it."

"I think he does," Luke said. He and Mara had postulated a similar theory themselves, shortly after the war, when it began to grow clear that Ben was withdrawing from the Force. "And how, exactly, did you block this memory?"

"It's a form of Force illusion," Jacen explained. "The Adepts call it a memory rub."

Luke frowned. "That sounds pretty invasive for the Fallanassi," he said. "And I don't recall any White Current techniques that can permanently affect another person's mind."

Jacen smiled and spread his hands in a gesture of helplessness. "Well, Akanah *did* say I was only the second-worst student she ever had."

"It's good to know I'm still number one with her," Luke said, not laughing at the joke. He paused a moment, then continued, "I see why you blocked the memory. I'll probably even be grateful, when I've had time to think about it."

"I'm grateful now," Mara said. Luke could feel that she had already forgiven Jacen completely. "I hope you can teach me that technique."

"I'm not nearly the guide Akanah is," Jacen replied. "But I can certainly try."

"First, I want to know why you didn't just tell Mara and me what happened," Luke said. "I understand you wanted to protect Ben, but that doesn't make sense."

"That's right, Jacen," Mara said, forcing herself to be stern again. "There's no excuse for keeping secrets from *us*."

"I'm sorry," Jacen said, shame crawling up his face. "I should have told you, but it was reckless of me to put him in that position."

"And so you decided to hide what happened from us?" Luke demanded.

"I don't know why, but I sense that he needs *me* to guide him into the Force," Jacen said. "And I thought if you knew what had happened, you wouldn't trust me with him."

"Jacen!" Mara's voice was incredulous, but her relief flooded the Force. "How could you think that?"

Jacen looked a little confused. "I'm not sure. I just thought—"

"You thought wrong!" Mara said. "You've been wonderful for Ben, and there's no one else I'd rather trust with him. But no more secrets." She glanced over at Luke. "Okay?"

"We'll see." He was a little less inclined than his wife to forgive all. There was no doubt about the effect Jacen had on Ben, but Luke remained uneasy about the way his nephew continued to shut his emotions off from the Force. "You're *still* hiding something from us. And I want to know what it is."

"I know you do," Jacen said. "But telling you any more would betray a confidence, and I won't do that."

"Jacen, if you're going to continue being a Jedi, you have to put the order first," Luke said. "We can no longer have divided loyalties."

"I understand that, and I'll leave the order if—"

"Nobody wants *that*," Mara interrupted. Luke shot a blast of irritation her way through their Force-bond, but she ignored it and continued, "We just need to know that this secret won't interfere with your duties as a Jedi."

"It won't," Jacen said, relief showing on his face. "In fact, I can promise that it makes me even *more* determined to be a good Jedi— and to keep our order strong."

Jacen revealed just enough of his presence to confirm he was telling the truth—that whatever the nature of this secret, he saw the Jedi order as the best means of protecting it.

"I guess we'll have to trust you on that." Luke's tone was measured. "Don't let us down."

Luke was about to dismiss his nephew when a guilty heaviness began to weigh on the Force from the direction of his inner office. He went to the door and found Ghent lying under the work station in the corner, affixing something to the underside of the writing table. Mara slipped through the door past Luke.

"Ghent!"

The slicer sat up, banging his head, and the guilt in the Force changed to fear. His gaze shot across the room toward R2-D2, then he pulled a tiny electronic device off the underside of the table and swallowed it.

"Have you been planting listening devices in Luke's office?" Mara demanded.

The tattoos on Ghent's face darkened with embarrassment. "S-s-sorry."

She used the Force to pull the slicer out from under the table, then began to go through his pockets, pulling out a truly impressive assortment of eavesdropping bugs.

"Did Chief Omas put you up to this?" Mara asked.

Ghent nodded. "He said it was for the good of the Alliance." He plucked one of the bugs out of Mara's hand and began to fidget nervously with the tiny wire antenna. "And he said that I couldn't help you with Artoo any more unless I did it."

"I see," Luke said, joining them.

He looked around for a moment, eyeing an out-of-place datapad on the surface of his work station, a recording rod that had mysteriously turned itself on, a holocube of Ben and Mara that was facing the wrong way on the shelf.

"Were you finished?"

Ghent looked confused. "N-n-not really."

"Well, then." Luke waved Mara and Jacen toward the door. "I guess we had better leave you to your work."

"You're going to let him *finish*?" Jacen asked.

"Of course." Luke nudged his nephew toward the outer office. "Didn't you just tell me that spying builds trust?"

TEN

Three jumps after departing Lizil, Han was running a systems check while Leia plotted the course to the Rago Run, the long hyperspace lane that would take them back into Galactic Alliance territory. So far, the *Swiff* had performed flawlessly, even reminding them to eat when the ship's droid brain noticed that none of the processing units in the galley had been activated in twenty hours.

"I don't like it," Han said, studying the nacelle-temperature history. "No machine is this reliable."

"To the contrary, Captain Solo," C-3PO said. "When properly maintained, operated in the appropriate environment, and not pushed beyond performance parameters, machines are *very* reliable. Malfunctions most often result from a biological unit's inattentiveness. I can tell you that has been true in my own experience."

"Watch it, Threepio," Leia advised. "It's not smart to insult the hand that oils you."

"Oh," C-3PO said. "I certainly didn't mean to imply that you or Captain Solo have *ever* been neglectful. I have had other owners, you know."

"Other owners? Now *there's* a thought." Han looked over to the copilot's station, where Leia was seated in one of the cockpit's self-adjusting, supercomfortable Support-Gel flight chairs. "How are those jump coordinates coming along?"

"Almost done," she said. "The navicomputer's a little slow, at least compared with the *Falcon*'s."

Han felt a small burst of pride. "That surprises you? The *Falcon* has top-notch—"

He was interrupted by the sharp pinging of an alarm.

"I knew it!" Han said, looking for a flashing indicator on the hyperdrive section of the expansive control board. "That warp stabilizer was running a couple of degrees hot at the end of our last jump."

"Actually, Captain Solo, the *Swiff*'s systems status remains at optimum," C-3PO reported. "Aboard a *Dray*-class transport, that chime indicates a proximity alert."

Han shifted his gaze to the sensor area of the console and found the flashing beacon.

"*That* can't be good." He reset the alarm, then activated the intercom. "Be ready back there."

The Noghri replied that they were *always* ready, and a bank of status beacons turned amber, indicating that the *Swiff*'s weapons systems were coming online.

Han brought up his tactical display and saw that a space–time hole had opened behind them. An instant later, the distortion closed and a bogey symbol appeared in its place.

"I *knew* getting out of there was too easy," Han said. After putting Tito and the Verpine off the ship, they had simply lifted the *Swiff*'s boarding ramp and pushed through the air lock membrane before the confused Killiks had a chance to stop them. "Someone must've slapped a homing beacon on our hull."

"Maybe," Leia said. After departing Lizil, they had done a security sweep of the interior of the vessel as a standard precaution, but there had been no time to do an external search without actually landing somewhere. "It's not going to do them much good, though. We'll be ready to jump in thirty seconds."

"As long as they don't start shooting in twenty." Han went to work on the sensors, trying to determine what kind of vessel was following them. "When it comes to a fight, this thing is no *Falcon*."

Before Han could get a sensor readout, the vessel's transponder code appeared, identifying it as a Mon Calamari *Sailfish*-class transport named *Real Deal*. A moment later, a chirpy Squib voice began to hail them over the open comm channel.

"Solo, you there?"

The *Deal* fired its ion engines and began to approach.

Han glanced over at Leia, who appeared just as surprised as he did, then activated his comm. "We're here."

"What are you doing?" asked a second Squib, probably Grees. "You're going the wrong way."

"We were starting to feel unwelcome," Han said. "And that's close enough, you three. The Noghri are still a little sore about those hit-bugs you sent."

"Hey, we *knew* they didn't stand a chance against you," Sligh said. "But we had to try."

"That was good, the way you turned Tito on us." Grees sounded more angry than admiring. "He got Krafte and Seneki before we could stop him."

"But no hard feelings, okay?" Emala asked. The *Deal* finally decelerated, but continued to drift toward the *Swiff*, slowly closing the distance. "We're the ones who started it, so fair is fair."

"Sure," Leia said. "But why do I doubt you followed us out here to mend partition barriers?"

"*That's* what we like about you guys," Sligh said. "Nothing gets past you."

"We could use someone like you in this thing of ours," Emala added.

The Squibs paused expectantly.

"You're trying to *hire* us?" Leia scoffed.

"*Recruit,*" Sligh corrected. "*Hire* is such an ugly word."

"War is very good for business," Emala added. "And this one is just going to keep getting bigger and better. Trust me when I say that we can have a very profitable relationship."

"Not a chance," Han said. He checked the weapons systems and found all of the status beacons green. If the Squibs continued to close, they were going to be in for a big surprise. *Real Deal* might be better armed than the *Swiff*, but the *Swiff* had Noghri gunners—and Han Solo in the pilot's seat. "But thanks for the offer."

"Let me put it to you plainly, Solo." Grees's voice was low and menacing. "This isn't an offer you want to refuse."

"I just *hate* it when someone tells me what I want." Han looked over and, seeing that the calculations for the next jump were complete, signaled Leia to transfer the coordinates to the guidance system. "So why don't you—"

"You're really not getting this, are you?" Grees interrupted. "Jaina is still in Colony space. We can help you get to her—or we can get to her ourselves."

Leia's finger hovered over the transfer key. "Are you threatening our daughter?"

"Not at all," Emala said. "We're giving you a chance to protect her."

Han's rage boiled over. "You try *anything,* and not only will I stop you, I'll personally drag you out of your fur and feed you to a Togorian."

"Now who's making threats?" Grees asked. "You think you're too good for us, so what choice do we have?"

"It's your own fault," Sligh said. "*We're* not responsible for what happens."

"That's it!" Han grabbed the yoke and throttles, preparing to bring the *Swiff* around to attack. "There's not going to be enough left of you—"

Leia reached over and pulled his hands off the yoke. "Han, no."

Han frowned. "No?"

"Think about it." Leia deactivated the comm microphone. "Why did they *really* come after us? Why did they put a death mark on us?"

Han thought about it. "Right. They still haven't come clean with the Killiks about Juun and Tarfang—"

"No." Leia shook her head. "The Squibs vouched for us to Lizil. If we tell the Alliance what the Colony is planning, it's on *their* heads."

Han let out a long breath. "So they're trying to distract us."

"Exactly," Leia said. "They don't need to hire us or kill us. If they can just delay us for a while, maybe even get lucky and actually put us out of commission—"

"We're going to keep going, aren't we?" Han interrupted.

Leia nodded. "We have to."

She transferred the jump coordinates to the guidance system, and Han's heart suddenly felt as heavy as a black hole. Even if the Squibs talked their way out of being held responsible for "Lord Rysto's" betrayal, they were sure to lose a fortune when the coups failed—and Squibs *hated* losing money. They would do their best to make good on their threat.

The *Deal* began to accelerate, then the lock-alarms began to chirp, announcing that the *Swiff* was being scanned by targeting sensors. Sligh's voice came over the comm channel.

"I can't believe you're making us do this, Solo. Don't you love your daughter?"

Han tried to ignore the Squib, but the question was too painful. *Of course* he loved his daughter. He would move stars to protect both of his children, to keep from losing them as he and Leia had lost Anakin. But that was growing more difficult every day. First Jaina had become a Jedi, then a Rogue Squadron pilot, and now she and Zekk were Joiners, fighting on the wrong side of a war that might never end. When you had a daughter as headstrong as Jaina, there was only so much a father could do—even when that father was Han Solo.

"They're not bluffing, Leia," Han said, leaving his comm microphone off. "You know they'll do it."

"They'll try," Leia said. "Jaina can take care of herself."

"Yeah, I know." Han pushed the throttles forward and began to accelerate away from the *Deal*. He knew Leia was right, that any assassin the Squibs sent after Jaina would be sorely outmatched—but that did not make it any easier to place the Alliance's welfare ahead of her safety. "I guess it runs in her blood."

"What runs in her blood?" Leia asked.

"Being a Jedi," Han answered. The attack alarms began to screech as the *Deal* opened fire. "Whatever Luke does with the order, it's pretty clear you'll be staying in it. Duty always comes first with you."

Leia looked hurt, but reluctantly nodded. "I'm not the only one, Han."

"I know, Princess." The *Swiff* shuddered as the *Deal*'s first salvo hit the rear shields. Han activated the hyper-drives, and the stars stretched into an opalescent blur. "And Luke won't even give *me* a lightsaber."

ELEVEN

The convoy was only minutes from the Verpine capital, arcing over the distant yellow dot that was the Roche system's sun, on final approach to the glow-speckled lump of asteroid Nickel One. With their underpowered ion drives and puffed-wafer silhouettes, the Slayn & Korpil Gatherers looked more like a long line of returning foragers than a deadly assault force. Mara could sense only a dozen presences aboard each ship, but some of those presences were a little too diffuse to be Verpine, and there was an electric hum in the Force that reminded her of one of those hot jungle nights when all creation seemed ready to erupt into war. There was definitely *something* wrong with that convoy.

She slid her StealthX into attack position behind the last vessel in line, then waited patiently as Luke and Jacen worked their way forward, using the Force to redirect the attention of the belly gunners as they passed beneath the ungainly Gatherers. Despite the diffuse presences they sensed aboard the transports, Luke was pouring caution into the battle-meld, urging Mara and Jacen to show restraint.

The holo the Solos had sent warning of a massive insect coup had been so flickering and distorted that even R2-D2 could not confirm that the voiceprint was Leia's. Luke and several other Masters had immediately suspected that the message was a forgery, designed to trick the Jedi into attacking legitimate convoys. Luke had decided to dispatch a team to each insect culture belonging to the Alliance, but with strict orders not to engage in battle unless it grew clear that the Killiks were indeed staging a coup.

That was why Mara was so confused when a flash of white brilliance erupted at the front of the convoy. It looked like a shadow

bomb detonation, but there had been no warning from either Luke
or Jacen, nothing on the tactical display to suggest that a coup was
actually under way.

The convoy began to cluster—standard procedure when the leader
wanted overlapping defenses—then continued toward the asteroid.

"Nine," Mara asked her astromech droid, "is there any sign of a
battle down there?"

The droid reported that a very large baradium explosion had just
destroyed a light transport on final approach to Nickel One.

"I *saw* the shadow bomb," Mara said. "I mean, is there anything
on the surface . . ."

The meld suddenly stiffened with shock, then abruptly collapsed
as Luke withdrew. Mara could feel his anger through their Force-
bond, a searing pressure that meant he had already answered the
question she had been about to ask her astromech. There was no hint
of a battle on the surface of the asteroid.

Jacen had attacked without provocation.

Mara looked down to find a long list scrolling up her display:
SHIELD PROJECTORS, AIR LOCK ENTRANCES, BLASTER CANNON EM-
PLACEMENTS, DEFENSIVE BUNKERS, TRANSPARISTEEL VIEWING PAN-
ELS, GUIDANCE LAMPS . . . everything her astromech could identify
on the surface of the asteroid.

"That's enough, Nine," Mara said. "I think I have my answer."

She reached out to Jacen and found him filled with impatience,
determined to stop the Gatherers before they reached Nickel One.

Mara urged him to withdraw.

Another shadow bomb detonated at the head of the convoy,
spraying specks of flotsam and torn hull in every direction.

Mara grew so angry that she had to break off contact. Anger
was too dangerous to share during a battle. It corrupted the discipline of everyone it touched, tainted their judgment and made the
killing personal.

A Verpine belly gunner caught a glimpse of Mara's StealthX and
began to stitch the surrounding darkness with cannon bolts. She
rolled away without firing and sensed Jacen trying to establish the
meld again, reaching out to her and Luke in confusion and frustration. One of the StealthXs' drawbacks—and the reason only Jedi
could fly them—was that the rigid comm silence protocols prevented
actual conversation. Instead, pilots had to communicate using the
combat-meld, which relied on emotions, impressions, and the occa-
sional mental image.

The convoy had pulled into a tight, three-dimensional diamond formation and was continuing to approach Nickel One, its gunners firing indiscriminately toward the surface. Whether the gunners were trying to suppress the asteroid's defenses or were simply reacting to Jacen's attack was impossible to say. Like Luke, Mara kept her own weapons silent.

A moment later, she felt Luke opening himself to the battle-meld again, and Jacen's relief flooded the Force. He renewed his call to the attack, sharing his alarm and fear through the meld. Luke responded with disapproval and condemnation, urging Jacen to withdraw.

A sudden spark of understanding flashed through the meld, followed by a sense of hurt and indignity. Mara guessed that Jacen had finally realized that his wingmates doubted his judgment, that they did not believe an attack was appropriate simply because he initiated one.

The thought had barely flashed through Mara's head before the gaping rectangle of a hangar entrance appeared in her mind's eye. The turbolaser batteries in its four corners all sat quiet, their turrets ripped open by internal blasts. A single Gatherer sat on the asteroid surface next to the hangar, with a line of pressure-suited Killiks streaming out of its air lock.

"Nine!" Mara was practically shouting. "Didn't you tell me there were no signs of battle on the asteroid?"

The droid replied that there *were* no signs of a battle.

"Then what about those turbolaser batteries?" Mara demanded. "And the Killiks?"

Nine reported that the turbolaser batteries were nonfunctional. And the Killiks appeared to be debarking, not attacking.

"Never mind." Mara felt at once relieved and ashamed—relieved that Jacen had attacked for good reason, ashamed that she and Luke had allowed their reservations—which now seemed unjustified—to compromise the team's effectiveness. "Select targets by expediency, Nine."

The droid illuminated a transponder symbol near the back of the convoy, and Mara swung in behind the Gatherer it represented. She launched her first shadow bomb and immediately peeled off, accelerating toward the next target. An instant later, space brightened behind her, and her tactical display filled with static. She launched her second shadow bomb without even bothering to glance back and check the damage caused by the first. The light transport had not been built that could withstand a direct hit by a Jedi shadow bomb.

More shadow bombs detonated near the middle of the convoy as Luke joined the battle. The StealthXs swirled around the Gatherers, attacking from all directions. Unable to catch more than a glimpse of the darting Jedi ships, the convoy's gunners set up rolling walls of laserfire. The Jedi, in turn, let the Force guide their moves, slipping around and under these barrages until they had obliterated another half a dozen vessels.

Finally, the convoy pilots seemed to recognize they were fish in a barrel. They dispersed, each Gatherer continuing toward a different corner of an imaginary square. As they fled, their gunners continued to blindly spray bolts into space, and now many of Nickel One's surface batteries joined in, trying to provide safe lanes of approach for their surviving "friends." That was the beauty of a coup: confusion worked in favor of the attacker.

Mara took out two more Gatherers and felt Luke destroy another one, then realized that she had lost track of Jacen. She could still feel him in the meld, but his presence had become cautious and furtive. She reached out to him, curious and concerned. His response seemed at once cocky and defiant, as though he was daring her to doubt him again.

"Whatever you're doing, hotshot, just don't screw up," Mara muttered aloud. She was counting on Jacen to keep nurturing Ben's interest in the Force, but that was not going to happen if her nephew continued to behave like a rogue Jedi. "Too much depends on you."

Jacen seemed puzzled by the sentiment, then a sea of turbolaser fire flowered between Mara and her next target, and her astromech began screeching for her to evade. She juked but continued toward her mark, then took a glancing strike on her flank and lost all her shields at once.

"Shhhhubba!" she hissed, still unwavering from her course.

Nine began to bleep and whistle frantically, filling the display with all manner of dire warnings about what would become of them if she failed to withdraw from combat at once. Mara ignored him and launched her last shadow bomb.

The attack caught the Gatherer just above its wing and punched through the shields in a blinding eruption of white. The StealthX's blast-tinting darkened, and she felt a terrible ripping in the Force as the vacuum tore the crew from its ruptured ship.

The StealthX shuddered as something large thumped into its canopy. Mara cringed and held her breath, half expecting to hear the curt *whoosh* of a catastrophic vacuum breach. But when the blast-tinting returned to normal a moment later, the only thing wrong with the canopy was that the exterior was so smeared with bug guts, that she could not find the nose of her own starfighter.

Mara immediately felt Luke reaching out to her in concern. She assured him she was fine, then switched to instrument flying and was relieved to discover she was telling the truth.

"Nine, can you do anything to clear the canopy?"

The droid promised that he would activate the defogger.

"Don't you dare!" Mara ordered. "That stuff is disgusting enough without having it run all over!"

Mara checked the tactical display and saw that only three Gatherers remained, two on Luke's side of the asteroid and one on hers. She swung her StealthX after the nearest target, trusting the Force to guide her safely around the faint streaks of color that were flashing past her blurry canopy. Her astromech droid posted a polite but urgent message on the display, reminding her that they had lost their shields.

"Relax, Nine," Mara said. "I never take more than one hit per sortie."

The droid chirped doubtfully, then asked if she usually flew blind.

"I'm not blind," Mara reminded him. "I have the For—"

Nine interrupted her with a shrill whistle, reporting that they were receiving a desperate message from the Nickel One hive mother.

"Then put it on the comm speaker," Mara ordered.

Nine replied that the message was not coming in over standard comm channels. Instead, it was being transmitted via radio frequencies that the Verpine used to communicate organically.

"Fine. What's she saying?"

A message appeared on Mara's display. HELP! THE HEART-CHAMBER IS UNDER ATTACK BY OLD ONES AND VERPINE MEMBROSIA-TRAITORS!

"Old Ones?" Mara asked.

Nine believed the hive mother was referring to Killiks.

"Tell her to lock herself in," Mara said. "We'll be there as soon as we can."

Almost instantly, a question appeared on her display. WHO?

"Just tell her we're Jedi," Mara replied. "The ones who have been attacking the convoy."

The droid tweeted an acknowledgment, and the hive mother's reply appeared on the display half a second later. THE HIVE ASKS THAT THE UNSEEN JEDI HURRY. THE MEMBROSIA-TRAITORS HAVE ALREADY INVITED THE OLD ONES INTO THE HEART-CHAMBER, AND THE MALES-WHO-DIE-FOR-THE-HIVE-MOTHER ARE ALREADY IN BATTLE.

Nine added a message of his own, noting that the ground emplacements were now targeting the Gatherers and suggesting that the Jedi would only get in the way if they continued to attack the same targets.

Mara checked her tactical display; the Verpine weapons emplacements *did* finally seem to be attacking the convoy—what was left of it, anyway.

"This had better be legitimate, Nine," she said. The R9 series was notorious for self-enhancing their preservation routines. "If you're altering data just to get me to turn back, I'll schedule you for an op-system reinstallation faster than you can count to a million and ten."

The droid reassured her that he was only reporting the truth, and as evidence, he pointed out that the salvos had stopped exploding around their vessel. Realizing that Nine was probably right—at least, she could no longer see any streaks of color flashing through the thick gunk on her canopy—Mara decided to believe him. She reached out to Luke, calling him to her side.

"Okay, Nine," she said. "Tell the hive mother we're coming in."

The hive mother's reply appeared on the display almost instantly. YES, YOU ARE VERY FAST. WE CAN SEE YOU NOW, CUTTING THE OLD ONES DOWN WITH YOUR CRYSTAL-FOCUSED BLADE.

"She can see us?" The reason occurred to Mara as soon as she had voiced the question. "Jacen!"

The happy swell of pride that suddenly filled her Force-bond with Luke told Mara that her husband had reached the same conclusion. While the two of them had been fretting over Jacen's trustworthiness and nearly blowing the mission, Jacen had been doing what needed to be done—and preventing the coup. He was already in the heart-chamber.

Jacen was, indeed, a *very* good Jedi.

"Ask the hive mother if it looks like we need any—"

Mara was interrupted by the chime of an arrival alarm, and the transponder codes of a Galactic Alliance task force began to appear on her tactical display. Nine ran a message across the screen, informing Mara that he was not altering *this* data, either.

A moment later, a familiar age-cracked voice came over the speaker in Mara's cockpit. "This is Supreme Commander Gilad Pellaeon aboard the Galactic Alliance Star Destroyer *Megador,* advising Nickel One that we are here on a peaceful mission. Please acknowledge."

Mara's droid reported that the hive mother was acknowledging, though it might take the *Megador* a moment to realize this, since she was still using Verpine radio waves.

"This is Supreme Commander Pellaeon aboard the *Megador*," Pellaeon continued. "I repeat, we are here to aid you. We have reason to believe that a hostile force may attempt to overthrow your government."

It was Jacen's voice that answered, sounding over his personal comlink. "Consider your suspicions confirmed, Admiral Pellaeon," he said. "But there is no reason for alarm. The Jedi have matters well in hand."

"The Jedi?" Pellaeon asked. He sounded relieved, perturbed, and not at all surprised. "I should have known."

Mara felt Luke's curiosity pour into the meld, and Jacen asked, "Why's that?"

"Because I've been getting reports that there were Jedi waiting almost everywhere that the Killiks have attacked so far."

This time, Luke did not even have to pour his curiosity into the meld. Jacen simply asked, "Almost?"

"I'm afraid so, Jedi Solo," Pellaeon said. "I *am* speaking to Jedi Jacen Solo, am I not?"

"And the Masters Skywalker," Jacen replied. "We're here together."

"Yes, that's what Master Horn reported," Pellaeon said. "Regretfully, our garrison intercepted his team before they could prevent the Killiks from landing on Thyferra."

The meld filled with alarm, though Mara could not say whether it was hers or Luke's or Jacen's, and Jacen asked, "You don't mean to say—"

"I'm afraid I do," Pellaeon replied. "The Killiks have taken control of our bacta supply."

TWELVE

A thousand fingers of silver fire stabbed down from orbit, slicing through the emerald rain clouds. The downpour turned as bright as the Core, and the ground shook so hard that the view in the periscope jumped like a bad holo signal. Still, the image remained clear enough to tell that the last wave of drop ships—at least those few Jaina could actually see through the deluge—had landed almost unchallenged. Their passengers were already debarking in armored hover vehicles, streaming forward to join the hundreds of thousands of troops already massing behind the defensive shield at the drop-sector perimeter.

But the Chiss success was not the cause of the icy knot between Jaina's shoulder blades, nor the reason her stomach refused to settle. UnuThul had always known the Colony would not be able to stop the enemy landing. After all, Tenupe was the linchpin of the Killik front, the gateway to the Sparkle Run and the Colony's heart, and the Chiss had committed two-thirds of their offensive forces to its capture. So there was nothing unexpected about the success of the landing, nor even all that alarming. Jaina was reacting to something else, something the Great Swarm had not yet discovered.

Jaina pulled away from the periscope and blinked for a moment as her eyes readjusted to the dim shine ball light inside the rustling tunnel. The air was hot and humid and filled with the bitter smell of battle pheromones, and the Force was charged with the same pre-combat anxiety common to soldiers of every species. The passage was literally packed with Killiks: millions of thumb-sized Jooj, an endless line of massive Rekkers, a scattering of knee-high Wuluws. There were also a few dozen volunteers from other insect species—

mostly mantis-like Snutib hunters, shriveled-looking Geonosian warriors, and a handful of Kamarians who kept asking about her father.

Jaina even saw a pair of greasy black-furred Squibs, armed with repeating blasters and thermal detonators, who seemed unable to take their big eyes off her. She smiled and reached out to them in the Force, trying to offer reassurance and calm their fears. She was not very successful; they merely curled their lips and continued to watch her.

Jaina eyed them suspiciously. It was hard to imagine why a couple of young mercenary Squibs would join this fight—unless they were desperate *and* stupid. On the other hand, it was hard to imagine them posing much of a threat, either. More likely, it was something else prickling her danger sense—something to do with the Chiss.

Jaina would have liked to know whether Zekk sensed anything unusual, but he was posted on a mountain more than a hundred kilometers away, too far away for her to share what was in his mind. With their own nest—the Taat—still trapped inside the Utegetu Nebula, their mind-link only functioned when they were within a few dozen meters of each other.

Jaina reached out to Zekk in the Force, communicating in the clumsy way Jedi usually did. When she felt nothing unusual, she withdrew from his presence and turned to a knee-high Killik standing beside her.

"Wuluw, inform UnuThul that we, er, *I* am having danger ripples." As she spoke, Jaina was absentmindedly running her wrists along its antennae. "Ask him if Unu is *sure* the scouts have found all of the Chiss reserves."

Wuluw acknowledged the order with a curt "*Urbu*." With yellow, oversized eyes and chitin so thin that it could be cracked by a stiff wind, the Killiks of the Wuluw nest hardly made ideal soldiers. But Wuluws mind-shared over a much greater distance than most Killiks—nearly half a kilometer, compared with a typical range of a few dozen meters—and so they were posted throughout the Great Swarm to serve as a communications net.

A moment later, Wuluw reported that UnuThul did not sense any danger in the Force. He wanted to know if she and Zekk were trying another trick like she had at Qoribu—

"No," Jaina interrupted. "We want to destroy the landing force, too. Maybe a big defeat will make the Chiss rethink the wisdom of pressing this war."

Wuluw relayed an assurance from UnuThul that they would soon teach the Chiss to respect the Colony. Then a murky Force pressure rose inside Jaina's chest, urging her and the rest of the Great Swarm to action. The tunnel filled with a loud clatter, and Wuluw rumbled a more specific order from UnuThul, telling Jaina to prepare her horde for the assault.

Jaina looked down a side tunnel to a large underground chamber, one of hundreds that the Killiks had been excavating since the drop ships landed. A steady shower of moist jungle soil was pouring down from the ceiling, partially obscuring the pale white chitin of the four Mollom burrowers already digging their way toward the surface.

"Tell UnuThul we'll be attacking the command craft any moment," Jaina said. She opened herself to the battle-meld—primarily with Zekk, but she knew UnuThul would also be monitoring it—then motioned to her insect troops and started down the side corridor. "We'll hit—"

"Ur ruub," the lead Rekker rumbled. "Uuu b ruu."

"Right," Jaina said. "We just need to be sure the volunteers—"

"Fassssst and 'arrrrrd," a Snutib whistled.

"UnuThul told us," a Geonosian added.

"Good," Jaina said, wondering why UnuThul had bothered to name her and Zekk subcommanders if he wanted to run the entire battle himself. "Ask if you have any questions."

She stopped just inside the entrance and waited in silence for the Mollom to break through to the surface. Thankfully, the jungle soil was too moist to raise dust as it fell, but as the burrowers neared the surface, the dirt changed to mud, and the chamber floor quickly grew slick. Finally, the Mollom boomed a warning down the shaft, and a loud sucking noise sounded from the surface.

An instant later the heat-blackened nose of a drop ship crashed down into the chamber, its shield generators overloading and exploding as they struggled to push back the cramped shaft the Mollom had dug beneath it. Rain began to pour down the hole, and the craft's forward beam cannons continued to fire, filling the room with heat and steam and color, and blasting bantha-sized craters into the walls and floor.

Jaina made a scooping motion with her hand, using the Force to hurl a huge mass of soil at the cannons, driving the mud down the emitter nozzle and packing it tight around the galven coils. The weapons exploded an instant later, blowing off the turret and leaving a five-meter breach in the top hull.

The Killiks rattled forward in a boiling wave, the tiny Jooj swarming along the walls and ceiling, the mighty Rekkers springing directly onto the drop ship. The Rekkers boomed their thoraxes in glee and dived through the breach left by the destroyed turret. A few seconds after the first insects had entered, the drop ship's hull began to reverberate with muffled sizzles and dull pings.

Jaina clicked her throat in approval, then reached out in the Force to see if she could sense Jagged Fel's presence aboard the vessel. They were enemies now, but she did not want him to die. As a skilled tactician and a high-ranking Chiss officer, he would be a great asset to the Colony—assuming he could be captured and brought into a nest.

And if Jag became a Joiner, she mused, the Dawn Rumble would be so much more—

"*R u u buruub!*" Wuluw burst out. The little Killik started to turn and flee back down the tunnel. "*Bur!*"

"No!" Jaina caught the insect by an arm. "This way."

If the Chiss were arming the drop ship's self-destruct mechanism, the last place they wanted to be when the shock waves hit was underground. Dragging Wuluw along, Jaina Force-leapt onto the drop ship's hull, then sprang again, leaping half a dozen meters to the surface.

She found herself standing in the heart of the Chiss landing zone, a clearing of mud and ash surrounded by a circle of blast-toppled mogo trees. A hundred meters away, the landing zone abruptly gave way to a skeleton jungle, a leafless tangle of trunks and limbs stripped bare by Chiss defoliating sprays. In the distance, barely visible through the pouring rain and the naked timber, she could see the upended tail of another drop ship, rising out of a hole similar to the one from which she had emerged.

A flurry of shrill sizzles erupted as a Chiss squad opened up with their charric rifles. Wuluw tried to dive back underground, but Jaina jerked her in the opposite direction.

"I told you, this way!" Jaina started across the clearing, dodging and weaving and dragging Wuluw along. "It's safer!"

"*Bur ub bbu!*"

"*Of course* they're shooting at us." Jaina reached the edge of the clearing and dived for cover. "They're the enemy!"

They landed between a pair of fallen mogo trees, and the sizzles became crackles as the charrics began to chew through the speeder-sized trunk.

"*R-ruu u-u b-b-burr,*" Wuluw stammered.

"Don't worry." Jaina unslung her repeating blaster. "We're Jedi, aren't we?"

Wuluw thrummed her thorax doubtfully.

Jaina popped up and began to pour bolts back across the clearing. The nearest drop ship—the one she had bounded up—had not yet self-destructed, and the Jooj were swarming up the hull and pouring out across the landing zone. The Rekkers were coming, too, springing out of the pit by the dozens, booming their thoraxes in glee and spraying shatter gun pellets in every direction.

But the Chiss were recovering from their shock and making their presence known. Nearly half the leaping Rekkers tumbled back into the hole, their thoraxes trailing arcs of gore or their heads vanishing in the flash of a maser beam. And many of those who *did* reach the jungle floor landed in pieces or limp, oozing heaps.

Jaina did her best to cover them, but the Chiss troops were camouflaged in color-shifting, fractal-pattern armor that made them nearly impossible to see. She reached out in the Force and felt perhaps a hundred enemy soldiers scattered throughout the area, all confused, frightened, and—typically for Chiss—still resolute. She began to rely on the Force rather than her eyes to find targets and saw a bolt strike what appeared to be a mogo limb—until it dropped its charric rifle and whirled away clutching a wounded shoulder.

Then a powerful jolt shook the ground. The nearest drop ship's tail erupted into a ball of shrapnel and orange flame, and the Force shuddered with the anguish of a mass death. Jaina dropped back behind the tree and turned to pull Wuluw down beside her. She found only a shard of white-hot durasteel, lodged in a blood-sprayed mogo trunk behind where the Killik had been standing.

Jaina had seen—had *caused*—so much carnage in combat that she had believed herself numb to the storm of emotions it spawned. But the loss of the frightened little Wuluw brought it all back—all the fear and the anger and the guilt, the despair and the loneliness and the soul-scorching rage that had been lurking just beneath the surface since the deaths of Anakin and Chewbacca and so many others.

Jaina leapt up again, eager to blast a hundred Chiss, to make the invaders pay for the deaths of Wuluw and so many others, but apart from her own fading battle cry, the area had fallen suddenly quiet. All that remained of the drop ship was the black smoke streaming out of the pit and a few shards of white-hot metal embedded in fallen mogos. Chiss and Rekkers alike remained tucked down among the tree trunks around her, momentarily too stunned to continue killing, and even the surviving Jooj seemed disoriented, swirling across the ground in rambling swarms of brownish green.

In the distance, Jaina could make out more columns of smoke

rising toward the emerald sky. Every few moments, a fresh thud sounded somewhere in the rain, marking the destruction of another drop ship. Each detonation brought the death of thousands of insects, but an entire drop fleet of detonations would not change the battle's outcome. What the Chiss failed to understand—what they would refuse to understand until it was too late—was that they could not win a war of attrition against the Colony.

A Killik could lay a thousand eggs a month, and within a year, those eggs would be battle-ready nymphs. In two years, the survivors would lay eggs of their own. Kill one Killik, and ten thousand would take its place. Kill ten thousand, and a million would take *theirs*. If the Chiss wanted to survive this war, they had only one choice: withdraw to their own borders and sue for peace. It was that simple.

After a moment, the Jooj started to find their way into the fallen trees the enemy was using for cover. Chiss soldiers began to leap out of hiding, screaming and ripping their armor off, slapping and even shooting at the thumbnail-sized insects that had slipped past their defenses. Jaina understood their panic. The Jooj were not attacking so much as feeding, injecting their prey with a flesh-dissolving enzyme and sucking the liquefied flesh back into their mouths. Supposedly, victims felt as if they were being burned alive.

The surviving Rekkers began to take advantage of the enemy's panic, pounding them with shatter gun pellets the moment they showed themselves. Other Chiss returned fire, and soon the battle was in full swing again. Jaina stretched into the Force and poured blasterfire at soldiers she could sense but did not see. The sharp *phoots* of insecticide grenades began to detonate all around her, and she felt Killiks dying slow, anguished deaths as their respiratory spiracles swelled shut.

Finally, Killik reinforcements began to pour out of the smoking pit again, the Rekkers springing into view with their weapons blazing, the Jooj scuttling over edges and spreading outward in all directions. The Chiss, disciplined even when it was clear they had no chance of survival, responded with a desperate assault, hurling vape charges and insecticide grenades into the hole in a futile effort to turn back the Killik tide.

Jaina felt an enemy presence behind her and turned to find a trio of Chiss soldiers leaping over a mogo trunk. Their charric rifles were already swinging in her direction. She swept her hand across her body, using the Force to redirect their aim. Maser beams sprayed harmlessly past, filling the air with smoke, splinters, and heat.

The leader was on Jaina instantly, his red eyes shining with hatred behind his helmet as he clubbed at her head with his rifle butt. She ducked, using the Force to pull him over her back and send him crashing into the trunk behind her.

The other two Chiss arrived a step later, one bringing an armored knee up at her face. Jaina blocked with her blaster, at the same time squeezing the trigger and pumping fire into the stomach armor of her other attacker. The bolts ricocheted away and sent the soldier stumbling back, but not before he slammed the barrel of his own weapon down on the back of her head.

Jaina found herself kneeling on the ground, her vision narrowing, her hands empty, and the deafening crack of the blow still echoing inside her skull. She tried to stand and felt the strength drain from her body.

No!

Zekk touched her through their battle-meld, pouring strength into her through the Force, urging her to stay conscious.

Jaina fell flat to the ground—then unhooked her lightsaber and activated the blade as she rolled away, slicing both soldiers at the knees. They screamed and crashed down behind her. She felt her blade move and recoil as a maser beam crackled into it. Her vision cleared, and she found herself facing the first Chiss who had attacked her.

She deflected the next shot back into his helmet visor, sending him tumbling backward over a mogo trunk. His body lay still and silent, the small plume of smoke that rose from it stinking of charred flesh.

Jaina spun on a knee and found the other two Chiss lying on their bellies in front of her, groaning in pain as they struggled to prop themselves on their elbows and open fire. She used the Force to rip their weapons from their hands, then stood and raised her lightsaber to finish them off.

Only the revulsion that Zekk poured into the meld stayed Jaina's blade. She was still so filled with battle lust that she had not even realized she was about to kill the two Chiss in cold blood. It was happening again. She was surrendering to the rage that had consumed her after Anakin died—giving herself to war, with no thought to anything but vengeance and victory.

Shuddering in disgust, Jaina deactivated her lightsaber and knelt next to the two soldiers. Her blade had cauterized their wounds, so they were not losing much blood. But they were both shivering and much too quiet. She rolled them onto their backs, then removed the first soldier's helmet. His blue skin was covered with perspiration, and his red eyes were distant and unfocused.

Jaina shook him by the chin, trying to bring him back to alertness. "Where's your medkit?"

The Chiss clamped a hand weakly over her arm. "Why?"

"You're going into shock," she explained. "You need a stim-shot, or you'll die."

"You?" the second soldier gasped inside his helmet. "Trying . . . to save us?"

"Isn't that what we just said?" Jaina demanded.

"No!"

The first soldier pushed her away, surprising her with his strength.

"Don't be afraid." Jaina poured soothing emotions into the Force, trying to calm and comfort the pair. "The Colony will take care of you. We'll even give—"

The second soldier snapped a vape charge off his utility belt and pulled the activation pin. "We know what you'll . . . do."

"Hey!" Jaina did not dare use the Force to yank the canister from his hand—the charge would detonate the instant he released the trigger. "You're not getting this. The Colony is *good* to prisoners. You'll hardly know—"

"That your bugs are eating our insides?" The Chiss nodded to his companion, then said, "We'll be waiting on the other side, Jedi—"

Jaina sprang into a backward Force flip and tumbled away in a high arc, thumbing her lightsaber active again and batting aside a flurry of maser beams as she came down in the murky ribbon of a jungle stream.

The vape charge detonated as she splashed into the water, a dazzling flash of white that tore the air itself, stealing the breath from her lungs and leaving her half blind, shaking, and confused. She was not all that surprised the two soldiers had refused to surrender—but the reasons they had given distressed her. Could they really believe the Colony fed its prisoners to its larvae?

Jaina had no time to debate the question, for another cold shiver of danger sense was racing up her back. She brought her lightsaber up and spun around to block . . . and found the two Squib volunteers peering down the streambank at her, their dark heads and power blasters poking out from beneath the trunk of a fallen mogo.

"Take it easy, lady," the one on the left said. His muzzle was a little longer and sharper than that of his companion, who had a crooked streak of white fur tracing an old scar down one cheek. "We just came to see if you were still alive."

"Apparently so," Jaina said. She lowered her lightsaber, but did not deactivate the blade. "Be careful. I sensed something dangerous up there."

"You don't say?" Longnose exchanged glances with Scarcheek, then said, "Then I guess it's a good thing we came along."

"Yeah," Scarcheek agreed. "You're real lucky to have us looking out for you."

THIRTEEN

Deep beneath the new Defense Force command compound on Coruscant—already known among military personnel as "the Dark Star"—there lay a dozen planning facilities so secret that Luke had never officially been informed of their existence. At the moment, he was in PaAR Five—*PaAR* being the acronym for "Planning and Analysis Room." That Cal Omas had actually summoned him—and Mara and Jacen—into one of the secret rooms, he took as a good sign. Perhaps the Chief of State was ready to put the trouble between the Jedi and the government behind them.

Their escort led them along a dimly lit walkway past a projection pit displaying a three-meter hologram of the planet Thyferra. Around the edges of the pit were arrayed several banks of work stations where dozens of communications officers, intelligence analysts, and system operators labored to keep the information displayed on the hologram up to the minute. From what Luke could see, the situation wasn't good. The green swaths of continental rain forest were speckled with colored lettering that showed the dispositions of various villages, forces, and facilities. The planet's largest city, Zalxuc, and most of its villages had already turned red, indicating they were known to be under enemy control.

At the end of the walkway, the Skywalkers and Jacen were admitted onto a secure command platform where Chief Omas stood poring over holofeeds with Admiral Pellaeon. Han and Leia were already there as well, studying a second bank of holodisplays along with a Vratix—one of the mantiform insects who inhabited Thyferra. When the guards announced their arrival, Omas pretended to be engrossed in a holofeed of the Thyferran rain forest, leaving a surprised Pellaeon to wave them toward the holobank.

"Masters Skywalker, Jedi Solo, please join us." Despite his aged face and bushy white mustache, Pellaeon—an ex-Imperial admiral—continued to look the part of the shrewd command officer he was. He gestured toward the insect at his side. "Do you know Senator Zalk't from Thyferra?"

"Only by reputation." Luke inclined his head to the Vratix. "I'm sorry the Jedi weren't able to prevent the coup on Thyferra, Senator Zalk't."

Zalk't scuttled over and greeted Luke by rubbing a massive forearm across his shoulder. "The fault was not *yours,* Master Skywalker." His speech was filled with whistles and clicks. "Thyferra thanks the Jedi for their efforts on our behalf."

"As does the entire Galactic Alliance," Pellaeon added. "Had the Jedi not responded so quickly, we would have lost far more than the Thyferra system." He cast a meaningful glance in Omas's direction. "Isn't that correct, Chief Omas?"

Omas finally tore his attention away from the holo and met Luke's gaze. He looked even more careworn than usual, with ashen skin and bags beneath his eyes as deep as those of a Yuuzhan Vong.

"Yes, it was a relief to find the Jedi serving the Galactic Alliance for a change," Omas said.

"The Jedi have always served the Galactic Alliance, Chief Omas." As Luke spoke, he was pouring goodwill into the Force. He could sense the anger that Omas's comment had raised in Han and Leia and even in Jacen, and he could not allow this meeting to degenerate into a shouting match. "But the issues have not always been clear, and sometimes we have taken the long view without talking to you. I apologize for our mistakes."

Omas's jaw dropped, as did those of Han, Leia, and Jacen. Only Pellaeon and Mara did not seem surprised—Pellaeon because the Galactic Alliance and the Jedi order clearly needed each other to deal with the Killiks, and Mara because she was the one who had suggested to Luke that it was the duty of the Jedi order to support the Galactic Alliance. Imperfect as it was, the Galactic Alliance remained the galaxy's best hope for achieving a lasting peace.

Omas finally recovered from his shock. "Thank you, Master Skywalker." There was more suspicion in his words than relief, and he quickly turned back to the bank of holofeeds. "I trust the Jedi won't find the issues too confusing today."

Almost all of the holofeeds showed a small squad of Killik commandos leading a few Vratix "tarheads"—insects addicted to black membrosia—into a village of graceful, multibalconied towers. The tarheads would enter one or two of the towers, then return with a few Vratix and present them to the Killiks, who did not even bother lining the prisoners up before spraying them with shatter gun pellets. Sometime during the process, the holo would usually show a Killik approaching the holocam, and the signal would go to static.

"The traitorsss are bringing out the village anirs," Zalk't explained in his whistling Basic. "But the coup actually began in Zalxuc. Before we realized what was happening, tarhead traitors had slain our high canirs and their assistants, and the Killiksss were hunting down every noninsect in the city."

"Cutting off the head so they can control the body," Leia said. "Standard coup strategy."

"Yeah, but this one has a twist," Han added. "Black membrosia will be running in the streets. Half the population will be addicts—and the bugs will be their suppliers."

"It gets worse," Leia pointed out. "If the Killiks hold Thyferra long enough, the Vratix will become Joiners."

Luke nodded. "*If* the Killiks hold it long enough." He turned to Jacen. "How long would it take for the Vratix to start becoming Joiners?"

"It doesn't matter," Jacen said, shaking his head. "The Killiks are trying—"

"That's *not* what I asked," Luke snapped. He could feel in the Force that Omas remained too suspicious of the Jedi to take advice from Jacen. "Just answer my question."

Jacen scowled at the rebuke. "Cilghal would have a better idea than I do," he said. "Normally, an outsider has to spend several months in a nest to become a full Joiner, but it might go faster for insect species."

"In the meantime, our bacta supply is cut off," Omas said. "And if we launch a counteroffensive, the damage could be even worse."

"The fighting will be widespread, and the xoorzi crop will suffer," Zalk't said.

"Xoorzi crop?" Han asked. "I thought bacta was made out of a couple of kinds of bacteria."

"It is," Zalk't replied. "Xoorzi fungus is the growth medium for the alazhi bacteria. It occurs only in the wild, in the deepest shade of the forest floor. The slightest disturbance will cause it to release its spores and shrivel."

"As you can see, a conventional battle would be devastating,"

Pellaeon said. "We were hoping the Jedi would be able to handle the situation a bit more delicately." He turned to Omas, his expression carrying an unspoken demand. "Weren't we?"

Omas swallowed hard, then said, "Yes. The Galactic Alliance would be very grateful for the Jedi's help."

Luke kept a sober expression, but inwardly he was smiling. The Jedi's quick response to the coup attempts had regained some measure of respect from Chief Omas, and now he was asking for the Jedi's help—albeit reluctantly.

"Of course." Luke felt a bolt of alarm shoot through the Force as Han, Jacen, and even Leia grew worried that he was allowing political concerns to undermine his judgment. "The Jedi would be delighted to help."

"If you and Admiral Pellaeon think that's best," Mara added, obviously sensing the same objections from their companions.

Omas frowned at her. "We do."

"Then that's what we'll do." Luke noticed Pellaeon's brown eyes studying Mara with their usual shrewdness. He nudged the admiral through the Force, feeding Pellaeon's doubt and urging him to question the situation. Outwardly, he simply bowed to Chief Omas. "If you'll excuse me, then, I'll start recalling our Jedi Knights—"

"Not yet," Pellaeon said. His gaze flickered briefly between Luke and Mara, and Luke knew the admiral had figured out that he was being played. That did not prevent him from asking the right question. "You don't think sending the Jedi to Thyferra is a good idea, do you, Master Skywalker?"

Luke kept his gaze fixed on Omas. "The Jedi are willing to go wherever Chief Omas feels we are needed."

"Blast it, Luke!" Pellaeon barked. "That's not what I asked. If you know something we don't—"

"It's not anything we *know*," Leia interrupted. "It's just experience."

"*What* experience?" Omas looked suspicious, but he was clearly unwilling to deny his Supreme Commander the leeway to pursue his own line of inquiry. "With the Killiks?"

"Precisely," Leia said. "I'm sure it hasn't appeared this way from your position as the Chief of State, but the Jedi are convinced that much of the Colony's aggression since Qoribu has actually been directed at the Jedi order."

"That wouldn't surprise me in the least," Omas said icily. "As I'm sure you recall, I didn't want the Jedi involved with the Colony in the first place."

"I don't see how that has any bearing on the current situation," Pellaeon said sharply. "And you feel these coups are directed at the Jedi *how*?"

"Not *at* us," Luke said. "They're diversions, to keep us on the defensive instead of destroying the Colony's strength at a crucial time."

"The Killiks are launching something major," Leia said. When Omas's brow rose, she raised a hand to forestall his question. "I can feel it through Jaina—there's a big battle going on, one she seems confident of winning."

This was news to Luke, who had not been able to get a clear Force reading on his niece since she became a Joiner, but Pellaeon nodded in agreement.

"Bwua'tu feels they're preparing another breakout attempt in the Utegetu," the admiral said. "And they certainly wouldn't want the Jedi interfering in *that*—not after the role you played in spoiling their first attempt."

Omas looked at Pellaeon with a dropped jaw. "You believe them?"

"I do. The Colony can't fight the Alliance and the Chiss at the same time. I never believed the coups were meant to be anything more than a diversion—and I'm certainly willing to consider the possibility that it wasn't the *military* they were trying to distract." Pellaeon turned to Luke. "Can the Jedi really destroy the Colony's strength?"

Luke nodded, using the Force to project more confidence than he felt. "We can."

"You'll forgive me if I want to know how," Omas said.

"Simple." It was Jacen who said this. "We take out Raynar Thul."

Pellaeon and Omas exchanged uneasy glances, then Omas asked, "By 'take out,' you mean—"

"We mean do whatever is necessary to remove him from power," Luke said. He was still not ready to commit to killing one of his own Jedi Knights—at least not publicly. "But to destroy the Colony, we can't stop there. I'll have to find and kill Lomi Plo."

Pellaeon's eyes narrowed. "And you can do that? I thought she was invisible."

"She won't be invisible this time," Luke said. "And we have a backup plan."

"We do?" Han asked, raising his brow.

Luke nodded. "Something Cilghal developed while you and Leia were scouting Lizil."

Luke avoided any reference to the mission being unauthorized. Despite Leia's misgivings about him assuming sole leadership of the Jedi, she was obviously still dedicated to the Alliance and the order— she had proved *that* when she and Han returned to sound the warning about the coups instead of continuing after Jaina and Zekk.

When Luke did not elaborate, Pellaeon grew impatient. "Master Skywalker, you obviously have a plan to end this entire crisis. Would you please stop wasting the Chief's time and tell us?"

Luke smiled. "Of course."

He laid out the basics of the plan that he and Mara had been developing for some time, outlining what he would need from the Defense Forces, how the Alliance's Jedi would be used, and what they would need from Chief Omas. By the time he finished, there had been a clear shift in the mood on the command platform.

"Just so I'm sure I understand," Omas said. "This will destroy the Colony, but not the Killiks?"

"That's right," Luke said. "And even if the Colony does somehow form again, it won't be able to expand."

Omas nodded, then caught Luke's eye and held it. "And you really said 'the Alliance's Jedi'?"

Luke laughed, trying to keep hidden the sense of loss he felt inside. "I did," he said. "The Jedi serve the Force—but we can't serve it in a vacuum. We need the Galactic Alliance as much as it needs us."

"Well, then!" Omas's face brightened, and he turned to Pellaeon. "What do you think of our Jedi's plan?"

Pellaeon grew thoughtful, absentmindedly twisting the ends of his mustache, then frowned in approval. "It's sneaky," he said. "I like it."

FOURTEEN

A terrible ripping noise growled down out of the clouds, and Jaina looked up to see another flight of Chiss missiles arcing through the downpour. It had been days—more than a week—since the Great Swarm had boiled out of the ground beneath the enemy's drop ships, and the missiles had not stopped. They came day and night, painting streaks of white fire across the sky and trailing green plumes of insecticide, grating nerves raw with their endless growling.

Jaina made a sweeping motion with her hand, using the Force to hurl three missiles back toward their launchers. The other two dropped into the defoliated jungle behind her and detonated in a blinding pulse, hurling trunks in every direction and flashing killer radiation through the naked trees for a hundred meters.

Killiks died by the hundreds in an instant, and they would die by the thousands as the plumes of poisonous vapor settled to the jungle floor and began to take their toll. It did not matter. UnuThul was urging the Great Swarm onward, filling every thorax with the same irresistible compulsion to *attack, attack, attack* that Jaina felt hammering inside her own chest. The Killiks had to overrun the Chiss lines; they had to do it now.

There was just one problem.

Already, the jungle floor lay buried so deeply beneath dead Killiks and pieces of dead Killiks that Jaina could barely walk. In places, she was literally wading through pools of insect gore or scrambling over mounds of broken chitin, and the enemy lines remained as unattainable as ever. For every hundred meters the Great Swarm advanced, the Chiss pulled back a hundred and one. Eventually, of course, they would run out of room to retreat—but Jaina was beginning to worry that the Colony would run out of Killiks first.

Jaina slipped behind the trunk of a giant mogo and dropped to her knees, keeping one eye on the flickering battle ahead as she uncapped her canteen. The problem was not that the Killiks were failing to kill the enemy. Jaina could see half a dozen panicked Chiss ripping at their armor to get at the Jooj underneath, and every few moments, a Rekker would spring over a breastwork and send a Chiss soldier bouncing off the trees—often in pieces.

The problem was that—with UnuThul's Will compelling them to attack almost mindlessly—the Killiks were a lot less efficient than the Chiss. They were running headlong into walls of charric fire, while the enemy remained concealed and protected behind their temporary fortifications, exposing themselves to attack only when there were so many Killik bodies piled in front of them that they had to withdraw to a clear position.

Jaina turned, looking for her newest communications assistant— she lost at least one Wuluw a day—and found only the two black-furred Squibs who had assigned themselves to watch her back.

"Wuluw?" she called.

A soft clatter sounded from the base of the mogo tree, and she looked down to find the little brown Killik crawling out from beneath a root-knee. "What are you doing down there?"

"*Ubb.*"

"Okay." Jaina sighed. "Just don't disappear entirely."

Wuluw withdrew back under the root, leaving visible the tiniest tip of one antenna.

The rain-soaked Squibs snickered openly, mocking Wuluw for being a coward—until a passing charric beam singed a hand-wide band of fur off the side of Longnose's head.

"*Rurub,*" Wuluw thrummed from her muddy hole.

"I know you're not laughing at *me,* bug." Longnose started to raise his repeating blaster. "Because you aren't that brave."

"Knock it off," Jaina said. She used the Force to push both Squibs away, then addressed herself to the mouth of Wuluw's hiding place. "Tell UnuThul this isn't working. We have to slow down and fight from position—"

"*Bb!*" Wuluw relayed.

"We *have* to," Jaina said. "At this rate, the swarm will run out of soldiers!"

"*Bruu ruu urubu,*" Wuluw thrummed, still relaying UnuThul's message. "*Ur bu!*"

"Even the Colony's army isn't that big!" Jaina protested. "The Chiss are slaughtering us by the millions."

"*Ur bu!*" Wuluw repeated. "*Urub bub ruuur uur.*"

"What do you mean you're going to be out of touch?" Jaina demanded. "You're the commander, UnuThul! You can't just leave the battle!"

"*Ru'ub bur,*" Wuluw relayed. "*Ur bu!*"

The "trust me" command was accompanied by the dark pressure of UnuThul's Will, urging Jaina to continue the attack, to overrun the Chiss lines. Everything depended on that.

"What choice do we have?" Jaina grumbled. "But before UnuThul goes, there's something he should know about the Chiss."

"*Ub?*"

"They're not surrendering," Jaina reported. "Even when they have no way to keep fighting, they make us kill them."

"*Uuuu,*" Wuluw rumbled. "*Bu?*"

"They seem to think we're laying eggs in them," Jaina reported, "and letting our larvae eat them, like what the . . ."

Jaina could not remember the name of the nest that had been doing those terrible things at Kr.

"Like what happened at Qoribu," she finished.

Wuluw relayed UnuThul's response quickly—too quickly. "*Buub urr bubb.*"

"It's more than a rumor," Jaina objected. "We saw what happened at Kr. So did you, UnuThul."

"*Ubbb ruur?*" Wuluw asked for UnuThul. "*Burrubuur rububu ru.*"

"Maybe," Jaina said. The pressure to attack had turned to a dark weight now, pressing down inside her chest, urging her to reexamine her memories. "It was dark in the grub cave. We could have misunderstood what we were seeing."

"*Buuu ururub,*" Wuluw relayed. "*Rbuurb u rubur ruu.*"

"That's probably it," Jaina agreed.

She knew that UnuThul was forcing the conclusion on her, that somewhere down inside she remembered events another way. But Zekk was still hiding in the mountains with the airborne swarm, too far away to share her thoughts and bolster her resolve, and without him, she simply lacked the strength to resist UnuThul's Will.

"It would be just like the Chiss to make that up," Jaina said. "That must be what happened. They must be afraid their soldiers will surrender and join the Colony."

"*Bur.*"

Wuluw went on to reiterate UnuThul's orders, instructing Jaina to continue pressing the attack on all fronts. Of course, it was not actually necessary for her to issue the order herself. The entire swarm simply felt the same pressure in their thoraxes that Jaina did in her chest, and they began to redouble their efforts, the Rekkers springing over the Chiss breastworks in waves, the Jooj swarming through the jungle in a droning brown-green cloud.

Taking care to make certain Wuluw stayed with her—and that she always knew where those Squibs were—Jaina started toward the mountains in the distance, hidden though they were by rain and mist. She could have turned toward any quadrant, since the swarm was attacking the Chiss from all directions inside the perimeters. But the mountains were where Zekk was waiting, and Jaina longed to be as near to him as possible. With Taat still trapped in the Utegetu Nebula, he was her entire nest now—the words that completed her thought, the beat that drove her heart—and if she was going to die today, she wanted to do it near him.

Suddenly, the sizzle of the charric rifles began to fade and the swarm began to advance more rapidly. Jaina finally waded free of the Killik gore and saw nothing ahead but scurrying limbs and fanning wings. There were no Chiss anywhere, no beams of death flickering out to slow the Colony. Jaina could not believe they had actually broken the legendary Chiss discipline, that UnuThul's last exhortation had been all that was needed for the swarm to push through the enemy lines.

Something was wrong.

Jaina stopped and turned to Wuluw. "Halt! Tell them to stop. It's a—"

The crackle of an incoming barrage echoed through the trees, then the jungle erupted into a raging storm of detonating artillery shells and splintering wood. Whole treetops began to crash down from above, crushing thousands of unlucky insects, and wisps of green vapor began to spread through the mogos and sink toward the forest floor.

The Killiks stopped and drummed their chests in alarm, working their wings and trying to keep the mist from settling on their bodies, but the artillery shells continued to come. The wisps of vapor turned into a ground haze, then the haze to a fog. The rain only seemed to make the fog grow thicker, as though the insecticide was water-activated. The river of Jooj stopped advancing, the jungle floor grew crowded with convulsing Rekkers, and Jaina began to gag on the sickly-sweet smell of the deadly gas.

She used the Force to clear a hole through the green fog. Before she could pull the electrobinoculars from her utility belt, the hole grew congested with charging Rekkers. She started to hop up on a mogo trunk so she could see over them, then realized how exposed that would leave her and thought better of it.

"Tell those soldiers to wait!" Jaina said to Wuluw. "I need to see."

Wuluw had barely acknowledged the order before the Rekkers dropped to the jungle floor. Jaina set the electrobinoculars to scan and peered down the tunnel she was keeping open through the green cloud. Even with all the foliage stripped away by Chiss defoliators, it was nearly impossible to see very far through the thick timber. But eventually, she did glimpse a muzzle flash from beside a fifty-meter mogo. She gave the tree a fierce Force shove and sent it crashing to the jungle floor.

A flurry of Chiss charric beams reduced the upended roots to a spray of dirt and smoking splinters, but Jaina wasted no time searching for the attackers. The fire had been quick and precise, which meant it had come from dismounted infantry, and that told her much of what she needed to know.

The rest Jaina discovered when another muzzle flash filled the viewfinder of her electrobinoculars. She centered the flash, magnified the image, and found herself looking at the blocky silhouette of a MetaCannon, one of the Chiss's largest drop-deployable field pieces. The MetaCannon could fire maser beams, blaster bolts, or even primitive artillery shells with a "quick-and-easy" change of the barrel.

What it could not do, however, was react quickly to changing tactics.

"Everybody into the treetops," Jaina ordered. The Chiss insecticide would not be as effective in the jungle canopy, since it would rapidly be dispersed by the wind or sink to the ground. "Advance rapidly until the enemy starts to fire into the jungle canopy, then drop to the ground and continue. Expect small-arms fire in—" She checked her range-finder. "—approximately one kilometer."

Having already relayed the orders, Wuluw started up the nearest mogo. The Squibs followed close behind. Jaina returned her electrobinoculars and lightsaber to her utility belt, then started after them, giving orders as she climbed.

"Report to all nests that it looks like the Chiss have brought their heavy artillery back to stop us."

Wuluw stopped climbing and spun her head around backward, her mandibles spread in alarm as she looked down her back at Jaina. *"B-b-bu?"*

"Really," Jaina said. "Don't worry. We're not going to let any-thing happen to you."

Wuluw flattened her antennae doubtfully. *"Buur urbu ruub u."*

"I mean it this time." Jaina fluttered her hand, using the Force to whisk away a bank of insecticide drifting their way. "Just keep climbing . . . and do your job! The other nests need that report."

Wuluw expelled air through her respiratory spiracles, then turned her head around and resumed climbing. A moment later, she began to drum her chest, relaying the other nests' pleasure at how well the battle was progressing. Kolosolok would be attacking the perimeter soon.

They finally climbed above the vapor layers into the remains of the jungle canopy. All the foliage was gone, of course, leaving the great mogos scratching at the rain clouds with the crooked fingers of their naked crowns. The artillery barrage had opened surprisingly few holes in the gray expanse, and there were even a few confused birds still circling low over the wet treetops.

To Jaina's relief, thousands of Rekkers had survived the danger-ous climb from the jungle floor. They were already advancing through the rain, springing from treetop to treetop with a power and grace that even Wookiees would have envied—had they been able to overlook the Rekkers' six limbs, antennae, and long pendu-lous abdomens.

The Jooj were advancing somewhat differently, winding across the treetops in huge sinuous blankets, circling gaps in the canopy or creating long boiling bridges out of their own bodies. The Chiss ar-tillery continued to savage the jungle below, occasionally sending the crown of a mogo plummeting into the poisonous tangle while pan-icked Killiks leapt to safety in adjacent treetops.

But mostly, the Colony's advance was unhindered. Rekkers and Jooj continued to rise into the canopy behind Jaina, and as far as the eye could see ahead, an unstoppable tide of insects was boiling across the jungle top toward the Chiss lines.

Jaina turned to Wuluw. "How good are you at jumping?"

"Bub bu," the insect admitted.

"That's what we thought," Jaina said. She turned her back to the Wuluw. "Hop on."

The Killik leapt up and wrapped all six limbs around Jaina's body.

"What about you two?" Jaina asked the Squibs.

They folded their wet ears flat. "Don't worry about us, doll," Scarcheek said. "We'll be right behind you."

"Sorry—didn't mean to insult you," Jaina said. She nodded them toward the Chiss lines. "Why don't you lead the way?"

They fixed their dark eyes on her for a moment, then slung their repeating blasters across their backs and scampered away on all fours. When they came to the end of the limb, they spread their arms and glided nearly twenty meters into the crown of the next tree.

When they stopped to wait for Jaina, she paused to speak over her shoulder to Wuluw.

"What do the nests know about those two?"

"*Urubu bubu rbu,*" Wuluw answered.

"I know they're Squibs!" Jaina said. "What are they doing *here*?"

"*Bubuu urrb.*"

"*Besides* killing Chiss," Jaina said.

"*Ruubu bu,*" Wuluw answered. "*Ub rur uru.*"

"It's *not* enough," Jaina said, exasperated. "People don't cross most of the galaxy just to fight in someone else's war—especially not Squibs."

"*Urub r buur.*"

"What thing sent them?" Jaina demanded.

"*Urub u ur r* Buur."

"Just *The Thing*?" Jaina asked. "We've never heard of The Thing."

"*Rburubru uburburu buu,*" Wuluw explained. "*Urb u?*"

"Okay."

Jaina clicked her throat in irritation, but knew there was no sense in interrogating Wuluw any further. Insects had unsophisticated motivations, so if a trusted transacting partner offered to send someone to help fight the Chiss, the Killiks were not likely to ask a lot of questions. She warned Wuluw to hold on tight, then began to Force-leap after the Squibs.

They were perhaps halfway to the MetaCannons when a descending whine broke over the jungle. Jaina looked toward the sound and saw the dark flecks of an AirStraeker squadron approaching through the rain.

"Son-of-a-Sith-harlot!" Jaina cursed.

Zekk and his swarm had visited a battering on the AirStraekers during the initial landing, so she had not expected the Chiss to risk what remained of the wing in the middle of a downpour.

Jaina pointed at the center of the formation, then reached out in the Force and began to shove one of the AirStraekers toward a wingmate. The second evaded, and the first aircraft began to struggle against her grasp. The rest of the squadron opened fire a second later. A wall of smoke erupted in the jungle canopy and began to roll toward her.

"Tell Zekk to get the Wing Swarm down here, *now!*" Jaina said over her shoulder.

"*Bb.*"

"No?" Jaina screeched. "We've got fireflies!"

Wuluw explained that UnuThul's orders had been clear. The airborne swarm was not to attack until the Chiss began to evacuate.

"The Chiss aren't *going* to evacuate if we don't stop those AirStraekers!" Jaina protested. "They won't have any reason to, because all that's going to be left of the Great Swarm is a jungle full of maser-popped bugs!"

"*Rruub uru bubub,*" Wuluw reported. "*Ubbuburu buub.*"

"I don't care if the Kolosoloks *are* attacking," Jaina said. "That's not going to do us much good up *here,* is it?"

"*Urbuubur, buubu ururbu.*"

"Oh." Jaina was quiet for a moment, still struggling to Force-shove the AirStraeker into a wingmate. "When you look at it that way, maybe we are expendable."

A fireball erupted over the jungle canopy as Jaina finally succeeded. With any luck, one of the AirStraekers she had downed had been the commander, but she knew better than to think that this would throw the squadron into disarray. The Chiss were far too organized to let a little thing like casualties disrupt their plans.

Wuluw began to tremble on Jaina's back. "*Uuuu buuuu . . .*"

"Ah, don't be that way," Jaina said. The squadron was so close now that she could see the droop-winged silhouettes of individual AirStraekers. "Maybe it's not that bad."

"*Bu ubu ru—*"

"Look, you shouldn't believe everything we say," Jaina said.

"*Urbur?*"

"Really," Jaina replied. She fixed her gaze on the AirStraeker squadron, then reached out to Zekk, concentrating hard and trying to make him feel her alarm through the battle-meld. "Humans *do* exaggerate."

Wuluw stopped shaking and remained curiously quiet for a moment, then reported, "*Burubu rurburu.*"

"He is?" Jaina gasped, feigning surprise. "Well, Zekk's StealthX isn't going to give anything away, is it? The Chiss can't even see that."

"*Ur!*" Wuluw clacked her mandibles in delight, then began to rub her antennae over Jaina's face. "*Burrb u!*"

"All right! That's enough!" Jaina laughed. "If we're going to get out of this, I still need to see."

Wuluw folded her antennae back immediately.

As soon as her view was clear again, Jaina realized that she had lost sight of the Squibs. Probably, they had dropped back into the jungle as soon as the AirStraekers appeared, preferring to take their chances with the MetaCannons. There was no time to worry about it. She could see the AirStraekers sweeping back and forth now, spraying a wall of maser beams ahead of them and setting aflame a kilometer-wide swath of jungle canopy.

Jaina reached out and tried her Force shove again, but the Chiss learned quickly. Her target simply peeled away from the squadron and climbed, fighting against her Force grasp until he entered the clouds and she lost sight of him. Thinking that disruption was as good as destruction, she began to Force-shove the rest of the squadron. They all vanished into the clouds—then dropped back into view a few moments later, in perfect formation and closer than before.

"Hurry, Zekk!" Jaina said under her breath.

"*Ubr?*"

"I said we need to keep pressing the attack," Jaina replied, not wanting to alarm her Wuluw again. "Let's see if we can find a good observation post."

Jaina Force-leapt into an especially tall mogo, then used the Force to make herself light and ascended high into the smallest twigs until she had clear view all the way to the mountains. Through the tangle of barren tree limbs, several MetaCannons were visible on the jungle floor, about half a kilometer ahead. Jaina retrieved her electrobinoculars and saw that the crews were busy changing the configuration of their weapons, replacing the ballistic barrels with fan-tipped beam emitters more suited to close-in fighting.

"Have the Rekkers jump those MetaCannons now!" Jaina instructed Wuluw. "If they don't get there in the next thirty seconds, those maser fans will tear them apart."

"*Ru.*"

Jaina checked on the progress of the AirStraekers and found them so close now that she could see the underwing emitter fans flashing individual maser beams—and she could hear the wood cracking as mogo trees burst into flame. She tried her Force-shove attack again, and again she succeeded only in sending the entire squadron into the clouds for no more than three seconds.

Jaina reached out to Zekk again, urging him to hurry. In response, the meld filled with reassurance.

Jaina returned the electrobinoculars to her eyes and began to scan the rest of the battlefield. Five kilometers beyond the MetaCannons, the Chiss perimeter shield was glowing through the battle smoke, a golden wall that flickered and flashed as the Colony's hordes attacked with catapults, magcannons, and other primitive field pieces. The Chiss were responding with maser cannons mounted on armored personnel carriers, directing most of their fire at a line of about fifty moss-covered hillocks that seemed to be ambling slowly forward.

Kolosolok was attacking.

Jaina watched in awe. More than fifty meters long and ten meters high, the enormous insects resembled freightersized spider-roaches, with broad, slightly humped carapaces that covered their entire backs. Their heads were slightly beetle-like, however, with a thicket of stiff black antennae that looked more like horns.

Though the Kolosoloks appeared sluggish and torpid, they were covering so much ground that the throngs of Killik soldiers following in their wake were having trouble keeping pace. Maser cannons were useless against them. The beams ricocheted harmlessly off their thick head chitin, or blasted craters three meters deep into the green, spongy moss that covered their thoraxes. And when a cannon strike did penetrate their chitin, the brief geyser of brown blood seemed to go unnoticed—at least by the victim.

The crackling of the fires in the jungle canopy became a building roar, and Wuluw began to tremble on Jaina's back again.

"Rurb u brubr ub."

"Can't leave yet." Jaina did not lower her electrobinoculars. "Those MetaCannons should be opening up with their maser fans about—"

A tremendous roar erupted down in the jungle, shaking Jaina's tree so hard that she had to Force-stick herself to the limb on which she was sitting.

"—now!" she shouted. "Hold on!"

A flurry of loud, long crashes began to sound from the area near the MetaCannons, and ancient, hundred-meter mogo trees began to drop to the jungle floor, their bases heat-blasted from beneath them.

Jaina continued to study the perimeter shield. That was the key, the place where the battle would be won or lost. The Chiss defenders changed tactics, standing atop their personnel carriers to launch gas grenades and vape charges. The gas grenades seemed to sicken the

Kolosoloks, causing them to shudder and stumble when one actually struck them. The vape charges opened gaping holes in their chitin, sometimes resulting in a flood of blood and organs large enough to drop them to their bellies. Even then, the huge warriors continued to crawl forward.

The Chiss weapons were simply too light to stop Kolosolok. More than half of the nest reached the perimeter alive and began to butt into the curtain of energy, snapping at the relay pylons with their mandibles, clawing huge pits into the ground, serving as siege towers for the rivers of Killik soldiers who streamed up their backs.

A cold prickle rose in the middle of Jaina's spine. She lowered the electrobinoculars and spun on her heel, staring down into the jungle toward the spot that seemed to be the source of the feeling. She saw nothing but shadow. She started to stretch out in the Force, but then the whine of an approaching AirStraeker became a scream and the heat of the burning canopy began to warm her face, and she knew Zekk had not made it in time.

Jaina spun back toward the sound and found herself looking through the canopy bubble directly into the red eyes of a Chiss pilot. There was no emotion in the woman's face as she twisted her control stick, swinging the maser fans in Jaina's direction.

Wuluw screeched, and Jaina felt her own hand rising as though to ward off a blow. But instead of turning her palm toward the emitter fans, she flicked her fingers sideways, reaching out with the Force to bat the AirStraeker's control stick out of the pilot's hand.

The Chiss's eyes widened in surprise. She lunged after the rebellious stick, and Jaina did not see what the woman did after that. The AirStraeker simply dipped into the jungle canopy and vanished, and an instant later an orange plume of fire boiled up through the trees. Jaina felt a gush of heat in the soles of her feet, and Wuluw shrieked again and clung to her even more tightly.

The rest of the squadron roared past, spraying crimson curtains of death fifty meters to either side, filling the Force with the anguish of thousands of dying Killiks, instantly turning the air so hot that Jaina's throat stuck closed.

Then the prickle between Jaina's shoulder blades became a cold shiver. She leapt without taking the time to look and found herself dropping through the smoke-filled jungle with no idea what lay below—no idea beyond the danger that she sensed. She was in someone's sights, and she knew it.

A flurry of blaster beams began to stitch the air around her, forcing Jaina into an ungainly Force tumble that sent Wuluw flying. She twisted around, reaching out to draw the Killik back to her . . . and saw Wuluw's thorax shatter as a blaster bolt tore through it.

Jaina felt the Killik's death as though it were her own. A terrible fire blossomed inside her and began to crackle on her fingertips, longing for release, for vengeance. A mogo limb appeared out of the smoke below, and she reached for it in the Force, pulling herself over to it and lighting on it as gently as a feather.

A handful of blaster bolts tore into the tree's trunk, then abruptly stopped when her attackers realized she was protected. Jaina snapped her lightsaber off her belt and Forceleapt to the branch above, then crept close to the trunk and peered around it, toward the source of the blaster bolts. As she had suspected, Longnose and Scarcheek were crouching in a trunk notch in the next tree, their large dark eyes scanning the area where she had disappeared.

Jaina scowled. *Hit-Squibs.*

She began to scan the surrounding branches, planning a route that would take her behind the two assassins, unsure in her anger whether she meant to capture them or simply take her vengeance.

That was when Zekk touched Jaina through the meld, wondering if she was hurt, urging her to focus. Vengeance was not important—it was *never* important. The battle was all that mattered now. She had a responsibility to the Colony.

Jaina glanced skyward. The smoke was so thick that she could barely see the green rain clouds above, but they were still there, still pouring water down onto the burning jungle.

Jaina wondered what had taken Zekk so long to reach her, and the image of attacking clawcraft filled her mind. Of course—the Chiss would never attack without top cover. She returned her lightsaber to her utility belt, then used the Force to snap a small branch about thirty meters behind Longnose and Scarcheek.

The two Squibs leapt out of their hiding place and started down the tree headfirst, moving so fast that Jaina wondered if they were falling. Once the pair had vanished from sight, she whispered after them, using the Force to carry her hard-edged voice.

"We'll finish this later," she said. "If you stay alive that long."

A pair of startled screams echoed up through the smoke.

A moment later, the hum of a StealthX's repulsor drives passed by overhead. She looked up to see a black streak flashing after the AirStraekers, its laser cannons ripping the sky open.

The MetaCannons were continuing to chew through the jungle, but now Jaina could hear other sounds, too—the wail of enemy voices, the pinging of shatter gun pellets on metal armor, the chain-thunder of exploding ammunition. The Rekkers had reached the Chiss lines.

Seeing that the lower levels of the jungle—at least in the direction of the fighting—had erupted into a solid wall of flame and smoke, Jaina returned to the canopy. She could see Zekk's StealthX in the distance as it hunted down the AirStraekers, but not much more.

Jaina retrieved her electrobinoculars, then used the Force to clear a hole through the smoke. The MetaCannons had cut a trench three hundred meters into the jungle. A solid wall of smoke and steam was pouring out of this trench, while thousands of Rekkers and millions of Jooj were swarming into it. Clearly, the situation at the MetaCannons was under control.

The battle at the perimeter was going more poorly. The Chiss had massed opposite the Kolosoloks, flinging vape charges and gas grenades at the great insects and firing their charric rifles from the roofs of their personnel carriers. The Killik tide pressed the attack, pouring shatter gun pellets over the shield or simply leaping into the horde of defenders.

The Chiss were too disciplined to panic and too well trained to break. Support units poured in by the squad, by the platoon, by the company. Bodies, both insect and Chiss, began to lie three and four and then ten deep. Personnel carriers exploded or became so riddled with shatter gun fire that the crews could be seen lying in pieces inside. The Kolosoloks were butting the shield, filling the air with golden sprays of discharge sparks, recoiling stunned and unsteady, then hitting it again and again . . . and still the perimeter held.

Then Jaina saw a Chiss vape charge fly astray when the soldier who had thrown it was hit by a line of shatter gun pellets. Responding more by instinct than by plan, she reached out for the vape charge in the Force. Her control at such a distance was almost non-existent, so she simply nudged it toward the nearest relay pylon and watched in surprise as the distant speck struck the post—then dropped to the ground and simply lay there.

Jaina cursed under her breath, then lowered her electrobinoculars. "The rodder didn't thumb the—"

A brilliant detonation dot appeared through the smoke, and a sudden jolt of surprise shot through the Force. Jaina raised the electrobinoculars again, then cleared a viewing hole through the smoke and was astonished to see that the relay pylon had disappeared after all. Killiks were pouring through the gap in the perimeter shield, enveloping a company of Chiss defenders and fanning outward in an unstoppable tide.

The Colony had broken the enemy line. Now the Chiss would *have* to evacuate.

FIFTEEN

The vastness of the *Megador*'s Hangar 51 rumbled with activity as a small army of technicians, droids, and support personnel rushed to ready the entire wing of Jedi StealthXs for combat. The StealthXs were temperamental craft with specialized equipment, so even simple tasks like fueling and arming required twice as much work and made three times as much noise as the same work on a standard starfighter. And the systems checks caused a cacophony in their own right, as furious bleeps and tweets flew back and forth between the StealthXs' security-conscious astromechs and the *Megador*'s self-important diagnostic droids.

As a result, Jacen could not overhear what Luke and Mara were saying to Saba and to his parents at the *Falcon*'s boarding ramp. But he doubted it was a problem. They were all holding hands and embracing, and he could feel their concern and warm feelings in the Force.

Probably, Luke had just called Jacen over to say good-bye before his parents departed on their mission against the Chiss. Jacen would have liked to save them the trip—to make them see that the Chiss would keep attacking the Killiks whether Luke's crazy scheme worked or not. But he did not dare.

Lowbacca and Tesar's accusations had left him in a tenuous position with Luke and Mara, and Jacen could not risk aggravating the situation by openly opposing Luke's plan. Everything depended on the Chiss winning this war, and he had to remain in a position to make certain they *did*.

Jacen reached the foot of the *Falcon*'s boarding ramp and stopped, waiting his turn to embrace his parents and wish them a good journey. Despite his father's graying hair and the crow's-feet creeping out from the corners of his mother's eyes, he did not think of them as old. They were just experienced—*vastly* experienced.

They had been going on missions like this together for over thirty years—since long before he and Jaina had been born—and Jacen was just beginning to truly understand the sacrifices they had made, the risks they had taken. How often had they faced dilemmas like the one he faced now, had to choose between a terrible evil and an absolute one? How many secrets like Allana had they kept hidden—how many were they *still* hiding?

The time had come for Jacen and his peers to take up the beacon his parents and their friends had been carrying all these years—not to push aside the previous generation, but to carry the burden themselves and allow the old heroes a well-deserved rest. He knew he and his fellows were ready; a group of Jedi had not been as carefully selected and prepared since the days of the Old Republic. But when Jacen looked at his parents and recalled how they had changed the galaxy, he found himself wondering whether he and his generation were *worthy*.

Sometimes, given their secure childhoods and formal training, he even wondered whether the new Jedi were too soft. Compared with the filthy, overcrowded freighter that his father had called home as a boy, or the dusty Tatooine moisture farm that had shaped his uncle Luke's early life, the Jedi academy on Yavin 4 had been luxurious. Even his mother, raised in the Royal Palace of Alderaan, had understood true danger as a child, with the deadly gaze of Palpatine always turned her family's way.

"Jacen?"

Jacen felt his father's eyes on him and realized everyone was looking in his direction.

"You here?" Han asked. "You're not having another of your visions, are you?"

"No, just . . ." He was surprised to find a lump in his throat. ". . . just thinking."

"Well, stop it," Han ordered. "You're scaring me."

Jacen forced a smile. "Sorry. I wouldn't want that." He turned to his mother. "You can't talk him out of this?"

Leia must have sensed something despite his defenses, because she ignored the joke and said, "Is there a reason I should?"

Jacen rolled his eyes, but silently cursed his mother's perceptiveness. "It was a joke, Mom." He spread his arms and wrapped her in a tight hug so she would not be able to examine his face too closely. "I just came to wish you a safe trip."

He released her and turned to embrace his father. "Good . . ." Had Jacen realized he was going to have such a hard time concealing his emotions, he would have found an excuse to be busy doing something else when his parents departed. ". . . bye, Dad."

"Take it easy, kid. We're coming back." Han suddenly stiffened, then pulled back and eyed Jacen nervously. "Aren't we? You haven't seen something—"

"You're coming back, Dad—I'm certain of it," Jacen said. "Just be careful, okay? Raynar isn't going to believe you—and it won't help that you're telling the truth."

"Is *that* what you're worried about?" Han sounded relieved. "Look, kid, we've been over this about a—"

"We'll be fine, Jacen," Leia interrupted, finally warming to him and squeezing his hand. "This is the only way to make the Chiss understand how difficult it would be to win a war against the Killiks."

Saba stepped up behind Leia, looming over her the way Chewbacca used to loom over Han. "Everything will be fine, Jacen. Your mother is a powerful Jedi—az strong in her way as you are in yourz."

Jacen nodded. "I know that." He leaned down and kissed Leia on the cheek. "May the Force be with you, Mom."

"And with you, too, Jacen," Leia said. "*We're* not the ones who'll be attacking Gorog's nest ship."

Han's face suddenly fell. "*That's* not what you're worried about—is it?" he asked. "Did you see—"

"I didn't see *anything,* Dad," Jacen said. "Really." He shooed his father up the ramp. "Go on. I'll meet you when this is over."

Han studied him for a moment, then finally nodded. "I'll hold you to that, kid. Don't let me down."

He took Leia's hand and started up the ramp.

Saba remained behind, one slit-pupiled eye fixed on Jacen, and began to siss in amusement. "You are alwayz full of surprisez, Jacen Solo." She started up the ramp. "Alwayz so full of surprisez."

Jacen had to fight down a moment of panic. He knew that Ben found the Barabel Master frightening, and he was beginning to understand why—she was just so hard to *read.*

Before starting up the ramp after Saba and the others, C-3PO paused in front of Jacen and tapped him lightly on the shoulder. "Pardon me, Master Jacen. But did whatever you saw have anything to do with me?"

Before Jacen could answer, Han's voice sounded from the top of the boarding ramp. "Threepio! If you're still on that ramp in three seconds, you'll be riding to Tenupe cargo-clamped to the hull!"

"Threats are hardly necessary, Captain Solo!" C-3PO clumped up the ramp after Saba and the others, his golden hands paddling the air. "I'm coming, I'm coming!"

Jacen smiled and waved a last farewell to his parents, then retreated to safe distance and watched with Luke and Mara as the boarding ramp retracted and the *Falcon* slipped out of the hangar. The ship hung below the *Megador* for a moment, a mere teardrop of white durasteel framed by the hangar's huge mouth, then spun toward the Star Destroyer's stern and streaked off deeper into the Unknown Regions.

Luke's hand suddenly clasped Jacen by the shoulder, and Jacen barely stopped himself from cringing. He could not afford to show any hint of surprise . . . or guilt.

"I'll bet it seems like they've been doing that your whole life, doesn't it?" Luke asked fondly.

"It does," Jacen said, nodding. "And I couldn't be prouder."

"No?" Mara slipped a hand through his other arm. "Well, neither could they."

"Uh, thanks." Jacen felt the lump forming in his throat again and swallowed it into submission. "Maybe I ought to get back to my fighter. Neufie has been giving those diagnostic droids—"

"In a minute," Luke said. "First, I'd like you to come with us."

"Sure." Jacen's heart began to pound so hard he had to use a Jedi calming exercise to quiet it. "Where?"

"Ghent is ready to show us the rest of Artoo's secret files," Mara said. "But he still hasn't finished duplicating the omnigate, so this may be the only time anyone gets to see the holos of your grandparents. Luke and I thought you'd like to be there."

"You did?" Jacen said, almost allowing his relief to show. "I mean, yes—of course!"

"It's okay—I'm nervous, too." Luke laughed uneasily, then added, "Scared, even."

"Well, *I'm* not."

Mara's tone was a little too light. The Skywalkers joked openly about Alema Rar's insinuation that Mara might have played a role in the death of Padmé Amidala, but Jacen knew how hurt his aunt had been by the whole incident.

The question had to be answered—and it had to be answered before the Jedi attacked the Gorog nest ship. Luke could not face Lomi

Plo otherwise. She would find any trace of doubt—especially *that* doubt—and use it to veil herself completely.

That was one of the reasons Jacen believed *he* ought to be the one to confront Lomi Plo. He had no doubts—of any kind. Vergere had scorched them out of him in a crucible of pain.

They found Ghent in a small briefing salon that overlooked Hangar 51, sitting on the floor beside R2-D2, surrounded by the usual litter of tools, circuits, and snack wrappers. The lanky slicer was peering through an access panel with his magnispecs flipped down, manipulating a micrograbber in each hand and muttering to himself in a high-pitched, staccato manner that sounded alarmingly like machine code. Afraid to cause a mishap by startling him, they stopped just inside the door and waited for him to remove his hands from inside the droid's casing.

"What are you standing there for?" Ghent asked without looking away from his work. "You won't see anything from the door."

"Sorry." Luke led the way forward. "Are you ready?"

"Don't I look ready?" Ghent asked. "All I have to do is snap the omnigate back in place."

"Oh," Luke said. "When I saw all the circuits—"

"Standard maintenance," Ghent interrupted. "No wonder this droid acts up. Some of those circuits haven't been cleaned in twenty standard years. They had carbon molecules stacked a hundred moles high."

As they drew closer, Jacen realized the slicer must have been working on R2-D2 for a couple of days straight—at least it smelled that way. In any case, Ghent had clearly not found time for a decent sanisteam lately. They stopped several paces away and watched as he snapped a circuit board back in place.

"All set." He rocked back on his heels, then looked up and said, "I don't think you should do this, you know."

"You told us already," Mara said.

Ghent's brow rose. "I did?"

"Several times," Luke said.

"Oh." Ghent ran a hand over his tattooed head, then said, "It's just that I've almost got the omnigate figured out. Another three weeks—no more than six, really—and I'd have it for sure. Then you could look at these files anytime you liked."

"We don't have six weeks." Luke checked his chrono. "We're due to launch in six *hours*."

Ghent's eyes widened. "That soon? I thought we had three days!"

"It *has* been three days," Mara said patiently.

Ghent looked around him in a daze, then said, "I guess he was in worse shape than I thought."

"Ghent, we really need to see that holo now," Mara pressed gently. "A lot depends on it."

"Yeah, I know," Ghent said. "But I don't think you understand. That's the Intellex Four designer's original back door. If we fry it before we've copied it, we're destroying a whole sub-era of computer history."

"Ghent, it's really important," Luke said.

The slicer sighed, then flipped R2-D2's primary circuit breaker without saying anything more.

The droid came to life with a startled bleep, then swiveled his dome around, carefully studying the stacks of tools and discarded circuit boards around him. After a moment, he began to roll back and forth on his treads, extending various utility arms and whistling in approval.

Then R2-D2's photoreceptor swung past Ghent's face. He gave a startled buzz, then looked at Luke and began to back away.

"Artoo, stop it!" Luke ordered. "Come back here. We need to see what happened to my mother after my father came back from Mustafar."

R2-D2 tweeted an explanation in machine code. Jacen was not really surprised when Ghent translated it.

"He says Anakin Skywalker didn't come back."

"He didn't?" Luke frowned. "What happened?"

R2-D2 remained silent for a moment, then abruptly blurted out an explanation.

"Padmé went to see your father," Ghent reported.

"Then show us *that*," Luke said to R2-D2. "And no tricks. I need to see this."

R2-D2 whistled doubtfully.

"He says—"

"Artoo, just do it," Luke interrupted. "We're going into combat soon, and you need time to calibrate yourself with the StealthX."

The droid trilled an excited question.

"*If* Ghent thinks you're up to it," Luke said. "And *if* you don't keep stalling."

R2-D2 tipped forward and activated his holoprojector. The image of a green starfighter appeared on a landing platform on some distant world that could not be identified from the image. A young man in a dark robe appeared, running into the image from the direction of the starfighter. As he drew closer, it grew apparent that he was Anakin Skywalker. He appeared tired and grimy, as though he had just come from battle. That fit what he had told Padmé in the last holo that Jacen and the Skywalkers had seen together: that he was going to Mustafar to end the war.

"Padmé, I saw your ship," Anakin said.

Padmé appeared, entering the image from the opposite direction, and they embraced.

"Anakin!" Her back was to the holocam, but it was clear that she was trembling.

"It's all right, you're safe now." Anakin looked down into her eyes. "What are you doing out here?"

"I was so worried about you!" Padmé's voice was somewhat muffled, since she was still facing away from the holocam. "Obi-Wan told me terrible things."

Anakin's face clouded with anger. "Obi-Wan was with you?"

"He said you've turned to the dark side," Padmé continued, avoiding a direct answer. "That you killed younglings."

"Obi-Wan is trying to turn you against me," Anakin said darkly.

Padmé shook her head. "He cares about us."

"Us?"

"He knows." Padmé paused a moment, then said, "He wants to help you."

"And you." Anakin's voice was full of jealousy now. "Don't lie to me, Padmé. I have become more powerful than any Jedi dreamed of, and I've done it for you . . . to protect you."

"I don't want your power." Padmé pulled away from him. "I don't want your protection."

Anakin drew her back to him. "Is Obi-Wan going to protect you?" he demanded. "He can't . . . he can't help you. He's not strong enough."

Padmé's head fell, and she was silent for a long time.

Perhaps R2-D2 had attuned his communications routines to Luke's moods over the years, because he seemed to sense the dread in Luke's presence as clearly as Jacen did. The droid took advantage of the long silence to whistle a long, worried-sounding question.

"He's afraid this is going to overload your circuits," Ghent reported. "And I know we're stressing his. Do you hear that warble in his interrogative pitch?"

"Keep going." Luke's tone grew a little softer. "It's all right, Artoo. I'm fine."

Jacen nodded his approval. There was an irrational and dangerous edge in Anakin's voice, and Jacen understood why R2-D2 had
been so reluctant to show these holos to Luke. But pain was only
dangerous when it was feared—that had been one of Vergere's first
lessons. Luke *needed* to see the end of the holo. He needed to embrace the pain.

After a moment, Padmé raised her head again in the holo.

"Anakin, all I want is your love."

"Love *won't save you,*" Anakin snarled. *"Only my new powers
can do that."*

"At what cost?" Padmé demanded. *"You're a good person.
Don't do this."*

"I won't lose you the way I lost my mother." Anakin's face belonged to someone else now, someone angry and frightened and
selfish.

Padmé did not seem to see the change—or, if she did, she remained determined to bring the other Anakin back again. She
reached for him.

"Come away with me," she said. *"Help me raise our child.
Leave everything else behind while we still can."*

Anakin shook his head. *"Don't you see? We don't have to run
away anymore. I have brought peace to the Republic. I am more
powerful than the Chancellor. I can overthrow him, and together
you and I can rule the galaxy . . . make things the way we want
them to be."*

"I don't believe what I'm hearing!" Padmé backed away, stumbling as though she had been struck.

Luke sighed audibly, clearly dismayed at the arrogance that had
led his father down the dark path of the oppressor. But Jacen found
himself responding to his grandfather far more sympathetically, almost with admiration. Anakin Skywalker had understood his own
strength, and—at one time, at least—he had tried to use that strength
to bring peace. Vergere would have approved. Power unused was
power wasted, and whatever had happened to him later, Anakin Skywalker had at least attempted to use *his* for a good end.

For a moment, R2-D2's hologram began to flitter, and everyone
held their breath. Then the droid gave a click and a whir, and the
scene continued.

Padmé had stopped retreating from Anakin.

"Obi-Wan was right," she said. *"You've changed."*

"I don't want to hear any more about Obi-Wan!" Anakin

started after her. "The Jedi turned against me. The Republic turned against me. Don't you turn against me."

"I don't know you anymore," Padmé said. "Anakin, you're breaking my heart. I'll never stop loving you, but you're going down a path I can't follow."

Anakin's eyes narrowed. "Because of Obi-Wan?"

"Because of what you've done! What you plan to do!" Padmé's voice grew commanding. "Stop now." She was silent for a moment, then her tone softened. "Come back. I love you."

Anakin's gaze shifted, and he seemed to be looking over Padmé's shoulder toward the cam. "Liar!"

Padmé spun around, and for the first time it grew clear just how advanced her pregnancy was. Her jaw fell in dismay. "No!"

"You're with him!" Anakin's gaze had returned to Padmé. "You've betrayed me!"

"No, Anakin." Padmé shook her head and started toward him again. "I swear . . . I—"

Anakin extended his arm, his hand shaped into an arc. Padmé cried out, then grabbed her throat and began to make terrible gurgling sounds.

Luke cried out in disbelief, and the Force grew heavy with grief and outrage. Even Jacen—whose time among the Yuuzhan Vong had taught him never to be surprised by the brutality one being could inflict on another—felt his stomach turn at the sight of his grandfather using the Force to choke the woman he supposedly loved.

An ominous but barely audible whine arose somewhere inside R2-D2. The holo began to flicker again, and a familiar voice spoke from outside the holo frame.

"Let her go, Anakin."

Arm still extended—and Padmé still choking—Anakin turned to sneer at the speaker. "What have you and she been up to?"

Obi-Wan Kenobi stepped into view, wearing the sand-colored robes of a Jedi. Though his back was to the camera, his shape and bearded profile were clearly recognizable.

"Let . . . her . . . go!"

Anakin whipped his arm to one side, and Padmé flew out of the holo.

Anakin started forward to meet Obi-Wan, saying, "You turned her—"

A sharp pop sounded from R2-D2's interior, and the holo dissolved into static.

Ghent flipped his magnispecs down, then peered through R2-D2's access panel and cried out as though a blaster bolt had pierced his heart. He lowered his micrograbbers through the opening and clicked something, then retrieved what appeared to the naked eye to be a smoking dust speck.

"I knew this would happen!" the slicer cried. "It's an omni*ash* now!"

No one answered. Luke was stiff and ashen, fighting back tears. Mara was staring at the spot where Padmé's limp form had vanished from the holo. Jacen was trying to decide where his grandfather had gone wrong, trying to puzzle out what flaw had made him a slave to his temper. Even R2-D2 remained silent, continuing to project a column of holostatic onto the floor.

After a moment, Ghent seemed to realize that the loss of the omnigate was not the most serious one of the day. He laid his hand on Luke's shoulder and gave it a comforting squeeze.

"Well, at least we know it wasn't *Mara* who killed your mother."

"Ghent!" Mara's eyes looked ready to loose a flight of blaster bolts.

"What's wrong?" Ghent seemed genuinely confused. "Isn't that what we were trying to find out?"

"Drop it," Mara ordered.

Tears were escaping down Luke's cheeks now, and Jacen could sense him struggling with the anger he felt toward his father. It left a fiery, bitter taste in the Force, all the more powerful because of the forgiveness that Luke had already granted Anakin Skywalker.

Ghent remained entirely unaware of all this history, of course. "But now we know," he insisted. "It wasn't Mara!"

Jacen sighed. "Ghent, we really *don't* know that," he explained. "We only saw Anakin throw Padmé. We don't know that my grandmother actually died."

R2-D2 trilled a series of sad notes.

"You see?" Ghent asked, as though everyone else could understand what the droid was saying, too. "Do you want to see it?"

"See what?" Mara demanded.

"Her death," Ghent replied. "This is what Artoo has been trying to protect Luke from, but now that the secret is out—"

"No—I've seen everything I need to." Luke rose and wiped his face dry, then added, "We have a battle to prepare for."

Jacen did not like the hollowness in his uncle's voice. Luke was retreating from his pain, avoiding that last file because he knew how devastating it would be to watch his mother die. And pain you feared was pain that could be used to control you. Luke was not ready to face Lomi Plo, would not be ready until he accepted the tragedy that had befallen his parents—until he *embraced* it.

"Are you sure?" Jacen asked. "It couldn't take long, and who knows when Artoo is going to be this cooperative—"

"I'm sure!" Luke snapped. "Don't you have some flight checks you should be doing?"

Mara nodded toward the door, but Jacen remained where he was. "This is more important. We need to talk about it."

Luke sighed, then went over to a briefing chair and sat down. "Okay, Jacen. Let's hear it."

Mara cringed, then closed her eyes and touched Jacen in the Force, urging him not to press the matter.

Jacen took a deep breath, then said, "I'm not sure you're ready to win this fight, Uncle Luke."

"That's not your decision to make, Jacen." Luke's tone was stern. "But go ahead."

Jacen did not hesitate. "You haven't committed yourself yet," he said. "You're afraid to look at the last file—"

"I don't *need* to look at it," Luke said. "I know what happened. I knew the instant that I saw my . . . that we saw *Darth Vader* raise his hand to my mother."

"You're afraid of the pain," Jacen accused.

"Pain isn't always good, Jacen," Mara said. "Sometimes it's just distracting."

"And I *don't* need to be distracted right now." Luke pointedly started to rise. "What I need is to prepare myself for combat . . . and so do you, Jacen."

"It's not only the file," Jacen pressed. He was certain now that *he* should be the one to face Lomi Plo; that he was the only one who had no doubts about what they must do. "You're not going to kill Raynar, either."

"I haven't decided anything yet," Luke said.

"You may think you haven't decided," Jacen said. "But you're not going to—and it's a mistake."

Luke cocked his brow. "I see." He fell silent for a moment, then returned to his chair. "I don't know what you've foreseen, Jacen, but I can promise you this—regardless of Raynar's fate, the Colony will be destroyed. The war in your vision won't come to pass."

"I'm sorry, Uncle Luke, but promises aren't good enough," Jacen said. He would not trust Allana's life to good intentions. "We must be *sure* the Colony dies—and that means we must act."

Mara came and sat beside Luke in front of Jacen, then asked, "So you're going to kill a man—someone who was once your friend—just to be certain?"

"I won't enjoy it," Jacen said. "But it's necessary."

"I know you think so, Jacen," Luke said. "But I'm not convinced. Not yet."

"We can't afford to doubt ourselves," Jacen insisted. "We must decide . . . and act."

Luke sighed in exasperation. "Vergere again." He shook his head. "Look, I know her instruction saved your life—"

"And helped us win the war with the Yuuzhan Vong," Jacen pointed out.

"And helped win the war against the Yuuzhan Vong," Luke admitted patiently. "But I'm not sure we should embrace her ideas as the core of our Jedi philosophy—in fact, I'm sure we *shouldn't*."

"Why not?" Jacen demanded.

"Because we're no longer at war with the Yuuzhan Vong, for one thing," Mara said. She shook her head, then pointed at R2-D2's holoprojector. "Didn't you learn anything from what you just saw?"

Jacen scowled, genuinely puzzled. "I don't know what you mean."

Luke's voice grew sharp. "There's more to being a Jedi than being effective, Jacen." He looked away, then continued in a gentler tone. "Since the war ended, I've been growing more and more troubled by Vergere's teachings, and I think I finally understand why."

Jacen lifted his brow. "Why?"

"Because their ruthlessness reminds me so much of what my father believed." Luke turned and looked into Jacen's eyes. "Of what the Emperor *taught* him to believe."

Jacen was astounded. "You can't be serious!"

"I'm not saying Vergere's teachings are immoral," Luke replied. "In fact, they don't concern themselves with morality at all. They provide no guidance."

"Exactly!" Jacen said. "They're about ridding ourselves of illusions, about seeing that nothing is ever truly dark or light, completely good or evil."

"So a Jedi is free to take any action necessary to achieve his goal?" Luke asked. "His only duty is to be effective?"

"His first duty is to *choose*," Jacen said. "Everything follows from that."

Mara and Luke looked at each other, and something passed between them that Jacen barely perceived.

Finally, Luke said, "But Jacen, that isn't what a Jedi *is*."

Jacen frowned. He could not understand what his uncle was trying to tell him, except that it had to do with principles and responsibilities—with those ancient shackles that Vergere had taught him to open. Could Luke really be saying that the Jedi should don them again; that they should let the opinions of others dictate their actions?

"Very well," Jacen said cautiously. "What *is* a Jedi?"

Luke smiled. "I suggest you spend some time meditating on that," he said. "In the meantime, just remember that we *aren't* bounty hunters, okay?"

Jacen nodded. "Yes, Master." He understood that he was being told in no uncertain terms not to assassinate Raynar—at least not without Luke's permission. "I understand, but I sense that you still have doubts about the morality of your plan. Perhaps *I* should be the one to confront Lomi Plo."

Luke's face showed his astonishment. "Is *that* what this was about?"

"I might be the better choice," Jacen said. "*I* don't have any doubts about this plan—or anything else, for that matter."

Luke stood, a smile of relief spreading across his face, and clapped Jacen on the shoulder.

"Jacen, you *are* a good Jedi," he said. "Thank you."

"Uh, you're welcome." Now Jacen was really confused. "Does that mean you agree with me?"

"Not at all—you're mistaking fairness for doubt," Luke said. He motioned R2-D2 to follow, then pulled Jacen toward the door. "I *am* going to kill Lomi Plo."

SIXTEEN

The Chiss survivors had withdrawn to a chain of islands in the great river, a defensible position but not an impregnable one. For days, the defoliated jungle had been reverberating with the crashing of the Colony's field artillery. The trebuchets were flinging rough-edged boulders, the catapults hurling waxes filled with hanpat incendiary. Every now and then, the Killiks even sealed a few thousand of their smaller fellows into a flight of wax balls and cast *them* onto one of the islands.

Nothing shook the Chiss. They remained hunkered down behind their breastworks, smothering the flames, tending to the wounded, picking off any Killik foolish enough to show itself outside the soil-works that shielded the field artillery. The Chiss still numbered nearly a hundred thousand, more than enough to prevent an assault across the river's swift current. After so many weeks of constant, raging battle, even the Colony was beginning to run low on soldiers, and Jaina knew that any attempt to seize the islands would end in the destruction of her army.

But a Chiss relief force might be arriving at any time, and Un-uThul was growing impatient. He remained out of mind-touch with the ground forces and did not understand what was preventing the final push. His Will had become a constant dark pressure inside Jaina's breast, urging her to press the attack and force the enemy's hand. Soon, she feared, he would grow weary of waiting for her plan to work and simply exert his Will over the Killiks. She needed to find a way to dislodge the Chiss *now*.

Jaina slipped a few meters down the muddy embankment, then spun around so she was facing the trebuchet it protected. Several dozen meter-tall Sotatos Killiks were crewing the piece, working the windlass with such coordination that the firing arm looked as though it were being retracted by a power winch. The weapon was being supplied with boulders by a long line of Mollom, who were quarrying the stones from a rare outcropping of stone, then carrying them two kilometers and loading them directly into the trebuchets. Despite being from two different nests, the two groups were so well coordinated that the trebuchet never sat idle, and no Mollom ever had to stand waiting to load a boulder.

Jaina's fragile Wuluw communications assistant joined her when she reached the bottom of the embankment. *"Rubbur bu uubu,"* she reported. *"Urr buur rrububu."*

"Tell Rekker to *unmass*," Jaina ordered. "Even if they can jump over to the islands, now is no time for a leap-charge. We can't get anyone there to support and exploit."

"Bur u buuur rrub," Wuluw objected.

"I *am* doing something!" Jaina snapped. "These aren't Imperials we're fighting, they're Chiss! They're not going to fall apart just because we throw a few million bugs at them!"

A sudden silence fell over the jungle, and Jaina realized that every Killik in sight had turned to stare at her.

"Blast it!" Jaina shook her head at the temperamental insect ego. "Don't be so touchy—we're fighting a war!"

She went into the jungle behind the trebuchet, then slid down a muddy bank into a shallow stream beside the emplacement. Wuluw followed behind her, landing on all six limbs and never breaking the surface of the water.

"Ruburu ubu?"

Jaina started downstream, circling back around the trebuchet toward the Chiss islands. "Doing something."

An approving drone arose in the jungle, and Wuluw skated along on the surface of the stream beside her.

"Ubu?"

"Don't know yet," Jaina answered. "But it'll be good."

As Jaina waded through the water, she was careful to keep her eyes level with the terrain next to the stream, her gaze always turned in the direction of the islands. The jungle floor was piled high with shriveled foliage and splintered mogo wood. Thousands of dead Killiks—perhaps tens of thousands—lay in the detritus, sometimes in twisted pieces and sometimes with their thin limbs reaching toward the sky, always stinking in the jungle heat, always with their insides spilling out through a huge burn hole in their body chitin.

Finally, only a narrow spit of jungle floor separated Jaina from the great river. The Chiss islands lay on the other side of a fast-moving channel, beneath the still-constant hail of boulders and burn-balls from the clacking catapults and booming trebuchets of the Killiks. At this distance, Jaina could barely make out the barricade of felled trees that the enemy had erected at the edge of the river. The island was too flat and smoke-swaddled to see the terrain beyond the breastworks, but Jaina knew the Chiss well enough to be certain that there would be a second and a third line of defense beyond the first—probably even a fourth.

Still being careful not to show her head above the streambank, Jaina brought the electrobinoculars to her eyes and found a mass of red eyes and blue faces peering out from between the mogo logs, scanning her side of the river for any hint of Killik activity. Here and there protruded the long barrel of a sniper rifle, surmounted by the dark rod of a sighting sensor. She continued to study the breastworks, wondering if Jag was out there somewhere, reaching out to see if she could sense his presence. She was not sure why she cared.

Wherever he was, Jagged Fel certainly hated Jaina for taking the Colony's side in this war—and for starting it in the first place. And truthfully, she could hardly blame him. Had he led a team of Chiss commandos against the Galactic Alliance, she would undoubtedly have hated *him*. That's how humans—and Chiss—were. Only Killiks fought without hate.

Jaina continued to study the Chiss defenses. She was not sure what she hoped to find—maybe someplace where the defensive lines did not have a clear view of the river channel, perhaps a cluster of mogo trunks that could be brought down atop the heads of the defenders. Twice, she thought she spotted weaknesses where the Chiss did not have clear fields of fire. They turned out to be traps, one designed to channel the attackers into a large expanse of quicksand, the other protected by the few pieces of field artillery that the Chiss had managed to salvage during their retreat.

Jaina's gaze reached the end of the first island. She turned her attention to the near riverbank, this time looking for a natural place to launch a crossing—then felt somebody looking back at her.

"Cover!" Jaina warned.

She pulled the electrobinoculars away from her face and dropped down behind the streambank—then saw a pair of bright flashes explode into the slope in front of her. The attack was coming from *behind* her.

Jaina dropped underwater. Her ears filled with a fiery gurgling as blaster flashes lit the muddy stream around her, instantly superheating liters of water and sending it skyward in a thin cloud of steam. She pulled herself along the silty creek bed, moving upstream and reaching out in the Force in the direction of the attack.

She felt two presences, both very familiar. *Squibs.*

Blast it! Couldn't those two wait until *after* the war to try killing her?

When Jaina judged she had traveled far enough upstream to be out of the Chiss line of fire, she yanked the lightsaber off her utility belt and rose out of the water. The air around her immediately erupted into a storm of flashing and zinging, but she had already activated her lightsaber and brought it up to block. She batted half a dozen bolts aside, several times narrowly escaping injury when her blade had to be in two places at the same time.

After a couple of moments of frantic parrying, Jaina finally sorted out the source of the attacks and realized the Squibs had her in a crossfire. She began to redirect their bolts toward each other, forcing them to worry about their own cover as well as attacking her, and it was not long before she found the chance to extend a hand and Force-jerk one of her attackers out of his tree.

The Squib's alarmed squeal was followed by a soft thud—then by a shrieking storm of maser beams as the Chiss sharpshooters reacted to the disturbance in the manner of most soldiers under stress: by shooting at it. Fortunately for the Squib, their angle was poor and he was far enough from the river to be well protected by the trees, but the attacks did at least force him to keep his head down.

Jaina used the Force to wrench his blaster away, then flung it into the jungle and turned her attention to the second Squib. She batted five or six blaster bolts straight back into the tree root behind which he was hiding, and when a big chunk of wood flew skyward, he finally stopped firing. Then she Force-jerked him out of his cover and pulled him straight to her—not minding that the Chiss sharpshooters did their best to pick him off as he passed between trees.

As the Squib approached—it was Longnose—he tossed his repeating blaster aside and reached for a thermal detonator hanging from his utility harness. Jaina flicked her fingers, and the silver orb sailed away before he had a chance to arm it.

Longnose's shiny eyes widened in surprise, then grew squinty and hard. "It don't matter what you do to me, girlie. You're—"

"If you had any brains, you'd watch who you called girlie," Jaina said. She dumped the Squib into the muddy water, then held the tip of her lightsaber so close to his nose that it melted his whiskers off. "Don't move—don't even breathe."

Longnose's eyes crossed as he focused on the tip of Jaina's blade, and she slowly let him sink.

"C-c-can I t-t-tread water?"

"If you can do it with your hands over your head," Jaina said.

Longnose's hands went over his head, then he sank so far into the stream that he had to tip his head back to keep his chin above water. Satisfied, Jaina turned her attention back to Scarcheek and was relieved to find him firmly in the grasp of a handful of Mollom, threatening and flailing as he tried to free himself.

Jaina turned to tell Wuluw to have the Squib brought over—and found the little Killik floating a few meters downstream, bobbing lifelessly in a slick of gore and shattered chitin.

Longnose tipped his head. "Sorry."

Jaina eyed the Squib sternly. "Jedi can sense when you're lying, you know."

Longnose's ears went flat. "Hey, it's not our fault!" he protested. "We were aiming for *you*."

Jaina risked sticking her head above the streambank long enough to call the Mollom over with the second Squib. As the Killiks dashed from tree to tree, dodging maser beams, she pushed Longnose up onto the bank. She unbuckled his utility harness and tossed it—and the hold-out blaster and vibroknives hidden on the underside—back into the water.

"Hey!" he demanded. "Those are my clothes!"

"It's warm," Jaina retorted. "We're on a jungle planet."

She studied Longnose for a minute, touching him through the Force to make him uneasy, then deactivated her lightsaber and leaned in close.

"Why are you trying to kill me?" she demanded.

"I'm not talking," Longnose retorted.

"Are you sure about that?" Jaina asked. She used the Force to press him into the muddy bank. "Because you and your friend get to live if you answer my questions."

"You're bluffing," Longnose said. "You can't kill us in cold blood. You're a Jedi!"

"You're right—but there's no time to watch you, either." Jaina cast a meaningful glance toward the approaching Killiks. "So your fate will rest in Mollom's hands. What do you want me to tell them?"

Longnose's lip curled into a sneer. "You wouldn't dare. I know about the dark side. If you . . ."

Jaina made a pinching motion with her fingers. Longnose's mouth continued to work, but his voice fell silent.

"If you're not going to say anything useful, there's no use in your talking."

Jaina turned her attention to Scarcheek, whom the Mollom were bringing down into the stream. The Killiks had been none too gentle with their prisoner, tearing off an ear and leaving him half bald. They deposited him in the mud next to Longnose, then took up encircling positions and stood there clacking their huge mandibles.

Jaina snatched Scarcheek's utility belt off him and tossed it into the water with Longnose's. "How about you?" she asked. "Feel like answering a few questions?"

"No."

"Too bad," Jaina said. "Because if you do, you leave here alive. Otherwise, I'll let Mollom deal with you."

Scarcheek glanced at his Killik tormenters and could not suppress a little shudder. Then he shrugged and tried to appear unintimidated. "Depends on the questions, I guess."

"Fair enough," Jaina said. "Why are you trying to kill me?"

"Dumb question," Scarcheek retorted. " 'Cause we took a contract. What do you think?"

Longnose rolled his eyes and began to shake his head.

"Don't listen to your buddy," Jaina said. "He's got a death wish."

Scarcheek nodded. "Goes with the business."

"Who put out the contract?" Jaina asked.

Longnose continued to shake his head, now drawing his finger across his throat.

"Why not?" Scarcheek demanded of her. "Nobody said nothing about keeping quiet. They just want her dead."

"You see?" Jaina gave them both a little Force-nudge, then locked eyes with Scarcheek. "Who wants us dead?"

"The Directors," Scarcheek said. "And it's just you. They said to leave your boyfriend out of it, unless he got in the way."

"Zekk isn't my boyfriend," Jaina said. "And you haven't answered my question—not really. Who are the Directors?"

Longnose rolled his eyes again and tried to speak, but could only choke.

"Ready to say something useful?" Jaina asked. When he nodded, she released his vocal cords. "Let's hear it."

"It'll go bad if you make them send someone else," Longnose said. "You'd be better off just letting us do you now."

"Yeah," Scarcheek agreed. "We'll make it real painless."

"I'll take my chances with the next crew," Jaina said. "I'm sure they wouldn't be any better than you."

Longnose perked his ears in pride. "You're a smart girl, Jedi. We like that in a target."

"Then how about telling me who these Directors are?" Jaina made a pinching motion with her thumb and forefinger. "Or is your partner the only one getting out of this alive?"

"I guess there's no harm—it's not like you're going to live long enough to go after *them*," Longnose said. "The Directors are the head of the family—our great-great-great-grandparents."

"Grees, Sligh, and Emala," Scarcheek finished. "Your parents had some dealings with them on Tatooine."

Jaina nodded. "I've heard about that. Why do they want me dead?"

Longnose shrugged. "Didn't say."

"You owe them money?" Scarcheek asked.

Jaina shook her head.

"Your parents owe them money?" Longnose asked.

"I doubt it," Jaina said.

The two Squibs glanced at each other, then Longnose nodded. "Well, you're costing them money somehow. That's the only reason the Directors *ever* put out a contract."

"Or maybe your parents are," Scarcheek added. "If they ignored a warning."

Longnose nodded enthusiastically. "That's usually what it is when they send us after the kids."

"Dad never heard a warning he took seriously, so that part makes sense." Jaina was more mystified than ever. "But I still don't know how my parents could be mixed up with your, uh, the Directors. What business are they in?"

"What business *aren't* they in?" Longnose snorted.

"But right now it's a lot of war stuff," Scarcheek said. "Double-billing supplies, gouging for fuel deliveries, vouchering meals that were never served—"

"You know: the usual stuff," Longnose continued. "War is always good for a few billion credits in off-the-book profit."

"Okay—now it makes sense," Jaina said.

If she knew her parents—and her uncle Luke and the rest of the Jedi—they would be working to end this war as quickly as possible.

And if their efforts had upset these "Directors" enough to put a hit on a Jedi, then whatever they were doing was effective. Maybe her parents actually had a chance of stopping the war.

Jaina shifted her gaze to the hit-Squibs' Mollom guards. "Get these two out of here. Turn them loose."

"*Burrub?*" boomed several of the Mollom together.

"A deal's a deal," Jaina said. She shifted her gaze to the Squibs. "But your contract is finished, you understand? If we see you again—anywhere—you're speeder-kill. Okay?"

The Squibs' muzzles fell open in surprise, and they both nodded enthusiastically.

"Yeah, sure."

"Whatever you say, doll."

"And *don't* call me doll," Jaina hissed. She motioned to the Mollom to take the Squibs away. "Tell Wuluw I need a new—"

"*Bu.*"

Jaina turned around to see a new Wuluw communications assistant standing on the water behind her. She smiled at the little Killik.

"What took you so long?"

Wuluw flattened her antennae in apology. "*Urru bu, urbru, uu bu ru—*"

"It was a *joke*," Jaina said. "Don't any of your nest's Joiners have a sense of humor?"

"*U,*" Wuluw answered. "*Bu urb r urubu bubu ur burbur?*"

"No, *that* was serious," Jaina said, feeling guilty about the number of Wuluws she had lost. "I'll—*we'll* try to do a better job of protecting you this time."

Wuluw rattled her mandibles in gratitude, then asked if Jaina had a plan to exterminate the Chiss on the islands yet.

"The plan's coming along," Jaina exaggerated. "We—just need to check out a few last details." She started down the stream, waist-deep in water and crouching to keep her eyes level with the top of the streambank. "Stay low. Those sharpshooters are good."

Wuluw splayed her limbs, lowering herself to within a few centimeters of the water, and followed close behind. The banging of the catapults and trebuchets continued unabated, filling the jungle with the simmering pressure of a star waiting to go nova. When the enemy islands came into view, Jaina stopped and lifted the electrobinoculars to her eyes again.

This time, she was doing more thinking than observing. After hearing about the trouble her parents had been causing the Squibs, she found herself wondering whether she really *did* need to develop a plan. If her parents were close to ending this war, perhaps the best thing to do would be to stall. The lives she saved would number in the millions—and that was Killiks alone.

But if Jaina was wrong about the reason the Squibs had put a hit on her—or if her parents failed to move quickly enough—a relief force would arrive to spoil UnuThul's trap. The Chiss would grow even bolder and attack deeper into Colony territory. Trillions of Killiks and millions of Chiss would die, and the war would continue more ferociously than before.

Fortunately, Jaina had a way to find out. She reached out to her mother in the Force and felt a jolt of happy connection—not as clear as a battle-meld, but stronger and more permanent. She filled her mind with thoughts of peace, then added curiosity. Her mother seemed at first relieved, then puzzled, then worried.

Clearly, Leia did not understand at all. Jaina tried again, this time filling her mind with hopefulness. Her mother seemed more confused than ever, and Jaina gave up in exasperation. Some things never changed.

She felt Leia touching her through the Force, urging patience, and suddenly Jaina had the feeling that she would be seeing her parents again soon.

That was all she needed to know.

Jaina lowered her electrobinoculars and turned to Wuluw. "Have the trebuchets start dropping short, into the water," she ordered. "We're going to fill that channel with boulders—and we mean that literally."

"Burubr?" Wuluw demanded. *"Ubru urb uburb!"*

"Then we'd better get started, hadn't we?" Jaina said.

Actually, Jaina thought it would take even longer than a week to fill the channel with stones. But if she could make it appear to Wuluw and the rest of Great Swarm that she was preparing a foolproof attack across a broad front, she hoped UnuThul would sense the swarm's confidence and be patient.

But the banging of the trebuchets continued to echo through the jungle. Boulders continued to sail over the channel onto the Chiss islands, and the pressure inside Jaina began to grow more powerful. She found herself on the verge of ordering an all-out assault. Her plan had created more impatience in the Great Swarm than confidence, and now UnuThul was warning her to get the assault going— or he would.

Jaina took a moment to perform a deep-breathing exercise, gathering herself to oppose UnuThul's Will.

Her meditations came to an abrupt end as a series of high-pitched squeals echoed down from the treetops. At first, she thought it might be a missile or a bomb dropping from orbit, but then she realized that the squeals were moving *across* the sky, flying from the direction of the Killik trebuchets toward the Chiss islands.

Jaina spun around in time to see a pair of spread-eagled forms spinning through the air toward the Chiss islands.

"What are those?" Jaina demanded.

"*Burru.*"

"I *know* they're Squibs." Jaina watched as the two figures arced down toward the island and landed about thirty meters inside the Chiss breastworks. "Why did they fly across the sky like that?"

"*Ruru bu rur,*" Wuluw reminded her.

"Trebuchets!" Jaina gasped. "I didn't mean get them out of here like *that*. Wait here."

Jaina climbed out of the stream and started up a mogo tree, staying on the back side where she would be protected from Chiss snipers. When she judged she was high enough to see over the breastworks, she used the Force to stick herself in place, then raised her electrobinoculars and cautiously leaned out to peer around the trunk.

To her surprise, Jaina found both Squibs back on their feet, staggering around, wiping their eyes and spitting something dark from their mouths and nostrils. She thought for a moment that both rodents had suffered grievous internal injuries when they landed—until a squad of Chiss came staggering up to take them prisoner. The soldiers were smeared head-to-foot with mud, and every time they took a step, they sank knee-deep into the wet ground.

The island was practically underwater.

A circle of coldness suddenly formed between Jaina's eyes, and she pushed off the mogo, launching herself into a backflip just as a maser beam scorched past the trunk. She sensed more beams flying in her direction and dropped the electrobinoculars, snatching her lightsaber off her belt and activating it in the same swift motion.

Jaina's wrists flicked three times, intercepting and redirecting three maser beams in less than a second before she splashed feet-first into the stream. The sniper attack stopped as abruptly as it had started, and suddenly it sounded as though a tremendous wind were blowing through the jungle, rustling leaves that no longer hung on the trees. Jaina had to listen a moment before she realized that she was hearing the clicking of millions of stick-thin legs.

The Great Swarm was on the march.

"Wait!" Jaina turned to find Wuluw.

The insect was floating down the stream, pressed flat to the water with a huge dent in the chitin where the electrobinoculars had bounced off her delicate thorax.

"No!" Jaina used the Force to draw the wounded insect back to her, then rubbed a forearm along her antennae. "We're sorry!"

Wuluw tried to thrum something and succeeded only in pumping a long gush of insect gore into the water.

"Don't try to talk." Jaina started back upstream. The rustling had become a murmur now, and she could see the first Rekkers springing through the trees toward her. "We'll get you some help, but first you have to stop the Swarm. Attacking now is a terrible mistake!"

Wuluw managed a barely audible mandible tap, and the murmur of the Swarm's advance rose to a drone.

"I have a plan!" Jaina cried. "A good one."

All six of Wuluw's limbs stiffened and began to tremble, and a milky tint appeared deep inside her eyes.

"Hold on, Wuluw—tell the others we're going to dam the river." Jaina began to pour Force energy into the insect, trying to keep her alive long enough to complete the message. "Tell them we're going to flood the Chiss off those islands!"

SEVENTEEN

The pearlescent blur of hyperspace had barely winked back into the star-sparkled velvet of normal space before the *Falcon*'s proximity alarms began to scream. Han hit the reset so he could think, and the alarms screamed again.

"What the blazes?" Han demanded. There was nothing ahead but the swirling disk of a cloud-swaddled planet that he assumed to be Tenupe, and it was still no larger than his fist—far too distant to have triggered the first proximity alarm, much less a repeat. "What's out there?"

"Working on it!" Leia's hands were flying over the control board, adjusting static filters and signal enhancers. "These sensors don't calibrate themselves."

"Okay, take it easy," Han said. "I didn't mean anything."

He hit the reset again, and again the alarms reactivated themselves. The repeats could mean that more hazards were appearing, or that the original hazard was drawing rapidly closer. Seeing nothing between them and the planet, he began to accelerate. Tenupe swelled rapidly to the size of a Bith's head, and the azure blots of hundreds of cloud-free inland seas began to mottle its creamy disk.

"Is it wise to accelerate while we're sensor-blind?" Juun asked from the navigator's station. At Luke's request, Pellaeon had arranged for him and Tarfang to serve as the Solos' guides to Tenupe. "We still don't know where—"

"You see something in front of us?" Han interrupted.

"Only Tenupe."

"Same here." Han reset the alarms, then cursed as they instantly reactivated. "So whatever keeps triggering those alarms is coming at *us*."

"And we are *running*?" Saba was incredulous. "We do not even know from what!"

"Think of it as getting out of the way," Han replied. He activated the intercom so he could speak to the Noghri. "Get into the cannon turrets and let me know if you see anything suspicious."

Tenupe had swollen to the size of a bantha's head now. Hanging to one side of the planet, Han could see a shadow-pocked lump that might be a small red moon. On the opposite side, a cluster of tiny, wedge-shaped specks were circling above the clouds.

"That doesn't look good," Han said. "Leia, how are those sensors—"

Han's question was interrupted when Meewalh and Cakhmaim announced that there were ion trails closing on the *Falcon*'s stern from all directions.

"Chisz?" Saba asked.

Tarfang chuttered something sarcastic.

"Tarfang believes so," C-3PO translated helpfully. "He points out that Killik fighters still use rocket propulsion."

"Of all the luck!" Han complained. "The Chiss are already here—and we enter the system in the middle of a patrol!"

A trio of crimson bolts flashed past barely a dozen meters above the canopy. Then a gruff Chiss voice came over the hailing channel.

"*Millennium Falcon*, this is Zark Two." The woman's Basic was thick-tongued and awkward. "The Chiss Expansionary Defense Fleet demands that you bring to a dead stop your vessel. Stand by for boarding."

Han activated his comm microphone. "Uh, just a second." He glanced over at Leia, then pointed at the control panel and raised his brow. When she gave him a thumbs-up and began to bring the sensors online, he continued, "Sorry. You'll have to say again. Your Basic is a little—"

Another flurry of energy beams flashed past the cockpit, this time so close that they left spots in Han's eyes.

"That is clear enough, *Falcon*?" Zark Two asked. "This is a war zone. If you disobey, we fire for effect."

Han's tactical display came up, and he saw that the *Falcon* had an entire squadron of clawcraft on her tail. The fighters were escorted by two heavy gunboats and an assault shuttle—a standard package for a boarding company.

But it was what Han saw near the planet that really alarmed him.

As he had suspected, the wedge-shaped flecks circling above the clouds were a huge Chiss battle fleet, clustered together over one tiny area of the planet.

"Leia, see if you can—"

"Working on it," Leia said.

A moment later, the image from a cloud-penetrating sensor scan appeared on Han's display. Most of the planet's land surface seemed to be covered by lowland jungles or mountain rain forests, but the area directly beneath the Chiss fleet was a brown smudge. A huge river ran through one edge of the smudge, and a tiny area along one bank shined red with thermal energy.

The lock-alarms began to chime incessantly, announcing that the *Falcon* was being targeted by her pursuers.

"*Millennium Falcon,* this is our final warning," Zark Two commed. "Bring your vessel to a dead stop."

Han pushed the throttles to the overload stops and dropped into an evasive corkscrew. Laser bolts instantly began to streak past on all sides, and the cabin lights flickered as the *Falcon*'s shields began to take hits.

"Captain Solo, the squadron leader's accent must be confusing you," C-3PO said. "She ordered us to *stop*."

"I heard." Han's eyes remained fixed on the image of the river-bank. "But that looks like a battle down there. A big one."

"How do you know that?" Juun sounded more amazed than doubtful. "I thought it was a jungle fire!"

"A jungle fire? With a fleet to provide space cover?" Saba reached over from the comm station and slapped the Sullustan's back. "So funny!"

Tarfang rushed to help Juun off the floor, then whirled on Saba and chittered so angrily it made the Barabel's scales ripple.

"Sssorry," she said. "This one did not know he was serious."

A depletion buzzer activated as the Chiss continued to pound the rear shields. Realizing he would never escape a dozen clawcraft with fancy flying alone, Han activated the intercom again.

"Are you two taking a nap back there?" he demanded. "Shoot something!"

The *Falcon* shuddered as the Noghri immediately cut loose with the big quad cannons.

Leia's eyes widened. "Han, I don't know if this is a good idea," she said. "Killing Chiss is only going to aggravate—"

"Look, *I'm* not the one setting the stakes here," Han said. "If I know my daughter, she and Zekk are in the middle of that battle down there, and that means the Chiss are trying to kill *them*. So pardon me if I return the favor."

"Han, I feel the same way," Leia said. "But we have to think of the mission. Luke wanted to do this without killing more—"

A damage warning began to scream, and suddenly the yoke felt like an angry snake, snapping from side to side and forward and back, twisting right, whipping left, then kicking and bouncing like a kid on his first bound-stick. The *Falcon* went into a shuddering vortex, and more alarms screamed as delicate systems began to take secondary damage from the violent shaking.

"Sh-sh-shut down n-n-number four n-nacelle!" Han ordered. At least he thought it was number four—with all the quaking and shaking, it was hard to be sure which status light he was seeing. "And if that doesn't work, try the others!"

Leia's fingers were already stabbing at the control panel, trying to catch the correct glide-switch. In the midst of it all, a synthesized boom reverberated from the control panel speaker, and Han glimpsed a Chiss designator-symbol vanishing from the tactical display. Even with all of the shaking and spiraling, one of the Noghri had hit a clawcraft. Han was not that surprised.

Leia finally managed to shut down the number four nacelle. The *Falcon* stopped shuddering, but her acceleration slowed and the yoke grew stiff and sluggish. Han struggled to bring the ship's wild spiral back under control.

"Han?" Leia's voice was brittle with fear. "You know what I was saying about aggravating the situation?"

"Yeah?"

"Forget it," she said. "They're already mad."

"Yesssszz." Saba's hiss had an air of thoughtfulness. "Master Skywalker did not know how far the situation has deteriorated."

"Thanks for your opinions," Han grumbled. "Now could someone get back there and disconnect the number four vector plate? We're handling like a one-winged manta right now!"

"Mantaz can fly with one wing?" Saba gasped.

"No, Master," Leia explained. "That's the point."

"Oh." Saba jumped up and tapped Tarfang on the shoulder, then started toward the back of the flight deck. "Why did you not say it was so bad?"

A jolt ran through the *Falcon* as they took another hit, and Han saw on the tactical display that the clawcraft were beginning to close the distance more rapidly.

"Jae, how long before we're in the clouds?"

"We won't reach them," Juun announced immediately.

"What are you talking about?" Han demanded. "Of course we'll reach them!"

Juun shook his head. "I've done the calculations. By the time we decelerate to enter the atmosphere—"

"Who says we're decelerating?" Han demanded.

Juun's voice grew even more nasal. "We're not going to decelerate?"

"Captain Solo never decelerates in these situations," C-3PO reported. "He seems to enjoy seeing how close we can come to crashing without actually doing so. I can't tell you the number of times that we have been statistically doomed, only to escape at the last possible mo—"

Another boom reverberated from the control panel speaker, announcing the destruction of a second clawcraft.

"You see?" C-3PO continued. "But I *am* pleased to report that our odds of survival have increased by three one-thousandths of a percent."

The boom had barely died away before the hailing channel grew active again.

"Captain Solo, that is *quite* enough!" The voice this time was male . . . and very familiar. "Come to a dead stop at once!"

"Sorry—someone's shooting at us." Han continued to corkscrew toward Tenupe, which was now so large that its cloud-blanketed face filled the entire forward viewport. "Is that you, Jag?"

"It is," Jagged Fel confirmed. "And I will *not* tolerate any more casualties."

"Then I advise you to order Zark Leader to stop pursuit," Leia retorted.

"I *am* Zark Leader," Jagged replied coolly. "And I am not at liberty to end this pursuit. If you do not stop immediately, there is only *one* way this can end."

"You're a *squadron* leader now?" Han asked, ignoring Fel's threats. "What'd you do to get busted down that far?"

"*Nothing.*" The cockpit speaker crackled with Jagged's indignation. "My rank remains intact. Bring the *Falcon* to a—"

"You're the same rank?" Leia broke in. "Are you telling me a *commander* is leading this squadron?"

"Captain, actually," Jagged replied.

"*Captain?*" Han began to feel sick to his stomach. The Chiss Expansionary Defense Fleet used the naval system of ranks, so captain was a command-grade rank—the equivalent of colonel in terms of

Galactic Alliance ground forces—and Han could think of only one reason a command officer would fly a patrol mission. "You're here because of us! You *knew* we were coming!"

"I should have thought that was obvious, Captain Solo," Jagged said.

Han did not respond. He was too busy trying to bring the *Falcon* out of her spin . . . and silently promising a painful death to whoever had betrayed them to the Chiss. Only a handful of people outside the Jedi order had known of the Solos' destination, so it would not be difficult to track down the spy and put a blaster bolt through his head.

"But now that you understand," Jagged continued, "perhaps you see how hopeless your situation really is."

"Hopeless?" Han scoffed. "I'm not even worried!"

He shoved throttles one through three past the overload stops. The *Falcon* began to spiral even more wildly, and a slight tremble returned to the yoke.

"Han," Leia said.

"Yeah?"

"*I'm* a little bit worried."

"Rel-l-lax." The yoke was vibrating so hard in Han's hands that it made his teeth chatter. "Those are rain clouds down there."

"So?"

"So when we pull up under them," Han explained, "they'll put out the entry burn."

"You're entering a gravity dive?" Juun's voice was filled with awe. "May I have permission to record? We should document how you pull out—especially given the damage to our controls."

"*If* we pull out," Leia groaned. She *hated* gravity dives. "But go ahead. What can it hurt?"

"We'll pull out," Han said, "assuming Saba and Tarfang get that vector plate disconnected. And we'll need to know if there are any mountains in that mess. Better run a terrain scan."

"I'll *try*," Leia said. "It's difficult to get a reading while we're spiraling out of control to our deaths like this."

"Who's out of control?"

Leia began to activate the imaging scanners, struggling to keep her hands on the appropriate switches as the *Falcon* bucked and shook. Zark Squadron continued to zing cannon fire at their stern, but the Noghri's accuracy seemed to have a chilling effect on the Chiss. Despite the renowned speed of their clawcraft, Fel's pilots were closing the distance much slower than Han had expected—and not nearly fast enough to keep them from reaching the planet, as Juun had calculated.

"Wait a minute!" Han said. They were so close to Tenupe now that all they could see ahead was pale mass of green clouds, marked here and there by a blue blob of cloudless sea, spinning past the forward viewport ever more quickly. "Something's not right."

"You can say that again." Leia sent the terrain scan to his display. "Look at this."

The map showed a rugged jungle planet of high mountains and vast drainage basins, with no large oceans, but rivers wide enough to see from orbit. It also showed a dozen cruisers converging on the *Falcon*'s point of entry, their course and original locations clearly outlined by the huge vapor trails they were leaving in their wakes.

"Get a tactical readout on those—"

The data appeared on Han's tactical display. As he had expected, they were drop cruisers—terrible in space combat, but ideal for supporting planetside operations. And the energy blooms on their hulls suggested they all had fully charged tractor beams.

"This is a setup!" Han pulled the three functional throttles back to three-quarter power—not suddenly, but enough to buy a little reaction time. "Jag is trying to drive us into a trap!"

"*Trying*, Han?" Leia asked.

"*Trying*," Han growled. "Nobody traps Han Solo."

Han waited until the Tenupe's little red moon showed through the top of the canopy, then jerked back on the yoke. A series of muffled crashes rumbled up the access corridor—the inertial compensators could not quite neutralize the high g forces—but the planet's cloud-swaddled face vanished from the forward viewport.

Jagged Fel's voice came over the cockpit speaker immediately. "I *told* my superiors that trap wouldn't fool you. But if you check your tactical monitor, you'll discover your situation has only grown more hopeless."

Han checked his display and had to agree. A pair of Chiss Star Destroyers had appeared on Tenupe's horizon, eliminating all hope of escaping around the curve of the planet. Zark Squadron was cutting the corner behind the *Falcon*, approaching at an angle and continuing to fire.

"Don't force me to destroy you and the Princess, Captain Solo," Jagged said. "Things didn't work out between Jaina and me, but I still remember you all fondly."

"Do what you have to, kid." Han pushed the three functioning throttles back past their overload stops. "I always liked Kyp Durron better anyway."

Leia slapped the comm microphones off. "Han! Are you crazy?" she demanded. "*Kyp?*"

"Relax." Han gave her a crooked smile. "I'm just trying to make him mad. I know Kyp's way too old for her."

Leia closed her eyes and shook her head. "Do you really think *now* is a good time to make Jag angry? He has an entire *fleet* at his disposal."

"Nothing to worry about," Han said. "He's bluffing."

"Han, Jagged was raised by *Chiss*. They don't know how to bluff."

"Must be why they're so bad at it." Han winked at her. "Send Meewalh and Cakhmaim to help Saba and Tarfang with that vector plate. I don't think we're going to need them in the turrets much longer, but it would be nice to have control of this tub again."

Leia activated the intercom and relayed the order. The laser cannons had barely stopped firing before Jagged's voice came over the comm again.

"You have stopped firing on us—thank you." He sounded genuinely relieved. "But I cannot stop firing on *you* until the *Falcon* comes to a dead stop."

"Jagged, we all know that if you were serious about this, we'd already be space dust," Leia replied. "What I can't figure out is *why* you're going to so much trouble to save us."

"Your confusion surprises me, Princess," Jagged said. "I should think the reason would be obvious to someone of your diplomatic and military background. You and Captain Solo will be valuable prisoners—and so will Master Sebatyne and Bwua'tu's master spies, the Ewok and the Sullustan."

"You're very well informed, Jag," Leia said. "But not well enough. If you knew our mission, you'd know we're trying to *end* the war. You would be helping—"

"I know you and Captain Solo came here to find Jaina and her, ah, *companion*," Jag retorted. "I also know you want to help them smuggle a Killik commando squad into one of our command and control centers. I know your brother believes—wrongly—that this maneuver will prove to us how difficult it would be to win a war against the Killiks. He also believes it will make it easier for him to persuade the ruling houses to accept the peace that he intends to impose on the Colony. Is there anything *else* about your mission that I should know?"

"No, that about covers it," Han said, speaking through gritted teeth. He had assumed that some spy eavesdropping in a hangar or briefing room had betrayed them. But clearly, it been someone a lot closer to the Jedi order than that—someone close enough to know Luke's entire plan. "You think it'll work?"

"No," Jagged said icily. "I'd have to kill you first."

"Yeah, that's what I figured," Han said.

Zark Squadron continued to pour fire after the *Falcon*. Another damage alarm started to scream—prompting Juun to take C-3PO and rush aft—but the clawcraft began to drift back on the tactical display. The Star Destroyers began to lay barrages of fire ahead of the *Falcon,* trying to channel her into tractor beam range, or force her to stop and wait for boarding.

Still fighting a sluggish yoke and an out-of-control spiral, Han dropped them back toward Tenupe and continued toward the planet at an oblique angle.

"Uh, Han?" Leia sounded worried. "What are we doing?"

"This d-d-doesn't make any ssssense," Han said. The yoke had started to shake again, and he was fighting to keep it from swinging around at random. "They know our plan. They ought to be coming after us hard."

"Han, this *is* hard." Leia's gaze was fixed firmly forward, where a green sliver of planetary horizon was slowly rolling around the edge of the viewport as the *Falcon* spiraled toward Tenupe. "There's a whole task force after us."

"That's what I mean," Han said. "You saw that battle down there! Do you think the theater commander really wants Jag wasting his time chasing *us* right now? They should just blast us back to atoms and be done with it."

"They won't *need* to," Leia said. "Han, we're heading for—"

"Whoever double-crossed us made them promise to take us *alive*," Han continued. The boiling red curtain of a Star Destroyer barrage blossomed ahead, jolting the *Falcon* and spreading spots before his eyes. "Leia, it had to be someone close to us."

"Okay, Han!" Leia pointed forward, where the hazy blur of Tenupe's atmosphere was whirling around the center of the viewport. "But what are you *doing*?"

"Just what it looks like—a planet-skip." Han activated the intercom. "Hold on back there!"

An instant later, tongues of red flame began to flicker over the viewport as they entered the thin gas of Tenupe's upper atmosphere. The *Falcon* bucked so hard that Han slammed against his crash harness, and the clamor of flying gear echoed up the access corridor. Han fought against the sluggish controls, struggling to keep the ship's spiral from growing any tighter and faster . . . and *that* was when the yoke went loose.

Before Han realized it, he had pulled it completely back against his thigh, and the *Falcon* was flipping out of its spiral in a weld-popping wingover. He quickly moved it back to center . . . and the wingover gradually slowed.

The *Falcon* stopped about three-quarters of the way through her roll and hung there, then languidly began to drift back toward upright—now headed straight for a rolling barrage of megamaser blossoms. Han pushed the yoke all the way forward, trying to dive under the fiery wall of death, and could only grit his teeth as the *Falcon* dropped her nose a mere five degrees.

Leia leaned over and grabbed Han's hand. "Han, I love—"

The barrage vanished as suddenly as it had appeared, leaving nothing ahead of the *Falcon* but the blotchy red surface of Tenupe's moon.

"Yeah, me, too." Han pulled the throttles back to the overload stops, gripping the handles tightly to keep his hands from shaking. "See what I mean? They killed that barrage to keep from vaping us."

"Yes. Okay. I believe you." Leia's voice was still shaky. "They promised *someone* not to kill us."

"Yeah." Han's tone was bitter. "I wonder who *that* could have been?"

"You're thinking Omas?"

"That's the only thing that makes sense," Han said. "Cal Omas would sacrifice us in a minute if he thought it would convince the Chiss that the Alliance isn't at war with the Ascendancy."

Leia shook her head. "Why would he bother making them promise to keep us alive?"

"Because he needs the Jedi, too," Han said. The moon ahead had swelled into a lumpy, fist-sized ovoid laced with a spidery web of dark rifts. "And if his double cross ever comes out, Omas would never be able to make peace with Luke if we were dead."

Leia frowned. "Maybe . . ."

"Look, it's either him or Pellaeon or someone in the Jedi," Han said. "And Pellaeon never double-crossed anyone, even when he was an Imperial."

"I guess, when you put it like that."

Leia still sounded doubtful, but their discussion was interrupted by Jagged Fel's astonished voice.

"I'm finally starting to understand Jaina," he said. "Insanity runs in her family. Only a madman would attempt a planet-skip in a damaged ship."

"Han's not crazy," Leia said. "Just good."

"I'm sure you believe that, Princess Leia," Jagged said. "But I'm warning—no, I'm *advising*—you not to attempt taking refuge in that moon cluster."

"Moon cluster?" Han peered more closely at the red lump ahead and saw that the rifts might, indeed, be interstitial spaces. He deactivated his comm microphone, then asked, "What the blazes *is* that?"

"I'll find out," Leia said, reaching for the terrain mappers. "In the meantime, stall."

"Stall *Jag*?" Han turned his microphone back on, then commed, "Thanks for the advice, Jag, but we were planning on going around anyway."

"Really?" Jagged sounded smug. "Then the *Falcon* must be even faster than Jaina always claimed."

Han glanced down at his tactical display and saw that the Zark Squadron had taken advantage of his planet-skip to put on their own burst of acceleration. They had stopped firing—a sign that they now felt certain of a successful capture—and were arrayed in a semisphere around the *Falcon*. The squadron's escort was not far behind, and the Star Destroyers had already closed to within tractor beam range of the moon cluster's near side.

Han cursed under his breath, but said, "Just watch, kid. You'll be surprised."

"I have no doubt," Jagged said. "But please believe me about the moon cluster. It's gravitationally unstable. Every one of our scoutships has been smashed flat. You'll be much safer surrendering to us, and I give you my word that we won't torture or humiliate you during your interrogations."

"Thanks, that's real good of you," Han said. "Let me think it over for a second."

Han closed the comm channel, then experimented with the yoke, pushing it around and feeling almost no reaction from the *Falcon*.

"How bad is it?" Leia asked. She was still staring at the terrain mapper, frowning and adjusting the controls.

"Bad," Han said. "How about those moons?"

"Even worse than he said." Leia looked out at the moons, which were close enough now for her to see that they were all shifting around, bumping against each other. "It looks like something shattered the old moon into fifty or sixty pieces. It must still be in there, because I'm detecting . . ."

Leia let her sentence trail off, then gasped and stared out the viewport.

"Yeah?" Han asked.

Leia raised her hand to quiet him, then closed her eyes in concentration.

Han frowned and leaned over to look at the terrain scanners. He saw only the shattered moon she had described, with a density reading near the center that suggested a metallic core—probably whatever had shattered it in the first place. He tried to be patient, waiting for Leia to do whatever Jedi thing she was preparing, but they were running out of time. The two Star Destroyers had activated their tractor beams and were already reaching out toward the moon cluster, trying to block any chance the *Falcon* had of slipping into one of the crevices.

Han activated the intercom. "Somebody back there get to the repulsor beam now! We've got some rocks to move out of—"

"Han, no!" Leia opened her eyes and turned to him, shaking her head. "We have to surrender!"

Han frowned. "Look, I know the yoke's a little sloppy—"

"It's not that." Leia reached over and pulled the throttles all the way back. "It's Raynar and the Killiks—those moons are teeming with insects!"

EIGHTEEN

The Jedi StealthXs appeared—as always—as though by magic, an entire wing of dark X's hanging against the crimson veil of the Utegetu Nebula. They floated there for just an instant, then drifted over to the black ribbon of a stellar dust cloud and vanished, darkness merging into darkness. It all happened so quickly that any picket ship pilots who happened to be looking in that direction would blink, question what they had seen, and check their instruments. And their instruments would assure them that their eyes had been mistaken.

The StealthXs continued their approach in full confidence that they remained undetected, and soon the bright disk of the yellow planet Sarm began to swell in the forward panels of their cockpit canopies. The Jedi pilots kept a careful watch for sentries—both on their sensor screens and by reaching out in the Force—and easily avoided a single inattentive blastboat operated by pirates. The StealthXs reached Sarm unobserved . . . and unsettled. The Jedi knew better than to underestimate a foe—especially during a war. The Killiks would not leave themselves exposed like this without good reason.

As the wing drew nearer the yellow planet, a network of ancient, world-spanning irrigation canals grew visible on the surface—all that remained of the beings who had inhabited Sarm before being blasted from the galactic memory by the Utegetu Nova. The Jedi had time to ponder those channels as they closed on their destination, reflecting on the destiny of civilizations in a violent universe, glimpsing the anonymous end to which every culture ultimately came. What did battles matter when a galactic burp could erase whole civiliza-

tions? Could any amount of killing ever change the fundamental brutal transience of existence?

Perhaps the Killiks knew the answers. After all, they lived in harmony with the Song of the Universe, killing and being killed as the
melody demanded, abounding and vanishing, fighting and dancing as
the mood moved them. They did not concern themselves with right
or wrong, feelings of love and hate. They served the nest. What ben-
efited the nest, they desired. What hurt the nest, they exterminated.

Not so with the Jedi. They struggled with their fates, worried
over whether something was moral or immoral, peered into the future and tried to bend it to their desires. And then, when their grasps
slipped and the future snapped back in their faces with all the force
of an impacting meteor, they were always so surprised, always so
shaken, as though their wills should have been strong enough to steer
the course of the galaxy.

And so the Jedi continued toward Sarm in their StealthXs, silent
and grim of purpose, readying themselves to kill and be killed, to
sing in their own way the Song of the Universe. Their targets came
into view just as Admiral Bwua'tu's intelligence officer had promised, eleven pale spheres in orbit around the planet, each the size of a
Super-class Star Destroyer, all but one enveloped by the diffuse Force
presence of a Killik nest.

The StealthXs swung wide around the planet, positioning themselves to descend on the nest ship with no Force presence. It was in
the lowest orbit, where it would be screened from attack by the rest
of the fleet. That was the Dark Nest's vessel, the one where Lomi Plo
would be hiding, and Luke's plan was simple. The Jedi would sneak
into position around the vessel and wait for Admiral Pellaeon to arrive with the *Megador* and the rest of the Alliance strike fleet. When
he did, they would destroy any craft attempting to leave the Gorog
nest, and then they would go inside and flush Lomi Plo from her den.

But Sarm was too quiet. There should have been smugglers and
membrosia runners flitting in and out of the nest ship hangars, and
an entire flotilla of pirate vessels hanging in orbit. There should have
been maintenance barges hovering over the nest ships, repairing the
damage the Jedi had inflicted at the Murgo Choke. Instead, the fleet
looked almost abandoned. Save for the presences they felt in the
Force, the Jedi would have believed it was.

Then blue halos of ion efflux appeared around the sterns of the
nest ships, and the vessels began to accelerate. Now the Jedi understood the reason Sarm was so quiet. The Killiks had already repaired

their battered fleet. They were breaking orbit and deploying to challenge the Alliance blockade.

Luke dropped into a power dive, swinging wide around two nest ships to avoid the sharp eyes of the Killik sentries. Mara and Jacen and the other Jedi followed close behind, grasping the change of plan through their combat-meld. Kenth Hamner took his squadron and circled back behind the first two nest ships, decelerating so their attack would hit at the same time as Luke's. Kyle Katarn's squadron peeled off and started for the far side of the planet. Tresina Lobi and her squadron broke in the opposite direction, heading for the front of the Killik fleet.

The remainder of the wing continued toward the original target: the Dark Nest of Lomi Plo. As they descended, Luke allowed his alarm to fill his thoughts and reached out to Cilghal in the Force, trying to impress on her the urgency of the situation. She was still aboard the *Megador* with Tekli and the collection crews, and Pellaeon would listen if she told him the attack fleet had to jump *now*. She seemed at first surprised by Luke's contact, then worried, but quickly focused on what he was trying to tell her and returned his touch with reassurance.

The Gorog nest ship grew steadily larger in Luke's forward viewport as he drew nearer, and soon its pale ovoid began to obscure Sarm's yellow surface. The planet took on the appearance of a huge, golden halo behind the immense vessel. Luke pointed the nose of his StealthX straight at the ship's heart, using its own shadow to shield his squadron from Sarm's planet-glow.

The strategy did not prove very effective. Insect eyes were especially adept at detecting movement, and barely a moment passed before R2-D2 scrolled a warning across Luke's display.

TARGET ENERGIZING WEAPON BATTERIES.

"Thanks, Artoo," Luke said. The three squadrons broke in different directions, then broke again and split into shield trios. "Good to have you riding the socket again, old friend."

IT'S ABOUT TIME, R2-D2 replied. YOUR SURVIVAL HAS BEEN IMPROBABLE WITHOUT ME!

"There *have* been a few close calls," Luke admitted.

The nest ship was close enough now that Sarm had completely disappeared behind its pale orb. Luke could see a double row of turbolaser barrels protruding up from among the knobby heat sinks that covered its hull. The smaller weapons that would be attacking the StealthXs remained concealed in a grid of dark shadows.

Luke began evasive flying, leading his shieldmates on a random, wild descent toward the target. Mara and Jacen followed as though their controls were linked to his, entering each roll almost before he did, coming out behind him so quickly their transponder codes looked like a single entry on his tactical screen.

A burst of elation filled the battle-meld as Kenth Hamner's squadron attacked. The tactical display showed repeated detonations in the sterns of three nest ships, and a string of white flashes erupted in a high orbit behind Luke's squadron. But none of the vessels seemed to be slowing down.

"Artoo, are they deploying—"

A sharp whistle filled the cockpit as R2-D2 warned that the Gorog had opened fire. Luke was already dodging, his hands and feet reacting even before he saw the laser bolts flashing up from the shadows. He rolled away from the burst and took a flak-shell in the forward shields. Mara reached out to him in concern, ready to move into the lead.

No need. R2-D2 already had the shields back at 90 percent. Luke followed the line of laser bolts visually down to their source, then reached out with the Force and shoved the cannon barrels aside. The deadly stream of color changed direction and began to pour harmlessly into space.

Mara made Luke's day by seeming impressed—at least that was what it felt like through their Force-bond. Then Jacen redirected a stream of mag-pellets and somehow located the flak-guns and pushed those aside, too. Mara seemed almost awed.

Luke sighed, then checked his tactical display. He saw no indication that the nest ships were doing anything except continuing to accelerate.

"Artoo, any sign of dartships?"

R2-D2 trilled a sharp response.

"Take it easy," Luke said. R2-D2's testiness made him wonder whether the droid truly was ready to return to combat service. "I just wanted to be sure."

R2-D2 beeped a promise to make certain Luke knew the instant a dartship appeared, then scrolled an additional message across the display: YOU HAVE NO REASON TO DOUBT ME. I WAS ONLY FOLLOWING MY OWNER-PRESERVATION ROUTINES.

"I know that, Artoo," Luke said. "But you can't protect people from the truth."

WHY NOT? THERE ARE NO TRUTH EXCEPTIONS IN MY PARAMETER STATEMENTS.

A turbolaser strike erupted ahead, bucking the StealthX so hard it felt like they had collided with the nest ship—which they soon would, if the squadron did not launch its attack quickly.

"I'll explain later," Luke said. "Right now, arm the penetrator."

R2-D2 beeped an acknowledgment, and Luke sensed the rest of his squadron lining up behind him. Basically a Jedi shadow bomb with a trio of shaped-charge warheads, the penetrator had been specifically designed to unleash a series of powerful, focused detonations toward the interior of a Killik nest ship.

A message appeared on the display announcing that the penetrator was live. Luke dodged past the fiery blossom of a turbolaser strike, then saw a pair of laser cannons flashing up from the dark crevices between a pair of spitcrete heat sinks. He Force-shoved the barrels aside, then released the penetrator and simultaneously used the Force to send the weapon smashing into the nest ship's hull.

His canopy blast-tinting went black with the first detonation, but the two explosions that followed were so bright that they lit the interior of the cockpit anyway. Luke rolled away, then did a wingover and flew back along the attack line.

With no dartships to worry about, he was free to watch on his tactical display as Mara, Jacen, and the rest of his squadron released their penetrators in one-second intervals. Each bomb disappeared into the crater left by the previous one, driving the hole deeper down through the nest ship's layered decks, wreaking increasing amounts of destruction and exposing more and more of the vessel's interior to the cold vacuum of space.

By the time the last weapon detonated, the Gorog were in such a state of shock that all defensive fire had ceased within a kilometer of the impact area. Luke swung his StealthX around and found a cloud of steam, bodies, and equipment tumbling from the crater, so thick it obscured the ship's hull. He could sense by the exhilaration in the meld that Kyp's attack on the stern of the ship had also gone well, but there was a certain heaviness in Corran's squadron that Luke knew all too well: a Jedi had fallen in the assault on the bow.

R2-D2 whistled an alarm, and Luke looked down to see swarms of Gorog dartships pouring from the vessel's hangar bays.

"Thanks, Artoo," he said. "What's the rest of the battle look like?"

The tactical display switched scales, and Luke saw that the other nest ships were bleeding dartships and dropping into lower orbits to support Gorog. Clearly, the Killiks had aborted their attack on the blockade. It was more important to protect the Dark Nest, and the Dark Nest had been wounded.

Luke reached out to Kenth, Kyle, and Tresina, calling them back to the initial target. When Pellaeon arrived with the main attack fleet, there would be fewer casualties from friendly fire if the Jedi were doing their best to follow the original plan.

Once Luke sensed that his squadron had re-formed behind him, he continued forward, using the Force to clear a path through the cloud of flotsam and bodies still pouring from the Gorog nest's interior. He knew by the growing tension of the meld that Corran and Kyp were also returning to begin the second, more dangerous phase of the assault. And he shared in their hope that the Alliance battle fleet would arrive soon. Once the Jedi began the final destruction of the Dark Nest, they were going to need all the support they could get.

Luke reached the breach in the outer hull and activated the imaging system in his helmet visor. The dark interior of the nest ship was immediately transformed into an eerie hologram of vibrant colors, with white-hot lumps of spitcrete rubble and glowing red pieces of Killiks streaming up a long, seemingly bottomless shaft before they tumbled out into the void.

The StealthXs shut down their ion drives and descended into the hull breach under the power of their maneuvering thrusters alone. As much as Luke would have liked to, there was no time to look for traps or counterattacks as they descended past each deck in the bombed-out shaft. The success of their assault depended on speed and ferocity, and their best hope lay in keeping the enemy off balance.

When the squadron had descended ten decks, the rear trio of StealthXs peeled off and glided toward the edge of the shaft. A few moments later, a series of blue flashes spilled out of the darkness as the three pilots came to an air lock and used their laser cannons to blast it open. Luke glanced over his shoulder and saw more flotsam streaming up the shaft behind him. The nest ship's artificial gravity generator had either been destroyed or shut down to conserve power, because even the heaviest pieces showed no sign of dropping toward the center of the ship.

A second trio of StealthXs peeled off after the squadron had descended twenty decks, and a third after thirty. By then, the combat-meld was charged with excitement as the Jedi blasted their way deeper into the enormous ship from three sides, cutting down waves of vac-suited Gorog warriors with their laser cannons, blasting open air locks and using the Force to hide shadow bombs at critical locations.

Luke and Mara and Jacen passed the fortieth deck and continued down to the fiftieth, the shaft narrowing to barely more than the spread of a StealthX's wings. The excitement in the meld turned to fear and anger and all the other emotions that boiled to surface in the midst of a pitched battle, then Kenth and Kyle and Tresina Lobi began to radiate alarm, warning Luke and Kyp and Corran that trouble was on its way.

Luke was not worried. Dartships were far less maneuverable than StealthXs and would be next to worthless in the twisting wreckage . . . but that thought came to an abrupt end when R2-D2 trilled an urgent warning.

"*B-wings?*" Luke asked. Armed more heavily than XJ-3s, B-wings were some of the most dangerous and maneuverable starfighters in the galaxy. "Are you sure?"

R2-D2 piped an annoyed affirmative.

Luke tore his gaze away from the dust-filled murk ahead just long enough to check his tactical display. At this point, the image showed only the shaft behind them, a flared column of space packed with descending starfighters.

"*Ours?*"

That question was answered when the blue streak of an approaching proton torpedo appeared on the display. Luke instantly poured on some speed and ducked into the exposed decks, leading Mara and Jacen away from the detonation area. The torpedo streaked past behind them, then reached the bottom of the shaft and exploded.

Luke and his wingmates were partially shielded by several layers of deck, but the blast reached them with enough power to beat down their rear shields and hurl them into the next bulkhead. Their forward shields absorbed most of the impact, but their cockpits broke into a cacophony of damage alarms and depletion warnings.

Luke spun his StealthX around while it was still wobbling. The wings banged into a ceiling on one side and the floor on the other, but at least his targeting systems seemed unaffected. A constant stream of laserfire flashed down the shaft as Kyle Katarn and two members of his squadron attacked the approaching B-wings from behind.

Although the hull breach was considerably larger than it had been just a few minutes ago, with the nest ship's artificial gravity nonfunctional, it was so choked with floating dust and rubble that the storm of cannon bolts was barely visible. Luke glanced over and found Mara and Jacen already using their attitude thrusters to move away from him, spreading out to lay an ambush.

As they waited, Luke silenced his alarms and wondered idly, "Where did *Killiks* get B-wings?"

R2-D2 ventured the obvious opinion. After all, B-wings were manufactured by Slayn & Korpil—one of the best known of the Verpine hive companies.

"All right—forget I asked," Luke said. All the Killiks would have needed to arrange a third-party sale was a single highly placed tarhead. "How are the rear shields? Can you get them back up?"

R2-D2 let out a falling whistle, then a pair of B-wings appeared in the storm of laser bolts pouring down the shaft breach. With their head-like cockpits mounted atop a crossshaped wing structure, the craft had a vaguely human profile, like a man standing with his legs crossed and his arms outstretched. The first B-wing was descending in the upright position, slowly spinning around to search the adjacent decks for StealthX infiltrators. The second was flying on its back, firing back up the shaft at Kyle Katarn and the other attacking Jedi from behind.

The first craft started to spin more rapidly, trying to bring the torpedo launcher on its tail assembly to bear on Luke's StealthX. He grabbed the vessel in the Force and held it in place, then opened fire with his laser cannons. The startled B-wing pilot applied more power, trying to break free. Luke drew on the Force more heavily to counter the maneuvering thrusters, and all of the energy flowing through his body began to make his skin nettle.

Mara and Jacen began to fire, too. The B-wing's shields emitted an overload flash, then went down in a storm of discharge static. An instant later the starfighter itself simply came apart under the combined fury of the StealthX cannons.

The second B-wing gave up trying to hold Kyle and his companions at bay and dropped its tail to bring its torpedo launcher to bear. Luke started to Force-grab the fighter again, but Jacen had already caught it and was holding it in place while cannon bolts pounded its shields from above.

This B-wing did not even try to break free. The pilot simply launched the proton torpedo in the direction it was pointed. Suddenly the electronics in Luke's cockpit were popping and spewing acrid smoke, and the spitcrete ceiling was crashing down on his StealthX, and Mara was touching him through their Force-bond, surprised and worried but somehow confident they were not going to die—not yet.

Then Luke and his StealthX became just so much flotsam, the laser cannons and broken wings tumbling away into the dust and the rubble, the fusial engines banging against the fuselage, still connected by a few twisted shreds of metal. R2-D2 was screeching warnings over the cockpit speaker, his voice barely audible over the roar of escaping air.

Luke sealed his vac suit and activated his helmet comm unit. "I'm okay, Artoo. Prepare to abandon the craft."

R2-D2 ran a message across the heads-up display inside Luke's visor. THE SELF-DESTRUCT CHARGE IS MISSING—AND THERE *IS* NO CRAFT.

"I know. Just unhook yourself."

Luke could feel that Mara was not injured, either, but Jacen was more difficult to read. He had drawn in on himself and vanished from the Force.

Luke opened a comlink channel. "Jacen?"

"Over here." Mara's concern filled their Force-bond. "His canopy is smashed, but his visor is down and I can tell that his vac suit is pressurized. He may still be alive."

Luke's breath left him in a rush of fear. *Not again.* He could not tell Leia that he had lost another of her sons.

"Get him out!"

"I'm *trying*," Mara commed. "Just calm down."

But Luke could not calm down. He felt as though he had been punched in the stomach by a Wookiee. It was bad enough that he had sent Anakin to his death, but this time Jacen had been with *him*. He looked in the direction from which he sensed Mara's presence.

It took a moment to pick out her blotchy red image through all the rubble displayed by the imaging system inside his visor. But she was already wearing her combat harness, and she had her bulky G-12 power blaster slung over one shoulder. The battered remains of her starfighter were bobbing along in the rubble beneath her, and she was hanging on to the empty droid socket behind the shattered canopy of Jacen's StealthX.

Now that he saw that Mara was already with Jacen, Luke began to calm. What could be done, she was doing—but he did not understand how she had gotten there so fast. Before the explosion, she had been on the other side of him.

"How'd you get over there?"

"Bounced," Mara said. She took the lightsaber off her utility belt. "You coming?"

"Be right there."

Luke popped his canopy, then grabbed his own combat harness and slipped out of his darkened cockpit. He pulled the massive power blaster out of the carrying sleeve behind his seat, connected the powerfeed to the energy pack on his combat harness, and slung the weapon over his shoulder.

A trio of Jedi presences arrived behind him, about fifty meters away. Luke glanced back and saw three empty spaces about the size of StealthXs amid all the dust and spitcrete floating in the penetration crater. Even this close, the imaging system inside his helmet was as blind to the starfighters as any sensor system.

"Master Skywalker?" Kyle asked over the helmet coms.

"Jacen's out—we don't know how bad." Luke used the Force to pull R2-D2 out of the astromech socket and used a utility clip to attach the droid to the back of his combat harness. "We'll need a hand evacuating . . ."

Luke let the sentence trail off when an icy knot of danger sense formed between his shoulder blades. He dropped behind his StealthX and felt the fuselage vibrating beneath a hail of shatter gun pellets. He peered under the belly of wreckage, but his attackers were too well covered for his helmet's imaging system to pick them out from the surrounding rubble.

Luke worked to quiet his mind, to sense only the Force holding him in its liquid grasp, lapping at him from all sides. He began to feel a mass of ripples coming at him from the emptiness ahead, from the shifting voids of beings hiding themselves in the Force. There were hundreds of them, Gorog warriors rushing to the attack, pouring into the battle zone through a choke point hidden somewhere deep in the sea of floating rubble.

And there was more, a stillness so fixed it was frozen, a cold hole that seemed to be drawing the Force into *it*.

"Lomi Plo is here," Luke commed. At the same time, he was reaching into the battle-meld, calling Kyp and Corran and the rest of the Jedi to his side, letting them know it was time to close the trap. "She came after *us*."

Shatter gun pellets began to stream through the fuselage on Luke's side of the cockpit, and he knew that his protection was disintegrating fast. Still peering under the StealthX wreckage, he pulled the heavy power blaster off his back, then used the Force to send a speeder-sized block of spitcrete tumbling toward an even larger one where he had detected the nearest group of Gorog.

The two blocks collided in silence and tumbled away in new directions. The shatter gun fire stopped instantly, and images of warm bug gore and crushed pressure shells began to drift across Luke's imaging system. He spotted a trio of Gorog tumbling through the rubble, all six limbs flailing as they struggled to bring their carapace suits back under control.

Luke swung the barrel of his power blaster around and fired one bolt at each insect, using the Force to steady himself against the blowback caused by the weapon's massive energy discharges. Unlike the lighter blasters that Luke and Mara—and Han and Leia—had been carrying the first time they fought the Gorog, the big G-12s had more than enough power to punch through the thick chitin of a Killik pressure carapace. As each bolt struck, it literally shattered the protective shell—and the bug inside.

When no more shatter gun pellets came his way, Luke turned toward Mara. She was crouching on the other side of Jacen's StealthX, trying to use her lightsaber to cut him out of the cockpit. She was not having much success. A small tangle of Gorog were floating toward her through the rubble, spraying Jacen's crippled starfighter with shatter gun pellets as they bounced from block to block.

Luke extended a hand and sent them all tumbling with a violent Force shove. As they struggled to right themselves, he pulled a thermal detonator off his harness, thumbed the activation switch, and sent it after them.

A sharp crackle came over his comlink as the weapon detonated, and his imaging system went momentarily dark. Luke squeezed the trigger of his power blaster anyway, spraying bolts toward the empty ripples in the Force that he could still feel approaching from deeper in the rubble.

By the time the imaging system cleared again, Mara had cut Jacen's canopy open and was depressing a button on his wrist to activate his suit's automatic stim-system. Luke started toward them, somersaulting through the dust and laying suppression fire into the rubble. He no longer needed to search for ripples in the Force to find Gorog—he could see them coming, a growing tide of egg-shaped carapaces springing from one hunk of spitcrete to another, spraying shatter gun pellets as they approached.

Luke reached Jacen's StealthX just as Mara was pulling his limp form out of the cockpit. "How is he?"

"Still alive," Mara said. A string of shatter gun pellets tore into the fuselage, blowing Jacen's R9 unit apart and filling the air with sparks. "For now!"

R2-D2 flashed a message across Luke's visor suggesting that without evasive action, none of them would be alive in a moment.

"Don't worry." Luke pulled a trio of thermal detonators off his harness and thumbed the activators. "I still have a few tricks left."

He tossed the detonators toward the oncoming wave of Gorog, then used the Force to spread them across the head of the entire swarm. This time, the crackle inside his helmet was ear popping. But Luke was looking in the opposite direction as the detonation occurred, pulling himself over Jacen's StealthX, and his imaging system did not darken.

Luke retrieved his nephew's combat harness and power blaster from the cockpit, then caught up to Mara and took an arm. As they Force-pulled themselves toward a slowly tumbling chunk of spitcrete, Luke's imaging system showed a StealthX-sized bubble pushing past through the flotsam. Kyle Katarn touched Luke through the battle-meld, reassuring him, letting him know reinforcements were on the way.

A moment later, the StealthXs turned the battle zone as bright as day with their flashing laser cannons.

Luke and Mara slipped behind the spitcrete with Jacen. Luke used the Force to hold the block steady so they could hide behind it. Mara opened the status display on the forearm of Jacen's suit and checked his vital signs.

"Everything reads okay," she said. "Maybe it's just a compression blackout."

"Or a concussion." Luke could hear the relief in his own voice. Neither type of injury was likely to be a fatal—as long as they could get him to help. "Turn up his comm volume."

Luke started to grab Jacen by the shoulders, but Mara pointed him toward the edge of the block. "Stand watch. I'll handle—"

An incoherent groan came over the comm channel, then Jacen's face grew suddenly pale inside his helmet visor. His eyes blinked open, and he nearly sent them all tumbling by trying to sit up.

"No, Jacen." Mara pushed him against the spitcrete. "Stay put."

He looked confused for a moment, then turned to Luke. "She's here, isn't she?"

Luke nodded. "I think so."

"Can you see her?" Jacen demanded.

"I don't know," Luke said. "I haven't—"

A deafening pop came over the comm channel, and an orange flash briefly lit the battle zone. Luke felt the sudden anguish of a young Jedi's fiery death, then saw the wings and cannon mounts of a StealthX spinning past along with the gravel and smoke. He slid over and peered around the edge of their spitcrete hiding place and discovered that he could, indeed, see Lomi Plo. The Dark Queen.

She floated about a dozen meters away, surrounded by Gorog

warriors and encased in a somewhat cylindrical Killik pressure carapace. A pair of long, crooked arms were still extended from her stooped shoulders, pointing toward the twisted skeleton of smoking durasteel that had been a StealthX just a moment earlier. A second pair of shorter, more human-looking arms protruded from the middle of her body, while one spindly leg jutted out from the side of her hip, giving her an appearance more insectile than human.

Intending to take her out with a sniper shot, Luke started to reach for his power blaster, but Lomi's danger sense was as acute as Mara's. A lightsaber immediately appeared in her lower set of arms, and she started to turn in a slow circle, scanning the rubble and looking for her would-be ambusher.

Realizing there was only one way to do this, Luke snapped the lightsaber off his own belt. "Mara, keep the bugs off me."

"Luke?" Mara came his side. "What are you—"

"Lomi's over there," Jacen said, joining them. "At least I think it's her."

"*You* can see her, too?" Mara asked.

"Sure," Jacen said. "Either that or I'm still unconscious."

"You're awake," Luke assured him. He shrugged out of his combat harness and sent it toward Jacen. "Keep an eye on Artoo—"

"I'm not *that* fuzzy," Jacen said. "I'm coming with you."

There was no time to argue, for Lomi Plo had spotted Luke and was staring right at him. The face inside the carapace was the same one Luke had glimpsed during their fight a few months earlier: a half-melted, noseless face with bulbous multifaceted eyes and a pair of stubby mandibles where there should have been lower jaws. The mandibles moved behind the faceplate, and the Gorog warriors raised their shatter guns and started to turn to fire.

Luke sprang toward Lomi Plo, at the same time grabbing her in the Force and pulling her toward him. She launched herself into a backflip, trying to wrench free, but Luke had her too tightly. It was all she could do to bring herself back around before he was on her, igniting his blade and thrusting at her abdomen.

She brought her purple blade down and blocked—then Luke glimpsed a white flash sweeping toward his helmet and had to throw himself sideways. Her second lightsaber swept past his shoulder, barely missing. Luke used the Force to accelerate his spin, whipping his feet up over his head. He landed a Force-enhanced kick to her faceplate, the tip of his blade tracing a smoky curve up the side of her carapace.

Lomi Plo whipped both lightsabers around in a counterstrike, the short purple one driving for Luke's abdomen, the long white one sweeping toward his knees. He switched to a one-handed grip, meeting the white blade with his own and blocking the other attack by spinning inside and striking across her elbow, forcing her to lock her arms with both blades extended. She countered by bringing her knee up into his helmet, sending him flipping away, and then they fell into a vicious contest of strike and counterstrike, neither one probing for weaknesses or trying to set up a fatal trick later, both of them fighting just to survive two more seconds, all their attention focused on blocking the next blow, pouring all their strength and speed and skill into landing their next attack just a little quicker, hitting their foe's blocks just a little harder.

Luke was vaguely aware of the larger battle raging around him. He could feel Mara and Jacen protecting his flanks, keeping Lomi Plo's bodyguards at bay with blasters and detonators and the Force. He could sense more StealthXs gliding into the battle zone, lighting it up with their laser cannons and penetrating deeper into the rubble, preventing more Gorog from reaching their queen. He could hear Kyle Katarn issuing commands over the suit comms, ordering Jedi Knights to leave their StealthXs and form a protective ring around their Grand Master.

Then Mara set off the first dazer. A shrill whine filled the comm channels, and the battle zone shimmered with a rainbow iridescence. The air inside Luke's helmet suddenly smelled like fresh-cut pallies—a side effect, he knew, of the aura-deadening pulse Cilghal had developed to disrupt the collective mind of the Killiks.

Deprived of the thoughts and feelings of their nest-fellows, the Gorog warriors froze or launched suicidal attacks or simply collapsed in trembling heaps. And Lomi Plo hesitated, her white lightsaber hanging above her shoulders for a heartbeat too long, her lower blade caught out of position defending a flank attack that was not coming.

Luke launched a furious assault, slipping under her upper lightsaber and catching her lower guard on the backswing, then driving forward and slashing at her midsection. She pivoted, dropping one side back, and Luke switched to a lunge, driving the tip of his blade deep in the belly of her carapace.

For a breath, the queen did not seem to realize she had been hit. Seeing Luke stretched forward and off balance, she snapped her mandibles in delight and brought her short blade around to attack his arm while her long blade descended on him from above.

Luke thumbed off his lightsaber and rolled away sideways,

watching in alarm as her long blade slashed past his head just a centimeter from his visor. He rolled once more and saw vapor billowing from the abdomen of Lomi Plo's pressure carapace, then brought his feet up over his head . . . and found himself hanging upside down, caught in a net of golden Force energy.

Luke knew what was coming next: the Myrkr strike team had described how Lomi Plo had used a similar net to dice a Yuuzhan Vong captor into bits. Luke began to push out with the Force, stopping the net from constricting any further and slicing through this vac suit. But he was not strong enough to break the attack outright. Cilghal's Dazer had cut Lomi Plo off from the collective mind of the Gorog, but not from the Force. She could still draw on her nest to enhance her Force potential, and as strong as Luke was, he was not strong enough to overpower an entire nest of Killiks. He would simply have to hold on—and hope she ran out of air before he ran out of strength.

A black, tarry substance began to boil from the puncture in Lomi Plo's pressure carapace, and the vapor plume disappeared. The queen had plugged the hole. She turned and started to float toward Luke, the mandibles on the other side of her faceplate spread so wide he could see the smiling row of human teeth they concealed.

There was no question of reaching out to Mara or Jacen for help. They were busy fending off Gorog warriors, somersaulting and spinning and Force-deflecting shattergun pellets. Instead, Luke risked a split in his concentration and used the Force to send a Wookiee-sized lump of spitcrete hurling toward Lomi Plo's head.

The attack never reached her, of course. She sensed it coming and raised her hand, deflecting it straight into Mara.

The impact sent Mara spinning, and a Gorog shatter gun pellet slammed into the small of her back. A puff of vapor shot from the hole, then quickly vanished as the vac suit sealed itself.

Luke still felt Mara's jolt of surprise, and to some extent even the numb, deep ache of the wound itself. A fierce rage boiled up inside him, and perhaps that was what gave him the strength to break Lomi Plo's Force-net . . . or perhaps she had just been distracted by the boulder Luke had hurled at her.

It did not matter. Luke pushed, and the net dissolved. He flew at Lomi Plo, determined to finish this *now*, but terrified that he would not be fast enough . . . that he was not good enough to kill the Unseen Queen in time to save Mara.

Lomi Plo turned to meet him, and suddenly she seemed the size of a rancor, with bristling bug arms three meters long and reflexes so quick that her whirling lightsabers were nothing but a blur. Luke drew up short, trying to shake his head clear, trying to calm himself so he could determine the truth of what he was seeing.

But it was no use. Luke was too frightened for Mara. He could feel her starting to slip, feel her fighting to control the pain . . . and the Gorog were still attacking. Luke hurled himself at Lomi Plo again. It did not matter that he would never get past her guard, or that he did not understand what he was seeing. He just had to kill her.

But Lomi Plo had grown weary of fighting Luke. She spun away, her long upper arms lashing out toward Mara. Luke locked his blade on and drew his hand back to throw—then found that his arm would not come forward. Nothing would move at all; his mouth would not even open to voice the scream that rose inside him as Lomi Plo's white lightsaber came arcing down toward the crown of Mara's helmet.

Then Jacen was there, slipping in front of Mara, his lightsaber flashing up to block. He caught the blow above his head and whipped his blade over Lomi Plo's and sent her white lightsaber spinning away into the rubble.

But Lomi Plo had two lightsabers, and she brought the second one up under Jacen's guard, pushing it into the abdomen of his vac suit. The purple tip came out through his back, and still Luke could not move. If anything, he was more paralyzed than ever; he could not breathe, could not blink . . . it seemed to him that even his heart had stopped beating.

The tip of Mara's power blaster appeared under Jacen's upraised arm, and Luke could feel the anger that was driving Mara, the rage at what had happened to their nephew. A blinding bolt flashed from the barrel, taking Lomi Plo full in the chest and sending her tumbling head over heels, leaving her purple lightsaber hanging in Jacen's body.

And suddenly Luke could move again. He used the Force to pull himself over to Jacen and Mara, then deactivated Lomi Plo's lightsaber and tossed the handle aside. By the time he had finished, Mara was already placing a patch over the holes in Jacen's vac suit.

Kyle Katarn arrived in the same instant, emerging from the flotsam with half a dozen other Jedi. They quickly drove the last of the Gorog warriors away, lacing the darkness with blaster bolts and flinging thermal detonators around like confetti, using the Force to create a protective shell of rubble around the Skywalkers and Jacen.

"Where's Lomi Plo?" he asked. "I can't see her. Is she still here?"

Luke barely heard. He could sense that Mara was in pain but still strong, and she remained lucid enough to have applied a pair of emergency patches to Jacen's vac suit. But Jacen's presence had grown as elusive as when he had been knocked unconscious, and the pattern of dark spray around the suit patches suggested that he had lost a lot of blood.

"Jacen?"

"Don't . . . worry about . . . me!" Jacen's voice was anguished but calm, and his words carried the sharp edge of command. "You're showing Lomi . . . your weakness!"

"It's okay." Luke peered over his shoulder, but saw no sign of Lomi Plo or her Gorog anywhere. "Mara drove her off."

"I *did*?" Mara asked. Obviously, she had not been able to see Lomi Plo, either. "You're sure?"

Jacen shook his head. "We don't . . . know." He grabbed Luke's sleeve and pulled him closer. "You showed her . . . your fear, and she used it . . . against you."

Mara caught Luke's eye, then nodded past his shoulder. "I'll take care of Jacen," she said. "You take care of Lomi Plo."

Luke took Jacen's power blaster and slowly turned around, quieting his own thoughts and emotions, surrendering himself to the Force so that he could feel its currents and search for the cold stillness that would be Lomi Plo. He felt nothing, not even the telltale ripples of her Gorog warriors.

"I think she's gone," Luke said. "I can't see her anymore."

NINETEEN

Interrogation cells were the same the galaxy over: dark, cramped, and stark, usually too hot or too cold. The interrogator usually had a breathing problem, some wheeze or rasp or even an artificial respirator that suggested he had been cuffed to a chair a time or two himself. This interrogator, a blue-skinned Chiss in the black uniform of a Defense Fleet commander, spoke with a wet snort. It was probably caused by the old wound above his black eye patch, a thumb-sized dent deep enough to have collapsed his sinus cavities.

As the officer approached, Leia's nostrils filled with the harsh stench of charric fumes—probably what passed for deodorant aboard a Chiss Star Destroyer. He stopped a meter and a half from her chair, running his good eye over her as though contemplating what a Jedi woman looked like beneath her robes. Leia pretended not to notice. The "undressing" was an old interrogator's trick, designed to make a prisoner feel more powerless than she really was. Leia had endured such scrutiny more times than she wanted to remember—and that applied especially to the time the interrogator had been Darth Vader.

Finally, the interrogator met her gaze and said, "You're awake. Good."

"I'm glad one of us thinks that's good," Leia said. "Frankly, I would've preferred to sleep until my head stops hurting."

The interrogator's red eye glimmered as he filed this tidbit away for future use. Again, Leia pretended not to notice. She intended to lay a trail of such tidbits for him . . . a trail that would lead straight to the identity of the person who had betrayed their mission.

"Yes . . . the knockout gas." The interrogator's impediment

caused him to pronounce *gas* as *khas*. "After the trouble we had taking Jedi Lowbacca into custody, we felt it necessary to be prudent with you and Master Sebatyne."

"You could have asked politely."

The interrogator offered her a thin smile. "We did. You destroyed two of our clawcraft."

Leia shrugged. "There was a little misunderstanding."

"Is that what you call it?" His voice remained steady, but there was an angry heat to it. "Then perhaps we should make certain there are no *more* misunderstandings."

He stepped back and gestured toward a sizable display screen hanging in the corner. On cue, an image appeared, showing Han cuffed into a chair similar to Leia's. Another Chiss officer, younger than the one in Leia's cell but with a harder blue face, stood next to Han. On a nearby table lay an array of nerve probes, laser scalpels, and electrical clips—a virtual smorgasbord of torture.

Leia gasped, her heart suddenly hammering hard. She turned to her interrogator, struggling to regain her composure. "Captain Fel promised there would be no torture."

"*If* you surrendered." A wet rumble sounded from the back of the interrogator's mouth as he inhaled. "Instead, you continued your attempts to escape until he trapped you against the Shattered Moon."

"A *Chiss* is going to hide behind a technicality?"

Leia knew that the contempt in her voice only confirmed to the interrogator that he had found his leverage, but she could not help herself. After discovering that the moon cluster was filled with Killiks, she had been the one who argued against making a run for the planet. With a faulty control system and Zark Squadron and two Star Destroyers ready to blast the *Falcon* to space dust, it had just seemed wiser to surrender and escape later. Now she wasn't so sure. To be willing to break promises and threaten torture, the Chiss had to be in desperate circumstances—and a desperate foe was the most dangerous kind.

The interrogator remained silent, giving Leia's emotions time to build, trying to move her from fear to anger to hopelessness as quickly as possible.

But Leia had already regained control of her feelings and hid her fear behind a cool voice. "I see I'll have to revise my opinion of the Ascendancy."

The interrogator spread his hands in a gesture of helplessness. "That is entirely up to you . . . as is your husband's fate."

On screen, the young officer picked up a laser scalpel and acti-vated the blade. Han responded with a sneer, but Leia could see the fear beneath his show of disdain. The officer brought the blade close to Han's eye, then made a very precise serpentine cut down Han's cheek—just proving that there were no rules for this interrogation. The letter S appeared in faint crimson, and blood began to dribble down Han's face.

Han held his sneer, not even flinching. "I can only get prettier."

Please, Han, don't provoke him, Leia urged silently.

"It's just a scratch," the interrogator said. "As long as you coop-erate, it's the worst your husband will suffer. But if you refuse, my protégé will be required to demonstrate his skills."

A surge of hatred rose inside Leia, and she had the sudden urge to show this little man who was really in control here, to reach out with the Force and squeeze his throat shut. Instead, she swallowed her anger and settled for narrowing her eyes.

"This may surprise you, but I'm willing to tell you whatever you wish to know." She turned toward the hidden vidcam she sensed to one side of the display screen. "You're already aware of the *Falcon*'s mission, and the Jedi have nothing else to hide."

The interrogator followed her gaze and smiled. "Impressive. Others might guess that a cam exists, but not its precise position. I'm sure you have many such talents, Jedi Solo." His smile faded abruptly, and he leaned in close, breathing fetid air in her face. "But I must warn you against using those talents to escape. Regardless of whether you succeeded, your husband will be in no condition to join you."

He glanced at display screen again. When Leia looked, the cam panned back. Behind Han stood two Chiss guards, their charric pis-tols pointed at his head. Leia took this in, her hatred of the inter-rogator now growing to include his superiors and all the others whom she knew were watching, and she expanded her Force-awareness around her.

As expected, she felt two Chiss guards standing behind her, as well. But she also felt a more familiar pair of presences lurking above and behind the guards, approximately where a ventilation duct might be. Cakhmaim and Meewalh had escaped custody—or, more likely, they had never been captured in the first place.

Leia turned her attention back to the interrogator.

"I don't appreciate your threats," she said. It was a code phrase that would alert the Noghri to the fact that she was about to give an order. "But threats *are* sometimes effective. While Master Sebatyne and I can take care of ourselves, I would be very unhappy if any harm were to come to Han or the other members of our crew."

The interrogator frowned, confused by what seemed only an indirect response to his warning. "If you are asking for a guarantee of their safety—"

"I'm not *asking* anything, Commander . . ." Leia paused, waiting for the interrogator's name to rise higher in his thoughts. ". . . Baltke. I'm *telling* you that whatever happens to Han and the others, I'm going to do the same to you." She turned to the hidden vidcam. "And to *you*."

The tightening of Baltke's lips was barely perceptible, but Leia knew that his superiors would point it out to him later as the moment he had lost control of the interrogation. For now, however, he seemed to believe he was still in charge. He spent a moment trying to stare Leia down—snorting softly with each breath—and she felt the Noghri withdrawing to carry out her instructions.

Finally, Baltke stepped to Leia's side and extended a hand toward one of the guards behind her. The hand returned holding a hypoinjector.

"Don't be afraid, Princess." Baltke pulled up the sleeve of her robe and reached down to press the hypo to her forearm. "This is only something to help you relax . . . and assure that the answers we receive from you are true."

"Oh, I'm not afraid, Commander."

Leia created a loud Force-thunk in the corner behind her, then used the Force to redirect the hypo into Baltke's thigh and depress the injector. He gave a startled cry and pulled the hypo away so quickly that even Leia barely saw what had happened. Given that the vidcam's view had been partially obscured by the commander's back, she hoped the monitors in the control room had not seen it at all.

"Commander?" asked one of the guards behind her. "Is something wrong?"

"Nothing's wrong," Leia said reassuringly. Normally, she could influence only weak minds with the Force—but the drug was *designed* to make minds weak. She just hoped that it was fast. "I flinched, and Commander Baltke nearly injected himself instead of me."

Baltke frowned and looked at the hypo in his hand.

"Commander?" the second guard asked.

"She flinched." He passed the hypo back to the guard. "I nearly injected myself."

Leia let out a long breath. "The drug must be working, Commander. I'm feeling more relaxed already."

"Good. Slo am I." Baltke's slur was barely perceptible, but it was there. He stepped back in front of Leia, wobbling slightly. "I think we're ready to begin."

"There's no need to stand, Commander," Leia suggested. "Sit down and make yourself comfortable. You're going to find me very cooperative."

"She's going to cooperate." Baltke looked to one of the guards. "Bring me a chair."

Leia felt a growing wave of concern from the two guards, and she did not hear either of them move to obey.

"Forgive me for inshruding." Leia slurred her words to reinforce the impression that she was not fully under control. "But washn't that an order?"

"That's not for you to say, prisoner," the guard retorted.

" 'S not my fault," Leia retorted. "*I'm* not the one who injected me with a truth drug."

"That was indeed an order," Baltke scowled at the guards. "Do I have to vocode it?"

"No, sir."

The door whirred opened, and a moment later a black-uniformed guard placed a chair behind Baltke.

"Thank you."

Baltke sat down and studied Leia, snorting softly, his brow furrowed as though he was having trouble remembering what he wanted to ask her. She was going to have to work fast. It would not be long before his superiors realized something was wrong and relieved him.

"I imagine you want to know what the Jedi's plans are," Leia prompted.

Baltke shook his head. "Already know 'em."

Leia frowned. "You do?"

"Aaaaffirmative." He nodded for emphasis. "We want to know *why*."

"Why what?"

"Why the Jedi are forcing the Galactic Alliance to side with the Colony against us."

"We're not," Leia said.

Baltke snorted sadly, then twisted around to look up toward the display screen in the corner. He clicked the comm unit on his lapel. "She's lying. Cut something off this time."

The officer in the vidimage smiled. Then he activated his laser scalpel and pressed the tip to the base of Han's ear.

"I'm not lying." Leia put the Force behind her words. "It's the truth."

"The truth?" Baltke seemed confused, and Leia realized that the belief she was fighting was deeply ingrained. "But the Killiks ambushed us with a brand-new *Alliance* Star Destroyer at Snevu!"

"Yes, I know," Leia said. "It was the *Admiral Ackbar*. The Killiks captured her in the Murgo Choke. That was shortly before Admiral Bwua'tu prevented the Colony's battle fleet from leaving the Utegetu Nebula."

"The Killiks? *Capturing* an Alliance Star Destroyer?" Baltke was clearly having trouble believing this, even under the influence of the mind-weakening drug. "That doesn't seem very likely, Princess."

The officer in the display began to cut into the skin around Han's ear, prompting Han to clench his teeth and tense against his restraints. His head—wisely—remained still.

"You stupid rodder!" Leia yelled. It required all her willpower to keep from Force-choking Baltke to death, but she held herself in restraint. The Noghri had not yet reached Han, or what she was seeing would not be happening. "I saw it with my own eyes. I was there!"

"You were there?" Baltke continued to watch the display screen, his face blank and disinterested, as though he saw someone's ear get detached in slow motion every day. "I'm sure that's why the *capture* looked so convincing in news-holo footage."

Leia groaned. "Look, *I'm* never going to convince you that it wasn't staged." She could not take her eyes off Han's anguished face. "So why don't you stop cutting and ask your source?"

"Our source?"

"The person who told you about the *Falcon*'s mission!" Leia said. Whoever *that* was, he—or she—was also going to pay for what Han was suffering now—assuming Leia could trick Baltke into revealing the traitor's identity. "You clearly have good reason to trust your source."

"An excellent suggestion." Baltke nodded a little too enthusiastically. "I'll pass it along to Commander Fel."

"Maybe you should stop torturing Han until you can confirm my answer." Leia used the Force again, trying to make Baltke think that was a good idea. "I *am* telling the truth."

Baltke stood and pressed his comlink. "Wait."

Han's torturer glanced over his shoulder, then stopped, the laser scalpel still held to Han's ear.

Leia exhaled in relief. "Thank you," she said. "By the time you get a message to Coruscant, there wouldn't have been enough left of him to—"

"Coruscant?" Baltke asked, looking confused.

"That *is* where your source is, isn't it?" Leia focused all her attention on Baltke, alert to any hint of deception . . . in his face or in the Force. "Or is he with the fleet?"

"You'd have to ask Captain Fel." Baltke's tone was helpful, as though he really believed Jagged might tell them. "He's the only one who knows who the source is."

Baltke cocked his head and frowned, no doubt listening to instructions over a hidden earpiece, and Leia tried not to choke on the growing lump of disappointment in her throat. Even if Baltke was somehow defeating his own truth drug, there was no hint of deception in either his face or the Force. As far as *he* knew, Jagged Fel was the only person who knew the identity of the mission's betrayer.

Baltke's face turned a lighter shade of blue. "You're very clever, Princess—but cleverness carries a price." He depressed his comlink again. "Finish it."

The officer resumed cutting, removing Han's ear, then stepped back with the appendage pinched between his thumb and forefinger. Han's mouth opened in a roar, and he shook his head, spraying a line of blood across the man's blue face. Leia grew so angry and sick inside that she had to fight to keep from retching.

"I hope you remember my warning, Commander!" Leia snarled. "Because I certainly do."

"Of course," Baltke replied pleasantly. "And I hope *you* remember what will happen if you attempt anything so foolish." Again, the display screen showed the two guards pointing their charric pistols at the back of Han's head. "Now perhaps we should discuss your daughter's activities."

"There's no point—you know more than I do," Leia said. She was still in shock from what she had just seen. The Chiss were tough, cunning soldiers, but she had not believed they would actually torture a prisoner—especially not when one of their command officers had promised otherwise. Of course, the fact that Jagged had felt it necessary to *make* such a promise suggested that Leia was being a bit naïve. "But I'm sure you won't believe *that,* either."

Baltke looked confused. "I *want* to believe you, Princess. Just tell us why she is leading the Killik ground swarm."

"How do I know?" Leia snapped. "Because she's a Joiner."

Baltke snorted loudly and cocked his head, and Leia began to regain control of herself, to realize that she was not going to help Han or the Jedi by allowing her fear and frustration to control her. She turned toward the hidden vidcam.

"And even if Jaina wasn't a Joiner," Leia said slowly, "the Jedi can't condone speciecide. We're *all* opposed to what you're doing here. Any help we're giving to the Killiks—*that's* the reason." She glanced toward the display, and when the officer remained standing next to Han's bleeding figure, she added, "All the Jedi are trying to do is end the war."

"By defeating *us*," Baltke retorted.

Leia shook her head. "No—by destroying the Colony and restoring the Killiks to their prior state of disorganized nests."

Balkte scoffed. "Perhaps you and Captain Solo are not getting along these days." He glanced toward Han's bleeding image. "Perhaps that is why you keep lying."

Leia used the Force again. "I . . . am . . . not . . . lying."

"You aren't lying?" Even under the power of a mind influence, Baltke sounded unconvinced. "Then the Jedi are fools. What you suggest can't be done."

"We think it can." Leia turned to the vidcam again. "You asked why the Jedi are opposing you. Let me explain."

The floor and interrogation chair began to shudder with a sudden acceleration tremor. Baltke furrowed his dented brow and remained silent for a moment, listening to his earpiece and snorting softly every time he inhaled. The Force became charged with anticipation . . . and with a strange, stoic fatalism.

Leia waited until Baltke's attention returned, then asked, "Something wrong?"

"Not at all," he said smugly. "Everything is going quite well, as a matter of fact."

Leia sensed no deception in his answer. "Then how come you're so ready to die?"

Baltke's eye widened in surprise, but he said, "Because I am a soldier, Princess Leia." He returned to his seat and gestured for her to continue. "But please don't waste our time with more lies. Our session will soon be cut short."

"Very well," Leia said. The vessel continued to tremble, suggesting they were accelerating into battle. "You already know what the *Falcon*'s mission was."

"Yes. Your assignment was to rendezvous with your daughter and her mindmate." Baltke was speaking a bit rapidly now, the truth drug and the excitement of the coming battle serving to agitate him. "Then you were to enter Chiss space and attempt to infiltrate our command and control centers with teams of Killik commandos."

"Not quite," Leia said. "Actually, the plan was to attack only *one* center, using a variation on the same tactic the Killiks used to capture the *Admiral Ackbar*."

Baltke arched the brow above his red eye, then asked in an interested voice, *"Really?"*

"The idea was to get the *Falcon* captured," Leia explained. "While you were interrogating us, a swarm of Killik commandos—they're about the size of your thumb—would be sneaking out of the *Falcon*'s smuggling compartments to infest your facility and take control at an opportune moment."

As Leia explained this, Baltke frowned and pressed a finger to his earpiece without seeming to realize he was doing it.

"Don't worry—your vessel is safe," Leia said. "That part of our plan relied on winning Jaina's cooperation. Since we haven't rendezvoused with her, we haven't picked up any Killiks yet."

"You'll understand if we want to check for ourselves."

"Go ahead," Leia said. "If you give me a comlink, I'll instruct See-Threepio to show you how to open the compartments."

Baltke started to reach for his comlink, then seemed to catch himself and smiled.

"Nice try, Princess." He glanced at one of the guards behind her. "Bring a vocoder. We'll have her *record* the message."

The guard acknowledged the order, and the door whirred open behind Leia. A moment later the vessel began to buck and shudder more noticeably.

"We're entering the atmosphere!"

"So it seems," Baltke replied calmly. "We're still confused about this plan of yours. How did you expect capturing one of *our* command and control centers to destroy the Colony?"

"We didn't," Leia said. "That was just to get your attention. Luke is destroying the Colony himself."

"Now I *know* you're a fool," he said. "How could one Jedi do that?"

"By destroying the Dark Nest and its Unseen Queen," Leia said. "That should be completed by now."

"You tried that at Qoribu," Baltke pointed out. "You failed miserably."

"This time, we're better prepared," Leia said. "Our scientists have developed a few weapons to disrupt the Killiks' collective mind—and we have an Alliance attack fleet to support us."

Baltke's voice grew derisive. "And once the Dark Nest is gone, you think the Killiks will become 'good bugs' again?"

"Not at all," Leia said. "That's only the first part of Luke's plan. He should be arriving here very soon to complete the second."

"Which is?"

"Destroying Unu and removing Raynar Thul from his role as the Colony's leader," Leia said. "It may take a little time, but our scientists are certain that once Raynar is no longer able to control the nests by exerting his Will through the Force, the Colony will grow disorganized and enter a self-regulating cycle again. Then it won't be a threat to anyone."

"An interesting theory," Baltke said. They began to buck harder than ever, and the cell began to grow warm—an indication that they were descending so fast that the vessel was having trouble dissipating the heat of atmospheric friction. "What exactly do you mean when you say 'remove' Raynar Thul?"

"Whatever it takes," Leia said. "Luke has never liked the idea of a Jedi leading any government, and this is a good example of why."

"So you're going to assassinate him?" Baltke asked.

"That's one possibility, but I don't know what Luke has decided," Leia said. "I can promise you this, though: Raynar Thul is a Jedi problem, and we'll do whatever it takes to fix it."

Baltke considered all this for a moment, then said, "It does sound plausible." He stood, shaking his head and turning to the display screen. "But I can see we're going to have to cut something else off your husband."

"*What?*"

The display screen showed a Chiss medic bandaging Han's ear—and, by the looks of it, enduring the cussing-out of his life.

"Your story doesn't hold together," Baltke told Leia. "Attacking *one* of our command centers contributes nothing to this plan."

"That's because the Jedi don't see the Chiss as an enemy," Leia said. "Luke never wanted to cause the Ascendancy harm—only to make a point."

"Is that so?" Baltke asked. "I'm afraid we fail to see it."

The lights flickered as the vessel began to fire its heavy weapons. Leia checked the display screen again, wondering why Han was still there. The Noghri should have had him free by now.

She turned her attention back to Baltke. "The point was to show that the Killiks are capable of infiltrating even your most secure facilities. The Alliance learned that the hard way with the *Ackbar*. The Killiks stole it right out from under the nose of our best fleet admiral."

"Bwua'tu might be *your* best," Baltke said. "But I can assure you that no Chiss admiral would make such a mistake—if, indeed, it *was* a mistake."

"I don't think you're very sure of that," Leia said. In the display screen, the medic stepped away and made some sort of joke that caused Han's tormenter to laugh. "If you were, you wouldn't have been so curious when I described the *Falcon*'s mission."

"Merely being prudent," Baltke countered. "An abundance of caution is never wasted."

"If you really believe in caution, then you'll think about what I'm telling you," Leia said. "Killiks can sneak into anyplace. They're *insects*. All they have to do is lay eggs in a few wounded soldiers and let you take them home aboard a medical frigate, and a whole base will be infiltrated. Or they could stow away in a returning supply freighter and then infest an entire planet. Before you know it, your whole society will be swarming with Killiks—and I don't have to tell you what that means. You'll become an empire of Joiners."

"And the Jedi think we would be better off letting the Colony mass nests on our border until they are ready to attack?"

"We think the Chiss would be better off ending the war *our* way," Leia said. "You'll never win the war your way. It's not *possible* to wipe out the Killiks. They were building nest cities on Alderaan twenty thousand years before the Chiss empire was born, and they'll be building nest cities on your frontier twenty thousand centuries after it's gone."

A confident smirk flashed across Baltke's face, and Leia felt something disturbing in the Force—something cold and menacing and final. Deciding to give up on the Noghri, Leia reached out to Saba, concentrating on the bloody image of Han in the display screen, allowing her alarm to flood her thoughts.

Saba's emotions were oddly reassuring—at least for a Barabel—and Leia received the distinct impression that Han was safe. Unfortunately, Leia was not assured.

Baltke cocked his head again and briefly turned toward the hidden vidcam, then faced Leia. "I'll pass your warning on to my superiors." He started toward the door. "But now I'm afraid I must be off to my duty station. We'll be expecting casualties soon."

"You're a medic?" Leia could not conceal her surprise.

"A battle surgeon, to be precise." Baltke removed his eye patch, revealing a perfectly sound organ underneath, and started toward the door. "Interrogations are a secondary duty."

"Wait!" Leia commanded.

Baltke stopped—clearly in spite of himself. He glared at her angrily.

"When I told you the Killiks would outlast the Ascendancy, you smirked," Leia said. "Tell me why."

"What are you doing? Using a Jedi mind trick?" Baltke demanded. "It will be your fault if I have to hurt Captain Solo again."

Leia glanced at the display screen and saw that the medic was still standing next to Han, laughing with the torturer. Something did not make sense. Saba had clearly meant to reassure her about Han, and yet Leia could see that he had not yet been rescued—in fact, that he did not even look close to being rescued.

The remaining guard started to step forward behind Leia. She grabbed him in the Force, then hurled him into the corner with the vidcam. He hit headfirst with a loud *thunk,* then dropped to the floor and did not move.

Leia looked back to Baltke and put the power of the Force into her voice. "*Why* do you think the Killiks can't win?"

Baltke's face twisted into a mask of resistance, but the truth drug made it impossible for him to lie.

"Because *we* have developed our own solution to the Killik problem," he said. "And *our* plan will work."

He tried to go to the door again, but Leia Force-shoved him up against the wall. "What kind of solution?"

"A p-permanent one." Baltke cast a longing look toward the display screen, then said, "It's not too late to save your husband. Just release me."

"Han's going to be just fine." Leia used the Force to begin working the locks of the cuffs holding her in the chair. "You, on the other hand, are in trouble—or have you forgotten what I said about anything that happened to Han?"

"I remember."

"Good." The first cuff came loose. "You might want to be a little more informative about this 'permanent solution.'"

Baltke shook his head, but he could not resist the power of his own drug. "P-p-parasites."

"Parasites?" Leia asked. The second cuff came undone. "You're going to infect them with parasites?"

Baltke nodded. "Any minute now," he said. "After the Killiks spring their trap."

"Trap?"

"You know," he said. "Isn't that why you turned back from the Shattered Moon?"

Leia's jaw fell. "You know about the Killiks hiding there?"

"We suspected." Baltke seemed almost proud. "We're counting on them to ambush us."

"I don't understand." Leia stretched her hand toward the unconscious guard and summoned his charric pistol to hand. "Counting on their ambush for *what*?"

A low boom rolled out of the air vent behind Leia, and the whole room rocked.

"To deliver a resounding defeat to us," Baltke said.

Leia understood the rest of the Chiss plan. "And tomorrow, all of the nests will have a huge victory dance."

"That's right," Baltke said. "The Killiks aren't the only ones who can play the infestation game."

"How long?" Leia asked. When Baltke did not answer, she asked again, this time using the Force. *"How long?"*

"We'll have to keep fighting for a while," Baltke answered. "The parasite won't be fatal for a year."

"And by then, it will have spread throughout the whole Colony."

Baltke smiled. "You see? We *can* win the war our way."

"Are you mad?" Leia cried. "That's speciecide!"

She used the Force to open her ankle restraints—then heard the cell door whirring open behind her. Thinking the other guard had returned with the vocoder Baltke had requested—or the officers watching from the control room had sent reinforcements—she threw herself out of the chair and rolled across the floor, then spun around, brought her captured charric pistol around . . . and found herself pointing it at the handsome face of her favorite scoundrel.

"Han?"

"Whoa—take it easy, Princess!" Han raised his hands. "I know I'm late, we had to take care of the control room first."

"I don't care!" Leia cried, recovering from her shock. She threw herself into Han's arms, barely noticing as Cakhmaim and Meewalh slipped past to take control of Baltke and the unconscious guard. Then she reached up and touched his ears. "They're both there!"

"Honey, are you okay?" Han moved her back from him and studied her with a concerned look—until he noticed the display screen in the corner, which continued to show the medic and the torturer standing beside Han's bloody head. "Hey! That poor rodder looks like *me*!"

TWENTY

A familiar voice echoing down a long tunnel . . . a hammer pounding inside her head, a centrifuge spinning her through the darkness . . . aching cold below the knees, aching cold from the shoulders up.

Nothing between. Just numb.

Then the voice again, calling Mara back, commanding her attention.

Luke giving orders . . . too fast. Not quite near enough to follow. *Slow down, Skywalker!*

Luke continued. "Nothinghaschanged. We're burruburrub," he was saying, "uruburruplan. Cilghalwillbe in urburbubu collection teams, thenserveas Kyle's scientific adviser urburub dispersal operations inside the Colony proper."

Mara opened her eyes and found herself staring up at a blinding white blur. Everything smelled of stericlean, and there were machines hissing and whirring all around. She tried to sit up and found herself held tight by a strap across her chest.

"Just how volatile *is* this nanotech?" a deep Duros voice asked from somewhere to her right. "Is it going to turn our StealthXs into dirt right under us?"

"Only if you let it escape the stasis jars," Cilghal replied. Her voice and the Duros' sounded somewhat muffled. "Even then, you would have plenty of time to go EV before the damage grew critical."

The brightness overhead came into focus, and Mara recognized it as the softly lit whiteness of an infirmary ship ceiling. It took her a moment to understand why she was here, then she turned her head and saw the tangle of IV lines hooked into her arm and she remembered: the shatter gun pellet that ripped through her vac suit and abdomen. It had destroyed one of her kidneys, and no healing trance could repair *that*.

The huge head of her Bith physician, Ogo Buugi, appeared above her. "Good, you're awake. How are you feeling?"

"Hararrg oooo aiiig meeeffffing?" Mara croaked. It was supposed to have been *How do you think I'm feeling?* but her throat was as dry as a Tatooine swamp and her tongue was too heavy to lift. "Ooggaf."

Buugi nodded approvingly, his smile half hidden by the epidermal folds hanging from his cheeks. "Good. That's what I was hoping."

Mara considered using the Force to slam him against the ceiling.

"The operation went very well—no complications at all," Buugi continued. "We already have a new kidney growing in the cloning tank. We'll insert it in a couple of weeks, and in a month you'll be ready to start your rehabilitation."

"A *month*?" Mara cried. "Are you a doctor or a—"

"Better let me take over, Doctor Buugi." Jacen appeared at Mara's bedside, seated in a hoverchair with a drainage bag hanging from his side. "Aunt Mara can be a little testy right after she wakes up."

Buugi smiled more noticeably and nodded. "So I see." He placed a delicate, long-fingered hand on Mara's forearm, then said, "You need to be patient with this. Even a Jedi can't grow a new kidney overnight."

"Thanks for the advice, Doctor," Mara answered, softening her tone. "And thanks for patching me up." Mara waited for Buugi to leave, then turned to Jacen. "Shouldn't you be in a bacta tank?"

"With the Killiks still holding Thyferra, the fleet is running short on bacta," Jacen explained, moving his chair closer to her bedside. "I'm out of action for a couple of weeks anyway, so I thought I'd save it for someone who doesn't have a healing trance."

Mara nodded her approval. "Good idea—very thoughtful." She pointed at the drainage bag hanging from his side. "How is it?"

"Inconvenient," Jacen said. "I've got holes in three different organs, and I can't move well enough to fight until I fix them."

"I know the feeling," Mara said. She reached for his arm and winced at the dull ache that the effort sent shooting through her lower back. "Thanks, Jacen. She would have gotten me."

"She nearly *did*," Jacen said. "If you hadn't been so fast with that blaster, neither one of us would be here."

"All the same." Mara squeezed his arm, then asked, "Do we know what happened to her?"

Jacen's expression turned sober. "Pellaeon's intelligence staff has been reviewing the battle vids. A skiff left Gorog just before we blew it. Nobody challenged it—nobody even seemed to see it, including the combat controllers."

Mara had a sinking feeling. "Lomi Plo."

"That's what Uncle Luke thinks."

Mara used the Force to operate the bed controls and raise her upper body. The shift of position sent another dull ache through her lower back, but she pushed the pain aside and looked out the door into the infirmary lobby, where Luke was meeting with Cilghal and the other Masters.

"And he's sticking to his plan?"

Jacen nodded.

"Who's taking our places?"

"No one," Jacen said, a slight frown betraying his disapproval. "Cilghal offered to lead a team herself so that Kyp, er, *Master* Durron could back Luke up, but Uncle Luke wouldn't hear of it. According to the intelligence maps that Juun and Tarfang left, the collection teams only need to harvest nanotech from fifteen different environments inside the nebula, but they're going to have to seed more than a thousand worlds in the Colony. Tresina Lobi is out of action with some crash burns, and Uncle Luke didn't want to take another Master off the dispersal teams. He thinks it's the nanotech environmental systems that will keep the Killiks in check—in the long run, anyway."

Mara's heart sank. "So he's going after Raynar alone?"

"Admiral Pellaeon is taking the fleet to Tenupe," Jacen said. "Wraith and Rogue squadrons will be assigned specifically to support him, and he'll have a company of Lando's bugcruncher droids—but we both know they won't be able to do much once the Force duel starts."

"And Lomi Plo isn't going to give up, either," Mara said.

"Not likely," Jacen said. "Unless that blaster shot you got off kills her first."

Mara gave him a sour look. "What do *you* think the chance of that is?"

"About the same as you do," Jacen confessed. "He'll have to take both of them out. Lomi Plo and Raynar."

Mara's stomach began to ache with fear. "Jacen, we can't let him do that alone."

"I don't think we have a choice in the matter," Jacen said. "Have you tried to stand up yet?"

Out in the lobby, Luke dismissed the Masters and turned to enter Mara's room, the faithful R2-D2 trailing close behind.

They had barely crossed the threshold before Mara demanded, "Are you *crazy?*"

Luke stopped and cast a sheepish look back toward the departing Masters before he returned her gaze. "You heard."

"You'd better not have been thinking you'd keep *that* from me, farmboy."

"Of course not." Luke came to her bedside and took her hand, then gave Jacen a stern look. "But I *had* hoped to tell you myself."

"Luke, the Colony isn't going to win this war overnight," Mara said. "Wait until Jacen and I can back you up. Raynar is inexperienced, but he's powerful."

Jacen nodded his agreement. "And Lomi Plo will be—"

"I can't," Luke said, cutting them off. He clasped a hand on Jacen's shoulder. "I've been feeling something urgent from Leia. This war is coming to a head *now*."

"Do you know *how?*" Jacen asked.

Luke shook his head. "All I can tell is that things didn't go well at Tenupe. The *Falcon* never connected with Jaina. I think maybe the Chiss were already there attacking."

Mara's heart skipped a beat, but the corners of Jacen's mouth rose in a near smile.

"Then we shouldn't interfere," Jacen said. "If Mom and Dad can recover Jaina and Zekk, staying out of the Chiss's way might be the best thing for the galaxy."

Luke frowned. "Jacen, you're as bad as your father," he said. "You think the answer to every insect problem is to start stomping."

"Not every insect problem," Jacen said. "Just this one. I thought I'd made that clear."

"You have," Luke said. "You also made it clear that you'd follow the order's leadership in this matter."

"It was only a suggestion," Jacen retorted. "Can't a Jedi Knight express himself around here anymore?"

Luke's expression softened. "Of course," he said. "But half a dozen times should be sufficient. I'm very aware of your opinion about the Killiks, and believe it or not, I *have* given it consideration."

"Okay. Sorry to bring it up again." Jacen looked more disappointed than apologetic—which suggested to Mara that he was sincere about following the order's leadership, even if he disagreed with it. "But I still think you should wait until Aunt Mara and I can back you up. You won't solve anything if Raynar kills you."

"Or if Lomi Plo does," Mara added. She had been growing more impressed with Jacen every day since Luke took sole leadership of the order, and she was even beginning to wonder if he might make a suitable second in command someday soon. "I don't think you can take them both, Luke."

"Then I'll have to take them one at a time," Luke said. "Because if I wait for you two to recover, Lomi Plo will have time to recover, too—and so will Gorog. Lomi is never going to be weaker than she is right now."

Luke's tone was as firm as Mara had ever heard it, and she could feel through their Force-bond that he would not be moved from his plan.

But Jacen, bless him, was determined to try. "And you're *still* not ready to face her."

Luke's eyes flashed with resentment—or it might have been self-doubt. "*I* will be the judge of that, Jacen."

"Of course." Jacen spread his hands in a gesture of surrender, and Mara thought she saw something bright, like moonlight dancing on a river, flicker in the depths of his brown eyes. "You *are* the Grand Master."

"Thank you, Jacen," Luke said. He turned to Mara, and she felt the faintest tingle of Force energy washing over her body. "And now, if you'll excuse me, I'd like a . . ."

Luke's jaw dropped, then he frowned in confusion. "Padmé?"

"Padmé?" Mara repeated. "Luke, what are you talking—"

"Mara?" Luke sounded disappointed. He shook his head as though to clear it. "I don't understand."

"Neither do I," Mara said.

"Mara?" Now Luke's voice was frightened. "What's wrong?"

"Good question," Mara said.

She turned to Jacen, but he only held a finger to his lips and moved his hoverchair closer to Luke. R2-D2 emitted a confused whistle and raised a hydraulic extension with a medical sensor at the end.

"*Mara!*" Luke turned and hit the emergency summons button next to Mara's bed, but Jacen made a motion with his hands and the button did not depress. Luke did not seem to realize this. He turned back to Mara and placed his fingers to her throat, checking her pulse. "I can't feel a pulse. Artoo, call an EmDee droid. Tell her to hurry!"

R2-D2 spun toward the data jack to obey, but Jacen used the Force to disable the power to the droid's treads.

Mara caught Jacen's gaze. "All right, Jacen. This has gone far enough."

Not yet. The message reverberated without words inside Mara's head. *He must learn.*

Mara felt another wave of Force energy pass over her, and Luke cried out in horror and looked toward R2-D2.

"*Artoo,* what's taking you so long?"

R2-D2 issued a frustrated whistle and spun an accusing photoreceptor toward Jacen. Luke could take it no longer. He raised a hand and began to fill it with life-giving Force energy.

"Jacen, we can't wait. We have to revive her ourselves." He pointed at the emergency respirator hanging on the wall. "Get the respirator."

Luke leaned over Mara and started to place his hand on her chest—until Jacen raised an arm and pushed him away.

"*Jacen!*" Luke screamed. "What's wrong with you?"

"Nothing," Jacen said calmly. "And there's nothing wrong with Aunt Mara."

Luke's gaze swung back to Mara, and she could not decide whether he looked more stunned or relieved. "You're . . . you're alive again!"

"I was never dead," Mara said. "I think Jacen is trying to make a point."

Luke turned back to Jacen, still too confused to be angry. "I don't understand, Jacen. What's she—"

"You're not ready to face Lomi Plo again," Jacen interrupted. "And you just proved it."

Luke's confusion started to fade, and his anger quickly began to build. "*You* did that to me?"

Jacen shook his head. "You did it to yourself," he said. "Your fear betrays you."

Mara suddenly understood what Jacen had done—or rather, what he had *not* done. "Luke, I think you'd better listen to him." She reached out to her husband through their Force-bond, adding a private plea that she knew he would not refuse. "For me."

Luke snorted, but turned to Jacen. "Okay, I'm listening," he said. "And it had better be good. Saving Mara's life does not give you the right to manipulate me."

"I didn't do that," Jacen said. "All I did was bring your fear to the surface. You created the illusion yourself."

"Remember what happened in the nest ship?" Mara asked. "After I got hit, you couldn't move. Luke, you froze."

"And then I couldn't see Lomi Plo anymore," Luke said, growing calmer. He turned to Jacen. "*You* did the same thing to me?"

"I doubt it." Jacen grew uncomfortable, and his gaze slid away. "That was just a mirror illusion I learned from the Fallanassi."

"But it does prove you're still vulnerable to Lomi Plo," Mara said.

"You don't fear for yourself," Jacen said. "You fear for others—and now Lomi Plo knows that. She'll use it against you."

Luke nodded, and a glimmer of recognition came to his eyes. "Fears aren't so different from doubts. I have to face mine—"

"No," Jacen said. "You have to *eliminate* them."

"Eliminate them?" Mara asked. "That's a lot to ask—especially before we reach Tenupe."

"But I *can* do it," Luke said. "I have to."

"How?" Mara demanded. "You can't give up caring about your family."

"He doesn't have to," Jacen replied. "He just has to surrender."

"Surrender?" Mara asked.

"Vergere taught me to embrace my pain by surrendering to it." Jacen turned to Luke. "I made that pain a part of me—something I would never fight or deny. You have to do the same thing with your fear, Uncle Luke. Then it will have no power over you."

"That may be easier said than done," Luke said.

"Not at all—I know just where to start." Jacen used the Force to lift R2-D2 over to them. "The first thing your fear showed you was your mother's face. And before the battle, you refused to see what happened after your father Force-hurled her."

"So I need to see that now?"

"Only if you want to kill Lomi Plo," Jacen said.

Mara wanted to discourage Luke, to spare him the pain of seeing his mother die by his father's hand. But he was determined to kill Lomi Plo and end this war on Jedi terms, and she knew that Jacen was right, that Luke could not succeed until he embraced his fears as Jacen had learned to embrace his pain.

"Jacen's right. If you're going after Lomi Plo, you need to do this." Mara reached for his hand. "You can't change what is in that holo. You can only accept it."

"That's a lot different from accepting you being hurt—or dying," Luke pointed out. "I couldn't do anything to stop what happened to my mother, but when you were hurt, I was there."

"And you still couldn't stop what happened to *me*," Mara countered. "You were pretty busy with Lomi Plo, as I recall."

"I was barely holding my own," Luke acknowledged.

"Some things you can't control," Jacen said. "If you fear them, then those things control *you*."

Luke shook his head. "I'm not sure we have time for this," he said. "And what if you're wrong? What if Lomi Plo's wounds are enough to distract her?"

"I'm not wrong," Jacen countered. "Look, you may think you push your fears aside when you go to battle—that you bury them. But you'll never bury them deep enough to hide them from Lomi Plo, no matter what her condition is. So you'll have to deal with this problem *now*. Because as you've pointed out, Lomi Plo is healing as we speak."

Luke let out a long breath. "Okay." He turned to R2-D2. "Show me the holo where my mother dies."

R2-D2 issued a questioning trill.

"We're going into battle either way," Luke said. "If you don't want to end up navigating slave ships for Lomi Plo, you'd better start where we left off last time."

R2-D2 gave a plunging whistle, then rocked forward and activated his holoprojector. The image of Padmé, Anakin, and Obi-Wan Kenobi appeared on the floor, Padmé choking, Anakin extending an arm toward her, and Obi-Wan approaching Anakin.

"Let . . . her . . . go!" Obi-Wan was ordering.

Anakin whipped his arm to one side. Padmé flew out of the holo, and Anakin started forward to meet Obi-Wan.

"You turned her against me!" Anakin accused.

Obi-Wan shook his head. "You did that yourself."

The pair left the holo as R2-D2 retreated and turned away from them. For a moment, their voices could be heard arguing in the background, slowly fading as Obi-Wan accused Anakin of falling prey to his anger and his lust for power. Then their voices faded entirely as Padmé's crumpled form returned to the holo, lying on a metal deck.

A lump of sorrow formed in Mara's stomach, and she felt Luke shaking with grief. R2-D2 extended a grasping appendage and started trying to drag Padmé's unconscious form to safety.

From somewhere out of the holo, C-3PO's voice called, *"What are you doing? You're going to hurt her. Wait!"*

The distant sounds of a lightsaber fight arose somewhere outside the holo, then C-3PO appeared and carefully took Padmé in his arms. He started toward the slick-looking skiff they had seen in the last holo, with R2-D2 following close behind, beeping.

"I am being careful!" C-3PO said. *"I have a good hold on her, but I'm worried about my back. I hope it's able to hold up under this weight."*

C-3PO entered the skiff and laid Padmé on a bed in a stateroom. The holo blurred as R2-D2 advanced it quickly through several minutes of watching her lie there; then Obi-Wan arrived to check on her and brush her hair back.

The holo flickered off for an instant, then restarted in the observation room of an operating theater. Obi-Wan was there with C-3PO, Yoda, and a tall, swarthy human. Mara recognized the man as Bail Organa—someone she would later spy upon when she became the Emperor's Hand. A medical droid entered the observation room and began to speak to Obi-Wan and the others.

"*Medically, she is completely healthy.*" *The droid's voice was tinny, but surprisingly sympathetic for a machine.* "*For reasons we can't explain, we are losing her.*"

"*She's dying?*" *Obi-Wan sounded as though he did not believe the droid.*

"*We don't know why,*" *the droid replied.* "*She has lost the will to live. We need to operate quickly if we are to save the babies.*"

"*Babies?*" *This from Bail Organa.*

"*She's carrying twins,*" *the droid said.*

"*Save them, we must,*" *Yoda added.* "*They are our last hope.*"

The medical droid returned to the operating room, and one of R2-D2's beeps sounded in the holo.

"*It's some kind of reproductive process, I think,*" *C-3PO said softly.*

After a few minutes, Padmé whispered something to the medical droid, and Obi-Wan was summoned into the operating theater. He went to her side, and his voice came out of R2-D2's holospeaker sounding even more tinny and distant than usual.

"*Don't give up, Padmé,*" *he said.*

She looked up at him, seeming very weak. "*Is it a girl?*"

"*We don't know yet.*" *Obi-Wan looked toward the droid operating on her midsection.* "*In a minute . . . in a minute.*"

Padmé winced with pain, then the medical droid lifted a tiny bundle into view.

"*It's a boy,*" *he announced.*

Padmé's voice was so weak that it was barely audible. "*Luke . . .*" *She smiled faintly, struggling to extend a hand to touch the baby on the forehead, then repeated,* "*. . . Luke.*"

The medical droid produced another bundle. "*And a girl,*" *he announced.*

"*Leia,*" *Padmé said.*

Obi-Wan leaned closer to her. "*You have twins, Padmé. They need you . . . hang on!*"

Padmé shook her head. "*I . . . can't.*"

She winced again and took Obi-Wan's hand. There seemed to be a necklace dangling from her fingers as she did this, but the holo was not clear enough to see what kind.

"Save your energy," Obi-Wan urged.

Padmé's gaze grew distant. "Obi-Wan . . . there . . . is good in him. I know there is . . . still."

She let out a sudden gasp, then her hand dropped out of Obi-Wan's, leaving the necklace dangling from his fingers. He gathered it into his palm, then turned his hand and began to study the jewelry with a shocked expression.

The holo ended, and R2-D2 tweedled a question.

When Luke did not answer, Jacen said, "Thank you, Artoo. That's all we needed to see."

R2-D2 tipped himself upright again, then swiveled his photoreceptor toward Luke and issued an apologetic whistle.

"There's nothing to apologize for, Artoo," Mara said. Although Luke looked outwardly composed, she could feel how hard he was struggling to contain his grief, to keep his anguish from erupting in an explosion of fury and pain. "It had to be done."

Jacen took Luke's elbow, then squeezed until Luke's blank gaze finally turned toward him. "Master, can you change what you saw in the holo?"

Luke shook his head. "Of course not."

"That's right. You can only accept it," Jacen said. "Some misfortunes you can prevent, and you will. But others . . . sometimes all you can do is embrace the pain."

Luke laid a hand across his nephew's. "I understand. Thank you."

"Good," Jacen said. "Now use what you are feeling. Your anger and your grief can make you more powerful. Use them when you meet Raynar and Lomi Plo, and you *will* defeat them."

A sudden wave of disgust rolled through the Force-bond between Mara and Luke, and Luke frowned and pulled his arm away from Jacen.

"No, Jacen," he said. "That's Vergere's way of using the Force. It won't work for me."

Jacen's face grew worried. "But you're one against two, and they'll have the Force potential of the entire Colony to draw on. You'll need all the power you can get!"

"No," Luke said. "I'll need *strength*—and that comes from my way of using the Force."

Jacen cast a worried glance toward Mara, and she began to grow fearful as well.

"Luke, I understand your hesitation," Mara said. "But I'd feel better if you took another Master or two—"

"I've made my decision." Luke smiled and squeezed her arm gently. "Don't fear. *Accept*."

TWENTY-ONE

It had grown clear that—for once—Han and Leia Solo would not arrive at the crucial moment. A ceaseless storm of megamaser fire had turned Tenupe's green sky into a flashing sheet of crimson and the endless downpour into a hot, foul-smelling drizzle. A dozen different kinds of rescue shuttles were hovering over the flooded river, trying to pluck the half-drowned Chiss survivors off their submerged islands. Clouds of fist-sized Qeeq and meter-long Aebea were droning out of the jungle to attack, clogging intake turbines with their puréed bodies and massing on hulls until their weight alone dropped the vessel like a stone into the river.

The crucial moment was past. Maybe Jaina had misinterpreted the situation when she reached out to her mother in the Force, or maybe something had delayed the *Falcon*. It hardly mattered. The battle could no longer be stopped. Zekk was descending out of the jungle's defoliated canopy with her StealthX slaved to his, and all that remained now was to spring UnuThul's trap and watch the Chiss die.

As the StealthXs drew near, Jaina and Zekk's mindlink was restored. It was not as all-embracing as it had been when they were with the Taat—living with other nests had weakened it—but the connection remained strong enough for Jaina to know the sense of urgency that filled every fiber of Zekk's body, and to understand the reason for it. UnuThul was coming with the Moon Fleet.

The struts had barely touched the jungle floor before Jaina's astromech was opening the canopy and tweedling a welcome.

"Nice to see you, too, Sneaky," Jaina said. "All systems go?"

The droid gave an affirmative whistle, and Jaina felt a wave of concern from Zekk. She looked battered and exhausted and bloody. Maybe she was not ready to start flying missions.

"You think the Chiss will wait while we take a nap?" Jaina retorted. Without waiting for a reply, she turned to her Wuluw communications assistant and reached down to rub a forearm along an antenna. "Sorry for getting you killed so many times, Wuluw."

"*Burru,*" Wuluw thrummed. "*U bru.*"

"You be careful, too," Jaina said. "Someday, the Song will have a verse about your bravery at the Battle of Tenupe."

"*Rrrr.*" Wuluw's mandibles clattered in embarrassment, then she waved all four arms in modesty. "*Uburr.*"

Jaina and Zekk laughed, then Jaina stepped over to her StealthX, retrieved her flight suit from the cockpit and gladly changed out of her mud-caked combat utilities.

She was just climbing into the pilot's seat when her mother suddenly touched her through the Force. Leia seemed terribly alarmed and was clearly trying to warn Jaina and Zekk about something, but the feeling was too vague to tell more.

Then Jaina and Zekk felt Saba reaching out to them as well, opening herself to a battle-meld. They did the same, and the situation immediately grew clearer. Saba and Leia were here, somewhere near Tenupe, and they needed Jaina and Zekk in the air. Something terrible was coming, something that had to be stopped.

Jaina hastily buckled her crash webbing, then glanced out at Wuluw, and she and Zekk wondered if this was something they should warn the Killiks about.

Yes! The impression came from both Saba and Leia, so strong that Jaina and Zekk heard it inside their minds as an actual word. *Must!*

Wuluw started to turn around and leave, but Jaina caught her in the Force and floated her back to the StealthX.

"*Urubu rububu!*" the Killik drummed as Jaina suspended her next to the starfighter. "*Brurb!*"

"Don't worry, you're not coming with us," Jaina said. "And even if you were, I really doubt you'd burst. StealthXs have inertial compensators."

"*Urb?*"

"You need to warn the swarm," Jaina said. "Something bad is coming."

"*Rr?*"

"We don't know. My . . ."

Jaina stopped, unsure whether she should reveal the source of her foreboding. She had heard how her parents had interfered with the

Utegetu evacuation, and she knew the Colony would disapprove of any effort to end the war, so she and Zekk both thought it was probably best not to mention Leia and Saba.

"We're getting a strong feeling from the Force." Jaina returned Wuluw to the ground. "Warn the swarm—and alert UnuThul!"

Jaina lowered the StealthX canopy and energized the repulsor drives, then followed Zekk up into the top of the jungle, where the defoliated mogos were now shattered and burning. Chiss megamaser strikes were lancing down through the clouds like a Bespinese lightning squall, igniting kilometer-long columns of flash fire and turning the lower sky into a region of flame-storm and hot, buffeting winds.

The two Jedi ascended toward the cloud ceiling half blinded by alternating instants of crimson brilliance and stormy dimness, trusting their stick hands to the Force, weaving and rolling their way through a forest of crackling energy. They were dimly aware of a quiet area by the river, where an erratic stream of Chiss shuttles was diving into the mass of Killiks swirling above the islands. But they did not even consider entering the enemy's rescue corridor. As nerve racking as it was to ascend through a barrage, it was far better than the alternative: being spotted by a rescue pilot and having a squadron of clawcraft jump them.

The cloud cover made the ascent especially challenging. The megamaser beams did not seem to descend so much as manifest from the mist. Jaina and Zekk constantly found themselves reacting rather than anticipating, rolling away from a fading column of flame only to find a new one erupting ahead. To make matters worse, their tactical displays revealed two squadrons of clawcraft circling through the clouds around them—enough to make even Jedi grind their teeth and curse under their breaths.

Zekk wanted it known that he was only responsible for the teeth grinding. Until he had become Jaina's mind-mate, he had never even *heard* most of the curse words that were now ricocheting around inside his head.

As they broke out of the clouds into the emerald vastness of Tenupe's upper atmosphere, both exhaled in relief. A blinding torrent of energy was still crackling down around them, but now that they were above the rain and the clouds, the situation looked a little more like the battles they had grown accustomed to in space—with an emphasis on *little*. The megamaser beams were fanning down from about fifty points overhead. The vessels that fired them were still so distant that they were barely flecks against the sky, but they *were* descending fast, following each other down in a large open spiral and trailing long plumes of gray entry smoke that gave away their positions.

Jaina wrinkled her brow. A military fleet dropping out of orbit with batteries blazing might be terrible, but it was hardly something that Leia and Saba would expect Jaina and Zekk to stop with a pair of StealthXs. The warning had to point to something else—something the two Jedi Knights had not yet seen.

"Sneaky, give me a full tac on that fleet," Jaina ordered. "I'm looking for something that doesn't fit the attack profile."

Sneaky tweedled an acknowledgment, then scrolled a message across the display: A SPACE FLEET PERFORMING CLOSE GROUND SUP-PORT DOES NOT FIT ANY ATTACK PROFILE IN MY RECORDS.

"Your records don't include the Battle of Bogo Rai," Jaina said.

AND YOURS DO?

"ReyaTaat's do," Jaina said. ReyaTaat had once been a Chiss in-telligence officer named Daer'ey'ath. "It's a famous Chiss battle. The Colony learned about it when Taat found Daer'ey'ath spying on us and received her into the nest."

OH.

The fleet deployment appeared on Jaina's tactical display. The en-emy's ground-support task force consisted of thirty Star Destroyers and their escorts, a truly awesome flotilla capable of incinerating the jungle from canopy to roots for kilometers around. But the Chiss were being oddly careless, leaving only a handful of Star Destroyers and their escorts in orbit to provide top cover. When UnuThul arrived with the Moon Swarm, he was going to do more than bloody the en-emy fleet and drive it off—he was going to smash it against Tenupe.

The Chiss have made their last mistake, Zekk said through their mind-link. *After UnuThul destroys their fleet, they will not be able to press the war.*

The Chiss will be weakened, Jaina agreed. Somewhere deep in her mind, she knew that the total destruction of the fleet was a two-edged sword, that weakening the Chiss too much would only em-bolden the Colony and prolong the war—but it did not seem that way to UnuThul. She could sense his excitement through the Force. It was a dark momentum inside her, growing more powerful each moment and carrying her inexorably into bloody total war. *The tide will change, and the Colony will crush them like bugs.*

Zekk chuckled at the insult, and the sensation of his amusement made Jaina feel a little sad. There had been a time when the chuckle would have erupted from her lips, too, and neither of them would have known—or cared—who laughed first.

Then Jaina sensed something else from Zekk—a sudden surge of alarm—and they quickly dropped back into the clouds where they would be difficult to see. Four squadrons of clawcraft had started to descend ahead of the main task force, escorting a pair of Chiss defoliators and swinging wide to avoid the megamaser barrage.

Jaina and Zekk reached out to the defoliators in the Force and suddenly felt sick and cold. *Those* ships were what Leia and Saba had wanted them to intercept. There was something terrible aboard those two defoliators, something so sinister and deadly that it had overwhelmed their danger sense from nearly a hundred kilometers away.

Navigating by instruments, they swung onto an interception vector, and shortly afterward they escaped the barrage area. UnuThul soon felt the threat, too. A dark pressure arose inside their chests, pushing them after the two defoliators, compelling them to attack *now*. It was all they could do to resist his Will, to remain in the clouds until they were actually in a position to succeed.

Finally, when the two defoliators had moved so close that the main fleet would not risk firing into the fight, Jaina and Zekk raced forward. They remained in the clouds until they were directly beneath their targets, then pulled back their sticks and climbed straight up. Jaina armed a pair of proton torpedoes—the Colony could no longer acquire the baradium needed to make shadow bombs—then designated the defoliator on the right.

"We'll take that one, Sneaky. Let me know when we have a target-lock."

The droid chirped an acknowledgment, and for a moment it looked like their StealthXs might reach attack range unseen.

Then clawcraft from the two trailing squadrons began to drop down to meet them. They seemed to be moving in slow motion, since the atmosphere even this high was thick enough to slow down a starfighter and tear it apart if it maneuvered too sharply. But the distances were also smaller—dozens of kilometers instead of hundreds—and within a few heartbeats, the dark specks of the first Chiss fighters came into view and began to rain cannon bolts down on the StealthXs.

Sneaky reported that they had a target-lock. Jaina confirmed that it was the correct vessel, then sensed Zekk doing the same. They launched their torpedoes together and watched the white dots of the propulsion tails vanish into the green sky.

A second later the first laser bolt slammed into Jaina's forward shields, spilling orange flame in front of her canopy and reverberating inside the cockpit as shield hits never did in space. Zekk slipped in close and slightly ahead of her, buying time for her shields to recover by placing himself between her and their attackers. They continued to climb like that, barely five meters apart, juking and jinking as one, pouring fire back up at the clawcraft.

Then Sneaky chirped in surprise, and Jaina checked her tactical display to find both sets of proton torpedoes detonating twenty kilometers from the defoliators—well short of where any countermeasures should have taken effect.

"What the Hutt happened?"

The tactical display replayed the last several seconds, and Jaina saw four clawcraft come streaking in to intercept the proton torpedoes head-on. One of the pilots was lucky enough to blast his target out of the air with cannon fire, but the other three missed and stopped the torpedoes by crashing into them.

That's spaced—even for Chiss! Zekk said through their shared mind.

Maybe the defoliators don't have countermeasures, Jaina suggested.

Or maybe the Chiss just want to be really *sure those ships deliver their payloads,* Zekk said.

Zekk took a hit in his shields, then Jaina slipped into the forward position. The enemy squadrons were coming head-on, a mad tactic as dangerous for them as it was for their targets. They were coming in waves of four, the leaders already so close that they were the size of fists. Jaina and Zekk picked the second one from the left and fired together, pounding through its shields by landing five cannon strikes simultaneously.

Before the fireball died away, Jaina and Zekk switched targets. The first wave was so close now that they could see the laser bolts streaming from the tips of the forward-pointing "claws" that gave the starfighters their nicknames. The Jedi fired again, aiming where the Force told them the craft was going rather than where it was. The pilot accommodated them by jinking into their line of fire, and the starfighter vanished in a flash of yellow flame.

Jaina and Zekk were just turning their attention to their next victim when the crash of a triple cannon strike shook Jaina's cockpit. Her instrument panel lit up with depletion lights and damage warnings, but she could not hear the alarms—or Sneaky's tweedling—over the roar of the explosion.

Zekk slipped into the lead position, and they began to pour cannon bolts at the next clawcraft. The two survivors from the first wave had swollen in apparent diameter to the size of a Bith's head, but they were barrel-rolling and bobbing and weaving so hard now that, at such short range, the StealthXs could not aim their laser cannons quickly enough to hit the targets.

Sneaky scrolled a message across Jaina's display. IT IS IMPERATIVE THAT WE TURN BACK IMMEDIATELY. WE HAVE LOST OUR FORWARD SHIELD CAPACITOR!

"So?" Jaina asked. "We still have shields for now, right?"

UNTIL WE SUFFER THE NEXT HIT, Sneaky replied. AND IF WE ARE FORCED TO EJECT, I DON'T HAVE A PARACHUTE!

"Relax," Jaina said. "I have the Force."

The Chiss finally rolled the wrong way. A trio of hits punched through his shields and took off an attack claw, sending him into an uncontrolled spin. He vanished into the roiling gray-green clouds below, and then the last clawcraft was on them, not evading, just coming straight at the StealthXs with all four cannons blazing.

Zekk's shields overloaded and flashed out in a second. Before Jaina could move into lead position, his StealthX took a hit in the nose and another in an upper wing, and still the clawcraft kept coming.

Then Jaina realized the pilot had no intention of veering away. With her and Zekk flying in overlap formation, the explosion from a midair collision would be enough to take them both out.

The thought had barely entered Jaina's mind before Zekk was breaking left. Jaina broke in the opposite direction, trying to force a hesitation by making the enemy choose between targets.

The Chiss was too good to hesitate. He smoothly switched targets and took aim at the side of Jaina's StealthX, pounding through her shields and blowing head-sized holes into her fuselage. Unable to shoot back, she used the Force to tip his clawcraft downward, redirecting his fire and forcing him into a dive that carried him beneath her starfighter instead of crashing into it.

As the starfighter streaked past, the Force fairly crackled with the pilot's frustration—with his very *human*-feeling frustration. Jaina reached out to him and felt an all-too-familiar presence. "Blast," she muttered. *Jagged Fel.*

Knowing better than to let a clawcraft pilot—particularly *this* clawcraft pilot—get behind her, Jaina pivoted the StealthX over its wing and started after him.

"Sneaky, open a hailing channel to our target."

The droid squeaked a long objection, which Jaina could barely hear over all the damage alarms—and which she could not read because her display was out.

"Comm protocols don't apply right now," Jaina said, taking a guess at what her astromech was upset about. "The enemy already knows where we are. They can *see* us."

Sneaky whistled in refusal.

"If I have to do it myself, I'm ejecting you," Jaina said.

The channel was open by the time she fell in behind the clawcraft. "Jag, what are you doing here?" she demanded.

"Trying to shoot you down," Jag said. "But I forget—that's supposed to be a military secret. Now I guess I have to kill you."

Jaina probably should not have been surprised by the bitterness in Jag's voice, but she was, and he nearly broke free by rolling to the left. Fortunately, Zekk was there pouring laser bolts into the clawcraft's exhaust tail, and Jag had to slip back into Jaina's sights when overload static began to snake across his shields. He tried to escape again by breaking hard to the right, but this time Jaina was ready and forced him back by sending a stream of cannon bolts past his flank.

"Jag, you shouldn't take this so personally," Jaina said. She noticed that he was gradually turning, trying to draw them away from the defoliators. "You and I were over a long time before Zekk and I met Taat."

"You think I *care* whose antennae you rub?" Jagged retorted. "You betrayed your honor."

"Our honor?" Jaina was confused. "We haven't made you any—"

"I guaranteed Lowbacca's parole at Qoribu," Jagged reminded her. "And you returned my courtesy with betrayal at Supply Depot Thrago and the Battle of Snevu. My family's reputation has suffered."

As had its finances, if Jaina recalled the terms of the guarantee correctly. Aristocra Formbi had said the Fels would have to repay any damages Lowbacca caused if he violated the parole—and before returning to the Alliance, he had taken part in the destruction of not only several million liters of space fuel, but also dozens of clawcraft and a couple of capital ships.

"Jag, I'm sorry," Jaina said. The second wave of clawcraft reached visual range and—ignoring the possibility of hitting Jagged by accident—opened fire on the StealthXs. "In the urgency of the situation, the parole just didn't occur to us."

"Don't apologize. The fault is all mine." Jagged continued his turn and started to climb, trying to set up Jaina and Zekk for his wingmates. "I should never have made the mistake of thinking Jedi had honor."

The rebuke hurt more than it should have, perhaps because Jaina and Zekk knew it was justified—and because Jaina knew that it reflected Jagged's current disdain for her. But this was war, and they could not allow personal feelings to interfere with stopping those defoliators—not when whatever the vessels were carrying felt so malevolent and deadly.

"Jagged, we—I—want you to know that I still love you. And I always will." Jaina activated her attack sensors and locked Jagged's clawcraft as the primary target. "But if you can eject, you should do it now."

Jaina and Zekk opened fire.

But Jagged had already gone into the Clawcraft Spin, whirling his starfighter around its ball-shaped cockpit and spraying laser bolts in every direction as he fell away in an erratic spiral impossible to target. It was a popular tactic in space combat, but in an atmosphere it was so dangerous and difficult that most pilots would have preferred to take their chances with no shields and one engine. Yet Jagged Fel somehow managed to keep the air resistance from tearing his craft apart, and by the time he vanished into the clouds, he was already emerging from the spin and starting to pull up.

Maybe we shouldn't warn him next time, Zekk suggested.

You're just saying that because you're jealous, Jaina joked.

Yeah, but not over you, Zekk replied. *No one can fly like that without the Force!*

A cannon bolt flashed past Jaina's cockpit—so close that it raised a heat blister in the canopy—and she and Zekk turned and dived. With their forward shields down and the Chiss behaving more like Killik suicide fliers than clawcraft pilots, their only chance of stopping the defoliators lay in catching the two vessels in the clouds, where their StealthXs could remain hidden until they attacked. The clawcraft pursued, but both Jaina and Zekk still had their rear shields and were able to endure the short pounding they received before reaching cover.

They had barely entered the clouds before the dark pressure began to build inside their chests again. UnuThul did not want them to wait. He wanted them to attack *now*. Jaina and Zekk reached out to him in the Force, trying to make him see that they could not possibly succeed, that their StealthXs were barely holding together and their only hope of success lay in concealment.

UnuThul did not understand—or care. The dark pressure grew unrelenting, until they thought their hearts would collapse. Still, they remained in the clouds, calling on each other for the strength to resist UnuThul, Jaina using the Force to steady Zekk's hand when his StealthX began to drift upward, Zekk reaching out to push her stick forward when she began to pull it back. Because Jaina's displays were not working and Zekk's sensor pod had been blasted away, they had to navigate by feeling alone, always keeping the noses of their battered starfighters pointed toward the menace they sensed in the Force.

And even as Jaina and Zekk closed on their targets again, they sensed Leia and Saba struggling with their own troubles far above. Sometimes, her mother felt tense and worried, and other times she and Saba were clearly in combat, filling the battle-meld with fury and fear and determination. Jaina and Zekk ached to help, but they were too well disciplined to ignore the defoliators—even without the influence of UnuThul.

A shock wave of astonishment rolled through the battle-meld, and suddenly Leia and Saba seemed confused, hopeful, and terrified all at once. The dark pressure inside Jaina and Zekk grew more powerful than ever, and they found themselves poking their canopies out of the clouds in spite of themselves.

The defoliators were only a few kilometers above, so close now that Jaina and Zekk could clearly see their hawkish silhouettes—and the drop-shaped outlines of two enormous bombs hanging beneath each wing.

Each of the vessels was tightly ringed by a defensive cordon of clawcraft, with another six starfighters arrayed farther out in intercept position. There would be another dozen Chiss ambushers even farther out, circling low over the clouds, ready to pounce the instant the StealthXs showed themselves.

Far above the defoliators, a distant web of light was flashing back and forth between the descending Chiss fleet and the lower reaches of space. With both of their tactical displays nonfunctional, it was impossible for Jaina and Zekk to tell exactly what was happening . . . but they could guess. UnuThul had arrived with the Moon Swarm and launched his attack prematurely, probably hoping to divert the Chiss's attention and make it easier for them to bring down the defoliators—and judging by the feelings in the battle-meld, Leia and Saba and the rest of the *Falcon*'s crew had gotten caught in the middle of it.

The tactic changed nothing as far as Jaina and Zekk were concerned. Their best chance of success, as small as it was, still lay in the . . .

A new presence joined the meld—the dark, oddly familiar presence of a Twi'lek Joiner. *Alema Rar.*

A wave of revulsion rose inside Jaina and Zekk—and inside Leia and Saba, as well. Alema was the holochild for all that worried Master Skywalker about the Jedi's new view of the Force. She was living proof that there *was* a dark side, for she had ventured into that darkness and lost her way so completely that even Luke had given up hoping of redeeming her. She had become a twisted and angry thing that cast off vows like boyfriends, that turned her back on faithful comrades and betrayed sacred trusts and viciously attacked those who had shown her nothing but kindness.

And none of that mattered, because there she was in a StealthX, hiding in the clouds a few kilometers behind Jaina and Zekk. The Chiss had no idea she was there, and Jaina and Zekk understood now why the dark pressure inside them had grown so strong, why UnuThul was so eager for them to sacrifice themselves in a futile gesture.

They were nothing more than a diversion. Alema—Night Herald of the Dark Nest—was the true firepower. To UnuThul, this was the surest way to stop the evil hanging beneath the defoliators' wings.

Leia and Saba reached out in the Force, urging Jaina and Zekk to resist UnuThul's Will, to stick to their own plan and attack in the clouds.

Jaina and Zekk pushed their throttles forward, then pulled their sticks back and began to climb in a wild corkscrew that made their astromechs shriek structure-stress warnings. With no forward shields left to share, it made no sense to fly in close formation. Instead, they climbed in parallel spirals, angling across the bows of the defoliators to cut off their descent.

The Chiss moved quickly to stop them, the defensive rings shifting to remain between the two StealthXs and their targets, the interceptors diving to confront them with laser cannons flashing. Jaina and Zekk returned fire effectively but without enthusiasm, destroying a clawcraft apiece and knowing that those pilots were being sacrificed to a diversion—just as they were themselves.

"Sneaky, can you get a torpedo lock on either of the defoliators?" The bombs—four on each vessel—were identical to the prototype that Jag had destroyed in the dunes above the Iesei nest.

The droid replied with an affirmative tweet, but added a long descending whistle that suggested he questioned the wisdom of this attack.

"Don't argue!" Jaina armed all of her proton torpedoes, and sensed Zekk doing the same. "Just let me know when you're ready."

The droid emitted a brief whistle.

Jaina fired her next two proton torpedoes and watched in horrified

THE SWARM WAR   869

fascination as a pair of clawcraft dropped down in front of the shrinking efflux dots. A moment later, she was momentarily blinded when a
pair of dazzling flashes lit the sky between her and the defoliators.

Guessing that she must be in range by now, Jaina began to pour
laser cannon fire into the defoliator Sneaky had targeted. The defensive ring tightened even more, bunching up to absorb the attacks on
their own shields and leaving the stern of the vessel badly exposed to
a proton torpedo.

Still, Alema did not attack. Was she waiting for the Chiss ambushers to show themselves . . . or for Jaina and Zekk to be blasted
out of the sky? The spite Leia and Saba were pouring into the meld
made clear what *they* thought.

Two proton torpedoes streaked from Zekk's StealthX toward
the second defoliator. A Chiss clawcraft dropped down and obliterated the first torpedo with a volley of cannon bolts. The pilots trying
to intercept the second torpedo were blinded by the explosion, and it
slipped past the defensive screen to detonate against the defoliator's
belly shields. Almost immediately, Jagged Fel and a dozen other ambushers emerged from the clouds to begin hammering Jaina and
Zekk's rear shields.

Trapped in a devastating crossfire and badly outnumbered, the
only sensible thing for Jaina and Zekk to do was to roll out. Sneaky
began to whistle and toot, no doubt extolling the wisdom of presenting their shielded tails to the enemy and fleeing while they still could.

Instead, Jaina launched her last set of proton torpedoes and accelerated toward her target, pouring a constant stream of cannon
bolts ahead of her and doing her best to make it appear that she intended to ram the defoliator. Zekk mirrored her every move, heading
toward the second defoliator. Four clawcraft defenders quickly
moved to block their torpedoes. The interceptors raced forward on a
collision course with Jaina and Zekk, while Jag and his ambushers
poured fire into the StealthX tails with no concern for hitting their
own starfighters.

Then Jaina and Zekk sensed Alema streaking up out of the
clouds, coming up behind the defoliators where there were no longer
any clawcraft to challenge her. Jaina's rear shields went down, then
one of her fusial engines flamed out, and Sneaky began to trill warnings that she could not understand. She continued to pour fire at the
belly of her defoliator, ignoring the pending collision with the clawcraft interceptors and using the Force to dodge what she could of the
mad storm of bolts.

One of Zekk's wings came off. His StealthX entered a spin and tried to nose over into a dive, but Jaina felt him using the Force to pull it back into a climb. He continued toward his target, his spiral more erratic than ever and firing with only two laser cannons, but holding the Chiss rapt.

You have nothing to be jealous of, Jaina said through their mindlink. *Even if Jag had the Force, he couldn't do that!*

Who's using the Force? Zekk replied. *This is fear!*

Alema finally launched her first set of proton torpedoes, targeting the nearest defoliator. She was so close that the vessel had no chance to deploy countermeasures. The first torpedo overloaded the vessel's shields and blasted its tail into shards. The second vaporized the entire ship, bombs included, leaving nothing behind but a white flash.

The Force roiled with shock and confusion, but the Chiss reacted with remarkable swiftness, instantly abandoning Jaina's StealthX to rush back toward Alema.

They were too late; Alema had already sent another set of torpedoes toward the remaining defoliator. One exploded just as the defensive ring arrived at the vessel's stern, and Jaina and Zekk felt a dozen lives wink out in an instant. The other torpedo smashed into a sacrificial clawcraft, but it was so close to the defoliator that both vessels took the hit. The defoliator's fuselage and one wing vanished in another white flash.

But one of the wings survived.

It went fluttering planetward, its silver skin flashing brightly in the blue sun, the two bombs still intact and the clouds below coming up fast.

TWENTY-TWO

High above Tenupe, *Fell Defender* was still shuddering from the Killiks' opening salvo when a grim calm came to the battle-meld, and Leia understood what Jaina and Zekk were about to do.

"We can't waste any more time being sneaky," she whispered. Alema Rar had just joined the meld. Leia could sense the Twi'lek in the atmosphere below, hovering behind Jaina and Zekk, calculating and resolute and slightly amused by the idea of using them for bait. "We need to board the *Falcon* now."

Tarfang chortled something that sounded a little like "impossible." He was the only one in the group who could stand upright in the oily-smelling conveyance tunnel, and he took advantage of the fact by bracing his hands on his hips and vehemently shaking his head as he chittered.

"Tarfang is right." Juun pointed into the bustling hangar, toward an out-of-the-way corner where about fifty Chiss troopers in black deflection armor stood in a tight cordon around the *Falcon*. "They know we're coming. That security platoon is clearly waiting for us."

"Ssso?" Saba rasped. "Maybe they will give us a good fight—for a change."

"Yeah, maybe *too* good," Han said. He was looking out across the gleaming vastness of the Star Destroyer's hangar, studying what had to be an entire maintenance brigade rushing to launch the *Defender*'s starfighter wing. "We can probably take the security platoon, but those maintenance guys are all carrying—"

"Han, Alema Rar has joined the battle-meld," Leia said. "I

think Jaina and Zekk are going to serve as her decoys, to pull the escorts off—"

"What are we waiting for?" Han raised the T-21 repeating blaster that Cakhmaim and Meewalh had liberated from the detention center's contraband vault—along with the rest of the group's weapons—then started to duck-walk out of the conveyance tunnel. "Let's go get my ship back."

Saba used the Force to stop Han in his tracks. "A plan would be good."

"You want a plan?" He pointed at Saba and Leia. "Okay, you two make a distraction. Cakhmaim, you and Meewalh sneak aboard and take out the squad I'm sure they've got waiting to ambush us. Tarfang, you and I blast anyone who even looks our way." He glanced back to Saba. "How's that for a plan?"

"Good," Saba said.

"It's vague and incomplete!" Juun objected.

"So?" Han demanded.

"So what am *I* supposed to do?" Juun demanded.

"Keep up," Han replied. " 'Cause the *Falcon*'s not waiting around for anyone."

"Of course not," Juun replied. "In *Spy Primer,* Kyle Katarn makes it clear that every member of an espionage team . . ."

Leia stopped listening as Cakhmaim and Meewalh crept out of the conveyance tunnel. They slipped behind an empty missile rack waiting to be sent back up the tunnel for reloading, then began to work their way along the wall toward the *Falcon.* They were so adept at camouflaging themselves that even Leia lost sight of them within five steps.

Saba pointed at one of the overhead storage gantries where clawcraft were moored before they were prepped for flight. One of the starfighters began to sway in its suspension rack, then suddenly came loose and fell to the floor with a deafening crash.

All eyes in the hangar turned toward the sound, and Leia led Han and the others out of the conveyance tunnel at a sprint, dashing between empty armament racks, crouching behind parked utility carts, hiding behind portable diagnostic units. Saba's distraction proved so dramatic that work came to a standstill as astonished technicians, pilots, and even the security platoon guarding the *Falcon* watched the emergency response team rush to investigate.

By the time the officers recovered from their own shock and began to fill the echoing hangar with shouted commands to return to work, Leia and her companions were kneeling behind a self-portable laser-cannon charging tank. The *Falcon* was only about twenty meters away, the security cordon about half that distance. She could feel the Noghri hiding somewhere in the shadows on the other side of the ship, waiting for their opportunity to slip aboard.

Leia signaled the others to be ready, then used the Force to create a loud creak in the storage gantries directly above the security platoon. The troops immediately looked up, already suspicious enough to raise their charric rifles.

Leia Force-grabbed a clawcraft hanging over their heads and began to swing it back and forth. The troops immediately began to back away from the *Falcon*—until their female officer started barking commands at them. In the next moment the officer was sliding across the deck with her arms flailing, still screeching orders in a panicked voice and gesturing at the gantries.

The soldiers stared after her in confusion, or looked up into the gantries and scowled. None of them noticed the slender, chest-high forms of two Noghri appearing out of the shadows behind them, then slipping up the *Falcon*'s boarding ramp.

Saba thumped her tail on the deck and began to siss uncontrollably.

"Quiet, Master!" Leia whispered. "You'll give us away!"

"Sssorry!" Saba replied. "She is juzt so funny, telling her soldierz to stay while she goes."

"Yeah, she's a laugh a millisecond," Han grumbled. He turned to Leia. "How about getting the rest of 'em to move so we can get out of here?"

Leia gave the swinging clawcraft a violent twist, and it came free of its mountings. The security platoon shouted the alarm and dived for cover, many of them zinging blind reaction shots into the gantries as they moved. An instant later the starfighter crashed down in their midst, scattering cannon arms and pieces of armor plating in every direction.

Leia and Saba were already leading the rush toward the *Falcon*, lightsabers in hand but not ignited. For a moment, the security troops continued to focus their attention overhead, thinking their attackers must be up in the gantries. Then one of them noticed Leia and the others racing toward the ship and shouted the alarm.

Leia and Saba Force-jerked half a dozen charric rifles out of troopers' hands and sent the weapons skittering across the floor. Han and Tarfang began to lay suppression fire, but that did not prevent the security platoon from launching a counterattack.

Leia and Saba activated their lightsabers and began to weave an impenetrable shield of light, synchronizing their movements through the battle-meld so that one blade was always in position to block without interfering with the other. Unlike blaster bolts—which carried little kinetic energy—each maser beam struck so hard that the blow nearly knocked the lightsaber from Leia's hand. Sometimes she called on the Force to reinforce her grasp and batted the beam back at her attacker, and other times she redirected the energy, using it to move her blade into its next position.

But no attacks penetrated their shield, and soon Leia and the others were all backing up the boarding ramp into the *Falcon*. Han raised the ramp, then winced at the sound of the maser bolts pinging into the ship's hull.

"Now that's just uncalled for," he said.

A pair of metallic feet came clanking down the corridor behind them, then C-3PO said, "Thank goodness you're here! They've been tearing the ship apart!"

"Who?" Leia asked.

"Lieutenant Vero'tog'leo and his subordinates," C-3PO replied. "They reactivated me and kept demanding that I tell them where the smuggling compartments were. When I explained that I wasn't authorized to reveal that information, they threatened to pour acid into my lubricators!"

"Where are they now?" Leia asked.

"Waiting with Cakhmaim and Meewalh in the aft hold, I believe."

Leia turned to Han. "Saba and I can handle that. You take Jae and get us out of here."

Han nodded and turned to go—then suddenly stopped. "Where *is* Jae?"

Leia looked around the boarding area and did not see the Sullustan anywhere. "Tell me we didn't leave him outside!"

Tarfang jabbered something angry.

"It's not her fault," Han said. "I warned him to keep up."

Tarfang chittered something else and pointed forward, and suddenly Juun's voice came over the intercom.

"Initiating emergency cold-start procedures," he said. "Secure all hatches."

They all let out long sighs of relief, then Han motioned to Tarfang. "Come on. We'd better get up there, or he'll still be doing circuit tests when the Chiss bring up their laser cannons."

Han and the Ewok started up the corridor at a run, and Leia and Saba went aft. As C-3PO had said, Lieutenant Vero'tog'leo had torn the *Falcon* apart, emptying stowage cabinets, disassembling the medical bay, even opening the service panels in the ceiling. By the time they reached the hold, Leia was mad enough to stow the lieutenant and his squad on the wrong side of a soon-to-be open air lock.

But when she saw how battered and bloody the Chiss already were, she decided that Cakhmaim and Meewalh had punished them enough. Leia herded the limping and slumping squad onto the cargo lift and simply off-loaded them.

The lift was still retracting when the *Falcon* rose from the deck and swung toward the hangar mouth. Chiss being Chiss, Leia was fairly certain that Vero'tog'leo had hidden a tracking device, a bomb, or both somewhere aboard. She sent Cakhmaim and Meewalh to do a security sweep, then she and Saba hurried to the turrets to engage the quad cannons.

Leia had barely buckled into her firing seat before Han had the *Falcon* shooting toward the hangar mouth. A handful of security troops pelted the hull with maser beams, but there was no question of anyone trying to stop them by sealing the barrier field. With the Killiks attacking, the Chiss had more important things to worry about than escaping prisoners. The *Defender* was gushing clawcraft as fast as she could, and the deck master was not going to interrupt the launch for anything.

Before venturing out into the tempest of energy erupting just beyond the *Defender*'s shields, the starfighters were using the shelter of her expansive belly to form up by squadrons. Han simply dropped the *Falcon*'s nose and dived, leaving Leia—whose turret happened to be facing aft—staring up into the flashing madness of the battle above. The sky was at once black with smoke and descending dartships and dappled with the blue brilliance of blossoming turbolaser strikes, and already the flaming hulks of two Chiss Star Destroyers were plummeting groundward in an uncontrolled gyre.

The *Falcon* suddenly veered out from under the battle, and Han announced, "Got 'em."

Leia checked her targeting display and saw that the *Falcon* was about five kilometers above a pair of Chiss defoliators and closing rapidly. The defoliator escorts were badly out of position, bunched up in front of the two craft as they fired at unseen targets that Leia assumed to be Jaina and Zekk. She could feel them through the battle-meld, grim and determined, driven by Raynar's Will and still focused on destroying the defoliators. She could also feel Alema— close by and just as determined.

Leia spun her turret around and touched Jaina and Zekk in the Force, urging them not to sacrifice themselves. Help was on the way. All they had to do was drop back into the clouds and wait.

But Alema Rar had never been patient. She continued to pour impatience into the meld, demanding that Jaina and Zekk keep attacking. Raynar's Will continued to weigh on the two Jedi Knights, and they began to exchange cannon bolts with the escorts.

Then the blinding dots of two torpedo detonations flared about three kilometers ahead the *Falcon,* and when the static cleared from Leia's targeting display, the trailing defoliator was gone.

"Han, get us there now!" Leia ordered over the intercom.

"Sure." The *Falcon* accelerated, and long tongues of flame began to lick past the turret canopy. "What's a little entry burn?"

By the time the second set of torpedoes detonated, they were close enough to see the thick cloud of clawcraft swarming around Jaina and Zekk's StealthXs—and to see how clumsily both craft were handling as they dived for the clouds. Even if Leia had not been able to feel it through the Force, she would have known just by looking that her daughter and Zekk were in desperate straits.

And there was no sign of Alema going to help them. The Twi'lek had vanished from the battle-meld as soon as she destroyed the second defoliator, and now she was doing nothing to help her decoys.

"Anybody see what happened to Alema?" Leia asked. "I'd like to send a few cannon bolts her way."

The *Falcon* shuddered as Saba opened up with the belly cannons. "Sssorry! This one misssed," she hissed. "She was on my side, diving for the cloudz."

"It looks like she's going after something," Han said. "And so are the Chiss."

Leia checked her targeting display and saw that eight clawcraft had entered a power dive, chasing something big and slow with an erratic flight pattern. "What is it?"

"A wing!" Juun was silent for a moment, then added, "With two huge bombs attached to it!"

Leia had a sinking feeling. "How close are they to the battle zone?"

"It doesn't matter," Han said. "This time, my daughter comes first. What do I care if her creepy friends get wiped—"

"Han!" Leia swung her turret around and began to pour laser bolts toward the clawcraft harassing Jaina and Zekk. "You do know StealthXs can eavesdrop on intercom transmissions at this range?"

"They can?"

"The StealthX'z primary mission is spying," Saba reminded him. She opened fire, too, and some of the clawcraft began to disperse and come after the *Falcon*. "But maybe they're not listening."

"Who cares?" Han asked. "Jaina knows I'm just worried about her."

"She also knowz that *you* know she can take care of herself," Saba said. "And that you would never let the Chisz rupture one of those parasite bombz. Even a few eggz might be enough to kill her friendz' species."

Han sighed. "You're saying we have to recover that wing, aren't you?"

"I'm afraid so," Leia said. The cold ache of disappointment in her stomach was only partially relieved by the feelings of encouragement and approval coming from Jaina and Zekk through the meld. "But nothing says you can't edge a little closer on the way past. Saba and I would enjoy some target practice."

The *Falcon* rolled into a dive so steep that it sent all the unstowed equipment and supplies flying around the interior of the cabin and holds. Leia ignored the crashing and banging and continued to fire. She also ignored the clawcraft now pouring cannon bolts after the *Falcon*. Instead, she used the Force to target the craft that continued to harass her daughter and Zekk, far below.

Even at that distance, even in an atmosphere, the *Falcon*'s powerful quad cannons were more than a match for the light shielding of a clawcraft. She sent one tumbling toward the clouds. Another burst into a ball of flame as it seemed to simply fly into a stream of Saba's bolts, then Leia hit a third starfighter with a series of glancing shots that forced it into an uncontrolled spin.

And finally, the two StealthXs had a clear lane down into the clouds. Jaina and Zekk dived into it, smoking and fluttering, with a dozen clawcraft hanging on their tails, but still in one piece. The meld grew warm with their gratitude; then the turret lights dimmed as the nearest clawcraft began to take a toll on the *Falcon*'s shields.

Han rolled again, causing even more crashing in the cabin, and the entry burn grew so intense that Leia could no longer see through the flames. She swung her cannons toward the clawcraft, then forgot about the targeting display and allowed the Force to guide her hand as she squeezed the triggers. The synthetic rumble of the fire-control computer announced one hit, then two, then one more, and suddenly she sensed no more targets.

Leia checked the display and found the thermal blossoms of a dozen dissipating explosions. Incredibly, for every starfighter she had destroyed, Saba had taken out two.

"Rodder!" Leia gasped. "Maybe I'll be able to do that when *I'm* a Master."

"Maybe?" Saba began to siss uncontrollably for some reason no one but a Barabel would ever understand. "Leia, now is no time for your jokez! This one must focuz."

The entry burn paled as the *Falcon* entered the clouds, then faded away altogether as they emerged into a downpour so fierce that Leia could barely see the freight-handling mandibles at the front of the ship. The targeting display showed the eight clawcraft that had followed the defoliator wing down. They were firing at the wing— which was catching updrafts and flittering back and forth so wildly that even Saba would have had trouble hitting it. They were also shooting at an empty area behind the wing, which Leia assumed to be Alema's StealthX. She felt no shame in wishing them good luck with the latter target.

C-3PO's voice came over the intercom. "How helpful!" he announced. "The Chiss appear to be shooting at their own bombs. Perhaps we should withdraw."

"They're not just shooting at them, chipbrain," Han said. "They're trying to detonate them."

"How odd," C-3PO replied. "Won't they detonate on impact anyway?"

"Only if they're armed," Leia interjected. "And obviously they're not. The pilots weren't on-mark yet when their defoliator was hit."

The fire-control computer began to designate targets in order of threat level, and Leia and Saba opened up with their quad cannons again. A trio of clawcraft erupted in flames before three of the others finally stopped attacking Alema and the wing and rolled out to come after the *Falcon*.

Saba switched to the *Falcon*'s attackers, leaving Leia to stop the other two from rupturing the parasite bombs. Her targets were clever, positioning themselves between the *Falcon* and the tumbling wing, so that she could not fire on them without running the risk of hitting the bombs. She looked out into the blinding rain and found one of the starfighters in the Force, then focused only on that and released all conscious control of her hand.

Leia felt the turret shudder as her quad cannons fired, then the fire-control computer announced the target's destruction with a synthetic rumble. She reached out to the other clawcraft in the Force— and was astonished to feel the familiar presence of Jagged Fel in the pilot's seat.

"Han," Leia said over the intercom. "That last clawcraft, it's Jag!"

"What? How do you . . ." Han caught himself. "Right—forget I asked."

Leia could tell by Han's tone that he was no more eager to kill Jagged Fel than she was, but they did not seem to have a lot of options. Saba was still exchanging cannon bolts with the clawcraft she had not yet killed, and they all knew that it would not be long before the squadron that had chased Jaina and Zekk into the clouds gave up their search and rushed over to help with the wing.

"I guess the shoe is on the other foot," Han said. "What are you going to do? We've got to shoot him down."

"I know," Leia said. "But give me a hailing channel."

"Go ahead, Princess," Juun said.

"Jagged Fel, I'm sure you know who this is."

"Princess Leia?" Jagged did not seem surprised. "I *told* them it's impossible to hold Jedi prisoners."

"Well, they know now." Leia placed her finger on the triggers. "If you can eject, I suggest you do it fast."

Jagged sighed. "I've been hearing that from a lot of Solo women lately."

Leia barely heard him. She was already deep in the Force, focusing all her attention on his starfighter.

She felt her finger twitch, and said, "Good-bye, Jag."

The turret began to shudder and did not stop. Leia felt her hand moving, following Jagged's evasion attempts, but he might as well have been trying to dodge light. She followed his juking and jinking through the Force for a moment, then began to anticipate him, and an instant later she heard the synthetic rumble of the fire-control computer.

But Leia did not feel the shock of his death.

She dropped her gaze to the targeting display and saw the fading blossom of his clawcraft explosion, but the image was not fine enough to determine whether some of the debris she saw fluttering away was an EV unit.

"Han, did he—"

"I don't know," Han cut in. "I might have seen an ejection flare before you fired, but we've got other problems right now."

A green blur, as vast as a planet, appeared out of the rain ahead, and then the *Falcon* pulled up, hard. Leia spun her turret around and glimpsed what was clearly a jungle canopy dropping away behind the ship's stern.

"Han, are you telling me—"

"Afraid so," Han said. "The bombs are down there somewhere."

TWENTY-THREE

Luke found Gilad Pellaeon alone in the *Megador*'s observation deck, his liver-spotted hands clasped behind his back and his gray-haired head tipped back slightly as he gazed out the center of the dome. His attention seemed to be fixed on the cloud-pearled planet ahead, where the red-flashing shadow of the Killik ambush swarm was spreading steadily outward. The insects were striving to keep the Chiss fleet trapped between them and Tenupe's surface, and by the looks of things, they were succeeding. If the Grand Admiral noticed his own huge armada sparkling out of hyperspace all around the edges of the observation dome, he showed no sign.

"I've never seen anything like this, Luke." Pellaeon spoke without taking his eyes off the planet. "The Colony must have a million dartships attacking down there. I can't imagine the logistics."

"*You* don't have a collective mind," Luke said, stepping to the admiral's side. "The Killiks are an extraordinary species. At times, I'm tempted to believe that they *were* the ones who built Centerpoint Station and the Maw."

Pellaeon studied him out of the corner of one eye. "And you don't think that now?"

Luke shook his head. "The nests have a habit of confusing their Joiners' memories with their own." He was surprised that Pellaeon seemed to take the Killiks' claim seriously. "And the technology does seem well beyond them."

"You think so?" Pellaeon returned his gaze to the dome, then pointed a wrinkled finger at the Killik fleet. "I wonder how long it would have taken the *Galactic Alliance* to build that navy."

"Good point." Luke studied Pellaeon carefully, trying to figure out what the cunning admiral was driving at. "But the Killiks don't even have a true science. How could they have the knowledge to build something like the Maw or Centerpoint?"

Pellaeon turned to face Luke. "A lot can happen in twenty-five thousand years, Master Skywalker. Sciences can be lost, knowledge can be forgotten, cultural imperatives can change. That *doesn't* mean we should underestimate our opponent."

"Of course not," Luke said, taken aback by the sharpness of Pellaeon's rebuke. "Forgive me, Admiral—I wasn't thinking on the same level you were."

Pellaeon's face softened. "No apology necessary, Master Skywalker. You had no way to know we were discussing our current attack strategies." He returned his attention to the Killik fleet, then added in a wry tone, "Since the Rebellion, I've become a bit fanatic about keeping an open mind toward my enemy's capabilities."

Luke laughed, then said, "I should have been more alert, especially since I *did* track you down to talk about our strategy."

Pellaeon nodded without looking away from the dome. "Go ahead."

"Thank you," Luke said. A burst of iridescent light flashed across the dome as the *Mon Mothma* and the *Elegos A'Kla* emerged from hyperspace and moved to either side of the *Megador*. "Our vessels appear to be deploying for an enveloping attack on the Colony fleet."

"We are." A hint of a smile appeared beneath Pellaeon's bushy mustache. "It's going to be a thing of beauty, Luke. The Killiks have absolutely no room to maneuver. We're going to smash them against the Chiss like, well . . . like bugs."

"Forgive me for spoiling your fun," Luke said. "But that's exactly what we *shouldn't* be doing."

"*What?*" Pellaeon tore his gaze away from the dome. "The Killiks might as well be dead already. They can't possibly escape us."

"Probably not," Luke agreed. "But we're not here to destroy an enemy fleet. We're here to stop this war."

"In my experience, they're one and the same," Pellaeon snapped.

"Yes, but your experience doesn't include Killiks." Luke's reply was blunt; he had to persuade the admiral to switch tactics *now*. Once the fleet started to deploy its fighter wings, changing battle objectives would become impossible. Not even Pellaeon was a good enough commander to recall several thousand starfighters, change formations, and continue the attack with any expectation of success. "Admiral, we have to concentrate our resources on retaking the *Admiral Ackbar* and neutralizing Raynar Thul."

Pellaeon arched his gray brows. "You know for a fact that Raynar is aboard the *Ackbar*?"

Luke nodded. "I'm certain. I feel it in the Force."

"Then you don't need an entire fleet to trap him," Pellaeon countered. "Admiral Bwua'tu's task force should be more than sufficient to support you."

"You're missing the point, Admiral," Luke said. "Destroying the Colony's fleet will delay the war, but it won't end it. The Killiks will only rebuild and be back with an even larger force next year."

"Then at least we will have bought ourselves some time." Pellaeon shook his head. "I'm not going to commit *everything* to neutralizing one man, Luke. If you fail—or if you're wrong, and removing Raynar *doesn't* cripple the Colony—we will have squandered the opportunity for a great victory."

"That's sound military doctrine, of course," Luke said. The *Mothma* and the *A'Kla* were now moving into shielding positions just ahead of the *Megador*. "But if you follow your plan, Raynar and Lomi Plo will defeat us—because we'll have lost sight of our true goals."

Pellaeon's eyes remained hard—perhaps even angry—but he did not interrupt.

"Let's assume I do neutralize Raynar and Lomi Plo without the fleet's full support," Luke continued, "and that you destroy the entire Killik fleet. Your strategy will only prolong the war."

"You're making no sense, Luke," Pellaeon retorted. "Without Raynar and Lomi Plo, the Killiks won't be *able* to rebuild their fleet. You've said yourself that neutralizing those two will destroy the Colony's ability to coordinate its nests. Are you telling me it won't?"

"I said removing Raynar would *eventually* destroy the Colony," Luke corrected. "And you're forgetting the Chiss. If you wipe out the Killik fleet here on Tenupe, what do you think the Chiss are going to do next?"

"Thank us," Pellaeon said. "Perhaps they'll finally believe that we're not siding with the Killiks."

"They'll know *that* if we focus on recapturing the *Ackbar* and neutralize Raynar and Lomi Plo," Luke said. "What they *won't* do is use that fleet down there to continue pressing the war against the Colony."

Pellaeon's eyes flashed in alarm; then he scowled and studied Luke as though they were meeting for the first time. Outside, the edges of the observation deck were laced with ion trails; the rest of the fleet was moving into attack formation.

Finally, Pellaeon spoke in a disbelieving voice. "Master Sky-walker, I do believe you're suggesting that we leave the Chiss fleet to its own resources."

Luke nodded. "It would be for the best," he said. "They were obviously willing to sacrifice much of it anyway."

"*Before* their parasite weapon was compromised," Pellaeon pointed out. The *Megador* had barely emerged from hyperspace before the *Falcon* had commed an update of the situation on Tenupe. "I suspect they're no longer eager to lull the Killiks into a false sense of security. This battle is going to be bloody."

"No doubt. But it might be wise to let the Chiss have a good taste of what the Killiks can do. Otherwise, the Ascendancy will continue pressing the war—they'll find another way to deploy their parasite weapon." Luke paused, then continued, "As excited as you are about this battle, I know you don't want speciecide on your conscience."

Pellaeon's eyes flashed, and Luke thought maybe he had gone too far.

Then the admiral sighed. "It isn't the killing, you know," he said. "It's the beauty of battles that I love—the choreography and the challenge of executing everything just right—and the challenge of matching your wits against a capable opponent."

Pellaeon's expression began to change from indignant to reluctant. "I guess I carry a little more Thrawn with me than I'd like to believe." He sighed again, then looked out toward Tenupe, now just as heavily blanketed with dartships as it was with green clouds. "The Chiss will lose a lot of ships, you know—and this is a dangerous part of the galaxy, even without the Colony."

"I know." Luke did not like the idea of abandoning so many Chiss to their fates, but the alternative would have meant *killing* even more Killiks. "The Ascendancy may have to rely more heavily on its friends for a while—and that will be good for the Alliance."

"Yes, I suppose it will be—provided they still consider us friends." Pellaeon stood staring out the dome for another moment, then sighed regretfully and turned toward the lift. "Come along, Master Skywalker. Before you join the boarding parties, I'll need a few minutes of your time in TacCon."

TWENTY-FOUR

The strength of the living Force in the jungle overwhelmed Leia's physical senses. Her ears hummed with its energy, her skin prickled beneath its warm pressure, even her vision had begun to cast the rain in a soft green glow. She found herself perceiving with her spirit rather than with her body, becoming a part of the jungle rather than a visitor to it.

Saba was reacting a little differently. She was creeping along the vine-swaddled mogo branches with all the stealth of a hungry rapard, barely stirring the thick foliage except when she suddenly fell on some hissing rodent or popped out of hiding to snatch a passing buzzbird.

Leia might have been bothered by the trail of death that her Master's predatory instinct was laying behind them had she not felt like half the jungle was trying to eat *her*. Through the Force, she could sense everything from tiny bloodbats to packs of Ewok-sized spiders—all of them on the hunt, stalking her through the canopy, watching and waiting for an opportunity to attack.

The prevalence of predators made Leia worry about Jaina and Zekk, who had gone down in their crippled StealthXs. She could feel them somewhere out there in this same ravening jungle, badly battered, but still alive, together, and apparently holed up in a safe place. They actually seemed more worried about Leia than she was about them, and they were pouring reassurance into the Force, encouraging Leia and Saba to deal with the parasite bombs first and them second.

That was easier said than done, of course. Han was doing his best to draw the enemy out of the area by flying top cover over a different part of the jungle, but it would not be long before the Chiss realized it was a ruse. Their sensor sweeps would eventually confirm that there was no metal—and therefore no bomb—in the area Han was protecting.

The soft beeps coming from Leia's scanner finally fused into a single long whine. She checked the display and saw that the metal signature she had been following for the last half hour was in the center of the small screen, indicating she was now on top of the source. She stopped and crouched down on the mossy mogo branch, her lightsaber in hand in case one of the predators stalking her decided to try its luck.

"Master Sebatyne," she called. "Perhaps you could tear yourself away from your fun?"

Saba popped out of a nearby bough, her mouth ringed by half a dozen bloody feathers.

"Do not be disapproving, Jedi Solo," she said. "This one can eat and search at the zame time. Who found Alema Rar'z StealthX?"

"You did, Master," Leia said.

Saba had found the starfighter hidden high in a mogo tree, camouflaged as a giant curtain of beard-moss and suspended nose-down with its rear landing struts carefully hung over a thick branch. They assumed that the Twi'lek was doing the same thing they were—trying to destroy the parasite bombs before the Chiss arrived to recover them—but it was not a task that either Master or student wished to entrust to someone else, especially not a Dark Nest Joiner.

"Have you checked your scanner recently?" Leia asked.

"Of course." Saba sneaked a look toward her utility belt, and her dorsal crest rose in surprise. She grinned sheepishly, then said, "This one was merely giving her student a chance to find the bombs first."

Allowing Leia no chance to challenge the statement, Saba leaned out of her hiding place and peered down into the jungle—then sissed in frustration. Leia clipped the scanner to her utility belt, then grabbed hold of an offshoot and leaned away from her own branch until she could see what Saba had found.

The defoliator's wing lay about twenty meters below, bent backward over a mogo branch. Both weapon mountings were empty, and the bombs were nowhere in sight.

"Bloah!" Leia yelled.

Her outburst sent a troop of long-armed monkey-lizards swinging away through the trees, screeching and hissing in alarm. Saba watched them go with a hungry leer, her long tongue flickering between her pebbly lips.

"*Focus,* Master," Leia urged. She pulled her scanner off her utility belt, then programmed it to ignore the wing and turned in a slow circle. She was about halfway around when the scanner began to beep again, and a contact-blip appeared at the top of the screen.

"Found something!" Leia reported.

"This one, too," Saba answered.

Leia glanced over her shoulder and saw Saba staring in the opposite direction.

"Of course—it would have been too much to ask that they fall *together,*" Leia complained. "We'll have to split up."

"It'z okay, Jedi Solo," Saba said. "This one is not afraid."

Sissing with laughter, Saba turned and Force-jumped down to an adjacent branch. Leia watched the Barabel vanish into the foliage, worried that perhaps she was absorbing more than Jedi wisdom from her Master. She actually understood the joke.

Leia took a bearing to her own contact, then selected a safe-looking branch to serve as her intermediate landing point and Force-leapt into the rain. She would much rather have used a repulsor pack, but Saba disdained technological "crutches" when the Force would do instead.

On the way down, a cold shiver of danger sense raced along Leia's spine, and she felt something hungry descending on her from above. The hiss of air rushing over wing scales began to rise behind her, and she rolled into a Force flip and ignited her lightsaber, bringing the blade up through the body of something huge, green, and musty smelling.

The snake-bird fell away in two pieces. Then Leia sensed her target branch coming up behind her—fast. She reached out to it in the Force and drew herself over to it, landing backward in the wet moss and nearly slipping off the branch.

Leia's danger sense continued to ripple.

She could hear a large river purling through the jungle somewhere far below, but she had no sense of where this new predator was hiding. She turned in a slow circle. When she saw nothing but clouds of emerald foliage, she reached out in the Force, but she felt only the same hunters as before. This danger was something different—something that could hide itself in the Force.

Leia stilled herself and began to search for an empty place in the gauzy fog of the living Force on Tenupe. It did not take long to find. There was an odd calm where her branch connected to the mogo's trunk, hidden behind a green curtain of strangle-vines. Still holding her lightsaber in one hand, she drew her blaster and began to fire into the vines.

The *snap-hiss* of an igniting lightsaber sounded from inside the mass of vines, then a blade so blue it was almost black sliced through the foliage and began to bat Leia's bolts aside. The tangle of vines quickly fell away, revealing a blue-skinned Twi'lek female with an amputated head-tail and one withered arm hanging useless beneath a sagging shoulder. She wore a StealthX flight suit two sizes too small for her slender figure, her front zipper open down to the navel.

Leia stopped firing and touched Saba through their battle-meld, trying to let her knew she had found something as important as the bombs. "Alema Rar. I should have known you'd crawl out of a hole around here somewhere."

Alema's unblinking eyes widened with anger, but she deactivated her lightsaber and bared her teeth in what looked more like an insect's threat display than a smile.

"Come now, Princess," Alema purred. "We are both here to destroy the bombs. Perhaps we should work together."

The Twi'lek's voice was so beguiling that Leia found herself thinking that Alema was not really such a bad girl; that anyone who had had such a hard life was entitled to make a few mistakes along the way. And besides, the suggestion *was* reasonable. The Dark Nest had even more reason than the Jedi to want those parasite bombs destroyed, and any time she and Alema spent fighting each other was time that would bring the Chiss closer to recovering them.

Then an image of Jaina and Zekk diving for the clouds in their battered StealthXs flashed through Leia's mind, and an icy knot of danger sense formed at the base of her skull. This was how Alema Rar—and probably the whole Dark Nest—worked, by offering the promise of something pleasant or reasonable to secure the target's cooperation. But in the end, it was the target who suffered—who played the decoy, or who had to stay and fight while the Twi'lek and the Dark Nest simply faded into the night.

"Thanks, but I'll pass," Leia said. "I've seen your kind of cooperation. It nearly got my daughter killed."

Alema gave a couple of throat-clicks, then said, "It was necessary for the good of the Colony. Jaina and Zekk understood that."

"They understand that you ran out on them," Leia countered. Now that she was alert to it, she could feel the Twi'lek trying to use the Force against her, to dampen her negative thoughts and bolster the positive ones. Fortunately, there *weren't* many positive ones. "And so do I."

"We had to destroy the bombs." Alema put a little urgency in her voice—and complemented it by pushing harder with the Force. "We still *have* to destroy the bombs."

"Okay," Leia said, deciding to switch tactics. She reached out in the Force, trying to make her own voice sound beguiling and reasonable. "I've never been one to hold a grudge. If you want to work together, Alema, just pass over your lightsaber and other weapons."

"Really?" Alema started to unbuckle her utility belt—then blinked both eyes in astonishment and let out a jagged little throat-rattle. "Nice try, Princess—but we don't think so."

"Good." Leia smiled, looking forward to the surprise she was about to visit upon the Twi'lek. "I was hoping you'd say that."

Leia charged, firing her blaster pistol with one hand and activating her lightsaber with the other. There was no question of giving Alema a chance to escape later by working with her now—even if it meant letting the Chiss recover the bomb. Eliminating the Dark Nest was the core of Luke's plan, and the Twi'lek was a big part of that nest.

Alema rushed to meet the attack, igniting her own lightsaber, wielding it with her one good arm and easily deflecting the stream of bolts. They met at a large burl where a smaller limb converged with its parent, their lightsabers coming together in a sizzle of sparks and color.

Leia jolted Alema with a one-handed power attack that hammered the Twi'lek's block down easily, then whipped her blade around in a buzzing backslash at a pulsing span of blue undefended throat. Alema dropped to her haunches and somehow snap-kicked from that impossible position, and Leia's middle exploded into pain.

The Princess exhaled hard, forcing the pain out, and did not yield a centimeter. She swept her blade down to attack the extended leg, but Alema had already drawn her foot back, and she ended up blocking the Twi'lek's blade as it came sizzling in at her knees.

Leia rolled her wrist and sent Alema's lightsaber flying, then brought her blaster pistol around and allowed herself a small smirk as she opened fire.

It was too soon to gloat.

Alema was already twisting away and launching herself backward in the air, her handed extended to recall her falling lightsaber. A pair of bolts burned past the Twi'lek's legs—so close that her flight suit began to smoke—but she rolled into an evasive Force tumble and landed unscathed on the adjacent branch . . . and slipped. She inhaled sharply and started to fall, then hooked the back of her knee over the branch and caught herself.

Leia fired at the knee, but Alema was already swinging around, facing her, deep blue lightsaber in hand, batting blaster bolts straight back at her. Leia stopped firing. The Twi'lek slipped back into the branch moss in a seated position, then brought her leg up and stretched it along the branch, staring at her boot.

Leia's earlier slash had not missed after all. The front half of Alema's boot was missing—along with half her foot. The Twi'lek turned toward Leia, her unblinking eyes wide in astonishment and anger, and that was when Leia's comlink earpiece crackled to life.

"How's it going down there?" Han asked.

"Busy!" Leia said into her throat mike.

"Any sign of the bombs?" Han pressed.

"Not really."

Leia watched in alarm as Alema rose and peered over the branch behind her—no doubt plotting an escape route.

"Gotta go," Leia said. "I'm sort of in the middle of something."

Determined not to let her prey escape, Leia Force-jumped from her branch toward Alema's.

The Twi'lek's withered arm swung up, reaching toward Leia. The princess tucked into an evasive somersault—then felt herself rolling the wrong way as her feet were Force-jerked in the opposite direction. She called on the Force to stop her rotation, but by then the back of her head was *thonk*ing into the side of the branch.

The moss was not as thick on the sides of the branches. The sound echoed inside her skull so hard that Leia thought she would never hear anything else. Then she felt her feet whipping down from above and sensed the darkness rising up to swallow hers and she knew she had come to one of those terrible instants when everything depended on willpower and the stubborn desire to live.

Fortunately, Saba had prepared her well for such moments. Leia found her arms lashing out behind her, one elbow hooking over the branch to stop her fall. Everything remained dark, but she knew she had to keep fighting, to keep her enemy . . . whoever that was—she was having trouble remembering . . . at bay.

Leia felt the blaster pistol in one hand and her lightsaber in the other . . . another of Saba's lessons ringing inside her head, never, *never* drop your weapon, *die* with your weapon sssstill in your hand . . . and Leia started to fire the blaster, pointing it down the branch where the trouble—who was it again?—seemed to lie.

A familiar voice sounded in her ear. "Hey, that sounds like blasterfire!"

Han.

"Yeah . . . it is." Leia started to recall the situation—a jungle, a Twi'lek, a fight—Alema Rar. "Now be quiet!"

Leia shook her head—*big mistake*—then whipped her leg up over the branch, still firing. The darkness faded from her eyes, but her blaster bolts were snaking toward their target in slow motion, while the target—a shimmering blue mirage that seemed to have three heads and six arms—was limping toward her behind a lightsaber moving so fast that it seemed to be weaving a shield of solid light.

Then one of the six blue arms moved. Leia's blaster flew from her own hand and vanished into the billowing greenness of the out-of-focus jungle.

The fight was not going exactly as planned.

Saba always said that planning would be Leia's downfall; that she planned too much and felt too little. She had also said that a shenbit always saves its deepest bite for last.

Leia pushed off the mossy branch and brought her feet up beneath her. The Princess had never met a shenbit, but Saba usually uttered the saying in sparring practice, right before she drove her student into the deck with a flurry of power strikes. Leia began to advance on her three-headed, six-armed opponent, weaving her blade through the frenzied slash-slice-and-rip of a Barabel rage attack.

To Leia's astonishment, the three-headed enemy suddenly stopped advancing, then began to retreat.

"Wait! This is silly!" Again, that beguiling voice and that furtive Force-touch, trying to dampen the negative thoughts and bolster the positive ones. Alema pointed her lightsaber over the side of the branch. "The bomb is right down there."

Leia stopped advancing—more to give her eyes a chance to bring her enemy into focus than because she was considering the offer—and glanced down. There *did* seem to be a big silver blur lying in a bed of green.

"It would be a shame to let the Chiss recover it," Alema said. "Can't we strike a truce long enough to destroy it—*then* finish killing each other?"

Leia pretended to consider the offer while her vision finished clearing, then—when Alema's extra heads and arms disappeared—she shook her own head.

"Let's do it now."

Leia started forward . . . and instantly regretted her decision when the branch bounced and nearly buckled her knees. She noticed it sagging beneath her weight and realized she was farther out on the end than she had perceived in her foggy-headed state. It was a mistake that would cost her dearly. With such unreliable footing, the Princess would be even worse off than her half-footed foe.

Alema was quick to press her advantage, hobbling forward to attack, launching a flurry of strike and Force-push combinations that drove Leia back even farther toward the tip of the bouncing branch. The Princess parried, but her reactions had been slowed by her head blow, and she had to retreat yet another step. She Force-shoved at Alema's knee, but the nimble Twi'lek—who had spent her youth dancing in the ryll dens of Kala'uun—simply lifted her bad foot and pirouetted forward on the good one, driving Leia back another, even longer step.

The branch sagged so precariously that the Princess had to Force-stick herself in place.

"Hey, those sound like lightsabers!" Han observed over Leia's earpiece.

"They *are*!" Leia growled. "Can you *just* hold on?"

Now the branch was bouncing even when the Princess wasn't moving, and her danger sense was covering her back with goose bumps. Had Alema launched a power attack—even a weak one— Leia's only choice would have been to drop off the branch and hope she could catch another one with the Force on the way down. Instead, the Twi'lek seemed content merely to hold the Princess in place with defensive swordplay.

Then comprehension finally burned its way through the concussion fog inside Leia's head. The danger she was sensing had nothing to do with Alema. A predator had landed behind her . . . something large enough to weigh down a limb the size of her thigh.

Alema smiled. "Dinnertime, Princess."

Leia's blood began to burn with a very Barabel-like rage. She would *not* die at the hands of some Twi'lek dancing girl—or at the claws of some jungle flunky. She went on the attack, forgeting her slow reactions and foggy head and uneven footing, and let the battle take her—let her lightsaber block and slash and stab of its own accord, let her feet dance back and forth over the bouncing limb.

Alema came at her just as strongly, kicking with her half foot, stretching out for long lightsaber lunges, pushing constantly through the Force—steadily driving Leia back toward the hungry presence that she could now sense coming up behind her.

Then a wisp of hot breath brushed the back of Leia's neck, and she knew it was time. The Princess tried a throat slash and swung wide, deliberately leaving herself open for a heart thrust. Never having been one to resist temptation, Alema could not help lunging for the kill.

Leia had already flexed her knees and was springing off the sagging branch, bringing her feet up over her head in an open Force flip. She saw the Twi'lek stretched out below her, not quite off balance— but not far from it—her neck craned back as she watched her target fly overhead.

Leia brought her lightsaber down, striking for the head. Alema could only whip her lightsaber up in a desperate block. The blades clashed in a growling shower of sparks and light, then the Princess was swinging down behind her, twisting around to plant one foot between the Twi'lek's shoulders and send her stumbling toward the shaggy mass that had been creeping up behind Leia.

There was no time to tell what kind of creature the thing was. All Leia saw was something the size of a bantha taking Alema's sword arm in its jaws. The Twi'lek screamed in pain; then four spiky pedipalps emerged from the side of the creature's mouth and began to feed her in.

Alema's legs were still outside, kicking wildly, when Leia felt the thing's attention fall on her and noticed six beady eyes peering out from beneath the mossy scales that covered its head. Before it could spring, the Princess brought her lightsaber down, cutting the branch away at her feet.

Instead of plummeting toward the jungle floor, the creature swung outward, hanging suspended by a thick, ropy tail that ascended more than ten meters to a branch above. It was even larger than Leia had first imagined, with a long slug-like body that had dozens of tiny feet wriggling on the underside. Alema remained in its mouth, kicking her feet and presumably screaming into its throat. Leia locked her lightsaber blade in the on position, then used the Force to send it spinning through the tail.

The predator—whatever it was—did not open its mouth or roar in pain. It simply plummeted groundward, filling the jungle with a terrific banging and cracking as it crashed through the mogo boughs, then finally splashed into the dark river below.

Leia called her lightsaber back to her hand, and had barely switched it off before Han's voice came over her earpiece again.

"Leia?"

"Don't worry, Han," she said. "I'm still here."

"That's good." Han sounded more impatient than relieved—or even surprised. "But about those bombs . . . you'd better hurry. The Chiss' scanners must have picked something up from that fight you and Saba were having, because you've got a bunch of clawcraft headed your way."

"Great." Leia sighed. "Can't a girl catch her breath?"

Still feeling a little unsteady from her fight—especially the head blow—Leia peered over the side of the branch toward the silver blur she had glimpsed earlier.

The blur was gone, and in place of the bough upon which it had been resting, there was only the jagged stub of a broken limb.

"Bloah!" Leia cursed. She snatched the scanner off her utility belt and found a very weak signal down at ground level, slowly moving away. "It's in the river!"

A loud sissing sounded behind her, and Leia looked back to see Saba standing near the mogo trunk, studying her own scanner and holding a thermal detonator in her hand.

"Nothing *ever* goes according to plan, does it?" the Barabel asked. "This one does not know why you bother with planz at all."

"It's a human thing, I guess," Leia said. "Did you destroy the other bomb?"

"Of course," the Barabel replied. "Not all of us were wasting our time fighting bughuggerz and knocking ourselvez in the head. The parasite bomb is destroyed."

"Then what are you doing just standing there?" Leia demanded.

"This one has been watching." Saba displayed her entire set of fangs. "She is very proud."

"*Proud?*" Leia cried. "I could've been killed!"

"No." Saba shook her head. "This one taught you too well."

Leia felt her jaw drop. "Is that a compliment, Master Sebatyne?"

"Yez." Saba thumped her hand against her chest. "This one did very well, given the material she had to work with."

"Gee, that's swell," Han said in Leia's earpiece. "But if you two can break up the mutual-admiration meeting for just a minute, what about that second bomb?"

"No problem." Leia checked her scanner again. The signal had moved perhaps fifty meters in the last few seconds, but it had grown so weak that she could barely find it anymore. "Blast—now it's sinking."

"Yez, that is what happenz when you drop something heavy in the river," Saba said. She activated her thermal detonator, then tossed it in the direction of the bomb and used the Force to guide it to the fading blip on their scanners. "You will have to be more careful next time, Jedi Solo."

The blip faded from the scanner. The tiny *bloop* of something small entering the water sounded from the same direction; then the sharp *wooosh* of an underwater detonation rose up through the trees.

"Did you get it?" Han asked.

Leia checked her scanner. There was still no blip on the screen. "Let's say we did—because even if we didn't, the Chiss will never find it, either." She motioned Saba to start climbing. "Let's go—it's time to go get my daughter."

TWENTY-FIVE

The interior of *Stomper One* filled with soft whirrings and electronic chirpings as the assault shuttle's passengers began their final systems checks. Each soldier worked his servomotors and confirmed the calibration of his targeting systems with two adjacent units, then executed a quick comm scan to be certain he was receiving on all channels. Because this platoon was assigned directly to the assault commander—Jedi Grand Master Luke Skywalker—they all performed a vocabulator check as well. The phrase "check sound, check Basic" reverberated through the passenger cabin thirty-two times—always in the ultradeep, ultramale version of Lando Calrissian's voice, which remained the standard for the entire line of YVH combat droids.

Sitting behind the controls of the assault shuttle, Luke found the mechanical symphony strangely isolating. As the sole biological unit in the assault brigade, he had already felt a bit out of place, and the stark efficiency of his YVH 5-S Bugcrunchers left him feeling more alone than he cared to admit. The droids would perform as well as— if not better than—living beings, but there was nothing like a little laughter to calm a soldier's nerves before combat.

As soon as the YVHs had finished their vocabulator checks, they began to spray vacuum-resistant lubricant into one another's joints. The whole assault shuttle was quickly filled with an oily-sweet odor that gave Luke watery eyes and a queasy stomach. He had never expected to miss the smell of another soldier's sweat quite so much.

The gravelly voice of the *Megador*'s Tactical Control officer came over the flight-deck speaker. "Task Force Stomper cleared for assault.

Be advised: Colony capital ships and dartship swarms attempting to return to support *Ackbar*. Time of breakthrough uncertain."

"Acknowledged."

Luke did not bother to check his tactical display for a tally of the enemy vessels—the number was going to be high, and it did not matter. In fifteen minutes, he would either be aboard the *Ackbar* fighting Raynar, or the eternal war that Jacen had foreseen would be erupting into full blossom.

Luke sealed his vacuum suit, then transmitted the attack order to the other fifty assault shuttles in his all-droid brigade and pushed his own throttles forward.

"Stomper in," he reported to the *Megador*.

"Good hunting, my friend." This voice belonged to Pellaeon. "And may the Force be with you."

Luke thanked the admiral for the good wishes and promised that his faith in the Jedi plan was not misplaced, then turned his attention to the assault.

The *Admiral Ackbar* lay only ten kilometers ahead, her bump-nosed silhouette surrounded by a swirling shell of Killik dartships that were rapidly being vaporized by Alliance turbolaser strikes. Her main engines lit space as she struggled to retreat toward Tenupe, but she was ensnared by the heavy-duty tractor-beams of half a dozen "piratenabber" Star Destroyers identical to herself.

Raynar would have been much wiser to send his fighter screen out to counterattack his captors, but he appeared to be holding the dartships back to deal with Task Force Stomper. That was what Admiral Bwua'tu had predicted he would do, and so far the Bothan seemed correct.

Beyond the *Ackbar,* dozens of what Luke thought of as *Shard*-class capital ships were abandoning the battle on Tenupe to rush to Raynar's aid. Somewhat chunky and conical, they ranged in length from a kilometer and a half to nearly ten, but each had one broad, rounded end and several jagged sides. It almost appeared that the strange flotilla had been constructed by shattering an asteroid or a small moon. Judging by the halo of dispersion flashes and fiery streaks around the vessels, each was also very well shielded and heavily armed.

The Battle of Tenupe itself continued to rage, a flashing red stain that now spread across a quarter of the planet. Most of the Chiss fleet was down in the clouds and hidden from sight, but some of the Colony's larger ships were silhouetted against the flickering brilliance below. The four nest ships that had escaped the Jedi at the

Murgo Choke were clustered near the heart of the battle, pouring a terrible rain of fire down upon the planet from one side of their hulls while the other hurled turbolaser potshots at the Alliance.

What impressed Luke most was the Killiks' inventiveness in completing their fleet. Arrayed around the edges of the battle were dozens of ancient megafreighters, their distinctive ring shapes surrounded by dark, swirling clouds that suggested the freighters were serving as staging areas for dartship swarms. Meanwhile hundreds of smaller vessels, visible to the naked eyed as triangular specks, were flitting around the center of the fight in erratic flight patterns, each pouring fire down from a single turbolaser. Chiss megamasers were blasting the gnat-like targets out of orbit whenever their gunnery crews could get a target-lock, but it would clearly take a while to exterminate them completely.

The *Ackbar*'s shields began to flicker with overload discharge, then collapsed in a string of bright, colorful flashes.

Control's voice came over the speaker in Luke's helmet. "Target is shields down. All main batteries switch to formation defense, all squadrons released for strafing runs."

The order had little to do with Task Force Stomper, but Luke was glad Control had included his channel in the transmission array. The sound of a nonelectronic voice reminded him that he was not attacking the *Ackbar* alone, that he and his bugcrunchers were merely the tip of a spear being driven by an entire attack fleet.

The Alliance batteries quickly obeyed Control's order and switched fire to the approaching Shard flotilla. The fighter squadrons left the safe stations where they had been waiting out the turboblaster exchange and streaked in to attack, painting whole swaths of space blue with their engine efflux. The *Ackbar*'s close-range cannons weaved a web of laser bolts in their paths, and the Colony's dartships drew back, creating an even tighter shell around the beleaguered Star Destroyer.

Bad mistake.

Bwua'tu had predicted the tactic. The Alliance fighter squadrons blew through the shell behind a flurry of proton torpedoes, then fell on the *Ackbar* like a thousand hawkbats, strafing her weapons turrets and clearing the way for Task Force Stomper.

A squadron and a half of starfighters—the eighteen craft that had been in the maintenance bays when the Killiks captured the *Ackbar*—dropped out of the hangar bay and turned to meet Luke's assault shuttles. Bwua'tu had predicted that, too. Rogue Squadron slashed in from its escort station and eliminated the interceptors in three fiery passes.

By then, Task Force Stomper had closed to within three kilometers of the *Ackbar,* with only the dartships to prevent them from reaching their target. The swarm peeled away from its combat with the starfighter squadrons and came after the assault shuttles.

Exactly as Bwua'tu had expected.

One of the Alliance's pirate-nabber Star Destroyers slid its tractor beam over and simply pulled the dartships away in a tumbling mass. Nothing remained between Task Force Stomper and its target but a thousand meters of laser-laced space. Every second or so, a blossom of color would flare somewhere in the task force as an *Ackbar* cannon bolt dissipated against a shuttle's shields or a stray dartship was destroyed by a YVH gunner. But for the most part, the starfighter squadrons and the pirate-nabber tractor beam did a remarkable job of deflecting the Killik attacks.

Luke activated his task force command channel. "We're on our own now. Fan out and get in fast."

Instead of acknowledgments, he was greeted by a static-filled pause precisely 1.2 seconds long—the standard delay a YVH droid allowed for a biological unit to finish an incomplete thought.

Then an ultradeep Lando Calrissian voice said, "Sir, 'fan out and get in fast' is not a clear order."

"Sorry." Luke sighed, wishing there had been room to add basic soft-logic interpretation to the YVH processing unit. "Disperse to assigned zones and penetrate target hull."

"Stomper Two acknowledging," the platoon's droid leader responded.

"Stomper Three acknowledging."

A long series of deep-voiced acknowledgments began to sound inside Luke's helmet—forty-nine other platoons in all. He passed the time by reminding himself that the bugcruncher brigade would prove well worth the irritation once Task Force Stomper entered the *Ackbar.* They were better armored and far more deadly than living commandos, and they would be immune to the Force-based influence attacks of Raynar Thul and Lomi Plo.

The assault shuttles were just beginning to fan out when one of them suddenly flew apart. There was no flash or fireball. The passenger cabin simply came apart at the seams, spilling its cargo of bugcrunchers out into the void.

As Luke was checking his tactical display to find the shuttle's number, another one came apart.

He frowned and opened a channel to the pilots. "Stomper Twelve, what happened to your shuttle?"

The reply came in the electronic tones of a voice synthesizer, since Stomper Twelve's pilot was currently floating through a vacuum and unable to produce any sounds with his own vocabulator. "It disintegrated."

"I can *see* that!" Luke said. "What caused . . ."

Luke let the question trail off when he suddenly felt the Force drawing in around him, as though gathering itself for a powerful, violent release. He had just enough time to create a bubble of counterpressure around himself before every damage alarm on his control panel came to life. The cockpit simply came apart around him, and he found himself tumbling through space in the midst of a flotsam cloud.

Raynar Thul.

An electronic voice sounded inside Luke's helmet. "Sir, if you were asking a question—"

"Disregard," Luke ordered.

Another assault shuttle came apart, spilling another platoon of thirty-two bugcrunchers into space. *This* was not an attack Bwua'tu had expected—but that hardly mattered, because the Bothan *always* planned for what he could not foresee. He had been the one who had insisted that the Alliance specify space-assault YVHs as the platform when it purchased its new Bugcruncher Brigade.

Luke opened a brigadewide channel. "All dismounted Stomper units continue toward original target zones under individual propulsion."

Again came the long string of acknowledgments. Luke used the Force to hitch a ride on a passing droid as his own platoon fired their thrusters and weaved through a blinding tangle of laser bolts, zipping starfighters, and rocket exhaust toward their target zone. They lost two units to lucky cannon strikes and three more to ramming dartships, but the Alliance starfighters were doing a good job of suppressing the enemy defenses, and Stomper One reached the *Ackbar*'s bridge in good order and with more than enough strength to perform their mission.

By then, much of the rest of the brigade had also reached the Star Destroyer and were dutifully reporting their successes as they breached the hull. The entire vessel had been declared a free-fire zone, so Luke really did not need to know more. He released the platoons to their own initiative and told them to report when they had taken their objectives.

Luke reached out in the Force and found Raynar reaching back, descending rapidly from the command deck atop the bridge structure. Raynar's presence was as murky and heavy as always, and as soon as Luke felt it, it began to press down inside, urging him to turn back.

Luke did not resist. He was *going* to leave, he *wanted* to leave . . . with Raynar. Luke began to exert his own will, pulling Raynar toward him, using Raynar's own power against him by binding their presences together with memories from their past: of how Luke had once helped protect Raynar's family from the Diversity Alliance, and how he had later helped Raynar's father destroy a terrible virus that could have caused a galaxywide plague. They were going to leave *together*. UnuThul wished Luke to go, Luke wished UnuThul to go with him, and so they would go together. *UnuThul* wished it.

The weight inside suddenly diminished as Raynar started to retreat. Luke tried to stop him, to find some part of his former student that he could hold on to. But UnuThul still had the power of the Colony behind him, and he called on that power to break the bonds of remembrance the Jedi Master had so quickly woven. His murky presence wrenched free, and the heaviness vanished from inside Luke's chest.

Stomper One and his assistant had already finished placing the breaching charges. The rest of the platoon was arrayed around Luke on the *Ackbar*'s hull, shielding him with their hulking bodies and firing their forearm-mounted blaster cannons at a flight of incoming dartships. Luke could see tiny divots forming in the droids' laminanium body armor as the enemy's weapons silently made their mark.

"What are you waiting for?" Luke commed Stomper One. "Detonate!"

But when it came to procedure, even war droids could not be hurried. "Stay clear!" Stomper One commed. "Fire in the hole!"

Then he detonated the charge.

Luke's faceplate darkened against the brilliance of the blast, but not so completely that he missed the flash of Stomper One's blaster cannons firing into the breached hull.

Then Stomper One pronounced, "Clear!" and began ordering, "Go . . . go . . . go . . ." at one-second intervals, sending a bug-cruncher through the hole with each command.

By the fourth *go*, Luke's faceplate had returned to its normal tint, and he could see a steady stream of captured food containers, membrosia waxes, and chunks of spitcrete gushing out the breach into space.

"Grand Master Commander?" the lead droid asked.

"Thanks."

Luke ducked through the hole into the interior of what had once been the junior officers' mess. The lights remained on, so he could see that the chairs that had once been bolted into place along the tables had been removed by the Killiks. The far half of the room had been converted to a nursery, and the larvae were lying half out of their cells, writhing in pain from the decompression blow. Membrosia waxes and Alliance foodstuffs were still tumbling out of their lockers—or rising out of spitcrete bins—and flying out the breach with the cabin's air.

Raynar's heavy presence returned, this time *summoning* Luke.

The Jedi Master started toward the interior exit, where the first bugcrunchers were already trying to override the decompression safety and open the hatch. He was happy to go to Raynar. Again, Luke exerted his own will through the Force, incorporating UnuThul's wishes, but turning them toward his own ends. He recalled his dinner with Aryn Thul, when she and Tyko had asked Luke to spare her son's life. It was time to stop the killing, to end this war, and the Jedi Master would gladly go to Raynar to accept his surrender. UnuThul wished Luke to come, and Luke wished to end the war, and so Luke would come and accept the Colony's surrender.

Again, Raynar withdrew, this time so violently that Luke had no chance to prevent it. UnuThul was coming—not *to* Luke, but *after* him. The Master would have to fight. He had known it would come to this, but knowing did not make his heart any less heavy.

The interior hatch finally irised open, and the decompression blow brought half a dozen Killiks tumbling out. The bugcrunchers opened fire with their blaster cannons, shattering the tough pressure carapaces before the bugs could react, then pushed through the doorway with weapons still blazing. By the time the fourth droid had gone through, a synthesized voice was already sounding the all-clear inside Luke's helmet.

Luke stepped through the hatchway and found himself in a narrow corridor littered with dead Killiks and pieces of shattered carapace. A closed hatchway sealed either end of the short passage. Two confused boxy little mouse droids were trying to make their way through the debris, determined to complete some errand that no longer mattered. A row of sealed hatches lined the opposite wall, which—if Luke recalled the *Ackbar*'s bridge schematic correctly—concealed storage lockers, officers' lounges, and exercise facilities. Each was a dead end, as well as a potential hiding place for ambushers.

The corridor was hardly the ideal place for a lightsaber duel, but it would have to do. Luke could already sense a furious Raynar Thul at the far end of the passage, using his brute Force-strength to wrest open the safety-sealed hatch.

As soon as the last of his platoon had entered the corridor, Luke pointed to the hatch through which they'd come. "Make that hatch airtight."

"Airtight, sir?" Stomper One asked. "Are you certain? As S-series droids, we enjoy a significant tactical advantage in a nonpressurized environment."

"But *I* don't." Luke plucked at the sleeve of his vac suit. "And I don't want to worry about ripping this. The fight is about to get rough."

"Rough?" Stomper One looked up and down the corridor, appraising their position and apparently reaching the same conclusion that Luke had: the corridor was a bad place for a firefight. "As you wish, sir."

The droids quickly went to work, sealing the hatch to the officers' mess and using their blaster cannons to spotweld the others closed so the platoon could not be ambushed. When Luke noticed they were leaving the hatch directly behind them open, he pointed to it.

"Fix that hatch, too." He started up the corridor toward the hatch at the far end. "We won't be retreating."

Stomper One's synthesized voice assumed a note of approval. "Very good, sir."

Luke felt the Force stir as Raynar made a final exertion. "They're coming. Prepare for—"

The far hatch suddenly ruptured inward, bringing with it a short-lived decompression squall that rocked Luke back on his heels and hazed the corridor with airborne dust. He glimpsed a tall figure in a black pressure suit.

Then the figure flicked one of his hands, and Luke found himself flying backward, bouncing off YVH droids and tumbling out of control. He reached out in the Force, grabbing at passing hatches, the ceiling, even Raynar himself, but he was whirling too fast to catch hold of anything.

He hit the end of the corridor with a tremendous *clung,* unsure whether he was upside down or sideways, then crashed to the floor struggling to remain conscious.

By the time his eyes came back into focus, the corridor had erupted into a crashing storm of cannon bolts and shatter gun pellets. The lower two-thirds of the corridor was blocked by a wall of laminanium bugcruncher armor, but the upper third of the passage belonged to Raynar's Killiks. Still in their pressure carapaces, they were scurrying through the smoke along the walls and ceiling, pouring shatter gun pellets down on the droids' heads, trying to get past so they could launch an attack from the rear.

Luke rolled to his feet . . . and watched in astonishment as his helmet dropped to the floor in two pieces. He glanced at the wall behind him and saw a fist-deep depression where its impact had dented the durasteel.

"Can't let him do *that* again," Luke groaned. He opened the seals on his vac suit gloves, shook them to the floor, and snatched the lightsaber off his belt. Then he averted his eyes and spoke into his throat mike. "Dazers!"

The corridor erupted in rainbow iridescence; then a piercing squeal came over Luke's earpiece and the smell of ripe hubba gourds filled his nostrils. Stunned by the Dazers' aura-deadening properties, several Killiks dropped off the ceiling into the midst of the bugcrunchers. The rest of the insects were soon spread overhead in yellow smears.

Luke had already rushed forward, only to find himself trapped behind his own bugcrunchers and unable to see the rest of the battle. "Make a hole!" he ordered. "Coming through."

Three bugcrunchers blocking his way obediently stepped aside, and Luke found himself staring up ten meters of corridor packed chest-high with Killik corpses and twisted YVH frames. At the other end, with his black helmet lying in a melted gob before him and the fingers of his vac suit gloves burned off by all the Force energy he had been throwing around, stood Luke's melt-faced opponent. Raynar Thul.

Luke jumped onto the pile of chitin and metal in front of him. Two of Raynar's Unu bodyguards immediately popped up and sent a burst of shatter gun pellets zipping down the corridor toward him.

Luke flicked his hand and Force-batted the projectiles into a wall, then the bugcrunchers at his back sent a stream of cannon fire down the hall. Raynar ignited a gold lightsaber and deflected most of the volley, but a few of the bolts made it through and splattered his bodyguards across the walls.

"It's not too late to surrender." Luke started forward at a walk. "I'm not eager to do this."

Raynar's burn-scarred lips twitched in a faint hint of a smile. "*We* are."

Raynar raised his lightsaber and jumped onto the carnage heap.

Luke ignited his own blade and raced forward, using the Force to keep himself from stumbling over debris. A loud crunching erupted behind him as his surviving droids raced after him, then half a dozen of Raynar's bodyguards leapt up from the other end of the pile and started forward, firing shatter guns with their lower set of arms and carrying flame tridents with their upper pair.

A flurry of cannon bolts zipped past Luke from behind and took out three insects. Raynar pointed at the attacking droids. A muffled thump erupted inside one of them, and it went down in a sizzling, popping crash of laminanium. Luke killed the last of Raynar's bodyguards by Forceslamming them into the wall so hard their thoraxes burst, then the two Jedi were on one another, their lightsabers flashing toward each other's heads with all the speed and might they could summon.

That was the trouble with powerful men—especially younger ones. Awed by their own strength, they so often believed strength was the answer to every problem. Luke was older and wiser. While Raynar swung, he pivoted.

As Raynar's gold blade sliced the air where Luke's head had been, Luke's boot was kicking him behind the ankles, knocking his legs out from under him and stretching him out flat.

But Raynar was a Jedi, and all Jedi were quick. He caught himself in the Force, levitating himself just long enough to bring his golden blade sweeping in at Luke's shoulder.

Luke had no choice but to block with his blade, and no place to block but the forearm. Raynar's lightsaber went spinning off, still securely in the grasp of his three-fingered hand, and caught one of Luke's bugcrunchers squarely in the back. The weapon sliced through six centimeters of laminanium armor before the severed forearm flew free. The blade deactivated, and the hilt disappeared into the tangle of death and destruction at the droid's feet.

The pain of losing an arm might have forced a common Jedi to stop fighting, but Raynar was no common Jedi. He had the Force potential of the Colony to draw on, and he did that now, swinging his remaining hand up to hurl Luke down the corridor as he had done before.

But this time, Luke was ready. He placed his own hand in front of Raynar's and rooted himself in the heart of the Force, and when he did that, he became the very essence of the immovable object. Nothing could dislodge him—not one of Lando's asteroid tuggers, not the *Megador*'s sixteen ion engines, not the black hole at the center of the galaxy itself.

Luke stood that way, waiting, dimly aware that his surviving bugcrunchers were moving into defensive positions, one at his back and the other just inside the burst hatch. Raynar continued to struggle, trying to hurl Luke down the corridor, trying to move him a single centimeter.

Luke did not budge, and finally Raynar stopped struggling and met his eyes with a stunned and anguished gaze.

The Master sighed and shook his head. "What am I going to do with you, Raynar Thul?" he asked. "You learn nothing from your mistakes."

Luke deactivated his lightsaber and picked Raynar up by the collar and slammed him against the wall. He used the Force to pin him there, waiting for an answer to his question, watching as the expression in his captive's pained eyes turned from astonishment to anger to calculation.

But when Raynar's free hand rose, it was not to summon the Force lightning that Luke had expected. It was to call his lightsaber back, to attempt to continue the battle that he obviously could no longer win.

It was in that moment that Luke finally decided that the life of Raynar Thul would be spared. He intercepted the weapon and used the Force to pin Raynar's remaining arm against the wall along with the rest of his body. Then he opened the hilt of the captured lightsaber and removed the focusing crystal. He held it up in front of Raynar.

"Someday I may return this—but for now, it's staying with me." He zipped the gem into a pocket of his vac suit, then reached out to Raynar in the Force and spoke in a softer voice. "Your days as UnuThul are done, Raynar. It's time to surrender and come home."

The eyes beneath Raynar's lumpy brow flashed with alarm. "The Colony *is* our home."

Luke shook his head. "That can't be anymore, Raynar," he said. "The *Colony* can't be anymore. If you stay with the Killiks, the entire species will die."

Raynar curled his scarred lip. "Lies."

"No." Luke touched Raynar through the Force. "You're still a Jedi. You can sense when a person is telling the truth. You can sense it in me, *now*."

Hoping to force his Will on his captor, Raynar accepted the contact—as Luke had known he would—then gasped in astonishment as he sensed the truth in what Luke was saying. *"How?"*

"Because as long as you are the Prime Unu, Lomi Plo will be the queen of the Gorog." Luke began to press, as though he were trying to force *his* will on Raynar. "And as long as there is a Gorog, the Colony will be a threat to the Chiss."

Raynar began to pull, learning from Luke's earlier tactics and trying to use Luke's own attack against *him*. "The Chiss are a *threat* to the Colony."

Luke went along with Raynar—in fact, he pushed even harder.

"That's right. The Chiss are a threat to the Colony," Luke said. "They have developed a weapon that can wipe out the entire Colony. They tried to use it here. Jaina and Zekk stopped them . . . but we both know they have more."

Backed by Luke's strength, the truth was too much for Raynar. His Will broke, and his resolve turned to panic. "We know," he admitted.

Luke continued to push. "And they'll use it—if you stay with the Colony."

Raynar shook his head. "We can't let them."

"Then you have to leave," Luke said. "It's the only way to save the Killiks."

A terrible sadness came to Raynar's melted face. He lowered his burned eyelids and reluctantly began to nod—then suddenly stopped and glanced toward the hatch through which he had burst earlier.

"Not the *only* way." Raynar's voice assumed a dark tone, and Luke knew his true target was finally preparing to show herself. "Maybe there is a weapon to kill the *Chiss*?"

Luke resisted the temptation to look toward the hatch. Lomi Plo would not show herself if she knew she was expected.

"Even if there was such a weapon, it wouldn't be right to use it," Luke said. "The Jedi won't permit speciecide against the Chiss—any more than we would against the Killiks."

"But you could . . . if it was self-defense." Raynar bared his jagged teeth in a try at a grin. "Destroying the Chiss would be self-defense, so you would *have* to permit it."

Raynar began to push back now, filling Luke's chest with the dark weight of UnuThul's Will.

"If it *were* self-defense, we might have to permit it," Luke said, playing along—and again using Raynar's own attack against him. "But even that wouldn't save the Colony. It cannot survive as it is. We know that."

"*How* do we know that?" Raynar demanded angrily. "We know no such thing."

"We *might*," Luke insisted, exerting his own will through the Force again, reeling Raynar in. "If the Colony grew too large, it would devour its own worlds and destroy *itself*."

"There are always more worlds," Raynar countered.

"Not always," Luke said. "Sometimes all of the other worlds are taken. That *could* have been what happened when the Killiks disappeared from Alderaan." He paused, then used the Force to pull as hard as he could, trying to draw Raynar into his own view of reality. "In fact, I'm *sure* that's what happened on Alderaan. The Killiks devoured their own world and tried to take someone else's. That's the reason the Celestials drove the Killiks into the Unknown Regions."

The fight finally went out of Raynar. "You're *sure*?" He folded his cauterized forearm stump across his stomach and cradled it with his other arm, his lips quivering in pain and tears welling in his eyes. "You know—"

The question was drowned out by the roar of a blaster cannon, and Luke glanced down the corridor to see the bugcruncher stationed there suddenly powering down. The droid fell out of the opening backward and crashed to the deck, then Lomi Plo scuttled through the hatchway on her mismatched set of legs—one human, the other insectile. She turned her bulbous eyes and noseless face down the corridor, then extended her crooked upper arms toward the lightsaber in Luke's hands.

The last remaining bugcruncher opened fire, forcing Lomi Plo to ignite the lightsaber in her lower set of hands. Her blocks and parries came so slowly that she was barely able to deflect the cannon bolts and she was forced to swing her upper arms toward the droid and drain its power. Raynar, thankfully, continued to stand dazed—and seemingly impotent.

Determined to reach Lomi Plo before she drained his lightsaber's power cell, Luke sprang down the corridor and leapt off the carnage heap to attack. Lomi blocked his first pass with her white lightsaber. Then, in place of the purple lightsaber she had left in Jacen at the end of their last meeting, she ignited a familiar-looking green blade—the lightsaber Raynar had confiscated on Woteba. *Luke's* lightsaber.

"Now you're just ticking me off," Luke said.

Lomi clacked her mandibles and hissed, then launched a deadly low–high–low combination with her flashing blades. Luke parried, ducked, and jumped, then brought an elbow up under her mandibles and sent her staggering back, all four arms flailing as she struggled to catch her balance on her mismatched legs.

Luke whipped his blade around, cocking it for a death slash across her middle—then had a prickle of danger sense between his shoulder blades and tried to spin away. He almost made it.

Something heavy and huge slammed into his shoulder—a shatter gun pellet?—and sent him tumbling across the floor past Lomi Plo's feet. He tried a reactionary slash as he rolled by, only to discover that was he was no longer holding his lightsaber, and he could not move his prosthetic hand—nor the rest of his arm.

Lomi Plo's two blades began to chop the floor behind him, so he used the Force to accelerate himself and continued to roll, then came to his feet two meters on the other side of her and called his lightsaber back to his good hand.

The weapon arrived just ahead of Lomi Plo, and suddenly Luke found himself on the defensive, being driven into a corner while Raynar Thul—not so impotent after all—used his other hand to fire more shatter gun pellets.

In lightsaber combat, Luke favored two-handed styles, but he could still fight single-handed—even with his weak hand—just as well as anyone in the academy. What he could not do, however, was fight wounded and weak-handed against twin blades while a second party fired a steady stream of hard-to-deflect shatter gun pellets at him.

In short, Luke was desperate.

So he dropped to his side and caught Lomi Plo's human leg in a scissoring motion between his feet. The knee bent backward and popped with a sickening crunch.

She fell, squealing in pain and clacking her mandibles—and redoubled her attacks, slashing so ferociously with her twin blades that Luke's lone hand barely had the strength to block.

Of course, Control picked that moment for an important announcement from the *Megador*. "Be advised that three Killik swarms are diverting to attack *Healing Star*."

Lomi Plo's attacks slackened for a moment, and Luke realized that she was gently probing him through the Force, searching for any hint of fear or doubt. He put the *Healing Star*—the fleet's main hospital ship—out of his mind and remained focused on the fight. Lomi Plo had almost certainly used the Dark Nest to divert those swarms, to try to create an opening that would give her power over his mind.

Still dodging shatter gun pellets, rolling back and forth on the floor and parrying madly, Luke glanced up the corridor and used the Force to reach into the carnage heap beneath Raynar's feet. He grabbed the largest, heaviest thing he could find—a disabled bugcruncher droid—and jerked it free.

The pile shifted and Raynar crashed down on his back, but Luke barely noticed. He was pulling the droid down the corridor straight at Lomi Plo.

She deflected it easily, of course—but she had to spin away from Luke and wave a hand, and that gave him the chance he needed to Force-spring up the corridor toward Raynar, who was just returning to his feet.

"As I was *saying*," Luke said, pointing his lightsaber down at Raynar's chest. "You never learn."

Raynar's eyes flashed with alarm and he rolled away—presenting the side of his head for a perfect knockout blow. Luke brought his lightsaber down, but deactivated the blade and flipped it around at the last second to strike at the base of the ear.

The blow landed with a sharp crack that suggested a breaking skull, but Luke had no time to worry about Raynar. Lomi Plo was dragging herself out the hatchway, trying to escape into the general confusion of the *Ackbar*'s recapture. He sprang after her, using the Force to drag her back into the corridor.

Lomi Plo whirled around, her lightsabers rising into a guard position but not attacking. Trapped on the floor with a broken knee, she knew as well as Luke did that she could not defend herself; that he could kill her any time he wished.

So Luke was half expecting it when Control's voice sounded in his earpiece again. "Be advised, Killik swarms are opening fire on *Healing Star*."

Lomi Plo's mandibles opened wide, and a long, gurgling hiss erupted from her throat. Luke did not need to speak Killik to understand what she was saying—or even to probe her meaning through the Force. *She* could call off the attack on the hospital ship.

All Luke had to do was let her go.

Luke snorted. "That's the trouble with you ruthless types—you're all so predictable."

Lomi Plo grabbed hold of the sides of the hatchway with two of her hands, then pulled herself up on her insect leg and cocked her head so that only one of her bulbous eyes was turned toward Luke.

"Mara and Jacen are in a hospital back on Coruscant," Luke explained. "There's nobody aboard *Healing Star* but a few mouse droids. Admiral Bwua'tu *said* you were going to attack it. And by the way, I have no doubts about Mara. She says hello, in fact."

Lomi Plo's reaction came so suddenly that Luke doubted even *she* was expecting it. She just came flying at him with both blades flashing, striking high and low from opposite sides in a desperate attempt to finish him off.

Luke, of course, had anticipated this, too. Lomi Plo had no

power over him. He simply stepped inside her attack and flicked his wrist twice, first sweeping his blade upward, then whipping it around in a backslash, and she landed at his feet in four parts.

Luke stood looking down at the pieces for a moment, half expecting them to turn to smoke and vanish, or to dissolve like a bad HoloNet signal. It was hard to believe that a woman of mere flesh and blood and chitin had caused so much trouble—had brought the galaxy to the edge of eternal war—but of course, beings of flesh and blood were *always* starting wars. That's why the galaxy needed her Jedi.

Luke reached down and retrieved the two lightsabers Lomi Plo had been wielding. He tucked the white one inside his flight utilities and hung the green one in its proper place on his belt, then returned to the side of his former student.

Raynar was still unconscious, but his vital signs were stable, and he did not seem to be in any great danger.

Luke broke out a medkit and started to work. "Let's get you patched up, son," he said. "We're going home."

EPILOGUE

The air had long since grown stale and the caf bitter, but the mood in the *Megador*'s cramped briefing room remained upbeat. Aristocra Formbi was more than two standard hours late for the long-distance conference, but no one was surprised. The Chiss had taken a battering even after the Alliance arrived, and the Jedi had prevented the deployment of their "secret weapon"—the insidious parasite bombs. Without a doubt, the Chiss were going to make their displeasure known, and Leia was just happy they were not doing it with megamasers.

Finally, Admiral Pellaeon's comm officer announced that Aristocra Chaf'orm'bintrano had opened a channel. Formbi's jowly blue face appeared on the giant vid display hanging at one end of the room. He did not bother introducing himself—or apologizing for his tardiness.

"The Ascendancy is ready to hear your peace offer," Formbi said. "But I warn you, we are not interested in any proposal that fails to eliminate the Colony threat."

"We understand that," Leia said evenly. "And we have already done so."

Formbi's eyes grew suspicious. "Really."

"As a matter of fact, yeah," Han said. He pointed a thumb at Luke, whose arm remained in a sling from the injuries he had suffered aboard the *Ackbar*. "Luke *killed* Lomi Plo, and Raynar's going back to the Galactic Alliance with us."

Formbi's face showed his alarm. "You're taking *Raynar Thul* into Alliance space? I thought you had killed him!"

"We've *neutralized* him," Luke said. "Raynar realizes that his continued presence can only bring more disasters like this one down on the Killiks."

"Besides, we have him buttoned up tight in a special brain hood Cilghal designed," Han said. "If he even *thinks* about a bug, he gets zapped with dazers."

Formbi frowned. "The Ascendancy would feel more comfortable if he were dead."

"He will be, if we find our measures are insufficient to keep him isolated until he recovers," Luke said. "Rest assured, the Colony has been destroyed. The Jedi will do whatever is necessary to ensure that Raynar Thul never troubles you again."

Formbi's brow shot up, but he quickly caught himself and assumed a doubtful scowl. "What of the Twi'lek Jedi?" he demanded. "This Alema Rar? Isn't she a Dark Nest Joiner?"

"She *was*," Leia said. "As of now, she is presumed dead."

Formbi's scowl deepened. "We Chiss prefer certainties to presumptions, Princess."

"As do we all," Leia said. "But I'm afraid that's impossible in this case. We were unable to locate her body, and I'm fairly certain that's because she was eaten."

Formbi was too shocked to feign disbelief. "By what?"

"Some sort of spider sloth," Leia said. "I can't actually name it. All I can tell you is that we were fighting on Tenupe when the creature attacked. I escaped and Alema didn't. The creature disappeared into the jungle with her upper body in its mouth."

"If that is what you Jedi mean by destroying the Colony, then I must inform you that your definitions are not acceptable to the Chiss," Formbi said. "If she survived and returns to the Dark Nest, she could restart the entire Colony."

"No, she couldn't," Luke said. "I assume you've been briefed on the nanotech environmental defense agents of the Utegetu Nebula?"

"Of course," Formbi smirked.

"Then you'll be reassured to know that as of our last report, Jedi teams have seeded more than half of the Colony's planets with the appropriate nanotech agents," Luke said. "Before we're done, that number will be as close to a hundred percent as our knowledge of Colony territory can make it."

"The Killiks won't be *able* to reconstitute the Colony," Leia said. "If they start to overpopulate, their own worlds will bring the nest down to a manageable level."

"You might say it's a failsafe," Han said. "It worked like a charm on Woteba."

"So you say," Formbi replied. "But I doubt your guarantees will be satisfactory to the ruling houses."

"They're going to have to be, Aristocra." Pellaeon spoke in a gruff, sharp voice that carried a subtle but definite threat. "The Galactic Alliance is ready to wash its hands of this matter, and our fleet will be returning to our own territory as soon as possible."

"You'll find no argument from us," Formbi said. "The Ascendancy never wanted you involved in the first place."

Pellaeon's voice grew even more steely. "Perhaps, but we need to deal with current realities. The war is over as of *now,* Aristocra. The Killiks have no reason to restart it, and very soon they'll lack the capacity to do so. Therefore, the *Ascendancy* has no reason to restart it, either."

"We Chiss are accustomed to formulating our own policies," Formbi sneered.

"We know that, Aristocra," Leia said. "But *you* know that those policies affect your relations with the Alliance—and the Galactic Alliance is not in the habit of tolerating aggressors and warmongers. Quite the opposite, as a matter of fact."

"Take a lesson from the bugs and don't hold a grudge," Han added. "*They* went home a week ago. You do the same, and we'll all be happy."

"The Chiss are not interested in what makes you happy, Captain Solo," Formbi fumed. He paused, swallowing a bit of his anger. "But we *are* beings who value peace above all else—and we are willing to take one more risk to achieve it."

Leia breathed an inward sigh of relief, and Pellaeon smiled beneath his mustache. That was nearly the exact statement that Bwua'tu predicted the Chiss would make—just prior to naming their terms.

"We're very glad to hear that, Aristocra," Leia said.

"Don't be," Formbi growled. "You haven't heard our terms."

"I assume you're prepared to remedy that situation," Pellaeon said, perhaps a bit too smugly.

"Of course," Formbi retorted. "The Chiss will agree to your terms, provided the Alliance will promise to come to our aid in the event of another unprovoked Killik attack."

Pellaeon frowned, pretending to consider a request that everyone in the briefing room already knew he was going to grant.

After a suitable pause, he nodded. "Very well. Done."

Formbi's eyes widened just enough to betray his surprise. "You agree? Just like that?"

"Why shouldn't we?" Pellaeon asked. "*We're* the ones who are promising there will be no Killik attacks."

Formbi frowned. "So you are," he agreed. "But this is a formal treaty. Don't you need authorization from Chief Omas?"

Pellaeon smiled broadly. "My dear Aristocra, I *came* with that authorization," he said. "There is nothing the Galactic Alliance desires more than a close relationship with the Ascendancy. You're welcome to send a team of diplomats back with the fleet when we leave, if you'd like to get started on the formal documents."

Formbi looked vaguely uncomfortable, like a sabacc player who just realized he should have called a bluff. "I'm afraid that will have to wait. We didn't bring any diplomats along on this campaign. We were under the impression we were going to war."

Pellaeon chuckled. "Well, war *can* be unpredictable."

"More so every day, it seems," Formbi said. "You may assure the Killiks—or whomever—that our fleet will be leaving within a day."

"Then you've completed your search-and-rescue operations?" Leia asked. Her heart was in her throat, for she was thinking of a certain young captain whom she had shot down.

"You would be safe in assuming that," Formbi replied with typical Chiss evasiveness about military matters.

"Would you happen to know if Jagged Fel was recovered alive?" Leia asked. "As you know, in the past, he has been a close personal friend of our family's."

"I also know that the *Falcon* was the vessel that shot him down," Formbi replied, a little bitterly.

"So he made it?" Han asked.

"I didn't say that, Captain Solo."

"You are not telling?" Saba burst out, speaking for the first time. "Jaina Solo will be a shenbit for a month!"

"I don't see why. It was my impression that their relationship was over long before her parents shot him down." Formbi grew thoughtful for a moment, then finally said, "Unfortunately, Commander Fel has not been recovered yet. His rescue beacon is transmitting from a rift valley inaccessible to recovery craft. We've sent in a team to search for him on foot."

"Perhaps the Jedi can help," Luke said. "We might be able to sense—"

"Your help would not be welcome," Formbi interrupted. "It has cost us too much already."

"I'm sorry you feel that way," Luke said. "Please let us know if you change your mind."

"We won't," Formbi assured him.

"Be that as it may, Jaina still regards Commander Fel fondly."

Leia did not mention Zekk; the Chiss were squeamish enough about Joiners without bringing a mind-mate into the love affair. "Jagged's status was the first thing she asked about after Han and I rescued her. If you *do* happen to recover him alive before you depart, please let him know that she and her wingmate are making an excellent recovery from their wounds. They'll be out of the infirmary tomorrow."

"I really don't see why Captain Fel would be interested. Assuming we *do* recover him." Formbi turned to Pellaeon. "You may assure Chief Omas that a diplomatic team will be arriving shortly to formalize the treaty."

With that, Formbi closed the channel and vanished from the vid display, leaving the mood in the briefing room slightly less jovial than before—despite the fact that they had just negotiated a successful end to the war.

After a moment, Han said, "Nice guy." He shook his head in disgust. "No wonder the Chiss get along so well with their neighbors."

"Out here, I'm afraid getting along with your neighbors means keeping them at arm's length," Pellaeon said.

An uncomfortable silence fell over the cabin—which Saba suddenly broke by snatching the lightsaber off Leia's utility belt . . . breaking the clasp in the process. Well accustomed to her Master's stern training exercises—and odd timing—Leia simply turned and bowed her head for the stern rap that she knew Saba was going to dispense for allowing her lightsaber to be snatched away.

When it did not come, Leia looked up to find the Barabel studying her lightsaber with a disapproving eye. "Master?"

"Jedi Solo, where did you get this lightsaber?" Saba demanded.

"I built it," Leia said. "Over twenty years ago."

Saba curled her lip in disdain. "This one thought so." She jammed the hilt into her belt, then added, "It is a terrible weapon, unworthy of your current skillz. You will carry it no more."

"What?" Leia gasped. "What am I supposed to do for a lightsaber?"

Saba blinked her slit-pupiled eyes in reptilian exasperation.

"Princesz Leia, you are a fine Jedi, the equal of any Jedi Knight in the order." She pointed a claw at the empty place on Leia's belt. "What do you think you should do for a lightsaber?"

Leia finally saw what the Barabel was driving at, then felt herself blushing at how long it had taken her to realize the answer. "Build a new one," she said. "A better one."

Saba closed her eyes. *"Finally."*

Luke laughed, then said, "Congratulations, Leia. I think that means you should consider yourself a full Jedi Knight."

"No kidding? A full Jedi Knight!" Han wrapped his arm around Leia's shoulders, then added, "But I don't see what the big deal is. I could've told you *that* a long time ago."

Leia slipped her arm around Han's waist, then stretched up to kiss him on the lips. "Thanks, flyboy. There's no one I'd rather hear say that."

Pellaeon cleared his throat and looked at the ceiling, obviously a bit uncomfortable. "That reminds me, Master Skywalker. I've had a messenger from Chief Omas. He wishes to convene a meeting of the Advisory Council as soon as we return. If I were Bwua'tu, I'd predict that he's eager to formalize the Jedi's new role in the Alliance."

Han groaned, and an empty feeling came to Leia's stomach. They had told Luke that they suspected Omas of betraying their mission. Unfortunately, they had no hard evidence of the Chief's treachery, and Luke did not want to damage the delicate relations between the Jedi and the government by making unprovable accusations. Besides, even if Omas *had* betrayed the Solos, it was not technically a crime, since he had been acting for the benefit of the Galactic Alliance.

Luke merely nodded. "I'll be happy to discuss that with Chief Omas myself," he said. "But I'm afraid the Jedi will be withdrawing from his Advisory Council."

By the look on the other faces in the cabin, Leia supposed that her brother's statement had surprised even Admiral Bwua'tu.

Finally, Pellaeon asked, *"Why?"*

"Because the Jedi should serve, not govern," Luke said. "In the Colony, we've seen again how badly matters turn out when Jedi take the reins of state—even with the purest of motives."

"But Jedi advice is important!" Pellaeon objected. "At times, I think you're the only disinterested representatives *in* the government!"

Luke raised his hand to calm the admiral. "The Galactic Alliance will have Jedi advice," he said. "I'm going to establish a new Jedi Council to help run the order, and I'll relay their advice to Chief Omas."

This declaration was received with the stunned silence that Leia would have believed it deserved—had she seen any better way to hold the Jedi order together.

Finally, Pellaeon said, "A workable organization, as long as you're at the head of it. But what happens if you're unavailable?"

An unfocused appearance came to Luke's gaze, and Leia had the impression that he was looking a long distance into the future.

"Good question," Luke said. "I wish I knew the answer."

TROY DENNING is the *New York Times* bestselling author of *Star Wars: Tatooine Ghost*, *Star Wars: The New Jedi Order: Star by Star*, and the *Star Wars: Dark Nest* trilogy, as well as *Pages of Pain*, *Beyond the High Road*, *The Summoning*, and many other novels. A former game designer and editor, he lives in southern Wisconsin with his wife, Andria.